## Praise for David Weber's Safehold Series

"Gripping . . . Shifting effortlessly between battles among warp-speed starships and among oar-powered galleys, Weber brings the political maneuvering, past and future technologies, and vigorous protagonists together for a cohesive, engrossing whole."

—*Publishers Weekly* (starred review) on
*Off Armageddon Reef*

"A superb cast of characters and plenty of action. . . . This fine book gives new luster to Weber's reputation and new pleasure to his fans."

—*Booklist* (starred review) on
*By Schism Rent Asunder*

"Like its predecessors in the Safehold series, the novel paints a vast, stunningly complex political and military tapestry, with wonderful battle scenes."

—*Kirkus Reviews* on *By Heresies Distressed*

"Vast, complex, intricate, subtle, and unlaydownable. This looks like the start of the biggest thing in science fiction since Isaac Asimov's Foundation series."

—Dave Duncan on *Off Armageddon Reef*

## TOR BOOKS BY DAVID WEBER

# HELL'S FOUNDATIONS QUIVER

## DAVID WEBER

A TOM DOHERTY ASSOCIATES BOOK
NEW YORK

This is a work of fiction. All of the characters, organizations, and events portrayed in this novel are either products of the author's imagination or are used fictitiously.

HELL'S FOUNDATIONS QUIVER

Copyright © 2015 by David Weber

All rights reserved.

Maps by Ellisa Mitchell and Jennifer Hanover

A Tor Book
Published by Tom Doherty Associates, LLC
175 Fifth Avenue
New York, NY 10010

www.tor-forge.com

Tor® is a registered trademark of Tom Doherty Associates, LLC.

ISBN 978-0-7653-6155-4

Our books may be purchased in bulk for promotional, educational, or business use. Please contact your local bookseller or the Macmillan Corporate and Premium Sales Department at 1-800-221-7945, extension 5442, or by e-mail at MacmillanSpecialMarkets@macmillan.com.

First Edition: October 2015
First Mass Market Edition: September 2016

Printed in the United States of America

0  9  8  7  6  5  4  3  2  1

For Sharon, Megan, Morgan, and Michael,
the four reasons I get up everyday.
I love you guys.

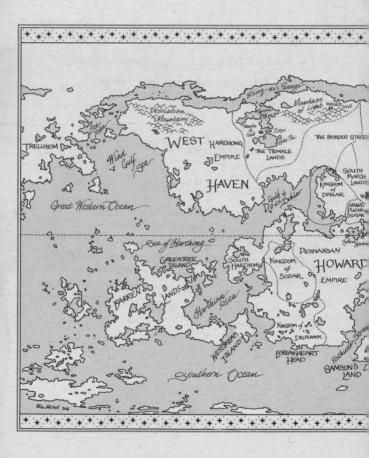

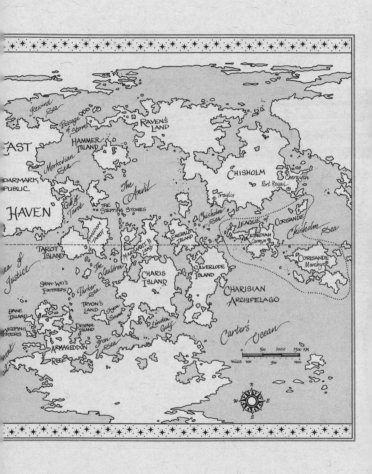

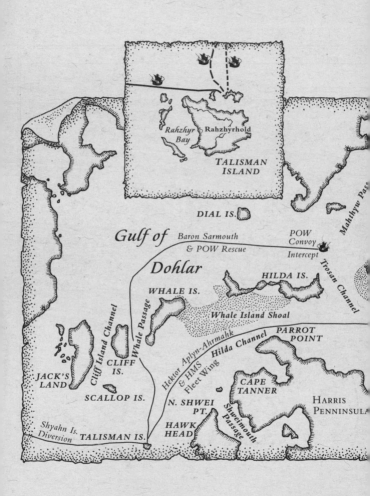

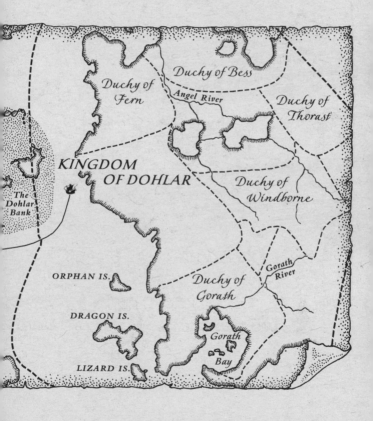

Duchy of Bess

Duchy of Fern

Angel River

Duchy of Thorast

KINGDOM OF DOHLAR

The Dohlar Bank

Duchy of Windborne

ORPHAN IS.

Duchy of Gorath

Gorath River

DRAGON IS.

Gorath Bay

LIZARD IS.

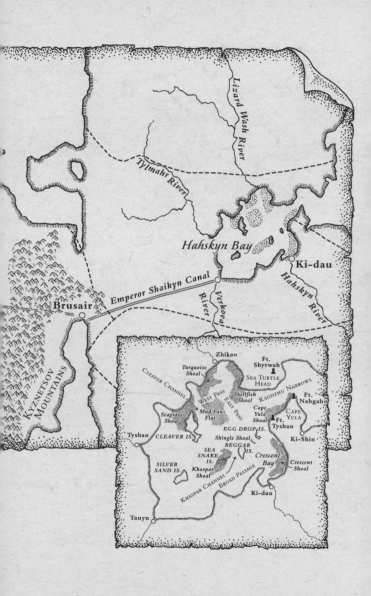

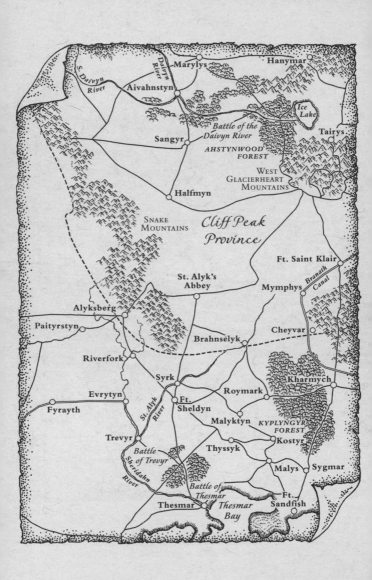

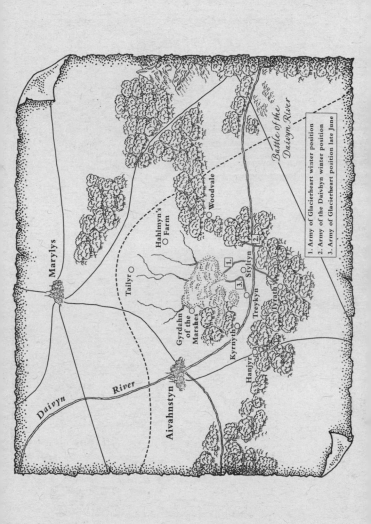

Marylys

Battle of the Daivyn River

Hahlmyn's Farm

Woodvale

Tailyr

Gyrdahn of the Marshes

Styltyn

Kyrnyth

Treykyn

Tyrath

Hanyr

Aivahnstyn

Daivyn River

1. Army of Glacierheart winter position
2. Army of the Daivyn winter position
3. Army of Glacierheart position late June

# MARCH
## YEAR OF GOD 897

·◆·

# . I .
## Merlin Athrawes' Chamber,
## Charisian Embassy,
## Siddar City,
## Republic of Siddarmark

The roaring, shingle-lifting bluster of snow-laden wind only made the sudden, profound silence more complete. The slight sound as a coal settled on the modest bedchamber's hearth seemed almost deafening, and Merlin Athrawes stood very still, shoulders against the door he'd just closed behind him, sapphire eyes gazing intently through the fire-flickered dimness at the slender woman in the single chair beside that hearth.

The woman who had just called him "Ahbraim."

Which, he reflected, made the question of how she'd managed to get by the alert sentinels guarding the Charisian Embassy here in the heart of Siddar City rather secondary.

The heavy, utilitarian coat hanging from his coat tree—like the boots and thick woolen stockings she'd slipped from slim, pedicured feet and set before the fire—was soaked with melting snow. The firelight cast dancing light and shadow across her brilliant, expressive eyes, gleamed on the gold and topaz encircling her aristocratic throat, and struck subdued highlights from hair that was almost as dark as Sharleyan Ahrmahk's own, and the gown she'd worn under that plain, serviceable coat was as exquisitely designed and cut as it was expensive. She was quite possibly the most beautiful woman he'd ever met and he could smell the subtle sweetness of her perfume, but none of those things were what held him so still.

"Why," he asked after a moment, in a tone which sounded considerably calmer than it should have, "did you call me 'Ahbraim,' Madam Pahrsahn?" He cocked his head, expression puzzled. "I assume it's a reference to Master Zhevons?"

"You really are *very* good," Aivah Pahrsahn—who'd once been known as Ahnzhelyk Phonda, among many other names—said approvingly. "Why, you could almost—*almost*, I say—convince me. But you can't, you know. I've been watching you for too long, and I have a *very* good memory for details."

"Watching me?" he repeated. "Watching me do what? I haven't made any special effort to keep my comings and goings here in Siddar City secret from you or the Lord Protector. Or from your agents, now that I think about it."

"Well," she said thoughtfully, leaning back and crossing her long legs elegantly. She propped one elbow on the chair arm and rested her chin on the palm of a perfectly manicured hand as she gazed up at him like a woman contemplating a problem to which she'd devoted much thought. "I'll concede that at least a part of what gave you away *were* things I could see working together with you and His Majesty here in the capital, but that wasn't really decisive. No, what finally convinced me my absurd suspicions might actually be well-founded wasn't so much the many interesting things you were doing *here* as it was the timing of all those occasions when you . . . *weren't* here, shall we say."

"In what way?" The tall, broad-shouldered Imperial Guardsman folded his arms across his chest and raised one eyebrow. "And while I'm asking questions, what sort of 'suspicions'—well-founded or not—are we talking about?"

"The world went the better part of a thousand years without a single verified *seijin*-sighting," Madam Pahrsahn replied. "Then, all of a sudden, *you* surfaced . . .

in Charis, of all places. During the War Against the Fallen, not a single *seijin*—not *one* of them, Merlin—was ever reported in remote, backwater, unimportant little Charis. Until Charis was neither little nor unimportant . . . and there you were, smack in the middle of Tellesberg."

She gave him a dimpled smile.

"Now, I realize you've always been careful to tell everyone you're not really a *seijin*—or to imply it as strongly as possible, at any rate—but no one's ever actually believed you. Quite reasonably, I concluded, once the reports of your activities came to my ears. Whatever you might choose to say, your accomplishments clearly established what you actually were, I'm afraid. And while the fact that a *seijin* had surfaced anywhere at this late date was remarkable enough, it became even more remarkable in light of the way you'd given your allegiance to the Church of Charis when everyone knew the *seijins* had always been *Mother Church's* champions. What, I wondered when I heard the first reports about your . . . astonishing capabilities, was a *seijin* doing in the service of a clearly heretical church and empire?"

"May I assume you eventually came up with an answer to that question?" he inquired politely.

"Well, given the difference between the heretical church in question and what that pig Clyntahn and his precious Group of Four had done to Mother Church, it didn't take me long to conclude that you represented a fairly emphatic statement of divine disapproval of their actions." Her smile disappeared. "And, to be honest, I found myself wondering what had taken God so long."

He inclined his head in a silent nod, acknowledging the point of her last sentence without responding directly to it.

"I kept as close an eye on you and your activities as I could," she continued after a moment. "Distance was something of a problem, but as I'm sure you've become aware, when I decide to keep an eye on something—or someone—I'm better at it than most. So long before *Seijin* Ahbraim ever entered my establishment in Zion, I'd come to the conclusion that despite all your protestations to the contrary, you were as genuine a *seijin* as ever walked the face of this world. And whether or not you chose to proclaim any semidivine status of your own, you were clearly on the side of God."

Her voice turned softer on the last sentence, and the wind roar behind the stillness gusted momentarily louder as their eyes met. She let silence linger for a long, quiet moment, then shrugged.

"That's one reason I was prepared to listen to *Seijin* Ahbraim when he turned up in Zion to warn me to expedite my plans. I think he probably would have convinced me anyway, but I happen to be something of a student of the lore about *seijins*, and I'd already had all of that time to draw my conclusions about you. Those conclusions applied by extension to him as your fellow *seijin* and . . . associate, and his advice turned out to have been remarkably good in the end. After all, it brought me here," she waved her free hand gracefully, as if to encompass the city beyond the bedchamber's walls, "where I was able to add my own modest efforts to those of all those people fighting openly to bring down Clyntahn and the others." She met Merlin's blue eyes very levelly. "For that privilege, that opportunity, I will be eternally grateful to . . . *Seijin* Ahbraim."

His nod was a bit deeper this time, almost a bow, and he crossed to the fireplace, opened the screen, and used the tongs to settle two more large lumps of coal into the fire. Fresh, brighter light flared, and he listened to the jubilant, hissing crackle as the flames explored the coal's surface, then closed the screen once more and turned back to Madam Pahrsahn. He raised his left arm, laying it along the small mantel above the hearth, and arched both eyebrows in a silent invitation to continue.

"I will admit," she said quietly, "that it took me some time to begin to suspect the truth—or at least *one* of the truths—behind your mask, Merlin. I'm quite certain I haven't perceived all of them even now. But something about you seemed very familiar when we first met here in Siddar City. As I said, I have an excellent memory, and a woman in my profession—or in Ahnzhelyk Phonda's, at least—learns to observe very small details about other people. Particularly, if we're going to be honest, about men. Especially about good-looking men who aren't simply courteous but gentle and even considerate with the women whose services they seek from someone like Ahnzhelyk. And Ahbraim and I—well, Ahbraim and Frahncyn Tahlbaht, I suppose—spent quite a lot of time together in Bruhstair Freight Haulers' warehouse and on the trip out of Zion.

"After I met you here in Siddar City, it gradually dawned on me that you reminded me a great deal of him. Oh," she waved her free hand again, "your hair's a different color, and so are your eyes, of course. Your voices and accents are very different, too, and Ahbraim's clean-shaven, whereas you have that dashing beard and mustache. Oh, and that scarred cheek, as well. But, you know, you're exactly the same height, your shoulders are the same width, and when I looked at you and mentally stripped away that beard and mustache, I realized the chin was almost identical. You really should have taken more care about that, and perhaps about the hands, as well."

"Oh?" Merlin held out his right hand, looking down at its back and then turning it to examine the long, strong fingers with their swordsman's calluses.

"I doubt anyone else has noticed a thing," she told him thoughtfully. "I mean, the entire idea's preposterous, isn't it? It took even someone who's been a student of the *seijins* for as many years as I have a long time to admit what I'd come to suspect. But when I did, I started keeping track of exactly when and where Ahbraim or any other *seijin* or suspected *seijin* made an actual face-to-face appearance rather than restricting himself to written reports. I started keeping track of any information I could find about their physical appearances, as well, and I discovered two fascinating things. First, every single one of those other *seijins* was quite tall, well above average in height . . . just like you. And, second, whenever I could positively nail down another *seijin*'s appearance, it always turned out that *you'd* left Siddar City on some mission—generally an unspecified and covert one—for Cayleb at exactly the same time. Aren't those interesting coincidences?"

"Obviously," Merlin said after a moment, "they aren't coincidences at all." He considered her thoughtfully, then shrugged. "I trust you'll understand if I don't rush to give you any more information in a sudden excess of enthusiasm?"

Madam Pahrsahn's sudden laugh was deep, throaty, and very real, and she shook her head.

"Merlin, somehow I don't really think of you as someone who's subject to sudden excesses of enthusiasm or anything else!"

"One tries not to be," he acknowledged politely.

"And quite successfully, too," she agreed. "But once I'd realized we weren't really seeing all that many *seijins* even now, and once I'd realized how your absence correlated so perfectly with every other verified sighting, I realized there really was only one of you. One of you who could change not just his outward appearance but who he actually *was* as easily as a mask lizard changes color in a flowerbed, and cover impossible distances with impossible speed. And that, my friend, was the final proof you truly were a *seijin*. Just as much as *Seijin* Kohdy."

Despite himself, Merlin blinked at her chosen comparison. *Seijin* Kohdy was deeply embedded in Safeholdian folklore, but unlike the double handful of "attested" *seijins* recorded in *The Testimonies* left by the Adams and Eves who'd survived Shan-Wei's Rebellion and the War Against the Fallen, there was no historical record of him at all. Not only that, but while the *seijins* of *The Testimonies* were all sober, focused, intensely disciplined warriors for God, Archangels, and Church, *Seijin* Kohdy swirled through the tales about him like some sort of traveling conjurer or laughing vagabond. Or an Odysseus, perhaps. His times had been anything but humorous, yet the vast majority of those tales related as much to his craftiness, his ability to gain his objectives through guile and subterfuge as much as by the deadliness of Helm Cleaver, his magic sword . . . and to his humor, his weakness for attractive women, and his fondness for a glass of good whiskey. Indeed, "*Seijin* Kohdy's Premium Blend," one of the most popular Chisholmian blended whiskies, was named for him, and its label featured not simply the magical sword which was inextricably bound up with his name but also an artist's impression of Kohdy himself . . . with not one but two scantily clad barmaids sitting on his lap.

The stories about him were full of laughter and warmth, stories about someone who was very, very different from the officially recorded *seijins*, and Merlin had come to the conclusion that he was, in fact, a fictional creation. A construct, fashioned by later generations from the legend of the "real" *seijins* and seasoned with more than a dash of the trickster DNA so many of Old Earth's mythologies had treasured.

It would appear, however, that Aivah was entirely serious, and that behooved him to move cautiously.

"Interesting you should bring up *Seijin* Kohdy," he said after a moment. "Especially since I don't recall him being mentioned in the official list of *seijins* who served the Church and the Archangels."

"No, he isn't," she agreed, and her expression was suddenly much grimmer, her tone darker. "All of those 'official' *seijins* are saints of Mother Church, and he's not listed there, either . . . now."

"Now?" Merlin's deep voice was gentler than it had been.

"Now," she repeated. She uncrossed her legs, sitting up straighter, and her nostrils flared as she inhaled deeply. Then she looked directly into his eyes.

"Who are you *really*, Merlin?" she asked. "Where do you truly come from? And don't just tell me 'the Mountains of Light.'"

"Where else might I come from, Aivah?" he asked in return, holding out his arms in a gesture which took in not simply the bedchamber, nor even the Republic's capital, but the entire world beyond them.

"I don't know," she told him very quietly, her eyes deep and dark in the fire-spangled dimness, "but I've come to suspect that wherever you truly come from is also where all of the Adams and Eves who awoke here on Safehold on the Day of Creation truly came from, as well."

. II .
# Charisian Embassy,
# Siddar City,
# Republic of Siddarmark

"She said *what?*"

It was getting on towards dawn—and *much* warmer—in Corisande. The eastern sky beyond the windows of Sharleyan Ahrmahk's guest suite in Manchyr Palace was ever so slightly less black than it had been, and she leaned back against piled pillows in a billow of sheets and filmy steel thistle silk nightgown. She'd actually been asleep for some hours before her husband's urgent com call awakened her, yet her huge brown eyes were anything but sleepy.

"Apparently, Jeremiah Knowles wasn't the only person who left a written record," Merlin told her wryly. "Mind you, the perspective's a lot different, according to what Aivah—" He paused, and the image of him projected on her contacts by Owl's communications equipment snorted and shook his head. "Oh, the hell with it! I'm going to call her Nynian from now on. I swear, that woman's the only person on Safehold with more identities to keep straight than *I* have!"

Someone laughed over the com net, despite the gravity of the moment. It sounded to Sharleyan like Domynyk Staynair, but it might have been Ehdwyrd Howsmyn.

"That does rather serve you right, Merlin," Cayleb observed from where he sat with the *seijin* in the lamp-lit sitting room of his own suite in Siddar City. He wore a fleecy robe over his own pajamas—his preferred habit of sleeping nude was contraindicated in Siddar City in winter—but unlike his wife, he hadn't quite dropped off to sleep before Merlin's knock pulled him back out of bed. "What's that cliché you used about that pain-in-the-arse Zhwaigair's improvement on the Mahndrayn?" he continued. "'Hoist by your own petard,' wasn't it?"

"Be fair, Cayleb," Merlin protested. "I've only been doing this for seven years. As nearly as I can figure out, she's been doing it since she was *fifteen!*"

"And damned well, too, it sounds like," Nimue Chwaeriau said soberly from her chair in Sharleyan's bedchamber. "Without, I might add, all of your—well, *our*, I suppose—advantages, either."

"I've always realized she was a remarkable woman," Archbishop Maikel Staynair said softly from his bedroom in Archbishop Klairmant Gairlyng's palace, across the square from Manchyr Palace. "I never imagined anything like *this*, though."

"None of us did, Maikel," Cayleb pointed out. "That's rather the point of this little conference. What do we do about her now?"

"I agree we have to decide that quickly," Rahzhyr Mahklyn put in from his Tellesberg study. The hour was later there than in Siddar City, though not nearly so late—or early, depending upon one's perspective—as in Manchyr, and the head of the Royal College cupped his mug of hot chocolate in both hands, gazing down into its plume of steam with a troubled expression. "At the same time, we need to consider very carefully how much of the full truth we share with her."

"I don't know that this is a moment for pussy-footing around, Rahzhyr," High Admiral Rock Point replied.

The archbishop's brother sat on the sternwalk of his flagship, gazing across the black mirror of Tellesberg Harbor towards the imperial capital's gas-lit wharves. Unlike Mahklyn, he'd opted for a glass of whiskey. Now he rolled a deep sip slowly over his tongue, swallowed, and shook his head.

"We already knew how dangerously capable this woman is," he continued. "Or we thought we did, anyway. What we *didn't* know was that there was actually an organization that's been around even longer than the Brethren *and* done just as good a job of keeping its existence a secret that entire time! Given this little bombshell of hers, I'm more convinced than ever that this is *not* someone you want deciding you can't be trusted because you're hiding things she needs—or obviously *thinks* she needs, at any rate—to know."

"I'd have to agree with that," Merlin said. "Both about her capability and how dangerous it could be to get on her wrong side. You might want to ask a dozen or so dead vicars in Zion about that. Or, for that matter, several thousand Temple Loyalist rioters—or another dozen dead assassins, for that matter—right here in Siddar City."

"Not to mention being someone whose principles are probably just a bit less flexible than Ehdwyrd's best armor plate," Nimue observed. "I don't know her as well as you do, Merlin—or you, Cayleb—but I'd come to *that* conclusion even before she laid this vest-pocket nuke on us." The slender, red-haired woman who shared Merlin's memories of Nimue Alban shook her head, blue eyes deep with wonder. "Now? This isn't someone who's likely to make any suicide runs, but she's not going to flinch from paying whatever price she thinks is necessary, either. And I'd hate to think of the kind of damage she and her organization could do to us if she put her mind to it. The last thing we need is for her to decide we're the enemy, too!"

Merlin nodded in sober agreement, and so did several of the others.

"You know," Maikel Staynair said after a moment, "I'd always wondered how a child from her background—a girl whose adopted parents were forced to send her off to the convent when her father became Grand Vicar—not only escaped that convent but became the Temple Lands' most successful courtesan! For that matter, I'd always wondered where she found the funds for it."

"Personally, I'd assumed it was a sort of under-the-table payoff to keep her mouth shut," Nahrmahn Baytz put in from his virtual reality in the computers of Nimue's Cave. "Oh, I was sure the primary reason she chose that . . . vocation was to put her thumb into his eye, but I'd also assumed she'd cheerfully turned the screws on him to get the cash to set herself up properly in the first place." He smiled puckishly. "It's the sort of thing *I'd've* done, after all!"

"I'm afraid my logic followed yours, Nahrmahn," Staynair acknowledged.

"All of us thought the same thing," Rock Point pointed out. "And I'm pretty sure all of us thought more power to her, too!"

"Granted," the archbishop agreed. "But I'm still trying to wrap my mind around just how wrong we were, and the more I think about it, the more likely it seems that she *wanted* anyone who figured out who she'd been born to think that. One thing is painfully obvious: this is a woman who not only plans decades—even lifetimes—in advance, but one who's lived her entire life like a Harchongese nest doll! No matter how many of the people she's been you take apart, there's always another one hidden inside it."

Staynair, Merlin thought, had a pronounced way with understatement upon occasion.

It had taken Aivah—*Nynian*—hours to tell her story, and he wasn't foolish enough to think she'd even begun to share all of it even now. He certainly wouldn't have, in her place. Not, at least, until he'd been certain the person he was telling it to was actually who and what she so obviously hoped Merlin Athrawes was.

"Owl has the entire conversation on record," he said now. "All of us can peruse it at our leisure, and I don't think Nynian really expects an immediate answer. She's obviously aware this is going to throw us for a loop and she doesn't know anything about SNARCs or coms, so she's going to give Cayleb and me at least some time to talk it over and decide what to do. But Domynyk's right about how dangerous it could be to give her *any* reason to distrust us."

His mind ran back over that same conversation, and he felt a fresh flicker of astonishment even now.

▼ ▼ ▼

". . . so while I was at the convent, Sister Klairah recruited me," Aivah said quietly, gazing down into Merlin's fire while the wind roared and buffeted about the embassy. "I don't know how much you know about the Convent of Saint Ahnzhelyk, but it's the sort of place parents and families send young ladies with rebellious streaks. It has a reputation for turning them around, and a remarkable number of them end up as sisters of Saint Ahnzhelyk's order. Of course, in my case there were several reasons for stashing me there, but I really didn't object to the order's austerity. I suppose I was young and impressionable—I'd just turned fifteen, for goodness' sake!—but I believed I had a true vocation, and so did Sister Klairah.

"She was careful about sounding me out, especially given who my father was and who'd raised me, but that very rebelliousness in the girls entrusted to Saint Ahnzhelyk's care had made the convent a good hunting ground for the Sisters of Saint Kohdy for many years. Not that most of Saint Ahnzhelyk's sisters knew anything about their activities . . . or that they could afford to run any risks that might expose them or tell the Inquisition they existed. The Sisters of Saint Kohdy were never actually proscribed, but they certainly should have been when Saint Kohdy was purged from

*The Testimonies*. In fact, if I had to guess, the only reason they weren't proscribed long before that was that the surviving Angels were waiting for the last of the Adams and Eves to die before they acted. It wasn't that difficult for them to edit *The Testimonies*, since all the originals were in the Temple's Grand Library, but according to the Sisterhood's journals, they'd waited to move against Saint Kohdy's official memory until none of the people with actual memories of his life were around to question the approved version."

Merlin Athrawes had no need to breathe, yet he inhaled sharply in muscle memory reflex as she paused and looked up from the fire at him. The matter-of-fact way in which she'd suggested—no, not suggested; *stated*—that the most important sacred writings of the Church of God Awaiting, outside of the *Holy Writ* itself, had been forged, or at least significantly "edited," was astonishing. Not so much because they had been, but because she was so obviously confident they had. In its own way, that was an almost greater surprise than Maikel Staynair's revelation of the journal of Saint Zherneau in Tellesberg had been.

But she clearly wasn't finished yet, and she smiled crookedly as he waved for her to continue.

"Saint Kohdy was a *seijin*, too," she went on after a moment. "I don't think he had all the abilities you have, Merlin, but he had quite a few . . . superhuman capabilities. And the stories about Helm Cleaver are true. I know they are, because I've handled it myself, used it to shave slivers off a solid block of granite." She smiled again, the expression softer yet somehow bittersweet, and shook her head. "I didn't realize when Sister Klairah recruited me—I was much more innocent and naïve in those days—that I would have suffered a very sad accident if she hadn't been able to convince me she was telling the truth." Her expression darkened. "Some candidates *have* 'suffered an accident,' and I never would've lived to see Helm Cleaver or Saint Kohdy's journal if Sister Klairah *hadn't* convinced me."

Merlin stiffened, and she nodded as if his reaction pleased her.

"We can't read some of it," she admitted. "It's not written in any language we can understand. According to the part of the journal we *can* read, *Seijin* Kohdy wrote that part of it in something called 'Español.' He didn't say why, but I've read the rest of it dozens of times, and I think he'd begun keeping his journal well before he began to feel any doubt about which side he was on. That's certainly how the first half reads, at any rate. The 'Español' portions are brief, initially, interspersed with the ones we can still read, but its last eight months are recorded entirely in 'Español.' I suspect he switched to that language when he wrote down things that might have done serious damage to the cause of Chihiro and Schueler if it had fallen into someone else's hands. Or perhaps they were things he might not have been certain of in his own mind at the time he wrote them down. From a handful of entries in the part I *could* read, I think it was a combination of the two. He wasn't certain, and if it turned out he'd been wrong to doubt and what he'd written were to fall into anyone else's hands, he didn't want it to draw others who might trust him because of who and what he was into the same error.

"I don't know that for certain, because he never explained his reasoning in the portions of the journal we can read. Until I encountered that 'Español' of his, it had never occurred to me another language might even exist! And however reasonable it may've seemed to him at the time, his decision to use it means even the Sisterhood's members are divided on at least a few points."

"Oh?" Merlin tilted his head, and Aivah smiled more than a little tartly.

"Some of us—myself included—have interpreted the passage in which he recorded his decision to begin using 'Español' to suggest that it came from some time or place which *predated* the Creation. Combined with a few other puzzling references, one could almost read that as saying all of the Adams and Eves were . . . somewhere else before Safehold was called into existence."

Her dark eyes were suddenly very intent, boring into him like twin blades, but she went on calmly, almost tranquilly.

"Even those of us who read it that way are divided about where that 'somewhere else' might have been. Most of us interpret it as evidence that not even an Archangel could create a soul—that God Himself must be the sole Creator in that sense—and that all those Adams and Eves were with Him while the Archangels prepared the world in which they would live. But a fair number of us think he might just as well have meant the Adams and Eves lived and breathed on an entirely different world and that God and the Archangels brought them here from that other world, rather than first giving them life on the Day of Creation. It's a substantial distinction, and one I've often thought we could have found the answer to if he'd written the 'Español' portions in something we could read. Or," she added, raising both eyebrows, "that the *Sisterhood* could read, at any rate."

"I might be able to do a little something about that," he acknowledged slowly. "I can't promise. And you'd have to trust me with the journal—or a true copy of it, at any rate."

"Either we're going to trust one another a great deal eventually, Merlin," she said, "or this is going to end very badly for someone."

She seemed extraordinarily calm for a woman who'd already acknowledged that the "Sisters of Saint Kohdy"—whoever the hell *they* were—had murdered an unknown number of young women to keep their secret. Then again, if they'd recruited her when she was only fifteen, she'd spent better than thirty-five Safeholdian years—thirty-two standard years—in that Sisterhood.

"At any rate," she said, "by the time the War Against the Fallen was winding towards a close, Saint Kohdy had come to question much of what he'd been told by the Archangels. We know from the parts we can read that he'd met someone—someone fighting to the bitter end on the other side—who'd convinced him that what had happened to Armageddon Reef didn't necessarily prove *Shan-wei* had fallen into evil. For that matter, after talking with him, Kohdy had come to question whether or not Langhorne himself had loosed the Rakurai on Armageddon Reef. The Fallen who'd taken up Shan-wei's struggle after the destruction of Armageddon Reef had insisted it was *Chihiro and Schueler* who'd turned to evil, not Shan-wei, but Kohdy had always brushed those assertions aside. After all, Shan-wei was the Mother of Lies, wasn't she?

"But according to his journal, not all the *seijins* fought under Chihiro and Schueler's banner, whatever *The Testimonies* might tell us today. Some fought for the Fallen, instead. They were called demons by the Archangels and by Mother Church, but Kohdy had met them sword-to-sword. He'd come to doubt their demonhood even before one of them defeated him, and his doubt grew still stronger after the 'demon' not only spared his life but revealed a totally different truth to him. I don't know exactly what that truth was—it was shortly after that point he began writing portions of his journal in 'Español'—but it made him question which side he was on. It took time for those questions to ripen, and by the time they did, the War Against the Fallen was almost over. The rebellious lesser angels had almost all been hunted down and destroyed. The servitors who'd fought for the Archangels had largely withdrawn to the Dawn Star, the last of the 'demons' fighting for the Fallen had been driven back to their final fastness in the Desolation Mountains, and the Archangels must have been preparing their final assault.

"And that's where the journal ends."

Merlin stared at her.

"That's where *it ends?*"

"Yes," she sighed. "He never wrote down his

intentions—unless he did it in Español—but the Sisters' tradition is that he'd decided to take his questions directly to the Archangel Schueler, the Archangel he most trusted to answer him fully. Whether that's true or not, he made a final trip to Zion . . . and died there."

"How did he die?" Merlin asked softly, and Nynian shook her head.

"We don't know. The Order of Saint Kohdy—the Sisterhood's parent order—was formed when his body was returned to his family. It was created and charged with preparing and maintaining his tomb, just as other orders had been charged to do for many of the other fallen *seijins*, and it was granted a benefaction for that purpose. I suspect if he hadn't fought so strongly, been in the forefront of the battle against the Fallen for so long, the Sisterhood would never have been formed at all. As it was, the Sisters quickly found themselves pushed to one side, largely ignored by the rest of the Church. This was in the period immediately after the Fallen's final defeat, you understand, after Schueler and Chihiro had departed in victory—the period in which I think the remaining Angels were waiting for the last Adams and Eves to die before purging *The Testimonies*.

"During that interval, the Sisters' original benefaction was exhausted, and the Church ignored or misfiled—intentionally, I'm sure—their requests for additional funds. So, left to their own devices, they solicited voluntary contributions, largely from members of their own families to begin with, and invested them. By the time *The Testimonies* were edited, their investments were returning an income comfortably greater than the Order required to maintain itself and Saint Kohdy's tomb.

"The Mother Abbess of the Order had realized Kohdy was going to be cast from Mother Church's canon of saints well before it actually happened, however. According to the Sisterhood's records, her brother was a vicar, as their father had been before him, and it would appear, even though she was careful not to say so in so many words, that her family's connections warned her of what was coming.

"She was very old by then, almost a hundred years old, and she was no Eve. Her health was poor, but that wasn't the reason she died when the Order was officially . . . disbanded."

Nynian's voice had gone very low, very quiet, soft enough a normal human ear would have had difficulty hearing her over the sound of the blizzard beyond the embassy's walls. But Merlin Athrawes had a PICA's ears. He heard the ancient grief—and the anger—in those words all too clearly.

She sat silent for endless seconds, staring down into the fire's incandescent heart once more, then shook herself and looked back up at him.

"Not all of the Sisters were prepared to abandon Saint Kohdy, even at Mother Church's command. They might have accepted the decree if any of the Archangels had issued it, but only the last of the lesser angels remained, and the Mother Abbess had known Kohdy, just as she'd known—had spoken with—both Schueler and Chihiro when she was a very young woman, before their departure. Neither of *them* had ever cast doubt upon Kohdy's sanctity, and that was enough for her. So she refused the decree, she and her sisters, and that, *Seijin* Merlin, is the reason there's no Abbey of Saint Kohdy today. And why no one ever bothered to officially proscribe the Order. When the Sisters proved . . . intransigent, the abbey—and everyone in it—was destroyed in the middle of the night in a 'blast of holy fury,' the last Rakurai of the War Against the Fallen. A blast which, strangely, was never recorded in any of Mother Church's official records."

Merlin stood very still, looking down at her, and her nostrils flared.

"But the fact that there's no *Abbey* of Saint Kohdy doesn't mean there's no *Tomb* of Saint Kohdy," she said quietly. "The Mother Abbess had moved the saint's body to a secret tomb well before the abbey's destruction, just as she'd moved duplicates of the Sisterhood's records . . . and Saint Kohdy's journal. And she'd taken advantage of the way in which she and her immediate predecessor had been forced to find alternate funding. A core of the Sisterhood was established in the secret abbey she'd created, and she'd divested the Order of a third of its investments. Those investments—and the income from them—were outside Mother Church's records, and they provided the surviving Sisters with the funds they required after the rest of their Sisters had been blotted away without warning or any opportunity to argue their case.

"They were made of stern stuff, those Sisters, and what had happened to the rest of their Order convinced them their Mother Abbess had been right to set a new path for their Order. It's followed that path to this day, with its Sisters individually members of Mother Church and yet apart from her. The Sisterhood's done a great deal of good over the centuries of its existence, *Seijin* Merlin, but always from the shadows, never admitting its existence."

"And today?" Merlin asked when she paused, and she smiled again, even more crookedly than before.

"Sister Klairah didn't recruit me simply because I wanted Mother Church to be what she's charged by God to be, Merlin. Many of the Sisters—most of them, really—have been called over the years for the same reason so many of my classmates were sent to Saint Ahnzhelyk's: because they were rebels. Because they had not simply the faith or the skills the Sisterhood needed, but because they had the fire, the need to *do* something with that rebellion—that touch of the *anshinritsumei* that comes down to us from Saint Kohdy. And in my case," her smile turned almost impish, "there was even more of that fire than I think Sister Klairah realized. I'm afraid I was never the most . . . dutiful of daughters, whether of my father or of Mother Church. And then, too," the smile vanished, "I had the example of my own father and of what was happening inside the vicarate.

"I knew better than most what had really happened to Saint Evyrahard, and I'd come to the conclusion there was precious little chance of the vicarate's ever reforming itself. The rot was too deep, the momentum building too steadily, for that to happen. Not without a little . . . push, at least. Which is why I became what I became. Oh, I'll freely admit I took a certain pleasure out of outraging my father and his family connections, especially since he couldn't openly object without admitting he *was* my father. But I also knew no one could possibly be in a better position to acquire the sort of . . . leverage that might inspire better behavior out of the worst of vicars than a courtesan—and later a madame—serving the most rarified heights of the episcopacy.

"Then I became aware of what Samyl and Hauwerd Wylsynn were trying to accomplish." She shook her head sadly, eyes darkening once more. "At first, I avoided them, since the last thing I wanted was for any of the vicars to see me coming and I was afraid an association with the Wylsynn family might come to light. But then it looked as if Samyl had a genuine chance of becoming Grand Inquisitor, and he was such a *good* man, and Adorai was already part of his circle. So I made myself a member as well, but only *as* myself, without ever acknowledging the Sisterhood's existence to anyone, even Adorai. Only he lost the election—almost certainly because Rayno manipulated the vote, though I could never prove that—and you know what happened from there."

She fell silent, and Merlin stood for several minutes, considering all she'd said.

"I assume the Sisterhood's secret investments explain where Ahnzhelyk Phonda found the capital she used to build that empire of hers in Zion? And the one here in Siddarmark, as well?" he asked then.

"You assume correctly," she acknowledged. "Except that the initial investments in Siddarmark are much older than I am. The Sisterhood's managed its portfolio well over the centuries, and until very recently its core expenses have been quite low. We've been active in charitable work for a long, long time, although we've had to be very careful about how we funded them without anyone's noticing us. The experience we gained in doing that for several hundred years was very useful when we started funding more . . . proactive endeavors."

"And your current Mother Abbess doesn't object to your more . . . secular activities, shall we say?" he asked, and she chuckled throatily.

"I'm afraid you don't quite have it straight yet," she told him. "The Sisters don't have a Mother Abbess anymore. We have a Mother Superior. She's the one who determines what the Sisters as a whole do in the world, and, no, she doesn't object to my 'more secular activities,' as you put it. That would be rather difficult for her to do, actually . . . since for the last twenty years or so, I've *been* the Mother Superior."

▼ ▼ ▼

"Trust me," Merlin Athrawes told the senior members of the inner circle as his attention returned to the com conversation. "Domynyk never said a truer thing in his entire life. Whatever else we may do, we *don't* want to turn this woman into our enemy."

. III .
HMS *Chihiro*, 50,
Gorath Bay,
Kingdom of Dohlar,
and
HMS *Destroyer*, 54,
Tellesberg,
Kingdom of Old Charis,
Empire of Charis

"Is that *confirmed*, My Lord?"

Commander Ahlvyn Khapahr sounded very much as if he hoped it wasn't, and Lywys Gardynyr, the Earl of Thirsk and the Kingdom of Dohlar's senior fleet commander, didn't blame him one bit.

"I'm afraid it is," he told the man who would have been called his chief of staff in Charisian service, and saw Khapahr's face tighten. He glanced around his day cabin and saw much the same reaction out of everyone else, as well.

Not surprisingly.

He pushed back his chair, rose, and crossed to the open quarter windows, looking out across the waters of Gorath Bay at the golden stone walls of the city of Gorath with his hands clasped behind his back. The late-afternoon sun hung barely above the western horizon, its rays slanting across the battlements and parapets, painting them with a deeper, more lustrous gold, and the kingdom's banners flew bravely above them.

Gorath Bay's temperature seldom fell below freezing, yet it could be bitterly cold in winter, especially for anyone out on its waters. The bay's cold snaps, with their raw, biting chill, might last for five-days, despite its southern location. That was what had caused so much sickness among Gwylym Manthyr's half-starved, half-

naked crews when they were confined in the prison
hulks.

*Oh, yes,* Thirsk thought. *The bay can be cruel, especially when human spite sees a chance to make it worse.*

His jaw tightened as he remembered that winter, remembered his shame and the way the Inquisition had
countermanded his orders to provide his prisoners—*his*
prisoners—with food and healers. That wind-polished
sheet of pitiless winter water danced before his eyes
again, and he felt the helplessness he'd felt then. Oh,
how he'd *hated* Gorath Bay throughout that cold, bitter winter.

But not today. He squared his shoulders and drew
a deep breath, forcing himself to step back from the
familiar rage, and looked out at the capital of his
kingdom.

Although it was the middle of winter, the breeze whipping across the bay today was little worse than chilly,
cold but not cutting, and the darkening sky was cloudless for the first time in several days. People in the city
were enjoying the last minutes of that sunlight, he
thought, possibly doing a little shopping as they hurried home. And the painters were probably out along
the Gorath River with their easels, catching that golden
light across the river that flowed through the heart of
the city as the sun gilded the Cathedral's scepters. He
wondered how many of those people had heard the
news? If they hadn't heard yet, they would soon
enough, even if Duke Salthar and Bishop Executor
Wylsynn attempted to conceal it. That would be not
only futile but particularly stupid, in Thirsk's opinion,
yet he'd seen ample examples of Wylsynn Lainyr's doing equally stupid things. Salthar was probably smart
enough to argue against it, but in this case Thirsk could
count on his own service superior, Duke Thorast, to
support any effort to hide the truth for as long as he
possibly could.

Although not, of course, for all the same reasons as
Lainyr.

"Do we know how it happened, My Lord?" Stywyrt

Baiket, *Chihiro*'s CO and Thirsk's flag captain, asked quietly. "I mean, they had over two hundred thousand men and Eastshare had less than *twenty* thousand!"

"The dispatches are less than detailed," the earl replied, never looking away from the harbor's soothing panorama. "Messages tend to be that way when people have to send them by wyvern, and the semaphore line was cut early in the Charisian attack. One thing they do make clear, however, is that the real threat didn't come out of Fort Tairys. It wasn't Eastshare; they got an entirely separate force down through eastern Cliff Peak past the Desnairian cavalry at Cheyvair. One big enough to block—and hold—the high road through the Kyplyngyr Forest." He shrugged heavily. "According to the message I've seen"—he didn't mention that he wasn't supposed to have seen it . . . and wouldn't have, if not for Bishop Staiphan Maik—"Ahlverez did his damnedest to fight his way through them. His attacks obviously hurt the Charisians badly, but they pretty much *gutted* our part of the army in the process, so Harless finally agreed to pull the majority of his own infantry back from Ohadlyn's Gap for a second attempt to clear the high road. That's when Eastshare attacked out of Fort Tairys, and with one hell of a lot more than twenty thousand men."

He gazed out over the harbor for another moment, then turned on his heel to face his subordinates.

"My best guess, reading between the lines, is that the Charisians and Siddarmarkians must've had a lot closer to *seventy* thousand men, probably more, and too many of the Desnairians were cavalry. Even an admiral knows that's *not* the sort of troops equipped or trained to take on entrenched infantry in the damned woods, and the Army of Shiloh was half starved and riddled with sickness. I doubt Ahlverez and Harless between them could actually have put much over half their official strength into the field. And let's face it—a fight with the Imperial Charisian Army at anything like equal numerical odds is a losing proposition."

Sir Ahbail Bahrdailahn, Thirsk's flag lieutenant,

looked uneasy at that remark. Not because he disagreed, but because that sort of frankness could be dangerous. Thirsk knew that, but if he couldn't trust these men there was no one on the face of Safehold he *could* trust. If one of them was prepared to inform the Inquisition that he was preaching defeatism when he shared the truth with them, there was no point even trying to stem the disaster he saw flowing towards his kingdom like some vast, dark tide.

"Do we have any idea of how severe our losses have been?" Baiket asked somberly, and Thirsk grimaced.

"Not really. Or if anybody does have an estimate, it hasn't been shared with me. I do know Hanth inflicted heavy casualties on the Army of the Seridahn when he attacked out of Thesmar, though."

The flag captain's eyes flickered at that, and Thirsk didn't blame him. Officially, Sir Fahstyr Rychtyr's command had been renamed solely as an honor, in perhaps belated recognition of the importance to the Jihad and the Kingdom of its accomplishments. But only an idiot—which Baiket was not—could have failed to note Mother Church's tendency to rename armies in what certainly *looked* like efforts to stiffen their morale in the face of unmitigated disaster. And *that*, the earl thought, did not bode well.

"The heretics've driven General Rychtyr almost all the way back to Evyrtyn," he continued. "I don't know what his losses were at Cheryk and Trevyr, but it doesn't sound good. And Ahlverez is probably going to lose a lot of whatever he managed to pull out of the Kyplyngyr. I don't see how anyone could've gotten a message to him yet to warn him Rychtyr's lost Cheryk, much less Trevyr, so he's probably marching straight towards Hanth right this minute. And we've lost touch with everything east of Syrk on the Saint Alyk, as well." He shook his head and puffed out his cheeks. "Frankly, I'll be astonished if we get as much as a third of Ahlverez's troops back, and I wouldn't count on *any* of his artillery making it out."

The only sound was wind and wave as his subordinates

looked at one another in dismay. Clearly the rumor mill had yet to catch up with how bad it truly was. Probably, he thought dryly, because the gossip mongers couldn't believe even a Desnairian could truly have proved as inept as the late and—in Dohlar, at any rate—*very* unlamented Duke of Harless.

"The good news—or as good as it gets, anyway—is that about a third of the riflemen headed up to reinforce Rychtyr are equipped with the new Saint Kylmahns," he wondered if his subordinates found that name as ironic as he did, given who'd actually designed the new rifle, "so at least they'll have breechloaders of their own. And if he can hang on for another few fivedays, he'll have at least a couple of batteries of the new rifled angle-guns, too. Combined with the weather and his entrenchments, he ought to be able to hold his position fairly well. Certainly against anything Hanth can throw at him."

The others nodded, as if he'd just said something hopeful, and he bit his tongue against an unworthy temptation to point out that the Army of Shiloh's disaster had revealed that unlike the Republic of Siddarmark Army or the Earl of Hanth's force of Marines and seamen, the Imperial Charisian Army was amply provided with the sort of cavalry—and highly mobile, new model field artillery—needed to work around a fortified position and cut the canal in its rear. Once the forces no doubt pursuing Ahlverez at this very moment reached Evyrtyn, Rychtyr was going to find himself in an even more unenviable position than the rolling disaster which had enveloped the Army of Shiloh. Unless, of course, he had both the wit and the intestinal fortitude to fall back along the Sheryl-Seridahn Canal faster than they could cut it behind him.

From what he knew of Rychtyr, he certainly had the wit, and he might well have the moral courage. Unfortunately, he might not have it, either. And even if he did, that was the sort of decision which could have fatal consequences. Lywys Gardynyr had had a little personal experience of his own in that regard, and the

Inquisition had grown even less patient with faint-heartedness in the service of Mother Church over the last few years.

"Sir Rainos always was a bit . . . heedless, My Lord," Baiket said. "You might say that runs in the family."

Thirsk's lips quirked in a sour smile at his flag captain's none too oblique reference to Rainos Ahlverez's cousin, Sir Faidel Ahlverez, the deceased Duke of Malikai. Malikai had also been a cousin by marriage of Aibram Zaivyair, the Duke of Thorast, who—like Ahlverez—held Thirsk personally responsible for Malikai's disastrous defeat off Armageddon Reef. It wasn't hard to follow Baiket's logic, and the truth was that much as Thirsk regretted what had happened to the Army of Shiloh, he was far from blind to the way in which any damage to Ahlverez's reputation and standing had to reflect upon the men who'd made themselves his patrons. And anything that weakened Thorast's grip on the Navy had to be a good thing from Lywys Gardynyr's perspective.

"I think we can all agree Sir Rainos was . . . overconfident before he set out for Alyksberg," he said out loud. "And if I'm going to be honest, I suppose I should admit the thought of his coming a cropper personally doesn't fill my heart with dismay," he added with a generous thousand percent understatement. "But I've read some of the dispatches he sent home to Duke Fern and Duke Salthar. On that basis, I have to say that however overconfident he may've been before Alyksberg, he did his damnedest to prevent most of Duke Harless' . . . questionable decisions, shall we say."

He decided not to mention the letters he'd received from Shulmyn Rahdgyrz, the Baron of Tymplahr. He hoped his old friend was still alive somewhere out there in the muddy, bloody wilderness of the South March, but according to Tymplahr, Sir Rainos Ahlverez had turned out to be remarkably unlike certain of his kinsmen. He'd actually learned from experience.

"Whatever part Sir Rainos may have played in bringing all this about, what's happened to his army's far too serious for me to take any satisfaction from how it may have damaged his reputation," he went on more soberly. "And not just because of the human cost. He had over half the Army's total field strength under his command, Stywyrt. That's probably entirely gone, for all practical purposes. Even if we get some of the regiments back, they'll have to be completely brought back up to strength, reorganized, and—undoubtedly—*reequipped* before they can possibly be effective fighting units again. And where do you think they're going to look for the manpower—and the weapons—for that?"

Baiket's blue eyes darkened and he nodded soberly. The Navy had been reduced to a much smaller slice of the kingdom's available resources in order to equip and field the army the Temple had demanded be launched into Siddarmark. Now that so much of that army had been destroyed and the threat of an enemy counterattack across Dohlar's eastern frontiers had become real, the Navy was only too likely to find itself on even shorter rations.

"My Lord," Khapahr said carefully, "they can't reduce our priorities too much. Not on the new projects, especially."

"They may decide they don't have any choice," Thirsk disagreed grimly. "When there's a slash lizard breaking down your front door, the great dragon raiding your neighbor's pasture has to take second priority, don't you think?"

"My Lord, the Charisians aren't loose in our *neighbor's* pasture; they're loose in *our* pasture, or they damned well will be soon enough. The Harchongians're going to be hit hard enough if they start sending raiding forces into the western Gulf again, but surely the Army has to understand the consequences if we lose control of the *eastern* Gulf!"

Thirsk nodded unhappily. His reports on the new armored galleons the Charisians had used to retake Claw Island were far short of complete. Out of Admiral Krahl's entire garrison, less than a dozen men—the most senior an army lieutenant—had escaped the debacle by commandeering a sixteen-foot sailing dinghy, somehow evading the Charisian pickets, and crossing the six hundred and seventy miles of stormy salt water between Claw Island and the Harchongese province of Kyznetzov.

In the winter . . . in an open boat . . . without a single trained naval officer to get them through it.

He was astounded they'd survived and profoundly grateful for what little they'd been able to report, but it would have been ever so much more useful if one of the *naval* officers had gotten away. All the actual escapees had been able to tell anyone was that at least two of the Charisian galleons had been invulnerable to the defending artillery. Obviously, they must have been armored, like the "smoking ships" the Charisians had sent rampaging through the canals and rivers in Bishop Militant Bahrnabai's rear last summer. The good news was that they'd been galleons, propelled by the masts and sails he understood, not whatever deviltry the river ironclads used. But to offset that smidgeon of sunlight, the artillery they'd ignored had been naval guns equipped to fire not only explosive shells but red-hot round shot—*heavy* round shot, not the lighter projectiles of the field artillery which had failed to stop the ironclads along the canals.

*At least there were only two of them*, he reminded himself. *So far, at least.*

"Ahlvyn's not the most diplomatic fellow in the world, My Lord," Baiket said, "but he does have a point. Admiral Rohsail knows his duty, and he'll do his best, but if the *batteries* couldn't stop those bastards . . . ."

"I know. I know!" Thirsk shrugged irritably. Not because he was angry at Baiket, but because the flag captain had such an excellent point. Still . . . .

"I agree with everything both of you've said. On the other hand, all the witnesses we have agree there were only two of those armored galleons in the attack. It's possible they're wrong, but I don't think so." The earl smiled tightly. "We've had a bit of experience of our own with how much iron it takes to armor even a relatively small galley. I realize the Charisians appear to be able to conjure iron and steel magically out of thin air, but it has to take even *them* a little time to produce enough armor for ships that size. From the description of their armament, they're a lot bigger than any ironclad small enough for river or canal use could possibly be, and not even Charisians could build and armor something like that with a snap of their fingers. They're *galleons*, too, not . . . whatever those damned smokepots are! What does that suggest?"

"That the inland ironclads are either too unseaworthy or too short-legged to make the trip from Corisande, My Lord," Baiket said, eyes narrowed in thought. "Or maybe both." He nodded slowly. "However those riverboats of theirs move, they're burning *something* to produce all that smoke, and there has to be a limit on how much coal or wood they can load into something that size, especially if they're also going to armor it and put guns into it."

"I think that's probably true." Thirsk nodded. "It's not something I plan to count on, but one thing we have to avoid is *overestimating* Charis' capabilities. I know it's better to be pessimistic than to be overly optimistic, but we can't paralyze ourselves with 'what-ifs.' Unless they have a hell of a lot more regular galleons based at Claw Island than reports suggest, we can meet their fleet on more than equal terms, and even an armored galleon needs spars to move. Between our own galleons and Lieutenant Zhwaigair's screw-galleys—and that other project of his—I think we'd have a pretty good chance of handing them a serious defeat if they were foolish enough to come out where we can get at them. And the fact that they seem to be staying close to home at Claw Island now that they've retaken it suggests they may feel the same way about it."

"For now, at least, My Lord," Baiket said, diffidently but stubbornly, and Thirsk nodded again.

"For now," he acknowledged. "That's always subject

to change. But it does suggest we have a little time in hand to continue to push Zhwaigair's projects. And in answer to the point Ahlvyn raised, I assure you the Army is aware of what'll happen to its supplies if the Imperial Charisian Navy comes east of the Narrows. Especially if they get as deep as the Gulf of Tanshar or Hankey Sound. Or, if it doesn't, at least it's not because Pawal Hahlynd and I haven't talked ourselves blue in the face explaining it to Salthar and the rest of them! So even though that slash lizard at the front door seems to have an awful lot of sharp teeth, they're still going to have to pay at least some attention to the great dragon in the pasture, and they know it."

He grimaced, his eyes bleak.

"We're not going to have the kind of priority we really need, but they can't cut us off completely, and they know it," he told his subordinates, and prayed he was telling them the truth.

▼ ▼ ▼

*No, they probably can't, My Lord*, Sir Domynyk Staynair thought. *I wish they would, but they won't . . . damn it.*

The high admiral sat back from his desk in his day cabin, listening to the nighttime sounds of his flagship, and busied his hands filling the bowl of his favorite pipe with tobacco while he contemplated the imagery he'd just watched. Nahrmahn might be dead, he reflected, but that hadn't affected his ability to recognize information other members of the inner circle needed to see.

The notion that Thirsk almost certainly would be able to make the case against cutting the Dohlaran Navy to the bone was less than palatable for several reasons. The earl was unquestionably Charis' most formidable naval opponent, and the time he'd had to train his fleet was rubbing off on his subordinates. Subordinates like Sir Dahrand Rohsail, for just one example. Rohsail, commanding the RDN's Western Squadron, had demonstrated a depressing level of competence, despite the loss of his base at Claw Island. Pawal Hahlynd, the man Thirsk had chosen to command Dynnys Zhwaigair's screw-galleys, was another case in point. And however outclassed those screw-galleys might be compared to the new steam-powered ironclads or even one of the sail-powered *Thunderers*, they were more than a match for any of the wooden galleons which still composed ninety-five percent of the Imperial Charisian Navy's total line of battle.

Rock Point's—and Cayleb Ahrmahk's—respect for Thirsk and the navy he'd built was the real reason Earl Sharpfield had been dispatched to retake Claw Island and establish a forward base—and coaling station—there. They'd sent him months earlier than they'd originally planned, and they hadn't been able to assign him all the firepower they would have preferred, but he'd done them proud. Claw Island would be a critical part of their end game strategy for the Gulf of Dohlar once the *King Haarahld VII*-class ships commissioned, but they'd hoped it might also serve as a support base for a squadron of the new *City*-class coastal ironclads. The *Cities* were too big to operate along the mainland canals the way the *River*- and *River II*-class ships were intended to, and they were over four knots slower, but that extra displacement gave them marginally thicker armor and almost twice the endurance. More to the point—and despite Halcom Bahrns' near miraculous feat of seamanship in the Tarot Channel—they were *far* better seaboats.

Unfortunately, they wouldn't be sending any of them to Sharpfield for quite a while after all, because while Thirsk might be their most *capable* opponent, he wasn't currently the most *dangerous*. That honor, difficult though any Charisian found it to believe, belonged to Sir Slokym Dahrnail, Duke of Shairn and navy minister of the Empire of Desnair, the least nautically inclined great power of Safehold.

Most Desnairians got seasick in a bathtub, but unlike the rest of Desnair, Shairn boasted an extensive fishing fleet which had dared the fish-rich waters off

Samson's Land and The Weeping Sisters for generations, despite their proximity to Armageddon Reef.
Their catch had provided the duchy with a valuable
export, and the House of Dahrnail had been smart
enough to recognize its importance. The last four dukes
had adopted policies which favored both the fisheries and the coastal trade, and when Duke Kohlman,
Desnair's previous naval minister, sought asylum in
Charis following the destruction of Ithryia, Sir Slokym
had struck Mahrys as his logical successor. The fact
that Shairn was a passionate Temple Loyalist, who
hated Charis with all his heart, had made him an ideal
successor in the eyes of the Church, as well, and the effective annihilation of the Dohlaran battle fleet at
Ithryia had allowed him to pursue a commerce raiding
strategy with all his resources.

Kohlman had wanted to do the same thing for years,
and he'd begun laying down light, fast cruisers as soon as
the Battle of the Markovian Sea demonstrated (to
anyone who could see) that fighting the ICN at sea had
become nothing short of suicidal. The Church had resisted that policy strongly, however, so Kohlman had
turned to issuing letters of marque to private shipown-
ers. Even that had been more than the Church wanted,
on the theory that it diverted resources from building
up the navy, but, ironically, Desnair's devastating defeat
at Ithryia had forced both Church and Crown to adopt
the "traitor" duke's proposals, and Shairn—who was
no fool, despite his religious bigotry—had driven them
hard ever since.

Which was why well over half of Sir Domynyk
Staynair's warships were now tied down in commerce
protection and convoy duties. There was a very good
reason he'd sent Payter Shain to wipe out the Gulf of
Jahras' privateer bases—hopefully for good, although
Rock Point was far from confident they wouldn't rebuild quickly if the pressure was ever taken off again—
but that left thousands upon thousands of miles of
additional coastline, especially along the stretch between Traykhos and Shairn. Scores of fleet, weatherly

schooners were swarming out to sea, and the situation was growing steadily more serious. Just six days ago, although Rock Point hadn't yet received official word, over a dozen of those cruisers—half of them navy ships, not just privateers, and acting with far better coordination than he cared to think about—had swamped a convoy from Tellesberg to Siddar City. The outnumbered escort had managed to prevent any of the half-dozen troopships under its care from being seriously damaged and had actually sunk two of the raiders, but no less than six cargo ships had been cut out despite all they could accomplish. One of the escorting schooners had been destroyed, as well, and two others—and one of the three defending galleons—had been damaged.

There'd been no survivors from any of the merchantmen or from HMS *Thistle*. The only "good" news from that perspective was that all of the wounded had been slaughtered out of hand rather than returned to Desnair for the Punishment. The captured cargoes, however, had provided Desnair with five thousand precious M96 rifles, almost a hundred three-inch mortars, and two entire batteries of four-inch rifled field guns . . . among other things. Charis was only lucky the damage hadn't been still worse—and that the overwhelmed escorts had been able to protect the troopships. But Rock Point couldn't count on that happening the next time around, and what had been a constant, niggling trickle of losses in other privateer attacks was growing steadily more serious.

Rock Point grimaced around his pipe stem, then struck a Shan-wei's candle and lit it. He took time to be sure it was drawing properly, savoring the sweet taste of the smoke, before he waved out the candle and dropped it into an ashtray. Then he sighed heavily and admitted the disagreeable truth.

Even with the Navy straining every sinew, he simply didn't have the escorts to put every merchantman into a convoy. Over a third of all Charisian merchantmen were still forced to sail independently, and while almost all of them were now armed, they were scarcely regular men-of-war. Nor did Rock Point have the ship strength to blockade such an enormous coastline in order to prevent the raiders from getting to sea to attack them. That was the reason Shain was in the Gulf of Jahras . . . and also the reason the high admiral wouldn't be sending the first new *Cities* off to Claw Island, after all. No, he was going to have a better use for those ships considerably closer to home. Or a more pressing one, at least. Sharpfield was just going to have to make do until more of the *Cities* were available, and it was entirely likely the *King Haraahlds* would be ready by then, as well.

Sir Domynyk Staynair didn't like it, but that was just the way it was. And however much he respected Thirsk's capabilities, at least when Sharpfield *did* receive his reinforcements, there wasn't going to be one damned thing Dohlar could do about it. And in the meantime . . . .

*Zhaztro's not going to like it, either,* he reflected, drawing on his pipe. *I imagine he's going to squawk about it—respectfully, of course!—when I break the news to him, too. But he'll get over it, especially when he considers the consolation prize. And*—the high admiral smiled grimly—*he'll do one hell of a good job once he does.*

. IV .
## West of Allyntyn,
## Northland Province,
## Republic of Siddarmark

The cold was bone-numbing.

At least there wasn't any wind, but even without the extra chill factor, the midday temperature had climbed no higher than twelve degrees on the Fahrenheit scale, and it was already falling steeply once more. After sunset it would drop to twenty degrees below zero—or lower—on the same scale, and the wind would be picking up once more as another arctic front began making its way through sometime after Langhorne's Watch. Snow lay horse knee-high and powdery on level ground; where any obstacle had offered the opportunity, drifts with sharply sculpted edges rose as high as a man's head or higher. The breath of the Raven's Land caribou hauling the heavy sleds rose like smoke in the frigid air, and the sturdy High Hallows under the mounted men jetted white vapor like the fumes of an Old Earth dragon. The sky was a polished blue bowl, harder and colder than steel, without a hint of cloud. It was only a few hours past midday, but the sun was already well to the west, dipping towards the peaks of the Meirstrom Mountains and promising that the brief northern evening—and much longer winter *night*— were not far away.

It was one of the coldest, bleakest vistas imaginable, Kynt Clareyk, the Baron of Green Valley, thought approvingly. He had no doubt the men of 1st Corps sorely missed the snug barracks they'd enjoyed at Allyntyn, but that was fine with him. And with them, too, if the truth be known. They were as impatient to be about their assigned task as he was.

He glanced to the northeast, where a party of Siddarmarkian engineers swarmed about the fire-charred skeleton of a semaphore station. There was no way to tell whether it had been fired by Temple Loyalists during the Sword of Schueler's initial onslaught or by Siddarmarkians loyal to their lord protector as they were driven from Northland by the rebellion, but whoever had set the blaze had done a less than thorough job of actually wrecking the station. Cables, pulleys, and the roof of the station crew's barracks had been destroyed, yet the towering masts and the barracks' stone walls remained, and the engineers would have it back in service by tomorrow afternoon. The stations were closer together across the bleak, rolling tableland of the Midhold Plateau because of how bad visibility became in the winter. Even with them restored to service, Green Valley's communications with Allyntyn were likely to be sporadic, given that same limited visibility, but they ought to be good enough. His communications with the rest of the *inner circle* couldn't care less about weather conditions, but since he'd left close to two-thirds of the Army of Midhold behind at Allyntyn under General Dymytryoh Brohkamp, who commanded his 2nd Corps, it behooved him to maintain the closest contact with Brohkamp that he could.

There was a reason he'd stripped Brigadier Wylsynn Traigair's 3rd Brigade, out of 1st Corps, transferred it temporarily to 2nd Corps, and left Brohkamp behind. Without Traigair, General Ahntahn Makrohry's 1st Corps consisted only of two battalions of the 1st Scout Sniper Regiment, 3rd Mounted Brigade, and General Eystavyo Gardynyr's 4th Division (Mountain). On the other hand, Makrohry himself had been raised amid the beautiful, bitter peaks of northern Chisholm's Snow Crest Mountains, and all of his units had been exhaustively trained in winter warfare at Raylzberg, perched high in the westernmost spur of the Lonely Mountains above High Hallow's Stonewater Lake. The Royal Chisholmian Army had made a point of acclimating all of its units to winter marches, but only about a third of the entire army had been trained in actual winter *war fighting*, which was a much more demanding regimen.

Even with their training, it would have been difficult or impossible for the new Imperial Charisian Army to have put this many men into the field this far north at this time of year without the manufactories of Old Charis. The Chisholmian experts had designed the necessary equipment, but their designs—tweaked here and there without their knowledge by an AI named Owl—had been *built* by Rhaiyan Mychail's textile manufactories and Ehdwyrd Howsmyn's foundries. Green Valley suspected that many of those foundry and manufactory workers in semi-tropical Charis hadn't quite been able to believe in weather conditions severe enough to require the items they'd been making, but that hadn't stopped them from churning them out in quantities no one on the Church of God Awaiting's side could possibly have matched.

The column of marching infantry swung along on their snowshoes with the practiced gait of men who'd spent the last several five-days regaining and sharpening their skills. It was unlikely many Army of God patrols would be out and about in the snow and cold (in fact, Green Valley knew from the SNARCs that none of them were), yet the scout sniper battalions ranged well out in front of the main column on cross-country skis. He couldn't exactly tell them there was no one in the vicinity, and he wouldn't have even if he could. There were limits to how many "inspired guesses" he could make, and however readily he could talk with the other members of the inner circle, he was limited to more mundane methods of communication with his subunit commanders . . . none of whom had the SNARC access he did. Even when the SNARCs told him exactly what they might be walking into, it wouldn't do any good unless he had some way to tell *them*, which all too often he would not. They needed the sort of reconnaissance which was the scout snipers' specialty, and it was best that they stay in the habit of making certain they had it.

Behind the infantry, caribou and snow lizards hauled heavy cargo sleds, loaded with food, fuel, forage, and ammunition. Each infantry support squad was accompanied by its assigned caribou, pulling its mortars and ammunition on dedicated sleds, and each twelve-man squad of infantry towed two sleds of its own. One normally carried the men's packs, sparing them that sixty-pound load, at least, while the other was loaded with the arctic tent assigned to that squad. The tent's outer layer was steel thistle silk—light, strong, and so tightly woven it was virtually impervious to wind. The inner layer was woven cotton, quilted with eiderdown, and when the tent was erected there was an insulating two-inch airspace between the layers. The same sled also carried a lightweight steel chimney and a relatively small but highly efficient oil-fired stove. In a worst-case scenario, a smoke hood could be rigged at the base of the chimney to permit other fuels to be used in an open fire pit, although that would be very much a second—or third—choice for the tent's occupants. It also would have posed a small problem for the tightly rolled caribou-hide sleeping mats strapped to the sleds to provide an insulating floor inside the tents.

Sleeping bags had been provided, as well, made in three layers—an inner removable liner, once again of steel thistle silk, followed by a thickly quilted insulating layer of eiderdown, followed by an outer layer of additional, insulated wind-resistant steel thistle silk. The liberal use of thistle silk was expensive, even for the Charisian textile industry, but it was no longer *prohibitively* expensive, and it also meant they were light enough to carry rolled and lashed to the top of a rifleman's pack. They were undeniably bulky, however, and because they made awkward loads, they were normally stowed on the sleds with the tents.

The men themselves wore white snow smocks over fleece-lined outer parkas and trousers of supple, well-tanned caribou hide. Inside that came inner parkas of steel thistle silk-lined, triple-knit wool over woolen shirts and corduroy trousers, and more steel thistle silk had been expended on each man's long-sleeved and legged underwear. That "layered" effect was essential for arctic clothing, and the silk served as a barrier against the menace of water vapor. Arctic air could accept less water as vapor, so moisture like sweat quickly condensed out of it. The steel thistle silk prevented perspiration from saturating the layers outside it, which would quickly have destroyed their insulating capacity.

To protect his hands, each man wore heavy, multilayered mittens or thick fleece-lined gloves over an inner glove of knitted wool and a separate liner of steel thistle silk. The mittens were warmer than gloves because they gathered and held the heat of the entire hand, not individual fingers, but they were clumsy, to say the least, and the gloves allowed greater manual dexterity when it was required.

Boots had been as carefully considered as the rest of the troops' gear. Made of sealskin and lined with fleece, they had double soles and an inner, moccasin-like liner which could be removed to dry, or worn as a sort of house shoe inside one of the tents.

The weight of all those garments was a significant burden, but one which allowed them to move and operate in temperatures far below freezing. Nature had provided the caribou and snow lizards with their own formidable insulation, and the High Hallows had been bred by centuries of Chisholmian breeders for conditions very similar to these. Nonetheless, arctic rugs had been provided for the horses as additional protection if the temperature plunged still lower.

The snow made marching difficult, even with snowshoes, but it provided easy going for the sleds which followed in the broad, beaten-down lanes the infantry's snowshoes provided. In many ways, conditions were actually less difficult than they might have been for dragons pulling conventional wagons cross-country in mid-summer.

*And best of all*, Green Valley thought, *no one on the other side has a clue of just how winter-mobile we are.*

If he'd ever entertained any doubts on that subject, the SNARC imagery of the Army of God's outposts would have put them to rest. Very few of those half-frozen men, shivering in inadequate clothing as they crouched around fires in whatever structures they'd found or whatever huts they'd been able to piece together, had any interest in going *anywhere* else. Nor would they survive if their shelters were destroyed, Green Valley reflected, his expression bleak under the two layers of snow mask—what would have been called balaclavas back on Old Earth—and the ski goggles he and every other man in the column wore. Freezing to death was a very unpleasant way to die, and the baron took no pleasure in the thought of inflicting that particular death even on his enemies.

Which wouldn't stop him from doing it for a moment.

.V.

Two Recon Skimmers,
Above East Haven,
and
Nimue's Cave,
The Mountains of Light,
The Temple Lands

"I never imagined clouds could look so beautiful from above," Aivah Pahrsahn said softly. She sat in the recon skimmer's rear seat, turned to the left to look down from the rear canopy over its wingtip as it banked, and the moon shining down through the thin, cold atmosphere turned the clouds' summits into shining silver and their gulfs into bottomless ebon canyons far below. "I always knew God was an artist, but this . . . ."

She shook her head, and Merlin smiled as he gazed out through his own canopy. They'd come two thousand miles from Siddar City in a little over three hours; they should reach their destination in the Mountains of Light in another hour and a half. He'd been a bit surprised by how calmly Aivah had taken the materialization of not one but two recon skimmers out of the snowy dark, but however calm she'd been, her sense of wonder had been obvious. If she'd felt any trepidation at climbing the access ladder into the needle-nosed, swept-wing skimmer, she'd concealed it admirably, and her enjoyment of the trip so far reminded Merlin irresistibly of Cayleb Ahrmahk's first flight.

He leveled the skimmer as he completed the turn, and glanced out over his starboard wing to where an identical skimmer kept meticulous station upon him. He hadn't initially anticipated needing both of them, but each could carry only a single extra passenger and Aivah had insisted upon being accompanied by Sandaria Ghatfryd, who'd been her personal maid for the last two decades. At first, he'd been surprised by the anxiety that seemed to indicate, but that lasted for only a very few minutes after the two women had joined him in the service alley behind Madam Pahrsahn's luxurious townhouse.

Sandaria was a good two inches shorter than Aivah, with mousy brown hair, a swarthy complexion, and an even more pronounced epicanthic fold than most Safeholdians, courtesy of her Harchongese mother. Merlin knew she'd been with Aivah for at least twenty years; what he hadn't known (until Aivah explained there in the alley) was that she'd actually been with her ever since Nynian Rychtair's convent days. In fact, Sandaria Ghatfryd had been a novitiate at the same time, and today she was a senior member of the Sisters of Saint Kohdy, not to mention Aivah's second-in-command . . . and closest confidante.

Sandaria, unlike Aivah, had evinced a little nervousness when they emerged from the city via one of Aivah's discreet routes and she discovered that she and Aivah would be aboard separate skimmers. She'd handled the silent appearance of the craft remarkably calmly; it was clearly the *separation* that concerned her. Unfortunately, except for the armored personnel carriers—and the full-sized assault shuttles—in Nimue's Cave, they were the only passenger vehicles available. The assault shuttles were about the size of an old pre-space jumbo jet, and hiding something that size in proximity to Siddar City would have been . . . a nontrivial challenge even with Federation technology. The APCs were smaller and more readily concealable than assault shuttles, but they were also much slower. Even on counter-grav, they were uncompromisingly subsonic, capable of only about five hundred miles per hour, and Merlin preferred to have a supersonic dash capability in hand, just in case. And while the far smaller air lorries were easier to conceal, they'd been designed to transport *cargo*. It had never occurred to anyone they might find themselves shuttling people back and forth from Nimue's Cave in job lots. Now that the possibility had suggested itself to them, Owl's remotes were busy converting two of those lorries into air buses at this very moment, but the process would require another day or so, and no one had wanted to wait the extra time.

Besides, the second recon skimmer had let him bring along a second pilot.

"How much longer will it take, Merlin?" Aivah asked now, and he looked down into the small display which connected him to the rear cockpit.

Aivah looked back out of it at him as if she'd been using coms all her life. She'd operated the controls he'd demonstrated to her with equal facility and confidence, and a smile tugged at the corners of his lips as he reflected on why she'd needed only a single demonstration.

*Yet another mystery solved*, he thought dryly. *No wonder the SNARCs and I never caught her decoding anything. She never* needed *to! And I do feel a little better about her remembering details of Ahbraim and Merlin to match against each other. "I have a very good memory," indeed!*

The rare gene group which produced true eidetic memory had been discovered (many skeptics had argued that "invented" was a better verb) in the mid-twenty-first century, and gengineering it into children had been something of a fad for the next fifty years. It had been far less damaging than *some* of those fads had proven before the whole field of human genetic design was brought under rigorous control, but with the development of direct neural interfacing and the cloud storage of memories, *everyone* had effective eidetic memory. Interest in the ability had waned, and far fewer parents had opted to build it into their offspring.

Nonetheless, it had remained far more common than it had been among earlier generations and it still cropped up occasionally—not often, but more frequently than on pre-space Old Earth—on Safehold.

Nynian Rychtair had it. She'd never needed to consult her codebooks when she wrote or read a message, because she carried them—*all* of them—in her head. Merlin and Owl had always known she smuggled a voluminous correspondence back and forth across the Border States, despite the war, but so far as they'd been able to tell, all of it was fairly innocuous: correspondence with the business managers she'd left behind, letters to some of the young women who had worked for Ahnzhelyk Phonda for so long, or messages from refugees to family and friends left behind, for example. They'd been unable to keep track of all of that correspondence once it flowed into Zion or other major Temple Land cities, and since they'd "known" none of it had been encoded—and that Aivah was on their side, at least for now—they hadn't actually tried all that hard, given all the other charges on Owl's surveillance ability.

"We should be there in about another ninety minutes," he said now. "We'll get there well before dawn, not that I expect anyone would be in a position to see us even at high noon. Not in the middle of the Mountains of Light in March."

"I imagine that would be . . . somewhat unlikely," she acknowledged, and he snorted.

"I think you can pretty much take it for granted. That's the real reason Nimue's Cave was located here in the first place."

"'Nimue's Cave'?" she repeated with a quirked eyebrow. "That's an odd name, even for a *seijins*' training camp. Does Captain Chwaeriau's name have anything to do with the person it's named for?"

"Actually, it does. Quite a lot, in fact. I can't explain exactly what the connection is—not yet—but I think you'll understand once we get around to explaining everything else to you."

"I'm looking forward to that . . . I think." Aivah's eyes gleamed with anticipation, yet his indirect reference to how little she still knew, how much faith it had required to come this far on the basis of so few hard facts, awakened an undeniable darkness under the anticipation. "I have to admit it was probably wise of you not to tell me quite how far we'd have to travel for that explanation until we were in the air. I won't guarantee I wouldn't have backed out and run for my life, despite Saint Kohdy's journal and his description of his *hikousen*, if you'd told me any sooner!"

She did not, he noticed, mention how much easier the isolation of their destination would make it if the inner circle ultimately decreed she must disappear.

"Oh, I think you're made of sterner stuff than that," he said out loud. "Still, honesty compels me to admit that my timing wasn't exactly a coincidence."

"No, *really?* I never would have thought anything of the sort!"

"Of course you wouldn't have," he agreed gravely. "On the other hand, I felt confident that someone of your . . . accomplishments would understand my thinking without taking it personally."

"I *think* that's a compliment."

"A very deep one, as a matter of fact. In many ways, you remind me a great deal of Prince Nahrmahn."

"Ah." She smiled. "I never met Prince Nahrmahn. For that matter, I never crossed swords with him professionally, either. Still, everything I've ever learned about him suggests he was one of the best at the Great Game. I deeply regretted his death. Is it true he died protecting his wife from one of Clyntahn's Rakurai with his own body?"

"Yes. Yes, it is."

"Then I regret his death even more deeply." Aivah sighed and turned to look back out through her canopy. "I've seen enough of cynicism, narcissism, and self-centeredness to last me two or three lifetimes. That's what happens when you grow up too close to the vicarate. Sometimes it's hard to remember there really are people willing to risk everything they have for the ones they love."

"Odd," Merlin said. She turned back to up at him from the display once more, and this time his smile was almost gentle. "As far as I can tell, you've spent your entire life risking everything for people you love even if you've never met them."

She opened her mouth, as if she meant to protest, then paused. Their eyes locked once again, and then, slowly, she nodded.

"You might have a point," she told him. "I won't say it's the way I've always thought of myself, and I won't pretend my motivation, especially in the beginning, didn't have a lot more to do with anger and revenge than with love. But at least I already knew there truly were people in the world who loved me—loved *me*, whatever my miserable excuse for a father was like— because I had Adorai and her parents. And I had Sister Klairah at the convent, and Sandaria, and the rest of the Sisters since then."

"Yes, you did. I don't doubt for a minute that the need for revenge—vengeance—was a huge part of what started you on this road. But I've worked with you pretty closely for the last year or so, and I've talked to Adorai. I think it was that love you're talking about that turned what you wanted into justice rather than personal vengeance."

"Somehow I don't think of myself as the new holy lawgiver," she said dryly.

"I remember something Nahrmahn said once," he countered. "We were talking about saints, and he said he suspected most of them had been pains in the ass." Aivah chuckled, and he grinned. Then he sobered. "For a lot of reasons—reasons I think will become clear to you shortly—the last thing *I'd* want to be is a 'holy' any-thing. That's not who or what I am, and I've seen where that kind of belief in your own infallibility can lead."

"So have I, Merlin. So have I. And I think you and Cayleb and Maikel Staynair are right. Even if we man-age to destroy the Group of Four we've got, the only way to prevent something just like it from reemerging is to break the Church's monopoly on God's own authority." She shook her head, eyes sad once more. "I don't like admitting that, because there's so much *good* in what the Church could accomplish—so many good things the Church *has* accomplished—and even as a Sister of Saint Kohdy, it's hard to reject the vicarate's authority. To decide the Grand Vicar doesn't speak with God's own voice. But if God's children are going to live together the way He wants them to, the thing His Church has become needs to be broken. I don't think Samyl Wylsynn could ever have accepted that in his heart of hearts, but I also think that deep inside he knew it was true, anyway. And I'm sure Hauwerd did."

Merlin nodded, his own eyes dark as he wondered how she was going to react to the full truth. Despite everything she'd said about Kohdy's journal, even her belief that the original Adams and Eves had been "somewhere else" while the archangels created Safehold, the depth of her faith—of her belief in what the Church "was supposed to be"—upheld her like a pillar of iron. How would she respond when she learned what the foundation of that iron pillar truly was? And how would *he* deal with what he'd have to do if she responded . . . poorly? The decision to take her and Sandaria to the cave would give him options he hadn't had far too many other times, yet even so . . . .

"Well, it won't be so very much longer before you and Sandaria are in a position to see exactly why *we* think that way," he told her.

▼ ▼ ▼

The recon skimmers grounded side-by-side in the vast main cavern of the complex Merlin had christened "Nimue's Cave" so many years before. The canopies retracted, and Aivah and Sandaria sat very still, gazing up at the towering, glass-smooth vault above them. In a way, Merlin suspected, they found the sheer size and sweep of that obviously artificial chamber even more impressive than the skimmers which had brought them here.

He climbed up out of his flight couch and dropped lightly to the cavern floor without recourse to the boarding ladder. As his boots hit the stone, he heard another pair of heels as Nimue Chwaeriau vaulted down from the second skimmer, and he grinned, despite his anxiety. Nimue was the next best thing to a foot shorter than he was, with dark red hair. That hair went well with the blue eyes they shared, but how would Aivah react when she discovered that eyes weren't the *only* things they shared?

"Welcome to Nimue's Cave, ladies," he said, looking up at their passengers as the skimmers' ladders extruded themselves from the fuselage sides. "If you'll come down and join us, we'll give you a short guided tour. That seems like the best place to start."

▼ ▼ ▼

For all her redoubtable personal toughness and resilience, Aivah's eyes were shadowed with wonder as she and Sandaria followed Merlin and Nimue up a long, wide flight of steps from the main cavern's floor. Merlin hadn't tried to explain everything they'd seen on their brief "guided tour," but what he had explained had been more than enough to stagger any Safeholdian. Even one who'd read Saint Kohdy's journal. What they were seeing at this moment was the actual reality of the *Holy Writ*'s descriptions of the archangels' *kyousei hi* and all the other "servitors" sprinkled about *The Testimonies* and the *Book of Chihiro*. Kohdy's journal had prepared them for the fact that the servitors had not, in fact, been alive themselves, but there was a vast gulf between knowing that—*believing* that—and actually seeing and touching the truth.

At least the tour had given her and Sandaria the chance to adjust a bit. Tension still drifted off of them like smoke, especially in Sandaria's case, but the worst, sharpest edge had been taken off it. Which meant it was time for them to be shown Nimue's sanctum sanctorum and told the *rest* of the truth, and Merlin's hands—faithfully mimicking a flesh-and-blood human's reaction to his emotions—were cold at the thought of taking their guests across that Rubicon.

*At least this time it doesn't have to turn into the Styx if they can't accept the truth*, he reminded himself. *At least I've got that much.*

They entered the largish—but still much smaller than the main cavern—chamber in which Nimue Alban had first awakened on Safehold twice. In preparation for their visit, Owl had manufactured an oval conference table of polished marble—or out of an advanced synthetic that looked and felt exactly like polished marble, anyway—large enough to comfortably accommodate a dozen people. The chairs around it were made of gleaming native hardwoods, with deep, comfortable cushions, and several wine bottles and a steaming carafe of hot chocolate had been set ready to hand.

"Please, sit," Merlin invited, and the Safeholdians obeyed. He waited until they were seated, then nodded for Nimue to sit, as well. "Wine? Or would you prefer chocolate?"

"Chocolate for me," Aivah told him, and smiled wryly. "I don't think I need alcohol complicating things just now."

"Of course." He picked up the carafe and poured into a cup. "Sandaria?"

"Chocolate will be fine for me, as well, Major."

He nodded, handed the first cup to Aivah, and poured a second for the "maid," then glanced at Nimue, who shook her head with a faint smile of her own.

He set the carafe back on the table, adjusting the cap rather more carefully than usual, then snorted quietly as he realized he was deliberately delaying the moment. He drew one of those deep breaths a PICA no longer required and settled into his own chair at the head of the table.

"As I'm sure both of you have realized by now," he said, "'Nimue's Cave' isn't the *seijin* training camp you thought we were taking you to, Aivah." His eyes met hers. "And, as I told you on the flight here, Captain Chwaeriau's first name does, in fact, have quite a lot to do with the reason we call all this"—he waved one hand in a gesture that took in the entire complex— "*Nimue's* Cave. But it's not because she was named for it. Actually, it was named for *her*. In fact, it was *created* for her over a thousand of your years ago."

Aivah's eyes widened, and he heard Sandaria inhale sharply.

"This chamber, these caverns, were here before the Day of Creation," he continued steadily. "They predate the Church, predate Armageddon Reef and the War Against the Fallen, predate even the first time the 'Archangel Langhorne' set foot on Safehold. You asked me once if I came from the same place all of the Adams and Eves had come from at the Creation, and the answer is that I did. So did Captain Chwaeriau. And so did the Archangels themselves, because they *weren't* Archangels. They were mortal men and women *pretending* to be Archangels."

Aivah and Sandaria were both staring at him now, their faces very pale.

"I know that's not what you expected, despite everything in Saint Kohdy's journal, but it's the truth. In fact, it's almost certainly what Kohdy had come to suspect—or to wonder about, at any rate—when he shifted to Español. And I'm positive it's the reason he died when he took his suspicions to Schueler."

"That's . . . that's not true!" Sandaria whispered. "It *can't* be true!"

"Yes, it can." Merlin smiled compassionately, even regretfully as he saw the shock in her eyes. "The Archangels were as mortal as you or Aivah, Sandaria. As mortal as Nimue and I used to be."

"What?" It was Aivah this time, her eyes just as huge, just as shadowed with shock and what looked too much like fear. "What do you mean '*used to be*'?"

"I know it's hard to believe," Merlin said gently. "But it's the truth. No, we're not demons, but Nimue and I used to be the same person, you see. And that person died over a thousand years ago."

▼ ▼ ▼

"I'm still not sure I can wrap my mind around it," Aivah Pahrsahn said several hours later.

The wine and chocolate had been supplemented by bowls of hot soup, accompanied by salads and thick slabs of hot, freshly buttered bread. By the time Owl's remotes had delivered the food, Aivah and Sandaria had been past the first stunning shock, and they'd watched in fascination as the soup tureen and bowls floated to the table on a counter-grav serving unit. There'd been more than a little fear in that fascination, perhaps, but the thick, tasty soup had become a solid, thankfully familiar, and thoroughly mundane anchor to the reality they'd thought they knew.

"It does take some wrapping," Nahrmahn Baytz told her. "You should try it from my side, though!"

The portly little prince's hologram "sat" in a chair at the foot of the table, looking up its length at Merlin. In deference to their guests' sensibilities, he'd walked in the door rather than simply appearing, and a hologram of Owl's black-haired, blue-eyed avatar sat to his left. Nahrmahn had been supplied with his own equally holographic bottle of wine in order to keep them company, and now he raised his glass in ironic salute.

"Sandaria?" Nimue said quietly from her seat across the table from Aivah's maid. "I hope you're feeling a little more . . . comfortable now?"

"That's not the word I'd choose," Sandaria replied. Her voice was harsh, her expression deeply troubled. "It's too much for me to even begin understanding at this point. We knew from Saint Kohdy's journal that there was a lot more than had ever appeared in the *Writ*, and we knew *The Testimonies* had been edited. But that *all* of it was a lie? That there's no truth in the *Writ* at all?" She shook her head, eyes dark, glistening with anguished, unshed tears. "I don't know if I can truly believe that. I don't even know if I *want* to believe it!"

"Sandaria—" Aivah began, her tone edged with alarm, but Merlin raised one hand, palm foremost, and shook his head.

"It wasn't *all* a lie, Sandaria. Nor was all of it evil. A lot of its consequences have been 'evil,' however you want to define the term, even judged solely by the *Holy Writ*'s own internal commands and obligations. But there's an enormous amount of *good* in the *Writ*, as well.

"I've read all of it, from end to end, and to be honest, one of the things I most hated about it, knowing what happened to Pei Shan-wei and all of my friends in the Alexandria Enclave, was that there was so much in it with which I completely and totally agreed. When someone like Sharleyan refers to the commands of the *Writ* today, when she says that God must weep to see us killing one another in His name, she's not being dishonest and she's not dissembling.

"I won't pretend that everyone who's learned the truth has simply gone merrily along still believing in God, because some of them haven't." Sandaria looked at him, her face showing how hard she found it to believe anyone could possibly think that way. "But the last thing I—or any other member of the inner circle—wants would be for you to stop believing in God simply because Langhorne and the others lied about Him. If you decide—if *you* decide—that God doesn't exist, that's your right, but do it on the basis of something besides the fact that Langhorne and Chihiro fabricated the story of what happened when human beings first came to Safehold. Make your decision based on your own reasoning, your own interpretation of the evidence and the universe, but don't let your belief in Him be destroyed by the actions of men and women who were terrified that the threat they'd escaped might someday threaten to exterminate the entire human race once more . . . and succeed."

"Merlin's right, Sandaria," Nimue said. "And I'm not saying that just because he and I used to be the same person!" She grinned impishly, then sobered. "But he and I both consider ourselves Christians. That's a religion, a God, you've never heard of, yet a huge part of the *Writ* is borrowed directly from the central, most sacred teachings of Christianity, and there are other parts of it borrowed from a religion called Islam, and one called Judaism. In fact, there are parts of it from almost every way in which mankind ever attempted to know God.

"The way he and I see it, the God in whom we believe's still there, Sandaria, still waiting for us to return to Him *if we choose to*. That's what Maikel Staynair's been saying from the very beginning. Like him, I believe God never walks away from anyone, but we have free will. That means anyone can choose to walk away from *Him* . . . and that anyone has the right to decide for herself that He doesn't even exist. In my opinion, they'd be wrong, but that's because of what *I* believe, and I have no right to require them to share my belief or to condemn them if they don't. That's really what this war is all about from the inner circle's perspective, giving human beings back the right to *choose*."

"But . . . but if it was all a fabrication, look at all the horrible things the *Book of Schueler* requires. How could God *let* them twist things that badly just to support a lie?!"

"When people have freedom of choice, some of them will make bad choices," Nahrmahn's hologram said quietly. "I speak from a certain personal experience. There are things I did before Cayleb and Sharleyan were kind enough to conquer Emerald that I look back upon with enormous regret. And I feel that regret *now*, Mistress Ghatfryd, long after learning the truth about Langhorne and the other 'Archangels.' The truth is, I feel it because learning the truth about them made me re-examine what I truly believed. What *I* believed, not what I'd ingested unquestioningly from childhood through Mother Church's teachings.

"Maikel believes that what we're seeing now here on Safehold is God moving in the world to restore the true knowledge of Him which was lost when all the rest of the human race was destroyed, and perhaps he's right. I think his brother, Baron Rock Point, is less certain God even exists, much less that He's taking a personal interest in anything that happens here on Safehold. If the two of *them*—brothers who grew up together, who love each other deeply, who would die to protect one another—can fail to see eye-to-eye on every aspect of faith, God, and God's will, certainly there's plenty of room for the rest of us to seek our own best understanding. Some of us will make mistakes, and some of us will willfully turn away from what we secretly suspect is the right thing to do, and that, too, is our right. Our *God-given* right. As Maikel says, either He doesn't exist at all, in which case whether or not we believe in Him is moot, or He's great enough to understand us in all our fallibility. But if He does exist and He didn't want us to exercise free will, He would never have given it to us in the first place."

"The truth is," Merlin said slowly, "as much as I hate to admit Langhorne might not have been a completely and totally vile human being. No one can read the *Writ* with an open mind and not see all of the *good* things it was also trying to accomplish."

Sandaria looked at him with manifest surprise, and he grimaced.

"Don't think it was easy for me to accept that. I *knew* the people—most of the people—the *Writ* demonizes. I know what happened to them, and I see all the lies incorporated into it. And despite that, there are whole chapters of the *Book of Bédard* and even the *Book of Langhorne* with which I find myself in complete agreement. Not just because they make internal sense, but because they represent exactly what *I've* always believed God wants of His children. Langhorne wanted to create a system, a structure, which would prevent humanity from ever developing the technology which might lead to a second encounter with the Gbaba. He was willing to do *anything* to accomplish that, and in the process, he robbed generation after generation of knowledge which might have prevented disease, prevented starvation, or taken millions of Harchongese and Desnairian serfs out of the worst sort of bondage. I can't even begin to describe all the things he stole from every single person ever born on Safehold. The recon skimmers that brought you here, all the things you've seen in the Cave—all of that is only a tiny part of what was denied to you, to your parents, to your grandparents and great-grandparents. To every generation ever born on this planet.

"Yet even as he did that, he tried to build a society in which men and women loved other men and women. In which they were supposed to treat one another as true brothers and sisters. In which the strong were to *protect* the weak, not prey upon them. The societies which grew up in places like Harchong and Desnair developed *despite* the teachings of the *Writ*, not because of them. When I first met King Haarahld, I asked him why his great-grandfather had abolished serfdom in Charis, and he replied 'Because it's what he believed God wanted of us.' I pointed out that serfdom and even slavery existed in other realms and that the Church tolerated it, and I asked how he could believe *God* didn't agree with serfdom if some men and women were bound to the land even in the Temple Lands, and he said 'The *Writ* teaches that God created every Adam and every Eve in the same instant, the same exercise of His will through the Archangel Langhorne. He didn't create kings first, or nobles, or wealthy merchants. He breathed the breath of life into the nostrils of *all* men and *all* women. Surely that means all men and all women are brothers and sisters.' "

Merlin paused, his expression touched with the grief he still felt over Haarahld's death. Then his sapphire eyes refocused on Sandaria's face.

"I didn't know then that he'd already read the Journal of Saint Zherneau. But the thing was that even though he had, everything he'd said about what the *Writ* taught was completely accurate. That *was* what it taught.

"In many ways, the *Writ* has what a Bédardist would

call a split personality. I have a copy of it from before the Rakurai strike on Armageddon Reef, and you're more than welcome to study it if you'd like to. But one thing you'll discover is that it doesn't have the *Book of Schueler* in it at all. In fact, much as I hated to admit it when Maikel pointed it out to me some time ago, if you read the *Writ* without the *Book of Schueler* and the *Book of Chihiro*, the God it speaks of is genuinely one of love and compassion. A God Whose plan for Safeholdians calls for them to love one another, to live in peace, to grow in experience and spirituality so that at the time of their mortal deaths they're ready to meet Him face-to-face and take their places as angels and archangels *themselves*. They're supposed to follow the rules set down in the *Book of Langhorne* and the *Book of Jwo-Jeng* because those rules are there for their own good and because they *want* to do what God wishes for them to do, want to live the lives He's ordained for them.

"Is there mass deception in it? Yes, of course there is. And is there coercion built into even the original *Writ*? Yes, there is, and it explicitly establishes an authoritarian church to preserve and enforce its teachings for all time. But it's not until after Armageddon Reef that the brutality, the iron-fist terror of the *Book of Schueler*, enters the Church canon. That wasn't written by Langhorne, and so as much as I find myself hating him for the friends of mine who he killed, for taking it upon himself to create the situation in which this monstrosity ever came into being, I've been forced to admit that what we face today isn't what he ever *intended* to bring into existence.

"Believe me, I'm about the farthest thing imaginable from an apologist for Eric Langhorne. The law of unintended consequences doesn't absolve someone from responsibility for the results he brings about, regardless of his *intentions*, and I have my own suspicions about where Langhorne's ended up. But the Church, the beliefs you and Aivah—you and *Nynian*—have given your lives to? Those are *good* things, Sandaria. No one's asking you to turn your back on them. No one wants to come between you and God. We want—we *need*—your help in destroying the perversion Zhaspahr Clyntahn's made not simply of the teachings of the God Nimue and I grew up believing in, but of the ones Langhorne wanted all of Safehold to believe in, as well.

"I don't doubt for a moment that Langhorne would approve of the Inquisition's effort to stamp out the 'heretical' knowledge and technology growing in Charis. But to do it *this* way? To torture and murder in God's name? To starve *millions* of innocent Siddarmarkians to death? Maybe the man who was willing to steal eight million human beings' lives, reprogram not simply their memories but their entire belief structure without their knowledge or consent, call down a kinetic strike on the Alexandria Enclave for daring to disagree with what he thought needed to be done—*maybe* he would agree no action was too extreme if it was the only way to prevent the emergence of the technology he dreaded so deeply. But the man who could approve the pre-Armageddon Reef *Holy Writ* would have seen that as a last resort, not a *first* resort. Would he have done it anyway in the end? Honestly, I can't tell you what he might have done today, a thousand years after the Federation's destruction. But much as I hate to admit it, I have to believe he would have tried everything else he could think of before resorting to the tactics Clyntahn embraced as his very *first* option."

He stopped speaking, and silence fell in the carven stone halls of Nimue's Cave. Sandaria Ghatfryd looked back and forth between Nimue and Merlin, as if studying the similarities between those two very different faces, looked deep into those identical sapphire eyes as if seeking the souls—or perhaps simply *the* soul—of a woman who'd died a thousand years before she herself was born. It was very quiet, and then, finally, she drew a deep, shuddering breath.

"I don't know if I can live with that," she said very, very softly. "I just don't know. All my life, ever since the convent, I've been dedicated to preserving the truth, and now you want me to believe everything I thought was true is really only another layer of deception. Oh," she waved one hand in a brushing away gesture, "I understand what you're saying about the goodness buried inside the *Writ*. But the truth remains that you're asking me to believe all of it, every single word—good or bad—is founded on falsehood. I don't know if I can do that. I don't even know if I *want* to be able to do that."

She met the PICAs' eyes levelly, fully aware of the consequences if she made herself a threat to the inner circle, and there was fear in her own eyes. But there was no hesitation, no readiness to lie, and Merlin looked back with equal steadiness. Then he smiled ever so slightly.

"People who abandon all they've believed in too easily make fragile allies, Sister Sandaria. Someone who forthrightly tells you they disagree with you is someone you can trust when they tell you anything else. There may come a time when they present a danger you have to neutralize, but they're always people to respect."

"Merlin," Aivah said, "don't do anything hastily."

Her eyes had flared with anxiety at the words "a danger you have to neutralize," and she reached out to grip Sandaria's hand firmly.

"I—" she continued, but Merlin shook his head at her gently.

"Neither Nimue nor I have any intention of doing anything hasty, Nynian." His tone was as gentle as his headshake. "There's no reason to, and no need." He returned his gaze to Sandaria. "No one will attempt to force you to believe or do anything that violates your own inner convictions. There's a reason Cayleb and Sharleyan have guaranteed the religious freedom of even Temple Loyalists in the Empire, and if they can do that there, how could they—or I—justify not respecting *your* religious freedom?

"Obviously, we can't allow someone to share what we've just revealed to you with the Group of Four," he said more somberly, "but at this moment, you couldn't do that even if you wanted to. You're here, in the Cave, with no way to communicate with anyone outside it. Under those circumstances, we're prepared to give you all the time you need to decide what you believe. In fact, that's the main reason we brought you and Nynian here in the first place; so that our hands *wouldn't* be forced if either of you decided you couldn't accept what we had to tell you.

"We're willing to leave you here where you can discuss the true history of Safehold with Owl and Nahrmahn, if you wish. To allow you unfettered access to Owl's libraries and the ability to discuss their contents with any other member of the inner circle—including Nynian—for however long you like. And if, in the end, you decide you can't become a part of the inner circle, we'll give you the choice between remaining what you might think of as a prisoner of state here in Nimue's Cave, in comfort and physical safety, with all the companionship we can provide, or of being placed in the same sort of cryo-sleep in which the colonists originally traveled to Safehold. No subjective time would pass for you from the moment you fell asleep to the moment you were once again awakened. The only thing we'd take from you would be the opportunity to actively *oppose* us, and that, I'm afraid, is a position at which, as Cayleb put it, 'We can do no other.' "

Silence fell once more, and he let it linger while a half-dozen slow, oozing minutes ticked into eternity. Then, still looking at her with that gentle smile, he said, "The choice is yours, Sandaria. We refuse to be one iota more ruthless than we *have* to, and this time, we have a choice, just as you do."

## . VI .
## The Seridahn River,
## The South March,
## Republic of Siddarmark

"What the hell is that?"

Lieutenant Ahrnahld Bryahnsyn stopped rubbing his hands together in a vain attempt to convince them they were warm and looked up, his expression baleful as he tried to identify the anonymous voice. It sounded like Corporal Kaillyt, who damned well ought to know better than to say something like that without identifying who was speaking.

That was his first thought. The second thought was that as reports went, it was a pretty piss poor excuse.

"Who said that?" Bryahnsyn snapped. "And what the hell are you talking about? What's 'what' and where did you see it?"

"Uh, sorry, Sir." Yes, it was Kaillyt. "It was me. And I don't know what it was. Something moved down there in the water—moved *up*stream, not down."

"What?"

Bryahnsyn climbed to his feet, careful of his footing in the icy darkness, and made his way towards Kaillyt's position. The corporal was perched on the muddy riverbank above the sunken river barge closest to the western edge of the Seridahn River, and slithering down the slick slope into the water wasn't high on Bryahnsyn's list of priorities. South March winters were considerably milder than those farther north, but the temperature hovered barely above freezing, and that gave the damp night a bone-gnawing chill. The current around the half-submerged hulk made soft chuckling and bubbling noises that seemed incongruously gay and cheerful under the circumstances. There were over a dozen more barges out there, stretching across the river in a more or less straight line, most of them in deeper water, where they'd been scuttled to block the navigable channel for reasons Bryahnsyn really didn't want to think about too closely. The last thing the Army of the Seridahn needed was for the demon-spawned armored ship reported at Thesmar to come upriver to support an infantry attack on its new positions the way it had ravaged the Army of the Sylmahn's rear areas last summer.

"Show me," he hissed, crouching beside Kaillyt.

"Don't see it now, Sir," the noncom said apologetically. "It was right about there, whatever it was."

The corporal was difficult to see in the darkness. The waning moon which had been visible earlier through the scudding overcast had all but set, but there was still enough light to burnish the low-lying river mist with silver, and Bryahnsyn jockeyed around behind Kaillyt until he could pick out the corporal's arm and pointing hand against the dim glimmer. That at least allowed him to orient himself, and he peered in the indicated direction, straining his eyes.

"Out there by the third barge?" he asked.

"Yes, Sir. Well, more between there an' number two, maybe. A bit closer in than that."

"Describe what you saw."

"Didn't rightly *see* anything, Sir. Not clear, if you know what I mean. There was something black, an' I thought it was a stick or a piece of driftwood. But then I realized it was movin' the wrong direction. It was goin' *against* the current."

Bryahnsyn glowered at the inoffensive river, staring until his eyes ached, but he saw no sign of anything Kaillyt might have seen, or thought he'd seen, or imagined, or whatever. He'd never thought of the corporal as a particularly imaginative individual, but the miserable light, the moving river, the thickening mist, the eyestrain, and the gnawing uncertainty were more than enough to make anyone start seeing things if he looked long enough.

"There was only the one of whatever it was?" he asked after a minute.

"Only *saw* one, yes, Sir. Might'a been more of 'em,

I guess. If there really was one of 'em to begin with, that is."

At least Kaillyt was honest, Bryahnsyn reflected. And it was better to have someone report things he thought he'd seen when he hadn't than keep his mouth shut when he truly had.

"Well, keep an eye peeled," he said finally.

"Yes, Sir."

The corporal watched the lieutenant disappear back into the shadows, then settled back down on his haunches, peering at the river. *Had* he seen anything? He truly didn't know, but he found himself hoping he hadn't. The longer things stayed quiet and unremarkable, the better he'd like it.

The heretics had punched a column out of the "besieged" port of Thesmar last month and driven southwest to take Somyr, cutting all overland connection between the Desnairian Empire and East Haven. Almost simultaneously, another column had stormed Cheryk without even slowing. True, the Cheryk garrison had been significantly reduced when the Army of Shiloh's primary supply line shifted to the St. Alyk River, but the defensive works had been formidable and there were ugly rumors the garrison had panicked when the surprise attack rolled in, supported by a hurricane bombardment from the small, mobile angle-guns no one had suspected Hanth had.

With Cheryk lost, General Rychtyr had ordered the batteries at Yairdyn on the Seridahn withdrawn and pulled all but a token delaying force back from his main position at Trevyr. The Yairdyn commander had been unable to block the entire river, but he'd scuttled a handful of barges in the deepest channel, which had been enough to prevent the heretic ironclad's passage at least briefly. There'd been another, heavier barricade twenty miles north of Yairdyn, as well, but the terrain at that point was flat as a table, totally unsuited to a serious defense even if there'd been some way to get enough men and guns there in time. The Yairdyn CO had kept right on retreating past it, using it to delay any riverborne pursuit, and it seemed to have worked.

But now Hanth's troops had moved up the Seridahn's western bank from the south, closing on General Rychtyr's new position, and there were reports they'd barged their artillery upriver with them. If *barges* could get that far upriver, could the ironclad be far behind?

Combined with what had happened at Cheryk and the disaster which had overwhelmed the Army of Shiloh, that possibility was more than enough to give anyone a few disquieting thoughts.

▼ ▼ ▼

"Headcount?" Lieutenant Klymynt Hahrlys whispered harshly.

"Everybody's back but Edwyrds, Sir," Platoon Sergeant Gyffry Tyllytsyn hissed back.

"Damn." Hahrlys muttered the single word quietly enough no one besides the platoon sergeant could have heard him. Then he inhaled deeply and thumped his senior noncom on the shoulder. "Well done. All the boys did well. Now get your arse back over to the warming tent."

"All the same to you, Sir, think I'll bide a bit. Wouldn't do t' let Edwyrds think I didn't care, now would it?"

The platoon sergeant's casual tone didn't fool Hahrlys, but he'd felt the icy wetness when he touched the other man's shoulder. Tyllytsyn hadn't been assigned as one of the swimmers, but clearly his own adventures hadn't gone exactly as planned, and Hahrlys heard the chatter of his teeth. He was shivering violently, as well, and the cutting wind wasn't making that any better.

"Trust me, he knows you care. Now get over there and warm yourself, damn it! Last thing I need is you going down sick on me."

There was a moment of silence, as if the platoon sergeant was weighing additional stubbornness. Then he drew a deep breath.

"Happen you're right 'bout that, Sir. I'll be over yonder if you need me."

"Fine. Now go get warm!"

Tyllytsyn touched his chest in a half-seen, half-guessed salute, turned, and made his way through the dense, ribbon-like fire willow leaves which screened the warming tent. Hahrlys watched him go, then pounded his gloved fists together and settled his chin deeper into his muffler, shivering as the wind keened across the river. It was out of the east, unusual for this time of year in the South March, and it wasn't very strong. He was grateful for the way it helped carry sounds away from the Temple Boys on the farther bank; he was *not* grateful for the effect of even a light wind's chill factor upon his men, and he felt a fresh stab of guilt. He knew it was irrational—he was the platoon's commanding officer and he swam like a rock, two very good reasons for him to have stayed right where he was—yet that impeccable logic did precious little to assuage his stubborn conviction that he should have been out there on the river leading his men.

*Oh, don't be any stupider than you have to be, Klymynt!* he snapped at himself. *All you'd've managed would've been to drown yourself. Assuming you didn't give away the entire operation splashing around before you went under. You could always've added that to your accomplishments. And wouldn't the Earl have been just delighted when you did?*

He took a quick turn along the bank, a dozen paces either way, elbows brushing the fire willows' leaves, eyes straining across the black water into the rising mist while he worried about his sergeant. Mahthyw Edwyrds was a good man, one of his best. He'd volunteered for his part of tonight's mission, and despite his present anxiety, Hahrlys was glad he had. There wasn't another man in the entire battalion as well qualified for it.

Most of the charges had been placed by four-man teams operating from the Imperial Charisian Army's folding canvas boats. Placing the charges themselves had been tricky—not to mention cold and dangerous—

in the darkness, but their experience clearing the channel at Yairdyn had helped a lot, and the boats had been effectively invisible.

There'd never been any possibility of using a boat—especially one that large—for the charge Edwyrds had volunteered to place, however. The outpost Hahrlys had spotted the day before was within thirty yards of where it had to go, and the pickets were undoubtedly alert, since the line of scuttled river barges was critical to Sir Fahstyr Rychtyr's defensive plans, and Rychtyr wasn't about to let anyone catch him napping.

Especially now.

He'd demonstrated his ability as one of the Church's better generals even before Duke Harless marched off to his rendezvous with disaster, and he'd clearly been informed of the arrival of HMS *Delthak* at Thesmar. That was almost certainly the reason he hadn't opted to hold Trevyr. The Seridahn was much narrower where it flowed through the town, but it was also deeper, with too strong a current to be blocked easily. It would have split his defensive position, and if *Delthak* had gotten into his rear it would have been impossible to withdraw his troops from the Seridahn's eastern bank under fire. Besides, the town's position at the Seridahn's confluence with the St. Alyk had lost its strategic importance with the fall of Brahnselyk.

That was why he'd pulled his main force another twenty miles upriver, to a point where the Seridahn broadened to the next best thing to a mile. The current was slower, the water was shallower, and the navigable channels were constricted. All of that had made it easier to sink blocking barges where he needed them, and the river narrowed once more as it passed between steep bluffs immediately upstream. He'd erected a massive twenty-four-gun battery atop the western bluffs, protected by a curved earthwork and positioned to cover the barricade with fire. Its height gave it good command, and the narrower river meant its guns could engage anything that got by the barge line at ranges of as little as a hundred yards.

It would be difficult to miss anything the size of an ironclad at that range.

Earl Hanth, however, had no intention of letting Rychtyr lock down the river, which was why Klymynt Hahrlys and his engineers were out here. It was also why Mahthyw Edwyrds had undertaken the riskiest part of the entire mission, because unlike any other member of Hahrlys' platoon, he was an experienced salvage diver. Not only that, he was an experienced *Chisholmian* salvage diver, and the water around Chisholm was at least as cold as the Seridahn River in March. Edwyrds had been instructed to bring his equipment with him when he deployed to the Republic, no doubt for moments just like this one, and he'd seemed confident he could handle tonight's mission.

*Of course he did*, Hahrlys thought bitterly. *If he wasn't confident, he'd never have* admitted *it. Besides, he knew as well as you did that he was the best man for the job. Just like he knew you were counting on him to be stupid enough to step up and volunteer.*

That was how it always was with the good ones. They stepped up, took the chances, and too damned many of them got killed doing it.

The lieutenant made himself stop pacing and raised one hand, shading his eyes as if that could help him see through the darkness.

Edwyrds had gone about his preparations calmly. In addition to his training as a diver, he was a skilled kayaker, like many Chisholmians, and he'd borrowed one of the light one-man craft from Major Mahklymorh's scout snipers for the mission. The scout snipers' kayaks were designed for stealthy incursions, made of black canvas which would be all but invisible in the darkness. After that, he'd enlisted two members of his squad to smear thick, insulating sea dragon grease over his tight-fitting canvas diver's coverall with its lining of Corisandian rubber, double- and triple-checked the seal of his diving glasses, and stood patiently while his assistants greased his face as well. Then he'd strapped the air bladder of heat-treated rubber to his back, checked the mouthpiece—the "regulator," he'd called it—and adjusted his weight belt and canvas and rubber gloves, climbed into his kayak, and paddled away into the night.

He couldn't take the kayak all the way across without being spotted by the Dohlaran sentries, so the plan had been for him to moor it in the shadow of one of the half-awash hulks farther from the bank, go over the side, and swim the rest of the way. That should at least get him close enough to reduce the total swim and the risk of hypothermia. But something must have gone wrong. He should have been back twenty minutes ago, and—

Hahrlys froze as something splashed. He strained his eyes, peering into the dark, and it splashed again. He stood a moment longer, then went tearing down the bank, wading out into the icy water. It was more than waist-deep, and he felt himself half-floating and half-wading, felt the dangerous pull of the current, but he refused to stop. Another step. Just one more, and then—

A gloved hand rose feebly from the water, and he grabbed hard with both his own hands. His right hand slipped on a thick layer of sea dragon grease, but his left hand caught the other man's glove and he heaved backward. Silt shifted treacherously underfoot and the current plucked at Edwyrds' body, prying, levering, trying to drag both of them out into the river's grasp. It was far stronger than Hahrlys was, and he felt himself being sucked deeper and deeper. The water was shoulder-deep now, slopping at his chin, but this was one of his men. If the river took one of them, then it took—

"*Hold on, Sir!*"

His head whipped around, startled out of the intensity of his battle with the river, as Platoon Sergeant Tyllytsyn grabbed his pistol belt from behind.

"Don't let go, Sir! Not yet!"

Something went around Hahrlys' body. The cold had already numbed his extremities, but he felt the rope jerk tight. Then—

"One more second, Sir!"

Tyllytsyn thrashed past the lieutenant. He was a shorter man. While Hahrlys' feet were still on the bottom, the platoon sergeant was swimming, but he stroked strongly and the lieutenant felt a sudden easing of the current's pressure as Tyllytsyn got a firm grip on Edwyrds' weight belt.

"Got him!" the platoon sergeant gasped. "Now let go and let them haul you in, Sir!"

"No." Hahrlys didn't recognize his own voice. Was that because it sounded so hoarse and breathless or because his cold-numbed brain wasn't working very well? "You'll need help pulling him out of—"

"Let go," Tyllytsyn repeated, the two words hard and unyielding. "Happen *I* can swim, Sir. An' I was smart enough t' tie onto a line *before* I went swimmin', too. Now let *go!*"

Hahrlys gaped at him for another moment, his brain churning sluggishly, then nodded.

"Whatever you say, Gyffry," he murmured, and released his grip. The rope around his waist plucked at him insistently, dragging him back the way he'd come, and he managed to grip the rope and turn in the same direction, holding onto the line and letting his legs and body float behind him.

By the time two of his men had hauled him ashore, three more had Tyllytsyn and Edwyrds within a few feet of the bank. Someone else floundered out into the water to help pull Edwyrds out, and Hahrlys managed to crawl to their side. He was probably more hindrance than help, he thought later, but he didn't worry about that at the time. He got a firm grip on Edwyrds and added his own feeble efforts to the fight to get the sergeant free of the water.

They dumped him on the muddy bank and Tyllytsyn peeled off the other noncom's swimming glasses. He pulled the bladder mouthpiece out from between

Edwyrds' tight-clenched teeth, and put his ear directly beside his mouth.

"He's still breathing!" he announced. "You three, get him up to the warming tent. Braishair, you and Wyltahn help the Lieutenant."

"And two of you help the Platoon Sergeant, too," Hahrlys said. Or that was what he tried to say, anyway. He was pretty sure afterward that all that actually came out was a slurred mumble, but that was all right.

That was just fine.

▼ ▼ ▼

"Yes, Pawal?" Halcom Bahrns looked up from the last of his scrambled eggs as Trynt Sevyrs, his steward, admitted Lieutenant Blahdysnberg to his day cabin. The overhead oil lamp cast shadows on the lieutenant's face, dusting the puckered scar on his cheek, picked up courtesy of a ricocheting rifle bullet during the Canal Raid, with darkness.

"The picket boat just brought word, Sir. The engineers say they got the charges placed."

"Did they?" Bahrns laid down his fork, reached for his hot tea, and sipped deeply. Then he lowered the mug. "How many did they lose?" he asked in a much quieter tone.

"None of them, apparently."

"*None* of them?"

Bahrns blinked. He hadn't been able to refute Admiral Hywyt's logic, and the advantages if the mission succeeded were amply worth the risk, but he'd never believed the engineers could pull it off without losing *someone*.

"According to the coxswain who delivered the message, they did come pretty close to losing at least one man, Sir," Blahdysnberg admitted. "But they got him back in the end and it sounds like he's going to be fine after all."

"And they got *all* the charges placed?"

"That's what they say, Sir. And I'm ready to take the word of anyone with big enough balls to even *try* setting them, myself. And the lieutenant in charge—a Lieutenant—" he glanced at the note in his hand, turning it to catch the lamplight "—Bryahnsyn, it says—lit all the fuses right on the dot at five-thirty."

"Can't say I disagree with you about the size of their balls," Bahrns conceded. Then he hauled out his pocket watch. "If he lit them off at five-thirty, I make it another forty minutes or so, assuming the fuses work the way they're supposed to." He closed the watch with a snap. "That being so, I suppose it's time we cleared for action."

▼ ▼ ▼

It was still dark when Bahrns stepped out onto HMS *Delthak*'s larboard bridge wing and into the bite of an icy breeze. The ironclad's superstructure was like an island rising from the thick river mist, and a trailer of funnel smoke wisped down across the dying night to greet him. The black gang had gotten steam up in ample time, and for once he envied the hot, oily cave in which they labored.

He could see precious little, but at least river currents were constant, not like the tricksy and capricious tide. He knew where his ship was, where she had to go, how the set of the current would try to prevent her from getting there, and what she had to do when she got there anyway. And Bryahnsyn's timing had been good. The eastern sky was already a tiny bit paler—unless that was his imagination—and he gazed upriver, waiting for the signal to begin.

He'd come to love his squat, unlovely command. There were times—a lot of them, actually—when the stink of funnel smoke was far from pleasant, or when talcum-fine black dust coated every surface after recoaling, that he longed for the days when all his command had needed was the pressure of clean wind on canvas. But those times came and went, and even at their worst, they were minor considerations beside *Delthak*'s speed, maneuverability, and power.

*And her pumps and propellers when the sea turns*

*bitchy, Halcom,* he reminded himself. *Let's not be forgetting those little advantages, either!*

He regretted the fact that he'd been forced to give up four guns in each broadside when they rearmed his ship before sending her to Thesmar, but there hadn't been any choice. The new breechloaders were twice a thirty-pounder's weight and over twenty feet long.

Unlike the thirty-pounders they'd replaced, the new mounts were fitted with handwheel elevation gear, and the toothed gears which rode the new, modified deck rails gave his gunners much more precise control of their pieces. The armored shutters had been bolted permanently closed over the empty ports, and the joints between the shutters and the casemate armor had been heavily caulked to prevent leaks. That had shown its worth during the storm-lashed voyage from Siddar City to Thesmar. But the Delthak Works had also fitted each of the new guns with a rounded gun shield that pivoted with the gun as it was trained around.

In many ways, Bahrns was as pleased by those shields as by the guns themselves. Most of *Delthak*'s casualties during the Canal Raid—like the scar on Blahdynsberg's cheek—had come when small arms fire found its way through the opened ports while the guns were run out. That wasn't going to happen now. In fact, he really wished he could simply leave the guns permanently run out, the way the new-build ironclads were designed to do. Running them all the way in was a backbreaking task, even with the auxiliary steam "donkey." Unfortunately, the shields, for all their virtues, weren't perfect. They leaked, and *Delthak*'s port sills were too close to the water. That was why the guns had to be run fully in so the original port shutters could be closed and secured before he risked taking her to sea in anything much above a dead calm.

But those long barrels, especially matched with the slower-burning "brown powder," gave them enormous power. The standard six-inch shell was almost four times the weight of a thirty-pounder smoothbore shell, and according to the Delthak Works, it struck with more than seven and a half times the energy. Theoretically, the new gun had a range of fifteen thousand yards at its maximum elevation of fifteen degrees, although no gunner could hope to hit another ship at ranges much in excess of four thousand. His own ship's motion would have made that impossible. Firing from the mill-pond smoothness of the Seridahn River, however, ought to be a rather different kettle of fish, and he was eager to try them in action for the first time.

Of course, first he had to get into position, and that was likely to prove . . . interesting.

He opened his watch again, holding its face to catch the light from a conning tower view slit. The eastern sky was definitely lighter. In fact, according to schedule, the festivities ought to have already kicked off, but he wasn't surprised they were running a little late. If *he'd* been in charge of cutting those fuses, he would have given himself a rather more generous margin of error than the nominal timetable required, and—

▼ ▼ ▼

"All right, you're relieved," Lieutenant Sandkaran growled.

As military formalities went, it was sadly lacking, Lieutenant Bryahnsyn reflected. On the other hand, Erayk Sandkaran was a surly fellow at the best of times, and he didn't like getting up before the crack of dawn any more than anyone else did. For that matter, Bryahnsyn couldn't for the life of him imagine why it was necessary for a sixteen-man outpost to be commanded by an officer in the first place. That was the sort of thing platoon sergeants were for, in his opinion, which Sandkaran obviously shared.

Not that he or Sandkaran were likely to raise that point with Colonel Sheldyn. That was usually a bad—

▼ ▼ ▼

Earl Hanth's command had been redesignated the Army of Thesmar in recognition of its defense of that city. Despite its magnificent new name, however, it remained lower in supply priority than its fellows. The Army of Shiloh had been shattered; the Desnairian Empire had lost eighty percent of its rifles and new-model artillery; and while the Royal Dohlaran Army had a greater potential to regenerate, it wouldn't be doing that anytime soon. So it was reasonable to give priority to the armies farther north, where heavy and decisive combat could be expected no later than May or June.

Because of that, Hanth had received none of the new bolt-action rifles and only a handful of the Mahldyn .45 revolvers. The 4th Infantry Brigade had brought along its organic mortars and field artillery; two additional batteries of four-inch muzzle-loading rifles had accompanied the same wave of reinforcements; and Hanth had a plenitude—indeed, an excess—of thirty-pounders on field carriages. They'd done him proud in his attack on Cheryk, and while the naval angle-guns Admiral Hywyt had landed to defend Thesmar were too immobile to take on campaign, the Delthak Works had compensated by supplying him with enough new mortars to equip five additional support platoons.

And as a consolation prize for the M96 rifles he hadn't received, Ehdwyrd Howsmyn had sent along eight hundred additional six-inch shells, with even more in the supply chain behind them . . . and just under a hundred tons of Sahndrah Lywys' newest brainchild. On a pound-for-pound basis, Lywysite was roughly two and a half times as powerful as black powder, because the shock wave of its detonation propagated at over twenty-three thousand feet per second while black powder's detonation velocity was less than *two* thousand. That gave Lywysite a much greater shattering effect, and since it weighed twice as much per cubic inch, the same weight charge could be packed into half the volume. And *that* meant it could be formed into neat sticks, ten inches long and one and a quarter inches in diameter, each of which weighed just under twenty ounces . . . and packed the effectiveness of over three pounds of black powder into barely fifteen percent of the black powder's volume.

▼ ▼ ▼

The explosions weren't simultaneous. That would have been expecting the impossible. But there were over a dozen of them, spread over a window of less than three minutes, which was very respectable timing . . . and a vast relief for all concerned. Especially for the engineers who'd placed the charges. They'd felt a certain trepidation at the knowledge that the fuses inside those charges had been lit even before the ominous, pitch-sealed packages were handed to the men responsible for putting them where they belonged before they blew the hell up.

Ehdwyrd Howsmyn and his minions had provided the engineers with a demolition fuse—a variant on the improved metallic time fuses he'd introduced for smoothbore artillery shells the year before—for those moments when it wasn't expedient to simply light a length of quick match and run for cover. Essentially, it was a solid, disk-shaped bronze casting whose upper surface bore a spiraling groove or channel packed with a very slow-burning compound that crept along the channel at a rate of only a foot an hour. It was sealed with a special varnish, then covered with a protective tin lid marked in increments, each equal to two minutes' burning time, which followed the line of the channel. When it was time to emplace the charge, an awl was punched through the tin at the appropriate time—up to a maximum of two hours—and flame was applied.

In theory, it provided a reasonably accurate—and reasonably *safe*—timing device. The only problem was that none of the engineers in question had ever before actually worked with the things, and no one could have blamed them for approaching their task a bit gingerly. Now they stood on the river bank, Sergeant Edwyrds still wrapped in a thick cocoon of blankets and leaning on Platoon Sergeant Tyllytsyn, and cheered each white-and-brown, mud-stained column of water as it erupted in the predawn gloom.

▼ ▼ ▼

"I do believe that's our signal, Crahmynd," Halcom Bahrns said, leaning in through the conning tower door as the final explosion roared. "I think we can proceed as planned, assuming that's convenient."

"Aye, Sir!" The flash of a white-toothed smile was just visible in Petty Officer Crahmynd Fyrgyrsyn's luxuriant brown beard.

"Ahead half please," Bahrns continued, glancing at the telegraphsman as Fyrgyrsyn turned the wheel, bringing *Delthak* around in a slow circle to point upstream.

"Ahead half, aye, Sir!"

The telegraphsman swung his polished brass handles and the ironclad quivered as her twin screws turned faster.

Bahrns stepped back onto the bridge wing while she gathered speed and folded his arms atop the bridge wing rail as white water began creaming back from her blunt bow. He could see quite a bit better in the slowly strengthening light—well enough to pick up landmarks on either bank above the mist—and he grunted in satisfaction as he realized *Delthak* was almost exactly on course. Not that accurate navigation would help a lot if Admiral Hywyt had gotten his calculations wrong. It was entirely possible he was about to damage his vessel severely, perhaps even sink her, although that was unlikely. Even if he did, the river was shallow enough that refloating her should be fairly simple, and it was far more likely those closely spaced explosions had shattered the sunken river barges as planned. In fact, he could already see broken sections of planking spinning downstream to meet him. Given that *Delthak* displaced twelve hundred tons and would be moving at approximately six knots when she reached the barrier, she should shoulder her way through whatever remained without too much trouble. The biggest risk, actually, was that one of her propeller blades might hit something big enough to damage it, and repairing *that* would be far more difficult than merely floating her once more. If she cleared the barrier, on the other hand, the Army of the Seridahn would suddenly find itself in what Emperor Cayleb liked to call "a world of hurt."

▼ ▼ ▼

Ahrnahld Bryahnsyn climbed back to his feet as the deluge of water, mud, shattered pieces of river barge, and dead fish finished thudding down around him. He didn't remember flinging himself facedown, although it had certainly been the right thing to do. Lieutenant Sandkaran hadn't, and he lay unconscious, bleeding heavily from a scalp laceration.

Bryahnsyn felt a distant pity for his fellow lieutenant, but it was buried under the sheer shock of that rolling series of explosions. At least he knew now what Kaillyt must have seen the night before, although Shanwei only knew how the heretics had managed to get boats or swimmers across that icy expanse of riverwater.

He was still in the process of working out *why* they'd managed it when a fresh thunder—this one the explosion of hundreds of mortar bombs and angle-gun shells—crunched down on the Army of the Seridahn's defenses like the heel of Chihiro's war boot. He crouched, wheeling towards the sound of the guns, then jerked back towards the river as something screamed impossibly.

A blazing limb of the sun reached above the horizon, touching the low-lying river mist—swirling in torment from the force of the explosions—with rose and gold. That was all he saw for a moment, but then something moved above the mist, like an island rolling arrogantly upriver, contemptuous of the current which tried to stay its progress.

The ironclad surged towards the cleared gap, huge and black, impossibly long guns protruding from its sides and across the front of its broad casemate, screaming its fury in a thick, white plume of whistle steam. A man in a watch coat stood on one bridge wing, peering upstream through one of the heretics' double-barreled spyglasses, and smoke streamed from its tall funnels. A growing mustache of white wrapped itself around the ironclad's stem, and as he watched, its bow smashed a splintered length of wreckage aside.

It went charging past, and he and his men clapped their hands over their ears as the dreadful shriek of the whistle crashed over them.

▼ ▼ ▼

Bugles sounded high and urgent, drums thundered, and Major Failyx Sylvstyr burst out of his hut in his shirtsleeves, hatless, napkin still clutched in one hand. His head whipped around to the southwest, where the bellow of enemy artillery laid a fiery surf of explosions, shrapnel, and shell fragments across the Army of the Seridahn's deeply entrenched front, and his jaw clenched.

That bombardment was entirely too ferocious to be anything other than the prelude to a serious attack, and he wondered how well the dugouts and entrenchments were standing up to it. They were considerably stronger than the ones which had protected Cheryk, but were they strong *enough*? The heretics' rifled guns—of which, thankfully, they seemed to have relatively few—had far more penetrating power and heavier bursting charges than anything his own twelve-pounders could produce. The engineers had done their best to dig deep enough and pile dirt and sandbags high enough to give the infantry a decent chance of surviving, but only time would tell whether or not they'd succeeded.

As one of the Army of the Seridahn's senior artillery commanders, Sylvstyr had been briefed on the new "Fultyn Rifles" which were supposed to become available "any day now." He'd believe they were coming when he actually saw one, but he hoped desperately that they really existed and might even perform as promised. He was proud of his gunners, of their efficiency and determination, yet that pride only made him even more bitterly aware of how outclassed their weapons were. And if the stories about Guarnak were true, nothing the Royal Dohlaran Artillery currently had could hope to stop the heretic ironclad if it got loose on the upper river. That was a point of significant importance to Failyx Sylvstyr, because it was his regiment that Sir Fahstyr Rychtyr had dug in atop the river bluff to keep just that from happening.

Sylvstyr didn't know how he'd drawn the short straw, but he'd done the only thing he could: saluted and then emplaced his guns behind the thickest earthen parapets he could throw up. In addition, he'd built four-foot-thick walls of sandbags between guns, putting each of them in its own protected bay, and roofed the entire position with heavy logs and four more feet of earth. Building those works in the midst of a cold, rainy South March winter had been no easy task, but at least—

Something shrieked, shrill enough to be heard even through the heretic guns, the drums, and the bugles. Failyx Sylvstyr had never heard anything like it in his life, yet he knew instantly what it had to be.

He turned back to the river, and his mouth was a thin, bloodless line as the ugly black carapace of the heretic ironclad surged through the golden glow of river mist, trailing twin banners of smoke.

"Stand to! *Stand to!*"

He heard other voices repeat the order. Then more bugles were sounding, calling his regiment to war, and he flung himself into the heavily sandbagged battery command post with a silent prayer to Langhorne and Chihiro.

▼ ▼ ▼

"There's the battery, Sir. 'Bout six points on the larboard bow."

Captain Bahrns swung his double-glass to the indicated bearing and grunted.

"Got it. Good eyes."

"Thank'ee, Sir!"

The lookout's pleasure at the compliment was obvious, but most of Bahrns' attention was focused on the battery itself. If their spy reports were as accurate as usual, it was likely to prove a tough slabnut to crack. On the other hand, his breechloaders had been designed to crack nuts just like it.

"Clear the bridge!" he commanded, still peering at the raw earthen face of the enormous battery. It was high enough its guns might just be able to score on the thinner armor of the decks and casemate roof, but the angle would be shallow if they did. "Inform Master Blahdysnberg that we'll be needing his gunners soon," he continued. "And bring her a point to starboard, if you please!"

Acknowledgments came back, and he felt the lookouts moving past him through the conning tower door. He stood where he was for a moment longer as *Delthak* swung slightly away, presenting her broadside more fully to the battery. Then it was his turn, and he stepped over the raised coaming and swung the armored door shut. One of the lookouts dogged the latches, and he nodded his thanks and stepped across to the forward vision slit on the larboard side.

The first furious gouts of gunsmoke blossomed from the heavily dug-in field guns, and he raised an eyebrow in ungrudging respect. They were quick off the mark, those gunners, and *Delthak*'s armor rang like a hammered anvil as twelve-pounder round shot ricocheted from her casing.

"Slow to one-quarter," he said. There was no point dodging about, and the lower speed would improve his own gunners' accuracy.

"One-quarter speed, aye, Sir!" the telegraphsman sang out, and Bahrns stepped to the voice tube, uncapped it, and blew down it to sound the whistle at the other end.

"First Lieutenant!" Pawal Blahdysnberg's voice acknowledged.

"I believe it's time you earned your princely salary, Master Blahdysnberg. You may open fire when ready."

"Aye, aye, Sir!"

Bahrns let the voice pipe cover snap shut and stepped back to the vision slit just as HMS *Delthak*'s six-inch rifles spoke in anger for the very first time.

▼ ▼ ▼

Major Sylvstyr felt a fresh, fierce surge of pride. Even surprised by the ironclad's appearance, his gunners had gotten off their first salvo before the heretics could fire. The waterspouts clustered around the ironclad were proof they'd taken time to aim, as well, and at least nine or ten had scored direct hits.

Which appeared to have been just as effective as the hits Bishop Militant Bahrnabai's gunners had registered at Guarnak.

He caught his lower lip between his teeth, peering out the observation slit through his spyglass, and his heart sank like a stone as he got his first really good look at his opponent.

Whatever those run-out guns were, they *weren't* the thirty-pounders the ironclad had used against Guarnak. Those barrels were longer than any gun he'd ever heard of, which suggested they were even more powerful than he'd feared. But how in Shan-wei's name did something that long run back in to reload? He couldn't imagine how it might be done, but however they did, the rate of fire must be incredibly slow. For that matter, how did they swab out and extinguish the sparks from the last round before loading the charge for the next into the muzzle? And—

The ironclad fired.

The muzzle flash was incredible, a bubble of fire raging out above the river's surface, burning away the mist, laying a ripple pattern of shockwaves across the water. The volcanic eruption of smoke was enormous, and it was *brown*—dark, dense, thick *brown* smoke!

That thought had just begun to register when six six-inch shells struck their targets almost simultaneously, and Sylvstyr staggered to their earthquake arrival.

*Sweet Langhorne! How the hell much powder are those things* filled *with?!*

The shells drove deep before they exploded, and even black powder could blow an enormous crater when there were eleven and a half pounds of it in each shell. At six thousand yards, *Delthak*'s armor-piercing shells would have penetrated four inches of solid, face-hardened steel armor. She wasn't firing armor piercing . . . but the range was less than two hundred yards, and she certainly wasn't firing at face-hardened armor.

One of her six shells drilled into the face of the bluff below the battery and ripped its hole harmlessly into the inoffensive dirt and clay. But the other five struck the parapet face, and Failyx Sylvstyr discovered that he hadn't made it thick enough, after all.

▼ ▼ ▼

Shell bursts erupted along the shore, and Bahrns showed his teeth as the earthwork between two of the gun embrasures blew heavenward in a vortex of fire, smoke, and dirt. The embrasure to the right of the point of impact disintegrated, and he thought he could see the muzzle of that field gun buried in the spill of earth and ruptured sandbags. He wasn't sure about the second gun; it might have survived, if its crew was unreasonably lucky. But there was no question about one of *Delthak*'s other shells. It landed almost directly under a third twelve-pounder's barrel and the explosion ripped open its emplacement and threw the shattered gun high into the air.

Down on the gundeck, the big rifles recoiled, then slid smoothly back into battery under the urging of the hydropneumatic recoil system. Gunners turned the heavy breech blocks and swung them open, and the waiting swabs hissed into the breeches to extinguish any lingering embers, followed by fresh sixty-eight-pound shells and twenty-pound bags of powder.

Twenty seconds later, they fired again.

▼ ▼ ▼

*Not possible. That's not* possible, *damn it!*

Failyx Sylvstyr stared in disbelief. Those preposterously long guns hadn't run back in at all! They'd merely surged backward several feet, then slid right back into firing position. And then, impossibly quickly, they *did* fire again. His twelve-pounders' maximum rate of fire was no more than four rounds per minute—one every fifteen seconds—even with a superbly trained crew. There was no way guns with the massive destructive power the heretics' had revealed could fire equally quickly! It simply couldn't be done!

But the heretics were doing it. Somehow, they must be loading the accursed things from the *breech* end, like their damned infantry's rifles!

Another hurricane of devastation ripped through his regiment's position, rending and shredding, setting off ready charges in a cascade of secondary explosions, and Major Sylvstyr's stomach was a frozen iron ball as he realized just how quickly that demon-spawned ironclad was going to tear his command apart.

And they weren't even scratching its paint.

Bile rose in his throat. His men were dying about him, and they were dying for *nothing*. Surely, whatever God demanded of them it wasn't to sacrifice their lives uselessly when their weapons couldn't even hope to damage the enemies who were killing them!

"*Get them out!*" he roared, staggering out of his command post and down the length of the earthwork, feeling his way through the smoke, the stench of explosions, and the shattered bodies of his men. "*Get the men* out *of here, damn it!*"

He collided with Captain Hylmyn, one of his battery commanders, in the smoke and chaos and grabbed him by both shoulders.

"Get your men out, Henrai!" he shouted, his voice frail in the tumult and the madness while he shook Hylmyn. "Get them out—and pass the word! We can't fight *that* with twelve-pounders!"

"But . . . but, Sir—!"

"Don't argue, damn you!" Sylvstyr snarled. "Get them out—*now!*"

Fresh thunderbolts unleashed new explosions and the screams of torn and broken men tore at their ears. Hylmyn stared at him for a single heartbeat longer, then jerked a choppy nod and spun away, shouting orders of his own.

Sylvstyr left him to it, fighting his way down the length of the earthwork through the confusion and the dying, bellowing the order to retreat again and again. Some of his men heard him and refused to obey. Others would never hear anything again, but most of his gunners—those who were still alive, anyway—heard and obeyed.

The major felt the shame of running away. He knew—he *knew*—it was the right order to give, but still he felt the shame. And he knew his men would, as well. He didn't know what the inquisitors might say about this day's work, but General Rychtyr would understand. He'd know there'd been no choice but to—

Another six-inch shell stabbed into the ruins of Failyx Sylvstyr's regiment. This one found a magazine, and the major felt himself flying through the air. Then he felt a shattering impact . . . and nothing else at all.

▼ ▼ ▼

"Secure the guns, Master Blahdysnberg," Halcom Bahrns said, and his voice was flat, his eyes dark. "Tell the crews I said well done."

"Aye, aye, Sir!" Pawal Blahdysnberg's jubilant voice came back up the voice pipe. "Thank you!"

"You're welcome," Bahrns replied. "You deserve it."

He closed the voice pipe, undogged the conning tower door, and stepped back out onto the bridge wing. The long, brown fog bank of *Delthak*'s gunsmoke rolled away on the chill, strengthening breeze. More smoke rose in a thick, choking plume above the plowed wreckage which had once been a battery of twenty-four twelve-pounders. There might be as many as five intact guns buried in those ruins, he thought grimly. There couldn't be more of them.

*I wonder how Pawal will feel about those compliments of mine when he has time to come above decks and really see what we've done? I know Baron Green Valley's right. You don't win a war by dying for your cause; you win it by making the other poor damned bastard die for* his. *And Langhorne knows the perfect battle from any CO's viewpoint is one in which none of his people die. But this—! It was like . . . like clubbing baby chicks. They couldn't possibly hurt us, and we . . . .*

He stared at his ship's handiwork, listening as the thunder of the army's artillery rolled and bellowed, and then he drew a deep breath and turned back to the conning tower.

"Come a quarter point to larboard and increase to half ahead," he said quietly.

"Quarter point to larboard and half ahead, aye, Sir!" PO Fyrgyrsyn responded, and if there was any doubt in his voice, Bahrns couldn't hear it. At the moment, that mattered. It mattered a lot, because *Fyrgyrsyn* mattered.

Captain Halcom Bahrns squared his shoulders and raised his double-glass again as he looked for the tow road along the top of the western riverbank. The one he was supposed to take under fire to deny it to the enemy and cover the landing of the Marine battalion Earl Hanth was sending upriver in *Delthak*'s wake. It was unlikely they'd be able to cut off Rychtyr's retreat entirely. The Dohlaran general had been too smart to dig in on the eastern side of the river. He'd probably believed—hoped, at least—that his barricade of river barges would protect his rear, but it was obvious he hadn't been prepared to risk his army's existence on that belief. And their spies reported another barricade across the river five miles farther north. However willing the engineers might be, they wouldn't be able to blow a gap through that obstacle before most of the fleeing Dohlarans were already past it on their way to

Evyrtyn. So, no, they weren't going to keep Rychtyr from falling back up the line of the Seridahn, but they could damned well make it a costly process.

And that, he reminded himself, glancing back at the shattered defensive battery, was what fighting a war was all about, wasn't it?

. VII .

# Fifty Miles East of Malys, The South March Lands, Republic of Siddarmark

"We're down eighteen more draft horses, Sir," Colonel Ahlfryd Makyntyr said wearily. "And another twelve-pounder broke an axle this afternoon, too. I think I can spread the remaining horses to keep the other pieces moving—for a while, at least—but I've lost two more dragons, as well."

Sir Rainos Ahlverez' expression was grim as he listened to his senior artillerist's report. Makyntyr wasn't telling him anything he hadn't expected. Or anything he hadn't already heard entirely too many times during the nightmare retreat from the Kyplyngyr Forest debacle. The general commanding what was left of an army which had once counted almost a quarter million men shouldn't have been worrying his head over the loss of a single twelve-pounder, but he no longer had almost a quarter million men. By the best estimate available to him, he was down to under forty thousand, including over ten thousand Desnairians.

And, allowing for Makyntyr's most recent loss, nineteen pieces of artillery.

"Do what you can, Ahlfryd," he said. There'd been a time when his relationship with Makyntyr had been icily formal, but that time was long past. One thing about unmitigated disasters, he thought mordantly;

they put pettier concerns and conflicts into perspective. "Go ahead and pull your remaining dragons off the ammunition carts. The guns are more important than they are, and we'll settle for the ammunition on the limbers. Once you've got the traction you need for all of them, turn the other dragons over to Shulmyn and lay fuses to the carts." He quirked a bitter smile. "No point leaving all that powder lying around for the heretics."

"Yes, Sir."

Makyntyr's unhappiness was apparent, but he didn't even try to argue. No artillerist liked to be told his reserve ammunition had become irrelevant. There was no point pretending it hadn't, however, and Sir Shulmyn Rahdgyrz' remaining supply wagons were vastly more important to the beaten army shambling its way towards what it hoped might someday be safety and survival.

A hunger-gaunt horse trotted up beside Ahlverez, and the captain in its saddle touched his chest in salute to his superiors.

"A courier just came in from Colonel Ohkarlyn, Sir," Sir Lynkyn Lattymyr said. "The Colonel's reached Malys. He says it's deserted, but he's pushing a section out towards Kostyr and one of his companies has established a blocking position on the road to Thyssyk."

"Any word from Colonel Tyrwait?"

"Not since this morning, Sir."

Ahlverez grunted in acknowledgment and unfolded his wretched excuse for a map, wishing for no more than the ten thousandth time that he had a better one. For that matter, that he had *any* maps of this Archangels-forsaken stretch of the South March. The best he had was this rough sketch, with an unreliable scale and so-called details in which he dared not place much trust. Worse, he had to assume any heretics hunting his command to finish off what was left of it had much better ones than he did.

What he did know was that the miserable, narrow, muddy tracks connecting the tiny hamlets thinly scattered across the almost three hundred straight-line miles between the village of Sygmar south of the Ky-plyngyr and the larger town of Malyktyn on the high road between Roymark and Cheryk were the closest thing to a road net the Army of Shiloh's remnants had. The only hope that any of Ahlverez' men might ever see home lay on the far side of Malyktyn, and they had precious little chance of getting there.

The farm tracks had never been intended for the traffic required to support even a routed army, especially in winter. They existed primarily to haul crops to market after harvest, when the weather was dry and the dirt roads offered firm going for farmers' wagons. In winter, soaked by the all too frequent rains and plagued by nights when the temperature dropped below freezing, the going had been anything but firm even before hundreds of thousands of feet and hooves churned it into muck. Even as their strength steadily diminished, the half-starved draft animals had to work twice as hard to haul wagons and guns over that treacherous surface, and men who were themselves half starved struggled to place each weary foot in front of another in mud which was often knee-deep.

Sir Rainos Ahlverez was a nobleman, accustomed to looking down his aristocratic nose at the commoners who provided the Royal Dohlaran Army's enlisted soldiers, yet every one of his surviving men—even the wretched Desnairians who'd attached themselves to his command—had become precious to him. Not simply because they represented the dwindling fighting power (such as it was) under his command, either. No. He knew what these men had done, what they'd suffered and given for God and king, how many others had lost their lives already. It was his responsibility to get them home again; he *owed* them that for the price they'd paid. And it was a responsibility he knew he was unlikely to meet.

But it wouldn't be because he hadn't tried, he reminded himself, inhaling deeply. He was just as happy none of the Army of Shiloh's senior Desnairian officers had made it this far. While it would have been intensely satisfying to be able to shoot them out of hand, he had at least a chance to get *some* of their men home without them to hinder him.

He frowned down at the dogeared sketch map. Malys lay southwest of the Kyplyngyr, at the intersection of no less than five of the pitiful, muddy excuses for roads available to him. The fact that Ohkarlyn, commanding one of his last two semi-full-strength cavalry regiments, had secured the road junction was good news. But to offset that, he'd still heard nothing from Tyrwait, who commanded the other one of those regiments. Tyrwait was doing his best to screen the main column's western flank, and he was supposed to be scouting towards the village of Zhonstyn, eighty miles south-southwest of Malys. Hopefully, he was also finding a place for at least a temporary blocking position on the farm road that led from Malys, through Zhonstyn, to Thesmar, although Ahlverez hoped to Langhorne it wouldn't be required. If it was . . . .

His position at the moment was over three hundred miles as a wyvern flew from Thesmar, at the mouth of the Seridahn River. Given everything else that had happened, he was certain the heretic Hanth had been heavily reinforced since Duke Harless' bloody failure to storm Thesmar's entrenchments at the very beginning of the Fort Tairys campaign.

It was obvious the Army of Shiloh had been not simply outfought but out-*thought*. It had been sucked into doing *exactly* what the heretics wanted. There was no point pretending otherwise, and the heretics who'd baited the trap would scarcely have overlooked the potential threat Thesmar represented to that army's rear. And as Makyntyr had quietly pointed out to him, the Charisian Navy could easily have landed another ten or twenty thousand men in Thesmar Bay.

Ahlverez still couldn't figure out how the heretics had managed it so smoothly, but it had become painfully evident that Bryahn Kyrbysh had died in the same massacre as the rest of the Fort Tairys garrison. All his dispatches detailing the starvation and demoralization of the heretic Eastshare's understrength army had clearly come from someone else, and Ahlverez felt his teeth grinding once more as he visualized the grinning heretic duke dictating those lying messages.

Just how inaccurate "Kyrbysh's" reports had been had become obvious when Eastshare's "starving, out-numbered" army attacked out of Fort Tairys to trap the Army of Shiloh between his healthy, well-fed, *numerous* troops and the *second* heretic army which had marched clear across Cliff Peak without being spotted.

The fact that the heretics had been able to produce that many troops—that many Charisian *regulars*—was frightening in more ways than one. A defeated army always tended to overestimate its opponent's numbers. Ahlverez knew that, but by his most conservative estimate, there must have been upwards of a hundred thousand men involved in springing that trap. Mother Church had assured him the Charisians had nowhere near that many available for service in Siddarmark, and if the Inquisition's information had been so thoroughly wrong about that, what *else* had it been wrong about?

There was no way to answer that question—yet, at least—and it didn't really matter as far as his current situation was concerned. What mattered was that he had no idea how many of those hundred-thousand-plus men were marching hard to overtake him. He had no better idea of what the Earl of Hanth might have been up to, but in the heretics' place Ahlverez would have been doing his utmost to crush what was left of the Army of Shiloh between the Thesmar garrison and Duke Eastshare's pursuit.

*Sure you would, Rainos,* he told himself, glowering at the bland, uninformative sketch map. *But how much of that is because you realize just how exhausted your men are? It's obvious to you that the logical step would be to finish you off, but you don't know what other problems might seem more urgent to* them. *There's still that arse-hole Hennet's cavalry at Cheyvair, for example. And truth be told, the Army of Shiloh's already* been "*finished off.*"

His stomach churned as he admitted that, yet truth was truth, and the one luxury he absolutely could not afford was self-comforting delusion. A third of his men no longer even had weapons. His artillery train—what little of it had escaped the heretics' initial trap and the destruction of the rearguard he'd left to delay the pursuit—was laughable. His men were sick, starving, with worn-out, leaky boots and uniforms indistinguishable from beggars' rags, and their fighting spirit was virtually nonexistent. The truth was, he admitted bleakly, that it might actually be to the heretics' *advantage* to let what was left of the Army of Shiloh go. The men who'd escaped the nightmare of the Kyplyngyr Forest had been brutally traumatized. Letting them go home to tell their fellow soldiers what they'd endured was probably the surest way to undermine the morale of any new army the Kingdom of Dohlar might put into the field.

*Stop that!* he told himself harshly. *Yes, you got reamed. They were three moves ahead of you—a dozen moves ahead of that idiot Harless—every step of the way, but that's no excuse to just throw up your hands and give up! You owe Mother Church and the Kingdom more than that. And however badly they may've outsmarted you this time, there's always the* next *time. There's that old proverb about the burnt hand, isn't there? Well, you got your hand burned right down to the* bone*, Rainos. What matters is what you learned from it.*

He looked at the sketch a moment longer, then back up at Lattymyr.

"All right, Lynkyn," he said, his voice level, "we'll keep pushing on to link up with Colonel Ohkarlyn at Malys. After that, unless Colonel Tyrwait reports that something's headed our way from Thesmar, I think we'll have to assume our good friend Hanth has other fish to fry. Probably General Rychtyr, I'm afraid." He grimaced. "If that's the case, though, they're going to be pushing towards Evyrtyn and then up the Sheryl-Seridahn toward Thorast and Reskar."

He paused, and both Lattymyr and Makyntyr nodded in grim understanding. It was barely three hundred and forty miles from Evyrtyn to the Dohlaran border.

"I don't see a lot we can do about that," Ahlverez admitted. "On the other hand, if that *is* what Hanth's up to, he won't be looking our way. In that case, our biggest worry is the damned Charisians moving down the high road from the Kyplyngyr towards Cheryk. And, of course, the possibility that there really is someone coming after us from Sygmar. There's not much we can do about that, either, except to keep moving as quickly as we can in this slop and be sure we've got the closest thing to an effective rearguard we can come up with."

Makyntyr was nodding more emphatically, and Ahlverez shrugged.

"The way I see it, our best bet is to strike northwest from Malys, through Thyssyk, across the high road, and then through Fyrnyst and on up to Fort Sheldyn. Once we cross the high road, we break almost due north for Alyksberg."

"That's a long way, Sir," Lattymyr pointed out in a painfully neutral tone, and Ahlverez barked a laugh.

"'A long way' is putting it mildly, Lynkyn. Or maybe I should say *tactfully!*" He shook his head and began rolling up the tattered sketch map. "Either we're going to find out I'm wrong, and the same bastards who punched out Brahnselyk and Roymark will be waiting on the line of the high road up ahead of us, or else we're going to march an extra two hundred miles or so with stragglers dropping the entire way. But at least this way we've got a chance of getting some of the men home again. If we march towards Trevyr or Evyrtyn, we'll be walking right into Hanth's arms. If this army were fit to fight a battle, coming up behind him might be the best thing we could do, but it isn't. And do any of us really think that after putting together what they did to us at Fort Tairys and Eastshare Cayleb wouldn't have provided Thesmar with the same damned sort of portable angle-gun they used on us? I hate to say it, but if I were Hanth, the one thing I'd want most in all the world would be for us to be stupid enough to attack him in the open field."

His two subordinates looked grim, and more than a little anxious. Not simply because of the additional miles he was proposing to march his exhausted army, but because marching to Alyksberg instead of moving to the sound of the guns might well be taken by the Inquisition as defeatism.

Ahlverez understood exactly what they were thinking, and they might be right. The last thing he needed as the senior surviving officer of the Army of Shiloh, *and* the one who'd handed the initial message from "Colonel Kyrbysh" over to Harless, was to give Zhaspahr Clyntahn additional ammunition when it came time to make examples. On the other hand, if that was how the Grand Inquisitor was thinking, there was already an enormous target pasted to his back. Nothing he did was likely to change that, and if the Inquisition was going to make an example out of him, then he would by God and all the Archangels save as many of the men under his command as he could first.

"I'll discuss it with Father Sulyvyn this evening," he continued, tucking the rolled-up map back into his saddle bag. "I feel confident he'll agree it's our best option, though, so go ahead and start passing the orders now."

"Yes, Sir. Of course." Lattymyr saluted again, turned his horse, and trotted squelchingly back the way he'd come.

"Sir," Makyntyr began, "I think—"

"I'm pretty sure I know exactly what you think, Ahlfryd," Ahlverez interrupted with a twisted smile. "Unfortunately, it's what *I* think that matters, isn't it?"

Makyntyr gazed at him for a moment.

"Yes, Sir. I suppose it is." He held Ahlverez' eyes for another moment, then inhaled deeply. "I'll just go see about redistributing those draft dragons, Sir."

His tone said something very different from his

words, and Ahlverez felt a faint stir of surprise as he realized how much hearing that approval from the ex-naval officer and ally of the Earl of Thirsk meant to him.

"You do that, Ahlfryd," he said, climbing up into his own saddle once more. "I'll see you at supper."

. VIII .
A Recon Skimmer,
Above the Mountains of Light,
and
Langhorne's Tears,
Mountains of Light,
The Temple Lands

"Do you think Sandaria's going to make the adjustment, Aivah?"

"I don't know." Aivah Pahrsahn's expression was troubled on the small cockpit screen. "Before you and Nimue took us to your cave, I would've bet almost anything that she'd be able to. But that was before I knew how much you were going to ask us to believe. Sandaria's one of the Sisters who've interpreted Saint Kohdy's journal to indicate the Adams' and Eves' *souls* had been somewhere else—with God—before they awakened here on Safehold, not that their physical bodies preexisted the Creation itself! What you're asking both of us to believe instead is so far outside anything we'd ever conceived of that I just don't know if she will. For that matter, I'm sure some of the other Sisters' initial reactions would be as bad as Sandaria's—or worse—if we told them the entire truth."

Merlin nodded, his own expression sober.

The problem, from the viewpoint of someone attempting to debunk the lie Langhorne and his command crew had crafted so carefully, was that literally nothing in the Safeholdian worldview offered a thread he could pull to unravel it. Safehold possessed a complete, continuous, seamless historical record from the very Day of Creation, with no breaks, no point at which any researcher or scholar could find a fundamental inconsistency. Unlike the historical record available to the theologians of Old Earth, there were no blank spots, no prehistoric eras, no sacred books whose authorship might be debated, and no civilizations which pre-dated writing, used a different alphabet, or even spoke another language. There were *no* periods which had to be reconstructed without contemporary, written sources—*primary* sources—of unimpeachable authenticity. Secular histories and even *The Testimonies* might disagree over minor factual matters or interpretations, yet that only strengthened the lie's foundation, because human beings *always* saw or remembered events differently. The fact that those differences were acknowledged within the body of the *Writ* and all of the Church's other histories only validated their integrity. And when he came down to it, those histories and firsthand accounts *were* absolutely honest. The people writing them truly had seen, heard, and experienced the events they set forth.

By the same token, the cosmology Langhorne had created, the explanation for natural forces and why things happened, was completely internally consistent. Worse, from Merlin's perspective, the "laws" the *Writ* laid down—Pasquale's laws for health and medicine, Bédard's principles of psychology, Sondheim's precepts for agronomy, Truscott's instructions for animal husbandry—*worked* in real life, and disobeying them produced exactly the consequences the *Writ* predicted. There were no inconsistencies between religious doctrine and the observations and experiences of forty generations of human beings.

Given that lack of inconsistencies, validated again and again throughout that enormous body of recorded history, the very concept of "atheism" had never even existed on Safehold. No one on the entire planet—outside the inner circle, at least—had ever doubted that God and the Archangels existed or that those Archangels had done every single thing the *Holy Writ* said they'd done. Some might be a bit lax in their observation of the *Writ*'s injunctions, some might attend the services of Mother Church only irregularly, yet every single one of them *believed*, with a unanimity that would have been almost more alien than the Gbaba to any citizen of the Terran Federation.

And, as Aivah had just pointed out, even the Sisters of Saint Kohdy believed in the integrity and truth of the *Holy Writ*. In that sense, they were fundamentally different from the Brethren of Saint Zherneau, because they lacked the equally ancient, equally first-person account and third-party documentation from the Terran Federation's past which Jeremiah Knowles had left the Brethren. Under those circumstances, it was far more remarkable that Aivah—Nynian—had been able to accept the truth than that Sandaria *hadn't* been. And Aivah was right about how dangerous that could prove if—when—other Sisters reacted the way Sandaria had.

"So you're certain this is the way you want to handle it?" he asked quietly. Aivah chuckled, and there was at least some genuine humor in it.

"I'm not *certain* about anything just at the moment! If you mean am I confident this is the best way to go about it, given what you've told me and how hugely that differs from what the Sisters have always believed, the answer is yes. If you mean am I confident it's going to *work* just because it's the 'best way,' the answer is I'll be damned if I know."

As responses went, that wasn't the most reassuring one Merlin had ever heard. But at least it had the virtue of frankness. And the bottom line was that if Aivah was to become a full partner of the inner circle, the inner circle had to trust her judgment about the best way to approach the other members of *her* circle.

"Well," he said, checking the navigation display, "we'll be on the ground in another fifteen or twenty minutes. I hope you're bundled up properly."

▼ ▼ ▼

The sun shone down from a sky of flawless, frozen blue. It wasn't far above the mountain peaks—it never got much above the horizon in these high northern latitudes in winter—but the brief day was bright.

Which was not to say it was particularly *warm*. In fact, the temperature hovered five degrees below zero, and the brilliant sun-sparkle off the deep, drifted snow was a sharp (and blinding) contrast to the blue dimness in the depths of the narrow alpine valleys. That snow was several feet deep—deeper than Merlin was tall, in places—and it wasn't going to melt before June. It would have provided heavy going for any flesh-and-blood human, although one might have been forgiven for concluding otherwise as the two travelers moved across it.

Merlin slogged along briskly in the practiced, swinging stride of an expert snowshoer. In fact, he was rather short of the years of experience he was displaying, but a PICA's ability to program muscle memory made up for a lot. Unlike the aforementioned flesh-and-blood human, he needed to perform an action properly only once in order to be able to perform it again, flawlessly, any time he had to. He could no longer count the number of times he'd found that capability useful here on Safehold, but if pressed, he would have been forced to admit he'd never anticipated doing what he was doing at the moment.

"You really are quite good at this, Merlin!" Aivah remarked. He turned his head and looked over his shoulder, and she grinned at him. "I'm a fairly good skier myself, but snowshoes and I have never gotten along. Even if we had, I'm so badly out of shape I'd be panting like a bellows by now."

"Which doesn't even consider how much you're enjoying yourself at the moment, does it?"

"It *is* rather fun," she acknowledged cheerfully. "I remember how Father—Adorai's father, I mean; not that miserable excuse for a human being who got my mother pregnant—used to take turns carrying both of us piggyback when I was a little girl." Her tone softened. "When he did, I knew what a *real* father was like. There's no way I could ever repay him and Mother for giving me the opportunity—the *gift*—to understand there truly is love in the world. Sometimes, when the decisions are especially hard, that's all that keeps me going."

"I know." Merlin's voice was as soft as hers had been. "I've been . . . damaged by a lot of things, Nynian, starting with the fact that I grew up knowing I was going to die before I was forty and that the entire human race was going to die with me. That . . . leaves a mark, and finding out what happened to Shan-wei and the Commodore and everything that's happened here on Safehold since I woke up didn't exactly make everything all better. But you're right about how much difference something as simple—and profound—as love makes. It's what keeps me trying and as close to sane as I still am."

"You seem almost insanely sane to me, given everything you've been through," Aivah objected.

"Appearances can be deceptive." He shrugged easily, despite her weight on his back. "Although I probably *am* a bit closer to sane since Nahrmahn chewed me up one side and down the other for floundering in self-pity after the Canal Raid. But I'm afraid I'm still a little more dubious about my sanity quotient than my friends are." His smile was a bit twisted.

"For what it's worth, I'm on their side." Aivah rested her mittened palm lightly against his cheek. "And I don't envy you. I always thought the task the Sisters and I had undertaken was hard enough, and we only wanted to *reform* the Church, not destroy it! That doesn't hold a candle to the one that got dumped on your shoulders."

"Maybe. But it didn't exactly get 'dumped' on me, you know. Or not on Nimue Alban, at least."

"But that's an important distinction," she pointed out as the two of them moved from brilliant sunlight into the deep shadows of the valley before them. "*You* didn't volunteer, whatever Nimue Alban might have done. You accepted the responsibility without any memory of having agreed to shoulder it, and the you you are today, Merlin Athrawes, is the product of that acceptance. You're not Nimue Alban; you're *you*, and from everything I've seen, you're quite a remarkable human being who just happens to live inside a machine."

"Nice of you to say so, anyway."

Merlin's light tone fooled neither of them, and she patted his cheek again before replacing her hand on his shoulder and adjusting her balance. Not so much to help him, as to position herself as comfortably as possible on his back.

Despite her slenderness and the fact that she was a foot shorter than he was, she knew she was no lightweight. Whatever disparaging remarks she might level at her own physical condition, vigorous exercise had always been a part of her life. She'd walked, run, and ridden horses whenever she could, and her Zion mansion, like her Siddar City townhouse, had boasted a well-appointed gymnasium to tide her over the winter months. Part of that was because she enjoyed the workouts, and part of it had been a courtesan's need to fine-tune—and preserve—her physical attractiveness. But for both those reasons, she was remarkably well-muscled, even more than Sharleyan Ahrmahk, and that made her a solid, substantial weight no flesh-and-blood human being, even one Merlin Athrawes' size, could have carried so effortlessly.

Or so long. Merlin had landed the recon skimmer on a mountainside above the northernmost of the alpine lakes Safeholdian geographers had named Langhorne's Tears. It was an inconvenient eight straight-line miles from their objective, which worked out to twice that distance on foot, but the landing spot he'd chosen had the advantage of a cave large enough to accommodate the skimmer. And as he'd been demonstrating for the last two hours, neither her weight, nor the altitude, nor the snow, nor the steepness of the slopes made any difference to him. In its own way, that was more impressive than all the other wonders he and Nimue Chwaeriau had demonstrated to her and Sandaria.

*And it never seems to cross his mind that he's actually better than a flesh-and-blood human,* she thought. *He comes from a place and a . . . technology*—she tasted the still unfamiliar word carefully as she used it—*none of us could possibly have imagined; he has knowledge most of us can't imagine, really, even now; and he's potentially immortal. Yet despite all of that, he treats us as his equals—in the privacy of his own mind, not just for public consumption—without even seeming to realize he's doing it. I wonder if he even begins to understand just how remarkable that makes him?*

She'd found Ahbraim Zhevons fascinating when they first met in Zion. She hadn't known the source of the understanding and compassion she'd seen in his brown eyes, yet they'd been intensely attracting qualities even then. Now that she'd been allowed a glimpse inside the life and soul of Merlin Athrawes, she found them far more than simply attractive. How did someone survive a lifetime's hopeless fight against the extinction of her entire race and then endure all the human being inside Nimue Alban's PICA had been through here on Safehold and still *feel* so deeply, without walling himself off?

Her own life had taught her too much about barriers and the price of survival, and she wondered if perhaps that was the reason she felt such an intense kinship with Merlin. Despite all the centuries in which his PICA had rested in its hidden cavern, *experientially* he was fifteen Safeholdian years younger than she. Yet his life had demanded even more sacrifice, dedication, and secrecy than her own. More than anyone else she'd ever known, even among the Sisters, he understood what she'd done with her own life . . . and what it had cost her.

She found herself snuggling more closely against his back—as closely as her parka permitted, at least—and rested her chin on his right shoulder, her cheek against the side of his neck, as he carried her smoothly down the valley.

▼ ▼ ▼

There was nothing particularly distinctive about the mountain above them.

It was steep—sheer in places—yet no steeper than many others. Its summit soared well above the tree line, its permanent snowpack gleaming brilliantly in the sunlight, but so did most of the others reaching upward around it. Merlin had gone back over the mapping imagery Owl had collected from orbit once Aivah told him where their destination lay, and the narrow track up from the valley floor could be picked out in the imagery from high summer. So could the gardens the Sisters tended during that brief warmth, yet now all those clues lay hidden under the featureless snow stretching away up the mountainside.

It was ironic, he thought, that the hidden Tomb of Saint Kohdy lay barely five hundred air miles from the cave in which his own PICA had slept away so many centuries. And that it, too, was concealed in a cave. The Church's lack of SNARCs probably made that degree of overhead cover redundant—these days, at least—yet that might not have been the case when the tomb was first established, for he had no idea what the "minor angels" who'd expunged *Seijin* Kohdy from the Church's annals might have been capable of. The fact that they'd commanded sufficient kinetic-energy weaponry to destroy the Order of Saint Kohdy's original abbey, even after the "Archangels'" departure, was not a pleasant thought, especially when he found himself wondering who else might have been left the equivalent of the Wylsynn family's Stone of Schueler.

At least Merlin had ample evidence that the *Group of Four* possessed no aerial reconnaissance assets. If it had had them, the Great Canal Raid could never have succeeded and the trap Duke Eastshare had sprung on the Army of Shiloh would never have worked. So presumably the only way the present-day Church could spot the Tomb of Saint Kohdy would be for someone to literally stumble over it on the ground, and that made the Abbey of the Snows, sixty-odd miles to the west on the Stone Shadow River, the Tomb's true protection.

Like the Tellesberg Monastery of Saint Zherneau, the Abbey of the Snows, overlooking the largest of Langhorne's Tears, had existed since the days of the War Against the Fallen. The imagery and radar mapping Owl's SNARCs had amassed since Aivah told them about it confirmed that it had been built on the site of an even earlier structure, although the Abbey contained no lingering trace of the technology Safehold had been forbidden to develop. The evidence of that technology was clear enough from the arrow-straight approach road cut up to it through the steep sides of the Stone Shadow's narrow valley and from the ceramacrete of which its ground floor had been constructed, however. It also accorded well with the Abbey's own traditions that it had been built on what had once been an earthly dwelling place of the Archangel Langhorne himself. The lakes took their name from his traditional association with them as a spot to which he'd retreated when he needed solitude and the severe serenity of their beauty to refresh his soul. They'd been called Langhorne's Joy before the Fall; they'd been renamed the Tears after his mortal body was destroyed by Kauyung's treachery.

Despite the spike of anger Merlin always felt when he encountered yet another charming legend about Langhorne, he understood exactly why an austere, contemplative order would find this the ideal place to build an abbey, and the Chihirite nuns who lived here and maintained the Abbey with loving devotion found a deep, sincere joy in sharing it with others.

During the summer months, it wasn't at all unusual for pilgrims to trek up the winding, narrow, steeply climbing Stone Shadow Valley to spend several five-days in retreat and introspection in the Abbey's guest quarters. Of course, by September, the snows for which the Abbey was named were already falling this high in the Mountains of Light. By mid-October, the only route in was closed by snow and ice, and it stayed that way until June. The nuns of the Abbey passed those winter months in study, prayer, and the calligraphy of the beautiful hand-lettered copies of the *Holy Writ* for which their scriptorium was famed.

What no one outside the Abbey knew was that for all its long association with the Order of Chihiro, the Abbey of the Snows had been thoroughly infiltrated by the Sisters of Saint Kohdy over six hundred years ago. Indeed, the process had begun even before that . . . about the time a forethoughtful abbess of the Order of Saint Kohdy had enlisted the assistance of the abbess of the Sisters of the Snows who'd happened to be her second cousin. The Sisters of the Snows had been instrumental in the secret construction of Saint Kohdy's first, simple tomb in the mountains east of Langhorne's Tears. Only a handful of them had known what was actually hidden there, but gradually, over the years, that had changed. By now, the entire Order of the Sisters of the Snows had been absorbed into the Sisters of Saint Kohdy. Or perhaps it would be equally accurate to say that the Sisters of the Snows had extended their membership—and their protection—over the Sisters of Saint Kohdy.

In either case, every Sister of the Snows was also a Sister of Saint Kohdy, and the Abbey of the Snows served as the protective gatekeeper of the cavern sanctuary which shielded the saint's mortal remains.

It was, Merlin acknowledged, a remarkably effective defense in depth, yet the Abbey of the Snows was too remote and inconveniently located to serve as the Sisters' operational headquarters. That was why the current mother superior had based herself in Zion—prior to her move to Siddar City—although Merlin doubted the majority of her predecessors had. Everything he'd learned from Aivah so far seemed to confirm his suspicion that young Nynian Rychtair had seen the Order's role rather differently from those who'd come before her.

The Sisters had been a persistent, quiet force for good within Mother Church from their inception, but Nynian had . . . radicalized them. That was the best way to put it, he supposed. It was possible some of her predecessors would have made the same decisions she'd made, if they'd lived to see the corruption of the vicarate Nynian had seen, yet he rather doubted that *any* of those previous mothers superior would have spent thirty years training a cadre of assassins and saboteurs in the name of their patron saint. The sheer size of the Order's network and its deeply embedded traditions of secrecy and anonymity had offered superb cover, concealment, and a support structure for Nynian's more . . . proactive preparations, although he had to wonder if she'd ever truly believed she'd be in a position to make use of those assassins and saboteurs.

Now he set her on her own feet—or, rather, on the second pair of snowshoes he'd towed behind them the entire way here—and gazed up that bleak, bare mountainside.

"Back on Old Earth, they used to say that real estate value was all about location, location, location," he remarked.

"The Sisters would certainly agree with that, *Seijin* Merlin." Aivah's eyes twinkled, but her tone was serious. "When the Angels themselves decree your extermination, there's no such thing as a location that's *too* remote."

"I can see how that might be the case."

"I'm sure you can, given what you've said about the bombardment platform and the capabilities of your own SNARCs. Of course, our true first line of defense hasn't been hiding from the Inquisition; it's been preventing the Inquisition from realizing we exist." She smiled thinly. "People don't look for things they don't know exist, and we've been careful to keep it that way where the Inquisition is concerned."

"Makes sense to me," Merlin acknowledged, and took her elbow as they began making their way up the steep slope. "I suppose that's the reason for the Bédardist chapel in the same cave?"

"Of course it is," Aivah replied, although the combination of thin air and exertion left her rather breathless.

He arched an eyebrow at her, and she chuckled.

"Like I said, there's no such thing as being too remote, Merlin, but we have to have *some* traffic in and out of the Tomb. And we normally have a dozen or so Sisters here, where their official job is to care for the Holy Bédard's chapel and live lives of deep meditation and prayer. We call them the Keepers, and you might not believe just how sought-after that duty is. Our veneration for the Saint's never precluded sharing his tomb with the Archangels, and the Sisters've always felt a strong kinship with the Bédardists, so there's nothing fraudulent about our devotion to her chapel. And few other houses of religion, including the Abbey of the Snows, offer such a wonderful opportunity for contemplation and prayer. All of us treasure that, and this is the very heart of what our Order was created to accomplish, a place where we can be who and what we truly are without fear of giving away the secret of our existence. It's a refuge we can return to, a place where we can be with our Sisters and rejuvenate both our purpose and our faith."

"The Brethren of Saint Zherneau feel the same way about their monastery in Tellesberg," he told her, and she nodded.

"We're like them in an awful lot of ways, I suppose, although I have to say that the way they accomplished so much . . . preparation in Charis before you ever arrived is more impressive than anything we've achieved. And I envy their ability to accept the truth about you so much more readily than many of my Sisters will be able to."

"Don't sell yourselves short!" Merlin shook his head and then half lifted her over a particularly difficult section of the putative trail they were following. "You've been at least as active for four hundred years longer than they have, and you've done it in the belly of the beast, as it were. Right here on the Mainland—even in the heart of Zion, for God's sake!"

"Oh, I know that." She smiled up at him and patted his parka-covered breastplate in thanks as he set her back on her feet. "What I meant is that they not only managed to survive after learning the truth—the full *truth* about the Archangels and the Church, which we never did—but to hang on to their own faith in God despite all the lies they knew had been told in His name. That's impressive, Merlin." It was her turn to shake her head. "I hope the Sisters can do the same thing."

"Really?" He gazed down at her, sapphire eyes dark.

"Of course I do." She met those eyes levelly. "I think Archbishop Maikel's entirely correct. Your waking up here, the corruption of the vicarate, the Group of Four's actions, the rise of the Reformists, King Haarahld's readiness to accept your help and defy Clyntahn, and the creation of the Charisian Empire—for that matter, the existence of two people as remarkable as Cayleb and Sharleyan to *lead* that empire . . . I genuinely believe all of that truly is God working to reveal the truth to His children once again, Merlin. I don't pretend to understand all His purposes, or why He's waited so long to act, and as an intellectual exercise, I'm prepared to admit I may believe all of this is part of His plan because I'm not brave enough to reject my faith in Him. But in here," she pressed her left hand against her own chest, "there's no doubt about Him or about His love for His children."

She grinned suddenly.

"I was prepared to topple the vicarate if the opportunity presented itself, Merlin, because I knew it couldn't possibly be doing His will, whatever it claimed. If I believed God Himself was calling me to do that when I also believed every sentence of the *Writ* was His own inerrant word, how can I possibly question this newer and far greater revelation you've shared with me?"

"You're a remarkable woman, Nynian Rychtair," he told her. "I don't imagine I'm the only one who's ever told you that, but I trust you'll acknowledge that I have a rather clearer perspective on that than most others do."

"Merlin, your perspective—not simply on the situation here on Safehold but on what it means to be *human*—has to be the closest thing to truly unique that's ever existed." Her grin faded into an intense, serious expression and she shook her head. "I've tried to imagine what that sort of perspective might be like, but I don't think I can. I don't think anyone else could."

He gazed at her for another moment, then looked back down at the slippery trail as he considered what she'd said. She probably had a point, yet her own life experience undoubtedly put her in a better position to understand his own perspective than anyone else on Safehold—outside Nimue Chwaeriau, at any rate.

"I—" he began, only to stop in mid-word.

"What?" she asked.

He looked up the slope for a second, then smiled crookedly at her.

"I've been monitoring the remotes Owl deployed around the Tomb. One of your Sisters just looked out the window, it seems. There appears to be just a bit of consternation raging up ahead."

"I can imagine," Aivah said dryly. "I suppose that under the circumstances, we should probably pick up the pace—pick up *my* pace, really—so we can set their minds at ease a little sooner."

▼ ▼ ▼

Sister Emylee, the senior Keeper, sat in the plain but comfortably cushioned wooden chair across the refectory table and watched Aivah and Merlin sip hot tea. She was in her mid-fifties, two or three years older than

Aivah, with dark hair beginning to show broad swaths of silver and eyes the color of a clear winter sky. At the moment, those blue-gray eyes were dark, filled with shadows and lingering questions.

She'd sent the other Keepers—there were only nine of them at the moment—back to their duties. It said a great deal for the Sisterhood's discipline that they'd gone without argument, although not even their obedience had been enough to prevent lingering looks over their shoulders. Only four of them had ever actually met their Mother Superior, and there'd been consternation in plenty when Aivah turned up in the depth of winter, on foot, with Merlin in tow.

Sister Emylee, Merlin thought, obviously shared that consternation in full.

"I'm pleased to see you, Mother," she said after several moments, "but I'm sure you can understand how . . . astonishing I find your arrival here. And yours, of course, *Seijin* Merlin."

"As I'm sure you've already realized, Sister Emylee, the *seijin* has quite a lot to do with my arrival," Aivah replied. "After all, you've read Saint Kohdy's journal."

The Keeper's eyes flickered as Aivah mentioned the journal in front of Merlin, but she only bent her head in acknowledgment. Aivah sipped more tea, then set the heavy mug on the table and met Sister Emylee's gaze levelly.

"*Seijin* Merlin is, indeed, a *seijin* in the old sense of the word," she said quietly. "I can tell you of my own personal observation that he has all of the capabilities Saint Kohdy had, and several I doubt even the Saint possessed. And," she smiled faintly, "I can now honestly say I understand the journal's references to being transported by the Archangels' *hikousen*. It's . . . not quite what we thought it was, but the actual experience is certainly miraculous enough."

"The *Seijin*'s been touched by the *kyousei hi*?" Sister Emylee's eyes widened, and Merlin shook his head.

"I would never make such a claim, Sister," he told her. "And, trust me, no holy fire burns about *me!*" He quirked a smile at her. "Madam Pahrsahn—well, Mother Nynian, really, I suppose—has a somewhat questionable sense of humor. I'm sure you've observed that for yourself."

Aivah shot him a humorous glare, and the nun chuckled. The byplay seemed to relax her, and she sat back in her chair.

"The truth is, Emylee," Aivah said then, "that when Saint Kohdy wrote about his *hikousen* he wasn't actually referring to the *kyousei hi* the way we thought he was. A *hikousen* was actually a . . . a *vessel* empowered by the mysteries of the Archangels, I suppose is probably the best way to describe it. *Seijin* Merlin can summon the same sort of vessel to his service when he requires it, but the *kyousei hi* which enveloped the *hikousen* of the Archangels themselves was visible to mortals only because they were the Archangels' own vehicles."

Sister Emylee's eyes widened once more, this time in wonder rather than shock, and Merlin nodded gravely. It went against the grain to give even passing credibility to the lie of the "Archangels," but it was scarcely the first time he'd had to tread the measures of a Safeholdian's faith carefully. And, as Sandaria Ghatfryd demonstrated, even a Sister of Saint Kohdy was likely to be ill prepared for the wholesale destruction of all she'd been raised to believe. If Sandaria found the truth difficult to accept even with the evidence of Nimue's Cave all about her, how could anyone expect Sister Emylee to accept it *without* that evidence?

*Aivah was right . . . again*, he acknowledged. *I may not like it, but it's clearly time for a variant on the "the* seijin *sees visions" gambit.*

And, as had been the case with King Haarahld and his councilors, that explanation was entirely true . . . as far as it went. That was important to him, and Aivah had agreed it was essential that they never lie to the Sisters. The potential consequences if those who'd trusted them discovered they'd been lied to were bad enough to contemplate, but for all the masks Aivah had been forced to assume, all the times she'd had no choice but to dissemble, her position was as driven by moral considerations as by pragmatism. She owed her sisters the truth; if she couldn't give it to them in its entirety, she would at least give them no falsehoods in its place.

"Even though *Seijin* Merlin has access to his own *hikousen*, he can't simply go dashing about the world in it," she continued now. "Not openly, at least. I'm sure you can imagine how Clyntahn and the Inquisition would denounce it as proof of his demonic origins, especially if it wasn't touched by the *kyousei hi* whenever it was seen!"

She rolled her eyes, and Sister Emylee nodded emphatically.

"Well, for the same reasons, I can't just suddenly appear in Zion—or anywhere else, for that matter—either." This time Aivah laughed softly. "Your Keepers' reaction when the *seijin* and I came hiking up the mountainside makes *that* clear enough, doesn't it?"

Sister Emylee nodded again, winter-blue eyes twinkling, and Aivah smiled back at her, then allowed her expression to sober once again.

"The real reason the *seijin* brought me here was to allow him to examine the journal, Emylee. As Saint Kohdy himself recorded, *seijins* are touched only by the *anshinritsumei*. For all their other abilities, they aren't Angels or Archangels, and he wishes to consult Saint Kohdy's account of the War Against the Fallen for whatever insight it may provide. And—" she met Sister Emylee's eyes levelly "—to read the sections of the journal we've never been able to."

▼ ▼ ▼

Saint Kohdy's tomb was beautiful.

The chapel dedicated to Bédard was lovely enough, although small. The simple chambers of the Keepers were half-built and half-carved into the stone of the cavern walls to either side of its entrance. That entrance had itself been closed by a stone wall, pierced by four beautiful stained glass windows which portrayed famous episodes from the Archangel Bédard's acts on Safehold. Little light came through them in the winter, but in the summer they must have turned the cavern's interior into a jewelry case of richly colored illumination. That light was also directed inward, to where the Archangel's chapel, dominated by a statue of her holding the lamp which was her symbol, sealed the end of the cavern.

Or what *seemed* to be its end, at any rate.

In fact, the cavern extended over a mile deeper into the mountain, and it was only part of an even larger series of caves which ran much farther, although the Sisters of Saint Kohdy had closed off his tomb from the rest of the cave system with a masonry wall. There were no stained glass windows here, but the native stone of the natural cavern had been smoothed and polished to form a perfectly circular rotunda, then carved with scenes from Saint Kohdy's life. Alternating, perpetually lit lamps of silver and gold, filled with perfumed oils, had been set into those walls at regular intervals. Centuries of lamp smoke and incense had darkened the rough stone roof of the cavern, and their light spilled over the carven panels and filled the hushed reverence of that chamber with honey-toned illumination.

The sarcophagus at the rotunda's center had been carved out of a single massive block of de Castro marble. That rose-colored stone, marked by dense swirling patterns and quarried from the de Castro Mountains in North Harchong, was the favorite medium of the Church's sculptors and architects. Exactly how the stone for the sarcophagus—over ten feet long and four feet tall—had been hauled to its present site was undoubtedly a story worth hearing, but Merlin already knew whose hands had created the larger-than-life recumbent effigy of the saint which adorned it. The detail of that incredibly lifelike image was breathtaking, and the sides of the sarcophagus were ornamented with a beautiful rendition of what appeared to be infinitely repeating patterns of highland lilies, the flower associated with martyrdom and the *seijins* who'd battled the forces of darkness in the War Against the Fallen.

Like the reliefs adorning the cavern's walls, the creation of that sarcophagus had been no an easy task. Nor had it been accomplished quickly, and every square inch was the work of the Sisters of Saint Kohdy, for no outsider had ever set foot here before Merlin himself.

There'd been no stonemasons or sculptors among the Sisters who'd first concealed Kohdy's body here. That had come later, as the hidden order slowly increased in number and some of its members with the talent for the task were trained for it in the great Zhyahngdu Academy in southern Tiegelkamp. Zhyahngdu had produced the Church of God Awaiting's sculptors for almost nine hundred years, and it was obvious that the Sisters whose hands had created the beauty around him could easily have been among the most famous of all Safeholdian artists. But they hadn't chosen to share their talent with the rest of Safehold; all of it had been lavished on this hidden, polished gem they'd known the rest of the world would never see, never even know existed.

He stood for a long, silent moment with the respect the faith and piety of the tomb's creators and caretakers deserved. The man buried here had been no more divine than the "archangels" who'd created the Church he'd served. But that took nothing away from his service, just as nothing could ever diminish the fidelity, belief, and devotion of those who revered his memory, and Merlin's nostrils flared as he inhaled the perfume of the lamps which burned perpetually in Kohdy's memory.

Then, finally, he turned from the sarcophagus to the equally beautiful golden reliquary which housed Saint Kohdy's journal. It sat atop a pedestal of gold-inlaid marble in a niche carved into the cavern's northern wall, flanked by an armor tree bearing an antique cuirass and helmet and a featureless block of de Castro marble impaled by a long, straight-bladed sword. The armor looked like bronze, and the sword like Damascus steel, but both were actually made of battle steel, and that sword could have been drawn from its stony sheath by anyone. For that matter, it could have been drawn *through* that block of stone, for its edge was every bit as keen as that of the *wakazashi* riding at Merlin's hip.

Aivah and Sister Emylee stood watching as he crossed to the reliquary and opened it. The volume which lay within it appeared to be bound in leather, but that, too, was deceptive. He lifted it gently from its velvet nest, opened the cover, and looked down at the strong, sharply slanted handwriting of its first page. Like the armor and the sword, the journal was made out of advanced synthetics, and its pages were as flexible as the day they'd been extruded.

"My name is Cody Cortazar," it began, "and I am an Adam, honored far beyond any mortal man might have deserved to stand beside the Angels and Archangels themselves against the forces of Darkness.

"My service began in the dark days of the opening battles of what has become the War Against the Fallen. Much of my memory of my early life has become unclear, almost as if it had been no more than a dream, but I remember volunteering to serve against the Fallen. And I remember awakening in the sacred sickbay, attended by the Archangels' servitors and with my mind filled by knowledge and skills far beyond the merely mortal, endowed by the very touch of God.

"The fight against Kau-yung's followers was not going well, and . . . ."

# The Delthak Works,
# Barony of High Rock,
# Kingdom of Old Charis,
# Charisian Empire

"Well, it's certainly *impressive*, Brahd."

Ehdwyrd Howsmyn folded his hands behind him as he walked down the length of the hulking "steam automotive" which sat silently on the gleaming steel rails. Brahd Stylmyn, the mastermind behind the project, walked beside him, followed by Stahlman Praigyr.

"The question, of course," Howsmyn continued, "is whether or not the damned thing will actually work."

"The models have all worked the way Doctor Vyrnyr and Doctor Mahklyn predicted, Sir," Stylmyn pointed out respectfully. "And Stahlman here swears the full-scale will work just as well."

"And very reassuring that is, too, I'm sure," Howsmyn said dryly, glancing over his shoulder at the small, tough-looking man behind them. "So I should take it you're confident enough to take it out on its first run, Master Praigyr?"

"Aye, Sir. That I am." Praigyr's wide grin showed his two missing teeth. "Those early models of Master Stylmyn's were fun clear through, but I'm really looking forward to seeing this 'un in action!"

Howsmyn shook his head, but he smiled while he did it. Watching Praigyr chuff around the circular path of the test track on the undersized models of experimental automotives had been a source of considerable amusement for the Delthak Works' labor force. Many members of the audience had spent their time laughing, in fact, but it had scarcely been the first time the baby steps of one of Delthak's offspring had generated amusement even among the people most devoted to making the contraption work.

The industrialist paused, looking up at the automotive's tall smokestack, then backed deliberately away until he could see the entire vehicle without turning his head.

For all its size, it had a curiously unfinished—or perhaps the word he wanted was "crude"—appearance compared to the imagery of last-generation steam locomotives from Old Earth with which Owl had provided him. By the same token, though, it looked far sleeker and much more sophisticated than its early-nineteenth-century predecessors ever had. It was built in what would have been called a 2-4-0 configuration back on Old Earth, with a two-wheeled front bogey followed by two paired drive wheels powered by two twenty-one-inch-diameter drive cylinders with a thirty-inch stroke. Unlike the marine engines which were Praigyr's first true love, the automotive used a fire tube arrangement, with the hot gases from the furnace carried through a water-filled boiler. It was, however, designed to run at rather higher pressure and temperature than most Old Earth locomotives prior to the twentieth century, and it incorporated both a superheater (tubes in which boiler steam passed through the hot furnace gasses in front of the boiler proper, which further heated it to produce "dry steam" for the cylinders) and a blast pipe using waste steam to boost the firebox draught to increase its efficiency. The superheater had been one of Praigyr's ideas, based on his work with the marine engines, but the blast pipe had been Howsmyn's suggestion, based on input from Owl and Doctor Dahnel Vyrnyr's suggestions. There was enormous room for improvement in the efficiency of both, since Vyrnyr's development of pressure dynamics was still at a very early stage, and there were still a few problems with the poppet valves which admitted steam to the cylinders. Despite that, the current design would produce about sixty-one dragonpower (over fifteen hundred Old Earth horsepower) by Owl's calculations and was probably already on a par with those of the last two decades or so of the nineteenth century.

The prototype before him had cost an enormous amount in terms of skilled labor and resources at a time when both were in critically short supply, but as with so many of the Delthak Works' other projects, the men (and women) responsible for designing it had kept their eye firmly on how to produce its progeny as efficiently as possible. While the prototype was essentially hand built, it was designed so that its successors could be constructed from a series of subassemblies, all sized and planned to facilitate rapid fabrication.

That would help a great deal if Howsmyn committed to putting them into production, but that would still require yet another expansion in his ability to produce the necessary large scale—*very* large scale—steel castings. In fact, he'd have to add a dedicated automotive works to his already enormous facility, not to mention an even larger one dedicated solely to rolling out rails for the eventual tracks. On the other hand, that sort of expansion was something Howsmyn had learned to take in stride, and the work Delthak had carried out in designing and building the Navy's steam power plants, armor, and new heavy guns would help enormously if he did. And he was pretty sure he would, given the personal interest Cayleb and (especially) Sharleyan were taking in the project.

*Of course, how I'm going to produce enough steel to keep all of my balls in the air at once is an interesting question,* he reflected dryly. *Thank God the Lake Lymahn Works are finally coming online! But even with that extra output . . . .*

He managed to suppress a shudder as he considered the additional strain this promised to place upon his steel works. Whatever Stylmyn and Praigyr—or Sharleyan, for that matter—wanted, railroads were simply going to have to take second or even third priority for the immediate future. He had the ironclads to finish, the *King Haarahlds* (and their guns) to complete, and all the artillery and small arms required by the Imperial Charisian Army to build first. After those minor matters were out of the way, he'd be able to give the automotive the priority Stylmyn clearly felt it deserved.

*And Brahd isn't far wrong about that, either*, he reminded himself. *It was railroads more than anything else that really drove the development of Old Earth's steel industry. And to be honest, railroads are going to go even farther towards breaking the Proscriptions' grip than artillery is. This is something anyone—especially any* land-based *power—who wants to compete industrially will simply* have *to have. Once they find out about it, anyway.*

"All right," he said finally, turning away from the automotive and meeting Stylmyn's gaze. "Father Paityr's coming by tomorrow or the next day for you to demonstrate your new monstrosity for him. So far, he seems comfortable with the idea, so please try to avoid blowing it up in front of him."

"We'll do that thing, Sir," Stylmyn assured him with a grin, and Howsmyn snorted.

"Easy enough to say *now*," he observed darkly. "If it does blow up, you'll get blown up right along with it, though. Which means *I'm* the one who'll have to explain it all to him after the fact!"

"Stahlman and I will do our best to avoid putting you to that sort of inconvenience, Sir," Stylmyn promised.

"See that you do," Howsmyn said sternly, then sighed. "And now I have to go have a few words with Master Mahldyn about the new rifle lines."

"Good luck, Sir," Stylmyn said, and Howsmyn snorted again and headed for his waiting bicycle.

Ehdwyrd Howsmyn's work force was the largest Safehold had ever seen. The Delthak Works alone employed more than forty thousand workers, which didn't include his army of miners or his gasworks—or his canal builders, bargemen, and shipyard workers, for that matter. Nor did it include any of his *other* foundries and manufactory sites. All told, he had well in excess of a hundred thousand workers in his employ, and the number continued to grow steadily. Delthak was, however, by far his largest single enterprise, and it was over two miles from the fledgling automotive shop to the Urvyn Mahndrayn Rifle Shop, the manufactory floor where the Imperial Charisian Army's revolvers and new rifles were produced. The permanent pall of smoke cast by the coking ovens and blast furnaces gave the air an acrid, sinus-stinging edge and the noise level and sheer, hurtling energy level were both daunting to the uninitiated and more than enough to impose caution on any cyclist trying to make his way through it.

He passed scores of other bicycles—they were becoming steadily more common, especially around Howsmyn's various manufactories—and he heard handlebar-mounted push bells chiming as their riders warned people they were coming. It was insufficient warning to prevent the occasional collision and fall, but most of his workers were acquiring the habit of nipping out of the way before they were run down by the new contraptions. They certainly made movement faster and more efficient, and if Nahrmahn Tidewater's proposal to manufacture pneumatic tires from Corisandian rubber worked out . . . .

He looked up at the smoke cloud with his customary mixed feelings. On the one hand, he hated what it was doing to his workers' lungs. On the other hand, it was the unavoidable consequence of producing the quantities of steel Charis needed for its survival. And whatever reservations he might have about it, those coking ovens and blast furnaces produced byproducts—from the coal gas lighting his manufactory floors and buildings and the Tellesberg waterfront to the creosote which would preserve the wooden sleepers Stylmyn's railroads would eventually require—that were of almost incalculable value. And in a very few more months, some of those same byproducts would be finding their way into the production of Safehold's first smokeless powder and artillery bursting charges.

In the meantime, the Lywysite manufactory west of the main Delthak Works had gone into volume production. At Merlin's urging, the initial pilot production had gone to Earl Hanth, who'd certainly used it to good effect, but producing it had scarcely been an efficient process. The new manufactory, on the other hand, incorporated dozens of lessons learned in the prototyping process, and it looked as if it was going to exceed Sahndrah Lywys' original output projections by at least ten percent. Howsmyn hoped that would offset her disgruntlement with what Cayleb and Sharleyan had insisted on naming the new explosive.

She'd wanted to call it by Alfred Nobel's original name, since most of her work had simply been the duplication of his Old Earth manufacturing processes. Unfortunately, no one had been able to come up with a reasonable explanation for a bizarre word like "dynamite," and she'd been less than delighted when her monarchs insisted on naming it after her, instead. The new manufactory's products were actually superior to Nobel's early accomplishments, but remained unsuitable as a shell filler for all the reasons most nitroglycerine-based explosives had: sweating, sensitivity, and its tendency to degrade in storage.

Nitrocellulose propellants were almost certainly going to be available before a suitable high-explosive shell filler, but Lywys was hot on the trail of military-grade TNT. She had all the ingredients (including toulene, extracted from the blue-needle pine, a tree which grew commonly in Charis and Emerald); it was mainly a question of producing them in sufficient quantity with the necessary safeguards against toxicity. And, Howsmyn admitted unhappily, with an eye towards limiting the long-term pollution volume production would create. As with so many other aspects of the Charisian version of the Industrial Revolution, they would do all they could to mitigate the consequences, yet they had no choice but to pursue the processes to create the weapons they needed to survive.

In many ways, picric acid was simpler to manufacture. It was also more powerful than TNT, but it carried serious stability and corrosion issues. For all of its other drawbacks, TNT was extraordinarily stable and far safer to store or handle, and its lower melting point made it much easier to fill shells with it.

The small arms cartridge production and filling assembly lines were in full swing at the Delthak Works, as well, although—like the Lywysite manufactory—the powder works had been located well clear of the main facility. Ultimately, however, the bulk of Charis' cartridge-filling capacity would be located at Howsmyn's Cahnyr Works, the satellite manufactory on Gull Inlet, just off Eraystor Bay in Emerald's Earldom of Bayshore.

More and more of the Empire's gunpowder production had already been moved to Emerald. Partly that had been to disperse production and decrease the Empire's dependency on the established Charisian powder plants, especially after the horrific explosion at the Hairatha powder mill. More of it had been simple rationalization, however, in light of Emerald's proximity to The Wyvernry. That craggy headland at the northwestern end of Silverlode Island, across Dolphin Reach from Eraystor, boasted immense, cliff-like deposits of wyvern guano which were the main reason Silverlode had been settled (if one could call its sparse population density "settled," even now) in the first place. They were also the reason the entire island had been claimed by the farsighted Ahrmahk Dynasty long before any of its members had ever heard of someone named Jeremiah Knowles, because of their value to the fertilizer industry. Zhaspahr Clyntahn's embargo had put a major crimp into the profitable nitrates trade with the mainland, but those same nitrates were just as important for the burgeoning munitions industry.

Given the quantities of powder Emerald was already producing and the fact that the Delthak Works' current case production was higher than could be filled locally, it made sense to ship the extra cases to Emerald. Eventually, as the Cahnyr Works' own case-drawing lines reached production, Emerald would also provide at least fifty percent of the Empire's total cartridge cases, and Cayleb and Sharleyan intended to locate much of the smokeless powder production in the island, as well. For that matter, they'd also begun installing case-drawing equipment at the Maikelberg Works, where the first of the new Chisholmian rifle- and pistol-making lines were already in operation. It was part of their plan to spread employment—and the heretical concepts of industrialization—as broadly as possible among their subjects.

And it would be a good thing when the Cahnyr Works hit their stride, Howsmyn reflected, pedaling steadily, because Kynt Clareyk's 1st Corps had been completely reequipped with the new cartridge-firing weapons. Every one of his scout snipers and every man of the 3rd Mounted Brigade had been issued one of the new revolvers (officially the "M96 Revolver, Caliber .45, Mod 0," but already known to the troops as the "Mahldyn .45," to the considerable embarrassment of Taigys Mahldyn), and one of the even newer M96 bolt-action rifles. Four thousand of the 4th Infantry Division's riflemen had also been issued M96s, while all the rest had been issued converted Mahndrayn breechloaders. Officially, those were designated the "Mahndrayn Rifle, Caliber .50, Mark II, Mod 2," but the troops, with their customary disregard for formal terminology, had adopted Mahldyn's own designation and called them simply "Trapdoors" from the design of their hinged breeches. The mounted infantry's cap and ball revolvers had been passed on to 1st Corps' artillerists, and the support squads' mortar crews and Artillery Support Party troopers had also been issued Trapdoors.

That meant 1st Corps' twenty-seven thousand or so men could lay down an awesome amount of firepower, but it also meant Howsmyn had been forced to ship the new weapons no later than the beginning of February if he'd wanted to get them into Green Valley's hands in time for his planned offensive, and cartridge production had run behind original estimates. They'd been able to ship two hundred rounds per revolver, three hundred rounds per Trapdoor, and three hundred and fifty per M96 rifle, but that wasn't a very generous supply, given the troops' need to familiarize themselves with the new weapons and carry an adequate ammunition supply into combat with them. More ammo was in the pipeline, already in transit to Siddarmark, but so were additional rifles and revolvers to use it. It was proving harder than he'd anticipated to build up an adequate supply of the new ammunition, and he strongly suspected that demand in the field would be higher than projected once the spring campaign season got underway, as well. All of which explained the sweat and worry he was expending over the new Emeraldian ammunition manufactories.

He grimaced at the thought, but if Green Valley was going to have to be careful about ammunition expenditures for the next month or so, his men would still be enormously better off than their opponents. The new M97 mortars would help offset any small arms ammunition shortages, as well, and while Lywysite wasn't a very satisfactory shell filler, Hanth had already demonstrated how useful it would prove to the Imperial Charisian Army's combat engineers. All in all, the Army of God was *not* going to enjoy the fresh fruits of Charisian inventiveness.

*Which is a damned good thing*, he told himself, his expression grimmer, as he reached his destination at last and dismounted from his bicycle. *Brother Lynkyn's proving even more irritating at St. Kylmahn's than Zhwaigair's proving in Gorath. And Duchairn's turning into an even bigger pain in the arse than he's been before. I hope whoever murdered Zhorj Trumyn and stole his briefcase finds an especially hot spit in hell. More to the point, I hope Aivah's agents catch him and drop him into Bedard Bay with a rock tied to his ankles.*

Lynkyn Fultyn's curiosity, imagination, and agile mind, like Dynnys Zhwaigair's, were doing exactly what Nimue Alban's original mission needed done . . . which was unfortunate from the perspective of what *Charis* needed. Fultyn had been smart enough to realize the pitch and shape of the new Zhwaigair-designed,

Fultyn-modified rifle's breech plug was likely to be critical. That being the case, he'd built no less than two dozen prototypes simultaneously, each with slightly different screws, and adopted the one which performed best.

Not content to stop there, he'd gone a step further than Zhwaigair and come up with an even better breech design *and* he was producing the new rifles in greater numbers—and more cheaply—than he'd predicted. He was even going to manage a greater degree of standardization, although that was only just phasing in. Worse, he'd leapt on the open-hearth steel production notes from Trumyn's briefcase like a drowning man onto a liferaft as the krakens closed in.

With Duchairn's backing, he'd translated the diagrams and instructions Trumyn had been supposed to deliver to Greyghor Stohnar's Council of Manufactories into detailed construction plans and directions for their operation and distributed them to every foundry in the Temple Lands, Harchong, Desnair, and Dohlar.

Desnair (predictably) had been much less receptive to the new concepts, and even Dohlaran foundry masters would take a while to get the new furnaces up and running. Winter weather wasn't helping construction, either. For that matter, Charis, thanks in no small part to Merlin's (and Owl's) input, had a huge head start on the art of making *good* steel, with alloys it would take the Church's foundries years (or even decades) to duplicate by trial and error. Even less-than-perfect steel was far better than cast iron, however, and the Church's production would rise enormously, with the very first of the new steelworks coming online around the Gulf of Dohlar in the next month or two.

It couldn't take much longer than that, given that Howsmyn himself had originated most of the new techniques as little more than systematic refinements of already existing practices. And, unfortunately, the directions he'd sent to Siddarmark for applying those refinements had been very clear, concise, and complete. They were simply lucky the other information in

Trumyn's stolen briefcase had been intended as a broad introduction to the *concept* of steam engines rather than building instructions with the diagrams and explicit directions about materials, dimensions, and practices which had been provided for the furnaces. The last thing they needed would have been to deliver what amounted to an actual working model of one of Praigyr's beloved steam engines to Mother Church!

Even Brother Lynkyn was finding the translation of general principles into actual hardware heavy going, but Howsmyn was glumly confident that, given enough time, he'd produce crude steam engines of his own. No doubt they'd be underpowered and prone to breakdown, not to mention offering plenty of chances for catastrophes like exploding boilers, but they'd still represent an enormous increase in the Church's capabilities. It would be bad enough just in terms of steam-driven blast furnaces and manufactories, but the thought of facing even relatively slow steam-powered warships was unappealing.

*Well, not even Brother Lynkyn and Lieutenant Zhwaigair are going to overhaul the Church's entire industrial plant overnight,* he reminded himself as he rolled his bicycle into the rack outside the Urvyn Mahndrayn Rifle Shop Number One. *And I don't think the Army of God has very many months left. Anything they want to do after we've kicked their army's arse up between its ears and convinced the Group of Four they never—ever—want to screw with Charisians again is fine with me.*

"Master Howsmyn!" Taigys Mahldyn greeted him with a huge smile, clasping forearms with him. "I see you're closer to on time than usual!"

"It's not a good idea to point out that I'm always behind schedule, Master Mahldyn," Howsmyn told him with a frown, and Mahldyn chuckled. He'd come a long way from the anxious but determined craftsman who'd sought an audience with the wealthiest man on Safehold to show him his concept for a new revolver. And so he should have, since he was well along towards becoming one of the wealthiest men on Safehold himself. Almost more important to Ehdwyrd Howsmyn, however, was Mahldyn's confidence in his own self-worth—and in his own inventive judgment—which had come along with the last furiously busy year or so of his life.

"Seems t' me there's no reason you should be different from those of us as work for you, Sir," Mahldyn pointed out now. "Every single one of us is trying t' do two hours' work in a single hour every Langhorne blessed day, aren't we?"

"I do believe you have a point," Howsmyn acknowledged as he released the other man's arm and twitched his head at the rifle works' door. "So why don't you and I go take a look at your latest effort to stretch the hours available to you?"

"I'm thinking it's something you might find a mite interesting, t' be honest, Sir," Mahldyn said, walking along beside him. "I've been giving some thought t' what you said t' other day 'bout the one advantage smoothbores have over rifles. Especially breech-loading rifles."

"Ah?" Howsmyn hid a smile behind a puzzled expression. He'd been looking forward to this conversation. "Oh!" He allowed his expression to clear. "You mean their ability to fire 'buck and ball' rather than just a single bullet when the range is short enough, like in the Battle of the Kyplyngyr?"

"Aye, Sir, that I do." Mahldyn nodded eagerly. "You see, I got t' thinkin' about that, and there's not rightly a reason we couldn't fire buckshot out of a cartridge, 'cept how much brass it'd use because the cartridge'd be so large. But then it came t' me. The *chamber* don't care what the cartridge's made of; its job's t' hold the charge, whatever we pack it in. So it came t' me that instead of usin' *brass*, there's other things we could be lookin' at. Like paper. You take the right cardstock, now, and you bind one end into a brass cup t' hold the primer, and all you'd have t' do'd be to—"

"Owl and I have completed our analysis."

Nahrmahn Baytz' holographic eyes tracked around the faces of the other members of the small group assembled—physically or electronically—at the table in Nimue's Cave. Actually, only Merlin, Aivah, and Sandaria Ghatfryd were *physically* present, but this time Owl had generated full holographic images of all of the attendees rather than simply projecting them onto the contact lenses of those scattered elsewhere around the planet.

"As the Sisters of Saint Kohdy had speculated," Nahrmahn continued, this time looking at Aivah and Sandaria, "the reason he decided to write in Spanish—in Español—was his concern over how far outside the bounds of accepted doctrine and theology his speculations might fall. Even the portions he recorded in English have given us considerable additional insight into what actually happened following the Rakurai strike on the Alexandria Enclave, though."

"Insight not already present in Saint Zherneau's journal?" Maikel Staynair asked, his sinewy hands folded on the table in front of him. Actually, they were folded on his desk in far-off Manchyr, where it was almost midnight.

"Quite a lot, really." Nahrmahn shrugged. "Jeremiah Knowles and his friends were hidden away in Tellesberg, Maikel. They had access only to whatever information reached what was basically a very small town at the back end of nowhere. That limited what they could really know about what was happening elsewhere, and their orders from Shan-wei to keep their heads down came into play, as well. There wouldn't've been much the four of them could've accomplished, cut off from Alexandria and isolated half a world away from all the rest of the colonists, even if they hadn't had Shan-wei's instructions to lie low, survive, and plan for the future. So in many ways, Saint Zherneau's perspective on the War Against the Fallen was as much that of an outsider as anyone else on Safehold had. Cody Cortazar, on the other hand, was right in the midst of that war. He saw a lot more of it, and from a considerably different perspective."

Staynair nodded slowly and thoughtfully.

"Thank you," he said. "I wasn't challenging your interpretation. I only wanted to be sure I understood the context."

"With all due respect, Your Eminence," Sandaria's expression was as dry as her tone, "I think 'context' is something we could all use at this point."

Several of the others chuckled, and Merlin smiled. Sandaria might continue to nourish reservations over the inner circle's version of the Archangels, but her sojourn here in Nimue's Cave had soothed those reservations' sharpest edges. And she'd obviously gotten over her initial discomfort at holding long conversations with people who weren't physically present . . . or happened to be dead.

She'd been skittish about Owl when Merlin and Nimue explained that his hologram was that of an individual who'd never physically existed outside the effectively "magical" confines of a computer. Still, that had been easier for her to process than the idea that the individuals she knew as Merlin and Nimue were actually a pair of machines, both of which contained the memories of a young woman—the same young woman—who'd died almost a thousand Safeholdian years before her own birth. She'd known—or been introduced to, at least—both Merlin and Nimue before that truth had been shared with her, however, and she related to them as the discrete and separate individuals they'd become in a way which pushed the fact of Nimue Alban's physical death back below the level of conscious awareness.

She couldn't do that with Nahrmahn Baytz. She *knew* he'd died, and he had no more of a physical body than Owl did. It had taken her many days to get past the idea that she was talking to a ghost whenever she and Nahrmahn spoke. In fact, for the first five-day after her arrival in the cave she'd *avoided* speaking to him whenever possible. She'd preferred to address any comments or requests to Owl and let the AI refer them to Nahrmahn if that turned out to be necessary.

*Maybe the fact that she's so much more comfortable with him now is a good sign,* Merlin thought. *I think her mind and her worldview have been . . . stretched in ways she still hasn't recognized yet. I sure as hell hope so, anyway.*

"Context is certainly critical in understanding what's actually been said, Sister," Maikel agreed. "And I suspect Saint Kohdy had a . . . unique perspective, to put it mildly."

"I think we could all agree with that," Nahrmahn said. "Actually, I found some of what he said even more interesting because of what it implies about the way in which the colonists' memories were reprogrammed."

"What do you mean?" Cayleb's eyes narrowed intently.

"Well, from the English portions of his diary, it was obvious that at least some of his memories were . . . rearranged a second time when he became a *seijin*. The references to his waking up in 'the sacred sickbay' and the lack of clarity of his earlier memories made that pretty clear. At first, we assumed they were unclear because they were *new* memories, like the ones Bédard implanted in all the colonists. But after a close reading and analysis, Owl and I came to the conclusion that that's not really what happened. Instead of new, fabricated memories, it appears the memories we thought Bédard had completely eradicated hadn't actually been destroyed. There are some passages which appear to contain references to at least partial memories of Old Earth. I suspect—" Nahrmahn looked at Sandaria again "—that those references are one reason the Sisters interpreted his later comments to indicate that the colonists' souls had been somewhere else before they awakened here on Safehold. They describe a world very, very different from Safehold, at any rate. For example, there's the one on page ninety which certainly seems to be a memory of a video call. He never actually calls it a communicator or a com—he uses the term *keitai*, which is apparently the word the Order of Chihiro used when it issued coms to the newly created *seijins*—but Owl and I agree that has to be what he was talking about. His memory simply wasn't clear enough to describe it fully."

"I remember the passage you're talking about," Sandaria said. "You mean the one where he's writing about his wife's ghost, don't you?"

"Exactly." Nahrmahn nodded. "From the way he describes seeing her 'as if in a mirror that lived and spoke' it's obvious he wasn't speaking to her face-to-face, and the only thing we could think of to explain it was a videoconference of some sort. We also checked the original passenger manifests, and we found Cody Cortazar and his wife Sandra listed as colonists in the Zion Enclave. According to Shan-wei's documentation, however, Sandra was killed less than three years after the colonists were awakened."

"Killed? How?" Nimue's hologram asked.

"By a slash lizard, but Kohdy apparently didn't remember any of the details of her death. In fact, there are several places where he comments on gaps in his own memories of Safehold, and he had no personal memory of the events immediately surrounding the Alexandria strike."

"Do you think those memories were deliberately suppressed?" Domynyk Staynair asked.

"No." Nahrmahn shrugged. "I suppose it's possible, but I don't see any reason for them to have done it on purpose. I think—and Owl agrees—that it was probably an unintended side effect of their effort to selectively undo some of the memory suppression they'd done when they turned him into an Adam."

"I noticed his early references to how readily he learned to control the '*hikousen*' they provided him with," Merlin said, "but I don't recall any place where he actually called it an 'air car.'"

Nahrmahn snorted, since Merlin—like Nynian Rychtyr (or any PICA)—had perfect recall.

"You don't recall it because he didn't do it," the plump little Emeraldian said. "He always referred to it as either a *hikousen* or simply 'my vessel.' You're right about how quickly he learned to handle it, though, and the same was true of a lot of the small high-tech items the 'Archangels' supplied to him. The med kit, the com, the low-light vision gear, and quite a few others, for example. It looks to us as if the command crew decided it would be simpler and faster—and probably more impressively 'miraculous'—for their *seijins* to simply 'have' whatever skills they needed without having to be taught. There could have been several ways to go about that—all the Adams and Eves still had their NEAT implants—but it looks like the one they opted for was to go back into their *seijin* candidates' memories and . . . reactivate those skills without any conscious recollection of where they came from or how they'd first been acquired."

"Well that was arrogant of them," Nimue murmured. All eyes turned to her, and she shrugged and looked across the table at Merlin. "Remember what Aunt Aeronwen said about disturbing deliberately suppressed memories?"

Merlin frowned for a moment, then nodded.

"You mean when she and Dad got into that knock-down, drag-out fight over the morality of suppressing traumatic memories?"

"Yes." Nimue returned her attention to the others. "Aunt Aeronwen was my—our, I suppose," her lips quirked a smile "—father's older sister. She was a psychiatrist, and like a lot of psychiatrists, most of her practice dealt with patients suffering from post-traumatic shock and the crushing depressive effect of how badly the war was going. The technology Operation Ark used to suppress the colonists' memories of

Old Earth was basically an application of therapies available to practicing psychiatrists, and I remember Aunt Aeronwen was very adamant that the proper verb was 'suppress,' not '*erase*' when she and Dad got into their fight. Dad thought it was immoral to steal someone's memories, even if they'd asked you to do it. Aunt Aeronwen thought he was full of crap, but in the course of the . . . discussion, she pointed out that it was impossible to truly erase a memory. All she could do was to suppress it and, in particularly serious cases, *supplant* it with a different, less traumatic memory.

"She was willing to concede that the supplanting was liable to abuse, but she was adamant that the suppression itself was entirely moral if the clinician thought it would be the most effective way to deal with the trauma and if the patient agreed after a thorough explanation of the procedure. And she also pointed out that the original memory was always in there somewhere. A therapist could recall it if there was some reason to do that later, so you could hardly call it 'stealing,' in her opinion. For that matter, it was standard practice for most psychiatrists to make a complete personality record that could be permanently stored and recalled at need as easily as uploading memories of a PICA's experiences to its organic original.

"What I'm thinking about right now, though, was that she pointed out that one reason for supplanting suppressed memories with manufactured ones was to prevent the patient from probing at a 'blank spot' in her recollections. And the reason for doing *that* was that if she poked at it too long and hard it was entirely possible for her to undo the original suppressing. Aunt Aeronwen would've been as horrified as Shan-wei and the Commodore over what Langhorne and Bédard did to the colonists, but if *she'd* been part of the command crew that signed off on it, she never would've gone in and poked those suppressed memories hard enough to bring them to the surface. Not unless she intended to restore the patient's original memories in their entirety, at any rate."

"I remember the conversation," Merlin said after a moment, eyes focused on something only he and Nimue could see, and smiled faintly. "Too bad Aunt Aeronwen *wasn't* part of the command crew; she'd've put a knife in Langhorne's ribs the instant he came up with his brainstorm! But I take your point."

His opened his eyes fully and refocused on the present.

"What Nimue's getting at is that if they started reactivating selected memories—or, at least, the memories of selected skills—they ran the risk of turning *other* memories back on, as well. And if they did, then 'Seijin Kohdy' may very well not have been the only *seijin* whose diary contained references to things no Adam or Eve was supposed to remember."

"That might explain why Owl and I couldn't find a single original copy of a diary or journal written by a *seijin* in any of the library catalogs we were able to check," Nahrmahn said thoughtfully. "If the Church—or the command crew's survivors, at any rate—realized the *seijins* were having unexplained flashes of 'false memory,' censoring them after the fact would make a lot of sense."

"And God only knows what mucking around in all those implanted and suppressed ones might've done," Nimue said, nodding slowly. "Especially to memories of actual events that occurred relatively soon after the colonists woke up here on Safehold. That could very well be why he didn't remember the details of his wife's death."

"If suppressed memories aren't genuinely erased forever, why couldn't Shan-wei bring back Jeremiah Knowles pre-Safehold memories?" Rahzhyr Mahklyn asked.

"She didn't have access to the stored memories—assuming Bédard ever bothered to record them," Nimue pointed out before Merlin could speak. "And from the records the Commodore left, I don't think they had a trained psychiatrist among the conspirators."

"That would've been critical to the problem?"

"Fairly critical, yes," Merlin said. "Without the proper equipment, or at least a trained psychiatrist to spend *years* working with regressive hypnosis, you'd get a hodgepodge of new, artificial memories and the old, genuine ones with no way to differentiate between them. It would be the equivalent of inducing an especially nasty dissociative memory disorder in the patient. From Kohdy's journal, it seems pretty clear he experienced at least a mild version of that despite the 'archangels' having had someone at least capable of turning the memories and skills they wanted back on again. That's one of the reasons Nimue said it was a damned arrogant thing for them to have done."

"This is all very interesting," Sharleyan said, "but is it really relevant to the contents of his diary?"

"In a way," Nahrmahn said. "You see, we found him in the original passenger lists, along with a description of what he did before Operation Ark. It seems that before he became *Seijin* Kohdy, and before he became a simple Adam named Cody Cortazar, he was *Sergeant Major* Cody Cortazar, Terran Federation Marine Corps, and he'd spent the better part of fifteen years as an unarmed and close combat instructor. He'd been first runner-up in the Fleet *moarte subită* competition twice and a championship fencer." He smiled crookedly as Nimue and Merlin both sat up straight, eyebrows rising in unison. "I think they might have been after more than his ability to fly an air car when they started poking around in Sergeant Major Cortazar's 'lost' memories."

"I believe you could safely assume that was the case," Merlin said dryly.

"That's what we thought, too." Nahrmahn nodded. "But one thing we're very sure of from having read the Spanish portions of his diary is that no one meant for him to remember his native language. It seems to've come back to him gradually, and he comments on his decision to keep that a secret."

"Because he was already considering the possibility

that the 'Archangels' had lied to him?" Rahzhyr Mahklyn asked.

"No, it was more as if he was afraid this strange, unnatural language might have been somehow implanted in his mind by Shan-wei and the Fallen. Or, at least, that his fellow *seijins* and the Archangels would *think* that was what had happened, at any rate."

"What about the 'demons'?" Sharleyan asked, her expression intent. "Where did *they* come from?"

"*Seijin* Kohdy's diary puts a rather different face on the histories of the War Against the Fallen," Nahrmahn told her. "You can see the same basic events in both accounts, but he fills in a lot of background that's quite different from the ones in the *Writ* or *The Testimonies*.

"For one thing, there were a lot more of the 'Fallen' than the *Writ* suggests. According to Kohdy, they weren't so much a faction of the command crew as they were the Navy and Marine personnel who'd served as the planetary police force under Commodore Pei once their warships had been discarded. He specifically refers to them as 'the Angels who looked to Kauyung before his Fall,' at least. We can't tell how many of them there were, but Owl and I both believe there were more than the *Writ* ever admitted.

"For another thing, they had more technological resources than we thought they had. There are all those references to 'servitors' in the *Writ* and *The Testimonies*, but it wasn't until we started reading the diary that we realized the Fallen were actually building additional 'servitors' for much of the war. Obviously, that meant they'd possessed a deeper manufacturing base than we'd assumed; one they must've spent some time hiding away in the mountains, a lot like the Commodore and Shan-wei hid Nimue's Cave."

"Why didn't the Commodore mention that in my—our—briefing?" Nimue asked.

"Probably because he didn't know about it," Nahrmahn said. "The *Writ* implies that the War Against the Fallen started immediately after the Alexandria strike—that the Fallen were found out by Schueler and

Chihiro at the same time Kau-yung killed Langhorne and the others. In other words, the War Against the Fallen was essentially a seamless continuation of a conflict that began with the destruction of Alexandria. But according to Kohdy, it didn't begin for at least two years *after* Armageddon Reef."

"The Sisters have always known that." Sandaria's eyes were intent, her expression deeply interested. "Saint Kohdy told us that much before he shifted to Español."

"Yes, he did." Nahrmahn nodded. "But according to the 'demon' who kicked Kohdy's arse without killing him, someone inside the command crew—someone Schueler and Chihiro *trusted*—diverted that capacity to the 'Fallen' from either the Zion Enclave or from *Hamilcar* itself only *after* the Alexandria strike."

Cayleb's lips pursed in a silent whistle, and Paityr Wylsynn's hologram leaned forward in his chair.

"Did Kohdy have any idea who that someone was, Your Highness?"

"No. In fact, it could have been almost anyone. It's clear from his diary that one thing the *Writ* didn't exaggerate was the extent of Chihiro's authority after Langhorne and Bédard died, and he'd obviously put an iron lock on any advanced technology. But by the time the War Against the Fallen flared up, the people opposed to him had access to enough capability to build those servitors of theirs and keep on fighting for over six years. That suggests some of them, at least, must've gotten their hands on industrial modules almost as capable as Commodore Pei and Shan-wei left for Nimue, and they could have come from only one source.

"That came as a nasty surprise to Chihiro and his associates. In fact, sort of reading between the lines of Kohdy's diary, it sounds as if the Fallen probably would've won if one of Chihiro's supporters hadn't stumbled across some sort of evidence that a storm was brewing before they were ready to strike. Kohdy—" Nahrmahn met Paityr's eyes levelly "—makes it pretty damn clear it was Schueler."

Father Paityr's jaw tightened. No one said anything else for several seconds, then Nahrmahn cleared his nonexistent throat.

"Anyway, the references in the *Writ*—and in Kohdy's diary—to 'fastnesses in the Mountains of Desolation' suggest the Fallen had been preparing for some time. Once the fighting began, however, any small industrial modules they'd managed to hide away in the mountains were enormously outclassed, because *Hamilcar* hadn't yet been disposed of. According to the English portion of Kohdy's diary, that was because Chihiro had been wise enough to be on the lookout for any of Shanwei's sympathizers who might've managed to hide among their unfallen fellows. According to the *Spanish* portion, however, Kohdy had started to suspect that Chihiro and his closest supporters had retained *Hamilcar*—although Kohdy didn't know what *Hamilcar* truly was; he refers to it throughout as 'the Dawn Star'—out of his own ambition to replace and supplant Langhorne completely."

"Excuse me?" Paityr sat back, his expression perplexed.

"We already knew from Aivah and Sandaria that the 'demon' who defeated Kohdy had suggested Langhorne might not've been the one who ordered the strike on Alexandria in the first place. There's no way to tell whether that was true, and Kohdy's diary doesn't tell us everything that was passing through his own mind. He was clearly unwilling to record some of his thoughts and doubts even in Spanish, so it's possible he'd actually found evidence one way or the other and simply not written it down. But from several of his comments, some oblique enough it took Owl's analysis to tease them out of the underbrush, he'd come around—slowly and unwillingly—to the belief that Chihiro was . . . significantly modifying Langhorne's original plan. That's the reason he went to Schueler."

"What did he expect Schueler to do about it?" Paityr Wylsynn's voice was calm, but there was something in his eyes, something almost desperate. Nahrmahn

Baytz recognized that something and shook his head sadly.

"He didn't write that down, Paityr. All he said was 'I must go to the one Archangel whose zeal has never faltered, who has always been in the forefront of the *seijins* fighting the Fallen. He has a will of iron, and I have served him faithfully from the beginning. He will not flinch before any test, and if I cannot trust him to tell me the truth, then I can trust no one.'"

"And he returned home from that meeting dead." This time Paityr's voice was harsh and flat. "So much for being able to *trust* him!"

"We don't know what happened, Paityr," Nimue said softly. He looked at her, his expression bleak, and she shrugged. "All we know is that he was killed. We don't know how, or by whom. All we really know at this point, I think, is *why*. And the why is that he'd become a threat to *Chihiro*, whether he was right about Chihiro's diversion from Langhorne's original intentions or not."

"That much definitely seems to be true," Nahrmahn agreed, drawing Paityr's attention back to him. "Another thing the diary does is explain how the struggle lasted as long as it did. For example, the *Writ*'s always admitted that many of the Adams and Eves went over to the side of the Fallen. From what Kohdy says, a smaller percentage of them joined the rebellion *actively* than the *Writ* suggests, but that was still a significant number, and even more seem to have been willing to lend it their passive support. That's one of the *Writ*'s explanations for why the war lasted so long . . . and also one of the justifications for the way the Inquisition's authority was increased afterward.

"In addition, the Fallen had apparently made hiding from Chihiro's sensors a high priority, and from some of the actions Kohdy describes, they obviously had SNARC capability of their own. They must've had some way to block or jam—or evade, at least—the other side's SNARCs, as well. They were *very* well hidden, and they only came out of hiding to launch guerrilla strikes against the 'Archangels.' Apparently the Adams and Eves who supported them hid them in the towns and villages between strikes, and their own industrial nodes were hellishly hard to find.

"Chihiro's people knew which members of the command crew had disappeared and gone over to the other side, but just finding them was extremely difficult, and that was largely where the *seijins* came in. They were the mortal interface between the Archangels and the rest of Safehold, equipped with special abilities and powers—like Kohdy's sword and the night vision gear which let a *seijin* see in complete darkness—and they served the faithful communities in a lot of ways. They were forest rangers, militia organizers, teachers, explorers, search and rescue personnel, policemen . . . It was a long list, and they did their jobs so well that their service won them those communities' trust and loyalty. It also put them in the best position to do their *real* job— spot the Fallen hiding among the villagers and townsfolk and form strike forces once a group of the Fallen or their sympathizers had been located.

"That's what Kohdy was doing when the 'demon' captured him and then let him go, and the experience shook him badly. The 'demon' in question was actually the mayor of the town in which he lived, and he had Kohdy dead to rights. More than that, Kohdy had known him for over two years. They'd been friends, and when his friend told him he was on the wrong side and provided evidence to support the allegation, it shook Kohdy's faith. Badly."

"Badly enough to send him to Schueler for an answer or reassurance," Merlin murmured.

"Exactly." Nahrmahn nodded heavily. "There's a lot more detail in here than I've summarized. I wish he'd been a little more specific about some of the evidence that convinced him his friend the mayor might have told him the truth, but that's the basic thrust of it. Owl's translated the entire Spanish section into English, and we've got hard copies of it for those poor souls among us who can't read the electronic version directly."

Merlin surprised himself with a chuckle as Nahrmahn elevated his nose with an audible sniff, and the atmosphere around the table lightened perceptibly. Then Nahrmahn looked directly at Sandaria.

"I think you should read it," he said quietly, almost gently. "Kohdy never knew the full truth, but this is the diary of a *good* man, someone who truly believed in what he was doing and only wanted to help other people. You might see some of your own journey in his, and I think you owe it to him, as well as to yourself, to *fully* meet the man behind the stories."

Sandaria looked back at him for a moment, then inhaled deeply.

"I think you're right, Your Highness," she said, equally quietly.

. XI .
# Esthyr's Abbey,
# Northland Gap,
# Northland Province,
# Republic of Siddarmark

It was warmer than it had been for the last couple of days. In fact, the temperature was barely ten degrees below freezing.

"Don't see much sign of movement," Corporal Paiair commented. He lay prone in the deep snow beside Sergeant Tahd Ekohls on a small but steep-sided hill, gazing down at the town of Esthyr's Abbey in the early—for a northern East Haven winter—morning light. Their hill rose above a thin belt of second-growth woodlot, between it and the river that supplied the town's water, which had somehow so far managed to avoid the woodsman's axe. Probably because woodlot in question was so far from the town and on the far side of the stream. The true object of their attention, however, was less the town than the bridge across that very same river.

"That's because there *isn't* any sign of movement."

Sergeant Ekohls' tone mingled satisfaction with sour disapproval of incompetence, and he raised his spyglass once more. A light dusting of frost, like an icy spider web, had been frozen along one edge of the objective lens, despite how careful he'd been not to expose it to the sort of temperature shifts that produced condensation in even the best-sealed spyglasses. The new double-glasses were better about that, he understood, but he was used to the old style and he rested the barrel on his forearm for steadiness as he studied the spot where he would have located the picket that should have been guarding the bridge.

*Be fair, Tahd,* he reminded himself. *Not like the entire damned river's not frozen solid enough for draft dragons t' walk across! Nobody really needs a bridge t' get over it, and they bloody well won't till spring. And the poor sodding Temple Boys'd freeze to death right fast if they* did *try t' picket the thing. Still and all . . . .*

He lowered the glass and looked at the lance corporal on Paiair's far side.

"Go back and tell the Lieutenant there's no picket on the bridge, and I don't see anything stirring within two hundred yards of the far bank. Probably at least some poor bastards're freezing their arses off playing sentry in the forward earthworks, but I can't see 'em if they are. There's smoke from a lot of chimneys in the town and at least a couple of dozen places right behind the earthworks—I'm betting it's those dugouts the *seijins* told Baron Green Valley about—but right now it looks like they're staying close to their fires."

"Right," Lance Corporal Fraid Tohmys, one of 3rd Platoon's runners, replied laconically.

The odds that anyone in the town might be looking their way at this particular moment, or that they might see anything at this distance even if they did, were miniscule, but Tohmys was a scout sniper. He pushed himself backwards through the snow, not rising to a crouch until he was certain his head and shoulders would be safely below the hill's crest, then scooted down the far slope to the skis he'd left standing upright in a handy drift. He tugged them free, shoved his boots into the toe straps, and pulled back the spring-tensioned cables to lock them behind his heels. The efficiency of the Imperial Charisian Army's cross-country skis had increased significantly with the widespread availability of the cable binding which had previously been available only to wealthy ski enthusiasts who could afford the hefty price tag. The Charisian steelmakers' ability to produce strong, powerful springs, capable of standing up to hard use under sub-zero field conditions, and to produce them in quantity, had changed that, however, and the corporal moved rapidly off across the snow, heading back the way Paiair's squad had come.

"All right, Zakryah," Ekohls said, turning back to Paiair. "Let's get somebody down into the riverbed. I want a couple of sets of eyes on the far bank."

▼ ▼ ▼

Baron Green Valley glanced at the caribou-drawn field kitchen as he trotted past it. Mounted on broad runners, the kitchen was fitted with a central island of cook stoves and framed with solid, boxlike wooden sides. For two-thirds of each side, the upper half of the outer wall formed a long, hinged panel which could be raised using cables running through pulleys at the peak of the kitchen's steep roof. In the horizontal position, those panels were about ten feet off the ground and offered at least some protection from rain or snow for someone standing under them. Counters built into the walls' inner faces gave the cooks working space, and the stoves featured metal plates which could be used as cooking surfaces or lifted aside to create wells into which specially fitted kettles could be slotted so the kitchens could cook soup or stew—or keep it hot—even as they moved cross-country. The runners turned the kitchens into sleds with excellent cross-country agility in winter, but they could also be fitted with wheels for mobility that was almost as good in summer.

The kitchen's design was one more example of the old Royal Chisholmian Army's forethought and careful planning, although the new manufacturing techniques coming out of Charis made them much cheaper and easier to build in quantity. Now, as Green Valley watched, lines of men of Company A, 3rd Battalion, 13th Regiment, 7th Brigade, of General Eystavyo Gardynyr's 4th Division (Mountain), passed smoothly along the field kitchen's sides. The cooks—in shirtsleeves, despite the icy temperatures, thanks to the heat generated by their stoves—ladled steaming tea into the tin cups held out to them and hot soup, thick with beef and vegetables, into the matching tin bowls.

Every ICA soldier was issued his own nested mess kit, which contained a skillet with a folding handle, a saucepan, individual fitted covers for both (curved so that they could be used as plates or bowls), and a steel knife, spoon, and fork. The entire remarkably compact package was closed with a leather strap that could be hooked to the canvas bread bag in which a soldier carried his combat rations and which, in turn, attached to his canvas web gear when he stripped down to combat order.

Even before the new mess kits, the Chisholmian Army's arrangements for feeding its men in the field had been better than anything available to the Army of God. As just one example, the huge iron kettles of the Church's commissaries were heavier, more cumbersome, and required far more fuel than their lighter Charisian counterparts. They were inefficient at the best of times, and if the commissary troops fell behind during troop movements (or simply got lost for a few days), the AOG troops were ill-equipped to cook their own rations. Nor did the Army of God have any equivalent of the mobile field kitchens which kept Green Valley's troops fueled with hot, nourishing food despite the arctic conditions.

And which saw to it that the men were well fed before going into battle. That was a tradition the ICA shared with the Imperial Charisian Navy, but it was even more important than usual under current conditions. The human metabolism burned energy like a furnace in arctic conditions. Good nourishment could become literally the difference between life and death when the cold bit, and that didn't even consider the morale factor inherent in being fed a hot, strengthening meal before plunging into the chaos of combat.

Green Valley looked away from the field kitchen, returning his attention to the SNARCs keeping watch over Saint Esthyr's Abbey and the farming town to which it had given its name. The SNARCs gave him an even better perspective than Sergeant Ekohls enjoyed, and their reports were both a source of profound satisfaction and one more coal for the furnace of his anger against Zhaspahr Clyntahn's "Sword of Schueler."

Located on the east-west high road where it passed down the center of the Northland Gap, between the Meirstrom Mointains to the north and the Kalgarans to the south, Esthyr's Abbey was the better part of three hundred and sixty miles from the nearest navigable river: the Kalgaran River, just south of the fork where it joined the Ice Ash. It was surrounded by a broad belt of farmland, which had been interspersed with occasional areas of woodlot, most of it second-growth terrestrial imports. More trees—mixed terrestrial and Safeholdian evergreens, mostly—had been planted as windbreaks around farmhouses and barns, along the edges of farm lanes, and as protection for pastureland and feedlots, and the fields themselves were separated by walls of the dry-laid stones centuries of plowing had brought to the surface.

It must have been a pleasant vista once upon a time, but "once upon a time" was long vanished.

While it had served as a natural center for farming, Esthyr's Abbey had never been as large as many another major regional town in Siddarmark because of its distance from water transport. Its pre-Sword of

Schueler population, never more than three thousand, had plummeted to little more than a thousand as those loyal to the Republic were killed or driven into exile—many of them to die of cold and starvation on the roads. Not that the Temple Loyalists had had it all their own way. The recent cluster of graves in the town cemetery indicated just how hard the loyalists had fought before their defeat. Nonetheless, it had still been home to almost thirteen hundred people the previous spring, and the survivors had greeted the Army of God's arrival enthusiastically. But then the Great Canal Raid devastated Bishop Militant Bahrnabai's logistics. Neither of Halcom Bahrn's ironclads had come within three hundred miles of Esthyr's Abbey, yet the raid had still given the town its deathblow.

Now less than two hundred of its original inhabitants remained; the rest had left voluntarily or been forcibly evacuated at Bahrnabai Wyrshym's orders the previous fall. The bishop militant hadn't liked giving that order—or the other orders that had effectively abandoned all of the Republic east of the Kalgarans and Meirstroms—but he'd had no option.

First, the state of his supply lines had forced him to commandeer every available scrap of transport to feed his own starving, freezing troops. That bitter truth had compelled his orders to evacuate not just Esthyr's Abbey but every other town between there and the Kalgaran River. There'd been nothing left to keep the civilians in those towns fed, and to give credit where it was due, the evacuees were both safer and better nourished in the refugee camps Rhobair Duchairn had established in the Temple Lands.

Second, it had been painfully clear the Army of God would require a heavy numerical superiority to defeat Green Valley's troops. Wyrshym had reached that conclusion on the basis of his experience in the Sylmahn Gap, but his original estimate of how great a superiority he would require had still been too low. Duke Eastshare's rout of the Army of Glacierheart and—even more—the cataclysmic destruction of the Army of Shiloh had made that brutally clear, and his original strategy had changed as a result.

His intention had been to reinforce the two divisions at Allyntyn with three more divisions before Green Valley moved in that direction. Unfortunately, when the Army of Midhold actually did move the previous fall, it had advanced more rapidly than even Wyrshym had anticipated. It had swept through central Midhold, driving out those loyal to Mother Church as it came, and its 3rd Mounted Brigade had closed in on Allyntyn before any reinforcements arrived.

In some ways, that had been just as well from Wyrshym's perspective, since his disastrous logistics made it impossible for him to sustain a force large enough to face Green Valley east of the Northland Gap. As Brigadier Mohrtyn Braisyn's mounted infantry advanced, they'd eliminated every cavalry regiment originally assigned to Bishop Qwentyn Preskyt, but before those regiments were destroyed, they'd managed to warn Preskyt that 3rd Mounted was coming. He'd semaphored the news to Wyrshym, in turn, and the bishop militant had immediately realized that Preskyt's unreinforced divisions could never hold Allyntyn. Bitter though the choice had been—and risky, in the face of Zhaspahr Clyntahn's wrath—Wyrshym had ordered Allyntyn abandoned to the advancing Charisians.

The bishop militant's decisiveness had deprived Green Valley of one of the prizes he'd sought, for Preskyt's prompt obedience had whisked the bulk of his command efficiently out of the envelopment Green Valley had planned at Allyntyn. It had been a very near thing, however, and his rearguard regiment had been trapped and destroyed when the town was captured.

Wyrshym's decision to abandon Allyntyn had transformed Esthyr's Abbey into the Army of the Sylmahn's most advanced position. Preskyt's St. Fraidyr Division and Bishop Zhaksyn Mahkhal's Port Harbor Division had dug in there, and Wyrshym had managed to replace the regiment lost in Allyntyn and find three more cavalry regiments—all understrength—to supply a little more mobility and reach.

The three divisions Wyrshym had originally earmarked for Allyntyn had been sent instead to the town of Fairkyn on the devastated Guarnak-Ice Ash Canal, and he'd scared up two more divisions to support them there, all under Bishop Gorthyk Nybar. Preskyt was instructed to keep Nybar fully informed of his situation but reported directly to Wyrshym at Guarnak. It was an awkward arrangement, yet Green Valley understood why it had been adopted, and he had to respect Wyrshym's reasoning. The bishop militant had arranged to keep Nybar out of the chain of command between himself and Preskyt in order to protect Nybar from the Grand Inquisitor if things went poorly at Esthyr's Abbey. Nybar would be fully informed about what was happening to Preskyt's command but free of any direct responsibility for it . . . and free to make his own decisions without looking over his shoulder at his own inquisitors and intendants.

The Army of God had no equivalent of the Charisian concept of organizing armies into corps, yet that was essentially what Wyrshym had done, and Nybar's command had been designated the Army of Fairkyn for administrative purposes. It wasn't very large as armies went: five infantry divisions and eight cavalry regiments, supported by a single regiment of artillery. If all his units had been at full strength, he would have commanded thirteen thousand men, including all of his artillerists, supported by only twenty-four twelve-pounders; in fact, he actually deployed less than eleven thousand, and keeping even that small a force adequately supplied had been difficult, although his situation had improved dramatically over the last three or four five-days.

Bishop Qwentyn Preskyt's, unfortunately, had not. Esthyr's Abbey was twice as far from Guarnak, and even though he was down to only forty-five hundred men, little more than seventy-five percent of his paper strength, keeping them fed over a thousand-mile-long winter supply line was still a nightmare.

Worse, from Wyrshym's perspective, the entire Army of the Sylmahn, including all detachments, counted barely sixty thousand men, less than eighty percent of the Army of Midhold's manpower, and its men had been more poorly armed even before the Canal Raid added starvation to the mix. True, its logistic situation had improved as Duchairn got the devastated canal net repaired with one temporary expedient after another. The entire line from East Wing Lake to Ayaltyn, a tiny town on the Hildermoss River south of Cat-Lizard Lake, was technically back in service, but Ayaltyn was still almost eight hundred miles from Wyrshym's primary forward supply center at Guarnak and the canals had already been freezing by the time Duchairn's engineers reached the town. By now they—and every river and lake north of Guarnak—were solid sheets of ice.

That had put an end to canal repairs until spring, but the ice did provide easier going for supply sleds, and Duchairn had gotten additional snow lizards and a handful of winter-hardy hill dragons forward to Wyrshym. The ragged state of his logistics prevented him from sustaining a bigger force at Esthyr's Abbey, but he'd begun building up supplies at Fairkyn to support Nybar and the heavier forces he'd earmarked to support him if Green Valley got past Esthyr's Abbey. As soon as winter released its grip and further improvements in his supply line allowed Vicar Rhobair to move up the promised reinforcements, he intended to massively reinforce Nybar. Indeed, he'd been promised a minimum of a hundred thousand fresh troops, many equipped with the new rifles and improved artillery the Church's foundries were frenetically turning out, which would give him twice Green Valley's strength and allow him to resume the offensive by early May.

In the meantime, Esthyr's Abbey was a forlorn and lonely place. With its civilian inhabitants dead or fled, Preskyt could probably have housed twice his actual troop strength in its houses and public buildings or in the homes, barns, and other outbuildings of the surrounding farms, if only it had been possible to feed them. As it was, the last of the abandoned livestock had been slaughtered months ago and most of Esthyr's Abbey's woodlots had been felled for firewood. For that matter, working parties had systematically pulled down the buildings of a steadily growing number of those outlying farms for fuel, as well, and more than a few unoccupied structures in the town itself had gone the same way.

The lack of clothing suited to North Haven's brutal winters was another problem for all Wyrshym's men, not just Preskyt's force, and no improvement in his transport capability was going to change that anytime soon. Everything left behind by Esthyr's Abbey's citizens had been combed through, looking for any additional warm clothing Preskyt's shivering troops could find, but the most optimistic observer couldn't have called them adequately clothed. They'd been driven increasingly to ground under the town's roofs, especially with the blizzards which had swept through the Gap in the last two five-days. The current warming trend would bring the temperatures up into the mid-thirties in a few days, which would encourage quite a bit of snow melt. But another bitter wave of arctic cold would follow the "warm snap" within less than two days, and the defenders of Esthyr's Abbey were going to find themselves far less well-suited to deal with it than they were now.

Green Valley smiled thinly at the thought and sent his sturdy High Hallow forging along the trampled slot where the scout snipers and most of Brigadier Zhorj Sutyls' 8th Infantry Brigade had moved up towards their objectives.

It was hard to pick out details of his men's deployment. Their snow smocks blended too well into the endless whiteness around them for that. It was actually easier to spot where they'd been than where they *were*, thanks to the tracks they'd left behind and the little islands where squads had parked their tent- and baggage-laden sleds while they stripped down to combat gear. The weather was warm enough (although, to someone of Green Valley's Old Charisian sensibilities, calling twenty-two degrees Fahrenheit "warm" came perilously close to blasphemy) that they'd been able to discard their heavy gauntlet-style mittens in favor of lighter gloves which would make handling weapons much easier, and each squad of the platoons moving forward into their jumpoff positions had left one man to keep an eye on its sled. Since the men had left their cumbersome caribou-hide outer parkas behind when they stripped down for combat, making sure those sleds and their burdens were close at hand would become critically important once the short winter's day slid over into twilight.

Other sleds were surrounded by a different set of acolytes. Those were the ones supporting the squat, menacing tubes of 1st Corps' mortars. Along with the influx of M96s and Trapdoor Mahndrayns, Green Valley had taken receipt of the Delthak Works' latest upgrade of the Army of Midhold's lethality in the form of a new four-and-a-half-inch mortar. Technically known as the "Model 97, 4.5" Mortar," the new weapon's standard explosive round had four thousand yards more range than the older M95 three-inch. The range increase for its rather heavier antipersonnel round was a little less than that, but its projectiles were three times as heavy as the M95s, with a proportionate increase in bursting charge and shrapnel which gave its rounds more than twice the lethal radius. It was, in fact, considerably more effective against concealed or semi-concealed targets than the artillery's four-inch muzzle-loading rifles, although the field pieces had a much deeper lethal zone against exposed enemies.

There weren't as many of the M97s as Green Valley could have wished, but there'd been enough to form them into additional support platoons, and he'd assigned one of those platoons to each of 1st Corps' regiments. At the moment, 7th Brigade had loaned its heavy mortars to 8th Brigade, and their gunners were opening crates of bombs and propellant charges while the lighter M95s continued to make their way closer to the town. Artillery support parties had already moved up close behind the deploying infantry, carrying their signal mirrors, signal rockets, and semaphore flags with them. Additional ASPs had been dropped off to serve as relays to the heavy mortars.

Green Valley reached the brigade command post and dismounted, passing his reins to Lieutenant Slokym as he slogged through the snow to where Brigadier Sutyls was deep in conversation with Colonel Ahlfryd Maiyrs, 16th Regiment's CO.

"So Colonel Gairwyl's regiment is swinging around the north side of town," Sutyls was saying, tapping the map between them. "There's more tree cover to get in the horses' way on that side, but it's almost all evergreens. That's actually kept the ground clear of snow, which means the mounted infantry can move pretty well, even through the trees, and they should keep anyone in town from spotting them."

The brigadier looked up as Green Valley arrived. He and Maiyrs began to come to attention, but the baron only shook his head and pointed at the map.

Sutyls nodded to acknowledge the unspoken command and bent back over the map, tracing positions with his forefinger as he continued speaking to Maiyrs.

"Colonel Hyndryks is moving up his First and Fourth Battalions down here," the brigadier indicated an arc around the town's southern approaches. Colonel Symohr Hyndryks commanded the 15th Infantry, the 16th's sister regiment in 8th Brigade. "He's using this line of hills for cover, and a company of Major Kharyn's scout snipers have outposts in these abandoned farms along here." The finger tapped again. "That should let Hyndryks move up to within a few hundred yards of their outer earthworks without anyone seeing him, and the rest of Kharyn's scout snipers've moved round to the west side with Colonel Yarith and the Sixth Mounted. The going's not as good around the southern flank, so Yarith's not in position yet, but his people got an early start and he's in heliograph contact with Colonel Hyndryks. Hyndryks'll pass the word when Yairley's cut the high road on the far side of town. At that point, the frigging Temple Boys are in the bag, with nowhere to go when your lads kick in their front door. Best current estimate is that Hyndryks and the Sixth ought to be in position in about another hour."

Green Valley glanced up at the sky. They were still an hour and a half or so shy of local noon, but the days were short this far north. They'd have no more than another four hours—five, at the outside—before darkness closed in once again. On the other hand, a quick check through the SNARCs agreed—for the most part—with Sutyls' time estimate. In fact, half of Colonel Symohr Hyndryks' 15th Infantry Regiment was already in place, close behind Fumyro Kharyn's scout snipers, making its final weapons checks while the other two battalions remained well back to form a reserve in the unlikely event that they were needed.

Sir Uhlstyn Yarith's mounted infantry and its accompanying ski-mounted scout snipers were a bit behind Sutyls' schedule, however. It had been a hard slog through deep snow, even for the Chisholmian-bred High Hallows and the caribou-drawn sleds of their assigned support element, but they were past the worst of it now. There'd be more than enough daylight left when they reached their positions, and the support element had already reached *its* position and begun erecting the first of the tents for their intended post-battle bivouac.

"Major Mahkylhyn and Major Tahlyvyr have moved up to this bank of the stream, Sir," Maiyrs told Sutyls, tracing his own line on the map. "I'll have Major Hylmyn in place on Tahlyvyr's left in thirty minutes, and then we'll just see about kicking that door down for you."

Sutyls grunted in satisfaction. Three of 16th Infantry's battalions—Tohmys Mahkylhyn's 1st Battalion,

Brygham Tahlyvyr's 2nd Battalion, and Samyl Hylmyn's 4th Battalion—were tasked as the primary assault units, while Major Rahnyld Gahdarhd's 3rd Battalion formed the regimental reserve and Colonel Hyndryks' infantry and the two mounted regiments prevented any breakout to the west by the AOG garrison. In theory, Brigadier Ahdryn Krystyphyr's entire 7th Brigade was available as a reserve or to exploit success, but Green Valley had no expectation of requiring Krystyphyr's men. Sutyls' brigade was almost fully up to strength, with the better part of nine thousand men present, compared to the barely forty-five hundred of all arms of Qwentyn Preskyt's understrength units, and trying to cram Krystyphyr's men into the operation would only have cramped the attack. That wasn't to say that 7th Brigade's men and officers weren't highly miffed at being told to sit this one out, but Green Valley had already promised Krystyphyr his brigade would be allowed to take the lead in the next stage of what the baron had dubbed "Operation Winter Vengeance."

He smiled with cold appreciation of his troops' determination to make that name fit, but the smile faded as he thought about the one thing none of his men or he would be able to accomplish. The nearest of the Inquisition's concentration camps was located at Hyrdmyn on the New Northland Canal, still seven hundred hopeless straight-line miles from Esthyr's Abbey. He probably had the logistical capability to reach Hyrdmyn, but he could neither have fed the camp's inmates after he got there nor evacuated them across that enormous distance. Those inmates were dying in dreadful numbers as cold and hunger—not to mention hopelessness and the Inquisition's brutalities—ate away at their fragile reserves of strength and endurance. Yet without a means to evacuate them, they would only have died still faster if he'd tried to mount a rescue operation.

Kynt Clareyk was no coward, but he could no longer bear to view the SNARC imagery of the camps. He'd left that heartbreaking task to Owl and to Nahrmahn Baytz, because he couldn't—literally couldn't—let his personal hatred and sense of helplessness compromise his ability to think about the tasks he *could* accomplish. He knew what was happening at Hyrdmyn, and in the camps at places like Gray Hill, Traymos, Lakeside, Sairmeet, Blufftyn, and Lake City, and the day of reckoning the Republic would demand of the Inquisition—the entire Church of God Awaiting—in the fullness of time would be terrible enough to fit the crime. For now, all he could do was try to speed that day.

"The scout snipers and the ASPs say the ice is more than thick enough to stand the recoil from the M95s," Maiyrs continued, "so I'm going to deploy them on the stream. They'll be closer to our lead units if we need to signal fire missions, and they ought to be able to get up the bank without even dismounting from the sleds to keep up close once we move off."

"Good," Sutyls said. "Good!"

Green Valley nodded in agreement. The lighter three-inchers packed less punch than the new M97, but they also weighed less than a third as much, which meant they—and their ammunition—found it easier to keep up close behind advancing infantry. And, perhaps more to the point, the M97s could handle their part of the operation just fine from their current locations.

"All right," the brigadier said. "It sounds to me like we're just about ready. Do you have anything you'd care to add, My Lord?"

He looked at Green Valley, who shook his head.

"It's your brigade, Zhorj, and it's all looking good to me. Besides, you know my motto. 'If it isn't broken—' "

He paused, and both of his subordinates grinned broadly at him.

"—'don't fix it,' " they finished in unison.

"Exactly." Green Valley smiled back at them, and it was a hungry, predatory smile. "On the other hand, I'm entirely in favor of your breaking something else."

▼ ▼ ▼

". . . about the size of it, Sir," Major Hahl concluded his report. Somehow, the major managed to look remarkably spruce and clean-shaven, despite his chapped face and hunger-sharpened cheekbones.

"Thank you, Lawrync," Colonel Bahstyk Sahndyrs said, acknowledging yet another clearly and concisely delivered report on the state of his 4th Infantry Regiment. It was scarcely Hahl's fault the report was so unpalatable.

The colonel turned away from the map tacked to his wall and gazed out the window at the snow-covered, slovenly streets of Esthyr's Abbey. The office in which he stood had been the dining room of one of the town's more affluent farmers, and its windows looked past the glistening icicles, some thick as Sahndyrs' wrist, which fringed the overhanging roof and ran across the aptly named Snow Dragon Square. Once upon a time, before the Sword, Snow Dragon had been one of Esthyr's Abbey's neatly maintained residential squares. Now its houses had been taken over to shelter Mother Church's infantry, and those half-frozen soldiers had more pressing worries than keeping things neat and tidy.

The only good thing about Major Hahl's report, Sahndyrs reflected, was that bad as things were, they were better than they *had* been. Only a drooling idiot could have argued the situation was good, yet the improvement was marked. He knew supplying Esthyr's Abbey used up far more of Bishop Militant Bahrnabai's precious snow lizards than the bishop militant would have preferred, and he sympathized with the Army of the Sylmahn's commander. But that didn't keep him from being grateful that at least nearly adequate supplies of food were finally reaching the town, and even more grateful for the fact that they'd received almost six hundred of the new St. Kylmahn rifles four five-days earlier than predicted. Of course, the rifles had been divided between St. Fraidyr and Bishop Zhaksyn's Port Harbor Division, but there were some advantages to being the division's senior colonel, and Bishop Qwentyn had seen fit to assign all of St. Fraidyr's share to

Sahndyrs' regiment. The good news was that that had been enough to completely reequip Sahndyrs' 4th Infantry; the bad news was that the only reason it had was that the regiment was at barely sixty percent strength.

From where he stood, looking across the square, the colonel could see the Church's green and gold banner flying from the roof of the house which had been appropriated for Bishop Qwentyn's quarters. Smoke plumed from both of the house's chimneys, and as he watched, the door opened, and Father Vyncyt Zhakyby—St. Fraidyr Division's intendant—stepped out of it. The Schuelerite upper-priest stood for a moment, clapping his gloved hands together against the day's cold while he exchanged a few words with the shivering sentry on a steamy spurt of breath.

Sahndyrs had come to know the divisional intendant fairly well, and, to be honest, he didn't much like him, because Father Vyncyt had a tendency to meddle in the management of the division's regiments. Still, the Schuelerite possessed both a powerful faith and enormous energy, and however much he might interfere in purely military decisions, he was also prepared to share any privation the troops under his care had to endure. He'd restricted himself to the same austere diet and the same cobbled-together grab bag of winter clothing, yet he'd sustained the pace of his visits, inspections, exhortations, and sermons at a level a peacetime priest would have found difficult to match. And unlike too many intendants and chaplains Sahndyrs could have named, he took time to actually talk to the men, to listen to their questions and concerns and *explain* things to them, not simply lecture them. Sahndyrs was prepared to overlook quite a lot of meddling as long as that was true.

He turned back from the window, and smiled at his executive officer.

"Yet another exciting day in Esthyr's Abbey," he said dryly, crossing to his desk and relishing the fire's heat against his back as he seated himself. "Should I assume

that with your customary efficiency you have that report about the men's boots?"

"Yes, Sir." The much younger Hahl inhaled deeply
and rubbed a forefinger across his mustache. "I don't
think you're going to like hearing it, though."

"Lawrync, I haven't liked hearing *most* of what I've
heard since the frigging heretics blew up the canals.
From your preface, however, I take it the Bishop Militant's quartermasters don't have any boots to send?"

Frostbite had become a deadly serious problem, inflicting more than half the division's total casualties
over the last two months, and it was worst of all for
the men's feet. Only a handful had been issued proper
winter boots, because there simply weren't enough of
them to go around. Most of the rest had wrapped what
boots they did have in straw from the many abandoned
barns and stables, bound in place with burlap or anything else they could find. Sahndyrs had been moving
heaven and earth to get his freezing men better boots
for more five-days than he liked to count, but it was
like trying to empty Lake Pei with a bucket.

"They've found us a few pairs, Sir." Hahl opened a
folder and looked at the top sheet of notes inside it.
"Unfortunately, I think the only reason they had them
on hand was probably the fact that they're too small
to fit most of our men. According to Lieutenant Khaldwyl, we'll be lucky if—"

▼ ▼ ▼

"The heliograph's just delivered a message from Colonel Hyndryks, Sir," Lieutenant Saith Zohryla announced.

Brigadier Sutyls and Baron Green Valley both looked
up quickly from the map and their quiet discussion of
the terrain between Esthyr's Abbey and St. Zhana, 1st
Corps' next objective.

"The Colonel says Colonel Yarith is in position," Sutyls' aide told them, and Sutyls' expression lightened. As
Green Valley had expected, it had taken Yarith longer to
reach his position than the brigadier had estimated, and
Sutyls had tried to hide his unhappiness as he felt

the precious winter daylight slipping away. "Colonel Yarith also reports he encountered a Temple Boy outpost where there wasn't supposed to be one," Zohryla continued. "He believes his men killed or captured the entire picket."

Sutyls' lips tightened once more at the word "believes," but Green Valley only nodded. The SNARCs had already told him about the collision between Yarith's men and the "outpost." In fact, the half-strength AOG platoon had been sent to inventory the contents of half a dozen abandoned barns and silos on the west side of the town which had been earmarked as future firewood. There'd been no way anyone could have predicted it would be dispatched on its mission, even with SNARC reconnaissance, but Yarith's scouts had spotted it in time and swept up its hapless infantry before any of them could fire a shot or escape to sound a warning.

Brigadier Sutyls wasn't privy to the information the SNARCs had reported to his superior, and it was obvious he was none too pleased by the encounter's potential to warn Preskyt's men there were enemies about. On the other hand, it wasn't like they weren't about to find out anyway.

"Very well, Saith," he said after a moment. "Pass the execute order to Colonel Maiyrs, please."

"Yes, Sir!"

Lieutenant Zohryla touched his chest in salute and strode purposefully towards the signals party, beckoning for one of the runners. A moment later, the runner departed on his skis, moving fast, and Sutyls turned back to Green Valley.

"I know it's more efficient this way, My Lord," he said with a wry smile, "but sometimes I sort of miss the days when I'd've been standing on a hilltop with a spyglass and personally organizing this entire attack!"

"If you think it's bad for a brigadier, you should try it as a *corps* commander," Green Valley agreed with feeling. "But it seems to've worked out pretty well so far."

"Langhorne send it keeps *on* working that way, Sir."

"I won't complain if he does," Green Valley said with complete sincerity, despite his feelings where Eric Langhorne were concerned. "Not one bit."

▼ ▼ ▼

"All right."

Colonel Maiyrs refolded the note from Brigadier Sutyls and shoved it into his parka's outer pocket, then put his gloves back on with slow deliberation. Once he had them adjusted properly, he turned to his own signal party.

"Fire the signal," he said.

▼ ▼ ▼

Lieutenant Byrtrym Azkhat was the commanding officer of the recently formed 23rd Heavy Support Platoon, which was currently assigned to the 16th Infantry's 1st Battalion. Now he looked up at one of his noncoms' shout and saw the signal rocket soar upward on its trail of smoke. The flash when it burst was pale in the daylight, but it was bright enough, especially when Azkhat had been waiting so impatiently to see it.

"*Now!*" he snapped.

▼ ▼ ▼

The new M97 mortars were big, ugly brutes with a barrel length of over five feet. Their explosive projectiles weighed thirty-three pounds, without propellant charge, and Azkhat's gunners had cursed them with sweaty sincerity in training. There weren't many of them, and Lieutenant Azkhat's feelings had been mixed, to say the least, when his platoon had been ordered to turn in their three-inch mortars and reequip with them.

They had a range of four miles, however, and at the moment they were emplaced just over *two* miles from the center of Esthyr's Abbey. There'd been ample time for Azkhat's men to dismount the weapons from their sleds and prepare solid, properly leveled foundations

on the eastern side of a long crest line, and the lieutenant and Sergeant Cahnyr Lynkyn, his senior squadron
commander, had positioned the range and bearing
stakes with finicky precision.

The crest of their concealing hill boasted a scattering
of northern spine trees. The spear-shaped evergreens'
branches were covered with the sharp, unpleasant
spines which gave them their name, but they were also
sturdy, and Azkhat had sent Corporal Shawyn Portyr
up the tallest of them. From there, he had an excellent
view of the town and of the actual abbey beyond it,
and he'd constructed a perch for himself and the map
on which a gridded overlay had been superimposed.
He'd long since located their initial targets' positions
from the map, and the rest of Azkhat's organic artillery
support party was prepared to pass his corrections to
the mortars. The ASP's position was also perfect—or
nearly so—for receiving and passing on fire requests
from other units.

The tubes themselves had been laid in on as close to
the correct bearings and elevations as they could come
without their own direct lines of sight. Now Sergeant
Ymilahno Fahrya, the sergeant in charge of 3rd Squad,
nodded sharply in response to Azkhat's one-word command and chopped one hand at Corporal Mahthyw
Khulpepur, the gun captain on 3rd Squad's number one
mortar.

"*Fire!*" Khulpepur barked, and Private Rahdryk
Nahkadahn, who'd been waiting, eyes locked on Khulpepur, dropped the first bomb down the rifled tube. The
M97 dispensed with the side caplock which had been
a feature of the original M95. The ICA had discovered
that the M95 had an unpleasant habit of "cooking off"
when a freshly loaded propellant charge hit an ember
left from the previous shot, so the Delthak Works had
modified its design to combine loading and firing into
a single, rapid motion. Now the priming cap fitted in
the simple retaining clip at the end of the rod projecting from the bomb's base hit the spike at the bottom of
the tube. The impact detonated the cap, its flash ignited

the powder-filled felt "doughnuts" fitted around the rod, and the mortar spat the bomb heavenward at over eight hundred feet per second.

▼ ▼ ▼

"—so Ustys is checking with the other regiments." Major Hahl shrugged ever so slightly. "It's not likely we're going to find many people with feet that small, but Ustys will probably turn up at least a few." The major smiled suddenly, although there was more than a hint of grimace in the expression. "I'm sure he'll drive a hard bargain for them!"

Colonel Sahndyrs chuckled in agreement. Technically, Lieutenant Ustys Khaldwyl was assigned to Rhobair Duchairn's quartermaster's corps, but Sahndyrs and Hahl had more or less kidnapped him and put him to work for 4th Regiment the better part of two months ago. He made a far better supply officer than they'd had previously, and while they knew they'd be forced to admit his whereabouts and give him up eventually, he'd been a gift from the Archangels in the meantime. Not only did he know how to work the official logistics system, but he was also an inspired scrounger and Sahndyrs' fellow colonels had begun muttering darkly about his depredations.

"I'm sure the Lieutenant will do us proud," the colonel said. "And, with that out of the way, I suppose it's time for lunch. Who are we messing with today?"

"Captain Myrgyn, Sir," Hahl replied, and Sahndyrs nodded. He made it a point to eat at least one meal a day with each of his company commanders in turn. The practice kept him abreast of their commands' readiness and morale, as well as the state of their rations.

"In that case, we should probably get started," he sighed, climbing out of his chair with an air of resignation. It was cold outside, and Captain Ahnthyny Myrgyn's 3rd Company wasn't what one might have called conveniently close to his own HQ. "At least—"

▼ ▼ ▼

Approximately three and a half seconds after Private Nahkadahn dropped it down the mortar's muzzle, the thirty-three-pound projectile came sizzling out of the clear winter's sky with a warbling wail that ended in a clap of thunder.

▼ ▼ ▼

Colonel Sahndyrs whipped back towards the window as something exploded like Langhorne's own Rakurai. A column of flame-shot smoke erupted from a roof on the far side of Bishop Qwentyn's headquarters, and Sahndyrs' eyes went wide with consternation as he tried to understand what had just happened.

▼ ▼ ▼

Shawyn Portyr peered through his double-glass, waiting . . . waiting . . . .

It was odd how slowly seconds could drag at a time like this, a corner of his brain reflected, eyes glued to the green and gold flag which made such a handy reference point. The wait really wasn't all that long, but it seemed far longer. There was always time to wonder if they'd gotten it right, how much it was going to miss by, whether or not—

The thunderbolt landed, and Portyr bared his teeth. The answers seemed to be yes, and not by much.

"Right fifty and down one hundred!" he called, never lowering his glasses, and heard the correction shouted back up in confirmation from his signalmen.

▼ ▼ ▼

"Right fifty and down a hundred," Sergeant Fahrya shouted, and Corporal Khulpepur's crew traversed the weapon slightly, using the ranging stakes, while the corporal himself turned the knob which adjusted its elevation.

"Right fifty, down one hundred, and . . . set!" he called back in confirmation, and Fahrya nodded.

"Fire!"

▼ ▼ ▼

*Was that a shell? No. That's ridiculous! How could it be—?*

Doors were beginning to open around Snow Dragon Square. Even through the window glass, Colonel Sahndyrs could hear sentries shouting the alarm, and Bishop Qwentyn appeared suddenly on the steps of the house across from Sahndyrs. He must have been about to leave his headquarters for an inspection, Sahndyrs thought, because he already wore his heavy coat and gloves, and there hadn't been time for him to don them in response to the explosion. But—

A second thunderbolt arrived from on high. It landed on the far side of the small, snow-covered circle of ornamental trees and frozen flowerbeds at the center of the square, almost on top of one of the stone benches where the square's residents were accustomed to sitting in warmer weather . . . and less than fifty feet from Bishop Qwentyn Preskyt.

The dining room window shattered on the wings of the explosion's shockwave, icicles and diamond-shaped panes blowing in like glass axe blades. One of those blades opened Bahstyk Sahndyrs' right cheek like a razor, but he hardly noticed. His ears were filled with thunder and Lawrync Hahl's choked-off cry of pain . . . and his mind was filled with the knowledge that he'd just become St. Fraidyr Division's commanding officer.

▾ ▾ ▾

"*Yes!*" Corporal Portyr shouted. He couldn't actually see down into Snow Dragon Square, even from his perch, but he could see well enough to know the second round had landed inside it. He looked down at the private at the foot of his tree. "Perfect. Tell the Lieutenant that was *perfect!*"

Eleven more M97 mortars duplicated Corporal Khulpepur's sight settings. Confirmations were called out. And then—

"*Fire!*" Lieutenant Azkhat barked.

▾ ▾ ▾

Kynt Clareyk stood with his head cocked, listening to the mortars' deep-throated coughs. His eyes were half closed, his expression intent, but he wasn't simply listening to the mortars, whatever his officers might think. No, he was watching through the SNARCs as their bombs came hurtling down all across Esthyr's Abbey, and unlike Corporal Portyr, he *could* see down into the town's squares and alleys.

He'd personally selected Snow Dragon Square as the target for Azkhat's heavy support platoon. Officially, he'd chosen it because it was close to the center of town and an easily identifiable target. Both of those reasons were true, but he'd also chosen it because he knew where Preskyt was headquartered. Chaos and confusion in the enemy's ranks were two of the deadliest weapons in any soldier's arsenal, and if he could decapitate the entire garrison . . . .

A dozen thirty-three-pound projectiles scorched across the sky, wrapping Snow Dragon Square in explosions, blasting roofs off of houses, setting fires. They were filled only with gunpowder, not the antipersonnel rounds' flesh-shredding shrapnel charges, but they scourged the town with fire and blast, and the garrison's troops—totally surprised, with no warning there was an enemy within a hundred miles—reacted with all the confusion Clareyk could have asked for.

The explosions shattered roofs and walls, and men who'd been huddled around fireplaces, or mending worn equipment, or asleep in their blankets under heaps of straw stumbled to their feet as the arctic cold swept in on the heels of destruction. Not just in Snow Dragon Square, either. More mortars had been positioned all around the town's eastern and southern perimeters. Most were M95s, but their lighter bombs were perfectly adequate, and there were a great many more of them. They targeted the outermost houses and barns which had been turned into barracks, directed by the ASPs embedded with the scout snipers and the forward companies of the 8th Brigade. Roofs disintegrated, glass and shutters blew outward as bombs exploded inside houses, stored hay—more precious than gold in the heart of a North Haven winter—caught fire, and cries of shock and screams of pain were everywhere. Men staggered out of the sudden inferno into the bitter cold, many only half-clothed, and a third of the M95s *were* firing antipersonnel bombs fused for airburst that sent cyclones of shrapnel through their bleeding ranks.

Each support platoon had its predesignated targets, and the mortar crews worked their way outward toward the town's edges, methodically shattering its buildings. Despite the carnage, the garrison's officers and noncoms managed to restore some sort of discipline and order. Leather-lunged sergeants bellowed orders, sending men into their assigned positions in the entrenchments which had been hacked out of the icy ground. Other sergeants and officers—the ones with the quickest minds, the ones who realized that even if they survived the attack they'd still have to face the winter—sent some of their men back to fight fires and rescue whatever of winter clothing and supplies they could snatch from the flames.

On the eastern side, the infantry racing for the forward trenches—most from St. Manthyr's Division's 3rd Regiment—came suddenly under accurate, heavy rifle fire. Two of Major Dyasaiyl's scout sniper companies had infiltrated to within thirty yards of the trenches under cover of the streambed and the eye-blurring effect of their white snow smocks. They'd lain patiently in the snow for hours, waiting without a sound, until the instant the first mortars fired. Then they'd come to their feet behind a hailstorm of hand grenades, bayonets fixed on their whitewashed M96 rifles.

The entrenchments were more rudimentary than anything the ICA would have tolerated. First, because it had been so difficult to hack them out of the frozen ground, but second—and more damningly—because no one had really expected to *need* them before spring. There would be plenty of time to deepen the trenches, build the shallow parapets higher, before the heretics could possibly advance this far. More effort had been expended on the dugouts threaded along the trenches, but that was mainly because they also served as snugger, better-insulated barracks for the infantry companies assigned to man them. It certainly hadn't been because anyone anticipated an actual attack, and the startled sentries, minds numbed as much by routine as by cold and hunger, never had a chance. They were swept away in the first rush, before most of them even realized they were under attack, and the infantry platoons sheltering in those dugouts for warmth had only a very little more warning. They were just beginning to pour out of them when the scout snipers arrived among them in a blizzard of bullets and bayonets. Men who normally would have stood their ground in the face of the most furious assault gave way, succumbing to a panic born of surprise, not cowardice. Dozens fell as the scout snipers' fire swept over them, others went down, screaming, as bayonets drove into them, and even as they died, the dreadful rain of mortar bombs doubled and redoubled in fury behind them.

The defenders fell back. They more than "fell back"; they routed. Many threw away the weapons which might have hindered their flight. Others fled back into the dugouts from which they'd come, only to discover the horrific depth of their error when scout snipers tossed grenades in behind them and turned their protection into charnel houses. And while one platoon in each scout sniper company dealt with that problem, the other three spread out along the captured trenches. They found firing positions among the defenders' bodies, and most of them removed the outer gloves from their right hands, retaining only the knitted glove liners, to improve their ability to manipulate bolt handles and triggers.

Each man had seventy rounds—one ten-round magazine already locked into his rifle's magazine well and six additional charged magazines in the ammunition pouches affixed to his web gear—and all along the captured trench line, scout snipers unbuttoned their ammo pouches and made sure those extra magazines were ready to hand. Behind them, the four infantry companies of Major Sethry Ahdyms' 2nd Battalion, 16th Infantry, slogged forward to reinforce them. And behind 2nd Battalion, more support squads dashed forward from the stream bank dragging their sled-mounted weapons up to the far side of the entrenchments, where the parapet concealed them from the defenders, to provide the close fire support which was so fundamental a part of Charisian tactics.

By the time the first counterattacking companies of Colonel Sahndyrs' 4th Regiment emerged from the smoke, dust, and flying snow of the bombardment, the scout snipers were ready. For the first time in Safeholdian history, magazine-fed, bolt-action rifles came into action on a field of battle, and the result was horrendous. The first savage volleys went home before the scout snipers' targets realized what was happening, while they were still moving forward in column formation under their officers' orders. They took a minute to grasp what was happening—to realize they were being killed by rifle bullets coming from in front of them rather than shrapnel and explosions from above—and they kept surging forward towards the illusory protection of the trenches they didn't know had been occupied by their enemies.

At least a tenth of them were killed or wounded before they understood what was truly happening. Worse, casualties were disproportionately concentrated among their noncoms and junior officers. Despite that, the majority responded by going prone and spreading out to make themselves poorer targets, not by simply turning around and pelting back the way they'd come in terrified retreat. Many of them did begin working their way back, crawling on their bellies towards the inner of the town's two lines of entrenchments, but 4th Regiment had been rearmed with St. Kylmahns. Two of its companies found cover in folds in the ground or behind sidewalks, planters, walls, trees—*anything* they could—and returned fire, trying desperately to cover their companions' retreat.

Single-shot breech-loading weapons were far from equal to the Charisians' M96s, but they were also far more effective than muzzleloaders would have been, and the scout snipers began taking casualties of their own, despite their protected positions. Still, they were taking many *fewer* casualties, even proportionately, and the mortars which had come up so close behind them began raining shrapnel on the defenders.

"Fall back! *Fall back!*"

No one would ever know who first shouted that command, but it was the right order to give. The decimated Church riflemen staggered toward the rear, moving in short dashes between inadequate bits of cover. They'd never been trained in the movement and fire tactics the ICA routinely employed, but sheer, dogged stubbornness prevented their retreat from turning into a rout, despite the confusion, chaos, and casualties. Men stopped to fire back again and again, effectively covering their fellows' movement even if no one had ever trained them to do so. The loss rate was unambiguously in the scout snipers' favor, but the differential was lower than it might have been. Almost half of 4th Regiment's two hundred riflemen made it back to the second trench line alive.

They flung themselves into position, looking around, realizing how many comrades they'd already lost, hearing the explosions and carnage ripping the town apart around them, and their eyes were wild. There were few cowards among them, but the certainty of eventual defeat had sunk its fangs deep into their bones, and they could see it in one another's faces.

"Reload!" a surviving lieutenant was shouting. "Keep your heads down, reload, and fix bayonets! This time it'll be *their* turn to come out in the open!"

The men of the Fourth obeyed; there was nothing else they could do.

Five minutes passed, then ten. Fifteen.

Cold gnawed into inadequately clothed bodies. The moans, whimpers, and sobs of the wounded faded quickly in the icy temperatures. The thunderous mortar bombardment went on—punctuated by a handful of much larger explosions when plunging bombs found the garrison's ammunition dumps—then tapered off. The crackling roar as flames consumed the shelter which spelled survival was like a dozen blast furnaces, and the shrieks of men trapped inside the inferno were the voices of souls condemned to Shan-wei's own hell.

Twenty minutes. Thirty . . . then another Charisian signal rocket soared into the heavens and, all the more terrible for the nerve-twisting wait, a hurricane of antipersonnel bombs shrieked down upon them.

Billowing smoke and blazing wreckage interfered with the Charisian ASPs vision, but they knew approximately where the second line of entrenchments had been dug, and each bomb was an airburst, fused to disperse its shrapnel over a circle fifty yards in diameter. The only overhead protection was in the dugouts spaced along the trenches at regular intervals, and many of the defenders retreated into them . . . which was exactly what their enemies had wanted.

The Imperial Charisian Army's signals capability was better than that of any other Safeholdian army, yet it remained almost entirely dependent upon visual signals. Whistles and bugles could be used to augment runners—and the new flare pistols just coming into service—at relatively short range. But audible signals were all too easily drowned out in the background roar of battle, and runners could too easily become lost. Although Charisian supporting fire could be coordinated and controlled with a sophistication no one else could match, signals were more likely to go astray than to reach their intended recipients once smoke began to obscure the battlefield. Initial fire missions could be preplanned, but "on call" fire was much more difficult and far more dangerous, given the high possibility of friendly fire incidents.

No one was better aware of that than Kynt Clareyk, who'd spent months developing the ICA's artillery doctrine. He'd stressed the need for concentration of fire, for exercising the tightest possible control yet recognizing that truly "tight" control would be impossible, and the artillerists had come up with several approaches to the problem. As much as possible, they released the mortars to specific rifle companies or even platoons, ready to put fire where it was requested by the units they were tasked to support but never firing in anyone else's support. That might mean they spent a lot of time standing idle, but it also decreased the chance of dropping rounds on friendly troops they hadn't known were there.

They'd also allowed for fire support at the battalion or regimental level, however, and devised standardized fire missions, like the one Major Sethry Ahdyms' 2nd Battalion had just called for. And for those sorts of missions, all of the units' mortars could be concentrated, with control temporarily reverting from the forward companies to higher authority. It could be difficult to get the word out when such a mission was required, and it relied more heavily on signal rockets than on runners, semaphores, and mirrors. It was also accepted that some of the support platoons who hadn't gotten the word would be unable to contribute to the mission, but it could be done.

Fire hammered down on the defenders, designed not simply to kill them but to pin them, drive them to earth—or down into the dugouts—in self-preservation. And as the mortars flailed them, the companies detailed to lead the Charisian assault moved out of the original trench line. They stayed low, close to the ground, easing forward while the supporting fire kept the defenders down.

It was a timed fire concentration. There was too much chance a ceasefire signal from the assault troops might be missed by some or all of the gunners supporting them, so the mortars fired steadily for fifteen minutes. It was the infantry's responsibility to be in position, waiting and ready when the fire mission ended as abruptly as a slammed door exactly fifteen minutes after it had begun.

The way 2nd Battalion was.

The handful of dazed, all too often wounded Church riflemen in the threshed and shattered trenches didn't understand why the fire had stopped. They didn't even realize for a second or two that it had.

But then a bugle blared, and suddenly white-smocked infantrymen were on their feet, erupting from the fog-banks of smoke like Shan-wei's own demons behind a thicket of bayonets and the high, piercing howl the ICA had adopted from the Royal Charisian Marines.

## . XII .
## St. Kylmahn's Foundry,
## City of Zion,
## The Temple Lands

"Thank you, Brother Lynkyn," Rhobair Duchairn said, cupping the heavy mug of hot tea gratefully between his chilled palms.

It was early afternoon, but the gloomy winter day was already sliding into dark and it was snowing outside Lynkyn Fultyn's office windows . . . again. A nasty wind gathered strength as it moaned about the eaves, too. It was entirely possible, the Church's treasurer thought, that he might end up spending the night in one of St. Kylmahn's guest chambers. It wouldn't be the first time, and while they were a far cry from his sumptuous Temple suite, at least they were weather tight and warm. That mattered in Zion in March. In fact, given the weather, Major Phandys, the recently promoted commander of his personal bodyguard (and the Inquisition spy Zhaspahr Clyntahn had personally assigned to report his comings and goings), had probably made provisional arrangements to quarter his Guardsmen for the night already.

"You're most welcome, Your Grace." The bearded Chihirite lay brother set the teapot on the small spirit burner beside his desk, picked up his own tea mug, and sat back. "Forgive me," he continued, "but I was under the impression Vicar Allayn would be joining us, as well."

"As far as I know, he will be." Duchairn sipped the hot tea, liberally sweetened with honey, appreciatively. "That was his intent this morning, at least. Considering what the weather seems intent on doing to us, however, I think we should probably accept that he may not make it after all."

Fultyn nodded. Winters in Zion were like winters nowhere else in the civilized world. Oh, winters in northern Harchong were even worse, but North Harchong scarcely qualified as "the civilized world," did it? It wasn't at all uncommon for snow, ice, and wind to disrupt meeting schedules in Zion this time of year. What *was* uncommon was for a member of the vicarate to stray beyond the Temple's mystically heated precincts to attend those meetings rather than summoning more lowly beings to the Temple. One could hardly expect such senior servants of God to expose themselves to the bitter cold, snow, and ice when they had so many more important and pressing matters to attend to.

Of course, the lay brother reflected, there were vicars, and then there were vicars. It was barely past midday, yet he knew St. Kylmahn's Foundry was Vicar Rhobair's second stop of the day, not the first. No, his *first* meeting, with Father Zytan Kwill, who administered the holy city's homeless shelters, had begun halfway across the city and no more than an hour past what passed for dawn in Zion, at Father Zytan's lakefront office, where the wind was even icier than here. And knowing Vicar Rhobair, it had probably ended no more than an hour or so ago.

"Excuse me, Your Grace," he said as that thought struck him, "but have you had lunch?"

"Lunch?" Duchairn looked up and arched his eyebrows. "Why, no, I haven't." He shrugged wryly. "My meeting with Father Zytan ran over, and I'm afraid we couldn't stop along the way if I meant to get here on time."

"I'd gladly have waited long enough for you to eat, Your Grace!" Fultyn gave the vicar a stern glance, then shook his head, reached up, and tugged the cord hanging from the ceiling. A bell jangled on the far side of his office door and, a moment later, that door popped open to admit his secretary, another Chihirite lay brother. The newcomer bent his head in a respectful bow to Duchairn, then looked at Fultyn.

"Yes, Brother Lynkyn?"

"His Grace hasn't eaten since breakfast, Zhoel. What's today's lunch menu?"

"I'm afraid it's only clam chowder," Brother Zhoel replied apologetically (and possibly a little anxiously), with a sideways glance at Duchairn.

"Clam chowder would be perfect on a day like this one, Brother," the vicar said, and smiled. "Especially if I could get a really *big* bowl of it."

"I'm sure we could manage that, Your Grace!" Brother Zhoel assured him.

"And some fresh bread?" Duchairn injected an edge of wistful longing into his tone, and the secretary smiled.

"They just finished baking, Your Grace. In fact, if you'd like, I could bring it to you in a bread bowl?"

"That would be marvelous, Brother. And if you could add a stein of Brother Lynkyn's excellent beer to it, I'd be forever in your debt."

"Of course, Your Grace!" Brother Zhoel bowed to him again, then looked at his own superior. "And for you, Brother?"

"Vicar Rhobair's menu sounds just fine to me, too, Zhoel."

"Very good."

The secretary dipped his head to Fultyn, then disappeared, and Duchairn turned back to the foundry director.

"Now that we've attended to that pressing concern—and thank you for asking, by the way—I suppose we should get some business done. Since Vicar Allayn may not join us after all, why don't you and I go ahead? If he does get here, we can bring him up to date on anything we've already covered. In the meanwhile, I'm sure there are things you and I need to discuss from the Treasury's viewpoint, anyway."

"Of course, Your Grace." Fultyn inclined his head in a sort of half-bow across the desk.

It wasn't as if the foundry was so busy that finding time for meetings was difficult. The tempo in Zion's manufactories always slowed, along with all the rest of the city, during the winter, but this year it had slowed much further than the winter before. The shipments of coal and iron ore which Mother Church's capital city and its foundries routinely stockpiled each autumn against the coming winter's needs, especially since the outbreak of the Jihad, had been hugely curtailed last year by the chaos in Siddarmark. As a consequence, Fultyn found himself with entirely too much time in which to do entirely too little, so making reports, even knowing he'd have to do it all over again whenever Vicar Allayn did arrive, was something of a relief from boredom. Besides, Vicar Rhobair was a frighteningly intelligent man. He was no mechanic or artificer, yet many of his questions had sent Fultyn questing down highly profitable avenues which might never have occurred to him otherwise.

"I realize it may not look like we're getting much accomplished just at the moment here at Saint Kylmahn's, Your Grace," he began, waving one hand at the ice frozen into the corners of his office windowpanes. "But we got quite a bit done before we froze over, and our shops are still turning out gauges and jigs to the new patterns. Of course, things are more lively at our less icy manufactories, but Brother Tahlbaht's taking advantage of our own lowered tempo to tweak his production circles' arrangements. The slower conditions let him move his workers around hunting for ways to increase their efficiency still further, and we're sending his suggestions out by semaphore whenever weather permits. I understand they've increased productivity by another three or four percent at the manufactories that are still operating at peak levels."

"Believe me, I'm fully aware of that, Brother." Duchairn smiled briefly. "The bills arriving at the Treasury would confirm it even if the letters coming back from the front didn't. Bishop Militant Bahrnabai's praises have been especially loud, and I assure you I'm equally well aware—probably even *more* aware—of how much the entire Church owes you and Lieutenant Zhwaigair."

Fultyn smiled back at the sincerity of the vicar's last sentence. He'd read many of the same letters from the Army of God's frontline officers, but the approval of a man like Vicar Rhobair was always welcome.

"Well," he said, "I have to admit I've been happily surprised myself by the production numbers. They're much higher than I'd anticipated, to be honest. And the conversion kits are working out better than expected, as well."

Duchairn's lips twitched on the edge of another, broader smile. He and Fultyn hadn't had this conversation previously, but Allayn Maigwair had waxed almost poetic making the same points to him, and never more so than about the modifications Lynkyn had made to Zhwaigair's original rifle design.

The sheer brilliance of the Dohlaran's deceptively simple concept had started the process, but the final design was as much Lynkyn's brainchild as Zhwaigair's. The lieutenant had designed an entirely new receiver as a separate unit that threaded onto the breech end of a rifle's barrel. The receiver was considerably broader than the rest of the barrel, and not just to accommodate the new breech and the multi-start screw which opened and closed it. The extra width allowed for a firing chamber, slightly larger in diameter than the rest of the rifle's bore, that tapered smoothly to meet the rifled portion of the barrel. It also meant the well in which the plug traveled was wide enough to admit the tip of a thumb. The idea was to load a paper cartridge through the well at an angle, using the tapering chamber to guide it, then push it fully home with a thrust of the thumb. That allowed the lieutenant's original design to be fired much more rapidly than any muzzleloader, but the loading motion was still a little awkward, and burned thumbs were inevitable, given how fiercely the breech heated in firing. The first experiments with the original design had demonstrated that very high rates of fire could be maintained once a rifleman was trained, yet Zhwaigair himself would have been the first to suggest there was room for improvement.

Lynkyn had provided that improvement, and his modification had been just as brilliant—and almost as simple—as Zhwaigair's initial concept. He'd simply observed that the screw sealed the breech when the threads on the front and sides of the screw engaged the threads cut into the face and sides of the breech . . . and that there was more than enough metal to either side—and above and below the axis of the bore—to hold the screw securely when it was closed. That meant metal *behind* the screw could be cut away. Or, put another way, the bore could be extended clear through the receiver and, with the breech screw dropped to the loading position, a cartridge could be inserted from the rear in a straight-line, natural path, exactly the same way the heretics loaded *their* rifles. The new receiver was a sturdy block of metal which contained the breech screw and trigger group, with the caplock mounted on its right side. It also formed a bridge joining the shoulder stock to the forestock and handguard without weakening the stock's wrist the way Zhwaigair had feared it might. In fact, the new rifle was even stronger than the old one had been.

"I wish we had more of the kits than we do," Fultyn continued, and his own smile vanished as his brain returned to a familiar frustration. "They're working better than trying to ship rifles back to the manufactories for conversion, but they're not working *enough* better."

"No one could possibly accomplish any more than you are, Brother Lynkyn. Vicar Allayn and I know that, even if *you* don't." Duchairn allowed a hint of sternness into his own tone. "And judging from his correspondence, Bishop Militant Bahrnabai clearly shares our opinion in that respect!"

Fultyn looked rebellious, but then he inhaled and nodded in agreement.

The field conversions were less sophisticated, both because of the armorers' limited facilities and because every St. Kylmahn receiver was going straight into a new-build rifle or into converting a muzzle-loading rifle which had not yet been shipped to the front. There simply wasn't sufficient foundry capacity to produce enough of them to convert weapons which had already been issued, as well. The best Fultyn had been able to do was send the field armorers breech screws, taps, and cutting heads. An armorer used the cutting head—essentially a half-inch drill bit—to bore a vertical hole through an existing rifle barrel, then used the taps to cut the female threads inside the hole to match those of the prefabricated screws.

Because the hole was so narrow, it was impossible to load a proper cartridge as Zhwaigair had originally envisioned. Instead, the rifleman had to insert the bullet and load loose powder behind it, which slowed his rate of fire badly. On the other hand, he could still fire twice as rapidly as he'd been able to manage with a muzzle-loader. Even more importantly, he could reload in a prone position, which had proven to be one of the heretics' greatest tactical advantages.

"I'm glad the Bishop Militant feels that way, Your Grace," Fultyn said after a moment. "That doesn't mean anyone here at Saint Kylmahn's is satisfied, though."

"Of course you aren't, but Vicar Allayn tells me that between a quarter and a third of Bishop Militant Bahrnabai's older rifles should have been converted by the time the weather makes campaigning possible again."

"That's true, Your Grace. But Bishop Militant Cahnyr

won't be able to say the same." Fultyn sighed. "We've gotten some new production rifles to him, but only five or six thousand, and all the conversion kits are going to the Army of the Sylmahn. We had to prioritize somehow, and Vicar Allayn instructed us to give precedence to Bishop Militant Bahrnabai."

"I know."

Duchairn understood the logic behind that decision. He wasn't sure he *agreed* with it—and he knew damned well Allayn Maigwair didn't!—but the logic in question, unfortunately, was Zhaspahr Clyntahn's.

By every normal rule of warfare, Cahnyr Kaitswyrth's Army of Glacierheart was likely to be attacked sooner than the Army of the Sylmahn, simply because the snow would melt so much earlier in Cliff Peak. Despite all that had happened to the Army of the Sylmahn, however, it remained little more than nine hundred miles from Siddar City itself, and the Sylmahn Gap was the only direct invasion route to the Siddarmarkian capital. If Wyrshym could hold his position against the heretics—*if* he could hold—the Army of God would be well placed to resume Mother Church's inexorable advance. Of course, it was entirely possible, perhaps even probable, Wyrshym *wouldn't* hold his position. What had happened at Esthyr's Abbey last five-day suggested the Charisians were much more winter-mobile than anyone had expected. Worse, the Church had no first-hand report on the battle because not one defender had escaped death or capture, which had to cast doubt on Wyrshym's ability to hold his other positions. But no one could expect Clyntahn to admit that, and he'd demanded that every possible resource be used to bolster the Army of the Sylmahn, no matter how problematical its chance to hold or how badly those resources might be needed somewhere else.

*On the other hand, even Zhaspahr can be right sometimes, can't he?* Duchairn reminded himself. *It may be more a matter of spleen and bile than logic, but that doesn't* necessarily *make him wrong.*

Even a rational human being could justify running

serious risks to sustain Wyrshym's army. The strategic advantages were obvious, and the sheer number of men under his command was another argument in favor of straining every sinew to preserve it. Although the Army of the Sylmahn had shrunk to little more than half its original strength, sixty thousand men were still sixty thousand men, and if Wyrshym *couldn't* hold his ground, his losses as he retreated were likely to rival those the Duke of Harless had suffered in the South March.

*For that matter, we could afford to lose Cliff Peak a lot better than we could afford to lose Hildermoss. And Kaitswyrth's supply lines are in better shape. We could move fresh troops more rapidly to respond to an attack there than anywhere else. So if we have to run a risk somewhere—which, obviously, we do—risking Kaitswyrth probably does make more sense. I only wish I had more faith in his ability to hold his ground. After what Eastshare did to him last summer, though . . . .*

The Treasurer gave himself a mental shake. Maigwair, he knew, shared his doubts about Kaitswyrth's mental state. The bishop militant's former brash confidence had been replaced by a querulous anxiety which saw a heretic hiding under every leaf and rock. It was bad enough when the soldiers of an army felt half defeated before the first shot was fired; it was far worse when the *commander* of an army felt that way, and Maigwair had tried repeatedly to ease Kaitswyrth out of command. Unfortunately, Kaitswyrth continued to enjoy the confidence of Sedryk Zavyr, the Army of Glacierheart's intendant, and the Inquisition because of his fiery devotion to purging the Republic of all heresy. Replacing him with someone else would have required a knock-down, drag-out fight with Clyntahn, who valued fervor even more than competence.

"One advantage of converting Bishop Militant Bahrnabai's rifles is that it gives him a degree of standardization the rifles we've been delivering to the Mighty Host don't really have yet," Fultyn offered after a moment.

There was probably a little sourness in that, Duchairn thought, given what a huge percentage of new rifle production had been poured into the task of rearming the vast Harchongese army wintering along the Holy Langhorne Canal. "The Host's rifles come from every manufactory with a rifle shop, whereas all the screws and all the taps and dies going to the Army of the Sylmahn are from right here at Saint Kylmahn's or from Saint Greyghor's. So if it's necessary to replace one of the screws, the Bishop Militant's armorers should find it a fairly simple task. For that matter, they'll have the dies to cut new replacement screws of their own, if they have to."

"That's good to know," Duchairn said, with a degree of understanding which would never have occurred to him before the last five or six months.

Of course, that had been before Brother Lynkyn explained the huge edge the heretics enjoyed because of the interchangeability of their parts. He and Lieutenant Zhwaigair had reached many of the same conclusions about those advantages independently, and ever since Fultyn had explained them to Duchairn and Maigwair, he and Tahlbaht Bryairs, his assistant, had bent their minds on ways to offset some of the enemy's advantages.

At least they'd had a few plusses of their own to help. The largest and most immediate was a massive increase in manpower—and *woman*power—thanks to Duchairn's non-discretionary directive that the great orders release at least twenty-five percent of their ordained members, lay members, and employees to the Jihad's needs. Those orders were by far the biggest employers in all of Safehold, yet even the Treasurer had been startled by the sheer number of warm bodies his order had produced. And to be fair, the orders had sent their fittest, healthiest people in almost every case. He hadn't really counted on their doing that without a little . . . encouragement from himself and the Inquisition, and the size of the workforce it had produced was one of the Jihad's happier surprises.

A large chunk of that workforce—much to its disgruntlement—had found itself assigned to the fields, to Duchairn's quartermaster's corps, or even to the canal repair crews, but even more had been assigned to the manufactories. Hands which had been soft from years of office work (or *no* work, really, in too many cases) had become hardened to actual toil in Mother Church's service, and Duchairn suspected it was doing their owners' spiritual health a world of good. Not that all of those owners would have agreed with him.

It had certainly done Mother Church's *manufactories* good, however. The influx of workers had found themselves incorporated into more of Bryairs' "circles of production," which were rapidly spreading beyond foundries like St. Kylmahn's to other areas of manufacturing, as well. Not without resistance. The Gunmakers Guild continued to protest (despite all evidence to the contrary) that so many "new and untried methods of manufacture must inevitably reduce our ability to arm Mother Church's defenders in the field," and some of the other guilds had joined them as they recognized the threat to their members' prestige and income. Unfortunately for the guildsmen, Zhaspahr Clyntahn found himself in the rare position of actually agreeing with the Treasurer and Captain General.

None of the new workers could have been considered masters of their new trades—the new "gunmakers," for example, each knew how to make only a single part, using gauges and jigs provided to them—but that was fine with Bryairs. He'd built his "circles" around numbers of workers calculated to produce each of a rifle's parts in the quantities needed to allow the circle's *other* workers to assemble complete weapons as rapidly as possible. None of them could have built an entire rifle, the way trained gunsmiths could, but each circle could turn out several times as many rifles as the same number of individual gunmakers could have produced using traditional techniques.

Not content with that achievement, Fultyn and Bryairs were now pushing to supply every circle, wherever it might be, with uniform gauges and jigs for as many parts as possible. They'd all been manufactured solely at St. Kylmahn's and St. Greyghor's, initially, but each shipment to one of the other manufactories was accompanied by a member of Fultyn's staff to oversee the fabrication on-site of still more of them from the master patterns. It would take time, but once the process was completed the parts made using those patterns should be interchangeable with parts from any other source. Not to the same degree or with the same precision as the heretics managed, unfortunately. All too often, they would still require some adjustment, some filing and shaping to fit. Overall, however, the improvement would be enormous.

They'd already achieved an unprecedented degree of standardization in the three central arms manufactories around Zion: St. Kylmahn's, St. Greyghor's, and St. Marytha's. All receivers, breech screws, trigger groups, and caplocks produced by those three manufactories were fully interchangeable. The bulk of the rifles being manufactured outside Zion—which, unfortunately, meant the majority of *all* rifles at the moment—still used locally produced and cut screws and breeches, but the new gauges, jigs, and dies were spreading more rapidly than Duchairn had allowed himself to hope they might. There was no way Mother Church's manufactories were going to match the heretics' ability to swap *any* parts between rifles, wherever they'd been made, yet if they could match that capability for the most *critical* components, that might be good enough.

And, in the meantime, they'd adopted yet another heretic innovation and every manufactory had begun stamping every part it made with its own identifying cartouche. At the very least, an armorer at the front would be able to identify the source of the original part at a glance, which would significantly speed repairs by telling him where to look for a replacement that would fit with the least possible adjustment.

"I think—" the vicar began, then paused as the office door opened once more and Brother Zhoel reappeared.

Fultyn's secretary was accompanied by another lay brother, pushing a wheeled cart covered by a snowy linen cloth and bearing two tall steins of beer, two large covered plates, a loaf of crusty brown bread, napkins, and silverware. The lay brothers bustled about, whipping off the covers to reveal two more loaves of bread which had been hollowed out to contain generous servings of clam chowder, rich with fresh cream, potatoes, and corn and dusted with grated cheese. By this time of year, the clams were canned and the corn had been desiccated for preservation, but it still smelled heavenly. One bowl was deposited on Brother Lynkyn's desk while the cart itself was wheeled over and parked conveniently in front of the vicar. Brother Zhoel whipped another cloth off the butter dish, took one more critical look at the food, then bowed to Duchairn and Fultyn before he and his fellow withdrew as wordlessly as they had arrived.

"I believe some of your staff might have futures in restaurant careers after the Jihad, Brother Lynkyn," Duchairn observed, and Fultyn chuckled.

"As long as the restaurant doesn't try to steal Brother Khalvyn or Sister Tabtha from our kitchens, Your Grace. I think you'll find the soup palatable."

Duchairn bent his head in silent blessing for a moment, then signed himself with Langhorne's scepter and picked up his spoon. He tried the chowder cautiously, then smiled in delight.

"You don't need to worry about any restaurants raiding your kitchens, Brother," he said. "I'll cheerfully anathematize anyone who tries! Now *my* kitchen, on the other hand . . . ."

Fultyn smiled back, pleased by the compliment—which, he admitted, was well deserved—and applied himself to his meal with gusto. He and Duchairn ate in a companionable silence which was made more peaceful and intimate by the increasingly angry wind-whine outside the office windows. By the time they finished, only crusts remained, and they sat back, nursing their beer steins as they returned to the matters which had brought the vicar to St. Kylmahn's.

"If I might ask, Your Grace," Fultyn said after a moment, "how well are the foundries outside Zion converting to the new steelmaking processes?"

His tone was wistful, and despite the gravity of the situation, Duchairn smiled. Winter had closed in too quickly for any of the foundries in the northern Temple Lands to construct the new "open hearth" furnaces before everything froze solid.

"The work's coming along well, Brother—thanks largely to *your* efforts. There's been some resistance, but most of our ironmasters are kicking themselves for not having come up with the same concepts themselves. As you pointed out to me, many of them are refinements of things we already knew—very clever, but not radically new inventions—that the heretics came up with before they occurred to anyone else. And where there *has* been resistance, Vicar Zhaspahr's overcome it handily. Five new furnaces will go into production in the Episcopate of Saint Grovair, on Fairstock Bay in Hayzor, and at Malantor in the Duchy of Malansath early next month, and a dozen or so more will be beginning operations a few five-days after that in Kyznetzov and Shwei. By May, we'll have several producing in Queiroz and even a few in Tiegelkamp and Stene. And, of course, once the thaw sets in, we'll be able to begin expanding and converting Saint Kylmahn's and the other northern foundries. By the end of May, according to my inspectors' reports, we ought to be producing almost as much steel each month, just in the new hearths, as we produced each month in all the crucibles in the Temple Lands combined last year. Actually, that's in *addition to* the crucibles' production, since they're staying in full operation until we can switch over to the new hearths completely, and output's going to increase steadily as we get additional furnaces into operation."

Fultyn's nostrils flared as he drew a deep breath of satisfaction. And quite probably of relief, now that Duchairn thought about it. He'd been the one ordered to produce the plans and directions from the captured heretic documents, and Lynkyn Fultyn was fully aware of the ambivalence with which Zhaspahr Clyntahn and the Inquisition regarded someone like him. Mother Church might need his ability to think outside the bounds of tradition, but that didn't mean the Proscriptions' guardians had to like it. Had those plans not worked . . . .

"That probably means we won't need to continue with the banded artillery designs," the Chihirite said after a second or two. "In fact, if we can produce steel in sufficient quantities, we may be able to abandon iron guns entirely, the way the heretics have. That's good."

"Possibly, but we'll have to see how that works out," Duchairn cautioned. "In the meantime, Vicar Allayn tells me reports from the artillerists who've been issued the new guns are highly favorable."

"The majority of them have been," Fultyn agreed. "Not all, though." He took a sip of beer and frowned, eyes focused on something only he could see. "Some of the guns are shedding the reinforcing bands, so obviously our present technique doesn't attach them as securely as I'd hoped. Brother Sylvestrai and I have had a few thoughts on ways to improve that, but without the ability to cast more guns and work on them here at Saint Kylmahn's, we can't test them properly."

"What sort of thoughts?" Duchairn asked curiously.

"Brother Sylvestrai's suggested that instead of cooling the reinforcing band of wrought iron from the outside after it's been fitted to the gun, we should pump cold water down the gun tube's bore and cool it from the *inside* while the band is being slipped over the breech," Fultyn replied. "The idea is to prevent the tube itself from heating excessively when the band is applied, and he's also suggested covering the reinforce with sand to insulate it once the inner layers have bound to the tube. That ought to keep the outer layers of the band from cooling more quickly than its middle layers, which is probably what's been causing the cracks we've observed. I think he's quite right about that, and while I was considering his suggestions, it occurred to me that if the gun is rotated on its axis—with the band in place but not turning with it, you understand—we could prevent the reinforce from binding first in a single place. The rotary motion would prevent *any* adhesion until the entire band shrinks enough to "grab" and it welds all around its circumference simultaneously. I think that should provide a far better weld and a stronger reinforce, and I've sent those recommendations to the foundries where the guns are actually being made."

Duchairn nodded wisely. He doubted Brother Lynkyn thought for a minute that he really understood what the Chihirite was talking about, in which case he was completely correct. But that was fine, because what the vicar *did* understand was more than enough. What mattered to him—and, he was pretty sure, to Allayn Maigwair—was that the new guns (already named Fultyn Rifles by the gunners who'd received them, although Zhaspahr Clyntahn seemed less than enthused by that) fired heavier projectiles to far greater ranges. The initial models had been built on altered twelve-pounder tubes, with the same bore dimensions but about a foot more length than the smoothbore weapons. With a thirty-pound solid shot fired at fifteen degrees elevation, they'd ranged to almost thirty-five hundred yards, twice the range of the standard twelve-pounder, and to *forty*-five hundred yards with a lighter twenty-pound shell carrying two and a half pounds of powder. Larger field guns, with bores of up to six inches and firing shells of up to two hundred pounds at even greater elevations, were under development as well, with ranges which might go as high as eight thousand or even ten thousand yards. Concerns about guns which shed their reinforcing bands, split, or even blew up occasionally were secondary in the minds of gunners when they were suddenly gifted with *that* increase in performance after being so mercilessly pounded by the longer-ranged heretic guns. And even larger and more powerful weapons were being developed for coastal defense, with an urgency driven by the heretic ironclads' apparent invulnerability to existing artillery.

"We're working on improving the shells' reliability, as well," Fultyn continued a bit fretfully, obviously unaware of the vicar's thoughts. "The new fuses give more consistent detonation times, but simply coating the projectiles in lead doesn't work as well as I'd hoped it would. Quite a few seem to strip out of the lead jackets on their way down the barrel, and they don't do it uniformly. Some of the lead stays attached on one side or the other, which unbalances them badly, at which point they actually become less accurate than smoothbore shot. I've come up with a possible solution—well, actually, Brother Sylvestrai and I have—but I'm afraid it's going to make them more expensive."

"Why?"

Duchairn tried not to sound wary, but he knew he'd failed when Fultyn's unfocused eyes narrowed and sharpened. There might even have been the slightest of twinkles in their brown depths, the Treasurer reflected.

"The cost increase won't be huge, Your Grace," the Chihirite soothed. "In fact, it'll cost less than the improvement Brother Sylvestrai originally suggested to me, although it *will* add an additional stage to shell manufacture.

"I think we're going to have to abandon my proposed lead jackets and go back to a variant of the heretics' practices. I'd hoped the jackets would let us avoid those 'gas checks' of theirs, but it's clear I was overly optimistic. We'll have to cast our projectiles with the same grooved bases and fit them with a seal, after all, but Brother Sylvestrai suggested we could still dispense with the rifling studs the heretics rely on if we used a wrought-iron skirt or shoe the same diameter as the shell but stamped around its rim to take the rifling. I suppose you'd call it 'pre-rifling,' and his idea was to combine the seal *and* the rifling in a single shoe. I think he's on the right track, but the additional wrought iron—though I suppose we could use steel, once it becomes available in quantity—would increase both cost and manufacturing time considerably. So I want to try using a more elastic material—bronze, probably—that expands when the propelling charge detonates. What I'm thinking is that bronze is tough enough it won't deform and strip the way lead does, especially if it takes the total initial force of the powder charge and transfers it to the projectile, instead of the other way around. On the other hand, it's enough softer than wrought iron that it should expand into the shallower rifling grooves we're using without the need for the pre-rifling Brother Sylvestrai's suggested *or* the heretics' studded shell bodies. It should actually produce a tighter seal, as well, which ought to drive up muzzle velocity and give us somewhat better range. Either way, it should be simpler than producing studded shells, and considerably less expensive than using wrought iron."

"I see." Duchairn frowned down into his stein, then shrugged. "I can't say I'm in favor of spending any more than we have to, but I've noticed most of your innovations work out even better than expected. I'll want to talk to Vicar Allayn about it, but if he agrees, the Treasury will just have to find the marks we need. And by the strangest coincidence," the vicar smiled suddenly, "you and Brother Tahlbaht are saving enough on the new rifles that I just happen to have quite a store of unanticipated marks on the books."

"I'm glad to hear that, Your Grace," Fultyn said slowly, "because I'm afraid I may've come up with yet another way to spend some of them, too."

"Oh?"

Duchairn's eyes narrowed—more speculatively than repressively—and Fultyn nodded.

"Some of the alternatives my artisans have suggested as answers to the heretics' portable angle-guns work, but none of them work *as well* as the angle-guns do. The spring-loaded catapult works best, but that's not really saying a lot, to be honest. It's badly outranged by the heretics' weapons, and slower firing, to boot. On the other hand, it's almost silent and there's no smoke to give away its position when it fires. Vicar Allayn assures me those are important advantages, but I have to confess that none of our original answers come close to matching the performance of the heretics' weapons.

"The estimates of steel production you've just given me make me more optimistic about our ability to produce the same sorts of angle-guns, eventually at least. On the other hand, a thought occurred to me last five-day. There *might* be a way to provide an even greater capability for the kind of . . . indirect fire, for want of a better term, the heretics are using on our own men. Something closer to the capabilities of their regular artillery's *heavy* angle-guns, but a lot more portable."

"How portable?"

"Less so than the heretic infantry's portable angle-guns, I suspect, Your Grace, but much, *much* more portable than most regular artillery pieces."

Duchairn frowned again, wishing Maigwair could have been present after all. The last time he'd spoken to the Captain General, Maigwair had waxed eloquent in his enthusiasm for the full-sized rifled angle-guns Fultyn had designed for the Army of God. Frankly, Duchairn doubted Fultyn's initial efforts would match the performance of the heretics' weapons, yet Maigwair obviously expected them to compensate for much of Church's present inferiority. At the same time, it was unlikely more than a few score of the new weapons could be gotten to the armies in the field before the spring thaw, and even if they could, the heretics and their infantry angle-guns had delivered a pointed lesson in the advantages of mobility.

"What do you have in mind, Brother Lynkyn?" he asked finally, and the Chihirite opened a desk drawer and extracted a circular disk of what looked like bronze. It was about four inches in diameter, Duchairn estimated, and perhaps a half inch thick, and pierced by a series of angled slots or holes.

"This is part of one of the heretics' rockets, Your

Grace." Fultyn laid it on his desktop and slid it across to Duchairn. "One of the Inquisition's agents managed to . . . acquire specimens of two or three of their new devices, including a signaling rocket and one that's *probably* what they used to illuminate Bishop Militant Cahnyr's troops on the Daivyn River. I'm not certain about that, but the top portion of it was packed with some compound I didn't recognize and fitted with a sort of folded parasol. I've experimented with it a little, and I think the parasol is what keeps the burning compound suspended as it drops down towards the ground, sort of like a dandelion seed.

"There are several other interesting aspects of their design," he continued in a very careful tone—one, Duchairn suspected, which was intended to make it very clear that while those aspects might be "interesting," they weren't "*fascinating*." The latter was the sort of word the Inquisition found unacceptable when applied to the heretics' demonically inspired devices.

"What sort of aspects?" the vicar asked in an almost equally careful tone.

"Well, I've wondered ever since I first heard about the heretics' rockets how they obtained such uniform performance. Our own efforts to duplicate them have been much more unpredictable and erratic in flight. Some of them have actually come around in complete circles to land right back where they were launched from, in fact! Initially, I assumed that was because our gunpowder burns less consistently than theirs, which means it delivers its pushing power more unevenly, and I still believe that's probably part of the problem. But when I started looking at *this*—" the Chihirite tapped the disk on his desk "—I realized that what it does is to . . . focus and direct the gasses spitting out of the back of the rocket. It *shapes* and regulates them, and I suspect the reason is to impart a spin to the entire rocket, the way rifling grooves spin and stabilize a bullet or an artillery shell. I'm virtually certain this is the main reason their rockets fly so much farther and so much straighter than ours do."

"And what exactly does that mean, Brother?" Duchairn picked up the disk and weighed it in his hand. It was heavy, although it still seemed preposterously light for something that could do what Fultyn had just described.

"What that means, Your Grace, is that if I'm right, and if we can duplicate this, we can produce rockets of our own . . . and not just for signaling purposes. I understand how important signaling and illumination are, but what I'm thinking about would be an actual weapon in its own right. I've sketched out a design for a rocket that would be five inches in diameter. All of my calculations are very rough, of course, because I haven't had an opportunity to actually try them, but if I'm right, we could put as much as ten pounds of powder into its head and fire it to as much as five or six thousand yards. Possibly even farther. They'd be two or three feet long, and they'd probably weigh somewhere around twenty-five or thirty pounds apiece, so an individual soldier couldn't carry more than three or four of them, and each of them could only be used once. But I think the rocket bodies could be made out of wood, which would make them much cheaper than any artillery shell. I might be wrong about that, but even if we needed to make them out of iron, they'd still use less of it and require much less labor than any other artillery weapon we have."

"I see," Duchairn murmured. "And how accurate would they be?"

"Even if I'm right about what the holes in that do," Fultyn replied, gesturing at the disk in Duchairn's hand, "and we can produce rockets as stable in flight as the heretics' are, they wouldn't be what anyone might call precision weapons, Your Grace. As individual projectiles, they'd be considerably less accurate than the new angle-guns' shells, for example. But they'd also be much more destructive, and we could produce a great many of them for the cost of a single angle-gun. That would let us use them in greater numbers, and if they were fired at a target in groups—twenty or thirty at a time, let's say—they could blanket its position even if none of them individually was all that accurate. In fact, a little inaccuracy might actually help by giving us more dispersion to cover a wider area. And if their heads were loaded with shrapnel and equipped with reasonably reliable fuses, they could provide the same sorts of aerial bursts the heretics' angle-guns are providing but over even larger areas. So if a few hundred of them were fired simultaneously and caught a heretic army in the open . . . ."

The lay brother's voice trailed off, and Duchairn tried not to shiver in a reaction which had nothing at all to do with the snow outside Fultyn's office as he attempted to envision what the Chihirite had just described. His imagination was unequal to the task, and he discovered that he was just as happy it was.

"I think I'll definitely avail myself of Saint Kylmahn's hospitality tonight, Brother Lynkyn," he said after a moment, laying the bronze disk back on the desk. "This is clearly something Vicar Allayn and I will need to discuss, and obviously we need you to be part of the conversation."

"Of course, Your Grace," Fultyn murmured, sliding the disk back into his drawer and closing it. There was something a bit odd about his voice, and when he looked up and his eyes met Duchairn's, the vicar realized what that oddity was.

*He's been thinking about this longer than I have. That means he's probably come a lot closer to imagining what those rockets of his might be capable of . . . and he doesn't like it one bit more than I do.*

It was strange, the Treasurer thought. The Inquisition would undoubtedly have all manner of reservations about Fultyn's proposal, since its most important design feature was copied directly from yet another heretical device, but it wouldn't matter. And the reason it wouldn't matter was that the one man in Zion who definitely wouldn't flinch from what the Chihirite was proposing—the one man who would positively *exult* in the slaughter it might produce, be its origins however heretical—was the head of that Inquisition.

*Oh, yes. Allayn and I won't have any problem at all convincing Zhaspahr to endorse this one . . . no matter how many dispensations he has to issue.*

. XIII .
Daivyn River,
Twelve Miles East of Stantyn,
Cliff Peak Province,
Republic of Siddarmark

The wind gusted down the long, frozen surface of the Daivyn River in a sullen roar of leafless branches, bitter enough to steal a statue's breath.

Well, that might be putting it a bit too strongly, Zhasyn Cahnyr conceded. The temperature was, after all, a mere four or five degrees below freezing, positively balmy after the last few five-days. But it was certainly more than cold enough to burn like an icy blade in the ancient lungs of an archbishop who'd seen more than seventy-five winters.

Cahnyr rode at the center of a mounted bodyguard much larger than seemed necessary to him. Not that anyone was particularly interested in his opinion. Not after how close he'd come to getting himself killed the *previous* winter. All very well for him to point out how the situation had changed, how much more secure Glacierheart and the neighboring portions of Cliff Peak Province had become, and how the Temple Loyalist guerrillas had been driven into hiding or killed. No one intended to allow him, even for a single moment, to forget his previous lapse in judgment, and his keepers—"loyal subordinates," he meant, of course—were none too shy about pointing out how enthusiastically the

Inqusition's Rakurais resorted to assassination. It had been all he could do to exert his paramount authority as God's steward in Glacierheart and refuse to make the trip along the river's ice in a snow lizard-drawn sleigh, wrapped to the nose in furs, blankets, and shawls and completely surrounded by a regiment or two of bodyguards.

*Which*, he acknowledged very privately, *might not have been so terrible an idea after all, deadly assassins or no deadly assassins. I can't decide whether my arse is frozen to the saddle or simply frozen.*

He grimaced at the thought, although the expression was fortuitously hidden by the thick, triple-knitted Angora lizard wool muffler which swathed his face to the eyes. Sahmantha Gorjah had knitted that muffler for him, and she'd personally wrapped it around his neck and tucked its ends down inside his parka before letting him out of Tairys, escort or no escort. At least this time he'd been able to convince her to stay behind herself . . . even if it had required him to take unprincipled advantage of the fact that all four of her children had joined their parents over the summer . . . and that she was three months pregnant with her fifth. It would, he had pointed out, be the height of unwisdom for her to expose herself to the potential rigors of such a trip under those circumstances.

It had, admittedly, been unscrupulous, but unscrupulous was fine with him, given the underhanded way all of them insisted on managing him. And he hadn't exactly gotten off unsupervised, anyway. Her husband, Gharth, rode to his left and Brother Laimuyl Azkhat, a very skilled Pasqualate healer, rode directly behind him. Brother Laimuyl was more than thirty years younger than Cahnyr, but age was no more protection against the healer's tyranny than the fact that he was a mere lay brother whereas Cahnyr was a consecrated archbishop who'd become the second ranking member of the Reformist Siddarmarkian episcopate.

Personally, Cahnyr was of the somewhat grumpy opinion that the ruby ring on his left hand and the broad, dove-tailed orange ribbon at the back of his priest's cap ought to have bought him at least a modicum of control over his own comings and goings.

*Oh, stop complaining!* he scolded himself. *It could be a lot worse, and you know it, you cantankerous old . . . gentleman.*

His lips quirked under the muffler as he remembered the way Byrk Raimahn had applied that noun to him the previous April. Sailys Trahskhat's additional adjectives after the near-fatal ambush on the Green Cove Trace had been far more colorful . . . and, he allowed, no more than he'd richly deserved. So perhaps his subordinates weren't being quite as unreasonable as it felt. And even if they were, it was no more of a penance than he deserved.

He reminded himself of that rather firmly as the ridiculous cavalcade trotted briskly along the snowy tow road atop the riverbank, paced by the cargo sleighs on the river ice below them.

▼ ▼ ▼

"You'd no need to come all this way in person, Your Eminence. I could've given you any report you needed by semaphore, or even messenger wyvern."

Somehow, Archbishop Zhasyn wasn't surprised by Ahlyn Symkyn's first sentence. He'd formed a tentative judgment of the stocky, gray-haired general after he'd been relieved as commander of the Charisian 3rd Division and passed through Tairys on his way to assume command of the Army of the Daivyn. Now that judgment was confirmed as the Chisholmian regarded him with exactly the same I-respect-you-but-you-shouldn't-be-allowed-out-without-a-keeper glower Fraidmyn Tohmys, his valet of far too many years, had bestowed upon him when he announced his intention to visit the front.

"Yes, my son," he replied tranquilly. "I'm sure you could have. Unfortunately, I've always found it just a bit difficult to visit the sick and bless the dying by semaphore or messenger wyvern."

Symkyn's cheeks colored ever so slightly, and he bent

his head in acknowledgment. Cahnyr wasn't deluded into believing the general's contrition would last long, however. Best to take as much advantage as he could before it dissipated.

"While I'm here," he continued, "I would, of course, like to inspect the army's positions and meet as many of your brave soldiers as I can." He touched his pectoral scepter and met Symkyn's eyes. "It seems the very least I can do for the men out here in the ice and snow protecting the people of my archbishopric. Believe me, General Symkyn. After the winter and summer just past, my Glacierhearters know exactly how important that is."

"Of course, Your Eminence. Happen I'll be happy to provide guides—and a suitable escort—to take you anywhere you like. Within reason, of course."

*Well*, that *window didn't stay open very long*, Cahnyr thought tartly.

He thought about arguing, but not very hard. He'd come over three hundred miles to make this visit, and he'd covered more than half of them before he warned the general he was coming. The delay hadn't been an accident, either. Whatever Symkyn might say now, the archbishop was certain that if he'd been so imprudent as to tell the army commander he was coming any sooner, the general would have found all manner of irrefutable reasons for him to turn right around and return to Tairys. From what he'd seen of Charisians and Chisholmians, Symkyn would have been fully capable of sending an armed escort to politely—but firmly—enforce his view of the matter, too. Under the circumstances, it was probably wiser to settle for any victories he could get.

Besides, once he was out from under Symkyn's eye, he should be able to browbeat whatever subordinate officer was assigned to command his escort into taking him wherever he really wanted to go. There were certain advantages to being a frail, white-haired, saintly looking, devious old cleric.

However resistant to them *generals* might be.

"Thank you, my son," he said meekly. "I'm sure you're the best judge of these matters."

Symkyn gave him a skeptical look, and Cahnyr didn't need to look at Father Gharth to know his secretary and aide had rolled his eyes heavenward.

"In the meantime, however," Symkyn said, "best we get you settled someplace warm and get some hot food into you. Once you've eaten and had a chance to rest for a few hours, I'll be happy to brief you on our situation here."

"That sounds like an excellent idea, my son. Thank you."

▼ ▼ ▼

The hot soup, fresh bread, and strong mountaineers' tea were even more welcome than Cahnyr had expected. They were also a far cry from the tight rations he and all of his flock had endured the previous winter and spring. His eyes darkened with the memory of how many of that flock had perished of cold and privation . . . and of how many had been so very young. They'd paid a bitter price for their loyalty to Republic and Protector—and to Zhasyn Cahnyr—his Glacierhearters. A price bitter enough to make any archbishop feel inadequate.

But the situation was far better this winter. Lord Protector Greyghor and his Charisian allies had moved heaven and earth to ship food up the canals and rivers from Siddar City. And even though far too many of Glacierheart's farmers and miners had either perished or been called to military service, they were a tough and resilient people, too stubborn for their own good and well accustomed to meeting the challenges of life head on. They'd managed to get the crops sown and the coal mined, despite everything, and at least this year they'd been spared savage guerrilla attacks and the threat of outright invasion. Their stony fields had answered their devotion with richer yields than usual. The gaunt, thin faces—even Cahnyr's hunger-hollowed cheeks—had filled out once more, and he no longer felt bitterly guilty when he sat down to a solid, nourishing meal.

He finished the last of the soup and sat back from the plain wooden table, cherishing the tea mug between his palms, and looked about him. He was certain his own august presence had displaced some major or colonel, and he regretted that, but there was no point thinking he could have convinced Symkyn and his subordinates to make any other sort of arrangement. Which was probably just as well, since Gharth and Brother Laimuyl would have pitched three sorts of fits if he'd argued that they should house him in the Charisian-provided winter tents they'd used on their journey here. They were actually warmer than the lodge from which he, Gharth, and Fraidmyn had made their escape from the Inquisition, but he doubted anyone would have been interested if he'd pointed that out to them.

His present quarters, however, were far warmer and snugger than his lodge had been and, truth be told, he was more than happy with that state of affairs. The room was part of a sturdy barracks built of peeled, squared, chinked—and blessedly draft-proof—logs, thickly roofed in shingles cut from the logs' bark. A row of back-to-back fireplaces were set into the stone wall which formed the structure's spine, a solid cliff of river rock that absorbed the fires' heat and radiated it back. The floor's wooden planks had been slabbed off by the Charisian engineers' water-powered sawmills, and he felt his eyelids trying to slide shut as he sat in warm comfort and listened to the wind moaning outside the walls.

Someone knocked lightly on his closed door and he started in surprise, then straightened in his chair, setting the tea mug back on the table.

"Enter!" he called.

The door opened far enough for Gharth Gorjah to poke his head through it.

"General Symkyn is here, if you're prepared to receive him, Your Eminence."

"Of course I am, Gharth!" Cahnyr stood. "Please, show the General in."

Gorjah dipped his head in acknowledgment and disappeared. A moment later, he reappeared, ushering Symkyn into the room, accompanied by a youthful captain with what looked like a rolled map tucked under his arm and a civilian who was probably midway between the captain and general in age. Cahnyr held out his hand, and Symkyn bent to kiss his ring of office, then straightened.

"Thank you for agreeing to see me, Your Eminence."

"No, thank you for *coming* to see me, General." Cahnyr smiled faintly. "I'm certain you have far more pressing tasks."

"Not so many as you might think, Your Eminence." It was Symkyn's turn to smile. "Once an army goes into winter quarters, there's not so very much for its general to do. Unless he's Baron Green Valley, of course."

The general's smile turned a bit tart with his last sentence, and Cahnyr nodded in understanding. He knew exactly what Symkyn meant, and he found himself rather in agreement with the Chisholmian's present, undoubtedly uncharitable thoughts about Green Valley. Not that he had anything at all against the baron, and it was well known that Symkyn and Green Valley were close friends. Unfortunately, supplies and capabilities had to be prioritized somehow.

Cahnyr was scarcely a trained military man, but he'd become unhappily familiar with the grim realities of campaigns, logistics, and winter weather. He was frankly astonished by the Imperial Charisian Army's ability to move supplies and men through the heart of a mainland winter, yet he'd come to realize even they were unable to properly support two winter offensives simultaneously, and so Symkyn's Army of the Daivyn had gone into winter quarters while Green Valley moved against the Army of the Sylmahn.

It must be especially galling to Symkyn given the way Duke Eastshare, with less than a quarter of the Army of the Daivyn's current strength, had driven the Army of Glacierheart over two hundred miles in reeling retreat. By the time Symkyn had moved up to reinforce the two lonely brigades—one Charisian and one of rifle-armed Siddarmarkian regulars—and militia Eastshare had left to keep an eye on Cahnyr Kaitswyrth's demoralized command, weather had ruled out any fresh offensive. According to their spies' reports, Kaitswyrth's men were enduring a far more wretched winter than Symkyn's, but they were immensely better off than Bishop Militant Bahrnabai's Army of the Sylmahn, and they'd had months to improve their present positions before the freeze set in.

"Please, be seated, all of you," Cahnyr invited.

He waved at the other three camp chairs around the table, but he wasn't surprised when only Symkyn accepted his invitation. The young, golden-haired captain stood at his general's right shoulder, while the civilian—shorter than either of the Chisholm-born officers—stood to the general's left with a faint smile. He was dark-haired and dark-complexioned, in distinct contrast to the Charisians, but his eyes were blue and even darker than the captain's.

"Allow me to present my aide, Captain Wytykair, Your Eminence." Symkyn gestured at the captain, who bent and kissed Cahnyr's ring. "And this is *Seijin* Ganieda Cysgodol, another of *Seijin* Merlin and *Seijin* Ahbraim's fellows."

"Your Eminence," Cysgodol murmured, bending to kiss the ring in turn. "It's an honor to meet you."

"The honor is mine, *Seijin*," Cahnyr replied seriously.

He was only too well aware of how much his own survival—and Aivah Pahrsahn's—owed to the intervention of other *seijins*, although this one seemed rather on the small side, compared to the descriptions of Merlin Athrawes and Ahbraim Zhevons. Indeed, he was almost diminutive next to the two Charisians, although there was nothing remotely fragile about him.

"Happens your timing was good in at least one respect, Your Eminence," Symkyn said. "I'd no idea

*Seijin* Ganieda was in the area. As you know," the general smiled thinly, "*seijins* come and go as they please. Or might be I should say they come and go as they're needed. Any wise, *Seijin* Ganieda's just brought us a fresh evaluation of Kaitswyrth's troops and their positions."

"Indeed?" Cahnyr cocked his head, raising one eyebrow at the *seijin*.

"Yes, Your Eminence." Cysgodol (whose name, Cahnyr reflected, was as outlandish as most *seijins*' names seemed to be) had a pleasant tenor with a pronounced Westmarch burr. "There isn't much change to report, but we like to keep an eye on the Bishop Militant." He showed his teeth in a smile even thinner than the general's. "Duke Eastshare gave him a pointed lesson in manners last July, and we want to be certain he took the instruction to heart."

"I'd gathered he had," Cahnyr replied. "From the reports reaching Tairys, however, it's sounded to me as if he's recovered at least some of his confidence since July."

"Aye, he has that," Symkyn acknowledged. "But *some* confidence's a mite different from *complete* confidence, as you might say, Your Eminence. And the men under his command, they're even more aware than he is of how badly the Duke mauled them." He shook his head. "He 'put the scare into them,' as Baron Green Valley likes to put it, the Duke did, and that 'scare' went deep in their bones. Happen they'll feel it again the next time they see Charisians and Siddarmarkians coming at 'em."

"The General's right, Your Eminence." Cysgodol's voice was firm. "Oh, Kaitswyrth's about finished reorganizing his forces. He's disbanded three entire divisions and used their remaining manpower to bring other regiments back up to strength, and despite the weather, his logistics are much better than Wyrshym's. He's received quite a few replacements and at least some reinforcements, even if our reports indicate he hasn't received anywhere near as many of the Church's new rifles. And while his supply situation's nowhere near as good as General Symkyn's, he's managing to keep his men reasonably well fed."

"Aye, that's true enough," Symkyn growled. "And those entrenchments of his'll make his muzzleloaders a lot more useful than they'd be out in the open where we could get at 'em. He's had time to throw up decent winter quarters, as well. According to the *Seijin* here, he's still losing men to frostbite, but nowhere near so many as the Army of the Sylmahn seems to be losing." He grimaced. "Now, I'd not wish frozen fingers and feet on any man—not normally, at least—but I've a bone to pick with the Temple Boys, and I'm finding it just a bit harder to feel the sympathy for my fellow man the *Writ* says I should."

"A failing I fear I share with you, General."

There was an edge of genuine regret in Cahnyr's tone, but only an edge. The *Writ* taught that the Archangels despised hypocrisy, and he'd gotten to know Mahrtyn Taisyn before the Charisian brigadier marched to his death defending Glacierheart. He'd been a dedicated and courageous man who'd laid down his life and those of the men he'd commanded in defense of the innocent, as the *Writ* itself enjoined, and Cahnyr had decreed a daily mass in Tairys Cathedral for the souls of all his men. It had shocked but not really surprised the archbishop when he'd discovered just how much vengeful satisfaction he'd taken from knowing how many of the inquisitors who'd overseen the massacre of Taisyn's men had suffered the penalty Cayleb and Sharleyan of Charis had decreed for them. And he'd discovered since that Symkyn had also known Taisyn well, if not as well as he knew Green Valley . . . which was going to be a very bad thing for the Army of Glacierheart in the fullness of time.

"The biggest problem, Your Eminence," the general went on, crooking the first two fingers of his right hand at Captain Wytykair, "is that there's a damned good reason—pardon my plain speaking—Kaitswyrth stopped where he did."

Wytykair unrolled the map under his arm in response to his commander's gesture. It showed considerably more detail of the two armies' positions than anything Cahnyr had previously seen. It was also too big for the young man to manage on his own once it was unrolled, so Cysgodol helped him spread it where it would be visible to both Symkyn and the archbishop.

"As you can see, Your Eminence," Symkyn continued, "Kaitswyrth's total frontage is broader than he'd like, I'm sure. It's about sixty miles, north to south, but his left is anchored on the marshes between Stylmyn and Gyrdahn and his right's anchored on Tyrath down here to the south." The general grimaced. "Those marshes're impossible for even our supply columns, and they cover his left for over thirty miles. And as for Tyrath, it's not much of a village, but it sits right on the only secondary road connecting the Haiderberg-Sangyr High Road to the Sangyr-Aivahnstyn High Road. Once the snow melts—or even sooner, might be, if I pushed hard—I could hook down to turn his right flank. But to speak truth, there's not so good a chance I could actually rupture his front the way the Duke did. And even if I flanked him, he'd still have the interior line to fall back on Aivahnstyn. Now, that'd be a sight better than leaving him where he is, but what we really want is to finish the bugger once and for all."

"That sounds like an excellent idea to me, General," Cahnyr murmured, and Symkyn flashed him a predatory grin.

"Well, I do believe we might be in the way of doing that little thing in another couple of months, Your Eminence." He tapped the map symbols indicating his own forward positions. "At the moment, I've only my First Corps all the way forward. That's the two infantry divisions and the Seventh Mounted. Well, and the one battalion of scout snipers, plus artillery. More than enough to keep those sorry bastards huddling in their holes after what the Duke did to 'em last summer, any road."

He did not, Cahnyr noted, apologize for his language this time. Which suited the archbishop just fine.

"Course, technically he's still got us outnumbered 'bout three-to-two, maybe a bit better, and according to the *Seijin* here—" Symkyn twitched his head at Cysgodol "—they've another thirty thousand or so marked to reinforce him from the reserve they've been building up and arming in Tanshar, as soon as ever they think his supply line'll support them. Meanwhile, he's digging in even deeper, and there's another thirty, maybe forty thousand militia and regulars gathering in Westmarch and the Border States—especially in Usher and Jhurlahnk—to support him. Mind, Your Eminence, they're the usual odds and sods with crappy weapons. Well, aside from the Jhurlahnkians and Usherites, at least. Prince Grygory's army's no more'n nine thousand strong, but Earl Usher's is probably half again that large, and both the Jhurlahnkians and Usherites're almost as good as Temple Boy regulars."

"Probably better than the units Kaitswyrth's put back together out of bits and pieces of other ones, actually, Your Eminence," Cysgodol put in with a grimace. "Their morale's a lot higher, anyway! And both of them have managed to hang on to more of their own rifles than the other Border States." The grimace turned into a smile. "Partly because Usher has more manufactories than almost any other Border State and built the rifles for Jhurlahnk as well as its own army, but mostly by pointing out—loudly—just how close General Symkyn here is to their borders. Of course, the other side of that coin is the Group of Four's insistence that they support Kaitswyrth in the spring."

"That's true enough, Your Eminence," Symkyn agreed. "And if we sit and let them do all that, Kaitswyrth'll be back up to somewhere above two hundred and fifty thousand men by the time they finish. Which'd be close to three times my strength, even with both corps up."

"I see."

Cahnyr hoped his tone didn't sound as . . . thoughtful as he was afraid it did. This was the first he'd heard of any Border State forces being placed under the Army of God's command. It was also the first he'd heard about the Army of the Daivyn being outnumbered by that large a margin. From the glint in Symkyn's eye, he felt reasonably confident the general had detected a certain trepidation on his part.

"As it happens, Your Eminence, that's one of the main reasons I don't plan on attacking the Bishop Militant until spring. We want those extra militia and all that Border State infantry up at the front."

"Excuse me?" Cahnyr blinked, and this time Symkyn actually chuckled.

"Your Eminence, there's a reason I've been sitting right here, and why I've kept half my strength far enough back Kaitswyrth couldn't see it even if he was trying to get patrols across the line. In fact, it's the same reason Duke Eastshare's headed north from the South March right this minute instead of moving on to the west behind Earl Hanth."

"He is?" Cahnyr wondered if he sounded like a village idiot, but surprise had startled the question out of him.

"Aye, that he is, Your Eminence. Happen he'll need to refit his troops over the next month or two—they've done some hard marching and fighting in rain and knee-deep mud—and we'll be using the rest of the hard freeze to sled more supplies up the rivers and canals from the coast before the mud sets in north of the Branaths, as well. We'll not have nearly so many of the new rifles as Baron Green Valley, but like the *Seijin* here says, Kaitswyrth's gotten damn all of the Temple Boys' new rifles, either. More to the point, though, happen that however many rifles he might get by then, betwixt the Army of the Daivyn, Earl High Mount's Army of Cliff Peak, and the Army of the Branaths, we'll have three times his present manpower—maybe more, if the Lord Protector's able to send up as many divisions as Lord Daryus hopes he'll be. Between us, we'll have four brigades of mounted infantry, as well. That means we'll actually have more troops than he does, maybe half again as many, even after his reinforcements come in, with Charisian artillery in support, and the equivalent of two full divisions of mounted infantry to sweep around his flanks and cut the roads and canals in his rear."

The general's smile was distinctly unpleasant now, and Cahnyr felt himself smiling back.

"Give us those numbers under the Duke's command, and that bastard Kaitswyrth'll never know what hit him, Your Eminence. Earl High Mount'll go north, around the marshes, send a column for Marylys, and take his main body straight for Aivahnstyn. At the same time, Duke Eastshare'll go south and flank Tyrath hard enough to pin Kaitswyrth's right. And while *they* do that, Your Eminence, happen the Army of the Daivyn will smash right through the bastards' front and the three of us'll do to the Army of Glacierheart what Duke Eastshare and Earl High Mount did to the Army of Shiloh."

The Chisholmian sat back in his chair, his eyes hard and bright.

"Happen even that rat bastard Clyntahn'll start to get the message once we've chopped another quarter million Temple Boys into sausage. And if it should happen he doesn't, well—" he shrugged "—there's always what's about to happen to Wyrshym to make it plain enough even for him!"

The bell mounted over the glass-paned door at the inner end of the air break vestibule jangled and a cold eddy swirled around the shop's interior.

Zhorzhet Styvynsyn paused in her conversation with Alahnah Bahrns and tried very hard not to frown. The shop's hours of operation were clearly posted, and customers who arrived ten minutes before closing on an icy April evening were not her favorite people. Any serious shopper should have known better than to arrive so late in the day, anyway. Not even the first-quality kraken oil for which Mistress Marzho's Fine Milliners paid exorbitantly was adequate to properly illuminate the shop's goods once darkness had set in, and darkness set in early in Zion in April. Besides, Zhorzhet had been looking forward to retreating to the snug apartment above the shop which she rented from her employer and curling up in front of her modest fire with a good book and a mug of hot chocolate.

*At least I'm not going to have to hike three or four blocks to get home the way Alahnah is*, she reminded herself, dutifully transforming her incipient frown into a smile.

From the look in the younger woman's eyes, Alahnah had been thinking about that walk herself, and Zhorzhet touched her lightly on the shoulder.

"I'll take care of it," she said. "Go find your coat and head home."

"Oh, thank you, Zhorzhet!" Alahnah said fervently.

She scurried off obediently, and Zhorzhet walked around a rack of expensive steel thistle silk towards the door.

The man who waited patiently for her wasn't one of their regular customers. Not surprisingly; regulars knew better than to come calling this late! He was a very tall man, however—well over six feet, she estimated—with gray eyes and a full beard. He'd removed his slash lizard fur hat to reveal a head of well-groomed fair hair, although his hairline was receding noticeably. He was well dressed, if not quite to the standards of Mistress Marzho's more upper-crust clientele, and she smiled as pleasantly as she could.

"Welcome to Mistress Marzho's, Sir," she said, extending one well-manicured hand in greeting. "How may we serve you?"

The customer took her hand and, to her surprise—and amusement—brushed his lips across its back. Then he straightened and beamed at her.

"You must be Zhorzhet." His voice was on the deep side, his accent that of a well-educated man, and she felt her smile turning more genuine as his left hand patted the hand he'd just kissed. "Actually," he continued, "a friend of mine asked me to stop by and pick up one of her purchases for her."

"I'll be happy to assist you with that, Sir," Zhorzhet said. "You understand, however, that I can't simply release one of our customer's purchases to you unless we've been authorized to do so."

"Of course—of course!" He smiled even more broadly and patted her hand again. "My name is Murphai, Zhozuah Murphai. I'm sure you'll find my cousin listed me in her account information with you."

"I'm sure she did," Zhorzhet agreed. "Could you give me her name, please?"

"Of course," he said again. "It's Bahnyta Tohmpsyn."

Zhorzhet's smile froze. She started to snatch her hand out of his grasp in sheer reflex, but she couldn't. It was as if her fingers were locked into a gentle but inescapable steel trap, and he patted it again, more gently, almost soothingly.

"I'll . . . have to check with Mistress Marzho," she heard herself say, and he nodded.

"I think that would be a very good idea," he told her,

and the gentle steel trap released her. "I'll wait right here."

▼ ▼ ▼

Marzho Alysyn, the proprietress of Mistress Marzho's Fine Milliners, was in her mid-fifties. She was dark-haired, brown-eyed, and very tall—within an inch or two of six feet, at least—and thin. She was not quite in the very first echelon of Zion's milliners, but she came close. Her exquisitely designed and executed hats had adorned the heads of the wives of dozens of bishops, archbishops, and even a handful of vicars over the years, and she was also one of the city's leading dress-makers. She carried herself with the pride and confidence befitting someone of her accomplishments, and her serene, regal smile looked almost—almost—natural as she extended her own hand to the man standing in her shop.

"Zhorzhet tells me you're here to collect a package for Bahnyta Tohmpsyn, Master . . . Murphai?"

"Indeed." Murphai bowed over her hand as he had over Zhorzhet's, but he made no attempt to retain possession of it when she gently withdrew it. "She's quite eager for me to retrieve it."

"I see." She regarded him for a moment, then shrugged ever so slightly. "I've checked our files, and I see that there's a balance due on Mistress Tohmpsyn's account," she said apologetically.

"She told me there would be." Murphai reached into the capacious pocket of his heavy fur coat and withdrew a glass object that gurgled. "She asked me to give you this," he said, looking directly into Marzho's eyes.

He held it out, and Marzho's nostrils flared as she recognized the bottle of *Seijin* Kohdy's Special Blend.

▼ ▼ ▼

"I'm sure you can understand why all of this makes me more than a little . . . nervous," Marzho Alysyn said twenty minutes later.

Zhozuah Murphai sat at the polished wooden table in the modest dining area of Marzho's apartment above the shop. She and Zhorzhet Styvynsyn sat on the other side, watching him with worried eyes while the teapot heated on her kitchen stove, and Murphai nodded soberly.

"I can't think of a single reason in the world why it *shouldn't* make you nervous," he said frankly. He reached out and ran an index finger down the whiskey bottle sitting in the center of the table, and his bearded lips flickered with a small smile. "I have to admit, though, it's an ingenious recognition sign."

"I always thought so," Marzho agreed. "Of course, I never really expected to see it."

Those worried eyes searched his face, and his wooden chair creaked as he leaned back in it.

"I can well understand that. To be honest, Arbalest made it quite clear to me that she'd never really expected for anyone else to use it, either. She *does* believe in contingency plans, though, doesn't she?"

*And this one* was *very clever*, he reflected.

According to his diary, *Seijin* Kohdy had named his *hikousen* "Bonita," which eight centuries of evolving dialects had transformed into "Bahnyta," and his closest mortal companion had been Kynyth Tompsyn. Bahnyta wasn't an unheard-of name in the Temple Lands, but it was rare—it was much more common to Dohlar or northern Desnair than anywhere else on the planet—which helped reduce the possibility of someone with that full name turning up in Marzho's shop as an actual customer. And while *Seijin* Kohdy's Special Blend had a modest following in Zion, it wasn't a very widely known or favored brand.

Marzho nodded emphatic agreement with his comment, and her expression was a trifle less wary, although Zhorzhet's didn't change. Not surprisingly, Murphai thought. Both of them belonged to Helm Cleaver, the covert action organization Aivah Pahrsahn had established decades earlier, but Marzho—*Sister* Marzho, to be more precise—was also a Sister of Saint Kohdy, which Zhorzhet was not. In fact, Zhorzhet had never heard of the Sisters of Saint Kohdy. She did recognize that any member of Helm Cleaver whose codename began with the letter "A" stood at or very near the apex of the organization, however. Marzho's codename was "Bracelet," and Zhorzhet's own codename was "Castanet." Her ability to place the source of Murphai's knowledge and authorization probably helped some, but she seemed to sense that there were even more levels of complexity about her than she'd expected. In some ways, he would have preferred for her not to be present, but she'd already met Murphai and already knew he was here on Helm Cleaver's business. She was also the senior member of Sister Marzho's cell, and if his visit resulted in any action by that cell, she'd have to know about it in the end, anyway.

"So Arbalest sent you personally?" Marzho asked after a moment.

"Yes," Murphai confirmed. "I'm not actually a member of your . . . organization, but I represent a group which shares your goals."

"Does that 'group' have a name we're allowed to know?"

"I'd prefer to simply say that we wish you every success and have no intention of putting any members of Helm Cleaver at avoidable risk," he said. Then he paused for a moment, as if thinking, before he shrugged. "On the other hand, Arbalest tells me she trusts you and Mistress Styvynsyn completely. Since that's the case, I can at least tell you that I share certain abilities with someone you've probably heard of by the name of Merlin."

Both women straightened in their chairs, eyes going wide.

"You're . . . you're a *seijin?!*" Marzho said after a moment.

"According to Arbalest, I'm as much a *seijin* as Saint Kohdy himself," Murphai told her. "As Merlin, I'm less inclined to claim that title for myself, but Arbalest tells me that's usually the case for *seijins* during their own lifetimes, and given how long, intensely, and . . . intimately"—he met Marzho's eyes once again—"she's studied the subject, I'm prepared to take her word for it."

"I can understand why you might be." Marzho's eyes had narrowed once more as she came back on balance. "But I imagine you won't be surprised if that raises almost as many questions in my mind as it answers."

"I seem to have that effect on people," Murphai said dryly.

"I don't doubt it." Marzho's tone was almost as dry as his own, then she twitched her shoulders. "Your bona fides are about as well established as they could possibly be, *Seijin* Zhozuah. Even if they weren't, I'm inclined to doubt the Inquisition would have come up with something this . . . bizarre as a means of infiltrating us. For that matter, if they know enough to provide you with the recognition signs, they've already learned more than enough to arrest all of us without all sorts of folderol. So, with that out of the way, what is it Arbalest wants us to do for you?"

"I need you to put me in contact with Barcor," he said.

Zhorzhet's anxiety clicked up perhaps half a notch, but Marzho only nodded, as if she'd expected his response. And she probably had, he thought. Nynian Rychtair hadn't chosen the head of her Zion organization at random, and Marzho Alysyn was a very, very smart woman.

Ahrloh Mahkbyth, codename "Barcor," was an ex-Temple Guardsman. He'd served loyally and with pride for almost fifteen years before retiring with a full and generous pension in the wake of a terrible personal tragedy. His nine-year-old son and unborn daughter had been killed in the same hit-and-run Zion traffic accident which had crippled his wife, and the Guard had fully understood his need to devote himself to her care.

What Sergeant Mahkbyth hadn't known at the time, however, was that the sporting carriage which destroyed his family had been driven by a distant relative of Vicar

Stauntyn Waimyan. The young man had failed to stop partly because he'd been so far gone in drink he hadn't realized he'd actually killed the boy and partly because he hadn't much cared, anyway. His only concern had been how to evade responsibility, and his groom—who never should have let him drive in his state—had moved quickly to hush up the scandal. He'd gotten the carriage safely into the family carriage house and immediately contacted the vicar . . . who'd promptly called upon a friend in the Order of Schueler.

A very highly *placed* friend by the name of Wyllym Rayno.

Because the family of a Temple Guardsman had been involved, the investigation, as Vicar Stauntyn had known it must, had come under the auspices of the Office of Inquisition . . . whose agents inquisitor had quickly determined what had actually happened. But the recently installed Grand Inquisitor had suppressed the report. Zhaspahr Clyntahn had already begun building his secret files, and it was unlikely Stauntyn Waimyan had even begun to suspect—then—just how much the "minor favor" he'd requested from Clyntahn would cost him over the years.

Unfortunately for the Group of Four, the Mahkbyth deaths had been one of the many cases of corruption within the vicarate which had drawn the attention of Samyl Wylsynn's circle of Reformists. There'd been no hope of reopening the investigation by that time, but Ahnzhelyk Phonda in her persona as Arbalest had used that information to recruit Sergeant Mahkbyth for Helm Cleaver six months after his wife's eventual death.

"I can do that," Marzho said after a moment. "It will take me a day or two to arrange it, though."

"In that case," Murphai said with a smile, "I suppose I'd better order a hat to come back and pick up when it's ready."

. XU .
Camp Chihiro,
Traymos,
Tarikah Province, and
Charisian Embassy,
Siddar City,
Republic of Siddarmark

She was cold.

She was always cold. In fact, she'd come to believe her memories of anything except cold were only dreams. Then again, dreams were all she truly had.

Her name was Stefyny Mahlard, and she was ten years old. On a planet which had once been known as Earth, she would have been only nine, and in her heart, she knew she would never see another birthday. Her older brother Rehgnyld and her mother Rose had already died; Rose on the nightmare trek from Sarkyn and Rehgnyld when he'd been foolish enough to attack the camp guard who'd sent Stefyny sprawling with the brutal, backhanded cuff which had cost her three teeth and broken her nose.

She remembered that day. Remembered the day her father Greyghor had done the hardest thing a father could possibly have done and watched, his arms around his sobbing daughter and younger son as his eldest child was murdered before his eyes. He'd turned Stefyny's bloodied, broken face against his filthy coat, holding her with implacable strength to keep her from looking, and his face had been carved from Tairohn granite.

Stefyny didn't understand about heresies and blasphemy, or about jihads. She only knew her world had been destroyed, that she was always cold, that she was always hungry, and that her father grew thinner by the day as he passed half of his own inadequate food to his two surviving children. No, she knew one more thing: the Church in which she'd been raised, which had taught her to love God and the Archangels, to love her family, had decided she and everyone she'd ever known were unclean and evil.

And that she was going to die.

It wasn't something a ten-year-old was supposed to know, but the past few months had taught her many things a ten-year-old wasn't supposed to know. They'd taught her to be terrified of anyone in a purple cassock, anyone in the purple tunics and red trousers of the Army of God. They'd taught her to hide behind the larger bodies of adults, hands clamped over her mouth, eyes huge when the camp guards drove the inmates out of their pitiful barracks with clubs and fists and whips and selected someone who would never be seen again.

Now she trudged through the snow, shivering under the multiple layers of too-thin clothing wrapped about her small, emaciated body, dragging the bucket in both hands, and tried to ignore her hollow, aching starvation. No one had ever explained to her that children were more vulnerable to hypothermia than adults, but the adults shivering around her knew it. And so, whenever someone died in one of the barracks—and God knew that happened all too often—and the bodies were stripped before the guards were notified, their clothing was distributed first to the children. It was little enough, but amidst the horror their lives had become, the inmates of Camp Chihiro clung to their own humanity. They would shiver, they would freeze, they would lose fingers and toes to frostbite, but whatever extra clothing, whatever scraps of food they could find, would go first to the children, then to the weak, and only last to the strong.

Greyghor Mahlard was no longer among the strong, and so he lay on his pallet in the barracks, watched over by eight-year-old Sebahstean with his pinched, frightened face, and hollow eyes, while Stefyny clutched all the courage within her and walked straight towards the kill line.

She knew what it was. They'd all been told when they first arrived, and anyone who might not have paid attention had seen it demonstrated since. It was marked with whitewashed wooden posts, although there were no rails or fence. Fences weren't needed with the rifle-armed troops in the guard towers under orders to shoot anyone who stepped across it. They'd done that just the day before yesterday. Stefyny had no idea what the man who'd tried to cross the kill line had thought he was doing, and no one had asked. They'd simply dragged his body away afterward and dropped it into one of the long trenches waiting among the other unmarked graves outside the camp's perimeter.

Stefyny knew the same riflemen were watching her now, but it didn't matter. What mattered was that her father was sick, probably dying, and that a ten-year-old girl had learned too much about what inadequate food did to someone who was ill.

▼ ▼ ▼

"Crap. She's not stopping."

Private Ahntahn Ruhsail's voice was as bitter as the icy wind when he saw the dark-haired girl trudging steadily towards the neat line of posts. The outer layers of the rags wrapped around her fluttered on that same wind, and though he couldn't see it from his place on the guard walk that circled the tower's enclosed top, he knew the cloth wrapped around her face was clotted with ice where her breath had frozen. It was a far cry from his own warm coat and the fleece-lined gloves and thick, knitted muffler his mother had sent him. She was a small, thin child, like all the others in Camp Chihiro—she couldn't have weighed much over forty pounds, fifty at the outside—and the bucket she dragged with her was half her own size. God only knew where she'd gotten it. It looked like one of the slop buckets used by the inmates drafted to clean and maintain the guards' barracks.

"What in Langhorne's name does she think she's doing?" Private Stahdmaiyr growled beside him.

"How in Bédard's name am *I* supposed to know?" Ruhsail shot back. His eyes were bleak as he gazed down at the girl, seeing the determination in those thin shoulders. "Whatever she's doing, she's not stopping, though."

"Oh, shit."

There'd been a time, Ruhsail knew, when Stahdmaiyr would have felt quite differently. A time when the other private's fervor and passionate faith—the same passion which had led him to volunteer for his present duties—would have been silently urging the girl on. When the old cliché that nits made lice would have been all the justification he needed. In fact, he'd said that very same thing when he'd returned from Sarkyn.

On the other hand, that had been before Sergeant Mahthyws and Sergeant Leeahm got their throats cut in their own barracks without a single soul seeing or hearing a thing. Stahdmaiyr's enthusiasm for smiting the heretic seemed to have cooled quite a bit since then. There were plenty of other guards, and plenty of inquisitors, whose ardor *hadn't* cooled, though. Who would happily have accepted the duty about to come Stahdmaiyr's way. Once upon a time, one of them might even have been named Ahntahn Ruhsail, but *his* ardor had cooled even before the cleansing of Sarkyn. Smiting the heresy, fighting the spawn of Shan-wei for the soul of God's own Church, giving all he had to serve the Archangels—that was one thing. What happened here at Camp Chihiro was something else entirely, and he'd found his soul lacked the iron to embrace that something else.

But that didn't change the standing orders, and Ruhsail found himself guiltily and unspeakably grateful that Stahdmaiyr was the tower's assigned marksman for the day. Of course if Stahdmaiyr screwed up, it would be Ruhsail's duty to finish the girl off. He prayed it wouldn't happen, but even as he prayed, he promised himself and the Archangels that if it did, he would make it as quick and as clean as he possibly could.

Stahdmaiyr checked the priming on his rifle, then

leveled it across the chest-high railing designed specifically to give the guards a steady shooting rest, and cocked the lock. The orders were clear enough. There were to be no shouted threats, no orders to go back the way an inmate had come. The kill line was exactly what its name proclaimed, and if anyone violated it, the consequences were to be visited upon him with no warning, no attempt to turn him back first, as a salutary lesson to his fellows. So the private settled in behind the rifle, his sights tracking the little girl as she marched steadily, unwaveringly towards her rendezvous with his bullet.

Three more strides, Ruhsail thought, his face like stone and his heart like iron. Three more strides and—

"What the *fuck* d'you think you're doing, Stahdmaiyr?!"

Both privates jumped so sharply that Stahdmaiyr almost squeezed off the shot. Then they whirled as Corporal Shain Fahbyan came storming out of the warm guardroom behind them. His dark face was like a thundercloud, and his eyes nailed Stahdmaiyr like matched arbalest bolts.

"I asked you a question!" he snapped.

"B-but . . . but—" Stahdmaiyr stammered, then stopped, looking imploringly at Ruhsail from the corner of one eye.

"One of the inmates is about to cross the kill line, Corp," Ruhsail said. In fact, he noted without seeming to look away from Fahbyan, she already had.

"So?" Fahbyan demanded.

"Standing orders." Ruhsail's anger and disgust at those same orders turned his reply curt, almost choppy, and Fahbyan's jaw tightened.

The corporal propped his gloved hands on his hips and looked back and forth between the two privates.

"That's a kid." His voice was flat. "It's not somebody trying to rush the line. It's not an escape attempt. Not even somebody old enough to know what the hell he's doing. It's a frigging *kid*."

Ruhsail and Stahdmaiyr looked at each other. Ruhsail understood exactly what Fahbyan was saying, but all three of them knew it made no difference. Orders were orders, and if they weren't followed . . . .

"Let her go," Fahbyan continued in that same flat voice. "Let the Fathers deal with her."

"Uh, whatever you say, Corp," Ruhsail said.

The noncom gave them both one more glare, then stepped back into the guardroom and slammed the door behind him. The privates looked at each other again, then drew deep breaths, almost in unison. They turned back to the compound below where a small, shivering girl child had just crossed the kill line without drawing a single shot, and as they did, Ahntahn Ruhsail felt a deep, complex stab of relief and guilt. Relief that she hadn't been shot, relief that she hadn't become yet more innocent blood on his own hands, and relief that he and Stahdmaiyr were covered by Fahbyan's orders.

And guilt that *he* hadn't been the one to make that decision.

▼ ▼ ▼

"Father."

Kuhnymychu Ruhstahd's head turned sharply at the single word. Brother Lahzrys Ohadlyn had stopped in mid stride and was looking to their left. Father Kuhnymychu followed the direction of the lay brother's gaze and felt his jaw tighten.

The ragged child had obviously seen them, as well. She'd stopped for a moment, and Father Kuhnymychu could almost physically feel the fear radiating off her like another, even icier wind. But then her spine stiffened, she turned, and she walked directly towards them.

Father Kuhnymychu watched her come and wondered why none of the guards had fired. But only for a moment, because deep inside, he knew exactly why they hadn't.

Her rag-wrapped feet crunched through the crusty snow bordering the path between the camp's buildings. She stopped, a few feet from them, and peeled the frost-stiffened cloth away from her face, and her gray eyes were huge in a gaunt, thin face. Her nose was misshapen, her bloodless lips chapped and split and crusted with scabs, and there was a century of bitter experience in those ten-year-old eyes as she looked up at them silently.

"Well, child?" he snapped.

Father Kuhnymychu hadn't meant to speak, but those silent eyes drew the words out of him like pincers. He shuddered deep inside as that thought went through the back of his brain, for he'd seen pincers used in deadly earnest all too often over the year just past.

"My father's sick."

The soprano was as thin as its owner, yet there was steel at its heart. There was fear—Father Kuhnymychu could hear it—but there was no hesitation. This child knew exactly what she was doing, what she was risking, and she'd chosen to do it anyway. It didn't matter whether it was courage or desperation—or love—or if there was any difference between those qualities. She knew, and the steely determination in that thin, shivering body touched Kuhnymychu Ruhstahd with shame . . . and something very like envy.

"And why do you tell me this?" he heard his own voice say.

"Because he needs food," she said flatly. "Hot food. *Good* food."

▼ ▼ ▼

Stefyny stared up at the tall, dark-eyed under-priest. She could tell he was a priest or an under-priest, because his priest's cap bore the brown cockade of his rank, and she tried not to show her terror, for that cockade was edged in the purple of the Order of Schueler. His face was as unyielding as the winter's cold as he looked down at her, and something even colder ran down her spine. She didn't know why she hadn't been shot crossing the kill line, but her shrunken stomach clenched within her as she smelled the half-remembered scent of hot food drifting from the mess hall behind the two warmly clad, well-fed men.

*They're going to kill me.* The thought ran through her, yet she never looked away. *They're going to kill me for trying to save Daddy's life. But I don't care. Not anymore.*

▼ ▼ ▼

Anger stirred under Father Kuhnymychu's shame. He was God's priest, consecrated to the Inquisition, sworn to eradicate heresy and to smite the heretic with the full power of Schueler's sword. His faith and determination, his courage, his dedication to God's will filled him with holy fire, fit to meet any challenge the Archangels might send him! How *dared* this ragged urchin—the very spawn of heresy, or she wouldn't have been here in the first place—*challenge* him this way? For that was what she'd done. In just eight words she'd defied every one of the Inquisition's actions—and him—and he felt his right hand clench into a fist and started to raise it.

"*Do not despise the wisdom of childhood.*" The words of the *Book of Bédard* flashed unbidden through his mind. "*Childhood is a canvas, pure in its innocence, awaiting the brush of experience. In time, that canvas will become the portrait of a life and the growth of a living soul. But that portrait may be rich with color, filled with the texture of joy, or gray and ugly, shrouded in the bleakness of despair. It is your responsibility to guide that brush as God would have it guided. Nor will the guiding leave your life, your faith, unchanged, for a child's eyes see what adults do not. A child's gaze is unblinkered by preconception, and children have not learned to look willfully away from truth. Do not be deceived! That searching gaze, those fearless questions, are God's gift to you. A child's questions require answer; answer requires explanation; explanation requires thought; and thought requires understanding, and so even as they ask, they teach. Learn from them, treasure the opportunity God has given you, and remember always that whenever one teaches, two learn, and there is no greater joy than to learn together."*

His hand fell back to his side and the cold air was a knife in his lungs as he inhaled deeply. He felt Brother Lahzrys standing behind him, felt the lay brother's eyes on his own back.

It was odd. He was a priest. That was all he'd ever wanted to be, and in that moment, he remembered the bright, burning day he'd first discovered he had a true vocation. It seemed much farther away and longer ago than it had actually been, and he wondered what had happened to that young man, so filled with joy and eagerness. Heresy *must* be stamped out among the children of God, with all the rigor the *Book of Schueler* prescribed, just as cancer must be cut from a living body to save the patient's life. Bishop Wylbyr was right about that, and Father Kuhnymychu couldn't argue with the logic of the Inquisitor General's conviction that anything which happened to a heretic in *this* life was but a foretaste of what awaited him in eternity.

He never doubted there were innocents imprisoned in Camp Chihiro. He regretted that, but it was the fault of Shan-wei and of heretics like Maikel Staynair and Cayleb Ahrmahk, like Greyghor Stohnar and Zhasyn Cahnyr, who had led so many others into corruption. Sin and apostasy could hide in the tiniest corner, and they would fester there like cankers, spreading their poison to even the most steadfast and faithful, if left uncleansed. Mother Church had no choice but to sweep every corner, sift every hint of heresy, if she was to purify the Republic of Siddarmark once again. Her servants must cut through the choke trees and rip out the wire vine strangling the garden entrusted to their care, yet they were merely mortal. They were fallible. Even with God's own guidance, they might well reap some of His flowers as they battled the noisome weeds seeking to choke the life from all of Creation. The Inquisitor General was right about that, too, and if the Inquisition erred, if the innocent perished as the price of combating the corrupt and the vile, then God and the

Archangels would gather those innocent souls in arms of love and soothe away the memory of their suffering in the joyous glory of God's own presence. Kuhnymy-chu Ruhstahd *believed* that, with all his heart. Yet it was hard to hold to the armor of his faith and the sword of his duty as he stared down into that thin, desperate face.

"What's your name, child?"

Even as he asked, he knew he shouldn't have. He shouldn't humanize this child, shouldn't allow his natural feelings to undermine the flinty steel of his calling and purpose. Shan-wei knew too well how to tempt and beguile by appealing to the goodness inside any man or woman, and the vilest of sins could wear the mask of innocence.

"Stefyny," she said. "Stefyny Mahlard."

"Where do you come from?"

"Sarkyn."

His nostrils flared, and he heard the extra fear in her voice as she admitted she'd come from the town which had been cleansed for its abhorrent act of sabotage. Bishop Wylbyr had singled out Sarkyn, both for the punishment it deserved and as an example to others who might be tempted by Shan-wei to undermine the Jihad. This child might not understand why the Inquisitor General had made that decision, but she clearly understood that Sarkyn and its people had been chosen for the Inquisition's special attention.

Of course, she probably didn't know what had happened to Hahskyll Seegairs, Vyktyr Tahrlsahn, and their lay assistants and army escort *after* the town of her birth had been cleansed . . . .

He felt Brother Lahzrys stiffen and wondered what the lay brother was thinking. Brother Lahzrys was a simple and direct servant of God and Schueler, with an unflinching readiness to do whatever the Jihad required. He knew the many ways in which Shan-wei and her servants distorted and violated the truth, yet not even Brother Lahzrys could be unaware of the broadsheets which had appeared in the Temple Lands' cities and towns. Which even appeared—somehow; no one could explain how—on barracks walls in places like Camp Chihiro. Nor was he unaware of the rumors those broadsheets had spread of what had happened aboard a barge in the Holy Langhorne Canal . . . and why.

*It doesn't matter*, Kuhnymychu Ruhstahd told himself. *Even if every one of those rumors is true, it still doesn't matter! We're God's warriors. If Shan-wei's servants strike us down, a thousand more will spring up in our place, and what fear does death hold for those who die obedient to God's will?*

Yet even as he thought that, a small, treacherous corner of his soul knew that it wasn't the death the false *seijin* Dialydd Mab had threatened which gnawed at his spiritual armor. No, that acid had been distilled in the charges Mab had hurled at the Grand Inquisitor himself, for if the man who spoke for Mother Church truly *was*—

He cut that thought off ruthlessly. This was neither the time nor the place for it . . . assuming there ever *could* be a time or a place to consider such faith-destroying corruption. But it was easier to tell himself to put it aside, pretend he'd never thought it, than to actually accomplish that task, and he forced himself to focus once again on the child before him.

▼ ▼ ▼

Stefyny's fear spiked as the tall priest's face hardened and his eyes turned to flint.

*I tried, Daddy*, she thought. *I really, really tried. I'm sorry.*

A single tear burned down her cheek in the icy cold, but she never looked away, never let her eyes fall. The winter seemed to hold its breath, and then, unexpectedly, the Schuelerite held out his hand to her.

"Come with me, child," he said.

▼ ▼ ▼

Two thousand miles from Camp Chihiro, Merlin Athrawes sat in his bedchamber in distant Siddar City, watching the SNARC's recorded imagery, and wished he could read Kuhnymychu Ruhstahd's thoughts.

Merlin seldom watched the SNARCs' take from the Church's concentration camps. His sense of duty insisted he ought to, yet he couldn't. That inability shamed him, but he literally couldn't. Intellectually, he knew Nahrmahn and Cayleb and Sharleyan were right, that it was both unjust and illogical—even arrogant—to blame himself for all the carnage and cruelty of the Church of God Awaiting's Jihad. He *understood* that. It just . . . didn't help, sometimes. And perhaps even more to the point, he couldn't afford the bitter, corrosive rage those camps sent roaring through his soul every time he so much as thought about them. If he went through them as his fury demanded, stalking through their guards in a whirlwind of steel, showing them the same justice he'd visited upon Tahrlsahn and Hahskyll Seegairs, it could only lend a damning credence to the Inquisition's charges of demon worship and summoning. That was why he'd been so careful to proclaim the *seijins'* mortality in Dialydd Mab's letter to Zhaspahr Clyntahn. He couldn't—*could not*—escalate beyond the capabilities *The Testimonies* and legend assigned to the *seijins* of yore, and what "Mab" and his fellows had already accomplished pressed all too perilously upon those limits.

Yet Nahrmahn had been right to ask him to view *this* imagery.

He watched the Schuelerite under-priest take the little girl's hand and lead her into the guards' mess hall. Watched Ruhstahd personally fill Stefyny's bucket to the brim with hot food, ignoring the stupefied and all too often outraged AOG privates and noncoms. Watched that same under-priest walk her across from the mess hall to the infirmary, watched him send one of the Pasqualate lay brothers back to Stefyny's barracks with her.

It was unthinkable. It *couldn't* have happened. The mere thought of what Father Kuhnymychu had laid up for himself when his superiors heard about this must be enough to shake the boldest heart, and its potential consequences for the Inquisition in Siddarmark were staggering.

*And the bastards will make an example out of that little girl and all that's left of her family, anyway,* he thought grimly. *They'll send all three of them to the Punishment. Unless . . . .*

▼ ▼ ▼

It was never really quiet in the barracks. There were too many sick, too many frightened, too many horrific memories and the nightmares they spawned for that. But darkness settled early this far north, and people who were chronically undernourished needed any sleep they could get.

It was bitterly cold, of course, for the miserly allotment of coal didn't allow for anything remotely like genuine heat, and Stefyny Mahlard lay curled tightly around Sebahstean, pressed against his back as he burrowed into their father's chest and Greyghor Mahlard's arms cradled them both. The outer layers of the rags they wrapped about themselves during the day had been spread across all three of them, treasuring the shared warmth of their bodies like a miser's gold. Her father's breathing was a little easier, yet she'd seen the fear—the despair—in his eyes when she returned with the Pasqualate and the bucket of food. He'd insisted upon sharing that food with the barracks' other inmates, although the Pasqualate had made him eat a hearty portion of it first. And afterward he'd sat with his arms wrapped around her, hugging her fiercely, whispering her name into her dirty, unwashed hair while Sebahstean nestled against her to share his embrace. He'd praised her courage, thanked her for all she'd done, told her how *proud* of her he was—how proud her *mother* would have been—and under the words and the love she'd tasted his terror. Not for himself, but for her.

She was no longer young enough to misunderstand that terror, but she didn't care. She told herself that fiercely as she lay unsleeping, warming her brother's thin body with her own, hearing the hacking coughs, the moans, the occasional dreaming cry of loss or whimper of fear in the icy dark. It had been worth it. Maybe the other priests and the guards *would* come for her in the morning. Despite all the bitter experiences of her young life, she didn't fully understand the concept of "making an example," yet she'd seen its consequences all too often, and she no longer believed all tales had happy endings. Maybe that *would* happen to her, as well. But if it did, then she would be with Mama and Rehgnyld and God, and that would be so much better than being *here*. And in the meantime, she'd helped her father, even if it was only for one single day. He'd taken care of her for her entire life, raised her, fed her, taught her, clothed her, always *been* there for her. He hadn't done all of those things just because he'd had to; he'd done them because he *loved* her, and she'd realized long ago how terribly that love hurt him now that he could protect her no longer. But she loved *him*, too, and she'd finally been able to share that love with him fully and completely. He'd taught her that you took care of the ones you loved, and this time, maybe just this once, she'd been able to do that for him as he'd so often done it for her.

That made anything that happened after today worth it.

She wondered what would happen to the priest who'd helped her. She didn't know his name, but she'd seen the way the soldiers looked at him—even the way the lay brother had looked at him, the expression of the Pasqualate he'd sent back to the barracks with her. He was an inquisitor, wrapped round with the terror that office had acquired since the Jihad began. He was one of the ones who made terrible things happen to people like Stefyny and her family. But this time he'd *helped* her, and how would the other inquisitors react to that? Part of her, the part which would never have been able to forgive the Inquisition even if she'd been allowed to live to old age, hoped they'd do something *horrible* to him. Hoped at least one of the people who'd helped destroy her entire world would suffer for it, even if he had helped her at the very end. But another part of her could only be grateful to him, and that part was bigger than the other one, and it hoped the others would remember that Langhorne himself had said, "I was hungry, and you gave me food; I was sick, and you gave me care."

But they wouldn't. That wasn't what inquisitors did, and—

Stefyny never felt the tiny remote that worked its way under the tattered heap of blankets. She never felt it scuttle gently, silently across her hair to the side of her neck. She *did* feel a tiny twinge—nothing strong enough to be pain or even discomfort—as the remote found the vein in the side of her neck, made the injection, and oblivion took her.

▼ ▼ ▼

The burlap robe was scratchy, and no protection against the bitter cold. At least the weather was a tiny bit warmer—it was actually above freezing, for a change—and he was going to be much warmer all too soon.

Kuhnymychu Ruhstahd—no longer *Father* Kuhnymychu, but simply Kuhnymychu the Apostate—stumbled through the snow in his bare feet, and wondered which was the greater terror: what was about to happen to him, or the eternity waiting on its farther side?

He'd already endured much of the Punishment, and he'd discovered the agony was even worse than he'd ever thought it was. There was a sort of justice in that, he supposed.

The Inquisition had always taught that a Schuelerite who betrayed his vows deserved no gentleness, although the truth was that he didn't think he *had* betrayed them. The child and her father hadn't yet been convicted of heresy, and there was nothing in the vows he'd taken which forbade him to minister to the accused before they were convicted. Yet whether or not he'd violated his *vows*, there was no question that he'd defied the Inquisitor General. That much he had to admit—*had* admitted, willingly, even before the Question. And it might well be true, even as Father Zherohm had declared when he was defrocked and handed to the inquisitors who'd been his brothers, that his actions had strengthened Shan-wei's power in the world. After all, if one of the Inquisition's own violated the regulations laid down for the governance of the holding camps—allowed misplaced leniency to encourage the heretical to maintain their defiance of God's plan and the Archangels' plain commandments rather than seek pardon and penance—it could only encourage others to do the same thing, which must inevitably undercut all Mother Church's effort to crush the heresy.

Once, Kuhnymychu would have agreed unhesitatingly with that damming indictment. Now he was . . . uncertain, and fresh fear filled him as the stake loomed before him. *Had* he failed God in the moment of his greatest test? Or had it truly been the Holy Bédard who'd moved his heart and guided his actions? One way or the other, he was about to learn the truth, and his lips moved in silent prayer—the only form of prayer left him, for they'd cut out his tongue lest he take this last opportunity to strike out at Mother Church's work in the world—as the chains went about him.

A tear surprised him, crawling slowly down his cheek, and he realized he wept not for himself, but for a little girl he'd met only once. A little girl whose courage and love had reached out and broken his armor of certitude and breached the fortress of faith about his heart. No doubt she'd been doomed from the moment she set out to find help for her father just as surely as *he'd* been doomed when he gave it, and it was God's own mercy she'd been spared what was about to happen to him. Yet even though all of that was true, he wished she might have lived.

God had willed otherwise, he thought. He made

himself raise his head and open his eyes once again, remembering the three still bodies which had been carried out of that prison barracks the very next morning. The inmates had brought them forth and laid them side-by-side, the children flanking the father, in the churned snow. They hadn't tried to conceal the deaths, as they usually did, in hopes the living would continue to receive their rations until the guards discovered they'd died. And they hadn't scavenged the pitiful family's garments the way they usually did, either. They'd laid them out as decently and with as much respect as they could. It had been their own act of defiance, and they'd watched in silence as the labor party of other inmates impressed for the duty carried them to the vast, unmarked graveyard where so many others had already gone.

They hadn't been buried immediately. Too many others died every day for that. Instead, they'd been laid side-by-side in the open trench. Then they'd been left, abandoned to the short northern day, the long northern night, and the sifting snow, waiting for the more tardy of the dead to join them, until the frozen chunks of dirt had been shoveled over all of them the following day.

No one had spoken any words for them, unless it had been the labor gang, praying as silently as Kuhnymychu prayed now. He hoped they had, and even as he stood among the piled faggots and gazed at the flaming torch, pale in the sunlight, a strange feeling of joy flowed through him when he realized he was praying for them just as much as for himself.

"You have heard the judgment and sentence of holy Mother Church, Kuhnymychu Ruhstahd," a deep voice intoned. "Have you anything to say before that sentence is carried out?"

He looked away from the torches, and he realized suddenly that he no longer questioned why he'd tried to help Stefyny. He knew Whose voice he'd heard in that moment. Knew it now, beyond any possibility of doubt or mistake. He'd heard the rumors about the heretic Gwylym Manthyr's execution, even seen one of the illustrated broadsheets, though he hadn't been supposed to. He hadn't believed the story that broadsheet had told . . . then. Now, as Father Zherohm Clymyns put that question to him, he knew it had told the truth.

And that meant Zhaspahr Clyntahn, and the Inquisition, and Mother Church herself had lied. Gwylym Manthyr *had* been silenced before his death, and for the same reason *he* had: fear. Fear that just as Erayk Dynnys had done in the Plaza of Martyrs itself, he would have spoken the truth from the very shadow of death. And the Inquisition he had served, Kuhnymychu Ruhstahd knew now, dared not face that truth.

He gazed at Clymyns, his eyes hard above the mouth which could no longer speak, and he knew why Clymyns had come. The upper-priest was Wylbyr Edwyrds' senior aide, taking more and more responsibility and authority upon his shoulders. He was the brain and soul of the Inquisition in Siddarmark, the very voice of the Inquisitor General, and he'd come to be that voice here, today, accompanied by Father Fhrancys Ostean and Brother Zhorj Myzuhno. Both of them were also members of Edwyrds' personal staff, and despite Myzuhno's relatively junior rank, all three were members of the Inquisitor General's inner circle. They were here to drive home the lesson of Ruhstahd's fate for any other Schuelerite whose ardor might falter or fail.

He could no longer speak, but as Clymyns' eyes met his, filled with scorn and the knowledge that he couldn't, he remembered again that broadsheet of Gwylym Manthyr's defiant death. It might not seem like much, here at the very end of all mortal things, but it was all he had, and there were far worse examples he might have followed.

He spat defiantly at Clymyns' feet and matched the defiance in his own eyes against the upper-priest's scornful contempt.

▼ ▼ ▼

Dialydd Mab lay on the hillside in his white snow smock and waited patiently, twelve hundred yards from the execution site. Over half that distance was deep virgin snow no one could get across in a hurry even after they figured out where he had to have been. The cross-country skis beside him would have taken him far away by the time they did, and no merely mortal pursuer was going to overtake a PICA on skis.

That was important, because it meant he'd been able to come himself, instead of dispatching one of Owl's remotes. And it meant there'd be ski tracks for those pursuers to find and follow—tracks which would prove a human being had been there and lead the inevitable pursuit well away from any town or village as they sped straight towards the Samuel Mountains and escape.

He found himself wishing there'd been a way to spirit Ruhstahd away, as well, but there hadn't been. That was another reason why he was here. He couldn't save the man, but there was one last gift he could give him.

Well, two, really, he supposed as he nestled his cheek into the stock of his rifle and prepared to deliver the first.

It looked like a standard M96, but appearances could be deceiving. Owl had built that rifle especially for Dialydd Mab. Its rifling was more precise than anything even Taigys Mahldyn's shops could have cut, the barrel lining was chrome plated, the stock was precisely tailored to his height and reach, and the cartridges in its magazine—loaded with a smokeless propellant centuries in advance of anything pre-Merlin Safehold could have produced—drove its massive bullets at well over two thousand feet per second, with a muzzle energy of better than five thousand foot-pounds. The pre-fired cases he'd brought to leave behind him had been filled with black powder to leave the proper residue for anyone who examined them, even though that precaution was almost certainly unnecessary. He'd also brought along a half-dozen black powder-filled squibs to produce the appropriate smoke cloud and be sure the camp guards found his position, the tracks leading them astray, and the letter to Wylbyr Edwyrds he intended to leave behind. But for this moment, on this day, he wanted the most precise instrument Owl could give him.

He didn't need any special sighting system to take advantage of that precision. Not when he had one of his own built in. Now pitiless sapphire eyes, far colder than their artificial origin could ever have explained, gazed over the rifle's open sights and his index finger stroked the trigger.

▼ ▼ ▼

"Very well," Zherohm Clymyns said flatly, hard gaze glittering with triumph as he nodded to the inquisitor with the torch, "if you have nothing to say, then—"

His head exploded.

The impact energy sent the corpse stumbling forward to sprawl on its belly. Sheer incredulity held the assembled audience motionless, trying to grasp what had happened, as the crack of the rifle which had delivered justice upon him—tiny with distance, yet sharp and clear through the icy air—reached them almost two seconds later.

The second round announced its arrival two and a half seconds after the crack of the first. It struck Fhrancys Ostean between the shoulder blades as he turned towards Clymyns, ripped through his heart and lungs in a spray of crimson, and wounded yet another Schuelerite.

The first ripples of panic washed through the spectators as understanding dawned. They began to turn, looking for the source of that deadly fire, and Zhorj Myzuhno collapsed with a hoarse, squealing shriek as the third bullet slammed its way through his liver and erupted from his back.

The panic became total, then. Faith was a frail shield against those heretical thunderbolts, and the warriors of Mother Church's Inquisition fled wildly towards the protection of Camp Chihiro's buildings. To their credit, a handful of the Army of God officers assigned to the camp's guard force kept their heads, going prone but scanning the hills until they found the telltale puffs of smoke.

Kuhnymychu Ruhstahd saw it all and somehow he knew who was behind that rifle. He knew it was the same rifle which had spoken from the bank of the Holy Langhorne Canal, and he, too, stared at that distant powder smoke, for he knew something else, as well. He knew the *seijin* behind that rifle—the true *seijin*, called by God as surely as any *seijin* of old, whatever Zhaspahr Clyntahn might claim—had one last gift for him. He watched that hillside, eyes bright and suddenly unafraid as he waited for that gift, and never heard the fourth and final shot that killed him instantly.

. XUI .
St. Tyldyn,
Northland Province,
Republic of Siddarmark

The bullet hissed by, not quite close enough to actually hit him but not so wide a miss as all that, and Traveler shied in protest.

"My Lord, will you *please* keep your head down!" Lieutenant Slokym snapped with rather more asperity than a mere lieutenant was supposed to use in addressing a general officer. "We really, *really* don't need anything . . . untoward happening to you!"

"I don't intend for *anything* to happen to me, toward or not, Bryahn," Baron Green Valley said mildly, and touched Traveler with a heel to encourage him to move smartly. It would be embarrassing, to say the least, to get himself killed by one of the zealots of the Temple rearguard.

*Impatience and frustration are piss-poor reasons for getting yourself killed by* anyone, *Kynt,* he reminded himself rather more tartly than he'd spoken to his aide. *And not even SNARCs will keep you from doing that if you insist on being stupid. Just like your nannies won't do a whole lot to keep you alive if you take a bullet someplace like—oh, the heart or the brain, maybe?*

A sudden crackle of fire, clearly from the 5th Mounted Regiment's M96s, answered the single shot which had whistled past his head and splinters flew from the stable loft where the marksman had taken his stand. Three more rifles cracked from inside the stable, smoke spurting from hastily hacked loopholes in its walls, and then another shot blasted out from the same spot as the first, far too quickly to have come from a muzzle-loading weapon.

"I'm getting just a bit tired of those newfangled rifles of theirs," he remarked to no one in particular as he swung down from the saddle in the shelter of a nice, solid stone wall. It looked as if it had once been part of a smithy. Of course, that had been before the retreating Temple Boys burned three-quarters of the town of St. Tyldyn to the ground.

"I can't say they make me very happy, either, My Lord," Slokym said sourly.

More of Colonel Gairwyl's riflemen were firing at the stable, but their initial rate of fire had eased and Green Valley nodded approvingly. Additional ammunition had come forward, and they'd expended less of it taking Esthyr's Abbey than he'd allowed for, yet the new cartridges remained in less than bountiful supply. He'd impressed the need to avoid wasting them upon his COs, and he was glad to see Gairwyl had taken his admonition to heart. The mounted infantry were still sending enough forty-five-caliber bullets the stable's way to encourage the Temple Boys inside it to keep their heads down, but they weren't simply blazing away when they had no clear target.

Green Valley peeked around one end of the wall at the sudden firefight, then glanced at his aide and his lips twitched at the lieutenant's expression. It was obvious that what the young man really wanted was to grab his idiot superior by the scruff of his oh-so-senior neck and drag him bodily back behind the wall.

"Forgive me, My Lord," Slokym continued after a moment, "but didn't our spies say they weren't supposed to have any of those damned rifles before mid-April?"

His expression, Green Valley noted, was not one of approval.

"Actually," the baron replied judiciously, one eye still on the stable, "our spies said they wouldn't have *very many* of 'those damned rifles' before April. And spies, alas, have been known to be mistaken, Bryahn."

Slokym scowled, and Green Valley didn't really blame him. The Empire of Charis and its allies had been rather spoiled by the quality of their intelligence reports. Getting those reports where they needed to be quickly enough was sometimes a problem, but they were accustomed to knowing the reports they did receive were accurate ones. And so they usually were. Not always, however. Even their allies might have become suspicious if Charis' "spies" never made a mistake. Worse, there were occasions on which no one could have come up with a credible explanation for how a particular bit of intelligence could be gotten to the recipient who needed it quickly enough to do any good. When that happened, it simply *didn't* get to that recipient, and that sort of problem had a particularly acute relevance for the Army of Midhold at the moment. Merlin Athrawes, even with Nimue Chwaeriau's assistance, could give faces to only so many *seijins*, and no one but a *seijin* would be operating in the bitter winter wastes of Northland Province.

*And we sort of painted ourselves into a corner with our initial appreciation of when Zhwaigair and Fultyn's toys were likely to arrive*, he reminded himself grumpily. *I don't suppose it's really Owl or Nahrmahn's fault, though. The real problem was that their information was too damned good!*

One drawback of the penetration the SNARCs and their remotes routinely accomplished—outside the Temple itself and the area of Zion immediately around it—was that the electronic spies reported what was actually being said. That had bitten the Allies more than once when the Group of Four (whose paranoia about heretic spies had become obsessive . . . justifiably, to be fair) used false orders to its own commanders as a disinformation technique. In this case, though, no one had deliberately set out to deceive them. They'd simply had access to Brother Lynkyn's own production estimates, and Brother Lynkyn had been overly conservative.

More powder smoke erupted from the stable. Clearly there must be the better part of two Army of God cavalry platoons inside it. And just as clearly, all of them were armed with St. Kylmahn conversions.

*Well, you knew there was going to be a rearguard, Kynt. And it probably made sense to give them the best weapons they could.*

He frowned as the SNARC specifically assigned to hover overhead whenever he was in the field inserted a couple of remotes into the stable and confirmed his estimate. The defenders were indeed cavalry—units of Colonel Hyndyrsyn's 42nd Cavalry Regiment who'd escaped the net at Esthyr's Abbey—although they were actually the remnants of *three* of the AOG's sixteen-man cavalry platoons, not two. They were thirty percent understrength, with barely thirty-three men between them, but there was no indication they intended to go easily. Which was no great surprise; if they'd been the sort to surrender, they never would have dug in inside the stable. They had to have known escape from their current position was effectively impossible when they chose to make their stand. For that matter, they didn't even have horses. But no one had ever said the Allies had a monopoly on courage. He would have preferred for those dismounted troopers to be less determined to die where they stood, delaying his advance, yet what bothered him more was that they were rifle-armed *cavalry*.

*We really don't need the Temple Boys to start developing the concept of mounted infantry of their own. But maybe this is more in the nature of an improvisation. A one-off effort because they're so focused on slowing us down.*

And maybe he was whistling in the dark, he told himself sourly. Safeholdian armies had used bow- and arbalest-armed dragoons for centuries; making the leap to issuing firearms instead shouldn't have been too difficult. But rifles had been far scarcer for the Army of God than for the Imperial Charisian Army and, up until very recently, they'd been reserved for the infantry. Every mainland realm knew the function of dragoons was to scout and skirmish, not engage in pitched firefights with enemy infantry, and he would be much happier if things stayed that way in the Church's book.

Bahrnabai Wyrshym had already demonstrated that he was less enamored of The Book than Green Valley might have preferred, however. The bishop militant had reacted to the threat to his flank with his customary firmness. Even before Esthyr's Abbey's fall, he'd dispatched a convoy of armorers to Gorthyk Nybar in Fairkyn, along with every St. Kylmahn conversion kit he'd had on hand. While it was true the converted breechloaders couldn't match the M96's rate of fire, or even fire as rapidly as the original Mahndrayn, it was also true they fired far more rapidly than any muzzle-loader ever made. And in some ways the conversions' crudity actually worked in the AOG's favor, since they were still flintlocks. They didn't depend on the primer caps of the new-build St. Kylmahns, which simplified problems of ammunition supply. But the really bad news was that those armorers in Fairkyn were turning out somewhere around two hundred conversions per day. At that rate, they'd provide Nybar with almost seven thousand more of the new weapons by the fourth five-day of April.

At that point, they'd have run out of conversion kits and undoubtedly been recalled to Guarnak. But by the *end* of April, the first shipments of new-build weapons from the Temple Lands manufactories would have reached Wyrshym at Guarnak ... and so would at least two additional artillery regiments with Fultyn's new banded rifles.

*The good news is that we're looking at a late thaw again*, he thought. According to Owl's meteorological data, they might see fresh snow accumulations north of the Kalgaran Mountains as late as the second five-day of May. *With a little luck, the extra bad weather may put their weapons deliveries behind Owl's current, revised estimates. And we're still a hell of a lot more mobile in the snow than they are. But it's going to run closer than I'd counted on.*

One of Gairwyl's captains was busy organizing an assault on the stable. Green Valley considered offering the youngster a better estimate of the strength inside it, but not very hard. First, getting to him without getting shot would be a nontrivial challenge, and there was that thought he'd had a little earlier about not getting killed doing something stupid. Second, while his officers and men were prepared to accept his observations and estimates as the next best thing to the *Holy Writ* itself, it might be just a bit awkward to explain how he was in any position to make a better estimate than Captain Mahnroh, whose men were already engaged with the stable's defenders. And, third, Gyairmoh Mahnroh was no one's fool and seemed to have matters well in hand.

One of the captain's platoons had worked its way around to the western side of the stable, where the charred ruins of the inn it had served offered protected firing positions within fifty or sixty yards of the defenders. That platoon's riflemen were engaged in a spirited, close-range exchange with their AOG counterparts, and more Temple Boys were being drawn into the firefight. They weren't leaving the stable's other walls unmanned, but the number of rifles protecting them was definitely being thinned.

Mahnroh's second platoon had crept cautiously into the snow-drifted paddock south of the stable without

firing a shot, and the fire of his third platoon, north of
the stable, was beginning to increase in intensity. The
defenders, who'd built thick hay-bale breastworks
along the inner sides of the stable's walls, squirmed
around to return the gathering fusillade, which reduced
the number of rifles in their western and southern defenses still further. And as Green Valley watched approvingly, one squad of Mahnroh's last platoon settled
into place behind a concealing haystack fifty yards east
of the stable and locked peculiar-looking cup-like tubes
onto their rifles' bayonet mounts.

*That's going to come as a nasty surprise*, the baron
reflected.

Only a few hundred of the newly developed "M97
Rifle Grenade Launcher, Model One"—officially abbreviated as the "RGL" but already known to the
troops as "Shan-wei's slingshot," which was in a fair
way to being shortened to "sling"—had reached the
Republic, and they'd been rushed forward to the Army
of Midhold. They'd arrived too late for the attack on
Esthyr's Abbey, so this would be the first time they'd
been used in action, which meant no one inside that
stable could have a clue what was about to happen.

Another bullet came his way. He was pretty sure this
one was a stray, not aimed specifically at him, but it
whined nastily as it ricocheted from the protective
stone wall.

"My Lord—!" Slokym began, but Green Valley
shook his head.

"Sorry, Bryahn. I need to see this."

Slokym looked less than convinced, but he clamped
his jaw on any further protest. In fact, he wiggled forward and joined his general in peering around the corner of Green Valley's wall, and the baron chuckled as
he made room for the younger man.

The RGL-armed squad had secured the launchers to
their rifles' muzzles. Now they inserted the grenades
into the cups. The black powder-filled weapons were
bigger and clumsier than grenades with high-explosive
fillers would have been, and aiming them was still

something of a black art. Howsmyn had cribbed the fundamental concept from Owl's libraries, however, and he'd moved directly to a "shoot-through" design which allowed the grenadier to use a standard rifle round instead of having to load a special blank cartridge. The bullet itself passed through a hole in the center of the grenade, igniting the grenade's fuse an instant before the expanding muzzle gases launched it on its way. Maximum range was only about a hundred and eighty yards, well short of what would become possible with the introduction of smokeless powder but much farther than anyone could possibly have thrown a grenade.

The squad members finished loading the launchers, knelt on one knee, bracing their rifle butts on the ground, and watched their corporal. He gave them a last, quick inspection and raised his right hand head-high. He held it there for a heartbeat, then brought it slashing down and the grenadiers fired.

The grenades arced toward the stable with a considerably higher velocity than a human arm could have imparted, but they were still far slower than a bullet. Like rifle grenades throughout Old Earth's history, that relatively low velocity resulted in a high trajectory and problematical accuracy, especially for first-time users who hadn't yet been issued proper sights for them. They trailed smoke from their ignited fuses, and a third of them went wide. Two more bounced off of the building's stout walls, three buried themselves in the stable's thatched roof, and two bounced off the closed stable door. But one of them sailed through a second-floor hay door into the stable's loft, directly into an AOG trooper's face, and the last—better aimed or extraordinarily lucky (or both)—drilled through the ventilation space under the stable's eaves.

The explosions sprayed shrapnel in all directions. The defenders' hay-bale breastworks absorbed most of the lethal balls, but three were wounded and two were killed outright. The morale effect was considerably worse; even men determined to die for God could be shaken when Shan-wei's own spite exploded in their midst in a blast of brimstone. They didn't *panic*, but shock and consternation paralyzed them, at least briefly, and the white smoke of burning hay added itself to the gray billows of powder smoke.

The grenadiers inserted fresh rounds into the launcher cups and a second salvo lofted towards the stable. Smoke poured from the burning thatch, at least two or three more grenades found their way into the building's interior, and the screams of wounded men answered.

The platoon which had infiltrated its way into the paddock had waited for the second wave of grenades. Now it leapt to its feet and charged. One of its squads charged with bayoneted rifles; the other three carried drawn Mahldyn .45s. None of the AOG troopers saw them for a moment or two. Then three rifles fired from inside the stable. One Charisian went down, but his companions carried through, rushing the closed double door in the middle of the stable's southern wall. It was barred from the inside, but there was a small, square window opening in the middle of each door panel. The sliding shutters which closed them were far thinner than the rest of the door's sturdy planks, and rifle butts smashed through them. Hand grenades were primed and tossed into the openings, more explosions thundered, and two revolver-armed Charisians took over each window, firing into the smoke-filled interior to keep the defenders' heads down while two more of the attackers assaulted the door bar with axes. The door resisted—briefly—but then the bar broke and the door panels flew open. Another mounted infantryman fell, but the others stormed past him, pistols firing and bayonets stabbing.

After that, it was over in a very few minutes.

Green Valley straightened slowly, then climbed back into Traveler's saddle. Slokym mounted beside him, and the two of them rode cautiously forward to join Captain Mahnroh's men.

▼ ▼ ▼

By midday, what was left of the town of St. Tyldyn was in Charisian hands.

There hadn't actually been that much fighting, Green Valley thought as he handed his reins to someone else and climbed the steps of what had once been the St. Tyldyn town library. Like every other building in town, it had seen better days, yet it was closer to intact than most of them.

Somehow the baron doubted that was because of the Army of God's deep respect for the printed word. More likely it had to do with how well the library's brick walls had resisted the flames. Most of the rest of the town—more of a largish village, really—had been built of more combustible materials. Aside from buildings like the stable which had been turned into defensive strong points, they'd been set ablaze as the rest of the retreating AOG cavalry fell back. Clearly, the Temple Boys understood the value of denying an enemy the shelter of unbroken roofs and walls.

"My Lord," Colonel Gairwyl greeted him, touching his chest in salute.

"Dahnyld." Green Valley nodded and reached out to clasp forearms with him. "I saw young Mahnroh's grenadiers in action. Impressive, but I think we need a little more work."

"He told me you were there, My Lord." Gairwyl's tone made it clear that the Army of Midhold's commanding general shouldn't have been close enough to the sharp end to see anything of the sort, and Green Valley smiled at him.

"I promise young Bryahn's already chewed me out for it."

"I knew he had a good head on his shoulders," Gairwyl replied, and the baron chuckled. Then his expression sobered.

"I wish we'd come closer to taking the place in one piece." He shook his head. "I'm less worried about you and your boys—or General Gardynyr's infantry, for that matter—but Second Corps is going to miss those roofs."

"They'll make out, My Lord," Gairwyl said. "Won't be their first snowstorm. Besides," he shrugged, "there were never enough roofs for more'n a regiment or two. They may not be as fond of playing in the snow as my boys or General Gardynyr's, but they know how to survive it and their tents're just as good as ours. Don't know about General Makgrygair's boys and their gear, though."

Green Valley nodded, because Gairwyl had a very good point. In fact, he had two of them.

The Charisian infantry of General Brohkamp's corps were far less suited to actual winter combat than Gardynyr's 4th Division and Brigadier Braisyn's 3rd Mounted Brigade, but all of them were equipped with arctic uniforms and tents. General Sulyvyn Makgrygair's 2nd Rifle Division, however, was Siddarmarkian. His infantrymen were tough and determined, and many were winter-wise, but they were far less well equipped and no one had ever trained them specifically for arctic warfare. That was why Green Valley had left Makgrygair to assure the security of Esthyr's Abbey while Brohkamp moved up from Esthyr's Abbey to St. Zhana, a hundred and fifty miles farther west.

The good news was that his snow lizard- and caribou-drawn sleighs were building up a major forward supply point at Esthyr's Abbey more rapidly than anyone in the Army of God would believe was possible. The bad news was that even so, he was going to have to hold his position at St. Tyldyn for at least a five-day or two. First Corps, and especially the engineers assigned to 4th Division, had been improving the high road as it went, but nature wasn't cooperating. There'd been a fresh blizzard—two days' worth of heavy snowfall—immediately after they'd taken Esthyr's Abbey, coupled with almost daily flurries since. Now another arctic front was on its way, and the additional snow would hamper anyone's logistics, even his. He doubted Brohkamp would be able to move even his Charisian infantry any farther forward than St. Tyldyn before the first day of April. Moving Makgrygair's Siddarmarkians under those conditions would be problematic, at best, and even 1st Corps was starting to feel the strain of the pace he'd demanded of it.

He followed Gairwyl to the library table where the colonel had spread out his maps and both of them frowned down at the uncompromising topography.

St. Tyldyn was barely a hundred and forty air-miles east of Fairkyn, but that was over a hundred and seventy miles for an army which followed the high road. That high road crossed to the western bank of the Ice Ash River ninety-plus miles from St. Tyldyn, at which point a spur road ran south along the river's bank to Fairkyn. The wooden spans of the drawbridges on which it had once crossed the Kalgaran and the Ice Ash had been burned, but the intact stone approach spans remained. Green Valley's engineers would be able to put them back into service quickly, and under what passed for good winter conditions in northern Haven—in other words, at least five days in a row without a blizzard—1st Corps' ski- and snowshoe-equipped infantry could have advanced almost thirty miles a day along the line of the high road. Much of that movement would have to be made in darkness, given how short those days were this far north, yet the road bed provided both a flat, graded path and a guide that would be hard to miss even in pitch blackness. But while 2nd Corps' supply train could match that rate of advance, it was unlikely its infantry could manage much more than twenty or so miles a day under the best of conditions.

The distance to Fairkyn was twenty percent shorter cross-country, but covering that kind of distance under arctic conditions would take at least seven or eight days even for Makrohry's 1st Corps, and he really couldn't justify sending Makrohry on his way until Brohkamp had reached St. Tyldyn. First Corps consisted of just over twenty-three thousand men, including its field artillery and attached engineers. Its actual combat formations, however, were down to a scant twenty thousand, barely seventy percent of their "paper" strength. While that was quite a lot more than Gorthyk Nybar commanded, it wasn't a lot more than Nybar would have shortly, because Wyrshym had pulled out all the stops after the loss of Esthyr's Abbey and St. Zhana. Nybar's units had been brought almost up to their official establishment with fresh replacements, and two more AOG infantry divisions were earmarked to join him over the next two or three five-days.

Worse, Nybar had kept his men busy improving their positions, despite the bitter weather, and Wyrshym had managed to squeeze out enough transport to stockpile two months' rations for Nybar's troops at Fairkyn. It hadn't been easy. Despite Rhobair Duchairn's improvements to the Army of the Sylmahn's supply situation, Wyrshym's entire command was still living hand to mouth. He'd run serious risks and pinched his own logistic capability at Guarnak to build up Nybar's supplies at Fairkyn, and he'd been forced to shave the rest of the Army of the Sylmahn's ration dumps dangerously thin, but he'd done it.

All of which meant Green Valley would shortly be looking at close to eighteen thousand well dug in, reasonably well-supplied infantry and cavalry. Their artillery would be weak, but Fairkyn sat at the top of a steep line of bluffs west of the Ice Ash. Those bluffs were the reason for the canal locks around which the town had grown, and the elevation would give the defenders the advantage of the high ground. Worse, Nybar—who was depressingly willing to learn from other people's experience, as well as his own—had built observation towers in Fairkyn itself and at regular intervals around his entire defensive position. His guns would be outclassed, in both numbers and capability, but Green Valley's artillerists would be unable to use their own weapons to full advantage because they simply wouldn't be able to see their targets. The last thing Green Valley wanted was to turn Fairkyn into some sort of deep-winter siege operation, and however superior to Wyrshym's his own supply capabilities might be, feeding the big guns' voracious appetite for any sort of lengthy artillery duel would impose a significant strain.

*We can still do this*, he told himself, looking down at the maps. *I can still get 1st Corps around Nybar's flank into the Ohlarn Gap, cut his direct connection to Guarnak, and there's no way in hell Wyrshym can move north and push me back out of the Gap before Brohkamp comes up through St. Tyldyn to invest Fairkyn from the east. But Nybar'll be able to hold out at least a month longer than I'd hoped he would, unless I want Brohkamp to pay the butcher's bill to storm his positions, and that'd gut 2nd Corps . . . at best. But if we let Nybar tie us down that long, Wyrshym'll have at least another month to improve his own supply chain and that pain in the arse Duchairn will spend it shipping in still more rifles, and this time they'll be new-build St. Kylmahns, not field conversions. Unless . . . .*

He gazed at the map, eyes measuring distances and considering the opponents' relative speeds. He didn't want to tie down and bloody 1st or 2nd Corps in a siege, no. That would sacrifice the priceless advantage of his Charisians' mobility and buy Wyrshym too much time, exactly as the bishop militant hoped. But if he was willing to let Makgrygair's *Siddarmarkians* invest Fairkyn with Charisian artillery support—and *if* he could get Makgrygair moved up quickly enough—then pass the rest of Brohkamp's corps north of Fairkyn, out of sight of Nybar's observation towers, while 1st Corps went *south* of Fairkyn . . . .

*Risky, Kynt*, he told himself. *Maybe even very risky. If Nybar gets feisty—or desperate—enough to come out of Fairkyn, Makgrygair would have his hands full. And if Nybar figures out what you're doing, and you already know he's no dummy, that's exactly what he ought to do. Because if you lose the high road through Ohlarn and then down through the Gap, you'll have sixty thousand hungry Charisians stuck in the middle of goddamned nowhere. No way even your supply trains could move enough food and ammunition forward cross-country to sustain them for very long.*

*But if you can pull it off and keep the boys fed long enough . . . .*

He sank into one of Gairwyl's camp chairs, leaning both elbows on the library table, propping his chin in his palms, and his eyes were dreamy.

He never even noticed the speculation in Gairwyl's eyes . . . or the resignation in Lieutenant Slokym's.

. XVII .

# Charisian Embassy,
# Siddar City,
# Republic of Siddarmark

"Well, what do you think of Kynt's latest brainstorm?" Cayleb Ahrmahk asked dryly.

He and Merlin Athrawes sat on a pair of well-stuffed settees, facing each other across the hearth in the sitting room of the emperor's suite. Aivah Pahrsahn sat comfortably at Merlin's side, her legs folded under her, and all three of them nursed glasses of *Seijin* Kohdy's Premium Blend. It was an excellent whiskey, and although Merlin actually preferred Sharleyan's favorite Glynfych, it had become the drink of choice whenever Aivah dropped by to confer with him and Cayleb.

"I think it's . . . audacious," he replied judiciously.

"'Audacious,' the man says!" Cayleb shook his head. "How about 'He's out of his frigging mind'?!"

"Now, that really isn't fair, Your Majesty," Aivah put in. Cayleb looked at her, and she shrugged. "I'm not a military person like you and Baron Green Valley, but he's never struck me as the sort who's likely to run off chasing wild wyverns. I don't pretend to understand all the movements he's talking about in this instance, but Owl and Prince Nahrmahn—and I, for that matter— all agree with his estimates of Nybar's and Wyrshym's supply situation. And whatever he does, he'll have the SNARCs to keep anyone from surprising him."

"The only problem, Aivah," Cayleb said in a considerably more somber tone, "is that seeing what's coming doesn't help a lot if you can't get out of the way. That's sort of what happened to us in the Markovian Sea two years ago. Even worse, it's what happened to Admiral Manthyr in the Gulf of Dohlar."

Aivah's expression tightened in understanding, but Merlin shook his head.

"You're right about that, Cayleb." His voice was gentler than usual, an acknowledgment of the pain he and Cayleb shared over what had happened to Gwylym Manthyr and his men, but his eyes were level. "On the other hand, Kynt's faster on his feet than anybody on the other side. Admittedly, Second Corps isn't quite as nimble as *First* Corps, but either one of them could march rings around anything the Church has, especially under winter conditions. So the odds are damned good that he *could* get out of the way in time if anything untoward came at him. And he'd have pretty close to parity with Wyrshym's entire army, to boot."

"A parity he'd be busy splitting at least three ways, counting Makgrygair's division," Cayleb pointed out.

"Fair enough. But the Army of the Sylmahn's *already* split three ways, and if Kynt pulls it off, Wyrshym won't be able to reunite his command in time to make much of a difference. For that matter, he won't be able to unite with Nybar *at all*, and frankly, given Nybar's capability, that would be a very good thing in a whole bunch of ways."

Cayleb's grunt might have signified agreement, or simple acknowledgment, or mere irritation, and he stared down into his whiskey for several seconds. Then his nostrils flared and he looked back up again.

"Are you seriously suggesting I should let him try this?" he asked quietly.

It was, Merlin acknowledged, a reasonable question, and he turned to gaze into the heart of the fire while he considered it.

Green Valley's original strategy had been to pinch out Gorthyk Nybar's command at Fairkyn, then move south through the Ohlarn Gap down the high road to Guarnak to threaten Wyrshym's primary forward supply head. Unfortunately, as Green Valley had pointed out, Wyrshym had thrown everything he could into reinforcing Nybar and Nybar had dug in too quickly and too damned efficiently. Like Green Valley, Merlin found himself respecting the Army of Fairkyn's CO more than he might have wished. Gorthyk Nybar was entirely too flexible when it came to tactical innovation and far too iron-willed when it came to hammering his plans through to success.

He'd lost better than five percent of his initial troop strength, mostly to frostbite, driving his men to fortify their position in the teeth of a North Haven winter, but he'd refused to flinch. And as they'd hacked entrenchments and dugouts out of the frozen earth, they'd also improved their quarters. Every one of those dugouts had its own crude chimney, and earthen walls and sandbags designed to be bulletproof also tended to be wind and weather proof, which had led to a significant decrease in subsequent frostbite casualties. That was scarcely a minor consideration, but from the Allies' perspective, what mattered most was that Nybar had already seen mortars and heavy Charisian artillery in action, and his fortifications reflected that experience. They might not be up to the standards of Old Terra's Western Front in 1918, but they were far better than any pre-Merlin fieldworks would have been, and black powder artillery was less effective *against* fieldworks than the high-explosive which had churned Flanders' fields into a moonscape. Even worse, perhaps, his own artillery had learned a few lessons of its own. It remained far from equal to its opposition, but it was better than it had been, and it was dug in where any assault would have to come to *it*.

The fortifications would go a long way towards redressing the imbalance between muzzle-loading and breech-loading rifles, as well. And that didn't even consider the minor point of how much of his current infantry force had been rearmed with breechloaders. All of which would make taking Fairkyn a much more unpleasant—and lengthier—proposition than anyone had anticipated when Green Valley formulated his original plan of campaign.

And, as Aivah had just pointed out, Green Valley was entirely correct about Wyrshym's improved logistics. Now that Nybar's needs had been seen to, the bishop militant's snow lizards and mountain dragons were busily hauling supplies forward to Guarnak from Five Forks, the Hildermoss River city where those supplies had been accumulating for the past two or three months. If Wyrshym was allowed to go on doing that . . . .

"If Kynt goes ahead with his original plan to crunch up Nybar, he's going to lose at least a month, Cayleb—probably more like two," Merlin said finally. "Now, at the moment, he's got something like a month and a half or even two months more of winter to work with, but once the thaw sets in he won't be a lot more mobile than the Temple Boys, at least until the snowmelt runs off, the rivers go back down, and the mud dries. *Nobody*'ll be moving anywhere except along the high roads—and not too damned quickly even there, given what spring flooding usually looks like north of Shiloh—until then. He'd probably take a lot of casualties punching Nybar out of Fairkyn, too, after how thoroughly the Temple Boys've dug themselves in around the town. But what's worse is that Wyrshym would have all that time to improve his own supply position. I figure the Army of the Sylmahn'll be short on food whatever happens, at least until sometime in late May or early June, but Wyrshym's already better off in that respect than he was in October. And if we don't do something about him before June, at the latest, he's going to've been heavily resupplied with the new rifles and those Parrott guns of Brother Lynkyn's, too . . . not to mention the damned rockets. We still don't know how well his version of the Katyusha's going to work, but I wouldn't hold my breath waiting for him to fail. He *probably* won't have any available in quantity until midsummer or early fall, but remember how low his—and our—estimates on rifle production turned out to be."

Cayleb grimaced sourly in acknowledgment of Merlin's points . . . especially the last two.

Lynkyn Fultyn's banded artillery concept had been bad enough by itself, but Sylvestrai Pynzahn had made it much worse. A lot of nineteenth-century ironmasters back on Old Earth had experimented with ways of banding cast-iron artillery pieces to strengthen their breeches, but few of them had been truly satisfactory. Until Robert Parrott's technique had come along, at least. Parrott Rifles had still been inferior to contemporary wrought-iron guns like the US Army's three-inch ordnance rifle, which hadn't needed to be banded at all, but Parotts had been available in much heavier shell weights, iron was *far* cheaper than wrought iron, his method had offered what was almost certainly the best combination of strength and affordability of any of the banded *iron* guns, and between them, Fultyn and Pynzahn had essentially re-created Parrott's methodology.

The new guns remained heavier for a given shell weight and range than Ehdwyrd Howsmyn's pieces, and no doubt the Church's gun founders would shift over to steel as soon as they got enough of the new hearths into operation. But the Fultyn Rifles which had already reached the AOG's artillerists had increased their range and lethality dangerously, and Fultyn clearly recognized that the same technique could go right on reinforcing existing iron cannon even after steel became available for new pieces. That meant many guns which would otherwise have been scrapped were likely to find themselves bored out, rifled, banded, and retained for service, instead. They might be inferior to the Church's new guns, far less the products of the Delthak Works, but they'd be one hell of a lot more effective than they *had* been, and there were a *lot* of them lying around.

The Church was unlikely to approach the sophistication of Charisian gunnery techniques for a long time to come, but the margin of superiority was narrowing. And until Charis managed to put the new propellants and shell fillers into production, the difference in range and effectiveness would be a lot lower than any of the Allies could wish, as well.

Yet Brother Lynkyn's proposed rocket artillery actually looked like being even worse news, especially since he'd put his finger so unerringly on the need to use the rockets en masse. In the absence of internal combustion engines they'd be less mobile than the rockets which had been used as area effect weapons during Old Earth's Second World War—in that sense, Merlin's reference to them as "Katyushas" was historically suspect—but over their effective range, they ought to be able to lay down devastating fire.

The Delthak Works had already started adapting its own rockets as artillery in response to a fresh Ehdwyrd Howsmyn inspiration, now that the concept had suggested itself to the AOG. They'd refrained this long simply because they hadn't wanted to draw Church attention to an idea so thoroughly within its means . . . and because properly employed rockets would offer far more advantage, proportionately, to Charis' foes than to its own forces. The new weapons would undoubtedly be useful to the ICA, yet they'd represent no more than an incremental increase in the power of its existing artillery while they'd confer a whole new order of capability upon the Church. One that was likely to kill a *lot* of Charisians before the smoke finally cleared.

None of which even considered what the receipt of several thousand more new-build St. Kylmahn breechloaders would do to the Army of the Sylmahn's effectiveness in the field.

*Or*, the emperor thought sourly, *exactly what all those damned Harchongians who already* have *St. Kylmahns are likely to be doing.*

"I hope you won't take what I'm about to say wrongly, Merlin, and I'm sure all the innovations coming out of people like Zhwaigair and Fultyn are exactly what we need to undermine the Proscriptions in the long run. But even bearing all of that in mind, I'm *strongly* tempted to apply the Nahrmahn Method to certain parties in Zion and Gorath."

"I don't blame you a bit," Merlin acknowledged. "But even if we decided it'd be a good idea, Fultyn and Zhwaigair are hardly the only ones on the other side who're pushing the envelope now. As you say, it's what we need to happen all over the planet eventually, and we'd need an army of assassins to take out *all* the people popping out ideas for them by now."

"Between you and Owl we *have* 'an army of assassins,'" Cayleb pointed out gamely. "A fact I believe you demonstrated at Camp Chihiro not so long ago."

"That's true, Your Majesty," Aivah put in. "On the other hand, if we started killing their more innovative thinkers, it would only underscore their importance to someone like Clyntahn. His Rakurai may be little more than single-shot terrorist weapons, but that's only because he's come to the conclusion that he can't coordinate targeted assassinations against our counterintelligence. He fully understands the value of that kind of operation, though, and even if he didn't, we've been underscoring it for him with Owl and Merlin's reprisals against the worst of his inquisitors. If we start picking off Maigwair's weapons developers, we'll only confirm to him how dangerous *we* think they are. That might be enough for a man of his mindset to decide to get behind them and push hard instead of dragging his feet the entire way."

"It might," Merlin agreed. "Mind you, some things are more likely than others, but he's never been shy about embracing pragmatism when he decides it's necessary, no matter how badly it flies in the face of the letter of the *Writ*. I expect that's only going to get even more pronounced as the Church's military position continues to deteriorate."

"And once he *acknowledges* that it's deteriorating, at least to himself." Aivah nodded, her expression serious.

"As of now, all indications are that he hasn't done anything of the sort. All of the Church's setbacks have been temporary in his mind because the power and the weight of her resources—*his* resources, really—is so great. I doubt he truly appreciates the implications Duchairn and Maigwair have obviously recognized about our comparative abilities to raise and equip armies. Once he does realize that—once it begins to percolate through his brain that he could actually *lose* this war— any remaining gloves will come off, Cayleb. He won't give a damn about the Proscriptions, or anything *else* in the *Writ*, once he realizes he isn't going to win his jihad if he tries to abide by them." She grimaced. "It's not like he really believes in anything besides the Church of Zhaspahr Clyntahn!"

"Wonderful," Cayleb said sourly, then shook himself. "All of that may be true, and you're both right that we need to be thinking about it. For that matter, I'm not *really* ready to break out the assassins yet myself. But the whole discussion's getting away from the matter actually at hand. And what you and Kynt are basically saying, Merlin, is that regardless of whether or not they decide to start producing rockets by midsummer, we need to take advantage of our better mobility while it's still winter—*before* the thaw—even if it means running some serious risks."

"More or less," Merlin conceded.

He dropped a command into the com net, and Owl obediently projected a map of the Ohlarn Gap onto Cayleb's and Aivah's contact lenses.

"Originally," Merlin said for Aivah's benefit, "Kynt's plan was to trap Nybar and his command as far forward as he could. What he really would've liked to do was to catch Nybar in an open field engagement, but there was never much chance of that, especially after Wyrshym pulled Nybar back to Fairkyn. So the fallback plan was to advance through Esthyr's Abbey, Saint Zhana, and Saint Tyldyn—which he's done now—to envelop Nybar at Fairkyn and crush that detachment in isolation. If Nybar hadn't been pulled back, and if Kynt hadn't been forced to take all three of those towns in order to clear the high road as he went, First Corps would already have dealt with Nybar, before he was so well dug in, and be on its way to Rankylyr."

A pointer appeared on the projected map, indicating a small, mountainous city on the northwest flank of the Ice Ash Mountains in the Ohlarn Gap. The high road from Fairkyn to Guarnak, which lay roughly three hundred miles farther to the southwest, ran just below the town's rocky perch. Artillery in Rankylyr could readily dominate the roadbed, although it couldn't possibly reach the line of the disabled Guarnak-Ice Ash Canal, almost fifty miles to the west. Wyrshym had already emplaced three precious batteries of twelve-pounders to do just that, and his fatigue parties had built emplacements for twice as many additional guns. He didn't have the pieces to put in those emplacements—yet—but the fact that he'd ordered their construction showed how clearly he appreciated the town's tactical importance.

"At the moment, there's only a relatively weak picket—just a couple of AOG infantry regiments and three militia regiments—actually in and around Rankylyr," Merlin continued. "There are enough artillerists to man the guns, but not enough infantry to put up a serious defense. What Wyrshym and Nybar have in mind is that if and when Nybar's forced to retreat from Fairkyn, he'll fall back to Rankylyr, bringing his own guns with him and putting them into all those empty emplacements. And if something nasty happens to Nybar, Wyrshym has two or three infantry divisions at Guarnak. Technically, they're his reserve for his forward positions down around Saiknyr—" the cursor swooped four hundred miles due south to Wyvern Lake in the Sylmahn Gap "—but he could also send them up to Rankylyr to deny Kynt the use of the high road while he either retreats, reorients his forces, or is reinforced by the Mighty Host of God and the Archangels. And if all of this is going on after the thaw's set in, Kynt won't be able to advance *without* the high road, whatever happens."

He paused, cocking one eyebrow at her, and she nodded to indicate that she was following him so far.

"All right. What Kynt's suggesting now is that he do basically what Duke Harless did with Thesmar . . . with the obvious difference that Fairkyn isn't a seaport and the AOG can't ship in supplies and reinforcements by sea. Instead of taking heavy losses capturing Fairkyn, what he wants to do is turn Fairkyn into a cage for Nybar's entire detachment. If Makgrygair's division can get into position, he'll come within a few thousand men of matching Nybar's field strength, unless Wyrshym gets the intended reinforcements to Fairkyn. Makgrygair's Siddarmarkians wouldn't have the strength to *take* the place, but especially if Kynt detaches Brigadier Tymkyn and the Fourth Mounted Brigade to support him and give him some extra mobility, he should have the strength to keep Nybar from pulling *out* of Fairkyn. For tactical and strategic purposes, the Army of Fairkyn will be as thoroughly out of action as if every man in it had been shot through the head."

"As long as General Makgrygair keeps the cork in the bottle," Cayleb put in a bit sourly, and Merlin nodded.

"As long as he keeps the cork in it," he acknowledged.

"And in the meantime, Baron Green Valley will do . . . ?"

Aivah's question trailed off and she arched her eyebrows at him.

"And in the meantime, Baron Green Valley and First Corps will head up the high road towards Fairkyn. But instead of diverting to his left after he crosses the Ice Ash, he'll continue along the high road and take Ohlarn, a hundred and forty miles to the northwest. At the moment, Ohlarn's garrisoned by only four regiments of militia, mostly still armed with arbalests and pikes. In order to keep Ohlarn from realizing he's coming,

Brigadier Braisyn's mounted brigade will continue to advance southwest towards Fairkyn while the rest of First Corps heads for Ohlarn. That should keep Nybar focused on the threat to his position without worrying about reinforcing Ohlarn.

"Hopefully, the first thing Nybar or Wyrshym will know about any threat to Ohlarn will be when the place surrenders. At that point, Kynt's on the high road only a hundred miles or so from Rankylyr . . . and a hundred and thirty miles closer to it than Fairkyn, with *Second* Corps already bypassing Fairkyn in his wake and General Makgrygair moving up to invest Nybar's position.

"From Ohlarn, First Corps takes Rankylyr. That should take about another five-day and a half. By then, Second Corps should've caught up with First Corps. At that point, General Brohkamp peels off someone to hold Rankylyr—probably Brigadier Traigair and Third Brigade—while First Corps takes advantage of its ability to move through deep snow and sets off cross-country for *here*."

The cursor swooped again, this time five-hundred-plus miles almost due west to the town of Five Forks.

"This is the part that's making Cayleb nervous," Merlin said. "Marching cross-country, Kynt can't count on moving more than twenty miles a day even with his snow lizards and caribou. In good, clear weather, he could probably come close to twenty-five or even thirty, for short bursts, with First Corps' ski troops and snowshoes. His supply echelons couldn't keep up with them, though, and in really bad weather, not even the Charisian Army's going to be able to move at all. So, call it an average of fifteen miles a day, instead. At that rate, it takes him thirty days to reach Five Forks. That *should* let him get there with at least a couple of five-days or so to spare, assuming Owl's long-range weather projections hold up and he doesn't get hit by an early thaw, on the one hand, or a series of blizzards, on the other. It'll be tighter for Second Corps, but with First Corps to break trail, Brohkamp's men should be able to stay pretty close behind Kynt's point. Barring those blizzards I mentioned, at any rate."

"But once he takes Five Forks, he'll be in the middle of enemy-held territory, with the Mighty Host north of him and Wyrshym *south* of him, won't he?" Aivah asked.

"Sure he will . . . with fifty thousand Charisian infantry with artillery support." Merlin's smile would have shamed a kraken. "Not only that, but whatever happens to the weather in New Northland and Tarikah, the thaw's going to come at least several five-days later along the Holy Langhorne Canal. That means the Mighty Host either won't be able to move at all, or else that it'll move very, very slowly. In the meantime, Nybar's trapped in Fairkyn, eating his way through his stockpiled supplies. Even if he somehow slips away from Makgrygair, *our* artillery will be emplaced at Rankylyr when he tries to move south to rejoin Wyrshym. And whatever happens to *him*, no more of those new rifles and new pieces of artillery'll be able to move past Five Forks to Wyrshym. For that matter, his entire existing supply line—such as it is and what there is of it—will be cut."

"And what about Kynt's supplies?" Cayleb asked sardonically.

"Kynt's supplies are . . . problematical," Merlin acknowledged with a crooked smile. "I did say I thought it was an 'audacious' plan, didn't I?"

"Yes, I believe you did," Cayleb replied affably.

"Well, according to his calculations, he ought to be able to haul along enough supplies to keep his men and his horses and draft animals reasonably well fed during his advance to Five Forks. It'll be a long way back to Ohlarn, which he plans to make his advanced supply head after Makgrygair seals off Fairkyn, but it ought to be doable. Things get dicier after that."

Aivah cocked her head.

"Somehow that doesn't sound incredibly reassuring, Merlin," she said. "What do you mean by 'dicier'?"

"He means Kynt's planning on eating his snow lizards and caribou," Cayleb told her flatly.

She looked shocked, and Merlin shrugged.

"It's always possible that if he moves quickly enough and the Church is in enough doubt about his actual objectives he'll be able to take Five Forks by a coup de main—sorry. That's from an Old Earth language called 'French.' It means 'a blow of the hand,' or a sudden strike that gets through your opponent's guard. Anyway, if he can take Five Forks before anyone thinks about destroying the supply center there, he'll have plenty of food and fodder. On the other hand, planning an operation which *relied* on doing that would be pretty damned stupid, so as Cayleb's comment suggests, Kynt's run his calculations on the basis that he *won't* capture Five Forks' supply dumps.

"To begin with, the caribou will find some forage even in North Haven. That'll help on the advance. The snow lizards, of course, are carnivores. That presents problems of its own, but if worse comes to worst, he'll be able to keep the snow lizards going by butchering some of the caribou as he empties the supply sleds they're pulling. After he takes Five Forks—assuming he didn't take the supply dumps intact—he slaughters the draft animals he doesn't need anymore and uses them to keep his troops and probably his snow lizards fed. If he slaughters the caribou first, it would ease his animal feed constraints and let him retain all of his available grain and fodder for his mounted infantry and his artillery draft animals."

From her expression, she didn't feel a lot better, and Merlin shrugged.

"Best-case scenario, Aivah, he takes the supply dumps, Second Corps closes up with him, and we get enough additional draft animals forward to him— we're expecting another convoy of caribou from Raven's Land in a couple of five-days, for example—that he doesn't have to do that. More probable scenario— assuming he *doesn't* take the dumps intact—he does have to slaughter somewhere around a third of his caribou. Maybe half. That reduces his mobility, but it should keep his troops fed through early June. By that point, the roads will be improving, we should have Fairkyn, and the ice on the Ice Ash will have broken up, which means we'll be able to move up the river from Ranshair and shift his primary supply head all the way up to Ohlarn, as planned. That would shorten his overland supply route from Grayback Lake by over eleven hundred miles." He shook his head. "That'll free up more than enough transport to keep Five Forks supplied even cross-country from Rankylyr, and by the *end* of June, the Navy'll be back in Spinefish Bay. With naval gunfire support, a couple of the new Siddarmarkian rifle divisions should be able to retake Salyk quickly, at which point we begin an advance up the North Hildermoss from the coast towards Cat-Lizard Lake. There're a lot of locks along the way that the Church can destroy to slow us down and make things difficult, but that's still going to pose a threat Maigwair has to take seriously."

Aivah was nodding now, her eyes intent, and Merlin shrugged again.

"With Kynt at Five Forks, Wyrshym would be in the same sort of trap as Nybar at Fairkyn. Except, of course, that if Nybar manages to hold out until the ice on the river breaks, we'll be able to send ironclads and additional troop transports all the way upriver to reinforce Makgrygair. For that matter, we'd be able to release another couple of Charisian divisions from the Reserve here in Old Province to create an additional army outside Fairkyn, probably under General Sahmyrsyt, because with the shorter supply line, they wouldn't overwhelm Kynt's available transport. At that point, Nybar either surrenders or we take the town away from him the hard way.

"It's unlikely Clyntahn will let Wyrshym retreat in time to escape what Kynt has planned for him. He'd have to pull out almost immediately, as soon as he figures out what's coming, and you know even better than we do how hard it'd be for Maigwair or Duchairn to convince Clyntahn to let him do that. If he doesn't, he's stuck at Guarnak and badly outnumbered by the forces we can bring to bear once we've taken Fairkyn and opened the lower reaches of the Ice Ash to our river traffic, and he's cut off from the Church's new rifles and artillery, as well.

"If the thaw comes as much earlier in eastern East Haven than along the Holy Langhorne as usual, the Mighty Host will still be stuck in ice, snow, or mud at that point. If they are, Kynt stays put at Five Forks to block any retreat while Sahmyrsyt or Makgrygair's Siddarmarkians advance through the Ohlarn Gap and General Stohnar comes north with the army the Republic's been building up in the lower Sylmahn Gap over the winter. The chance that Wyrshym's going to get out of *that* . . . isn't very good, let's say."

"And if we're unlucky about the weather and it thaws earlier than projected along the Holy Langhorne?" Cayleb asked quietly, and Merlin shrugged.

"If the Harchongians can move sooner than we're anticipating, and if they're able to coordinate with Wyrshym—and the Church is prepared to ignore the threat coming up the North Hildermoss *and* what should be happening to it about the same time down in Cliff Peak—we could be in trouble," he conceded. "At that point, Kynt has to hold Five Forks while the Siddarmarkians deal with Wyrshym and all of our supply calculations get a lot more . . . complicated. But he's absolutely right about the payoff if he can pull it off, Cayleb. And about the fact that Eastshare, High Mount, and Symkyn are going to be occupying just a *bit* of Maigwair's attention, come spring. You know he is."

"Yes, I do." Cayleb sighed. Then he managed a crooked, half-bitter smile and shook his head at Merlin. "I do, and if *I* were the one leading this . . . this 'calculated risk' of his, I'd probably be just as eager to try it as he is. But I'm not." He shook his head again. "I'm the one who has to authorize someone *else* to do it, and if it doesn't work—if it turns into a disaster because we get two solid five-days of blizzards nobody anticipated, or the thaw comes early in the Border States, or it comes late on the Ice Ash—I'll be the one who rolled the dice—because, in the final analysis, the responsibility's mine, whoever came up with the idea in the first place—and crapped out with the lives of sixty thousand men."

"I know." Merlin looked across at the emperor who was also his friend, and his blue eyes were almost gentle. "I know. But look at it this way, Cayleb. If you do decide to let him do this, you'll get to use your own dice, and the fellow you'll have actually rolling them has a pretty damned good track record."

"That's certainly true," the emperor admitted wryly. "And if he thinks he can pull it off, I don't suppose *I* ought to be telling him no. It still makes me nervous as hell, though. And I think before we make any decisions on this, we need to discuss it with Domynyk and Sharleyan, once they both wake up. And with Stohnar, for that matter, once Kynt's official dispatch gets to us here. Most of the Army of Midland's Charisian, but if we screw around and *lose* that army, he's the one whose northern flank's going to come apart all over again."

Merlin nodded and Cayleb took a long swallow from his whiskey glass. His expression was sour, but Merlin knew him too well to be fooled. The emperor still didn't like the idea, for all the reasons he'd just listed, yet he already knew he probably *was* going to sign off on it.

"Well," Aivah took another sip of her own—a far more delicate and ladylike one in her case—then set down her glass, unfolded her legs, and stood, "I'm just as happy to leave all those hard, sweaty military decisions up to you and the Emperor, Merlin." She swept Cayleb a graceful curtsey, and the emperor chuckled. "In the meantime, however, I have errands of my own to run. I appreciate your willingness to loan me your recon skimmer."

"You're welcome," Merlin said solemnly. "Just try not to break it."

"Since Owl's going to be flying it by remote while I keep *my* hands safely off the controls, perhaps you should take that up with *him*," she suggested sweetly.

"I guess any parent worries when his kids take the air car out without him," Merlin sighed.

"I shall endeavor to deliver it and Madam Pahrsahn to the Cave intact, Commander Athrawes," Owl said over the com link, and Merlin chuckled, although his humor was slightly forced.

Since the PICA Owl had built had been loaded with a duplicate of Nimue Alban's memories and personality, the AI had been forced to find a way to differentiate between the different iterations of her. Fortunately, it was a situation the Federation had faced before.

Under Federation law, it had been legal to emancipate electronic personalities. Indeed, quite a few of them— only a tiny number, perhaps, compared to the size of the Federation's total population, but almost a million overall—had been housed in PICAs free of the hard-wired time limit of Nimue's PICA. The ten-day limit in her case had been required because PICAs like hers *weren't* independent entities. They were extensions of an existing biological intelligence, and the limit was intended to do two things: first, prevent the cybernetic version of that intelligence from "going rogue," and, second, to establish legal responsibility for any of the PICA's actions.

The PICAs built for emancipated personalities lacked that limitation. Instead, *they* were hardwired to prevent any other personality from ever being loaded to them in the first place, and the question of whether those copies of flesh-and-blood humans were actually human— like the question of whether or not they had "souls"—had remained hotly debated. There'd been so few of them, and the ability to create last-generation PICAs had been so comparatively recent—and the threat of the Gbaba had provided such an enormous distraction from such concerns—that any sort of definitive philosophical consensus had been impossible to achieve. Merlin Athrawes found it rather bitterly ironic that

Nimue Alban had never thought too much about either of those questions. Or perhaps she had when she volunteered to die so that a PICA with her memories could awaken here on Safehold. If she had, however, neither he nor Nimue Chwaeriau would ever know a thing about it.

*Legally*, however, the Federation had concluded that—like the virtual personalities created for its military R&D—the electronic people living in those PICAs had the same legal rights as any biological entity. Many of them, in fact, had been members of the military, and a handful had even served as elected members of the Federation Assembly.

Owl had simply decided that both the PICAs running around Safehold were emancipated personalities, and since Nimue Chwaeriau was seven Safeholdian years younger than Merlin Athrawes, he was senior to her due to time in grade and so remained the senior TFN officer on Safehold. In order to avoid any confusion about whom he might be addressing at any given moment, however, Merlin had become "Commander Athrawes" while Nimue had become "Commander Chwaeriau." It made perfectly good sense and it was in perfect accordance—well, *almost* perfect, given the hacked state of Merlin's software—with Federation law, yet every time Owl used either form of address, Merlin felt a little more of the human being he'd once been slip away from him. If the truth be known, he thought of himself much more as Merlin now than he did as Nimue. Perhaps that would have been inevitable anyway, but the existence of his "younger sister" seemed to have driven the process both faster and farther, and he wasn't certain how he felt about that.

"Do that, Owl," he said after only the briefest of pauses. "And when you get there, Aivah, be sure to give my regards to Sandaria and our guests."

"I will," she replied, and then her own expression sobered. "I only hope we'll ever be able to let them *leave* the Cave."

"I think we will. And even if we never can," Merlin's

face hardened, and for just a moment Dialydd Mab looked out of those sapphire eyes at her, "it was still worth every single minute."

"You're right," she said softly, and laid one hand on his scarred cheek. Then she leaned close, kissed him on the forehead, and straightened with a gentle smile. "And I'll give them your love, as well as your regards," she promised.

. XVIII .
Camp Dynnys,
Lake Isyk,
Tarikah Province,
Republic of Siddarmark

"I've spoken to you about this before, Father," Bishop Maikel Zhynkyns said coldly. "I don't think you properly appreciate the gravity of your offense."

Father Aizak Mohmohtahny looked back across the desk at the man who administered Camp Dynnys. Zhynkyns was dark-haired and dark-eyed, and at the moment those eyes were chips of brown agate in a face of iron.

"The prisoners in this camp are here because Mother Church has excellent reason to suspect them of heresy and blasphemy," the bishop continued. "The vast majority of them—as you know as well as I—confess and acknowledge their sins in the fullness of time. You do them no favors by suggesting to them by your actions that Mother Church will not, in the fullness of time, demand a full and total accounting from all of them for their crimes against her, God, and the Archangels. Are you deliberately attempting to hamper the Inquisition's holy mission, Father? And are you prepared for the consequences if that is indeed your intention?"

He paused, glaring at the under-priest in the cassock of Pasqualate green, obviously demanding a response.

"My Lord," Mohmohtahny said, "I have no desire to hamper the Inquisition, but I have vows of my own. Those include healing any child of God."

"Heretics have cut themselves off from God of their own volition!" Zhynkyns snapped. "Mother Church will grant absolution for true contrition for any lesser sin, yet the Holy Schueler made it abundantly clear that there can be no absolution for heresy and violation of the Proscriptions. God may forgive those who repent, even from the lip of the grave, but that's because God is empowered to forgive what man is not. And heretics, Father, are excommunicate, cast out, and damned. We are *required* to give them to the Punishment, and they are not covered by your healers' vows."

"That may very well be true, My Lord. I'm a Pasqualate, not a Schuelerite, and I've never claimed to be an Inquisitor. Nor do I dispute your reading of the *Book of Schueler* and what it requires, and I would never set my judgment in opposition to Mother Church's. Yet Mother Church herself teaches that until someone is proved guilty and convicted as a heretic, that person must be considered *innocent*—as all of God's children must be presumed innocent until they be proven something else. And so I'm obligated to heal their hurts whenever possible until such time as they're fully sifted by the Inquisition and condemned for their crimes."

He met the bishop's fiery eyes unwaveringly, and Zhynkyns suppressed an urge to scream in the impertinent young bastard's face.

Part of the problem was that Aizak Mohmohtahny wasn't officially under Zhynkyns' direct command, despite the vast gulf in their priestly ranks. The young Pasqualate was attached to the Camp Dynnys guard force, drawn from the Army of God and technically responsible to Bishop Militant Bahrnabai Wyrshym, rather than directly to the Inquisition. The insolent son-of-a-bitch wasn't actually supposed to have any contact at all with Camp Dynnys' inmates, but he'd taken it upon himself to "improve their conditions." He'd actually drafted members of the guard force to work on sanitation in the camp—officially because disease that began with the inmates could readily spread to the guard force, as well. And Zhynkyns was certain he was quietly diverting rations from the guards' mess halls to the prisoners with the same justification: if starvation weakened their resistance to disease, the pestilence might well spread beyond their own numbers, exactly as the *Book of Pasquale* warned that it would.

No doubt it all seemed harmless enough to Mohmohtahny. It probably made him feel better in the face of the stern demands of the Punishment of Schueler, too. In the end, it was going to accomplish nothing where the true, spiritual well-being of the inmates was concerned, of course. Only the cleansing of the Punishment could hope to reclaim a heretic's soul from hell, and beside that, what could the fate of their physical bodies possibly matter?

But it *could* matter, and what neither Mohmohtahny nor Colonel Ahgustahn Tymahk, the camp guard force's commanding officer, seemed capable of grasping was just how destructive his actions truly were. Anything which might suggest to the inmates that the Inquisition would not, in fact, deal with them as sternly as the *Book of Schueler* required could only strengthen the perversity and corruption which had drawn them into the worship of Shan-wei in the first place. Their accursed mistress would whisper in their ears that they might yet evade the penalty their apostasy and heresy had laid up for them throughout all eternity. The "kindness" for which fatuous fools like Mohmohtahny patted themselves sanctimoniously on the back was actually the greatest cruelty they could possibly have shown the heretics consigned to Zhynkyns for sorting and cleansing!

The bishop hovered on the brink of ordering Mohmohtahny's arrest on charges of undermining the Jihad. There could scarcely be a more clear-cut case of defiance of the Inquisition's true mission, however it might be cloaked in the letter of Church law, and Zhynkyns had no doubt that Inquisitor General Wylbyr would support him fully. Yet he hesitated, and the reason he did only filled him with even more fury.

*The little bastard knows what happened at Camp Chihiro.* The thought grated through the bishop's mind like gravel through a manufactory's gears. *Somehow, those frigging broadsheets have gotten through into my camp, and this insubordinate little shit knows what happened to Father Zherohm, Father Fhrancys, and Brother Zhorj. That's what this is really about. He's running scared that the demonic "Seijin Dialydd" will get him if he doesn't lick the prisoners' arses!*

A trickle of cold arsenic ran under the magma of Zhynkyns' rage. Deep inside, he knew what that arsenic was, however fiercely he refused to face it. And in that same deeply hidden place, he knew Aizak Mohmohtahny wasn't driven by fear of the false *seijins'* retribution. The Pasqualate might be—was—tragically wrong about the consequences of the false kindness that encouraged a heretic to persist in his heresy, but he was sincere. It was Camp Dynnys' *inquisitors* who were terrified that Mab's bullets or blade might find them.

The way in which his fellow Schuelerites had allowed their purpose and resolve to falter in the face of a threat to their mortal bodies was enough to turn Maikel Zhynkyns' stomach. It was more than simply disgusting; it was a failure before God and a defiance of His most holy command through Schueler Himself. Despite all he could do, the tempo at Camp Dynnys had undeniably dropped. It was reflected everywhere he looked, from the rate of confessions from inmates to the catastrophic drop in summary judgments written up by his agents inquisitor as they sifted the evidence. They were careful to cover themselves by filling in all the blanks, dotting all the "i"s and crossing all the "t"s. They'd suddenly rediscovered all the petty legalisms Inquisitor General Wylbyr and the Grand Inquisitor himself had set aside in the face of the mortal threat the Charisian-spawned heresy posed to Mother Church and God's plan for all the world. It was the tactic of a law master more interested in sterile legalisms than the true purpose of the law, yet it gave them cover—at least until the Inquisitor General, Archbishop Wyllym, or the Grand Inquisitor denounced it—and at the moment, they were actually more afraid of the "*seijins*" then they were of Mother Church and the Inquisition.

And what truly stoked the vitriol of his fury was that deep, dark, never-admitted awareness that *he* was just as terrified of Dialydd Mab as any of them were.

*If I order Tymahk to arrest him, the bastard's likely to refuse. He'll say Mohmohtahny hasn't done anything against the Army's regulations. And he'll point out that that's why I have inquisitors. And that's the rub, isn't it? Because I* do *have agents inquisitor who would be required by their vows to obey me and arrest the little prick . . . and they might not do it.*

It was unlikely anyone would be stupid enough to defy him openly. Certainly not when word of their defiance would inevitably reach the Grand Inquisitor or Zion! But every single one of them would try to find a way to make sure someone *else* arrested Mohmohtahny and—at least in theory—nominated himself for Dialydd Mab's next bullet. The order would be passed along, misfiled, conveniently overlooked, or anything else they could think of to delay the inevitable. Eventually, Mohmohtahny *would* be arrested and almost certainly sent to the Punishment, but the simple fact that it would take days—possibly five-days—would undercut Zhynkyns' authority far more seriously than Mohmohtahny's present actions possibly could.

Unless the bishop wanted to *personally* arrest the Pasqualate. That would be one way to avoid that potentially poisonous delay.

And if Dialydd Mab truly existed—which he did—and if his demonic familiars carried word of Zhynkyns' actions to him—which they might—then *Maikel Zhynkyns'* name might just appear on one of the notes

Mab and his fellows left behind them, sealed in the blood of inquisitors.

The bishop drew a deep, steadying breath.

"Father Aizak," he said, "Mother Church is at war, and not just any war. This is *Jihad*, a battle for her very survival and for the souls of every man, woman, and child ever born or ever to *be* born. I understand the distinction you're making between the accused heretic and the *convicted* heretic, but this is no time for legal niceties or for false kindness which ultimately encourages the heretic to cling to his heresy rather than renounce it and seek the welcoming arms of God. If you persist in these activities, if you persist in going beyond your responsibilities to your comrades in the Army of God, then I will have no choice but to present my report on your actions—and their probable consequences— to the Inquisitor General himself. I don't think he'd find that report pleasant reading . . . or that you'd find his reaction to it particularly pleasant, either. Do you understand me, Father?"

"Of course, My Lord."

There might have been a tiny flicker of fear—or uneasiness, at least—in Mohmohtahny's eyes, but the young Pasqualate only nodded.

"Then go and consider very carefully what I've said to you today," Zhynkyns said icily, trying to pretend to himself that he hadn't just kicked the can down the road rather than dealing with it. "I would advise you most earnestly not to find yourself standing before me for the same reason again."

He held Mohmohtahny's gaze for a slow, measured ten-count. Then he nodded coldly.

"That will be all, Father."

. XIX .
Euyrtyn,
and
The Sheryl-Seridahn Canal,
The South March,
Republic of Siddarmark

*"Shit!"*

Private Lairy Ghanzalvez cowered in the bottom of his muddy hole as the rumbling, *ripping* sound of heretic shells snarled overhead. They sounded for all the world like a sail splitting in a high wind. That was a sound Ghanzalvez had heard the one time he'd been foolish enough to venture out to sea on his brother-in-law's fishing boat to trawl the Dohlar Bank. The memory of that stormy disaster—he and the brother-in-law in question had spent two days clinging to the keel of their overturned vessel before another trawler found them—was why he'd sworn he'd never go to sea again.

At the moment, a mere hurricane would have been a welcome diversion, however.

The shells sizzled onward, then hammered Ghanzalvez' bones with the shock of their explosions. The red-cored eruptions shattered the already battered church upon whose steeple one of Baron Traylmyn's signal parties had mounted their flagstaff. Shingles, bits and pieces of carved angels and archangels, sparkling shards of stained glass, and jagged chunks of building stone flew up and out in a fiery whirlwind, then crashed back in a lethal rain of debris, and the private clasped both hands over his helmeted head in a frail effort at self-protection.

There were bits and pieces of what had once been signalmen in that pattering, thumping deluge of wreckage, and Ghanzalvez tried—he really *tried*—not to think it served them right. He'd been none too pleased by the signal party commander's decision to use one of God's churches that way. He'd told himself he was being unreasonable. Surely God wouldn't mind, given who they were fighting against. It had still gone against the grain . . . and the fact that the church was barely two hundred yards west of his own position hadn't made him one bit happier. Shan-wei knew the heretic gunners were fiendishly accurate, but they weren't perfect shots, and he'd seen what one of that ironclad vessel's heavy shells could do when it landed right on top of a man's position.

And judging by what had just happened to the church in question, maybe God *had* objected to having one of His houses dragged into the middle of a war. Ghanzalvez couldn't think of any other explanation for how no less than three of the heretics' shells could have struck the same building in a single salvo. It was ridiculous! No one's artillery was that accurate, and—

The heretic guns thundered again, and that was another thing. Heavy cannon weren't supposed to be able to shoot that quickly, damn it! None of the Royal Dohlaran Army's could, anyway.

Apparently the heretic gunners didn't realize they'd already destroyed the church, he thought, trying to burrow still deeper as more explosions filled the universe. One was short of its target, and he swore again as shell splinters hissed through the air above his hole. One of those splinters actually sizzled *into* his hole and buried itself in the muddy dirt less than a foot from the private's right ear.

At the moment, a corner of Ghanzalvez' brain reflected, that fishing boat and that hurricane were sounding better and better. Almost homey, in fact.

▼ ▼ ▼

Whatever the limits of rifled guns' effective ranges on the high seas, they could shoot a long, long way against targets that didn't move. The Army's rifled angle-guns had already demonstrated that. And whatever other warships might do, HMS *Delthak* had been specifically designed *not* to fight on blue water. Brown water was her home, and as her engines throbbed gently, driving her propellers just hard enough to maintain her position against the Seridahn's current, she was a perfect, stationary gun platform.

She couldn't elevate her guns as high as the angle-guns, so her maximum range was lower than it might have been, but at this moment, every inch of Evyrtyn was within her seven-mile reach. And that meant that any target Earl Hanth's artillery support parties could see, Bahrns' ship could destroy.

"Signal from Colonel Ovyrtyn, Sir!" Ahbukyra Matthysahn announced.

Halcom Bahrns lowered his double-glass and turned his head to raise an eyebrow at the young petty officer.

"Support parties say 'Target destroyed,' Sir." Matthysahn spoke loudly enough to be heard through the earplugs they both wore, and Bahrns nodded, then looked over his shoulder through the open conning tower door.

"Cease fire!"

His order came too late to stop the next broadside, and he coughed as the dense brown cloud of smoke erupted across the open bridge wing. The concussion of the muzzle blast would have blown his hat off his head if he hadn't already removed it.

*You really don't have to be standing out here, you know*, he told himself. *In fact, it'd be a whole hell of a lot easier on you if you were smart enough to stay inside the conning tower with young Cahnyrs!*

Well, of course it would. He wouldn't have been able to see as well, and the interior of the conning tower left a little something to be desired in terms of comfort and breathability when the big guns were in action, but at least the armor would have prevented his feeling as if the Tellesberg Krakens had decided to use him for batting practice. All of that was true, yet it didn't really matter. He needed to be out here in the open, where he could see and hear. Where he could keep an eye out for obstacles in the water or any more of those powder kegs the Dohlarans had floated down the river to greet them.

"New target, Sir!" Matthysahn called out, peering at the shoreside signal party through a rail-mounted telescope he could steady with his good hand, and Captain Bahrns nodded with a smile of grim satisfaction.

▼ ▼ ▼

"Is this confirmed?" Sir Fahstyr Rychtyr asked, looking up from the semaphore dispatch. "*That* far?"

He stood on a hilltop above the Sheryl-Seridahn Canal, fifteen miles west of Evyrtyn, where the mounted courier had overtaken his small party. The wind was out of the west—again—and powerful enough to roar quietly through the leafless trees and winter grass, which probably explained why none of them had heard anything.

"I'm afraid it is, Sir," Colonel Mohrtynsyn said grimly, then glanced at Rychtyr's aide. "We need the Evyrtyn artillery map, Zhulyo."

"Of course, Sir." Lieutenant Zhulyo Gohzail thumbed quickly through the maps in his case for the one Mohrtynsyn wanted. "Here, Sir," he said, kneeling on the damp grass to spread the large-scale map. He weighted its corners with handy pebbles, and Rychtyr went down on one knee to look at it.

"Colonel Wykmyn isn't just guessing at the range, Sir." Mohrtynsyn, who headed Rychtyr's headquarters staff, drew his sword and used it as a pointer. "He's confirmed that the heretic ironclad is right here." He touched a point on the map, two-thirds of the way across the six-hundred-yard-wide river. "And he's also confirmed that it's not only destroyed the signal mast in Evyrtyn but also taken this twelve-pounder battery right here under fire." The sword tip tapped again, and his expression was grim when he looked up at his general. "They must have observers out somewhere who can see it, because the gunners aboard that ship sure as Shan-wei can't. But we don't have any idea where those observers are or what *else* they may be able to see."

Sir Fahstyr's jaw tightened. He glared down at the map for a moment, nodded, and stood once more. One hand brushed at the damp patch on his knee; the other had clenched around his own sword hilt. His eyes were unfocused for several seconds, staring at something only he could see. Then he drew a deep, nostril-flaring breath, and turned to the Schuelerite upper-priest at his elbow.

"It's even worse than I feared, Father," he said in a flat, toneless voice.

"What do you mean, my son?" Father Pairaik Metzlyr, the Army of the Seridahn's special intendant, looked back at him with a worried expression. "Surely we knew the heretics would bring every weapon to bear on Evyrtyn?"

"Of course we did, Father." Rychtyr nodded. "And we saw what that meant at Cheryk and above Trevyr."

Metzlyr's expression went from worried to bitter and it was his turn to nod. They had, indeed, seen what HMS *Delthak*'s guns could do at point-blank range. None of Major Sylvstyr's guns had survived to withdraw from his riverbank redoubt, yet so far as anyone knew, the ironclad, with its preposterously long-barreled cannon, hadn't lost a man, and it had continued to pour fire ashore afterward. Rychtyr's army had managed to retreat without disintegrating only because of the general's forethought in blocking the navigable channel with successive chains of sunken canal barges. He'd still suffered heavy casualties, and three of his regiments had sacrificed themselves holding the Marines Hanth had thrown across the river to cut off the rest of his army's retreat. But at least the blocked channel had prevented the infernal ironclad from continuing its bombardment once he disengaged and managed to fall back upriver towards Evyrtyn.

"I knew they'd come calling as soon as they cleared the obstacles," Rychtyr continued now, his voice heavy. "I'd hoped it would take longer than it did. Or that we might have gotten lucky with the explosion rafts."

The inquisitor nodded again, this time hard and

choppy—and not because he was angry at Rychtyr or the pessimism in the general's voice.

The thinly veiled contempt for Rychtyr's judgment which had permeated the late Duke of Harless' dispatches had infuriated Metzlyr. Given how spectacularly Harless had marched into the jaws of annihilation with an army six or seven times the size of Rychtyr's, the Desnairian duke's contempt should be considered a badge of honor!

True, Rychtyr's Cheryk garrison had been surprised by the heretics' sudden attack, but Cheryk had been demoted to little more than a forward screening post for Thesmar when General Ahlverez turned the St. Alyk into his primary supply route. Manning Cheryk heavily enough to stave off a serious attack from the south would have required reducing the Trevyr garrison to no more than four or five thousand men, and Rychtyr had decided it was more important to be certain he held what had become the Army of Shiloh's most vital supply point. With luck, the screening force Harless had detached for that specific purpose would keep Hanth and his heretics penned up in Thesmar and he would hold both; if he had to lose one of them, however, the one he (and General Ahlverez) simply *could not* afford to surrender was Trevyr. Not only that, but if the Imperial Charisian Navy ever got loose on the river, Trevyr itself was only too likely to prove impossible to hold, at which point any troops deployed east of it—like at Cheryk, for example—would be cut off and doomed.

The Desnairians, predictably, had turned up their noses and ridiculed their Dohlaran allies' timidity. They'd been at least reasonably careful not to express their views of Rychtyr's feckless cowardice openly, but Metzlyr and his fellow inquisitors heard everything, sooner or later. And in fairness, the Desnairians had had at least some justification for pointing out how important Cheryk was to *their* supply line. And if he was going to be honest, the intendant had to admit that even he had thought the general was being ... overly cautious, perhaps. The Seridahn, after all, was too shallow for the heretics' galleons or their accursed bombardment ships, and he hadn't quite been able to bring himself to believe the preposterous stories about smoking, self-propelled ships sheathed in iron even after the devastation of Bishop Militant Bahrnabai's communications.

But Rychtyr had been right . . . again.

No one was any too certain how the heretics had managed to blow a gap in that first river barrier north of Trevyr, but Rychtyr had already erected a second one farther north. There'd been less laughter about that one . . . and no laughter at all once the second row of sunken barges prevented the ironclad from steaming straight past and shelling the Army of the Seridahn as it retreated along the tow paths and country lanes which followed the river north.

Nor had the general settled for purely defensive measures, and the explosion rafts should have accomplished more than they had. Certainly the men who'd come forward, volunteering for the hazardous duty, had tackled their assignment with all the faith and courage the Archangels could have asked for, and conditions had seemed close to perfect. The night of the attack had been cloudy, rainy, cold, and moonless. The ten rafts—plank platforms laid across floating barrels—had each been loaded with half a ton of gunpowder, painted black, and smeared with pitch, both to make them harder to see and to protect the powder kegs from rain and riverwater, and they'd drifted with the current like darker, solider chunks of the night. Each raft had been manned by half a dozen men, working the stern sweeps and guiding the small flotilla towards its target. If even one of them had managed to get alongside the ironclad and detonate, it ought to have inflicted severe, probably crippling, and possibly fatal damage.

But the heretics had anchored a heavy boom between a trio of barges upstream from the anchored warship, and they'd positioned field guns and those infernal infantry angle-guns to cover the boom. Even worse, perhaps, they'd put riflemen aboard the barges, ready to sweep the river's surface with bullets, and one of their accursed illuminating rockets had burst overhead, revealing the rafts with pitiless clarity while they were still two hundred yards short of the boom. None of them had survived. The best the sixty men who'd given their lives for God and Mother Church had been able to do was to sink one of the boom-anchoring barges.

And now this.

Rychtyr had placed yet another barrier across the river below Evyrtyn, but the heretic engineers continued to show Shan-wei's own demonic energy. Heretic infantry, probing up the river, covered and supported by the ironclad's guns, had secured the eastern bank and dug in to provide their engineers with cover as they labored to clear the river. Despite more rain, fog, and the iciness of the riverwater, they'd dealt with the barrier—blown it to pieces just like the others, actually—in a bare two days, ripping yet another gap for the ironclad to creep through. And then, of course, Rychtyr's forward regiments had been forced to withdraw into the Evyrtyn entrenchments. Where . . . .

"Father, they're accurately engaging targets over three miles back from the river," Rychtyr said into the Schuelerite's thoughts. "To be honest, we don't have any way of knowing they can't reach even farther than that, and unless they screw up and let us get an explosion raft through after all, there's not a single thing we can do to stop that damned ship from systematically destroying all of the town's defenses." He met the upper-priest's eyes levelly. "By itself, the ironclad can't take Evyrtyn away from us. Hanth's *army*, though—that's another matter. And what the ironclad *can* do—what it's already *doing*—is massacre any artillery we try to use to defend the town. Our entrenchments offer good protection against rifle fire, but they're weak enough against field guns and infantry angles. Against the kind of fire that ironclad can hand out, they're death traps.

They'll knock out our own artillery so their infantry can get close enough to take us under fire with their angle-guns. They'll keep our men's heads down with their angles and field artillery, then work their troops forward until they can storm our trenches with grenades and bayonets. I can bleed them, but nowhere near as badly as *they* can bleed *us*, and you've read the dispatches from Gorath."

Metzlyr's face tightened, for he had, indeed, read the dispatches. It was unlikely Sir Rainos Ahlverez would ever reach home; it was even more unlikely more than a handful of the Army of Shiloh's troops would be with him if he did. The Royal Dohlaran Army had suffered catastrophic losses, and the stark truth was that the Army of the Seridahn was the only field force it had left. Duke Salthar and Duke Fern were laboring frantically to rebuild, calling up thousands of militia and enlisting even more thousands of new recruits. But while the militia could be integrated into existing, understrength regiments stationed at home in Dohlar, and while the depot companies each of the field regiments had left behind to train replacements could be expanded into full regiments in their own rights, *equipping* that militia would be a far harder task. And raising, training, *and* equipping entirely new regiments would be harder still. The ugly truth was that neither the Jihad nor the Kingdom of Dohlar could afford to lose the Army of the Seridahn. For that matter, they could no longer afford to exchange casualties with the heretics even on a one-for-one basis.

"What, exactly, are you proposing, my son?"

"Father, we *must* retreat from Evyrtyn. We have to get far enough from the river to be outside the range of the ironclad's guns, and we must destroy the locks behind us so that it can't follow us along the canal."

To his credit, Rychtyr's tone was completely level and he met Metzlyr's gaze squarely.

"And how far will be far enough, my son?" the Schuelerite asked softly.

"I can't say for certain," Rychtyr admitted, still holding Metzlyr's gaze. "I wouldn't've believed they could reach targets three miles from the riverbank, frankly. As it is, I think we have to assume they still have additional range in reserve. Operating on that assumption, I believe we should fall back for at least five miles."

"Five miles?" Metzlyr couldn't hide his dismay, but Rychtyr only nodded.

"At *least* five miles," he emphasized. "Father, giving additional ground to the heretics has to be disappointing to anyone. On the other hand, we're still over three hundred miles from the Dohlaran border. In my opinion, our best option at this time is to keep the canal open behind us but deny the heretics the use of it in *front* of us and be willing to retreat along it if they press us. With your permission, I'd like to request additional civilian laborers. At the moment, we don't have enough weapons to equip large numbers of new troops, but civilians can wield shovels as well as trained soldiers. If we have the workforce available, we can throw up an entire succession of strong points between Evyrtyn and the border—entrenchments and field works we can withdraw into at need."

"But if we fall back far enough to beyond reach of the ironclad's artillery . . . ."

"Father, the heretics have destroyed the Army of Shiloh. They didn't simply defeat it or drive it back—they *destroyed* it. That means every regiment they had tied down against Duke Harless and Sir Rainos is available to be used *somewhere else*." Rychtyr's face was carved out of iron. "If I were Eastshare or Cayleb or Stohnar, that 'somewhere else' would be driving directly along the canal and into Dohlar. Admittedly, I'm a Dohlaran, so perhaps that course of action seems more obvious to me than it will to them. After all, there's Silkiah and the Salthar Canal to the south, and there's also the Army of Glacierheart to the north. Either of those would certainly constitute worthwhile strategic objectives, and much as it pains me to admit it, it'll be months—probably even next year—before the Kingdom can field another army powerful enough to threaten the heretics."

He did not, Metzlyr noticed, comment on the Charisian galleons currently rampaging through the western reaches of the Gulf of Dohlar. Exactly what the heretics intended to do once they finished ravaging the coasts of Harchong remained to be seen, but no one expected it to be good for King Rahnyld. And if the Charisians could put together yet another army, one that could be transported east from Chisholm rather than west from Charis . . . .

"Very well, my son," the upper-priest said heavily. He reached out and laid a hand on Rychtyr's shoulder. "I know how little you must relish giving ground, whatever the strategic wisdom in doing so." He squeezed the general's shoulder, looking into his eyes. "I also know the courage it's taken for you to be this honest with me. And I agree about the need to fall back immediately. For that matter, I agree with the wisdom of your larger plan. I can't promise anything about the reaction in Gorath—or in Zion—when they hear your proposal, but I *can* promise you this: when they hear it, it won't be *your* proposal, it will be *ours.*"

"Thank you, Father." Rychtyr couldn't keep the gratitude out of his tone. For that matter, he didn't even try. He stood for a moment, looking back at the Schuelerite, then turned to Mohrtynsyn and Gohzail. "I think we'd better be climbing back into the saddle," he told them, his voice harsh. "We've got some orders to write, so we'd best get back to headquarters and get started."

. XX .
# Wyllym Rayno's Office,
# The Temple,
# City of Zion,
# and
# Nimue's Cave,
# Mountains of Light,
# The Temple Lands

Wyllym Rayno, Archbishop of Chiang-wu, frowned at Father Allayn Wynchystair. It was unlike the upper-priest to enter his office without arranging an appointment ahead of time.

Wynchystair managed to look nondescript even in his inquisitor's cassock; when he'd been an under-priest, that ability to fade into the background had served him well as an agent inquisitor who'd specialized in covert operations. These days, he spent most of his time in an office three doors down the hall from Rayno's own, and the record of successes which had put him in that office had also dumped responsibility for combating the "Fist of Kau-Yung" upon him.

From the expression on his face, he hadn't called upon the Inquisition's adjutant to announce a glorious success.

"I'm afraid you should see this, Your Eminence," Wynchystair said. One of his virtues was a willingness to bring bad news to his superiors without trying to dress it up in more palatable clothing. "We lost another agent inquisitor last night—a sexton assigned to the Vicar Sebahstean murder." His lips tightened. "That's bad enough, but they found this pinned to his cassock. It was brought to me still sealed and unopened. I took it upon myself to open it when I saw that it was addressed to you, however, in case its contents suggested there might be other information I should bring to you at the same time."

He extended an envelope marked with ominous reddish-brown stains.

Rayno looked at it for a moment. Those sorts of envelopes had become unhappily common over the past several months. The rest of them, however, had been left with inquisitors operating in Siddarmark, not right here in Zion.

"What was our man doing before he was killed?" he asked.

"According to his last report, he was looking into the possibility that the assassins"—even Wynchystair hesitated to use the term "Fist of Kau-Yung" in conversation with his superior—"had suborned one of the Vicar's bodyguards. The one who simply disappeared following the attack."

"And?"

"And as nearly as I can reconstruct it, he'd gone to speak with an informant without taking any backup." Wynchystair shook his head wearily. "I've warned all my men to be insanely cautious about that sort of thing, Your Eminence. But the truth is, if they want to turn up the information we need, they have to take chances."

Rayno grimaced in agreement. It hadn't always been that way, yet the Fist of Kau-Yung's record of successes—and its ability to vanish like smoke after one of its attacks—required riskier tactics. Worse, the Inquisition couldn't resort to open searches and manhunts without admitting to Zion's citizenry in general that someone was systematically assassinating the Grand Inquisitor's allies in the vicarate. And as long as they had to operate in the shadows, without drawing attention to the threat . . . .

"Understood," he said and, finally, held out his hand. He unfolded the letter, and his face tightened as he read it.

*To Wyllym Rayno, Archbishop of Chiang-wu and traitor to God:*

*This is to inform you that Brother Vyktyr will file no more reports about Vicar Sebahstean's unfortunate demise. We were tempted to send him back to you alive, lest you replace him with someone competent. Instead, however, we take this opportunity to inform you that your own security is less than perfect. Last Thursday, when you visited St. Evyryt's, you entered by the eastern door, as you always do. If you send one of your agents inquisitor to check, you will discover a twenty-pound charge of powder in the crypt below the walkway you used. We can't imagine how it might have gotten there.*

*While the attitude which has led your subordinates to dub us "the Fist of Kau-Yung" is no doubt flattering, we prefer another, more accurate designation. And so we inform you that, in time, the Fist of God will come for you as we have already come for so many of Zhaspahr Clyntahn's corrupt and venal tools in the vicarate. For now, however, it best suits our purposes to leave you exactly where you are . . . for the same reason we were tempted to send Brother Vyktyr back to you alive.*

Rayno made himself read it completely through a second time, then refolded it with meticulous care and laid it neatly on his blotter.

"This is a new departure," he observed in a toneless voice.

"It is, Your Eminence." Wynchystair nodded. "And there are three things about it which concern me most deeply."

He paused, and Rayno waved for him to continue.

"First, I did send three of our agents inquisitor to Saint Evyryt's, and I'm afraid they found the gunpowder exactly where the heretics said we would. Whether it was there *Thursday* or not is more than we can say at this point, but in my judgment, it would be wise to assume it was. In either case, Your Eminence, they're much too well informed about your own movements, even if only after the fact. I think we're going to have to begin taking greater precautions to ensure your safety. No doubt that's exactly what they want us to do, but I don't see that we have any other option."

Rayno's nod was noncommittal, an invitation to continue rather than a sign of agreement, but deep inside the archbishop felt a stab of fresh dismay. The Inquisition had been forced to take a more and more open role in policing Zion and the Temple. Officially that was because the Temple Guard had been cut to the bone to find the men the Army of God required, yet the real reason had been to be sure of the Inquisition's grip upon the city of God on earth. The regular city guard knew better than to challenge the Order of Schueler's authority, but the Grand Inquisitor had decided it was time to make sure of that. As for the Temple Guard, the Inquisition knew who its friends were within its ranks, and on Zhaspahr Clyntahn's orders, Rayno had assigned special intendants to the *Guard* as well as the regular army. Every bit of armed force in Zion was firmly under the Inqusition's control . . . and *still* the heretics had murdered Brother Vyktyr and gotten their gunpowder into Saint Evyryt's!

"Second," Wynchystair continued, "the fact that they know our agents inquisitor have begun referring to them, at least among themselves, as the Fist of Kau-Yung is troubling. There might be several explanations for how they came by that knowledge. I think, however, that we must assume they do, indeed, still have agents of their own in the ranks of the Inquisition. It's entirely possible that, as in the case of tightening your own security, that's exactly what they *want* us to assume. Unfortunately, I don't believe we have any other choice.

"But, third, Your Eminence—and what concerns me the most, frankly—is the way in which this note to you emulates the ones the false *seijins* have been leaving at the scenes of *their* crimes. It seems to me that this is a clear-cut declaration that this 'Fist of God' is in—or has entered into—a direct alliance with 'Dialydd Mab' and his accomplices."

Rayno considered Wynchystair's analysis for several moments, his expression far calmer than the icy fury and—little though he cared to admit it even to himself—the fear behind it. And then, slowly, he nodded.

"As usual, you've cut straight to the heart of the matter, Father Allayn." He picked up the letter and returned it to the upper-priest. "File this in the Level One files, but have a single copy of it made and returned to me first. No one other than your own document clerk is to see it or know of its contents."

"Of course, Your Eminence." Wynchystair tucked the letter into the sleeve of his cassock and folded his hands before him. "And then, Your Eminence?"

"And then I want you to begin a point-by-point consideration of my own and—especially—Vicar Zhaspahr's security. Clearly, this 'Fist of God' wants us to be . . . anxious about our safety. As you say, however, their accomplishments to date leave us no option but to take them seriously."

"I'll discuss that with Bishop Markys this very afternoon, Your Eminence. I'll take Father Byrtrym along to be sure he's briefed in, as well. I'm sure the Bishop will want his input," Wynchystair said, and Rayno nodded.

Markys Gohdard was one of Rayno's senior deputies, charged with the supervision and coordination of his own and Zhaspahr Clyntahn's personal security. Byrtrym Zhansyn had been one of Wynchystair's best agents inquisitor until he'd been wounded in a Fist of Kau-Yung ambush which had killed two other agents inquisitor. Zhansyn had been left for dead when the Temple Guard responded to the sound of the shooting. His injuries had left him with a permanent limp, and the fact that the terrorists had obviously figured out who he truly was had taken him out of the field. Since then, he'd been attached to Gohdard as Wynchystair's personal liaison.

"Good," the archbishop said. "And as soon as you've done that, Allayn, I want a complete analysis of this Brother Vyktyr's files. I want every report he ever wrote, and I want every agent inquisitor he ever worked with interviewed. I want to know exactly who he might have interrogated or interviewed about Vicar Sebahstean's assassination. It's most likely he got too close to something the heretics don't want us to know about, but it's remotely possible that something else—something that may have happened *years* ago but which they were afraid he or his superiors might put together—was behind it. Whatever it was, I want it found."

"Understood, Your Eminence." Wynchystair bowed, his nondescript face iron-hard. "If it's there to find, we'll find it for you."

▼ ▼ ▼

Snow fell silently, sifting onto the sidewalks of Mylycynt Court without the cutting winds which so often swept through the streets of Zion. Ahrloh Mahkbyth gazed out at it through the front window of his quietly elegant shop, watching the thick flakes settle as gently—and coldly—as a false lover's kiss. It was already dark and growing quickly darker. Other shops' windows glowed with lamplight, and he smoothed his guardsman's mustache with one index finger as he considered the time.

He wasn't as much a stickler as some of his fellow merchants about exactly when he closed shop, especially in the winter. His clientele was extremely well-heeled, including many members of the episcopate and more than a few vicars. Not that he often saw such exalted individuals in person here in the shop; that was what servants and wine stewards were for. He did see quite a few priests and upper-priests, though. He supposed some of that was a case of ambitious members of Mother Church's hierarchy being eager to be seen patronizing the "right" shops, but mostly it was because he was one of the half-dozen best in the entire city of Zion at his trade.

The fact that he was also an honorably retired Temple Guardsman didn't hurt, but he'd always had a refined palate. Twenty-two years ago, shortly after his son's death, he'd used the generous pension the Guard had extended to him, along with his savings and loans from a few people who'd believed in him, to open Mahkbyth's Fine Spirits and Wines.

He smiled—briefly—at the memory. Even his wife, Zhulyet, who'd loved him dearly, had been convinced he'd lost his mind. And, truth to tell, in some ways he'd come pretty close to doing just that after Dahnyld's death. But he'd proved the doubters wrong, and while the first major customers he'd secured might have been . . . ladies of negotiable virtue, their enthusiastic recommendation to their own clients had brought Ahrloh to the attention of his present ordained and quite often excessively wealthy customers.

He'd stayed in touch with his old comrades in arms, as well. At sixty-one, his physique remained powerful, kept that way by rigorous exercise that included regular fencing bouts with several current members of the Temple Guard. A dozen of his old friends had risen to senior rank in the last two decades, and he doubted their recommendations hurt his prospects with their ecclesiastic superiors, either. Whatever the explanation, business was brisk despite the unsettled times and life was about as good as a childless widower could have asked for.

On the positive side, Mahkbyth's Fine Spirits and Wines showed a very comfortable cash flow. Indeed, one of the reasons his hours could be as flexible as they were was that so many of his sales were special orders, with the price tags that implied these days. Perhaps even *especially* these days, since his cellars were deep and he'd laid in an extensive collection of the harder-to-get brands—especially from Chisholm—before the embargo had shut down legal commerce with the heretical Out Islands. There were some, mostly competitors, who suggested—quietly—that at least a few of those bottles and casks had found their way to Zion *after* the embargo was declared, but no one paid much heed to such libelous accusations. The mere thought that such illustrious individuals as Vicar Zahmsyn Trynair, Mother Church's own Chancellor, would patronize a common *smuggler* was preposterous! Why, even the Grand Inquisitor's wine steward had been known to nip into Mahkbyth's shop for the odd bottle of Vicar Zhaspahr's favorite Old Mykalym Grand Reserve, the single thing about Chisholm which had somehow escaped the Inquisition's anathematization.

On the negative side, when one of his special customers requested him to remain open a little later, he didn't really have much choice. Those sorts of people were accustomed to special treatment. They tended to get . . . surly when they didn't receive it, and the last thing anyone in Zion needed these days was to have high-ranking clergymen irked with him.

No one of such august stature had made any such request tonight, though, and so he stood there, watching the lights and thinking about the past, about his vanished family, about the future which would never have them in it, and about the things which made that future worthwhile anyway. A snow lizard-drawn trolley car rolled noisily past, the draft lizard's breath jetting like smoke, and he wondered how low the temperature was going to dip. Some of his fellow shopkeepers began to shutter their windows for the night, and the snow fell a little faster, and he stood there, watching it.

The bright, cheerful jingle of the silver bell above the shop's door was so sudden that Ahrloh twitched in surprise. Then he shook himself, straightened the subdued but well-tailored tunic that went with his professional standing, and turned to greet the last-minute customer.

"Good evening, Father."

"And good evening to you, Master Mahkbyth," the newcomer replied. He was a solidly built man, thirteen years younger and an inch or so taller than Ahrloh, who wore the purple-badged cassock of a Schuelerite priest under his heavy coat and carried a cane in his right hand. "I apologize for arriving so late, but I was delayed at the office."

"It's not a problem," Ahrloh assured him. "I was just standing here, watching the snow. Besides," his lips twitched a fleeting smile, "there's no one waiting for me to get home by any set time. Well, no one except my housekeeper, and she's used to my . . . irregular habits, let's say."

"If you're sure I'm not keeping you?"

"Well, to be honest, you are, Father." Ahrloh smiled at him. "As I just said, though, my time's my own, and you're one of my better customers. In fact, I only wish you could afford the *really* expensive brands."

"Ouch!" The priest raised his free left hand in a gesture of surrender. "You're already my greatest single monthly expense, Master Mahkbyth!"

"It's always a pity when the demands of someone's palette exceed the reach of his purse," Ahrloh observed with another smile, this one more of a grin, and glanced over his shoulder at Zhak Myllyr, his senior employee.

"I think the snow's going to pile deeper tonight than we expected, Zhak," he said. "If it does, the trolleys won't be running much longer, and you'll have a fair walk home in the cold. Why don't you go ahead and start now?"

"Are you sure, Master Mahkbyth?" Myllyr was about the priest's age, with hair and eyes as brown as the apron he wore. "I don't mind staying till closing."

"Oh, don't be silly!" Ahrloh waved dismissively. "You've already swept, there's no dust anywhere I *can* see it, and I can close up just fine. And unlike me, you've got a wife and two children still at home waiting to make your life miserable—or maybe *my* life miserable—if you're late getting home. On the other hand, if I decide to, I can easily bed down here for the night. That's why I've got the cot in the office, isn't it? Mistress Gyzail doesn't start my supper till she sees me coming this time of year, and if I don't turn up, she'll feed Chestyr for me before she turns in herself. Two good things about cat-lizards: they'll eat dry food, and they don't need to be let out as long as there's a pan handy. Of course, he'll make my life Shan-wei's own hell *tomorrow* night, but every so often a man has to remind his cat-lizard who's in charge."

Myllyr snorted, then shook his head and began removing his apron.

"In that case, I won't pretend I wouldn't like to get home while the trolleys are still running," he admitted. He hung the apron on a hook behind the counter; bundled into his coat, scarf, and gloves; and nodded to the priest. "Good night, Father."

"Good night, Zhak."

The bell jangled again as Myllyr disappeared into the gathering darkness, and the cleric turned back to Ahrloh.

"How do you manage to smile at him that cheerfully?" he asked, leaning on his cane.

"He's been with me for twelve years, and he really does know his spirits. He's worth every silver I pay him, and as for the rest—" Ahrloh shrugged. "I've had lots of practice. Besides, not all of Rayno's informants are evil at heart any more than all of Rayno's enemies are pure of heart."

"I suppose. Langhorne knows there are worse bastards out there," the Schuelerite acknowledged, and it was his turn to shrug. "I really am sorry to be dropping in on you this late, Ahrloh, but something's come up."

"That's what I figured when you sent your note around this afternoon," Ahrloh replied. "Let me lock up behind Zhak, then we'll go down into the cellar where we can talk and I'll pick you out a bottle of something nice in case anyone asks about it."

"Sounds good to me—you have so much better taste in these matters than I do, anyway."

"Byrtrym, with all due respect, I could scarcely have *worse* taste than you do! Everyone knows you've been trusting me to pick out your whiskeys for the last eight years."

"Yes, and I've been grateful to Arbalest ever since, even if you are a snob about it."

Ahrloh laughed, then twitched his head towards the cellar stairs.

"Should I assume this has something to do with that

little gift we left in the crypt at Saint Evyryt's?" he asked as he opened the door at the head of the stairs.

"You should indeed. In fact, it's had an . . . unanticipated consequence. Guess who Wynchystair's decided should coordinate with our esteemed Adjutant's and Grand Inquisitor's security staff?"

"Langhorne!" Ahrloh paused on the stairs, looking back over his shoulder, then whistled when the priest nodded. "Never saw that one coming." He shook his head. "Opens all sorts of possibilities, doesn't it?"

He started down the stairs again as he spoke, the priest following him, careful on his weakened right leg.

"Not as many as we might like," he said. "We could have gone ahead and gotten Rayno at Saint Evyryt's, you know. Now that he's been warned, he's going to be a lot more careful, and I'm only Wynchystair's liaison. It's not like I'm going to be involved in the day-to-day planning of his schedule, and you can be damned sure he and his bodyguards will be keeping that as close to their tunics as they can, especially after Saint Evyryt's."

"Point's not about killing Rayno—not yet, anyway," Ahrloh replied, turning up the wick on the lantern at the foot of the stair. "Mind you, I'd love to see the bastard dead, and his day'll come. But Arbalest's right. Killing Rayno before we get a clear shot at Clyntahn would produce the worst bloodbath Zion's ever seen—worse than when Clyntahn went after the Wylsynns and his other opponents in the vicarate. It would hurt the fat pig badly, at least for a while, but he'd find a replacement, and the cost to the innocent bystanders would be way too steep for such a short-term advantage. Scaring the shit out of all of them in the meantime's likely to be a lot more useful. Arbalest's right about that, too."

The priest nodded, albeit a bit grudgingly, and Ahrloh lit another lantern from the wick of the first and led the way down a narrow aisle between dusty bottles.

"Let's go get that bottle of the good stuff," he suggested. "In fact, let's get two of it. I think your news is worth cracking the seal for a wee dram or two of our own before you head back out into the ice and snow."

▼ ▼ ▼

"Hello, Stefyny."

Stefyny Mahlard opened her eyes at the sound of her name.

She was warm. That was her first thought, the very first thing she realized. She was *warm*, and her vision blurred as that blessed, glorious warmth flowed through her. And then she realized she wasn't hungry, either. And that she didn't hurt—not *anywhere*.

She blinked away the tears of gratitude and made her eyes focus.

She lay on a bed, warmer and more wonderfully comfortable than any bed she'd ever felt, in a nest of crisp, clean sheets and blankets. An arched stone ceiling soared above her, glassy smooth and gleaming as if it had been polished in the light of some sort of lamp. That had to be what it was, although she'd never imagined any lamp remotely like it.

A lady leaned over her—the most beautiful lady she'd ever seen—and a soft hand was gentle on her cheek.

"Are . . . are you an angel?"

Her voice sounded tiny, even to herself, and the lady smiled, then sat on the edge of the bed. The mattress didn't even dip, a corner of Stefyny's mind realized, and the lady shook her head.

"No, dearling." Her voice was as beautiful as her face. "No, I'm not an angel, and this isn't Heaven. I'm sure a girl like you will go there eventually, but not yet."

"I'm not dead?"

Somehow she felt almost disappointed, and she blushed as the lady laughed gently and smoothed the hair—the beautiful, clean, freshly washed hair—back from Stefyny's forehead.

"Not yet," she said. "And neither are your father and Sebahstean, although I'm afraid they're not awake yet.

I promise you, all of you are as safe as if you were cradled in the hand of God, but you and I need to talk for
a little bit before they wake up, all right?"

"All right," Stefyny agreed. It had to be a dream, she
thought. This couldn't possibly *really* be happening.
But if it was a dream, she hoped she would never, ever
wake up. "What do we need to talk about?"

"Well, that's just a *tiny* bit complicated, sweetheart.
First, though, I should introduce myself, I suppose."
The lady smoothed Stefyny's hair again, and smiled.

"You can call me Nynian," she said.

# APRIL
## YEAR OF GOD 897

·◆·

"What do you mean, you don't know where they are?" Zhaspahr Clyntahn glared at Allayn Maigwair. "How in Langhorne's name can you lose track of entire *armies?*"

It was evident from his tone, Rhobair Duchairn thought, that he'd found it very difficult not to insert the word "even" between the words "can" and "you."

"I could ask you how the Inquisition lost track of how many men were in the heretics' army to begin with," Maigwair shot back. "I believe you told us they couldn't have more than two hundred thousand men in the entire Charisian Army? And that they couldn't send more than a hundred thousand of them to Siddarmark without Corisande and Zebediah going up in rebellion behind them?"

"They were the best numbers I had!" Clyntahn snapped. "And," he added, rallying gamely, "Chisholm and Charis—*and* Corisande—are a hell of a lot farther away on the other side of a damned ocean. It's just a little harder to get accurate messages back and forth across all that saltwater!"

"Actually," Duchairn said in his most pacific voice, "the situation's a lot more similar than you seem to be suggesting, Zhaspahr."

Clyntahn's glare swiveled to the Treasurer.

"It's not saltwater that's the problem," Duchairn

continued. "It's distance . . . and snow. There never were many civilians in the South March, and most of them are gone now." He forced his tone to remain level and refrained from pointing out just whose fault that was. "The semaphores are down and there aren't any Faithful left to carry messages. As for the situation in Cliff Peak and the Sylmahn Gap, there are still at least a few people living in the area but the semaphore towers have been burned there, as well, and it's impossible for Allayn's people to patrol in the middle of winter. For that matter, they can't even get messengers through by courier half the time."

"Well, the *heretics* seem to be moving around like fleas on a griddle, snow or no snow," Clyntahn pointed out.

"Because they're better trained and—obviously—far better equipped for it than our people are," Maigwair said. "I doubt we would've trained our troops to the same extent, anyway, but the fact that we had to kick off the invasion before we'd had time to fully equip our regiments didn't help." His eyes met Clyntahn's hotly. "Rifles weren't the only thing we didn't have enough time to manufacture. Things like winter uniforms, skis, snowshoes, gloves, and boots would've been nice to have, too."

"Even stipulating that all of that's true," Zahmsyn Trynair interceded as Clyntahn's jaw muscles bunched, "the point at issue isn't how we got into this situation. It's trying to figure out what the heretics have in mind now that we're in it."

The Church's chancellor found himself in an uncomfortable position, outside the growing alliance between Duchairn and Maigwair and afraid to antagonize Clyntahn too openly. By the same token, though, he could sometimes act as a buffer between the others, and at the moment, Duchairn was grateful he could. The last thing they needed was to have the conversation segue back into another exchange over the "spontaneity" of the Sword of Schueler.

"That's true." The Treasurer jumped back in firmly.

"And the problem, Zhaspahr, is that we don't know, and we probably won't know for at least some time. And before you say anything else about that, I assure you that I'm no happier about our ignorance than you are. For that matter, I imagine Allayn's even unhappier than either of *us*!"

"Of course I am." Maigwair shook his head. "They've already demonstrated how dangerous it is to lose track of their formations. Admittedly, I doubt any of our remaining field commanders could match the towering pinnacle of incompetence Duke Harless managed to scale with the Army of Shiloh." Clyntahn's nostrils flared again, ever so slightly. He'd expected far more out of the Imperial Desnairian Army than Maigwair and Duchairn had warned him they were likely to get. "But even a competent general might've been surprised by the heretics' flank attack through southern Cliff Peak. And that's what worries me right now. Where *else* are the bastards headed?"

Duchairn considered the intricately detailed map on the council chamber's wall. It dated from the Temple's original construction, so many of those details were no longer accurate, but the markers indicating the positions of their own and the heretics' forces were placed with as much accuracy as mere mortals could attain.

"What's your best guess, Allayn?" he asked quietly.

"Well, the two places I'm pretty sure Eastshare *isn't* headed are Dohlar or Silkiah," the Captain General replied. "If he was headed for Dohlar, the Army of the Seridahn would already've been smashed. And—"

"Why d'you say that?" Clyntahn demanded.

From his tone, he was emotionally torn. Clyntahn had always regarded Dohlar with suspicion, given King Rahnyld's desire to emulate the Charisians' pre-Jihad wealth and merchant fleet. Deep inside, he continued to fundamentally distrust Dohlar's commitment to the Jihad, but at the same time, the kingdom had been, by almost any measure, Mother Church's most effective secular ally.

"Because he only has about forty-five thousand men,

even with all the reinforcements Duke Salthar's been able to scrape up. He's got maybe eight or nine thousand of the new rifles—the original Dohlaran design, not the one from Saint Kylmahn's—and a grand total of eleven of the new rifled artillery pieces. By our most conservative estimate, Eastshare must've had a hundred thousand men, all of his infantry armed with breech-loading rifles, and hundreds of field guns, not to mention those damned portable angle-guns of theirs." Maigwair raised both hands in front of him. "What do *you* think would have happened to Rychtyr if Eastshare had brought all of that along to reinforce Hanth, Zhaspahr?"

Clyntahn looked at him a moment longer, then grunted in irritated concession, and Maigwair shrugged.

"So, as I say, he's not headed for Dohlar. And if he were headed for Silkiah, he'd already be there, especially with the grip the heretic navy's established on the Gulf of Mathyas and the Gulf of Jahras. They could easily supply him by water, and, for that matter, they could put his troops aboard ship and land them anywhere along the grand duchy's coast, if that was what they had in mind. Mind you, I imagine they're going to do that as soon as they get around to it, anyway. I'm only saying it's clear to me that whatever else they have in mind for the immediate future is more important than the Grand Duchy is."

And that, Duchairn thought, was worrisome. Conquering Silkiah would deprive the Church of the rifles being produced in the grand duchy, which would represent a painful loss. Loss of the Salthar Canal would be more than merely painful, however. The Imperial Charisian Navy had already shut down its eastern terminus by moving their armored bombardment ships into Silkiah Bay and demolishing the defending batteries. They'd left a blockade squadron to make sure nothing moved out of the Salthar into the bay, and the heretic Hanth's capture of the town of Somyr had shut down the northern terminus of the Silk Town-Thesmar Canal, as well. There was a difference between losing the use of those transportation links for Mother Church's own use and losing them *to* the heretics' use, though.

They'd have to take the entire grand duchy to really control the Salthar, he reminded himself. And even if they did, the Dohlaran Navy was firmly in control of Salthar Bay at its western end.

*For* now, *that is*, he amended, thinking about the heretics' "steam-powered" ironclads. They had reports of at least six of them now, and Clyntahn's agents inquisitor promised still more would be arriving over the next several months.

"What worries me most," he admitted to the others, "is that I can think of only one target anywhere near the South March that might be more valuable to them than either knocking Dohlar out of the Jihad or securing a direct transportation link between Silkiah Bay and the Gulf of Dohlar."

"The Army of Glacierheart," Maigwair said flatly with a curt nod. "That's got to be where they're headed, even if we haven't seen them yet. I ordered Kaitswyrth to patrol as aggressively as he can, but I have somewhat less than lively faith in just how much aggressiveness he has left after last summer." Clyntahn's eyes narrowed for a moment, but the Captain General shrugged. "At the same time, I do have to admit that the snow's pretty damned deep in northern Cliff Peak and Westmarch, too," he said, instead of renewing the argument about relieving Kaitswyurth.

"Tell him to send that arsehole Hennet," Clyntahn growled, with an expression which boded ill for the Army of Justice's one-time cavalry commander.

"I'd love to." Maigwair's tone showed an increasingly unusual heartfelt agreement with the Grand Inquisitor. "Unfortunately, Zhamsyn won't let me."

Clyntahn looked at the chancellor, who shrugged.

"I'm no fonder of the man than either of you are. In fact, I'd be delighted to turn him over to *you*, Zhaspahr. Unfortunately, he's related to too many senior Desnairian nobles. Frankly, from the panicky tone of Archbishop

Ahdym's correspondence, our ability to keep the Empire in the Jihad is far from certain. Punishing Hennet the way we all agree he deserves wouldn't help a bit. In fact, I imagine at least some of his relatives would jump on anything that happened to him as a pretext to declare neutrality."

A sudden icy silence hovered in the wake of the word "neutrality."

"Are you seriously suggesting Desnair might . . . withdraw from the Jihad?" Duchairn asked after a moment. Not, he added to himself, that losing Desnair would necessarily be a catastrophe, if the Desnairian component of the Army of Shiloh was anything to go by. Aside from the contributions coming from its gold mines, at least.

"I think that's a question for Zhaspahr," Trynair said.

"It's not anything they're thinking about very hard . . . yet, at least," the Grand Inquisitor growled. "And I assure you my agents inquisitor are keeping a close eye on anyone who might be inclined in that direction. Unfortunately, they *are* reporting widespread panic after the Army of Shiloh's destruction, and there's been at least some talk—very *quiet* talk, for the moment—about how well that bastard Gorjah did for himself after Tarot went over to the heretics."

"Wonderful." Duchairn shook his head. If Clyntahn was prepared to admit that much, the situation in Desnair must be going from grim to dire even more rapidly than any of his own sources had suggested.

"There's nothing we can do about that right now," Maigwair said pointedly. "Which brings me back to what I was saying before. All of our spy reports, such as they are, agree that Stohnar's been steadily reinforcing his cousin in the Sylmahn Gap. Assuming that's correct, they're obviously building towards an all-out push against Bishop Militant Bahrnabai as soon as weather permits. But as far as we know, all of those reinforcements are Siddarmarkian regulars, not Charisians, which leaves the question of what *they're* up to.

We don't know exactly what Green Valley's going to do now that he's taken Saint Tyldyn; from the way he's probing around Nybar's positions, it *looks* like he's going after Fairkyn. But he's a devious bastard, and I'm not comfortable about concluding that's all he has in mind. Whatever he's planning, though, it'll be easy for the heretics to reinforce him as soon as the thaw sets in and they can push their ironclads up the Ice Ash. So I'm as confident as I can be that they're leaving Wyrshym to him—for now, at least—and sending Eastshare to deal with Kaitswyrth. Eastshare may not've moved up into Glacierheart or central Cliff Peak yet—if I had a choice between wintering there and wintering in the South March, I'd choose rain over snow and ice any day—but that's what he has his eye on."

"So we should concentrate our efforts on reinforcing Kaitswyrth?" Trynair asked.

"We've already earmarked enough fresh troops to bring him back up to close to two hundred and fifty thousand men as soon as the canals melt," Duchairn replied. "We don't have much more than that to send. And the truth is that if he's forced to retreat, his lines of communication are a lot better—and shorter—than anything Wyrshym has. That's why I'm so much more worried about the Army of the Sylmahn."

Clyntahn's expression turned instantly mulish. He remained as adamantly opposed as ever to giving up a single mile of Bahrnabai Wyrshym's advance.

"Zhaspahr," Maigwair said, "look at how aggressive Green Valley's been in the middle of the damned winter! I know he's operating with specialized troops who're obviously trained and equipped for exactly those sorts of conditions, but he's advanced over *seven hundred miles* in less than a month and a half. That's an *average* of almost eight miles a day, for Chihiro's sake! Once the rivers open and he can move his main supply head forward, all the rest of his army—plus anything else they send him from their reserve in Old Province *and* anything Stohnar and Parkair can dig up—will be just as mobile as he is. And at that point, he's going to swing south, close the door behind Wyrshym, and sit there while General Stohnar comes north. It's *going* to happen if we don't do something about it."

"No," Clyntahn grated. His shoulders hunched, and he shook his head. "We can't just cut and run, damn it! Think of the message that would send to all of the Faithful in Siddarmark!"

*And of the way it would threaten your damned concentration camps, Zhaspahr,* Duchairn thought coldly.

Which, unfortunately, didn't mean Clyntahn was entirely wrong. Duchairn lacked the Grand Inquisitor's army of spies, but he spent far more time than Clyntahn out in the city of Zion itself, actually speaking to Mother Church's sons and daughters. Despite the fact that he knew he'd become deeply beloved, especially by Zion's poor, he remained a vicar and one of the Group of Four, so no one was going to complain openly to him. But the Bédardists and Pasqualates who oversaw the soup kitchens and winter housing projects were another matter, and so he knew about the creeping malaise, the uncertainty—even fear—which had stolen through the hearts and minds of Zion on the heels of the stunning reverses the heretics had handed Mother Church's defenders.

*Maybe it has, but what does Zhaspahr think is going to happen if the heretics do to Wyrshym what they've already done to Harless and Ahlverez?*

"—a valid point," Maigwair was saying. "But if we suffer another—"

"We won't," Clyntahn said flatly. "You've just pointed out that the troops Green Valley's operating with are specialized, and that the heretics don't have many of them. By the time rivers like the Ice Ash start melting, the Harchongians will be able to move, too, won't they?"

"Probably," Maigwair conceded. "But they'll be moving overland, and—"

"And most of them are from *North* Harchong," Clyntahn interrupted again. "If we have a force anywhere that can move in winter conditions, it's got to be *them*, doesn't it?"

"Well, yes. But—"

"Haven't you and Rhobair been telling us how important it was to equip and train the Harchongians? And haven't we been getting all those glowing reports about how well it's gone?"

"We have," Maigwair admitted. "It would still be better to shorten Wyrshym's lines of communication, Zhaspahr. And I doubt very much that the Mighty Host"—he used the term quite seriously, Duchairn noted—"will be able to move before the heretics are able to attack in the Sylmahn Gap."

"If they attack out of the Gap, they'll be attacking directly into Wyrshym's entrenchments," Clyntahn riposted. "With Wyvern Lake in their way, they won't be able to move all of that damned mobile artillery of theirs right up in his face, either. At worst, he bloodies them first, then has to retreat along the high road, which means he damned well ought to be able to stay ahead of them. At best, he stands his ground and cuts them to pieces. By the time anybody could come in from *behind* him, the Harchongians *will* be able to move."

Maigwair darted a glance at Duchairn from the corner of his eye, and the Treasurer shrugged very slightly. No doubt Clyntahn's analysis rested far more on his prejudices and refusal to disgorge his prize than on logic, but he did have a point. And as he'd just reminded them, it was Duchairn and Maigwair who'd transformed the Mighty Host of God and the Archangels into an increasingly formidable weapon. He'd supported them only grudgingly, too well aware of how bitterly the Harchongese aristocrats who'd supported Mother Church so faithfully and for so long had opposed every step of the change to be happy about it. Under the circumstances, it shouldn't surprise anyone that he meant to call in his debt and insist the Harchongians be used where *he* thought they were most needed.

"All right, Zhaspahr," Maigwair sighed. "I'll tell

Wyrshym to hold his position, and Rhobair and I will do everything we can to improve his supply situation. But you need to be aware that the Army of the Sylmahn's our most exposed, vulnerable force. If the heretics come up with another surprise . . . ."

He shrugged, and Clyntahn grunted.

"In the meantime," Duchairn said, "I'd like to discuss Brother Lynkyn's latest report. In addition to the improved technique for banding the iron guns, he's achieved some initial success in duplicating the heretics' rocket throats. There are still some technical problems, and it looks as if it's going to take rather longer than he'd anticipated, but—"

▼ ▼ ▼

"I hope *you* have some good news for me," Zhaspahr Clyntahn growled, flinging himself heavily into the comfortable chair behind his desk. "If I have to put up with another meeting with that pair of—!"

He cut himself off with an angry gesture, and Wyllym Rayno nodded silently. The increasingly close partnership between Duchairn and Maigwair worried Clyntahn more than he would admit, even to Rayno. He might have a sound basis for that concern, too. Unfortunately . . . .

"I'm afraid there isn't a great deal of 'good news' available at the moment, Your Grace," he said.

Clyntahn's jowls darkened, but he pushed himself back in his chair and took a visible grip on his temper. He wasn't pleased with the Archbishop of Chiang-wu, not at all. Yet however tempestuous his passions might be, he still realized how badly he needed Rayno or someone like him.

"Tell me," he said flatly.

"I've completed my investigation of that business at Camp Chihiro," his adjutant told him. "It confirms the initial reports. The commander of the camp's guard force sent a pursuit after the murderer, but his men were unable to overtake him. They were able to confirm that there was only the one gunman, however, and according to the letter they found at the scene, it was Mab. And from the range at which the shots were fired, they could only have come from him or another of the false *seijins*."

Clyntahn's eyes flashed, despite his resolution to restrain his temper, but Rayno made himself return his superior's glare levelly. There was no point trying to skate around the truth. Especially since the contents of "Mab's" letter had already been made public throughout the Temple Lands.

Wyllym Rayno was not a man much given to despair, nor was he the sort who admitted defeat readily, yet the relentless appearance of blasphemous broadsheets bade fair to drive him to do both. There was no way whoever was posting them could keep evading his agents inquisitor this way. It simply wasn't possible! Yet it continued to happen, as inevitably as the rising and setting of the sun. If he watched nine hundred and ninety-nine walls or village bulletin boards, the broadsheets appeared on the thousandth one. It was as if the heretics posting them knew exactly where every single one of his agents was on any given night.

And even if *that* hadn't been true, how were they produced so well and how in Shan-wei's name did they get distributed so *quickly*? The engraved illustrations rivaled—or even surpassed—the finest plates from Mother Church's own Office of Engraving, the paper was first quality, and the printing itself was always crisp, clear, and clean. There were differences between the illustrations, differences in wording, and they were printed on different stock, yet it was as if every one of them had been produced in the same superbly equipped printing office. Except that they *couldn't* have been, because they appeared everywhere from Desnair the City to Gorath to Zion herself and as far north as some wretched village church in the Province of Pasquale. Not only that, but in addition to the content they all shared, each of them contained stories about purely local events—stories that proved someone in the city or the town or the village where they were posted was responsible for them. Yet try as he might, his agents inquisitor had never *once* intercepted a single person on his way to tack one of his poisonous assaults on Mother Church onto a handy wall somewhere.

They *had* snapped up—and made examples of— almost a hundred corrupted individuals who'd sought to *emulate* whoever was behind the master campaign. But there'd been no comparison between the smudgy, amateurish sheets those people had been carrying and the ones which had inspired their imitation. And, truth be told, he wasn't certain turning them into examples was the best solution. It made the point that people who posted such things were heretics and servants of Shan-wei, but it also made the point that people were doing it despite the promise of the Punishment if they were caught at it.

At least no one seemed aware of how broadly spread the damnable things had become . . . so far, at any rate. Not even all of his agents inquisitor realized that. Most of them, like the communities they were charged to protect, believed they were a purely local phenomenon. He'd gone to some lengths to keep it that way, but his most senior subordinates had to know the truth, and an awareness of how ubiquitous the problem had become was seeping steadily through the rank and file of the Inquisition's investigators.

*And that son-of-a-bitch Mab and the Fist of Kau-Yung aren't helping,* he thought bitterly.

It still worried Rayno more than he wanted to admit even to himself that the assassins had discovered the title his own agents inquisitor had bestowed upon them, even though Father Allayn's investigations had turned up no signs that the "Fist of God" truly had penetrated the Inquisition. Unfortunately, all that proved was that they hadn't *found* any penetration, not that it didn't exist.

At least, unlike Mab's accomplishments, none of their assassinations had made it into those pernicious broadsheets. Apparently even they shrank from the probable reaction of Mother Church's loyal children if they discovered someone was systematically murdering God's own stewards on Safehold. But there was no telling how long that restraint would last. And while word of the killings probably would inspire an outpouring of rage and fury—except, perhaps, among the handful of people who knew the truth about the dead vicars' personal lives—it would also be proof Mother Church could not protect even her own princes.

"I assume the contents of his latest letter are appearing in every realm?" Clyntahn said, biting each word out of solid granite.

"Actually, no, Your Grace." Clyntahn's eyes narrowed, and Rayno inhaled surreptitiously. "It doesn't appear to have been . . . generally distributed. Instead, it's appeared at each of the holding camps. And—" he sighed "—on the door of St. Edmynd's."

"What did you say?"

The question came out quietly, almost calmly, which was far more terrifying in its way than the most enraged of bellows. St. Edmynd's Church was the largest church in the Siddarmarkian city of Sairmeet. And Sairmeet was the central headquarters from which Inquisitor General Wylbyr Edwyrds administered the Inquisition in Siddarmark. In fact, the church was directly across the street from the mansion Edwyrds had requisitioned for his use.

"I'm afraid it's confirmed, Your Grace. It was posted on the church door in a blizzard, but the guards swear no one could have gotten past them. They've been relieved, of course, in light of the possibility that they themselves put it there. Personally, I'm strongly disinclined to think they were responsible, since they were the ones who found it and removed it—before anyone else had an opportunity to see it, fortunately. They'll be carefully interviewed, but I doubt anything will emerge to discredit their stories. Nonetheless, I'm sure rumors about it must've leaked out. Coupled with the broadsheets posted at the camps themselves, I'm afraid it's had a . . . significant effect on the morale of Bishop Wylbyr's Inquisitors."

"This has gone on long enough, Wyllym." Clyntahn's voice was still low, but "calm" was *not* the word Rayno would have chosen to describe it. "The only way this could be happening is that the false *seijins* truly are Shan-wei's demons reintroduced into the world by that Shan-wei's bastard Cayleb and his bitch empress. There's no other explanation. But the *Writ* and the *Book of Schueler* both teach us that demons cannot succeed against the holy. They may win battles, as they did in the War Against the Fallen, and even the Faithful may fall before them. But in the end—*in the end*—they must always fail before the *kyousei hi* of the Archangels and the wrath of God Himself. There can be no other outcome."

His eyes met Rayno's, and the archbishop saw a deep, burning determination that was far more frightening than Zhaspahr Clyntahn's customary fury.

"Call in however many agents inquisitor it takes." The words were beaten iron. "This so-called 'Fist of God' operates here in Zion. You've taken some of them, so we know that whoever and whatever they may be, they aren't these accursed false *seijins*. They're mortal and they can be killed—enough of them have killed *themselves* to avoid capture to prove that. I want this city flooded with your agents. I want these murderous bastards *found*, and I want some of them taken *alive*. I want them put to the Question, and then I want them put to the Punishment. We'll find out who's killing the vicars of Mother Church, and we'll reveal the depth of their sin to the Faithful and make our dead brethren a rallying cry for vengeance and justice. And at the same time we do that, we'll inform all of Mother Church's loyal children that there are among them agents of Shan-wei, like those godless murderers, spreading sedition and lies in the service of Cayleb and Sharleyan, aided and abetted by the demons Athrawes and Mab and all the others. We'll turn their own lying propaganda against them."

"Of course, Your Grace," Rayno murmured, even as his heart sank.

If the resources already hunting for the Fist of Kau-Yung were insufficient, merely adding more manpower was unlikely to produce success. He was convinced the Fist *could* be found and destroyed—as Clyntahn himself had just pointed out, they had proof its members were, indeed, mortal, however foul the evil to which they'd sold their souls. But he was equally convinced it would take time. That, ultimately, it would depend upon some unanticipated break, some mistake on the Fist's part which would yield to patient, meticulous investigation, rather than simply throwing additional bodies at the problem.

Clearly, however, this was not the moment to make that argument to the Grand Inquisitor. Nor was it the moment to suggest that an official authorization to . . . ease the rigor in the camps might be in order. Clyntahn's expression and flat, hard voice made that abundantly clear.

*On the other hand,* he thought, *the camp Inquisitors are* already *'easing the rigor' with which they're administered. None of them want to admit it's out of terror that they might be the next to find themselves in Mab's sights, but there's no use pretending that's not the reason.*

This wasn't the moment to mention *that,* either, but behind the customary tranquility of his own expression, Wyllym Rayno found himself deeply and unaccustomedly concerned. For the first time in his memory—for the first time since the War Against the Fallen—the Inquisition's aura of invincibility as Schueler's Rod in the world had begun to erode. It was still a small thing, and it was happening only slowly, yet it was happening not simply among the Inquisition's own ranks but in the eyes of Mother Church's children in general.

And, he thought, even the greatest avalanche began with the slippage of a few small stones.

"It's hard t' believe." Greyghor Mahlard's expression was troubled, but there was a hard light in his eyes. "Even after wakin' up here and all, it's hard t' believe."

"I don't doubt it," Merlin replied.

He wasn't physically present at the moment—another of those things Mahlard probably found hard to believe—but Owl had placed his hologram in one of the chairs around the conference table. Now he leaned back in the chair his PICA actually occupied in far distant Siddar City.

"In fact," he continued, "it may be even harder *because* of everything that's happened, especially to you and your family, Greyghor."

Mahlard snorted harshly.

"After what happened t' my family?" His voice was even harsher than his snort had been. "Trust me, I've a lot less reason t' put one damned bit o' trust in those bastards in Zion. I'd figured *that* much out even before you rescued us, *Seijin* Merlin!"

"I don't think that's exactly what the *seijin* means, Greyghor," Sandaria Ghatfryd said from her own place at the table. Mahlard looked at her, and she shrugged. "Of course you realized Clyntahn and the rest of them had betrayed everything they'd ever been taught about God! There are millions of people on Safehold who've realized that just by watching them in action; you and your family *experienced* the way they've twisted and broken every good thing in the *Holy Writ*. But there's a difference between that and rejecting the *Writ* itself, and the more we've seen people—*mortal* people, like Clyntahn and the other three—pervert the *Writ*, the more tightly we've clung to what it really says. Our anger and our hatred for them and what they've done is . . . framed in our outrage for the way in which their actions defy what we *know* is the will of God and the teachings of the Archangels. And that makes it even harder for us to accept anything that challenges the rock we've been hanging onto for dear life, far less something that breaks the rock up into tiny pieces of gravel and then throws it out the window!"

Mahlard looked at her for several long moments, then nodded slowly.

"Sandaria has a point," Nimue said from the chamber's doorway. Her hologram walked across to the table and took a seat between Sandaria and Aivah. "Sorry I'm late." She made a face. "Irys and Phylyp had a late session with Anvil Rock and Tartarian. And Koryn, of course. They're hammering out the final details for incorporating the Corisandian Army into the Imperial Army, and Tartarian's especially eager to get that out of the way." She chuckled. "Getting Corisandian officers into the Navy's the next step, and guess who wants his admiral's streamer back?"

"I don't blame him." Merlin shook his head, expression sour. "He's been stuck in council chambers ever since he ended up on the Regency Council, and I've had more experience of being stuck in an 'office job' of my own than I ever wanted!"

"I don't think you'd get a lot of sympathy from Cayleb," Aivah pointed out. "You do get out and about a lot more than you've allowed him to. Well, you and Sharleyan, anyway."

Mahlard looked back and forth between speakers, following the conversation, and his expression had changed from its tight anger into one touched with wonder. He'd been a woodworker in a moderately prosperous but small Border State town far from any thronerooms or palaces. Now he found himself sitting at a conference table, face-to-face with potentially demonic beings out to steal his soul, yet it was evident that he found such casual references to the two most powerful monarchs in the world almost more surreal.

"That may be true," Merlin said, "but it's getting a

little afield from Greyghor's point. And, frankly, how he winds up dealing with it is going to be significant for his future in more ways than one."

"I know." Mahlard leaned back in his own chair, rubbing his forehead with the fingers of his right hand. "Don't think for a minute I'm not grateful t' you—to *all* of you." He lowered his hand to wave at the individuals, flesh-and-blood and electronic, around the table. "Fact is, I'd be dead by now, and so'd Stefyny and Sebahstean, and that's the truth." His mouth tightened with remembered pain as the faces of the wife and son he'd never see again flowed through his mind. "Whatever happens from here'll be a lot better'n where we'd've been 'thout you. And I understand why you need t' be sure I'll keep my mouth shut 'bout just how you managed it."

Merlin nodded, watching the Sardahnian's expression thoughtfully. He'd been impressed by Mahlard's intelligence and resilience. It was impossible to miss the dark places experience had left behind the gray eyes he shared with his daughter, but Nimue Alban had seen those dark places behind many another set of eyes, even before her resurrection here on Safehold, and Merlin had seen a lot more since. Mahlard handled his better than a lot of those other eyes' owners had handled theirs, perhaps because his surviving children needed him to. And whatever else, they hadn't slowed his mental quickness. He wasn't a well-educated man, even by Safeholdian standards, but he possessed an abundance of common sense, and his horrific experiences hadn't dulled it.

That was good . . . probably. Merlin had seen no option but to transport him and the two children directly to Nimue's Cave after their rescue. The three of them couldn't reappear in Sarkyn—or anywhere else they might conceivably be recognized, for that matter—after they'd "died" in Camp Chihiro. Nothing in the Church of God Awaiting's theology supported the concept of physical resurrection, and even if it had, the Temple Loyalists would instantly have proclaimed the three Mahlards had to be demons. Nor could he have allowed them to simply awaken somewhere else—in Tellesberg, for example—with no memory or explanation for how they'd escaped the camp. Their confusion and disbelief would have driven Greyghor to ask the very questions no one could afford for him to ask.

In theory, he could leave the small family here indefinitely, just as he'd explained to Sandaria that he could leave her. At the moment, he rather suspected Stefyny and Sebahstean would have voted in favor of exactly that. He'd managed to visit the Cave physically three times since they'd awakened, and if the two of them had initially been a bit shy around him, they'd quickly gotten over it. At first, he'd been irked to discover that Sandaria and Aivah had explained to them—and to their father—that *Seijin* Merlin had personally rescued them. Telling them they'd been rescued by Merlin when Dialydd Mab had taken credit for the attack on Camp Chihiro's inquisitors as far as all the rest of the world knew had seemed an unnecessary complication. But he'd quickly realized how silly it was to worry about *that* "complication" when there were so many others to worry about where their rescue was concerned, and the kids were a joy.

Sebahstean was a solemn, sober little boy, and Merlin doubted that was going to change, given the appalling things he'd endured. But he was also bright and full of energy, and those experiences of his hadn't killed his ability to love. Stefyny seemed less outwardly marked by what had happened to them, yet she had a grave, thoughtful streak which was far older than her years. She didn't begin to understand the full truth about how she, her father, and her baby brother had been not only rescued but completely healed. Even her broken nose had been repaired and her missing teeth regenerated. That was quite enough for her, and Aivah had been wise enough not to even attempt the explanation which had been given to her father. As far as Stefyny was concerned, *Seijin* Merlin and his friends were simply magic. They didn't call themselves angels, and she was willing to let them pretend they weren't, but none of that affected the proof that miracles *did* happen and that one of them had happened to her, and her smile could have melted a Glacierheart canal in winter.

Since their rescue, the two kids had explored many of the safer sections of Nimue's Cave under Sandaria's and Owl's supervision, and Nahrmahn had introduced them to Owl's library of holodramas and electronic books. They'd taken the holograms and books in stride as just so much more "magic," and no one had tried to explain to them that Nahrmahn—or, for that matter, Merlin—was dead. Still, whether they realized it or not, they were as much prisoners here as they'd been in Camp Chihiro. It was a very different sort of imprisonment, but no less real, and they deserved better than that.

*Besides, my cave's getting a little crowded*, he thought. *I'll have to see about having Owl extend it a bit farther if I'm going to go on taking in boarders.*

"You're right that we couldn't afford to have the true story get back to the Temple, Greyghor," he said. "For that matter, having word of a *genuine* 'miracle' get back to Clyntahn would be . . . less than ideal from my perspective, if not for exactly the same reasons. Although," he smiled faintly, "I would love to watch our dear friend the Grand Inquisitor try to explain *that* one away!"

"That's because you have such a deep nasty streak," Nimue told him. Aivah smothered a laugh, and Nimue smiled. But then her expression sobered as she turned to Mahlard. "You do realize what Clyntahn would have to do if the three of you ever turned up alive anywhere the Inquisition could get its hands on you?"

"He'd shut our mouths one way or t'other," Mahlard said grimly. "Prob'ly torture us t' make us deny who we really were first, o' course. Doubt he'd lose much sleep over it, neither."

"No, he wouldn't," Merlin agreed. "But I don't think it's good for the kids to be locked away here forever, either, Greyghor. They need to be around other kids their own age, and to be honest, we need to get them there before their experiences here differentiate them too much from those other kids."

"Not too sure what 'differentiate' means, *Seijin*," Mahlard replied, "but I think I've a fair notion of what you're tryin' t' say, and you're right. Lord love you, Sister Sandaria, but those two were a big enough handful even afore they fell into your clutches!"

"They're lovely children, Greyghor Mahlard!" Sandaria scolded.

"Never said different. But if they're t' keep their mouths shut 'bout all this, best t' get 'em away from the 'magic' 'fore it soaks too deep into the bone, as you might say."

Merlin nodded again. Mahlard was right about that, too. In fact, Merlin would almost have preferred for Nahrmahn never to have crossed the children's paths. Unfortunately, that would have solved nothing in the long run, unless they'd been prepared to slap Stefyny and Sebahstean into cryo and leave them there until the time came for their hopefully reasonable father to take them elsewhere, and cryo wasn't good for children. A *brief* stint wasn't likely to do them serious physical harm, but cryo—especially prolonged cryo—could have a significant effect on the development of cognitive function in children as a side effect of two of the preparatory drugs. In fact, some kids had an immediate and severe reaction to them, and in those cases the damage could be massive. That was why there'd been no children among the original colonists, which had played into Langhorne's "creation" myth quite nicely. Merlin had used one of those drugs to simulate death in all three of the Mahlards, but he'd been unwilling to risk using *both* on the children, however small the possibility of inflicting harm. Even if he had been, he knew Sandaria and Aivah—not to mention Sharleyan!—would have fought him every inch of the way.

"It's not something we have to decide tonight, right this minute," he said. "I think we've got a little longer. Have you considered my suggestion, though?"

"Aye, I have, and seems t' me it makes sense. Never been t' Tellesberg—never wanted t' be, if you'll pardon my sayin' so—but it'd be good t' have some other folks around as know who we are an' how we came t' be there in the first place. These 'Brethren' of yours sound like decent folk, and I've never heard aught but good 'bout Archbishop Maikel from anybody—'cept those bastards in the Inquisition, o' course. And Tellesberg's far 'nough from home there's not much chance o' meetin' anyone's might know us. And I've no doubt you'd all feel easier in your minds knowin' you'd someone you trusted keepin' an eye on us."

"I won't deny there's something to that last thought," Merlin acknowledged. "But the Brethren—and Archbishop Maikel—would also be available to help you and the kids . . . keep it all in perspective. For that matter, Maikel will be leaving Manchyr for Tellesberg with Sharleyan next five-day, and I've discussed it with him. The Church has established enough orphanages and refugee camps—good ones, with proper housing, healers, schools, and counselors to deal with what's happened to the refugees and their families. Master Howsymn, Master Mychail, and their Council of Manufactories help maintain the orphanages and camps and find jobs—and training, where it's needed—in their manufactories for as many of the refugees as they can, and Maikel says he can easily slide your family into one of the camps if that's what you'd prefer. But he also says Archbishop's Palace could really use a good wood-worker. It would give you a place where no one would be asking any questions, and the kids would be under his personal protection. That means they'd have an opportunity for the best schooling in the world, among other things. Nimue could deliver you to Manchyr just before he and Sharleyan embark, and that would give you at least six or seven five-days aboard ship with them for you—and especially the kids—to settle back into something like a normal life before you reached Tellesberg."

Mahlard looked at him for a moment, then bobbed his head.

" 'Preciate it," he said, his voice gruff with the depth of his gratitude.

A brief silence fell, but then Sandaria shifted in her chair.

"Would it happen that I could get transportation back to Siddar City at the same time, Merlin?" she asked.

"If you're sure that's what you want, of course you can," he replied. "*Are* you sure, though?"

"Yes." She nodded firmly. "It took me a while to realize it, but I've been doing exactly what I just described to Greyghor. That's what Nynian's been trying to tell me all along." She smiled at Aivah, who reached out to take her hand and squeeze it firmly. "I've known the truth about Saint Kohdy for so long, hung onto it so firmly to keep me going in the face of people like Clyntahn, that I couldn't accept there might be another, even greater truth behind that one." She shrugged. "It's time I did."

"It's not so much *another* truth, as it is an expansion of the truth we already knew," Nimue pointed out gently, and Sandaria nodded.

"Oh, I know that. And Archbishop Maikel's helped a lot, too. He told me about something you'd said a long time ago, Merlin—that God can creep in through the cracks whenever He chooses to, despite any lies someone may have told about Him in the meantime. I wish He'd gotten around to doing it a little sooner in Safehold's case, but what Emperor Cayleb's so fond of calling the 'upside' is that this way, *I* get to be part of the process."

# .III.
## Kyznetzov Narrows,
## Kyznetzov Province,
## Harchong Empire,
## and
## Manchyr Palace,
## City of Manchyr,
## Princedom of Corisande

"What do you make of it?"

Captain Kahrltyn Haigyl, CO, HMS *Dreadnought*, sounded more than a bit impatient as his armored galleon heeled to the press of her canvas. It was a hot, bright morning, a far cry from the blustery cold *Dreadnought* had left behind in Chisholm, although the northwesterly wind—what seamen called a topsail breeze—gusting down the Kyznetzov Narrows at twenty miles per hour made it seem cooler. At the moment, that wind was perfect for Haigyl's purposes; it would be much less so when the time came to withdraw, however. Hence his impatience as Dahnyld Stahdmaiyr, his executive officer, stood on the breech of one of *Dreadnought*'s massive six-inch guns, braced his elbows on the top of the port bulwark, and peered through his double-glass.

Lieutenant Stahdmaiyr was a somewhat bookish sort, in sharp contrast to his commanding officer, and more than a little nearsighted. At the moment, his wire-frame spectacles were propped on his forehead to keep them safely out of the way. A ribband from one earpiece was also attached to one of his buttonholes, legacy of a lesson learned the hard way as a midshipman in a wave-tossed longboat.

"Hard to make out details from here, even through the glass, Sir," he said. "On the other hand, doesn't look like they tried to *hide* anything. Looks like a mix of old-style doomwhales and new-model guns, probably twenty-five pounders."

"Hrrumph!"

Haigyl scowled, nodded, folded his hands behind him, and resumed his interrupted pacing. Although *Dreadnought* was one of the largest galleons ever built, she mounted only thirty guns. That left a lot of deck space for pacing, and Haigyl normally spent an hour or two every morning using it for his regular exercise. *This* morning he had more than exercise on his mind, however, and his dark brown eyes were agate-hard. A casual observer might have read his pacing as nervousness or anxiety, but his crew knew him better than that. When Captain Haigyl started pacing like an irritated slash lizard, he had death and destruction on his mind.

Not a brilliant man, Captain Haigyl. Not very imaginative, either. But he was as capable as he was hard-bitten, with the roaring heart of a great dragon and a score to settle with the Royal Dohlaran Navy. At the moment, unfortunately, the Dohlarans were beyond his reach, so the Harchongese defenders of the Bay of Alexov would just have to do.

Still, it didn't take a brilliant or an imaginative man to recognize the risks inherent in his current mission. *Dreadnought*, the bombardment ships *Vortex* and *Firestorm*, and the transport *Tellesberg Bride*, escorted by ten unarmored galleons and five schooners of the Imperial Charisian Navy, were over a hundred and fifty miles from the open sea, just passing Symov Island at the halfway point of the Narrows. It also happened to be the narrowest point of the passage linking the Bay of Alexov to the Sea of Harchong, and while "narrow" was a purely relative term—the Narrows were better than twenty-five miles across, even here,—they had another six hundred miles to go to their objective. And a passage which was abundantly broad with the wind in their favor was likely to seem a great deal less so if they were forced to beat to windward the whole way out.

At the moment, Haigyl's squadron was well clear of any of the numerous defensive batteries covering the

Narrows. That was another thing that might change if his ships had to tack all the way back to the Sea of Harchong, however, which was rather the point of Stahdmaiyr's survey of the Symov Island batteries. The lieutenant knew his captain had to be sorely tempted to close the island, trailing *Dreadnought*'s coat just close enough to the batteries to draw their fire. That would be one way to be certain what they were armed with, and nothing in the Harchongese artillery park was likely to make much impression on *Dreadnought*'s two-inch steel armor. Unfortunately, their charts were less than reliable. The information they had suggested there were nasty shoals around Symov, and the Harchongians had removed the navigation buoys when the Imperial Charisian Navy retook Claw Island from the Dohlarans. All the armor in the world wouldn't do a ship much good if she ripped out her keel on a reef.

On the other hand, Stahdmaiyr thought cheerfully, still peering through his double-glass, that same armor was going to make any units of the Imperial Harchongese Navy they happened to encounter very, very unhappy.

▼ ▼ ▼

"It must be one of those armored ships the Dohlarans were yammering about," Captain of Foot Ruhngzhi Lywahn growled.

He stood on top of the battery's curtainwall on the west side of the Kyznetzov Narrows, gazing through the huge tripod-mounted spyglass at the line of ships sailing boldly past him. Not that there was any reason they *shouldn't* be bold. His fifteen old-model Great Doomwhales were monstrous pieces, weighing six tons apiece and firing seventy-five-pound shot. They were also antiques without even trunions, fired once every five minutes, and had a maximum range of not much over two thousand yards. His most effective pieces—a dozen new-model twenty-five-pounders—had twice that range, but the heretics were far beyond even their reach. He doubted the Charisians had any intention of coming *into* their reach, and if that was one of their armored galleons leading the way . . .

"Are you sure, Sir?" From his tone, Lywahn's executive officer couldn't make up his mind whether to be skeptical or worried. Which, truth to tell, summed up Lywahn's own feelings fairly well.

"It's a hell of a lot bigger than any other ship out there," he told Captain of Spears Haigwai Zhyng without taking his eyes from the spyglass. "And it's only got one row of gunports. What does that sound like to *you*?"

Zhyng made an unhappy noise of agreement, and Lywahn watched the Charisian warships bowling along on the stiff breeze for another minute or two, then straightened.

"Well, I'm sure everybody else has already sent word to Yu-kwau, but we might as well add our bit. Go to the semaphore office. Warn Baron Star Song and Captain of Seas Shyngwa they're coming. Tell him it looks to me like one of their armored galleons and twelve regular ones, plus a half-dozen or so schooners."

"Yes, Sir!" Zhyng touched his chest in salute and hurried off.

Lywahn watched him go, and wondered if he should have dictated a more erudite message. Most Harchongese nobles could have effortlessly tossed off a minor epic, with at least a dozen literary allusions which would have had the semaphore clerks cursing the entire time they transmitted it. Lywahn, however, was not a noble and had no desire to become one. Like the majority of militia officers in South Harchong, he was a merchant and the son of merchants. That was one of several differences between the southern and northern lobes of the Empire, and the militia's commoner officer corps—like the fact that the men in its ranks were free volunteers rather than conscripted serfs—offered the toweringly noble aristocrats of North Harchong yet another reason to look down upon their southern brethren.

They weren't alone in that. The bureaucrats who ran

the Empire weren't a lot happier with people like Ly-wahn than the nobility was, since the southern merchants knew where too many of the bureaucrats' bodies were buried . . . not always figuratively speaking. Worse, not even the imperial bureaucracy wanted to antagonize Mother Church, and every second son of a Kyznetzov merchant house was either a priest or a law master . . . or both. The bureaucrats knew there'd be no winners in a fight to the finish between them and the merchant families, so they settled for much smaller bribes than they would have expected in the North and, in return, the merchants of the South kept their mouths shut about any minor irregularities in government contracts.

So far, the Jihad had been good for South Harchong—aside from the bombardment of Yu-shai, at least. That had been ugly, but the city had been almost completely rebuilt since the heretic Manthyr's attack, and the abundant cashflow of the Jihad was what had made that possible. The southern foundries were far more efficient than their northern counterparts, and not just because of the more salubrious climate. And although many of the foundry owners resented the manner in which their businesses had been taken over by Church managers, they were still making money hand over fist. Best of all, the fighting—other than that unpleasant business at Yu-Shai—had been four thousand miles and more away from the Bay of Alexov.

Unfortunately, it looked as if that was going to change.

▼ ▼ ▼

"This is confirmed?"

Captain of Seas Ryangdu Shyngwa's voice was unreasonably calm, under the circumstances, but his eyes stabbed Captain of Winds Tsauzhyn like daggers.

"It's as confirmed as anyone could expect, Sir," Tsauzhyn replied. "Baron Star Song's received a score of semaphore messages. This—" he indicated the dispatch in Shyngwa's hand "—represents a compilation of the information in all them. Of course, they're all coming from militia officers, not Navy officers, but I'm afraid it probably is fairly accurate."

Shyngwa's face tightened. Then he inhaled deeply and nodded.

"Of course it is. Forgive me, Maidahng. I think I'm taking out my temper on you, and you deserve better than that."

"I don't recall hearing any complaints coming from me, Sir." Tsauzhyn smiled almost naturally.

"Of course you don't."

Shyngwa touched his flag captain on the shoulder, then crossed to the stern windows and looked out across the sparkling blue water at the grandly named Alexov Defense Squadron. Unlike Tsauzhyn, the captain of seas was distantly related to at least three noble families from the North, but his mother's family was one of the South's more prominent banking dynasties. He knew Lord Admiral of Navies Mountain Shadow had chosen him for his command because those family connections made him an acceptable political compromise, but he took his responsibilities seriously. He'd worked hard to make the squadron an effective force and, under most circumstances, it was a pleasant duty. The provincial capital of Yu-kwau was less than seven hundred miles below the equator, and it was summer in Safehold's southern hemisphere. The sun was already high overhead, beating down on the anchorage and softening the pitch in the deck seams of His Most Imperial Majesty's Ship *Celestial Music*, his fifty-six-gun flagship.

Captain of Winds Tsauzhyn was proud of his ship, and rightly so. Unlike too many of his better-born fellow captains, Tsauzhyn regarded his vessel as a weapon of war, not a personal possession. He'd drilled *Celestial Music*'s seamen and gunners to a level of competence rarely seen in the Imperial Harchongese Navy, and the flagship's example had spread to the rest of Shyngwa's squadron.

All five galleons and eighteen old-style galleys of it.

Shyngwa leaned forward, bracing his hands on the sill of the open stern windows, and looked beyond his ships at the crowded anchorage, thick with anchored merchant galleons which had fled to the supposed safety of the provincial capital's shore batteries. The Charisian light cruisers had made their presence felt quickly after the heretics drove the Dohlarans out of Claw Island once more. They'd turned the coastal waters of Cheshire, Boisseau, and Tiegelkamp into a wrecker's yard of burned and sunken shipping, and merchant traffic in the Harchong Narrows had come to a standstill. And while the heretics appeared unwilling to operate too deep into the Gulf of Dohlar—from the reports he'd received, fifteen hundred miles seemed to be the limit they'd decided upon—Kyznetzov, unfortunately, lay within their operational radius, and Shyngwa knew exactly where this Charisian squadron was headed.

He raised his eyes from the anchored merchant ships to the Yu-kwau docks and skyline.

Yu-kwau, the provincial capital and the gem of the Bay of Alexov. Its white walls and orange terra-cotta tile roofs gleamed in the sunlight. Windows—many of them stained glass works of art—flashed back the light, nearpalms shaded paved streets and walkways of crushed seashells, brilliant flowers glowed like so many jewels, and golden fire flickered from the scepters atop the city's cathedrals and churches. Shyngwa had never understood why the imperial capital hadn't been moved to the South long ago, but he supposed it must have something to do with tradition. Shang-mi, on Boisseau Province's Beijing Bay at the mouth of the Chiang Jiang River, was the ancient heartland of the Harchongese people. The capital dated from the very Day of Creation, whereas South Harchong was a mere appendage which had been captured and colonized hundreds of years later. It was a pity, however. Yu-kwau's climate would have made it a far more suitable imperial capital, and perhaps the imperial bureaucrats would have become less deeply embedded in the South.

And the vineyards, nearpalm plantations, and vast stretches of farmland in Kyznetzov and Queiroz must certainly be a welcome change from the frozen beet fields, potatoes, and hog farms of Cheshire, Chiang-wu, and northern Boisseau!

And capping its many other attractions, Yu-kwau had the Bay of Alexov. The Harchong Narrows might be closed to merchant shipping, but the bay wasn't, and the city's docks were crowded with coasters, many of them carrying loads of coal from Queiroz, others loaded to the deckhead with corn, grain, beans, apples, oranges, and sugar apples from the farms of Queiroz and Kyznetzov. They couldn't ship it by sea, but the St. Lerys Canal was one of the oldest on Safehold, carved through the heart of the Kyznetzov Mountains by the Archangels themselves to connect Yu-kwau (although the city had been little more than a smallish town—called "New York," or some other uncouth, barbarian name—at the time) all the way to Shwei Bay, fourteen hundred miles to the east. Indeed, the canal was the reason Yu-kwau had been built in the first place, and that traffic, especially the foodstuffs, had become more profitable and important than ever. Yet unthinkable though it once would have been, the heretics had amply demonstrated their readiness to destroy Safehold's canal systems in complete defiance of the *Holy Writ*'s commands.

*And I can't stop them.* The admission went through his brain like a cold wind, and he shivered, despite the morning's heat. *I couldn't have stopped them even if they hadn't brought along one of those armored monstrosities of theirs. With* it *added to the scales, not even the batteries will be able to stop them.*

That was a bitter, bitter thought, that last one, because unlike the batteries fringing the Kyznetzov Narrows, Yu-kwau's waterfront artillery had been completely overhauled. The new-model twenty-five-pounder and forty-pounder shell-firing cannon were products of Yu-kwau's own foundries, and they'd been sited with care. Few of the new guns had been wasted on the

Narrows' batteries for the simple reason that unless wind and tide cooperated, no enemy fleet was going to come into their range. They were positioned to cover likely landing beaches or handy anchorages blockaders might have used, and for that purpose, they were probably adequate, but no one had ever realistically expected them to drive off an attacking fleet.

The Yu-kwau waterfront batteries were intended to do just that, and until the heretics had produced their accursed armored galleons, that was precisely what they *would* have done. Now? He shook his head, his eyes bitter. If the Dohlarans' reports of what had happened at Claw Island were accurate, not self-serving lies intended to excuse their own defeat, the batteries stood no more chance of defeating this attack than his own ships did.

*None of which means I don't have to try anyway.*

"Well," he said, turning back from the white walls and orange roofs, "at least it'll take them another three days or so to arrive. I suppose we should spend them getting the men ready, Maidahng."

"Yes, Sir." Captain of Winds Tsauzhyn met his regard levelly. "I'll get started on that right away."

▼ ▼ ▼

"I see why Earl Sharpfield thinks so highly of Captain Haigyl," Sharleyan Ahrmahk said, watching the SNARC imagery projected on her contact lenses.

"So do I." Hektor Aplyn-Ahrmahk sat across the glass-topped table from her on the Manchyr Palace balcony, one arm around his wife's shoulders. The same imagery played itself across their contact lenses, as well, and the Duke of Darcos shook his head. "I know it has to be done, but Captain of Seas Shyngwa deserved better than he got."

"I suppose he did," Nimue Chwaeriau acknowledged. She and Edwyrd Seahamper stood outside Sharleyan's suite, protecting their privacy . . . and watching the same feed from the SNARCs. "At least Captain Haigyl rescued all of Shyngwa's people he could."

"I just wish Shyngwa'd been one of them," Hektor said. "I've seen enough ships sunk and enough men killed to last me a lifetime, Nimue."

Irys Aplyn-Ahrmahk put one hand on his knee. He looked down into her hazel eyes, and she smiled a bit sadly.

"Don't worry, love," he said, giving her shoulders a squeeze. "I'm not going all melancholy on you. It's just that when you come down to it, seamen are all the same under the skin. The sea doesn't play favorites, and all of us know it."

"I don't think your stepfather and Domynyk would agree with you entirely," Sharleyan said quietly. Hektor looked at her, and she shrugged. "Oh, I'm sure they'd agree with you where Shyngwa's involved. And they'd probably sign on about the sea not playing favorites. But they're not prepared to forgive and forget where *some* seamen are concerned." Her eyes were bleak. "There's still a bill waiting to be collected for Gwylym Manthyr and his men."

"I know. But, you know, even before Irys and I got access to the SNARCs, I never thought that was Thirsk's idea. I agree entirely with Cayleb and Domynyk that there's a price for something like that, whether it was his idea or not. But that doesn't mean I need to be looking forward to it."

They fell silent as *Dreadnought* sailed slowly across the Yu-kwau harbor under topsails and jibs, rifled six-inch guns bellowing one by one, steady as a metronome, each gun individually laid as it hurled its heavy shells into the shoreside batteries. The Harchongese gunners stood to their pieces with defiant courage, pouring fire back at her, but to no avail. *Their* shells bounced from her armor plating like so many baseballs; *her* shells smashed straight through their parapets, dismounting their guns in volcanoes of splintered stone and mangled flesh.

Beyond her, *Vortex* and *Firestorm* had come to anchor and rigged springs to their anchor cables. Now they rotated in place, bringing their high-trajectory angle-guns into action. To Haigyl's credit, Nimue thought, his ships were careful to keep their fire as far as possible from the provincial capital's residential sections. It was unlikely any Church fleet would have made the same effort. But, then, that was the difference between the two sides, wasn't it?

The waterfront and—especially—the canalfront were fair game, however. The warehouses were roaring infernos, belching dense clouds of black smoke. So were the wharves—those which hadn't already simply collapsed in shattered ruin—and launches and longboats from *Tellesberg Bride* and the regular war galleons were making short work of the anchored merchantmen. No doubt many of those would be burned in the end, as well, since Haigyl lacked the manpower to put prize crews aboard all of them, but many others—the ones with the most valuable cargos—would be returning to Claw Island when he left. And once the defensive fire was completely suppressed—which wouldn't take so very much longer—*Tellesberg Bride* would land her Marines under cover of the squadron's guns to complete the demolition of the St. Lerys Canal's waterfront locks. They hadn't brought along any of the Delthak Works' Lywysite, but enough gunpowder would do the job just fine.

"It's a tidy operation," she said over her internal com, never moving her lips. "I don't think Admiral Rohsail's going to bite, though."

"We can always hope," Hektor replied, and she chuckled.

"First, someone has to get him the word soon enough, Hektor, and that isn't going to happen. But, second, even if he found out in time to sortie and intercept Haigyl off the Crown of Queiroz, he's probably too smart to try it."

Hektor nodded just a bit sourly. The Crown of Queiroz, the arc of islands off the mouth of the Kyznetzov Narrows, enclosed the waters of Eevahn Sound and Hwangzhi Sound. They also offered the best opportunity Sir Dahrand Rohsail, who commanded the

Royal Dohlaran Navy fleet currently based on Whale Island, was likely to find to intercept Haigyl on his way back to Claw Island. That was why *Dreadnought*'s sister ship *Thunderer*, another twenty-five galleons, and four scouting schooners of the Imperial Charisian Navy were currently keeping station off Mahdsyn Island in hopes he'd attempt exactly that.

"Does it really matter whether or not Earl Sharpfield can draw Rohsail into an engagement?" Irys asked. "I mean, he's avoiding action, isn't he? And as long as he does that, we can go on doing things like *this*."

She waved one hand, indicating the cauldron of smoke and flame which had enveloped the Yu-kwau waterfront.

"Yes, and no," her husband said. "He's not avoiding action because he never plans to fight, Irys. He's avoiding action because he doesn't want to fight *yet*."

"But if we go on launching raids like this one, will it matter what he might plan to do to us sometime in the future? I mean, the damage will be done, won't it? And when the *King Haarahlds* commission, we'll be able to go as deep into the Gulf of Dohlar as we want!"

"That's not going to happen for months yet," Nimue pointed out. "And in the meantime, there's Zhwaigair and his damned spar torpedoes. Not to mention those screw-galleys of his!" She snorted over the com. "I'll be damned if I would've believed he could make that notion work."

"Lieutenant Zhwaigair has a nasty habit of making all sorts of notions work," Sharleyan agreed sourly.

The empress, Nimue thought, had a point. Zhwaigair had completed over a dozen of his armored screw-galleys now, with as many more under construction. When he'd first proposed the concept, Earl Thirsk had been forced to fight tooth and nail for every pound of iron diverted to them; after the Great Canal Raid, priorities had shifted radically, however. Once the Grand Inquisitor himself signed off on the project, the physical ability of Dohlar's foundries to produce iron plate had become the only limiting factor.

The schooner-rigged galleys weren't the sturdiest craft ever created, and their propellers were substantially less efficient than the ones fitted to Charis' steam-powered vessels. Despite that, with thirty-four men on each crank, the four-hundred-ton vessels were capable of eight knots. Even with a complete replacement set of crankers—or "cranksmen," as Zhwaigair had dubbed them—they could sustain that speed only for about forty minutes, but they could maintain *four* knots just about indefinitely, easily as long as any conventional galley's oarsmen could have managed. Under sail, they could make seven or eight knots in average wind conditions with their two-bladed screws rotated into a vertical position to minimize drag, and they could *combine* wind and screws for a really remarkable turn of speed.

Surprisingly, they were good seaboats, as well, despite the heavy weight of their iron armor. Or, more accurately, they would have been good seaboats if the weight of all that armor and the three ten-inch smoothbores—all mounted forward—hadn't placed such an incredible stress on a wooden vessel. Zhwaigair had never expected them to be blue-water warships, but he'd found out the hard way that their hulls strained badly, and however well they might *handle*, one of them had literally broken up in no more than six-foot seas. He'd done what he could after that misadventure to stiffen the hulls, but there was a limit to what he could accomplish without the steel and wrought-iron frames available to Sir Dustyn Olyvyr. And that restricted them firmly to coastal waters and moderate sea conditions. Against wooden galleons and under those conditions, however, they had lethal potential.

Their iron armor wouldn't stand up to *Dreadnought*'s rifled projectiles, but it was more than enough to resist the thirty-pounder smoothbores which were the ICN's standard heavy guns. And while eight knots might not sound blisteringly fast, it was twice the speed most galleons could maintain under fighting sail. Not to mention the fact that galleys could steer directly into the wind.

That was bad enough, but in some ways Zhwaigair's reinvention of the spar torpedo might well prove even worse. Conceptually, it was simple: put two hundred pounds of gunpowder into a watertight copper container; mount the container on the end of a spar; rig a detonator using the percussion caps now available to the defenders of Mother Church; and then put the entire contraption into a small, fast boat. The "torpedo galleys" Zhwaigair had come up with were conventional, oar-powered vessels for the most part, with the fifteen- or twenty-foot spars mounted so that they could be extended over their bows. They were essentially an ambush weapon, useless against a ship underway, but they could be deadly under the right conditions, especially against a ship at anchor. And since they attacked below the waterline, *Dreadnought*'s armor would be entirely ineffective against them.

"I have to admit, I'm worried," Sharleyan continued. "I can't forget what happened to Admiral Manthyr. I trust Earl Sharpfield's judgment entirely, but I'd feel a lot happier if he had the same kind of reconnaissance ability our land commanders do!"

"Duke Eastshare's done pretty well without SNARCs," Hektor pointed out.

"Yes, but '*Seijin* Ahbraim' gave Merlin a way to feed Ruhsyl intelligence at critical points in his campaign," Sharleyan responded. "That's a lot harder to do for a fleet commander." She snorted suddenly. "Not that I should have to tell *you* that!"

"No, you shouldn't," Nimue agreed. "On the other hand, it's a really valid point. There's not a good way for Merlin or me to drop in on Sharpfield whenever we need to deliver some hint he needs to hear. And he's already behind the information curve. Just for starters, Zhwaigair hadn't proposed his spar torpedo yet when he sailed from Chisholm."

"And Cherayth's over nine thousand miles from Claw Island. There's no 'legitimate' way to explain how spies could've gotten word of the torpedoes to Cherayth and it could've been sent forward to him across that much distance, either." Sharleyan sighed. "Not in time to be any use to him, anyway. It's that damned communications loop again."

"Merlin or I *could* arrange to go deliver that information to him, at least," Nimue suggested. "Admiral Manthyr got reliable intelligence from Harchongese fishermen when he was operating in the Gulf. In fact, the more I think about it, the more I think that would be a very good idea, assuming Merlin has the time or we can come up with a reason for Captain Chwaeriau to be somewhere else for a few days."

"I think you're right about that," Hektor said soberly. "But that's pretty much a one-time fix. As you say, there's no practical way to set up someone like *Seijin* Ahbraim or *Seijin* Ganieda as some sort of semipermanent fixture."

"If we can't, we can't," Sharleyan said gently. "And at least Nimue's right that we can warn him about the torpedoes."

"I know, and God knows it's important to do that, but we need more." Hektor's eyes turned grim, looking out of the face of a naval officer hardened by experience. When he looked like that, it was easy to forget he was only seventeen, Nimue thought. "I've been in situations like this with the Admiral."

Despite herself, Nimue's lips twitched. "The Admiral" referred to only one person when Hektor used the title with no name attached: Sir Dunkyn Yairley, Baron Sarmouth. Sarmouth was more than a respected or even revered flag officer to Hektor Aplyn-Ahrmhak; he was the mentor and second father who'd taken a newly ennobled midshipman under his wing and finished teaching him to be a man, as well as a king's officer.

"I can't remember how many times Sir Dunkyn's said it's not the things you don't know that kill you," Hektor continued. "It's the things you *do* know but you're wrong about. Generally speaking, I agree completely, but something like those spar torpedoes or how efficient the screw-galleys've turned out to be . . . those kinds of things can kill a lot of people if an admiral doesn't know about them. And that doesn't even consider the way the weather turned against Admiral Manthyr, or the fact that all Earl Sharpfield or Captain Haigyl really know about the enemy is what their own lookouts can actually *see* at any given moment."

"Isn't that true for any admiral on either side, though?" Irys asked. "And I may be prejudiced, but I think Admiral Sarmouth's done pretty well despite his lack of aerial reconnaissance. For that matter, all of your Charisian admirals have done pretty darn well!"

"Of course, but as Prince Nahrmahn says, if you aren't cheating you aren't trying hard enough, especially where men's lives are concerned," Hektor replied, and Irys nodded. Then her eyes widened suddenly.

"What?" Hektor asked, looking down at her. "I recognize that expression. What devious thing have you just thought of?"

"Actually, I was thinking about that advice of Nahrmahn's you just quoted," she said slowly. "I think it's time we started cheating a little more energetically."

"How?"

"Well . . . I know Admiral Rock Point's stuck in Old Charis because that's where high admirals have to be, not to mention how deeply involved he is in everything Master Howsmyn, Sir Dustyn, and Baron Seamount are up to. I'll be astonished if he doesn't come up with some excuse to hand those responsibilities to someone else as soon as the first *King Haarahlds* commission. But for now he can hardly go dashing off to Claw Island, and since Admiral Lock Island was killed, he's the only flag officer the inner circle has. At the moment, anyway."

"'At the moment'?" Sharleyan repeated, gazing at her stepdaughter-in-law intently.

"At the moment," Irys said again, firmly, and looked back at Hektor. "I know it's always a risk to bring someone else into the inner circle, especially from a standing start. Sometimes it still scares me when I think of the chance Archbishop Maikel and Merlin took when they told *us* the truth. I understand exactly why the circle's always been so cautious, always taken the time to consider—when there was time, at least—whether or not someone would be able to accept the truth. But it occurs to me that all of us—especially you, Hektor—know one admiral very, very well. And that admiral happens to be right here in Corisande at the moment, where Sharleyan—and Nimue—would be available to help convince him you haven't gone stark staring mad."

. IV .

Ice Lake,
Province of Glacierheart,
Republic of Siddarmark

It's good to see you again, Your Eminence," Ruhsyl Thairis said as Zhasyn Cahnyr stepped ashore from the iceboat. "Even if it does seem a bit chilly to be dragging you out in the cold." The Duke of Eastshare regarded the archbishop sternly. "*We* could have come across the lake to *you*, you know."

"Of course you could have, my son," the silver-haired archbishop who still preferred to think of himself as "lean" rather than "frail" agreed. "But if you'd done that, I would have been denied an exhilarating outing." His eyes twinkled. "Not even Sahmantha could object to a simple boat ride!"

Eastshare arched his eyebrows skeptically. He'd met Sahmantha Gorjah last winter on his way through Glacierheart to halt Cahnyr Kaitswyrth's advance.

"Well, she didn't object too long. That's what I *meant* to say," Cahnyr corrected himself, and the duke snorted.

"Now *that* sounds more like Madam Gorjah," he observed.

"I see you know my keepers," Cahnyr said. "One of these days, they'll even let me have a sharp knife to cut my food with. Perhaps."

He shook his head and turned to the other officers gathered at dockside to await him. It was an impressive collection, he reflected. In addition to Eastshare, there was Sir Breyt Bahskym, the Earl of High Mount, as well as Ahlyn Symkyn, and the three generals were accompanied by their chiefs of staff, personal aides, and—in Eastshare's case—his chief of artillery, Colonel Hynryk Celahk.

No, it was *Brigadier* Celahk, the archbishop thought, noting the crossed silver swords which had replaced the single silver sword of a colonel's collar insignia. For that matter, Eastshare's rank insignia had changed, as well. The single golden sword which denoted a general officer in the Royal Chisholmian Army had been replaced by crossed golden swords, marking the duke as the first *high* general in Chisholmian—or Charisian—history. Right off the top of his head, it was difficult for Cahnyr to think of anyone who'd deserved promotion more than either of them. Although, to be fair, Eastshare always had been the Imperial Charisian Army's senior uniformed officer. His new rank was more of a housekeeping detail than anything else, in that respect.

"Well," Cahnyr said, "now that I'm here, I'm sure the keepers currently in attendance—" he twitched his head at Zhorj Gorjah and Laimuyl Azkhat, standing innocently at his heels "—would prefer for all of us to get out of this wind. Somehow it seems less 'exhilarating' standing here at dockside than it did sailing across the lake."

"Imagine that," Eastshare murmured, then bowed slightly and waved at the waiting sleighs. "After you, Your Eminence."

▼ ▼ ▼

It wasn't a very long ride, although Cahnyr was grateful for the warm blankets and windproof, beautifully tanned snow lizard pelt his hosts had insisted upon tucking around him. It was the first time he'd ridden behind one of the Raven's Land caribou rather than a snow lizard, however, and he found the thick-shouldered, antlered beasts impressive. They passed quite a few other caribou—and snow lizards—along the way, and his eyes glittered with a light which was harder and far, far colder than they'd ever been in more peaceful times as he saw the artillery pieces many of those draft animals were towing. After the previous year's vicious fighting, he'd developed an appreciation for the weapons of war which once would have horrified him. Which *still* horrified him, actually, he reflected. It was just that there were other things which horrified him still more.

"That's impressive, My Lord," he remarked, twitching his head at a massive, bizarrely shaped cannon.

Like its smaller brethren, its wheels had been chocked onto long, broad runners to help it glide across the snow, but those wheels were much bigger than most and set farther back on its carriage. They made it look . . . off balance, he thought, and that was scarcely the only—or the most—odd thing about it. It was hard to make out details under the canvas tarp which shrouded it, but a large box-like framework beneath its barrel housed two side-by-side cylinders, almost like two additional, stubby guns. The actual barrel clearly moved along the top of the frame, and it had been run fully to the rear, so far back its muzzle projected no more than a few feet beyond the carriage axle. The breech seemed oddly angular under the protective canvas, as well, he thought. For that matter, the gun trail was different from any he'd ever seen before. It seemed to be made entirely out of steel, it was much longer than normal, and it had been split lengthwise into two legs joined by a massive hinge at the rear of the carriage and locked back into a single unit for towing purposes.

"It *is* impressive, Your Eminence," Eastshare agreed. "That's one of the new breech-loading angle-guns."

"Ah?" Cahnyr looked at it again. "I'd heard your Delthak Works were improving your existing artillery.

Improving it still further, I suppose I should say." He smiled briefly. "May I ask why the barrel seems so far . . . back?"

"That's to equalize the weight between the axles and the limber while it's being moved." Eastshare nodded at the two-wheeled cart—its wheels also on runners at the moment—hitched to the end of the gun trail. "When it's fired, though, the barrel recoils to the same position without moving the carriage. That's why the trail's split that way, so it can be spread and dug in properly to stabilize the gun."

"I see." The archbishop turned back to his general. "It seems quite substantial," he observed. "Much larger than the thirty-pounders Brigadier Taisyn was equipped with. It actually looks a bit larger than the angle-guns you deployed last year, for that matter."

"Because it is, Your Eminence," Eastshare agreed. "It's a breechloader—basically the same weapon the Navy's mounting in the heavy ironclads, just on a field mounting. It's the same caliber as our original angle-guns, and its barrel's about two feet longer, although the field version is still quite a bit shorter than the Navy's version, to keep weight down. It has more elevation than the Navy's pieces—or than our muzzle-loading angles, for that matter—but its maximum range is shorter than for the Navy because of the shorter barrel. Brigadier Celahk tells me it can still reach out to about twelve thousand yards, though, half again as far as our older angles could shoot, and it has a much higher rate of fire. We only have four of them, at the moment, and I'm glad to see them. Frankly, I didn't expect to have any at all before early summer."

"I can see why you'd be pleased," Cahnyr acknowledged, and shook his head, once more bemused—and possibly more than a little frightened—by the furious pace at which the Empire of Charis persisted in changing the face of war.

*So much killing*, he thought sadly. *So much blood and death and destruction. But terrible as it is, how much more terrible would it be if someone like Zhaspahr*

*Clyntahn had been left free to wreak whatever vengeance he chose upon anyone who dared to defy him?*

"In a lot of ways, I'd prefer old-fashioned cannon and matchlocks, too, Your Eminence." Eastshare's comment surprised the archbishop and drew his eyes back to the high general's face, and the duke shrugged. "There's nothing demonic about any of the new weapons. Father Paityr and Archbishop Maikel have both assured me of that, and Master Howsmyn's mechanics've described the principles to me often enough. For that matter, any general who doesn't embrace anything that saves the lives of his own men has no business commanding them in the first place. And I don't want to sound callous, but dead is dead, however a man's killed. But sometimes . . ." It was his turn to shake his head. "Sometimes the *number* of the dead is enough to keep me awake and on my knees all night."

Cahnyr reached out impulsively, laying one hand on the other man's knee.

"That's a good sign," he said. One of Eastshare's eyebrows rose, and the archbishop smiled. It was a little crooked, that smile, pulled off-center by the way Eastshare's admission resonated with his own thoughts of only a moment before. "It's a sign you have a conscience, my son. God and the Archangels gave you that for a reason, and it's good you still have it." His smile faded. "I only wish more of those who claim to serve Mother Church could say the same."

"I think you're right, Your Eminence. That it's good *we* still have consciences, whether or not the other side does. In fact, what worries me most is the number of good men I've seen *losing* their consciences to the need for vengeance. For that matter," he looked away, "I can't pretend *I* wasn't . . . grateful when Lairys Walkyr refused my offer of quarter."

"Not all wounds are of the flesh," Cahnyr said quietly. "And not all of them heal. But I think you should cherish the pain you feel when you think about Fort Tairys. Don't let it prevent you from doing what you must, but remember what makes you who you are."

"I'll try to bear that in mind, Your Eminence," Eastshare replied, turning back to meet his gaze levelly. Then he shook himself and smiled, pointing ahead as their sleigh rounded a bend. A line of artillery pieces had been deployed, Cahnyr saw, and his eyes widened in sudden understanding.

"I'll try to bear it in mind," the general continued, "but in the meantime, we have a small surprise demonstration to show you before we get you indoors and brief you on our current dispositions. They aren't as heavy as the angle-gun we passed on the way here, but I think once you've seen them in action you'll understand why I was so happy to see the heavy angles."

The new guns were . . . sleeker than the six-inch angle, Cahnyr thought, and fitted with sloped steel shields of some sort. They had the same split trails, however, and there were spades at the end of each leg, dug into solid earth. Gun crews stood waiting—fewer of them per gun than he would have expected—and he looked back at the duke questioningly.

"Master Howsmyn's christened them the 'M97 Field Gun, 4-inch, Model 1,' Your Eminence. Like the new angle-guns, they don't use studded shells anymore, and a trained crew can fire six or seven rounds a minute out to as much as five thousand yards. And I'm afraid," Eastshare's smile faded into an expression of grim satisfaction, "the Temple Boys aren't going to like them a bit."

# . V .
# Mahzgyr,
# Duchy of Gwynt,
# and
# The Ohlarn Gap,
# New Northland Province,
# Republic of Siddarmark

"I think you'll find this interesting, Your Eminence," Taychau Daiyang said, waving one hand at the infantry platoon marching through the snow towards them. "It was the suggestion of a young captain of spears in the Two Hundred Thirty-First Volunteers."

"Was it, My Lord?" Archbishop Militant Gustyv Walkyr turned to look in the direction the commander of the Mighty Host of God and the Archangels had indicated. "That would be Camp Number Four, wouldn't it?" The Harchongian nodded, and Walkyr smiled. "I understand several interesting suggestions have come out of that camp," he observed.

"True. And I, for one, am grateful for it."

There was quite a freight of meaning packed into that sentence, Walkyr reflected. Taychau Daiyang, the Earl of Rainbow Waters, had been appointed to the rank of lord of horse for his present assignment. An earl was rather junior for such an important post in the Imperial Harchongese Army, and lord of horse might be best described as an *elastic* rank. It was roughly equivalent to a bishop in the Army of God or to a general—possibly even a mere brigadier—in the Siddarmarkian or Charisian armies, but there was no formal step or title between it and lord of hosts, the highest Harchongese field rank. That meant it held whatever authority the emperor (or his bureaucracy, at least) decided it needed to hold at any given moment, and Rainbow Waters had been selected over the heads of at least a score of lords of horse whose seniority far exceeded his own.

He was also the fifth commander the Mighty Host had enjoyed since leaving Harchong. The first two had resigned in protest when they'd discovered what Allayn Maigwair and Rhobair Duchairn had in mind. The third had been removed in disgrace for incompetence and a degree of corruption not even the IHA had been prepared to tolerate. The fourth had also resigned, officially because he found it impossible to endure the arrogance and interference in his command's internal affairs by the Army of God "advisors" attached to it. Personally, Walkyr was confident his opposition to what those advisors were attempting to accomplish had had quite a lot to do with his decision, as well.

But Rainbow Waters was different. He was smarter than any of the others, for one thing, and far more pragmatic. The earl clearly had misgivings of his own, yet it was equally clear he understood *why* the Mighty Host had required such a massive overhaul. Unlike any of his predecessors, he'd gotten behind the effort and pushed both hard and competently, despite the passive resistance of at least a quarter of his own subordinates. He'd been remarkably ruthless about relieving the most obstructionist of those subordinates, too, despite the near certainty of bitter future feuds with their powerful families or patrons.

"What have the Volunteers come up with this time, My Lord?"

"I prefer to allow you to enjoy the surprise, Your Eminence."

"Ah?"

"I believe Captain of Swords Tsynzhwei deserves to have you approach it without . . . preconceptions, although I'm not at all certain he came up with the idea himself, initially." Rainbow Waters smiled faintly. "In fact, I rather suspect it came from one of his company commanders. Possibly even some lowly sergeant. I doubt the heretics are going to enjoy it, however."

The marching infantry had continued to approach

the covered reviewing stand on which Walkyr, Rainbow Waters, and half a dozen lower-ranking officers and aides stood, and Walkyr somehow managed not to roll his eyes as he realized the entire platoon was equipped with slings. The Imperial Harchongese Army was the only major army which still included slingers in its order of battle—mostly because peasants and serfs were prohibited by law from mastering any more sophisticated missile weapon. Despite the massive effort to reequip the Mighty Host of God and the Archangels, over sixty thousand of its million infantry were still sling-armed, which meant they were the next best thing to useless on a modern field of battle.

The archbishop militant sighed internally and prepared to find some way to express approval of whatever he was about to see without perjuring his immortal soul. Rainbow Waters might be more pragmatic than the majority of his peers, but he was still a Harchongese aristocrat which, by definition, meant proud, prickly, and deeply aware of his towering superiority to any non-Harchongian. Irritating as that might make him upon occasion, he'd made a massive sacrifice of his own honor—by Harchongese standards—simply to accept his current command, and it would never do to offend him. For that matter, he *deserved* a little diplomatic stroking. Chihiro knew more than a few of those peers of his back home were already plotting his assassination for his betrayal of his own kind!

*Besides*, Walkyr reminded himself, *useless or not, there are less than seventy thousand of them in the entire Host*. His lips twitched at the irony of using the adverb "less" about a number greater than the entire current strength of the Army of the Sylmahn, but the truth was that it represented less than six percent of the Mighty Host's manpower. *We can afford to let Rainbow Waters play with them any way that amuses him.*

The oncoming infantry came to a halt on the drill field, fifty yards from the reviewing stand and deployed into a single line, and Walkyr noted the polish of its drill with approval. It was twice the size of an Army of

God platoon, and its "uniforms" were a motley collection of civilian garments, but its men's movement was smoother—and quicker—than the majority of AOG units the archbishop militant had reviewed.

*Hmmm. Those aren't regular slings, either,* he realized. *They're staff slings. Now what . . . ?*

The platoon's formation was much more open than archers, arbalesteers, or riflemen would have required, which probably reflected the additional room a slinger must require. Walkyr had never really thought about it, since the sling had become obsolete in most of Safehold generations ago. In fact, it was practically unknown outside Harchong these days, and it had probably persisted there only because slings were incredibly cheap and because of the prohibitions the Empire placed on more advanced weapons. The only reason Walkyr knew the difference between simple slings and staff slings was the sheer quantity of paperwork which had crossed his desk during the Host's rearmament.

The slingers moved briskly, inserting stones into their weapons' leather-reinforced pouches. It was little wonder they were cheap, Walkyr reflected. They were little more than a staff, perhaps six feet long, with a relatively short length of tanned leather attached to its end. He was a little puzzled by the apparent size of their ammunition, however. According to the paperwork he'd seen—which included charges for cast lead "bullets"—they shouldn't have been that large. The bullets weighed between one and a half and three ounces which shouldn't have been much larger than an old-style matchlock bullet, and whatever they were using today was a lot bigger than that, close to the size of a man's fist. It wasn't spherical, either, which he'd always assumed sling bullets had to be. It was more . . . elliptical. Or perhaps the word he wanted was "ovoid." At any rate—

A crisp order rang out. The staffs whipped up with lightning speed, arcing through a sharply defined motion whose precision took the archbishop militant by surprise. Obviously, the men using those slings had begun learning how to handle them almost before they could walk!

His eyebrows flew up in even deeper astonishment as he realized just how far the slingers' projectiles could travel. He'd assumed they'd do well to reach a hundred yards, but they far exceeded that. In fact, their shots sailed well over *two* hundred yards, despite the size of the projectiles, before they thudded softly into the snow.

And exploded.

Archbishop Militant Gustyv stepped back involuntarily as flame, snow, and smoke erupted with absolutely no warning. The fountains covered a zone at least fifty yards across and ten yards deep, and the flat, staccato explosions hammered his ears. He felt his jaw drop, but there was nothing he could do about that. He could only stare at the clouds of snow and smoke rising higher and higher on the chill wind.

It took him at least ten seconds to close his mouth, shake himself, and turn back to Rainbow Waters.

"That . . . was remarkable, My Lord," he said. "It never occurred to me that slings could reach *that* sort of range. And as for the explosions—!"

"I don't doubt that, Your Eminence." The Harchongese officer shrugged slightly. "It's been my observation that Easterners significantly underestimate the range a trained slinger can reach. In fact, with a properly designed bullet, these men could reach at least twice the range they just demonstrated."

Walkyr started to object to such a claim, almost by reflex. Fortunately, he stopped himself in time.

"If they weren't using bullets, what were they using?" he asked instead.

"Hand bombs," Rainbow Waters replied. "We made them ourselves, based on the ones Mother Church is supplying to our infantry. They're individually smaller—they weigh only half as much and don't carry as much powder or as many shrapnel balls—but you've seen how far our slingers can throw them. Of course, these men are using *staff* slings, which have much more range than a standard sling, and they can't be used at short ranges. Their bullets—or bombs—have to travel in an arc without the flatter trajectories standard slings can achieve. On the other hand, they can reach two hundred yards with the full-size hand bombs; with the ones they used today, they can reach almost four hundred, although their accuracy falls off at that range. The hand bomb patterns become less concentrated the farther they have to sling them."

"I see." Walkyr looked at the earl for a moment, then back at the slinger platoon, which was now standing motionless, awaiting its next order. "Might I see them demonstrate that again, My Lord? And would it be possible for you to have them show me how well they can do with the full-size hand bombs?"

"By the strangest coincidence, Your Eminence, they happen to have a half dozen of each size with them."

Rainbow Waters smiled broadly at the archbishop militant, then nodded to one of his aides. The young man saluted crisply, hurried down the reviewing stand's shallow steps, and jogged towards the waiting platoon.

"I know we haven't been able to duplicate the heretics' portable angle-guns," Rainbow Waters said, his own eyes on the slingers as he stood beside Walkyr. "From the reports Bishop Militant Bahrnabai and Bishop Militant Cahnyr have shared with me, the best slinger in the world isn't going to be able to match those sorts of ranges. But once the range falls . . . ."

His voice trailed off, and Walkyr nodded as he watched the slingers reload.

▼ ▼ ▼

"I have to admit, My Lord," the archbishop militant said several hours later, sitting across a well-laden supper table from the lord of horse, "that I never anticipated anything like those slingers. You're right about the heretics' portable angle-guns' range advantage, but they don't have anywhere near as many of those as you have of slingers."

"The thought had crossed my own mind," Rainbow

Waters acknowledged, pouring fresh tea into Walkyr's cup with his own hands. "On the other hand, the specially designed hand bombs aren't the easiest things to make."

He raised one eyebrow across the teapot, still held in midair, and Walkyr nodded.

"I take your point, My Lord. And I imagine Vicar Allayn will be delighted to give them priority at the powder mills once he reads my report."

"Excellent!"

Rainbow Waters set the teapot aside, and Walkyr sipped from the tissue-thin porcelain cup. The smaller hand bombs the slingers preferred were, indeed, ovoid in shape. They also consisted of old-fashioned musket balls embedded in a matrix of pitch and cored with a small powder charge. The most effective ones used the new primer caps the Inquisition had approved for production, but caps were in short supply for the Mighty Host of God and the Archangels, and virtually all of the ones the Harchongians had received were earmarked for the new-build St. Kylmhan breechloaders they'd been issued. A second variety, like the standard hand bombs the Church had begun producing after the heretics used them against her defenders in battle, had to be lit with a length of slow match, instead. That worked, but it also meant that each slinger had to be paired with someone to light—and, if necessary, cut—the fuses before they were slung at the enemy.

"I'm glad I was able to see your demonstration in person," he said, setting the cup back on its saucer. "I don't think a written report would have done it justice."

"I admit I wanted you to see it without any . . . preconceptions, shall we say?" Rainbow Waters smiled. "That was how my nephew demonstrated it to me, in fact."

Walkyr smiled back. The lord of horse's nephew— Medyng Hwojahn, the Baron of Wind Song—was a captain of horse, roughly equivalent to an Army of God colonel. He was also Rainbow Waters' senior aide and adjutant. He didn't appear to be quite as intelligent as his uncle, but he possessed abundant energy and he was meticulously organized. Even more importantly, perhaps, he shared the earl's awareness of why it had been so vital to reorganize and rearm the Mighty Host. No wonder both he and his uncle had been so delighted by the possibility of demonstrating the effectiveness of their new technique.

But then, slowly, Walkyr's smile faded into a more sober expression. Rainbow Waters watched it happen and sat back in his own chair.

"May I presume, Your Eminence, that we're about to come to the primary reason for your visit?"

"You may."

The archbishop militant sighed, and Rainbow Waters chuckled softly.

"I suspect I might be able to guess at least a part of your purpose, Your Eminence," he said almost gently. "It's two thousand miles from Zion to Mahzgyr, after all. Not the sort of journey Vicar Allayn's chief assistant is likely to make in the middle of winter without some pressing motivation."

"I'm afraid you're right about that," Walkyr conceded wryly with a shudder which wasn't at all feigned. He was fortunate he'd been able to makc almost the entire journey across the frozen lakes, canals, and rivers by iceboat, but it had still been an exhausting—and frigid—ordeal. "And the distance I had to come is rather relevant to the *reason* I came, I'm afraid."

"You're worried about the heretic Green Valley," Rainbow Waters said, and Walkyr's estimate of the Harchongian's intellect revised itself upward yet again.

"Precisely," he acknowledged. "The fact is, unfortunately, that we're . . . less informed than we'd like about his movements. In fact, we don't have any idea where he is at the moment! Bishop Gorthyk's in communication with Bishop Militant Bahrnabai by messenger wyvern, but he reports that the heretic troops currently investing Fairkyn appear to consist almost entirely of Siddarmarkians. They're supported by at least some Charisian artillery, and some of the Charisians' mounted troops are in the area, as well, but Green Valley himself is nowhere to be seen. And that, My Lord, makes us nervous."

"If you'll forgive me for pointing this out, Your Eminence, you must have been well on your way to Mahzgyr before Bishop Gorthyk reported that."

"Once again, you're absolutely right." Walkyr shrugged. "The reason I was initially dispatched was to form a firsthand opinion of the Mighty Host's readiness for combat. The reports we've had from you and officers like Colonel Krestmyn have made it clear how hard the majority of your officers and men are working—and that they've made enormous progress—but I hope you'll forgive my frankness when I say they've also made it apparent not all of your officers are fully supportive of your efforts even now."

It was Rainbow Waters' turn to sigh, and he nodded. He obviously didn't like agreeing, but his atypical (for a Harchongese noble) willingness to admit the truth was one of the things Allayn Maigwair and Gustyv Walkyr most valued about him.

"That was only a part of the reason I came," the archbishop militant continued. "Frankly, one reason our current ignorance of Green Valley's position concerns us so deeply is the degree of mobility the heretics have demonstrated. We'd given some thought to ski-equipped or snowshoe-equipped infantry, but not on anything like the scale the heretics appear to have undertaken. Our men are neither equipped nor trained for movement in this sort of weather. In fact, the only troops who might be capable of that sort of movement—"

"—are my Harchongians," the earl said, and Walkyr nodded again.

"Vicar Allayn and Vicar Rhobair realize that sort of movement at this time of year was never anything they discussed with you or your superiors, My Lord. And the last thing either of them wants is for you to lose men to frostbite and freezing. But at this moment, your headquarters are the better part of four thousand miles from Guarnak. Even before Green Valley's heretics . . . disappeared, that meant it would take the Mighty Host over two months to cover the distance by canal boat. Obviously, trying to move you or any substantial proportion of your troops when everything's frozen will only make that even worse. But every mile closer to Guarnak that you could get before the canals thaw might well be priceless."

Rainbow Waters frowned thoughtfully, toying with his salad fork while he considered his response, and Walkyr sat back in his own chair. Maigwair's dispatches had overtaken him less than a five-day from Mahzgyr, and the Captain General's sense of urgency had come through clearly. Yet his instructions for Walkyr to be careful how he pushed Rainbow Waters had been explicit and very, very unambiguous. The Mighty Host of God and the Archangels had always been the largest single force at Mother Church's command. Now, against all logical expectation, it had been transformed into what was almost certainly also the most powerful and effective of those forces. The last thing Maigwair wanted was for a Harchongese Duke of Harless to overpromise what he could do and march the Mighty Host into the same sort of starvation, with frostbite as a garnish. If—*if*—Rainbow Waters could begin moving towards the front without killing his own men in the process, the Captain General wanted him underway as soon as possible, but there was no point marching a force twenty times the Army of the Sylmahn's size into exactly the same trap.

"It distresses me to say so, Your Eminence, but I couldn't possibly move any large proportion of the entire Host under these conditions." The regret in Rainbow Waters' voice was genuine, Walkyr realized. "While it's true my men are more winter hardened than the majority of Easterners, not even they could move with the sort of . . . facility of which the heretics appear capable. On the other hand, my own reading of the reports coming back from Fairkyn and from Bishop Militant

Bahrnabai suggest that not even the heretics' *entire* army is equally capable of movement and combat under these conditions."

His tone made the last sentence a question, and Walkyr nodded.

"Their entire force seems to be able to move far better than we ever anticipated, My Lord. But you're right. The reports we've received so far suggest that Green Valley used only a portion—probably less than half—of his total strength in his attacks on Esthyr's Abbey, Saint Zhana, and Saint Tyldyn. Whether that's because only the troops he's using are truly trained and equipped for arctic combat or because his ability to move supplies is more constrained than his ability to move *troops* is more than we've been able to determine, but Vicar Allayn is leaning towards the former."

"I'm inclined to agree," Rainbow Waters said. "And that's really the problem the Mighty Host would face. To be perfectly honest, Your Eminence, *none* of my men are truly trained to fight under these conditions. If I demanded it of them, they'd do their best and probably be more capable than my own fears suggest. But the problem of keeping them supplied isn't precisely a minor one, either. Especially not when it would be impossible to supply them by foraging."

Walkyr managed not to grimace. The mere thought of turning a Harchongese army loose to forage on the Temple Lands and Border States was enough to terrify anyone, especially at this time of year. Very few of the towns, villages, and farms in North Haven would have any food to spare this late into winter, and when starving civilians found themselves oppressed by a starving soldiery—especially a starving *foreign* soldiery—the only question would be *how* disastrous the outcome would be. And even if that hadn't been true, once the Host crossed into Siddarmark, there simply wouldn't be any towns or villages to be pillaged in the first place. Not in the Sword of Schueler's wake.

"So you don't believe it would be possible at this time?" he asked heavily.

"That's not precisely what I said, Your Eminence. I said I couldn't move any *large proportion* of the total Host under these circumstances. But even a very small proportion of a million men is a substantial force. I believe I could probably put as many as fifty thousand— possibly sixty thousand—into motion towards Guarnak within the five-day. That would be dependent upon Vicar Rhobair finding the additional snow lizards or mountain dragons to support their move, of course. And I doubt that even following the canals and rivers they could make good much over ten or twelve miles per day. It would also require me to divert a lot of my tentage and fuel, which would have consequences when it's time for the rest of the Host to advance. But it's now early April; it will be early June before the canal and river ice begins to break up. Even at only ten miles a day, my detachment could be six or seven hundred miles closer to Guarnak by then, and I could start with Baron Falling Rock. I'd like to be able to tell you we could accomplish more than that, and if we find we can, we certainly will. The last thing Vicar Allayn or Mother Church needs, however, would be for me to assure you I can accomplish more than I believe is possible and end up throwing away the weapon we've spent all winter forging."

Walkyr's eyes widened.

"That's far better than I anticipated you might be able to accomplish, My Lord," he said frankly. "With your permission, I'll transmit your comments to Vicar Allayn immediately."

"Of course, Your Eminence." Rainbow Waters gave the archbishop militant a seated bow. "The burden Mother Church and the Archangels have placed upon our shoulders is a heavy one, but it's also the most honorable and important burden which could ever be entrusted to mortal men. What I can do, I will, and so will the men of the Mighty Host."

▼ ▼ ▼

"—will the men of the Mighty Host."

*Well,* that's *certainly a pain in the arse,* Kynt Clareyk

thought grumpily as he finished viewing the SNARC report. *Bad enough the damned Host got itself reorganized and rearmed—did they really have to find it a competent commanding officer, too?*

He growled an unpleasant word under his breath and sat back in his camp chair, holding a mug of hot tea between his palms. A strong and still-strengthening wind blustered around his tent, and Owl's remotes promised at least thirty hours of fresh snowfall. Fortunately, while it might be steady, it didn't look as if it would be very heavy. The AI's forecast called for accumulations of no more than ten inches or so, but it was still going to slow his progress until it cleared.

At the moment, he was over two hundred miles southeast of Ohlarn, and the good news was that he'd pounced on the largely deserted town before anyone realized he was coming. His scout snipers and mounted infantry had snapped up its shivering, understrength garrison and the relative handful of remaining civilians—after cutting the semaphore chain west of the town—in the middle of the night. The astounded defenders had never managed to get a message out, and ski-equipped scout snipers, moving all but invisibly in the short days and poor visibility, had swept on ahead of his main body. They'd bypassed semaphore stations which might have seen them coming in daylight and struck repeatedly in darkness, chopping the chain into disconnected bits and pieces incapable of warning anyone else his main body was coming. It was unlikely he'd be able to keep that up forever, but it *was* likely he'd make good at least another couple of hundred miles before the Church realized what was happening.

*But they've done a better job of figuring out what* might *be happening than I like,* he acknowledged. *And Rainbow Waters is a hell of a lot smarter than anybody else they've tried in command of the Mighty Host. I think he's being a little pessimistic about how far he'll be able to move in a day, too. And if he* does *start with Falling Rock . . . .*

The sheer size of the Harchongese army had required

Rhobair Duchairn to split it up between encampments, if only because of hygiene considerations. There were over a dozen of those camps threaded along more than a thousand miles of canal and river, and Gwainmyn Yiangszhu, the Baron of Falling Rock, commanded the easternmost of them all, located outside the city of Watermeet, at the confluence of the Sabana River and the Holy Langhorne Canal. Even assuming Rainbow Waters' estimate wasn't pessimistic, Falling Rock would be more than two-thirds of the way across the Earldom of Usher by the time the ice melted. That was still a long way from Guarnak or Five Forks, but it was more than halfway to Lake City in Tarikah, and that was a lot closer than Green Valley wanted fifty or sixty thousand new-model Harchongese soldiers.

*Well, it's not the end of the world, Kynt,* he told himself after a moment. *You should still have time to deal with Wyrshym, and maybe it won't be such a bad thing if they decide to feed fifty thousand men into the furnace early instead of keeping the entire Host together in one big sledgehammer. Especially with those damned grenade-launching slings added to the mix!*

That was another potentially painful miscalculation, he acknowledged. Like Walkyr, he—and the rest of the inner circle, including one Merlin Athrawes—had allowed themselves a certain contempt where slings were concerned. As Rainbow Waters had pointed out to Walkyr, that was largely because none of them had ever seen them in use, and because they'd seriously underestimated the range and accuracy of which a *skilled* slinger was capable. Nor had they considered the effect of specially shaped ammunition. Owl and Nahrmahn had been back over the available information since Rainbow Waters' demonstration and discovered a point all of them had overlooked, probably because of the way they'd automatically dismissed such "obsolete" weapons. The same Harchongese laws which prohibited serfs or peasants from possessing those or firearms imposed bloodthirsty penalties for the possession of sling *bullets*, as well. Simple river rocks could never have matched a properly designed bullet's range or accuracy, and the greater surface area of a stone limited its penetrating ability.

The sling grenades the Harchongians had come up with, however, were the same shape as the bullets the IHA had always issued to *its* slingers, as opposed to the slingers it might oppose in the event of a peasant rebellion. They were fairly sharply pointed double-ended ovoids—in fact, they looked a lot like an ancient American football—and they oriented in flight to travel point first and spin rather like a rifled bullet. Owl had recomputed their range and potential accuracy, and the result had been astounding. An experienced slinger could actually hurl his bullet at an initial velocity of almost three hundred feet per second, forty-five percent faster than a crossbow bolt, which Owl calculated would allow him to attain a range of as much as six hundred yards with a "standard" three-ounce bullet.

The sling, he'd discovered courtesy of Owl's rather belated research, had enjoyed greater longevity than any other missile weapon in human history. In addition to its cheapness, it was easy to make and had been used in virtually every part of Old Earth except the continent of Australia. Its main drawbacks were that, even more than the bow, it required literally a lifetime's training—preferably, beginning in childhood—and that a slinger required a lot of room to use his weapon properly. Space requirements were fine for an *individual's* weapon, but far more bows, crossbows, or firearms could be packed into the same space and provide a much greater density of fire.

The substantially bigger and less dense grenades couldn't reach out as far as bullets from the same weapons, however. A standard Church grenade weighed two ounces more than its Charisian counterpart, and the best attainable range with one of them would be no more than a hundred and sixty yards or so. But three hundred yards should be well within the staff slingers' reach using the specially designed grenades, and even men equipped with standard slings could hurl grenades much farther than they could be thrown by hand. Under the wrong circumstances, that sort of deluge of grenades could prove extremely painful. On the other hand, slingers had to stand upright to launch their projectiles, and any massed formation that stood upright in the open within two or three hundred yards of Charisian riflemen in open terrain wouldn't do it twice.

*Brother Lynkyn's damned rockets are going to be more dangerous than slings,* he told himself. *It's just another factor you're going to have to take into consideration, and the rifle grenades will help. Or would help, assuming you had enough of them to match the sort of volume of fire* they'll *be able to put out.*

He grimaced at that last thought, then ordered himself to stop fretting about it. It wasn't as if he didn't have enough other things to focus on.

Besides, when the rest of them started giving him a hard time, he intended to point out that neither Merlin nor Owl had seen this one coming any sooner than he had.

It might not be much, but a good tactician maximized whatever advantage he had.

# . VI .
# Claw Island,
# Sea of Harchong,
# and Charisian Embassy,
# Siddar City,
# Republic of Siddarmark

Sir Lewk Cohlmyn, the Earl of Sharpfield, looked up at the sound of a discreet knock.

"Enter!" he called, and the office door opened to admit his flag lieutenant.

"Yes, Mahrak?"

"There's someone to see you, My Lord," Sir Mahrak Tympyltyn replied.

"'Someone'?" Sharpfield repeated quizzically, and Tympyltyn shrugged.

"I've never met the, ah, gentleman before, My Lord. He just sailed in through the North Channel in a fishing yawl . . . by himself. One of the guard boats intercepted him, and escorted him to Broken Tree Inlet, and Major Wyllyms interviewed him. He seems to be Dohlaran, which puts him a long way from home. He's rather insistent about speaking to you, however, and he asked me to tell you Clyffyrd sent him."

Sharpfield's eyes narrowed, and he straightened in his chair.

"I see," he said. "Does this visitor have a name of his own?"

"He says it's Cudd, My Lord. Dagyr Cudd."

From Tympyltyn's expression, the lieutenant recognized an alias when he heard one. On the other hand . . . .

"Please show Master Cudd in," the earl said, and Tympyltyn inclined his head in a brief bow and withdrew.

The door opened again a moment later, and the lieutenant ushered in a roughly dressed, sandy blond man of perhaps forty years and a bit less than average height. The newcomer's naturally fair complexion was darkly tanned and weather-beaten, his hands bore the calluses of hard work, and his eyes were dark brown under bushy eyebrows.

"Master Cudd, My Lord," Tympyltyn said.

"Thank you, Mahrak."

Sharpfield's tone conveyed both thanks and polite dismissal. Tympyltyn looked as if he might like to object, and his eyes dipped very briefly to the serviceable fisherman's knife sheathed at Cudd's right hip. They rose again to meet his superior's, one eyebrow raised, but the earl only smiled and twitched his head at the open door.

"Of course, My Lord," the lieutenant murmured, and closed the door behind him.

"So my good friend Clyffyrd sent you, did he, Master Cudd?" Sharpfield inquired pleasantly, leaning back in his chair.

"Aye, that she did, My Lord," Cudd replied in a pronounced Dohlaran accent. "Mind you, it's been a while since she sent me out here."

"I see."

The earl's eyes narrowed ever so slightly at Cudd's choice of pronouns and he propped his elbows on the arms of his chair and steepled his fingers across his chest as he considered the man in front of him. The fact that Cudd knew the codename he'd used to gain admittance to Sharpfield's office didn't necessarily prove he truly was a Charisian spy. But for the Inquisition to have provided that name to him—and for him to have known it referred to Empress Sharleyan herself—would have required near total penetration of the Charisian spy network. That seemed . . . unlikely, given the Inquisition's repeated failures against Charisian intelligence, and Master Cudd's outlandish name was its own bona fide, in an odd sort of way.

"Tell me, Master Cudd—would it happen that you're acquainted with a fellow named Merlin?"

"As a matter of fact, My Lord, I am," Cudd acknowledged, and Sharpfield's eyebrows arched as the Dohlaran accent vanished into one the earl knew very, very well. Harris Island, between Cherry Blossom Sound and Helena Sound, had produced the Kingdom of Chisholm's hardiest fishermen for at least the last two hundred years.

"I see," he said once more, in a rather different tone. "And may I ask why you're here?"

"Well, as to that, My Lord, there's a few things I think you should know about what Earl Thirsk's been up to. For example—"

▼ ▼ ▼

"That went rather better than I expected," Aivah Pahrsahn said as she, Cayleb, and Merlin reviewed the SNARC imagery.

"No reason why it shouldn't have gone well." Cayleb sipped from the whiskey glass in his hand and shrugged. "Nimue had the proper identification, and Sir Lewk's never been stupid. He recognized the truth when he heard it."

"And at least now he knows about the spar torpedoes and the availability of Zhwaigair's screw-galleys," Merlin pointed out.

"I only wish he could get the word out to all of his detachments more rapidly." Aivah shook her head. "I'd never really thought about the sheer distances involved in naval operations—or the fact that there're no handy semaphore chains in the middle of the sea—until I fell into my present evil company. Now . . ." Her shrug was almost a shiver. "Given the radius of his operations, it may take five-days just for his dispatch boats to find everybody."

"That's always true for naval operations," Cayleb replied. "And to be honest, given how . . . fragile the screw-galleys are and the fact that the spar torpedo's basically an ambush weapon, it's not likely they'll be able to threaten any of his ships at sea. He hasn't designated too many temporary anchorages, his captains are already pretty damned alert whenever they use one of them, and the dispatch boat skippers will hang around off the entrances to the anchorages they're using to make sure they alert anyone headed into them." He shrugged. "It's the best we can do, Aivah, and it ought to be good enough."

"I know," Aivah acknowledged. "And as you say, that'll probably be more than enough to prevent unpleasant surprises."

"I'm afraid surprises have a habit of biting people on the ass no matter how well protected against them they may think they are," Merlin observed a bit darkly. "Like those rockets of dear, sweet Brother Lynkyn's, for example. Or his damned artillery, for that matter!"

"Admit it, Merlin," Cayleb said with a challenging grin, "you're still pissed off by Zhwaigair's breech-loader, aren't you?"

"I decline to answer on the grounds that it might tend to incriminate me."

"So *that's* why you insisted we put that 'Bill of Rights' section into the Imperial Constitution!" Cayleb accused.

"I decline to answer on—"

"Personally," Aivah interrupted, "and without any intention of changing the subject before this conversation bogs down completely, I'd feel happier if we knew what Khapahr's up to." She grimaced. "I'd like to think whatever it is has to be good from our perspective, but as Merlin says, surprises have a habit of biting people no matter how careful they are, and there are too many unknowns for me to count on that."

Merlin nodded. Nahrmahn and Owl's discovery that Earl Thirsk's senior aide was quietly laying plans of his own had all sorts of potential implications—implications which could quite possibly be far more significant than ironclad galleys or spar torpedoes. Unfortunately, as Aivah had pointed out, they had no idea what Khapahr's ultimate objective might be. The possibility that he intended to *betray* Thirsk in some fashion didn't exist—his devotion to the earl was beyond question—and it seemed unlikely Thirsk was unaware of whatever he was up to. Yet they had no evidence of what the earl *was* aware of it—none at all—and that was troubling.

The fact that Khapahr was moving so carefully and covertly that Nahrmahn had almost missed it entirely, despite the close surveillance under which Owl kept Earl Thirsk, suggested that whatever he was up to was something he definitely didn't want the Inquisition or Thirsk's political enemies to know about. That ought to be good news from Charis' perspective, but no one was prepared to count on anything of the sort. All they knew at this point was that Khapahr had met with Mahrtyn Vahnwyk, Thirsk's personal secretary, and

Stywyrt Baiket, his flag captain, to quietly—and very obliquely—discuss the hypothetical possibility of "taking the earl's daughters for a cruise" aboard one of the Dohlaran Navy's galleons. Exactly how Khapahr intended to get them from their homes to the galleon in question was more than even their SNARCs could tell them—probably, in Merlin's opinion, because Khapahr himself hadn't been able to work out that bit yet. For that matter, they had no idea what Thirsk—assuming he actually knew anything about it, which he just about *had* to, didn't he?—thought he could accomplish by getting them aboard ship in the first place. Still, one thing they'd learned about the Dohlaran admiral was that he was accustomed to achieving the tasks he set himself.

"I think we'd all like to know that," he said out loud. "And I'm sure we'll find out, eventually. One way or the other," he added dryly, and Cayleb chuckled. Then the emperor sobered.

"Do you think it would be a good idea for *Seijin* Ahbraim to have a conversation with him?" he asked much more seriously, and Merlin shrugged.

"I'd say no. Not until we have a better feel for his plans—whatever they are—anyway. On the one hand, it might be all he'd need to break with the Church once and for all. On the other hand, though, it could push him in the other direction. And if we're wrong in hoping he might be considering some sort of defection, we could find him screaming for the guards the instant he realizes he's face-to-face with a *seijin*. That could get . . . messy. And it could wind up burning his bridges behind him, too." He shook his head. "No. If he gets to the point of dropping us a note like Coris did, or if we get a positive read on where he's planning on sending his daughters and his grandchildren, I think then it would definitely be time to send Ahbraim—or possibly even your humble servant—to have a conversation with him. For right now, though, as Aivah says, there are too many unknowns—and imponderables—for us to go mucking about."

"Well, in that case," Aivah set aside her own whiskey glass and rose, "would you care to accompany me to the Cave to fetch Sandaria?"

"You don't really need me as your chauffeur, you know." Merlin shoved himself up out of his chair with a slow smile. "Owl is perfectly capable of handling the air van for you now that it's in service."

"Besides which, Merlin doesn't like flying around in something so slow it can't go any more than three times the speed of sound," Cayleb pointed out. "I think he finds such plebeian transport beneath his dignity."

"I never said anything of the sort." Merlin looked down his nose at what was arguably the most powerful man on Safehold. "I merely said it was always a good thing to have a little extra speed in reserve when you needed it."

"Yeah, *sure* you did!"

Aivah folded her arms, looking back and forth between the two of them with the expression of an overtried governess.

"I don't really care how fast it is," she told them. "And I realize Owl is perfectly capable of piloting me there and back again. For that matter, I might actually enjoy spending a few hours discussing certain male parties with Sandaria now that she's decided how she feels about the Church and all those other weighty spiritual matters. I'm sure she'd enjoy the laughter."

Cayleb stuck out an unrepentant tongue at her, and her lips twitched. She brought them back under control, however, and added a slowly tapping toe to her governess impersonation.

"All of those things are true," she said sternly. "However—*however*, I say—there's the matter of Stefyny." Her expression softened suddenly and she looked up at Merlin. "She misses you, you know. And if we really are going to send her and her family to Maikel and Sharleyan in Manchyr, this is probably the best time to do it, since Sandaria won't be there in the Cave to keep them company any longer."

"I'm glad the two of them will be going home to

Tellesberg, but I really wish Sharley was coming here, instead," Cayleb said a bit sourly.

"I know you do," Merlin said. "And so does she. But one of you really does have to check in with Trahvys, Bynzhamyn, and Ahlvyno from time to time. It's how empires run . . . or so I understand. And at least Alahnah's turning into a bit better sailor. One of these days, she's actually going to realize she's a *Charisian*, isn't she?"

"I believe you're right. And at least they're going to have an interesting evening before they leave, aren't they?" Cayleb's smile was a bit crooked. "That being the case, I think Aivah has a point about your accompanying her. For that matter, why don't you go ahead and take the recon skimmer for the trip *to* the Cave? Then you could zip right back here—with Aivah, for that matter—while Owl flies the air van to Manchyr with the Mahlards. He could always drop Sandaria off here the *next* night."

"Actually, that might not be such a bad idea," Merlin said thoughtfully. "Assuming, of course," he glanced at Aivah, one eyebrow raised, "that Aivah won't mind being cooped up with me in the skimmer that long."

"The mere thought is unspeakably repugnant," Aivah assured him, lifting her nose with an audible sniff. Then she looked at him and smiled soulfully. "However, I am far too refined and proper to ever admit any such thing. So instead of being truthful, I will bend my neck to the yoke of good manners, smile, and say—lying through my teeth the entire time, you understand—nothing could possibly give me greater pleasure."

"You did that *very* well," Merlin said admiringly and offered her his arm. "Shall we go?"

"Good evening, My Lord."

Admiral Sir Dunkyn Yairley, Baron Sarmouth, paused as the red-haired, blue-eyed armswoman with the black, gold, blue, and silver blazon of the Charisian Empire on her breastplate bowed in polite greeting.

"Good evening, Captain Chwaeriau," he replied.

He'd come to know the exotically attractive imperial guardswoman at least slightly over the last several fivedays, since Hektor Aplyn-Ahrmahk—despite his marriage and his wounds—officially remained Sarmouth's flag lieutenant. Despite that, he still wasn't positive what to make of her. Given the stories about her and a certain Charlz Sheltyn, late of the Royal Corisandian Guard, there was no question in Sarmouth's mind that she was amply qualified for her present duties, and he made a conscientious effort to think of her as he would have thought about any other obviously competent officer of his acquaintance.

It was just that he found it difficult to picture someone whose head barely topped his shoulder—and who looked like one of his niece's schoolmates at St. Areetha's Convent—as a deadly warrior out of Safehold's most ancient lore.

Of course, that was also the mistake *Sheltyn* had made, now wasn't it? *Not* the company he wanted to be in.

"Her Majesty is expecting you," Chwaeriau continued, nodding to the graying sergeant standing watch outside the polished wooden doors with her. Sergeant Seahamper came briefly to attention and saluted her, and she pushed the door open and bowed Sarmouth through it.

"If you'll accompany me, My Lord," she invited.

▼ ▼ ▼

Sarmouth fought down a smile as Chwaeriau escorted him into the large, airy dining room. It was on the uppermost floor of Manchyr Palace, looking to the east across the harbor through a glass wall, and a large, sumptuous buffet had been arranged along its inner wall. The sun was sliding steadily down the western sky, and the palace cast tall shadows across the manicured grounds between it and the water battery which protected its eastern approaches. That wasn't what made him want to smile, however.

"Sir!" The Duke of Darcos shot to his feet, making no effort to hide his enormous smile, and held out his right hand. His left arm remained motionless at his side, but there was nothing weak or hesitant about the arm clasp he bestowed upon the admiral. "It's *good* to see you again, Sir!"

"Forgive me for mentioning this, *Your Grace*," Sarmouth said a bit pointedly, "but I understood that this was to be a social occasion. In which case, unless I'm sadly mistaken, a duke takes precedence over a mere baron and doesn't address him as 'Sir.'"

"Don't encourage him to become any snootier than he already is, please, Sir Dunkyn!" Irys Aplyn-Ahrmahk implored, coming forward to greet him in turn.

She didn't bother with any arm clasps, and Sarmouth hesitated as she hugged him with a familiarity which would undoubtedly have horrified eighty or ninety percent of her brother's subjects. It was only a brief hesitation, however, and he found himself hugging her back as the smile he'd tried to restrain broke free. He'd never married—it had always seemed to him that a serving sea officer had no business asking a woman to share his life when he'd be away at sea for half or more *of* that life—but thirty years' worth of midshipmen had given him ample sons. It would never have done to admit that that was how he saw them, of course, and especially not in the case of those who'd happened to belong to the royal family of Charis. But there was no point pretending to himself that Hektor Aplyn-Ahrmahk didn't hold a special place in his heart . . . or that the five-days Irys had spent aboard HMS *Destiny* hadn't given him a heart-*daughter*, as well.

"I hadn't observed any *snootiness* on his part, Your Highness," he observed, standing back from her with a twinkle. "Laziness, perhaps. But surely 'snooty' is putting it at least a *little* too strongly, isn't it?"

"You wouldn't say that if you'd been the one who caught him practicing looking down his nose at himself in the mirror," Irys assured him, tucking his left hand into the bend of her right elbow. She shuddered daintily. "It was quite horrible," she said faintly.

"Pay no attention to either of them, Sir Dunkyn," another voice said, and Sarmouth turned quickly, bowing deeply as Empress Sharleyan and Archbishop Maikel swept into the receiving room. "They've been practicing on me and the Archbishop all day. Please don't encourage them!"

"I'll . . . try to bear that in mind, Your Majesty." Sarmouth rose from his bow, then bowed again, not quite so deeply, as he kissed the ring Maikel Staynair extended to him.

"Your Eminence," he murmured.

"Admiral," Staynair responded. "It's good to see you looking so well, My Lord."

"Well, it's even better when I see His Grace and Her Highness looking as well as they do," Sarmouth said much more seriously. "The first reports we had in *Destiny* sounded . . . bad."

"Without Hektor, we'd both be dead," Irys said softly, and her husband looked down at her quickly. Shadows of memory stirred in her hazel eyes. He put his good arm about her and squeezed gently and she shook herself, then looked back up at him with a quick smile before she turned back to their guest. "I suppose that's the reason I keep him around. Well, that and this. So . . . expeditious, those Charisian seamen."

She touched her stomach, which was ever so slightly more domed than it had been, and Sarmouth heard Empress Sharleyan snort in amusement.

"Of course, if the cad had warned me that twins run in his family, I'd never have married him, of course."

"I *did* warn you!" Hektor said virtuously. "I even introduced you to two or three pairs of them."

"Don't try to squirm out of it, you scoundrel!" She smacked her husband, then blinked soulfully at Yairley. "You see what I have to put up with, Sir Dunkyn?"

"Ah, yes, Your Highness," the baron managed. "I, ah, understand the news was . . . received enthusiastically by your brother's subjects."

"Yes, it was, wasn't it?" Irys' eyes twinkled demurely. "It's not every girl who has cannons going off all over the waterfront when the world finds out she's pregnant. And aboard *Destiny*, for that matter, if I'm not mistaken. *That* happened pretty expeditiously, too, now that I think about it."

"Mercy, Your Highness!" Sarmouth raised his free hand in capitulation.

"I have no idea what you're talking about, My Lord." Irys raised her eyebrows in a politely questioning expression, and Hektor laughed, tucking her in tightly at his side.

"You'd almost think she was Charisian, wouldn't you, My Lord?"

"Because she is now, Your Grace, to Charis' great good fortune." The words came out quickly and lightly, but Sarmouth's brown eyes were serious.

"I think I agree with you, My Lord," Sharleyan said, then waved gracefully at the buffet. "As you can see, we're dining informally this evening. I rather regret that you won't be transporting the Archbishop and myself back to Tellesberg. Somehow, it seems wrong to be sailing aboard a ship other than *Destiny*. That's one reason—among others—we asked you to join us, and

Irys and Hektor were adamant that we could manage for ourselves without servants."

"I'm honored, Your Majesty," Sarmouth said sincerely. "May I serve a plate for you?"

"No, you may not, although I certainly appreciate the offer. Tonight we serve ourselves, and since you're the guest, please be good enough to get things started, My Lord."

Sarmouth considered arguing. He knew he *ought* to argue—that serving his own plate before the Empress of Charis was served was the height of impropriety. It was the sort of behavior which would have gotten the knuckles of any midshipman who'd ever sailed with him severely cracked . . . before another portion of his anatomy was thoroughly warmed by the boatswain. It was also the sort of behavior which made Sir Dunkyn Yairley acutely uncomfortable. Or would have, at least, under other circumstances. Sharleyan and Cayleb's informality with those they knew and trusted had long since become a byword—scandalously so, in some quarters—however. And this, he realized, was the empress' way of telling him she'd decided to include him in that select company.

It was, he decided, the greatest honor which had ever been bestowed upon him.

"Of course, Your Majesty."

He bowed deeply, took a plate from the stack at one end of the buffet, and began filling it with food.

▼ ▼ ▼

Sir Dunkyn Yairley sat back in his chair and sipped the excellent Zebediahan port after-dinner wine with a sense of pleasant repletion.

Corisande was much smaller than Old Charis, even though its total population was several million greater. Charis, however, had Howell Bay, which had been the true focus of the kingdom's growth and development. Its population was heavily concentrated along the bay's shores, whereas far more of the Corisandian interior had been turned into well-tilled farmland. That difference between the princedom and the kingdom undoubtedly explained the variance in their cuisines, as well, and he'd been very happily surprised by it. Charisian cooking, while delicious in its own right, tended to focus on seafood, whereas *Corisandian* cuisine merged the seafood to be expected from an island people with more "inland" foods. He doubted that combining mutton, chicken, wyvern, and shrimp with onions, mushrooms, bamboo, broccoli, carrots, and pineapple in a single stirfried dish would have occurred to most Charisians, but he'd already decided to get the recipe for his own chef aboard ship.

"That was delicious, Your Majesty," he said, and Sharleyan smiled at him. There was something just a bit odd about that smile.

"I appreciate the compliment, Sir Dunkyn," the empress said before Sarmouth really noticed that oddity. "The menu was Irys' choice, however, and the chefs are Prince Daivyn's, not mine. And so, alas, I can claim very little credit. Although," she added thoughtfully, "I did select the wines."

"Which were an excellent accompaniment for the meal," he said.

"I told you Sir Dunkyn had trained me properly, Mother," Hektor said from his end of the table. "See how adroitly he recovered after your correction?"

"Stop picking on the Baron," Irys said sternly, and poked her husband in the ribs. "He deserves much better treatment than that."

"In fact, he does." Sharleyan's voice was lower than it had been, almost solemn, and when Sarmouth turned back to her, her brown eyes were dark. "That's rather the point of tonight's dinner."

Sarmouth's eyes narrowed ever so slightly, and she nodded to him.

"The truth is, Sir Dunkyn," she said, "that this isn't a purely social affair after all. Mind you, it's *also* a social affair—an opportunity for Irys and Hektor and my entire house to thank you for your many services to us. While I'm sure Hektor would find it difficult to express in so many words, you've become very important to both him and Irys . . . and to me. Not simply as a loyal, courageous, and highly competent servant, but as an individual we treasure for *who* you are as much as for *what* you are."

Sarmouth felt his cheeks tighten with an unaccustomed heat, but the empress held his eyes levelly.

"All that's true," she told him softly, "yet tonight, we're about to ask something . . . extraordinary of you. Something you may not be able to give us, and something which—I'm afraid—places you in peril of your life. I hope you can forgive us for that."

She paused, and the baron set his wine glass down on the spotless white tablecloth.

"Your Majesty," he told her simply, "there's nothing to forgive. I *am* your servant, and the Empire's. It would be my honor to grant you any service within my power."

"Don't be too hasty, Sir Dunkyn."

Sharleyan smiled again, and this time he recognized the oddity, the edge of apprehension and . . . sorrow in that smile. She looked at him for a second or two, then glanced over her shoulder to where Captain Chwaeriau had stood post behind her chair for the entire meal.

"Nimue?" she said quietly.

Sarmouth's eyes snapped to the *seijin*, who bowed briefly but deeply to the empress, then stepped around the table to face the baron across it.

"My Lord," she told him, "when Her Majesty said she was about to ask you for something 'extraordinary,' she was referring to me. To your ability to accept who and what I truly am, and how *Seijin* Merlin and I came to serve Charis. We want you to know how that happened, what it truly means, and what the war against the Group of Four is truly about. Because what it's *truly* about is far greater than the corruption of the Group of Four and the current vicarate, and it goes back far, far farther in time than you could possibly know."

Sarmouth stared at her, then darted a quick look at

Sharleyan while his brain tried to grapple with what she'd just said. The empress' expression was impassive, and he flicked a look at Hektor and Irys. Their expressions were tauter than Sharleyan's, worried—possibly even frightened—yet he found that somehow reassuring. They were worried about *him*, he realized. Not about whatever the *seijin* was about to say to him, but about him, as someone who was as important to them as a *person* as Sharleyan had just told him he was. He looked into his flag lieutenant's eyes for a moment, then back at Captain Chwaeriau.

"I'm prepared to hear whatever it is you have to tell me, *Seijin*," he said without a quaver, and realized it was true.

She gazed back at him for a handful of heartbeats, then bowed across the table almost as deeply as she'd bowed to Sharleyan.

"I believe you are, My Lord," she said as she straightened. "I hope you'll still feel that way when we've finished."

She paused, as if drawing a deep breath, then squared her shoulders.

"My Lord, the truth is that everything you've ever been taught about the Church and the Archangels is a lie." He stiffened, but she went on in that same measured voice. "A thousand years ago, before human beings ever touched the surface of Safehold, there was a war. It was a war between something called the 'Terran Federation' and something called the 'Gbaba,' and it began at a place called Crestwell's Star when a ship named *Swiftsure* first encountered—"

▼ ▼ ▼

"You were serious when you said you were going to ask something extraordinary of me, weren't you, Your Majesty?" Sir Dunkyn Yairley said slowly the better part of four hours later.

His brown eyes were haunted as he looked back and forth between his empress and the blue-eyed, red-haired young woman who claimed to be more ancient than the Creation itself . . . and yet less than three months old. Those eyes traveled to the side table where the fireplace poker she'd tied into knots to demonstrate her strength lay beside the "communicator" over which Emperor Cayleb himself had spoken and the "hologram projector" which had shown him the fallen Archangel Kau-yung personally speaking to a woman a thousand years dead. He looked at all those items, remembered all those things, and he wanted, more than almost anything in the world, to lick his lips, but he refused to.

He sat very still, aware that even though they'd been very careful not to say it, his life hung by a thread. They'd told him too much, *shown* him too much, for it to work any other way. And deep within him a part of him wanted that thread to snap. Wanted to turn away, to wail a grief-ridden lament over the dead corpse of all he'd believed in, everything he'd ever known was true. What they wanted—what they *demanded*—that he believe instead turned the Archangels he'd trusted and revered for his entire life not simply into mortals, not simply into imposters and liars, but into *traitors*. Into betrayers and mass murderers on an inconceivable scale. And at the same time, it transformed Shan-wei and Kau-yung from the greatest traitors in history into the honorable and blameless *victims* of those murderous "Archangels" he'd loved so deeply. It was impossible, it simply couldn't be true, and his skin crawled at the thought of giving his service—and his soul—to Shan-wei herself.

Yet for all of that, it was also impossible for him to simply reject what they'd told him. It explained too many things about the present war, about the new weapons, the new concepts spilling out of Charis and the Royal College. Too many things about the capabilities of Charisian spies and how smoothly Sharleyan and Cayleb functioned as a coordinated team even when they were tens of thousands of miles apart.

*And then there's the Archbishop*, he thought, glancing at Maikel Staynair who sat in his own chair, hands folded before him on the table, looking back at Sarmouth with an expression that mingled understanding with compassion and a steel-hard fidelity. *There's not a more godly man in all the world, not one who could match Archbishop Maikel's gentleness and love, his fearless defense of his flock, or his tolerance and compassion even for those who hate him. And yet he wants me to believe the Church herself is nothing but a monstrous lie.*

"I don't know if I can believe all you've told me and shown me, Your Majesty," he said finally. "That the . . . *seijins* are capable of even more than I ever suspected they were, or that you—and they—truly possess all the miraculous powers you've demonstrated to me . . . *that* I have no choice but to believe. But that the Archangels, the Church, God Himself are *lies* goes far beyond that, and the *Writ* offers explanations in plenty for everything you've shown me."

"Of course it does, My Lord," the archbishop said simply, and Sarmouth's eyes returned to him. "It must offer those explanations—those demons and fallen archangels and all the unclean, blasphemous powers with which they tempt the children of God—in order to accomplish its own goals. And just as you fear at this moment that we may have interwoven truth and compassion and love for our fellow men and women into a false explanation in the service of Shan-wei, the *Writ* weaves truth, compassion, and love into a false explanation in the service of Langhorne and the rest of his command group. As you say, we can demonstrate our *capabilities* to you by demonstrating Nimue's marvelous strength, her pieces of equipment, our ability to communicate with Siddar City from this very room. Those are concrete things you can touch, hear, feel. The truth of what we *believe* and what we ask *you* to believe is far more difficult to demonstrate. Yet the *Writ* itself says you will know who and what a person is by what that person does in his or her life. At this moment, in this place, how will you judge Nimue and Merlin, Cayleb and Sharleyan, and Hektor and Irys by what they've done in their lives? And how will you judge Zhaspahr Clyntahn, Wyllym Rayno, the Inquisition, and all the hideous things Mother Church has done in their service?"

"If it were that simple, Your Eminence, there'd be no war on Safehold," Sarmouth replied. "*Men* can be evil, not matter their station. Mother Church has punished criminals among her episcopacy and even the vicarate before now. And the fact that men—or women—are *good* doesn't necessarily make them *holy*, either. How often has the Church taught that Shan-wei seduces men and women by appealing to their *goodness*, not to the darkness within them?"

"And how essential would it be to the Church we've revealed to you this night to teach precisely that, be it ever so dark and deadly a lie?" Staynair riposted softly.

Sarmouth closed his eyes, poised between two equally agonizing possibilities. His faith told him Staynair was lying, that the archbishop *must* be lying. Yet reason, his own eyes, his trust in his monarchs, and his own sense of duty all told him *Langhorne* must have lied. That he, like every other man and woman who'd ever lived on Safehold, had given his faith, his service, and his love to the greatest falsehood in human history.

*And whether they're telling the truth or not, they can't allow me to leave this room alive unless they're convinced beyond a shadow of a doubt that I believe them*, he thought coldly.

He opened his eyes again and found Nimue Alban watching him across the table through the calm, sapphire eyes of Nimue Chwaeriau. He looked back at her, and she tipped her head to one side and smiled at him almost compassionately.

"My Lord," she said, "I think I know at least one thing running through your mind right now, and you're right. If you choose to reject what we've told you, if you choose to place your loyalty and ability, all the things which make you so valuable to the Empire and to the fight against the Group of Four, in the service of the lie, we can't allow you to leave this room alive. But it would be a betrayal of all we ourselves believe and of the deep affection Hektor and Irys have for you if we were to repay your sense of honor with death. Until a year or two ago, that would have been our only option, yet that's no longer true. We still lack many of the capabilities the Federation took for granted, but shortly after Prince Nahrmahn's death, Merlin instructed Owl to produce new batches of the drugs used aboard the starships which brought humanity to Safehold, and one of them—you might think of it as a . . . sleeping draught—simulates physical death almost perfectly. If you're unable to continue to serve Charis with the same devotion and courage with which you've always served her in the past, I'm afraid you'll suffer a 'fatal stroke' this evening. And in about a five-day or so, you'll wake up again, none the worse for wear, in the Cave. You'll be imprisoned there, I'm sorry to say, but in conditions of comfort and respect. I hope that if that happens, in the fullness of time, you'll be able to accept that we've told you nothing but the truth, yet honesty compels me to admit that we could never return your old life. In that sense, you would, indeed, be dead, because you couldn't come back from the grave in the eyes of the world."

"Please, Sir," Hektor said, reaching out his good hand towards him. "I realize how unfair it is of us to ask this of you, but we truly have no choice. We *need* you, even more than we ever needed you before."

Sarmouth looked back at the youthful duke, his heart twisted by the conflict between affection—love—and a lifetime's faith. He *wanted* to believe Hektor and the others, he realized. He truly wanted to . . . but that was the snare Shan-wei always laid before men. That was—

"Sir Dunkyn."

Irys Aplyn-Ahrmahk stood. She walked around the table to stand in front of him and laid her hands on his shoulders, and her gaze met his unflinchingly.

"I owe you my life," she told him. "I owe you more than that. I owe you the chance to meet the man I love and the child I'm about to bear him, and I owe you my brother's—my Prince's—life. Those are debts I can never repay. But I tell you this now, with all the honesty within me.

"I knew none of this until the day Hektor sacrificed his life to save mine. That's precisely what he did, because neither of us dreamed it might be possible for him to be so terribly wounded and survive. I know that discovering he could be saved after all—and that he was—biases me towards believing the best about the people who restored him to me. But the chance they took—the risk they ran—in telling *me* the truth was even greater than the risk we've taken in telling you. It might have devastated everything they'd fought for years to accomplish here in Corisande. They knew that . . . and they never hesitated. That's who they are, who *we* are, and because we need you and because we love you—because *I* love you—I beg you to believe the truth. Long before I ever wed Hektor, before Sharleyan and Cayleb allowed Daivyn and me to return to Corisande and trusted us to do what was right, I knew where I stood. I discovered that aboard *your* ship between Charis and Chisholm, and it terrified me because I realized Archbishop Maikel had been right all along—that *I* had to choose what I believed. What I could give my life to accomplishing. And when I realized that, I knew I would rather stand beside people like Sharleyan and Cayleb—and beside the people who loved and followed them—in the deepest pit of Hell than stand in the highest Heaven with any God who could agree with Zhaspahr Clyntahn. You want that, too. I *know* you do, because I've come to know you. And if you read all the horrors in the *Book of Schueler*, if you read all the lies in the *Book of Chihiro*, then you know that Zhaspahr Clyntahn's God—the God of Mother Church—*does* agree with him."

Her hazel eyes looked deep, deep into his, and they were bottomless as the sea, dark with honesty and the depth of her own fearless belief.

"So the question, Sir Dunkyn," she said softly, "is whether or not *you* agree with that God."

# Sheryl-Seridahn Canal,
# West of Evyrtyn,
# The South March Lands

"Get *down*, Sir!"

Something hit Lieutenant Bryahnsyn from behind, wrapped itself around his knees, and sent him crashing facedown to the ground. He hit so hard his sinuses stung . . . just before the abbreviated whistle of one of the heretics' small angle-gun shells ended in a sudden explosion. It was an explosive round, fortunately, not one of the shrapnel-spewing airbursts, and it exploded only after hitting the ground, but shell fragments hissed nastily overhead.

He pushed himself cautiously up on his hands and looked over his shoulder at the nineteen-year-old private who'd tackled him.

"A simple shout might have done the job with less bruises, Symyn," he pointed out. "And without exposing both of us, now that I think about it."

"Sorry about that, Sir." Private Hyldyrshot didn't seem particularly crushed by his company commander's reprimand. "Didn't think you heard it coming," he added.

"Well, I appreciate your taking care of me," Bryahnsyn told him, choosing not to mention that Hyldyrshot was entirely correct. He *hadn't* heard the incoming shell, and he should have been paying better attention. Langhorne knew the heretic bastards chucked the things over often enough to keep the Army of the Seridahn from feeling bored! Most of his men had acquired the survival-oriented reflex to hit the ground whenever one of them arrived, and he supposed officers should set the example in that, as well. It would be a far better one than the "See how brave I am when I stand out in the shrapnel!" attitude some of his denser colleagues seemed to prefer to demonstrate.

Briefly, at least.

"Now get back under cover," he continued. "I promise I'll watch my own arse in the meantime." The private seemed to hesitate, and Bryahnsyn lowered his eyebrows and glowered. "If you get yourself shot full of holes for absolutely no good reason, Private, Platoon Sergeant Abykrahmbi will give me Shan-wei's own hell over it!"

"Yes, Sir."

Hyldyrshot grinned, touched his chest in salute, and crawled back into what someone in the Imperial Charisian Army would have called his slit trench. Bryahnsyn paused just long enough to nod in gratitude, then resumed his journey—more cautiously, exactly as he'd promised—across 5th Company's position.

The private's attitude was a welcome indicator of the state of the army's morale. Personally, Bryahnsyn wouldn't have been surprised to see the men cowering in their holes instead of worrying about what might happen to one of their officers who wasn't paying attention the way he ought to. Instead, they seemed well aware of the reasons they couldn't stand and challenge the heretics to a fight to the finish. They didn't *like* retreating, yet they understood why they were doing it, and instead of the sullenness Bryahnsyn might have expected, they'd decided to take a sense of pride out of conducting that retreat as skillfully—and as stubbornly—as possible.

They'd fallen back from Evyrtyn to get out of the ironclad's range, and before they'd left, their engineers had blown up the river locks between Evyrtyn and the town of Riverfork, a hundred and eighty miles farther up the Seridahn, as well. Personally, Bryahnsyn was inclined to think the river above Riverfork was probably too shallow for something the ironclad's size, but there was no way to be sure of that, so General Rychtyr had destroyed the locks anyway, just to be safe. Surely it would take even the heretics months to rebuild or replace them in mid-river, especially with the spring floods not so many five-days away! He hoped so, anyway; the last thing they needed was that monster getting as high as Alyksberg and severing the Dairnyth-Alyksberg Canal, as well.

There was damn all the Army of the Seridahn could do about Alyksberg, however. All it could do was fight its stubborn retreating action as slowly—and with as few casualties among its own men—as possible. That was how the lieutenant found his platoon thirty-five miles west of Evyrtyn, crouching in their muddy trenches while the rest of the army fell back to the much more substantial entrenchments waiting five miles beyond them. At least the labor gangs which had been sent up the canal from Dohlar had finished preparing the army's next main position in plenty of time. They were supposed to be working on the position beyond that one now, and as long as the heretics didn't bring up the *heavy* angle-guns . . . .

"Over here, Lieutenant!"

He looked up at the shout and saw Brynt Atwatyr, Captain Mahkluskee's company sergeant, waving to attract his attention. The company commander's hole, hidden from the heretics directing the angle-guns' fire by a dense thicket of second-growth timber, was rather larger than the one Bryahnsyn had left behind, and 4th Platoon was dug-in amid the trees to prevent any unwelcome guests from disturbing the captain's meeting.

Bryahnsyn waved back to Atwatyr and jogged the remaining fifty yards, then slithered down into the hole beside Lieutenant Aimohs Zhynkyns, who'd inherited 4th Platoon after Lieutenant Sandkaran's death.

"Glad you could make it, Ahrnahld," Captain Mahkluskee observed with a sardonic smile. It wasn't a reprimand. In fact, it was almost a compliment, since Bryahnsyn had had farther to come than any of the captain's other platoon commanders.

"Let's get to it," Mahkluskee continued more briskly, beckoning the lieutenants closer to his sketch map. They gathered around him, and he tapped it with a dirty finger. "We're here," he said, indicating a point on the Sheryl-Seridahn Canal while heretic angle-gun shells continued to explode in a sort of ragged rhythm in the background. Bryahnsyn didn't want to think about what would happen if one of them chanced to find its way into the hole with them by blind luck. "Colonel Sheldyn has Second and Third Company out on our flanks—here and here—but they're farther west than we are, and the rest of the army, except for Colonel Hahpkyns' regiment, has already fallen back. Basically, we're the head of the arrow right now, and our job's to stay where we are at least until dark. After the sun sets, I'll pass the order to begin pulling out. I'll be using runners, not whistles or bugles, since we'd just as soon not have the bastards realize we're moving in the open."

All of his lieutenants nodded in fervent agreement. A platoon caught in the open by a fusillade of shrapnel-charged infantry angle shells could be wiped out in minutes. They'd found that out the hard way since the heretic Hanth had taken the offensive.

"All right," Mahkluskee went on. "Ahrnahld," he looked at Bryahnsyn, "your people are the farthest east on the canal, so we're going to start by moving you back. When the runner tells you it's time to go, pull out *quietly*. We don't want the heretics to know we're going anywhere until we're already gone. Frankly, I'd prefer for it to be sometime next five-day before they figure it out, but I'm not going to bet my pension on it."

A couple of his platoon commanders chuckled, and he grinned tautly, then turned to Lieutenant Charlsyn Dahnel, 1st Platoon's CO.

"You'll be next to go, Charlsyn. Ahrnahld will send a runner to your position when the last of his men are out of their holes and headed west. Stay where you are until you hear from him. Then, I want you to move—"

▼ ▼ ▼

"We need more of the heavy angles, My Lord," Admiral Sympsyn said. "The mortars are good—they're a hell of a lot better than just *good*, in fact—but once the bastards get dug-in below ground level, especially with any kind of overhead cover, mortars just don't have the firepower to blast them back out again."

Sir Hauwerd Breygart, the Earl of Hanth, grunted in sour agreement. It wasn't as if his artillery chief was telling him anything he didn't already know. Unfortunately, there wasn't much he could do about it. More rifled six-inch angle-guns were supposed to be on their way to him "as soon as possible," but the unfortunate truth was that the Army of Thesmar's priority remained clearly secondary to the other forces Charis and Siddarmark had in the field. The fact that he understood the logic behind that state of affairs didn't seem to make it any more palatable, however.

"What we've got is what we'll have for at least another month, Lywys," he said as philosophically as possible. "In fact, I won't be all that surprised if we don't get them until some time in late June. And depending on how things go against Kaitswyrth, it could be even longer than that. Master Howsmyn's doing his best, but the Navy's had first priority on the heavy guns since the first ironclads were laid down."

It was Sympsyn's turn to grunt in acknowledgment of something he already knew.

"In the meantime," Hanth continued, "we need to keep the pressure on. I'm not planning on pulling a Harless and storming any of these earthworks. Our boys have better things to do than fertilize some farmer's fields! But we're actually more mobile than they are now, once we get away from the canal. So as long as we can keep working our way around their flanks, we can keep them moving steadily westward."

He turned to Major Dyntyn Karmaikel, his aide. Like Sympsyn, who'd been a naval captain when they arrived in Thesmar, Karmaikel had been promoted. He'd also found himself assuming the position of Hanth's chief of staff, which was a heavy load for a man who'd been a Marine lieutenant only months earlier. He'd risen to the challenge nicely, however, and in the process he might have begun laying the demons of hatred which had ridden him for so long, as well.

"Dyntyn," the earl said, "we need a dispatch to Brigadier Mathysyn. I want Major Mahklymorh's scout snipers and Colonel Brystahl's regiment ready to move out by morning. I'm pretty sure we're going to run into another damned set of entrenchments a few miles beyond the odds and sods in front of us right now. According to the maps, the terrain's better on the north side of the canal. That's why I want Mahklymorh and Brystahl to hook around to the *south*. If they've slipped up and left us an opening, it's more likely we'll find it on that side."

"Aye, My Lord."

"Draft me a dispatch to that effect. Then let me take a look at it before we send it off."

"Aye, aye, My Lord."

The Marine saluted and stepped into the command tent where Hanth's clerks waited at their portable writing desks.

It was nice to have a properly equipped field headquarters, at least, the earl reflected. It would be even nicer to get the heavy artillery he truly needed, but he wasn't about to complain. Not after the frayed boot lace upon which he'd been forced to operate the summer before.

Besides, the truth was that even without the heavy angles he was far, far happier with the way this year was shaping up. His army had advanced over four hundred and fifty miles from Thesmar following the high road—well over six hundred, up the course of the Seridahn—in less than three months and driven Sir Fahstyr Rychtyr from every position he'd tried to hold. Unfortunately, Rychtyr had figured out how to slow things up since then.

The key to his rapid advance had been HMS *Delthak*'s heavy guns. His mortars and thirty-pounders were effective enough in the open, but as Sympsyn had just pointed out, they weren't powerful enough to demolish properly designed entrenchments. *Delthak*'s six-inchers could do that . . . if the thoroughgoing destruction of the Evyrtyn locks hadn't barred the ironclad from the canal.

It would have taken Commodore Parkyr and his engineers five-days, at best, to repair the canal locks, and the effort would have been pointless. The town of Fyrayth, a hundred and ninety miles west of Evyrtyn, was the highest elevation along the Sheryl-Seridahn Canal. That made its locks the key to the entire eastern portion of the canal, and as long as they were in Rychtyr's hands, he controlled the water level in the canal.

Which explained why there was precious little water in it at the moment.

Without *Delthak* in support, and without enough of the Army's heavy angles to replace her firepower, pushing Rychtyr farther back promised to be an extraordinarily unpleasant task. Rychtyr couldn't stop the Army of Thesmar from ultimately working its way around the Dohlarans' flanks, but he could make any frontal assaults unbearably costly. It was going to be like some formal dance where everyone knew the steps; Hanth could already see that much. Unless Rychtyr was obliging enough to screw up and let the Charisians and their Siddarmarkian allies actually cut the canal behind him before he retreated, Hanth's troops were going to wear out a lot of perfectly good boots over the coming several months.

*And if the bastards keep getting more of those new rifles of theirs forward, it's only going to get worse,* he reflected grimly. *I'm not looking forward to seeing proper angle-guns in their hands, either. If the* seijins *are right about how soon they're going to start turning up we're going to have to be* damned *careful about how aggressively we go after them.*

He grimaced. The good news was that nothing he was going to face was likely to be better than his own men's weapons; the bad news was that what he was going to face was no longer going to be *inferior* to his own men's weapons.

*But we'll still be moving in the right direction, whatever the bastards come up with,* he reminded himself. *That's a hell of a lot more than* Rychtyr *can say!*

. IX .
HMS *Destiny*, 54,
and
Manchyr Palace,
City of Manchyr,
Princedom of Corisande,
Empire of Charis

"It's different this time, isn't it, Hektor?" Baron Sarmouth's voice was quiet as he stood beside Hektor Aplyn-Ahrmahk on HMS *Destiny*'s quarterdeck.

"Oh, in a lot of ways, Sir," Hektor replied, never taking his eyes from the towers and windows of Manchyr Palace. "Just being able to tell what the weather looks like ahead of us is going to be a huge advantage, isn't it?"

"I wasn't talking about *that*," Sarmouth said dryly. "And, frankly, if you want to talk about your Merlin's magic, I'm inclined to think *weather's* going to be the least of its advantages." He shook his head and let his left hand rest lightly on the youthful duke's right shoulder. "I'm talking about who's going to be waiting for you when you get home this time. And who's likely to be waiting *with* her, frankly," he ended much more gently.

"I know." Hektor glanced at him and smiled briefly, then returned his gaze to the palace falling slowly astern as *Destiny* and the rest of her squadron ghosted out into Manchyr Bay's broad waters on the fitful wings of a light topgallant breeze. They were making no more than a knot or two, which Lieutenant Aplyn-Ahrmahk had just discovered only made the slow, drawn-out process of separation even worse.

"I know," he repeated. "That's why I'd rather talk about 'Merlin's magic.'"

Sarmouth squeezed the shoulder under his hand and

nodded. What young Hektor was feeling at the moment was another reason he himself had never married, he reflected. And yet, despite the misery the young man beside him was experiencing, the admiral envied him, too.

Irys hadn't come out to *Destiny* to bid her husband farewell. Any one of the royal barges could have lifted her from the palace's water gate out to Sarmouth's anchored flagship, but the Regency Council's disapproval of any such notion had been remarkably firm. Sarmouth doubted they were going to be able to keep her wrapped up in cotton silk because of her pregnancy for very long, but that wasn't going to stop them from trying. Besides, Earl Anvil Rock and Archbishop Klairmant had played unscrupulously upon the fact that she was now Prince Daivyn's regent, as well. As such, her responsibilities to the Crown precluded her from running avoidable risks.

Despite that, she probably would have accompanied Hektor to *Destiny* if Empress Sharleyan hadn't added her own weight to the scales. Sharleyan had no fear the barge would suddenly sink amid the six-inch wavelets of Manchyr Harbor, but she'd had her own experience taking leave of sailors potentially headed in harm's way. It would be better all around, she'd said firmly, for Irys to kiss Hektor goodbye in the privacy of their own palace suite and then let him go.

And, Sarmouth felt certain, at this very moment Sharleyan, Sarmouth, and Nimue Chwaeriau were making certain the princess had plenty of company to keep her occupied. For that matter—his lips twitched on the brink of a smile—*Irys* was probably fully occupied consoling Prince Daivyn! The boy's misery when he'd discovered his brother-in-law was headed back to sea would have melted the hardest heart. No doubt many of his Corisandian subjects would have sneered at his sorrow over Hektor's departure and seen getting Hektor out of Manchyr as a major plus. The idea that their prince could actually burst into tears at the thought of being parted from a member of the Charisian imperial family would have struck those Corisandians as a self-serving pro-Charis lie.

But those scoffers hadn't watched that same prince and Hektor aboard this very ship following Daivyn and Irys' rescue from Delferahk. Or on the voyage from Charis to Chisholm and then on to Corisande, for that matter.

*True enough*, he thought, *but not really much to the point, is it? Hektor may be trying to distract himself from leaving Irys—and Daivyn, be fair—behind, but you're trying to distract yourself from "Merlin's magic" by focusing on that, instead, aren't you, Dunkyn?*

And he was. There were times—probably not more than two or three dozen of them a day, he thought wryly—when it all still struck him as more than he could possibly take in. He had no idea where his own beliefs would ultimately settle, and an occasional icy wind of doubt—doubt that what he'd been told could *really* be true—still blew through the marrow of his bones. In the end, he suspected, even more than duty, more than his own oaths to his monarchs, more than his devotion to his navy and his empire—more even than his faith that Maikel Staynair was a true man of God, whatever else he might be—what had truly carried him across the divide between rejection and belief had been the hazel eyes of a young woman who'd stolen her way into his heart.

*I wonder how many other hard-bitten, practical decisions have been made on just that sort of basis? And is it really such a bad way to do it? When it all comes down to a decision point you can't avoid—when you have to choose, yet the evidence before your eyes disproves all the things you've ever believed and all the things you've ever believed say the evidence must be false—isn't it the heart that matters? And if that young woman could rise above all the reasons she had to hate the House of Ahrmahk to give her allegiance to Cayleb and Sharleyan's true cause, how could I not give it mine, as well?*

He squeezed Hektor's shoulder again, then tucked

his hands behind him and began slowly pacing up and down the weather side of his quarterdeck.

▼ ▼ ▼

"Well, so far so good," Cayleb observed over the com. "As long as he stays converted, of course."

"Oh, he'll stay converted," Sharleyan reassured him.

She sat in a wicker rocking chair on one of Manchyr Palace's balconies with Alahnah dozing in her lap. The princess had celebrated her third birthday just before Hektor left for *Destiny*, and she'd exhausted herself thoroughly. Thoroughly enough to dissipate the sugar buzz of far too much chocolate cake, in fact, and thank God for it! Mother and daughter were shaded by the balcony awning and Sharleyan rocked her little girl gently as she simultaneously watched the image projected on her contact lens and the tan and gray sails moving slowly away from her.

"He's smart," she continued, "and deep inside, where it matters, he knows we told him the truth. We all come at it a little differently, but we've all been in the same place, haven't we? Whatever pain he's feeling right now is the pain of disillusionment—of bereavement, maybe—not of doubt. I don't know where he's ultimately going to come down on faith in God, but I'm pretty sure I know where he's going to come down on faith in the 'Archangels,' Cayleb."

"You're probably right. I have to admit, though, that I'm just as happy having Hektor along to ride herd on him, for a while at least. I wish it didn't mean parting him and Irys, though."

"Hektor's not much of a court lapdog, love. He'd stay and do his duty, and he didn't want to leave Irys any more than she wanted him to leave, but he's like you. He needs to be out and doing."

"Which I most definitely am not at the moment," Cayleb said sourly.

"That's because you know when you *have* to stay put and do your duty, instead." Sharleyan smiled at his grimace and shook her head. "It's only fair, in a way. I haven't seen you in a lot longer than Irys hasn't seen Hektor. And Mairah hasn't seen Hauwerd, either. We're *all* doing our duty where we have to be, and most of us would damned well rather be somewhere else."

"I know," he sighed. "I know."

They sat in comforting silence for several moments, then Cayleb shook himself.

"Speaking about doing our duty. Have you had any more thoughts about how you're going to be in three places at once?"

Sharleyan snorted in amusement, but he had a point. In fact, it was a very *good* point. It was well past time for her to return to Tellesberg as the imperial constitution required, but constitutional requirements didn't always leave much scope for *other* responsibilities involved in making certain the empire established by that constitution remained intact. And, at the moment, there were more political problem children—in this instance, named "Corisande" and "Chisholm"—than either of them could have liked. Corisande remained the newest and most fragile unit of the Empire of Charis, still in the process of integration, and certain nobles in the western portion of Chisholm were gradually working their way towards what could only be construed as open treason.

"Actually, I have," she told him. "I'm not too sure I'm not making virtues out of necessity in a couple of places, but it seems to me that I need to leave Manchyr and Cherayth to manage themselves and go home to Tellesberg. I know we can rely on Trahvys and Domynyk to keep an eye on things for us there, but there really is a Constitution, you know."

"Yes, I do," he agreed, and his tone was more than a little grumpy. "There are times I'm inclined to think Rayjhis was right about that 'brilliant notion' of mine, though."

"It made a lot of sense when we were talking just about Charis and Chisholm, love." Sharleyan smiled and shook her head. "If it *wasn't* a 'brilliant notion,' that's only because you weren't thinking big enough.

When you proposed it, though, it struck exactly the right note, and you know it. Moving the official seat of government back and forth was the surest way to reassure my Chisholmians that we weren't going to become just a Charisian appendage."

"Oh, I know that. At the same time, you have to admit that it could've turned into a colossal blunder if Merlin hadn't ended up telling us about Owl and providing us with coms. Even with those advantages, it's inconvenient as hell to have the two of us dashing around and continually leaving either Charis or Chisholm without a resident monarch. Or, in this case, leaving *both* of them without resident monarchs for months on end!"

"Admit it," she teased. "What really ticks you off about it is that the two of us haven't been in the same place since you left for Siddarmark and I left for Chisholm. Coms are all very well, but what you are really missing are the . . . less cerebral advantages of face-to-face 'conversations' when we're both in the same place."

"Well, I *am* a sailor," Cayleb pointed out. "And now that I think about it, Alahnah is three years old. I think it's time we provided a backup heir, don't you? Purely as a dynastic duty, I mean. Besides, she's going to be outnumbered sometime around November. We need to start catching up, especially if Irys and Hektor are going to specialize in twins like his parents! Unfair advantage, that's what it is!"

" 'Dynastic duty,' is it?" Sharleyan snorted. "What was that quote Nimue gave me the other day? The one from Queen Vyktohriah or whoever? Something about 'Close your eyes and think of England,' wasn't it?"

"She only told you about it because she was born and raised in that Great Britain place," Cayleb retorted. "Obviously that makes it the most important nation Old Earth ever had! And the other reason she told you is because she has a wicked, low, disrespectful, salacious sense of humor which is no respecter of our imperial dignity."

"Wonderful, isn't it?" Sharleyan agreed with a grin.

"But the other reason she told me was because she knows I miss those 'less cerebral' conversations as much as you do."

"I know she does. And we're lucky to have her and Merlin—especially to have both of them—even if there are times their so-called sense of humor makes me want to wring their cybernetic necks."

"You're a fine one to be talking about anyone else's sense of humor, Cayleb Ahrmahk!"

"Did I ever say I wasn't?" Cayleb riposted with a chuckle, but then his expression turned serious once more.

"Leaving aside any question about *seijins*' questionable senses of humor, I admit you have a point about the need to get back to Tellesberg. Our people are willing to cut us some slack about that particular constitutional provision because they realize we simply can't keep a regular schedule when the entire world's blowing up around our ears, but that doesn't mean they like it. And it really would be nice, you know, if we could come close to hitting that legally required schedule at least once every, oh, ten or fifteen years. I'm not sure that argument really overrules the ones in favor of leaving you in Manchyr or sending you back to Cherayth, though."

"Sooner or later, I'm going to have to leave Manchyr, unless we want people to start thinking Daivyn, Irys, and the Regency Council are simply our sock puppets," Sharleyan retorted, and it was Cayleb's turn to snort. Merlin had introduced the concept of sock puppets to Alahnah before she could walk, and somehow it had trickled out of the imperial nursery and wormed its way into the Charisian branch of Safehold's venerable traditions of puppet theater.

"In some ways, Irys and Hektor's marriage only makes that particular problem worse," she continued. "Those who are inclined to see us as puppet masters see their marriage as one more hook to help us manipulate her and Daivyn."

"We don't really need to 'manipulate' anyone,"

Cayleb pointed out mildly. "Daivyn's sworn fealty, and Corisande is now officially part of the Empire, if I remember correctly. I believe that means we can simply issue *instructions* without any manipulative shilly-shallying around."

"Of course he did, of course it is, and of course we could . . . in theory, at least. But we wouldn't be having this conversation, love of my life, if we didn't both realize it's still a new, fragile sort of union. There are still a lot of things that could go wrong, and that's where the perception of us as puppet masters comes into play. We don't need to give any fresh Paitryk Hainrees any more ammunition to distort for propaganda purposes than we can help, now do we?"

He shook his head, and she shrugged.

"I suppose I could make a case for hovering here until the children are born, but I'm sure those naturally suspicious people we've just been talking about would denounce that as only another cynical excuse to let me stay here and maintain my iron grip on everything."

"A point," Cayleb acknowledged. "But it doesn't change the fact that Corisande's still awfully new to the Charisian fold, as you just also pointed out. So there's something to be said for iron grips at the moment."

"Yes, there is, and that's one reason we've got to bring Coris into the circle," Sharleyan said positively. "If there's anyone in the world better equipped—and better informed—to keep an eye on things here than he is, I certainly can't think of who it might be! And if we're going to add him to the circle, we need to do it— and give him time to settle down with the new reality— before Maikel and I leave for Tellesberg. In fact, Maikel, Irys, Nimue, and I should probably see to that in the next day or two. Have the Brethren come around to our viewpoint?"

"Father Ahbel has, and so has Sister Ahmai." Cayleb twitched his mouth in sour amusement. "With the two of them signed on, I think we can consider it what Merlin and Nimue would call a 'done deal.' All that's left is the formal nose-counting, and frankly I think how strongly Sandaria's finally come around is working in our favor. For a while there it looked like we'd made a huge mistake in her case. I could almost hear some of them saying 'Act in haste and repent at leisure, young man!' " He rolled his eyes. "Now that she's made her mind up, their relief makes our judgment look a lot sounder to them again, and I think we should ride that for all it's worth. I won't say they're happy about the thought of adding Coris, because I don't think they are—still a bit of that 'But he worked for *Hektor!*' to be overcome, I think—and they weren't exactly overjoyed about approaching Sir Dunkyn on such short notice, either. They're about to jump in Coris' favor, though. And even if they weren't, this would be another of those times you and I together would have to jointly overrule them."

"In that case, I need to stay long enough to get him firmly on board. Once that's done, I can leave him—and Nimue—to support Irys and Daivyn. That should be more than enough support for anybody!"

"I wish there wasn't that element that resents the hell out of her pregnancy," Cayleb said a bit fretfully. "The sort of people who get their noses out of joint over something like that are just the sort of people likely to do something monumentally stupid!"

"They are, but there aren't that many of them. And they'd have to get past Nimue, Coris, Koryn, Anvil Rock, Tartarian, Charlz Doyal, Alyk Ahrthyr, and the Royal Guard, dear," Sharleyan pointed out. "I won't say they couldn't do it if all of those very capable people managed to screw up simultaneously. I will say there are more profitable things you might spend your time worrying about, though."

"I know. I know!" Cayleb shrugged. "I probably wouldn't be worrying about it as much if that bitch hadn't come so close to killing both of them on the cathedral steps. But you're right, and I know it."

"Well, in that case, I think we can agree Corisande

will do just fine even without my skilled hand on the tiller."

"Granted—assuming we bring Coris on board and it turns out he really can handle the truth. And I agree with you: you need to be there personally to tell him. It's not something we can or should delegate to Irys and Nimue, especially if it turns out he's *not* ready to handle it after all. If he has to suffer a sudden 'stroke' and be carted off to the Cave, we'll *really* need you there to put out the forest fires. But I'm pretty sure he will be . . . which brings us back to Chisholm, and I have to say I'm getting a little more worried about that. In fact, I'm a *lot* more worried than I was last summer, Sharley."

"I admit Rock Coast and Black Horse have put more thought and effort into it than I ever expected out of such less than brilliant conspirators," she conceded. "I think Ahlber, Sylvyst, and Braisyn are still on top of things though."

"Courtesy of the 'seijin network.' " Cayleb nodded. "But that's not the same as having one of us on the ground to act on that intelligence, and while I'm very happy about having recruited Dunkyn, Irys, and Hektor and I'll be *delighted* to add somebody as competent as Coris to the mix, we don't have *anyone* from the circle in Chisholm at the moment. That's something we should have taken care of long since."

"I know. But the main reason we haven't is that we didn't need anyone as badly as we need someone here in Corisande. I've known I could trust the people I had looking after things as long as we could provide them with the information they needed to make good decisions. I don't see how that's changed, Cayleb, and General Kahlyns has almost completed training the new regiments, so it's not like Braisyn won't have a big stick if he needs one. For now, at least."

Cayleb grunted unhappily. Like Sharleyan, he had great faith in Braisyn Byrns, Earl White Crag, her first councilor. Sylvyst Mhardyr, Baron Stoneheart, her lord justice; and Sir Ahlber Zhustyn, her spymaster, were also smart, loyal, and competent. For that matter, Sir Fraizher Kahlyns was as reliable as they came, as well. Kahlyns was of commoner stock—his grandfather had been a serf—totally unimpressed by the aristocracy's complaints, and as loyal and tough a soldier as Safehold had ever produced. He wasn't its most *brilliant* soldier, however, which was one reason he'd been left home to train the new recruits when Duke Eastshare took Kynt Clareyk, Ahlyn Symkyn, Sir Breyt Bahskym, and Bartyn Sahmyrsyt to Siddarmark. The other reason was that there wasn't a single man on Safehold Ruhsyl Thairis trusted more than he did Sir Fraizher Kahlyns.

But if Sharleyan was right about the men she could rely upon, she was also right about Duke Rock Coast and Duke Black Horse. They *were* working much more circumspectly and carefully than Cayleb would have expected, and the Grand Duke of Mountain Heart was listening even more closely to them than he had before. Worse, Rebkah Rahskail, the Dowager Countess of Swayle, had arranged a betrothal between her son, Wahlys, and the younger sister of Sir Bryndyn Crawfyrd, Duke of Holy Tree. That had to be a bad sign, and Cayleb wasn't the only one who thought so. Earl Dragon Hill, Rock Coast and Black Horse's customary partner in intrigue, seemed to be growing increasingly concerned over his colleagues' apparent intentions, but they were confiding less and less deeply in him. Which, of course, only made him even more nervous.

"We ought to go ahead and arrest Rydach, seize Lady Swayle's correspondence, charge them with treason, and break this entire thing wide open right now," he said. "We know what they're planning, and—"

"And we still couldn't prove everyone's involvement just from Lady Swayle and Rydach's correspondence," Sharleyan interrupted. "And we can't justify moving against a grand duke, three dukes, and an earl—all but one of whom are known to have been my political opponents for years—without ironclad proof of their involvement. You know that. And much as I'd like to see all five of them a head shorter, if we violate their rights on the basis of the skimpy evidence we could seize from Swayle and Rydach, we'd make a lot of disgruntled but not currently treasonous nobles wonder if they're next on our list. That would be true even if we were later able to prove every one of them was guilty of sin, and the truth is that Holy Tree *isn't* guilty of anything overtly treasonable. Not yet, at least."

"But if we wait, and even if Braisyn's ready to pounce the instant these bastards come out into the open, a lot of innocent people are likely to get hurt, Sharley. And I don't like what they seem to have in mind for Lady Cheshyr one bit."

Karyl Rydmakyr, the Dowager Countess of Cheshyr, was in her mid seventies. She was also the regent for her son, Kahlvyn, the current earl. The same carriage accident which had killed Kahlvyn's wife ten years earlier had left him paralyzed and incapable of speech, and the Royal Council had named his mother as his regent, at least until his son Styvyn, who was currently fifteen, attained his majority. Lady Cheshyr had been born and raised in the Duchy of Tayt and was one of Sharleyan's own distant cousins. She was also a shrewd, canny politician, as she had to be, with her none-too-wealthy earldom sandwiched between the duchies of Rock Creek and Black Horse. There was no question where her own loyalties lay, and most of the sparse population of Cheshyr was only too well aware of how much iron ore and coal was likely to flow through their earldom's magnificent natural harbors—and how much money was likely to flow into their purses—if Cayleb and Sharleyan's plans for Chisholm's future came to fruition.

That meant Cheshyr had precious little interest in treason, yet its position meant it separated Rock Creek from Black Horse, while the same harbors made Cheshyr Bay an ideal place for the Imperial Charisian Navy to land the Imperial Charisian *Army*, or even just the Imperial Charisian Marine Corps to deal with any . . . unruliness. And *that* was why Rock Creek and Black Horse felt compelled to add a few paragraphs dealing with Cheshyr to their master plan. It was unlikely Cheshyr could physically resist the much more heavily populated duchies if they came at her from both sides, but that would be messy and might suggest that the southwestern nobles weren't united in their principled stance against Sharleyan's tyranny and the "foreign influence and intriguers of Charis."

Fortunately, from their perspective, Lady Cheshyr's deceased daughter-in-law had been a Seafarer and a second cousin of *Zhasyn* Seafarer, the current Duke Rock Coast, and Styvyn Rydmakyr—not the most brilliant young man ever born by an unfortunately large margin—venerated his much older cousin Zhasyn, whom he regarded much more as an uncle than as a mere cousin. He was young enough to be malleable, trusting enough to be convinced, and inexperienced enough to think there could be something "romantic" in plotting against the Crown. In fact, he'd already been approached by the conspirators and told them he was prepared to support them. How much support a fifteen-year-old might be able to provide was questionable, of course, and it was probably as well for Styvyn's present peace of mind (if not his future) that he hadn't stopped to think how that might shift if someone helped an unfortunate accident happen to his grandmother.

"I don't like that either—not any of it, and especially not the risk to Lady Karyl." Sharleyan's eyes were dark, but her tone was flat and her expression was unflinching. "And I fully intend for Sylvyst and Sir Ahlber—and our '*seijin* network'—to beef up her security. But this is something that's been brewing ever since my father's death, and you know it. The Army and Mahrak Sahndyrs—and I—broke the aristocracy's *power*, but we never broke the aristocracy *itself*. Or, at least, we never made them *admit* we had. Ambitious nobles are like that Hydra creature Nahrmahn found in Owl's library files, and it's been less than twenty years since I took the throne. Most of the people involved in this remember me when I was only twelve years old, Cayleb!

Idiots like Rock Coast and Black Water can convince themselves that I'm *still* only twelve and that it was only Mahrak and Uncle Byrtrym who let me beat them the first time around. Well, Uncle Byrtrym's dead, and Mahrak's a retired invalid, and we both know it's only a matter of time until you and I have to deal with something serious coming out of the southwest, whatever happens. We can do it in a series of plots, attempted rebellions, and passive resistance that could go on for the next two or three decades, or we can do exactly what you did in Zebediah."

Cayleb pushed back in his chair in his Siddar City suite, looking out the windows at the snowy dark. He knew what she meant, and a part of him agreed with her, and yet—

"I don't like the thought of an actual uprising in Chisholm, Sharley," he said softly. "I don't like the thought of who's going to get hurt if that happens, and I'm afraid from their timing that that's exactly what they have in mind."

"I don't like the idea of that any more than you do, and I hope it won't actually come to that."

Sharleyan's scowl suggested she might be just a little less confident than she wanted to appear. Unfortunately, quite a bit of that circumspection coming out of Rock Coast and Black Horse was the result of the conspirators' calculations where the Imperial Charisian Army was concerned. General Kahlyns had indeed almost completed the training of the new regiments, and many of those new soldiers were Zebediahan and Tarotisian, with more than a smattering of unnatural Charisians who preferred dry land to the open sea thrown in for good measure. The Royal Chisholmian Army had always displayed a bedrock loyalty to the Crown, and those "foreign" recruits were even less likely to be swayed by any conflicting Chisholmian loyalties. But over half those newly trained soldiers would be dispatched to Siddarmark as reinforcements and replacements within the next month or two.

Originally, the conspirators had apparently intended

to make their move as soon as those units were shipped off and Kahlyns' troop strength had been drastically reduced. Unfortunately, from their perspective—and from Sharleyan's, if she was going to be honest—they'd decided they couldn't be ready in time. The implications of the fact that they were willing to wait, prepared to spend the additional time in laying their plans and preparing the groundwork to be sure they had it right before they struck, was bad enough. Worse, perhaps, they'd realized that Kahlyns' training programs would promptly begin training still more new troops once those reinforcements had been dispatched. That meant they had no intention of coming out into the open anytime soon, yet whatever happened this year, *next* year would see an even more desperate grapple and very probably a major Charisian and Siddarmarkian offensive on the mainland. Coming up with the forces needed for operations on that scale would require additional, massive reinforcements, far more than were likely to be shipped off this year. And when that happened, they'd realized, it would almost certainly reduce the Imperial Army's available troop strength in Chisholm to an even lower level than the one to which it had dipped the previous summer.

"I hope it won't actually come to that," she repeated. "But I also believe—no, Cayleb, I *know*—that it's time we cut off every single one of *this* Hydra's heads once and for all. We need to give them enough rope, let them proceed far enough that when we pounce, and when all these traitors face justice, no one will be able to doubt their guilt any more than they could doubt the guilt of Craggy Hill or any of the other conspirators in Corisande. Unless something changes their thinking radically, they aren't going to try anything overt until we actually ship all of General Kahlyns' troops off to Siddarmark next summer, so it's not like I need to rush home to put out any raging forest fires before then. If anything changes in that regard, we'll know about it as soon as they do, thanks to the SNARCs. And, frankly, they're a lot more likely to commit themselves that far, give us the evidence we need to cut out the cancer once and for all, if I'm *not* in Cherayth, and you know it."

Caleb looked into her eyes for endless seconds. And then, slowly, he nodded. He didn't like it, but Chisholm was her kingdom. It might be part of *their* empire, but she was the one who'd come to Chisholm's throne as a girl of less than thirteen years. She was the one who'd fearlessly broken Chisholm's nobility to the Crown's bit and bridle once. If anyone on Safehold could do it again—for the last time, this time—it was she. And she was also the one whose judgment he trusted above that of any other human being.

"All right," he said. "In that case, that's our policy. And that being so, I agree that where you need to be next is in Tellesberg."

"Good," she replied in a much gentler tone. Her eyes met his, still dark with the steel which had allowed that long-ago girl child to become a *ruler*, and not just a queen, yet warm. Warm with the knowledge—the understanding—that he wasn't simply acquiescing, not simply abandoning the argument. "I'll leave as soon as we have the Coris situation resolved. And at least once I get there, I'll be six thousand miles closer to *you*, too."

. X .

## HMS *Eraystor*, 22,
## Geyra Bay,
## Duchy of Harless,
## Desnairian Empire

"Let's come two points farther to starboard, Captain Cahnyrs."

"Aye, aye, Sir." Alyk Cahnyrs glanced over his shoulder at the helmsman. "Two points to starboard," he said.

"Two points to starboard, aye, Sir," the man at the

wheel responded, and HMS *Eraystor* turned obediently.

Sir Hainz Zhaztro nodded in satisfaction, stepped back out onto his flagship's bridge wing, and looked aft, past the smoke pluming from *Eraystor*'s single funnel. His 2nd Ironclad Squadron was still understrength, with only four of its six assigned ships present, but he watched with approval as HMS *Riverbend*, HMS *Cherayth*, and HMS *Bayport* followed his flagship around. He'd had time to drill his command rigorously, if not quite to his own satisfaction. All his captains understood the standard he expected from them, and their precise stationkeeping was all he could have asked for.

He smiled—more of a grimace than a smile, really—at how impossible a conventional squadron would have found it to match that precision. The Imperial Charisian Navy's standards of seamanship were the highest in the world, yet not even their skippers could have held such precise station under sail in such fitful wind conditions. Which was, although it would never do to admit it, why he was so much more comfortable with his present command than he'd ever been with a galleon.

His grimace smoothed back into a smile at that thought, yet it was true. As a ship-handler, he'd never quite made the leap from galleys to square-riggers. That was one reason he'd been so delighted when Prince Nahrmahn Gareyt had insisted on putting his own name into nomination when the Navy went looking for officers to command its new ironclads. He'd been pleased by the implied compliment—both by his current prince's recognition of his service to Prince Nahrmahn, and by Admiral Rock Point's enthusiastic acceptance of the nomination—but the fact that he didn't have to worry about managing sails any longer was a vast relief.

The truth was that galleys were actually better preparation for steamers than galleons would have been, and the fact that he was about to demonstrate just how dangerous the Empire of Charis' newest ironclad class truly was filled him with a solid, vengeful pride. His present objective wasn't *quite* as satisfying as bombarding one of the Temple Lands' port cities would have been, but the *City*-class was too short-legged for that; without additional coaling stations farther west than Claw Island, Zhaztro's ships could have operated no deeper into the Gulf of Dohlar than the western coast of Shwei. Personally, he'd rather have been doing exactly that, range limitations or no, but High Admiral Rock Point had been firm. And, Zhaztro admitted, he'd been right, as well. The privateers operating from the Desnairian coastal enclaves *were* a far greater threat to the war effort in Siddarmark. They needed seeing to, and if that seeing to was the task the Navy needed from him, he damned well intended to do a proper job of it.

Especially given exactly what *else* operated out of the city of Geyra.

He raised his double-glass and gazed through its lenses at the impressive but ancient—and obsolete— walls and battlements. His squadron had passed through the Nearpalm Passage, between Nearpalm Island and the mainland coast, then turned almost due west to steam through the sixty-mile-wide mouth of the magnificent Geyra Bay, at the northern end of a twenty-three-hundred-mile stretch of coastline which ought, by rights, to have made the Desnairian Empire one of the great seafaring nations of Safehold. Protected by a nearly contiguous chain of islands beginning with Nearpalm in the north and anchored by Crab Shell Island at the extreme southern end, it offered scores of protected anchorages, most of them with deep-water access. Three of Desnair's major cities—Geyra, Malyktyn, and Desnair the City itself—lay along that stretch of coast, and the Osalk-Sherkal Canal extended for sixteen hundred miles, connecting all three of them to the Sherkal River, barely four hundred miles from Iythria on the Gulf of Jahras.

Unfortunately for all that unrealized potential, it belonged to Desnairians, whose scorn for seafarers— not to mention merchants, manufactory owners, and bankers—knew no bounds. Worse, perhaps, for all its imposing length, the Osalk-Sherkal barely met the *Writ*-defined minimum standards for a *secondary* canal, far less a primary canal, like the Holy Langhorne or the Guarnak-Ice Ash. Its largest locks were barely eighty feet long and twenty feet wide, its maximum depth was barely eight feet, and its tow paths were poorly laid out and maintained, totally unsuitable for the sort of heavy, sustained traffic the primary canals routinely handled.

It was just like Desnairians, he thought disgustedly, to do a half-arsed job on something which might have provided such an enormous benefit to their economy. The Osalk-Sherkal was quite adequate for the needs of Eastern Desnair's serf-owning agrarian overlords, and those overlords weren't concerned about meeting anyone *else*'s needs. The only real exception to that was the Duke of Shairn. In addition to the rich fisheries in the waters east of Shairn, the locks in the Varna and Shairn rivers offered the sole water transport link between Eastern and Western Desnair. Those locks weren't up to the really heavy traffic of northern Haven, either, but they could handle much larger barges than the Osalk-Sherkal could. As a consequence, Shairnians were a less lubberly lot than Desnairians in general, which was undoubtedly the reason Duke Shairn had ended up running the Imperial Desnairian Navy.

Desnair's misfortune had been Charis' good fortune, however. The Osalk-Sherkal was virtually useless when it came to moving the quantities of timber, artillery, anchors, masts, and all the other paraphernalia which went into building ships of war. (Masts and spars were especially problematic, given their length, but they were scarcely the only bottleneck.) That, in turn, had split Desnair's shipbuilding capacity up between the Acorn Bay yards at Desnair the City, the Malyktyn yards on Harless Bay, and Iythria on the Gulf of Jahras. (Why no navy yard had been built at Shairnport initially was an interesting question whose answer undoubtedly had something to do with typically convoluted internal

Desnairian politics, but Zhaztro wasn't about to complain about it.) Thanks in no small part to the ICN, the squadrons built in those widely separated yards had never managed to combine into a single unified force, and the systematic elimination of all shipbuilding capacity in the Gulf of Jahras had disposed of everything north of Malyktyn and Geyra.

Disposing of the threadbare remnants of the Imperial Desnairian Navy promised to be a somewhat more difficult task, however. The interconnected waterways of Geyra Bay, Harless Bay, Hathor Sound, and—courtesy of the Empress Alysahndra Canal, the one real (if short) canal east of the Desnairian Mountains—Acorn Bay were one enormous maze, its flanks riddled with potential hiding spots for galleons, galleys . . . and privateers. (Shairn Bay, three hundred miles farther south and without the same plethora of islands and coves, was a separate problem which would have to be settled later.) The twenty-odd miles of the Empress Alysahndra Canal were too shallow for blue-water galleons, but it was more than adequate for small coasters and privateer schooners. And, just to make Zhaztro's task more interesting, the Desnairians had scattered dozens of pocket-sized building yards over the entire area to produce even more privateers.

*Of course they have. Not even the Church could really interest Desnairian noblemen in building a navy, but* privateers—! *Ah, that's different, isn't it? After all, that's a way for those same noblemen to make money without demeaning themselves by actually building up their own country or dirtying their hands with anything reeking of "trade."*

It was possible he was being unfair to the Empire's aristocracy. Possible . . . but not damned likely.

At the moment, however, he and his squadron were about to begin divesting those privateer-building nobles of their assets. It was a long overdue task, and the fact that he got to start with Geyra was simply icing on his personal cake. Emperor Mahrys II, the current emperor's great-grandfather, had decided to make the City of Geyra his winter capital eighty-two years before, when he married the grandmother of the current Duke of Harless. Zhaztro had visited both Geyra and Desnair the City during the winter in the service of Prince Nahrmahn, and he had to acknowledge that there'd been much to recommend Mahrys' decision from the viewpoint of both architecture and climate. Many of his imperial advisors had been adamantly opposed to the move, mostly because of the huge increase in prestige and political power it had bestowed upon the House of Gahrnet. Desnair the City had been even more bitterly opposed, for obvious reasons, but at least the imperial court had been located in Geyra for only three months a year.

Mahrys IV, however, had been raised in Geyra, not Desnair the City. His mother, the daughter of the previous Duke of Traykhos, had been the first cousin of Sir Ahlvyn Gahrnet, and she'd spent much of her own girlhood in Geyra. Not only that, she'd detested Desnair the City for a host of reasons, and she'd instilled the same feelings into her son. Emperor Mahrys vastly preferred his hometown to the official capital, and he spent no more than two or—at most, kicking and screaming the entire time—three months a year in Desnair the City. There were those who argued—very quietly and privately; they preferred their heads where they were—that Mahrys' preference for Geyra had directly contributed to the disaster the Army of Shiloh had suffered, since the present Duke of Traykhos, his maternal uncle, was his first councilor and he and Traykhos between them had selected their mutual cousin Sir Ahlvyn, the recently deceased Duke of Harless, to command the Emperor's armed forces in Siddarmark.

That move, unfortunately, had worked out poorly for a great many people, not all of them Desnairian. Now it was time to make the Empire of Charis' displeasure with such ill-considered decisions clear, and Sir Hainz Zhaztro had been chosen to deliver the message.

*I do hope His Majesty's in residence to receive it personally,* he thought cheerfully. *I'm pretty sure he won't like it. And I doubt the new duke's going to be any happier with Charis than the old one was, for that matter. Pity about that.*

The double-glass showed flickers of movement along the city walls and along the batteries built to cover the Geyra waterfront. His ships were still too far away for him to make out any detail, even through the double-glass, but that was fine. His targets weren't going anywhere.

He swung away from the city, making a quick but thorough survey of the rest of his command. Geyra Bay stretched over three hundred miles from east to west and was almost a hundred and twenty miles deep along its north-to-south axis. That offered plenty of scope for naval maneuvers, and his schooners and supporting galleons—and the trio of bombardment ships— lay hove-to like a vast, untidy gaggle of sea wyverns a good ten miles southeast of his abbreviated line of ironclads. They were waiting, handy if he needed them but safely out of harm's way in the meantime, and he nodded in satisfaction.

"We're coming up on the designated range, Sir Hainz," Lieutenant Ahdym Stormynt, his flag lieutenant, reminded him tactfully, and he snorted.

"Always a good thing to remember," he acknowledged, dropping the double-glass to hang from the strap around his neck. He dug into his tunic pocket for the earplugs and fitted them into place. He didn't like the sound-deadening effect, but he liked the thought of what *Eraystor*'s heavy guns would do to his hearing without them even less.

Once they were settled as comfortably as possible, he raised the double-glass once more, gazing at his intended target and licking his mental chops.

▼ ▼ ▼

Sir Haimltahn Rahdgyrz stood atop Duke Wahlys' Tower, feeling the ache in his neck as he bent over to peer through the powerful, tripod-mounted spyglass at the quartet of black, evil-looking vessels forging steadily closer to Geyra. The smoke streaming from them amply confirmed their heretical—and no doubt demonic—origins, yet other than that they didn't seem to match the descriptions he'd received. He couldn't tell anything about dimensions at this range, but the reports from Siddarmark all agreed that the ironclads looked like floating barn roofs with conventional gunports cut into their sides and paired smokestacks. These ships had definite superstructures, set back at least a few feet from the outer edge of the hull at deck level, and only a single smokestack each. Not only that, they had no gunports at all. Instead, the deckhouse which extended for three quarters of their length had . . . scalloped-looking sides. The black feelers of preposterously long guns projected from the scallops, and his mouth tightened as he abruptly realized what he was seeing.

He had no idea how anyone could load such ridiculously long weapons from the muzzle, but if the rumors about the heretics' new rifles—their *newest* rifles, he corrected himself grimly—were correct, he supposed there was no reason they couldn't load *cannons* from the breech end, as well. And the angled superstructure was shaped almost like a pair of triangles placed base-to-base while the gun barrels sticking out of those "scallops" disappeared into what appeared to be solid, rounded . . . shields, for want of a better word. If it was possible for them to be trained from side to side—and it certainly looked as if it was—then all of the guns on either side could be fired in a single broadside and *half* the guns on either side could be fired at a target which lay well ahead or astern of the ship.

And there were a *lot* of guns poking out the sides of those ships.

He straightened, rubbing the small of his back, and glanced at the youthful IDA lieutenant standing beside him. Sir Rhobair Gahrnet, the new and youthful Duke of Harless, had reconfirmed Rahdgyrz as the duchy's seneschal. As such, all Army units in Harless came under his control, and the present duke's father had chosen Sir Haimltahn for his duty less because of his distant kinship to the House of Gahrnet than because he'd known Rahdgyrz took his responsibilities seriously. A direct Charisian attack on Geyra or Desnair the City hadn't seemed very likely until the Empire began building and basing so many privateers and Navy commerce-raiders along the coast between there and Desnair the City, but Rahdgyrz believed in being prepared. Desnair the City's defenses hadn't been his responsibility, but he'd worked hard for over four years to improve Geyra's coastal batteries and train their gunners.

To be honest, those gunners hadn't been very good in the beginning. The heretics were said to be able to fire three broadsides in two minutes, and that was twice the rate of fire the Geyra artillerists had been able to attain. That was no longer the case, however, and the twenty-five-pounders and even heavier forty-pounders were lavishly supplied with exploding shells. And while there might be a lot of guns aboard the approaching ironclads, there were better than four hundred in Rahdgyrz's eighteen carefully sited defensive batteries, and all of those guns were on solid, steady, *unmoving* mounts. There was a reason warships had historically avoided well-sited land batteries, and while it was possible the heretics' introduction of armor plating might have changed that, it was unlikely it could have changed the balance between shore and ship enough. Especially given how much more powerful the forty-pounder was than anything they'd faced in any of their operations in Siddarmark. It had almost three times the range of the Army's twelve-pounder field guns, threw a solid shot *more* than three times as heavy, and would penetrate over four feet of solid oak at a thousand yards.

He was tempted to open fire as soon as they approached within four thousand yards—at five degrees' elevation, the forty-pounders reached to two thousand yards, but his gunners were well practiced at using ricochet fire to reach twice that far—yet he made himself suppress the temptation. Each bounding contact with the water would reduce the round shot's velocity and striking power, and he was going to need as much of that as he could get to deal with an armored target. Given the deep, soft earth berms of his batteries, his guns should be better protected than the ironclads, and—

▼ ▼ ▼

"Six thousand yards, Sir Hainz," Lieutenant Stormynt said.

"Very well." Zhaztro stepped back and around the solid horseshoe of armor which protected *Eraystor*'s conning tower. "Captain Cahnyrs, you may open fire," he said formally.

"Aye, aye, Sir. Lieutenant Gregori, open fire!"

"Aye, aye, Sir!"

HMS *Eraystor*'s fifteen-hundred-ton bulk heaved as she belched a huge bubble of fire that sent eleven six-inch shells sizzling across the water at twice the speed of sound—a far, far higher velocity than any Desnairian would have believed possible.

▼ ▼ ▼

Rahdgyrz stiffened in disbelief as the lead ironclad vanished into a vast, dense, *brown* cloud of smoke. What in Shan-wei's name could the heretics think they were doing opening fire at that range?! They had to be three and a half miles from their target! Surely they couldn't—

The other three ironclads belched fire and smoke, and then the first of the heretics' shells came screaming out of the sky ahead of the noise of their own passage. There was no rumble, no warning sound. One instant, Rahdgyrz was staring at the cloud of smoke, trying to understand what had happened. Six and a half seconds later the sixty-eight-pound shells reached their targets and the seneschal stumbled three steps backward in simple, unadulterated shock as they exploded.

The range was long, even for Charisian gunners equipped with the first axial telescopic sights ever affixed to Safeholdian artillery. And, for all their advantages over the defenders, the ironclads' artillery and ammunition only began to approximate the weapons of the last decade or so of Old Earth's nineteenth century. Pinpoint accuracy was beyond them, especially with each gun crew firing individually, relying upon its gun captain's judgment of the ship's roll.

Despite that, only two rounds went long. Three more slammed into the water short of the battery and exploded, throwing up huge mud-tinged columns of white, but the other six found their target.

▼ ▼ ▼

Sir Haimltahn Rahdgyrz was over two miles away from the point of impact as the heretics' fire smashed into the St. Gwythmyn battery, but his eyes went huge as the pattern of volcanoes erupted. He'd seen the explosion of his own forty-pounder shells, but that was *nothing* compared to these! Most of them were absorbed by the protective earthen berm, yet that was scant comfort, given the vast craters they ripped out of it. Two of them, though, cleared the berm and landed among the battery's guns. Rahdgyrz groped for the spyglass—not because he wanted to see the carnage those two hits had wreaked, but because he *needed* to—and then, just under ten seconds behind the shells, came the rolling thunder of the guns which had fired them.

▼ ▼ ▼

*Riverbend, Cherayth,* and *Bayport* opened fire as well, and Admiral Zhaztro bared his teeth in satisfaction. Even with the earplugs, the bellow of *Eraystor*'s guns was like being clubbed across the head, and the enormous banks of smoke turned the bright afternoon into twilight before the brisk breeze cleared them, but what was happening where those shells landed was far, far worse, and he knew it.

On the gundeck, behind the four-inch armor, the

massive guns recoiled, but only for about four feet.
Smoke swirled inboard, yet there was far less of it than
the choking clouds of smoke which had filled *Delthak*'s
gundeck whenever she fired her thirty-pounders. The
guns returned to battery, the breech blocks spun and
opened, soaked swabs extinguished any embers, fresh
shells and bagged powder charges slid into the breeches,
the blocks closed, and each gun captain bent back to
the sight mounted to the recoil cylinder. Crewmen bent
over the big brass traversing handles, following the
captains' hand signals as they compensated for *Eraystor*'s forward movement through the water.

"*Clear!*" the gun captain shouted, simultaneously
waving his right arm in the signal to clear the mount's
recoil path. His Number Two checked visually to be
sure the rest of the crew had obeyed the signal, then
slapped him on the shoulder in confirmation. The captain waited an instant longer, peering through the
sight, waiting for the roll to be exactly right. Then he
straightened and jerked the firing lanyard.

The gun roared and recoiled, the deck surged underfoot, and the deadly ballet began yet again.

▼ ▼ ▼

"Sir Haimltahn!"

It was the Army lieutenant, and Rahdgyrz turned
like a man in a nightmare to face him. The other three
ironclads' broadsides had arrived, each of them seeking out a separate defensive battery. The pattern of
their shells' explosions didn't seem quite as tight as for
the first ironclad, but the explosions echoed and roared,
and the heretics were firing not simply from an impossible range and with impossible accuracy, but with
equally impossible *speed*.

"What are your orders, Sir?!" the lieutenant asked
urgently, and Sir Haimltahn Rahdgyrz stared at him,
wondering what order he could possibly give in the
face of such unmitigated disaster.

▼ ▼ ▼

Hainz Zhaztro watched those savage explosions, remembered the day when the corrupt butchers who'd seized control of Mother Church had sent his flagship and seventy other Emeraldian galleys into the nightmare cauldron of the Battle of Darcos Sound. His flag captain—his younger brother, Ahntahn—had died that day, along with more than two hundred and thirty of the galley *Arbalest*'s seven-hundred-man crew. He and *Arbalest*'s fourth lieutenant, her senior—and only—surviving officer, had somehow sailed that shattered wreck seven hundred miles home to the city his current flagship was named for . . . and once they reached it, despite all they could do, she'd slowly settled to the bottom, too exhausted to fight any longer after the bitter struggle to bring her surviving people home.

Zhaztro had never blamed Haarahld or Cayleb of Charis for that. Not really. It had been their guns, but he'd always known who'd delivered his crew, his brother, and his Navy into the jaws of destruction. Even if he hadn't known then, he'd had ample proof since of just how many human beings, how many of their fellow children of God—women and children, as well as soldiers and sailors—Zhaspahr Clyntahn and the rest of the Group of Four were prepared to slaughter in the name of their own foul ambition.

He couldn't reach the Group of Four, or even the Temple Lands. Not now, not yet. But he *could* reach the Desnairian bastards who'd signed on to do Clyntahn's will, and as he watched those explosions, he found himself hoping the Geyra garrison would be too stupid to haul down its colors.

"What was that?" the shivering Army of God private said suddenly.

"What was *what*?" the equally cold corporal in charge of the guard post demanded, looking up from the charcoal brazier over which he'd been warming his hands.

"I heard something," the sentry replied. "Sounded almost like a voice . . . or something."

His own voice trailed off under the corporal's skeptical gaze. Wind-driven snow flurries filled the night, and that branch-tossing wind wasn't simply icy; it was also noisy enough to drown out most sounds without any effort.

"Well, *I* don't hear anyth—"

That was as far as the corporal got before a white, snow-smutted apparition appeared out of the night and drove a bayonet through his throat.

▼ ▼ ▼

"*Langhorne!* What morons," Corporal Graingyr growled in disgust, standing ankle-deep in the bodies of the late corporal's detail.

"Now, Charlz," Platoon Sergeant Edwyrds replied. "Poor bastards didn't have a clue there was anyone within ten miles of them. Not too surprising they weren't the most alert bunch in history."

"Yeah?" Graingyr looked sidelong at 3rd Platoon's senior noncom and snorted. "So next time we're sure there's no one within ten miles, you're gonna let *me* sit on my arse looking into a charcoal fire and wiping out my night vision?"

"Not so much," Edwyrds told him, and the corporal snorted again, louder.

"What I thought," he said, then gathered up the other members of his squad with a jerk of his head.

"Don't get comfy 'round that fire. We've got another bunch of morons sitting around another fire 'bout four hundred yards thataway. Let's go help 'em sleep as sound as this bunch."

▼ ▼ ▼

Baron Green Valley stood in the miserable, windy, snow-clotted, subzero, *beautiful* night and held up his watch as Lieutenant Slokym opened the slide on the bull's-eye lantern to let him check the time. The baron glanced dutifully at the watch face before nodding for his aide to close the slide once more, but he wasn't really worried about the timepiece. He was too busy watching the SNARC imagery projected on his contact lenses while Platoon Sergeant Edwyrds, Corporal Graingyr, and the rest of Major Ahrkyp Dyasaiyl's scout snipers swarmed over the rest of the Colonel Kholby Somyrs' pickets.

*Graingyr's got a point*, he reflected as the corporal's squad dispatched yet another detachment of Somyrs' 111th Infantry Regiment. This one hadn't had anyone even pretending to be alert; the scout snipers caught them in their bedrolls, huddled around the fire, with only two of them even awake . . . briefly.

*There's no way my boys would tolerate something that sloppy. But Edwyrds is right, too. They never had a clue we were coming, thank God.*

It wasn't Allayn Maigwair's fault they hadn't. He and Bishop Militant Bahrnabai had seen to it that every commander of every post in the Army of the Sylmahn's operational area knew the Army of Midhold had disappeared somewhere in New Northland. Somyrs, the senior regimental CO and the senior officer in command at Five Forks, had dutifully acknowledged the information, and the sentry posts Dyasaiyl's scout snipers were busily eliminating represented his response to it. It was about to prove pathetically inadequate, but he'd never truly believed Charisians might appear more than six hundred straight-line miles from Ohlarn.

*Sylvaio probably had a little something to do with that, too,* Green Valley acknowledged. *After all, he told Somyrs where we "really" were, didn't he?*

General Sylvaio Dymrohv's 2nd Division had been the last Charisian unit to move through Ohlarn, and his 4th Brigade had executed a perfect pounce on the blocking position at Rankylyr, which Bahrnabai Wyrshym had counted on to delay any advance along the Ohlarn-Guarnak High Road. No one in Guarnak—or Five Forks—had realized the bulk of the Army of Midhold's Charisian infantry had already passed well north of Rankylyr, following the line of the canal and taking out the semaphore line as it advanced, and a particularly generous critic might have excused Somyrs for assuming 4th Brigade represented Green Valley's entire army.

Like Corporal Graingyr, however, Kynt Clareyk was not a generous critic where the lives of men under his command were concerned.

*Well,* he thought, turning to watch a purposeful, bayonet-bristling column from Brigadier Ahdryn Krystyphyr's 7th Brigade move steadily and swiftly through the icy night's wind-roar on its snowshoes, *I don't suppose the good Colonel's going to get a lot of sleep tonight. Too bad.*

▼ ▼ ▼

Kholby Somyrs leaned back in his comfortable chair and enjoyed another swallow of the brandy one of his contacts in Lake City had forwarded to him. Colonel Somyrs was a conscientious man who'd avoided sneaking special items for his own use into the supply train for months, and not simply because both Bishop Militant Bahrnabai and the Inquisition had made it clear such practices would not be tolerated. But now that the Army of the Sylmahn's worst supply problems had been largely—not completely, but largely—dealt with, he was prepared to relax that restriction just a bit, not simply for himself but for the other senior officers here in Five Forks.

It wasn't as if the odd cask of brandy or case of canned delicacies was likely to displace anything critical these days. A few months ago, yes—then every pound, every cubic foot had been precious to the starving, overstrained Army. And to be honest, Guarnak's supply levels remained well below anything Somyrs would have considered genuinely adequate. But that was because of the difficulty in getting those supplies forward from Five Forks, not because the problem in getting them as far as Five Forks in the first place remained insuperable. The truth was, the supply depot under his command probably contained enough provisions by now to feed the bishop militant's entire field force for two or three months, possibly even as many as four. Moving them where they were needed was still a problem—supplies were stacked in mountains under snow-shrouded tarpaulins or piled high in barrels and casks under an open sky, waiting for the transport to shift them the remaining four hundred and fifty miles to Guarnak—but even that situation was improving and—

Colonel Somyrs' head jerked up, he surged to his feet, and the brandy glass fell from his hand as a sudden eruption of explosions and the vicious crackle of small-arms fire shattered the night.

▼ ▼ ▼

The rest of Five Forks' garrison was just as surprised as its sentries had been. Like its commanding officer, its men had never imagined the enemy might be anywhere in the vicinity. Now they tumbled out of bedrolls, struggled up out of sleep, and found the next best thing to four thousand men armed with hand grenades, repeating rifles, and revolvers storming mercilessly into the tiny town they'd transformed into a massive supply depot. Four thousand more men were ready to follow the assault battalions, and less than a quarter of the defenders even reached their weapons. Of those who did, barely half reached their assigned defensive positions, and they were still trying to figure out what was happening when the Charisians stormed over them in a surf of hand grenades and a storm of bayonets.

## . XII .
## The Temple,
## City of Zion,
## The Temple Lands

"How bad is it?"

Rhobair Duchairn's voice was quiet but tension burned in its bones, and Allayn Maigwair gave him the sort of expression that soured milk.

"Bad? It's a frigging disaster, that's how *bad* it is!" he snarled. "Shan-wei take it! I've been telling Zhaspahr and the rest of you for *five-days* that—!"

"I know you have," Duchairn interrupted. Maigwair glared at him, and the Church's Treasurer shook his head. "I *know* it, Allayn. For that matter, I've been helping you say it, remember?" Maigwair glared a moment longer, then nodded grudgingly. "So what I'm asking you now is how bad it really is. I need to know if there's anything my people can do about it."

The Captain General inhaled deeply, closed his eyes for a moment, and gave himself a shake.

"All right," he said in a calmer tone. "The truth is that I don't know how bad it is, but I'm confident it's worse than anything I *do* know. We only found out about it because eleven men—eleven men out of an entire supply convoy's mounted escort—made it back to Guarnak when they were ambushed three miles outside Five Forks. I'm not sure what happened when the heretics attacked the supply depot itself. We haven't heard a damned thing from Colonel Somyrs or anybody else in the garrison, but I do know the heretics have cut the semaphore chain twenty miles north of the town. And I know because of what happened to the supply convoy that they're firmly in control of the southern approaches, as well. Given that information, I have to assume Green Valley and his bastards have the town and probably got most of the supplies intact."

"I agree it's better to be cautious than overly optimistic, but why are you assuming Somyrs and my people in Five Forks didn't manage to destroy the supply dump first?"

"Because if they'd had time for that, *someone* in the garrison would've had time to get out, too." Maigwair shook his head, his face like iron. "Everything points to the heretics having attained complete surprise, Rhobair. And, frankly, 'destroying' a supply depot is a hell of a lot more difficult than most people realize. The only practical way to do it is by burning the place—or blowing it the hell up. Stores of powder can be blown up fairly quickly . . . if you know you have to. Otherwise, it's usually stored in ways specifically designed to *prevent* it from all blowing up by accident. Most provisions, on the other hand, don't actually burn all that well without a lot of effort and fuel, and it takes time and planning to arrange something like that. Without at least a day or two of warning, especially with all the snow piled up around Five Forks to help smother any fires, there's no way Somyrs pulled it off. No." He shook his head again. "Green Valley's sitting on top of enough of our supplies to keep his entire army fed for at least a couple of months, and that assumes he didn't bring along *any* of his own." The Captain General bared his teeth. "Would you like to make a little wager on the possibility of someone like Green Valley *not* making sure he had an adequate cushion of supplies before he advanced cross-country over seven hundred miles of snow?"

"No." It was Duchairn's turn to shake his head. "No, I wouldn't. I don't suppose we have any sort of estimate for how big his force is?"

"No, we don't. I'm in contact with Wyrshym over

the Hildermoss semaphore chain, and he's trying to get a patrol far enough north to give me at least some idea of Green Valley's numbers. Unfortunately, the chance of his managing to pull that off under the current weather conditions and against somebody who's obviously so much better at moving in arctic conditions than we are is somewhere between zero and less than that. He'll keep trying, but we'd be fools to think he's likely to succeed. Under the circumstances, I think we have to operate on the assumption that it's basically all of Green Valley's Charisians, minus the seven or eight thousand men he has at Rankylyr."

"You don't think he left any of them around Fairkyn?"

"No. I think he played us for fools there, too." Maigwair's voice was bitter. He'd cautioned the rest of the Group of Four that what they actually knew about Gorthyk Nybar's situation was dangerously threadbare, yet even as he'd issued the warning, he'd believed Nybar's estimates were substantially correct. Until Rankylyr had fallen, at least. "I think he left his Siddarmarkians to keep Nybar penned up in Fairkyn, probably with his own heavy artillery to support them . . . and to fool us into thinking the *rest* of his army was there, too, of course. Not that leaving the guns didn't make sense for a lot of other reasons, as well. I doubt even Charisians wanted to haul heavy angle-guns overland in the middle of winter!"

"In that case, is there any possibility of Nybar breaking out to the south? Could he retake Rankylyr and rejoin Wyrshym?"

"No way in hell," Maigwair said flatly. "First, because if there really are seven or eight thousand Charisians dug-in at Rankylyr—and that's been pretty thoroughly confirmed—he'd never have the firepower to take it back from them. That's a *tough* defensive position, Rhobair; that's why Wyrshym chose it in the first place. And, second, because he's under orders to hold Fairkyn until he's relieved and reinforced. In theory, if he could break out of the siege lines, he could retreat past Rankylyr without actually engaging its garrison. He'd have to abandon his artillery and supplies, but he could do it. Except for the fact that we can't get word to him to tell him he has to. And notice that I said 'in theory.' Those Siddarmarkians of Green Valley's may not be as good at running around in the snow as his Charisians are, but they're damned tough, their supply situation's one hell of a lot better than Nybar's is, and after what the Sword of Schueler did to the Republic, I think they're about as motivated as anyone could be."

Now there, Duchairn thought, Maigwair had a point.

"All right. I assume you're telling me this before we have to face Zahmsyn and Zhaspahr so we can be more or less on the same page when we do?"

"Damned right I am!" The Captain General's expression was more snarl than smile. "Wyrshym's already made it clear that his position's even shakier than we thought it was. I didn't really need him to tell me anything more than that we've lost Five Forks to realize that for myself, you understand. He's got whatever supplies he had on hand, which may—*may*—be enough for six five-days. I'm sure he's already reinstituted rationing, probably even more stringently than before, but we're not going to get any more food—or any more of the new rifles or any more of the new artillery—through to him unless we can retake Five Forks. And that," he said grimly, "isn't going to happen, Rhobair. Green Valley's already had almost a full five-day to dig in, and I'm guessing he must have at least forty thousand men to do the digging with. Wyrshym's chance of taking Five Forks back under those circumstances doesn't exist."

"All right." Duchairn's face was drawn, but he nodded. "So what does that leave us as options?"

"Damned few."

Maigwair took an angry, frustrated turn around Duchairn's private office. He stood for a moment, gazing out that office's window at the heavy snow falling across Zion, then wheeled back to face the Treasurer.

"Zhaspahr's downplayed it, just like he downplays *anything* he doesn't want to face, but we've been receiving spy reports—and rumors—that Stohnar's been reinforcing his cousin in the Sylmahn Gap since at least October. And while no one's told me about it, I have to assume the bulk of the Army of Shiloh's rifles have now found their way into heretic service."

The two vicars' eyes met, and, after a moment, Duchairn nodded unhappily. The Army of Shiloh had been equipped with over eighty thousand rifles; Sir Rainos Ahlverez had reached Alyksberg with thirty-two thousand men, five field pieces, and fewer than *twenty* thousand rifles. Frankly, it was incredible he'd managed to salvage that many men from the debacle and hold them together through that nightmare march, although Duchairn knew that view of things was far from universal. Ahlverez was presently on his way back to Gorath to account to his own superiors—and, the Treasurer was sure, to the Inquisition—for the disaster, and Duchairn devoutly hoped the general would survive the trip. They needed men who could work miracles like that.

But assuming that even no more than half of the rifles the Army of Shiloh had lost had been captured intact and appropriated for the Siddarmarkian Army's use, they would suffice to arm another fourteen infantry regiments for Greyghor Stohnar. They wouldn't be as good as the Church's new breechloaders, but the heretics had captured quite a few St. Kylmahns by now. There was no reason they couldn't convert the captured muzzleloaders to the same design—and probably a lot more quickly and efficiently than the Church could have done it—if they chose to.

"That being the case," Maigwair resumed, "and assuming Stohnar and Cayleb are at least smart enough to pour piss out of a boot—which I believe they've demonstrated is the case—they're going to build up their troops in the Gap and move fresh troops up to Fairkyn, and as soon as the ice melts they're going to use their damned navy to open a new, short supply line up the Ice Ash. And as soon as the weather's good enough for the Siddarmarkians, they're going to close in on Guarnak from the south and from the east, and Green Valley's position at Five Forks's going to mean there's nowhere Wyrshym can go."

"So we're going to lose his entire army the same way we lost the Army of Shiloh?"

The question came out more harshly than Duchairn had intended, and Maigwair's eyes flashed for a moment. But then he shrugged.

"If he stands where he is, yes. That's exactly what's going to happen. The only way to prevent it—the only way to save *some* of his army—is for him to start moving units back through Hildermoss and Westmarch." The Captain General met the Treasurer's eyes again, unflinchingly. "He doesn't have the transport to move anywhere near all of his men that far cross-country. At best, I estimate he might get sixty to seventy percent— *maybe* as much as seventy-five percent—of the Guarnak garrison out, but to do that, he'd have to sacrifice the rest of that garrison and everyone he's got holding Saiknyr. And it would automatically write off Nybar's detachment at Fairkyn. But Fairkyn's already gone, for all intents and purposes, and if Wyrshym doesn't start falling back now—immediately—he's not going to get anybody out, Rhobair."

"What about the Harchongians?"

"Yes, that *is* an interesting question, isn't it?" Maigwair scowled. "Baron Falling Rock's moving forward along the canal, exactly the way Rainbow Waters promised Gustyv he would. He's moving a little faster than Rainbow Waters estimated, too. But even so, he's barely into Usher by now; he's still a long way from Lake City, far less Five Forks. We've got around twenty thousand of our own men already garrisoned in and around Lake City, but even that's six hundred miles away by the shortest route. At this point, I'm afraid the best thing we can do with Falling Rock's army is to reinforce *Lake City*. If the heretics get their damned ironclads back into Spinefish Bay and head south along the Hildermoss at the same time they're moving north from Five Forks . . . ."

Duchairn nodded slowly, and Maigwair turned back to the window.

"And then there's Kaitswyrth," he said over his shoulder, never looking away from the snow. "He's heard about Five Forks, too, and he's heard about what Hanth's doing to Rychtyr along the Sheryl-Seridahn. His 'patrols' are a piss-poor excuse for the sorts of patrols the heretics send out, especially this time of year, but he's insisting there are over a quarter million men ready to attack him any moment now. Frankly, the tone of his reports is panicky enough I'm disinclined to believe his estimates, but I've got damn-all from any other source to confirm that. For all I *know,* he might even be right. On the other hand, nobody's captured any critical depots in his rear. His supply line down the North Daivyn's still secure, which means his line of retreat *up* the North Daivyn is also secure . . . and that the Mighty Host could relieve him a lot sooner than it could get to Guarnak. And if worse came to worst, he ought to be able to retreat up a shorter, intact river line faster than even Eastshare could follow him up."

"And as long as he holds his current position, any troops who manage to retreat through Hildermoss could reinforce him?"

"Of course they could. And if I had my way, Wyrshym would relieve him in command as soon as he got there."

Duchairn nodded again. Not that it was likely to happen. Even if Maigwair was allowed to pull out as much of Wyrshym's army as possible, Zhaspahr Clyntahn remained stubbornly unwilling to acquiesce in replacing a onetime favorite like Kaitswyrth—even if Kaitswyrth hadn't exactly covered himself with glory the previous summer. The Grand Inquisitor was even more unlikely to agree to replacing him with a "defeated" commander he'd never fully trusted in the first place.

"All right," he said finally. "I think I've got the picture,

Allayn, and I promise I'll do what I can to support you. I can certainly point out how grim Wyrshym's logistical position is now that we've lost Five Forks. And everything else you've said makes good sense to me."

Maigwair turned to face him again, and the Treasurer saw the same recognition in the Captain General's bitter gaze. What made good sense to *them* might not make the same sort of sense to Zhaspahr Clyntahn. In a reasonable world, the united front of the Army of God's commander and its quartermaster ought to carry more weight than the passion and fury of the Grand Inquisitor. In the world they actually had, however . . . .

*It's the two of us against Zhaspahr on this one,* Duchairn thought grimly. *Zahmsyn's collapsed completely where anything remotely connected to the military's concerned since we found out about the Army of Shiloh. The news out of Geyra and Malyktyn aren't doing anything to stiffen his spine, either. I think he can see what's coming from Desnair, and he figures Zhaspahr's going to lay that at his door, since he's Chancellor.*

The Treasurer grimaced at the direction of his own thoughts. There'd been times he would cheerfully have cut Trynair's throat for his part in enabling this madness, and the Chancellor's total lack of moral courage was enough to turn his stomach. But there was no point pretending Trynair was going to change course now. And, in some ways, given the alternatives, it was hard to blame the other man. At the same time, he was a vicar of Morth Church. That meant he had *some* responsibilities to God and God's children, and—

Duchairn cut off that line of thought and inhaled deeply.

*He was already frightened of Zhaspahr,* he reminded himself. *Now that the Inquisition's officially taken over all the "security functions" here in Zion from the Temple Guard, Zahmsyn's too terrified to cross him over anything, and not without reason, to be fair. Zhaspahr's never been what anyone might call "reasonable," and it's getting a hell of a lot worse. He's not telling us everything, either. He never did—Allayn's got a point about his "downplaying" inconvenient bits of news— but it's been five-days since he gave us any kind of progress report on the holding camps. That's a sort of report in its own right, given the way he's always gloated over them in the past. I don't believe him when the says Rayno's making progress against the Fist of Kau-Yung, either, and I'm damned well sure those propaganda broadsheets worry him one hell of a lot more than he's willing to admit!*

Zhaspahr Clyntahn's belief in the iron rod and the power of terror was how this years-long nightmare had begun in the first place. What he'd never believed, in the beginning at least, despite whatever reverses he might encounter along the way, was that he could actually *lose*. Whatever might happen in the short term, in the long term victory had been certain, and with it the destruction of all those enemies, real or imagined, who'd dared raise their hand against Mother Church . . . and him.

But now, for the first time, Mother Church no longer faced simply one more failure to crush Charis and the schism for him. Now she was face-to-face with the very real possibility that *they* would defeat *her* . . . and with her, Zhaspahr Clyntahn. Duchairn doubted the Grand Inquisitor was prepared to admit that even to himself and even now, but beneath anything he might be willing to face openly, the uncertainty, the doubt— the fear—was like acid gnawing its way through the armor of his arrogance.

*And because it is, he's getting more and more desperate . . . and fanatical*, the Treasurer thought. *Any suggestion—any* hint *—that we have to give ground, even temporarily, is automatically unacceptable to him. So how in Langhorne's name do we make him see reason* now?

▼ ▼ ▼

"The whole idea's ridiculous!" Zhaspahr Clyntahn snapped, his heavy jowls mottled with fury. "Wyrshym's not even under *attack*, and you already want him to *retreat?!* Never!"

"Zhaspahr, Allayn's explained it to you in the simplest possible terms." Duchairn kept his tone as reasonable as he could. "It's not a matter of *wanting* him to retreat; it's a matter of saving what we can."

"*Dragon shit!*" Clyntahn slammed one meaty hand on the polished table then glowered around the council chamber, the power of his wrath filling the air like curdled thunder. "That's dragon shit! You want him to abandon his position, give up almost everything we gained in last year's campaign—*that's* what you want!" His lips worked as if he wanted to spit. "That's defeatism. That's abandoning the Jihad, handing victory to God's own enemies! If you think I—if you think the *Office of Inquisition*—is going to stand by and see that happen, you are *sadly* mistaken, Rhobair!"

"No one's being defeatist," Allayn protested. Which, Duchairn reflected, was less accurate than he might have preferred. "I want to *preserve* Wyrshym's army and add it to Kaitswyrth's, Zhaspahr! Assuming Kaitswyrth's estimates of the heretic forces massing against him are remotely accurate, he's going to need all the reinforcements he can get, and Wyrshym's too far forward for us to support him. I know you don't want to give up the ground he's taken, but we need to . . . readjust our own positions. Let me do that. Let Rhobair finish re-equipping our Army, as well as the Harchongians, with the new rifles and the new artillery. Let Dohlar rebuild at least some of its strength. For that matter, Harchong's already raising another five hundred thousand men to add to the mix and the Emperor's promised still more! Once we've done that, we'll be in a position to resume our own offensive without worrying about shattered supply lines and armies we can't even feed."

"No," Clyntahn said flatly, and his eyes were slits of rage. Zahmsyn Trynair sat silent, eyes on the table, face pale, and the Grand Inquisitor glared at the other two members of the Group of Four. "Wyrshym is staying right where he is."

"Zhaspahr, I'm Mother Church's Captain General," Maigwair said, meeting that glare. "And this is a military decision."

"It's only *partly* a 'military decision,'" Clyntahn sneered. "If you pull back Wyrshym, you expose all of Inquisitor General Wylbyr's camps. You give up all the territory we've reclaimed for Mother Church—territory the *Inquisition*, not the Army, is responsible for restoring to God. You abandon your responsibilities *as* Captain General at the time of God and the Archangels' greatest need in the world since the War Against the Fallen itself! *That's* what happens if you order Wyrshym to retreat, Allayn. Are you prepared for the consequences if you betray God Himself that way?"

Maigwair had gone almost as pale as Trynair. He refused to back down, but his gaze flicked sideways to Duchairn, and Clyntahn turned those furious eyes upon the Treasurer.

"I'm tired of hearing complaints about why we can't do this, and why it's impossible for us to do that, and how we can't possibly sustain Wyrshym where he is," the Inquisitor said flatly. "If a quarter of the effort you've spent explaining all the reasons for all the things we've failed to do, or we're still unable to do, had been spent *solving* the Shan-wei-damned problems in the first place, we wouldn't be in this mess! Well, if the Army and the Treasury aren't prepared or able to do their duty, the Inquisition's prepared *and* able to do its, no matter who it has to call to account!"

Duchairn felt the moment humming in the council chamber's air as the iron gage of Clyntahn's challenge hit the floor, and the need to take it up burned in him like a fire. It was time—it was far *past* time—to reclaim the vicarate and Mother Church herself from the likes of Zhaspahr Clyntahn. And yet—

The Treasurer never broke eye contact with the Inquisitor, but his mind saw the guards in Schuelerite purple standing outside the chamber's door and the other inquisitors seeded throughout Zion and the Temple. If he let this moment pass, if he and Maigwair didn't defy Clyntahn now, when all sanity was so over-whelmingly on their side, the Grand Inquisitor's control would become absolute. But if they *did* defy him he wouldn't hesitate to have them arrested and turn both of them into examples. It wouldn't be the first time he'd murdered fellow vicars to make a point, and the public execution of the only two members of the Group of Four willing to confront him would make him, not the nonentity sitting on the Grand Vicar's throne, the unchallenged dictator of Mother Church.

*Face him!* a voice cried out deep inside. *Face him now, because if you don't, you may never have another chance! Why have you been making preparations all this time if you're never going to* use *them?*

But that was the problem, wasn't it? He *had* made preparations, and he knew their strength, knew how deep they went, yet he also knew they relied not on weapons of war or the might of legions. They were no match for Clyntahn in a direct confrontation, especially not since the Inqusition's imposition of outright control over the city of Zion and all its guardsmen.

No sword, no spear, no army is more powerful than the will of God. No shield, no armor, no fortress is greater safety than trust in Him who created all the universe. No shackle, no fetter, no prison can lock a child of God away from the love of God. Put not your trust in principalities or worldly powers, for principalities fail and any man is easily killed. But the word I have brought you from Him, the truth I have taught you as His messenger—that is invincible. It will endure more ages than the world itself, and he who places his faith in it, even though he taste of death, shall never know defeat.

The words of the *Book of Langhorne* ran through him, and he knew they were true. The truth of God *was* invincible . . . and any man *was* easily killed. The inquisitors outside the council chamber would obey whatever order Zhaspahr Clyntahn gave them, and if he and Maigwair died, they would accomplish nothing but their own martyrdom. There were times when Rhobair Duchairn longed for exactly that, if only as a way to lay down his burden. But even as Langhorne had promised the invincibility of God's truth, he'd also warned that God knew how to measure a man's task.

> God will show you the path set before your feet. God will teach you the task He has laid upon you. It will not always be easy, and you may groan beneath its burden. Yet you will know the task which bears your name, written upon it in words of fire. You will know it, and you will lift it up, and you will walk every weary mile of the road. You may falter, you may long to turn aside, but you will not, for you are God's, as this whole world is His, and as He will not fail you, you will not fail Him.

What other burden, what other task, had God set before him than to repair the frightful wounds of His own Church? It wasn't simply his task—it was his duty . . . and his penance. His life was not his own to lay down before that task was finished. He might yet die in its doing, but he had no right—he'd *forfeited* the right—to let himself be killed *unless* that accomplished the charge God's will and his own guilt had laid upon him.

He faced that bleak awareness, and then another passage flowed through him, this one from the *Book of Bédard*.

> Be patient. Wait upon God, for be you ever so heavy laden with sin, He will show you all good things in His own time. His Love is forever, He does not abandon those who do not abandon Him, and He will search through all eternity for any who are lost.

No darkness can hide you from His eye, no sin can place you beyond His forgiveness, and they who return to Him and take up their tasks once more will rise up upon the wings of wyverns. That which hinders them today, He will remove in the day of His own choosing, and that which bears them down He will cause to lift them up in the morning of His victory.

"Zhaspahr," he said, still refusing to look away, "we may disagree about the best way to accomplish what lies before us, but whatever you may think, the Army and the Treasury have always been prepared to do their duty. As Allayn's said, he and I want to *preserve* the Army of the Sylmahn. We have no more desire than you to give ground to heresy and schism. We simply believe that in order to resume the offensive successfully and carry God's banner to victory we need to reorganize, rearm, and reequip His forces. And as part of that reorganization, we need to extract as much of Bishop Militant Bahrnabai's army as possible from the trap the heretics have built around it."

"Reorganize and rearm all you like," Clyntahn said coldly. "We've seen in the case of the Mighty Host what you can accomplish when you truly set your hearts as well as your minds to your task, trusting in God for success. But we will not betray our duty to Him or to the complete cleansing of heresy in Siddarmark in the process. The Army of the Sylmahn is the shield for that cleansing; it will *not* be removed, and however much mortal men may despair of accomplishing what God has called them to do, there's *nothing* He cannot accomplish through them so long as they keep faith with Him. The Mighty Host's vanguard is already in motion, and if we can't prevent the accursed heretics from reentering the Ice Ash, we can certainly destroy every river lock south of Spinefish Bay to deny them access to the Hildermoss! You may be right about the noose about the Army of the Sylmahn's neck. Maybe it *is* doomed if it stands its ground. But if it *doesn't* stand, even at the price of its destruction, we abandon all of Siddarmark west of Tarikah to Shan-wei and dark damnation. The Mighty Host will either relieve it or avenge it, but it will not betray God by abandoning the position He's called upon it to defend in His name!"

"All right," Duchairn heard himself say. "All right. I think you're wrong, Zhaspahr. I want that clearly understood between us. But you may not be, and I can't dispute anything you've said about Siddarmark or God's ability to accomplish what fallible mortals believe is impossible. So Allayn and I will do everything humanly possible to support the Army of the Sylmahn, to expedite the movement of the Holy Host, and to prevent the heretics from using the rivers against us. But I want something from you in return, Zhaspahr."

"What?" Clyntahn half sneered.

"I want your promise that your inquisitors will back off while we do it." Duchairn's eyes bored into the Grand Inquisitor's. "We need—our people in the field need—the freedom to do their jobs without having one of your people who may know everything there is to know about the *Writ* but doesn't know *squat* about logistics or strategy or troop movements looking over their shoulders and hampering them every step of the way. I can't guarantee we'll succeed even with that freedom, but I can guarantee we *won't* succeed without it."

Something flickered at the back of Clyntahn's eyes. Duchairn didn't know what that something was, but he didn't much care, either. Silence hovered for a moment, and then Clyntahn nodded once.

"Very well. Your 'people in the field' will have the 'freedom' you say they need. See to it that they use it well."

. XIII .
HMS *Chihiro*, 50,
Gorath Bay,
Kingdom of Dohlar,
and
HMS *Destiny*, 54,
Great Western Ocean

"Thank you for coming so promptly, Pawal."

"It's not like I had anything else to do this afternoon," Pawal Hahlynd observed dryly, reaching out to clasp arms with the Earl of Thirsk. "Except worry, of course," he added rather more somberly.

"There's a lot of that going around," Thirsk agreed.

Lieutenant Bahrdailahn had withdrawn after ushering Hahlynd in, leaving the two admirals alone in Thirsk's day cabin. Which might be just as well, given Hahlynd's last remark . . . and his own, Thirsk reflected.

"Come on."

He twitched his head at the open glass doors to *Chihiro*'s sternwalk and Hahlynd followed him out into the cool spring morning. They stood side-by-side, leaning on the railing, gazing out across the blue harbor at the warships lying to anchor and the bevy of merchant ships and coasters gliding in and out under their more martial sisters' watchful eye.

There were a lot of those merchant vessels crowding the harbor and its wharves, far more even than before the Charisian privateer onslaught with which the war had begun. Virtually every one of them was no more than two or three years old, built to replace the privateers' depredations in mass construction projects in the shipyards the Church had created to build her navy, and the building pace had redoubled since the Sword of Schueler had been loosed against Siddarmark. The

Jihad's voracious appetite for the supplies which truly were the sinews of war had seen to that, and with winter still gripping northern Howard and Haven, a huge percentage of that traffic was passing through the Gulf of Dohlar's eastern ports. The pressure would ease a bit in the next couple of months, as the northern canal systems began to thaw once more, but for the moment Gorath was probably the only port in the world which could rival heretical Tellesberg's normal volume of shipping, and protecting it and keeping it flowing was the responsibility of the two admirals gazing out across it.

After a minute or two, Thirsk straightened, pulled his pipe and tobacco pouch out of his tunic pocket, and began methodically filling the pipe's bowl.

"Funny how peaceful it all looks, isn't it?" he said, pausing to wave the hand holding his pipe at the panorama before them. "Especially given what's happening elsewhere."

Hahlynd grunted in agreement and hauled out his own pipe. The two flag officers fussed with the implements of their addiction with all of the ritual tradition demanded of them, but Hahlynd's eyebrows rose as Thirsk took an unusual-looking device out of his pocket. The earl smiled at his friend's expression, then flipped up a tight-fitting, hinged metal cover on one end of the device to reveal what looked like a lamp wick with a milled metal wheel bracketed in front of it. Thirsk's thumb spun the wheel, and Hahlynd stepped back half a pace in surprise as a fountain of sparks leapt from the wheel to ignite the wick.

The earl only smiled again and applied the flame to his pipe, drawing until the tobacco was nicely alight. Then he extended the device to Hahlynd, who leaned cautiously forward to light his own pipe. He straightened, and metal clicked as Thirsk closed the device, extinguishing the flame.

"Handy," Hahlynd said after a moment. "Another of Lieutenant Zhwaigair's ideas?"

"No." Thirsk held the device up between them,

sunlight gleaming on its semi-polished surface. "No, actually this is something Ahlverez brought back with him. Some of his men came across it during the fighting in the Kyplyngyr. We're not sure what the heretics call it, so we're simply calling it a 'lighter,' since that's what it does. Young Dynnys *did* recommend changing the fire vine oil the heretics used in it for something a little less poisonous if I was going to insist on lighting my pipe with it, though."

The earl gazed at the "lighter" for a moment, then slipped it back into his pocket and met Hahlynd's gaze levelly.

"I'm sure this thing"—he tapped his pocket lightly—"has all sorts of military applications, but think about it for a minute. The Charisians don't really *need* it, but they produced it anyway. That means their ability to manufacture weapons and the ammunition those weapons need is so great that they have surplus capacity to produce things like this just because they're . . . what did you call it? 'Handy,' I think? It sort of puts our current problems into perspective, don't you think?"

Hahlynd looked back at him without speaking for a second. Then he nodded, although his expression was wary.

"Don't worry, Pawal!" Thirsk shook his head. "I'm not going around making that point to just anybody. Ahlvyn and Ahbail—and Stywyrt, of course." Hahlynd nodded at the earl's reference to his senior aide, flag lieutenant, and flag captain, then tensed again as Thirsk added, "And Bishop Staiphan. He's the one who gave me the lighter in the first place. We spent several minutes discussing the military implications of its existence."

"I see. And the Bishop . . . shared your view about them?"

"Actually, he raised them with me, first."

Hahlynd nodded slowly, looking back out across the bustling harbor, and blew a smoke ring as he digested that. The ring floated away on the breeze, shredding as it went, and he frowned, wondering if that was some sort of oracle.

"I didn't ask you here just to show you my new toy, though," Thirsk said, and Hahlynd turned back towards him, resting his left elbow on the sternwalk rail. "I'm afraid you and your squadron are about to begin earning your pay."

"Are we?"

The question came out calmly enough, but Hahlynd's pulse accelerated slightly. He and Thirsk were lifelong friends. There'd never been any question in the earl's mind who he wanted in command of Dynnys Zhwaigair's armored screw-galleys, and Hahlynd had spent months working out doctrine and training his officers and crews to apply it.

"You are," Thirsk confirmed. "I wish it could be under better circumstances, but the truth is that what happened to the Army of Shiloh and . . . certain reports from northern Siddarmark have quite a lot to do with the timing."

"What sort of reports?" Hahlynd asked cautiously.

"Let's just say that what happened to the Army of Shiloh could be about to happen to the Army of the Sylmahn, as well." Thirsk's expression was grim. "I don't know that that's the case, but from a few rumors Bishop Staiphan and I have picked up, it seems . . . possible, at least."

Hahlynd's jaw tightened. The Kingdom of Dohlar was still reeling from the Army of Shiloh's destruction. Everyone knew Sir Rainos Ahlverez was in a fight for his professional life as his role in the disaster was debated by his superiors, and rumor had it that Ahbsahlahn Kharmych, the Kingdom's intendant, was deeply displeased with Ahlverez, too. There were even rumors the intendant was almost equally displeased with Father Sulyvyn Fyrmyn, Ahlverez' intendant. If any of that was true, Ahlverez might lose more than simply his *professional* life before it was over.

It must be hard for Thirsk to decide how he felt about that, Hahlynd thought, given the long-standing hatred between himself and Ahlverez. But whatever the earl felt, the mere suggestion that yet another of

Mother Church's armies might face the same sort of calamity . . . .

"I'm not happy to hear that," he said out loud. "And I'm afraid I don't quite see how anything my squadron might do could have any effect on what happens to Bishop Militant Bahrnabai, Lywys."

"It won't." Thirsk exhaled a jet of smoke. "The problem is, Pawal, it looks to me as if the Charisians and Siddarmarkians are working to a grand plan. I think they intend to crush the Army of God's formations—*all* its formations, not just Wyrshym's—in the field before the Harchongians can come forward to reinforce them. I know they're pushing Rychtyr steadily back along the canal, but that's going slowly enough it'll be high summer, at the earliest, before they reach the Kingdom. By then, we'll have largely rebuilt the Army, and it's pretty obvious their spies are so damned good they have to know that's going to happen. The fact that none of the forces they used to pulverize that stupid bugger Harless are helping hammer the Army of the Seridahn suggests they're about to be used doing something else. Something they think is even more important than finishing *us* off before our Army does that rebuilding. So after pondering what that 'something else' might be, I'm guessing Bishop Militant Cahnyr'll see them in Cliff Peak before very much longer."

Hahlynd nodded slowly, his eyes intent as he followed Thirsk's logic. The earl's access to information about the larger war was more extensive than his own, and he suspected Staiphan Maik was showing Thirsk even more than his own religious superiors might have preferred. It was sad that Mother Church had decided to keep so much secret from her own defenders, but there seemed little chance that was going to change anytime soon.

"Unfortunately," the earl continued, "the mere fact that they aren't reinforcing Hanth doesn't mean they don't have some *other* plan to deal with us."

"Beyond taking Claw Island back from us?"

"Oh, *definitely* beyond that." Thirsk smiled with no humor at all. "They've been a little more cautious than I really would have expected out of Charisians, to be honest. As far as Rohsail's been able to determine, they haven't been operating in any sort of strength east of the Narrows, but I think that's about to change."

He paused for a moment, gazing up at the white clouds drifting above the harbor, then looked sharply back at Hahlynd.

"How much have you heard about what happened at Yu-kwau?"

"I heard it was bad," Hahlynd said slowly. "Why?"

"Because it was a hell of a lot worse than 'bad.'" Thirsk's expression was grim. "They took their time kicking the shit out of the Bay of Alexov, and there wasn't a damned thing the Yu-kwau squadron or the shore batteries could do about it. They brought along one of their armored galleons to take out any battery that might've threatened their regular galleons and backed it up with a couple of those bombardment ships. The Yu-kwau waterfront's a total loss, and it's going to take over a month to reopen the Saint Lerys Canal. And they paid visits to all of the Bay's other ports, as well."

Hahlynd's face tightened, and Thirsk nodded.

"They spent more than a five-day doing the job right. And I'm sure you can figure out as easily as I could how badly that's going to hurt the Jihad. The good news is that they didn't have enough troops to get far enough inland to take out most of the foundries, and apparently at least some of the coasters on the bay managed to dodge around and evade them. For all intents and purposes, though, Queiroz and western Kyznetzov are completely cut off until either we push the Charisians back out of Claw Island or they get the canal open again. Oh, they could still move some material south out of Su-shau and up Anvil Bay to Brusair, but not enough to do any good. And even if the Harchongians get the canal fully back into operation, there's nothing in the Bay of Alexov to stop the Charisians from coming right back and wrecking it all over again."

It was Hahlynd's turn to nod in bleak understanding. The damage was more severe than even the worst rumor he'd heard. And he also knew what Thirsk hadn't said. Even if the St. Lerys Canal was fully restored to service, it could handle only a fraction of Queiroz and Kyznetzov's shipping needs. It was one of the primary canals, built in accordance with the *Writ*'s instructions, yet even the broadest and deepest canal was a narrow, shallow substitute for the open sea. Vicar Rhobair and his carefully trained specialists, in conjunction with the Canal Service, had done wonders to streamline and improve canal traffic, but even at their best, the canals had never been intended to meet the transport needs of a Jihad which had enveloped the entire world.

"I'm afraid, however," Thirsk continued, "that the Charisians—actually, the admiral they sent out to seize Claw Island is Earl Sharpfield—are well enough satisfied with what they've done to the Bay of Alexov to begin looking farther afield. According to Rohsail's dispatches, their schooners and light cruisers are operating west of Saram Bay. In fact, they've been reported as far west as Jack's Land and Whale Island. And given what they did to Yu-kwau, I have to think a return visit to Shwei Bay might strike them as a worthwhile excursion."

"That's . . . not good," Hahlynd observed, and Thirsk snorted.

"You could put it that way. I won't say Shwei Bay's stark naked, but it's not a lot better than that, especially given all the other threats Rohsail has to deal with. He's a good man, but he doesn't begin to have the hulls—or the right *sort* of hulls—to be everywhere he needs to be."

Hahlynd considered mentioning the fact that the Earl of Thirsk was not one of Sir Dahrand Rohsail's favorite people, but he thought better of it. It was typical of the earl that he was able to recognize the capability of an officer whose politics differed so radically from his own. And, to be fair, Rohsail's attitude towards Thirsk seemed to have mellowed somewhat under the corrupting influence of the earl's sheer competence.

"He's got forty-two galleons," Thirsk went on, "and we've just dispatched ten more to reinforce him, but you know as well as I do how quickly ships get used up when it comes to commerce protection. It looks like at least some of Sharpfield's original galleon strength's been recalled, although I wouldn't want to count on that too heavily. It'd make sense—despite what just happened to Geyra Bay, there are a *lot* of Desnairian privateers making their merchant galleons' lives miserable. But even if the reports are accurate, his *light* units are still a pain in the arse, and with the Charisians raiding that far east, Rohsail's had to organize local convoys. That eats up a lot of *his* available strength, especially his lighter units. He's managed to keep thirty or so of his galleons concentrated—enough to prevent the Charisians from dispersing their own line of battle too broadly—but he can't engage armored ships at sea. Certainly not ships whose armor is thick enough it could shrug off our Claw Island batteries or the guns at Yu-kwau!"

Hahlynd nodded again, and Thirsk shrugged.

"Part of me's inclined to take the entire Home Squadron west, combine it with Rohsail's force, and go hunting the Charisians on the theory that we'd have to have enough cannon to handle their ironclads. There has to be some reason none of the steam-powered ones have come forward, so theoretically, if we destroyed the two they have based on Claw Island, we'd be free to deal with the rest of their galleons. Unfortunately, we'd lose far more of our fleet than they'd lose of theirs. And unless we could go back in and retake Claw Island ourselves, which seems unlikely, they'd still have a secure forward base. Worse, I'm inclined to doubt they only built two of the damned things, so losing a third of the

Navy beating the ones we know about strikes me as pretty poor tactics. By the same token, while your screw-galleys would stand up to their guns better—and longer—than our galleons would, you and I both know they aren't the most seaworthy ships ever built."

That was a tidy piece of understatement, Hahlynd reflected. However—

"I can't disagree with you about that, but if the situation's that bad, my captains and I can sail for Saram Bay tomorrow, Lywys."

"I appreciate that offer—deeply. But given the weather this time of year, I doubt you'd get as far as the Dohlar Bank before a half-dozen of you broke up and went to the bottom."

"Maybe so, but we're not accomplishing anything sitting in the harbor, either," Hahlynd pointed out. "I don't want to lose any of them to weather, either, but if we're the only ships that have any chance against those armored galleons, I don't think you have any choice but to send us. It's all very well to think about defending Hankey Sound when the heretics finally get around to attacking it, but if we lose the rest of the Gulf and get driven solely back onto the canals . . . ."

He waved at the crowded harbor, and Thirsk grimaced.

"As it happens, I agree with you," he said. "On the other hand, a thought occurred to me when all of this came up. We've been thinking in terms of operating the screw-galleys only in company with the Home Squadron, but we don't *have* to do it that way. And if all I want is to send your squadron to reinforce Rohsail, I don't have to send you via the Gulf at all, do I?"

Hahlynd looked at him in puzzlement for several seconds. Then, slowly, he smiled in understanding.

▼ ▼ ▼

"*That*'s profoundly irritating," Admiral Sarmouth remarked.

The admiral and his flag lieutenant sat on HMS *Destiny*'s sternwalk with their chairs cocked back and their heels resting on the rail while a spectacular tropical sun settled into the sea off the galleon's larboard beam. Sarmouth, to the extreme displeasure of Sylvyst Raigly, his longtime steward and valet, had developed a taste for the cigars which were a Corisandian specialty. The Duke of Darcos agreed with Raigly. Unlike the majority of sea officers, Hektor had never felt any inclination to smoke, and he understood why the steward was less than enthralled by the cigar ash which had invaded his world.

"Cayleb's always said Thirsk's the best commander the Church has," he agreed now, grateful for the brisk northeasterly that blew his admiral's smoke out to disappear far, far from him. "I asked him once if he meant the Church's best *naval* commander, and he told me, no—he meant best commander, period."

"I think there are a few army commanders who could give the earl a run for his money," Sarmouth demurred. "On the other hand, His Majesty has a point. Worse, Thirsk seems to have a gift for training up additional good commanders. Rohsail, for example. And Hahlynd, for that matter. I never actually realized how true that was before—"

He waved his cigar in a gesture which somehow indicated the imagery he and Hektor had been watching on their contact lenses, and Hektor nodded.

"I know what you mean, Sir. It *is* sort of . . . addictive, isn't it?"

"That's certainly one way to put it," Sarmouth replied dryly.

Clearly, the baron remained in two minds about the earthquake which had reordered his world, yet he was too good a sailor not to recognize the staggering value of Owl's SNARCs. Simply knowing about weather changes in advance was a huge advantage for any seaman, yet the advantages for any *naval* officer were still greater. And that didn't even consider the ability to actually sit in on his opponents' conversations. On the other hand . . . .

"I can see why you wanted someone with this sort

of access out with Earl Sharpfield," he said now. "But I'm still trying to figure out how I can make best use of it. I suppose it's human nature to always want more than you have, but I'd give two or three fingers to be able to hand coms to each of my captains."

Hektor snorted.

"At least you've got signal flags, Sir," he pointed out. "And I suppose if we really needed to, *Seijin* Dagyr could pay another visit on Earl Sharpfield. I know accounting for the time for him to have gotten to Gorath and back to Claw Island quickly enough might be tight, but still . . . ."

Sarmouth drew heavily on his cigar while he considered that.

The reports on the Dohlaran screw-galleys had emphasized their small size, yet until he'd gotten access to the SNARCs and "seen" them for himself the implications hadn't truly registered.

*And they damned well should have*, he thought. *The frigging things're twenty feet shorter and thirty percent narrower than* Delthak. *If Merlin could decide to send Bahrns up the Guarnak-Ice Ash to trash Wyrshym's logistics, why shouldn't someone as sneaky as Thirsk see the advantages of being able to fit his ironclads into the canals? And why am I so surprised he did?*

Like most Charisians, Sarmouth had a tendency to overlook the mainland canal system's ubiquity. Because of that, he'd never considered that Thirsk could send Hahlynd's ironclads from Gorath to Saram Bay—or, in this case, Shwei Bay—without having to traverse the Gulf of Dohlar to get there.

*It'll be a longer trip, but less than half of it'll be over saltwater.*

The screw-galleys would have to cross six hundred and fifty miles of Hankey Sound to the Desnairian port of Ershalla, at the mouth of the North Hankey River, but from that point, they could travel well over two thousand miles "overland" to Hahskyn Bay, which connected in turn to Shwei Bay. The entire trip would take at least five five-days, as opposed to the sixteen days for a galleon to reach the same destination, but it would get the fragile screw-galleys there safely.

*And they'll reach Yu-shai a five-day before we get to Claw Island . . . without the possibility of their being spotted by any of Sharpfield's cruisers.*

"I'm afraid we do need to dust off *Seijin* Dagyr," he said. "Sharpfield needs to know about this—and get warnings to his squadrons—as soon as possible."

"Yes, Sir." Hektor pursed his lips in thought while he did the mental calculations. "If we assume he finds out about Thirsk's plans at least a few days before Hahlynd leaves Gorath, he could reasonably reach Claw Island at least two five-days before the screw-galleys get to Yu-shai. I don't see any way we could legitimately get the information to Earl Sharpfield any faster than that."

"Actually," Sarmouth exhaled a long streamer of smoke, "that ought to be more than soon enough, since Yu-shai's thirty-six hundred miles from Claw Island and over a thousand beyond his cruisers' current operational area. It might not be a bad idea for *Seijin* Dagyr to just 'happen' to encounter one or two of those cruisers on his way, though. Having the Earl's forward elements informed of what's happening even before he is couldn't hurt."

# MAY
## YEAR OF GOD 897

⟡

# . I .
## Jarith,
## Sylmahn Gap,
## Hildermoss Province,
## Republic of Siddarmark

General Trumyn Stohnar contemplated the enormous map of the Sylmahn Gap on his office wall.

The colored pins marking the known and estimated positions of the Church's Army of the Sylmahn hadn't moved very much over the past several five-days. The pins marking the positions of *his* troops had changed considerably, however. The biggest difference was that there were far more of them than there'd been the previous year, and he smiled thinly as his eyes drifted back to them once more.

A discreet knock sounded on his office door, and he turned to face it.

"Come!" he called, and Lieutenant Sahlavahn, his personal aide, escorted Colonel Aivahn Yazhuhyro into the office.

"Aivahn." Stohnar clasped forearms with the colonel and nodded to Sahlavahn. "Thank you, Dahglys. Don't forget to remind Colonel Kohmandorsky and Commander Parkmyn that Colonel Yazhuhyro and I will be joining them in Commander Parkmyn's office at fourteen o'clock."

"Of course, Sir," Lieutenant Sahlavahn murmured, and withdrew.

"Am I right in remembering his birthday's coming

up, Sir?" Yazhuhyro inquired as the door closed behind him, and Stohnar snorted.

"No, it happened yesterday, actually. He just turned twenty-three."

"Twenty-three?" Yazhuhyro repeated, and shook his head. "Langhorne! They get younger every year, don't they?"

"Actually," Stohnar's smile faded, "Dahglys is a lot more than a year older than he was this time last year."

"We all are, Sir," the colonel pointed out, and Stohnar grimaced in agreement, then pointed at the empty chair in front of his desk.

"Have a seat," he invited, and opened his desk's bottom drawer. He extracted a bottle of Old Province brandy, poured two glasses, and handed one of them across before he settled into his own chair facing the colonel.

Yazhuhyro raised his glass to touch Stohnar's gently, then sipped appreciatively. Stohnar followed suit, letting the liquid fire spread its comforting warmth through him before he sighed and shook his head.

"The inspections went well?"

"Very well, in fact, Sir." Yazhuhyro waved his glass under his nose, inhaling the bouquet. "The frontline units are in good shape and there's no indication anyone on the other side of the lake's noticed a thing. The ice is still awfully solid and a lot thicker than it ought to be by this time of year, but it won't stay that way much longer."

"Good." Stohnar nodded slowly, his eyes thoughtful. Yazhuhyro had just returned from a personal inspection of the Army of Hildermoss' forward units dug into their winter quarters around and below the ruins of Malkyr, well south of Wyvern Lake's normal shoreline. What with the previous year's flooding, an incredibly rainy autumn, and a winter even colder than the last, the lake currently stretched virtually the entire width of the Sylmahn Gap and over ten miles farther south than usual. A more formidable natural barrier would have been difficult to imagine, and both armies had entrenched artillery to cover their own sides of the swollen lake.

"That's good," the general repeated, and took another sip of brandy. Then he smiled at the colonel. "I'm sure Dahglys, in his usual efficient manner, told you why I wanted to see you as soon as you got back?"

"Well, not in so many words." Yazhuhyro sat back, cradling his glass in both hands. "He did say you'd just received a clutch of dispatches, though. And since you and I are apparently about to slog through the snow down to the canal—*not* something I'm looking forward to after the last five-day—I'm assuming they said basically what we've been hoping they'd say?"

"They did indeed," Stohnar confirmed. This time his smile was hungry, and the gray-eyed, dark-haired Yazhuhyro smiled back.

The Republic of Siddarmark Army had borrowed a new position from its Charisian allies, and Yazhuhyro was the Army of Hildermoss' chief of staff. Over the last several months, he'd gone about organizing the command structure of the steadily growing army with so much driving efficiency that a part of Stohnar had actually resented his focused, ruthless energy.

There was very little left of the army with which Trumyn Stohnar had fought his brutal, bloody delaying action down the length of the Sylmahn Gap the previous spring. His obscenely outnumbered men had known their defense was hopeless, yet they'd fought anyway. They'd fought until eighty percent of them were dead or wounded. Until they were no more than a thin line of musketeers and artillery pieces, with no reserves and even less hope. Until, beyond hope or prayer of salvation, a single reinforced Charisian brigade had arrived on the eve of their destruction and smashed the Church back up the Gap in rout and ruin.

Every single survivor was precious to him. What he'd really wanted, after they'd been relieved by Baron Green Valley, was to give them the rest their courage and sacrifice so richly deserved. Yet whatever he might have wanted, Yazhuhyro had done what he'd *needed*, instead, and driven those survivors to integrate the flow of desperately needed replacements and reinforcements into their decimated companies and regiments.

"According to the Seneschal's dispatch, the latest convoy from Tellesberg reached Siddar City three days ago," the general continued. "We'll be receiving just over ten thousand of the new 'Trapdoor Mahndrayns' and enough mortars to bring us up to establishment across the board. And we should be seeing at least three more batteries of heavy angle-guns, as well."

"That's good to hear, Sir." Yazhuhyro's eyes brightened. "Assuming, of course, that we've got enough ammunition for the Mahndrayns!"

"The Seneschal says we'll have fifteen hundred rounds for each of them." Stohnar shrugged. "We won't be seeing any more of the *rifles* for a while; General Mahrkohne's going to draw the dragon's share of them before he moves his corps up to support Green Valley. The Charisians appear to've solved that ammunition 'bottleneck' of theirs, though. At any rate, I've been assured additional cartridges will be forthcoming when we need them."

"Good!"

Yazhuhyro's eyes narrowed as he considered how best to utilize the new weapons. Ten thousand would be enough to reequip two entire brigades, or they could use them to rearm twenty-two companies and give each of the army's current regiments one four-hundred-and-fifty-man Mahndrayn-armed company of its own. He and Stohnar had discussed both approaches, but they hadn't made a hard and fast decision because no one had been certain when—or if—any of the new breechloaders might become available to them.

Or how *many* they might see, either.

"In addition," Stohnar continued, "the Seneschal's informed me that between new production weapons and rifles captured from the Army of Shiloh, he's been able to arm five more divisions than anticipated, and three of them are earmarked for us."

Yazhuhyro twitched upright in his chair. They'd

hoped for *one* more division . . . and hadn't really expected to see it. Three of them would be a gift from Chihiro himself! True, it sounded as if they'd be armed primarily with muzzleloaders, but a muzzle-loading rifle was one hell of a lot better than *no* rifle, and forty thousand more men would *double* the Army of Hildermoss' strength.

"How soon, Sir?" he demanded.

"They're en route now. We should see their advance elements within the month. Hopefully, all three divisions'll have come forward by the time the ice actually begins breaking up."

"And Baron Green Valley?" There was an anxious edge in Yazhuhyro's question this time, and Stohnar shrugged again.

"Getting dispatches from Five Forks to Rankylyr's no walk in the park even for Charisian ski troops. As of the Baron's most recent message to the Seneschal, he was well dug-in, with 'ample'—that was his word, not the Seneschal's—supplies and was confident of holding his position for at least another full month or six fivedays."

"I've never met the Baron myself, Sir."

The colonel's tone was almost painfully neutral, and Stohnar showed his teeth in something a bit too hungry to call a smile.

"I have, Aivahn," he said flatly. "If that man says he can hold for a month, Kau-yung himself won't push him out of position one day sooner than that."

Yazhuhyro nodded, satisfied by the answer to his unasked question, and the general tipped back in his chair.

"Duke Eastshare's almost done reequipping his troops, as well," he observed. "Which means all we're really waiting on at this point is the weather."

"Aren't we always, Sir?" Yazhuhyro replied wryly.

The colonel was a native of Rollings Province, born in the foothills of the Black Hill Mountains, and he'd always done his best to discharge his God-given duty to sneer at the effete citizens of such balmy provinces as Glacierheart, where snow accumulations were measured in mere yards. Still, even he had to admit the winter which had theoretically ended two five-days ago had been brutal. The ice on Wyvern Lake was still thick enough to support cavalry charges, and it wasn't going to be melting by the day after tomorrow.

It was too bad, really, that it hadn't been possible to build up the Army of Hildermoss soon enough to take advantage of that ice. Still, they'd always known that was probably going to be the case. That was why Commander Zhorj Parkmyn of the Imperial Charisian Navy held the acting rank of colonel in the Republic of Siddarmark Army. He and the seamen Admiral White Ford had drafted from the galleons in Bedard Bay were the card tucked up the Army of Hildermoss' sleeve.

"Does Duke Eastshare have any estimate about the weather in Cliff Peak and Westmarch, Sir?" the chief of staff asked after a moment.

"Things are a little better there than here. There are some signs the spring thaw's about to set in, especially south of the Daivyn River, but not much change north of it. His position's a lot like ours, actually, at least from a timing viewpoint. His troops're almost ready, but they aren't quite going to complete their preparations before the river ice begins breaking up. And once that happens—"

"They'll have to wait out the worst of the flooding," Yazhuhyro sighed.

"Exactly." Stohnar nodded. "Of course, in our case a little flooding may actually be a *good* thing, don't you think?

His chief of staff nodded back with a most unpleasant smile, and Stohnar finished his brandy, pushed back his chair, and stood.

"Dahglys has complete copies of the latest dispatches for you," he said. "In the meantime, though, I think you and I should go share the good news with Parkmyn and Colonel Kohmandorsky."

"It's always nice when an operation goes exactly as planned," Sir Bruhstair Ahbaht observed, gazing through one of the angle-glasses bracketed to HMS *Thunderer*'s armored bulwark while rainwater ran down his oilskins. "That's what I've always heard, anyway," he added, wincing as a pair of surf boats collided in a centipede confusion of thrashing oars.

"It's not really *that* bad, Sir," Lieutenant Kylmahn, *Thunderer*'s first lieutenant pointed out. He stood beside his captain, bent at the waist to peer through an open gunport which happened not to have a six-inch rifled cannon poking out of it at the moment.

"Much as it pains me to disagree with you, Daivyn, it *is* that bad," Captain Ahbaht replied. *Thunderer*'s commanding officer was an Emeraldian, five inches shorter than his senior lieutenant, with the typical dark hair and eyes of his birth princedom. "If there was anything remotely resembling organized resistance waiting for them, it'd turn into outright disaster pretty damned quickly."

Kylmahn started to reply, then stopped himself. His diminutive captain was a naturally humorous man, but that sense of humor was conspicuous by its absence this afternoon. Not without at least some justification, unfortunately.

The heavily overcast sky deposited a steady, soaking rain on all and sundry, and the customary smoothness of the Imperial Charisian Navy's ship-to-shore operations was even more conspicuously absent than Captain Ahbaht's sense of humor. Much of that was undoubtedly due to the speed with which their mission had been planned and implemented. The storms they'd endured on their way here hadn't helped, and the present heavy downpour wasn't making things any better, yet none of that excused the landing's sloppy execution.

The lieutenant used one hand to shade his eyes from pelting raindrops and returned his attention to the thoroughly unimpressive island Captain Ahbaht had been ordered to secure. Talisman Island was roughly triangular and only about twenty miles long on its northwest-to-southeast axis. Its terrain was rugged, to say the least, and their reports said its limited water supply was barely sufficient for the year-round needs of the small fishing community of Rahzhyrhold. Yet Talisman's two enormous advantages trumped all those difficulties: Rahzhyr Bay and the island's location off the coast of Shwei.

The deepwater bay, a pocket of water twelve miles across on Talisman's west coast, offered a secure, almost totally sheltered anchorage. Protected from easterly winds by the bulk of Talisman itself, it was shielded from the north and west by even smaller, half-awash islets and rocky, barely submerged shoals which formed a natural breakwater. The mainland of Howard, less than ninety miles to the southeast, provided a bulwark against bad weather from that direction, as well. Talisman's unforgiving terrain and the treacherous band of shoals stretching around its circumference everywhere outside Rahzhyr Bay made the bay itself the only practical spot for troop landings, which promised to make the island an extraordinarily tough defensive target, as well. In many ways, it was Claw Island in miniature, and it was also barely three hundred miles from Shwei Bay and under a thousand from the Royal Dohlaran Navy's base at Saram Bay in North Harchong's Stene Province. Perhaps even more to the point, it was barely four hundred miles from the advanced anchorage Sir Dahrand Rohsail had established for the RDN at Stella Cove on the large island of Jack's Land at the eastern end of the Harchong Narrows.

Kylmahn understood the logic behind acquiring Talisman. It would have made sense under any circumstances he could think of; after the near-hurricane gale which had ravaged the Narrows in late April, however, it had taken on even greater point.

"Do you think this is going to cause Rohsail to change his tactics, Sir?" the lieutenant asked after a moment.

"Hard to say."

Ahbaht straightened and turned his back on the angle-glass. He folded his hands behind him and began pacing back and forth across his quarterdeck while raindrops bounced off his oilskins and Kylmahn kept station beside him.

"It ought to make him more nervous, anyway," the captain continued. "I expect he'll feel at least some compulsion to keep more of his line of battle concentrated in case we get adventurous and decide to raid Jack's Land, for example. For that matter, he has to be worried about our attacking Saram Bay itself, given what Captain Haigyl accomplished in the Bay of Alexov."

Kylmahn nodded. He suspected that Sir Bruhstair would have already sailed into Saram Bay and reduced it to rubble if he'd been allowed to. Unfortunately, Admiral Rohsail was clearly determined to protect what had become his primary forward base after the loss of Claw Island. Their most recent spy reports indicated that he had several score of the Dohlarans' new "spar torpedoes," and he'd placed batteries on every rock and islet—and on floating batteries with massive bulwarks reinforced with anchor chains and sandbags—to cover the bay's entrances. The lieutenant knew Earl Sharpfield wasn't especially concerned by the possibility that even the heaviest Dohlaran guns could penetrate his two ironclads' armor, but he had a very lively concern over what might happen if the enemy managed to dismast one of them with spar torpedoes in the vicinity.

*And the fact that Captain Haigyl damned nearly lost* Dreadnought *in that gale doesn't help any,* he reminded himself grimly.

There were those in the Imperial Charisian Navy—including himself, Kylmahn admitted—who were less than impressed by Captain Kahrltyn Haigyl's abilities as a seaman, yet he'd done himself and his command proud last month. The storm had moved in far too quickly for anyone to seek shelter, especially when the nearest available harbor had been Claw Island itself, and more than one of the Charisians in Earl Sharpfield's squadron had remembered the disastrous hurricane which had doomed Sir Gwylym Manthyr the *last* time a Charisian squadron entered the Gulf of Dohlar.

This one hadn't been as bad as that one, according to the handful of officers who'd survived both, but it had been quite bad enough for Daivyn Kylmahn. Two of Sharpfield's galleons had been lost. One had gone down with all hands, which meant no one knew exactly what had happened to her. The second had been driven ashore on Martyn's Point, barely three hundred miles from Saram Bay, with the loss of eighty-three men, although her consorts had rescued the rest of her company before the Harchongians realized what had happened. A third galleon, so badly damaged she'd had to be towed back to Claw Island, had been effectively written off Earl Sharpfield's effective strength. Unwilling to risk her at sea in her crippled state, he'd stripped her of her guns and turned her into an anchored receiving ship. One of the earl's schooners had vanished at sea in the same storm, along with her entire crew, and another had lost every spar, although she'd survived.

*Dreadnought* had also survived, despite having found herself trapped in the gale's direct path. She had, however, suffered heavy damage aloft, and her armored hull had strained badly. All her damage was repairable, and the service galleons Sharpfield had brought along for the purpose were confident they'd have her back in full commission shortly. In the meantime, however, the earl's available strength had been severely reduced. He'd already dispatched five of his original unarmored galleons back to Chisholm, escorting his withdrawing transports to protect them against privateers, as his original orders had required. That had reduced his total galleon strength to twenty-eight, counting both ironclads. After the storm, he was down to only twenty-five, at least a half dozen of which had to be kept at Claw Island, and he had no intention of running any avoidable risk with his single remaining ironclad.

"I really hate to ask this, Sir—given how smoothly the landing seems to be proceeding, and all—but how soon do you think you'll be able to hand matters over to Commander Makgrygair?"

"Not soon enough to make me happy," Ahbaht said a bit sourly.

The captain, Kylmahn knew, had a lively respect for Commander Symyn Makgrygair, the officer Sharpfield had selected to command the base facilities on Rahzhyr Bay. He also liked and respected Major Qwentyn Ohmahly, who would command the Marine garrison. It was scarcely their fault that things were proceeding . . . less than smoothly, but Sir Bruhstair's irritation was apparent.

"Actually," Ahbaht said, stopping and peering up at the sodden masthead pendant, "I imagine we'll have most of the Marines landed by evening. Another five-day or so to sway the guns ashore and land supplies. Then another five-day, say, to get the batteries emplaced and make sure the anchorage's been properly surveyed. So I could probably make a fairly good case for turning command over to Makgrygair by the twelfth, let's say."

Kylmahn brightened slightly. That was better than he'd expected, and he wondered if Ahbaht's own desire to be off and about was influencing the captain's estimate. He dismissed the thought almost instantly. Sir Bruhstair Ahbaht wasn't the sort to engage in wishful thinking, no matter how great the temptation.

The lieutenant pulled out his pocket watch and checked the time.

"With your permission, Sir," he said, snapping the case closed, "I promised the Bo'sun I'd oversee that sail room survey this morning. I think he's concerned about the storm sails after last month."

"I find myself in rather strong agreement with him on that particular point," Ahbaht said with a smile.

"Then I'll be about it, Sir."

Kylmahn touched his chest in salute and strode off briskly. Ahbaht watched him with an approving smile, then shrugged and resumed his pacing once again.

In all fairness, Kylmahn had a point—it wasn't *really* going as badly as it seemed to him it was—and he strongly suspected that the real reason for his disgruntlement were the orders keeping him tethered here until the defensive batteries were in place, sighted in, and fully manned.

*But once I can sign off on their readiness . . . .*

His lips twitched in a hungry smile at the thought.

Sir Dahrand Rohsail, in Sir Bruhstair Ahbaht's considered opinion, had entirely too good a grasp of his own responsibilities and his resources. Nothing he had could possibly stand up to *Thunderer* or *Dreadnought* in a ship-to-ship action. By the same token, any attempt to retake Claw Island could end only in disastrous defeat, and once Major Ohmahly's batteries were in place, any attack on Talisman Island would be equally costly. But if Rohsail wasn't stupid enough to match his own unarmored ships against heavy batteries, and if he couldn't engage the ironclads at sea, nothing prevented him from engaging any *other* Charisian ship he encountered, and he'd already destroyed three of Sharpfield's schooners. There were no reports of survivors from any of them, which might say something about Rohsail's willingness to offer quarter. It might just as easily say something about the Charisian Imperial Navy's unwillingness to *ask* for quarter from the Navy which had delivered Sir Gwylym Manthyr and his crews to the Inquisition. Ahbaht's mental jury was still out on that point, but there was no denying that Rohsail's ships' companies were well drilled and tough. And unlike any other Safeholdian fleet, they respected the Charisian Navy's reputation without being overawed by it. They were quite prepared to engage on anything remotely like equal terms, and that aggressiveness had severely hampered Earl Sharpfield's operations against the Gulf of Dohlar's merchant shipping.

Once Talisman was secured and ready to support the earl's light cruisers, and once *Dreadnought* was returned to service, Ahbaht and Haigyl would take themselves off to Saram Bay to do a little something about that unhappy state of affairs. With Talisman to fall back on for supplies, fresh water, and shelter from bad weather, they should be able to maintain an effective blockade of the bay. For that matter, one of them might keep watch over Saram Bay while the other did the same for Jack's Land. With any luck, they'd catch all or a substantial portion of Rohsail's galleons in the harbor when they began patrolling the approaches. If the Dohlaran wanted to come out and fight, that would be fine with Ahbaht. And if he *didn't* want to come out and fight, his ships could sit at anchor and rot while Sharpfield's cruisers wreaked havoc on the commerce they were supposed to be protecting.

*We'll get the job done, one way or another*, the captain promised himself. *It may not be pretty, and it damned well won't be as* quick *as we'd hoped it would, but we'll get it done. And once the* King Haarahlds *are ready, that won't be the* only *thing we get done, either.*

. III .

# The Temple,
# City of Zion,
# The Temple Lands

"Archbishop Wyllym, Your Grace," the Schuelerite under-priest murmured as he ushered Wyllym Rayno through the mystic sliding door of Zhaspahr Clyntahn's office. The office walls' ever-changing mirror of God's handiwork showed a forest glade today, the straight white and gray trunks rising from a drift of ground mist as golden bars of sunlight shone down through holes in the canopy. Another golden streamer, from no discernible source, struck down to illuminate Clyntahn's actual work space, distant birdsong and wyvern whistles came quietly, quietly from the forest, and every so often a nearbadger or some other small creature scurried through the hushed stillness of that woodland cathedral.

No one seemed to notice. The Grand Inquisitor only responded to the announcement with his customary grunt of acknowledgment and jabbed an index finger at the chair on the other side of his desk. The under-priest disappeared, the door closed once more behind him, and Rayno seated himself obediently, folded his hands in the sleeves of his cassock, and regarded his superior calmly.

"You wished to see me, Your Grace?"

"No, I damned well didn't *wish* to see you," Clyntahn growled. "There are a hell of a lot of other things I'd wish for before *that!* Unfortunately, what I wish and what I need are two different things at the moment."

Rayno allowed himself a slight nod of acknowledgment. The Grand Inquisitor snorted, yet he seemed uncharacteristically loath to come to the reason he'd summoned the archbishop. He straightened a sheaf of notes on his desk, then adjusted the pen holder on his blotter, before he finally tipped back in his chair and regarded the Order of Schueler's adjutant.

"I'm worried about Maigwair," he said abruptly, and paused, obviously inviting a response.

"In what way, Your Grace?" Rayno asked obediently, and Clyntahn's face tightened.

"He's accepted that Wyrshym can't retreat—for the moment, at least—but he's one hell of a long way from being happy about it and I'm none too sure he won't do what he can to get Wyrshym's orders changed. Or even to quietly circumvent them, if he thinks he can get away with it! And he might just decide he *could* get away with it, because I doubt he's the only member of the Army of God who feels that way, and he knows it. All any of them can see is the frigging *battlefield*. Not one of them seems to understand what's really at stake here, not the way you and I do! For all I know, it might even make some sort of *military* sense to let Wyrshym retreat—assuming he could, under the circumstances, and I'm not so sure it would be possible in the first place!—but giving that ground would be disastrous for the cause of crushing the heresy in Siddarmark. What *really* matters beside accomplishing that?"

Rayno nodded, partly in sincere agreement and partly in understanding of the real cause of at least half of Clyntahn's ire. Despite any effort on Inquisitor General Wylbyr's part to put a good face on things, the Inquisition's own internal reports all pointed to the extent to which the inquisitor general's own inquisitors had allowed the rigor with which they approached the heretics in his holding camps to . . . erode. That was bad enough in the Grand Inquisitor's view; the possibility that every unsifted heretic in one of those camps might be rescued by their fellow heretics was intolerable.

"You'd never guess from his deployments that that was important to Maigwair, though," Clyntahn continued in a tone that was more than half a snarl. "He spends a lot of time talking about reinforcements and replacements, but he never seems to *do* anything with them! Just look at the way the Army of Tanshar's sitting on its arse—and not because Bishop Militant Tayrens *wants* to be sitting there, either!"

Rayno's expression never flickered, but his jaw clenched. Tayrens Teagmahn commanded the Army of Tanshar, the reserve army Allayn Maigwair had raised over the past fall and winter and drawn upon for the reinforcements sent forward to Cahnyr Kaitswyrth's Army of Glacierheart. At the moment, it was located in the Princedom of Tanshar, from which it took its name, just over the Temple Lands border from the Episcopate of Klynair, where the relatively moderate climate had allowed the needed drill and training even in the heart of winter. Unfortunately, it had critically few rifles and field guns at the moment for the very good reason that Maigwair had stripped out its best trained and equipped formations to reinforce Kaitswyrth.

It was perhaps unfortunate that the Grand Inquisitor had never let his ignorance of the realities of finance or logistics get in the way of his demands for weapons and equipment. He deeply resented any niggling reality that thwarted his desires, and the fact that Teagmahn, like any good general, wanted his troops to be properly equipped only increased the Grand Inquisitor's frustration. The bishop militant had submitted request after request to Allayn Maigwair and Rhobair Duchairn for the weapons to arm his *entire* command, and when they informed him that the weapons he wanted simply weren't available, he hadn't been shy about turning to his intendant, Auxiliary Bishop Rhobair Makswyl. Makswyl was as fervent an intendant as a man could wish for, and he'd passed every one of Teagmahn's requests along to his own superiors, which had brought Clyntahn into repeated conflict with his fellow vicars even before Teagmahn was forced to disgorge Kaitswyrth's reinforcements.

Normally, Rayno found his superior's tendency to brush over the Jihad's physical limitations one of the most frustrating aspects of serving him, but in this case he was even angrier than the Grand Inquisitor, if not for exactly the same reasons.

The Rayno family was powerful enough—and had sufficiently distinguished itself in Mother Church's service—that Mother Church had set aside her customary policy of assigning senior priests or bishops to parishes and bishoprics outside the lands of their birth in the case of one Wyllym Rayno. That was how he came to be Archbishop of Chiang-wu . . . and it was also why he'd been bitterly opposed to rearming and—especially—retraining the Mighty Host of God and the Archangels. The last thing he wanted to see was an army of experienced, well-trained serfs returning to his family's ancestral home polluted by all sorts of radical ideas picked up from other lands . . . and equipped with the military training to do something about them.

The Grand Inquisitor, unfortunately, saw only the monumental reliability of Harchong. He was delighted by the sledgehammer into which Allayn Maigwair and Rhobair Duchairn had transformed the Mighty Host, and Rayno knew better than to argue the point with him. Instead, he'd limited his opposition to quiet, covert efforts to undermine the Earl of Rainbow Waters while making certain any intendant assigned to the Mighty Host had the proper fire in his belly.

Still, he understood the point Clyntahn was making, and if it offered an opening . . . .

"Do you believe Vicar Allayn and Vicar Rhobair are deliberately starving Bishop Militant Tayrens of weapons, Your Grace?" he asked carefully.

"I believe Vicar Allayn is deliberately withholding as much of Teagmahn's entire army from Siddarmark as he can get away with," Clyntahn grated. Despite himself, Rayno felt his eyebrows rise slightly, and Clyntahn glowered at him. "Think about it, Wyllym. If Teagmahn had received forty or fifty thousand of the new rifles, Maigwair would have had an *effective* reserve sitting there in Tanshar instead of the miserable thirty thousand he came up with to send the Army of Glacierheart! He could've sent *all* of it across the Gulf of Tanshar and up the Fairmyn River to reinforce Kaitswyrth, or he could've sent Kaitswyrth the troops he's actually getting and used the Dairnyth-Alyksberg Canal to send the rest of them south to hit that bastard Hanth in the rear. Either of those would put more pressure on the heretics and draw at least *some* weight off Wyrshym, wouldn't it?"

"I see your point, Your Grace," Rayno murmured.

The truth, of course, was that it would have accomplished nothing of the sort. An advance south *might* have compelled the heretic Hanth to abandon his steady, grim advance along the Sheryl-Seridahn, but it would never have diverted Greyghor Stohnar and Cay-leb Ahrmahk's unwavering determination to destroy Bahrnabai Wyrshym's army once and for all. The Army of the Sylmahn was simply too vulnerable, especially now, and Cayleb and Stohnar were resolved to liberate the Inquisition's camps in northern Siddarmark at the earliest possible moment. However . . . .

"I see your point," he repeated. "Unfortunately, you're also correct that, at the moment, Bishop Militant Tay-rens could accomplish very little simply because his men lack the arms to meet the heretics in battle. Perhaps it would be wiser to transfer at least some of the rifles and field pieces en route to Earl Rainbow Waters to the Bishop Militant, instead." He shrugged. "I'm no military man myself, Your Grace. Nonetheless, it seems evident to me that there's little point in raising and training an army if you then fail to *arm* it."

"*Exactly* the point I've been making to Maigwair and that sniveling cretin Duchairn!" Clyntahn growled. "And I intend to *go on* making it, I assure you. But the truth is I'm actually more concerned about Bishop Mil-itant Ruhsail. I have some nasty suspicions where he's concerned."

"I beg your pardon, Your Grace?"

Rayno cocked his head in genuine surprise. Bishop Militant Ruhsail Symmyns' command, in winter quar-ters in the Episcopate of Schueler on the southeastern shore of Lake Pei, was far smaller than the Army of Tanshar. In fact, he commanded barely thirty thousand men, and he was one of the most ardent supporters of the Jihad Rayno could think of.

"Oh, I'm not concerned about *Symmyns'* loyalty." Clyntahn waved a beefy hand. "I'm a little less confi-dent about some of his regimental and division commanders, though. His intendant's reports seem to in-dicate all of them—even Symmyns, to some extent—are strongly in agreement with Maigwair's desire to pull Wyrshym back. None of them are actively criticizing the decision *not* to withdraw the Army of the Sylmahn, but it strikes me that they have just a bit too much confidence in the 'Captain General' and his judgment."

Rayno felt no temptation to point out to the Grand Inquisitor that most armies considered it a good thing when their officers and troops had confidence in their commanders' judgment.

"Are you concerned about their . . . reliability, Your Grace?" he asked delicately.

"I don't know." Any admission of uncertainty was most unlike Zhaspahr Clyntahn, and Rayno's eyes narrowed slightly. "I just know Maigwair's managed to get a higher percentage of rifles to Symmyns' command than he has to the Army of Tanshar. He *says* that's because Symmyns is so much closer that the logistics are simpler—and he's pointed out that the Army of Tanshar was originally supposed to be armed with Dohlaran-built rifles before that disaster in the South March. Now Dohlar's hanging on to every rifle it can manufacture while it rebuilds its own army. According to him, that's the reason Teagmahn's standing around with his thumb up his arse waiting while Symmyns is getting at least a trickle of rifles and artillery. I haven't been able to *prove* he's lying to me, but . . . ."

The Grand Inquisitor's voice trailed off, and Rayno's eyes narrowed a bit more. Then they widened, and his expression went completely blank as he realized what he'd just seen in *Clyntahn's* eyes.

Uncertainty. Possibly even fear.

*Schueler! It* is *fear,* the archbishop thought, and an icicle ran down his spine.

The one emotion he'd never seen Clyntahn display—or not more than briefly, at any rate—was fear. And certainly he'd never seen uncertainty. The Grand Inquisitor's power was the core of his personality. The ability to destroy his foes, to smite them with all the invincible power of God and Mother Church, was the lens through which he saw the entire world. Other people feared *him;* any other arrangement was unthinkable. And while he might occasionally be *wrong* about some problem or decision, he was never *uncertain*; that was another fundamental hallmark of his character. But now—

*He's more worried about Wyrshym and the Army of the Sylmahn than he wants to admit even to himself,* Rayno thought. *He could wave his hands over what happened to the Army of Shiloh, but not this one. The Army of Shiloh was a* secular *army, with secular commanders who obviously screwed up by the numbers, so he could dismiss what happened to them. Besides, Shiloh and the South March were secondary theaters, as far as he was concerned.*

*But it's different when he starts talking about the Army of God. He's pinning a lot of faith on the Mighty Host, but how much of that is because he* has *to? Because he's got no other choice? Because the truth is, the only army he truly trusts is Mother Church's own. That's the real reason he's so pissed off that Maigwair and Duchairn keep telling him we simply don't have enough weapons to equip armies the size of the ones he wants to throw at the heretics, too. He feels things slipping out of his control, and those Shan-wei-damned broadsheets going up all over the Temple Lands, the Fist of Kau-Yung, and the way even our own inquisitors are backing off in the camps—all of that—only makes it worse.*

*He's actually beginning to think Mother Church might* lose *the Jihad.*

Wyllym Rayno had seen frightened men many times in his life. Indeed, the archbishop who was the Inquisition's second-in-command was accustomed to seeing fear. But not in Zhaspahr Clyntahn. Not in the Grand Inquisitor himself.

"Do you truly believe Vicar Allayn would deceive you about something like that for some reason, Your Grace?" he asked in a painfully neutral tone.

"I believe he's never had enough steel in his spine for Mother Church's Captain General at a time like this," Clyntahn said flatly. "He's always been ready to jump at shadows, to hide in his corner when the going got a little rough. And I believe he has enough spider rat in him to start thinking about 'exit strategies' to save his worthless skin."

A Bédardist, Rayno reflected, would probably have called that "projection," although he had no intention of pointing that out.

"What sort of 'exit strategy,' Your Grace?" he asked instead.

"I think one reason he's been sucking up to Duchairn is the hope that the two of them might be able to form a united front against me," Clyntahn replied. "He'd probably prefer Trynair, but Zahmsyn's learned his place." The Grand Inquisitor smiled nastily. "Our esteemed Chancellor isn't going to cross *me* whatever happens. So Allayn's looking to Rhobair, and so far it's been working for him, because however little I trust either of them the Jihad needs *both* of them. For now, at least. But the truth is that Allayn's the more . . . expendable of them. I can always find someone else to run the Army, but Rhobair's the only one who begins to understand how to keep the bills paid. Mother Church won't *always* need him either, though, and when the time comes . . . ."

Rayno nodded. He and Clyntahn had discussed the Grand Inquisitor's post-Jihad plans for Rhobair Duchairn often enough.

"The thing is that Allayn's getting too big for his britches," Clyntahn said. "And however much I trust Symmyns, some of his officers might obey Allayn even if that meant mutinying against their immediate superior. That wouldn't bother me too much—they're still six hundred miles from Zion, after all—but they're the *closest* standing military force. If they did mutiny in Allayn's support, they could reach the city—or the *Temple*—before anyone else."

"Do you seriously believe Vicar Allayn is contemplating some sort of coup, Your Grace?"

"If he isn't contemplating one now, he's likely to start contemplating one soon enough." Clyntahn's expression was grim. "I don't expect him to try anything overt unless the situation in Siddarmark goes even further into the crapper. That'd take more guts than he's ever had in his life! But if he manages to fuck up this summer's campaign the way he did *last* summer's, he may just decide he has no choice but to throw the dice, especially if he thinks he can convince Rhobair to support him. Under the circumstances, I think it's time we began taking a few small precautions, don't you?"

. IV .
# Larek Shipyard,
# and
# The Delthak Works,
# Earldom of High Rock,
# Kingdom of Old Charis,
# Empire of Charis

Coal smoke and the smell of saltwater, paint, oil, and hot metal filled Ehdwyrd Howsmyn's nostrils. The clangor of old-fashioned hammers and new-model pneumatic rivet guns was deafening, but it was scarcely the only sound assaulting his ears as he stood at dockside and gazed at the mammoth ship floating against the thick fenders. HMS *King Haarahld VII* was one of the three largest vessels ever built on Safehold. She measured four hundred and thirty-five feet on the waterline, with a beam of seventy-seven feet, and her normal displacement would be over fourteen thousand tons when she was completed. With a deck load of coal, she would be able to make the entire voyage from Tellesberg to Claw Island without refueling in just over a month and a half. If she went by way of Cherayth and coaled there, the trip would be five hundred miles longer but she could steam twice as fast and reach her destination in barely twenty-four days.

She was the first Safeholdian ship to be formally designated a "battleship," and when she went into commission, not a warship in the world—not even *every* other warship in the world, combined—could stand up to her.

"You and your people are doing us proud, Eysamu," he said to the stocky, solidly built man standing beside him.

Eysamu Tahnguchi had been one of Howsmyn's assistant foundry foremen before he'd moved over to the design of the Delthak Works canal barges. He'd had a major hand in converting four of those barges into the original *Delthak*-class ironclads, and he'd supervised the construction of the first of the *City*-class coastal ironclads before moving over to the *King Haarahlds*. Along the way, he and Sir Dustyn Olyvyr had invented entirely new construction techniques . . . and modified those techniques on the fly as still newer and better capabilities—like the rivet guns—became available.

"Thank you, Sir," Tahnguchi said now, his own eyes watching the hordes of workmen swarming over *King Haarahld VII* and her two sister ships. "We're still a long way short of done, though."

"Yes, you are," Howsmyn agreed in a severe tone. "I believe you're only three five-days ahead of schedule at the moment. What sort of slackers do you have working for you?"

Tahnguchi chuckled, but he also shook his head.

"With the *Cities* diverted to Desnair, Earl Sharpfield *needs* these ships, Sir. We aim to get them to him, too."

"I never doubted it," Howsmyn said simply.

The industrialist donned his hard hat and the two of them began walking towards one of the half-dozen gangways connecting *King Haarahld VII* to the building wharf. Workmen stood aside to let them pass, and Howsmyn smiled at each of them in passing, stopping every few yards to chat with them, tell them how much he and the entire Empire depended upon—and appreciated—their nonstop work. They deserved his praise as much as Tahnguchi did, and he knew it.

They reached the ship's deck at last, solid teak planking over an inch and a half of "Howsmynized" steel armor, and he looked around. At the moment, the ship resembled an unfinished manufactory more than a warship, and it looked nothing like any galleon or galley ever built. Bits and pieces of equipment lay strewn about the deck, the armored barbette which would eventually mount the forward ten-inch guns loomed like a rusty steel fortress, and the massive casing for the ship's forward funnel floated overhead, drifting downward in the snorting grasp of a steam-powered crane. Hand ropes formed a warning barrier around a gaping hole where neither deck armor nor the planking to cover it had yet been put in place, and Tahnguchi guided his guest towards the opening.

"The ladder's a bit steep, Sir," he cautioned. "I'd hoped to have this closed in by now, but two of her boilers failed final inspection." He grimaced. "Unless we're damned lucky, that's going to use up every minute of those five-days you were talking about. In the meantime, though, it's the shortest route to the machinery spaces. Your letter said you wanted to see the boiler rooms first, so I thought we'd start there. After that, we can work our way back to the engine rooms, and from there I thought we'd take a look at the after magazines and the hydraulics for the gun training gear. Then—"

▼ ▼ ▼

"I see you survived the trip," Brahd Stylmyn said dryly as Howsmyn climbed down the boarding steps.

"No fault of your fiendish contraption," Howsmyn replied.

"You're the one who chose the route for the trial line, Sir," Stylmyn pointed out. "*I* wanted to run it to the mines, if I remember correctly."

"And you know damned well why we didn't," Howsmyn replied, and Stylmyn raised his hands in surrender. Although, Howsmyn reflected, for a man who'd lost an argument he seemed remarkably cheerful about it.

Paityr Wylsynn had indeed signed the attestation for Stylmyn's "steam automotive," and despite all the other endless demands for steel, Stylmyn had pressed hard for constructing an actual working rail line. After all, he'd said, it was the only way to really prove the concept . . . and let him see his new toy in operation.

His proposal to build a freight line to supplement the barges hauling coal and iron ore down the Delthak River had been a nonstarter, however. The sheer length of the line—not to mention the amount of grading, excavation, and bridge-building which would have been required—made it impossible at the moment, even with Sahndrah Lywys' Lywysite. The line between the Delthak Works and the city of Larek, however, was both much shorter and offered terrain which was mostly flat and unmarred by any rivers or valleys. It had provided a far more suitable route for Safehold's first railroad, and its sixty-five-mile length had officially opened to traffic only three days ago. There were still a few minor bugs to be worked out, in Howsmyn's considered opinion—there was one two-mile section he was damned well going to have ripped out, regraded, and re-ballasted—and the passenger cars could use more human-friendly suspensions. But it certainly worked, and hordes of spectators had come out to see it in operation. They'd cheerfully paid to ride it, as well, and he had to admit he could readily become addicted himself to making a sixty-five-mile trip in barely an hour.

Now the only problem would be fending off Stylmyn's desire to build still more railroads. And the fact that Sharleyan Ahrmahk was going to lend him her vociferous support as soon as she got home and officially found out about this one's existence wasn't going to make his life any simpler, Howsmyn reflected.

*But there's only so much steel* available, *damn it,* he thought. *For that matter, Sharley knows it, too. The real reason she's going to be supporting him so vocally is that she figures putting the imperial imprimatur on the whole notion of railroads will bring potential investors out of the woodwork to pay for them. She's probably right about* that, *too.*

He snorted at the thought as he and Stylmyn walked across the first Safeholdian railroad station's boardwalk towards their waiting bicycles.

"What?" his henchman inquired.

"Just thinking about something a friend of mine said," Howsmyn replied.

They pulled their bicycles out of the rack, climbed into the saddles, and began pedaling their way towards the main works. Morning was easing into afternoon, and Howsmyn found himself pedaling a bit harder in hope of reaching their destination before shift change inundated them in a sea of humanity.

*Besides*, he thought with a mental chuckle, *it'll do Brahd good to keep up with me. He doesn't get enough exercise, anyway.*

Actually, Stylmyn kept pace without any sign of undue strain or even breathing heavily. Which, Howsmyn discovered a bit grumpily, was more than he could say for himself.

"I hope this won't take too long," he said, looking across at Stylmyn. "God knows I don't want to cut Taigys short, but Zhain and I haven't had dinner at the same time in the same place in almost a five-day. If I'm late again, she's going to have my ears. Besides, I've got a surprise for her."

"If she collects any ears, it won't be *my* fault," Stylmyn replied. "*I'm* not the one who suggested an entirely new weapon to him. *I'm* not the one who inspired him to design a completely different cartridge to make it work. *I'm* not the one who's going to insist on taking the damned thing out to the range and blazing away until I've used up every one of the cartridges he's already made. *I'm* not—"

"Shut up and pedal, or you won't be the one who has a *job* anymore, either!"

Stylmyn laughed, remarkably un-cowed by the threat, and Howsmyn shook his head. Not that Brahd didn't have an excellent point. Several of them, in fact.

Taigys Mahldyn had persevered with his cardboard cartridges and effectively reinvented the shotgun. The current version was something someone from Old Earth might have called a 10-gauge, with a .75 caliber barrel, and he'd started with a simple break-barrel design. Howsmyn had spent several enjoyable hours perforating targets on the range behind Mahldyn's rifle shop with it, but Taigys—inevitably—had been convinced he could improve it, and he had. In fact, he'd produced his own version of a pump-action shotgun, and he was already tinkering with a design to apply the same sort of slide action to a modified M96 rifle.

Howsmyn doubted that the Imperial Charisian Army would be adopting slide-action rifles anytime soon. The current M96 already provided it with an enormous firepower advantage, and the additional complexity would offer more opportunities for soldiers to break things. That was never a good idea, and the new action would drive up cost substantially. Besides, before Duke Eastshare signed off on any new weapon, he was going to seek Baron Green Valley's opinion, and Green Valley was fully aware of the semi-auto and full-automatic actions Sahndrah Lywys' smokeless propellants would make practical.

*But in the meantime*, he told himself with a grin, *you're going to enjoy the hell out of blazing away with the thing. Don't pretend you're not! And don't think you can get away with telling Zhain it was all Taigys' fault, either. She knows you even better than Brahd does, and she'll have a right to be pissed if you drag in late and covered with burnt gunpowder!*

True, all true, he thought. Of course, she might cut him a *tiny* amount of slack when she found out about the other news he was bringing back from Larek.

It had never bothered Zhain Howsmyn that she, the daughter of the Earl of Sharphill, one of the Kingdom of Charis' most senior nobles, had married a mere commoner who was eight years older than she. It had probably helped that the "mere commoner" in question had been one of the wealthiest men in the Kingdom and had since become the wealthiest man in the world, period. But that hadn't really mattered to her, either. Still, their anniversary was coming up next month, and she was only human. Caleb and Sharleyan Ahrmahk had decided what to give the Howsmyns as an anniversary gift, and the word he'd been awaiting had finally officially reached Tellesberg from Siddar City and been forwarded to Larek.

*Duke and Duchess Delthak.*

He rolled the title over his mental tongue, and smiled as he pictured her reaction after he dragged in late and just offhandedly dropped the news on her when she began to read him the riot act. When she got done goggling at him, then finished laughing, then finished whacking him about the head and shoulders, she would undoubtedly drag him off to bed where he would receive an early anniversary gift of his own.

*Yes*, he reflected, *it looks like being a very good night all around.*

. V .

## HMS *Thunderer*, 30,
## Gulf of Dohlar

Sir Bruhstair Ahbaht turned from the wide stern windows of HMS *Thunderer* as his steward showed the compactly built, sandy-haired fisherman into his day cabin.

"Master Cudd, Sir Bruhstair," the steward said, with what might have been the slightest possible edge of disapproval. Mahrak Chandlyr had been with Sir Bruhstair Ahbaht for almost twenty years, but he hadn't quite reconciled himself to the sorts of disreputable people with whom the captain of an imperial warship was forced to hobnob.

"Thank you, Mahrak," Ahbaht replied gravely, and the steward bowed slightly—to him—and withdrew.

*Thunderer*'s captain smiled after him, shaking his head, then turned to his visitor. "I trust Mahrak wasn't too rude, *Seijin* Dagyr."

He reached out to clasp forearms with Cudd, and the *seijin* smiled back at him.

"I'd say he was less rude than . . . wary, perhaps. As was Lieutenant Zhaksyn when my boat came alongside, although I think my accent probably helped with him."

Ahbaht snorted. Ahlber Zhaksyn was *Thunderer*'s second lieutenant. He was also just twenty-nine years old and a native of Chisholm, so he probably had found Cudd's Harris Island accent reassuring.

"Well, fortunately, Earl Sharpfield mentioned your meeting with him when he sent me out here. It would appear it was a good thing he did."

Ahbaht released Cudd's arm and waved the roughly dressed *seijin* into one of the wingback armchairs sitting on the square of carpet under the skylight. He poured whiskey into two glasses, handed one to his visitor, and then settled into the second armchair and leaned back.

"I trust you won't take this wrongly, *Seijin* Dagyr," he continued, "but it's rather a relief to encounter a *seijin* of merely mortal dimensions."

"Not all of us are as tall as Merlin or Ahbraim," Cudd agreed with what was undeniably a grin this time, not a smile. He was no more than an inch or two taller than Ahbaht.

"No, I don't suppose you are." Ahbaht sipped whiskey for a moment, regarding the *seijin* levelly. Then he shrugged. "It would seem, however, that all of you are . . . equally gifted at turning up unanticipatedly. Would it be violating any secret *seijin* lore to ask how you came to happen across us?"

It was, Cudd acknowledged, a reasonable question. At the moment, *Thunderer* was about midway between Hilda Island and Parrot Point, over nine hundred miles east of Talisman Island. Ahbaht was doing exactly what he was supposed to be doing, now that Talisman been secured and the coastal batteries were in place, by deliberately showing the ironclad so far east of the Harchong Narrows. Whether or not he would succeed in drawing any substantial portion of Sir Dahrand Rohsail's squadron away from Saram Bay and Jack's Land was an open question, at best. Frankly, Cudd thought there was relatively little chance of someone as canny as Rohsail obliging Earl Sharpfield that way, but it was certainly worth trying.

"Actually, no special arcane *seijin* lore was required, Sir," he replied almost, but not quite, honestly. "I'd heard rumors of Charisian ships having seized Talisman Island and it seemed reasonable to assume they might be operating farther east than they had been. For someone who doesn't want to come any closer to Admiral Rohsail than I had to, the Hilda Channel would seem like the best route from Gorath to Claw Island." He shrugged. "All I had to do was keep a close lookout on the way through, and your ship's not exactly hard to recognize, Sir Bruhstair."

There was, he decided, no need to mention that Owl had used one of the air lorries with a heavy-lift tractor to deliver his fishing boat to just outside visual range of *Thunderer* before he started keeping a close lookout for her.

"I see." Ahbaht nodded, although he suspected it hadn't been quite as simple as the *seijin* seemed to imply. "On the other hand," he continued, "I rather doubt you stopped by simply to exchange observations on other people's height."

"You doubt correctly." Cudd's expression sobered. "In fact, when I heard you'd been sent to take possession of Talisman, I decided it was even more important for you to have this information than Earl Sharpfield." Ahbaht raised his eyebrows politely, and Cudd grimaced. "It seems Earl Thirsk's had an inspiration where his screw-galleys are concerned, Sir Bruhstair. In fact—"

▼ ▼ ▼

"Thank you both for coming so promptly," Captain Ahbaht said as Daivyn Kylmahn, his first lieutenant, showed Horayshyo Vahrnay and Lywelyn Pymbyrtyn into his day cabin.

Nine days had elapsed since his meeting with Dagyr Cudd, during which *Thunderer* had made her laborious way back to Talisman Island against persistent headwinds. A Charisian officer—especially a Charisian *naval* officer—was supposed to exercise his own judgment in the absence of specific orders from his superiors, and Ahbaht had spent those days considering the implications of the *seijin*'s information. All of his squadron was now gathered in Rahzhyr Bay, taking on fresh water from the water hoys sent forward from Claw Island, and he'd signaled for the other two captains to repair aboard the ironclad almost before her anchor had hit the bay's sandy bottom. They had to be afire with curiosity over the sudden, peremptory summons.

Vahrnay commanded HMS *Vengeance* and Pymbyrtyn commanded her sister ship *Vindicator*. After *Thunderer*, the pair of sixty-eight-gun galleons were the two most powerful units of Ahbaht's entire squadron, and Vahrnay was his second-in-command. He was also a consummate seaman, and one of the finest warship commanders Ahbaht had ever seen, but Pymbyrtyn was even more interesting in many ways. He was a subject of Old Charis, but he spoke with a heavy Tarotisian accent, because until five years ago, he'd been a subject of King Gorjah of Tarot rather than Haarahld VII. When King Cayleb and Archbishop Maikel decided to bid defiance to the Group of Four, however, Pymbyrtyn had abandoned everything he owned in Tarot, resigned his commission in the Tarotisian Navy, and traveled to Tellesberg to offer his sword and his loyalty to Charis. An ardent Reformist and a skilled seaman, he'd also become a fervent Charisian patriot who thoroughly deserved his powerful command.

"Your signal did indicate a certain urgency, Sir

Bruhstair," Vahrnay answered for both of them, and Ahbaht nodded.

"Yes, it did. We have a problem, gentlemen." Ahbaht tapped the map spread across his dining table with a pair of brass dividers. It wasn't a nautical chart, and his visitors wondered why he was looking at a map showing features as much as a thousand miles inland. "In approximately twenty-five days, Admiral Pawal Hahlynd of the Royal Dohlaran Navy will be arriving at Yu-shai with at least twelve and possibly as many as fifteen of Thirsk's armored screw-galleys."

The other two captains stared at him for a moment, then turned their heads in unison to look at each other before turning back to him.

"Excuse me, Sir Bruhstair?" Pymbyrtyn said, and Ahbaht showed his teeth.

"I don't blame you for wondering if I've lost my mind, Lywelyn, but I'm serious. And, no, they aren't going to try to sneak them through the Shweimouth Passage past us." He tapped the map again, the dividers' points touching the thin blue line of the Sherach Canal. "They're sending them by canal."

Pymbyrtyn's eyes narrowed, then widened in sudden understanding.

"Shan-wei!" he muttered, and shook himself. "They *are* small enough for that, aren't they?"

"They are, indeed," Ahbaht agreed, "and we're very fortunate certain spies of ours were able to get word of it to us this quickly. The same word's on its way to Earl Sharpfield. Unfortunately, it won't reach him for another two five-days. Even after it does, it would take at least another ten days for any reinforcements he might send us to reach us here. For that matter, he only has ten galleons of his own, so there's not a lot he *could* send us. And there's always that bastard Rohsail to worry about. We didn't see any sign of him east of Whale Island, no matter how assiduously we trailed our coats. That may suggest he has something else in mind. If he knows Hahlynd's coming—and I trust nobody thinks Thirsk's stupid enough to have sent this sort of reinforcement without informing Rohsail about it—and the two of them combine forces, the only ships we've got that could hope to stand up to them would be *Thunderer* and *Dreadnought* . . . and the last we've heard, *Dreadnought*'s still on the binnacle list. That's probably changed by now—in fact, I'm confident it has—but we can't be certain of that. And even if she's on her way to us right this moment, what happened to her indicates we could always lose one or even both of the ironclads all over again, at least temporarily. For that matter, Hahlynd's supposed to be bringing along a sizable supply of those 'spar torpedoes' Earl Sharpfield warned us about. If his screw-galleys reach Yu-shai, especially with those damned torpedoes, they could make any attack into Shwei Bay prohibitively expensive. For that matter, if the Saint Lerys Canal's been repaired, Hahlynd could send some of them all the way to Yu-kwau to cover the Bay of Alexov."

Both of the other captains were back on mental balance now, gazing at the map intently.

"I'm sure you're telling us this for a reason, Sir Bruhstair." Captain Vahrnay's tone suggested he had his own suspicions about what that reason might be, and Ahbaht smiled at him.

"I am indeed, Horayshyo. I am indeed."

He dropped the dividers on the map and beckoned for the other two captains to join him on *Thunderer*'s sternwalk. They stood under the hot afternoon sun, watching seabirds and wyverns soar against a cloudless blue sky, and gazed out across the thicket of masts. It was a peaceful scene, and all of them conscientiously reminded themselves of the Dohlaran ships based on Jack's Land, less than five hundred miles away.

"If Hahlynd's supposed to reach Yu-shai basically this time next month, then they'll be reaching Symarkhan, where the Hahskyn-Varna Canal enters the Hahskyn River, seventeen days from now," Ahbaht said, "and unlike most Harchongese rivers, the Hahskyn's navigable for blue-water ships as high as Symarkhan. It's not anything I'd call an easy channel, but it's navigable.

"If we were to sail today, assuming average wind conditions, we could reach Ki-dau, where the Hahskyn enters Hahskyn Bay, in nine days. It's a hundred and seventy miles upriver from Ki-dau to Symarkhan, and assuming a fair wind, we might be able to make three knots against the current. That means we could be there in eleven or twelve days from the moment we weighed anchor here at Talisman. Taking *Thunderer* and the other galleons or the bombardment ships that far up the river, especially without local pilots, would run some pretty serious risks, but if we had that much time in hand, we could use the schooners and our own small craft to find us a way through. And if we were to do to the Symarkhan canalfront what Captain Haigyl did to the *Yu-kwau* canalfront, Hahlynd and his screw-galleys would be stuck fourteen hundred miles from Yu-shai and even farther than that from the Gulf of Dohlar."

"If you took the entire squadron, we'd leave Talisman unprotected behind us, Sir," Vahrnay pointed out after a moment.

"And if the wind didn't cooperate, we might not reach Symarkhan in time to keep the screw-galleys bottled up," Pymbyrtyn added. He shook his head, although his expression was thoughtful, not one of disagreement. "I don't like to think about what they could do to us if they caught us in a river where we couldn't maneuver freely."

"First, you're absolutely right about leaving Talisman exposed, Horayshyo," Ahbaht agreed. "They'll send word to Rohsail the minute they spot us passing through the Shweimouth on our way south, and I don't think any of us believe Rohsail's going to just sit there with his thumb up his arse. He might decide to attack us here, but, frankly, I wouldn't be all that concerned if he did. First, because I'm fairly confident Major Ohmahly and Commander Makgrygair between them would be able to stand him off, and secondly, because *Dreadnought*'s repairs should be pretty much complete by now. That means Captain Haigyl will be coming forward, which means he'd be available to help defend the anchorage.

"Bearing all that in mind, I think it's more probable Rohsail would come in pursuit of us, especially if he already knows Hahlynd is on his way. Depending on his deployments when he came after us, he could have a substantial numerical advantage. In fact, I imagine he wouldn't pursue us in the first place if he *didn't* have a heavy numerical edge, but even if he does, I'm not too concerned about our ability to handle him out on Hahskyn Bay without the screw-galleys to support him. He'd still have to deal with *Thunderer*, and the rest of you aren't likely to be standing by doing nothing in the meantime.

"I'd be more concerned about his arriving close enough on our heels to hold the rivermouth against us before we could get back to the bay after attacking Symarkhan. But even his Jack's Land squadron would be at least four days behind us, and that's assuming he's ready to sail the instant he gets word we've entered the Shweimouth, without calling in any additional galleons from Saram Bay. That would cut down on the numbers he could bring to bear, and we should still have enough of a lead to hit Symarkhan and get back out of the river again even if he did it. No one can guarantee that, of course, but I plan on leaving a few of our schooners in South Shwei Bay to watch our backs.

"As for encountering the screw-galleys in the river, I'm no more interested in that sort of foolishness than either of you are. If we get to Ki-dau and it's clear we won't have time to reach Symarkhan before Hahlynd does—or even if it's simply not clear that we *would* have time—I'm perfectly ready to turn around and go home again. Let's be honest, keeping those screw-galleys out of Shwei Bay—and out of the Bay of Alexov, for that matter—would be highly beneficial. Keeping them from getting up to anything adventurous, like attacking Talisman while the rest of us were at sea, would be even more beneficial. But it's not exactly critical to High Admiral Rock Point's long-term plans for the Gulf and for Dohlar. This is eminently worth doing; it's not *worth* losing valuable ships and men if the timing goes belly-up on us. If that looks like happening, I *will* turn around in a skinny Siddarmarkian minute."

"Can't say I'm sorry to hear you say that, Sir," Vahrnay said. "I realize I'm the only Old Charisian in this little conversation, but the truth is, I get nervous when there's anything besides saltwater under the keel. Fresh water's all very well for drinking and even the occasional bath, but it's no place for a Navy man, if you'll pardon my saying so."

"I don't think Lywelyn or I would disagree with you under normal circumstances," Ahbaht replied. "On the other hand, as I say, this is definitely something worth doing if we can pull it off. And if we decide we can't, and if Rohsail *has* tried to follow us, we might just snare a consolation prize. I think we'd all enjoy an opportunity to engage an isolated portion of his squadron with *Thunderer* to lead the way, don't you, gentlemen?"

. VI .
# Guarnak,
# Mountaincross Province,
# Republic of Siddarmark

"Have you seen Colonel Fyrgyrsyn's latest report?" Bishop Militant Bahrnabai Wyrshym asked.

Icy wind whistled around the eaves of the mansion he'd commandeered as his headquarters, and it was cold in the splendidly furnished dining room. He and Auxiliary Bishop Ernyst Abernethy sat at a small table across the hearth from the frugal fire which was all Wyrshym permitted himself as the Army of the Sylmahn's stocks of fuel and food dwindled once more. The spartan breakfast before them—little more than two bowls of porridge, sweetened with the last of Wyrshym's chef's jealously hoarded sugar and enormously out of place on the expensive, polished table—was another sign of that army's tightening belt.

"I haven't seen one in the last day or two," Bishop Ernyst replied. "I'm sure if I had it would've made depressing reading, though."

"Depressing, but not surprising," Wyrshym agreed. Colonel Tayrens Fyrgyrsyn was the Army of the Sylmahn's senior quartermaster. He was intelligent, good at his job, and only in his early fifties, but anyone looking at him would have guessed his age at at least sixty-five or seventy, and for good reason.

"They slaughtered the last draft animal yesterday. Assuming nobody has to burn up energy marching around or performing heavy labor—and that the mortality rate keeps climbing the way it has—he and Father Zherohmy estimate they can feed what's left of the Army through the second five-day of June. Which, of course, means for another four five-days, total. After that, we'll be well below Pasquale's minimums, and it'll only get worse. If their numbers are accurate, the Army will literally starve to death by the end of next month."

Abernethy sighed heavily and closed his eyes in brief, silent prayer. Then he opened them again and looked back across the table at the bishop militant.

"Is there anything else we can do?" he asked quietly.

"Not without violating our orders to stand fast," Wyrshym replied, with far more candor than most AOG commanders would have exposed to their army's intendant. "I realize the Mighty Host's supposed to be marching to our rescue, but, frankly, there's not a chance in hell it could get here before mid-June or early July even if it didn't have Green Valley to worry about at Five Forks. And if it doesn't get here by the end of next month, the heretics won't have to *attack* us at all; they can just sit where they are and let us starve."

"Do you really think they'll do that?"

"If I were in their boots, that's *exactly* what I'd do." Wyrshym's expression was grim. "Why take casualties when they can let hunger win the battle for them? It's worked in enough sieges, and that's effectively what this is, as long as we stand fast. On the other hand, we can't be sure what Green Valley's situation is at Five Forks, and they may be feeling a little nervous about having him stuck out at the end of such a long limb. For that matter, we don't know what's happening south of Wyvern Lake, either, really."

His lips twisted and he patted them with his napkin, then folded the fabric over precisely and laid it on the table.

"My boys are doing their damnedest to keep an eye on Stohnar, but let's not fool ourselves. They're cold, they're hungry, they're more poorly armed than the enemy, and the heretics hold the high ground. I'm sure you've seen even more chaplains' reports than I have, Ernyst. All the faith in the world can't compensate for empty bellies, frostbite, and lack of fires. They're trying, and they'll fight hard to hold their ground, but there's a big difference between that and pressing home patrols—and taking casualties—looking for information they figure won't make much difference in the end. So Stohnar could've been reinforced by eighty or a hundred thousand men without us knowing a thing about it. As for Fairkyn, Nybar's down to his last few messenger wyverns, but his last report indicates the heretics've settled for keeping him pinned, at least for now. They may be figuring to starve *him* out without losing men, either, but it's also possible they're simply waiting until their own reinforcements come up before they go ahead and assault.

"If they do decide to come at us from the south, though, they need to do it pretty quickly. The ice on Wyvern Lake's going to start breaking up any day now. It may already be too thin for them to come straight across it, and that's going to leave them with the same bottleneck they faced last fall. I should at least be able to pull some of our regiments back once that happens, not that I have any brilliant ideas for where else to use them, I'm afraid."

Abernethy sat silent for several long moments, gazing down into his porridge bowl with hooded eyes. Then he raised his head and gazed across the table at the bishop militant.

"*If* those regiments were here at Guarnak," he said in a very careful tone, "and *if* the heretics took Fairkyn and advanced down the line of the canal towards Guarnak, would their presence help you . . . conduct a fighting retreat towards Jylmyn and the Hildermoss?"

Wyrshym's face froze for just a moment. He sat very still, looking back across the table at Zhaspahr Clyntahn's personal representative in his headquarters. He knew exactly what Abernethy was painstakingly *not* suggesting, and if Wyrshym gave that order—and Abernethy didn't instantly countermand it—both of them would face the Inquisition.

*But it might also save at least part of this Army*, a quiet voice said in the back of the bishop militant's brain. *These men have been through Shan-wei's own hell for Mother Church, and for that fat bastard sitting in the Grand Inquisitor's chair. They damned well deserve a chance—just a* chance! *It wouldn't be* much of *a chance without better supplies, especially at this time of year, but it'd be more than they'd have sitting here while the heretics' artillery blows them apart . . . or every one of them starves, anyway.*

"Yes, Ernyst," he said, after a moment. "A few more regiments might make the difference between holding the Army together and watching it break up. That's something worth bearing in mind. Thank you for pointing it out to me."

He smiled at his intendant, and Abernethy smiled back. They weren't joyous expressions, those smiles, and yet Bahrnabai Wyrshym drew enormous comfort from them.

# JUNE
## YEAR OF GOD 897

·✦·

# Delthak Works,
# Barony of High Rock,
# Kingdom of Old Charis

"I think that's just about everything," Ehdwyrd Howsmyn sighed, rolling his swivel chair back from his desk and stretching enormously. It was as close to dark outside his office windows as it ever got at the Delthak Works, but the gaslight illumination inside that office, for all its brightness, could be hard on weary eyes and the hour was late. "I hope it is, anyway. I promised Zhain I'd be home in time for supper tonight . . . if she agreed to serve it an hour or so later than usual. And since she *did*—"

He grimaced, and Nahrmahn Tidewater and Zosh Huntyr chuckled. Zhain Howsmyn's husband's demanding schedule would have tried the patience of a saint. She didn't really like the hours he worked—more because of how hard he drove himself than for any other reason—but she also tried not to place even more demands upon him. Still, she did insist he come home for supper and get something remotely like a good night's sleep at least two nights out of every five-day. He'd been forced to disappoint her in that regard more times than he liked to think about, but he tried hard to avoid doing it any more often than he absolutely had to. And when he *promised* her he wouldn't, he moved heaven and earth to keep his word.

"Mind you," he told his senior artificers as he closed the last production report folder and climbed out of his chair, "she's been willing to cut me a little more slack since she found out about the dukedom. I'm not inclined to press my luck, though. So, if you gentlemen will excuse me?"

"Personally, I'm in favor of keeping Mistress Zhain happy," Huntyr told him. "Especially if that keeps her from taking out her *un*happiness on us!"

"Zosh, I'm *shocked!* Are you seriously suggesting I would attempt to blame *you* for *my* tardiness? How could you even think such a thing?!"

"Probably has something to do with the fact that you did just that when you got home late after playing with Taigys' latest toy," Tidewater suggested.

"Well, I see no point in standing around here being insulted!" Howsmyn said with a grin, starting for the office door. "So on that note—"

He broke off as an unearthly, shuddering wail froze him in mid stride. His eyes went wide, and Tidewater and Huntyr bounced up out of their chairs with shocked expressions. A second high, keening wail joined the first, and all three men turned as one and ran for the door.

▼ ▼ ▼

It was like looking into a volcano.

The roar of the flames was like one of the blast furnaces, but this was no blast furnace. The thick, black pillar of smoke rose into the night like a foretaste of Hell, lit from below by lurid billows of flame, and the heat radiating from the blaze was like a physical blow.

Manufactories, especially ones like the Delthak Works, were always dangerous places. No one knew that better than Ehdwyrd Howsmyn, and he'd invested as much time thinking about ways to protect his workers—and his workshops—from the endless chain of disasters just waiting to happen as he'd ever spent on ways to speed production. The people in his employ knew that, and they appreciated it deeply, even though he himself was never satisfied. Intellectually, he understood that all the precautions in the world couldn't keep accidents from happening. He even understood that despite the size, scope, and furious pace of the Delthak Works, his workers suffered far fewer injuries than were common in much smaller manufactories whose owners had spent less time thinking about safety procedures and organizing emergency response crews.

At the moment, that was extraordinarily cold comfort.

The fire brigade had responded at the first wail of the sirens. They'd been on-site, already coupling their hoses to the fire mains that crisscrossed the Delthak Works, and the first streams of water had gone hissing into the flames even before he reached the disaster. But there were limits in all things, and his jaw clenched as he realized where the fire was and just how huge the blaze had already become.

"Master Howsmyn!"

He turned as someone called his name. It was Stahnly Gahdwyn, the Delthak Works Fire Brigade's commander. Gahdwyn had been the assistant commander of the Tellesberg Fire Brigade before Howsmyn stole him away for the Delthak Works, and the commander had embraced the new and improved firefighting equipment available here like a miser diving into a knee-deep pile of gold coins. He was a squared-off plug of a man, with dark hair and brown eyes and a left hand badly scarred from a long-ago Tellesberg blaze, and he regarded fires as a personal enemy, not some impersonal act of nature.

"What happened, Chief?"

"Don't know yet, Sir." Gahdwyn removed his steel helmet and ran his fingers through his hair. "I'm afraid it may've been the gas lines."

"I didn't hear any explosions!"

"No, Sir." Gahdwyn shook his head. "I'm thinking we had a major rupture, but not an explosion. When my first lads got here, there was a column of fire blasting right up out of the middle of it all. Standard procedure's to shut down the gas mains whenever we have a fire, and given how quickly that 'column' went away when we did, I'm thinking that had to be the source. And if it was, it's Langhorne's own grace we *didn't* have an explosion. By now, though, it's deep into the structure itself, and Shan-wei knows there're enough oil baths and other flammables in there—not to mention wooden joists, beams, and rafters—to keep it burning all night."

"*Shit*," Ehdwyrd Howsmyn said with quiet, heartfelt intensity.

"Yes, Sir." Gahdwyn put his helmet back on and squared his shoulders. "I've called in all of the backup crews. I think we can keep it from spreading, but I'd be lying if I said it looked good here."

"I know." Howsmyn rested one hand on the fire brigade commander's powerful shoulder. "I know. Do what you can, Chief."

▼ ▼ ▼

"My God!" Brahd Stylmyn said. "My God, what a disaster!"

Howsmyn doubted Stylmyn even realized he'd spoken aloud. The engineer sagged with exhaustion in the gray predawn light as he watched the firefighters working to extinguish the last of the blaze. Like Howsmyn himself, he was covered with soot and his clothes were spotted with burn marks, but Stylmyn's badly burned left hand was wrapped in a filthy bandage, as well.

"It could've been worse," Howsmyn told him. Stylmyn turned his head to look at him, and the industrialist shrugged resignedly. "We could've lost the entire foundry."

Stylmyn grimaced, his soot-streaked face bitter, and Howsmyn shrugged again.

"I said it could've been worse; I didn't say it was *good*," he said. "And we won't really know how bad it is until the rubble cools and we can do a thorough inspection. Whatever happens, though, it's going to play hell with the *King Haarahlds*."

"You never said a truer word, Sir . . . *damn* it," Stylmyn agreed. Then he squared his shoulders. "Best

you go home and get a hot shower, Sir. Eat some breakfast, too, while you're at it. By then, maybe I'll have a
better idea of the damage for you."

"You've got assistants of your own, Brahd." Howsmyn looked at his chief engineer sternly. "Get that hand
looked at by the healers, and get a shower of your own.
I don't want to hear about you being back here for at
least four hours. Understood?"

Stylmyn's expression tightened. For a moment, he
hovered on the brink of defiance. But then he shook
himself and drew a deep breath of still-smoky air.

"Happen you've got a point," he agreed wearily.
"Meet you back here at . . . nine o'clock or so?"

"That sounds good to me." Howsmyn patted him on
the shoulder. "And now, I need to go home and explain
to my wife where I've been all night."

▼ ▼ ▼

"You were right when you told Stylmyn it could've
been worse, Ehdwyrd," Merlin Athrawes said several
hours later.

"Unfortunately, I was also right that 'could've been
worse' isn't remotely the same thing as 'good,'" Howsmyn said bitterly. "I can't *believe* I let this happen!"

"Don't be silly, Ehdwyrd!" Sharleyan said sharply
over the com link. Her image frowned ferociously in
Howsmyn's contact lenses. "It's a miracle we haven't
had more accidents like this, given how frantically
we've been—*you've* been—expanding your facilities!"
She shook her head. "When I think of all the things that
*could* have gone wrong over the years . . . !"

"Sharley's right," Cayleb said firmly. "And at least
we can be pretty sure this really was an accident, not
something like the Hairatha Works happening all over
again."

"And at least no one was *killed*, Ehdwyrd," Paityr
Wylsynn said very quietly. "Your evacuation procedures and your fire brigade and fire mains saved a lot
of lives last night. I think you need to bear that in mind
when you get ready to start kicking yourself. Industrial

accidents happen, no matter how careful we are. I'm just grateful it happened where someone like you had put enough thought into dealing with it to prevent a disaster from turning into a catastrophe."

"Agreed," Domynyk Staynair said firmly from the sternwalk of his flagship.

"How bad a hit are we actually going to take?" Nimue Chwaeriau asked from her modest but comfortable bedchamber in Manchyr Palace.

"Fortunately, the barrel foundry for the Army contracts is practically undamaged," Howsmyn said after a moment. "We're probably going to lose at least a couple of five-days while we clean up the mess, strip everything down to inspect it, and then get everything back up and running, but I doubt it's going to be much worse than that.

"The bad news is on the Navy side." His expression was grim. "All but two of the ten-inch mounts were caught in the fire. I've got the pair of barrels we used for the initial trials and proof firings that I could put with the one the shops had already finished, but I'm really not comfortable at the thought of using them aboard ship. Even we did, we'd still only have the main battery for one *King Haarahld*. The other mounts' recoil cylinders are going to have to be torn down and rebuilt, at the very least, and we'll need to go over every inch of the gun tubes themselves. That's bad enough, but we had half the ten-inch and at least half of the eight-inch still in the production queue, and until we rebuild the machinery, we can't complete them. For that matter, the buildings themselves will almost certainly need to be torn down and rebuilt." He grimaced. "We may be able to salvage some of the barrel shop, but the entire roof's gone, and every bit of wooden framing—rafters, studs, floors: *everything*—is pretty much shot. We can *probably* use canvas tarps for temporary roofs and get the machinery—or *replacement* machinery, more likely—back up and running on the old foundations while we build a completely new shop next door, but it's going to be a mess however we tackle it."

"Probably a good thing Ahbaht's decided to take those screw-galleys in hand, then," Rock Point said philosophically. "We need to keep the Dohlarans pruned back until we're ready to take an axe to Gorath Bay itself."

Howsmyn grunted in sour acknowledgement and climbed out of his chair, swaying just a bit with fatigue. He walked to the window that let him look out over the charred skeleton of his barrel foundry. From this elevation, looking down on the damage, it seemed impossible that it could ever be repaired, but he shook his head stubbornly and reminded himself how many other "impossible" things he and his people had already accomplished.

"Best guess," he said finally, "this is going to push the completion on the *King Haarahlds* back by at least three months, probably more like four, or even five." He tasted the admission's bitterness, made even worse in some ways as he remembered his last conversation with Eysamu Tahnguchi. "I'll have a lot better idea in a couple of days."

"Well, if that's the way it is, then that's the way it is," Cayleb said, much more philosophically than any of them actually felt, and smiled tightly. "It's not like we don't have other things to do while we wait, is it?"

. II .
# HMS *Defiant*, 56,
## Jack's Land,
### and
# HMS *Dreadnought*, 30,
## Gulf of Dohlar

"You sent for me, Sir?"

"Yes," Sir Dahrand Rohsail said, turning from the stern windows' panoramic view of Stella Cove, the Royal Dohlaran Navy's anchorage on the west coast of Jack's Land. His flagship, *Defiant*, lay to her anchor between Ribbon Island and the cove's shore, her stern towards the larger island as the steady westerly wind blew into the anchorage. That was the one true weakness of Stella Cove; although the smaller islands offshore offered some protection against heavy weather out of the west and Ribbon offered additional shelter inside the anchorage itself, it was far from perfect.

"Yes, I did, Markys." He gestured at the thin sheet of paper lying on his desk's blotter. "Take a look at that."

Markys Hamptyn, his flag captain, gathered up the sheet—the sort that wyvern-carried messages were written on—and unfolded it. He recognized the handwriting of Admiral Caitahno Raisahndo's secretary, and one eyebrow rose. Raisahndo and Rohsail cordially disliked one another, but they'd also learned to respect each other, and Raisahndo was Rohsail's second-in-command. At the moment, that meant his flagship, *Demonslayer*, was stationed at Saram Bay with the other half of Rohsail's Western Squadron to protect the southern coast of North Harchong and the Border States.

He scanned the tersely written message quickly, then read it through a second time, much more carefully, before he looked up at his admiral.

"I see why you wanted to see me, Sir."

He laid the dispatch back on the desk and crossed to stand beside Rohsail at the windows. Twenty-five more galleons shared the anchorage with *Defiant*, all but two of them purpose-built war galleons rather than the converted merchantmen which had composed the majority of the Royal Dohlaran Navy the last time the Imperial Charisian Navy had come calling in the Gulf of Dohlar. Two of them, including *Defiant* herself, were prizes which had been taken from the Charisians upon that occasion. In fact, HMS *Defiant* of the Royal Dohlaran Navy had once been HMS *Dancer*, of the Imperial Charisian Navy, the flagship of the heretical admiral who'd led that incursion. It had taken months to repair all of the damage she'd suffered in the Battle of the Harchong Narrows, but Dohlar's shipwrights had learned quite a bit from analyzing her construction. Among other things, they'd finally learned the secret of how to copper their own ships below the waterline, and shared that information with the rest of Mother Church's shipyards and their secular allies.

"From the sound of it, they must've taken everything they had at Talisman," Hamptyn said after a moment.

"Agreed." Rohsail folded his hands behind him, pursing his lips as he considered the information the messenger wyvern had borne from Saram Bay. "In some ways, it's a pity the Harchongians didn't have any of our Jack's Land messenger wyverns. We'd have found out a lot sooner if they'd been able to send us word directly."

"Yes, Sir, we would have," Hamptyn agreed. "On the other hand, *Admiral Raisahndo* wouldn't have known about it as quickly. There's something to be said for that, assuming we're going after them."

"That *is* the question, isn't it?" Rohsail said dryly.

He looked out at the anchored ships for several more seconds, then sighed and turned away from the windows. He crossed to his chart table and stood frowning down at it with Hamptyn at his shoulder.

"You're right that assuming the Harchongians got

their sums right—of course, we *are* talking about Harchongians, so let's not get carried away counting on that—this is everything we think they had at Talisman. And if that's true, then we do have twenty-six galleons to their fifteen. Unfortunately, two of that fifteen are those bombardment ships of theirs, and another is one of their damned ironclads."

"Yes, Sir. But one ship can only be in one place and engage one or two other ships at a time," Hamptyn pointed out. "And if Admiral Raisahndo weighed anchor as soon as he indicated he intended to, he and the rest of the Squadron are already a full day out of Saram Bay headed this way."

Rohsail nodded. Caitahno Raisahndo remained as stubbornly low born and uncultured as ever, and he was still far too soft when it came to disciplining common seamen, but much as it irked Rohsail to admit it, he had a good head on his shoulders otherwise. There was no doubt in his mind that Hamptyn was right and that Raisahndo was on his way with twenty-four additional galleons, three-quarters of them purpose-built ships. Pulling them out of Saram Bay posed a nontrivial risk if the Harchongians were right and only one of the ironclads had accompanied the force headed into Shwei Bay, but it would probably be survivable. According to the documents they'd salvaged from the wreck of HMS *Turbulent* when the heretic galleon was driven ashore on Martyn's Point, Sharpfield could have no more than eight to ten additional galleons at Claw Island. He was unlikely to get *too* adventurous with such a small force, even if it did include one of the ironclads.

In theory, then, Raisahndo could safely join him and bring his force up to forty-nine galleons as opposed to the heretics' fifteen, and three-to-one odds should prove crushing even if they did have one of their accursed ironclads in company. The problem would be bringing them to battle, since even now less than half his own ships had copper-sheathed bottoms. After so long at sea, those which hadn't been coppered were sadly foul and at least twenty percent slower than the heretics', *all* of whom had been coppered. There was a reason the handful of schooners the heretics had lost since retaking Claw Island had each fallen prey to one of his own copper-sheathed galleons and even then only in heavy, blowing weather where the larger Dohlaran ship had been able to carry more sail than the schooner.

"I wonder . . . ." he said slowly, tapping his lower lip with one index finger while he looked at the chart.

"Wonder what, Sir?" Hamptyn asked after he'd stood silent for over two minutes.

The admiral shook himself and snorted. It was a sign of how long Hamptyn had served as his flag captain that the other was willing to break in on his thoughts. Or perhaps it would be more accurate to say that the flag captain had learned to recognize when he was lost in his thoughts and needed to be recalled to the world about him.

"They've passed through the Shweimouth," he said. "The question is where they're headed."

"The most reasonable target would be Yu-shai, Sir."

"Perhaps. And I suppose it would make sense for them to secure an emergency anchorage at Talisman before their regular war galleons ventured into the Yu-shai Inlet and risked taking damage from the shore batteries. It would also explain the presence of the bombardment ships. But what if they had something else in mind?"

"There are a lot of potential targets around Shwei Bay—around *both* Shwei Bays," Hamptyn said. "Yu-shai's probably the richest one, though."

"Only because it's the collection point for everything passing through the Shweimouth and across the Gulf," Rohsail pointed out. "If the heretics are serious about shutting down the entire western half of the Gulf, Yu-shai's going to be about as useful as teats on a bull dragon."

Hamptyn frowned. The Western Squadron's job was to see to it that the heretics did nothing of the sort, and he was more than mildly surprised that Rohsail would mention the possibility so calmly, even to him.

*On the other hand, there's nobody here to hear him except me. And, come to think of it, he's not saying the heretics are going to succeed; he's only saying that's what they seem to intend. Because if it is what they mean to accomplish, they'll be choosing their coastal targets based on that outcome, won't they?*

"You're thinking about what they did in the Bay of Alexov, aren't you, Sir?" he said out loud.

"Yes," Rohsail acknowledged. "What I'm really wondering about, though, is whether or not they know Admiral Hahlynd is on his way to Yu-shai?"

"How could they, Sir?" Hamptyn asked reasonably. "We've only known about Earl Thirsk's plans for three five-days ourselves."

"One thing we've learned the hard way is to never underestimate heretic spies," Rohsail said grimly. "What I find . . . interesting about this is that if they *do* know about Admiral Hahlynd, and if they have the sheer gall to penetrate that deep, they've given themselves more than enough time to reach Ki-dau. For that matter, if they're really ballsy—and Shan-wei knows, the heretics've never seemed especially short in that category!—they might actually have time to get as deep as Symarkhan before Admiral Hahlynd gets there."

"Take galleons that far upriver, Sir?" Hamptyn rubbed his chin. "I suppose they might. And Admiral Raisahndo reported they have a half-dozen of their schooners along. They're fitted to row, which would make them handy in a river under most circumstances. What sort of defenses does Symarkhan have? Could they put Marines ashore using just the schooners?"

"I don't imagine Symarkhan is fortified at all." Rohsail shrugged. "With so many potential targets so much closer to the coast, why would anyone in his right mind fortify a town almost two hundred miles inland? Fortunately, Raisahndo says the Harchongians sent messengers and semaphore messages off in all directions as soon as they spotted the heretics in the Shweimouth. What we need to do is to send off a few messages of our own."

"Yes, Sir. What sort of messages did you have in mind?"

"I realize Raisahndo's already at sea, but I want wyverns off to Captain Kharmahdy within the hour." Hamptyn nodded; Captain Styvyn Kharmahdy commanded the batteries and shore facilities at Rhaigair on Saram Bay. "He's to use the semaphore to pass a priority message to Earl Thirsk informing him of the heretics' movements, warning him the Harchongians should expect the possibility of an attack on the canal head at Symarkhan, and urging Admiral Hahlynd—and the Canal Service—to expedite the ironclads' movement as much as possible."

"Yes, Sir," Hamptyn replied.

It was a pity *Defiant* hadn't been supplied with messenger wyverns that could have carried the warning directly to Yu-shai. Still, the semaphore system could transmit the message all the way from Saram Bay to Gorath around the northern shore of the Gulf of Dohlar in less than eight hours—in daylight and under normal weather conditions—and any order from Thirsk to Hahlynd would move along the semaphore stations which paralleled virtually every major canal behind the screw-galleys at the same speed.

"As soon as we've seen to that," Rohsail continued, "I want all ships in company ready to weigh anchor within four hours. We'll drop a boat with a message to Governor Cloud Shadow on our own way through the Shweimouth. He's smart enough to move heaven and earth to prepare Symarkhan. We'll just have to hope the local militia has enough artillery to at least hold those damned schooners at bay. If the heretics *have* to use their ironclad, just getting that beast up and down the river will buy us at least three or four more days to catch up with them."

"Yes, Sir. I'll see to it."

"I know you will, Markys. And while we're worrying about what the heretics may want to do to us, let's not overlook the possibilities of what *we* may get a chance to do to *them*. They've got time to get there, as long as the wind doesn't decide to screw them over. But if Admiral Hahlynd's able to expedite his movement and get *his* ironclads into the river before they get to Symarkhan, they'll make mincemeat out of their damned schooners. For that matter, they'll kick the arses of their regular galleons! And if we can turn up close enough on their heels and the wind lets us pin them against the coast somewhere . . . ."

Hamptyn nodded again, because his admiral was right about the potential opportunity. The flag captain didn't like to think about how many Dohlaran galleons that single ironclad would smash before they managed to overwhelm it. In fact, it was more than possible that it would be able to cut its way through their entire squadron. But the conventional galleons with it *wouldn't*, and the Royal Dohlaran Navy had a bone to pick with the heretics.

▼ ▼ ▼

"North Shwei Point bears four points on the starboard bow, Sir," Lieutenant Stahdmaiyr said, and Captain Kahrltyn Haigyl grunted in satisfaction.

"Thank you, Dahnyld."

The captain stood beside HMS *Dreadnought*'s binnacle, rubbing the patch over his left eye socket with an index finger while he peered down at the illuminated compass card. Then he lifted his head, gazing up at his ship's canvas.

Kahrltyn Haigyl was not the finest ship handler ever to serve in the Imperial Charisian Navy, and the truth was that he would have felt more confident—or happier, at least—threading his way through the Shweimouth Passage in daylight. The Harchongians had removed all of the Shweimouth buoys as soon as Earl Sharpfield's light cruisers started raiding their shipping in the Gulf of Dohlar. Admittedly, the passage was seventy miles wide at its narrowest point, but the sky was covered in clouds, there was no moon, the deepwater channel was far narrower than that, he had no local pilot, and there was always the odd shoal, mudbank, or unbuoyed rock.

*Dreadnought*'s armor wouldn't do her very much good if he managed to poke a hole through her bottom.

Time was more important than caution, though. He'd reached Talisman Island considerably sooner than he'd expected, barely a five-day after Captain Ahbaht's departure, to discover the message Ahbaht had left for him. In fact, Commander Makgrygair had sent the message out to him in a small boat before *Dreadnought* had fully entered Rahzhyr Bay, and Haigyl had turned back to the open Gulf within ten minutes of reading it.

He understood exactly what Ahbaht was up to, and Kahrltyn Haigyl always approved of taking the battle to the enemy, especially if it meant keeping those armored Dohlaran galleys out of the squadron's hair. It couldn't hurt to provide the dapper little Emeraldian with some additional support, though. And even if that hadn't been true, Haigyl had no intention of allowing Ahbaht to have all the fun.

Still, he would have preferred daylight. Shot, shells, and cold steel he could deal with; rocks and shoals were something else entirely.

"Steady as she goes, Dahnyld," he said calmly.

. III .

Aivahnstyn,
Cliff Peak Province,
Republic of Siddarmark,
and
Stahlberg,
Earldom of Usher

The servant topped off Bishop Militant Cahnyr Kaitswyrth's cup of tea and withdrew silently. The bishop militant raised the cup in both hands, holding it close enough to inhale the fragrant steam, and tried not to think about the rain pounding on the townhouse roof. He would have vastly preferred for it to be more snow and ice.

"Have you heard anything more from Vicar Allayn, Cahnyr?" Father Sedryk Zavyr asked from the other side of the breakfast table, and Kaitswyrth grimaced as he heard the worry in Zavyr's tone. Obviously his intendant's thoughts were following his own.

"Not since last Thursday," he said, in less than cheery tones. There was no point dissembling with Zavyr. They'd been together for far too long—and thought far too much alike—for that. "I'd be a lot happier if we had heard something more, but let's face it, from what he said in his last message, there's not much more he can send us until the canals farther north thaw. And it sounds to me like somebody in Zion's pushing for anything that *becomes* available to go to Wyrshym."

He'd tried hard to keep any edge of complaint out of his voice, but he knew he'd failed, and Zavyr's cheek muscles tightened. The upper-priest sympathized completely with him, yet his ultimate loyalty was to the Grand Inquisitor, and both of them knew who was behind the effort to divert resources from the Army of Glacierheart to the Army of the Sylmahn.

"In fairness," Kaitswyrth made himself say, "Vicar Allayn points out that between the draft from the Army of Tanshar and Baron Wheatfields' Jhurlahnkians and Usherites, he's already sent us the next best thing to fifty-three thousand men and another sixty guns. He agrees it's . . . unfortunate that he can't send us any more artillery, but fifty-three thousand rifles are fifty-three thousand rifles when all's said, Sedryk."

"But if your estimate of the strength the heretics are amassing is accurate," Zavyr began, "you don't—"

"Given how hard it's been to get any sort of hard count on the heretics, I'm afraid our estimate's probably actually low," Kaitswyrth said somberly. "And I strongly doubt Cayleb and Stohnar are finding it quite as hard to scrape up additional artillery for Symkyn." He showed his teeth in a humorless grin. "They've

damned sure made it one of their top priorities, though—
I'll promise you that! And with good reason, Shan-wei
take them." He shook his head. "I'm inclined to think
that some of our superiors in Zion who haven't personally experienced heretic artillery are underestimating
the threat."

"If they are, it's not because I haven't fully endorsed
your reports." Zavyr took a sip from his own teacup
and grimaced. "I hate to say it, but I think you're right
about how . . . out of touch certain parties in Zion are,
though."

"At least the canals *are* finally beginning to thaw,"
Kaitswyrth said in a determinedly more cheerful tone.
"I could wish the entire Mighty Host wasn't strung
along the Holy Langhorne like beads on a string, given
how much later the thaw comes farther north, but it is
coming. And we can always hope the rain and mud will
keep the heretics home in their nice, snug barracks
until someone gets us enough reinforcements we'll actually have a chance of holding our position."

▼ ▼ ▼

"I have that Canal Service report for you, My Lord,"
Wynshyng Pahn, the Baron of Crystal Sky, said in a
white puff of breath as he drew rein beside Lord of
Horse Gwainmyn Yiangszhu, Baron Falling Rock.

"Am I going to want to hear it?" Baron Falling Rock
asked him.

"Probably not," Lord of Foot Crystal Sky admitted.
"It's still a solid block of ice north of Mhartynsberg."

"You're right. I didn't want to hear that. Not that it
comes as any great surprise." Falling Rock smiled thinly
and waved his off hand at the flurries of snowflakes ed-
dying down out of a heavy pewter sky.

"At least we'll be able to get you under a roof tonight, My Lord," his senior brigade commander and
second-in-command pointed out. "That's something."

"But the men in the ranks won't be able to say the
same thing."

"No, I'm afraid they won't," Crystal Sky agreed.

It always surprised him just a bit when Falling Rock said something like that. The lord of horse was eighteen years older than Crystal Sky, and tough as an old boot. He was also a noble of the old school, who'd never been noted for his solicitude for the serfs bound to his substantial estates in Maddox. In fact, he'd obviously been a little dubious, initially, about having Crystal Sky under his command, given the younger baron's reputation as a liberal who'd actually been known to suggest—hypothetically, of course—that a free peasantry might actually be preferable to serfs permanently and legally bound to the soil. Yet he'd embraced the effort to rearm and retrain the Mighty Host of God and the Archangels, and he clearly recognized that those "men in the ranks" were an essential component of the Jihad. In fact, Crystal Sky suspected he'd come to feel a responsibility for their welfare that went beyond keeping his weapon sharp, although he doubted Falling Rock would ever admit anything of the sort.

"I think we'll at least get them bivouacked in time for them to cook a hot meal, tonight, Sir. And at least the canal's thawing *south* of us. If the flooding doesn't slow the rest of Host too badly, it should start catching up with us within the next few five-days."

"And I'll be glad if that happens," Falling Rock acknowledged. "But we're still a long way from the Army of the Sylmahn, and the truth is, we're not going to make it in time."

Crystal Sky's head snapped around more quickly than he'd intended, and his eyes had widened ever so slightly as he looked at his commander.

"There's no point pretending differently, Wynshyng," Falling Rock said heavily. "Oh, I'll keep on pushing the pace. We *are* fighting in God's name, so I'm not going to foreclose the possibility of a miracle. But short of that, the heretics are going to hit Bishop Militant Bahrnabai at least a solid month before we could reach him."

"If that's true, Sir—and I'm only surprised to hear

you say it, not surprised that it probably is—won't Vicar Allayn allow the Bishop Militant to fall back?"

"If it were up to Vicar Allayn, he'd already have fallen back," Falling Rock said bluntly. "It's not, and you and I both know it." He held the younger man's eyes until Crystal Sky nodded, then shrugged. "From a military perspective, it's the wrong decision; from the perspective of the Jihad, it may be the right one. If nothing else, the time it takes the heretics to deal with him will be that much more time for the Host to move up the canal to meet them head on. And given the Bishop Militant's supply situation, he's probably too short on rations and draft animals to get more than a tithe of his army out at this point, anyway."

Crystal Sky's nostrils flared, but then, slowly, he nodded again.

"Oh, don't look so down in the mouth, Wynshyng!" Falling Rock reached across and punched the lord of foot gently on the shoulder in an unusual gesture of affection. "God never promised us it would be easy, and if Shan-wei wasn't loose in the world and doing everything in her power to help the heretics, there'd never have been a Jihad in the first place. And however much it may hurt to think about losing it, Bishop Militant Bahrnabai's entire army's barely a tenth the strength of the Host and Earl Rainbow Waters will have every man and gun we've got coming up this canal behind us. Whatever happens to the Army of the Sylmahn, the heretics will have *us* to deal with long before they get to the Border States' frontier, and we'll have the entire summer to show them that not even Shan-wei can save them from the wrath of God."

## . IU .
## HMS *Thunderer*, 30,
## Shwei Bay;
## HMS Destiny 54,
## Sea of Harchong;
## and
## Charisian Embassy,
## Siddar City,
## Republic of Siddarmark

"Good morning, Sir."

Lieutenant Zhaksyn saluted his captain as he came on deck. Sir Bruhstair Ahbaht returned the salute gravely, then nodded to the lieutenant, walked to the taffrail, and stood gazing back to the southeast as the morning sunlight gilded the topsails of his squadron. They were seventeen days out of Talisman Island, and the cloudless sky was a polished blue dome: clear, bright, hot . . . and the next best thing to windless.

The squadron was more spread out than he might have wished, but that bothered him less than the way the ships' sun-burnished canvas hung slack or flapped languidly. At the moment, *Thunderer* was ghosting through the water at less than one knot, with barely a sigh of water around her stem, and several of her consorts were slowly but steadily overtaking her. Ahbaht loved his ship, and in any sort of wind her lofty rig made her fleet-footed and surprisingly handy for a vessel of her size and tonnage. In light airs like this it was as if she were dragging an anchor astern of her, and the clock was ticking.

He folded his hands behind himself, rocking gently on his heels, feeling the enervating equatorial heat. It was already in the seventies; by afternoon, the squadron's seamen would be looking for any hint of shade they could find, and he'd already ordered awnings rigged to shield *Thunderer*'s decks. There wasn't going to be much breeze to help cool them, though, he thought grimly.

*Oh, don't be an old woman, Bruhstair!* he told himself. *Yes, you're running behind your most optimistic schedule, but you've still got a full five-day in hand. And just like you told Lywelyn and Zheryko, you can always turn around and head home if you don't make it in time.*

He looked up at the unhelpful sky again for a moment, then turned to Zhaksyn.

"I think we'll advance gun drill this morning, Ahlber." He smiled ever so slightly. "Let's get it out of the way before it *really* gets hot."

▼ ▼ ▼

"This is starting to make me a little nervous," Cayleb Ahrmahk acknowledged.

Eight in the morning on Shwei Bay was thirteen o'clock, the Safeholdian equivalent of noon, in Siddar City, and the remains of lunch sat on the table between him and Aivah Pahrsahn. They awaited the arrival of Henrai Maidyn and Daryus Parkair, the Republic's Chancellor of the Exchequer and Seneschal, who were en route to the embassy to discuss the latest dispatches from General Stohnar and Duke Eastshare. Although Maidyn did his dead level best—generally successfully—not to resent the efficiency of the Charisian spy network which provided the vast bulk of the Allies' intelligence, there was no point pretending his own agents had anywhere near the penetration and reach Charis did. Cayleb—well, more precisely *Seijin* Merlin and his far-flung web of spies—and Madam Pahrsahn were far more effective, and the Republic had come to rely upon them heavily.

"It's not precisely causing me to turn handsprings of delight either, Your Majesty," Sir Dunkyn Yairley said over the com from his flagship as HMS *Destiny* and her small squadron continued to drive steadily eastward across the Sea of Harchong under the pressure of a far more lively westerly. It was only three in the morning aboard *Destiny*, but he and Lieutenant Aplyn-Ahrmahk had roused early for the conference. "I understand exactly what Sir Bruhstair is doing, and I think he's right. I also like to think I'd've made the same call in his place, and it's true that anyone who refuses to run a risk guarantees he can never win. But Rohsail's better coordinated than he'd expected—than *I'd* expected, for that matter—and with the wind conditions he's been encountering . . . ."

His voice trailed off and he shook his head.

"I believe you've had a little experience of your own with . . . adverse wind conditions, My Lord," Merlin observed.

He stood gazing out the window of the conference room in which Cayleb, Aivah, Maidyn, and Parkair would shortly gather. Ostensibly, he was conducting the routine security check he and the other members of the Imperial Guard carried out before any meeting of such august personages, but the imagery he was actually watching was a display of Harchong's Shwei Province. Small green and crimson icons crept slowly across it, moving steadily south, and there were far more of the red ones.

"Yes, I have," Baron Sarmouth acknowledged. He was still new enough to the inner circle to feel a flicker of uneasiness talking to the fearsome *Seijin* Merlin through a medium all previous training and experience insisted had to be demonic, but his mouth quirked in a smile. "In fact, Hektor and I both have. It was a rather different sort of adverseness, however."

"Agreed," Cayleb said. "On the other hand, even though you and he didn't know it at the time, Sharleyan and I were both watching through the SNARCs the whole time you were fighting that hurricane. When I told you afterward how much I admired your seamanship, especially after that anchor cable snapped, I was speaking from a more . . . informed perspective than you probably realized."

"You should've seen it from his quarterdeck, Cayleb," Hektor put in. "I don't think any of us would've believed he could pull it off if there'd been time to stop and think about it." The lieutenant shrugged. "Fortunately, there wasn't. We were too busy doing what he told us to do to worry about whether or not it was the right thing!"

"Well, that may be true," Sarmouth's embarrassment at their praise was evident, "but it doesn't change the fact that Rohsail's managed to make up at least a full day's sail on them. Or that between them he and Raisahndo have better than three times Ahbaht's strength."

"No, it doesn't," Merlin agreed. "And I wish there were a way we could tell him all of that." He grimaced unhappily. "I keep telling myself this isn't going to be Gwylym Manthyr and the Battle of the Harchong Narrows all over again, but it's not the easiest thing I've ever tried to convince myself of."

"I don't see any sign of the sort of heavy weather that crippled Gwylym's rigging, and neither does Owl," Cayleb pointed out. "And Rohsail may have made up time on them, but so has *Dreadnought*. Haigyl ought to catch up with Ahbaht well before Rohsail could overtake either of them, and I can't think of a captain I'd rather have supporting me. As long as those damned screw-galleys aren't part of the equation, *Thunderer* and *Dreadnought* between them ought to just about equalize the odds. And don't forget about *Tumult* and *Turmoil*; they aren't armored, but those rifled angleguns are going to blow great big holes through any galleon that gets in their way."

"Forgive me for asking this," Aivah said, "but I'm not as informed about boats as all you Charisians are." Cayleb winced at the word "boats," and Aivah's eyes twinkled at him briefly. "But how dangerous *are* those 'screw-galleys'?"

"That's the thousand-mark question," Merlin replied. "The six-inch rifles ought to punch through their armor, but it's thicker than we originally projected the

Dohlarans would be able to produce. At least it's iron, not steel, and it isn't face-hardened the way Ehdwyrd's armor plate is, but it's going to stand up to thirty-pounder shells all day long. Even solid thirty-pound round shot probably won't be able to break through without pounding a lot of hits into the same piece of plating, and I'm none too sure *standard* six-inch shells will penetrate it as readily as we'd all like, either. I'm confident the armor piercing can handle it, but neither of the ironclads have as many rounds of that as I'd like, and the bombardment ships have even less of it."

"But only the forward parts of their hulls are armored, aren't they?"

"For all intents and purposes," Merlin agreed. "They have some light plating to protect their helmsmen from small-arms fire and wolves, but aside from that, two-thirds of their hulls are unarmored. The problem is that between their schooner rig and those damned propellers, they could easily keep their bows towards our ships in weather conditions like this. For that matter, they could manage it even in considerably heavier winds, under the right circumstances. And to make bad worse, they can work upwind of any of our galleons under sail alone with that fore-and-aft rig, which doesn't even consider their ability to move directly into the wind under power. When you add that to the weight of the guns they carry forward, you get something a lot more dangerous than it ought to be."

"And they're faster than they ought to be, too." The frustration in Hektor's tone was obvious. "They should barely be able to move 'under power' without steam!"

"Propellers are more efficient than oars, although I didn't really expect Zhwaigair to give the cranks such a heavy gearing advantage," Merlin said philosophically. "And they built the things light enough to give them decent 'sprint' capability. On the other hand, the gears're a potential weak spot—they've certainly had enough of them break in training exercises—and that light build of theirs is why they're so fragile, and *that* means that out on blue water they'll be even more use-less than Dohlar's galleys were off Armageddon Reef."

"Which would help a lot if we weren't talking about an inland bay," Cayleb pointed out sourly. He glowered at the same map imagery Merlin was looking at, then shook himself. "Well, there's not anything we can do about the situation from here, anyway." His lips twisted for a moment. "Something I've had a lot more experi-ence with than I ever wanted. And in the meantime, Henrai and Daryus will be here any minute. Which brings us to the ice on Wyvern Lake and our good friend Bishop Gorthyk."

His lips twitched again, in a far more unpleasant smile.

. V .

# The Sylmahn Gap,
# Mountaincross Province,
# Republic of Siddarmark

General Trumyn Stohnar checked his watch again.

It was, alas, only seven minutes later than the last time he'd looked, which didn't seem possible, given the iron will with which he'd stopped himself—dozens of times, surely!—from pulling it back out of his pocket in the interim.

He snorted at his own anxiety, wondering how it felt for the men under his command who were waiting for the same event. The Army of Hildermoss was a far cry from the desperate, outnumbered, and dwindling force he'd commanded the previous spring. The handful of starving, exhausted regiments had been transformed into six rifle divisions, supported by six regiments of Siddarmarkian dragoons, and if their equipment re-mained inferior to that of their Charisian allies, it was enormously better than the Republic of Siddarmark

Army had ever before boasted. Every one of its eighty thousand infantrymen was equipped with a bayoneted rifle, over a third of them breechloaders; every one of its twelve thousand dragoons was equipped with a rifle or a rifled carbine; and his divisions were equipped with over two thousand mortars and almost six hundred field guns. Admittedly, the field guns were still the naval thirty-pounders and fourteen-pounders mounted on field carriages Charis had provided, rather than the four-inch rifled guns equipping more and more of the ICA's field artillery regiments, but they still gave his artillery park a massive punch.

And if *he* didn't have any of the Charisians' rifled field guns, he knew where he could—

A rocket soared upward out over the predawn blackness of Wyvern Lake.

▼ ▼ ▼

"*Sir!* Colonel Olyvyr!"

Bryntyn Olyvyr's spine snapped upright in his camp chair, sloshing half his meager cup of precious hot chocolate over his tunic. It was only five o'clock, still well short of sunrise this far north this early in the year, and he'd been half drowsing over his spartan breakfast, allowing his mind to dream of home, of his wife and three sons.

He swore softly but with feeling as he spilled the chocolate, but more at his own clumsiness than at his aide. Lieutenant Dahntahs had been with him since the St. Yura Division marched east the previous summer. He didn't interrupt his colonel on a whim, and whatever had startled that tone into his voice probably foretold something far worse than a chocolate-soaked tunic.

The door of his headquarters hut opened, and young Dahntahs half flew through it. His brown eyes were wide, and his normally unruly hair seemed to bristle in all directions as he skidded to a halt.

"What is it, Taydohr?" Olyvyr asked sharply.

"A signal rocket, Sir—out over the lake!"

A chill which owed nothing to the cold, damp morning started somewhere around the nape of Olyvyr's neck, ran down his spine, and took up residence in his perpetually hungry stomach. Every officer in the Army of the Sylmahn knew the heretics would attack as soon as the weather permitted them to move, but Wyvern Lake's ice had been melting for five-days, hastened by the beginning of the spring floods. Olyvyr, like most of Bishop Militant Bahrnabai's senior officers, remembered those same spring floods from last year. Langhorne knew the Sylmahn Gap had been a nightmare of mud and chest-deep water this time last year! Surely that meant the heretic Stohnar was as mud-bound as the Army of the Sylmahn and the anticipated attack would have to come from the west along the Guarnak-Ice Ash Canal.

Apparently, however, it meant nothing of the sort.

He set his cup back down, took one swipe at his tunic with a napkin, reached for his coat with his other hand, and headed for the door. Behind him, Dahntahs tarried just long enough to collect his colonel's sword belt, then hurried after him.

Olyvyr bolted out into the open, still shrugging his arms into his coat. The signal rocket Dahntahs had reported drifted high in the heavens, fuming and smoking in blue fury under one of the parasols the heretics used to hold them up. The sudden eruption of light made the darkness over the lake even more impenetrable, yet the thing had obviously been launched from no more than a few thousand yards from 1st Regiment's muddy, half-flooded entrenchments. That meant it had been fired from somewhere out *on the lake*, and the colonel shaded his eyes against the glare with both hands, staring into that blackness for what he knew had to be out there somewhere, wondering what the heretics intended.

*What the hell are they doing over here on the* east *side of the lake, anyway?* The thought burned through his brain. *They ought to be hitting Bishop Zhasyn, not* us!

The narrow water gap which connected the eastern

and western lobes of Wyvern Lake was barely six miles wide where the bridge and causeway had crossed it before Bishop Militant Bahrnabai ordered them destroyed. Even now, with all the flooding, it couldn't be much more than eight miles across, whereas it was the next best thing to thirty-five miles from the closest heretic-held point on the southern shore of the lake to St. Yura's position. Bishop Zhasyn Howail's St. Thadyus Division held the wreckage of the causeway, and he'd been heavily reinforced from the Army of the Sylmahn's straitened artillery park precisely because it was the most vulnerable point. Despite the current high water, the demolished roadway's piers still rose above the surface, a priceless advantage for infantry trying to assault across the water gap or engineers attempting to bridge that same gap on the infantry's heels. So why—?

"*Sweet Chihiro!*"

Olyvyr staggered back a full step in sheer surprise as a dozen more rockets—no, *dozens* more rockets!—streaked into the heavens. They erupted in an arc which must have been at least four or five miles across, blazing in the darkness like a bevy of curses as they howled upward on steeply slanting trajectories. The colonel wanted to fling himself facedown, cowering against the ground like a rabbit or near squirrel before the cry of a hunting wyvern. He managed not to only because he knew every eye which wasn't glued to those rockets was watching *him*, instead. And so he made himself straighten, watching those fuming lines of light climb, even though he doubted he was fooling anyone.

And then the rockets began to burst, and Bryntyn Olyvyr's blood turned to ice. These weren't signal rockets; they were the heretics' *illuminating* rockets, and their light streamed down across his regiment's position.

"Stand to! *Stand to!*"

At least his sergeants and junior officers were on their toes, he thought distantly. The bone-deep reflex of training and responsibility had them by the throat, driving them to their duty . . . whether it was going to do any good at all or not.

He shook himself. If they could do their duty, then he could damned well do *his*, and he turned and dashed for his command post with Lieutenant Dahntahs at his heels.

▼ ▼ ▼

"All right, boys!" Commander Zhorj Parkmyn shouted. *"Tell the bastards we're here!"*

It was hardly the proper, professional way to pass the order, but Parkmyn didn't really care. He'd taken over the preparations Colonel Mhartyn Mkwartyr had set in train long before Baron Green Valley pulled out of the Sylmahn Gap and headed for Grayback Lake the previous August. It was a bizarre sort of thing for a naval officer to be doing eight hundred miles and more from the nearest saltwater, but that was just fine with Zhorj Parkmyn.

The flotilla of brigs, schooners, and assault boats he and his parties of seamen and Siddarmarkian carpenters had spent the winter building spread out on either hand in the darkness. In the end, it had been simpler to build a sawmill and a boat yard at Ananasberg, eighty miles above the Serabor Dam, instead of portaging them around the dam. Dragging the heavy naval angle-guns up past the dam had been a sufficiently monumental task, although it had been more arduous than difficult once Mkwartyr had the sheer legs rigged to do the heavy lifting. From there, they'd been barged forward to Ananasberg, where the shallow-draft gun vessels awaited them.

A rifled six-inch angle-gun, or one of the even heavier ten-inch smoothbores, was a massive weight of ordnance for anything shallow enough to thread its way through the mainland canals, but the stoutly framed and planked brigs were equal to the task. None of them could carry more than two of the huge pieces, but he'd built twenty-five of them. Every one of those twenty-five was anchored in an only slightly ragged line stretching out to east and west of *Grenade*, his hundred-foot-long flagship. They were anchored on springs, and they'd adjusted their aim carefully as the blazing rockets illuminated their targets ashore. The gun crews were ready, waiting impatiently for *Grenade* to open fire, and *Grenade*'s gunners had been waiting only for Parkmyn's permission.

▼ ▼ ▼

Colonel Olyvyr was barely halfway to his command post when the lake exploded.

A long line of searing muzzle flashes—huge, fiery tongues of light, lashing upward from the surface—shredded the darkness. He knew instantly what the heretics had done; he simply couldn't understand how they'd gotten away with it without anyone noticing. He paused, sick at heart, watching the bright streaks as the heretics' shells arced upward. They seemed to move almost slowly as they climbed, but then they reached their maximum height and came howling downward, faster and faster, until they slammed into the earth and erupted with Kau-yung's own fury.

His eardrums cringed under the rolling thunder of that bombardment, and through the sound and fury of the heretic shells, he heard shouts of alarm and the bloodcurdling screams of the wounded. He'd dug his regiment in as deeply as he could, but his heart sank as the sheer weight and power of the explosions washed about him. His men's bunkers and dugouts couldn't stand up to that sort of punishment for very long. Even if they could, the heretics wouldn't be shelling them this way unless they intended to come calling in person, and men who were crouched in dugouts were men unable to man the parapets of their works.

And then it got worse.

▼ ▼ ▼

Parkmyn peered through his double-glass, trying to make out some sort of detail as successive waves of angle-gun shells plummeted out of the heavens onto the Temple Boys' positions. He couldn't see much, despite the illuminating rockets, what with the darkness, the smoke, and the blinding flashes of gun muzzles and shell explosions, but it looked as if his gunners were hitting their targets even more accurately than he'd hoped they could.

He bared his teeth as he lowered the double-glass and watched the wave of canal barges fitted as mobile, oar-powered mortar platforms row past *Grenade*. The smallest of them carried twelve of the original three-inch weapons; the larger carried the far heavier M97s with their four-and-a-half-inch bombs. The thirty barges carried a total of just over three hundred mortars, and the combination of the illumination rockets still bursting overhead and the angle-guns' heavy shells should give them plenty of light to see their targets.

▼ ▼ ▼

Colonel Olyvyr never made it to his command post. An M97 mortar bomb detonated almost directly above him, and the cone of shrapnel balls tore him and his aide to pieces. Less than two minutes later, a ten-inch angle-gun shell exploded almost directly on top of his body.

Two men's deaths were little enough against the scale of the disaster reaching out to engulf the Army of the Sylmahn. Elahnor Olyvyr and her children would never know for certain how their husband and father had died, and Agtha Dahntahs would never know what had happened to her son, but thousands of other families would be able to say the same. Yet one thing *was* different about Olyvyr's death: any chance his regiment might have had of holding its ground died with him. It probably would have happened anyway, but his company commanders were as confused and terrified as any of their men. They did their best, and two-thirds of them died in the doing, but without Olyvyr's steadying, *trusted* voice, their best simply wasn't good enough.

First Regiment routed under the lash of that hurricane

bombardment. Surprised, frightened men, who'd already sensed the inevitability of ultimate defeat in the miserly rations and grossly inadequate clothing their quartermasters issued to them, panicked. Too many of those who might have stemmed the panic, like Colonel Olyvyr, were dead, and the survivors fled the holocaust . . . only to run into its very heart. Out of their dugouts, without even the protection of slit trenches, they were naked before the lash of shrapnel and sizzling steel splinters as the enemy's shells and mortar bombs exacted the penalty always demanded of troops who broke under fire.

▼ ▼ ▼

"All right!" Parkmyn shouted thirty minutes later, loud enough to make himself heard through the thunder of artillery. "Let's send General Mahklymorh his invitation, Charltyn!"

"Aye, aye, Sir!" Lieutenant Charltyn Vynchozy, *Grenade*'s commanding officer, touched his chest in acknowledgment and nodded to a waiting signalman. The petty officer lit the rocket's fuse from a length of slow match and it streaked into the heavens to burst in a cascade of red and green fire.

Parkmyn watched it climb, watched it erupt, then looked back to the south as the first wave of assault boats rowed powerfully through the thick, drifting fogbanks of powder smoke and the thunder and lightning of the bombardment. General Tobys Mahklymorh's 8th Rifle Division had waited months for this moment, and he could hear the wail of their pipes and the high, wild howl they'd learned from the Charisian Marines even through the bedlam of the guns.

He snatched off his hat, waving it overhead as his gunners returned the infantry's cheers, and his lips drew back in a hungry snarl. The Temple Boys had a lot to answer for, and Mahklymorh's men were about to collect the first down payment.

Zhaspahr Clyntahn's tight, angry expression was hard enough to chip stone. His eyes glittered with the deep and bottomless rage which had become ever more a part of him in the last few years, and danger radiated off of him like a curse. Wyllym Rayno could almost smell the blood and smoke as he stood quietly waiting while Clyntahn scrawled his signature across half a dozen arrest orders, tossed them back into his secretary's hands, and jerked his head curtly in a gesture of dismissal.

The secretary didn't offer to kiss the Grand Inquisitor's ring in formal leavetaking. He simply darted a quick, frightened bow and disappeared like smoke from last winter's fires, leaving Rayno alone with his master.

"Sit."

Clyntahn jabbed a forefinger at Rayno's normal chair, and the Archbishop of Chiang-wu settled into it with his briefcase in his lap.

"You brought the documents?"

"Yes, Your Grace." Rayno opened the briefcase and extracted a half-dozen well-stuffed folders. He laid them on Clyntahn's desk. "All of the officers whose files you requested, Your Grace."

Clyntahn stretched out his hand and dragged the folders closer, like an angry cliff bear swiping a salmon out of a stream. He scowled as he sorted through them until he found the two he obviously wanted. Then he shoved the others to one side and opened the selected pair one after the other, flipping rapidly through their contents. Finally, he closed them again, sat back in his chair, and bent that dangerous, fiery glare on Rayno.

"I assume you've confirmed the initial reports?"

It came out in a half-snarl, but Rayno had expected that. He simply nodded, his own expression grave.

"I'm afraid so, Your Grace." He shrugged slightly. "Communications are difficult, you understand, and the agents inquisitor we have reporting from the field—the ones whose orders don't require them to clear their messages with Abernethy before transmission—are in relatively junior positions. In fact, most of them have cover identities as regular Army personnel. That means their access to the semaphore or other methods of communication is limited at the moment. I do, however, have three separate confirming messages, all delivered by wyvern."

"Those *bastards*."

The two words were hissed, almost whispered, which gave them even more power than Clyntahn's more habitual bellowing fury. Rayno had seen the Grand Inquisitor in every conceivable mood, from genial good fellowship when things were going well to incoherent, furniture-smashing fury when things went . . . less well. At the moment, he would have preferred one of Clyntahn's shrieking, gobbling tantrums to the icy cocoon of so much tightly focused rage. These were the moments when the vicar was least inclined toward restraint and most powerfully impelled toward . . . extreme responses. His tantrums were dangerous enough, but the cold, *focused* passion of his present mood was far more perilous.

The archbishop waited. Not so much to learn what Bahrnabai Wyrshym's and Ernyst Abernethy's fates might be as to learn how those fates were going to overtake them. Their dooms had been sealed from the moment they ordered Colonel Clairdon Mahkswail to lead twenty-five thousand men westward from Guarnak in a desperate bid to escape the juggernaut hammering mercilessly up the Sylmahn Gap towards what was left of the Army of the Sylmahn. It was unlikely the fugitives could actually escape—they were all infantry, without any cavalry among them, according to the agents inquisitor's reports—and both Wyrshym and Abernethy had remained behind with the rearguard, trying to buy them a little more time.

And because it kept them out of the Inquisition's reach, no doubt. Although that was a mixed blessing in Abernethy's case, given the heretics' declared policy towards inquisitors.

"I want them arrested," Clyntahn said flatly. "Send the order to Father Ahndair."

"I'll certainly attempt to, Your Grace." Rayno managed not to flinch as those fiery eyes narrowed. "As I said, however, communications are . . . chaotic. I may not be able to get the instructions through to him. And, frankly, even if we succeed in getting them to him, he may not be in a position to act."

Clyntahn showed his teeth. Ahndair Seegairs was officially the senior member of Ernyst Abernethy's staff. In fact, he was also Zhaspahr Clyntahn's eyes inside the Army of the Sylmahn, and he'd been reporting for the last two months that that army's morale was less than reliable. Obviously, he'd been right.

"Why shouldn't he be in a position to act?" the Grand Inquisitor asked in a dangerously calm tone. "This is one of the things he was specifically put into place to deal with, and he has my personal commission to act in the Inquisition's name."

"I realize that, Your Grace. But such flagrant disregard for orders on Wyrshym's part argues that this is something he's been thinking about for some time, exactly as Father Ahndair warned us he might be. For him to have *succeeded* in it, however, argues that Abernethy has to have decided to support him—passively, at the very least. And whatever else may be true, neither Wyrshym nor Abernethy are stupid enough to think the Inquisition wouldn't be keeping as close an eye as possible on both of them. I'm sure they've taken precautions—to the best of their ability, at any rate—to preclude interference from someone like Father Ahndair, and to arrest them, he'd have to rely on regular Army officers to carry out the Inquisition's orders.

Normally, that wouldn't concern me; in a fluid situation like the one the Army of the Sylmahn faces at this time, even the most loyal regular officers are likely to be too . . . preoccupied to rally to the Inquisition as they ought."

"You mean the rot's spread so far they'd take Wyrshym's orders over Father Ahndair's," Clyntahn grated.

"Not precisely, Your Grace," Rayno replied, although he strongly suspected that that was exactly what would happen if push came to shove. "What I meant is that although Father Ahndair carries your personal warrant, no one outside the Inquisition is likely to recognize it—or your signature, for that matter—when they see it. If Abernethy countermands the order while combat is still raging, regular officers are likely to decide his higher priestly rank and his official position as the army's intendant give his orders more weight than a mere upper-priest's." The archbishop shrugged again. "Honestly, Your Grace, under the circumstances it would be unreasonable to expect any other reaction out of laymen faced with such . . . conflicting levels of priestly authority."

"I see."

The two-word response was chiseled out of Lake Pei's winter ice and Clyntahn's nostrils flared. His face, already flushed with anger, got a little redder, but the explosion Rayno had feared failed to put in an appearance.

"All right," he said finally, like granite crumbling into gravel, "you may be right. And the last thing we need to do is to order their arrests and fail. But I want to see every word of every order, every bit of correspondence, that went back and forth between our good friend Allayn and Wyrshym since the decision was made for the Army of the Sylmahn to stand its ground. Every word of it, Wyllym!"

"Of course, Your Grace." Rayno produced a seated bow. "I anticipated you might desire that, and my confidential clerks are pulling it together now. I'm afraid it will be quite extensive."

"I don't care. Have it checked for any evidence of unauthorized ciphers or codes, as well."

"Yes, Your Grace."

In truth, that had already been done. During a jihad, the Inquisition's oversight of Mother Church's semaphore system became even more inclusive. Copies of *every* semaphore message, including those of the Army of God and the Navy of God, were filed with Rayno's office, and all military communications were routinely inspected for any sign that someone other than the Inquisition might be passing secret messages back and forth. The archbishop had seen no evidence that Allayn Maigwair had conspired with Wyrshym to evade the Army of the Sylmahn's order to stand its ground, but he was confident that a sufficiently painstaking search— and the use of carefully selected excerpts—could prove Maigwair's complicity in the bishop militant's ultimate decision.

Assuming that was what Clyntahn wanted to prove, at any rate.

"And in the meantime," the Grand Inquisitor finished coldly, "I want the names of Wyrshym's and Abernethy's immediate families."

## . VII .
## Fairkyn,
## New Northland Province,
## Republic of Siddarmark

Bishop Gorthyk Nybar rode out the sally port and headed down the steeply sloping road, accompanied by Colonel Bahrtalymu Hansylman, the officer who would have been called his chief of staff in the Imperial Charisian Army, and Captain Teagmahn Fhrancys, his youthful aide. A cold wind whipped into their faces from the northeast, but it wasn't cold enough, he thought grimly. Snow still lingered, piled deep in places, where it was shadowed by the sun, but elsewhere it had melted. In a normal year, the Guarnak-Ice Ash Canal would have overspread its banks by now, despite the many and ingenious provisions for flood control on mainland canals. This year, the canal bed was barely half full, and all of that was snowmelt, for the locks between Guarnak and Fairkyn had yet to be repaired.

The Ice Ash River, on the other hand, swirled brown and angry below the bluffs upon which what was left of Fairkyn perched. The city's location had been dictated by terrain considerations; it lay at the head of a valley running northwest into the rugged foothills that penetrated into the higher tableland west of the Ohlarn Gap. That valley offered a natural canal route into the central Republic which required the minimum number of locks to reach the New Northland Plateau, but the Fairkyn bluffs had presented the canal builders with a formidable challenge. They formed a barrier, almost a natural escarpment, almost eight miles wide between the valley and the Ice Ash River. Getting through it had been an arduous task, yet the shortest alternative route would have added over a hundred miles to the length of the canal and required almost as many locks in the end, anyway.

Fairkyn itself lay on the narrow spine at the center of the high ground where the locks themselves were located. Because of that, it had been built on two levels, with High Town's canalfront docks, at the head of the valley above the locks, serving the barge traffic moving through the canal proper. Low Town, below the locks to the southeast, backed up against the bluffs, but most of it was barely above or actually below the river's flood plain, built there to serve the traffic headed into or arriving from the river, despite the perennial risk of flooding. The ground broke sharply away from High Town to both southeast and northwest—the locks raised barges over a hundred and eighty feet from the Ice Ash and then lowered them sixty feet to the level of the canal—because gunpowder had been unavailable for blasting away the intervening bedrock when the canal was first constructed. As a result, High Town formed a natural strongpoint, close to two hundred feet higher than the approaches from the river and almost half that far above its western and northern approaches.

Nybar had always known Low Town couldn't be held against a serious overland attack, however, so he'd never intended to try. Instead, he'd withdrawn his entire defensive force to High Town, blown gaps in Low Town's protective levees, and systematically demolished its buildings to deny their use to the heretics.

Thanks to the breached levees, at least half of Low Town—like most of the six and a half miles of the low ground between it and the river—was currently submerged. The only exceptions were a few low hills and a couple of connecting ridgelines rising from the foam-streaked water, too cramped for either side to use as worthwhile military emplacements. The heretics had occupied much of the low ground earlier, but only a handful of infantry remained to picket the hilltops now that they were isolated by the water, and it was difficult to pick out the line of the submerged canal where it crossed the lowlands.

There was no flooding away from the river, unfortunately, and Nybar's eyes hardened as he saw the Charisian and Siddarmarkian banners flying above the heretical earthworks which encircled Fairkyn on every side except the south. The redoubts and batteries erected to seal Nybar's besieged command into the town didn't form a contiguous line of fortifications, but they were more than close enough together to sweep the spaces between them with rifle and artillery fire. They were also far enough from the city's perimeter to deter Nybar from wasting any of his slender stock of irreplaceable artillery ammunition against them. They were not, unfortunately, far enough out to prevent the heretics' longer-ranged artillery from bombarding Fairkyn whenever they chose to, although they hadn't done much of that. The city's (and Nybar's fortifications') high perch meant their artillerists would be firing blind, and until recently the weather must have made it difficult for them to haul huge amounts of ammunition this far forward, as well.

On a planet named Earth, those emplacements would have been called a work of circumvallation; on Safehold, they were simply called "siege works," but the function was exactly the same, and they were manned by a dismayingly powerful army—a fact which explained why Gorthyk Nybar was making this ride this chill June morning without Father Charlz Kaillyt at his side.

The bishop's jaw tightened as he contemplated Kaillyt's absence. He didn't like the reason he'd had no choice but to leave the cleric safely in Fairkyn, but there was no use pretending, just as there was no use pretending he had any choice about accepting the parley summons in the first place. Sir Bartyn Sahmyrsyt, the heretic commander, had phrased his written message with at least marginal courtesy, but the iron fist inside the rather threadbare silk glove had been there for any to see. And if anyone had missed it the first time around, Sahmyrsyt's flat rejection of Nybar's counteroffer that they meet inside his position—a rejection which had included words like "treachery" and "murderers"— would have made it abundantly clear.

*And I don't have any choice but to go meet with the arrogant, heretical son-of-a-bitch wherever he chooses.* The thought burned harshly through Nybar's brain as he neared the designated redoubt. *I wonder if he knows how short our rations really are?* He snorted grimly. *I guess I may find out about that in the next half-hour or so.*

A group of horsemen rode out to meet his small party as it approached the redoubt, and Nybar was uncomfortably aware of the riflemen manning the earthen parapet. Neither they nor the redoubt's half-dozen field guns were aimed directly at him, but that minor detail could be quickly corrected.

*At least the bastards were polite enough to meet us*

*outside their own hidey hole*, he reminded himself. *Of course, that probably has more to do with their not wanting me to see anything on the other side of their damned entrenchments than it does with courtesy.*

The heretics drew rein about fifty yards from the redoubt and waited for the trio of Army of God officers to reach them. Nybar continued straight ahead at an unhurried pace, only too well aware of how his own mount's hunger-thinned gauntness compared to the heretics' well-fed, well-cared-for horses.

*A message in that, too*, he thought. *I wonder if that's why they bothered to mount up in the first place instead of just walking out to meet us? Or are they making sure they didn't find themselves looking up to us at some sort of psychological disadvantage?*

He drew his own horse to a halt a few feet from the dark-haired, dark-eyed heretic with the single gold-sword collar insignia of a Charisian general who had to be Sahmyrsyt. He was a big man, at least two or three inches taller than Nybar's own five feet and eleven inches and yet stocky for his height, with powerful shoulders, a deep chest, dark hair and eyes, and eyebrows that formed a single thick bar across the bridge of his nose.

Sahmyrsyt was flanked on his left by a much younger man with the twin silver crowns of a lieutenant and the look of someone who'd been born on the island of Charis itself. He also looked as if he was perhaps fifteen years old ... until someone got a look into those steady brown eyes of his. The man on the general's right had a pair of silver swords on his collar and offered the visual antithesis of the lieutenant, with fair hair, blue eyes, and a full, well-kept beard. All of them, Nybar noted, were immaculately groomed and obviously well fed. Well, he hadn't been able to do anything about his own officers' semi-starved appearance, but at least they were as perfectly turned out as the heretics.

He tried not to think about any words like "thin pretense."

"Bishop Gorthyk." Sahmyrsyt's voice carried a strong Chisholmian accent and sort of deep power one might have associated with that thick chest.

"General Sahmyrsyt." Nybar kept his tone brusque and clipped in response, and his fingers tightened on his reins when Sahmyrsyt smiled ever so slightly, as if that terseness amused him somehow.

"Brigadier Silkiah, my chief of staff," the Chisholmian said, indicating the blond officer to his right. "And Lieutenant Mahkgrudyr, my personal aide. I see you've brought Captain Fhrancys and Colonel Hansylman along."

He nodded to Nybar's subordinates with something which might have been mistaken for courtesy under other circumstances, and Nybar felt his expression go briefly blank. How in Langhorne's name had Sahmyrsyt known who Fhrancys and Hansylman were? Fhrancys had been with him since the Army of God marched out of the Temple Lands, so he supposed it was possible prisoner interrogation might have provided his name and rank, even his description, to the heretics. But Hansylman had been detached from the St. Emylee Division to serve as his equivalent of the heretic Silkiah less than three months ago, when Nybar consolidated the skeletons of the division's four original regiments into three regiments which were merely badly understrength.

*It doesn't matter how he knows, Gorthyk*, he told himself flatly, banishing surprise's blankness. *He probably got it from some fucking deserter. It sure as Shanwei doesn't mean they've got* spies *inside Fairkyn, anyway! And it's obvious the only reason he dropped the names was to make you worry about it exactly like this*, so stop.

"You requested the parley, General," he said, looking Sahmyrsyt in the eye, and the Charisian nodded.

"Yes, I did. It occurred to me that this might be a moment to recall the *Book of Langhorne*'s injunctions. Chapter Seventeen's to be exact—verses twelve through fourteen. I realize no one seems to have been reading that passage very much from your side lately, but I think it applies."

Nybar heard Hansylman inhale sharply and sensed young Kaillyt's stiff-faced anger, and his own jaw clenched as Langhorne's words went through his mind.

The time will come when violence mars the peace God Himself has created for His children, and He will weep to see it. Yet there is no virtue in attempting to deny that truth, for Truth is Truth, and God has given all of you freedom of will to choose your own course. Let no man forget that God breathed the breath of life into all Adams and all Eves at the same instant, in the same minute of the same day under the same sun. Whatever the anger you may feel, whatever the fury which impels you to raise hands against one another, you are all equally His children in His eyes and love. So on the day when you face one another with anger in your heart and weapons in your hands, keep that memory in your minds and souls. If war you must, then let mercy stay your hand against the helpless and compassion for the defeated keep you clean of the spiritual poison which must destroy any whom it touches.

"So I should assume your purpose today is to demonstrate your 'mercy' and 'compassion,' should I?" he asked after a moment, the words bitter in his mouth.

"Something of the sort," Sahmyrsyt agreed.

"But something rather less than that for our inquisitors, I imagine," the bishop said harshly.

"'As he sows, so shall he reap, and the mercy he denies to others shall be denied to him in his turn,'" Sahmyrsyt quoted softly. "The sermon was Archbishop Maikel's, but the words are Chihiro's, and in this case rightly applied. You know my Emperor and Empress' policy, and so do any inquisitors in your army who've chosen not to leave that bastard Clyntahn's service."

"And you expect me to turn consecrated priests over to you to be murdered, is that it?" Searing anger burned in the question, but Sahmyrsyt only nodded. "And what in Shan-wei's name makes you think I'd do that?!"

"In some ways, I don't really care whether you do it or not," Sahmyrsyt said calmly. "I'm a simple man at heart, Bishop Gorthyk. I honor Emperor Cayleb and Empress Sharleyan, and my orders from them are pretty clear, but I prefer simple solutions, myself. That means I'm perfectly all right with what happened at Fort Tairys last winter, if that's the way you want to handle it instead of accepting terms. But you might want to think about the other eighteen or nineteen thousand men trapped in that spider rat hole with you."

"You think any of my men are afraid to die for God?" Nybar sneered.

"For God?" Sahmyrsyt shrugged. "Maybe not. For that fat, fornicating pig Clyntahn?" He rolled his eyes under the solid barrier of his eyebrows. "Anybody willing to die for him is so frigging stupid we should go ahead and cull him now, before he reproduces!"

Nybar's face went first red and then white with fury. Yet even as the rage went through him, a part of him knew Sahmyrsyt had a point. Little though he wanted to admit it, even to himself, the very foundations of the Jihad had begun to quiver. Even in the Army of God, there were those beginning to differentiate between the Grand Inquisitor and Mother Church. He and his chaplains and inquisitors jumped on that sentiment with both feet whenever it reared its head, but it was like trying to quench a grass fire in high summer. Each flame they extinguished threw out its own fiery embers before it died, and the realization that the Army of Fairkyn had been left to die in place had fanned them like a high wind.

"If you expect to goad me into some . . . intemperate response," he bit out, "I have no intention of obliging you. And whatever your murdering friends may have done at Fort Tairys, I think you'll find Fairkyn a much bloodier and harder to chew mouthful."

"Whether or not you surrender now is up to you,"

Sahmyrsyt replied. "What happens in the end if you *don't* surrender is another matter. At the moment, you have just over fifteen thousand infantry, twenty-seven hundred cavalry, and eighty-three guns. No, wait." He shook his head. "It's eighty-*two* guns after that Fultyn Rifle burst Friday in Captain Zakrai's battery, isn't it?" His smile was a razor. "I, on the other hand, have the next best thing to eighty thousand infantry and cavalry, and over two thousand angle-guns, field guns, and mortars." He shrugged. "I'll grant you most of them are mortars, not angle-guns. I'll even grant that we won't be able to target your positions as accurately as we'd like and that assaulting uphill is never easy. I don't have any doubt about the outcome if my army *has* to assault, however. And while I don't plan to be playing 'The Pikes of Kolstyr' on the way up, I tend to doubt many of my men will be remembering Langhorne's injunctions about mercy and compassion once we get to the top. They'll have their orders about giving quarter and taking prisoners, of course. But given the Army of God's outstanding record of restraint after victory, I'm sure you'll understand how it is that sometimes the troops get out of hand."

An icy cannonball congealed in Gorthyk Nybar's belly as Sahmyrsyt catalogued his own strength so calmly . . . and so accurately. There was no way—no way under God's golden sun—Sahmyrsyt could have those numbers, yet he did. And as badly as Nybar wanted to believe he'd exaggerated his own strength, he was sickly certain the Charisian hadn't.

"I suppose we'll just have to find out then, won't we?" the bishop heard himself say.

"I suppose we will." Sahmyrsyt glanced up at the sun. The morning was ticking away, the shadows shortening, and he looked back at Nybar. "In that case, this parley's over. The truce extends until thirteen o'clock. I'd recommend that you and your chaplains spend the time in prayer. You may not have another opportunity."

He twitched his head at his companions, and the

three of them turned away and trotted back towards the redoubt without another word.

▼ ▼ ▼

"Are you sure this is going to work, Sir?" Lieutenant Mahkgrudyr asked quietly as Sir Bartyn Sahmyrsyt checked his watch. He and the general stood in the shadow of the looming observation tower, and the lieutenant shrugged when Sahmyrsyt glanced at him. "It sounded really good when Colonel Ahlgyrnahn proposed it, Sir, but that was then and this is now."

"I have a great deal of confidence in Colonel Ahlgyrnahn and his men, Cayleb," Sahmyrsyt said mildly. "And *Seijin* Ahbraim's friends were good enough to confirm the accuracy of his navigation in addition to keeping tabs on Nybar's troop and artillery strength for us. Major Sahndyrsyn's men went exactly where they meant to go. So is there some other reason you don't *expect* it to work?"

"No, Sir. But I can't help remembering what Emperor Cayleb said in Corisande. He and General Chermyn even coined a term for it: the KISS Principle."

"'Keep It Simple, Stupid,'" Sahmyrsyt said with a nod. "Baron Green Valley's fond of the same phrase. But when you come down to it, Colonel Ahlgyrnahn's suggestion was about as simple as they come. Hard work, true, but certainly *simple*."

Mahkgrudyr didn't—quite—glare at his general, but he was clearly less than amused by Sahmyrsyt's ironic tone. And, his superior reminded himself, young Mahkgrudyr was both older and much more experienced than his boyish appearance might suggest. He'd been a Marine sergeant for Emperor Cayleb's Corisande campaign, and when the bulk of the Royal Charisian Marine field force transferred to the new Imperial Army, Mahkgrudyr had come with it. He'd been all but functionally illiterate before he enlisted, but he'd caught the eye of his superiors in Corisande and been recommended for a commission before the transfer. The Army had agreed with the recommendation, and the

Royal Chisholmian Army, with its tradition of recruiting commoners, had more experience than most at filling any holes in its volunteers' education. That was how he'd been sent off to the Imperial Officers School—which had previously been the *Royal* Officers School—at Maikelberg and emerged as a shiny new lieutenant just in time for Sahmyrsyt to snap him up as an aide. He'd also emerged as a committed bibliophile, determined—apparently—to catch up on the last several centuries' worth of the reading he'd missed earlier in life.

"Seriously, Cayleb," the general said now, reaching out to rest one hand on the lieutenant's shoulder, "I think Ahlgyrnahn came up with a perfectly workable idea that's going to save a lot of lives . . . assuming it works. And given his men's experience and Colonel Mahknail's input, I think it *will* work. If it doesn't," he shrugged, "we'll just have to do it the hard way after all."

Mahkgrudyr looked back at him for a moment, then nodded, and Sahmyrsyt started the climb up the observation tower's steep zigzag stairs with his aide at his heels.

▼ ▼ ▼

"Get ready," Colonel Kynt Ahlgyrnahn said, looking at his own watch, and Major Bryntwyrth Sahndyrsyn, CO of the 63rd Infantry's 4th Company, smiled and reached for the brass ring.

Major Sahndyrsyn was three years younger than his colonel, and like almost all of the 63rd's men, he'd been born in New Province. In fact, Sahndyrsyn had been born and raised in Irondale, and his family had been miners for generations. A lot of Ahlgyrnahn's men could have said that about their families, and at least half of them had been miners themselves before volunteering when Ahlgyrnahn's regiment was recruited back up to strength after its losses to the Sword of Schueler. The original 63rd, a New Province-based regiment of regulars, had suffered well over fifty percent casualties in that first dreadful winter, and the majority of its new personnel had enlisted to avenge brothers, fathers, or cousins. They brought a certain practicality to the pursuit of that vengeance, however, and when Baron Green Valley had left General Makgrygair's 2nd Rifle Division to keep an eye on Fairkyn pending General Sahmyrsyt's arrival, they'd found themselves with time on their hands.

Colonel Ahlgyrnahn, who'd been the regiment's senior surviving company commander after the Sword, was a firm believer that idle hands were Shan-wei's workshop, so when Sahndyrsyn—whose long-armed, short-legged physique and sloping forehead concealed a frighteningly acute brain from the casual observer—approached him with the suggestion, he'd leapt on it. In fact, he'd authorized the regiment to begin work even before taking the idea to General Makgrygair.

Makgrygair had been at least a little dubious, but he, too, was a regular who recognized the negative consequences of too much idleness. He'd allowed the 63rd to continue its efforts and even championed their idea to Sahmyrsyt when he arrived. Fortunately, Colonel Thyadohr Mahknail, Sahmyrsyt's chief engineer, had embraced it enthusiastically when the rest of the Army of New Northland came up. In fact, his surveyors had helped materially in directing the effort and he'd sent back to Siddar City for something a bit more . . . energetic than gunpowder.

Not all of Fairkyn's bluffs were solid bedrock. That was especially true on their southern edge, where the ex-miners had toiled away for two and a half months, and the result was a three-thousand-yard tunnel extending into them from the south. The 63rd had managed to finish the excavation just in time to avoid the flooding threat of the spring floods—that time pressure had been a large part of General Makgrygair's original skepticism—and the site chosen for its mouth was on the reverse slope of one of the low hills which was still above water level, completely concealed from even the defenders' observation towers. But the tunnel itself climbed steadily as it angled to the east and ended in a two-hundred-foot-long perpendicular gallery, like the crossbar on a capital "T," directly under the outermost of Gorthyk Nybar's defensive earthworks. The miners had hoped to drive it deeper into Nybar's position, but they'd encountered solid rock well short of their planned endpoint. That gallery lay seventy feet below the entrenchments, however, and they'd packed it with seven thousand pounds of the Charisians' new "Lywysite." After that, the last thirty yards of the approach tunnel had been refilled with hard-packed earth to focus the blast upward by preventing it from blowing back out the mouth of the mine when the moment came.

Ahlgyrnahn wasn't certain he really believed the Charisians' estimates of the new explosive's effectiveness, but he figured three and a half tons of anything ought to make a satisfying bang, And since Sahndyrsyn's company had come up with the idea, it was only fair the major execute its final stage. Now Ahlgyrnahn watched the sweep hand bite off the last few seconds. Then he looked up.

"Go," he said simply.

Sahndyrsyn hooked his index finger through the ring on the polished wooden box and drew a deep breath.

"*Fire in the hole!*" he announced, and pulled firmly.

▼ ▼ ▼

"Perhaps you *should* consider surrendering, Gorthyk," Father Charlz Kaillyt said somberly. He stood gazing out one window of Gorthyk Nybar's office in Fairkyn, and the bishop looked at his sword-straight spine incredulously.

"You can't be serious, Charlz! *Surrender* to a slew of godless heretics before they've even fired a single shot?!"

"If you don't surrender, the men are going to starve to death," Kaillyt replied flatly. "The only thing you'll accomplish by *not* surrendering is to get even more of them killed in the end."

"No, that *isn't* the only thing I'll accomplish." Nybar's tone was equally flat. "If those bastards assault us here, then by Chihiro we'll kill a lot of *them*, too."

"And achieve what?" Kaillyt wheeled from the window and glared at the bishop.

They'd known one another for years, and Kaillyt—originally the senior chaplain of Nybar's Langhorne Division—had become the Army of Fairkyn's acting intendant. He was a Schuelerite, although he'd never been a formal member of the Inquisition, and he was less fiery than many. Yet Nybar had never doubted his quiet, determined opposition to the heresy. Now Kaillyt raised a right hand which had lost its thumb and two fingers to frostbite over the winter and pointed at his bishop with his ring finger, in the gesture he'd acquired since his mutilation.

"However deep you stack the bodies, you aren't going to stop them, and you aren't going to save Bishop Militant Bahrnabai—assuming the heretics haven't already overrun him, as well. It's obvious the Inquisition completely underestimated how many men the Charisians can put into the field, Gorthyk. I don't doubt for one moment that Sahmyrsyt gave you accurate numbers—why in Shan-wei's name *shouldn't* he have? It's not like we'll be telling anyone, is it? And the truth is that if he has *half* the strength he says he does, this army is already completely screwed, so why inflate the numbers? And we already know the Siddarmarkians are putting fresh regiments into the field as quickly as they can get rifles into their hands, as well. You can't possibly kill enough of them to keep them from taking your position away from you, and I don't want to see any more of our men dead. My God, Gorthyk! Look what they've already given us! They deserve a chance to live."

The last sentence came out slowly, deliberately, and Nybar's face tightened. Father Charlz wasn't saying anything he hadn't already thought. His command was already lost, as far as the rest of the Army of God was concerned. Whether they were prisoners or dead, they would be equally off the field, yet in the brutal calculus of war, every heretic they killed would be one less to continue the attack afterward. It was a cold, despicable logic—the sort to appeal to a Zhaspahr Clyntahn—but that didn't mean it was *invalid* logic.

And if he did surrender . . . .

"I can't turn you and the other inquisitors over to them, Charlz," he said quietly. "I just can't."

"Much as I despise the heretics," Kaillyt told him, "Sahmyrsyt has a point. They gave us fair warning two years ago. We can't pretend—*I* can't pretend—we didn't see this coming, and the bitter truth is that it's far better for a handful of God's priests to die for Him than for an entire army to be put to the heretics' equivalent of the Punishment. And another truth is that if I were a heretic and truly believed I was obeying God's will, I'd be every bit as angry they are over how many of their fellow heretics have already suffered the Punishment." He shook his head, eyes dark. "I know it doesn't seem that way, but they really are being merciful if they're willing to settle for so little vengeance. And the *Writ* tells us Mother Church is sustained by the blood of martyrs. I have no more desire to die than the next man, but there are far worse ways—and far worse causes for which—a man could surrender his life."

"But I don't thin—"

A roll of thunder like the end of the world cut Nybar off in mid-syllable.

▼ ▼ ▼

A volcano blasted its bowels into the heavens.

It was larger and louder by far than the greatest, most deafening explosion any of the witnesses had ever imagined—ever *could* have imagined. The Lywysite-packed gallery disappeared into a vast mushroom-headed cloud and a crater over two hundred yards wide, four hundred yards long, east-to-west, and the next best thing to eighty feet deep. Of the six hundred infantrymen and seventy artillerists manning that stretch of works at the moment of detonation, seventeen survived; the others were either killed instantly, mortally wounded, or buried alive to die a slower and more terrifying death.

Unlike the Army of God, the Army of New Northland had known what was going to happen . . . and the Republic of Siddarmark Army's 2nd Rifle Division had awaited this day with hungry anticipation. They had a debt to settle with the Army of God and Zhaspahr Clyntahn, and so far, they'd had to watch their Charisian allies exact most of that debt's payment on their behalf. In fact, the fact that Sir Bartyn Sahmyrsyt knew exactly how they felt had driven much of his decision against allowing starvation to defeat Gorthyk Nybar's army without firing a shot. Time was of the essence, as well, but that had been only a part of the decision-making process, and not the largest one. It was essential to blood the new Siddarmarkian formations—to give them actual battlefield experience, and the confidence which went with it, with their new weapons and their new doctrine—just as it was essential to demonstrate to the Army of God that someone besides Charis was fully capable of demolishing it in battle. All of that was true, yet the bottom line was that Sahmyrsyt—and Cayleb Ahrmahk and Greyghor Stohnar—would have made exactly the same choice anyway.

It was time the Republic of Siddarmark Army got some of its own back.

Makgrygair had tasked his 1st and 3rd Brigade with the actual assault, with 2nd Brigade in reserve, and they'd begun their preparation over a month earlier, out of sight of Fairkyn's defenders. They'd rehearsed the attack no less than five times, although it had been impossible for them to accurately project the exact size and shape of the eventual crater, and the one thing their commanders had insisted upon again and again was the need to stay *out* of the crater itself. The mine was a means to an end, not an end in its own right. The very last thing the Army of New Northland needed was for the assault element to flow into the crater and attempt to use it as a defensive bridgehead rather than continuing to drive the attack aggressively home.

There were over four thousand men in each assault column, and they headed up the bluffs' steep slope, assisted by the debris which spilled down from the crater's lip. It was a hard, exhausting slog even with that assistance, but sixty six-inch angle-guns opened fire on the defensive positions to either side of the crater. The defenders in those positions were so stunned—physically, not simply mentally—by the stupendous force of the explosion and the almost equally sudden bombardment that the attackers had crossed the no-man's-land between besiegers and besieged and climbed the heights before Nybar's men could even consider any sort of organized response.

First Brigade was on the south, 3rd Brigade on the north. The guns went silent as they reached the top of the bluff into which the crater had been blown, and each brigade faced *away* from the crater. They swept outward with bayonets and grenades, bursting into the trenches which had been abruptly flanked. Rifles and pistols crackled spitefully, grenade explosions sent shrapnel into the faces of panicked, confused defenders, and those defenders crumbled.

There was nothing wrong with the Army of Fairkyn's courage, but its men were perpetually hungry and already oppressed by the knowledge that the siege could have only one ultimate outcome. Nor were even men prepared to sell their lives dearly in God's service immune to the effects of shock, cataclysmic violence, and surprise. At least half of them simply fled, falling back before the attack, seeking some fresh position where they might hope to reorganize and hold. Others dove into bunkers or dugouts, repeating the same instinctive mistake the St. Fraidyr Division had made at Esthyr's Abbey and Colonel Somyrs' regiment had made at

Five Forks . . . and with the same result. Grenades turned what should have been defensive strong points into slaughterhouses, and the assault stormed on past them.

By nightfall, half of the Army of Fairkyn's outer defenses were in Allied hands.

. VIII .
City of Zion,
The Temple Lands

"Yes, Your Eminence?" Bishop Markys Gohdard's tone was slightly surprised and he started to rise as Wyllym Rayno entered his office unannounced, but the archbishop waved him back into his swivel chair.

Gohdard was a distinguished-looking man, with elegantly groomed silver hair, blue eyes, and a taste for expensively tailored cassocks. He'd been a youth pastor many years ago and remained active in the Inquisition's youth outreach ministries even today, and he was a doting father of three whose eldest son had recently been ordained as an upper-priest in the Order of Schueler.

He was also the man in charge of Rayno's and Zhaspahr Clyntahn's personal security details, and he'd lost track long ago of how many of their potential—and personal—enemies he'd . . . dealt with.

"I'm sure you've heard rumors about Fairkyn by now," Rayno said without preamble and without even extending his ring of office to be kissed. His tone suggested that a man in Gohdard's position damned well should have heard them if he hadn't. "Well, they're true. Nybar surrendered two days ago. His last message reached Maigwair this morning—he got a carrier wyvern to Lake City and the semaphore sent it on from there—and that's probably where the rumors are coming from, but Maigwair still hasn't informed the Grand

Inquisitor of that tiny fact. In fact, he doesn't seem to have informed *anyone*."

Gohdard's eyes narrowed. He didn't ask how Rayno knew what had happened at Fairkyn, the better part of five thousand miles from Zion, if Maigwair hadn't informed anyone at all. It was the Inquisition's business to know things, and Gohdard was more familiar than most with the arrangements which made sure that happened. He simply sat, hands folded on his desk, waiting.

"The Grand Inquisitor is . . . perturbed by the Captain General's silence on this minor matter," Rayno continued. "He feels it may indicate a certain dereliction of duty, or even something more serious. Because of that, he feels it's time to begin considering all of Mother Church's options where her Army is concerned. Accordingly, he's decided to convene a meeting of a small, select group to begin that process."

He extracted a folded sheet of paper from a cassock pocket and extended it to Gohdard. The bishop unfolded it, and only his many years of experience prevented him from pursing his lips in a silent whistle as he scanned the fifteen names written on it. There were nine vicars on the list—the other six were archbishops—and all of them had been closely associated with planning for or actively organizing the Army of God. At least seven of the vicars were personal friends of Allayn Maigwair and four of them sat on the Council of Vicars' Army Oversight Committee. All of the archbishops headed or sat on various sub-committees associated with manning and managing the Army of God and Navy of God, and three of them had been Maigwair's protégés prior to the Jihad.

"This needs to be handled discreetly," Rayno said. Gohdard looked back up, one eyebrow arched, and his superior smiled thinly. "I'm afraid Vicar Allayn is unaware that all of the men on that list have quietly—and privately—assured Vicar Zhaspahr of their loyalty to Mother Church. Not all of *them* are aware the others have done so either, however, and the Grand Inquisitor believes it's time they were made aware of one another's positions vis-à-vis the Army—and its command structure—and the high regard in which he personally holds each of them. Under the circumstances, it might be best to find a venue outside the Temple in which they might convene for a quiet gathering under Vicar Stauntyn's guidance. One in which he might acquaint them with the many difficult but necessary decisions which may have to be made in Mother Church's name."

"I understand, Your Eminence."

Gohdard bent his head in a seated bow and laid the list of names on his blotter. Stauntyn Waimyan had been one of Zhaspahr Clyntahn's allies on the Council of Vicars long before the Jihad. Gohdard was fairly confident that Waimyan's loyalty to the Grand Inquisitor had less to do with principle than with the sorts of deals, debts, and secrets which fueled so many of the vicarate's relationships. What mattered in this case, however, was that his name wasn't on the list Rayno had just handed him, because Vicar Stauntyn had never had a hand in the creation of the Army of God. He knew nothing at all about strategy, tactics, logistics, or recruiting. In fact, Gohdard was none too sure Waimyan even knew what a bayonet was or what a soldier was supposed to do with one of them! If he was supposed to "guide" this meeting, he'd be there as Zhaspahr Clyntahn's personal representative, and every other man on that list would know it. Any message or instructions he delivered would come straight from Clyntahn . . . with the advantage that Clyntahn wouldn't have to deliver them personally.

And any instructions Zhaspahr Clyntahn delivered to *this* group could only be the first step towards removing Maigwair from his offices. And since the vicar was a member of the Group of Four, he would have to be removed both very publicly and for rather . . . spectacular cause. Something which would justify the Grand Vicar acting swiftly, unilaterally, and above all decisively, in a way which made it clear this was not a case of simple factionalism or the elimination of someone who'd become a rival for power but a decision forced upon him by his supreme responsibility to Mother Church and the Jihad. That sort of cause would just happen to require the sort of punishment which would dissuade anyone else—and especially anyone in the Army who might have delusions of loyalty to the fallen vicar—from following in Maigwair's tracks. Setting the stage for that would require some delicate maneuvering, and if the vicars and archbishops on Rayno's list were unaware that all of them were Zhaspahr Clyntahn's men, getting them together somewhere out of the public eye while they got their marching orders—and making sure all of them had those orders *straight*—had much to recommend it.

"Will you be attending, Your Eminence?" the bishop asked.

"No." Rayno shook his head. "Under the circumstances, Vicar Zhaspahr's of the opinion that it would be unwise for me to drop out of sight at a time like this. He believes Vicar Allayn might draw an unwarranted conclusion if I seemed to be evading him. In fact, he intends to call for a meeting with Vicar Allayn, Vicar Rhobair, and Vicar Zahmsyn—at which I'll be in attendance—to discuss the situation in New Northland and Hildermoss. I'd appreciate knowing how quickly you'll be able to arrange this matter—" a tiny finger flick indicated the list of names on Gohdard's desk "—so that we can set a time for that meeting."

"Of course, Your Eminence. I'll try to have that information for you by this afternoon. Will that be soon enough?"

"It will indeed. In that case, I'll leave you to your duties."

This time, Rayno did extend his ring hand, and Gohdard stood and bowed across his desk to kiss it.

▼ ▼ ▼

"Excuse me, Your Grace."

Zhaspahr Clyntahn looked up from the memo he'd been dictating with a flicker of annoyance. He hated being interrupted, but the annoyance vanished quickly as he saw Wyllym Rayno's expression.

"A moment, Father," he said to the secretary, and pointed at his office door. "We'll finish that after I've dealt with whatever brings Archbishop Wyllym here. I'm sure it won't take long."

"Of course, Your Grace," the under-priest murmured. He withdrew with a courteous and respectful bow to both of his superiors, and Clyntahn sat back.

"Well?"

"Markys has submitted his recommendation to me, Your Grace. Before I approve it, I thought it best to get your view on it."

"Well?" the Grand Inquisitor repeated a bit more impatiently.

"Markys suggests Second Pasquale's as the venue, Your Grace. He believes it would lend itself well to security, from several perspectives, and if the location is agreeable, he proposes to arrange the meeting itself for early tomorrow afternoon. He was thinking of about fifteen o'clock so that none of them would be conspicuous by their absence during luncheon."

Clyntahn frowned, not in disapproval but thoughtfully.

Second Pasquale's—more formally known as the Second Church of the Holy Pasquale of the Faithful of Zion to differentiate it from the original, older, and more prestigious Church of the Holy Pasquale of the Faithful of Zion—was located several blocks outside the Temple's precincts in a relatively quiet area of Zion. Despite the fact that it lay outside the Temple proper, however, its location backed up against a section of townhouses and luxurious apartment buildings in which many of the archbishops and senior bishops too junior for quarters in the Temple itself had their lodgings. As such, primary responsibility for security in its vicinity had become the business of the Inquisition rather than the Temple Guard over the last two or three years.

He could have wished for a little more physical separation from the Temple, yet he understood the advantages which had drawn Gohdard to that location. The vicars and archbishops should find it relatively simple to arrive at Second Pasquale's without drawing attention to their movements, and the Inquisition already controlled the patrols in the area. Gohdard would have no problem clamping the necessary tight security into place.

"That sounds reasonable," he said after a few moments' consideration. "Tell him I approve. Then inform Waimyan that he's to dine with me tonight. He and I need to go over exactly what needs to happen."

"At once, Your Grace." Rayno bowed slightly. "Should I also inform Vicar Allayn and the others that you need to meet with them after lunch tomorrow?"

"No." Clyntahn shook his head. "I don't want that bastard to get even a sniff that anything special is going on. I'll have one of my clerks draft the invitations this afternoon and send them through the regular channels." He smiled coldly. "Given the debacle in New Northland, I don't imagine any of the others will find it too difficult to set aside a little time on their calendar."

▼ ▼ ▼

Father Elaryn Ohraily sat on the bench while he finished his wyvern breast sandwich. It was a bright day and he was grateful for the sunlight's warmth—anemic though it might still be this early in June in Zion—yet he frowned ever so slightly as he wiped his lips with his napkin. This meeting was supposed to be . . . inconspicuous. Bishop Markys had made that abundantly clear. No one had explained why that was so important, but Ohraily hadn't served the Inquisition for fifteen years without understanding the need to keep secrets closely held. He'd also recognized at least six vicars among the participants who'd already arrived, and he understood security needed to be tight for such exalted individuals, particularly given the Fist of Kau-Yung's recent activities. He wasn't supposed to have heard about that affair at St. Evyryt's, but he'd been one of Bishop Markys' senior troubleshooters for almost ten years now. There were very few things he didn't hear about eventually.

So, yes, he understood the need for a strong security cordon, but if they were going to be "inconspicuous," the guards needed to be a bit less obvious.

He rose from the bench where he'd been calmly eating his lunch, tucked his napkin into his lunch sack, and strolled across the tiny tunic-pocket park, beer bottle still in hand, toward one of the people who were supposed to be looking inconspicuous. He paused behind the other man, examining the blossoms on a flowering shrub, and cleared his throat quietly.

"Yes, Father?" Major Walysh Zhu said politely, turning to face him.

Well, at least he hadn't come to attention or saluted, Ohraily thought. That was something.

"Major," he said, trying not to sound overly patient as he abandoned his examination of the shrubbery, "we're not supposed to draw attention to the church."

"Yes, Father. I know that."

Zhu was a shortish, blocky man who'd probably just turned forty or so. He was also a Harchongian, very devout and very orthodox, who'd spent half his life in the Temple Guard. That made him a treasure in the Inquisition's eyes, and it had called upon his services more than once in the past, but in some ways he was a very blunt instrument of a treasure.

"In that case," Ohraily said, "could you please ask your men not to stand in such neat, militarily correct lines? They're supposed to be . . . scattered. That's why they're in civilian clothing, so that they can stand around, enjoy the shade, admire the flowers," his tone hardened very slightly on the last three words, "be having a casual conversation—that sort of thing. Anything besides being obvious sentries stationed around the church."

The major's face tightened for just a moment, but

then he nodded. His right hand twitched as if he'd forcibly restrained the reflex to salute.

"I'll have a word with them, shall I, Father?"

"I think that would be a splendid idea," Ohraily congratulated him.

He watched the major move off, then returned to his original bench and pulled his personal copy of the *Holy Writ* out of his cassock pocket, found his place, and began scanning the familiar words with a tiny corner of his attention while the rest of it kept watch over the Second Church of the Holy Pasquale of the Faithful of Zion.

▼ ▼ ▼

"Well, this is a fine mess," Zhaspahr Clyntahn observed sourly. He looked around the conference table and his gaze settled on Allayn Maigwair. "Took you long enough to tell the rest of us about Fairkyn, didn't it, Allayn?"

"The entire situation in New Northland and Hildermoss is in turmoil," Maigwair replied more calmly than Clyntahn had anticipated. "I'm getting all sorts of reports, at least half of which are wholly inaccurate and another quarter of which are wildly exaggerated. If you'll recall, I warned everyone that Wyrshym wouldn't be able to hold his position if we didn't withdraw him. I believe I also mentioned Fairkyn was already gone, for all intents and purposes. So, yes, I did take the time to try to confirm Nybar's dispatch before I distributed it. If you've read through that, Zhaspahr," he gestured at the folder on the conference table in front of the Grand Inquisitor, "then you know I sent you not only his original message but also the best estimate I could put together of everything *else* happening in that theater yesterday afternoon."

"Yes, you did," Clyntahn conceded in that same sour tone. "I don't see any explanation in here of why Wyrshym decided to violate his orders to stand fast, however. Which he obviously did."

"Zhaspahr, we've already been over that entire situation," Rhobair Duchairn put in. The Grand Inquisitor glowered at him, and the Treasurer shrugged. "I know the Army of the Sylmahn was ordered to hold its positions no matter what. I think it's obvious from the sheer weight of the attack, however, that Wyrshym *couldn't* have held his forward positions for more than a day or two no matter what he did, and it's not as if he ordered his entire army to retreat. Surely he was justified in trying to save at least *something* out of the wreckage."

"Not when neither he nor his intendant ever suggested they meant to do anything of the sort he wasn't," Clyntahn said harshly. He held out one meaty hand, and Wyllym Rayno placed another, much thicker folder in it. "In fact, that's what disturbs me the most. I'm not happy with Wyrshym, and I'm not delighted with the fact that Allayn here didn't keep him on a short enough rein to prevent something like this from happening. But what actually concerns me more is that Bishop Ernyst didn't breathe a hint of any of this to *me*, either. This isn't just a case of Wyrshym falling back too precipitously, Rhobair. It looks like it's a case of active *collusion* between him and his intendant—collusion aimed at keeping his superiors, you, me, Zhasyn, and Allayn—ignorant of their intentions, and that cuts at the very heart of the reason our commanders have intendants."

He opened the folder and began handing out paperclipped copies of semaphore dispatches.

"I submit we *all* have a problem here," he continued, "and it's one we'd better get a grip on quickly. If I'm right, then I obviously didn't have Abernethy on a tight enough rein, either, did I?" The corner of his eye noted the surprise Maigwair couldn't quite hide as his reasonable tone registered. "These are copies of the last reports he filed with my office. I'd like to go over them with all three of you, because I think we can all agree that if we have field commanders who really are making private arrangements with their intendants without our knowledge, we need to put a stop to it *now*."

▼ ▼ ▼

Major Zhu's guards still looked like guards, but at least they looked *less* like guards, Father Elaryn reflected wryly. His own agents inquisitor did a far better job of projecting their harmlessness; even so, if he was going to be honest, there were too many of them standing around to be totally unobtrusive.

Well, Bishop Markys had been around the block a time or two. No doubt he'd realized from the beginning that no one could put guards around a church in the middle of Zion without anyone at all noticing that he'd done it. On the other hand, there were guards around at least two dozen of the city's churches at this very moment, for one reason or another, so there was nothing to draw *special* attention to Second Pasquale's.

At least all of the attendees had arrived. Vicar Stauntyn had put in his appearance last, of course. That was only to be expected of someone of his seniority. Especially if, as Ohraily suspected from one or two things Father Byrtrym had carefully *not* said, none of the others had known he was coming in the first place. No one had told Ohraily how long this gathering was supposed to run, either, but he rather suspected he'd be sitting down to a late supper. A meeting of such senior prelates, especially at this particular time, wasn't going to race through its work and—

The Second Church of the Holy Pasquale of the Faithful of Zion disappeared in a mind-numbing roar that fountained fire, shattered stone, and dust into the peaceful afternoon sky.

. IX .
HMS *Thunderer*, 30,
Kaudzhu Narrows,
and
HMS *Dreadnought*, 30,
South Shwei Bay,
Shwei Province,
Harchong Empire

"Thank you, Mahrak. I think that's all we'll need for a while. Leave the teapot, and I'll call for you if I need you."

"Of course, Sir Bruhstair."

Mahrak Sahndyrs came briefly to attention, nodded respectfully to both Captain Ahbaht and Lieutenant Kylmahn, and withdrew, leaving the pot behind. Lieutenant Kylmahn looked as if he might be in two minds about that. Ahbaht, like quite a lot of Emeraldians, preferred cherrybean tea, made from the roasted and ground seeds of the cherrybean tree. Kylmahn couldn't deny that cherrybean did a much better job of keeping him awake than hot chocolate or most of the other teas he'd ever tried, but he really couldn't understand why Sir Bruhstair and the other cherrybean gourmands liked its *taste*. Personally, he preferred to bury it under copious quantities of cream and sugar.

Ahbaht smiled slightly, thoroughly aware of his first lieutenant's views on the subject of cherrybean, and poured two cups. He passed one across the breakfast table to Kylmahn, then sat back with his own.

"We should raise Cape Longzhi by the turn of the watch," he remarked.

"Assuming the wind holds, Sir," the first lieutenant agreed as he began spooning powdered milk into his cup.

Ahbaht tried not to shudder. He'd never understood

why so many people insisted on adulterating cherry-bean with milk or cream, and—unlike most mariners—he'd never developed a taste for dried milk, anyway. Others might insist that it tasted just like fresh milk and be glad to get it after five-days or months at sea, but Sir Bruhstair Ahbaht wasn't one of them. He was glad it was available to help satisfy the dictates of Pasquale's Law, he'd drink it when he absolutely had to, and he was grateful to the Archangel for teaching men how it was made, yet the rotating heated drums on which the liquid was evaporated always left a bit of an off taste, in his opinion. It was true the Imperial Charisian Navy insisted on first-quality dried milk, without any of the browning which resulted if it was left on the evaporating drums too long before being scraped off, which improved its taste considerably, but not enough that he would ever dream of contaminating perfectly good cherrybean with it!

"I could wish for a bit more of a breeze myself," he acknowledged, his voice tranquil despite the barbarity before him as Kylmahn added sugar to the powdered milk and began gently stirring the light-brown brew.

At the moment, the squadron was spreading out a bit again in a light topgallant breeze and *Thunderer* was making good no more than a knot and a half with all sail set to the royals. The wavelets were short and glassy, without any break, banners and streamers flapped halfheartedly, and the sun beat down mercilessly. The weather was atypical for this time of year, to say the very least, and it was all Ahbaht could do to project the semblance of serenity required from a captain. They were eleven days out of Talisman Island, passing through the narrows between South Shwei Bay and Hahskyn Bay, and by his original timetable, they should have reached Ki-dau by tomorrow morning. At their current rate of progress, it would take them another four days.

And if it did take them four more days . . . .

He watched Kylmahn sip his so-called cherrybean tea with apparent pleasure and shook his head.

"If we don't get a better wind than this by midday tomorrow, I'm turning back," he said.

Kylmahn stopped sipping and lowered his cup, eyes suddenly intent, and Ahbaht smiled humorlessly.

"The last thing anyone needs is for me to go plowing onward like a gambler shoving his last pile of marks onto the table in hopes of throwing triple-six, Daivyn. If we can't get to Symarkhan before the screw-galleys do, there's no point going at all, and I'm not a lot more eager about facing them even out here on the bay without more wind in my pocket than this. That might not be the proper attitude for a captain imbued with true derring-do, but personally, I'd rather bring the squadron back intact."

"I don't think you'll hear any argument out of me about that, Sir," Kylmahn replied. "The men will be disappointed, though." He shook his head affectionately. "They're Charisians, you know, even the Chisholmians and the Emeraldians amongst them—no offense intended, Sir."

"None taken," Ahbaht said affably. He sipped cherrybean. "After all, at some point all that salt in you Old Charisians' blood always seems to dry up your brains. It does seem to happen more quickly among first lieutenants than to anybody else, though, doesn't it?"

"Ouch!" Kylmahn raised his free hand in the fencer's gesture which acknowledged a touch. "I suppose I had that coming, Sir."

"You suppose correctly. On the other hand, you have a point. They *aren't* going to be happy if we turn around and 'run for home.' Even the ones who understand why we're doing it are going to be pissed off, and I imagine they'll be just a *bit* grumpy about it. Still, I'd rather have them feeling pissed off because they're too aggressive than relieved because they're too timid!"

"Oh, I don't think that's something you need to worry about very much, Sir."

▼ ▼ ▼

"Any more sign of that damned schooner, Dahnyld?"

Lieutenant Stahdmaiyr looked up quickly, the sunlight through the open skylight flashing brief silver off the lenses of his spectacles, as Captain Haigyl stepped back into his day cabin from HMS *Dreadnought*'s sternwalk.

"No, Sir. Not since last night," the lieutenant replied and gestured at the chart he'd been updating. "I've laid in our current position. Master Gyllmyn and I concur that we're about eighty miles from the mouth of the Narrows."

Haigyl nodded. His own navigation skills were more than adequate ... but not a *lot* more than adequate. Both Stahdmaiyr and Ahlahnzo Gyllmyn, *Dreadnought*'s sailing master, were more proficient at it than he, and he was confident enough in their ability—and in his own judgment of their ability—to trust the positions they gave him. Not that Stahdmaiyr's estimate made him happy.

Wind conditions could vary widely even over relatively short distances; every sailor knew that, and it was entirely possible Bruhstair Ahbaht's squadron had already reached its destination, carried out its attack, and headed home. By the same token, it was possible *Dreadnought* had made up so much time that his lookouts would spot Ahbaht's topsails before lunch. The *probability*, however, lay somewhere between those two extremes, and he wasn't happy about the schooner whose topsails those same lookouts had spotted the evening before.

He stepped up beside Stahdmaiyr, rubbing the patch over his left eye socket as he considered the chart. He'd already decided that if he reached Ki-dau after Ahbaht had headed upriver, he wasn't going to follow. Instead, he'd lie off the estuary's mouth, watching Ahbaht's back and not getting his own ship tangled up in the narrow channels, mudbanks, and potential groundings of a river. The truth was, he was perfectly content to leave that sort of business to the undersized Emeraldian.

But that schooner . . . . That schooner bothered him.

Even a Harchongian should recognize a Charisian warship's lofty rig, yet the schooner had held its course, following along in *Dreadnought*'s wake until darkness fell. No merchant skipper would have done that, although, to be fair, the chance of the ironclad's turning around and overtaking a schooner in these weather conditions didn't exist. So maybe he was being too paranoid. Maybe a merchant skipper *would* tag along, see where the Charisian warship in question was going and what it was up to before turning and running for port somewhere. But he didn't think so. He couldn't have said why, but he didn't think so.

"Make sure the lookouts keep their eyes peeled," he said, still rubbing his eye patch and frowning at the chart. "If that lad has friends along up to windward, I want to know about it."

"Aye, Sir." Stahdmaiyr nodded soberly. "I'll do that thing."

. X .

## Cliff Peak Province, Republic of Siddarmark

"—still got one brigade moving to the front, but Rhandyl and Brigadier Dahmbryk'll have everything buttoned up right and tight between 'em by the time I get back there," Ahlyn Symkyn said. "Truth to tell, I'd not've thought we'd be this close to ready this close to on time."

"Most battle plans work just fine until the enemy turns up, Ahlyn," Ruhsyl Thairis pointed out. The Duke of Eastshare stood at the enormous table, looking down at the contour map his staff cartographers had constructed out of papier-mâché. Green-headed pins indicating the positions of three Allied armies stood out of it like clustered rows of strange topiaries, spread wide in a rough crescent reaching towards the elongated clump of sullen red-topped pins representing the Army of Glacierheart. "I'm rather fond of the one we've worked out in Kaitswyrth's honor, but it *is* a bit complicated."

"Not so much complicated as just . . . large, Your Grace," Sir Breyt Bahskym, the Earl of High Mount, observed. "I don't believe anyone's ever tried to coordinate the attack of over three hundred thousand men across a front more than eighty miles wide. Bound to be a little slippage in there somewhere. In fact, I'll guarantee there's some we don't know about right this minute and more we won't find out about till months after."

"You're always such a comfort to me, Breyt," Eastshare observed, and the other two army commanders chuckled.

The relationship was good, the duke thought—immeasurably better than the internal dogfight the Church's Army of Shiloh had turned into last winter. Symkyn had been born a commoner and might well die that way; the Bahskym family had held the High Mount title since the founding of the Kingdom of Chisholm; his own father had earned the Duchy of Eastshare less than forty years ago, fighting for King Sailys against his own distant kinsman; yet there was none of the supercilious jockeying for position which had wracked the Army of Shiloh's command structure.

Or, for that matter, he thought far less happily, that marked the attitude of far too many of Chisholm's present nobles when it came to matters political. He didn't much care for what Sir Fraizher Kahlyns' latest dispatches from home had to say about certain well-born gentlemen in southwestern Chisholm. On the other hand, those dispatches had taken the best part of three five-days to reach him, even with the Raven's Land semaphore chain back up and running. Lots of things could have happened in that much time, and, he reminded himself firmly, there wasn't one damned thing he could do about whatever might have.

"I'm sure you're right about the slippage," he continued out loud, "and the truth is, we don't have to co-ordinate things perfectly. Whatever happens, we're going to be a hell of a lot smoother than the bastards on the other side, and I'll put our regimental and company commanders up against any general that fat prick in Zion can come up with!"

The others bared their teeth, obviously as grateful as Eastshare himself for Zhaspahr Clyntahn's interference in the Army of God's internal organization. The results produced by that sort of meddling had revealed themselves only too clearly in the Army of Shiloh's disintegration, and he supposed it was greedy of them to hope for still more of the same. He didn't intend to rely on their getting it, either, but all indications to date—from his own patrols, as well as the *seijins*' spy reports, not to mention his own experience against the Army of Glacierheart the previous fall—suggested that Kaitswyrth was as big a disaster waiting to happen as the Duke of Harless had been. And he was clearly *Clyntahn's* choice at this point, not Maigwair's. Every single spy report agreed on that, and Eastshare had spent many a night thanking God for it.

"Well, I suppose it's time the two of you got back to your own headquarters," he said. "If anything slips—anything major, I mean—on the schedule, let me know by semaphore and I'll adjust from here if that seems necessary. Use your own judgment deciding if anything's that important." Symkyn and High Mount nodded, and he nodded back. "In that case—"

"'Scuse me, Your Grace," a voice said . . . with rather more diffidence than it usually used addressing Eastshare. He turned to find himself facing Corporal Slym Chalkyr, his batman of far too many years. Chalkyr was the only man besides his personal aide, Captain Lywys Braynair, who would have dared to interrupt a meeting of six generals, eight brigadiers, five colonels, and all their aides, and Braynair was already in the group gathered around the map table. Anyone other than Chalkyr would have anticipated being annihilated on the spot, but very few things fazed Slym Chalkyr, and Eastshare knew he wouldn't have interrupted on a whim.

"Yes, Slym?"

"Beggin' your pardon, Your Grace, but Archbishop Zhasyn's here."

Eastshare's eyebrows rose, but he only nodded.

"Give the Archbishop my respects and ask him if he'd care to join us."

"Aye, Your Grace."

Chalkyr disappeared. A few moments later, the door opened again, and Zhasyn Cahnyr stepped through it.

"My Lord," Eastshare said with a slight bow, then bent to kiss the bishop's extended ring. "This is an unexpected pleasure. I didn't expect to see you until day after tomorrow."

"I finished the current round of the paperchase earlier than I'd expected, Your Grace," Cahnyr said, "and the roads are much better—muddy, but otherwise better—than the last time I visited the front. I didn't expect to get here myself before General Symkyn and General High Mount returned to their own commands, but I hoped I might." He smiled at the other two generals and raised a hand, signing Langhorne's scepter in a general benediction for the three dozen officers around the table. Then his expression sobered. "On the eve of such an endeavor, I very much wanted the opportunity to speak to all of you briefly, if I may."

"Of course you may, My Lord. Please—it would be our honor."

"That's gracious of you, as always, Your Grace, but the truth is that the honor is mine." The archbishop let his eyes track across the gathered officers and his voice was as serious as his gaze. "If not for you and your countrymen, Duke Eastshare, Kaitswyrth and his army would have swept across Glacierheart last summer, and we know from what happened at Aivahnstyn what would have happened in Glacierheart, as well. Thousands of my parishioners—and I—owe our lives to Brigadier Taisyn . . . and you. And now you're going to take the offensive back to Kaitswyrth, and after him to all the other butchers Zhaspahr Clyntahn's launched at the throat of the world. I've followed the semaphore reports. I know what's already happened to the Army of the Sylmahn, and I know—I *know*, my sons— what you and your men, your Charisians and the Siddarmarkians serving with them, will soon do to the 'Army of Glacierheart.' But I also know that however superior your weapons, however superior your men, you are about to pay a price in blood to liberate soil that was never yours. For that, 'gratitude' is far too small and shabby a word."

"My Lord, half of Brigadier Taisyn's force was Siddarmarkian," Eastshare said after a moment into the silence Cahnyr's words had produced, "and your own Glacierheart Volunteers fought superbly before, during, and after the assault on Fort Tairys. They and General Wyllys' division will be at the heart of this fight, as well, right beside us, and while we may be about to liberate *Siddarmarkian* soil, this is as much or more *our* battle than it could ever be yours. As you say, Clyntahn launched his butchers against the whole world, against every single one of God's children who refused to bow down and worship him instead of God or the Archangels. We know that. Our *men* know that, and none of us will stop or turn aside until the sort of corruption which has poisoned Mother Church at her very heart can never happen again."

"As your Emperor said," Cahnyr murmured, "'Here you stand,' Your Grace."

"His Majesty is more eloquent than I am. He has a much better way with words. But, yes, My Lord. Here we stand."

"In that case, may I send all of you back to your duties with my prayers?"

"We would be honored, My Lord."

Heads bent all around the map table, and Cahnyr sketched the scepter once again and raised both hands.

"O God, Creator and Judge of all that is, has been, and ever shall be, look down upon these Your servants, called to the stern task of war against the captors of Your Holy Church. Be with them in the hurricane as they take up the sword against Your enemies. Guide them, inspire them, *guard* them. Bless the strength of their arms, the courage of their hearts, and lead them to victory in Your name and in defense of all Your children. Fill them with fortitude as they face the test of battle, and inspire them to remember that true justice resides in mercy, not brute vengeance. Be with them in the furnace, gather those who may fall into Your loving arms, and give Your comfort to those who loved them. And finally, as the Archangel Chihiro prayed so many centuries ago, You know how busy they must be in the coming days about Your work. If they forget You, do not You, O Lord, forget them. Amen."

▼ ▼ ▼

Bishop Militant Cahnyr Kaitswyrth pushed back the light blanket, sat up, and swung his legs over the edge of the cot. He stood, stretching and yawning, then rubbed the small of his back. The funny thing was, the camp cot was actually more comfortable than the soft, luxurious bed he'd left behind in Aivahnstyn.

He smiled, but the amusement was brief as he reflected on why he'd left Aivahnstyn. He didn't trust the reports from his own scouts, for a lot of reasons. For one thing, too many of them said exactly the same thing day after day, and that same thing described a uniform lack of activity on the heretics' part. The main reason for that . . . unvarying report, he suspected, was that none of his scouts were willing to push home a reconnaissance effort against the heretics. In some ways it was hard to blame them, given the casualties they suffered whenever they ran their noses into the heretics' accursed scout snipers or the Kau-yungs the heretics left strewn in their wake. But there was a reason the heretics were so determined to prevent him from getting a look at whatever was gathering behind their lines, and he was grimly certain of what that reason was.

He knew Allayn Maigwair was skeptical of the

numbers he was reporting in his front, and if the Captain General knew how his scouts' aggressiveness had suffered, it was hard to fault his skepticism. For that matter, Kaitswyrth was unhappily aware that all of his estimates were based on the flimsiest possible pieces of information. His own strength was almost 220,000 men, supported by over a thousand guns, yet whether anyone in Zion believed him or not, he knew—*knew*—there had to be at least twice that many, more probably three times as many, men and guns on the other side. And the roads were clear. The high roads were in only too good a condition, and even the secondary roads' mud was beginning to dry. It couldn't be long before—

He made himself draw a deep breath, backing away from the familiar paths worry and concern had worn through his brain, like a hamster racing around and around its exercise wheel. If it happened, it happened, he told himself, and Father Sedryk was right. They *were* God's warriors, and God would not suffer Himself to be defeated in the end, whatever transitory victories Shan-wei and her followers might win.

His jaw tightened with resolution, and he reached for the bedside bell to summon his servant. Dawn was still two hours away; there was plenty of time for breakfast before another round of inspections of front-line positions, and—

Thunder rumbled, and Kaitswyrth frowned. The sky had been clear when he'd turned in, and it was early in the year for a thunderstorm. Besides—

More thunder rumbled—a *lot* more—and a sudden cold stab of apprehension went through him. Surely that couldn't be . . . ?

He dropped the bell and charged barefoot across the outer area of his command tent. He threw back the flaps and charged out onto the hilltop . . . and froze, staring southeast, as the entire rim of the world blazed with light.

▼ ▼ ▼

Cahnyr Kaitswyrth had hugely overestimated the total numbers of the three armies aligned against him, yet his count on artillery had actually been low. Ruhsyl Thairis hadn't deployed three thousand guns against him; he'd deployed almost *five* thousand, thirteen hundred of them six-inch angle-guns. And that didn't even count the three-thousand-plus mortars assigned to his brigades and regiments.

No one in the history of Safehold had ever seen or imagined or *dreamed* of the huge, brilliant tongues of flame leaping from the muzzles of over a thousand heavy guns. They blazed against the blackness of the predawn dark, hurling their glowing skeins of shells in an endless cascade of lightning bolts, lacing the heavens with livid fire. The sky above them burned, set alight by the incandescent, smoke-spewing fury of their rage, and then those shells came plummeting down to explode upon the earth.

Illuminating rockets soared from the Charisian front lines, streaking across no-man's-land to burst in brilliance above the Army of Glacierheart's forward positions. Their glare stripped away the night, revealing the entrenchments to pitiless eyes, and signal lanterns glowed like blink lizards. Corrections for the fall of shot flickered to the rear . . . just as the heavy mortars dug in behind those same frontline positions added their own wrath to the fiery sledgehammer smashing down upon the Army of God with absolutely no advance warning.

Craters blasted themselves into the shuddering earth. Trees flew apart, adding their own lethal splinters to the tempest seething across the entrenchments and dugouts. Men who'd been mustering for breakfast screamed in agony as blast and shell fragments ripped through fragile flesh, and the men who'd planned that bombardment had paid special attention to the artillery emplacements marked on their maps. Those maps had been compiled and updated by their own observers and patrols and corroborated by *Seijin* Ahbraim's agents' reports, and an avalanche of destruction crashed over them.

From where he stood, Cahnyr Kaitswyrth could see only a tiny fragment of the chaos and the confusion and the death. But as he stood on that hilltop and stared at that blazing sky, as he saw the fountains of fire marching across his entrenchments and felt the earth itself trembling in terror underfoot, he knew he looked into the fiery maw of Shan-wei herself.

And it was coming for his army.

## . XI .
## The Temple,
## City of Zion,
## The Temple Lands

Rhobair Duchairn looked up from the paperwork he'd spread across his end of the conference table as Zhaspahr Clyntahn finally arrived. The Treasurer wiped the nib of his pen, recapped his ink bottle, then gathered up his notes and jogged them neatly together while Clyntahn strode to his own chair, dropped his briefcase heavily on the floor beside it, and flung himself into its embrace.

One of Duchairn's eyebrows rose ever so slightly as Wyllym Rayno followed Clyntahn into the conference chamber. It was unusual for Rayno to attend a meeting of the Group of Four, although he'd done it upon occasion in the past. And given the current situation, Duchairn supposed he really shouldn't have been surprised to see him here today.

*Still*, he thought, studying the Archbishop of Chiang-wu's expressionless face, *the fact that he is here says interesting things about the probable state of Zhaspahr's mind.*

"I suppose we should go ahead and get started," Zahmsyn Trynair said after a moment. The chancellor's once smooth voice had become increasingly tentative over the last couple of years, like the blade of a master swordsman who'd lost his surety and balance . . . and knew it. Now there was an actual quaver at its core, and his hands played nervously with his pectoral scepter.

"I agree," Allayn Maigwair said crisply. Unlike Trynair or Clyntahn, the overwhelming emotion in Maigwair's voice was neither confusion nor fear; it was anger, and that same anger blazed in his eyes. "I'm sure I have another mountain of semaphore reports already waiting for me. I'd just as soon not let it get any taller before I get back."

"Under the circumstances, I don't see a great deal you can do to improve the situation from here," Clyntahn said a bit spitefully, and Maigwair turned a flat, level gaze upon him.

"I don't try to tell you how to run the Inquisition, Zhaspahr. Perhaps we might all be doing just a tiny bit better if you'd return the compliment and let *me* run the Army without constantly interfering."

Clyntahn's head snapped up, his expression as astonished as if a cat-lizard had turned into a slash lizard and launched itself at his throat, and even Duchairn blinked in surprise.

"Yes, we're getting hammered . . . again," the Captain General continued. "The heretics pounded the piss out of Kaitswyrth's main positions with a hell of a lot more guns—and heavier ones—than the Inquisition told us they had. They taught us another lesson in using them, and Kaitswyrth's falling back all across his front. He's trying to put a good face on it, and I think his men really are fighting hard, but there's no use pretending he isn't getting the crap kicked out of him. But from the sound of things, he's got a new line stabilizing—maybe—along some of the rivers west of his original position and the damned heretics seem to be—*seem* to be—finding it hard to drag their frigging guns forward to deal with that. I'm not happy about his flanks, and I've warned him to watch out for those Chihiro-damned Charisian dragoons, but he's a long way from dead, and he spent half the winter mining the locks in the Daivyn and the Charayn Canal all the way back into Westmarch. They're going to push him back; that's a given, since we can't get any of the Harchongians there in time to support his present positions, and I'm not going to spin any fairy tales about it. I don't know how much of his army will be intact by the time he's as far back as Lake Langhorne, and I'm not making any optimistic predictions about *that*, either. But I'll guarantee you those mines *will* be blown. Whatever else, Eastshare won't be barging any troops or supplies up the rivers and canals after him while he retreats!"

"And your point is?" Clyntahn's answering anger over the dig at the Inquisition's fresh intelligence failure was obvious. "Excuse me for pointing this out, but you're in the process of losing *another* fucking army, aren't you? Would it happen that any of your commanders have any intention of ever *winning* a goddamned battle?!"

The Grand Inquisitor seemed to have forgotten whose choice to command the Army of Glacierheart Cahnyr Kaitswyrth had originally been, Duchairn observed. For that matter, he seemed oblivious to his systematic efforts to block Maigwair's desire to replace Kaitswyrth after the previous summer's debacle. From the Captain General's expression, *his* memory was excellent, but he didn't rise to the bait, if that was what it was.

"The Army of the Sylmahn and the Army of Glacierheart were never the only forces we had in the field, Zhaspahr," he said instead, icily. "There's Teagmahn and Symmyns, just for starters, plus Rainbow Waters' entire army. Even assuming Kaitswyrth's estimate of the numbers against him was accurate—which I damned well don't think it was—and taking the worst-case estimate for *everything* reported in New Northland and Mountaincross, plus everything Hanth has in the South March, the heretics—Charis and Siddarmark combined—have no more than six hundred to seven hundred thousand men in the field right this minute. The Harchongians have over a million, with another four hundred and fifty thousand plus following along behind them, *plus* the seven hundred thousand men we're raising right here in the Temple Lands and the new regiments Dohlar's raising while we're talking. Not only that, but we've got a hell of a lot more rifles and artillery—not to mention Brother Lynkyn's rockets—coming out of the foundries now, so we'll actually be able to *arm* all those new troops within three or four months."

The Captain General shook his head, his eyes grim.

"They've hurt us, and it's going to get worse. But Kaitswyrth's not dead yet, we have an enormous defensive depth, we'll wreck the canals in their faces every mile of the way to slow them down, and the Harchongians are directly between them and the shortest route to Zion. No, Zhaspahr—this Jihad's far from lost, and I'd like to get back to work and keep it that way. Besides," those grim eyes narrowed, "it seems to me you've got a few problems of your own right here in Zion. I'd think you'd want to get back to *them*, too."

Duchairn drew a deep breath as Clyntahn flushed angrily, but Maigwair's gaze never wavered. The Treasurer wondered if Clyntahn was as startled as he'd been to see Maigwair take the offensive, especially with the reports of fresh disaster coming back from the Army of Glacierheart. From the sound of things, Kaitswyrth would be fortunate if his command survived, far less held its ground, and a catastrophe on that scale should have put Maigwair firmly on the *de*fensive. Even more surprising than Maigwair's bellicosity, though, was Clyntahn's failure to launch into a furious tirade in reply.

*Of course, his own position's less than enviable at the moment. Allayn's right about that. And it's even worse after the way he's spent the last couple of years trying to conceal the 'Fist of Kau-Yung's' activities. Well, he can't hide them anymore, can he?*

The cratered ruins where the Second Church of the Holy Pasquale of the Faithful of Zion had once stood were far too big to conceal, especially since the apartments of so many bishops and archbishops overlooked them. A half-dozen of those bishops and archbishops had suffered cuts and lacerations as the explosion shattered their windows and sent knife-edged glass splinters flying. Closer to the actual site of the church, the damage was far worse. Ornamental trees and shrubbery had been shattered, their broken branches stripped naked by the blast, and at least thirty-five members of the Temple Guard and "several"—Clyntahn and Rayno still refused to issue an official number—agents inquisitor had been killed along with every single person in the church.

And the list of the dead made interesting reading, especially for anyone with an un-trusting turn of mind. Duchairn hadn't discussed it with Maigwair, but he knew the Captain General must have his own suspicions about how those particular vicars and archbishops, who just happened to represent over half the prelates involved in overseeing the Army of God's operations, happened to have gathered in that particular church on that particular day. The fact that the only vicar present who *hadn't* been associated with the Army of God had been one of Zhaspahr Clyntahn's closest allies had to lend those suspicions a certain pointed edge.

*I wonder if Zhaspahr and Rayno think* Allayn's *the one who blew them up?* The thought gave Duchairn a certain mordant amusement. *Rather a case of the biter bit, wouldn't it be? And how delightful if Allayn had put it together.*

Only he hadn't. The entire Group of Four had been sitting in this very conference chamber when the massive explosion's thunder rolled through Zion. The sound had been clearly audible even here, and Duchairn had seen the Captain General's expression. Maigwair hadn't expected anything of the sort, and his reaction when the Inquisition grudgingly announced the names of the dead had been revealing. It was clear to Duchairn that he'd had nothing to do with their deaths . . . and equally clear he'd never expected Clyntahn to be able to reach so many of the men he'd worked with and relied upon for so long.

"I assure you my inquisitors are dealing with those . . . problems even as we sit here, Allayn." Clyntahn's tone was icy when he finally spoke, but far removed from the savage, cutting edge it would normally have carried. "We *will* find out who did it, and how. And when we do, they'll answer for it, whoever they are."

From the glitter in his eye, he still hadn't abandoned the possibility of Maigwair's involvement.

"In the meantime, however, I'm afraid the situation here in Zion's going from bad to worse, Zhaspahr," Trynair said. It should have come out sharply and assertively; instead, it sounded querulous. Clyntahn looked at him, and the chancellor shrugged irritably. "I don't doubt the Inquisition will get to the bottom of it eventually. But I have semaphore queries coming in from secular rulers from Shang-mi to Gorath to Desnair the City. All they have so far are rumors from their ambassadors here in Zion, but it won't be long before . . . well, you know."

Trynair's voice trailed off, and he shrugged unhappily as Clyntahn's glower turned into a glare. The broadsheets and leaflets Clyntahn and Rayno had never managed to get ahead of had appeared all over Zion within a day of the explosion. They'd listed the names not simply of the vicars and archbishops the Inquisition had officially admitted had died, but also of the senior aides who'd accompanied them, the Temple Guardsmen who'd been killed, and twenty-three names listed as agents inquisitor. Nor had they stopped there. They'd also included a message from something calling itself the "Fist of God" which claimed responsibility for Second Pasquale's . . . and listed another fourteen vicars, six archbishops, nine bishops, and eleven upperpriests it claimed to have killed over the last three years. Even worse, it listed the "crimes" for which they'd been executed, just as it did for the prelates who'd died in Second Pasquale's.

The damage to the Inquisition would be almost impossible to exaggerate, Duchairn thought. Not only had Clyntahn's aura of invincibility been shattered, but if the "Fist of God" was telling the truth—and Duchairn knew it was—the Grand Inquisitor had been caught lying, for it had announced that almost all the previous assassination victims had died of "natural causes." With that glaring proof of dishonesty in front of everyone's eyes, Clyntahn's efforts to deny that the dead prelates had been guilty of the offenses leveled against them rang hollow, to say the very least.

A quiver had run through the bedrock of the Inquisition's foundations—proof of present weakness and promise of greater damage to come—and the fact that the united power of the Inquisition and the Temple Guard couldn't prevent the broadsheets and leaflets from circulating only underscored Clyntahn's ineffectuality.

"I don't pretend to know how the bastards behind that lying propaganda are managing to spread it all over the city," Clyntahn growled, "but I'm not about to rule out the possibility of outright demonic activity. Notice that none of it's appeared here on the Temple's grounds. There's a reason for that, and I can only think of one. So I wouldn't go investing too much faith in its accuracy, if I were you, Zahmsyn."

"I wasn't talking about any . . . disinformation here in Zion." Trynair was obviously trying to pick his way through a field of verbal Kau-yungs. "I'm talking about inquiries from heads of state and first councilors coming back over the semaphore in response to messages from their ambassadors to the Temple. They want to know what's happening, and I need to know what to tell them."

"Tell them Shan-wei is active in the world," Clyntahn said flatly. "Tell them men who've sold their souls to her have every reason to murder true servants of God and then lie about their victims to justify their bloody actions."

That, Duchairn thought, was an amazingly accurate self-portrait, although he doubted Clyntahn saw it that way. In fact, from his expression and his tone, the Grand Inquisitor might actually believe what he was saying.

"Remind them of *Chihiro*, Chapter Seven—the first verse!" Clyntahn snapped. "'The service of Shan-wei is the service of lies. Why, therefore, should one expect truth in anything her servants might say or do?' And if that's not enough, tell them to read the *next* two verses!"

Trynair seemed to wilt before the fiery conviction in the Grand Inquisitor's voice, and Duchairn frowned as his own memory supplied the entire reference:

The service of Shan-wei is the service of lies. Why, therefore, should one expect truth in anything her servants might say or do? There is no truth in them, their mouths speak only deceit, and they will beguile the godly into damnation with convincing words and facts manufactured from falsehood and poison. Do not be deluded! He who opens his ears to the blandishments of the Mistress of Hell sets his own feet upon the path to her front door. Be they ever so reasonable, ever so plausible, yet still they are the daggers of the soul, and he who heeds them cuts himself off from God and the last hope of redemption.

Was it truly possible for Zhaspahr Clyntahn to not realize that passage was the very mirror of his own soul? Or to believe the heads of state seeking guidance wouldn't see it that way? Yet what else did the Grand Inquisitor have? The assassins had proven they could reach into the heart of Zion and be as deadly as Clyntahn's Rakurai ever had been in Tellesberg or Cherayth or Manchyr. And unlike *Clyntahn's* killers, the "Fist of

God" had killed anything but indiscriminately. They were executioners, not mass murderers, and how long did Clyntahn expect it to take for people to recognize that difference?

*And this man is the guardian of Mother Church?* The Treasurer's thought was bitter with disgust. *We're to believe* he's *the keeper of her truth, her protector and champion—the man chosen by God to preserve her foundations against all the powers of Hell?*

"As Allayn just said about the Army," Clyntahn continued in a voice like crushed gravel, "Mother Church's cause has been hammered here in Zion, as surely as on any battlefield. But she's *Mother Church*, Langhorne's Bride, God's true daughter and servant! We who serve her are mortal. We can die. *We* can fail, but *she* cannot! And, as God and Langhorne are our witnesses from the very Day of Creation, she *will not* fail—not then, not now, not *ever*! So you tell anyone who has doubts, who takes counsel of his fears, who opens his ears to Shan-wei's lies and distortions, that the Archangel Schueler knows how to deal with traitors to God, and we of the Inquisition are Mother Church's servants in this world just as he and the threshing floor of Hell will be in the next."

▼ ▼ ▼

"Banister," Ahrloh Mahkbyth said, "allow me to introduce you to Master Zhozuah Murphai."

Byrtrym Zhansyn leaned on his cane, looking at the tall, fair-haired man with gray eyes. He was more than a little nervous about meeting a stranger—even one Mahkbyth vouched for—when he was officially dead. He'd actually been in the church less than fifteen minutes before the explosion, and his name was on the "Fist of God's" list of casualties. It was a perfect cover for his disappearance . . . as long as the Inquisition didn't discover the lie, and his left hand touched his pectoral scepter. He took a sort of grim reassurance from the poison capsule it contained. If he should fall into the hands of his erstwhile Inquisition colleagues, they'd make certain he truly was dead, but not until they'd wrung every single thing he'd ever known about the "Fist of God"—and organization called Helm Cleaver—from his screaming body.

"Don't worry," Mahkbyth said, reaching out to clasp the priest's shoulder, and there was something about his eyes. They'd flickered with a dark, hungry light when Vicar Stauntyn Waimyan's death had been confirmed, but this was different. Now they glowed with dancing blue fire, alight with a joyous certainty Zhansyn hadn't seen in his old friend in far too long.

"Don't worry," he repeated. "I should have offered to introduce you to *Seijin* Zhozuah, not Master Murphai, because he *is* a *seijin*, Byrtrym—as much and as true a *seijin* as Saint Kohdy himself."

It was Zhansyn's eyes' turn to widen, and they darted back to the bearded man standing in the shadows of the warehouse space Mahkbyth leased.

"I'd planned to get you out the regular way," Mahkbyth continued, "but then the *seijin* turned up. It's not the first time, either. Didn't you wonder how Arbalest got those explosive sticks to us? Seijin Zhozuah delivered them for her, and she sent him specifically to fetch you afterward."

Zhansyn swallowed hard. His older sister Tyldah was a Sister of Saint Kohdy, as his Aunt Claudya had been. "Arbalest" had found it easy to recruit him straight out of seminary, and he was one of the very few men who'd ever read Saint Kohdy's diary. It was the truth in that diary which had sent him into the Inquisition as Helm Cleaver's spy, and now—at last—he found himself face-to-face with a true *seijin*.

"The *seijin*'s brought his *hikousen*, Byrtrym. He's going to get you out of the Temple Lands. By this time tomorrow, you'll be reporting directly to Arbalest and *Seijin* Merlin." Mahkbyth smiled, shaking the priest by the shoulder, and shook his head. "I *envy* you, Byrtrym, but at least I'm not the one who's going to have to keep his mouth shut about an actual trip in a *seijin*'s *hikousen!*"

"Speaking of which," Murphai said in a deep, pleasant voice, "I'd really like to take advantage of the darkness to get out of the city. So I'm afraid we're going to have to move right along, Father. I hope you've got everything packed."

. XII .
HMS *Thunderer*, 30,
Kahskyn River,
Shwei Province,
South Harchong Empire,
and
Village of Kyrnyth
and
Aivahnstyn,
Cliff Peak Province,
Republic of Siddarmark

"It's time," Sir Bruhstair Ahbaht said.

His voice was flat, and Lieutenant Kylmahn turned quickly. He hadn't heard the captain come on deck, and he touched his chest in quick salute. Ahbaht returned it, but his expression was less than happy.

"Time for what, Sir?" Kylmahn asked, although he strongly suspected what his commanding officer was going to say.

"Time to turn around and get our arses back downriver," Ahbaht confirmed, and snorted as he saw the combination of disappointment and relief which flashed across Kylmahn's expression and remembered an earlier conversation. "I know. The men're going to be pissed. Well, they aren't going to be any more pissed than I am," he said. "Hopefully, they'll get over it, but whether they do or not, it's time we turned around, Daivyn."

"I wish I could disagree with you, Sir," Kylmahn said after a moment. "Unfortunately, I can't." He shook his head. "We tried, Sir Bruhstair."

"And the men've done us proud," Ahbaht agreed in a marginally more cheerful tone. "Almost makes it worse, doesn't it?"

He looked up at the late-morning sun and then out across the Hahskyn River's brown water at the schooners moving steadily—if slowly—up it, directly against the current under oars. They were fitted to row on the berthdeck, which meant their guns—mounted on the weather deck—could be worked at need; that was the main reason they'd taken the lead. If opposition turned up, they had the maneuverability to deal with it, despite their lighter armaments and lack of armor, where the galleons would not. Ahead of them, launches and gigs spread out across the broad river, watchful in case the Harchongians felt adventurous enough to try any boat attacks but mostly busy with lead lines, running lines of soundings. Others had temporarily anchored themselves, marking shallows and mudbanks in place of the navigation buoys the Harchongians had removed once they realized the squadron was coming.

They were sixty miles from the coast, a third of the way to Symarkhan, but it was the twenty-fourth day of June, and by Ahbaht's estimate Admiral Hahlynd and his screw-galleys should reach Symarkhan no later than the twenty-seventh. And despite how hard his men were working, the wind—fitful and fluky at best—had veered around from the northeast to almost due east, almost directly into the squadron's teeth. The galleons' best speed against the current had been no more than a single knot even with a fair wind; now, it would be even lower, and they'd be forced to tack. That would have been risky enough in a well-buoyed river. Under the current conditions, it would be madness.

Despite all that, Ahbaht was tempted to continue. He and his men had invested too much effort in the attempt for him to feel any other way, especially given his own natural aggressiveness. Yet he'd always known everything depended on the weather—every seaman learned that lesson early—and that he would have no right to risk his valuable ships and the men for whose lives he was responsible if the weather turned *unfavorable*.

"Hoist the signal, Daivyn," he said heavily.

"Aye, aye, Sir."

Kylmahn saluted rather more formally than usual and turned away to call for the signal midshipman of the watch.

▼ ▼ ▼

"Well, that's a relief," Baron Sarmouth said, thirty-four hundred miles west of the Hahskyn River and three hours earlier than the crew of HMS *Thunderer*. His flag lieutenant sat across the breakfast table from him, a cup of hot tea in his good hand, and Sarmouth grimaced. "I know exactly what Ahbaht's feeling just now, but I can't tell you how delighted I am that sanity governed in the end."

Lieutenant Aplyn-Ahrmahk nodded in full agreement. If he'd been in Ahbaht's place, he knew, sanity would have had a harder time overruling his own desire to press on. Sarmouth, he suspected, would have made the same decision Ahbaht had. Indeed, he might have turned back sooner, not because there was a cowardly bone in his body—the baron was one of the most courageous men Hektor had ever known, although he'd come to realize Sarmouth didn't see himself that way—but because he calculated odds even more keenly than Sir Bruhstair Ahbaht had. In this case, though, both of them knew something Ahbaht didn't; Pawal Hahlynd was better than two days ahead of schedule, having expedited his movement in every way humanly possible.

Worse, unless the weather changed drastically—and that wasn't going to happen, according to Owl's meteorological projections—Sir Dahrand Rohsail would reach Hahskyn Bay no later than the twenty-sixth. Sailing with the current, rather than against it, and with the wind out of the east, however, Ahbaht should reach Ki-dau by early next morning. He'd be well out into the bay by the time he ran into Rohsail, and Kahrltyn Haigyl and *Dreadnought* should have joined him before that happened.

"Do you think Rohsail will attack, Sir?"

"I'm positive he will," Sarmouth said in a grimmer tone. Then he sat back in his chair and took a deliberate sip of tea. He set the cup back on its saucer and shrugged. "Whatever else Rohsail may be, he's no coward, and he has to realize this is absolutely the best chance he'll ever have. By the same token, though, I doubt any of his captains will be what you might call eager to get to grips with *Thunderer* or *Dreadnought*." He smiled briefly. "So it's possible—especially since he knows Hahlynd and those damned screw-galleys will be arriving on Ahbaht's heels—that he won't rush straight in to attack. If he blocks the Kaudzhu Narrows with his galleons long enough for Hahlynd to bring his galleys up, the odds would shift heavily in his favor. On the other hand, somehow I don't see Ahbaht—or especially Kahrltyn Haigyl—sitting on their thumbs and letting him get away with that."

▼ ▼ ▼

Rain fell steadily.

It wasn't heavy, pounding rain, yet it was damnably persistent, Colonel Zhandru Mardhar reflected. The day limped towards evening, the local water table rose relentlessly under the steady, soaking rain, and it wasn't as if the heavily forested terrain between Kyrnyth and the village of Gyrdahn, thirty-eight miles to the northeast, wasn't already swampy enough. They didn't call Gyrdahn "Gyrdahn of the Marshes" for nothing! And Shan-wei knew spring in Cliff Peak could be thoroughly cold and miserable enough without rain. As it was, the soupy mud and raw, humid chill weren't doing a single thing for his men's morale.

*Morale!* he snorted and shook his head. *They don't have any morale any longer—not really. And how in Langhorne's name do I blame them for that?*

"The guns are getting louder," a voice said quietly, and he turned to look behind him.

Father Zhames Tymkyn, the 191st Cavalry Regiment's chaplain, had followed him out of what passed for the village of Kyrnyth's local inn into the rain, and Mardhar smiled thinly. Father Zhames was a Langhornite, not a Schuelerite, and he'd been Mardhar's personal chaplain before Mardhar was assigned to command of his regiment.

"I don't know if they're getting louder or only closer," he said, with a frankness he would have shown to very few others. "Treykyn's not much of a strong point when you come down to it, Zhames."

"But surely Bishop Sebahstean can hold a little longer." Tymkyn's protest came out sounding more like a prayer than a prediction.

"To be honest, I can't figure out why the bastards haven't already overrun him." Mardhar gazed off towards the village of Treykyn, twenty-seven miles southeast of his present position. "I wish I could believe it was because the Bishop's position was strong enough to stop them, but we both know it's not. Not with the amount of artillery they can bring to bear!"

"The softness of the ground has to be making it difficult to drag those really big cannons forward, though," Tymkyn objected, and Mardhar nodded.

"Yes, it does. And I know the latest dispatches from Aivahnstyn say that's what's slowing the heretics down. But I don't believe it." The colonel shook his head grimly. "One thing that bastard Eastshare showed us last summer was that he knows how to drive an attack home. And much as I respect Bishop Sebahstean, I don't see any way he could have dug in deeply enough to keep the heretics from pushing him farther back if they really wanted to. They've got too many of those portable angle-guns and too much regular field artillery to do the job even without the heavy angles."

"Then why haven't they overwhelmed the Bishop yet?"

"That's what worries me," Mardhar admitted. "There has to be a reason, and I don't think we're going to like it when we find out what it is."

▼ ▼ ▼

"We've got trouble, Sarge!"

Platoon Sergeant Zhykohma Kahldonai looked up from his hoarded cup of hot tea with a sour expression. He had a well-deserved reputation for the zealousness of his faith and he was always ready to do his duty, but getting a fire to burn at all in this sort of weather was no inconsequential challenge. Finding a place to light one where it wouldn't betray one's position was even harder. The thought of being obliged to move away from it did not fill him with pleasure, but he didn't even consider saying so—not when Corporal Crahnstyn gave him that sort of news in that sort of tone.

"What sort of trouble, Shadow?" he asked.

"*Bad* trouble," Lairmahnt Crahnstyn replied grimly. The corporal was Company A's most accomplished scout by any measure. He'd earned his nickname for his ability to pass through even dense underbrush almost noiselessly, he had eyes like needles and the ears of a catamount, and he and his section of cavalry had a sort of roving commission. Major Grausmyn, Company A's CO, had learned to give Crahnstyn his head, although he did like to suggest certain areas—tactfully of course—in which he might like the corporal to expend his efforts.

"There's a shit pot of heretic cavalry three miles northwest of us," Crahnstyn continued, "and sure as Shan-wei they're heading for the Kyrnyth Road."

Kahldonai put down his cup and stood abruptly.

"How many?" he asked urgently.

"Couldn't tell you," the corporal replied. That was another thing about Crahnstyn; he never reported anything he wasn't *certain* of. "There's a lot of 'em, though—that's for sure! If I had to *guess*," he stressed the verb, "what I saw was probably the head of one of those big-assed regiments of theirs." He shrugged. "I figured it was more important to get back and tell somebody about them than get myself killed trying to get close enough to actually count them!"

"Can't argue with that." Kahldonai gripped Crahnstyn's shoulder for a moment, thinking hard.

At the moment, he and his platoon were spread along the road between the small town or large village of Hanjyr and Bishop Sebahstean's headquarters at Treykyn. But if Crahnstyn was right—and he usually was—and the heretics had gotten far enough around the company's right flank to reach the road between Hanjyr and *Kyrnyth*. . . .

"Right," he said decisively and tapped Crahnstyn's breastplate. "Lieutenant Oraistys is about two thousand yards that way." He pointed. "Go find him and tell him what you just told me."

"Gotcha." Crahnstyn sketched an abbreviated scepter in salute and headed off at a quick jog, despite the mud and his tall cavalry boots, and Kahldonai turned to another member of Crahnstyn's section.

"Zhakky, I want you back on your horse and headed for Treykyn five minutes ago. You tell them exactly what you and Shadow saw. I'm guessing the Lieutenant or the Captain're going to send a written dispatch, too, but Bishop Sebahstean needs to know about this fast!"

"Right, Sarge!" Private Kyndyrs saluted, vaulted back into his saddle, and disappeared down the muddy track to Treykyn in a spatter of mud.

"As for the rest of you," Kahldonai took time to gulp down the last of his tea, "saddle up. I'm sure the Lieutenant will have something he'd like us to be doing pretty damned soon."

▼ ▼ ▼

"They're *where?!*"

Bishop Militant Cahnyr Kaitswyrth stared at Colonel Maindayl.

"According to Colonel Mardhar, at least an entire regiment of Charisian dragoons is on its way to Kyrnyth," the colonel replied. "In fact, they may already *be* at Kyrnyth. It looks like Mardhar got his dispatch off the instant his scouts reported the movement. For that matter, one of his company commanders sent a separate dispatch carried by the corporal who spotted them." Maindayl's expression was grim, but there was approval in his tone. "He wanted us to have the best information available. The corporal says he heard firing from behind him before he was a mile past Kyrnyth, though."

"*Shan-wei.*" Kaitswyrth muttered the curse, staring down at the map table in his Aivahnstyn headquarters, and his heart was a lump of ice as he realized Allayn Maigwair's suspicions had been better taken than he'd wanted to believe.

He knew Maindayl was thinking the same thing. For that matter, the colonel had already expressed his own concern that the Captain General might be onto something. Kaitswyrth and Father Sedryk had preferred to think Maigwair was being alarmist, and the heretics' relatively slow progress against the Army of Glacierheart's ferocious defense after their initial, crushing bombardment had seemed to support that belief.

Or it had seemed that way to *him*, at any rate, he admitted harshly, wishing fervently that Sedryk Zavyr hadn't chosen this particular night to tour his army's frontline positions.

"All right," he said, rubbing his hands together while he thought. "All right. If this corporal heard firing at Kyrnyth, then we have to assume Mardhar was also right about what was coming at him. And they wouldn't have sent just the one regiment—not into Taylar's rear." He grimaced and made the bitter admission. "It sounds like Vicar Allayn was right to worry about our flanks. But how in Chihiro's name did they get all the way to Hanjyr—and from there to Kyrnyth—this damned quickly without going through Tyrath?"

That, Maindayl had to acknowledge, was an excellent

question. Even passing through the village of Tyrath, the southern anchor of the Army of Glacierheart's original position, it was over a hundred miles—thirty of them cross-country through dense woods—from the heretics' pre-attack position on the Daivyn to Hanjyr. Going farther south, the high road would offer much better going by way of the city of Sangyr, but the cross-country portion of the trip would rise to almost fifty miles and the total distance to over two hundred, and Sangyr was picketed by a garrison of almost six thousand Faithful militia. So how *had* Charisians reached Hanjyr so quickly . . . and without being spotted until they were already there?

"They must've gone by the high road, Sir," he said. "They could've saved forty miles by cutting across between the Sangyr-Glacierheart High Road and the Sangyr-Aivahnstyn High Road south of the forest. It'd be slower going cross-country in this kind of slop, but they might have made it by now, especially if they actually started before they began the initial bombardment."

*Or they might have gone straight* through *Sangyr without our knowing a thing about it,* he thought to himself. *I never was happy about "General Klaibyrn's" scouting, and Charisian regulars'd go through his militia like shit through a wyvern. Damned Siddarmarkians can't do* anything *right!*

He might be being unfair to General Zhames Klaibyrn, the loyal Siddarmarkian militia commander to whom Kaitswyrth had entrusted responsibility for Sangyr, but he doubted it. More to the point at the moment, he didn't care.

"However they did it, though," he said urgently, stepping to the bishop militant's side and tapping Kyrnyth's position on the map, "they're squarely across Bishop Sebahstean's most direct line of retreat from Treykyn to Aivahnstyn, and that threatens the entire army."

His finger traced the line of the Army of Glacierheart's current front. Treykyn lay thirty miles west of

its over-winter position, on the far side of the large
town of Styltyn, where the heretics had punched a
deep, triangular salient into the Church's starting position. The Army of Glacierheart had been driven back
for as much as twenty miles, but it had fallen back sul-
lenly, contesting every inch of ground after the initial
ferocious heretic bombardments. He knew the heretics'
casualties had been minute compared to the Army of
Glacierheart's, despite the fact that it was Mother
Church whose troops were fighting from defensive positions. But Kaitswyrth's battered, disheartened men
had refused to give up, and the Border States contin-
gent under Baron Wheatfields' command had fought
like heroes at the northern end of the Army of Glacierheart's lines. They'd clung stubbornly to the line of the
West Black Sand River, flowing out of the Gyrdahn
Marshes to the Daivyn, high and brown, laced with
furrows of yellow foam as the drenching rains filled it
to overflowing. And the Army of God's divisions had
fought equally hard, spearheaded by Sebahstean Taylar's own St. Zhudyth Division, to hold the almost
equally over-full Cow Ford River to the south. They'd
been pushed back everywhere—especially in the center,
towards Treykyn—but the heretic Eastshare had
seemed unwilling to pay the cost in blood to drive his
way through like a bull dragon.

*We thought it was because now that he had all that
artillery he was trying to husband his manpower, and
maybe he was. But what if Vicar Allayn was right about
what* else *he had in mind?*

"If they've taken Kyrnyth and they're able to hold it,
they've got a quarter of Bishop Sebahstean's total
strength—basically everything south of the Treykyn-
Hanjyr Road—in a pocket, Sir," he continued harshly.
"The only line of retreat still open to them would be
that miserable track from Treykyn to Gyrdahn. And if
he has to fall back, then everything *north* of Treykyn
would have to go the same way, as well."

"Then they'd better not have to retreat at all!"
Kaitswyrth snapped.

Maindayl looked up quickly, but bit back what he'd been about to say. The bishop militant's expression told him everything he needed to know. Whatever Kaitswyrth might say, he knew the truth. It might take a while longer, but in the end, he'd face that truth. The question was, how much of the precious time Sebahstean Taylar's men no longer had would it take for that to happen?

"Sir," he began—

"Excuse me, My Lord."

Kaitswyrth and Maindayl turned quickly as the door opened. A lieutenant, one of the bishop militant's junior aides, stood there, his face anxious, and an exhausted-looking, mud-coated courier in the colors of the Earl of Usher stood at his shoulder.

"What?" Kaitswyrth snapped.

"I apologize for disturbing you, My Lord," the lieutenant said quickly, "but this messenger's just come in from Baron Wheatfields."

Maindayl's nostrils flared and his stomach muscles tightened. He looked at as much of the Usherite's face as he could see through the mud, and in that man's iron expression he read the message he'd come to deliver.

"I'm afraid . . . That is . . ." The lieutenant drew a deep breath. "My Lord, Baron Wheatfields reports that heretic infantry have seized Gyrdahn of the Marshes. They're digging in with infantry angle-guns and field guns. He estimates there are at least eight thousand of them, My Lord."

# JULY
## YEAR OF GOD 897

✦

# . I .
## HMS *Thunderer*, 30,
## Hahskyn Bay,
## Shwei Province,
## Harchong Empire,
## and
## Guarnak,
## Cliff Peak Province,
## Republic of Siddarmark

Sir Bruhstair Ahbaht stood by the binnacle, smoking his pipe and listening to the fiddle scrape away on *Thunderer*'s foredeck. The ironclad's long, slender bowsprit was a lance, pointed directly at the sun settling into the broad blue waters of Hahskyn Bay in a smother of crimson ash and golden clinkers, and the day's oppressive heat was settling into the cool of evening along with it. His crew was just as disappointed at turning back as he'd expected them to be, but they were seamen—*Charisian* seamen, as Daivyn Kylmahn had pointed out to him—and it never occurred to them that his decision might have anything to do with lack of confidence. Still, as blue-water sailors were wont to do, they approved of captains with prudence, and they'd felt nothing but relief when the smell of salt-water welcomed them back to their natural habitat once more.

He shook his head with a half-smile as he watched the off-watch crew dance to the fiddle. It wasn't the hornpipe it might have been back on Old Earth, but it was just as exuberant and exhausting, and just as faithful a sign of the crew's morale.

It spoke for his own morale, as well, he decided. The passage downriver had gone more smoothly than he'd feared it might, actually—mostly because they'd already located most of the shallows where any of his galleons might have run aground. And he had to admit he'd felt a certain satisfaction as they sailed past Ki-dau without drawing a single shot. The squadron had demolished the port's rudimentary defenses on its way up the Hahskyn Estuary. There'd been no time for the Harchongians to rebuild, and even if they'd had the time, none of them would have been foolish enough to challenge *Thunderer* and the bombardment ships a second time.

They'd cleared the southern end of Crescent Shoal almost four hours ago, and the wind which had defeated his drive up the Hahskyn was perfectly suited to his present heading. He could wish there was more of it, but in another four hours, they'd enter Egg Drop Passage, the twenty-six-mile-wide channel between Beggar Island and Egg Drop Island. It was the widest and safest of Crescent Bay's four entrances, which was a non-trivial consideration, given the general unreliability of Harchongese charts and the absence of any buoys. By dawn, they'd be into the southern end of the Kaudzhu Narrows, and he couldn't pretend he wouldn't be a lot happier once they were back into the broader waters of Shwei Bay.

He stood a while longer, smoking his pipe, respectfully ignored by the seamen and officers who'd realized how he treasured such moments, and watched the sun's fiery orb snuggle back under its rippled blue blanket for the night.

▼ ▼ ▼

"You did notice that I had the king of diamonds, didn't you, Ahndru?" Sir Bruhstair Ahbaht asked pleasantly.

The youthful-looking cleric in the green cassock

badged with Pasquale's caduceus in the brown of an under-priest looked back across the table at him with guileless gray-green eyes. Ahndru Graingyr doubled as *Thunderer*'s chaplain and healer, and Ahbaht knew how fortunate the ship was to have him. Graingyr had been born in Siddarmark's Tarikah Province but assigned by his order to the main Pasqualate hospital in Cherayth three years before the battle of Armageddon Reef. Like many Pasqualates, he'd leaned strongly towards Reformism, and when Sharleyan accepted Cayleb's proposal of marriage, he'd declared firmly for the Church of Charis. He was only thirty-three (and just over nine inches taller than his captain), but he had the gift, the knack for convincing even the most grizzled old salt to trust his soul in his chaplain's hands, and he was one of the most skilled and compassionate healers Ahbaht had ever encountered.

He was also an expert spades player, a master of what had been the traditional game of the Royal Charisian Navy for at least the last hundred years, although the last hand might have led some people to doubt that particular credential.

"Oh, I'm sorry, Sir Bruhstair. Did I cut your king?"

"Yes," Ahbaht said with commendable restraint. "You did. It was fortunate you were able to make that jack of hearts good. Otherwise, I might have been forced to . . . speak more sharply to my spiritual shepherd than I really ought to."

"We could never have that!" Graingyr said earnestly. "I'll try to do a better job of remembering which cards've been played in the next hand, I promise."

"Father," Lieutenant Tymythy Mahgrudyr said to no one in particular while he shuffled, "mendacity is unbecoming in a man of the cloth."

Mahgrudyr, *Thunderer*'s purser, was a native of Tellesberg, with eyes so darkly brown they were almost black and a very swarthy complexion. He was only about six years younger than Ahbaht, which would have made him a bit elderly for a lieutenant with a line commission. He was actually rather young to have attained that rank as a supply specialist, however, and unlike most Emeraldian pursers Ahbaht had known before his transfer to the Imperial Charisian Navy, he was scrupulously honest.

"That's a rather serious charge—or allegation, I suppose I should say—my son," Graingyr said austerely.

"No, it's a simple observation of the truth, Father," Daivyn Kylmahn said. He was the customary fourth for the captain's thrice a five-day spades games, and while he was above average by most people's standards, he was outclassed by the other three players and knew it.

"What he meant to say," the first lieutenant continued, "is that you're not fooling anyone. Not even me. You knew exactly what you were doing, and you and the Captain might as well stop trying to sharp me into thinking you didn't."

"I am cut to the quick," Graingyr said, with a noticeable lack of sincerity. "How could you possibly think such a thing of me? I agree that I'm the product of one of the best Temple Lands seminaries, so I suppose I might be a *little* suspect on that basis, but I've been a good, bluff, unimaginative, depressingly honest—one might almost say *dull*—Chisholmian for almost nine years now! After all that time exposed to such a merciless barrage of stolid righteousness, all of that seminarian logic chopping and equivocation's been thoroughly beaten out of me!"

"I think the noun I used was 'mendacity,' not 'equivocation,'" Mahgrudyr observed as he offered the shuffled deck to Ahbaht. The captain cut and the purser began dealing. "I believe there's a distinct difference between the two. One even those of us deprived of a Church education can recognize."

"Just remember who's going to be in charge of assigning your penance at this Wednesday's confessional, Tymythy," Ahbaht advised, gathering his cards and sorting them as they were dealt. "I wouldn't want to suggest that the good Father might—"

The universe heaved suddenly. The overhead lamp

swung wildly. Lieutenant Kylmahn had been tipped back in his chair, balancing it on the rear legs; now it crashed over, dumping him on the deck, and the sounds of breaking glass came from the captain's whiskey cabinet and Mahrak Chandlyr's pantry.

Ahbaht dropped his cards, surging to his feet, just as another jerking shudder ran through the ship. Voices were raised on deck—initially in alarm, and then, almost instantly, in sharp, disciplined commands. Bare feet rushed across the deck overhead, there was a sudden, thunderous avalanche of sound, and Ahbaht paused only long enough to extend a hand and yank Kylmahn back upright before he went thundering towards the deck himself.

▼ ▼ ▼

"Well, I suppose it could be worse," the captain sighed two hours later.

He stood beside the binnacle once again, Kylmahn at his shoulder, but there was no one on the wheel this time. There was no point; *Thunderer* was firmly aground, listing perhaps three degrees to larboard, on a shoal which appeared on none of their charts. It seemed to be at least four or five miles long, and it lay ten miles off Egg Drop Island's southern shore. That put it almost squarely in the middle of the deepwater channel indicated on those same charts, and the fact that no court of inquiry would ever find Sir Bruhstair Ahbaht's judgment faulty made him feel absolutely no better. However good his *judgment* might have been, everything about *Thunderer*—and, in this instance, his entire squadron—was his *responsibility*.

"At least it's mud, not rocks, Sir," Kylmahn offered. "We've started a few seams, but a rock would've ripped the guts right out of her, hard as we hit."

"That's what I meant about its being worse. Unfortunately, that's about the *only* way it could've been," Ahbaht replied, then gave himself a mental shake.

*Let's not wallow in too much despair, Bruhstair!* he told himself. *And it's all right to let your guard down*

*with Daivyn as long as you don't do it where anyone
else can hear you. Now stop kicking yourself and figure out what you do next.*

The problem was that there wasn't a great deal he
*could* do. Kylmahn was right about one thing. *Thunderer* had been bowling along at almost five knots on
that favorable wind he'd been so happy about. If they'd
hit an uncharted rock at that speed it *would* have ripped
a potentially enormous hole in her hull. As it was,
she'd slid up onto the mudbank at a relatively gentle
angle and the carpenter and his mates reported that
there was no serious underwater damage.

The same couldn't be said above decks. The sudden
stop had snapped the fore topmast right out of her before the sheets could be let fly to empty the huge fore
topsail of wind. How the main topmast had failed to
follow suit was more than Ahbaht could say, and he
intended to have it very carefully inspected as soon as
there was light. The falling fore topmast had taken the
fore topgallant and royal masts with it, and at least two
hands had been missing and unaccounted for after the
wreckage was cleared away. The captain was grimly
certain they'd been crushed and taken over the side by
the plunging spars, and nine of their shipmates had
been injured—three of them seriously—at the same
time.

The worst aspect of it was that they'd grounded on
a rising tide, very close to high water, and tides this far
inland were nothing much to write home about. That
meant the next flood tide was unlikely to float them
neatly off the shoal. The speed at which they'd hit made
bad worse in that respect, since he was certain the ship
had driven deeply into the mud. That was going to create a powerful suction effect, which could only make it
still harder to work her off.

*Just be grateful those damned screw-galleys won't
reach Symarkhan for another two days*, he told himself.
*Or that they're not likely to, anyway. That gives you
some time to deal with this, and you've got a whole
squadron worth of boats and other galleons to help get*

*you off this Shan-wei-damned mud pile. Between them, they've got enough anchors to kedge* Eraystor *out to sea!*

"All right, Daivyn," he said briskly. "First we need to get a boat off to the *Vengeance* to tell Captain Vahrnay he's now the acting senior officer afloat. We need to get some of the schooners out to make sure no one sneaks up on us while we're stuck here like a wyvern waiting to be skinned. Then I want both launches rigged to carry anchors. Unless the wind backs clear around to the west, there's no way in Shan-wei's hell any of the other galleons'll be able to tow her off, so let's go ahead and get the hawsers run aft, too, since the only way we're going to kedge her off is astern. Obviously, we're not going to do that until the top of the flood, but we might as well get the anchors laid out now. Next we need to see about lightening ship. We're not throwing any guns over the side just yet, but I think it's time to see about pumping the water tanks. I don't like it, but we can steal some of it back from the squadron's other ships once we get her back afloat. See what else we might be able to jettison without compromising our fighting ability, too; if it comes to it, I'll be willing to drop solid shot over the side or lower it into the boats where we can reclaim it later. Next—"

▼ ▼ ▼

General Trumyn Stohnar rode slowly along the street, surrounded by his staff, his aides, and what seemed to be at least half a company of Siddarmarkian dragoons. With so many bodyguards, he felt free to examine the damage as they threaded their way deeper into the city of Guarnak.

There was a lot of it to examine.

The Guarnak canalfront had been devastated by the Charisian Navy's Great Canal Raid. Most of the warehouse district had burned during and after the ironclads' bombardment, and the replacement structures the Army of the Sylmahn had hurriedly thrown up to protect its supplies over the winter had a raw, slapdash, temporary look to them. At least a quarter of *them* had burned in the most recent fighting, anyway. Other parts of the city—near the canalfront—had suffered significant damage from overshooting Charisian shells or Army of God artillery fire which had bounced off Halcom Bahrns' armor and ricocheted into the streets.

That was nothing compared to what had happened to what had once been Mountaincross Province's largest city over the last few five-days, however.

The troops Bahrnabai Wyrshym had tried to get out had covered no more than a hundred miles, less than half the distance to Jylmyn, before they'd been run to earth by the Army of Hildermoss' Cavalry Corps: five regiments of dragoons armed with rifled carbines under General Fraidareck Shyrbyrt. That could have turned extraordinarily ugly, Stohnar conceded, since Shyrbyrt had been born in Westmarch Province and his family had a tradition of Army service and fierce loyalty to the Republic. They'd also been virtually wiped out over the past year and a half—first by the rebellious Temple Loyalists, then by the advancing Army of God, and finally by Wylbyr Edwyrds' Inquisition. Fortunately, Shyrbyrt was a professional and a decent man who clearly intended to do his best to go on being both of those things, despite the volcanic fury banked up inside him. There was little chance he'd shy away from any atrocities for which the Republic's enemies gave him a reasonable pretext, however, and Colonel Clairdon Mahkswail had come perilously close to doing just that.

Shyrbyrt commanded just over twelve thousand troopers, whereas there'd been closer to twenty-five thousand in Mahkswail's column. On that basis, the colonel had rejected Shyrbyrt's first summons to surrender—possibly out of fear of Zhaspahr Clyntahn, possibly in an attempt to protect the inquisitors Wyrshym had attached to his column in an effort to get them out of Guarnak, or possibly for some other reason. Unfortunately for him, while there might have been little better than half as many men in the Cavalry

Corps, there'd also been two hundred and forty mortars, and Shyrbyrt had seen no reason to lose any of his troopers to AOG rifles when he could stand out of range and kill them all with mortar bombs. He'd made that point to Mahkswail with cold, savage precision . . . and then informed the colonel that four of his cousins had been massacred by the Army of God when Cahnyr Kaitswyrth overran General Charlz Stahntyn's fifteen-thousand-man force south of Aivahnstyn the previous summer.

Mahkswail had taken one look at Shyrbyrt's icy eyes and understood exactly what the Siddarmarkian was saying. And so he'd surrendered, although at least half the inquisitors in his column had committed suicide before the Siddarmarkians got their hands on them.

*I can live with that,* Stohnar thought coldly. *Stupid of them—unless they figured we'd give them to the Punishment the way they damned well deserve, whatever we might say before we got our hands on them. I doubt hanging or beheading hurts any more than some of the ways they did themselves in. I can hope not, anyway.*

Personally, after what he'd seen last year in the Sylmahn Gap, there were times he wished his cousin hadn't agreed with Cayleb and Sharleyan of Charis about limiting reprisals and counter-atrocities. He was perfectly prepared to assume the Inquisition and the Temple Loyalists had applied Langhorne's Golden Rule to their enemies as the *Writ* enjoined and were prepared to have the same done unto them. It was hard, sometimes, to remind himself that he'd have decades to live with whatever he did or ordered done.

His thoughts had carried him even deeper into battered, broken Guarnak. Shattered walls, smashed buildings, burned-out ruins, and listless, weary plumes of smoke stretched out in every direction. The street down which he and his bodyguards rode was half choked with rubble, and he could see at least twenty or thirty bodies at any given moment. Wyrshym and his rearguard had stood their ground and fought hard. In fact, he could still hear the crackle of rifle fire, the thud of mortars, and the thump of grenades from the northern end of the city, where the last of Wyrshym's command—penned up in a steadily contracting pocket—continued to fight back. It was all but over, though. The Army of the Sylmahn was down to no more than six or seven thousand wretched, starving men, as hungry and as short on ammunition—and hope—as the defenders of Serabor had been fifteen months ago, before Stohnar marched to their relief. Only there was no one to relieve Guarnak.

According to Lieutenant Sahlavahn, there was an intact—or mostly so—townhouse somewhere ahead which had been earmarked for Stohnar's HQ. It was hard to believe *anything* in this sea of wreckage could possibly be considered "intact," but young Sahlavahn was a truthful sort whose judgment was usually sound. Stohnar was prepared to take his word for it, at least until personal experience proved otherwise. In the meantime—

A rider came cantering down the street—recklessly fast, considering the state of that street—and the dragoons of his bodyguard closed in around the general protectively. They relaxed at least slightly as they realized the oncoming horseman wore the uniform of the 1st Siddarmarkian Scout Regiment.

The youthful lieutenant slowed to a trot when he saw the general's party, then drew rein as he reached Stohnar and touched his breastplate in salute.

"Colonel Tymythy extends his respects, General," he said.

"Thank you, Lieutenant—?"

"Kahlyns, Sir. Abernethy Kahlyns," the lieutenant replied, and Stohnar's ears pricked as he recognized the accent of Siddar City's Charisian quarter. Young Kahlyns was obviously Siddarmarkian-born, but from the sounds of that accent, at least one of his parents had been born in Old Charis.

"May I ask why—besides to extend his respects, of

course—Colonel Tymythy's sent you my way, Lieutenant Kahlyns?"

"Yes, Sir!" Kahlyns straightened in the saddle, his eyes bright and fierce. "The Colonel instructed me to tell you, Sir, that we've received an envoy under a flag of truce. He says Bishop Militant Bahrnabai requests a cease-fire to discuss the terms of his surrender."

. II .
### Shingle Shoal,
### Hahskyn Bay,
### Shwei Province,
### South Harchong Empire

"At least the wind should be better next time, Sir." Lieutenant Kylmahn tried to sound purely professional, not hopeful. "Captain Kahrltyn seems confident he can tow us off if it continues to back."

Sir Ahbaht Bruhstair nodded, although he was rather less confident than Captain Zoshua Kahrltyn had sounded when he'd come onboard *Thunderer* to discuss the situation.

Like *Thunderer*, Kahrltyn's HMS *Firestorm* mounted only thirty guns, yet she was also the largest unit of Bruhstair's squadron after *Thunderer* herself. A member of the ICN's second (and last) class of unarmored bombardment ships, she was armed with a longer, harder-hitting version of the navy's six-inch muzzle-loading rifles and her sail plan was at least as powerful as a *Rottweiler*-class ironclad's. That made it considerably *more* powerful than *Thunderer*'s was at the moment, actually, given her jury-rigged repairs. If any ship of the squadron was likely to be able to tow *Thunderer* off the mudbank upon which she'd stranded herself, it was *Firestorm*, and Kylmahn was correct about the current wind. It had backed steadily around from the easterly which had driven them onto the shoal. By now, it was coming from the north-northeast; if it continued backing at the same rate, it would be out of the north-west or possibly even directly out of the west by the time the tide was full once more.

That, unfortunately, wouldn't happen for another eleven hours.

Bruhstair folded his hands behind him and walked to the nearest gunport to gaze out across the gentle waves. They were a little steeper and a lighter color where they swept across the mudbank, yet even there they were little more than a foot and a half in height. They were almost listless looking, as if they were wilting under the mid-morning sun's heat, which was pretty much par for the course, now that he thought about it.

He tried to shake off the pessimism creeping into his bones, but the truth was that the "flood tide" wouldn't be all that much of a tide even when it was next full. Hahskyn Bay was a large body of water, yet it was far smaller than Shwei Bay or South Shwei Bay, and its only connection with the open sea was indirect, to say the very least. Unlike Chisholm or Old Charis, it experienced only two tides per day, not four, and they were far feebler, as well. In Cherry Blossom Sound off Chisholm's east coast, the range between high tide and low tide was just under nine feet, and in the Sea of Charis it was almost six; in Hahskyn Bay, there was a bare two-foot difference between high water and low. That didn't prevent a nasty tidal set from pouring through the Kaudzhu Narrows when the ebb tide added its force to the current already flowing out of Hahskyn Bay to South Shwei Bay, but it meant the flood tide wasn't going to provide the sort of lift which would float *Thunderer* effortlessly out of the mud into which she'd driven herself. On the other hand, it would be the only chance he got in the next twenty-six hours.

He looked up at the sun and grimaced as he made himself face an unpleasant truth. It wouldn't be the only chance he got in the next twenty-six hours; it was all too likely to be the only chance he got, period. If he couldn't get *Thunderer* off the shoal on the upcoming high tide, such as it was and what there might be of it, the Dohlaran screw-galleys would almost certainly arrive before the next one. And that meant . . . .

He sighed, shook his head, and turned to face his first lieutenant.

"We'll have to lighten her more," he said unhappily. "Call all hands, Master Kylmahn. We'll jettison the first six guns in each broadside and bring the next three aft."

Kylmahn's face tightened. He hesitated briefly, as if tempted to argue, but then he squared his shoulders and nodded.

"Aye, Sir," he said and reached for his speaking trumpet.

Ahbaht left him to it, moving a bit farther to one side to get out of the way and deliberately continuing to look out across the cheerfully sparkling waters. Not that he found the view particularly enthralling. It was, however, one way to keep his people from seeing his expression as they set about obeying him.

He'd hated giving that order as much as Kylmahn had hated hearing it, but there was really no choice. In fact, he should have given it before the first attempt to work his way off the mud. Knowing that made him no happier about sacrificing forty percent of *Thunderer*'s firepower, though. He'd hoped he'd be able to claw his way clear with the kedge anchors, and for a while, it had seemed he might. *Thunderer*'s boats had laid out four anchors from her own capstans, and three of his other galleons had laid out kedges of their own and passed towing hawsers to the ironclad. As the tide had reached its highest point, all four ships had manned their capstans simultaneously, their crews heaving at the capstan bars with every scrap of muscle and sinew they possessed in an effort to drag Bruhstair's ship bodily out of the mud.

It hadn't been enough, and he berated himself silently for hoping it might have been instead of accepting that it wouldn't. He'd pumped water overside, jettisoned provisions and every extra spar left over after repairing the damage aloft, and lowered every boat to reduce weight. But he'd tried desperately to hang on to the guns, and he shouldn't have.

*Thunderer* had run just over a third of her length up onto the gently rising mudbank before crunching to a stop. There were barely three feet of water under her sternpost at low tide; even at high tide there would be no more than five and a half, and the suction between the mud and the ship's hull was enormous. Breaking that suction's grip clearly called for more draconian measures, and each of *Thunderer*'s six-inch guns weighed almost four tons. With their carriages added, they weighed over five tons apiece, and jettisoning twelve of them and moving six more aft would concentrate the full weight of her artillery in the *after* third of her length. Altogether, it would reduce the weight bearing down upon the ironclad's forward section by about ninety-five tons and *increase* the weight aft of the point at which she'd taken the ground by thirty-two tons. That should turn the ship's length into a lever, prying upward against the shoal's suction at the same time *Firestorm*, having passed a tow to her flagship, gradually set every scrap of canvas she had. With *Thunderer* backing her own sails at the same moment, the two galleons would exert far more force than the merely mortal flesh-and-blood leaning against the capstan bars had been able to produce, even in a light breeze like the current wind. Of course, that assumed the wind did continue to back and *didn't* drop still further.

Once they had her afloat once more, they could redistribute her remaining guns to adjust her trim, but first—

"Deck, there! *Sojourn*'s repeating a signal from *Restless!*"

Ahbaht's head snapped up. He shaded his eyes with one hand, looking up at the midshipman perched in the maintop, paging quickly through the signal book while his signalman assistant peered through a telescope at the eighteen-gun schooner five miles southeast of *Thunderer*, reading off the signal hoists.

"Number Eleven, Sir!" the midshipman called, his voice cracking slightly, and something clenched inside Sir Bruhstair Ahbaht.

Number Eleven was "Enemy in sight."

▼ ▼ ▼

"*Cutlass* confirms *Lance*'s signal, Sir," Captain Mahgyrs said as Pawal Hahlynd came on deck. HMS *Sword*, Mahgyrs' command and Hahlynd's flagship, drove swiftly through the water, all sail set while the deck underfoot vibrated gently but perceptibly.

"Thank you, Ahlfryd," Hahlynd acknowledged the report. "Any more detail from Commander Snelyng?"

"Not yet, Sir. But *Lance* is closing quickly. I'm confident Snelyng's going to have a more complete report for us shortly."

Hahlynd nodded and walked to *Sword*'s bulwark. He looked over the low-slung screw-galley's side at the water creaming away from its hull. The schooner-rigged vessel could come far closer to the wind than any square-rigged ship, and the twin screws spinning away at the ends of their crankshafts added at least four knots to her speed. When they *weren't* turning, their drag probably stole that much speed from her, even when they were locked in the vertical position behind their skegs. That wasn't the case just now, however, and he smiled thinly as he considered what that might mean in the next several hours. The day was hot, the light wind was turning increasingly fitful, and what little there was of it would favor his schooners far more than any square-rigged galleon. When the advantage of his screws was added to that equation . . . .

He'd heaved a sigh of relief when the semaphore messages from Symarkhan informed him the Charisians had turned back a full day before he'd reached the Hahskyn River himself. Yet that relief, for all its strength, had been flawed, as well. He was grateful the

Charisians' mission to wreck the Symarkhan end of the Hahskyn-Varna Canal had failed, but their withdrawal had also meant there was very little chance even his screw-galleys were going to overhaul the retreating galleons. Still, there'd always been *some* chance, especially with Admiral Rohsail coming along behind the Charisian squadron. If Rohsail could force them to stand and fight long enough, or even simply convince them to dodge around trying to avoid action, Hahlynd's armored ships might yet overtake them on the inland waters of Hahskyn Bay or South Shwei Bay.

What he hadn't counted on even for a moment was encountering the Imperial Charisian Navy less than seventy miles from Ki-dau. He'd expected the poor wind conditions to slow them *some*, but by his most optimistic calculations they ought to have been at least entering the Kaudzhu Narrows by now. In fact, he'd been so certain of the lead they must have built up after reaching saltwater once more that he'd been proceeding under sail alone, resting his cranksmen.

Until Tymythy Snelyng's *Lance* reported sighting a Charisian schooner, at least.

*There has to be some reason they're still this close to Ki-dau,* he thought. *I suppose it might be some sort of elaborate trap, although exactly how it's supposed to work is a bit hard to see. Fifteen galleons is still only fifteen galleons when all's said, and I doubt they've managed to sneak a bunch more of them through the Shweimouth without anyone's sighting them and mentioning it to me.*

He frowned down at the water as he considered the numbers. Any one of the Charisian galleons outgunned his flagship by a factor of five-to-one or better, and they had at least one of the armored monsters which had crushed the batteries at Claw Island. And done the same thing to Ki-dau's defenses, for that matter, he reminded himself, thinking about the shattered gun emplacements he'd passed on his way through the heavily damaged port. He had only fifteen vessels of his own, and despite their armor, his screw-galleys were fragile and vulnerable from the flanks or rear. A single full broadside into the unarmored portion of their hulls from one of the Charisian galleons would probably send one of them to the bottom. Two broadsides certainly would.

*But conditions are almost perfect*, he thought, rubbing one palm up and down the bulwark rail like a man gentling a prized but nervous mount. *Langhorne himself couldn't have designed a better day to test Zhwaigair's brain children. Now it looks like he's even arranged an opportunity for us to do just that.*

There'd been more times since Armageddon Reef than Hahlynd cared to admit when he'd found himself wondering what God and the Archangels could be thinking to allow the heretics such a devastating succession of victories. It wasn't that Pawal Hahlynd believed God's champions needed any sort of "unfair advantage," yet there'd been those times when he'd questioned why God couldn't at least stop allowing the *heretics* those sorts of advantages.

*That's what He did in the Harchong Narrows, Pawal,* he reminded himself, *and Lywys kicked the Charisians' arses there. No reason you can't do the same thing here. Just don't get so carried away you screw up the opportunity. The bastards on the other side can probably replace entire galleons quicker than we could replace screw-galleys—or their armor, at least. And don't forget Rohsail's coming along behind them. You don't need to lose ships because you decided to wade into them all by yourself!*

All of that was true, and he knew it. Just as he knew he and his youthful screw-galley commanders were going to rip out the Charisian Navy's throat if the opportunity offered.

▼ ▼ ▼

"We're not getting her off—not in time," Sir Bruhstair Ahbaht said flatly. Daivyn Kylmahn's jaw clenched and

Ahbaht saw the desperate need to argue in the lieutenant's eyes, but the arguments died unspoken. Kylmahn could judge time and the tide as well as anyone.

"Signal to Captain Vahrnay," Ahbaht said more briskly. "Inform him that I'm passing command of the squadron temporarily to him. He'll know what to do with it."

"Aye, aye, Sir."

"Then we need signals to *Wanderer*, *Sojourn*, and *East Wind*. Instruct them to close with *Thunderer* and prepare to pick up our boats. And after that—" he met Kylmahn's eyes levelly, his own bleak "—inform Master Muhlkayhe that I'll require a fuse laid to the magazine."

▼ ▼ ▼

"You're joking," Pawal Hahlynd said, staring at Sebahstean Traivyr in disbelief. Traivyr, the admiral's flag lieutenant, shook his head emphatically.

"No, Sir. Captain Mahgyrs checked by signal twice. He even sent Lieutenant Haystyngs up to the masthead to look for himself."

Hahlynd laid down his napkin slowly, his mind trying to grapple with Traivyr's news. He wondered if the reason it seemed so hard to believe was because he wanted so desperately for it to be true. Was he simply unwilling to believe it for fear of the disappointment if he found out it *wasn't* true?

"I see," he said. He made himself finish his glass of wine, then pushed back his chair and reached for his tunic. "In that case, I suppose I should come back on deck."

The trip from the oven of his miniscule cabin's sweltering heat to the scorching sunlight of *Sword*'s cramped quarterdeck didn't take long, given the ship's diminutive dimensions, and Mahgyrs was waiting for him when he arrived.

"I understand we've had an unexpected windfall, Captain?" the admiral said, cocking his head, and Mahgyrs nodded.

"I sent Jyrohm here up to see with his own eyes, Sir," he said, touching his first lieutenant's shoulder lightly. "Jyrohm, why don't you tell the Admiral what you saw?"

"One of them's hard aground, Sir," Lieutenant Haystyngs replied. "That's what it looks like, anyway."

"I'm thinking it must be Shingle Shoal." Mahgyrs' forefinger tapped the Harchongese chart unfolded atop the binnacle. "I doubt anyone'd go as far as calling this chart *reliable*, but it's a Shan-wei of a lot closer to that than anything the heretics're likely to have, Sir. Probably never even saw it coming, and with the pissant tides on the Bay . . . ."

His voice trailed off, and it was Hahlynd's turn to nod as he gazed down at the map. It was easy enough to understand how a ship might drive herself onto the mudbank in the middle of Egg Drop Pass as Mahgyrs had suggested, and the captain was right about the difficulty in getting a ship back off it again. But the Charisians had clearly realized he was coming—he still couldn't figure out *how* they'd known, but that was the only reason he could think of for them to have started up the Hahskyn River at this particular time (and to turn back when they had)—so why hadn't they simply burned the grounded galleon and continued their retreat? No squadron commander wanted to abandon one of his units without a fight, but given the odds against getting it off the mud before the screw-galleys swooped down upon it, any tough-minded flag officer (and Langhorne knew *all* Charisian flag officers seemed uniformly tough-minded) should have bitten the bullet, burned the ship, and headed for South Shwei Bay. Unless . . . .

"You saw her yourself, Lieutenant?" he asked, turning back to Haystyngs.

"Yes, Sir. I did."

"Could you make out any details?"

"Not at this distance, Sir. She's almost stern-on to us, so there's damn-all, begging your pardon, I could see. She does have a list to larboard; that's one reason I'm sure she's fast aground. But other than that—well, that and the schooners and boats around her—I really couldn't see anything."

"I see." Hahlynd rubbed his chin for a moment, then looked back up at the set of *Sword*'s sails and inhaled sharply before he turned back to the flag captain.

"Signal *Lance*," he said. "I want Captain Snelyng to continue closing until he can get a better look at our friend on the mud. In particular, I want to know how many armed decks she has." He saw Mahgyrs' eyes narrow in understanding and speculation, but the flag captain didn't interrupt as he continued. "After you've signaled Snelyng, hoist Number Sixty-Three."

"Aye, aye, Sir!"

Mahgyrs touched his chest in salute and turned away to begin volleying orders. The Royal Dohlaran Navy's signals vocabulary remained rather primitive compared to that which had been developed for the Imperial Charisian Navy, but Number Sixty-Three had been assigned to one of the Galley Fleet's preplanned—and well practiced—battle plans.

The necessary signals soared to *Sword*'s masthead while *Lance* continued towards the Charisians at her best speed, making good almost eight knots now despite the fitful breeze, sailing close-hauled with both cranks fully manned. Astern of her, the other fourteen screw-galleys slowed as they maneuvered into four columns, two of three ships and two of four, and began to spread into a pattern aligned like the four fingers of an outstretched hand. *Sword* was the first ship in the four-ship column in the "ring finger" position, and as the formation settled down, Mahgyrs started the entire squadron moving forward once again, quite a bit more sedately than *Lance* but still faster than any pure sailing ship could have managed.

*It helps that we're all coppered, too,* Hahlynd thought, watching with profound satisfaction, despite the hollow, singing sensation in his midsection, as his well-drilled crews headed towards the enemy. *Nimbleness and speed—those're going to be our real weapons today, although the hundred-and-fifty-pounders aren't going to hurt a thing.*

The three massive guns mounted in each screw-galley's armored citadel each weighed four tons, exclusive of their carriages, and fired a round shot ten inches in diameter. Each time one of them fired, the recoil was enough to jar a man's teeth right out of his head. It was also sufficiently severe that Hahlynd had decreed that the guns had to be fired individually—in succession, rather than simultaneously—and the cloud of smoke could have choked a dragon, but their hitting power was incredible. He didn't know if they'd penetrate one of the Charisians' ironclads, but he'd seen what they did to *unarmored* galleons, not to mention stone walls or other handy obstacles, in test firings. He doubted they'd have any opportunities to use the spar torpedoes each screw-galley carried in addition to its gun armament, but he also doubted that they'd need to.

"Signal from *Lance*, Sir," Lieutenant Traivyr told him. Hahlynd looked up from his thoughts, and his flag lieutenant's smile seemed to split his face. "Captain Snelyng's lookouts've gotten a good look, Admiral! She's showing only one line of gunports."

Hahlynd smiled back, and Captain Mahgyrs looked at him wonderingly.

"How'd you guess, Sir?"

"It was more of a hope than a guess, really, Ahlfryd," Hahlynd admitted. "Still, if I'd been whoever's in command over there, I wouldn't have hung about unless I had a really good reason. They've got plenty of regular galleons—God knows they took enough prizes in the Markovian Sea and at Ithryia!—so it almost had to be one of their bombardment ships."

"Or the ironclad, Sir?" Mahgyrs' brown eyes blazed, and Hahlynd shook his head.

"Let's not get too greedy, Ahlfryd. If Langhorne's seen fit to give us a bombardment ship, that's good enough for me."

"But if it *is* the ironclad, Sir?" Mahgyrs pressed, and

the admiral's smile was far, far colder than his flag lieutenant's had been.

"Why, in that case, Ahlfryd, I think it's time we took
advantage of the opportunities God sends us."

▼ ▼ ▼

"Everyone's clear, Sir. Everyone but you and your boat
crew."

Lieutenant Kylmahn had not mentioned himself or
Edwyrd Muhlkayhe, *Thunderer*'s gunner, Ahbaht noted
with grim humor.

"In that case, Daivyn, I think it's time you and Master Muhlkayhe were over the side, as well," he said.

"All the same to you, Sir Bruhstair, I'll be leaving the
same time you do," Kylmahn replied flatly.

Ahbaht considered making it a direct order, but
then he looked at his first lieutenant's face and thought
better of it. A glance at Muhlkayhe showed the same
stubbornness—and unhappiness—and the captain
shrugged.

"Very well, then we'll all leave together," he said, and
waved his two subordinates towards the entry port.

Kylmahn gestured for Muhlkayhe to go first, and the
gunner started down the battens attached to *Thunderer*'s tall side towards the barely bobbing cutter lying in
the ironclad's lee. Ahbaht watched him go, then
watched Kylmahn start the same descent. He moved to
the entry port himself and took one last look around
his ship's deserted deck through eyes which refused to
focus somehow. He rubbed them angrily and drew a
deep breath.

*My fault*, he thought harshly. *All my fault. The whole
operation was my idea, and then I ran her onto the
mud.* A corner of his mind knew he was being unfair
to himself, but the rest of his self-flagellating brain
didn't care. *I should've jettisoned the guns yesterday,
gotten her off last night. But, no! I was so damned sure
I'd have time. The bastards shouldn't've been here until
tomorrow, but I should've remembered Charisians
aren't the only ones who can move quickly when they*

*have to, and* they *didn't have to worry about the wind while they did it.*

Ahgustahs Sahlahmn, his coxswain, called quietly from below, and Ahbaht shook himself free of his bitter thoughts. He swung out through the entry port and started down the battens himself, pausing six feet below deck level while he groped a Shan-wei's candle out of his tunic pocket. At least there was too little wind to snuff its flame, he thought, and struck it against the ship's armor. It sputtered to life, and he applied it to the length of a slow match hanging down *Thunderer*'s side.

The little speck of fire moved up the fuse in a thin plume of smoke, burning its steady way towards its rendezvous with the ironclad's magazine.

*Just my luck the damned fuse'll go out.*

He considered climbing back aboard, ordering Sahlahmn to stand off while he made certain the fuse reached its destination. Unfortunately, he doubted that was an order the coxswain would obey, and Kylmahn was even more problematic.

*Besides, Muhlkayhe knows his business*, he told himself, *and he knows how important this is. That's why he laid five separate fuses.*

Ahbaht lingered just long enough to see the climbing eye of fire reach the junction point of those five fuses and go hissing along each of them. One of them was certain to reach the magazine, he told himself, and dropped down into the waiting boat.

"All right, Ahgustahs." His voice was harsh, angry, although he was confident Sahlahmn knew that anger wasn't directed at him. "Get us away."

"Aye, aye, Sir," Sahlahmn said quietly, then raised his voice. "You heard the Admiral, boys. Put your backs into it!"

The oarsmen knew where those fuses were headed and needed very little encouragement. The oar blades dug deep and the cutter went scooting towards one of the waiting schooners.

Sir Bruhstair Ahbaht sat facing aft, watching his magnificent ironclad as she lay forlorn and abandoned behind her fleeing crew and five fiery worms ate their way into her belly.

▼ ▼ ▼

"It *is* the ironclad, by Langhorne!" Captain Tymythy Snelyng muttered to himself in disbelief. HMS *Lance* was close enough to Shingle Shoal for him to be certain of that now, however impossible it might seem. And the heretics had clearly abandoned the ship, which meant—

"They must've set a fuse, Sir."

Snelyng looked over his shoulder at Ahldahs Zhaksyn, *Lance*'s gunner. Zhaksyn was at least twice Snelyng's age, but he also held a warrant rather than a king's commission, which meant he would never command a ship of the Royal Dohlaran Navy. That didn't mean his brain wasn't just as keen as the next man's, however, and Snelyng fully realized how valuable a resource Zhaksyn and his experience were.

And he wasn't saying anything Snelyng hadn't already deduced for himself. On the other hand . . . .

"But how *long* a fuse?" he said. "That's the question, isn't it?"

"Too damn short for what you're thinking, Sir," Zhaksyn said bluntly. "They'd be keeping closer to her, elsewise."

Snelyng knew the gunner was almost certainly correct. The grounded Charisian vessel was still at least two thousand yards distant, and the closest enemy schooner was a thousand yards farther away from it than *Lance*; on the far side of the shoal. In fact, the entire heretic squadron was headed up the Egg Drop Passage directly *away* from the ironclad. Snelyng very much doubted they'd have been doing anything of the sort if they'd thought there was a single chance in Shanwei's hell that anyone could get boarders onto the ship before the fuse undoubtedly burning in her magazine blew her to perdition. Heretics or no, no one who'd been at the Battle of the Harchong Narrows—or who'd seen the state of the ships who'd fought there afterward—

would ever make the mistake of doubting Charisian courage, and the Charisians had to be even better aware than Snelyng of how vital a prize one of their ironclads would prove.

There was no question what a Charisian captain would have done before abandoning a ship like that. Unfortunately, there was no question in Tymythy Snelyng's mind about what he had to do anyway.

"Hold your course," he said to the helmsman, and looked at Lieutenant Seevyrs, his first officer. "Drop the gig. I want a volunteer crew—*real* volunteers, Alyk, and make sure they understand what they're volunteering *for*."

▼ ▼ ▼

"They're dropping a boat, Sir," Daivyn Kylmahn said quietly, lowering his double-glass and looking at Ahbaht.

"Gutsy bastards," Ahbaht muttered with a bitter scowl far removed from his normal expression. Then he raised his voice. "Captain Cupyr!"

"Yes, Sir?"

Lieutenant Commander Aizak Cupyr, HMS *Sojourn*'s commanding officer, was a fellow Emeraldian. He was also barely half Ahbaht's age, with the sort of corsair confidence the commander of a sixteen-gun schooner required. There was a difference between "confidence" and "recklessness," however, and young Cupyr had demonstrated that it was a difference he grasped. *Thunderer*'s ship's company had been split between three of the squadron's schooners, and *Sojourn* had taken aboard the last sixty men and officers. She was packed to the gunwales—this time the phrase was literally correct, not figurative—and low in the water with all the extra weight, and he obviously had no desire at all to expose that vulnerable, fragile target to the heavy guns aboard the rapidly approaching screwgalley.

Which didn't mean he wouldn't do it anyway if he had to.

"Clear away your pivot, Captain," Ahbaht said flatly. "We may need it."

▼ ▼ ▼

"You're in command now, Alyk," Snelyng said as the last of the volunteers scrambled down into the boat towing alongside. "Don't bring her within a thousand yards. That's an order."

"But, Sir—!"

"There's no *time*," Snelyng said sharply, chopping off Seevyrs' protest as he strode towards the ship's side himself. "And I'm not interested in any arguments. Understood?"

"But—" Seevyrs began again, then cut himself off.

Clearly, there was no point in reminding Snelyng that this sort of lunatic adventure was why captains had first lieutenants. The captain understood just how little chance there was of getting aboard that ironclad in time to extinguish any fuses . . . and how *good* a chance there was of getting himself and his entire boat's crew blown up for his trouble. And Tymythy Snelyng agreed with Earl Thirsk: a good officer *led* his men, he didn't drive them.

"Understood, Sir," he said heavily, instead. "A thousand yards. Langhorne bless, Sir."

"I won't say it wouldn't be welcome."

Snelyng smiled tightly, clapped Seevyrs sharply on the shoulder once, and dropped over the side. The bowman unhooked almost before the captain's feet hit the floorboards, and the coxswain put his helm over, veering sharply away from the still-moving screw-galley. The five oarsmen were poised and ready, and the oars bit deep the instant they were far enough clear of the ship.

The captain didn't have to tell them how short time might be, and they pulled their oars as if they were in one of the fleet-wide rowing races. Four or five knots was normally a realistic sustained speed for the twenty-four-foot boat, but twice that was possible for short bursts, and it cut through the water like a kraken, spray flying despite the light breeze and short, gentle waves.

▼ ▼ ▼

"Fire!"

*Sojourn* twitched as the pivot-mounted thirty-pounder just forward of her foremast belched a bubble of flame and a cloud of smoke. The round shot screamed away, cutting a line of white across the wavelets. It missed the Dohlaran boat by a generous margin, and Sir Bruhstair Ahbaht made himself stand motionless instead of slamming the schooner's rail with a frustrated fist.

*Thunderer*'s orphans were packed belowdecks like sardines to clear *Sojourn*'s deck, and he considered instructing Cupyr to engage with his broadside guns. Unfortunately, the carronades on the broadside carriages were shorter-ranged, and closing to use them would have required the schooner to close to no more than five hundred yards or so of her target. Her draft was shallow enough she could *probably* get that close without taking the ground herself, but there was no certainty of that. It would also require her to close *Thunderer* once again, which would have been risky enough, given the lit fuses burning away aboard her. Perhaps even more to the point, however, it would have required her to close with the oncoming screw-galley, and that would have been little short of suicidal. The two vessels were very nearly the same size, and *Sojourn* was far more seaworthy and carried twice as many guns, but she was much slower than *Lance* under the current conditions, and her guns would be effectively useless as long as the screw-galley kept its bow towards her.

Ahbaht frowned as the Dohlaran boat seemed to accelerate. It had well over a mile to go, yet at its present speed, it would reach *Thunderer* in no more than another ten or fifteen minutes.

*"Fire!"*

▼ ▼ ▼

Snelyng swore as the second round shot slashed through the waves just astern of the boat, close enough to soak them all with spray.

"Lucky shot, boys!" he called, hoping to Langhorne it really had been.

If that was one of the Charisians' rifled pieces, though, luck might have had very little to do with it. Reports said they were fiendishly accurate, and in calm conditions like this, with so little ship's motion to throw the gunners off . . . .

"Pull, boys—*pull!*"

Fresh, deeper thunder rolled, and he darted a glance back at *Lance* as the screw-galley disappeared behind a thick cloud of gunsmoke.

▼ ▼ ▼

Ahbaht's eyebrows rose as the screw-galley fired. The range was at least three thousand yards, and Dohlaran gunpowder and gunfounders alike were inferior to their Charisian counterparts. Despite that, three massive projectiles came bounding across the waves towards *Sojourn*. None of them passed within fifty yards of their target . . . but they continued skipping from wave crest to wave crest for almost five hundred yards *beyond* the schooner. There were no explosions; either they'd been round shot or their fuses had been extinguished. If it was the latter, the same thing was likely to happen to any additional shells that ricocheted into their target, but there was no reason Ahbaht could see for them to be using shells. Projectiles that size didn't *need* to explode to inflict devastating damage on a ship *Sojourn*'s size.

*And if the bastards really want to bring us into their range, they damned well can*, he thought grimly, watching the screw-galley slice through the waves.

At least those mammoth guns had to be slow-firing, and Cupyr's gun crews were displaying the practiced gun drill which was a Charisian hallmark. They were getting off three aimed shots every two minutes, and the Dohlarans would be fortunate to manage half that rate of fire.

*With* three *guns instead of one, of course*, he reminded himself.

He dragged out his pocket watch and checked the time.

▼ ▼ ▼

"Come on, lads! *Move* your frigging arses!" Ahldahs Zhaksyn shouted. "The Captain *needs* us, damn your eyes!"

Lieutenant Seevyrs was a devout man and something of an oddity in naval service in that he never swore. He felt no temptation to rebuke *Lance*'s gunner in this instance, however. He stood on the screw-galley's quarterdeck, peering at the heretic schooner through his spyglass while he raged inwardly against Captain Snelyng's order to keep *Lance* at least a thousand yards clear of the grounded ironclad. His heavy guns' maximum range was a bit over twenty-five hundred yards. With seas this calm, they could reach out another thousand or even another fifteen hundred yards with ricochet fire, but the ironclad lay almost directly between him and the schooner.

"Come another point to larboard!" he snapped.

"Aye, aye, Sir!"

*Lance* angled a bit farther away from the ironclad, circling around it along the thousand-yard arc Captain Snelyng's orders imposed. There were limits to how far round her guns could train, even on their Zhwaigair-designed carriages, and the angle meant Seevyrs' larboard hundred-and-fifty-pounder could no longer bear on the enemy, but it let him take advantage of the screw-galley's greater speed—she had to be moving two or three times as fast as the schooner—without transgressing the captain's limit.

The Charisian's pivot gun roared again, spurting smoke that was darker and far browner than *Lance*'s, and another round shot went ripping through the water, missing the cutter by little more than its own length.

▼ ▼ ▼

"Enough," Ahbaht said.

He had to repeat himself in a far louder voice before Cupyr heard him and turned to face him.

"That's enough, Captain," Ahbaht said then. "It's time to go."

Lieutenant Commander Cupyr's expression turned mulish. For a moment, Ahbaht thought he was going to argue, but then Cupyr looked at the screw-galley cutting through the water and grimaced.

"Yes, Sir," he said quietly.

▼ ▼ ▼

Seevyrs grunted in mingled satisfaction and disgust as the Charisian turned away. He'd more than half expected it, and he was grateful that the enemy could no longer fire on Captain Snelyng's boat on her new heading. Unfortunately, that same heading also meant the schooner would rapidly draw out of *Lance*'s range. He was sorely tempted to turn straight after her in pursuit, but that would have required him to pass within much less than a thousand yards of the ironclad. Even if that hadn't been true, the Charisian was on the far side of Shingle Shoal. At high tide, *Lance* could have passed directly over the mudbank; at the moment, she'd probably run aground the instant she tried to cross it.

"Avast cranking," he ordered. "Bring her hard to larboard."

▼ ▼ ▼

"Good lad," Tymythy Snelyng murmured as he watched *Lance* turn farther away.

Young Seevyrs had come perilously close to the thousand-yard limit he'd set, but he supposed he shouldn't complain about that, since *Lance*'s fire had probably contributed to the Charisians' gunnery problems. With that threat alleviated, Seevyrs was doing the smart thing and putting additional distance between his ship and the enormous potential bomb waiting on the mudbank.

*If I had the sense God gave a wyvern, I'd be doing the same thing*, the captain thought. *Unfortunately, I don't.*

"Come on, boys!" he called. "I thought you lads could *row!*"

Two of the panting, red-faced oarsmen bared their teeth at him in fierce grins, and he grinned back, then returned his attention to the ironclad. They were close now. No more than another two or three minutes.

▼ ▼ ▼

*"Yes!"*

Alyk Seevyrs snatched off his hat to wave it overhead as Captain Syngyltyn's boat went alongside the ironclad. He didn't need a spyglass to know who the first man up the Charisian ship's side was, and he bared his teeth in a fierce grin of satisfaction. They'd done it! Now if there was just ti—

▼ ▼ ▼

HMS *Thunderer* lived up to her name one final time.

She vanished in an enormous blast of fire, smoke, spray, and mud. It wasn't a single explosion; it was a chain of them, so close together they sounded as one savage drumroll of detonations. Wreckage arced high above the water, reaching out, plummeting back down into the sea in an irregular circle of white splashes, and the column of smoke towered against the sky, standing for long, dreadful minutes before the light breeze began to disperse it.

Sir Bruhstair Ahbaht closed his watch with a snap and returned it to his pocket. He stood staring at his ship's funeral pyre until the smoke began to fray. Then he drew a deep breath, shook himself, and looked at Lieutenant Kylmahn.

"Less than a minute off," he said quietly. "Remind me to compliment Master Muhlkayhe."

# . III .
## South of the Kaudzhu Narrows, Kahskyn Bay, Shwei Province, South Harchong Empire

"Our friends still there, Master Trymohr?" Kahrltyn Haigyl asked as Ahlyn Trymohr stepped past the Marine sentry into HMS *Dreadnought*'s day cabin with his hat under his arm.

Sweat gleamed on the fair-haired midshipman's forehead, and Haigyl wiped sweat from his own forehead as young Trymohr came to attention. The cabin skylight was open, wind scoops had been rigged, the stern door and scuttles—and every internal doorway and scuttle, as well—stood wide, and the cabin was still hotter than the hinges of Shan-wei's hell.

"I'm afraid they are, Sir." Trymohr grimaced. "In fact, the lookout thinks there may be at least one ship beyond them. It's awfully hazy, though, Sir."

Haigyl grunted in sour acknowledgment and pushed his chair back from his desk. It wasn't as if he'd found the routine paperwork enthralling, and his sweaty hands were sticking to it. The paper didn't seem to want to take the ink, and the ink seemed determined to transfer itself to his hands anyway, so the hell with it. He'd deal with it later . . . if he absolutely had to and couldn't find a semi-legitimate way to dump it on Zhasyn Skryvnyr, his clerk, instead. Skryvnyr had been a tutor for over fifteen years before joining the Navy after the Battle of Darcos Sound, and Haigyl was guiltily aware that the clerk had found himself saddled with more responsibility than he really ought to have.

*Of course, I don't feel all* that *guilty about it,* he acknowledged. *Hell, Zhasyn's a lot better at it than I'd be, anyway!*

He started to reach for his tunic, then thought better of it. His dignity would survive going on deck in his shirt sleeves, and there'd probably be at least some breeze on deck, despite *Dreadnought*'s tall, armored bulwarks. He was damned if he'd miss out on any of it if there was.

"After you, Master Trymohr," he said gruffly, and the midshipman headed for the cabin door.

There *was* at least a bit of breeze across the deck. It wasn't much—as Haigyl had expected, the seven-foot bulwarks blocked a lot of its strength—and the canvas overhead seemed weary, hanging heavily from the yards. There was little wind to fill the sails, and it came fitfully, letting the canvas go slack entirely too often for Haigyl's peace of mind. *Dreadnought* had set a veritable mountain of canvas ... and it was doing her damned little good. In fact, he doubted they were making much more than three knots with all sail set to the royals and studding sails rigged, as well.

He gazed up in disgust. If he could have found a place to set a single additional scrap of canvas without blanketing *another* scrap, he damned well would have. Unfortunately, there wasn't one.

He stepped to one of the after angle-glasses and raised it, and his lips tightened as he peered aft. There was no question that *Dreadnought* was being shadowed now. The head of the angle-glass was no more than twenty-five feet above sea level, but even from that low a vantage point, he could see the topsails of what had to be a fairly large schooner and what looked like a brig in company with her. They were even closer than they'd been yesterday, and in airs this light they could run down the bigger, heavier ironclad easily.

What they'd do with her after they caught up with her was another matter, but he'd long since realized they must have friends along. If they hadn't, at least one of them would have run off to report the Charisian intruder's course and position.

*There's something nasty on the other side of that*

*horizon, Kahrltyn, my boy*, he told himself. *Those bastards're talking to* someone, *even if we haven't been able to spot any of their signals from here. And whoever it is wouldn't be coming after you if he didn't figure he could do something with you after he caught up!*

He didn't much like that thought. On the other hand, just because someone thought he was big enough to get a job done didn't necessarily mean he was. The Dohlarans had bitten off more than they could chew on more than one occasion, and there was no reason to think this one would be any dif—

"Deck, there!" The call floated down from the foretopmast crosstrees. "Gunfire! Gunfire from the southsoutheast!"

▼ ▼ ▼

"God *damn* those fucking galleys!" Commander Bryxtyn Dahnvyrs snarled as fresh gunfire rumbled across the water.

"Bastards're a hell of a lot handier'n *I* ever thought they'd be," Dahnel Mahkneel, his first lieutenant, agreed bitterly. They stood on HMS *East Wind*'s quarterdeck, watching the Dohlarans' gunsmoke roll slowly downwind, like a lost, woolly fog bank, and the sun was hot overhead.

"Faster, too."

Dahnvyrs' tone was even bitterer than Mahkneel's. He'd commanded *East Wind* for almost a year and a half, and he was proud of the schooner. She was fast, maneuverable, and her sixteen thirty-pounder carronades and pair of thirty-pounder pivot guns gave her a devastating punch, especially firing explosive shells. He loved her dearly, and she'd never failed him, never faltered before any demand he'd made upon her. But while she barely ghosted along under every scrap of canvas he could set, the damned screw-galleys—*galleys*, damn it!—pursued her at at least twice her own best speed.

"Our turn next," he told the lieutenant. "Pass the word to load the carronades with shell. We'll use round shot from the pivots to pound their frigging armor while they close, but if we get a chance to pop a hit in *around* the damned iron, I want those bastards *hurt*."

▼ ▼ ▼

Sir Bruhstair Ahbaht stood on HMS *Broadsword*'s quarterdeck and watched the sudden smoke billow up from HMS *Restless*. The relentlessly pursuing screw-galleys had gotten close enough to engage Zheryko Cumyngs' schooner almost two hours ago. It said unflattering things about the Royal Dohlaran Navy's gunnery that it had taken them more than ninety minutes to score their first hit. After that, though, as more of them came into range, the hits had come quickly, despite a low rate of fire which undoubtedly reflected the weight of the screw-galleys' guns. According to *Seijin* Dagyr, they mounted pretty damned massive pieces in those armored citadels of theirs, and he was pretty sure at least one of them had burst. *Something* had certainly started a massive fire forward on one of the Dohlarans before the vessel had blown up, and it was highly unlikely that it had been a Charisian shell.

He'd felt a wave of vengeful satisfaction as the galley exploded, but so far the exchange rate had been entirely in the Dohlarans' favor. The single ship which had exploded was their only loss, which was far more than *he* could say. In addition to *Thunderer*, he'd lost *Restless* and her sister ship *Foam*, and absent a miracle, *East Wind* would be joining them shortly. At least the slow speed imposed by the miserable excuse for a breeze had allowed boats pulling between the squadron's other units to redistribute *Thunderer*'s seamen among the rest of his galleons. He hadn't lost all of them along with the schooners' companies, which didn't make him one bit happier at the thought of all the men he *had* lost.

*And unless the wind comes up, it won't be so very much longer before you start losing something a mite bigger than a schooner*, he told himself harshly.

Every instinct demanded that he stop running, that

he reverse course and go to *meet* the screw-galleys with his far more heavily armed galleons. If he hadn't already lost *Thunderer*, he'd probably have given in to that demand, but cold logic told him it would have been a mistake even then. Now, with *Thunderer* gone, *Firestorm* and *Catastrophe*, his two bombardment ships, were the only ships who could probably penetrate the screw-galleys' armor. The others would be targets, not warships, unless they could somehow get around the Dohlarans' flanks and avoid that armor. And that, unfortunately, was something they simply weren't going to do under weather conditions that let them move at no more than three knots while the screw-galleys could make twice that speed . . . at least.

No. No, he had to keep the range open for as long as he could, hope a wind came up, hope he could avoid them until darkness fell and then, possibly, give them the slip. It galled him bitterly to avoid action with such small opponents, but the Imperial Charisian Navy itself had demonstrated that size and combat power weren't always synonymous.

He started to pull out his watch, but he made himself glance up at the sun instead rather than stare at the watch face and demonstrate his anxiety to anyone watching him. At least another five hours, he calculated, and looked back at the oncoming screw-galleys.

They'd be within range of his rearmost galleon in no more than *three* hours, and what did he do then?

▼ ▼ ▼

"That's three of their schooners, Sir!" Captain Mahgyrs announced exultantly as the shattered, dismasted hull of HMS *East Wind* vomited flames and smoke. "We'll be up with their galleons in another hour or two."

At least some of the Charisians' crew had managed to take to the boats once the hammering shells of no less than three of the squadron's screw-galleys had set her ablaze, and Pawal Hahlynd was just as glad they had.

*Or am I? We had Charisian prisoners once before. If I take these people home, what's Lywys going to do with them? It stuck in his craw sideways last time, and somehow I doubt handing them over to Clyntahn's going to go down any easier this time.*

Fortunately, that wasn't his decision, he told himself, trying not to feel like a coward. And Mahgyrs was right; they *would* be close enough to engage the fleeing galleons soon, although he suspected his flag captain's estimate was at least a bit overly optimistic.

So far, the screw-galleys' armor had stood up well to the Charisians' fire. As far as he could tell, not a single shell or round shot had penetrated it yet, although he couldn't absolutely rule that out in *Pike*'s case. Given the timing of the explosion, however, it seemed more likely that one of *Pike*'s hundred-and-fifty-pounders had burst catastrophically. Dohlaran gunfounders had improved the quality of their products enormously, but guns with ten-inch bores crowded the very limit of what they could accomplish, and cast iron was still far more brittle than bronze or steel. The guns being cast for the additional screw-galleys building in Gorath would be banded like the army's Fultyn Rifles. Hopefully that would improve the situation, but for the moment, he and his men had to fight with the weapons they had.

*And at least you won't be firing them with double charges, the way you'd've done against one of their ironclads*, he reminded himself grimly, and shook his head.

*Lance* had passed close enough to *Sword* for Lieutenant Seevyrs to inform Hahlynd what had happened to Tymythy Snelyng. He was going to miss Captain Snelyng. He'd been the squadron's third ranking officer, and Hahlynd had come to know him well. He would have expected nothing less out of Snelyng, given even the remotest possibility of capturing one of the ironclads intact. Which was unlikely to be much comfort to the captain's widow and two young children.

"Let's reduce the tempo, Captain Mahgyrs," he said.

The flag captain seemed a bit surprised, and the admiral shrugged. "We're faster than they are in this wind, even without the cranks," he pointed out. "We'll overtake them well before dusk whatever happens, and I'd prefer to have the cranksmen as fresh as possible when we do, so go to standard tempo."

▼ ▼ ▼

"Sir! Sir Bruhstair!"

Ahbaht turned as Lieutenant Zhaksyn called his name. *Thunderer*'s second lieutenant had stepped into an illness-caused vacancy in Captain Tydwail Zhaksyn's chain of command when Ahbaht and twenty-five of the ironclad's company had come aboard the sixty-gun galleon. Now the lieutenant pointed up at *Broadsword*'s maintop.

"Captain Pymbyrtyn's just signaled, Sir! It's *Dreadnought!*"

"What?" Ahbaht blinked.

Lywelyn Pymbyrtyn's *Vindicator* was leading his line of galleons, if one could call the untidy, clumped formation—the best even Charisian captains could manage under such fluky wind conditions—a "line." Any signal from him must have been relayed through at least two other ships to reach *Broadsword*, here at the rear of that formation. That was his first thought. Then the ship's name penetrated.

"It's *Dreadnought*," Zhaksyn repeated, eyes blazing. "It's Captain Haigyl! Captain Pymbyrtyn estimates he'll rendezvous with us within four or five hours."

▼ ▼ ▼

"Well, damn," Kahrltyn Haigyl said mildly, gazing down at the written copy of Sir Bruhstair Ahbaht's message.

In a way, he really wished the Emeraldian had waited rather than pass the news by signal, where every signalman with a spyglass could read it and undoubtedly share it with his own ship's company. He grimaced at his own thought. It wasn't like all the rest of Ahbaht's squadron didn't already know, was it? And Ahbaht was damned well right that it was more important to get the news of *Thunderer*'s loss into his hands as rapidly as possible than to worry about how his message might affect people who already knew about it.

*Wish I could blame this all on him,* Haigyl thought grimly. *Not his fault, though—I'd've done exactly the same damned thing every step of the way in his place. But we're in one hell of a mess now, and I'm senior. At least the frigging wind's picked up a little. Of course, that brought along its own little complication, didn't it?*

Relative seniority wasn't really something he'd spent a lot of time thinking about as he pursued Ahbaht towards Hahskyn Bay, but it wasn't something he could *avoid* thinking about now. Ahbaht was junior to him. That meant it was up to him to decide what they were going to do, and he didn't see a lot of good options lying about.

He dropped the message on his desk and looked across it at Lieutenant Stahdmaiyr. The lenses of the lieutenant's spectacles gleamed as a sunbeam found the skylight and penetrated the day cabin's dimness.

"Hell of a mess, Dahnyld."

"One way to put it, Sir," Stahdmaiyr agreed. "I have the latest count, if you want it?"

"Might's well tell me." Haigyl shrugged. "I'm going to find out anyway soon enough."

"Well, in that case, the masthead's counted at least twenty-five galleons. There's more behind those, though; we just can't make out how many."

"Are they still overhauling?"

"I don't think so, Sir, and Master Gyllmyn concurs." It was Stahdmaiyr's turn to shrug. "They must've brought the wind down with them to've made up on us this way. Now that we've got the same wind, I believe we're actually opening the range a bit again."

"But unless the wind picks up even more, we're still

going to be a hell of a lot slower than these goddamned screw-galleys," Haigyl pointed out. "And that's a lot of galleons, Dahnyld."

"Yes, Sir. It is."

Haigyl scowled at the chart, but there were no answers there, either.

If that was only Rohsail and the Jack's Land squadron behind him, then it would be Ahbaht's surviving galleons plus *Dreadnought* against no more than twenty to twenty-five Dohlarans. Stiff odds, but not too stiff to handle with *Dreadnought* to lead the Charisian line. But if Rohsail had combined with Raisahndo's Saram Bay squadron, there could be at least forty or fifty galleons coming down upon him . . . and the screw-galleys were in *front* of him. The wind hadn't picked up enough to pose any sort of problems for them—not yet—and he was caught squarely between them and a superior number of conventional galleons.

It was not a winning situation.

He folded his hands behind him and began pacing, rubbing the patch over his empty eye socket with one forefinger while he wondered how adventurous the screw-galleys were likely to feel overnight. They were smaller than the Charisian galleons, closer to the water and undoubtedly harder to see. Would they feel emboldened by that and try to actually penetrate his formation under cover of darkness? That was what *he'd* do in their place—get in close and blaze away with those heavy guns at point-blank range. Maybe even try a run with those "spar torpedoes," if they'd brought any along.

But despite his reputation as a bull dragon with a toothache, Kahrltyn Haigyl really did think before leaping straight into the fire. Sometimes, anyway, and this was damned well a time for thinking first. And for not assuming the other fellow would do what *he'd* do in the same situation.

He was well aware that he tended to be more aggressive than most. Not everyone was as likely to charge in as he was, and those screw-galleys had just proved they represented the closest thing to a winning card any of the Imperial Charisian Navy's opponents had come up with yet. True, their present success owed a great deal to the fact that they'd found themselves with ideal weather conditions. Had Ahbaht been given a lively breeze to work with, one that would have allowed his heavier galleons to maneuver while simultaneously making heavier going for the fragile galleys, things could have been different. For one thing, he probably wouldn't have destroyed *Thunderer* and run for it. But that lay in the world of might-have-been; in the world that actually was, he'd done exactly the right thing, as the screw-galleys had unfortunately demonstrated all too clearly since. So far, they'd cost Ahbaht's squadron—*Haigyl's* squadron now, he supposed—four schooners and HMS *Sickle*, a fifty-four-gun galleon.

He paused in his pacing, gazing at the bulkhead-mounted barometer for a moment, then started walking again.

It was hard to be certain from Ahbaht's tersely worded signal, but it sounded as if Raimahnd Tohbyais, *Sickle*'s captain, had deliberately turned back into the midst of the pursuing Dohlarans once he realized he was going to be overtaken anyway. If he had, more power to him. His ship had been pulverized by the screw-galleys' heavy shells, and in the end she'd caught fire, as so many wooden ships did when shells began tearing them apart. In the process, though, Tohbyais had forced them to concentrate on him, maneuver to keep their armored citadels facing his guns rather than flow around him and pursue Ahbaht's other ships. They hadn't dared to expose their vulnerable flanks to his gunners, and Haigyl wondered how hard it had been for Ahbaht to resist trying to come to *Sickle*'s aid. He knew how hard it would have been for *him*, and he found himself respecting Ahbaht's decision not to turn upon the screw-galleys even more because he did.

*He might've gotten a couple of them, but not if the Dohlarans fought smart. They only closed in on* Sickle *because they could. If Ahbaht'd tried to concentrate his galleons against them, they'd have backed off, stayed out at a range where he couldn't hope to fire at anything except their armor. And whether they know it or not, he knows what's coming up behind me.*

But the key point was that the screw-galleys had beaten *Sickle* to death in less than forty-five minutes of close action . . . and without losing a single one of their own.

He stopped pacing again and strode back to the chart, glaring down at it.

"The wind is going to pick up," he said.

Dahnyld Stahdmaiyr blinked at him. It hadn't been a question, and it hadn't been a prayer. It had been a statement, and Haigyl bared his teeth as he looked up and caught the lieutenant's expression.

"Haven't lost my mind yet," he said, "but the glass is falling and the wind's been strengthening for the last three hours now. Not a lot, I'll grant, but it's been picking up *steadily*, Dahnyld, and the temperature's dropping, too. I'd give one of my balls for a good heavy storm, but I'm sure as Shan-wei not going to count on that. What I think *will* happen, though, is it'll come up enough we can dance with the fucking screw-galleys. I don't know what *they'll* do if that happens. Doesn't seem likely they'd just turn around and go home after coming this far, but whatever they do, they won't do it as well as they've *been* doing it. Probably won't have anywhere near the same speed advantage, either."

"*If* the wind comes up, Sir," Stahdmaiyr conceded.

"Well, if it doesn't, we're so screwed nothing else'll matter," Haigyl replied. "So I'm going to figure it will. Oh," he waved one hand, "I'll allow for the chance that it won't, but you know as well as I do that if it doesn't, all the planning in the world's not going to change what happens. Way I see it, we might's well plan for the best."

"Can't argue with that, Sir," Stahdmaiyr agreed.

"Of course, 'best' isn't always all that damned good, is it?" Haigyl glowered at the chart some more, then looked back up at his lieutenant. "Even if the screw-galleys're more or less out of it, that still leaves us with Rohsail. More likely, we'll have both of 'em on our arses, assuming each of 'em figures out the other one's there. Most probably they don't have a clue about that—yet—but you can be damned sure that'll change soon's they get close enough to hear each other's gunfire."

He paused, and Stahdmaiyr nodded in grim agreement.

"Well, in that case we've got some signals to send, and it's going to take a while, because we're going to have to spell a lot of it out instead of relying on the vocabulary," Haigyl said. "And we've got to get them all passed before it gets too dark for Ahbaht to read them, so let's get Zhasyn and Master Trymohr in here and start figuring out what to tell him."

. IV .

# The Kaudzhu Narrows,
# Hahskyn Bay,
# Shwei Province,
# South Harchong Empire

"Is this going to work, Sir?"

Dahnyld Stahdmaiyr's eyes were level and there was no second-guessing in the lieutenant's quiet voice. There was a clear, knife-sharp edge of tension and more than a little regret, perhaps, and a steely core of purpose, but what sounded most clearly at that moment was honest curiosity and something almost like . . . whimsy.

"Don't know," Captain Haigyl replied equally honestly, then smiled a brief, ferocious smile. "Wind's actually made up a bit better'n I expected, but I just don't know. Still, I expect it'll at least come as what Earl Sharpfield likes to call 'an unpleasant experience' for the bastards. Whether or not we get anybody out, though—"

He shrugged, and Stahdmaiyr nodded. Then he touched his chest in salute and headed for his normal battle station at the foot of the mainmast.

Haigyl watched him go, then glanced up at the pale streaks beginning to appear in the eastern sky. Dawn came quickly in these latitudes, once it started, and he spent a moment hoping to all the Archangels that most of the Charisian ships would be at least approximately where he wanted them to be when that happened. Frankly, it was unlikely, given the difficulties sailing ships faced in just finding one another, far less keeping station on each other, in a pitch-dark, moonless night, but he could hope.

He'd managed to get his signals passed before darkness closed in, and Captain Ahbaht had acknowledged them. Given what he knew of Ahbaht, Haigyl was certain the other captain hadn't liked his orders, but that was too bad. Haigyl didn't much like his own part of the proposed battle plan, either. In fact, he'd have given just about anything he could imagine to avoid it.

He inhaled deeply and looked around *Dreadnought*'s immaculately neat and tidy deck once more, realizing how much he loved this ship and her crew. Then he nodded to Ahmbrohs Lywkys, the ship's chaplain.

"I think it's time, Father," he said softly, his voice almost lost in the sounds of wind and water, and the Bédardist under-priest nodded and signed himself with Langhorne's scepter.

"Let us pray, my sons!" he called. The deck went silent but for that same sound of wind and wave, and a single, lonely wyvern whistled somewhere in the darkness above the ship's wake as heads were bared and bowed and he raised his hands in benediction. "Oh God, we ask Your blessing upon us this day as we face the enemies of Your will. The battle will be hard. Losses will be heavy, and we are but mortal. We are sore afraid of that to which we are called, yet we know what it is we must do, and we face it supported by the knowledge that You will be with us, whatever the cost, and that there is no better cause for which those who love You could contend. Be with us in the dark valley of death as You are always with us, and welcome into Your loving arms those who this day give up their lives in Your service. Amen."

▼ ▼ ▼

"Sunrise in another twenty minutes, Sir," Lieutenant Traivyr said.

Pawal Hahlynd nodded, and the flag lieutenant handed him a hot cup of tea. Nights were seldom what one might call "cold" on Hahskyn Bay—they were less than five hundred miles below the equator—yet the darkness was cool and breezy, and the admiral took a grateful sip. The wind had gathered strength steadily during the night. By now, it was a stiff topgallant breeze, blowing out of the northwest and raising four-foot waves. It wasn't enough to worry him—yet, at least. What *did* worry him was that that westerly wind carried clouds on its breath. The stars to the west had disappeared steadily over the last few hours, and the glass was still falling.

*Sword* rolled uncomfortably as she moved through the steeper waves with the rest of her squadron close about her. Hahlynd hadn't liked breaking off the action to reassemble his formation, but sometimes discretion truly was the better part of valor. He'd caught up with the Charisian galleons later in the day than he'd anticipated, and he blamed himself for reducing the crank tempo to rest his cranksmen earlier. The wind had come up more quickly than he'd expected, which had allowed the Charisians to make more speed. Coupled with his own decision, that had stretched out the time until his ships could come in range of the heavily armed galleons, and HMS *Sickle*'s decision to turn directly into the pursuing galleys had stretched it out still longer.

The screw-galleys' armored citadels had been sorely tested as the galleon poured twenty-five-gun broadsides into them—firing solid shot, not shell. They'd stood up to the punishment better than Hahlynd had really expected, but that didn't mean they hadn't suffered broken plates and shattered bolts or that their supporting timbers hadn't been wracked and twisted by the pounding. Only *Carbine* had actually been penetrated, but he suspected some of the others had taken more structural damage than their captains were prepared to admit. The delay to deal with *Sickle* without exposing their unarmored sides to the galleon's grimly determined gunners had cost at least another full hour—more like an hour and a half—of daylight and badly disordered Hahlynd's formation.

It had also taught the screw-galleys the limits of their armored protection when one of them *had* inadvertently exposed her flank. *Sickle*'s captain had obviously reserved at least a few guns, loaded with shell rather than shot, for exactly that chance, and a pair of thirty-pounder shells had ripped effortlessly through *Bayonet*'s larboard side and exploded inside her.

She'd survived the experience, but the damage had been brutal and the resultant fire had been extinguished only with difficulty. She was clearly unfit for further action after only the two shells, yet *Sickle* had taken at least twenty direct hits from the screw-galleys' massive forward guns before *she*'d finally been driven out of action. Despite the screw-galleys' tough iron carapaces, their opponents could clearly withstand far more damage than they could once enemy fire got past—or around—that protection. The lesson had reinforced Hahlynd's determination to present nothing but the armored aspects of his vessels to the enemy, and if that slowed the pace of the battle, so be it. His screw-galleys were too effective, too expensive, and too damned hard to replace for him to take avoidable losses.

He'd caught up with the enemy's main body just before dark, despite the delay *Sickle* had imposed, and two of his columns had gotten in among the rearmost galleons. Moonless night had fallen before they could drive home their attack, however, and the engagement had come apart in a wild confusion of guns firing at point-blank range. The incandescent fury of heavy guns fired in near-total blackness had made it almost impossible for cringing human eyes to actually *see* anything, and the choking palls of powder smoke had obscured what little they might have seen anyway. The fact that *Sword* and her column had fallen behind the others hadn't helped, but even if he'd been right in the heart of the action, no one could possibly have kept track of the furious melee under those conditions, far less exerted any sort of control. Unfortunately, his smaller, more agile screw-galleys *required* more control at the best of times, and especially when they had to engage at such brutally short ranges. They needed to work as coordinated teams, combining their firepower and protecting one another's vulnerabilities.

That was why Hahlynd had fired the signal rockets, calling the rest of his ships back to rendezvous with *Sword* and regain their formation. He'd seen yet another enemy galleon turned into a torch, blazing against the darkness behind them until the flames reached the waterline, as they fell back, and he knew many of his captains had obeyed his signal only with rebellion in their hearts. He didn't fault them for that . . . but he'd also declined to renew the action until he could sort out the state of his own squadron and at least see the enemy once more. He had enough speed advantage to overtake them by midday, no matter what they did, and he intended to be able to maneuver effectively against them when he did.

*Bayonet* was in danger of sinking by the time he recalled his other units, and her captain had jettisoned her guns in his struggle to keep her afloat. *Dagger* and *Halberd* had taken damage as well, although in their case it was minor. *Carbine*, on the other hand, was taking on water forward. Not only had her armor been breached by at least three round shot, but the recoil of her guns appeared to have started her seams badly. He was fairly certain her captain, like several of his other captains, had ignored his standing orders *not* to fire all three of her heavy guns simultaneously. He couldn't say he was surprised they had—or that he wouldn't have done the same thing in their places—but the screw-galleys really were ill suited to stand that sort of re-peated recoil force again and again. Whether or not that was what had opened *Carbine*'s seams, however, her pumps were hard-pressed to keep ahead of the flood-ing, and it was only likely to get worse if she reengaged the enemy.

He'd decided to send her and *Bayonet* back to Ki-dau, which had left only eleven ships under his com-mand. They'd spent most of the night regaining their formation—now only three columns, with just three ships in the one to windward. Just finding one another had been a challenge, even with the section command ships in each column showing different colored lan-terns at masthead and stern to help sort things out, and he blessed the endless hours of drill they'd carried out in Gorath Bay before ever starting out.

Now it was time to do something with them once again.

"Deck, there!" the cry floated down from above. "*Waraxe* is signaling!"

Hahlynd turned reflexively towards the east, where Captain Haarahld Stymsyn's *Waraxe* led his outermost column, a thousand yards to starboard and a mile or so ahead of *Sword*. He realized he was straining his eyes against the darkness, and snorted at his own fool-ishness. At that distance, especially from deck level, no one short of an Archangel could have seen the signal lantern flashing laboriously from *Waraxe*'s maintop!

The RDN's lantern signals, adapted from the army's heliograph, were short-ranged and even more cumber-some than flag hoists, and the brightness beginning to streak the sky beyond *Waraxe* made it no easier for anyone to read the feeble flickers of light. Hahlynd knew all of that, yet he found his toe tapping the deck as he waited impatiently for the signal midshipman of the watch to decipher this one. Finally, after what seemed far longer than he knew it actually was—

"*Waraxe* signals 'One enemy galleon in sight, bearing northeast-by-north, range five miles,' Sir!"

"North*east*," the admiral repeated. He turned to Captain Mahgyrs with raised eyebrows and realized the flag captain's frown was actually visible in the gathering predawn light.

"Does seem a bit reckless of them, Sir. Assuming they're all still in company and didn't just scatter overnight, that is," he said, and Hahlynd nodded in agreement.

The Kaudzhu Narrows were forty-four miles wide at their southwestern end, but they narrowed steadily. They were barely eighteen miles across at their northeastern end, and the southern side of the passage was lined with treacherous shoals and shallows. He would have expected the Charisians—especially after losing one of their precious ironclads to grounding—to have stayed as far as possible from that hazard to navigation. Apparently he'd been wrong. And it wasn't all bad. If they were to the east, they'd be silhouetted against the dawn whereas his own ships would be much more difficult to pick out against the darker western sky.

For a while, anyway.

"Well, we know where at least one of them is," he told Mahgyrs, "and I doubt they scattered." He shook his head. "No, *Waraxe*'s found a trailer, not a stray. The rest of them are ahead of us somewhere fairly close to hand, and I think it's just about to be light enough for us to go find them."

▼ ▼ ▼

Sir Bruhstair Ahbaht stood on HMS *Broadsword*'s quarterdeck and drummed the fingers of his left hand slowly, steadily on the hilt of his sword.

He stood in the bubble of open space his rank created as the galleons' officers and men prepared for what all of them knew was coming. They'd been fed a hearty breakfast, in keeping with the Charisian tradition, but the messdecks had been unusually quiet. Now he heard muted voices as orders were passed—and as friends spoke softly to one another—and heard the knowledge in them. They were grim, those voices, yet they were far from defeated, and he wondered how much of that was genuine confidence and how much was a thin shell of false bravado over something very different. In fact, he wondered how much of his own confidence—the confidence it was his duty to project, whatever he actually felt—was exactly that.

*It doesn't matter,* he told himself. *You know what your job is now. The least you can do after getting all of them into this crack is to pretend you know how to get them back out of it.*

He grimaced at the thought, and again, more deeply, as he contemplated Kahrltyn Haigyl's orders. He didn't like them, not one bit, but there'd been no time to debate them, especially when the argument would have depended on passing signals slowly and cumbersomely by signal flag to a ship he hadn't even been able to see. Besides, under the circumstances, those orders had made sense, however bitter that sense might be . . . and he'd been too busy executing his part of them to argue.

Thank God the wind had strengthened! With that stronger northwesterly coming in across his ships' larboard quarters, his copper-bottomed galleons could make good better than five knots—almost six. The screw-galleys would still be faster, but their speed advantage had probably been cut by at least a third and the squadron's galleons would be far more maneuverable than they'd been the day before. That was going to make the Dohlarans' task much harder.

With the loss of *Sickle* and *Relentless*, the squadron had been reduced to eleven galleons and *Sojourn*, his sole surviving schooner, and he was grateful the enemy had given his ships time to find one another and settle into something approaching the formation Haigyl had wanted. There'd never been much chance of achieving exactly the desired alignment—not in the dark with wind-powered ships. But *Relentless'* blazing funeral pyre had provided a grim yet useful navigation beacon, and at least she hadn't exploded. There'd even been time for some of her people to take to her surviving boats and find refuge aboard her consorts, and *Broadsword* was approximately where she was supposed to be, the second ship in Ahbaht's line.

Now the only thing that remained was to see if Haigyl's desperate plan worked.

▼ ▼ ▼

"Any sign of the heretics, Markys?"

Markys Hamptyn turned quickly to salute Sir Dahrand Rohsail as the admiral came on deck.

"No, Sir. Not yet," he said.

"Any more of those signal rockets?"

"No, Sir. One of the lookouts did report a 'glow' to the south, but no one else saw it."

"Was it a reliable man?" Rohsail asked, eyes sharpening, and his flag captain shrugged.

"One of my best, actually, Sir. That's why I'm inclined to take his word for it. He might be mistaken, but he's honest as the day is long. If he says he saw something, then I'm pretty damned sure he actually did."

"But he can't tell us anything except that it was a 'glow'?" the admiral asked skeptically.

"No, Sir," Hamptyn admitted.

"Umpf."

Rohsail nodded and walked to *Defiant*'s taffrail. He leaned on it beside one of the stern chasers, gazing out into the darkness and willing the dawn to hurry. The increased wind was welcome, but he didn't like the overcast creeping in from the west. The last thing he needed was rain! Low visibility was far more likely to help the fellow trying to run away than to assist the other fellow trying to catch him, and if this turned into the sort of action he expected it to . . . .

He couldn't be certain the solitary Charisian galleon he'd been pursuing for so long truly was one of the heretics' ironclads. It seemed likely, given its sail plan, the fact that his scouts' best estimate was that it had only a single row of gunports, and the fact that it was wandering around all alone and unsupported. If so, however, he was about to find himself face-to-face with *two* ironclads, and that was a sobering reflection. On the other hand, he had fifty galleons, and they'd have only sixteen.

He would have preferred to overtake the singleton, whatever it was, before it rendezvoused with its consorts, but he'd never had the wind to do that. It was possible he might have managed it with his coppered galleons, but that would have required him to leave half his strength behind, and there'd never been any way of telling how close the rest of the Charisians were. Besides, the damned heretics ultimately had to get back past him one way or the other, whatever happened or however long it took. Under the circumstances, prudence had suggested keeping his entire force concentrated until the moment he really needed it.

Now that moment had come, and he waited impatiently for the sun to break the eastern horizon. It was time to show the heretics they weren't going to get past him after all.

▼ ▼ ▼

"Sail ho!"

The call floated down from *Dreadnought*'s masthead, and all conversation and movement on deck froze as men looked up at the lookout's lofty perch. Kahrltyn Haigyl did the same, waiting tensely for the rest of the report. Whoever it was, it wasn't going to be an unexpected friend, he thought grimly. Captain Ahbaht's galleons had already been spotted and identified—a bit farther south than he'd hoped they'd be, but close enough to work with—so anyone else had to be—

"Looks like at least thirty 'r forty galleons, four points off the larboard bow!" the lookout shouted down after making the best estimate he could. "I make it about twelve miles! Course sou'west, but they're alterin' to leeward!"

*So they've seen* us, *too,* Haigyl thought grimly. *Well, it could've been worse . . . assuming that's everything they've got, anyway. And still headed* southwest, *for the moment at least. Looks like we aren't exactly where they expected to find us. Pity about that.*

"Lubberly lot not to've seen us sooner," he grunted, just loud enough to be certain he'd be overheard, and carefully paid no attention to the grins he saw around him. "And I've time for my morning constitutional before we have to worry about them."

He tucked his hands behind him and began pacing slowly up and down the weather side of the quarterdeck with a calm, thoughtful expression. There was nothing he could do at this point except wait.

▼ ▼ ▼

"Not *quite*, you bastard," Sir Dahrand Rohsail muttered.

He stood about thirty feet above deck level in *Defiant*'s mizzen ratlines, shading his eyes against the fierce light of the newly risen sun as he peered almost directly into it. He'd expected to find the heretics farther west of him, or trying to *get* farther west of him, at any rate. In their place, he'd have fought hard for the wind gauge, holding position up to windward where his pursuers would have found it all but impossible to close with him. The last thing he'd have done would have been to deliberately accept the *lee* gauge, where the enemy would be free to sail down upon him, especially when he was pinned against a coast as dotted with shoals and mudbanks as the southern side of the Kaudzhu Narrows.

They were also a good bit farther north than he'd anticipated, though. He'd deliberately reduced sail overnight on the assumption that the galleon he'd been pursuing had made rendezvous with the rest of the Charisian squadron. It was always possible the other ship's signal flags had been a bluff, an attempt to convince Rohsail it had friendly support close enough to read its messages. They'd gone on for a very long time, however, and he'd been forced to assume there really were additional Charisians in the vicinity. If there were, their only sane course of action, given the numbers, was to avoid action if at all possible, which would mean running for home. They might have chosen to run in front of him, *away* from the narrows, but that was ultimately a losing game as long as he stayed put and blocked the only exit from Hahskyn Bay against them.

At the same time, if he'd pursued too eagerly and blundered into them unexpectedly, the confusion of a night action could only have aided the heretics. All *they* were likely to want was to escape, and it was far easier to simply hold a chosen heading in the darkness than it was to pick enemy from friend and be sure one wasn't firing into one's own consorts instead of the foe.

All those considerations had strongly suggested the enemy would turn back towards South Shwei Bay as soon as possible after darkness fell. They probably wouldn't *want* to fight, but they'd be more willing to accept a night battle than to fight in daylight. By preference, though, they'd avoid engaging at all if they could, which meant they'd work their way as close as possible to the Narrows' *northern* shore in order to take the weather gauge if they could. That was why he'd slowed his own rate of advance and edged up towards the west overnight to stay outside and up-wind of them.

"Clever bastard, aren't you?" he murmured. "Figured out how I'd think and took advantage of it, hey? But you're not far enough north yet, friend."

He gazed at the nearest enemy ship, no more than ten miles clear now. From his current perch, all he could see of the line of additional galleons five miles beyond her were scraps of sail on the horizon. His masthead lookouts had a hard count on them, though, although the numbers seemed to have come up a little short. And there was no doubt about the identity of that single ship between *Defiant* and the other Charisians. It was clearly one of the ironclads, and he rather doubted she was so far to windward of her consorts because of bad navigation. No, she was there specifically to offer battle.

It seemed unlikely, to say the least, that even she could defeat fifty conventional galleons. She could hammer the shit out of anyone who tried to get *past* her, though, and from that perspective, her captain had positioned her almost perfectly. Rohsail was far enough north to intercept the entire Charisian force, but at least two-thirds of his squadron was southwest of the ironclad, where it would have to get past her to reach her consorts. What had been the rearmost third of his own formation had already turned to intercept the head of the heretics' line, and he'd deliberately concentrated his coppered ships to the north, placing his fastest galleons in the best position to pursue the enemy if they'd somehow managed to get past him during the night. Now they should be able to pass ahead of the ironclad to attack the ships it obviously intended to protect. Of course, it was almost certain that the *second* ironclad was somewhere in the midst of those other galleons, preparing to exact a painful price when they *were* intercepted. On the other hand . . . .

*Is it possible they've lost the other one? They're down four galleons for some reason, which means they've taken losses somewhere . . . unless I want to assume they just got scattered for some reason. That's certainly possible, but the weather's been too moderate for them to've been driven apart and what I can see of their formation's too tight to make it anything I'd call likely. Still, I've been assuming those were heretic signal rockets last night, a beacon to guide the ship we've been chasing to the rest of their squadron. What if they weren't, though? What if Hahlynd got here even sooner than I expected he could? Could that "glow" the lookout reported have been a burning ship below the horizon? Is that where the other ironclad went?*

The desire to believe that was greater than any temptation he'd ever felt before, and he forced himself to step on it firmly. A pessimist was disappointed far less often than an optimist, he reminded himself. And either way, he still had to deal with the ironclad he knew about. But if it was true . . . .

He climbed down the ratlines to rejoin Captain Hamptyn on deck.

"It's going to be ugly," he said, "but the bastards aren't getting away from us this time."

"Good!" Hamptyn's eyes glittered. "Ugly or not, the men're eager to be about it, Sir."

"I know they are." Rohsail gazed into the sunrise for a few more moments, then looked back at his flag captain. "Signal the schooners to search to the southwest. I've got a feeling we might just find a few friends in the neighborhood."

▼ ▼ ▼

Sailing ships were neither slash lizards nor race horses at the best of times. Even though the wind continued to slowly and steadily increase in power, the best speed Dahrand Rohsail's ships could make good on their current heading was no more than five and a half knots with all sail set. Once they reduced to fighting sail, they'd be lucky if they could make half that, and because the Charisians continued sailing resolutely northeast, the Dohlarans were forced to sail the hypotenuse of a very long right triangle if they wanted to engage. Even the rearmost Dohlaran galleons had to cover over eighteen miles to reach Captain Ahbaht's line; for Rohsail's van it was closer to twenty-five.

And, of course, his *rearmost* ships were the ones which would be forced to deal with *Dreadnought*, first.

There were few cowards in the Imperial Charisian Navy, yet the gnawing wait as the Dohlarans inched closer with agonizing slowness ate at the courage of even the stoutest heart. Rohsail's squadron wasn't a fleet; it was a forest of titan oaks, a dense and impenetrable thicket of masts, spars, and canvas rumbling down upon them. The ICN knew its worth, knew no other navy in the world was its equal, yet there were odds no qualitative skill could even, and the men in those Charisian galleons recognized the avalanche rolling across the water towards them.

And between the two lines sailed HMS *Dreadnought*.

Kahrltyn Haigyl stood on his quarterdeck, hat low on his forehead to shade his eyes, hands clasped behind him, and watched his enemies come. Unlike the unarmored galleons in Ahbaht's line, *Dreadnought* had set no studding sails or staysails. There was no haste aboard her, and he raised his voice.

"We'll have that signal now, if you please, Master Trymohr!"

"Aye, aye, Sir!"

The midshipman saluted and turned to his signal party. An instant later, the flags went soaring to her mizzen yard and broke to the breeze. A moment longer the silence held, and then it tore apart under the weight of five hundred fierce, baying voices.

"Remember King Haarahld," *Dreadnought*'s signal said, canvas vanishing from her yards as she furled her courses, reducing to topsails and topgallants alone while her speedier wooden sisters forged steadily by on her starboard side. And as they passed, every one of them in turn dipped her banner in salute.

▾ ▾ ▾

"Well, that's a hell of a surprise," Pawal Hahlynd said dryly as he read the smudgy pencil message the signal midshipman of the watch had just handed him.

"Beg your pardon, Sir?" Captain Mahgyrs said from the other side of the table, setting down his stein of beer.

Hahlynd looked up from the note, then smiled crookedly and patted his lips with a napkin. He and his flag captain had decided to make it an early lunch, given how active their afternoon was likely to prove, and they'd been joined by Lieutenant Traivyr and Lieutenant Haystyngs.

"It seems the Charisians are even more popular than we thought they were," the admiral said. "We've just received a signal from *Scourge*, one of Admiral Rohsail's schooners."

His three dinner guests stiffened in their chairs, and he passed the note across to Mahgyrs. He picked up his wine glass and sipped while the flag captain read it. Then Mahgyrs looked up and their eyes met.

"Puts a bit of a different perspective on it, doesn't it, Sir?"

"It does, indeed, Ahlfryd." Hahlynd set down the wine glass and stood. "I believe I feel the need for a bit of fresh air."

The others followed him up on deck, and he held out one hand to the officer of the watch. The lieutenant put his spyglass in it, and the admiral raised the glass, peering at the Charisians they'd been pursuing since dawn.

They'd had farther to go than he'd initially thought, and even with a speed advantage, a stern chase was always a long chase. With no desire to exhaust his cranksmen before he even reached the enemy, he'd settled for pursuing them under sail alone, since his smaller vessels were capable of half again their speed under the current conditions of wind and sea. At that rate, he'd expected to come into long cannon shot of them within the next hour or so, but it seemed he'd been looking in the wrong direction.

He swung the glass away from the Charisians, and there were *Scourge*'s sails.

"Remind me to have a word with our lookouts," he heard Mahgyrs murmur to Lieutenant Haystyngs, and his lips twitched in amusement.

He wouldn't care to be the unfortunate lookouts in question, the admiral thought, although Mahgyrs had a reputation as a humane CO. And he understood how it had happened. Like every other man aboard *Sword*, the lookouts had known exactly where the enemy was—they could damned well *see* them—and the thought of engaging that many galleons—especially *Charisian* galleons—was enough to dry any mouth. Little wonder they'd been so focused on the enemy that they'd failed to note a friend's approach. Still, however understandable, it was also inexcusable for them to allow *any* ship to get this close without being spotted, and he had no doubt Mahgyrs would make that point abundantly clear to his entire ship's company.

"Sir, the masthead reports additional sails beyond *Scourge*," a midshipman told the flag captain very carefully, and Hahlynd was careful to keep the spyglass to his eye, peering out to sea where no one could see his smile. "It, ah, appears to be an entire fleet."

"Why, it's very obliging of them to share that information with us, now that it's come to their attention, Master Walkyr," Mahgyrs replied. "Be so good as to give them my personal thanks for the news."

"Uh, of course, Sir."

Young Walkyr faded away and Hahlynd lowered the glass and turned to raise one eyebrow at the flag captain.

"'An entire fleet,'" Mahgyrs murmured.

"Well, Admiral Rohsail's dispatches did say he was bringing the whole Western Squadron with him," Hahlynd pointed out. "And if he did, that means we have the Charisians trapped between us and fifty galleons."

"Not quite *between* us, Sir," Mahgyrs corrected respectfully.

"Point taken," Hahlynd conceded. "On the other hand, we do have them at what I think we could legitimately call a significant tactical disadvantage."

"Oh, yes, Sir. I imagine we could call it that."

Hahlynd smiled, but then he looked back towards the west, into the eye of the wind, and his smile faded. The clouds weren't coming on all that rapidly, but they *were* turning steadily darker and piling steadily higher. It wasn't just an overcast; it was an oncoming storm, and he could almost hear the thunder already. With a little luck, it would hold off until evening, but if it didn't, his screw-galleys could be in serious trouble.

At the moment, they were just passing Fort Tyshau at the southern end of the Cape Yula Shoal. The name was something of a misnomer; the Harchongese fortifications which had once guarded the Kaudzhu Narrows had decayed into ruins long ago, following the minor unpleasantness during which the Empire had wrested the remainder of Hahskyn Bay and the area about it away from the hapless Kingdom of Sodar. The Harchongians had no longer seen any need to control the Narrows, now that they'd deprived Sodar of the only thing approaching a seaport it had ever had, and the fortresses hadn't been manned in almost a century and a half. Most of the stone and brick of which they'd been built had been appropriated for other uses in the meantime, turning them into little more than heaps of rubble. Three of their names remained, however, appended now to small fishing ports. It was possible he might be able to get the shallow draft screw-galleys into the tiny harbor that served Fort Tyshau, but it was also possible he wouldn't. And even if he could, it afforded poor protection against a powerful westerly.

Fort Nahgah, at the tip of Cape Yula, the southern headland at the head of the Kaudzhu Narrows, would offer a much better anchorage, but it was also the better part of fifty miles from Fort Tyshau . . . with a minor obstacle called the Imperial Charisian Navy between them and it. It was only about ten o'clock and nightfall was still over nine hours away, yet he had to admit he'd feel a lot more comfortable with better protection against foul weather closer to hand.

But the weather wasn't what mattered now.

"I believe it's time we called the cranksmen," he said. "If we can get close enough to nip at the Charisians' heels, perhaps we can encourage them to slow down to maneuver against us. I imagine Admiral Rohsail would appreciate any small effort in that direction on our part."

▼ ▼ ▼

"The screw-galleys are coming up from astern, Sir," Lieutenant Pahrkyns said quietly. Kahrltyn Haigyl turned his head to meet his second lieutenant's eye.

"How far astern?" he asked.

"About five miles, Sir. And it looks like they're making at least ten or twelve knots."

"Impressive," Haigyl observed, then nodded. Pahrkyns touched his chest in salute and moved back towards *Dreadnought*'s wheel while his captain contemplated the news.

Twelve knots was just over twice his own ship's present speed, and quite a bit faster than he'd expected them to be. He supposed he shouldn't be too surprised by that. His information on them had been fragmentary, to say the best, and there'd been no way for Ahbaht to pass him any sort of report on his own experiences against them. If Pahrkyns' estimates of distance and speed were accurate, however, the screw-galleys would overtake *Dreadnought* in a little less than an hour.

That could prove unfortunate. Unhappily, it wasn't the only thing that might be said of, and he turned to Paityr Gahnzahlyz, *Dreadnought*'s gunner.

"It's time to try the range, Master Gahnzahlyz."

▼ ▼ ▼

"About another hour till Admiral Hahlynd overtakes them," *Defiant*'s third lieutenant said.

Lieutenant Parkyr appeared to be speaking to himself, probably without even realizing it, but Admiral Rohsail nodded. By his own estimate, the first of his galleons, HMS *Scepter*, would come within her extreme range of the ironclad in no more than another twenty minutes. Another four or five of the Western Squadron's galleons would be close enough to engage it shortly thereafter, but he cherished no illusion that taking down that ominous, black-hulled monster would be an easy task. He wouldn't object at all if some of Hahlynd's screw-galleys were available to add their weight to the effort.

"I think—" someone else began, but a sudden clap of thunder cut whoever it was short.

▼ ▼ ▼

Captain Zherohm Spryngyr chewed the stem of his unlit pipe as he watched the gap between his ship and the heretic ironclad narrow.

The day had turned into a fittingly spectacular setting for what was about to happen. It was just past midday, the sun at the very start of its western descent, yet the wind out of the west had grown steadily cooler. It had picked up a little more strength, as well. *Scepter* had reduced to topsails and jib in anticipation of what was to come, but that wind was strong enough to heel her to starboard, despite the reduction in sail area. Some of the waves had developed foamy white crests, and the green water around the galleon shaded into a sapphire blue so intense it almost hurt the eye as one looked out towards the horizon. The cliffs along the southern shore of the Kaudzhu Narrows were a steep wall of dark gray and brown stone topped with long, blowing grass, and the sky to the west was an even steeper wall of still darker gray, black-bottomed below and blindingly white above. The sunlight was even more brilliant against that slow-moving mountain range of cloud, and he had an unpleasant suspicion about what the night was going to be like.

*Of course, first we have to survive until nightfall, don't we? I know it's an honor to be the first to engage, but just this minute I wouldn't mind having someone else in closer support.*

He snorted, drawing on the cold pipe. The others would be along soon enough. *Archangel* and *Holy Saint Tyldyn*, the next two ships astern of *Scepter*, hadn't begun reducing sail yet. The additional speed that bestowed upon them would bring them to his support within another ten or fifteen minutes, well before he was likely to need them.

*About three thousand yards,* he estimated. *Need to close to about two thousand to have much chance of reaching the bastard with a twenty-five pounder, so call it another fifteen or twenty minutes. Of course, we won't do much good against his frigging armor until we get a lot closer than that.*

He'd already made up his mind to hold his fire until *Scepter* was within five hundred yards of her target, and he'd loaded with round shot rather than shell. There was no point thinking he could punch shells through the heretics' armor—not from beyond yardarm-to-yardarm range, anyway. From what he could see, it wouldn't even help all that much if he could somehow cross the bastards' stern. The ironclad had a sternwalk, but he'd studied it carefully through his spyglass. There was a single central doorway; aside from that the only other openings in the rounded stern that he could see were gunports or relatively small circular scuttles. The scuttles were probably sufficient to admit light and air, but he doubted very many cannonballs were going to find a way through them.

*Sneaky bastards*, he thought with a tinge of admiration. *Turned the whole frigging ship into an armored battery, didn't they? That thing's going to be Shan-wei's own bitch to take, but the lads should—*

His teeth sank deep into the stem of his pipe as the ironclad's side abruptly belched brown smoke.

▼ ▼ ▼

*"Fire!"*

Paityr Gahnzahlyz' command was swallowed up in the sudden thunder of HMS *Dreadnought*'s number two six-inch gun. The squat, massive cannon recoiled on its Mahndrayn carriage, and the rifled projectile howled away in a choking eruption of foul-smelling smoke.

Kahrltyn Haigyl stood at the larboard broadside's aftermost angle-glass, watching the Dohlaran galleon, and his lips drew back from his teeth as the shell struck the water at least two hundred yards *beyond* the Dohlaran and exploded.

*Dreadnought*'s shells were equipped with what Ehdwyrd Howsmyn's manufactory called "base-mounted percussion fuses." Master Gahnzahlyz had explained their operating principles to him, but Haigyl hadn't worried too much about the details. All he needed to know was that the shells didn't arm until they were fired, and that they relied upon impact, not a lit fuse, to explode.

The white fountain thrown up by *this* shell's explosion was certainly impressive.

"I see we're in range, Master Stahdmaiyr!" he called. "Show them we care!"

▼ ▼ ▼

*"Shan-wei seize them!"* Dahrand Rohsail snarled as the column of water rose, whiter than snow in the sunlight and well over thirty feet tall.

He'd expected to be outranged, but by *that* much?! The ironclad's reach exceeded his own guns' range by at least half. That meant they'd be able to start pounding his galleons as much as half an hour before they could engage it. It also meant the ironclad could cover a far broader zone than he'd allowed for, which would make it even harder for any of the ships from what had become the rear of his column when he turned back to the north to get past it and engage the fleeing conventional galleons. And the sheer size of the water column told him the heretics' shells were going to be far more destructive than he'd anticipated. All of which meant the cost of attacking that ship was going to be far higher than he'd allowed for.

For just a moment, he considered breaking off. But, no, damn it! If there were *ever* going to be circumstances under which the Royal Dohlaran Navy would be able to engage one of the heretics' ironclads, they had to be today's!

"General signal," he snapped. "'Make more sail'!"

▼ ▼ ▼

Captain Spryngyr needed no signals from the flagship. He'd reached exactly the same conclusions as his admiral, and more canvas blossomed abruptly along *Scepter*'s yards as seamen raced to obey a volley of orders. The galleon leaned more sharply to starboard, gathering speed under the press of the extra sail, and Spryngyr turned back towards the ironclad.

They had to get closer as quickly as they could, had to get into their own range of the enemy before the heretics could—

▼ ▼ ▼

*Dreadnought*'s entire larboard side erupted in smoky, rolling thunder. Despite their rifling, her guns were still muzzleloaders. They were wire-wound steel cannon, yes, yet they were little more advanced in terms of accuracy than those of Old Earth's mid-nineteenth-century rifled guns, with none of the advanced fire control systems a later age would have taken for granted. They were individually fired by hand, and all the gunners had to compensate for the motion of ship and target was an experienced eye. The range was thirty-two hundred yards, almost two miles, and HMS *Scepter*'s hundred-and-sixty-foot length made a very small target at that distance.

There were sixteen guns in *Dreadnought*'s broadside, and only one of them actually hit its mark.

▼ ▼ ▼

*Scepter* heaved indescribably as Langhorne's own Rakurai slammed into her.

The elongated, cylindrical shell drilled effortlessly through her stout wooden side. It weighed two and a half times as much as *Scepter*'s own shells, and its eleven-and-a-half-pound bursting charge was six times as heavy. It exploded in the sailing master's small cubbyhole of a cabin, one deck down and twenty feet forward from Captain Spryngyr's cabin, and the blast shredded the gundeck immediately above it.

Eighteen of the galleon's men died in the explosion. Eleven more were wounded, three seriously, and two of her twenty-five-pounders were dismounted. Blast and concussion stunned everyone in the immediate vicinity, but the ominous smell of woodsmoke jerked them back into action. Spryngyr's crew had laid out buckets of water and rigged pumps and hoses in anticipation of the sort of fire hazard posed by exploding shells, and his specially detailed damage parties hurled themselves towards the shell hole. They'd just reached it and begun dousing the smoldering wreckage when *Dreadnought* fired again.

Sixteen more shells snarled through the air. This time, three of them hit their target, and *Scepter* staggered. One shell punched entirely through the galleon before it exploded harmlessly, throwing up a tall, white column well beyond her; the other two were less kind.

▼ ▼ ▼

Admiral Rohsail's face was stone as the heretics' shells hammered *Scepter*. Zherohm Spryngyr's ship continued to close upon her more powerful foe, but she had yet to enter her own extreme range of the Charisian, and he watched through his spyglass as the explosions ripped through her. She wasn't going to make it into effective range, he thought harshly, but she refused to break off. She'd go right on trying, attracting the heretics' fire onto herself, soaking up their shells until her sisters could get close enough to avenge her.

Until she sank or blew up, at least.

He lowered the spyglass. Most of his galleons had begun reducing sail in preparation for battle; now, in obedience to his signal, they were crowding on every scrap of canvas. It would make them more vulnerable to damage aloft, and the additional sails increased the danger of fire, but speed was more important than anything else now. They had to get in close, crowd the bastards, hammer that Shan-wei-damned ironclad from every angle they could. But it was going to hurt them while they tried. Langhorne, but it was going to *hurt* them!

"Signal to Admiral Hahlynd. 'Engage the enemy more closely'!"

▼ ▼ ▼

Pawal Hahlynd had needed no signals. He'd been as appalled as Rohsail by the reach and power of *Dreadnought*'s guns, and he was suddenly sinkingly certain that his screw-galleys' armor wasn't going to stop shells like *that*.

But they'd still have a better chance of surviving than Rohsail's galleons did.

All eleven of his surviving vessels went driving through the steeper waves in bursts of spray, vibrating to the urgent tempo of their cranks. He'd planned on striking his sails when he engaged, the way conventional galleons had for centuries, but now he changed his mind. At least until he was into knife range, he'd need all the speed he could get, both to reach the enemy in time and to make his ships fleet enough to be at least slightly more difficult targets.

▼ ▼ ▼

Sir Bruhstair Ahbaht looked back.

Like Dahrand Rohsail earlier, he stood in *Broadsword*'s mizzen rigging. *Dreadnought* was invisible from deck level now, but he could still see her from his loftier perch. She looked like an exquisitely detailed toy boat in the distance. A toy boat manned by men who were only too much flesh and blood, thundering out thick clouds of brown smoke as she hurled defiance at her enemies while the Imperial Charisian Navy's battle cry flew above her. It was harder to see her target, but the Dohlaran galleon had lost her foremast and was beginning to belch a column of white woodsmoke. Unless she was very, very fortunate, she was doomed, and something deep inside Ahbaht snarled in satisfaction.

He looked away, and his mouth tightened.

Haigyl's plan was working . . . so far at least. As nearly as Ahbaht could tell, at least half of the Dohlaran galleons were driving in on *Dreadnought*. He didn't know whether it was a calculated bid to get inside her reach and overwhelm her quickly or simply that she'd drawn their attention and their anger, and it didn't really matter.

Haigyl was about to find himself engaged at odds of over twenty-to-one, which didn't even count the screw-galleys . . . just as he'd intended. And in the doing, he'd reduced the odds against Ahbaht and the conventional galleons to little more than *two*-to-one. Those were scarcely the numbers any sea officer would have chosen, but they gave his squadron at least a chance. He'd considered hoisting the same signal Haigyl had, but he'd decided against it. The honor of flying that defiant challenge on this day belonged to only one captain, only one ship.

The Dohlarans steering to intercept his own battle line must all have coppered bottoms, judging from their speed, and they'd had the positional advantage from the very beginning, since he was pinned against the coastline to the south. He had to hold his own course, allowing them to close with him if they had the speed for it, and he could visualize exactly what was going to happen, as if he were looking down at markers on a chart. They'd enter engagement range of one another just about . . . *there*, a spot two miles ahead of HMS *Stormbird*, leading the Charisian line directly ahead of *Broadsword*.

He looked aft. Horayshyo Vahrnay's *Vengeance* followed in *Broadsword*'s wake, with Zoshua Kahrltyn's *Firestorm* directly behind her. Combined with *Stormbird*, they were Ahbaht's mailed fist, his battering ram, designed to open a path for the ships behind them. Whether they could hold that path open was another question, of course.

More artillery rumbled and rolled, more than *Dreadnought*'s guns could account for, and he raised his double-glass once more.

At least four of the Dohlaran galleons, and probably more, had opened fire. The range remained long enough he was confident none of those round shot and shells were penetrating *Dreadnought*'s armor, but the pack was closing in. Peering through the smoke, he could just see a cluster of schooner-rigged screw-galleys charging up from the southwest to add their own weight and fury, and he lowered the double-glass and closed his eyes for just a moment.

*Mother Church teaches You love the brave, Lord*, he prayed silently. *Be with them now . . . and be with us in this, our moment of need. Spare my men, please.*

His eyes opened again, and he turned to *Broadsword*'s captain.

"About fifteen more minutes, I believe, Captain Zhaksyn. Be good enough to load and run out, if you please."

▼ ▼ ▼

*"Heads below!"*

Kahrltyn Haigyl had no idea how he heard the warning shout through the bedlam raging all about him, but he ducked instinctively backward . . . just in time to avoid the length of broken spar thundering down from above. He fetched up painfully against the wheel and nearly fell, but one of the helmsmen caught him in time.

He said something in thanks out of pure reflex, but his remaining eye was cold and bleak.

The end couldn't be long in coming now.

He looked the length of his command. The deck was littered with broken rigging and broken men, although there were remarkably few of the latter, given how long the engagement had raged. *Dreadnought*'s armor stood undaunted against her enemies' best efforts, defying full broadsides delivered from as little as a hundred yards' range. The *face* of that armor had been dimpled by literally hundreds of rebounding round shot, and some of those round shot had found their way inboard through gunports. That was what had killed or wounded most of the forty or fifty men he'd already lost—those who hadn't been killed aloft. Three of her guns had been dismounted by direct hits, another was out of action with its slide jammed by another round shot, and a messenger from Paityr Gahnzahlyz had warned him they were almost out of bagged charges for the guns. Gahnzahlyz and his gunner's mates were frantically preparing more, but at the rate his men were firing . . . .

One of the stern chasers roared suddenly, and he wheeled in that direction. He peered through the aftermost angle-glass, and his lips drew back in a slash-lizard smile as he saw a screw-galley swerve to starboard, shuddering in agony while her mainmast went toppling over the side and smoke belched from the wreckage. Two of the galleys had already been sunk, yet his smile faded as nine more of them poured fire into *Dreadnought*. He didn't know what those damned guns of theirs were, but they were one hell of a lot heavier than anything their galleons mounted. They were slower firing, but they hit with enormous power. So far, none of them had managed to penetrate *Dreadnought*'s armor, but they'd found one of her potential weak spots and started pounding away at her rudder. It was a difficult target at the best of times—which the steadily rising waves and strangling clouds of blinding smoke definitely weren't—but if enough of them fired at it long enough, someone was bound to get lucky.

Something screamed through the air above the deck, and Haigyl swore viciously. Chain shot. Chain shot was the only thing that made that unearthly, vicious screaming sound. It wasn't the first time this bloody day he'd heard it, either, and he knew why he was hearing it now. Someone aboard one of those attacking galleons had realized they couldn't defeat *Dreadnought*'s steel-clad sides, so they were trying to kill her mobility exactly like those screw-galleys attacking her rudder. Other galleons' captains had had the same idea earlier, but anyone who got close enough to use the short-ranged anti-rigging ammunition had to come close enough for *Dreadnought*'s six-inch guns to demolish his ship even more rapidly than he could take down her rigging.

Unfortunately, her rate of fire had dropped as exhaustion clawed at her men and it took longer for shells to reach the remaining guns from below. More of the enemies crowding in around her were staying in action longer, getting off more fire of their own before they could be crippled or driven off, and her rigging had already been severely damaged. Her fore topgallant mast had been shot away over an hour ago, taking the fore and main royal masts with it. Thirty feet of her jibboom had been shot away, as well, and the flying and working jibs had gone with it. Now, as the chain shot wailed overhead, a tearing, ripping sound came from above as the mizzen topmast disintegrated just below the topmast cap. The broken spar fell like thunder, and this time the main topgallant came with it. The mast ripped through the protective netting rigged above the decks, crushing half a dozen men, fouling three more guns in the starboard broadside, and then plunging over the side like a sea anchor.

He felt it like a blow to his own body, and swiveled the angle-glass in the direction from which the chain shot appeared to have come. It was hard to even estimate where it might have come from in the wild confusion of smoke, muzzle flashes, and burning galleons, but his eye narrowed as he suddenly saw a familiar profile cleaving through the smoke.

That was no Dohlaran-built ship! That was a *Charisian* galleon, one of the ships Dohlar had taken from Gwylym Manthyr, and Kahrltyn Haigyl snarled.

He'd known from the beginning that *Dreadnought* couldn't escape. The entire purpose of his plan had been to draw as many of the enemy down upon his own command as he could, sacrificing his ship—and his men—so that as many of Ahbaht's ships as possible might escape. And he'd also known from the beginning that his ship could not be allowed to fall into the enemy's hands. Every man aboard her had known what that meant, yet he'd seen no disagreement in any of their eyes . . . not after what had happened to the last Charisians to surrender honorably to a Dohlaran admiral. He'd made sure Stahdmaiyr and all *Dreadnought*'s other lieutenants understood their duty to prevent that from happening and personally supervised the laying of the fuses.

But *this*. He hadn't hoped for this final gift, and his single remaining eye was a fiery coal as he flung himself across the deck.

He tripped, almost falling, and his mouth tightened as he looked down and saw Dahnyld Stahdmaiyr's body. One lens of the lieutenant's spectacles had been shattered by the splinter, blasted from the ironclad's rigging, which had driven through his eye socket and into his brain. Even through the bedlam and the screams and the thunder of the guns, there was room in Kahrltyn Haigyl for a burning stab of regret. But he'd be along to join his first officer soon enough, and he shook himself free and grabbed the shoulder of the midshipman in charge of the nearest three-gun division.

*"Sir?!"*

The youthful midshipman stared at him, eyes wild in a filthy, powder-stained face, and Haigyl pointed at the topsails edging closer behind another howling salvo of chain shot.

"There's your target, boy!" he bellowed, his mouth inches from the youngster's ear. "Mark her down and then *sink the bastard!*"

The midshipman stared at him a moment longer, then looked at the looming topsails and nodded fiercely.

"Aye, Sir!" he shouted back, and turned to his gunners.

Another rending, tearing crash from above announced the destruction of the main topmast. The massive spar crashed downward, and Haigyl felt *Dreadnought* falter under his feet as she was progressively lamed and crippled.

*Not much longer now, girl,* he thought. *Hold together for me!* Please *hold together just long enough, and then, I promise, you can rest.*

The ironclad's guns bellowed again, and again. The Dohlaran ship which had once been Charisian reeled as the six-inch shells slammed into her. Explosions ripped and tore at her planking, and splinters—shell splinters and pieces of her hull, alike—sliced through her crew, spattering her decks with their blood. Haigyl peered through one of the angle-glasses, watching her come apart under his ship's devastating fire, and exulted in her destruction.

*This one's for you, Gwylym! I won't be burning Gorath to the ground for you after all, but this one's for you, but—*

Another salvo of massive ten-inch round shot slammed into *Dreadnought*'s stern from Pawal Hahlynd's screw-galleys, and the ironclad bucked in anguish . . . and then fell off, her tattered remaining sails spilling their wind as her rudder disintegrated and her helmsmen lost control. Haigyl looked up from the angle-glass as she pivoted slowly and majestically, turning downwind, and timber shrieked and splintered as she ran hard alongside one of the Dohlaran galleons.

The enemy ship rolled as the far heavier ironclad drove into her. Her damaged mainmast snapped off two or three feet above the deck level and came down in an avalanche of shattered timbers and shredded canvas. It crashed across *Dreadnought*'s armored bulwark, hung for a moment on the ironclad's already truncated main topmast, then brought both sets of spars down in tangled ruin.

*Dreadnought*'s mainmast was a hundred and twenty feet long and almost forty inches in diameter, made of the finest seasoned nearoak, and immensely strong. Despite that, it snapped cleanly as the massive weight of the Dohlaran's rigging smashed into it. It came crashing to the deck, broken into pieces by the impact, and buried thirty-one of the ironclad's crew in its shattered ruin.

The fragment which landed on Kahrltyn Haigyl was twenty-three feet in length . . . and weighed "only" four tons. He never heard the fierce, savage baying of the Dohlaran crew as it swarmed across the wreckage and onto his ship's deck.

. V .
# West Black Sand River
# and
# Treykyn,
# Cliff Peak Province,
# Republic of Siddarmark

"It's Baron Tryfeld, My Lord."

Sir Clairync Dynvyrs, Baron Wheatfields, looked up quickly from the urgent conference with his senior Jhurlahnkian regimental commander. He waved curtly, putting the other man on hold, and then held out his right hand to clasp forearms with the newcomer who'd just been ushered into the miserable hut serving as his command post.

Sir Daivyn Wynstyn, the Baron of Tryfeld, was only fifty-three, eight years younger than Wheatfields, and bald as an egg, with a fierce, hooked nose which hinted only too accurately at the pugnacity of his personality. He was the senior Usherite commander attached to the Army of Glacierheart, which made him Wheatfields' senior subordinate, and he was also a close personal friend.

"Daivyn," Wheatfields said, his eyes searching the other man's face while the rumble of heretic artillery swelled, crested, then eased—a little, at least—in the background. There was dried blood on Tryfeld's tunic, but it didn't look as if it was his own.

"Clairync." Tryfeld gripped Wheatfields' forearm tightly. "Sorry to break in on you like this."

"What do you need?" Wheatfields asked simply, and the other baron smiled. It was a fleeting smile, and a bitter one, yet there was the warmth of friendship in it, as well. Then the expression vanished, as quickly as it had come.

"What I need, you can't give me," he said flatly, like a surgeon giving a family the last news it wanted to hear. "The heretics've thrown a column across the Black Sand seven miles north of Styltyn. The Third and the Fifth are gone. We can't hold them."

Wheatfields' jaw clenched. He'd hoped—against hope, and in the face of all indications (and experience) to the contrary—that their flank of Cahnyr Kaitswyrth's Army of Glacierheart might somehow hold its ground long enough for him to retake Gyrdahn of the Marshes and open a path of retreat. But if the heretics had fought their way across the West Black Sand River, and if they'd routed or destroyed two of Tryfeld's regiments in the process . . . .

"I came to tell you personally," Tryfeld said, and shook his head. "I'm sorry. The boys did their best, and a hell of a lot died doing it. It was the artillery that did it." His nostrils flared bitterly. "Their regular field guns'd already done for our abatises—frigging river's less than a hundred yards wide, even with all the damned rain, so it wasn't like they couldn't see their targets!—and their small angle-guns pounded the piss out of us until the instant before their assault boats hit our bank. They were firing a mix of explosives to rip open the trenches' overhead and shrapnel to kill everyone in them once the cover was breached. And they've got a new shell—*another* new shell, I guess I should say. This one makes smoke when it lands—a *lot* of smoke. Our field guns couldn't even see to lay down fire on their boats until they were right on top of our own men."

"Shit," Wheatfields muttered.

"I don't know what's happening south of the Fifth," Tryfeld admitted. "I don't think it's good, but that's only a guess. What I do know is that they're pushing as many men as they can across now that they've got a foothold. According to what the Third's survivors're saying, they've got at least two pontoon bridges across by now, and they're rolling my boys up as they push north. I'm trying to form a new position here—" he leaned over Wheatfields' map and tapped a point on the West Black Sand roughly ten miles north of Styltyn . . .

and less than two miles south of where they stood in Wheatfields' command post, located in what had been the middle of his area of responsibility as the Army of Glacierheart's left flank commander "—with the Seventh, but the best Colonel Tylbor's going to manage is slow them down a bit."

Wheatfields nodded, his expression grim, and looked up. He couldn't see the sky from inside the hut, but he knew what he would have seen if he could. Somewhere above the heavy clouds sweeping in from the west, the sun was no more than an hour or two from setting. It was going to be a wretched, miserable night of rain and wind, the last thing men trying to find defensible solid land in this Langhorne-forsaken swamp needed.

"I'm going back to try and find Tylbor enough men to hold at least until nightfall," Tryfeld said. "I don't think we'll last much longer than that. It's time for that breakout of yours."

"Stay here," Wheatfields said. "I'm going to need your advice, and the rest of your—"

"Screw that!" Tryfeld snapped. "Those're my boys out there doing the dying right now. That's where I belong. Besides," he managed something almost like a grin for a heartbeat or two, "they'll hang on longer if they know I'm there to kick their arses if they don't!"

Wheatfields closed his eyes for just a moment. The real reason Tryfeld's men would "hang on longer" was because so many of them would die where they stood rather than disappoint their commander. Tryfeld was that kind of man . . . that kind of friend.

He considered ordering the Usherite to remain, but not very hard. The only way he could enforce an order like that would be to arrest the man. Besides, he was right.

"Daivyn, I—"

"I know, and there's no time to say it, anyway." Tryfeld gave his arm another squeeze, then stepped back. "Frankly, I don't think there's much of a chance for a breakout, anyway, Clairync. But if anybody can pull that off, it's you. So I'll buy all the time I can for your next miracle. Try to get as many of my boys out with you as you can."

"Of course I will," Wheatfields promised. His voice was husky and he cleared his throat harshly. "God bless, Daivyn."

"You, too," Tryfeld said, then turned and shouldered his way back out of the hut, shouting for his horse.

▼ ▼ ▼

Bishop Militant Cahnyr Kaitswyrth's face was drawn and gaunt as he stood beside Sedryk Zavyr and stared down at the pitiless map. The lamp overhead shivered and danced, swaying, casting queasy shadows across the map and its tokens, and dust sifted down from the bunker's heavy log roof. Rain poured from the inky-black heavens, leaking down the earthen steps and sending muddy tendrils across the dirt floor, but the thunder rumbling across the rainy night and setting that lamp aquiver had nothing to do with the weather.

"Have we heard anything more from Bishop Sebahstean?" Zavyr asked anxiously.

"No, Father," Colonel Maindayl said shortly, never looking up from the stack of hurriedly scrawled dispatches.

"What about Bishop Khalryn? Or—"

"Father, we haven't heard anything from *anyone* in the Angle in over three hours," the colonel interrupted, "and we're not going to."

Zavyr looked up quickly, his pinched face flushing angrily. The "Angle" was the east-pointing triangular salient just west of Styltyn which had drawn in more and more of the Army of Glacierheart's troop strength . . . before the Charisians punched through Bishop Sebahstean Taylar's lines north and south of the town. Zavyr had insisted that the position *had* to be held, despite Maindayl's warning that it couldn't be. Now he glared at the colonel and opened his mouth to denounce his "defeatism," but Maindayl only shook his head.

"I'm sorry, Father," he told the Army of Glacierheart's

intendant, his voice hard and yet oddly gentle, "but that's the way it is. This—" he waved the scribbled note the most recent runner had delivered "—is from Bishop Chestyr. He's fallen back to the Swamp Grass, and the heretics're pressing him hard. If they haven't already completely crushed the Angle, they will as soon as they get around to it, because they've got everything in it locked into a pocket it's not getting out of."

Kaitswyrth's stomach was a frozen lump of lead. He wanted to scream at the colonel, but there was no point, and it wouldn't make anything Maindayl had just said any less true. The Swamp Grass River was six miles west of Taylar's headquarters . . . and only five miles *east* of Treykyn.

"We're done, Sedryk," he heard himself say. Zavyr wheeled back to face him, and he shook his head like an exhausted pugilist. "Unless Wheatfields did manage to get some of his men out through the swamps, the Shan-wei-damned heretics have *all* of us in a 'pocket.' " He slammed his palm down on the map and swept viciously across it, scattering the useless tokens, and his lips drew back in a sudden snarl. "*Langhorne!* I told them—*we* told them—we couldn't hold against a *half million* men without more reinforcements! But would anyone *listen?* Of course not!"

"Cahnyr, surely there has to be—"

"There isn't," Kaitswyrth cut the intendant off. "There's not one damned thing we can do, aside from making them use up more ammunition killing what's left of us. And, I'm sorry, Sedryk, but I can't do that."

"What do you mean?" Zavyr said sharply.

"I mean I can't have any more of my men killed pointlessly if there's any way to prevent it . . . and there is. I know what that means for all of our inquisitors— for *you*—but that's going to happen anyway when they move in to finish us off. I can't justify getting more of our people killed trying to prevent something we can't prevent anyway."

The color drained out of Sedryk Zavyr's face. He

looked at Kaitswyrth for a long, silent moment. Then he turned—slowly, like a man moving in a nightmare—and looked at Maindayl. The colonel looked back, his face carved of stone, and the intendant drew a deep breath.

"I see."

His voice quivered ever so slightly, and he swallowed hard. Then the inquisitor who'd ordered the massacre of Charlz Stahntyn's entire command not more than a dozen miles from where he stood that very moment nodded like a poorly strung puppet.

"I see," he repeated. "I think we should fight on, trusting in God and the Archangels to save us, but I understand what you're saying. How long do we have?"

"I need to send the parley request to Eastshare as soon as I can," Kaitswyrth replied unflinchingly. "As heavy as the firing is out there, we probably can't expect them to see a truce flag before dawn, but as soon as the sun rises . . ."

He let his voice trail off, and Zavyr nodded.

"I understand. Well, then." He squared his shoulders and inhaled sharply. "I suppose I'd better go inform as many of my inquisitors as possible, shouldn't I?"

He looked at the two other men in the shivering lamplight, then turned and started up the bunker steps into the rain without another word.

Kaitswyrth watched him go. Then he sat down heavily on one of the stools beside the map table, pulled out his personal notepad, and jotted a half-dozen lines on it. He looked down at them, reading them over, nodded, and dashed his signature across the bottom with a sort of weary finality.

"Here, Wylsynn," he said, tearing off the sheet, folding it, and handing it to the colonel.

"My Lord?" Maindayl raised his eyebrows as he reached to accept it.

"Your orders, Colonel." The bishop militant managed a corpse-like chuckle, but there was no humor in his eyes. "Your last orders, as it happens."

"My Lord?" Maindayl repeated, his tone suddenly taut and cautious.

"Pick a good, reliable man to take the truce flag to Eastshare," Kaitswyrth told him. "Someone you can rely on to keep his head. I think that'll probably be important."

"Of course, My Lord. I think Colonel Zhames would probably be our best choice. I'll inform him you need to speak to him."

"That's probably a good idea," Kaitswyrth agreed in a curiously tranquil voice. "Why don't you go get him now?"

"Certainly, My Lord."

Maindayl nodded and started up the mud-slick steps in Zavyr's footsteps.

He'd made it halfway up when he heard the single pistol shot behind him.

. VI .
# Charisian Embassy,
# City of Siddarmark,
# Republic of Siddarmark

"What do you think of Ruhsyl's surrender terms, Merlin?" Cayleb Ahrmahk asked, looking across the quiet study at Merlin Athrawes.

Merlin stood at the open glass doors to the study's small balcony, one shoulder propped against the lintel, and gazed upward. The night outside the Charisian Embassy was breezy and cool, the heavens speckled with stars no Old Terran would have recognized, with a moon too small for Merlin's memories, but that wasn't what he was actually watching, anyway. His attention was on the imagery from the SNARC hovering above the rubble of what had been the small town of Styltyn, where the Duke of Eastshare had just delivered his terms to what was left of the Army of Glacierheart. Owl's best estimate was that the better part of a hundred and eighty thousand men had been trapped inside Eastshare's net. Less than three thousand others had escaped through the swamps on Kaitswyrth's left under the command of Baron Wheatfields, and they were unlikely to get far with sixteen thousand mounted infantry from the Earl of High Mount's Army of Cliff Peak in hot pursuit. Taken altogether, the Army of God and its secular allies had just lost over a quarter million more men in killed, wounded, and—now—captured, plus the Army of Glacierheart's total artillery park.

"Well," he replied, "they're better terms than the ones he gave that bastard at Fort Tairys last winter. They're about the same as he gave the survivors of Army of Shiloh, really."

"They're also better than the ones General Stohnar gave Wyrshym," Aivah Pahrsahn pointed out from the comfortable, overstuffed armchair in which she sat. She grimaced. "I'm not sure the vengeful side of me approves of that, especially given the difference between Wyrshym and Kaitswyrth—and between Abernethy and Zavyr, for that matter."

"It's not really about some kind of fairness, Aivah," Baron Green Valley said from his hcadquarters at Five Forks. "Having said that, *my* 'vengeful side' agrees with yours."

"I think all of us could agree with that," Baron Rock Point put in from Tellesberg. The high admiral's tone was colder and bleaker than Green Valley's. He'd taken what happened to Sir Bruhstair Ahbaht's squadron—and especially to HMS *Dreadnought*—hard, and it was difficult for him to find much sympathy for the Church's armed forces at the moment. But then he grunted sourly. "Still, I suppose the real question is how it's likely to affect the Army of God's attitude towards future surrenders."

"They aren't really all that *much* better than the ones Wyrshym got," Nimue Chwaeriau pointed out from

Manchyr. "In fact, I think the Duke's a lot sneakier than General Stohnar, when you come down to it. Offering to 'exchange' Kaitswyrth's senior officers for future Charisian prisoners?" She shook her head. "Assuming Clyntahn was willing to contemplate anything of the sort, what do you think would happen to those senior officers once the Inquisition got its hands on them? Not exactly conducive to future loyalty on *other* senior officers' part, I imagine. And what happens to the rest of the Army's morale when captured senior officers who could have gone home *refuse* to be exchanged?"

"Which they will, unless they're stupid enough to think they'd escape the Punishment for their 'failures' once they got back to Zion," Earl Pine Hollow said. The Empire's first councilor sat in his private office, his desk strewn with paperwork, with a whiskey glass in his hand. "I suppose there probably are some who really are that stupid, and that'd probably make handing them over an even better idea. If by some chance they did manage to avoid the Punishment, they might actually end up in command again somewhere they could screw up all over again. Unfortunately, anyone stupid enough to trust Clyntahn is probably dumb enough he forgets to breathe without a reminder."

"Probably." Merlin turned back from the balcony to face Cayleb and Aivah, and his expression was grim. "Of course, Ruhsyl didn't realize when he made the offer that the Temple was really likely to have Charisian POWs to exchange for them, did he?"

Silence fell. It lingered for a few seconds, and then he shrugged.

"Sorry. I didn't mean to be the ghost at the banquet. It's just—"

He broke off with another shrug.

"I know what you mean," Rock Point said harshly, scowling out his flagship's stern windows at the reflections of Tellesberg's waterfront lights. "It's like Gwylym all over again, but with twice the men."

Merlin nodded heavily, except that the Battle of the

Kaudzhu Narrows had actually been far worse than the Battle of the *Harchong* Narrows. Sir Bruhstair Ahbaht had fought his way through to South Shwei Bay, but with only four of his galleons and the single schooner *Sojourn*. The entire remainder of his squadron had been taken or destroyed, and the only reason the survivors had escaped was the concealment they'd found in the sequence of storms sweeping across Hahskyn Bay and South Shwei Bay.

It was bitterly ironic. If those storms had arrived only two days earlier, Ahbaht and Haigyl would very likely have gotten the majority of Ahbaht's squadron— and probably *Dreadnought*—to safety. If not that, the Dohlarans at least would have paid an even higher price for their victory.

Not that they'd gotten off lightly. Sixteen of Admiral Rohsail's galleons had been destroyed, six of them with all hands, and four more were almost certainly beyond repair, which amounted to forty percent of his total pre-battle strength. Rohsail's flagship had been sunk along with them, and Rohsail himself had been badly wounded. In fact, it was unlikely the healers would be able to save his life, which filled Merlin with a vengeful satisfaction. And so did the fact that even though Kahrltyn Haigyl hadn't lived to see it, his ship had sent Gwylym Manthyr's old flagship to the bottom.

Eight of Admiral Hahlynd's fifteen initial screwgalleys had also been lost, most to a combination of battle damage and the stormy seas which had followed the savage engagement. And four of Rohsail's light cruisers—a trio of brigs and a single schooner—had stumbled into Ahbaht's surviving galleons the night after the battle. None of them had survived to inform Admiral Raisahndo, commanding the Western Squadron now that Rohsail was out of action, of where he might find the fleeing Charisians. Of course, even if he'd had that information, it would have taken him the better part of a full day just to sort out which of his remaining thirty-galleons were fit enough to be sent after them. He probably couldn't have come up with more than a dozen of them.

All told, Rohsail and Hahlynd between them had lost twice as many ships as Ahbaht, although many of them had been individually smaller and lighter, and only four ICN galleons had been taken intact—or close enough to it to be repaired, at any rate. One of them, unfortunately, was HMS *Vortex*, one of Ahbaht's two bombardment ships. *Firestorm* had made it out, along with *Broadsword*, *Vindicator*, and HMS *Thunderhead*. That was it, aside from *Sojourn*, and every one of the galleons was severely damaged. And far worse, what no one aboard Ahbaht's handful of battered ships yet knew was that *Dreadnought* had also survived.

No one would ever know exactly how that had happened, since not one of Kahrltyn Haigyl's officers—aside from a single wounded midshipman—had survived the battle. Paityr Gahnzahlyz would probably have fired the fuse on his own initiative if he'd realized the ironclad had been boarded by the companies of no less than three Dohlaran galleons. Perhaps he *had* realized, but if so, there hadn't been enough time between the moment that he did and the moment some idiot of a Dohlaran Marine dropped a lit hand grenade down the main companion just as Gahnzahlyz was headed up it. That grenade had exploded within less than twenty feet of *Dreadnought*'s magazine, which should by rights have carried out Haigyl's last order for him. Somehow, by some perverse miracle, it hadn't. It *had* killed Gahnzahlyz, however. Merlin had no idea where the gunner had been going or why—not even Owl and the SNARCs had been able to sort the last savage minutes of the fight aboard the ironclad into a coherent picture—yet it seemed likely that Gahnzahlyz' death explained why the charges in the magazine had never been fired. The officers fighting for their own and their men's lives on *Dreadnought*'s deck had known he was waiting to fulfill that last, grim duty; quite probably they'd left that to him and abandoned themselves to killing as many Dohlarans as possible before they went down themselves and Gahnzahlyz' gunner's mates had hung on too long waiting for orders from their officers.

No one would ever know, and the why of it didn't matter. What *mattered* was that the Royal Dohlaran Navy was now in possession of the only seagoing ironclad on the Gulf of Dohlar or any of its surrounding waters. And that Dynnys Zhwaigair was about to have six-inch rifled guns on Mahndrayan carriages to examine. God only knew where *that* was likely to lead!

And then there were the five hundred Charisian seamen and officers who'd been captured.

That wasn't all that many, really . . . given that there'd been just over seven thousand men aboard the ships which had been captured or destroyed. Ninety-three percent of the seamen and officers manning those ships had died fighting; that tended to happen when the men in question knew what would happen to them if they were surrendered to the Inquisition. At least four or five hundred of them had been killed out of hand when they could fight no more, although the SNARC imagery suggested many of those deaths had been mercy killings, not cold-blooded murder. Despite the ferocity of the Dohlarans' attack, it was clear some of Rohsail's officers and men had found they had no stomach for repeating what had happened to Gwylym Manthyr and his men.

"I don't know how you could stand to watch that," Aivah said softly. Merlin looked at her, and she gave him a sad smile. "I know you thought you owed it to them, and I suppose it's only right that someone keep watch over them. They deserved it, I know. But even the little of it that I did watch was terrible. If I'd watched all of it, I think it would've destroyed me."

"You live with what you have to live with," Merlin told her, and managed a smile of his own. "Nahrmahn reminded me of that rather . . . forcefully. And you were right, bless your rotund little heart, Nahrmahn."

"I wouldn't want to say anything about how frequently that turns out to be the case, since I'm such a naturally modest sort, with an instinctual aversion to using words like 'infallibility.' Especially where Ohlyvya might hear about it." Nahrmahn replied from his virtual reality, and several members of the conference surprised themselves with chuckles.

Cayleb wasn't one of them, although even he smiled. But then he shook his head.

"This time I want those men back," he said flatly. "Not another Gwylym *this* time. This time we damned well find a way to get them back."

"If we can, we will," Merlin told him, his tone equally flat. "And if we can't, Nimue and I will damned well arrange a magazine explosion to send any ship they're aboard to the bottom. But if they send them overland again—"

"I think that's unlikely this time," Nahrmahn said. All of them looked at his image, and he shrugged. "Clyntahn's going to want them in Zion as quickly as he can get them there. He'll want the biggest, most spectacular auto-da-fé imaginable to flaunt 'his' triumph—especially after what happened to the Army of God—and to be sure he provides a suitable object lesson for anyone whose devotion to the jihad might threaten to waver. Besides, the way he'll see it, Dohlar's just destroyed any Charisian naval presence which could prevent it from shipping them to him across Gorath Bay."

"That," Rock Point conceded sourly, "is entirely too close to true. Once Sarmouth gets to Claw Island, Sharpfield will have a total of ten galleons—none of them ironclads—under his command. And that's assuming all four of Ahbaht's can be repaired out of local resources."

"What do you think Sharpfield will do when Ahbaht gets back to Claw Island?" Pine Hollow asked.

"If he listens to Sir Dunkyn, the Earl will convene a court of inquiry, find that Ahbaht acted in the highest tradition of the Charisian Navy, and return him immediately to command," Nimue said crisply. "We need captains like him, and *he* needs to be put back up on the horse as quickly as possible."

"I don't think Lewk's likely to need Dunkyn's advice

to come to that conclusion on his own," Rock Point said. "I think the real problem's going to be whether or not Ahbaht can come back from this in his own head."

"That's why I said he needs to get back onto the horse," Nimue agreed.

Rock Point nodded. Sir Dunkyn Yairley and Hektor Aplyn-Ahrmahk weren't participating in the present conference for the same reason Sharleyan wasn't. All three of them were at sea, where it was even later at night (or earlier in the morning, depending on which time zone they happened to be in), and all of them were asleep. It was equally late for Nimue, but she had certain unfair advantages where the need for sleep was concerned.

"All right, we can't do anything more about that, at least until Ahbaht gets back to Claw Island and Sharpfield finds out what happened," Cayleb said briskly. "So, getting back to Ruhsyl's surrender terms. Should I take it from what's already been said that there's general approval?"

"I could point out, Your Majesty, that there doesn't need to be *general* approval as long as *you* approve," Pine Hollow said. "Since I'm far too dutiful a first councilor to do anything of the sort, however, I'll just say that they seem to make sense to me. Leaving aside the exchange provision—which we're all perfectly well aware he intended primarily as a political and psychological ploy—the only other thing he could have done with them was to carry out reprisals against the rank and file for what happened to General Stahntyn. If Kaitswyrth hadn't killed himself, I'd recommend executing *him* for that, at the very least. But with him and Zavyr—and two-thirds of his division commanders and *all* of his inquisitors—already dead, I don't really see a point in piling the bodies any deeper, Cayleb. Besides, all those strong backs will come in useful for the harvest. And we're going to have some canals to repair, for that matter. Ahlverez and Harless' waifs seem to be working out quite well in that regard. I don't see any reason the Army of God shouldn't make a similar contribution to the cause."

"You've got that part right, Trahvys," Merlin said, amid a general nodding of heads.

The Army of Shiloh's survivors had been allowed to surrender, for which most of them were pathetically grateful, given what had happened to the Fort Tairys' garrison and the wretched, ragged semi-starvation to which they'd been reduced even before Eastshare sprang his trap upon them. The Safeholdian rules of warfare permitted prisoners who hadn't been paroled to be employed at forced labor, with the proviso that they be properly fed. Accordingly, the Desnairian and Dohlaran POWs had found themselves in southeastern Siddarmark—which included eastern Shiloh, the province which had been their destination—working on the massive farms which had sprung up to replace the western cropland lost to the Sword of Schueler.

Those farms would more than replace the food supply which had been so brutally interrupted that first winter, which was a good thing, considering the half million or so prisoners who had to be fed, as well. None of the guards and supervisors riding herd on the POWs were inclined to be overly gentle, especially in Shiloh, but there was very little overt brutality. Discipline was tough, the hours were long, and the work was hard, yet probably not a great deal longer or harder than the conditions most of the Desnairian serfs would have faced back home. And while the prisoners' freedom of conscience was respected and Temple Loyalist clergy were made available to them, the Church of Charis had seized the opportunity for a little missionary work. Men who'd been as utterly defeated as the Army of Shiloh, the Army of the Sylmahn, and now the Army of Glacierheart might be excused for wondering if God had truly been on their side to begin with, and the Charisian clergy had made some significant inroads among those who'd been in custody longest.

"Do you think Stohnar and Parkair will object to their 'leniency,' Aivah?" Cayleb asked.

"I think Daryus would prefer to collect their heads and let the rest of them rot, to be honest," Aivah replied. "And, frankly, now that I think about it, it occurs to me that he and Greyghor are going to insist that any Army deserters who mutinied during the initial insurrection and then went over to the Army of God should be turned over to face court-martial."

"Oh, damn! She's right, Cayleb." Merlin's expression was chagrined. "I never even thought about that, and I damned well should have—we *all* should have. I guess it didn't occur to me because his cousin pretty much took care of that with the Army of the Sylmahn and it never came up for discussion. But now that someone with a working brain's suggested the possibility, I'm sure just about everyone in the Republic—the part that stayed loyal to Stohnar, at least—would stand up and cheer if the mutineers in the Army of Glacierheart got the same treatment. For that matter, they're not covered under your and Sharley's promise not to seek reprisals against anyone but inquisitors, and they damned well are guilty of mutiny *and* treason under the Republic's law."

"Ruhsyl did include them—at least provisionally—in the terms he offered to the Army of God, though." Pine Hollow sounded faintly troubled. "Or he didn't draw any distinctions *between* them and the AOG regulars, anyway. If we 'go back' on the terms he stipulated—and they accepted—docs that create bigger problems down the road?"

"No," Cayleb said firmly. "First, because Aivah and Merlin are right. They are mutineers and they are traitors, and if Greyghor and Daryus want them, then they damned well get them. And, second, because any military commander's terms are always subject to confirmation by his political superiors, just like Thirsk's terms to Gwylym were." The emperor's mouth twisted around the bitter taste of his own words, but he continued unflinchingly. "In this case, the political superiors in question are our allies, and they and their country have paid a pretty damned horrible price. We ought to've given him specific instructions about this before he ever launched his attack, and I'm frankly surprised—now that I think about it—that the Siddarmarkians didn't insist on our doing exactly that."

"I think they may have taken it as a given that any mutineers taken in enemy service would automatically be handed over to them," Green Valley said after a moment. "Which means it's a good thing Ruhsyl's dispatch will be coming to *you* before it goes to Stohnar or Parkair. We've got time for you to get out in front and point out to them that this was an oversight and that, obviously, mutinous members of the Siddarmarkian Army aren't covered by it."

"That sounds like a very good idea to me, Cayleb," Pine Hollow said firmly. "We don't really owe the traitors in question anything, and any problems we may have with the other side 'down the road' are a hell of a lot less important than making sure we don't offend our allies. Especially over something like this."

"I agree," Cayleb said, and glanced at the clock on the study wall. "And on that note, I hereby declare this com conference adjourned."

. VII .

HMS *Chihiro*, 50,
Gorath Bay,
Kingdom of Dohlar,
and
HMS *Destiny*, 54,
Claw Island,
Sea of Harchong

The Earl of Thirsk sat back from the report on his desk with a face of stone. He was alone in his day cabin. He'd deliberately sent Mahrtyn Vahnwyk, his personal secretary, off on an invented errand to ensure that he would be alone when he read Caitahno Raisahndo's report. He'd read the brief initial dispatch the semaphore had transmitted immediately after the battle, so he'd already known a great deal of what this follow-on, detailed report was going to say when the dispatch boat delivered it, just as he'd known why it was from Raisahndo rather than Sir Dahrand Rohsail. And because he'd known what it was going to tell him, he'd also known the last thing he'd needed was for anyone else to see his reaction when he actually read it.

He tried to feel regret that it had been left to Raisahndo to write the final report of the Battle of the Kaudzhu Narrows, but it was difficult. Although Rohsail had adapted far better to the realities of the reformed Dohlaran Navy than Thirsk had once believed would have been possible, he remained rebellious where many of Thirsk's reforms—primarily those relating to the discipline of enlisted personnel and the earl's prohibition of capricious use of flogging and the cat—were concerned, and no one would ever mistake him for a Thirsk partisan. His reflex arrogance didn't exactly endear him to those about him, either. Thirsk un-grudgingly acknowledged the determination and initiative which had made possible the Royal Dohlaran Navy's greatest victory in at least the last half-century, but he still couldn't bring himself to *like* the man.

*And berating yourself for that is another way to postpone dealing with what's staring you right in the face, isn't it, Lywys? But it's not going to go away, however much you want it to.*

He shoved up out of his chair and stalked aft to stare grimly out *Chihiro*'s stern windows. The bright, late-afternoon sun beaming down on the city of Gorath, the colorful banners popping and snapping against the blue sky and puffball white clouds, and the white horses following one another across the harbor on the wings of the sharp northwesterly wind were a stark contrast to the darkness swirling about within him. He tried to recapture the emotions he'd felt when news of Rohsail's great victory first reached Gorath. There'd been no report then of enemy casualties . . . or prisoners. He'd been free to think about—*feel* about—the battle the way any secular admiral might have felt, and what he'd felt had been exultant elation . . . and somber, proud pain for the price his reformed and reorganized navy had paid to win it.

Yet even then, the exultation had been flawed, for he'd already known (whether he'd wanted to admit it yet) there would be prisoners. Or, if there weren't, there'd be the knowledge that his navy had slaughtered its defeated foes rather than offering quarter. And the truly hellish part of it, before Raisahndo's report put the doubt to rest, was that he'd almost hoped it would be the latter.

It hadn't been. Reading between the lines, he knew quite a few of those defeated Charisians *had* been killed out of hand, and he found himself wondering how many of the men behind those killings had done it out of fury and hatred . . . and how many had done it for the same reasons *he* would have? He'd never know, but he knew now that there were five hundred and twenty-three Charisian prisoners headed back down the canals towards Gorath, and his jaw clenched against the need to curse out loud.

*Damn you, Caitahno*, he thought harshly. *Oh*, damn *you for doing this to me! Don't I have enough innocent blood on my hands already?!*

He leaned his forehead against the glass, closing his eyes, and forced the bitter, bitter anger to subside. He knew exactly why Raisahndo had opted to send the Charisians back to Gorath via the canals, and he wondered if Zhaspahr Clyntahn's wrath would descend upon the other admiral. No doubt the Inquisition would be of the opinion that they should have been dispatched directly to Zion by the fastest possible route, and he rather doubted Clyntahn would accept Raisahndo's reasoning for not doing exactly that.

The admiral who'd inherited command of the Western Squadron had pointed out that more than half his surviving ships were badly damaged. He'd needed every hand he had to deal with their repairs and to reinforce ships' companies which had been brutally winnowed in the battle. He would have been able to provide—by his estimate; Thirsk more than suspected that estimate was purposely low—no more than half a dozen galleons to transport the prisoners, and he knew at least four Charisian galleons had escaped. It was entirely possible additional Charisian ships had been dispatched to reinforce Earl Sharpfield at Claw Island, as well, and there was always the possibility that his six galleons might have been intercepted en route to Saram Bay or Malantor. In that case, both they and the prisoners might very possibly have been lost to the enemy. Sending them to Gorath by canal barge would take longer—they wouldn't arrive until the middle of the month—but in the long run, it would be safer and more secure, at least until they knew the Charisians *hadn't* reinforced Sharpfield.

It was nonsense, although if Raisahndo and Thirsk both insisted the logic was sound—and there truly was a *smidgen* of logic to it—and both of them kept their faces straight while they did it, they might make it stand up. But Raisahndo's real reasons were perfectly clear to Lywys Gardynyr.

*You watched me send Gwylym Manthyr and his men to Zion, didn't you, Caitahno? Oh, it was the Inquisition who transported them there, but you watched me let the fucking inquisitors take them. Watched me stand there like a gutless coward while men who'd surrendered honorably—surrendered honorably to you and me—were handed over to be tortured to death by that fat, sick, sadistic bastard. And you couldn't do it again, could you? You couldn't be the one who personally sent these men to Zion to die exactly the same way. So you're sending them here, instead . . . so I can be the one to do it all over again.*

Caitahno Raisahndo was a good man, a loyal officer, even a friend, and Thirsk tried hard—*hard*—not to hate him for what he'd done. And the truth was that Raisahndo was completely justified, both legally and morally. The Earl of Thirsk was the Royal Dohlaran Navy's senior uniformed officer and King Rahnyld and his entire government were located right here in Gorath. In the absence of standing orders on the subject of prisoners of war, his decision to send them home to his superiors was perfectly correct.

And it left Lywys Gardynyr face-to-face with the horror of his own past blood guilt, the hideous prospect of culpability in yet more acts of murder, and the terrible decision about what to do about it.

▼ ▼ ▼

The midmorning sun was climbing towards noon as HMS *Destiny* and the rest of her squadron made their way close-hauled on the larboard tack between Hardship Shoal and Hog Island. The wind was out of the north-northwest, which would have been dead foul for an attempt to use Snake Channel, farther to the south, but once they rounded the tip of the shoal and made the turn into North Channel they could make the anchorage with a leading wind—what was often called a "soldier's wind"—from just abaft the beam.

It was a beautiful day, if more than a little hot—days were always hot at Claw Island—and clouds of seabirds and wyverns gusted and eddied about the galleons. The squadron made a brave sight under its towering pyramids of canvas, with banners starched stiff by the wind, pushing through the moderate seas in bursts of spray. Baron Sarmouth's squadron had been reinforced before he left Manchyr, and the ten powerfully armed ships of his command would be welcome additions to Earl Sharpfield's command.

In fact, the baron thought bitterly, no one on Claw Island had any concept of just how welcome his squadron was going to be.

He glanced sideways at the profile of the youthful lieutenant at his elbow and recognized the tension no one else would see behind those calm, watchful eyes. Young Hektor had taken the Kaudzhu Narrows hard. In fact, he'd reported sick and retreated into his cabin for two full days, and Sarmouth had envied him. He'd wanted to do the same thing, but he hadn't had that option. No doubt some of his subordinates wondered why his temper had been so short, why his attention had seemed to stray so readily. A part of him had been angry at Hektor for "hiding" instead of doing his own bit to shore up the illusion of normalcy, but he'd realized even then that it was irrational. Perhaps he should have tried to order Hektor not to watch the engagement, but that would have been irrational, as well. They both would have known it was being fought, whether they'd watched it or not. They were only fortunate that the timing had required both of them to be about their duties, interacting with the other officers and men around them for so much of it. Neither of them had been able to watch the fight as it happened under those constraints . . . which hadn't prevented both of them from viewing the recorded imagery afterward.

*And as hard as it hit him, it was so much better to have him "sick" in his cabin,* Sarmouth admitted. *He's a good lad—a good man—and that's the very reason he couldn't have pretended nothing had happened until he'd had a chance to deal with it.*

The fact that he'd been able to spend so much of that time talking with his wife—and with Maikel Staynair—over the com had helped, Sarmouth knew. Yet he'd found himself wondering how well Hektor would be able to dissemble over the next endless five-days. It would be at least fifteen or sixteen days before word from Sir Bruhstair Ahbaht could reach Claw Island. How would Hektor—how would *he*—manage to conceal their knowledge of what had happened in the meantime?

*I thought I'd realized how damnable a curse knowing things like this might be when Her Majesty and Nimue explained it to me, but I was wrong. It was all still theoretical for me. Now it's* real, *and God how it hurts!*

Like Hektor, he'd known all too many of the men

serving aboard some of those ships. Not all that huge a number against a navy size of the ICN, perhaps, but it was big enough to rip a bleeding hole deep within him. The grief—and rage—had eaten at him like acid, and he'd wondered how in God's name he was supposed to smile his way through the traditional meals ashore and afloat which always greeted the arrival of a new squadron at a foreign station.

*You're* not *going to be able to . . . so it's a damn good thing you won't* have *to after all. Here, at least,* he told himself flatly, and reached out to rest one hand lightly on Hektor's shoulder.

"Sir?" Hektor turned towards him, one eyebrow raised over a brown eye dark with the same sorts of thoughts his admiral had been thinking.

"I know you're going to be brokenhearted at spending so little time in the garden spot of the Sea of Harchong," the baron said, twitching his head at the sun-beaten hillsides reaching out to them. "Unfortunately, our orders don't leave us much leeway, do they?"

"I suppose not, Sir," Hektor said. "Her Majesty *was* pretty emphatic, wasn't she?"

Sarmouth's mouth quirked in a smile.

"Yes, she was," he agreed. "And, on balance, I think she was wise. Captain Haigyl and Captain Ahbaht have been doing an excellent job, but we really should have a flag officer forward deployed to Talisman. And it won't hurt to strengthen our forces west of the Narrows."

"No, Sir, it won't."

Hektor nodded firmly, although Sharleyan had said nothing of the sort before they'd sailed. It wasn't as if she would have disagreed with what Sarmouth was now suggesting, even before the Kaudzhu Narrows. It was simply that it hadn't occurred to her to jostle Sharpfield's elbow with any explicit suggestions about how he ought to manage the ships committed to his command. All things were subject to change, however, and Sarmouth was still a bit bemused—grateful, but bemused—by what some of those changes meant.

It was entirely possible Sharpfield would have wanted them back underway to Talisman Island within twenty-six hours of their arrival, given the numbers and the need to maintain as powerful a forward presence as possible. It was also possible, though, that he'd want to retain them for three or four days, being certain Sarmouth was thoroughly updated and informed before he assumed his new duties. After all, the baron had to be five-days, probably months, behind on events since the recapture of Claw Island and the Charisian Navy's return to the Gulf of Dohlar. And, under normal circumstances, Sarmouth would have been perfectly content to spend those days at anchor, if only for the opportunity to establish the proper rapport with the earl.

Unfortunately, circumstances were anything but normal after the Kaudzhu Narrows disaster. He needed to get forward as rapidly as possible . . . which made it fortunate that he now had written orders, signed and sealed by Empress Sharleyan herself, to do just that. Of course, they'd arrived onboard *Destiny* only night before last, delivered by one of Owl's remotes, and Sharleyan had never actually personally touched them. Owl was quite capable of writing orders—or anything else—in just about anyone's handwriting. In this case, though, he'd at least had the supposed author's permission to write them, which was seldom the case in his other forgeries.

What mattered, however, was that Sarmouth had them now and they told Earl Sharpfield the Empress wanted him deployed to Talisman Island as rapidly as possible. Which meant Sharpfield would do just that.

*And that*, the baron thought, nodding back to his flag lieutenant and returning his own attention to the winged escorts scolding and whistling about his flagship, *will be a very good thing indeed*.

"Well, at least they've decided *something*," Lord of Horse Taychau Daiyang, Earl of Rainbow Waters, said sourly, laying the thin sheaf of pages on the tabletop and setting the paperweight to hold them down. "Even if the something in question does leave quite a bit to be desired. To say the least."

The commander of the Mighty Host of God and the Archangels sat in the small, exquisitely carved and painted gazebo outside his rather more utilitarian office with an eggshell-thin porcelain teacup steaming in his hand. His nephew, Baron Wind Song, sat on the other side of the lacquered tea table and raised one eyebrow a fraction of an inch.

"Oh, don't worry yourself, Medyng," Rainbow Waters said. "I'm not likely to discuss it quite this . . . frankly with anyone else. But I smell the stink of desperation in our latest orders."

"I'm . . . less surprised to hear that than I might have wished, Uncle," Wind Song said after a moment.

The baron was twenty years younger than the earl, which made him a bit on the youthful side for his position as what amounted to the Mighty Host of God and the Archangels' chief of staff. He was, however, more intelligent than most and meticulously organized, and he had a great deal of energy. In addition to which, of course, he had the noble birth required for his position. In public, he was always careful to address his uncle by his title or military rank; in private, there was little point pretending the familial bond wasn't at least as important as any of his other excellent qualifications.

"Are you not, indeed?" Rainbow Waters' smile was thin. "Well, your mother always told me you were a clever lad."

"Odd that she never shared that opinion with me,

Uncle." Wind Song's eyes gleamed with brief but genuine humor. "I believe the exact way she put it to *me* was that I was an *overly* clever lad who was bound to come to a bad end someday."

"My sister always was an excellent judge of character," Rainbow Waters agreed. Then his own smile faded. "In this case, however, and with all due respect for your mother's opinion, the amount of cleverness required to recognize disaster probably isn't all that great."

"Is disaster not too strong a word at this point?" Wind Song asked a bit delicately, and Rainbow Waters snorted.

"That depends upon who uses it and to whom he applies it." The earl sipped tea then lowered the cup. "In the case of the Army of God at this moment, I think it can be fairly applied. The question before us is whether or not the Jihad can recover from the . . . less than brilliant decisions which have led to that disaster."

"I see."

The baron sat back in his rattan chair and crossed his legs. He reached into his belt pouch and withdrew a chamberfruit foamstone pipe and a leather tobacco pouch. The chamberfruit—a native Safeholdian plant similar to Old Terra's calabash gourd—had been carefully shaped while it grew, then carved and further shaped to receive its foamstone bowl. Deceptively simple figures ran down the outside of the chamberfruit, which was bound in silver filigree, and Wind Song's fingers moved nimbly as he filled the bowl.

"Is the situation truly that bad, Uncle?" he asked as he finished the time-buying task and puffed the tobacco alight with a splinter ignited in the spirit lamp heating the teapot. "It seems sufficiently . . . grave to me to cause considerable concern, but you seem to be suggesting the situation is even .worse than I'd assumed."

"I may be overly pessimistic," Rainbow Waters conceded as his nephew's fragrant pipe smoke drifted across the table to him. "The less than stellar performance of every other commander who's faced the heretics in battle doesn't precisely offer much to induce and sustain *optimism*, however." He took another sip of tea. "The problem which currently concerns me most, though, is twofold. First, I believe the Inquisition is underestimating the heretics' actual present troop strength and being . . . overly sanguine about their *future* troop strength. Second, I fear the decisions being dictated to us are . . . militarily suspect, shall we say?"

"Overly sanguine?" Wind Song repeated. "Uncle, there's no way Bishop Militant Cahnyr could possibly have faced the half million men he *claimed* had been massed against him. I know you've seen the reports and my own people's analysis of them. The heretics' total field strength couldn't possibly have been much in excess of two hundred and fifty to three hundred thousand."

The baron forbore to mention that he and his uncle had assembled their own staff of analysts—recruited primarily from the scholars and the sons of merchants and bankers who'd somehow found themselves serving with the Mighty Host—precisely because they no longer trusted the sorts of numbers they were getting from people like Cahnyr Kaitswyrth. Or from the Inquisition, for that matter, although they'd been *very* careful to avoid mentioning *that* to anyone else.

"No, it couldn't," Rainbow Waters agreed. "And in our latest dispatches from Zion, his estimate's been reduced somewhat. I believe they're now placing the heretic Eastshare's total troop strength at perhaps the three hundred thousand your own analysis had already suggested. Their total estimate for the strength the heretics have in the field is now approximately five hundred thousand, or somewhat less than half the Mighty Host's strength. However, I believe they're still significantly underestimating the heretics' artillery support, and that they're making insufficient allowance for how much of the heretics' infantry is mounted. That much, at least, should be clear from what happened to the Army of Glacierheart! More to the point—and much more dangerous for the future, Medyng—I believe they continue to underestimate the rate at which the heretics are able to produce the arms needed to stand up additional fresh formations. In other words, even if their current estimate for the total number of infantry and cavalry currently facing us is reasonably accurate, their estimate of the *combat power* of the heretics' present armies is low and I believe their estimate of the combat power the heretics will be able to put into the field *next* year."

Wind Song smoked in silence for several seconds, reflecting upon his uncle's analysis. Much as he would have liked to, he couldn't dismiss Rainbow Waters' reasoning. Still . . . .

"Our own weapons production rates are continuing to climb, Uncle," he pointed out. "And the latest reports on the performance of Brother Lynkyn's . . . rocket artillery arc promising."

"Oh, I'm not attempting to argue that we won't be able to equip our armies with new and better weapons of our own. Nor am I unaware of the way in which Mother Church's new manufactory techniques should help to close at least some of the gap between the heretics' accursed productivity and our own. However, the events of the past few months make it evident—to me, at least—that the initiative lies presently with the heretics. Prudence suggests that we . . . reassess our own strategy and operational methods in light of the fact that the heretics will almost certainly launch fresh offensives as soon as they possibly can."

"Forgive me, but isn't that what these—" Wind Song's index finger tapped the pages on the tabletop "—are intended to do?"

Rainbow Waters nodded, because his nephew was entirely correct.

Baron Falling Rock's fifty thousand men had reached Lake City the five-day before. The rest of the Mighty Host was only beginning to stir into full movement now that the canals were available once more, however. He didn't like the lateness of their start, but there'd been little he could do about it. And little as he liked his involuntary tardiness, he liked the Temple's requirement that he send a third of his total strength—four hundred thousand men—to shore up the Church's southern flank in Westmarch and western Cliff Peak even less. He couldn't argue with the need to bolster that flank as quickly as possible in the face of the Army of Glacierheart's destruction, and he'd already selected Lord of Horse Zhowku Seidyng, the Earl of Silken Hills, to command the about-to-be-formed *Southern* Mighty Host of God and the Archangels. The problem was what the Temple wanted to do with the other *eight* hundred thousand men of the original Mighty Host.

"The canals and roads in Bishop Militant Cahnyr's rear are either already demolished or will be destroyed before the heretics can capture them," he said, with a silent prayer of thanks that Baron Wheatfields had been able to pass the order to execute Cahnyr Kaitswyrth's plans in that regard. Exactly how the baron had managed to get that order out of the Aivahnstyn Pocket was more than Rainbow Waters was prepared to guess, but he was profoundly grateful.

"The destruction of the transport system will severely degrade the heretics' supply capabilities as they try to follow up their victory," he continued. "I think it would be a mistake to underestimate their ability to work around the difficulties it's likely to impose, but it will definitely hamper them. However, we both agree that at the moment somewhere around two-thirds of their total combat power is concentrated under Eastshare in Cliff Peak, whereas we're proposing to face it with only *one*-third of our own strength. The preponderance of the Mighty Host is under orders to advance to join Baron Falling Rock at the extreme end of our own intact—*presently* intact—transport system. At the same time, the heretic navy is once more operating throughout the eastern half of Hsing-wu's Passage, they've reoccupied Spinefish Bay and retaken Salyk, they're in the process of restoring the Guarnak-Ice Ash Canal, and their ironclads are once again operating up the Hildermoss River."

He sat back, regarding his nephew levelly, and Wind Song drew heavily on his pipe as he considered his uncle's last two sentences. The Holy Langhorne Canal offered secure communications as far forward as Lake City . . . at the moment. The addition of that qualifier sent an uneasy shiver through him as he contemplated the flipside of that particular coin. *Without* the canal—or if that canal were somehow cut behind them—they couldn't possibly keep eight hundred thousand men fed and supplied. For that matter, they'd just experienced the difficulty of moving a force barely six percent that size along the Holy Langhorne when it was frozen, so what happened when winter closed the brief northern campaigning season once more in October?

"These orders," it was Rainbow Waters' turn to tap the sheets of paper under the paperweight, "are obviously weighting our left wing to advance beyond Lake City while effectively holding our ground—at best—with our right. I think, frankly, that Silken Hills will require more than four hundred thousand men to be confident of holding, or at least significantly delaying, the sort of army Eastshare's just demonstrated he commands. And the thought of launching twice that many men into Icewind, New Northland, and Hildermoss when the heretics are already in control of the existing roads, rivers, and canals . . . does not fill me with overwhelming confidence."

"Our instructions say nothing about advancing beyond Lake City," Wind Song said slowly.

"No, they don't. Yet, at least."

Rainbow Waters poured fresh tea into his cup, inhaled the fragrant steam, and sipped appreciatively. Then he lowered the cup once more.

"Medyng, when Eastshare has just very convincingly demonstrated the threat he represents, yet only a third of our strength is being deployed against him while all the remainder of it's funneled along the Holy Langhorne, Mother Church clearly contemplates using that strength for something besides sitting in Lake City and digging entrenchments around it. What do you suppose that 'something' might be?"

Wind Song drew on his pipe, and that uneasy shiver went through him again, stronger this time.

*The camps*, he thought. *He's talking about the Inquisition's camps.*

Despite Bahrnabai Wyrshym's defeat and the destruction of the Army of the Sylmahn, the Army of God and its Temple Loyalist militia allies still had perhaps two hundred thousand men under arms in Tarikah, Icewind, eastern New Northland, and northwestern Hildermoss. Scattered over that vast an area, they couldn't possibly resist the sort of offensive the tightly concentrated heretic armies could throw against them. In fact, the baron suspected, many of them wouldn't even try very hard, as disheartened and demoralized as they must be after the one-two punch the heretics had just delivered.

But those two hundred thousand AOG troopers and militia hadn't been distributed to resist major heretic attacks in the first place. They were there to suppress any local sentiment towards returning to loyalty to Lord Protector Greyghor . . . and to protect Inquisitor General Wylbyr's camps. But those camps were distributed over a dozen widely dispersed locations. The forces already in position couldn't hope to defend them against a serious heretic effort to liberate them.

*And neither can the Mighty Host. Not really. And if we get pulled too far forward from Lake City . . . .*

"What we ought to be doing," his uncle said quietly, "is ordering every man who can to fall back into Tarikah Province. And they ought to be destroying every canal lock and every bridge behind them as they retreat. We can turn Lake City into a canal head covered with entrenchments even the heretics won't penetrate easily, especially with the new artillery to support us. If we use the summer to stockpile supplies at Lake City, we can create a supply point capable of sustaining our entire force for five-days or even months, even if the canal is somehow cut behind us. In the meantime, we ought to take at least half of the strength we've been ordered to send to Lake City and either attach it to Earl Silken Hills or create an additional reserve in Jhurlahnk or Usher, where it would be available to reinforce either wing and simultaneously reduce the logistical strain on the Holy Langhorne. We need to stabilize our own front, be sure of our own supply lines, and concentrate on equipping the new armies Mother Church is currently raising. Then, next spring, we need to *use* those new armies and weapons to resume the offensive—hopefully before the heretics can overcome our numerical advantage. *That's* what we ought to be doing . . . militarily speaking, of course."

"Of course, Uncle," his nephew repeated.

They sat gazing at one another across the gazebo in the warm sunlight, and Baron Wind Song wondered how the July sun could feel so cold.

### . IX .
### Camp Dynnys,
### Lake Isyk,
### Tarikah Province,
### Republic of Siddarmark

White smoke billowed up, sinus-tearing and choking whenever the wind blew it back into someone's lungs. It was amazing how hot a paper-fed fire could burn. It was seldom what one might have called scorchingly hot this far north even in early July, but the fierce heat radiating from the fire pit was like a blast furnace's breath.

"Faster!" Father Zheryld snapped at the ragged, laboring line of inmates he'd impressed for the task. "*Faster*, Shan-wei take you!"

Brother Ahlphanzo Metyrnyk coughed harshly, despite the wet cloth he'd tied over his face and nose, as he stirred the fire with a long-handled rake to encourage the flames. The heat seemed to be singeing every hair on his head, his garments stank of smoke, and perspiration greased his face with a skim of ash and soot. Two more members of Father Zheryld's staff had quietly disappeared night before last, and Metyrnyk wondered where they thought they were going to go. Obviously they wanted to be somewhere else before the heretics arrived, but things seemed unlikely to end well for them, wherever they went. He was only twenty-six years old and a mere lay brother of the Order of the Quill, but he'd seen and learned enough over the last two years to have a pretty shrewd idea of how the Inquisition would deal with anyone who deserted his post at a time like this.

*Of course, that's going to happen to them somewhere in the future*, he reflected glumly. *They're probably worried more about the* immediate *consequences if they* don't *disappear*.

Well, he was worried about those consequences, too, but he couldn't quite bring himself to just cut and run that way. He wondered if that was because he could imagine those future consequences more clearly than the deserters (and preferred to take his chances with the heretics, all things considered) or if it was something else, something innately crossgrained about his nature.

"*Idiot!*" Father Zheryld barked. A whip hissed and cracked and someone cried out. "Get up, you clumsy cow!"

Metyrnyk looked over his shoulder and grimaced under the protective concealment of the water-soaked bandanna. He'd never much liked Zheryld Cumyngs. The under-priest and he might be members of the same order, but Cumyngs was a pale, colorless, petty tyrant of a man. Metyrnyk had done his duty as part of Camp Dynnys' administration, but he'd never liked it. Some of the things that went into the records and files he helped maintain had been enough to chill a man's blood, and there'd been nights—many of them—when he'd found it damnably hard to sleep. He doubted Cumyngs had ever missed a single wink. There was something almost . . . banal about him. He never questioned anything he was told to do—or believe—by his superiors, and the consequences of his actions never bothered him at all, as far as Metyrnyk could tell. To him, Camp Dynnys' hapless inmates were no more important, no more human, than a farmer's cattle or draft dragons, and Metyrnyk suspected that was exactly how he saw them . . . in more ways than one.

Now he kicked the inmate he'd lashed, driving the young woman who looked three times her age thanks to starvation and casual brutality back to her feet, and punched her as she staggered erect.

"Pick it up—*now!*" Cumyngs barked, and she began gathering up the scattered sheets of the files she'd dropped when she fell. One of the Army of God privates guarding the labor party looked unhappy as blood streamed from the nose the under-priest's fist had crushed, but he only turned his head and looked away as she managed to claw most of the pages back together, carried them to the fire pit, and flung them in.

Apparently Cumyngs had at least a little more imagination than Metyrnyk had ever believed he possessed, after all. He had enough of it to account for the terror in his eyes, at least, and Metyrnyk wondered if he had some special reason to feel that terror.

▼ ▼ ▼

"No, My Lord," Colonel Ahgustahn Tymahk said flatly.

Bishop Maikel Zhynkyns stared at the colonel incredulously. The dark-haired, swarthy Schuelerite was clearly unaccustomed to being told "no" by a subordinate.

"That wasn't a *request*, Colonel!" His voice was icy. "It was an *instruction*—Inquisitor General *Wylbyr*'s instruction. Do you intend to tell *him* you refuse to obey it?"

"With all due respect, My Lord," the one-armed colonel replied, "the Inquisitor General isn't here, and I've seen no written confirmation of that 'instruction.' Without having it in writing, I can't in good conscience obey it."

"How *dare* you?!" Zhynkyns snapped. "Are you calling me a *liar*, Colonel?"

"Not unless you choose to construe it that way." Tymahk returned the bishop's glare with cool, level eyes. "I'm simply saying that instructions and intentions can be misunderstood or misconstrued—" he stressed the last word ever so slightly, eyes glittering "—when they aren't written down. And that I have no intention of asking my men to commit wholesale murder when the only orders I've received are verbal ones from someone who's already had his horse saddled."

Zhynkyns swelled with fury and his hand clenched at his side. The colonel's insolence was intolerable. The consequences for him once Zhynkyns reported it would be severe, but that was precious little consolation at the moment.

"You can carry out the order—the *Inquisitor General*'s order, whether or not you choose to believe that—or you can face the penalty under Army regulations for disobeying a superior's orders, and then the penalty for defying Mother Church's Inquisition in the midst of a Jihad!"

He felt a stab of satisfaction as Tymahk's face tightened under the threat. The Punishment would be all but certain for anyone who defied a bishop of the Inquisition at a moment like this one, and it was entirely possible the Inquisitor General and Grand Inquisitor might choose to make an example of the colonel's family, as well. Tymahk was silent for several seconds, his eyes blazing like molten glass, then he inhaled sharply.

"My Lord, I'm not *disobeying* a superior's orders. I'm requesting that they be put into writing, which is my right as an officer in the Army of God. Unless they are, I'm under no obligation to accept their validity, which means I'm under no obligation to obey them."

Zhynkyns' jaw clenched, but the colonel's stony face refused to flinch. The bishop had commanded Camp

Dynnys from the day its gates first opened, and he'd sorted out thousands—*scores* of thousands—of heretics and sent them to the Punishment over the last year and a half. He'd been infuriated enough when his own inquisitors started finding excuses to slow the processing of the camp's inmates after the Sarkyn fiasco and—especially—after that disgraceful incident at Camp Chihiro four months ago, and Tymahk's attitude had only made that worse. The colonel had been transferred to Camp Dynnys the previous autumn, while he was still recovering from the loss of his arm in the Sylmahn Gap fighting, and it was obvious his heart had never truly been in the performance of the Inquisition's stern duty. He'd obeyed direct orders, but he'd found ways to . . . mitigate their stringency whenever he thought he could get away with it, even before the godless murderer Mab had started slaughtering Mother Church's defenders. And now *this*.

The bishop realized his teeth were grating together and forced his jaw muscles to relax. He had no time to deal with this, not when the heretics' lead elements were likely to reach Camp Dynnys any time. He expected them no later than tomorrow, and given the number of barges they'd probably captured at Five Forks, they might well be here sooner than that. The last anyone had heard, the garrison at Syairnys, the small town where the Hildermoss River entered Lake Isyk, was still holding and the heretics hadn't yet come into sight, but that report was a full day old. Besides, the garrison was only a few hundred men strong, drawn from the Camp Dynnys guard force and placed under the command of one of Tymahk's lieutenants, who was probably as feckless as Tymahk himself!

If the heretics had taken Syairnys, they were less than sixty miles away by water. If they had sailing barges and knew how to use them—and they were Shan-wei-damned *Charisians*, weren't they?—they could probably reach Camp Dynnys within another ten or fifteen hours. If they had to come overland, around the eastern edge of Lake Isyk, they'd have twice as far to go, but Zhynkyns had precious little faith in the reliability of the pickets Tymahk had thrown out. They'd probably be too busy taking to their heels to save their own worthless skins the instant the heretics came into sight to even think about sending warning to the camp.

So, yes, the heretics could be arriving at any moment now . . . and there was their godless, blasphemous decree about the fate of any of Mother Church's inquisitors who fell into their hands to bear in mind.

He glared at Tymahk, but then he made himself straighten his shoulders and draw a deep, cleansing breath. Very well, if it was the only way to carry out the intentions the Inquisitor General had expressed to him verbally, so be it.

He stalked over to his desk, flung himself into the comfortably padded chair, and snatched a pen from the stand. He scribbled the note quickly, signed it with a flourish, then shoved himself up and stamped around the desk to hand it angrily to Colonel Tymahk.

The colonel looked down at it. It was short and to the point.

> To: Colonel Ahgustahn Tymahk—
>    *The inmates of Camp Dynnys must not be allowed to return to the heresies they have embraced. It is the Inquisition's duty to see to it that they do not, and your duty to assist the Inquisition in all ways necessary. You are therefore ordered and instructed to prevent those inmates from falling into the hands of the heretics' armed forces by any means necessary, including their execution.*
>                    *Bishop Maikel Zhynkyns,*
>                    *Camp Dynnys, commanding.*

"There!" he snapped. "I trust that's clear enough?"

"Yes, My Lord." Tymahk folded the sheet of paper carefully and put it into his tunic pocket. "It's perfectly clear. Thank you."

Zhynkyns' eyebrows rose at the odd note of . . . satisfaction in the colonel's tone. Then his eyes widened in disbelief as the same hand which had put the order into Tymahk's pocket continued to the double-barreled pistol at his side. The pistol rose, one hammer came back, and Zhynkyns found himself staring into the weapon's gaping bore.

"What do y—?"

The pistol's deafening explosion rattled the office windows. It also cut the bishop off in mid-word and flung him back across his desk in a graceless sprawl with a dark, black-edged hole in the center of his forehead.

Tymahk stood looking at him through the thick fog of gunsmoke, pistol still up and extended, then turned as the office door opened behind him. A short, compactly built Army of God captain stepped through it and glanced at the bishop's body and the grisly crimson and gray pool spreading across the desk blotter from the shattered head.

"He wrote it down, then, Sir?" Captain Lywys Rahmahdyn, Tymahk's second-in-command, asked calmly.

"Yes, he did." The colonel patted the pocket containing Zhynkyns' final order. "I don't know how much good it will do, but we can always hope the Charisians, at least, will see reason."

"Hope is a good thing, Sir," Rahmahdyn agreed. "But truth to tell, I don't think I could've done it anyway."

"Me either." Tymahk looked back at the body again for a moment. Then he shrugged. "Go find Father Aizak. Tell him it worked—so far, at least. Then send someone to collect that poisonous snot Cumyngs and make sure no more of the records get burned."

"Cumyngs won't like that," Rahmahdyn observed with a certain satisfaction, and Tymahk smiled thinly.

Zheryld Cumyngs had grown wealthy by extorting money and property from the families of prisoners in Camp Dynnys in return for false promises to smuggle their loved ones out or at least get them better food and medicine while they remained incarcerated. He'd allowed prisoners to write letters home and smuggled them out, too—for a price from the recipients—and he'd kept the official inventories of the property which had been confiscated from prisoners on their arrival at the camp. Those official inventories had been somewhat less than accurate, since they failed to list the property he and his accomplices had diverted to their own use, and Tymahk knew he'd been careless enough to leave evidence of his actions in the camp files. Probably because he'd been confident no one but him would ever see those particular files. Or not, at least, until he'd had ample time to tidy up.

"Even the Inquisition would've hanged him if they'd found out what he's been up to," the colonel said now. "I'd hate for the Charisians to pass up the opportunity to do the same thing. Now go."

"Yes, Sir!"

Rahmahdyn signed Langhorne's scepter in salute and disappeared back out the office door. Tymahk looked around for a moment, then crossed to the desk, grabbed the corpse by the collar of its cassock, and dumped it on the floor. The blotter followed, and he used a swath of cloth ripped from the cassock to mop up the scattered splashes of blood and brain tissue the blotter hadn't caught.

Father Aizak was going to need someplace to work, after all.

▼ ▼ ▼

Baron Green Valley watched the SNARC imagery as Brigadier Braisyn's 3rd Mounted Brigade trotted steadily along the road from Five Forks to the mostly ruined buildings of what had been the town of Lakeside. Braisyn would reach that destination well before nightfall. By tomorrow morning he'd reach Camp Dynnys, the first of the Inquisition's concentration camps to be liberated.

It would be a long time before Green Valley or anyone else forgave themselves for how long it had taken, but they'd had to deal with the Army of the Sylmahn—and

the Ice Ash and North Hildermoss Rivers had had to
be opened and free of ice once more—before he could
have assumed the logistical burden of simply feeding
the camps' half-starved inmates. Even now, that burden
was going to significantly impact the ability of Army
of Midhold and the Army of New Northland to press
the offensive. In terms of cold-blooded military logic,
he ought to be striking directly for Lake City and the
eastern terminus of the Holy Langhorne Canal rather
than allowing himself to be diverted from what was
currently the biggest strategic prize of northern East
Haven, but there were times cold-blooded military logic
had to be ignored.

This was one of those times.

His own forces were about to liberate Camp Dyn-
nys. A column from Bartyn Sahmyrsyt's Army of New
Northland was already en route to Camp Lairays near
the town of Hyrdmyn, two hundred miles northeast of
Ohlarn, and Trumyn Stohnar's Army of Hildermoss' entire cavalry corps was on its way down the Jylmyn-
Waymeet High Road to Camp Shairys. From Lairays,
Sahmyrsyt's mounted infantry would drive another
three hundred miles to reach Camp Chihiro, while
Green Valley continued down the Hildermoss to Cat-
Lizard Lake and Camp St. Charlz. The number of inmates per camp varied from a low of 20,000 to just
under 110,000. The average was about 70,000, which
meant that over the next half-month or so, they were
going to liberate the next best thing to 310,000 sick,
starving, desperate people. The weather—thank God—
promised to remain mild while they went about trying
to evacuate them and move them to safe areas deeper
into the Republic, but their numbers would actually exceed the number of men in the liberating armies, which
explained the serious impact it was going to have on
his logistics. That number also explained why Cayleb
and Greyghor Stohnar—and Sharleyan, if Stohnar had
only known—had decreed that this time humanity had
to trump military expediency.

It remained to be seen how many of the other camps'

garrisons would emulate Colonel Tymahk and his men. The SNARCs had suggested Tymahk intended to try *something* to prevent the wholesale massacre of the Camp Dynnys prisoners, but the decisiveness—and effectiveness—of his actions had still surprised Green Valley. Tymahk wasn't making any strenuous efforts to prevent the camp's inquisitors from fading away— aside from that rat-bastard Cumyngs and his immediate accomplices, at any rate—and Green Valley rather regretted that. Still, he supposed they'd end up catching quite a few of Wylbyr Edwyrds' loathsome minions before they were done, and Tymahk *had* hung onto the cream of the crop from Camp Dynnys. The written instruction from Bishop Maikel was a nice touch, too. It didn't really *prove* anything, but it would be at least circumstantial evidence that Tymahk and his guards had refused direct, written orders to execute the camp's inmates rather than allow them to be rescued. The colonel couldn't know Green Valley had actually watched the entire confrontation and knew every word he planned to say in defense of his soldiers was the literal truth, nor did Green Valley intend to suggest anything of the sort. Despite which, Colonel Tymahk and Father Aizak were going to find themselves being treated quite a bit better than they'd probably dared to hope.

*Decency's too rare a commodity on the Church's side for me to let it go to waste,* the baron thought with a sense of profound satisfaction, shutting down the imagery and returning his attention to the paperwork on the desk before him. *Tymahk and Mohmohtahny have managed to thread the moral needle without compromising themselves. That's one hell of an achievement, under the circumstances. I suspect we're going to see more of that, too, and not all of it out of people who do it because they genuinely are decent human beings. The bastards' morale's starting to crumble; the trick is to keep the process moving . . . and accelerating.*

# The Temple,
# City of Zion,
# The Temple Lands

The atmosphere in the luxurious council chamber could have been chipped with a knife, assuming someone could have found a knife strong enough and sharp enough for the task. The faces of three of the vicars sitting around the enormous table might have been masks carved from frozen marble. The fourth radiated the heat and fury of molten lava, instead, driven by what might possibly be the dawning awareness that his power was less than absolute after all. It was at least remotely conceivable that the man behind that fury had actually realized he could no longer simply hammer aside anyone who opposed him and make the truth be whatever he needed it to be.

*And it's always conceivable that he* hasn't, *too*, Rhobair Duchairn thought bitterly.

He didn't feel that bitterness because he gave a single solitary damn about what Zhaspahr Clyntahn thought he needed, and he would have been more than human if he hadn't felt an enormous caustic satisfaction at watching the Grand Inquisitor come face-to-face with the consequences of his own vicious arrogance and cruelty. No, he would shed no tears for Zhaspahr Clyntahn or his minions like Wyllym Rayno or Grand Inquisitor Wylbyr. But that didn't prevent him from recognizing catastrophe for Mother Church, as well, when he saw it.

"So General Rychtyr believes he'll be able to hold his position on the Sheryl-Seridahn at Fyrayth for the rest of the summer and fall, now that the new artillery's come up in sufficient numbers," Allayn Maigwair was saying. "By the beginning of September, he should have another forty or fifty thousand men under his orders, as well. It's possible he's being overly optimistic, but I'm inclined to believe his appraisal is realistic."

The Captain General paused and looked around the table. Clyntahn jerked an impatient nod, but it was obvious he wasn't particularly concerned about the threat to *Dohlar* at the moment, and Maigwair looked back down at the file open on the table in front of him.

"Farther north, Earl Silken Hills will be in position at the southern end of the Black Wyverns within another five-day," he continued. "Baron Falling Rock is already in place at Lake City, and Earl Rainbow Waters' vanguard will join him there no later than next Thursday. Of course, it will take considerably longer—at least two five-days, and more probably three—for his entire force to come up, given the congestion on the Holy Langhorne."

He glanced at Duchairn, his eyes opaque, and the Treasurer looked back with matching impassivity. Neither of them bothered to look at Zahmsyn Trynair. The Chancellor hadn't said a word in the last hour and a half and it was unlikely he intended to say one now. He'd washed his hands of military and logistic decisions, retreating into the narrow, increasingly irrelevant sphere of Mother Church's diplomacy. There was no longer any pretense that the Church was doing anything besides issuing orders to the secular states, which turned Trynair's diplomats into little more than messengers. The only place anything remotely like true diplomacy mattered was in the efforts to keep Desnair actively involved in the Jihad at all, and given the state of Desnairian arms and industry, failing in that regard would have little real negative impact. Still, it let Trynair push notes back and forth while resolutely removing himself from any of the Group of Four's truly important decisions.

Neither Duchairn nor Maigwair had that luxury, however. For all practical purposes, the Group of Four had become the Group of *Three*, and that new power relationship was still . . . fragile. None of its members knew precisely where the limits currently lay. Clyntahn clearly held the whip hand where the power of suppression was concerned, but however much he hated admitting it, he *needed* the other two. His ability to ignore inconvenient truths would lead quickly to outright military disaster; even *he* realized that, somewhere deep inside, although he would die before admitting it. And unlike him, both of them were only too well aware of the way in which the Holy Langhorne Canal had become *the* vital lifeline of the Mighty Host of God and the Archangels. That would have been bad enough under any circumstances; as it was, the strain of simultaneously moving the Mighty Host forward and somehow bringing up the supplies to establish a sufficient forward magazine at Lake City was perilously close to unsustainable. It would get better—probably, at least a little—once the personnel movements had been completed, but it was never going to be anything Duchairn would have called *good*, and he shuddered to think what another disaster like the one at Sarkyn the previous autumn might do to them all.

"Then why isn't Falling Rock already advancing?" Clyntahn demanded harshly . . . and entirely predictably, Duchairn thought.

"Because we'd sort of like him to *survive*, Zhaspahr!" Maigwair snapped.

The Grand Inquisitor locked fiery eyes with him, but the Captain General refused to look away. The meeting which had been preempted by the Fist of God's attack on Second Pasquale's had . . . clarified his relationship with Clyntahn. It had also cost Clyntahn his most valuable tools within the Army of God's senior hierarchy, and Maigwair had moved rather more effectively than even Duchairn had expected to capitalize on those unexpected vacancies by putting men he trusted into those positions. And he'd been a great deal more careful about just whom he decided he *could* trust while he'd been about it.

"He's only got fifty thousand men," the Captain General continued now. "If he advances beyond the line of the Hildermoss River, he'll be massacred!"

"No, he won—"

"Yes, he *will!*" Maigwair slammed his open hand down on the table—rather gently, actually, all things considered, in Duchairn's opinion. "Your own agents inquisitors' estimate gives Sahmyrsyt better than eighty thousand men. Green Valley has at least that many more men, and that bastard Stohnar's got close to a hundred thousand of his own. What d'you think'll happen to fifty thousand men who find themselves under attack in the open field by the next best thing to *three hundred* thousand men with superior weapons?! And that doesn't even consider the fact that the heretics control Hsing-wu's Passage as far west as Saint Phylyp's Bay! Or the fact that their ironclads are operating as far up the North Hildermoss as the Darailys locks. Thank God the captain commanding the Darailys picket had the gumption to blow the locks without waiting for authorization from someone higher up the command chain! At least we've got them stopped there—for the moment, at any rate—but if Falling Rock marches out into the middle of all that, the heretics will *annihilate* him."

Clyntahn's face was clenched in rage, but he slammed himself back in his comfortably upholstered chair. The struggle to control the stream of vituperation locked behind his teeth was obvious, yet it was equally obvious Maigwair was correct.

Charisian galleons and schooners had flooded into Hsing-wu's Passage as soon as the ice melted, and they'd been accompanied by more of the new sort of ironclads which had effectively demolished the harbors of Geyra, Malyktyn, and Desnair the City. In fact, Duchairn suspected they were the *same* ironclads; surely, not even the heretics had an unlimited supply of them! The good news (such as it was and tattered though it might be) was that they clearly lacked the endurance of the sail-powered vessels, but a Marine landing force, covered by the ironclads' heavy guns, had gone ashore in Regyr's Cove and seized the small coastal city of Seryga in the Episcopate of St. Phylyp.

They hadn't just *raided* Seryga, either. They'd come to stay, throwing up fortifications and establishing a depot under the protection of the ICN's artillery to provide the ironclads with coal.

*And Seryga's barely three thousand miles from Temple Bay,* the Treasurer thought grimly. *That's halfway from the Icewind Sea, and who's to say they couldn't go the rest of the way before winter closes the Passage down and they have to pull back again?*

It was a terrifying thought, and he reminded himself—again—of the danger of assigning invincibility to the heretics. But he rather doubted Clyntahn was thinking about it the same way he was. No, what *Zhaspahr* was thinking about was the fact that the river town of Darailys was barely eighty miles from the confluence of the North Hildermoss and the Tarikah River. That put the Charisian Navy within little more than three hundred miles of Lake City . . . and less than a hundred and forty of Camp St. Charlz. The heretics hadn't seized the camp—yet—according to their latest reports, but Duchairn would be astonished if that remained true for very much longer. St. Charlz was barely two hundred and eighty miles from Camp Dynnys, after all. For that matter, it was entirely possible the heretic Green Valley had already seized St. Charlz and Zion simply hadn't heard about it yet thanks to the disruption of Mother Church's communications. The confusion and chaos in Icewind Province and eastern Tarikah as Faithful refugees fled west, followed by heretic mounted columns, would be almost impossible to exaggerate.

"All right, Allayn," Clyntahn grated at last in an ugly voice like crumbling limestone. The effort it took to exert even that much control was only too evident, and he glared at Maigwair and Duchairn. "I realize there are all those dozens of *military* reasons for Falling Rock to sit on his arse in Lake City. I'm sure you and Rhobair can describe them to me in excruciating detail, no matter what argument I put forward about our responsibilities to God and Mother Church."

The hatred in the Grand Inquisitor's eyes boded ill for Maigwair, Duchairn thought, but the Captain General met them coldly. The Treasurer wondered how much of that courage was bravado, how much was the result of growing confidence in his own power base, and how much of it was simply the determination of a man who was resolved to deal with a crisis and no longer *cared* what Clyntahn might say or do.

"But if there are all of those goddamned reasons why we can't move Falling Rock and the rest of the Harchongians *forward*, then you and Rhobair had fucking well better find a way to pull the inmates of every damned camp in Tarikah and northern Hildermoss back into the Temple Lands before the Shanwei-damned heretics reach them!" Clyntahn continued harshly. "*Understand* me, both of you. If the Army and the Mighty Host simply stand there with their thumbs up their arses and watch my Inquisitors lose those camps and all the unsifted heretics in them, whoever— *whoever*, and I don't give a single fucking *damn* who that whoever might be—is responsible for that decision will face the Punishment right here in Zion! *Whoever* it is."

His meaning was abundantly clear as he glared at Maigwair and Duchairn, and a chill ran through the Treasurer. This was the most openly Clyntahn had threatened the only two members of the Group of Four who still had the will to question *his* will. The polarization within the Group of Four was now complete, and Duchairn wondered if Clyntahn realized the totality with which he'd just driven him and Maigwair into one another's arms.

"You're talking about thousands of inmates, Zhaspahr," he said in a deliberately calm tone. "I know you don't want to hear about 'military reasons' why we can't do things, but we don't have anywhere near the capacity to move that many people back along our remaining transportation routes. It's not that we have it and we're refusing to make it available to you for some reason. It simply doesn't exist."

"Then Allayn had better find the troops to march the bastards back into the Temple Lands on their own feet!" Clyntahn snarled. "Or else, he'd better find the troops—troops who will goddamned well obey their orders instead of hiding under their beds for fear of 'Dialydd Mab' and his assassins!—to execute every single one of those prisoners where they stand."

"Inquisitor General Wylbyr's own reports make it clear his inquisitors haven't had time to sift the guilty from the innocent, Zhaspahr!" Duchairn protested. "That's why they're still in the camps."

"And better a thousand innocent children of God return to Him and the Archangels than that a single servant of Shan-wei be rescued by her vile, corrupt servants and returned to the struggle against Mother Church!" Clyntahn shot back. "God will know His own, and He'll welcome them to His arms as the martyrs they'll become!"

Duchairn began a hot retort, then made himself shut his mouth. At the moment, Clyntahn's agents inquisitor and the Temple Guardsmen and city guardsmen who'd been coopted into the Inquisition's security forces had a near total monopoly on armed power in Zion. Maigwair had a few thousand men in the city's vicinity, but the majority of them were in staff and administrative positions. Even if that hadn't been true and all of them had been combat forces, they were easily outnumbered by close to ten to one by the armsmen available to Clyntahn and Wyllym Rayno. For that matter, it was far from certain they would defy the Inquisition if Maigwair asked them to, and Clyntahn's goaded irrationality was only too plain to see. If Duchairn and Maigwair chose to challenge him openly, he *would* launch that armed force against them. In fact, that was probably exactly what he wanted to do.

The Fist of God's continued strikes in and around Zion—and the way the broadsheets and pamphlets reporting those strikes continued to proliferate—were an intolerable challenge to his personal authority which fed his steadily increasing frustration, anger, and hatred. For that matter, however little he wanted to admit it, his inability to crush the Fist or even find the printing presses churning out all that anti-Inquisition propaganda was probably terrifying to him. So, yes, no doubt he did want to lash out at whatever enemies he *could* find.

"Allayn?" The Treasurer looked at Maigwair. "Do we have the troops to do that?"

"I don't know." Maigwair's tone was flat. "Marching thousands of prisoners cross-country is an entirely different challenge from guarding them inside a prison camp. It would require a lot more men than the camps do. And even if I can find the troops, managing to keep them—and the prisoners—fed while they march hundreds of miles is going to be . . . problematical, at best."

"Well, you'd better find both of them somewhere," Clyntahn said. "If you can't, or if you can't find me the troops to execute the heretics we can't march back to the Temple Lands, then the Inquisitor General and I will issue the orders to put them all to death through our own chains of command. And if we have to do that, I think it's going to be time for the Inquisition to think very hard about taking complete direction of the Jihad." He showed his teeth in a cold, vicious smile. "Perhaps it's time to demonstrate just how much men of true faith can accomplish without worrying about all those technicians and specialists we've been relying on so long. After all, they've done a wonderful fucking job *this* far, haven't they? Maybe it's time the Inquisition relieves them of their onerous responsibilities before they lose the *rest* of the Jihad!"

"That would be a particularly unwise thing for the Inquisition to do, Zhaspahr," Duchairn told him levelly. "No doubt you could . . . motivate any of Mother Church's children to give their all for the Jihad, and it's true that sometimes faith, devotion, and energy can achieve miraculous results. But trust me on this. Without Allayn's officers, and without my manufactory workers and my Treasury workers, Mother Church's ability to arm, clothe, and feed her defenders will evaporate. If you want the Army of God and the Mighty Host to face the heretics with what amounts to bare hands, then you go right ahead and 'take complete direction of the Jihad.' No doubt the consequences would be very unpleasant for Allayn and me, but they'd be a frigging *disaster* for *you*. I'm just a little tired of running around with you throwing out your threats and your promises of dire consequences. However we got here, we—we and *Mother Church*, Zhaspahr—are looking straight into the face of defeat. Understand that. We . . . are *looking* . . . at *losing* . . . the Jihad!" The Treasurer glared at Clyntahn. "If we do, then everything we've done, all the sacrifices and the bloodshed and the dying, will've been for nothing. Everything I've tried to accomplish, that Allayn and Zahmsyn have tried to accomplish, and everything *you've* tried to accomplish, will be *destroyed*. And all of us will face God and the Archangels with that failure in our hands. Is that what you want? Because if it is, then you go right ahead and 'take complete direction of the Jihad.' "

Clyntahn stared at him, and Duchairn felt a tremor of astonishment run through him. He wouldn't have thought the tension in the conference chamber could actually increase, but he would have been wrong. He felt Maigwair's taut presence across the table from him and realized just how thin a thread supported their lives at this moment, and the truly amazing thing was that in that instant of time, neither of them really cared.

"Don't think I won't if you push me to it, Rhobair," the Grand Inquisitor said finally, his voice soft. "Because I will. *Believe* me, I will. You may even be right about what will happen if I do, but if I look around and all I see is that we're going to be defeated anyway, that decision will make itself. You and Allayn and all of your 'technicians' may believe you're indispensable to the Jihad's victory, but I know better. *I* know that God will not suffer Himself to be defeated. Yes, He wants His mortal servants to live up to His law and shoulder the tasks He sets before them. And, yes, the Jihad may be His way of testing our worthiness. But in the final analysis, He *will* have the victory, whatever He must do to bring that about. So if it comes to the decision point, if I'm—if the *Inquisition* is—forced to take complete direction of the Jihad because the rest of you have failed Him and my Inquisitors, then I know—I *know*—God will do *whatever* it takes to give Mother Church the victory."

He sat back from the conference table, his eyes hard and flat, and silence enveloped the richly appointed chamber.

. XI .

HMS *Chihiro*, 50,
Gorath Bay,
Kingdom of Dohlar

"Captain Hamptyn is here, My Lord."

Lywys Gardynyr turned from the stern windows as Paiair Sahbrahan appeared diffidently in the stern cabin's doorway. The earl had already heard the routine challenge of the sentry outside his quarters, and he nodded.

"Show him in, Paiair," he said, and returned his attention to the harbor, where an extremely large galleon lay to its anchor. The stark black of its hull was relieved only by a white strake along its single line of gunports, and the green wyvern on a red field of Dohlar fluttered proudly from its mainyard above the silver and blue checkerboard of the Imperial Charisian Navy.

"My Lord," another voice said, and Earl Thirsk turned once more to face a swarthy, dark-haired man in a captain's uniform. Hamptyn bowed, his hat clasped under his left arm while the palm of his right hand rested lightly on the hilt of his sword to steady it.

"Captain," Thirsk replied, with a shallower answering bow, and extended his right hand as both men straightened. They clasped forearms, and Thirsk indicated the two chairs on either side of the small table. Sahbrahan had already laid out the whiskey decanters and glasses. Now, at a brief nod of Thirsk's head, the valet disappeared, leaving the officers alone.

Hamptyn waited until the earl had seated himself before he settled into the facing chair. Their positions—not by accident—let both of them look out through *Chihiro*'s stern windows at the ironclad galleon he'd sailed back to Gorath Bay.

"I've studied your report with some interest, Captain," Thirsk said as he poured whiskey into both glasses. "It was impressive reading. I was sorry to hear about your ship—and about Admiral Rohsail's injuries, of course—but your squadron did well. *Very* well. And on behalf of His Majesty, I thank you all. I feel confident he'll add his personal thanks to mine once he's had time to read it, as well."

"It was . . . chaotic, My Lord." Hamptyn appeared to be searching for exactly the words he wanted, and he sipped the whiskey as if to buy time while he considered them. "There wasn't anything remotely like formal tactics or formations," he continued after a moment. "Not in our part of the engagement, anyway. Admiral Raisahndo was able to maintain his line better than we could, but when it came to *Dreadnought* . . . ."

His voice trailed off as he gazed at the ship he'd been given to bring home, and Thirsk nodded. He'd already concluded that Kahrltyn Haigyl had done precisely what he'd clearly intended to do. The prize—and threat—of the powerful ironclad had been too much for Rohsail or his captains to resist. They'd closed in on *Dreadnought* like starving wolves, concentrating three-quarters of their total combat power on a single ship, and a part of the earl wanted to be furious with them for allowing themselves to be manipulated that way. But as he'd told Hamptyn, he'd already read the captain's report. For that matter, he'd already read Pawal Hahlynd's, and there was no question in his mind that *Dreadnought*'s sheer might had made that concentration inevitable.

In terms of cold-blooded logic, Haigyl might well have made the wrong decision. If he'd concentrated on cutting his own way out, his ship's combination of armor and fighting power would almost certainly have allowed him to do that. Instead, he'd deliberately chosen to sacrifice any chance of escape to cover the conventional galleons. Given how much damage *Dreadnought* had inflicted in her single-handed stand against the entire Western Squadron *and* Pawal Hahlynd's Galley Fleet, sacrificing her to save less than half a dozen unarmored galleons had to be considered a questionable exchange. At the same time, Thirsk knew he would have made exactly the same decision in Haigyl's shoes. There was a time and a place for cold-blooded logic; there was also a time and a place to meet a man's responsibilities to the other flesh-and-blood men who fought with him. Haarald of Charis had set that standard for his navy at a place called Darcos Sound, and given what Haigyl must have known would happen to any Charisian prisoners foolish enough to surrender . . . .

"You seem to have taken her remarkably intact," he said.

"More because of her armor than any care we took in that respect, My Lord, and only after she'd lost her rudder and been completely dismasted." Hamptyn's lips twitched in a fleeting smile. "I understand your Lieutenant Zhwaigair's going through her from keel to main truck, but I can already tell you her armor's much tougher than our own. It's impossible to be certain, but from counting the dents, my best estimate is that we must have hit her at least two hundred times. But even though we cracked her armor in half a dozen places—thanks to Admiral Hahlynd's guns, not our own—we never actually *penetrated* it. In fact, most of the cracks seem to've resulted when the timber backing of the armor was driven in; the plates' faces just sneered at the heaviest shot we had."

"So I'd already gathered from your report." Thirsk shook his head. "Lieutenant Zhwaigair's also read your report—and Admiral Hahlynd's—and his preliminary conclusion is that the Charisians are using steel armor, not iron, and that they've managed to harden its face even further somehow." He grimaced. "That's not something I wanted to hear, you understand, especially since not even the Lieutenant can figure out how they've managed to harden such large plates. For that matter, the largest single plate we can produce, even out of iron, is only two feet on a side; theirs are four times that size and half again as thick, to boot. That's the sort of news I *really* didn't want to hear."

"I don't blame you, My Lord." Hamptyn sipped more whiskey. "*Their* guns punched right through any of our galleons they hit. The screw-gallcys stood up to them better than anything else we had, but at least seven of them were penetrated cleanly, and virtually all the survivors have cracked and broken plates."

"We've already dispatched replacement armor and bolts down the canals," Thirsk told him. "And we've placed three more screw-galleys in commission since Admiral Hahlynd's departure. We'll have at least two more before the end of next five-day, as well. I'd like to send all five of them forward, but there's considerable pressure to retain them here to protect Gorath Bay."

"Admiral Rohsail and I discussed that before I sailed for home, My Lord. He was still in considerable pain, and the healers were increasingly of the opinion that they'd need to amputate the remainder of his arm, but he was quite clear and . . . forceful in his own view."

"Which was?"

"Which was that it's essential we maintain pressure on the heretics in the western Gulf rather than retreat into some sort of citadel east of Jack's Land, My Lord. To be honest, he'd really prefer for *Dreadnought* to be placed back into full commission and returned to the Western Squadron, but he understands that we need an opportunity to examine her thoroughly and learn what we can about her construction and armament. He still hopes to have her returned as quickly as possible, and in the meantime, it's his view that Admiral Hahlynd should be reinforced as quickly and powerfully as possible. And whatever the heretics' ironclads may be capable of, the screw-galleys have certainly proved their usefulness against their conventional galleons."

Thirsk nodded slowly. However little he liked Sir Dahrand Rohsail, the man's strategic instincts were sound, and Thirsk was impressed by his ability to think clearly after the loss of most of his right arm and all of his right leg. The truth was that Thirsk probably should have ordered him back to Gorath for medical treatment, but the Order of Pasquale had enormously enlarged and improved the Order's hospital at Rhaigair on the northern shore of Saram Bay. It was unlikely he could have received better treatment in Gorath, and Thirsk had decided it was better to send him to Rhaigair and spare him the voyage home until he'd recovered—*if* he recovered—from his wounds. At the moment, however, the fact that his judgment coincided with Thirsk's was rather more important than where he was hospitalized.

The earl leaned back in his chair, contemplating the younger man on the other side of the table. Captain Hamptyn was a competent and courageous officer. His ship had been brutally savaged by the Charisians, no doubt because they'd recognized her as one of their own. Caitahno Raisahndo's *Demonslayer* had been almost as badly damaged as *Defiant*, although she'd also been luckier. Her crew had faced a grueling, epic battle to keep her afloat, and from the preliminary damage survey, it seemed likely she was beyond repair this time. But at least *she* hadn't caught fire under the pounding she'd taken from the Charisian shells. *Defiant* had . . . and she'd burned to the waterline, despite her crew's heroic efforts to extinguish her fires. And one of the last orders Hamptyn had given as Rohsail's flag captain, before notifying Raisahndo that command of the Western Squadron had devolved upon him, had been for two of Pawal Hahlynd's surviving screw-galleys to tow her clear of *Dreadnought* lest her magazines explode and take the hard-won prize with her. That was a significant indication, especially combined with how doggedly Hamptyn had fought his ship up to the very end, of the kind of officer—and man—he was, and he clearly got along well with his admiral. It probably said something for Rohsail that he engendered that sort of loyalty in that sort of man, although Thirsk didn't truly understand how that could work. On the other hand, he didn't *need* to understand the relationship to appreciate its value to the Royal Dohlaran Navy, and Hamptyn had clearly been the right man in the right place.

"You were lucky you were able to get *Defiant* clear, Captain," he said, voicing a part of his own thoughts. "If *Dreadnought* had caught fire as well, you would've lost both of them."

"That wasn't the only way we were lucky, My Lord." Hamptyn shook his head. "The heretics had laid a fuse in her magazines." Thirsk stiffened slightly. That minor fact hadn't been included in the reports he'd read. "I'm still not clear on why they didn't fire it," the captain continued. "I don't think there's any doubt that was part of their plan from the very beginning, and if she'd gone up, we'd probably have lost at least another two or three galleons of our own in the blast, given how close alongside they were. The only thing I can think of is that once we managed to board we swarmed her so quickly—and she'd lost so many of her own men in the fighting—that the order simply didn't get passed. The only one of her officers who survived was a midshipman, and *he* was wounded and unconscious when she finally surrendered." Hamptyn grimaced. "For that matter, we took less than thirty of her entire crew alive."

"So I understood." Thirsk kept his own voice level, but it was hard, because he knew exactly why so few Charisians had been captured rather than killed. And he didn't doubt for a moment that Kahrltyn Haigyl had intended to blow up his own ship as much to save any of her remaining crew from the Inquisition as to deny her to the Royal Dohlaran Navy.

*And he damned well deserved to succeed at both of those*, the earl thought grimly. *But he didn't. So now what do I do?*

It was a question he was going to have to answer. He couldn't—and had no desire to—deny the pride he felt in what his navy had accomplished. The numerical odds might have favored Sir Dahrand Rohsail and Caitahno Raisahndo overwhelmingly, but the actual *combat* power had been far more evenly balanced. And returning one of the Charisians' ironclads for study and eventual employment under the Dohlaran flag was a huge accomplishment. For the moment, at least, Dohlar—not Charis—enjoyed a monopoly on armored warships in the Gulf of Dohlar, and it was the navy Thirsk had built and trained which had made that possible.

Yet despite that, and despite the many things he was certain Dynnys Zhwaigair would learn from examining her, he was grimly confident the Charisians would get around to replacing her far more quickly than Dohlar could have duplicated her even if they'd had the technical capability to do that.

*And when they* do *replace her, whoever's in command of their navy's going to be making his decisions where* our *Navy's concerned based not just on what happened in the Kaudzhu Narrows but also on what happened to their people* after *the battle. And the truth is that he should damned well do* exactly *that.*

He felt it coming, could almost smell its stinking, carrion breath, and this time it was going to be worse. There were more Charisians this time, and this time he couldn't even pretend he didn't know *exactly* what would happen to any of them who were surrendered to Zhaspahr Clyntahn. And if—*when*—Cayleb and Sharleyan Ahrmahk were in a position to demand justice for their murdered sailors . . . .

A fresh wave of despair flooded through him. No matter what he did, no matter how brilliant Lieutenant

Zhwaigair might be, the relentless tide of Charisian innovations and the constantly swelling volume of their manufactories' production loomed before him like some unstoppable avalanche.

He'd tested the new Fultyn Rifles, and the heaviest one yet manufactured in a Dohlaran foundry—an eight-and-a-half-inch monster with a fourteen-and-a-half-foot tube that weighed over ten tons—could reach a maximum range of almost ten thousand yards, although he had his doubts about its ability to actually *hit* something at that distance, even from a stationary fortress mount. And it had effortlessly punched a solid two-hundred-and-seventy-five-pound shot straight through the best armor plate they could produce at a range of five hundred yards. That was impressive performance, but according to the preliminary reports on *Dreadnought*'s guns, her shells weighed less than half as much yet had come terrifyingly close to matching that performance. That suggested they were capable of substantially higher muzzle velocities, and according to the reports of what had happened to the Empire of Desnair in Geyra Bay, the *breech-loading* cannon mounted in their new steam-powered ironclads were far more powerful than *Dreadnought*'s muzzle-loading weapons.

They also fired much more rapidly, and that was a far from insignificant point. The tests of the new Fultyn Rifle had already demonstrated the significant problems involved in working a muzzleloader approaching fifteen feet in length. Indeed, length was much more critical in that regard than the simple size and weight of the enormous projectiles it fired. Just swabbing the barrel between shots was difficult and time-consuming, yet if it wasn't swabbed properly, if there was a single spark or ember waiting when the next powder charge was rammed home . . . .

The gun founders were promising him a ten-inch weapon with a gigantic four-hundred-pound shot and a shell weight of well over *three* hundred pounds. Their estimates suggested it would be even longer ranged than the eight-and-a-half-inch weapon, and shot that heavy might well be able to penetrate even *Dreadnought*'s armor. But each gun would weigh almost seventeen tons, and the barrel length would be over *sixteen* feet, which was going to slow its rate of fire even further.

Any unarmored ship that challenged those weapons would be doomed, yet that thought was scarcely reassuring, given that the Charisians were certain to have more—and better—*armored* ships than anyone else in the world. And producing guns of that size and power took time—*lots* of time. The Charisians could obviously produce *their* guns far more rapidly than the Church's foundries could produce Fultyn Rifles. And as vast an improvement as the banded rifles clearly were, they were still cast iron and their bore pressures pushed the limits of their endurance every time they were fired with full-powered charges. Any battery commander and—especially!—his gun crews could be excused for feeling a totally justified nervousness under those circumstances.

The foundries were working on smaller, lighter six-inch weapons which could be mounted on shipboard, and that would increase the Royal Dohlaran Navy's combat power considerably. It might even be possible to mount a shorter and lighter version of the new ten-inch weapon in the screw-galleys' armored citadels, where it could conceivably survive long enough to do some good. In the end, though, they weren't going to be able to match the Charisian artillery's performance, and that was simply the way it was. So whenever Cayleb and Sharleyan Ahrmahk decided they could spare the effort from the liberation of the Republic of Siddarmark, the Dohlaran Navy was doomed. He had no doubt its men would fight as courageously as Captain Hamptyn's men had fought in the Kaudzhu Narrows, but it wouldn't matter.

And that brought him right back to the question of those Charisian prisoners of war.

*It shouldn't come down to that*, he told himself yet

again, his mental voice weary and raw. *I shouldn't have to even think about arguing that torturing and killing the other side's sailors and soldiers when they fall into our hands is "bad policy" because it can only justify the Charisians in taking reprisals against our own sailors and soldiers. People fighting on the side of God should understand that it's wrong—wrong morally and religiously, from every possible aspect—to treat honorable enemies that way even without the fear of reprisals!*

He turned his head, staring out the stern windows at Hamptyn's ship to prevent the captain from seeing his face as the dull, searing flood burned through him yet again. But there was no point pretending. He'd already discussed it—obliquely and very carefully, in private—with Staiphan Maik, and the bishop's eyes had been as bleak as his own. Yet Maik had been able to offer no comfort. In fact, the conversation had only made it worse.

Because they'd become so close, the bishop had shared his confidential reports about the Inquisition's concentration camps in Siddarmark . . . and the orders the Grand Inquisitor had issued. That was why he knew the hapless inmates of four of those camps were already marching across western Siddarmark towards the Border States, driven ruthlessly to keep them ahead of any possible rescue. And why he knew that Inquisitor General Wylbyr had decreed the execution of every prisoner in three other camps too far from the Border States to be evacuated before they were liberated.

Bishop Staiphan's expression had been grim as he told the earl how those orders had been followed to the letter in one of those camps, despite the warning notices its guards had found posted inside their own fences by the *seijins* allied with the notorious Dialydd Mab. In the other two camps, though, at least some of the guard force had decided to resist the order. In one of them, the mutineers had been ruthlessly suppressed and the executions had been carried out anyway, although at least some of the prisoners had managed to escape during the fighting. In the other, however, the *mutineers* had won. Most of the camp's inquisitors and quite a few of the guard force had faded away during the fighting, but the victorious mutineers had marched its inmates *east*, not west. Detachments of Army of God cavalry had been dispatched after them, but Maik's sources suggested that the pursuit wasn't being pressed very hard.

Thirsk hoped those sources were correct. In fact, he'd gone down on his knees to *pray* that they were. Bishop Staiphan's most conservative estimate was that another hundred and twenty thousand Siddarmarkian civilians had been butchered, exactly as the Inquisitor General had ordered. Given that close to three million people had already perished at the Inquisition's hands, that might not seem like all that many additional lives. But it was. It was a horrific number, piled onto a vaster, even more horrific number, and if the "heretics" and their allies won in the end, their demands for vengeance—for *justice*—would be fiery, merciless, and totally justified.

So what was Lywys Gardynyr going to do when Zhaspahr Clyntahn demanded that the Charisian survivors of the Kaudzhu Narrows be delivered to Zion? It was "only" another five hundred lives, after all. They wouldn't even be noticed when the death toll was totaled up at the end of this madness. Except by those who'd loved them—by wives and daughters, by sons and brothers and sisters, and by fathers and mothers.

And by Lywys Gardynyr, who would know their blood was on *his* hands, however truthfully he might tell himself he'd had no choice.

Baron Sarmouth stood on HMS *Destiny*'s quarterdeck, hands folded behind him, and watched calmly as his squadron made its way into Rahzhyr Bay. They made a brave show under the clear July sky with their severe black hulls, gray and tan sails, and the blue, silver, black, and gold of the imperial Charisian standard rippling from their yardarms.

There were only four galleons anchored off Rahzhyrhold, but the water around them was busy with launches, gigs, and other small craft. At this range it was difficult to decide what all those boats were so industriously doing, even with one of the new doubleglasses, and the admiral waited patiently in the shade of the awning stretched across the quarterdeck while *Destiny* forged steadily towards them.

"Seems to be an awful lot of boat traffic, Sir Dunkyn," Captain Rhobair Lathyk remarked, standing to Sarmouth's right. "And I wonder where the rest of the squadron is?"

"No doubt we'll discover all of that soon enough," the admiral replied serenely.

"No doubt," his flag captain agreed, yet there was more than an edge of concern in Lathyk's tone.

It was the concern of an experienced naval officer with an itch he couldn't quite scratch, the sense that something he was seeing wasn't quite what it ought to have been. That sort of itch was the gift of instinct and hard-won skill, and it was invaluable. It was also a gift Sir Dunkyn Yairley possessed in abundance . . . and one he didn't need on this hot, beautiful day.

"Deck there!" The call floated down from the masthead. "Cutter broad on the starboard bow!"

"I see it, Sir," a voice said from Sarmouth's left. The

baron glanced over his shoulder and saw Lieutenant Aplyn-Ahrmahk holding a double-glass in his good hand while he peered through it. "I think . . . yes, she's definitely flying a dispatch boat pennant."

"You see, Rhobair?" Sarmouth said with a slight smile, quirking an eyebrow at the flag captain. "As I promised. All is about to be revealed."

▼ ▼ ▼

There were no smiles in the admiral's day cabin as Sir Bruhstair Ahbaht stood facing Sarmouth the better part of two hours later. The Emeraldian captain was perfectly groomed, despite the sling supporting a left arm encased in plaster, but there was no sign of his habitual dry humor.

"So after returning to Talisman, I dispatched my full report to Earl Sharpfield at Claw Island by courier vessel. I thought it wisest to remain here while *Vindicator* and *Broadsword* completed their repairs. I'm actually a bit surprised the Dohlarans haven't already moved against us here, and I felt we'd be most useful assisting Commander Makgrygair and Major Ohmahly in the event that they did."

He fell silent, looking the taller Charisian admiral in the eye. His own eyes were level, yet somehow he had the look of a man facing a firing squad . . . and convinced that he ought to.

Sarmouth leaned back in his chair for several seconds, gazing at the officer on the far side of his desk, then he inhaled deeply.

"I see," he said. "And now that you've completed your report, Captain, be seated, please."

His voice was calm, but it was also insistent, and he pointed his right index finger at the chair beside Ahbaht. The chair he'd invited the Emeraldian to take upon his arrival. Ahbaht had declined the invitation then, preferring to stand as he described the debacle into which he'd led his squadron. Now he started to decline once more, but Sarmouth's expression stopped him. Instead, he settled into the chair, although he didn't seem to relax noticeably as he sat.

Sarmouth nodded in satisfaction and raised his voice. "Sylvyst!"

"Yes, My Lord?" Sylvyst Raigly appeared like magic.

"Please pass the word for Captain Yairley and Lieutenant Aplyn-Ahrmahk to join us. And be so good as to bring the whiskey, as well. The Glynfych, I think."

"At once, My Lord."

The valet bowed and disappeared once more, and Sarmouth returned his attention to Ahbaht. It was strange, really. Somehow he'd expected the fact that he already knew what had happened in the Kaudzhu Narrows to make Ahbaht's report easier to listen to. It hadn't. If anything, it had made it harder, and not simply because he had to watch his responses lest he say or do something that might suggest that everything Ahbaht was telling him wasn't coming at him cold. It was because he *had* already seen it, he reflected. Because he had the actual images and sounds, all the carnage and fury, to go with the words of Ahbaht's description. And because he had those things, he also knew Ahbaht had been far harder on himself than anyone else would have been. There was no way he could tell the captain that, however, and so he only shook his head.

"I know that at this moment you blame yourself for every ship and every man we've lost, Captain," he said quietly. "In your place, I'm sure I'd feel exactly the same way. On the other hand, I would have made precisely the same decisions you made, had I been in your position and in possession of the same information. You acted with the boldness we expect of officers in the Imperial Charisian Navy. It's unfortunate that the weather turned against you, yet it's clear to me that you'd allowed sufficient cushion against that possibility. But for the shoal you encountered, the Dohlaran galleys would never have had the opportunity to engage you, and I'm strongly of the opinion that with both *Thunderer* and *Dreadnought* you and Captain

Haigyl would have cut your way out through the Dohlarans with far lighter losses. It's not given to us to command the wind or the vagaries of fortune, Captain Ahbaht. All any mortal man can do is make the best decisions he can based on the information he actually has. It's my opinion that that's exactly what you did in this instance."

"I . . . appreciate that, My Lord." Ahbaht stopped and cleared his throat. "I appreciate it," he continued, his voice just a bit husky, "but I'm not sure I agree with you. If I'd passed my information on to Earl Sharpfield, or not taken it upon myself to—"

"If you'd done either of those things, you *would* have been culpable, Captain!" Sarmouth interrupted with an edge of sharpness. "Their Majesties' Navy doesn't select captains or flag officers who shirk their responsibilities or take counsel of their fears.

"I said it's not given to us to command the wind, and that's true. It's also not given to us to simply command victories, either. We do what we must in the service of the Crown and the defense of Their Majesties' subjects. That is our greatest honor, and you're as aware as I am of what it demands of us. Emperor Cayleb described a captain's responsibilities to me once. He said, 'A captain has to sail to meet the enemy; he doesn't have to come home again.' That's what you did. You sailed to meet the enemy, exactly the way *I* would have—exactly the way *His Majesty* would have, and *did* in the Armageddon Reef campaign—and this time some of your ships and too many of your men than either of us will find easy to live with didn't come back. Neither did King Haarahld, at Darcos Sound."

He held the captain's eye for a moment.

"Sometimes we live, sometimes we die; the one thing we *always* do is keep faith with our honor, our duty, our monarchs, and our God, and that's *precisely* what you and all the men under your command did this time. Whether you agree with that or not, I know exactly what His Majesty would say to you at this moment. Since he's not here, I'll say it for him. You reacted wisely, resolutely, and quickly, based upon the best information available to you, in the best traditions of the Imperial Charisian Navy, and so did every one of your officers and men. The operation didn't end in a victory, but you—and they—have *nothing* for which to be ashamed or to blame yourselves. I retain full confidence in you, just as I'm certain Their Majesties will when news of this reaches them, and I'm not prepared to entertain reproaches against you—or the men under your command—from *anyone*. And to be perfectly clear about this, Captain Ahbaht, that 'anyone' includes *you*. Is that understood?"

"I—" Ahbaht began. Then he stopped, and his nostrils flared as he inhaled deeply. "Yes, My Lord. It's . . . understood."

"Good!" Sarmouth said more briskly as Lathyk and Hektor Aplyn-Ahrmahk entered the cabin. Sylvyst Raigly followed them in, carrying a large silver tray laden with glassware. He set the tray on the end of Sarmouth's desk and began pouring amber whiskey into the waiting glasses.

"Good," the baron repeated. He picked up his own glass and raised it, holding it there until Ahbaht and the other two officers had raised their glasses to meet it.

"I'm glad it's understood," Sarmouth said then, holding Ahbaht's gaze with his own, "because I have no intention of allowing the Dohlarans to savor this victory one second longer than I have to. That means you and I have a great deal of work before us, Captain. All of us do. So let's be about it, shall we?" He smiled thinly and glanced at his flag lieutenant with a nod.

"I give you Their Majesties," Hektor said, lifting his own glass just a bit higher. "The toast is loyalty, honor, victory . . . and damnation to the enemy!"

# AUGUST
## YEAR OF GOD 897

·✦·

# . I .
## Royal Palace,
## City of Gorath,
## Kingdom of Dohlar,
## and
## Tellesberg Palace,
## City of Tellesberg,
## Old Charis

Soft cooing and the rustle of pigeons' wings floated in through the open window. It was an incongruously gentle combination of sounds, given the place and the occasion, but not one the Earl of Thirsk found soothing. In fairness, that had more to do with the reason for this meeting than with the sounds themselves, yet he couldn't avoid the thought that there was a certain irony in it. Or perhaps what he meant was that there was a connection *between* those sounds and the reason he was sitting in this room at this moment.

King Rahnyld IV of Dohlar was not the most competent monarch in the history of Safehold. Thirsk didn't especially like admitting that even to himself, since he was Rahnyld's sworn vassal and a man who took his oaths seriously. That didn't make it untrue, however, although to be honest it probably wouldn't have mattered, given the madness which had gripped the entire world, if Rahnyld had been a political genius rather than a ruler of . . . erratic notions and enthusiasms. The fact that he'd come to the throne thirty-six years ago as a boy of only fourteen had probably contributed to his uneven record, and Thirsk knew the King resented the demands his crown placed upon him and his family. Clearly, Rahnyld would have been much happier in a less stressful role, and that had become only more evident since the beginning of the Jihad. In fact, rumor said he'd discussed abdication with Duke Fern on more than one occasion.

Those rumors might well be true, Thirsk thought. Yet however ill-suited to his role he might be, he couldn't simply step down. Crown Prince Rahnyld wouldn't be sixteen until next month, and the last thing Dohlar needed at a time like this was a four- or five-year regency for a minor king. If abdication was out of the question, though, the King seemed determined to avoid as many of the Crown's day-to-day responsibilities as he could.

That was why the sounds drifting in through the window irritated Lywys Gardynyr rather profoundly. They came from the elaborate pigeon coop mounted outside the window, and it was mounted there because King Rahnyld raised racing pigeons. In fact, he concentrated on that hobby with a focused intensity Thirsk couldn't help wishing he'd spend just a little of on the affairs of his kingdom. It was . . . disconcerting, to say the least, when a crowned king spent his time leaning out the council chamber window to putter with his pigeons during meetings of his Royal Council rather than actively engaging with the advisors and councilors inside the chamber.

Although, the earl thought now, the King's absence actually might not be a bad thing today, given the agenda.

"—so I'm afraid Father Ahbsahlahn's hints are becoming rather more pointed," Sir Zhorj Laikhyrst, Baron of Yellowstone, said now as he wrapped up his initial report. "He hasn't presented any formal communiqués about it yet, but I don't think it will be much longer before he does. And I'm certain he's going to make Mother Church's view abundantly clear and explicit the moment the prisoners arrive in Gorath."

Yellowstone was almost seventy years old with thinning silver hair, faded blue eyes, and a weedy neck. He'd sat on the Royal Council longer than any of its other members, and he functioned effectively as the kingdom's foreign secretary. He was also quite a bit more intelligent than his unprepossessing physical appearance might lead the unwary to conclude, and his anxiety was obvious.

"Then we ought to go ahead and give him an answer now, before we do receive any 'formal communiqués,'" Aibram Zaivyair, the Duke of Thorast, replied sharply. Technically, Thorast was Thirsk's political master, although fortunately for Thirsk, Samyl Cahkrayn, the Duke of Fern and King Rahnyld's first councilor, had effectively stripped him of day-to-day oversight of the Navy. Now Thorast glared at Thirsk. "There's no question whose authority is paramount in this case. Why are we even discussing it?"

"Aibram has a point," Shain Hauwyl, the Duke of Salthar and commander of the Royal Dohlaran Army, put in with a scowl. Salthar was considerably more intelligent than Thorast, but he was also a fervent son of the Church and, despite the serious defeat the Army had suffered, one of the Jihad's strongest supporters. "Even if Mother Church's authority didn't override anyone else's, what conceivable reason could we have for even considering refusing her demands at a time like this?"

"Actually," Fern said, leaning back in his chair at the head of the table beside the empty throne where King Rahnyld should have been sitting, "as Sir Zhorj's just finished telling us, we haven't had any demands from Mother Church on this matter. Not yet. That's rather the reason for this meeting, Shain."

"Does that really matter if Kharmych's dropping all those *hints*?" Salthar retorted. "Since he happens to be the Kingdom's Intendant, I imagine we can consider them a fairly clear indicator of the direction of Mother Church's thinking, don't you?"

"Of course we can." The First Councilor's tone was astringent. "The question before us is how *we* want to approach the problem. After all," his eyes swept the other faces around the table, and there was something guarded in their depths, "there are certain other . . . pragmatic considerations involved."

The sounds from the pigeon coop seemed much louder suddenly in the profound silence his words produced, and Thirsk inhaled deeply. He hadn't expected Fern to allude even indirectly to those "pragmatic considerations," and he suddenly found himself wondering if he might not have been wrong when he'd assumed he'd been summoned to this meeting simply to hear the Council's decision.

He let his gaze drift to his left for a moment. The man seated beside him had far better family connections than Thirsk, despite the fact that he held no title beyond a simple knighthood, but the earl had wondered about *his* presence, as well. Sir Rainos Ahlverez had faced the very real possibility of being handed over to the Inquisition after the previous winter's disastrous Shiloh Campaign. Personally, Thirsk had assumed that Ahlverez' close relationship with Thorast explained his survival, but the earl had seen very few smiles directed at him by the duke since this meeting began.

"What sort of 'pragmatic concerns' would that be?" Salthar asked now, eyes narrowing at Fern across the table.

"The pragmatic concern that the heretics currently hold far more of our men prisoner than we hold of theirs, for one," the first councilor replied flatly, with a candor which astonished Thirsk. It obviously took Salthar aback, as well, and the Army's commander sat back in his chair with arched eyebrows.

"I would never advise against meeting Mother Church's legitimate demands," Fern continued. "However, we owe it to the Crown, as well as to Mother Church, to look realistically and honestly at our own position and what may be best for the prosecution of the Jihad. For us to stand at Mother Church's side in this fight, we first have to *survive*, Shain. We need to fight as effectively as we can, we need the best strategies and tactics, and the best weapons we can give our soldiers and sailors, but we also need to survive. And at the moment General Rychtyr is at Fyrnach, barely a hundred and twenty miles from our frontier."

He looked away from Salthar long enough to give the naval minister a very level look indeed, since the hundred and twenty miles in question was actually the distance to the eastern border of the Duchy of Thorast. Then he turned his gaze back to Salthar.

"I shouldn't have to point that out to you, Shain, given that just day before yesterday you and I discussed that very point. I've been very impressed with General Rychtyr's determination, but it's clear the canals and highways out of Cliff Peak and into Westmarch have been thoroughly demolished after the Army of Glacierheart's . . . defeat. That means the heretics have somewhere in the neighborhood of half a million men within nine hundred miles of our frontier, with no means of moving them rapidly *north*, and winter's coming on in the next few months. You may have observed the previous winter that campaigning is far easier closer to the equator, and the heretics have secure communications which would allow them to pull as many of those half-million men as they want back from Westmarch and ship them by water to Thesmar. And from there, it would be absurdly simple for them to add their weight to the heretic Hanth's Army of Thesmar."

He paused, and the stillness in the chamber was intense.

"In addition to that consideration," he continued after a moment, "there are the thousands of our soldiers already in heretic hands. At the moment, those prisoners appear to be receiving relatively humane treatment. How long that will continue may well depend upon some of those other 'pragmatic concerns.' Of course, the heretics hold even more of the Desnairians' men than they do of ours, but that's probably becoming rather less of a 'pragmatic concern' to Emperor Mahrys at the moment, isn't it?"

He showed his teeth in a thin, humorless smile. There was no need for him to be any more explicit, Thirsk thought. After the devastating bombardments of Geyra, Malyktyn, and Desnair the City, the Desnairian Empire was in a state of virtual military collapse. The Desnairians' total—and understandable—focus on self-defense had taken them completely out of the field and seemed likely to keep them there indefinitely. In fact, Thirsk strongly suspected that Emperor Mahrys and his advisors intended to stay out of the field for as long as they possibly could. It would probably be an exaggeration to say Mahrys was *grateful* for the damage his capital—both of his capitals—had suffered, but he definitely *was* grateful for the excuse it gave him to avoid any fresh adventures in Siddarmark.

*I wonder if Fern's suggesting Dohlar might go the same way?* the earl thought suddenly. *Surely not! For one thing, we're in a lot better shape than Desnair was even before the Charisians blew the piss out of their capitals. And for another, we're a hell of a lot closer to Zion than Geyra is . . . .*

"My point," Fern continued, "is that our paramount responsibility to Mother Church is to adopt policies which permit us to continue as her champion in the Jihad. That means, among other things, advising the Council of Vicars of those considerations which will have a direct effect upon our ability to do that. Admiral Rohsail's victory in the Kaudzhu Narrows has enormously enheartened the entire Kingdom." He nodded across the table to Thirsk. "The prisoners taken in that battle are presently on their way to Gorath and will be arriving within the next five-day. While no loyal son of Mother Church could question her legitimate right and responsibility to deal with those taken in impious and heretical rebellion against her, it would not be inappropriate for us to advise the vicarate about how best—and most effectively—the treatment of those prisoners might enhance rather than weaken our own Kingdom's ability to support and sustain the Jihad."

"What are you suggesting?" Salthar asked.

"Before I answer that question, I'd like to ask Sir Rainos to speak to the fashion in which the men and officers of the Army of Shiloh responded to the heretics' announced policy where *their* prisoners were concerned," Fern replied. "I submit that we need to consider both the positive and the negative consequences of delivering the captured Charisians to the Punishment they undoubtedly deserve. It's not a matter of *refusing* to surrender them to the Inquisition, of course. If that should be Mother Church's decree, then as her loyal sons we would obviously have no option or desire to resist it. If, however, there's the possibility of a decision—even a temporary one—which seems likely to us to yield a greater short-term, purely *tactical* advantage, then I believe it's obviously our responsibility to respectfully share our analysis with Father Ahbsahlahn and Bishop Executor Wylsynn."

He paused, clearly inviting a response, but no one spoke. He waited another handful of heartbeats, then returned his attention to Ahlverez.

"Could you give us your impression of how the Army of Shiloh's rank and file responded to the heretics' announced policy where prisoners of war are concerned, Sir Rainos?"

▼ ▼ ▼

"Do you really think they're going to argue with Clyntahn?" Sharleyan Ahrmahk asked.

She sat in a private council chamber with Earl Pine Hollow, Baron Rock Point, Maikel Staynair, and Ehdwyrd Howsmyn. She and the archbishop had returned to Tellesberg only three days ago, and news of the Kaudzhu Narrows catastrophe had arrived—overland by semaphore to Windmoor Province, then across the Tarot Channel to Tranjyr, across the Tranjyr Channel to Margaret's Land, and on to Tellesberg—four hours before she had. Nothing could have prevented her Old

Charisian subjects from greeting her, their beloved archbishop, and the heir to the throne with enthusiasm, yet the battle—and especially the loss of both *Thunderer* and *Dreadnought*—had cast an undeniable pall over her return.

Which was fair enough, she thought, given the pall it had cast over the entire inner circle well before anyone else in Tellesberg had heard a word about it. Now she gazed at her husband's image, projected onto her contact lenses, and her own expression was anxious as she thought about the prisoners headed along the long line of canals towards Gorath. Or perhaps "anxious" wasn't precisely the right word. Perhaps the word she wanted was "anguished."

"*Argue* with Clyntahn?" Cayleb shook his head, his own expression somber. "No, they're not going to do that. But I think it's possible they really will suggest an . . . alternative disposition of their prisoners."

"Salthar and Thorast sure as hell aren't going to sign on to any 'alternate dispositions' willingly," Rock Point said flatly. "And despite the fact that Ahlverez is directly related to Thorast, I don't think Fern's scoring any points with the Duke by asking for Ahlverez' opinion."

"He's not really asking Ahlverez' *opinion*, Domynyk," Merlin put in over the circuit. At the moment, he was in his Dialydd Mab persona, moving through a rain-soaked forest towards one of the columns of concentration camp inmates being driven towards the Border States. "In fact, what he's trying to tap dance his way around to is even more problematical than that. He wants Ahlverez to suggest that his own men were less willing to fight to the death in a hopeless position because they knew it was our policy to treat prisoners humanely so that *he* can suggest to Kharmych—*not* Clyntahn—that our people might react the same way if they thought they wouldn't be handed over for the Punishment. I think he hopes the Group of Four may be desperate enough to embrace at least a little rationality after what's just happened to the AOG in Siddarmark. He's not doing Ahlverez any favors by asking him to say anything of the sort, though, and I have to say I'm a little surprised that Ahlverez seems willing to answer the question honestly. He has to know he's putting his neck right back into the noose—potentially, at least—if he takes a position that ends up pissing Clyntahn off."

"A noose might be the least of his problems if he pisses off Zhaspahr Clyntahn," Aivah Pahrsahn observed ironically from the study of her Siddar City townhouse.

"Personally, I think what's most significant is that Fern is even considering suggesting, however diffidently, that it might be wiser to not give our people to the Punishment," Pine Hollow said. "Consider how completely silent he was when it was Admiral Manthyr's turn." The Charisian Empire's first councilor shook his head. "I'll bet you're entirely right about the way what happened to Kaitswyrth and Wyrshym—and even more what's been happening to Rychtyr, too, now that I think about it—is driving his position, Cayleb. There's no way he'd be doing this if he was remotely as confident as they're all trying to pretend they are about just how their 'Jihad' is going to work out in the end."

"You're right about that," Nimue Chwaeriau said from her post outside Princess Irys' bedchamber. Irys was going to be irritated at having missed this conference, but Nimue was recording the entire conversation for her and she needed her sleep. Her advancing pregnancy was taking a lot out of her, and Nimue wasn't going to wake her for something like this. Besides, it wasn't as if Irys was still the only Corisandian cleared for the discussion.

"To be honest, I wasn't all that surprised when Desnair effectively bailed on the jihad after what happened to the Army of Shiloh and the way Zhaztro hammered Geyra and Desnair the City. I wasn't too surprised Mahrys weaseled his way around the decision with all those earnest promises to 'return to the field as soon as humanly possible,' either. It's a bad sign for Zion when an emperor begins deliberately lying about his intentions to support the jihad, but Mahrys and Desnair in general have always had a lot of cynicism in their devotion to Mother Church. More than I think even they realized, to be honest. And, frankly, how big a loss to the Group of Four does Desnair's military collapse really represent? They can still squeeze gold out of Mahrys, and it's not as if the Desnairian Army—or Navy—covered itself with glory, is it? No." She shook her head. "This is potentially a lot more significant, I think."

"Agreed," Phylyp Ahzgood said firmly.

The Earl of Coris might be the inner circle's newest member, but he'd taken the revelation in stride. His familiarity with the Group of Four's tactics and ruthlessness had made it much easier for him, and like the princess he served, he'd decided any God who agreed with Zhaspahr Clyntahn was no God of his. Now he sat beside his bedchamber's window, gazing out into the Manchyr night, and nodded crisply.

"Dohlar's been the Group of Four's most effective secular supporter from the beginning—at least since Armageddon Reef, anyway. I think that probably surprises the Dohlarans as much as it surprises *us*, frankly, but it's true. So if Fern's looking for ways to mend fences with us, that says some really unpleasant things from Clyntahn's perspective."

"The problem is how Clyntahn chooses to take any suggestions coming out of Gorath," Sharleyan said. "From his track record, any suggestion that he might not get his own way is only likely to make him even more furious."

"I don't think that really has a downside as far as we're concerned," Cayleb said somberly. "Pissing him off isn't going to make things any worse for any of our people he gets his hands on, after all. It *can't*. But if he responds to any perceived criticism from Dohlar the way he very well might, the consequences for the *Dohlarans* could be . . . severe. And from our perspective, anything that reduces Dohlar's effectiveness—like, oh, a situation in which the members of the entire Royal Council find themselves desperately looking for ways to protect themselves and their families from the Inquisition—has to be a good thing. And, frankly," the emperor's expression was grim, "after what happened to Gwylym and his men, it won't break my heart to find them having to do exactly that."

"I have to admit I'd feel a lot better if Dohlar's relationship with the Temple came a little unraveled, too," Howsmyn said. "Something that buys us a couple of more months for the *King Haarahlds* would be really, really welcome just now."

"It certainly would," Rock Point agreed. "On the other hand, now that we've officially gotten word about what happened in the Kaudzhu Narrows I can dispatch a couple of more *Rottweilers* to back you up, Dunkyn. Unfortunately, they'll have to come from Tellesberg, so it'll still be at least a couple of months before we can get them there."

"Speaking solely for myself," Baron Sarmouth replied from his sleeping cabin aboard *Destiny*, "I'm in favor of anything that gets us something with the armor to stand up against *Dreadnought* as quickly as possible. At the same time, I don't think they're going to be using her very aggressively against us anytime soon. They're too busy still figuring out what they've got, and Kahrltyn had expended most of his ammunition before they took her. That means Thirsk and Zhwaigair are going to have to figure out how to produce more of it for her. Mind you, now that that clever bastard Fultyn's producing shells for his own rifled guns that may not take them as long as we'd all like for it to. But for now, she's more of a long-term threat than an immediate problem."

"What about diverting the *Cities* from Hsing-wu's Passage?" Cayleb asked.

"I don't think we can," Rock Point replied. "Dunkyn's probably right about how long it would take Thirsk to get *Dreadnought* back into action, and Kynt needs the *Cities* up there on his right flank. For that matter, we need those bastards in Zion worrying about where they might go next. I could probably pull out the ones keeping an eye on Desnair, but they're all the way on the other side of the Sea of Justice. That's damned near five five-days for a dispatch boat, even if we use the semaphore to pass the message to Tarot and send the dispatch from Brankyr Bay. That'd cut a thousand miles or so off the voyage time, but by the time I got a dispatch boat to them with orders to leave their present station, I could have *Lightning* and *Seamount* a solid month on their way. And even after we got any of the *Cities* moving, they'd be limited to the speed of the galleons carrying their coal along with them. I think it's entirely worthwhile to think about redeploying them eventually, especially with the delay to the *King Haarahlds*, but it'll be faster to send the *Rottweilers* first."

"Agreed," Cayleb said after a moment. "We'll do it your way, Domynyk. And in the meantime, if anyone has any spare time on his or her hands, I think it might not be a bad idea to spend it praying Fern does suggest that 'alternate disposition' of their prisoners and Clyntahn actually listens."

"I'll see to that," Archbishop Maikel promised, then smiled a bit sadly. "We're already holding daily masses of intercession for the prisoners, after all. On the other hand, I'm afraid some miracles are more likely than others."

. II .
# The Temple,
# City of Zion,
# The Temple Lands

"If this continues, Wyllym, there are going to be some *changes*," Zhaspahr Clyntahn said coldly. "You can tell Wynchystair and Gohdard that. And—" his eyes were frozen flint as he glared across his desk "—it might not stop there."

"Your Grace, I entirely understand your sentiments, and if you truly wish me to pass that . . . warning on to Father Allayn and Bishop Markys, I will, of course," Wyllym Rayno replied levelly. "Unfortunately, removing them from their posts—or removing *me* from *my* post—isn't going to defeat these heretic terrorists." He returned the Grand Inquisitor's icy glare without flinching. "The Inquisition has no servants better at their jobs or more aware of their duty than Father Allayn or Bishop Markys. I'll leave your estimate of my own capabilities and loyalty to your own judgment. Replacing any of us, however, is more likely to create confusion among our agents inquisitor than to have any beneficial effect."

"I don't see how it could have any *detrimental* effect," Clyntahn half snapped. "It would be rather hard to accomplish *less* than a total lack of progress or success, don't you think?"

"We have made some progress, Your Grace," Rayno said in that same level voice, working hard to make his expression reflect both an awareness of Clyntahn's rage and just the right amount of confidence. It was rather more difficult to project the latter. "Over the last six five-days, we've intercepted two assassination attempts and killed a half-dozen of the heretic terrorists," he pointed out.

"Yes, and *failed* to intercept the assassination of Vicar Styvyn and Archbishop Samyl," Clyntahn shot back. "And unless my memory of your reports is in error, all but two of those terrorists killed *themselves* when they realized they couldn't escape. Which brings another minor point rather forcibly to mind. It's all very well to *kill* the bastards, but without someone to interrogate, we're learning fuck-all about who they are and how they've gotten their hands on such fiendishly accurate intelligence!"

Rayno began to reply, then stopped himself, partly because contradicting his superior was always risky when Clyntahn was in this sort of mood and partly because the Grand Inquisitor had a point.

A very *good* point, as a matter of fact.

"Your Grace," he said instead, after a moment, "I'm afraid I'm coming to the conclusion that your earlier belief that we were confronting more than merely mortal foes may very well have had merit." He watched Clyntahn's jaw muscles bunch but continued unflinchingly. "I'm not speaking here of the terrorists and assassins themselves. I believe we've amply demonstrated that even though they've sold their souls to Shan-wei, they, at least, are mortal. Whether or not they have demonic direction and sources of information, but when they're shot or stabbed, they bleed, and when they poison themselves, they die.

"Yet having said that, I can find no other explanation than active demonic intervention for our complete inability to so much as *see* whoever's spreading those damnable broadsheets throughout the Temple Lands. Your Grace, five-day before last, Father Allayn had twenty—*twenty*—of his best-trained and most reliable agents inquisitor surrounding Saint Ahnthyny's Church. He had reason to suspect Saint Ahnthyny's senior priest might have become involved with the so-called Fist of God."

Rayno knew how much Clyntahn hated that name; unfortunately, the Grand Inquisitor hated hearing anyone call it the "Fist of Kau-Yung" even more.

"Why? And why wasn't I told about it?" Clyntahn demanded, leaning belligerently over his desk towards Rayno.

"Because the evidence was very scant and because anything which might lead us to these murderers is kept very, very closely held, Your Grace. Unless there's some reason to share such information, we don't . . . even with you. As you say, the terrorists seem fiendishly—*demonically*—well informed, so we've adopted the same policies you established for the Rakurai. Unless someone *needs* to know critical information, he isn't made aware of it.

"Moreover, in this case, I believe—and Father Allayn

concurs—that the priest in question has not, in fact, had any contact whatsoever with Mother Church's enemies. The informant who suggested he might have has disappeared as tracelessly as the terrorists themselves, and we believe the information laid against Father Sairahs was actually fed to us *by* the terrorists."

"And why should they have done *that?*" Clyntahn fairly bristled with suspicion, and Rayno sighed.

"Because, Your Grace, Father Sairahs is Vicar Zakryah's cousin," he said.

Clyntahn sat back in his chair, his expression one of surprise. Vicar Zakryah Hahlcahm was one of his closer allies in the vicarate. A Chihirite of the Order of the Quill, Hahlcahm had been a seminary classmate of Rhobair Duchairn, and until the beginning of the Jihad, he and Duchairn had remained close. Clyntahn had found that quite useful upon occasion. More importantly, perhaps, Hahlcahm had given Clyntahn his allegiance without any of the blackmail or extortion the Grand Inquisitor used to control so many of his "allies." Hahlcahm was a strong supporter of Clyntahn's policies where heresy was concerned, which might very well explain a Fist of Kau-Yung attempt to undermine Clyntahn's trust in him by falsely implicating his cousin in acts of blasphemy and treason.

"And you didn't see fit to mention this to me?" he asked after a moment, his voice still hard but without the edge of distilled fury it had carried earlier.

"Your Grace, I've already explained why we're holding critical information so closely, but to be honest, there was more than one reason you weren't informed in this case. One of my responsibilities is to . . . to serve as your filter. If I'd brought this information to you, especially before Father Allayn and I found the opportunity to sift the 'evidence' against Father Sairahs, it must have planted a seed of doubt in your mind. It was my judgment that Vicar Zakryah is too important to the Jihad—and to you personally—to allow that to happen unless there was other, supporting evidence of the allegations made against him. Afterward, when I'd determined there was no such evidence, I still saw no reason to inform you of it lest some lingering doubt cloud your trust in the Vicar. If I erred in doing so, I ask your forgiveness, but you have far too many other and completely valid things to worry about. If I can spare you from things you *needn't* worry about, I see that as one of the duties of my office and as the Adjutant of the Order."

Clyntahn frowned, but he also seemed to settle just a bit, and Rayno drew a deep, surreptitious breath of relief. What he'd just said was true, and despite the Grand Inquisitor's volcanic temper and near-paranoid suspicion of his many real (and imaginary) enemies, Clyntahn knew just how valuable Rayno was in that regard. In his calmer moments, at least; he found it unfortunately easy to forget such things when his fury was fully engaged. Despite that, he had no idea how many potential victims of that temper and suspicion Rayno had preserved by simply not mentioning their names to him until after the archbishop had investigated them thoroughly. Rayno, on the other hand, had a very clear notion of what that number was, and he wasn't at all averse to reminding Clyntahn just how valuable he was and in how many ways that was true.

"Very well," the Grand Inquisitor growled after a moment, waving one hand dismissively. "But if this Father Sairahs was innocent, then what do the agents inquisitor around his church have to say about demonic assistance for the heretics?"

"Only this, Your Grace. That church was surrounded all night long. No one entered or left it after Father Sairahs retired to his rectory. Father Allayn has twenty agents inquisitor who will all swear to that, and I've personally walked every inch of Saint Ahnthyny. There is no way any mortal being could have entered that church unseen. Yet in the morning, one of the heretics' broadsheets had been nailed to the *inside* of the church doors."

He sat very still, hands folded in the sleeves of his

cassock, and watched Clyntahn's expression. It was clear his superior didn't care for the implications.

"Under the circumstances," the archbishop continued into the silence, "I'm forced to the conclusion that it required more than mortal abilities to accomplish that, Your Grace. And that means you were correct. The heretics *are* being aided by demons, and it seems very likely '*Seijin* Merlin' and the others of his ilk are, indeed, Shan-wei's own demons."

"But actually *inside* a consecrated church?" For once, even Zhaspahr Clyntahn sounded subdued, almost frightened. "How could a demon penetrate that sacred ground?"

"There *are* reports of demons violating sanctified ground during the War Against the Fallen," Rayno reminded him quietly. "I realize tradition holds those reports were inaccurate. However, the first Grand Inquisitor saw fit to include them in the official archive for some reason, and he actually lived through the last few years of that struggle. Perhaps tradition's been wrong all these years."

"But—"

"Even if those accounts were accurate, Your Grace," Rayno said almost gently, "there are no reports of demons *ever* actually penetrating Zion herself or the Temple. Saint Ahnthyny's is technically in Zion, but it lies a good ten miles beyond the original boundary of the city. We have no evidence of any of these mysterious broadsheets appearing closer than five miles from the Temple. So even if the heretics are being aided by demons, they clearly can't penetrate the holiest ground in the world. I remind you also that we have no reports of these so-called *seijins* operating within the Old City, either."

"But if they can operate freely elsewhere . . . ."

"Your Grace, however widely they may operate, there are clearly limits on both their numbers and how *overtly* they may operate. If, indeed, demons are distributing the heretics' broadsheets, then why have they not done so openly? Surely the appearance of a demon walking the streets of our cities, laughing at our efforts to stop it, would have an even more terrifying impact upon Mother Church's sons and daughters than the mysterious appearance of propaganda, the half of which is rejected out of hand by those who read it. Yet they haven't done that, and none of the '*seijins*' have dared to show themselves here, either. It seems evident to me that, for whatever reason, they're forced to go about their accursed work even more circumspectly than they did during the War Against the Fallen. And just as they were unable to deliver the entire world to Shan-wei then, they'll fail now."

For once, there was no slightest trace of calculation in Wyllym Rayno's voice, no sign of it in his eyes, and Zhaspahr Clyntahn sat a bit straighter in his luxurious chair.

"You're right, Wyllym." He nodded. "You're right. But if your suspicions about demonic interference are correct, then it's more important than ever that we get our heel on these terrorists' necks!"

"Agreed, Your Grace." Clyntahn's calmer, more intent tone was a tremendous relief, but Rayno allowed no sign of that to color his voice or his expression. "In the meantime, I think—"

A soft chime sounded and Clyntahn scowled at the interruption. He started to ignore it, but then he snorted and touched the glowing God light on the corner of his desk. The door slid open and one of his senior clerks stepped through it.

"I beg pardon for interrupting you, Your Grace," the man said nervously, "but Vicar Zahmsyn sent you this by special courier. It's . . . it's marked 'Urgent,' Your Grace."

"Then give it to me," Clyntahn growled.

The clerk handed it to him, kissed his extended ring, and disappeared quickly enough to raise Rayno's hackles. None of Clyntahn's subordinates were foolish enough to linger when their intrusion might have irritated him, but they seldom vanished quite that abruptly. Not unless they had reason to believe that whatever had prompted the intrusion was likely to prompt an eruption, as well.

Clyntahn slit the thick, official envelope with an ornamental letter opener. He withdrew the folded sheets, opened them, and scanned Zahmsyn Trynair's cover letter quickly.

His face darkened and his lips tightened, drawing back from his teeth. He stripped the cover letter angrily from the rest of the correspondence, tossing it to one side, and began reading the rest of the document. He got perhaps halfway through the first sheet before—

"God *damn* those bastards!" He slammed the document down on his blotter and exploded to his feet. "Those *cowards!* Those Shan-wei-damned *traitors!* Those puking, fornicating, ball-less, *weaklings!* How *dare* they?! I'll have every one of them put to the Punishment!"

Wyllym Rayno recognized the signs. He knew better than to ask any questions, and at least Clyntahn's office was less filled with the sort of priceless treasures so many of his other tantrums had demolished.

Unfortunately, that office was occupied by one Wyllym Rayno, and any effort to withdraw could only have . . . unfortunate consequences.

"That fucking, backbiting, lying *cretin!* The fucker thinks his goddamned navy's so damned important he can get away with *this* kind of crap?! I'll have him and his Shan-wei-damned family here in Zion so fucking fast his arse won't catch up to the rest of him for three fucking five-days! *Then* we'll see about coddling men taken in active rebellion against Mother Church, God, and the Archangels! I'll—"

It went downhill from there.

. III .

HMS *Chihiro*, 50,
Gorath Bay,
Kingdom of Dohlar,
and
The Glydahr-Selyk High Road,
Princedom of Sardahn

I'm afraid we have no choice, Lywys," Bishop Staiphan Maik said heavily.

Night lay over Gorath Bay. The wind was into the bay, out of the west, and Earl Thirsk's flagship moved gently as she lay to her anchor. Lamplight gleamed warmly on his cabin's fittings, and the breeze blowing in through the open scuttles and funneled down the skylight by the canvas wind scoop was cool for this time of year. Beyond the galleon's stern windows, the bay was a sheet of rippled glass, touched with dancing, reflected paths of moonlight, and the distant lights of the city of Gorath gleamed through the darkness.

It was a restful sight, but Lywys Gardynyr felt anything but restful as he stared at Maik. The bishop sat in one of his armchairs, facing him across a low coffee table, gripping a large glass of whiskey in both hands, and his expression was that of a man about to take a bullet.

"My Lord, we can't—" the earl began, but Maik raised an open hand in a stopping gesture.

"Lywys, the orders are as clear and unambiguous as I've ever seen." He shook his head. "And reading between the lines—and given the way Kharmych gloated when he passed them to me—I don't think Duke Fern's suggestion was . . . well received in Zion. I'm instructed to dispatch every prisoner taken in the Kaudzhu Narrows directly to Zion. And I'm also instructed that if anyone—*anyone*, Lywys—argues about those instructions or attempts to dissuade me from them in any way, I'm to send *him* to Zion, as well, to . . . explain his objections to Zhaspahr Clyntahn in person."

The auxiliary bishop paused, then shook his head.

"From the fact that they directed those orders specifically to *me*, I don't think they're talking about Fern, Lywys. Too many people in Zion have figured out how *you* feel about this matter. I fear—I very *much* fear—that no matter who signed the letter to Vicar Zahmsyn, they think you were the instigator."

An icy wind blew through the marrow of Thirsk's bones as he looked back at the special intendant who'd become his friend.

"I suppose I should be relieved you haven't already been instructed to send me to Zion, My Lord," he said after a moment.

"Perhaps you should be," Maik agreed. "I can't be positive, of course, but I suspect someone had to talk very fast to convince Clyntahn not to do just that."

"And why should anyone bother to do that?" Thirsk couldn't keep the bitterness out of his voice. In fact, he didn't try very hard, and Maik sighed.

"Probably not because they love you so much," he said. "If I had to guess, somebody pointed out that your Navy's won the Jihad's only victory since the heretics demolished the Guarnak-Ice Ash Canal and stopped the Army of God's advance across Siddarmark in its tracks. You may not fully appreciate just how much of a hero—a talisman of victory—that's made you with the Faithful, but I assure you other people do. Mother Church's children have been desperate for some sort of good news; your Navy gave it to them.

"Admiral Rohsail and Admiral Raisahndo get much of the credit, of course—and rightly so. But you're the man who reorganized the Navy, built the fleet, and trained the men Rohsail and Raisahndo used, and *your* Navy is the only one to have *twice* defeated Charisian squadrons in battle. My guess is that someone—probably someone on the Council of Vicars itself—pointed out to Clyntahn that delivering the man who made that possible to the Punishment might have ... negative consequences for the morale of Mother Church's loyal supporters. In fact," Maik looked at him very levelly, "it might make some of those Faithful question who truly ordered it ... and what his *personal* motives might be."

Thirsk snorted harshly. He pushed himself up out of his chair and stalked across to the stern windows, gazing out them at the lights of Gorath. They looked so pure, so innocent, from here. But he knew the truth, knew he would never feel clean again if he simply stood there and let this happen.

Yet he also knew Maik was right. In fact, however accurate the auxiliary bishop's analysis might be at this instance, he himself was almost certainly the only reason Thirsk hadn't been summoned to Zion to face the Inquisition long since. A part of him almost wished he had been, since it would have taken the burden from him. Only they wouldn't have summoned him alone; Zhaspahr Clyntahn's Inquisition had made its theory of "collective responsibility" only too clear.

*Strange*, he thought, sipping whiskey as he gazed at those distant lights. The thick, liquid fire rolled over his tongue and down his throat, and he shook his head. *Strange to think that somehow my people and I have become the one bright spot in the darkness. How did we ever come to this? And can God truly care about His plan if he lets this happen in His world? What have we done? How have we made Him so angry that He leaves us in this abyss? Lets someone like Zhaspahr Clyntahn rip away our honor, shred it like garbage? Trample on what the* Writ *itself tells me to do? And what am I to do about it? Tell me that, God! Surely You can tell me that much!*

But God was silent, and Thirsk threw back another swallow of whiskey while he cursed the day of his own birth.

▼ ▼ ▼

Dialydd Mab sat quietly on the rock outcrop near the crest of the hill.

That hill rose above the bridge on which the Selykr-Glydahr High Road crossed the North Daivyn River, seventy miles east of Selkyr, and he'd been waiting patiently there for almost six hours. He'd waited the better part of two days for the proper combination of weather and location, however; he didn't begrudge a few more hours.

It was raining again, hard enough to cut visibility significantly, and thunder muttered as distant lightning illuminated the bellies of the clouds. It wouldn't be long now, he thought, watching the take from the SNARCs. Another forty-five minutes—an hour, at the outside—before the encampment settled down enough for his purposes.

Nimue Chwaeriau had offered to join him, but he'd turned her down. He wasn't sure why he'd done that, really. Officially, he'd argued there was no point having two of the known *seijins* mysteriously out of sight at the same time, especially when he already had all the help he was likely to need. But both of them had known how weak *that* argument was. More probably, he'd decided, it was because he still felt compelled to protect his "younger sister" from all the ugliness with which *he'd* had to deal.

*And maybe you just didn't want to* share, *either,* he told himself bitingly. *This is your private little crusade, isn't it? And how much of it—how much of* tonight, *right here*—*is because you had to sit and watch without doing anything about it for so damned long?*

He didn't have a good answer for that question, but that didn't bother him as much as perhaps it ought to have. Maybe he should discuss that with Archbishop Maikel. The Bédardist was actually a very good psychiatrist, after all.

He checked the imagery again. No one had bothered to provide anything remotely like adequate tentage for the inmates being marched from Camp Tairek in

Westmarch to the new camp prepared for them at Glydahr in the Princedom of Sardahn. They'd managed to throw together crude, leaky lean-tos for the weakest—and sickest—of their number, but most of them were huddled together in the rain, crowded around the smoky, raindrop-sputtering fires. Many of them had taken off their ragged clothing and used it to throw at least a fragile roof over the fire pits, but keeping those fires alight was a bitter struggle on a night like this.

He was, frankly, surprised the guards had permitted even that, but it hadn't really been left up to them. Major Lainyl Paxtyn, the commander of the guard detachment, was Zhaspahr Clyntahn's kind of officer. He'd invested his own sadism in the jihad, and he'd volunteered to march these prisoners to their new home. He'd also gone out of his way to make the journey a misery for them, and no doubt he would have ordered those fires extinguished in a heartbeat, if it had been his decision. And it was likely Father Trynt Dezmynd, the Schuelerite upper-priest in charge of the prisoner transfer and a man cut from very much the same cloth, would cheerfully have agreed with him . . . normally. But Father Zhames Symmyns, Dezmynd's assistant, had other ideas. A less brutal man by nature—and one who seemed to have taken Dialydd Mab's promises to heart—Symmyns had managed to mitigate the worst of Dezmynd and Lohgyn's natural inclinations, if only by convincing Father Trynt that their ecclesiastic superiors would frown on a march which killed two-thirds of the prisoners en route.

"Is this really going to be a good idea, Merlin?" a voice asked over the com.

"It can't hurt anything," he growled back.

"It may not *help* anything, either," Cayleb Ahrmahk pointed out. "You're seventy miles behind the Harchongians' front. Whatever you do to the guards, these people aren't going to be able to walk to safety. And not even you can guide nine thousand people, half of them sick and all of them malnourished, through the woods to our lines without being overhauled by *someone*."

"That's not my object," Mab said bleakly. "I know we can't get them out. That doesn't mean I can't give the guards a . . . pointed suggestion that they ought to at least treat them like human beings."

There was an almost-sound over the com, as if Cayleb had begun a response and then stopped himself, and Mab smiled thinly. His mission tonight was probably as quixotic as Cayleb had suggested, but that didn't mean it wasn't worth doing. He would count it a bonus if the guards at the new camp were wise enough to learn from Major Paxtyn's example, yet he wasn't going to pretend he really expected that to happen. No, this had far more to do with Lainyl Paxtyn and the handful of particularly brutal noncoms and enlisted men he'd handpicked for this march.

It was a pity they wouldn't live long enough to learn from their own object lesson, but he could live with that.

"Do you think Clyntahn's likely to let Thirsk survive very much longer?" Cayleb asked in a rather different tone, and Mab's lips twitched at the emperor's obvious bid to change the subject.

"I think Bishop Staiphan's theory about the only reason Thirsk hasn't already been hauled to Zion was pretty close to spot on, actually," he said. The SNARC permanently assigned to Lywys Gardynyr had caught the entire conversation. "And I very much doubt Zhaspahr Clyntahn's the least bit happy that someone whose loyalty he distrusts so profoundly is currently the Temple Loyalists' hero." He shrugged. "If I were Thirsk, I'd be worrying about daggers in my back—especially if Clyntahn tries his favorite trick of blaming the assassination on *us*. And I'd for damned sure figure Clyntahn would be taking steps to get rid of me as soon as there's been a little time for my Kaudzhu Narrows' halo to wear off."

"Do you think Thirsk's thinking the same way you would in his shoes?"

"I'm not sure. I know he's thinking *something*—Khapahr's activities've made that pretty clear. Kartyr may be one of Thirsk's spies, and Khapahr's the logical person to get any reports from him or tell him about any little missions the Navy needs him to undertake, but that's not what's going on here."

"I'd have to agree," Cayleb said. "I suppose it *could* be some sort of genuine clandestine operation for the Navy, but it sure doesn't *sound* like one."

Mab nodded in the rainy darkness. Lazymyr Kartyr was a merchant captain, of sorts. The extraordinarily obese and self-indulgent sailor owned and commanded the twin-masted schooner *Mairee Zhain*, which had been caught running contraband—better than seventy thousand marks' worth of Chisholmian whiskeys and Charisian luxury goods—into Gorath in defiance of Zhaspahr Clyntahn's embargo and King Rhanyld's own decrees. The punishment for that was death, but Khapahr had convinced Thirsk and Staiphan Maik he would be more valuable as a live spy than as a dead smuggler. And, to be fair, he'd provided quite a bit of useful intelligence to the Royal Dohlaran Navy, courtesy of his contacts with his Chisholmian suppliers. He'd even inserted half a dozen Dohlaran spies and two agents inquisitor into Chisholm by sending them back up his chain of contacts. Of course, none of those spies or agents inquisitor had prospered after *reaching* Chisholm and the agents Sir Ahlber Zhustyn had had waiting for them, courtesy of warnings from the *seijin* network. In fact, four of them had been sending back information Zhustyn and First Councilor White Crag *wanted* Dohlar to have.

So, yes, there *could* be a legitimate reason for Khapahr to visit Kartyr and tell him to hold the *Mairee Zhain* in readiness for another, as yet undisclosed mission. Unfortunately, they had no idea what that mission might be. It was tempting to assume it must have something to do with getting Thirsk and/or his family out of Gorath, except that there was exactly zero evidence that Khapahr—or Thirsk—had ever said so much as a single word about any such possibility to any of the earl's daughters or either of his sons-in-law.

"Damn it!" Cayleb growled after a moment. "We *know* he's up to *something*, and we know it has to be for Thirsk! And we *still* don't have a clue what the two of them are planning. I just wish we'd had a SNARC on them when they organized whatever the hell it is they've organized! For that matter, I'd like to know how the hell they did it *without* our having a SNARC on them, given how carefully we've been monitoring Thirsk!"

"I've been thinking about that," Mab said. "And it's occurred to me that we may have been coming at this the wrong way. I don't think *Thirsk's* organized anything with Khapahr; I think *Khapahr's* been doing all the organizing."

"What?" Cayleb blinked in the imagery floating before Mab's eyes. "That's ridiculous!" he said, although there was a suddenly thoughtful edge in his voice. "Khapahr's his chief of staff—oh, I know he's not allowed to use the term, but that's what he is. Are you trying to tell me Commander Khapahr is slinking around—probably to organize the flight of his admiral's daughters and grandchildren—without Thirsk knowing anything about it? That's crazy, Merlin!"

"I didn't say that was what was happening, either," Mab pointed out. "What I said is that Khapahr's been doing all the organizing. Nahrmahn and I—well, more Nahrmahn and Owl, even if I did help out—have been back over all the take from the SNARC monitoring Thirsk. We didn't realize Khapahr was up to anything until April, but Nahrmahn and Owl found a conversation between him and Thirsk from early March—you can have Owl play it for you later, if you like—which was very interesting. He and the Earl were eating supper together, and Thirsk looked across the table at him and said, 'I used to take the girls for sails, you know, Ahlvyn. They always liked to pretend we were sailing to an exotic foreign land. I wish I had the time and opportunity to do that with them again, maybe even get the grandkids out on the Bay again.'"

"All right," Cayleb said after a moment. "I admit it's an . . . interesting exchange, given what we think is going on now. But so what?"

"So Ahlvyn Khapahr is intensely loyal to Earl Thirsk, Cayleb," Mab said very seriously. "And both he and Thirsk know the Inquisition has to be watching the Earl like cat-lizards stalking a spider rat. I think he understood exactly what Thirsk was saying to him, and that he's been working at it on his own without any formal direction from the Earl. And I think Thirsk trusts him enough to leave that entirely in his hands, because both of them understand that the farther away from anything remotely like an escape plan Thirsk stays, the less likely anyone is to notice the planning is underway."

"I suppose there could be something to that," Cayleb conceded slowly. "*I'd* hate to have Sharleyan and Alahnah's lives depending on someone else's planning, though."

"Of course you would, and I don't doubt for a moment that Thirsk does. But assuming we're right and he really is thinking along the lines of getting his family out of the line of fire, I don't think he has any choice but to trust Khapahr to get it done."

"Um." Cayleb made a noncommittal sound and his image's eyes were unfocused as he considered Mab's argument. Then they sharpened again.

"Actually, now that I think about it, I'd be perfectly willing to leave Sharley and Alahnah's lives in *your* hands, so maybe there's something to your ridiculous theory after all. But whatever's going on with Thirsk, do you think Dunkyn and Hektor will be able to pull it off?"

"Unless the weather screws them over as thoroughly as it screwed Ahbaht over, I think they've got a damned good chance," Mab said.

"Good."

The single word came out of the emperor like something between a prayer and a curse. It lay between him and the *seijin* for a long moment, and then he gave himself a shake.

"I know we didn't have a choice, didn't have this sort of an option, when it happened to Gwylym," he said very quietly. "But I've still never forgiven myself for being so damned helpless."

"Well, we're not helpless this time, Cayleb." Mab's voice was just as quiet. "And if Dunkyn Yairley can't 'pull it off,' I don't think there's anyone on the face of Safehold who could. For that matter, it's not going to hurt a thing that no one in Gorath knows Dunkyn and his squadron have reached Talisman. Sort of hard to plan for threats you don't know exist, now isn't it?"

He and the emperor looked at one another, with smiles any shark might have envied. Then he consulted his internal chronometer and stood.

"I think it's about time," he said in a voice whose calm fooled neither of them. "Owl?"

"Yes, Commander Athrawes?" the AI's voice replied instantly.

"Are we ready?"

"Yes, indeed," the AI said, and no one could have missed the grim anticipation in that artificial person's voice.

Owl had been designed as a tactical computer, a weapon of war. Constraints had been built into his software to prevent him from acting without human authority, yet when reduced to his most basic self, he'd been created to kill. Since he'd become fully self-aware, he'd internalized an entire set of philosophical, moral, and ethical constraints about how and when killing was justifiable, but they hadn't changed his original function. What they *had* done was to teach him to hate Zhaspahr Clyntahn and the Inquisition with a pure and searing passion for the casual atrocities and deliberate murder they'd wreaked upon the people of Safehold. In retrospect, Mab thought, it shouldn't have been particularly surprising that he'd reacted that way, especially after spending so much subjective time with

Nahrmahn Baytz. After all, Nahrmahn had a very *direct* attitude towards people who killed or injured the innocent, and while Owl might have been built as a killer, that killer had also been built as a protector, a champion of the human race in its extremity. That was his function, as much as it had ever been Nimue Alban's, and in this moment, Owl and Dialydd Mab were as one.

"Then I suppose we'd better get started," Mab said now. "Be sure to leave Mahafee and his sergeant intact."

"I'll remember, Commander Athrawes. And—" there might actually have been a suppressed chuckle in the mellow voice "—I'll endeavor to be certain none of the remotes are seen by any survivors, as well."

"I think that would be an excellent idea," Mab agreed, drawing a revolver with one hand and unsheathing his katana with the other. "Let's go."

He started down the hill, and as he did, a dozen combat remotes—manufactured in Nimue's Cave but also armed with black-powder rifles instead of the more advanced weapons they might once have mounted—drifted out of the rain-soaked woods behind him and floated down the slope in his wake.

▼ ▼ ▼

"—and I don't want to have this frigging conversation *again*, Mahafee! It's our job to move these motherless bastards to their new home as quickly as possible, and any of them who drag arse along the way need to be *encouraged* to move along smartly. That's your fucking job, and if I have to discuss this with you again, I'll have your guts for boot laces when I'm finished! I hope that's clear enough even *you* can understand it?!"

Major Lainyl Paxtyn glared up into the face of the taller lieutenant. The major's left fist was propped on his hip while his right hand rested—not coincidentally, Lieutenant Ansyn Mahafee felt confident—on the hilt of his sheathed sword.

"Yes, Sir," he bit out.

"And another thing," Paxtyn snarled. "I don't give a damn *how* wet the frigging wood is or how late we stop. I see you letting another work party wander out into the woods—in the dark—with only two guards, you and I'll just have to have a little talk with Father Trynt. If they can't drag in enough wood for themselves, as well as the guard force, then that's too fucking bad. They can damned well *freeze* to death overnight, for all I care, but they are *not* going to have a chance to sneak off in the dark. Is *that* understood?!"

"Yes, Sir," Mahafee repeated woodenly, and the major glared at him for another thirty seconds. Then he snorted, hawked, and spat contemptuously on the ground and stalked off. The lieutenant watched him go and wondered, distantly, how he'd kept his hand away from his own weapons. He'd known Paxtyn for less than two five-days, and it already seemed a lifetime spent in hell.

*And if it's bad for* me, *what about all these poor bastards we're dragging to Glydahr? This sadistic son-of-a-bitch is—*

He made himself bite that thought off. Whatever he thought of his present superior, Paxtyn was doing exactly what Father Trynt Dezmynd wanted him to do. And Dezmynd was no mere major in the Army of God; he was a Schuelerite upper-priest, handpicked by Inquisitor General Wylbyr for his current mission. Mahafee had seen enough in the last year or so to be less than confident that God or Langhorne could truly have approved the Inquisition's actions here in the Republic of Siddarmark, but that was an even more dangerous thought, and he backed away from it with spinal-reflex quickness.

He felt like a coward for reacting that way, yet what could he do about it? He was the most junior officer of the entire prisoner escort. He and his platoon had been assigned to guard a canal lock south of Selyk. They'd seen that assignment as a well-deserved rest after the ferocity of the combat they'd experienced against the heretic Duke of Eastshare the previous summer, but they'd stood their duty alertly. And when the order came in to destroy the lock and fall back to Selyk, they'd executed those instructions with equal efficiency.

And their reward had been to be assigned to *this*.

His lips worked. He wanted to spit to clear the foul taste from his mouth, but he couldn't know who was watching. Even in the dark and the rain there was bound to be *someone*, some set of gimlet eyes just waiting to report his attitude to Paxtyn or Father Trynt or to Father Zhames Symmyns, Father Trynt's assistant. Although, to be fair, Symmyns might not care all that much. He'd enforced his superior's orders for the guards to "encourage" the prisoners with their whips and clubs, but it seemed to Mahafee that he hadn't gone out of his way to find opportunities for fresh brutality the way far too many of the guards did. And whatever else his faults, Father Zhames had at least allowed—indeed, encouraged—the guards to give the prisoners time to erect what pitiful shelters they could at each stop. For that matter, he'd even convinced Father Trynt that it would be wise to allow the prisoners to gather firewood each night, as well. He'd pointed out that with so many prisoners in the column, there were thousands of hands to gather the wood the guards needed, and if they used married prisoners, or those with children—or parents—in the column, they were unlikely to flee into the wilderness and abandon their family members. And if they were gathering wood for the guards, anyway, they might as well be allowed to retain at least some of it for their own use.

It was a cold, calculating sort of logic, but Mahafee had seen Father Zhames watching the prisoners huddled around their own fires when Father Trynt was in his tent. The lieutenant suspected Father Zhames had . . . shaped his logic to appeal to his superior.

Even if that was true, however, it wouldn't do Mahafee one damned bit of good if Paxtyn and Father Trynt reported him to the Inquisition for continuing to "mollycoddle" the heretics in the column.

*No*, he thought almost despairingly. *Not the heretics*

*in the column; the* accused *heretics in the column. Am I the only officer in this whole Archangel-forsaken march who remembers that not one of them has been* convicted *of heresy or blasphemy yet?*

He drew a deep breath and turned on his heel, squelching off through the mud towards his platoon's bivouac. They were due on watch in less than an hour.

"Who goes there?!"

The challenge stopped Mahafee, and he felt a stir of pride. Whatever the rest of the guard force might have allowed itself to become, his platoon were still *soldiers*.

"Lieutenant Mahafee," he replied to the sentry.

"Was getting a little worried about you, Sir," another voice said, and Mahafee smiled faintly as a shadow detached itself from the night beside the sentry. "Beginning to think you might've forgotten we had the duty," Sergeant Ainghus Kohrazahn said dryly.

"You know, it *had* slipped my mind, Ainghus. I appreciate your reminding me."

"What a sergeant's for, Sir," Kohrazahn told him, but the sergeant was close enough now for Mahafee to see his expression at least dimly in the light of one of the encampment's rain-sputtering torches. That expression was far more worried than the sergeant's tone . . . or any expression Kohrazahn would have allowed any of the members of his platoon to see.

"I had a brief conversation with Major Paxtyn," Mahafee told him. "It's under control, though."

"Good to hear, Sir."

Mahafee heard the wariness—and the warning—in those four words. Ainghus Kohrazahn was no shrinking flower of delicacy, but the lieutenant knew the sergeant was as sickened by the constant brutality as he was himself. And he also knew Kohrazahn was worried—deeply worried—about him. They'd been together since Cahnyr Kaitswyrth's army had marched out of the Temple Lands. Along the way, they'd saved each other's lives at least a half-dozen times, and Mahafee was uneasily aware that the bonds between the two of them—and, for that matter, between all of the platoon's members—had more to do now with their loyalty to one another than with their loyalty to the Army of God. There were times he thought that mutual loyalty might well be stronger than their loyalty to Mother Church, as well. Or even to the Archangels themselves.

And because that was so, he could not—*dared* not—defy Paxtyn, because if he did, Kohrazahn and the platoon would almost certainly support him. And if they did that . . . .

"It's all good, Ainghus," he said reassuringly, even as he wondered if *anything* would ever be "good" again. "It's all good."

▼ ▼ ▼

Dialydd Mab paused under the leaves of the dripping trees. If he'd still been human, he would have drawn a deep breath to settle himself. Indeed, he *did* draw that deep breath, but it was only remembered reflex.

He checked the icons Owl had projected across his vision. The last of the AI's remotes was settling into position, and he smiled coldly as he remembered a conversation with Nahrmahn Baytz in his Siddar City bedchamber. Everything he'd said then was true. There were times when the thought of the millions of dead the jihad had already claimed, and of the hundreds of human beings whose blood he'd personally shed, came down upon him like one of Ehdwyrd Howsmyn's steampowered drop hammers. As he'd told Nahrmahn then, it was worst when he thought about how easily he could turn into a monster even worse than Zhaspahr Clyntahn. It wasn't just the killing; it was the fact that for a PICA, it was almost like some obscene VR game, because even though the carnage was completely real, his victims had no chance at all of killing *him*.

Every bit of that was true, yet what haunted him wasn't really the killing itself, or even his own effective invulnerability. It was the fact that so many of his victims were simply doing the best they could in accordance with what they'd been brought up and taught to believe. It was the knowledge that so few of them truly deserved the label of "evil," and that the reason they'd died was simply that they'd been in the wrong place and crossed his path at the wrong time.

But sometimes . . . oh, yes—*sometimes*.

"Are you ready, Owl?"

"Yes, Commander Athrawes."

"Then let's go."

▼ ▼ ▼

The windy dark was flayed by a sudden eruption of lightning.

Ansyn Mahafee had been winding his watch while Kohrazahn headed off to turn out the duty section. Now he dropped the expensive timepiece and spun towards the trees, reflexes already throwing him flat, as long, livid tongues of flame exploded between the trunks. There had to be at least a dozen riflemen out there . . . and every one of them had to be equipped with one of the heretics' new multi-shot rifles!

Bullets hissed overhead, and he heard cries of shock—and screams of anguish—as they found their marks. He couldn't understand how anyone could possibly see to shoot under these conditions, but the attackers seemed to be doing just fine.

The men of his platoon began to return fire. He and Ainghus Kohrazahn had seen to it that they didn't forget the habit of digging trenches every night. Now they rolled into them, splashing into the water which had gathered in their bottoms, and took their rifles with them. Their rate of fire was hopelessly lower than that of whoever was attacking them, but at least they had protection while they reloaded and he could hear Kohrazahn's deep voice holding them together, coordinating their fire.

Mahafee started crawling towards his platoon sergeant, then stopped, staring in disbelief as a single human being came out of the trees.

He was tall, with an oddly curved sword in his right hand and one of the heretics' "revolvers" in his left hand. Muzzle flashes—from the prisoner guards as well as from the trees behind him—picked him out like spits of lightning even before he entered the uncertain illumination of the torches and the campfires. As far as Mahafee could tell, he was unarmored, but that didn't seem to bother him at all. He moved quickly—inhumanly quickly—and the pistol in his left hand tracked like some sort of mechanism. He fired on the run, which should have made it impossible for him to hit a thing, yet a guard went down with every shot.

Then the revolver was empty. It disappeared into its holster, and a second blade, perhaps half the length of the sword he'd already drawn, materialized in his left hand in its stead.

One of the guards came at him with a bayoneted rifle. The short blade blocked the thrust; the long blade hissed in a blood-flaring arc and the guard's head leapt from his shoulders.

*That's not possible*, a small voice said through the madness and the chaos in the depths of Ansyn Mahafee's brain.

He'd seen enough combat by now to know how ridiculous the bards' tales of one-handed decapitations truly were. *Real* combat was far uglier and far more brutal than any of those stories ever admitted, and real soldiers couldn't simply lop heads off with a single sidearm blow. It couldn't be done.

Yet the charging shape of nightmare in front of him could do it. And whoever it was, he did it again as a second guard came at him. Dozens—scores—of the guards were firing at him now, probably because they couldn't see a single target under the trees, and it did no good at all. Mahafee had been astounded by how many shots could be fired in a battle without hitting anyone, but surely not *all* of those bullets could be missing him!

Only they were. Somehow, they were, and he heard screams of terror as the attacker waded through that storm of fire to get at the men behind it.

"Demon! *Demon!*" someone wailed, and something

clicked in Mahafee's mind. Mother Church and the Inquisition might call them "demons," but there was another name for them, as well, and he knew now that they'd meant every single word of the messages they'd left behind in their bloody work. "De—!"

The cry cut off abruptly, and then that single attacker—that single *seijin*—was at the center of at least a dozen men.

They had as much chance against him as a stand of bamboo against a grazing dragon. They didn't just die. They *flew* away from him, not as intact bodies but as bits and *pieces* of bodies. No man could come within his reach and live.

The *seijin* forged steadily toward the tents set aside for Father Trynt and the rest of the clergy, cutting his way through anything in his path like the wrath of Chihiro itself, and the rifle fire pouring out of the trees crashed over the wavering, terrified defenders like the sea. Every instinct told Mahafee to stay exactly where he was, but some stubborn spark of duty shoved him to his feet, instead.

"*Lieutenant!* Lieutenant—*Ansyn!* What the *hell* d'you think you're doing?! Get *down*, Goddamn it!"

He heard Ainghus' voice behind him, even through the tumult and the deafening thunder of rifles, but it didn't matter. Whatever he thought about the Inquisition, he had his duty. If he abandoned that, he had nothing, and it was only now that he truly realized how desperately he'd clung to that concept as his lifeline in a world turned to horror. Duty, honor, loyalty to his comrades and the men under his command—whatever one chose to call it, it was a far more complex concept than he'd ever realized before the Army of God marched into Siddarmark, and it was the only thing he had left. In this moment he saw that with a clarity he'd never before attained, and he knew that he would rather die than surrender the one thing which had allowed him to remain someone he recognized.

He started to run, drawing his own sword as he went, hearing more bullets than he could possibly have counted hiss by him from those lightning-shot woods. They couldn't possibly all be missing *him*, either, yet his life seemed as charmed as the *seijin*'s. He half stumbled over dead and dying men, left in the ruin of the *seijin*'s wake, and he knew beyond any shadow of a doubt that his own body would be joining them soon.

He ran faster.

*There!*

Major Paxtyn raised his own pistol as the men between him and the *seijin* went down . . . or threw away their weapons and ran. The major's face was twisted in fear, his eyes huge and disbelieving, and he gripped the pistol in both hands. Flame exploded from the barrel, the muzzle flash almost touching the *seijin*'s unarmored chest. He *couldn't* have missed at that range, yet the *seijin* never even slowed, and Paxtyn cried out in raw terror—then screamed in agony—as that dreadful sword disemboweled him. He went down, shrieking, trying to hold his butchered belly together, and the man who'd killed him simply vaulted over his body and left him to finish dying behind him.

Mahafee tasted the sour burn of vomit at the back of his throat and hurled himself after the *seijin* as the other man—or the demon; Mother Church's claims of demonhood seemed far less problematical at the moment—reached the tents just as Father Trynt darted out of one of them, staring about him in horrified panic and disbelief.

"There you are, *Father!*" The deep voice cut through the tumult almost effortlessly, yet it was impossibly calm, almost conversational. The *seijin* wasn't even breathing hard! "I've been looking for you. You should have heeded my warning."

"*Demon!*" Father Trynt screamed, signing Langhorne's scepter against him, and the *seijin* laughed.

It came through the chinks in the gate to hell, that laugh. And then, with blinding speed, he dropped the longer of his two blades, caught the front of the priest's cassock in his suddenly empty hand, and snatched Trynt Dezmynd from his feet.

"Give my regards to Father Vyktyr," that deep voice said. "Tell him Dialydd Mab sent you."

Dezmynd screamed in horror, feet kicking as he twisted like a terrified cat-lizard kitten in the *seijin*'s grip. Then that shorter blade buried itself in his belly and butchered its way upward. It exploded back out of the upper-priest's chest, and Dialydd Mab tossed him away to die.

Mahafee drew in a sobbing breath that mingled horror, fear, and desperation in one and drove his sword into Mab's back in a powerful lunge backed by all the momentum of his running pursuit.

It never connected.

The *seijin* reached back with his empty hand, without even looking—without ever having so much as seen Mahafee coming—and caught the naked blade. It was as if Mahafee had driven the keen-edged steel into a brick wall. The thrust simply *stopped*, with a violence that half numbed his own hand. And then the *seijin*—Mab—twitched his wrist, and the sword flew out of the lieutenant's grip.

Mahafee snatched at his dagger, but now Mab turned to face him. The same hand which had stopped his sword, the hand that should have lost fingers to it sharpness, *flicked* downward. It caught his own hand before it ever reached his dagger, and he cried out in anguish as it twisted his arm, forcing him up onto his toes.

Time froze.

He found himself staring into the rock-hard brown eyes of a man five inches taller than he was. A man whose arm didn't even tremble as his steely fingers gripped Mahafee's wrist with crushing force.

"Lieutenant Mahafee," that same deep voice said calmly, cutting through the tumult—the ongoing screams, the continuing crackle and bellow of rifle fire—with utter clarity. "I've been looking for you, too."

Mahafee stared at him, feeling his complete helplessness in that inhumanly strong grip. The *seijin* flicked his blade with a snapping motion that cleared most of the blood from it. Then he sheathed it, and something tugged at the lieutenant's belt as the other man's left hand plucked Mahafee's dagger from its sheath. He knew he was about to die, and the terror of that thought choked him, yet at least it would be an end.

"You may not believe this, Lieutenant," Mab told him, "but this is actually for your protection."

*Protection?* Mahafee blinked. That was the most insane thing he'd ever—

Anguish flared like white-hot fire as the blade in the *seijin*'s hand—Mahafee's own dagger—stabbed effortlessly through his own upper left arm. The pain was incredible, and yet the thrust was clear, clean, economical, and impossibly quick—the blade recovered almost before the hurt was given.

"You're going to want to have Sergeant Kohrazahn take care of that, Lieutenant," that deep voice said. "And just to be on the safe side . . . ."

Mahafee cried out again as the hand on his right wrist moved upward to his forearm, tightened, and twisted. Bone snapped, and he felt his knees collapsing.

His thoughts flickered and flashed in a welter of confusion, pain, and shock, and somehow the strangest thing of all was how gently the man who'd just broken his arm eased him to the ground. He knelt there, still supported by the *seijin*'s right hand and unable to do anything else, and Mab tossed the bloody dagger over his own shoulder. Then he lowered Mahafee the rest of the way and knelt beside him on one knee while he ripped open the lieutenant's bloody sleeve and tied a rough but efficient bandage around the deep, wicked wound with flashing dexterity.

"There," he said, resting one hand lightly, almost companionably, on Mahafee's breastplate. "That should handle the bleeding until Kohrazahn finds you. He's headed this way now, so I suppose I'd best be going before I have to leave *him* proof of how hard the two of you fought, too."

The lieutenant blinked up at him, his mind slow and sluggish, and Mab smiled ever so slightly. Then the smile disappeared.

"You're the senior officer of this moving atrocity now," he said. "Don't make me regret that I put you in command."

Mahafee blinked again, hammered by too many shocks, too many impossibilities in too brief a time, to do anything else, and Dialydd Mab patted his breastplate.

"Do your best to survive this jihad, Lieutenant," he said through the crackle and roar of the other *seijins*' gunfire. "The Church is going to need men like you when it's over."

Then he vaulted back to his feet, caught up the sword he'd dropped, and disappeared into the night.

. IV .

# HMS *Destiny*, 54,
# Talisman Island,
# The Gulf of Dohlar

"So my intention," Baron Sarmouth said, looking around his rather crowded day cabin at the twenty-odd officers packed into it like sardines, "is to make our presence felt. On the other hand, I'd like the actual strength of our squadron to come as as nasty a surprise as possible to the other side, and I have a few *specific* surprises I'd like to share with them . . . eventually."

He showed his teeth, and something between a chuckle and a snarl answered that thin smile.

"It helps that they haven't—hadn't—been keeping a very close eye on us here," he continued. "Very considerate of them, that was. Of course, we owe Commander Lywys and Commander Cupyr a certain debt of thanks in that respect, as well."

The snarl was a bit more pronounced this time. It also carried a note of profound satisfaction, and Cupyr, who was both young and amazingly blond and blue-eyed for an Emeraldian, colored ever so slightly. His *Sojourn* was the only survivor of the schooners which had sailed for Hahskyn Bay with Sir Bruhstair Ahbaht, and he'd taken that hard. The loss of his close friend Zheryko Cumyngs hadn't made that any easier—the ICN's small-ship captains tended to be a close, tight-knit fraternity—although there was scarcely anyone in Sarmouth's squadron who hadn't known *someone* who'd died—or, far worse, been captured—at the Kaudzhu Narrows. Grief hadn't prevented Cupyr from doing his duty, however. In fact, it had sharpened his edge, and he and Commander Fraizher Lywys' *Foam* had pounced on the pair of brigs the Royal Dohlaran Navy had sent to take a look at Rahzhyr Bay in the aftermath of that savage battle.

The Dohlarans had been considerably later getting around to that minor detail than a Charisian squadron commander would have been.

Sarmouth was grateful for that tardiness, yet he reminded himself not to confuse it with lethargy. Admiral Caitahno Raisahndo was a generally vigorous and capable officer, but he had a lot on his plate just now, and all of his intelligence reports agreed there couldn't be any large number of additional Charisian galleons that far forward. Not yet. Even assuming there'd been enough of them at Claw Island for Earl Sharpfield to send them east in strength, the earl couldn't have learned about Ahbaht's defeat soon enough to have already dispatched them to Talisman Island. More to the point, Raisahndo had a fairly accurate estimate of what Sharpfield's initial strength had been, and he knew exactly how many ships had been lost at the Kaudzhu Narrows. He also knew—courtesy of spies operating out of Port Royal—that no reinforcements had been dispatched from Chisholm, at least as of three five-days previously. Unfortunately for his intelligence estimates, however, Sir Ahlber Zhustyn knew all about the Port Royal spy. In fact, that spy had been carefully left in place while his counterpart in Manchyr had been quietly eliminated. As a result, even though Raisahndo knew exactly what *hadn't* sailed from *Chisholm*, Corisande was rather a different matter. There was no way for any Dohlaran even to know Sarmouth and his squadron had departed Manchyr, far less that it had reached Claw Island and that "Empress Sharleyan's orders" had inspired Sharpfield to send him forward as rapidly as possible.

By the time Raisahndo did get around to dispatching a pair of his light cruisers to check up on Talisman, Sarmouth had arrived, and he'd stationed his own light vessels—all of them, including *Sojourn*—to patrol as aggressively as possible on the island's eastern approaches. *Foam* and *Sojourn* had been waiting, almost perfectly placed and with a favorable wind, when Raisahndo's scouts finally arrived, and they'd captured both brigs after a short, vicious action.

Less than a third of the Dohlaran crews had been taken prisoner. That probably said a few unfortunate things about the Imperial Charisian Navy's present attitude towards the Royal Dohlaran Navy, but there was little evidence the schooners' companies had simply massacred people trying to surrender. It was more a matter of how . . . vigorously they'd gone about the business of boarding their enemies.

The consequence of their neat little engagement, however, was that Raisahndo still didn't know—and *couldn't* know, for five-days at the very least—that Sarmouth's squadron had reached Talisman or how powerful it actually was.

"Since we don't want them to realize we're coming until we're ready to invite them to our picnic," the baron went on, "it would be very helpful if they don't *see* us until then. Bearing that in mind, here's what I intend."

He nodded to Hektor Aplyn-Ahrmahk, who stood with a pointer in his good hand while Sylvyst Raigly and Trumyn Lywshai, Sarmouth's secretary, held up a large, unrolled chart so that everyone in the cabin could see it. Lieutenant Aplyn-Ahrmahk put the tip of his pointer on the tiny symbol labeled "Talisman Island" and looked at his admiral expectantly.

"The Squadron will depart Rahzhyr Bay with the morning ebb," Sarmouth said. "We'll shape our course to stay well clear of Scallop Island, and we'll time our transit through Whale Passage to pass between Cliff Island and Whale Island during the hours of darkness. That assumes, of course, that the wind allows us to do so, which it probably will." Hektor's pointer traced the line of the baron's proposed course as the baron spoke. "We'll have approximately twelve hours of darkness; with a normal westerly, we can make the entire transit in only ten. We're most likely to be spotted by fishing boats, especially in our approach to Whale Passage. On the other hand, fishermen have a well-known aversion to encountering enemy warships—for that matter, *any* warships—at sea."

The soft sound from his assembled officers was much more chuckle than snarl this time, and he smiled back at them.

"Just to be on the safe side, however, we'll expect Commander Cupyr, Commander Lywys, and their associates to . . . shoo away any fishing boats that seem slow about taking to their heels. They'll also be responsible for spotting those fishing boats before the fishing boats spot the rest of the squadron's sails. It's always possible someone will get a glimpse of us and get away from them, despite their best efforts. However, it seems most likely to me that the majority of the Dohlaran squadron is still in Hahskyn or South Shwei Bay, or—at worst, from our perspective—en route back from there."

In fact, he knew from Owl's SNARCs that all but five of the surviving Dohlaran galleons remained at anchor—most of them in the Yu-shai Inlet—while they awaited replacement personnel and the worst damaged underwent repair in Yu-shai itself.

"So even if someone spots us and runs for Jack's Land or Saram Bay to report our presence, the word isn't going to get to Admiral Rohsail—" at the moment, Sarmouth and his flag lieutenant were the only two

Charisians in the Gulf of Dohlar who knew Rohsail had been too badly wounded to exercise effective command "—before we want it to. Even if it does, however, there's no way he could have *Dreadnought* back in service under Dohlaran colors yet, and in her absence, I'm *more* than willing to encounter what's left of *his* galleon fleet after Captain Haigyl and Sir Bruhstair got done with it."

Heads nodded throughout the cabin with a certain grim satisfaction. Even without benefit of SNARCs, most of those officers could do the math for the Royal Dohlaran Navy's probable losses and damages. Which wasn't to say they didn't approve wholeheartedly of their commanding officer's precautions.

"Once we've passed Whale Island," Sarmouth went on as Hektor's pointer continued to move across the chart, "we'll shape our course to the east." Several people were leaning forward now, their eyes intent. "We'll be penetrating farther into the Gulf than anyone's gone since Admiral Manthyr withdrew from Trove Island. As of our last reports, the majority of the enemy's shipping is using the Trosan Channel—" Hektor's pointer swooped down to tap the hundred-and-forty-mile-wide stretch of water between the eastern tip of Hilda Island and the Dohlar Bank "—or staying even farther east and skirting the Dohlaran coast through the Fern Narrows. That's probably due to the way in which Captain Ahbaht's people have made themselves so thoroughly unpleasant in the *western* Gulf."

He nodded slightly in Sir Bruhstair Ahbaht's direction, and the diminutive Emeraldian nodded back. It was a stiff gesture, without the edge of relaxed humor which had characterized him before the Kaudzhu Narrows, but it also acknowledged the validity of Sarmouth's analysis. There would undoubtedly be a lot of pressure for shipping patterns to move farther west again to shorten transit times now that Ahbaht's squadron had been destroyed, but there would also be a lot of resistance. Charis still held Claw Island, and Ahbaht had taken less than half of Sharpfield's schooners with him. The rest were still available to continue their depredations against enemy commerce, and the officers and crews of the merchant ships involved would have a pronounced distaste for encountering those schooners until and unless their own navy was in a position to provide escorts once more.

"My intention," Sarmouth said, letting his eyes sweep the other officers' faces, "is to position our galleon strength somewhere in this area." Hektor's pointer tapped the water midway between the northeastern tip of Hilda Island and the Fist of Schueler, the southernmost headland of the border state of Erech. "Rather than tip our hand prematurely by attacking any ports or revealing the presence of our main strength, we'll begin by letting the schooners have their head in this area." Hektor's pointer swept a circle over the Dohlar Bank, Trosan Channel, and Mahthyw Passage. "I imagine their presence that far east will come as a nasty surprise to the other side, especially after the Kaudzhu Narrows. Hopefully they'll have at least a five-day or so of good hunting before anyone gets himself well enough organized to send his own light cruisers or galleons to chase them away.

"Of course, someone *will* send those galleons to see to that chasing eventually. Most likely, they'll draw a half dozen or so of them from the Dohlarans' home fleet, and when they arrive, the first of our schooner captains to sight them will break and run. Right through *here*."

Hektor's pointer tapped the area between Hilda Island and the Fist of Schueler again, and there was no chuckle at all in the snarls that answered him.

Sarmouth smiled fiercely at his assembled captains, treasuring that sound. And treasuring even more something he knew but they didn't about just who would be passing through the Trosan Channel about the time they got there.

"Do you think they're really coming, Sarge?"

Sergeant Laijah Kaspahrt of the Army of God stopped and turned to face the questioner. Private Tohmys Fhranklyn had just turned nineteen. He had untidy straw-colored hair, a prominent Adam's apple, and a bad case of acne. He also had very worried brown eyes, and he licked his lips nervously as Kaspahrt looked at him expressionlessly.

"Is who really coming?" the sergeant asked after a long, slow moment, and the private's Adam's apple bobbed as he swallowed hard.

"*Them*, Sarge," he said. And swallowed again, harder. "The . . . the heretics."

"I think the only heretics you'd better be worrying about, boyoh, are the ones in *there*." Kaspahrt jerked a thumb over his shoulder at the ragged clusters of prisoners inside Camp Chihiro's fences. "You just let the Bishop and the Major worry about any *other* heretics. Got me?"

"Yeah, Sarge. I mean, sure!" Fhranklyn nodded in jerky agreement.

The sergeant held him with a cold, beady eye for another fistful of heartbeats, then nodded back much more firmly and resumed his walk. Behind him, young Fhranklyn turned to look disconsolately not at the camp's inmates, but southeast, down the Gray Hill-Hyrdmyn High Road.

▼ ▼ ▼

"Somebody just got on the wrong side of Sergeant Kaspahrt," Private Ahntahn Ruhsail remarked. Lewshys

Stahdmaiyr looked up from the not especially tasty sandwich he was eating and raised an eyebrow.

"Whatcha talking about?" he asked a bit indistinctly, and Ruhsail twitched his head at the pimple-faced private peering down the road.

"You want to bet Fhranklyn was dumb enough to ask Kaspahrt if the heretics're about to come calling?" he asked.

Stahdmaiyr grunted, swallowed, and washed the mouthful down with a swig from a jealously hoarded—and none too good—bottle of beer.

"Nothing I wouldn't wanna lose," he said then. He stood and walked to the guard tower rail at Ruhsail's side. "Boy's 'bout four cards short of a full deck, you ask me. On t'other hand, though," he scratched his chin thoughtfully, "hard t' blame him fer worryin', isn't it?"

"Oh, I think that's fair enough," Ruhsail agreed. He looked to the southeast himself. From his higher vantage point he could look past the rudimentary defensive works Bishop Failyx had insisted the camp guards throw up outside the perimeter and see considerably farther down the high road than Fhranklyn could see from ground level. So far, there was nothing *to* see, however, and he was torn between gratitude for that absence of oncoming, vengeful heretics and resentment of the pincers of anticipation twisting him as he waited for them.

"Fair enough," he repeated softly. "Fair enough."

▼ ▼ ▼

"So, everyone's clear?"

Brigadier Dairak Bahrtalymu, CO, 10th Mounted Brigade of the 1st Corps of the Army of New Northland, scanned the faces of the other three officers gathered around his map. Major Stywyrt Malikai, his chief of staff, stood at his left shoulder. Colonel Mahkswail Veldamahn, CO of the 19th Mounted Regiment, and Colonel Saisahr Bailukhav, who commanded the 20th Mounted, Bahrtalymu's second regiment, stood on the far side of the folding desk.

"I think so, yes, Sir," Veldamahn said, glancing at Bailukhav. The other colonel was both four years older and senior to Veldamahn.

"And you, Saisahr?" Bahrtalymu asked.

"Clear, Sir."

Bailukhav's accent still sounded a bit strange in the Imperial Charisian Army. He was an Emeraldian, from the capital city of Manchyr itself, who'd been sent off to the Imperial Army by the late Prince Nahrmahn's Uncle Hanbyl, the Duke of Solomon. One didn't normally think of the words "Emeraldian" and "cavalry" in the same sentence, but Duke Solomon had been right about Bailukhav. He was tough, flexible-minded, and the sort of officer to whom mobility was second nature.

He also looked just a bit disgruntled at the moment, and Bahrtalymu didn't really blame him. Of course Bailukhav wanted to be in at the kill, but it was just as important to circle wide of the objective and snap up anybody headed west, towards Cat-Lizard Lake and the Temple Boys. Well, towards the *Harchongians* now, really, but it was the same thing.

"It's important that you and your boys cut the high road between Gray Hill and Traymos," he said now. "And I want you keeping a sharp eye out to the *west*, too. So far the Harchongians haven't shown any signs of rushing forward, but if the *seijins'* reports are accurate, they're probably under orders to move at least as far forward as Cat-Lizard, and that's less than three hundred miles from Gray Hill. The last thing we need is for them to start feeling adventurous and us not realize they're coming."

"Understood, Sir."

Bailukhav nodded just a bit more cheerfully as Bahrtalymu gently stressed the importance of his mission, and the brigadier turned back to Veldamahn.

"The main thing as far as you're concerned, Mahkswail, is that we don't want a bloodbath here. The Inquisitors are for the high jump, no matter what, and they damned well know it. Frankly, if one of them wants to cut his throat or hang himself before you get your hands on him, the bastards have my permission. But if they know they're going to die anyway, some of them may decide to take as many of the prisoners—or of your boys—with them as they can. So I want you to emphasize the need for everybody to watch his arse. And remind them that for now, at least, the order's to let any of the Temple Boys who want to give it up surrender."

Neither colonel looked very happy at that, and Bahrtalymu shrugged.

"I don't like it, either," he said flatly.

His brigade had been the first Charisian troops into Camp Lairays at Hyrdmyn, and even Charisian discipline had wavered—snapped, actually, in a couple of cases—when his troopers saw the state of Camp Lairays' inmates. General Sahmyrsyt had had a few stern words to say to Bahrtalymu about that, although to be fair, they'd been extraordinarily mild stern words compared to some of Sir Bartyn's more famous and inventive tongue lashings. The general's heart hadn't really seemed to be in it.

"I don't like it, but as Sir Bartyn pointed out to me some few days ago, *we* aren't the Group of Four and we're not going to behave as if we were. Unless, of course," he smiled thinly, "the motherless bastards give us an excuse."

▼ ▼ ▼

"Bishop Failyx is concerned about the state of your troops' morale, Major," Father Aizykyal Trynchyr said.

"Is he, Father?"

Major Zhefytha Chestyrtyn's question came out almost mildly but his face tightened with anger. Trynchyr was Bishop Failyx Mahkgyvyrn's second-in-command here at Camp Chihiro. The Schuelerite upper-priest was a fair-haired native Siddarmarkian with muddy blue eyes who was ten years older than Chestyrtyn and seemed to have about as much imagination as Chestyrtyn's left bootheel.

And considerably less empathy than that.

"Yes," Trynchyr said now. "More and more of your men are . . . creeping away in the middle of the night. That won't do, Major. It won't do at all."

Chestyrtyn bit his tongue firmly against the temptation to point out that two-thirds of Camp Chihiro's *inquisitors* had already crept away "in the middle of the night." In fact, over half of the ordained clerics and at least that many of the lay brothers who'd been attached to Camp Chihiro were nowhere to be seen. Bishop Failyx wasn't one of them, unfortunately, and he was determined that Chestyrtyn and his men—his *remaining* men—would defend the concentration camp to the death.

*I suppose I should count myself fortunate that he hasn't already ordered us to execute every single inmate, like those lunatics at Camp Fyrmahn. And this idiot's worried about the troops "creeping away" like his own frigging inquisitors?*

"I'll make a personal inspection this afternoon and impress that upon all of them, Father," he said, once he was confident he had control of his tone. "Was there anything else?"

"No. No!" Trynchyr shook his head. "Just . . . just see to it they do their duty, Major."

He waved one hand in a tossing-away gesture, turned, and headed back towards the camp's administrative block. Chestyrtyn watched him go with a sense of relief, then turned and resumed his own walk across the parade ground.

Captain Mohrtyn Ahdymsyn, his own youthful second-in-command, was waiting for him—or had damned well *better* be waiting for him—in his office. Ahdymsyn wasn't the sharpest arrow in the quiver by a long chalk, but at least that very lack of imagination made him unlikely to come up with any bright ideas—or with *any* ideas, really—of his own. It was a sorry note when someone who couldn't be trusted to think for himself was a more desirable subordinate than someone who could do that thinking. In this instance, though, obedience to orders was going to be far more important than initiative.

*And the wrong* sort *of "initiative" could damned well get us all killed*, the major thought grimly.

Zhefytha Chestyrtyn was devout, he was orthodox, but whatever else he might be, he was no fool, and he had no death wish. He'd made certain—unobtrusively, of course—that every man of his remaining guard force had heard what had happened to the guards and inquisitors who'd overseen the forced march of the Camp Tairek prisoners to Sardahn. The *prisoners* had made it in the end, but almost two-thirds of the guard force and *every* ordained inquisitor who'd set out from Camp Tairek had been less fortunate. The nightmare reports of the survivors had made it clear—far clearer than the Inquisition undoubtedly wished—that the attacking "terrorists" had reserved their greatest fury for the priests and guards who'd been most brutal during the march.

Not that Chestyrtyn and his men had needed those reports. Chestyrtyn himself had been present when Zherohm Clymyns, Fhrancys Ostean, and Zhorj Myzuhno were shot down like so many prong bucks at Kuhnymychu Ruhstahd's execution. He'd been there when the note signed "Dialydd Mab" was opened, and his company had been dispatched to "chase down" the killer. Which—thank Langhorne!—they'd been unable to do. Chestyrtyn had paced off the distance from which Dialydd Mab had taken those shots, and he'd wanted no part of what a marksman like that could have done to his pursuers.

It was remarkable, really, how Camp Chihiro's inmates' treatment had improved after that object lesson. It was also remarkable how many of the camp's more senior officers—especially those with strings to pull—had been transferred to other duties over the next couple of months. Major Chestyrtyn had been only one of the Camp Chihiro guard forces' officers at the time Dialydd Mab had paid his visit. Now he'd inherited command, and he wished with all his heart that he hadn't.

▼ ▼ ▼

"All right," Major Symyn Zylwyky said. "Colonel Veldamahn's been what one might call abundantly clear about the need to let these bastards surrender if they want to. I have to assume that's because Brigadier Bahrtalymu made that point to him. I trust all of you will bear it in mind?"

It wasn't really a question. Major Zylwyky commanded 1st Company of the 19th Mounted Regiment, and he was a no-nonsense sort of officer. He let the silence linger for several seconds, then grunted in satisfaction.

"Good," he continued. "In that case, Shaimus, your platoon has lead."

Lieutenant Shaimus Dahnvyrs, commanding 1st Platoon, nodded in understanding.

"Dunkyn," Zylwyky turned his attention to Lieutenant Dunkyn Murphai, 3rd Platoon's CO, "you'll have Shaimus' back. Once he's secured the gates and the guard towers on the eastern perimeter, you'll move straight for the administrative block. After that—"

▼ ▼ ▼

"Oh, *shit*," Ahntahn Ruhsail muttered.

"What?" Private Stahdmaiyr said, turning quickly. Then his jaw tightened.

"Oh, shit," he agreed.

"Better find the Corporal," Ruhsail said, watching the long, broad column of extremely well-armed horsemen trotting up the high road towards him.

▼ ▼ ▼

"They're here, Sir," Sergeant Kaspahrt announced grimly.

"Wonderful," Chestyrtyn sighed.

He looked down at the report on his desk, then smiled crookedly and tossed it over his shoulder. The individual sheets of paper separated, fluttering like awkward ghosts, and he shoved his chair back from the desk.

"Go find Ahdymsyn," he said. "Sit on him—respectfully, of course. If he even *looks* like doing something stupid, hit him over the head with whatever you can find."

"Yes, Sir!"

The sergeant sketched Langhorne's scepter in salute, turned on his heel, and disappeared out the office door. Chestyrtyn watched him go, then picked up his sword belt and buckled it around his waist.

▼ ▼ ▼

"Company, halt!"

The command—and Major Zylwyky's raised hand— brought the entire column to a halt. The major's eyes narrowed as a single man in the uniform of the Army of God with a major's insignia stepped out of Camp Chihiro's gates and stood alone, facing the Charisians.

The earthworks which had been thrown up outside the camp's fence were sturdy enough to offer the certainty of painful casualties if they were defended. They seemed a little extensive for someplace which was supposed to have the garrison the Army of New Northland's intelligence reports estimated Chihiro had. It was always possible that strength estimate had been in error, but now, as he studied them in the early-afternoon sunlight, he realized there'd been absolutely no rush to man those fighting positions. In fact, the guards he could see in the watchtowers on either side of the gate were rather ostentatiously looking anywhere but at his column.

After a moment, Zylwyky touched his horse with a heel and started slowly forward, followed—without orders, he thought dryly—by Zhaikyb Presmyn, his company sergeant major. Presmyn was almost twice his major's age and trusted any Temple Boy about as far as he could have walked across Cherry Bay. Zylwyky didn't need to look over his shoulder to know that the retaining strap on Presmyn's holster had been unbuttoned.

He stopped his horse six feet from the Army of God major and sat there, looking down at the other man from the height advantage of his saddle.

"Major Chestyrtyn, Army of God," the Temple Boy said.

Zylwyky had heard an accent like his before. It came from the border area between the Harchong Empire and the Desnairian Empire, and Zylwyky's eyes narrowed as he heard it. People from the Harchong-Desnair border had a well-earned reputation for devout orthodoxy. Some might have preferred the phrase "foaming fanaticism," in fact.

"Major Symyn Zylwyky, Imperial Charisian Army," he replied flatly.

"I assume you're here to take possession of Camp Chihiro," Chestyrtyn said.

"I am, in the name of Their Majesties and Protector Greyghor."

Zylwyky's tone was even flatter, and Chestyrtyn nodded.

"Major," he said, "I have strict orders from Bishop Failyx Mahkgyvyrn not to surrender my post. However—"

He drew his sword very carefully by the quillons and held it up, offering Zylwyky the hilt.

. VI .
## Lake City,
## Tarikah Province,
## Republic of Siddarmark

"So, Nephew," Taychau Daiyang said, porcelain wine cup nestled between his palms as he sat on the shaded veranda and enjoyed the cool afternoon breeze blowing in off East Wing Lake, "ought I to assume that you bring me yet more tidings of gladness and joy?"

The wine cup in the Earl of Rainbow Waters' hands did not contain wine, and he raised it slightly, nostrils flaring as he inhaled the scent of the whiskey it *did* contain. The remains of a light luncheon lay on the wicker table in front of him, and he raised one mobile eyebrow at Captain of Horse Medyng Hwojahn, the Baron of Wind Song.

"'Gladness and joy' are not the precise terms I would have chosen, My Lord," Wind Song replied.

"For some reason, I fail to find myself overwhelmed by surprise," Rainbow Waters said dryly. He took one hand from his wine cup and gestured at another of the chairs on the broad veranda. "Sit and tell me what fresh non-gladness brings you here."

"Thank you, My Lord."

Baron Wind Song settled into the indicated chair and, at his uncle's gesture, poured some of the truly excellent Chisholmian whiskey into another of the all-but-priceless wine cups. He took a moment to savor the first small sip, then squared his shoulders and looked across the lunch table at the earl.

"There *is* some good news, My Lord," he said. "Earl Silken Hills reports that he's established his positions as directed by Vicar Allayn. At this time, all I have is his preliminary semaphore message to that effect, but Captain of Horse Hywanlohng assures me that a complete written report, including maps, will arrive by courier as soon as possible."

Falling Waters nodded. Wind Song was correct; that *was* good news, and if Captain of Horse Hywanlohng promised the complete report would arrive shortly, Silken Hills could be confident that it truly would. That wasn't something he could have taken for granted from all of his subordinates, unfortunately. Too many of them were imbued with the philosophy that it was better to fend off unpleasantness today by promising their superiors whatever they wanted to hear for tomorrow. That, the earl had been forced to admit to himself many years ago, was an attitude endemic to much of the Harchongese aristocracy.

Unlike most officers of his rank, however, Kaishau Hywanlohng neither held an aristocratic title nor stood heir to one, although he was related to several noble families. In fact, he was some sort of remote cousin of the Duke of Yellow Dragon, although Silken Hills doubted that even Harchongese genealogists could have determined the exact degree of kinship. However low-ranked he might have been in the Empire's nobility, Hywanlohng was a hard-bitten military professional who'd served for over a quarter century in the Imperial Harchongese Army before his assignment to the Mighty Host of God and the Archangels. At present, he was Earl Silken Hills' equivalent of Baron Wind Song, the effective chief of staff of what had now officially become known as the Southern Mighty Host of God and the Archangels.

"I have the impression from Captain of Horse Hywanlohng's message," Wind Song continued a bit delicately, "that some considerable portion of Earl Silken Hills' line east of the Black Wyverns consists of fortified posts screened by patrols rather than a solid line of entrenchments."

"Given his strength and the width of the front he's been instructed to hold, I find that not surprising," Rainbow Waters said after a moment. "It seems reasonable enough to me. Unless Captain of Horse Hywanlohng's fuller report shows some reason to reconsider that, I see no reason to trouble Archbishop Militant Gustyv or Vicar Allayn with an overabundance of details." He smiled briefly. "They have so many details to keep track of already, after all."

"Of course, My Lord," Wind Song agreed.

Officially, Silken Hills had been instructed to fortify his entire front in sufficient strength and depth to withstand the sort of whirlwind attack which had overwhelmed Cahnyr Kaitswyrth's Army of Glacierheart. In fact, that would have been impossible, and Wind Song knew his uncle was confident Archbishop Militant Gustyv Walkyr had been well aware of that when he passed on Allayn Maigwair's instructions to that effect. He also knew that the Mighty Host's commander strongly suspected those instructions had been issued more to placate Zhaspahr Clyntahn than because Maigwair had believed for a moment that they could actually have been obeyed by mortal men.

"And now for the less good news," Rainbow Waters prompted, and Wind Song nodded.

"We have official confirmation that the heretics have liber—" The baron paused in mid-word and cleared his throat. "That is to say, we have official confirmation that the heretics have *captured* Camp Chihiro," he said instead and was rewarded by an even briefer smile from his uncle.

"While news of any reverse must be less than welcome to any loyal son of Mother Church, it would be foolish to deny that this particular reverse simplifies our own situation somewhat," Rainbow Waters remarked after a moment.

Wind Song let the observation pass without comment. Bishop Merkyl Sahndhaim, the Mighty Host's official intendant, would be . . . less than happy to hear about Camp Chihiro's fall. The baron suspected he would be even less happy when he heard *how* Camp Chihiro had fallen, but there wasn't any actual confirmation that the camp guards had surrendered themselves, the prisoners, and Camp Chihiro's inquisitors without firing so much as a single shot.

Hopefully, there wouldn't be.

In the meantime, however, the official loss of Camp Chihiro should mitigate the pressure on Rainbow Waters to somehow race the almost five hundred miles between Lake City and Gray Hill to prevent its loss. Wind Song was pretty sure Sahndhaim had recognized the impossibility of doing anything of the sort, but the intendant had been under immense pressure from the Grand Inquisitor and the Inquisitor General. On the other hand, he'd been far less insistent about it than he might have been, given that pressure from above. Bishop Merkyl's support for Vicar Zhaspahr's policies was well known, but he was an intelligent man. More than that, he had more than enough faith in the Mighty Host's orthodoxy and zeal to be willing to accept Rainbow Waters' military analyses and arguments, even when those analyses weighed against the . . . overly impetuous fulfillment of the Grand Inquisitor's designs. He was also intelligent enough to accept Rainbow Waters' judgment without openly arguing against the Grand Inquisitor's instructions. It was an often tricky tightrope, but Sahndhaim was well acquainted with the techniques Mother Church's bureaucrats had evolved over the centuries to protect their own backs.

They were almost as skilled in that regard as *Harchongese* bureaucrats.

"The other bit of news on that front," the baron continued after a moment, "is that the column from Camp Saint Charlz will be arriving by barge tomorrow or the next day."

"I see."

Rainbow Waters sipped whiskey. Despite his own deep faith and belief in the Jihad, the earl had been much more than simply dismayed by the conditions he'd discovered at Camp St. Tailahr, the Inquisition's camp outside Lake City, when he first saw it. Harchongese aristocrats were seldom squeamish, but the brutality of the camp guards—especially directed towards those whose heresy had yet to be proven—had struck him as excessive. And that had been before he discovered that conditions in St. Tailahr had been still worse until Archbishop Arthyn Zagyrsk personally intervened. Primate of Tarikah or not, it had required more intestinal fortitude than most mere archbishops were willing to display to risk the ire of Inquisitor General Wylbyr or Zhaspahr Clyntahn, but Zagyrsk had insisted that since the camp inmates were being used as a labor force by Mother Church, Mother Church had a moral obligation to see to it that they were at least adequately fed and received minimal medical care. And moral considerations aside, he'd pointed out acidly, if the inmates were simply worked to death, they would no longer be available as a labor force.

Rainbow Waters wasn't looking forward to receiving the prisoners evacuated from St. Charlz and discovering what the inmates of camps who'd lacked an Archbishop Arthyn had endured. Not even the splendid whiskey in his cup was enough to kill the taste that was likely to put into his mouth. On the other hand . . . .

*Yes, there's always an "other hand," isn't there, Taychau?* he thought dryly.

"If the camp's been successfully evacuated," he said serenely, lowering the cup once more, "then the pressure to defend Traymos has . . . somewhat decreased."

Wind Song nodded.

"In that case," the earl said rather more briskly, "we will reinforce our forward observation force at Mardahs, and also the one at Ayaltyn. A cavalry picket at Camp Saint Charlz' position—*former* position— should suffice to cover the approaches from Cat-Lizard Lake, for the moment at least. Sanjhys will become the northern anchor of our main position."

"Yes, My Lord."

Wind Song forbore to point out that the Mighty Host of God and the Archangels' orders were to hold a position as far east as possible. In fact, they were to hold the line of the North Hildermoss River, a hundred and fifty miles east of East Wing Lake, if at all possible. It was evident from the correspondence from Zion that with the heretic navy's armored riverboats stymied on the line of the north Hildermoss—so far at least—by the demolished locks at Darailys, the Captain General (or at least the Grand Inquisitor) wanted the entire river line south from Darailys held. It was equally obvious from what his uncle had just said that Rainbow Waters had no intention of doing anything of the sort. Sanjhys, one of the villages and small towns—very small towns, this far north—strung along the Tarikah River between East Wing Lake and the Hildermoss, was barely sixty-five miles east of the lake. It was also, however, only about a hundred and twenty miles from the Great Tarikah Forest which would form the *southern* anchor of Rainbow Waters' proposed defensive line.

The Tarikah Forest stretched six hundred miles, north-to-south, and most of it was trackless, virgin, unconsecrated forest. No doubt the heretics would be able to get through it more readily than Mother Church's defenders—they'd demonstrated their accursed mobility clearly enough by now—but not in great strength. And as long as the Mighty Host held blocking points along the canals, rivers, and limited road net, they wouldn't be getting any supply wagons or *artillery* through it.

It would also prevent Rainbow Waters' right from dangling in midair and inviting yet another of the heretics' devastating flank attacks.

"Were the year not quite so advanced," the Mighty Host of God and the Archangels' commander continued calmly, "I would, of course, prefer to advance to the line of the Hildermoss, at least as far south as Lake Mayan, with an eye towards taking the offensive should the heretics' present preoccupation with capturing Mother Church's holding camps offer an opening. Under the circumstances, however, and given the damage done to the transportation system, it would clearly be rash to advance too precipitously with winter no more than a month and a half away. Our ability to supply the forces necessary to hold the occupied—*reoccupied*—territory would be problematical at best, once winter sets in. Far better to select a line we can be confident of holding and spend the next month or two building up our supply magazines here at Lake City in order to assure us of the ability to launch a powerful and *sustained* offensive in the spring."

"Of course, My Lord," Baron Wind Song agreed.

## . VII .
## St. Zheryld's Abbey,
## Episcopate of St. Shulmyn,
## The Temple Lands

"I hope you'll feel this was worth the trip, Your Grace," Lynkyn Fultyn said, bending to kiss Allayn Maigwair's extended ring as the Captain General stepped off the gangplank from the heavily escorted barge. "I know we're a long way from Zion," he continued as he straightened, "but—"

"But I'm the one who insisted on moving the project out here for development, Lynkyn," Maigwair interrupted. "And it's not that bad a trip by water. I'd hate to make it overland, of course, but the trip across the lake was almost like a vacation of sorts. To be honest, I enjoyed it."

Brother Lynkyn nodded. The largish town of St. Zheryld's Abbey lay almost four hundred miles east of Zion. Aside from the modest foundries which had called St. Zheryld's Abbey home, there'd been nothing particularly worth making the journey before the Jihad. The St. Zheryld River was a brawling and tempestuous stream where it came spilling down from the southern end of the Mountains of Light—well suited to driving the waterwheels of the pre-Jihad foundries but completely unnavigable above the town. Below the town, it was considerably deeper, but also narrow, navigable only by barges far smaller than those which normally plied Safehold's rivers and canals. That limitation was the reason St. Zheryld's Abbey hadn't been chosen as a site for one of Mother Church's newer, larger foundries, but it also explained why the town— out of sight and out of mind—was ideally suited to Maigwair's present purposes. He could make the trip across Lake Pei and then up the lower St. Zheryld's in less than three days (and in relative comfort), but it was isolated enough to allow for tight security, and its existing foundries were fully capable of producing the necessary metalwork under Fultyn's skilled supervision.

"Well, with that out of the way," the Captain General continued cheerfully, resting one hand on Brother Lynkyn's shoulder, "why don't we get on with the demonstration?"

"Are you certain you don't wish to go to your quarters, first, Your Grace?" Fultyn looked a bit anxious. "It's past lunchtime. Couldn't we feed you and let you rest a bit?"

"Lynkyn, I've been sitting on my arse for the last two and a half days," Maigwair pointed out with a smile. "This barge," he gestured one-handed at the vessel from which he'd just debarked, "although a bit on the small side, is very comfortably appointed, I assure you. And my cook's seen to it that I've been reasonably well fed since leaving Zion. Unless, of course, there's some reason you're trying to *delay* me . . . ?"

"No, Your Grace! Of course not!" Fultyn began quickly, then paused as Maigwair's smile turned into a grin.

"Very well, Your Grace," the Chihirite said after a moment, his own lips quivering on the edge of a smile, "you got me. If you'd be kind enough to step this way, that demonstration is waiting for you."

"Somehow I was certain it would be," Maigwair replied, squeezing the lay brother's shoulder affectionately.

▼ ▼ ▼

"As you know, Your Grace," Fultyn said as Maigwair followed him up the observation tower's stairs, "getting what we've dubbed the 'exhaust nozzles' properly designed was a more difficult proposition than I'd hoped, despite possessing the example we'd captured from the heretics. That gave me a model to work from, but actually figuring out how to cast and machine them properly—and *uniformly*—was rather challenging. In addition, the bronze used in the heretics' rockets melts or erodes in flight. Clearly, that hasn't been a problem for them, but since they've been using them primarily as *signaling* devices, whereas we want to use them as weapons, we need a longer . . . burn time, for want of a better term, out of *our* rockets. We also need a greater degree of accuracy. Rockets are never going to be as accurate as rifled bullets or shells, but we need to be confident all of them will fly to at least approximately the target we want to hit, and that makes the nozzles' performance—and durability—even more important. Bronze lasted *almost* long enough, but in the end, we had to convert to steel. Fortunately, the new hearths are producing so much of that that it's actually cheaper than bronze would have been. Harder to machine, which costs us a little on the labor side, but overall it costs a lot less."

"That's good."

There was an unwontedly fervent note in the Captain General's response, and Fultyn glanced back over his shoulder. Maigwair grimaced slightly but said nothing, only waving his hand for the lay brother to continue climbing. There was no point explaining to Fultyn just how parlous Mother Church's finances had become. The revised revenue measures had increased receipts from the Harchong Empire by almost thirty percent and more than doubled those coming from the Temple Lands. Desnair's tithes, however, had tumbled disastrously even before the Empire had been driven effectively out of the Jihad, and Dohlar's had actually been cut to the bone to reflect the enormous amounts Rahnyld found himself forced to spend on his own armed forces. Even the more affluent Border States found themselves in situations very similar to Dohlar's, and Siddarmark's were, of course, gone in their entirety. Rhobair Duchairn estimated he could continue to fund the Jihad for perhaps another year, even fifteen months. At that point, however, the Church would be effectively bankrupt.

Clyntahn, predictably, downplayed the Treasurer's gloomy "defeatist" warnings, pointing out that Duchairn had managed to overcome every one of the other disasters he'd predicted. Besides, the Grand Inquisitor was perfectly prepared to rely on the Inquisition's ability to impose an economy based upon barter—or even purely upon Church requisitions—if worse came to worst. Personally, Maigwair more than suspected Clyntahn was overestimating the extent to which even the Inquisition could compel men and women faced with feeding their children and providing for their families to cooperate in such a draconian scheme.

*And meanwhile, the damned* heretics *are rolling in gold*, he thought resentfully. The Inquisition's first reports on the massive gold and silver strike in the Mohryah Mountains of Silverlode Island had started coming in last month. Clyntahn was doing his best to downplay *those*, too, the Captain General reflected bitterly.

Maigwair suspected there were two reasons for that. First, Clyntahn had his blinders on where the simple economic consequences of the newly opened mines were concerned. He didn't want to admit to himself that even as Mother Church's economy tottered towards collapse, the heretics—no, the *Charisians*—were not only finding expanding market opportunities in Siddarmark and throughout their own empire, but now they were literally shoveling gold out of the ground. The implications of that if the war lasted another year or so—especially without Mother Church finding some way to reverse her fortunes on the field of battle—were nothing the Grand Inquisitor wanted to contemplate, so he simply refused to do so.

But secondly, and even more to the point, Clyntahn was determined to avoid any question of divine favor. Mother Church's children would have been more than human not to question the implications of the new, massive infusion of gold into the *heretics*' economy at the very moment when they themselves confronted largely stagnant wages, ever higher tithes, and the ever mounting costs of food, fuel, and clothing. No doubt the Inquisition would eventually proclaim that the newly opened gold mines were *Shan-wei*'s work, not

God's. Clyntahn would insist it was an indication of her desperation that she'd been forced to shore up her servants by providing them with so much additional gold, whereas God knew His faithful children required no such intervention to accomplish His will. Maigwair expected many of the faithful would find that persuasive, at least initially. But sooner or later, inevitably, someone was bound to point out—very quietly, as far from the Inquisition's ears as possible—that if God was truly on Mother Church's side, He could at least have *prevented* Shan-wei from bestowing such largess upon her servants.

From there to the conclusion that perhaps God wasn't supporting the Jihad because he wasn't on the *Group of Four's* side would be only a very small step. And Zhaspahr Clyntahn still wouldn't—

He shook his head angrily, then made himself inhale deeply as the stairs topped out on the observation tower's platform. He followed Brother Lynkyn to the sturdy rail and stood gazing out across the foothills which rolled away to the west.

The Army of God sergeant who'd been waiting for them went to one knee, kissing the ring Maigwair extended to him, then stood once more, looking expectantly at Fultyn.

"I think we can begin now, Sergeant," the lay brother told him.

"Yes, Brother!" the sergeant replied, and reached for the staff of the large red flag leaning against the tower's railing. He raised it over his head and swept it around in a tight circle.

"There, Your Grace," Fultyn said, pointing out across the nearest hillside, and Maigwair's eyes narrowed as he saw what looked like three large, articulated dragon-drawn wagons. They were little more than four hundred yards away, but they were covered in canvas tarpaulins, which would have made it impossible to see into the wagon beds even with the powerful telescope mounted on the observation tower's rail.

They moved steadily, however, and judging by their speed, they were only lightly loaded.

"We're cheating a little bit here, Your Grace," Fultyn acknowledged as the dragon drovers maneuvered their vehicles. They were lining up in a straight row, with their left wheels—the ones away from the observation tower—on a broad white line that looked like powdered lime. "In the field, they probably wouldn't have the advantage of a precisely surveyed firing line or exact range measurements. In this instance, though, I thought we might as well use every unfair advantage we could to impress you with how splendidly our new weapon works."

The lay brother smiled almost slyly at the vicar, and Maigwair smiled back.

"I promise to be just as trusting and credulous as you could possibly desire, Lynkyn," he said. "As long as it really works, of course."

"Oh, I think you'll agree it *works*, Your Grace," Fultyn said, and pointed at the drovers as they unhooked the dragons from the traces. "In the field, we might not have time to unhook the draft animals," he said in a somewhat more somber tone. "We'll either have to do that or else put them down before we fire, though, I'm afraid. Any dragon still harnessed to one of those wagons is guaranteed to panic the instant the rockets begin firing, and the firing sequence takes long enough that a panicked dragon could easily disturb the aim of the entire volley."

"Really?" Maigwair looked down at the somewhat shorter Fultyn. "I know we had that reaction out of all of the dragons—and the horses, for that matter—when we first introduced field artillery. You're saying we can't train dragons to stand steady with these rockets the way we already have with the field guns?"

"I don't think there's much chance of that at all, Your Grace," the Chihirite said. "For that matter, it would probably be a bad idea to even make the attempt in this case. I believe you'll understand why in a moment."

The dragons and their drovers were over a hundred yards clear of the parked wagons and continued moving steadily away as three-man teams of AOG artillerists swarmed over the vehicles, stripping off the tarpaulins, and Maigwair bent to the telescope, peering through it at what the canvas had covered.

Each wagon consisted of two six-wheeled sections, each of them twenty-five feet long and eight feet wide, but rather than the standard four-foot-tall sides, the wagon boxes were little more than eighteen inches high. Instead of the heavy wooden strakes which would normally have sided them, they'd been fitted with an iron frame that formed cells five or six inches across. Each cellular structure was perhaps five feet tall, with framing members something less than an inch in cross-section, and they were supported on the right side—the near side, from where Maigwair stood—by uprights that could be adjusted to raise or lower that side of it. The far side was hinged or pivoted in some way, so that when the near side was raised, the entire frame changed angle.

Each of the six wagon sections carried twelve rows of cells, thirty-seven cells long, for four hundred and forty-four per section, or a total of just over twenty-six hundred between them. And every one of those cells contained a white-painted object five inches in diameter and six feet in length with a sleek, rounded nose.

"To be honest, Your Grace, we're using up quite a lot of rockets in this demonstration," Fultyn said as the vicar straightened and looked up from the telescope. "I wanted to be sure you got to see the full effectiveness. The first few test shots actually seemed a bit disappointing, compared to what I'd anticipated. When they're used properly, however, in sufficient numbers, well . . . ."

He shrugged, and Maigwair nodded. He also made a resolution to avoid being overly easily impressed. He wanted—needed—for this weapon to perform as effectively as possible, and he trusted Lynkyn Fultyn completely. At the same time, the Chihirite would have to be one of the true *seijins* of old if he hadn't wanted to stack the deck as spectacularly as possible for this demonstration.

The tarpaulins had been removed completely and the soldiers moved smartly away from the wagons, aside from a single noncom who stood waiting with a lit torch in his hand.

"The wagon beds are sheathed in iron, as well, Your Grace," Fultyn said, "and there's about ten inches of water in each of them as protection against the backblast."

Maigwair's eyebrows rose, but he only nodded for Fultyn to continue.

"If you'll look to your right, beyond the wagons, I think you can see the target area fairly clearly with the spyglass," Fultyn said, pointing to the northeast, and Maigwair swiveled the rail-mounted glass to peer in the indicated direction.

The target area—an open field a thousand yards from the launchers—was a rectangle, five hundred yards on a side. A half-dozen additional articulated freight wagons had been parked at its center, surrounded by the square, post-mounted targets used to train the Army of God's riflemen.

"I see it," the Captain General confirmed. He left the telescope trained on the target but straightened, returning his attention to the readied rocket wagons, and Fultyn nodded in satisfaction.

"All right, Sergeant," he said.

"Yes, Sir!"

The sergeant swept his flag in another circle, and the other noncom, standing near the parked wagons, touched the torch to the waiting fuse. Then he dropped it, spun on his heel, and sprinted after the other rapidly departing members of his detachment and the dragons and drovers, who were now close to five hundred yards away.

The fuse burned steadily, branching away from the initial ignition point so that a small, sputtering line of smoke moved towards each of the wagon sections.

"We've come up with a better system for firing them in the field, Your Grace," Fultyn said, gazing through the calm afternoon sunlight at the silent wagons. "Actually, we've come up with two. One uses a friction primer, while the other uses primer caps. Both systems use fuse hose, which protects against inclement weather and also speeds up—"

He was still speaking when those burning fuses reached their destinations. They hadn't been cut perfectly, which meant the rockets failed to fire in perfect synchronization, but it didn't matter.

Despite himself, Allayn Maigwair stumbled back three full paces as the massive wagons seemed to explode. Only that wasn't actually what they did. It wasn't an explosion, it was an *eruption*, and his eyes went wide as two-thousand-plus rockets screamed out of their launch cells at the rate of three per wagon section every half second. The entire massive volley launched in the space of less than nineteen seconds.

Those nineteen seconds were the *longest* nineteen seconds Allayn Maigwair had ever experienced. The rockets shrieked into the air with a terrible keening scream, like a thousand demons breaking the chains of hell. They rose in an incredible pillar of smoke—and no doubt steam—on tails of flame that sent more smoke sheeting across the sky in a smothering canopy. A small corner of his mind realized that any dragons who'd still been tethered to those wagons would have been killed almost instantly, but it was a distant reflection as he stared at those terrifying rockets. They arced upwards, spreading out slightly as they went, howling through the heavens, climbing higher and higher. Then they reached the top of their arcs, plummeted back towards earth, and landed in a terrible, re-echoing roll of thunder even worse than the fiendish clamor of their passage.

The entire target area simply vanished, disappeared in a maelstrom of explosions, while a hurricane of smoke and pulverized dirt rose like a canopy from a vortex of utter destruction. The dreadful, terrifying sound seemed to continue forever, for the rockets took just as long to land and explode as they had to ignite and launch. The dreadful cacophony lasted almost forty seconds—forty seconds of the pure, unadulterated rage of Shan-wei herself—and then, suddenly, it was over. The final explosions echoed back from the hillsides beyond the target zone, until, finally, silence crept back, hovering in the choking clouds of smoke as if afraid of itself, and Lynkyn Fultyn spoke.

"Maximum range is over four thousand yards, Your Grace," he said softly while the breeze began thinning the incredible smoke canopy. "Minimum range is approximately eight hundred." There was something about the Chihirite's tone. Something Maigwair's still numbed brain wasn't quite able to parse. "And as you can see, Your Grace," Fultyn continued, pointing at the telescope, "it's . . . quite effective."

Maigwair bent back to the telescope's eyepiece. He was surprised to discover a tremble in the fingers adjusting the focus knob, but he had plenty of time to correct it before the smoke dissipated enough for him to see through it. Finally, it did, rising and lifting like a fog bank, and the vicar inhaled sharply.

There was nothing left in the target area. Just . . . nothing at all. It was one huge, overlapping sea of craters, without a single one of the scores of targets which had filled it. He saw a single intact axle from one of the freight wagons; but for that, there were only splinters, overlapping craters, and the still-drifting clouds of smoke. And as he stared at that barren spectacle of devastation, Allayn Maigwair realized exactly what he'd heard in Lynkyn Fultyn's voice.

▼ ▼ ▼

"Well, *that* was certainly impressive," Sharleyan Ahrmahk said dryly from her Tellesberg bedchamber.

"I'd go a lot further than just 'impressive,' Your Majesty." Aivah Pahrsahn's voice over the com was much more somber than Sharleyan's. "'Terrifying' comes to mind, really."

"And with good reason," Nimue Chwaeriau put in from Manchyr. She stood on a Manchyr Palace balcony where Irys, who'd discovered the joys of morning sickness, was sharing a late breakfast—of dry toast and tea in Irys' case—with the Earl of Coris. "That's the most concentrated destruction anyone's ever seen out of a purely Safeholdian weapon system."

"Can they produce enough of them to use in that sort of quantity on the battlefield?" Coris asked.

"Yes and no," Ehdwyrd Howsmyn replied. "Yes, they can manufacture them in large enough numbers to use on the battlefield. No, they can't manufacture them in large enough numbers to use them with that . . . density of effort on a regular basis. For set piece battles, where they can make preparations and manage their logistics well in advance, yes. As a routine 'on call' artillery application, probably not."

"And if they put them into production and stockpile them over the winter?" Cayleb Ahrmahk asked from Siddar City.

"In that case, yes," Howsmyn acknowledged. "At least for next year's opening battles. On the other hand, without the machine tools we've been able to build and power—both hydraulically and pneumatically—their production rate's going to be *slow* compared to ours, Cayleb. They still aren't going to be able to produce millions of these things. Thousands, yes. Even tens of thousands. But not in the sorts of quantities the Russians used back on Old Earth."

"Someone's been studying his military history," Merlin Athrawes observed with a chuckle. "Someone who didn't know what the Mississippi was the first time I mentioned converted ironclads to him."

"Self-defense, Merlin," Howsmyn retorted. "You—and Nahrmahn, now, damn him—keep dropping these obscure references on us. I've had to do a little studying, in my copious free time, to protect myself. I'm just grateful Nimue doesn't abuse us poor, backward Safeholdians the way you two do!"

"I'm a much nicer person than he is," Nimue said

primly. "Besides, I don't want to confuse you with too many distractions at once."

"I *think* that's an insult," Howsmyn said.

"No, just an explanation," Merlin said before Nimue could respond. Then his voice turned more serious. "Actually, I think your estimate's probably pretty close to accurate, Ehdwyrd. I'm not going to count on that, given Brother Lynkyn's record for bettering even his own projections, but I think you're definitely in the ballpark. The problem as I see it is that those smaller, hundred-and-fifty-cell launchers he's working with are actually more dangerous than the ones he just demonstrated to Maigwair. They need a shorter logistics tail, they're faster and more maneuverable, they can operate in terrain where those monster freight wagons can't, and they'll be a lot harder for anyone without SNARC reconnaissance to spot when they move up."

"And they'll use up rockets at a lower rate, which means production may be able to stay in front of usage," Cayleb acknowledged gloomily.

"What are the chances of his succeeding with that bigger coast defense variant he and Maigwair discussed?" High Admiral Rock Point asked.

"Those could be nasty," Merlin replied. "They're not going to have the kind of armor penetration a ten-inch shell does, of course. On the other hand, they'll be plunging fire whenever they hit a target, and even the *King Haarahlds'* deck armor is a *lot* thinner than their side armor. And if he really does start producing ten- or fifteen-inch rockets, even with gunpowder warheads they'll be a handful. That's not going to happen tomorrow, or even next five-day, though. His emphasis is going to have to be on battlefield applications, at least until he knows about the *King Haarahlds*."

"He'll have production problems when he tries to scale up that far, too," Howsmyn put in.

"Well, what about our answer to them?" Earl Pine Hollow asked.

"Sahndrah?" Howsmyn invited.

"Our rockets will outperform their rockets by a

substantial margin," Doctor Sahndrah Lywys responded. "We're finally getting the smokeless propellants into volume production, although the 'volume' part of that description is still smaller than I'd really like, and we'll have a lot more power and a much more consistent burn time, as well. That should translate into both more range and better accuracy than anything they can build. And unlike artillery shells, rockets are perfect vehicles to deliver *dynamite*—" she used the term deliberately, and several members of her audience smiled "—warheads, so even with black powder propellant, each of our rockets will be much more destructive than one of theirs."

"And we can manufacture them much more quickly," Howsmyn agreed. "And, as Sahndrah says, we ought to be able to get better range performance out of them, as well. But everybody needs to understand that this is going to be a situation in which we have an advantage in *degree*, not in *kind*."

"Ehdwyrd's right about that," Baron Green Valley interjected from his headquarters at Lakeside. "And that means it's going to improve their capabilities more than it's going to improve ours. Their starting point was so far behind ours that it's a much greater incremental increase in their combat power than fielding an improved version of rocket artillery's going to be for us." He grimaced. "I've been doing a little research of my own, and if they manage to recruit up and train all of the reinforcements Maigwair and Duchairn are planning on, then equip them with these damned rockets, someone as smart as Rainbow Waters is likely to hit on the notion of duplicating the Red Army's World War Two tactics."

"Another research student, I see," Nimue said.

"I've been tutoring him," Nahrmahn Baytz told her from Nimue's Cave. "Owl and I have had a lot more of that 'copious free time' of Ehdwyrd's than you flesh-and-blood—well, the *other* flesh-and-blood—types do."

"It wouldn't happen to be that you've been 'tutoring' Ehdwyrd, as well, would it?" Merlin asked suspiciously.

"Nonsense." Nahrmahn's image grinned at the rest of them. "All I did was answer a few questions for him."

"And, I might add, answer them with insufferable smugness," Howsmyn said.

Several people chuckled this time, including Merlin. But then he shook his head, his expression more serious.

"I hate to say it, but it sounds to me as if we don't have much choice but to put our own version of Brother Lynkyn's Katyushas into production as a counter."

"With all of our other production requirements, we're not going to be able to exceed their production *volume* despite our greater production *rate*," Howsmyn warned them. "We may not even be able to *match* their production volume, now that they're getting all of those open-hearth steel plants up and running."

"They've got production constraints of their own," Cayleb pointed out. "And everything we've seen indicates their finances are in even poorer shape than we'd thought."

"Cayleb's right," Green Valley said. "And since Sahndrah'll have the new propellants into something approaching volume production by spring, Ruhsyl and I should have the capability to deal with Brother Lynkyn's little surprise."

"The keywords there are 'something *approaching* volume production,' Kynt."

"Agreed. But they will be becoming available, along with more of the breech-loading artillery. That's going to restore a lot of the artillery advantage those damned Fultyn Rifles have pared away, and our artillery tactics are already a lot more flexible than theirs are. So if Nahrmahn's little brainstorm about fire control works out anywhere near as well as he keeps assuring us it will, we ought to be able to cope with anything the Temple Boys come up with over the winter."

"You're probably right," Cayleb said after a moment. "I hope to God you are, at any rate. I'd still prefer to be able to bloody Rainbow Waters' nose before snowfall, though."

"Not going to happen, I'm afraid," Green Valley said regretfully. "He's too smart to come out where we can get at him, and our logistics have taken too big a hit with the concentration camp inmates and the Temple Boys' scorched-earth policies where the transportation system's involved."

"I know that, and liberating those camps was the right trade-off to make," Cayleb acknowledged. "That doesn't mean I don't regret the lost opportunity."

"That's the way wars are," Merlin observed sadly. "You never have the resources to do everything you'd like to do, and then the fellow on the other side comes along and screws up the plans you've already made for what you think you *can* do."

"Like the Kaudzhu Narrows, you mean?" Rock Point's voice was bitter, and Merlin shrugged.

"Exactly like the Kaudzhu Narrows, Domynyk. Or like Rainbow Waters' refusal to come out and play with Kynt and Duke Eastshare. Or like the frigging Sword of Schueler, for that matter."

"And with all due respect, Domynyk," Baron Sarmouth said, entering the conversation for the first time as he stood with his flag lieutenant on *Destiny*'s sternwalk, "we intend to do our modest bit to . . . compensate for the Kaudzhu Narrows very shortly now."

# SEPTEMBER
# YEAR OF GOD 897

·◆·

# . I .
# Trosan Channel, Gorath Bay

"Anything to report, Zhorj?" Lieutenant Cahnyr Ahlkofahrdoh asked.

"No, Sir." Lieutenant Zhorj Symmyns saluted HMS *Tide*'s first lieutenant as he came on deck to relieve him. "That fishing boat the lookout reported headed off to the northwest just before sunset, but that's about all."

"Can't blame her for that." The first lieutenant snorted. "Probably out of Erech, not Dohlar, so I don't suppose there's any reason he should trust our intentions. For that matter, if I were a fisherman, I'd stay well clear of *any* warship, if I could!"

"Me, too," Symmyns agreed. "Aside from that, though, we haven't had any excitement all afternoon. And so far, it's been a pleasant evening, too."

"For some, at least," Ahlkofahrdoh said. He regretted the comment the instant he made it, but he couldn't un-say it, and Symmyns grimaced in agreement.

Very few of *Tide*'s company were pleased with their present duty. That wasn't to say any of them would have considered protesting their orders, but there was a difference between that and eagerly obeying them. Even Captain Ohkamohto, who was firmly of the opinion that any heretic deserved whatever he got, had been less than delighted when Earl Thirsk selected him as the senior officer in command of the small, heavily escorted convoy.

Ahlkofahrdoh walked to the taffrail and stood beside the post supporting the center stern lantern's three-foot-tall, glassed-in housing. The lantern itself was a good three feet above his head, and he shaded his eyes against its illumination as he looked astern through the darkness from *Tide*'s high poop deck at *Prodigal Lass*, the merchant galleon the Royal Dohlaran Navy had taken into service temporarily as a transport. She was easy enough to find, picked out of the night not just by her masthead lights but also by the lamplight spilling from the scuttles and skylight of her large, midships deckhouse. The glow reached upward, gilding her lower masts and rigging with a faint patina of gold, and he grunted in satisfaction. Commander Rubyn Mychysyn, in command of her naval crew—including the gunners for the dozen wolves which had been hastily mounted along her rails—was an excellent ship handler. The merchant ship wasn't the handiest vessel Ahlkofahrdoh had ever seen, but Mychysyn, as always, was maintaining meticulous station astern of the escort flagship.

HMS *Truculent*, the regular Navy transport carrying the rest of the Charisian prisoners, was a bit farther astern of *Prodigal Lass* than she ought to have been. Not badly so—she'd started closing up again as the daylight faded, and Ahlkofahrdoh could pick out her masthead lights without much difficulty, as well, although her deck lights were impossible to see from here—but Commander Urwyn Guhstahvsyn's seamanship had impressed him less favorably than Mychysyn's over the last seven days.

*You'll only have to worry about Guhstahvsyn's ship handling for another five-day or so*, he reminded himself. The convoy was just under two-thirds of the way from Gorath to the port of Esku on the Bay of Erech, where the heretics would be handed over to the Temple Guard detachment responsible for moving them the rest of the way to Zion. At that point, the Royal Dohlaran Navy would wash its hands of the prisoners and *Tide* would return to more normal duties.

*And don't pretend getting shut of Guhstahvsyn's the only thing you're looking forward to when that hap-*

*pens, either*, he thought grimly. *Or that you're going to feel clean again afterward, whatever you do. Heretics or no, they're sailors—just like you and all of your men—and they fought for what they believe in and for their emperor and empress exactly the same way you fight for Mother Church and your king.*

He reminded himself not to discuss that with Captain Ohkamohto and turned his attention to the rest of the escort.

Captain Fraidareck Chalkyr's *Challenger* had lost her fore and main royal masts in a sudden squall three days after leaving Gorath. Chalkyr had been mortified, yet it was scarcely his fault. Ahlkofahrdoh knew that because he'd been on deck when the squall came raging down on the convoy. *Challenger* had been well up to windward, and the savage gust front had hit her first, with no more than a minute or two's warning. Chalkyr had done well to avoid being completely dismasted, under the circumstances, and what had happened to *his* ship had warned her consorts of what was coming. Without that, they would undoubtedly have suffered severe damage of their own.

The sudden blast of fury that had cost *Challenger* her royals had also carried away her main topgallant and sprung her main and fore topmasts, however, seriously compromising her ability to carry sail. Given their orders to deliver the prisoners as quickly as possible, Ohkamohto had ordered him to return to port for repairs rather than slowing the rest of the convoy, which had reduced the escort squadron from five galleons to only four. Ahlkofahrdoh knew he hadn't liked doing that, but the Inquisition's orders had left little choice. Besides, four ought to be more than enough, given what had happened to the heretics' navy, and Ohkamohto had deployed them carefully.

Captain Zhorj Kurnau's *Saint Ahndru* led *Tide* by four or five ship lengths, all four of her stern lanterns burning brightly through the night. *Saint Ahndru* was a fifty-four, marginally more heavily gunned than *Tide*, but Captain Sir Lywys Audhaimyr's fifty-six-gunned

*Riptide* was the most powerful unit of the escort and Captain Ohkamohto had her positioned up to windward. She was close enough Ahlkofahrdoh could just see the lantern light gleaming from her scuttles and the half-dozen gunports which had been opened for ventilation, even from deck level, whenever waves lifted both of them simultaneously. She was well placed to come down on the wind if anything untoward happened, and Captain Bryxtyn's *Saint Kylmahn*, one of *Tide*'s sister ships, was somewhere astern of the transports, watching the small convoy's back. Ahlkofahrdoh couldn't see her lights at all, but Honshau Bryxtyn was one of the most reliable officers he'd ever met. In fact, even though every officer in the Royal Dohlaran Navy knew Earl Thirsk was bitterly opposed to their current mission, whether he'd been foolish enough to say so this time or not, he'd still picked five of his best galleon captains to carry it out.

*And we'll all be glad to get back to Gorath Bay . . . the sooner the better*, Ahlkofahrdoh thought.

▼ ▼ ▼

Baron Sarmouth took the cigar from his mouth, blew a smoke ring for the stiff breeze to shred, and nodded.

"I think it's about time, Rhobair," he said.

"Aye, aye, My Lord!" Rhobair Lathyk touched his chest sharply in salute and turned away. "Pass the word—*quietly*," he said. "Hands to sheets and tacks."

The captain's fierce anticipation echoed in the half whispered acknowledgments which came back to him, and Sarmouth replaced his cigar, folded his hands behind him, and positioned himself by the aftermost quarterdeck carronade, where he'd be as out of the way as possible.

He looked across *Destiny*'s starboard bulwark to where the fishing boat *Snapdragon* held station on his flagship. The small schooner-rigged vessel wasn't much to look at. At thirty-two feet, she was little more than three times the length of her namesake, and her previous owners had spent no more on her upkeep than they'd absolutely had to. Yet that unprepossessing craft was Lieutenant Hektor Aplyn-Ahrmahk's first independent command.

Sarmouth smiled at the thought. And again, as he considered the fishing boat's name. No living Safeholdian had any idea why the snapdragon—the warm-blooded, oviparous mammalian Safeholdian analogue to Old Earth's leatherback sea turtle—had received that particular name, but Sarmouth knew now, thanks to Owl's records.

Pei Shan-wei's sense of humor had occasionally gotten the better of her, and she'd bestowed the name partly because of the snapdragon's rather dragon-like head but mostly as a private joke because of its improbable looking, multi-hued leathery carapace. However whimsical the name, however, form followed function, and aside from its extra set of fins, the snapdragon's body form was quite similar to the leatherback's, although it was much larger. Fully mature body lengths of nine feet were common, and occasional examples closer to eleven feet had been recorded. Despite the humor in the name Shan-wei had given it, it was a formidable predator, even more dangerous than most species of krakens, and so perhaps the fishing boat's name had been aptly chosen after all.

His smile faded as he considered the real reason Hektor had been placed in command of her. They'd needed a scouting vessel which wouldn't arouse apprehension in any Dohlaran who happened to spot it, and *Snapdragon*—acquired from her previous Erechian owners two days ago in what might aptly be described as a hostile takeover—fitted that bill perfectly. She'd been able to get close to the convoy Sarmouth and Hektor had known was coming without sounding any alarms, which had provided the baron with a plausible, clearly non-demonic means of "discovering" the opportunity sailing towards his squadron. And Hektor's access to the SNARCs had allowed him to con his vessel into exactly the right position to "happen across" the prisoner convoy at exactly the right moment.

This time they hadn't even needed a *seijin!*

*Of course, they aren't exactly flying a huge banner that says "We're a prisoner convoy!"* he reflected.

Still, he'd allowed himself to leap to at least one intuitive conclusion. Hektor's report had made it clear that at least three galleons of the Royal Dohlaran Navy were escorting a pair of lightly armed transport galleons *somewhere.* (Actually, he'd known there were four, but HMS *Saint Kylmhan* had been too far astern for him to obtain a sighting on her.) Given the timing, it had seemed permissible for Sarmouth to conclude that the transports might—*might*—be carrying prisoners captured at the Kaudzhu Narrows to Zion. He'd made it quietly clear to Lathyk and to Sir Bruhstair Ahbaht even before setting out from Talisman Island that he'd hoped to encounter something like this, but he'd also cautioned both of them that the odds of a successful interception were no better than moderate. Now that *Snapdragon* had reported them, he'd seen to it that every man aboard every ship under his command knew that he hoped their targets were transporting those prisoners.

It would never have done to tell them he *knew* they were . . . or that he'd also known exactly where those transports had been at any given moment over the last seven and a half days.

His face hardened, with no trace of a smile, as he thought about what else the SNARCs had shown him.

Father Ahndyr Brauhylo, the Schuelerite under-priest assigned to *Truculent* to oversee the prisoners packed into her hold, was determined to see them delivered to their destination and consigned to the Punishment, but he was disinclined to be any more brutal about it than he had to. He even allowed them out on deck for exercise—only five at a time and chained together, but still on deck—on a daily basis. Father Tymythy Maikyn, aboard *Prodigal Lass,* was a very different sort, however. A personal favorite of Ahbsahlahn Kharmych, the Dohlaran intendant, he had a sadistic streak he was prepared to allow free rein. For the most part, he'd restricted himself to petty cruelties, close and perpetual confinement, occasional beatings, and psychological torment, but only because Kharmych had personally cautioned him to avoid fatalities on passage. The previous batch of heretics had lost too many to attrition en route from Gorath to Zion, and Zhaspahr Clyntahn wanted as many candidates for the Punishment as he could get. No doubt he was looking forward to a grand auto-da-fé, with hundreds of heretics to burn for their sins, as a way of convincing the Church's capital city the Jihad was well in hand, regardless of what those lying broadsheets tacked up on the walls of Zion might claim about disastrous reverses in the field.

Sarmouth suspected that if not for the restrictions Kharmych had imposed, Maikyn would have killed at least a third of them on the twenty-seven-hundred-mile voyage to the Bay of Erech.

*And if he thinks there's a chance of their being rescued, he'll do whatever the hell he can to make sure we rescue as* few *of them as possible*, the baron thought grimly.

*Destiny* changed heading, altering course to the southwest. Eighteen more galleons of the Imperial Charisian Navy followed in her wake, cleared for action with every gun loaded and run out and showing not a single gleam of light, aside from their shaded stern lanterns . . . and the tiny glow of the single cigar which was one of rank's privileges. Sir Dunkyn Yairley drew on that cigar, settled back on his heels, and waited.

▼ ▼ ▼

"Captain on deck!"

Lieutenant Trumyn Vyrnyn, third lieutenant in HMS *Saint Ahndru*, turned and came quickly to attention as Captain Kurnau appeared on deck. Kurnau was a calm, methodical man, the sort who didn't feel constrained to spend his time looking over his subordinates' shoulders. It wasn't unheard of for him to take a turn on deck before retiring for the night, but it wasn't exactly a habit of his, either.

"Captain," Vyrnyn greeted him, touching his chest in salute.

"Trumyn."

Kurnau nodded in recognition of the courtesy, then tilted his head back, gazing up at the dimly visible masts and spars. It was difficult to make out his expression in the uncertain light cast by the binnacle's lit compass card and leaking up through his cabin's skylight to illuminate his face from below, but he seemed . . . thoughtful, Vyrnyn thought. The lieutenant started to ask him if he had any instructions, but the captain hadn't invited conversation. If he did have any orders, he'd pass them when he was ready. In the meantime, Vyrnyn returned his own attention to his watch standers.

The captain walked to the weather side of the poop deck. He wasn't a very tall man, and he had to rise on the balls of his feet to look over the bulwark. He gazed out into the night for the better part of a minute, then squared his shoulders and walked back across to the wheel. He looked down at the glowing compass card, glanced around the deck one more time, and nodded to Vyrnyn.

"Keep them on their toes, Trumyn," he said.

"Of course, Sir." Vyrnyn tried hard to keep any surprise out of his response, but Kurnau snorted and smiled briefly.

"I don't know anything you don't know, Master Vyrnyn," he said, resting one hand on the younger man's shoulder for a moment. "I'm just . . . feeling an itch I can't scratch. It's probably nothing, but keep them on their toes."

"Yes, Sir."

Kurnau gave him another nod, squeezed his shoulder, and went back below.

▼ ▼ ▼

"Cap'n!"

Rhobair Lathyk turned quickly at the soft-voiced call. Bosun's Mate Ahntahn Selkyr grinned hugely and pointed southeast.

"Lookout's spied lights a quarter-point off the larboard bow, Sir," Selkyr said. "Masthead lights, looks like. Least two ships, but prob'ly more, he says. Makes the range 'bout eight thousand yards, but it's only a guess."

"Good man!" Lathyk nodded sharply.

Admiral Sarmouth had ordered that all commands and messages aboard the squadron's ships were to be passed as quietly as possible. Now the flag captain crossed swiftly to the admiral's side, the sand scattered on the deck for traction when *Destiny* had cleared for action crunching quietly under his shoes.

"Don't know how you knew, Sir, but you've hit this nail right on the head," he said admiringly. "Must be something that comes with that admiral's kraken on your cuff."

"Are you suggesting this was something I couldn't have done when I was a mere captain, Rhobair?"

"No, My Lord! Not in a million years. Although," Lathyk smiled at him, "I don't *recall* your ever doing anything quite like this back in those days."

"That's only because you weren't watching closely enough," Sarmouth said. Then he twitched his head to the southeast. "Now that you've been suitably dazzled by my superb seamanship and unfailing instinct, however, I think it's time we saw about those gentlemen."

"Aye, aye, Sir!"

▼ ▼ ▼

Sir Bruhstair Ahbaht turned to face Lywelyn Pymbyrtyn as HMS *Vindicator*'s captain materialized on her quarterdeck at his side.

"*Destiny*'s shown the signal lanterns, Sir Bruhstair," Pymbyrtyn said. "Two yellow above one blue." The captain shook his head. "Damned if the Admiral hasn't done it after all!"

"A remarkable man, Admiral Sarmouth," Ahbaht agreed. "We'll alter to starboard and get the topgallants on her, if you please. And be good enough to repeat *Destiny*'s signal to the rest of the detachment."

"At once, Sir!"

Pymbyrtyn saluted and turned back to his crew. Orders flowed in a low-voiced stream, the shaded signal lanterns rose to her mizzen yard, visible only from behind her, and canvas flapped overhead as the courses and topsails were trimmed. *Vindicator* leaned more heavily as her topgallants blossomed unseen in the darkness and she took the wind over her starboard quarter and gathered speed.

*A truly remarkable man*, Ahbaht reflected. *I never really thought he could do it. Maybe I didn't want to think he could because it would have hurt so badly when it turned out I'd been wrong to think he could.*

He strode to *Vindicator*'s taffrail, gazing aft as Tydwail Zhaksyn's *Broadsword*, Captain Dahnyld Mahkeen's *Cherry Bay*, and Captain Sebahstean Hylmyn's *Dynzayl Tryvythyn* followed on *Vindicator*'s heels, and thought about what else that remarkable man had done. Ahbaht had been astounded by Sarmouth's reaction to the Kaudzhu Narrows fiasco. He'd expected to be relieved pending a court of inquiry, at the very least; instead, Sarmouth had endorsed his decisions and retained him as his second-in-command. His present division consisted of only four galleons, but every one of those galleons was rated at at least sixty guns, making them four of the six most powerful units of the entire squadron.

There was no way in the world he deserved that command, not after what he'd let happen to his last squadron, but Sarmouth had given it to him anyway, and he was unspeakably grateful to have it. And to be entrusted with his current mission.

The shaded lights from *Destiny*'s stern—two yellow over a single blue—meant the flagship had sighted the enemy bearing almost due southeast. And those lights also meant it was Ahbaht's job to sweep south, then come in across the Dohlarans' base course, hopefully well astern of the convoy. Anyone who tried to run from Sarmouth's attack would break to the south, back into the Trosan Channel, and it was virtually certain that any transports actually carrying Charisian prisoners would be ordered to do just that, trying to escape back to Gorath Bay under cover of darkness while the escorting galleons covered them.

*It would've been simpler if we'd been able to catch them in daylight,* he thought. *Except for the minor problem that they'd've seen us coming at least two or three hours before we could get to grips with them. No telling what the Inquisition's butchers would do to our people with that much time.*

He didn't know how long he'd have to make his drive to the south. Baron Sarmouth would give him as much time as possible—the other thing the combination of lights told him was that the rest of the squadron was *reducing* sail to slow the rate of closure—but it wasn't likely to be as much time as he really needed. The night was clear, and he'd been told the human eye could see the light of a single candle at up to ten miles under the right conditions. Even so, lights could be hard to pick up at any sort of distance, and—

"Lights on the larboard bow!"

The announcement was relayed to the quarterdeck, and Ahbaht sprang up into the mizzen shrouds to gain more height and peered in the indicated direction. He found the lights quickly—masthead lights well above the sea and a row of illuminated gunports dipping in and out of sight as the two ships rose and fell relative to one another—and his jaw tightened. The other ship was no more than a mile downwind, which was perilously close. If there'd been even a trace of moon tonight, her lookouts *must* have seen his galleons' sails against it. But there was no moon, and he watched the lights unblinkingly.

If the commander of that convoy had been given any hint that the Imperial Charisian Navy was anywhere in his vicinity, not one of those lights would have been lit, Ahbaht thought. But he *didn't* know that. Indeed, he had every reason to believe there were no Charisian galleons east of Claw Island, and even if that hadn't been the case, the odds against Charisians stumbling into contact with him in the middle of the night were staggering. Ahbaht wasn't one bit surprised by his ships' illumination; given what he knew, it only made sense to light them up in order to help them maintain station on one another in the darkness.

The diminutive Emeraldian wondered if that convoy commander's superiors would share that opinion if he lived long enough to file an after-action report.

After a moment, he was certain: the other galleon was heading northwest, on an almost exactly reciprocal course. That was good . . . as long as she kept going, at any rate. Their relative motions would let him sweep in astern of her sooner. On the other hand, the convoy was headed almost directly towards Baron Sarmouth's main force, which also meant the Dohlarans would run into Sarmouth more quickly. And that would shave time *off* of how long Ahbaht had to get into position.

He climbed back down to deck level, where only the masthead light was visible, and his brain whirred as he computed relative ship speeds, probable positions for the transports he hadn't yet seen, and the strength of the wind. After a moment, he felt Pymbyrtyn standing at his shoulder and turned his head. *Vindicator*'s captain's expression was invisible in the darkness, but Ahbaht knew he was staring at that illuminated masthead with hard, hazel eyes. There was a reason Sarmouth had assigned *Vindicator* and *Broadsword* to their part of the mission. If Captain Kahrltyn's *Firestorm*'s damages had been less extensive, she would have formed part of Ahbaht's division as well instead of remaining anchored in Rahzhyr Bay to continue her repairs.

"How much longer do you think, Sir?" Pymbyrtyn's Tarotisian accent was more pronounced than ever, and something *hungry* lurked in the depths of his voice.

"Probably not long enough," Ahbaht replied softly. "I'll take every minute we can get."

"Understood, Sir. But—"

Pymbyrtyn broke off with a shake of his head, and Ahbaht nodded in understanding. *Vindicator*'s commander knew they needed all the time they could steal to get into position, yet he was as eager to be about it as Ahbaht himself.

"Another ten minutes, Lywelyn," he said, touching Pymbyrtyn's elbow lightly. "Another ten minutes. That's how long we need to come in cleanly behind that bastard. If they'll just give us that long, I'll be a happy man."

▼ ▼ ▼

"Ship on the larboard bow!"

The sudden, startled shout came down from *Tide*'s masthead. Cahnyr Ahlkofahrdoh spun towards the mainmast, eyes widening in astonishment. The lookout had to be imagining things! There couldn't possibly be a—

"*Galleon* on the larboard bow!" the lookout bawled. Then, a moment later, "Oh, Sweet Langhorne! *Many* galleons on the larboard bow!"

"Clear for action!" Ahlkofahrdoh shouted. "*Clear for action! Someone call the Captain!*"

For just an instant, nothing happened. Then the drums began to roll, ripping startled shouts from *Tide*'s crew, and bare feet pattered across planking as the ship's company rolled out of its hammocks and dashed for its action stations.

*This is impossible*, a voice like ice said in Ahlkofahrdoh's mind. *It's not* possible! *No one could sail straight to us in the middle of the frigging dark!*

Or at least no one could do it without supernatural aid, he thought, and felt the hairs on the back of his neck trying to stand on end.

▼ ▼ ▼

The shouts of alarm were faintly but clearly audible, and Sir Dunkyn Yairley grunted in mingled satisfaction and irritation. He and the rest of his column had covered almost four miles since sighting the convoy's lights. He'd hoped to get even closer—preferably clear across the Dohlarans' bows before he was spotted—yet he'd always known the odds were against that. Even though he knew precisely where his opponents were, his ability to communicate with his captains was too cumbersome, too limited, for him to achieve the exact placement he'd wanted. What he had would simply have to do . . . and, in fairness, it ought to be good enough.

"Well, they know we're here, Rhobair," he said calmly to his flag captain. "Let's shed a little light on the subject."

"Aye, aye, Sir!"

▼ ▼ ▼

Captain Frahnchesko Ohkamohto dashed out onto the main deck and raced up the short ladder to *Tide*'s raised poop deck. Bangs, thumps, the squeal of gun trucks, and volleys of orders filled the night as his men cleared for action. They were as well drilled a crew as any captain could have asked for, yet he heard—and felt—the edge of confusion as they raced to prepare for battle, and he couldn't blame them for it. This had to be a mistake—it *had* to be! There was no way the heretics could *really* be out there and—

Something hissed and shrieked its way into the night, rising in a pillar of flame from less than a mile away, and Ohkamohto swore viciously. He'd read the Army of Shiloh's after-battle reports, or as much of those reports as he'd been able to get his hands on, at any rate. That had to be one of the heretics' rockets, and if it was, when it burst, it was going to—

Then *another* rocket howled heavenward, this time from starboard, well to the east and downwind of *Tide*'s position. They soared upward, arcing toward one another, dazzling the eye, killing any night vision. And then they burst in rapid succession, and the pitiless, eye-tearing light of the heretics' flares blazed down from above.

▼ ▼ ▼

Sir Bruhstair Ahbaht's slitted eyes glowed in the parachute flares' brilliant illumination. The first rocket had come from *Destiny*; the second was from HMS *Intrepid*, one of the ICN's schooners. *Intrepid*'s skipper wasn't exactly where he was supposed to be—not surprisingly, given that the precise location of the Dohlaran convoy had been impossible to predict when his ship was sent off—but he was close enough. He'd seen *Destiny*'s rocket launch and fired his own promptly, hopefully after taking due precautions to avoid setting his ship's sails alight with its exhaust. Now it burst in splendor, stripping away the darkness and telling the Dohlarans there were enemies to the east of them, as well.

Of course, there weren't very *many* enemies to the east of them, but there was no way they could know that, was there?

"There!" he said, pointing as the flares showed him the single Dohlaran galleon whose lights *Vindicator* had already sighted. *Vindicator* had let the other ship sail past her, then Pymbyrtyn had worn ship to follow her, still upwind and on her larboard quarter while the other ships of Ahbaht's division continued to the south for another fifteen minutes. By now, they would have turned almost straight downwind, running for the transports whose masthead lights *Vindicator*'s lookouts had finally sighted almost twenty minutes ago. Ahbaht would have preferred to be with them, but *Vindicator* had a different task to see to.

Estimating the enemy ship's size accurately was all but impossible under the current conditions, but she had at least two armed decks, and if he'd been the Dohlaran commander, he'd have placed one of his more powerful units in that spot. She was a mile and a half to windward and perhaps that far northwest of the transports, perfectly positioned to run down to them with the wind in case of emergency.

Now *Vindicator* turned sharply to starboard in a smother of white foam and a boom of canvas, coming onto the wind and bringing her larboard broadside to bear on the Dohlaran ship from a range of just over six hundred yards.

"Engage the enemy, Captain Pymbyrtyn," Sir Bruhstair Ahbaht said coldly.

▼ ▼ ▼

Captain Sir Lywys Audhaimyr was sound asleep in his cabin when the first Charisian rocket screeched into the heavens, but HMS *Riptide*'s company was as well trained as any crew anywhere. By the time he reached his cabin door, the drums were beginning to roll; by the time he reached the deck, breeching tackle was being cast off, gunports were opening, and powder monkeys were already dashing for the magazines.

And by the time his eyes found the blazing Charisian flares, hanging like curses above the sea, HMS *Vindicator* was already turning across his stern at a range of six hundred yards, hidden in the darkness while his own ship stood out starkly against the flares and with every gun run out.

"Sail on the weather quarter! *Sail on—!*"

▼ ▼ ▼

"Fire as you bear!" Lywelyn Pymbyrtyn barked.

The range was long, even for Charisian gunners, but the Dohlaran galleons' illuminated stern windows were about as visible as a target could be and *Vindicator*'s gun crews had been waiting for this moment ever since the Kaudzhu Narrows. They took their time to do it right. Division officers and gun captains waited, making certain every gun was fully prepared, judging the ship's motion, then—

"*Fire!*"

The powerful galleon's broadside tore the night apart like an erupting volcano.

▼ ▼ ▼

Despite all of the gunners' skill and all of their meticulous preparations, "only" eleven of *Vindicator*'s thirty-pounder shells found their target. But those shells crashed into *Riptide* while the Dohlaran crewmen were still racing to their stations, still trying to cope with the paralyzing surprise. It wasn't a perfect raking broadside; the angle was too acute for that. But it was close enough, and they arrived like demons, howling out of the night to rip into the ship, and exploded with all the fury of Shan-wei herself.

Captain Audhaimyr's ears cringed under the roar of explosions, and hard on their heels he heard the screams of wounded and dying men.

*"Hard to starboard and clear for action!"* he shouted. "Come on, boys! Get those guns cleared away—*now!*"

*Riptide* began to swing to starboard, turning her vulnerable stern away from her foe, and he heard scattered shouts of acknowledgment from the gun crews. But even as he urged them on, he knew it was futile. The turn would take too long, and it took at least fifteen minutes to clear for action from a standing start. A well-trained crew might manage it in as little as ten, but only if they knew the evolution was coming. Surprised in the middle of the night, with absolutely no warning, they'd be lucky to do it in twenty, and *Riptide* didn't have twenty minutes.

Another savage broadside screamed across the water, trailing the red streaks of burning fuses, and HMS *Riptide* shuddered in agony as the exploding shells savaged her.

▼ ▼ ▼

"Captain! *Captain Vahrnay!*"

Horayshyo Vahrnay opened his remaining eye as someone shook his good shoulder. It took what seemed an eternity for him to rouse in the foul, stinking hell-hole of *Prodigal Lass*' hold. Then he coughed, cleared his throat, and spat.

"What?" he asked. "What is it, Zhaspahr?"

Zhaspahr Shewmakyr had been HMS *Vortex*'s third lieutenant. He was also the second-ranking prisoner after Vahrnay himself. Only nine officers—three of them midshipmen—had survived to reach Gorath Bay. Vahrnay knew more than that had been captured initially, but the others had died of their wounds after the battle, and Shewmakyr was the only one of the survivors who hadn't been severely wounded. Instead, he'd had the misfortune to be knocked out by a falling block when *Vortex*'s mizzen mast went over the side. He hadn't recovered consciousness until the second day after the battle. And even then—

"Gunfire, Sir!" Shewmakyr's urgent voice cut through Vahrnay's wandering thoughts like a water-powered bandsaw.

"*Gunfire?!*" Vahrnay thrust himself upright, his right hand—the only one he still had—sliding in the noisome filth produced by men left permanently chained to the deck. He almost fell, but Shewmakyr's grip on his shoulder prevented that.

Surely the lieutenant must be mistaken! There was nothing left under the Charisian flag to be firing at the Dohlarans. It must have been thunder. Trapped down here, with the hatches battened, it was impossible to see the sky or evaluate the weather, after all, and—

Horayshyo Vahrnay froze as he, too, heard the long, rolling cascade of explosions which could never be mistaken for anything else by anyone who'd ever heard it.

▼ ▼ ▼

"*Heads below!*" someone screamed, and Captain Audhaimyr looked up just as *Riptide*'s mizzen toppled like a weary forest giant. The entire mast tilted with slow majesty, and he swore again with hopeless venom. It must have been cut away below deck level by one of those Shan-wei-damned shells, and the rending, tearing sound as the main topgallant mast snapped and followed it was dreadfully clear even through the bedlam.

Three of his spar deck gun crews had gotten their guns cleared away, but they had no target. The Charisian galleon had forged steadily across *Riptide*'s stern, guns blazing, pounding away, then ranged up beside her to leeward. The situation had been hopeless, and he'd known it, even before his ship lost her mizzen. Now, as he ducked to avoid the decapitating power of the snapping mizzen shrouds he saw his assailant, no more than two hundred yards clear of his ship. She'd backed her topsails, reducing speed, providing a steadier gun platform, and her guns belched flame, smoke, and death with metronome precision.

More of the heretics' rockets roared into the heavens, pouring their pitiless light down across a scene of horrors. At least three Charisian galleons hammered fire into Captain Kurnau's *Saint Ahndru*. She'd already lost her foremast, mainmast, and bowsprit, and although it was impossible to be certain at this range, it didn't look as if even one of Kurnau's guns was in action.

Two more of the Charisians had run alongside *Tide*, pounding her savagely from both sides simultaneously. Even as he watched, both of them crashed aboard Captain Ohkamohto's ship and grappling hooks flew. He couldn't hear the high-pitched, howling Charisian warcry—not from here, not through the unending bellow of the guns—but he didn't have to hear it to know what was happening aboard the escort's flagship. And after what had happened in the Kaudzhu Narrows, and given where the convoy had been bound, there would be precious little mercy behind that shrill, terrifying howl this night.

He looked around desperately, but the falling masts had taken *Riptide*'s banner with it. He had no colors to strike, and he was none too sure the Charisians would have paid any attention if he'd had them.

"*Fire!*" someone screamed. "Oh, dear God, boys! *She's taken fire!*"

Audhaimyr wheeled towards the cry and his belly turned into a knot of ice as he saw the first flames belching from the forward hatch.

"Abandon ship!" he shouted. "Abandon ship!"

Other voices took up the order, and men began plunging over the galleon's tall sides. Some of them— petty officers and senior seamen, for the most part—kept their wits about them well enough to cast floats to the men in the water. Others struggled to lower the surviving boats. But most of them simply went over the bulwarks or scrambled frantically out of her gunports, fleeing the madness and the terror . . . and the flames.

And even as they fled, the Charisian guns continued their pitiless thunder.

▼ ▼ ▼

"My God," Father Ahndyr Brauhylo murmured, signing himself with Langhorne's scepter, as the night astern of HMS *Truculent* dissolved into flaming chaos and nightmare.

The under-priest had no idea—couldn't imagine—how it could have happened so suddenly, with so little warning. One moment, it seemed, everything was calm, normal. The next instant those hideous blazing lights poisoned the heavens and the merciless, rolling broadsides began. Commander Urwyn Guhstahvsyn had obeyed his standing orders and immediately brought his ship about and headed southeast, back for the Trosan Channel, but *Truculent* was a transport galleon. No one had ever intended her as a genuine warship, just as no one had wasted the expense of a coppered bottom on her. The chance that she might outrun a Charisian galleon was minimal, to say the least. Even Brauhylo knew that.

"What's . . . what's happening now?" he asked.

"All due respect, Father," Commander Urwyn Guhstahvsyn said flatly, "we're getting our arses kicked. *Tide*'s done for, *Saint Ahndru*'s a wreck, and *Riptide*'s on fire. Must be at least twenty or thirty of the bastards, and it's only a matter of time until—"

The night in *front* of them tore apart in the sudden, rapid eruption of broadsides.

▼ ▼ ▼

Captain Honshau Bryxtyn had clapped on every stitch of canvas he could when the northern horizon turned into a cauldron of fire and explosions. Unlike the other members of the escort, he'd actually had time to clear for action—and douse every light—yet he was under no illusions about what must have happened. He had no more idea than any other Dohlaran officer of *how* it could have happened, but the "what" of it was devastatingly clear.

He had no illusions about what would happen if he sailed his ship into the midst of that cauldron, either, yet he had no option. It was his duty, and it was at least possible HMS *Saint Kylmahn* would survive long enough to cover the flight of *Truculent* and *Prodigal Lass*.

*"Ship on the larboard bow!"*

Bryxtyn wheeled in the indicated direction and swore as the courses and topsails of a Charisian galleon loomed against the fire-sick night. The other ship was boring straight in, leaving him no option but to meet her.

"Three points to starboard!" he told his helmsmen, and *Saint Kylmahn* began to pivot away from the oncoming Charisian, opening her broadside firing arc.

"Off topgallants and royals!" he shouted, and men dashed aloft to reduce sail as *Saint Kylmahn* stripped down for combat.

▼ ▼ ▼

"And now it's *our* turn," Sebahstean Hylmyn murmured to himself.

He'd always been proud of his magnificent ship. Named for King Haarahld's flag captain at the Battle of Darcos Sound, HMS *Dynzayl Tryvythyn* mounted sixty-eight guns, including a pair of pivot-mounted eight-inch muzzle-loading rifles on her upper deck. Hylmyn knew *Dynzayl Tryvythyn* was outmoded, already left behind by the Imperial Charisian Navy's breakneck pace of innovation. Armor, steam, and breech-loading guns were the ICN of the future, and he knew that, too. But his ship's namesake had commanded the Royal Charisian Navy's flagship in the last galley battle in history. It was fitting that *Dynzayl Tryvythyn* should be here for this one, as well.

"Not until the range drops, Bryahn," he said to Bryahn Mastyrsyn, his first lieutenant. "No more than half-musket shot. I want this over as soon as it's begun."

His voice was flat, hard, and his eyes were cold.

"Aye, aye, Sir," Lieutenant Mastyrsyn replied, and his voice was just as hard.

▼ ▼ ▼

"Make more sail! *Make more sail!*" Father Tymythy Maikyn half shouted, brown eyes wild.

"Father, there's no more sail to make!" Rubyn Mychysyn shot back. He waved one arm at the *Prodigal Lass*' masts and yards. "This is a merchant galleon, not a warship! If you see any place I could set another sail, show it to me!"

He knew his voice was dangerously hard for anyone addressing any inquisitor, far less one who was a member of Ahbsahlahn Kharmych's personal staff, but he really didn't care. The chance that he might survive to face Father Ahbsahlahn's anger ranged from slim to none, in his considered opinion. Besides, he hadn't liked Father Tymythy from the instant the Schuelerite came on board.

Maikyn stared at him, face pale. Clearly the Charisian policy towards inquisitors was running through his mind, and Mychysyn was surprised by the vicious pleasure he felt at that thought. The murder of any priest was impious blasphemy, yet he'd discovered there were some priests he'd miss less than others.

Maikyn whirled away from him, staring back at the carnage astern of them. The firing had begun to fade, and Mychysyn glanced back, knowing what he was going to see. The outnumbered and outgunned escorts, taken by surprise out of a moonless night, had never stood a chance. One of them was heavily on fire and two more were motionless wrecks, with Charisian galleons hard alongside. The burning ship and the rockets, continuing to burst overhead at regular intervals, lit that vista of devastation with hideous clarity, despite the distance between them and Mychysyn's command.

He had no time to spare for what was happening behind them, however. Not with a pair of galleons locked in mortal combat looming up *ahead* of them. The Charisian combatant was clearly much larger and more heavily armed than *Saint Kylmahn*. Even if she hadn't been, her guns were better served, each of them getting off at least three shots for every two *Saint Kylmahn* fired in reply.

He had no doubt there were plenty of Charisian galleons—or schooners—bearing down on *Prodigal Lass* from the north. Any one of them could overwhelm his command in a heartbeat. She was armed with a grand and glorious total of twelve one-pounder wolves in swivel mounts along her rails, and those had never been meant to resist an enemy warship. They were there in case the prisoners chained in the transport's hold had managed to break loose somehow and storm the hatches.

" 'Nother of the bastards, Sir!"

Mychysyn turned towards the shout and saw yet another Charisian galleon bearing down on *Truculent* from the northwest. The other transport was perhaps a mile upwind and three-quarters of a mile astern of *Prodigal Lass*, and the galleon swept down upon her like a storm.

▼ ▼ ▼

"What are you going to do, Captain?" Father Ahndyr asked quietly, and Commander Guhstahvsyn turned to face him.

"That ship mounts at least fifty-six guns, Father," *Truculent*'s commanding officer replied, "all of them at least thirty-pounders. We mount eighteen, all of them twelve-pounders, and all we have for them are round shot. We can't fight them. Not and win."

"That's not what I asked you, my son," Father Ahndyr said. "I asked you what you were going to do."

"You can't dump all of this on me, Father," Guhstahvsyn said. "I'm this ship's captain. My decision is final. But you're Mother Church's Inquisitor. *You* speak for her, not me. And you know as well as I do what the heretics will do if you fall into their hands."

"Yes, I do," Brauhylo said, far more calmly than Guhstahvsyn could have spoken in his place. "I imagine I'll be rendering my account to God and the Archangels quite soon now," the Schuelerite continued. "Whatever else, Captain, I won't be in any position to report you or your men for . . . lack of zeal."

Guhstahvsyn looked at him, and the under-priest smiled sadly, almost gently. Then he traced the sign of Langhorne's scepter between them.

"Go with my blessing, whatever your decision, my son," he said. "But if I were an officer of the Dohlaran Navy and not an inquisitor sworn to obey the Grand Inquisitor in all things, I would ask myself if I truly wished to stain my hands with the blood of the helpless. And I would also look to my own men's lives."

He held Guhstahvsyn's eyes for another moment, then turned and headed down the companion towards his cabin. Guhstahvsyn watched him go, then drew a deep breath and turned to his first officer.

"Strike the colors and heave-to," he said.

▼ ▼ ▼

"You can't let these accursed heretics escape their just Punishment!" Father Tymythy shouted as the leading Charisian galleon bypassed *Truculent*, leaving Guhstahvsyn's command to her next astern, and bore down swiftly on *Prodigal Lass*.

"And just how do you suggest I prevent that, Father?" Rubyn Mychysyn demanded harshly.

"You've got wolves on the rails!" The Schuelerite waved one arm in a wild sweep indicating the swivel-mounted weapons. "Use them!"

"They'd be less than useless against *that*!" Mychysyn shot back, jabbing an index finger at the oncoming Charisian.

"Not against the galleon—against the heretics in the hold! Load them with canister!"

"You're insane," Mychysyn said flatly. "They're mounted on the *bulwarks*, Father. I could sweep the decks with them, but there's no way anyone could aim them down into the hold! And even if we could, I can't think of a single thing which would be more likely to get my men massacred—and rightly so!"

"What does that matter beside our duty to *God?!*"

"I imagine it would matter quite a bit to their wives and children, Father. Besides," he turned back to the Charisian galleon, already beginning to reduce sail as she came charging up to starboard, "there's no time for any of that lunacy."

"Then blow the ship up—*burn* it!" the inquisitor demanded.

"There's no time to burn it, and probably not enough powder in the magazine—such as it is—to blow it up. And with all due respect, Father," he didn't sound especially respectful, "I don't see any reason I should ask my lads to do anything of the sort. They're not inquisitors, are they? Killing accused heretics is *your* job, isn't it?"

Maikyn stared at him, cheek muscles quivering, then darted another look at the galleon, now less than two hundred yards away and closing quickly.

"You're right, Shan-wei take you!" he shouted suddenly, and reached into the pocket of his cassock.

Mychysyn had no idea where the priest had gotten the hand grenade. He'd never suspected Maikyn had anything of the sort, but now the Schuelerite snatched it out and dashed towards the main hatch. There was a lantern above the hatch, placed there so that the watch on deck could be sure the barred grating remained securely locked. Maikyn reached for that lantern, opening its hinged front to light the fuse of the grenade before he dropped it through the grating. The glass was hot enough to burn his fingers badly, but he scarcely even noticed. His lips drew back in a snarl of anticipation as he raised the hand grenade and—

He never heard the single pistol shot from behind him.

"Fuck you, Father," Rubyn Mychysyn said flatly as the pistol smoke eddied away on the stiff breeze. He gazed at the shattered ruin of Tymythy Maikyn's skull for a moment, then flipped the pistol over the rail and stepped closer to *Prodigal Lass*' stern lantern, standing with his hands where they could be clearly seen.

▼ ▼ ▼

Horayshyo Vahrnay stared uselessly through the thick, stinking blackness of his prison. Even if he'd had both eyes, he would have been able to see nothing. Like every other prisoner chained to that filthy deck, all he could do was listen, try to discern what was happening by ear alone.

There were no more broadsides, no more explosions, and surely that had to be a good sign. But he and his men had endured too much at Tymythy Maikyn's hands to feel optimism. Whatever else he might be, the Schuelerite was as savage a fanatic as the Inquisition had ever produced, and he was already under sentence of death if he fell into Charisian hands. If he was in a position to—

Something exploded overhead. The solid deck muffled the noise, but it sounded like a pistol or a rifle, and Vahrnay felt his belly muscles tightening as he tried to understand what had happened. In that moment, he felt even more helpless than he had when he and his men were first chained here. They were so close, rescue was so near, but if their captors decided—

Something slammed into the ship, driving alongside in a grinding thunder of planking that shook *Prodigal Lass* to her keel. The entire ship staggered, and then there was the thunder of feet overhead, rushing across the deck. Dozens of feet—*scores* of them!

And then there was a single voice, a *Charisian* voice that shouted only four words:

*"The Navy's here, lads!"*

By rights, Horayshyo Vahrnay thought later, they should have heard the cheers from *Prodigal Lass*' hold all the way home in Tellesberg.

. II .
HMS *Chihiro*, 50,
Gorath Bay,
Kingdom of Dohlar,
and
The Temple,
City of Zion,
The Temple Lands

"—and I have the honor to remain His Majesty's most humble and obedient servant, et cetera, et cetera," Lywys Gardynyr finished, tipped back in his chair while Mahrtyn Vahnwyk's pen skittered across the sheet of paper in front of him. It was late, and the two of them had been working since mid-afternoon. The lamps hanging from the deckhead cast a mellow light over his day cabin and a well-earned half-empty glass of whiskey sat at the earl's elbow. He waited until Vahnwyk had finished writing, then let his chair come upright and leaned forward over his desk with his forearms on the blotter.

"Read that back, please," he said, closing his eyes to concentrate as he listened.

"Of course, My Lord."

Vahnwyk found the first sheet of the lengthy report and cleared his throat.

"From Lywys Gardynyr, Earl of Thirsk, aboard His Majesty's Ship *Chihiro*, lying in Gorath Bay, this Ninth Day of September, Year of God Eight Hundred and

Ninety-Seven, to His Grace the Duke of Fern. Greetings. Pursuant to your request, I write to inform you of the conclusions my officers and I have drawn from our examination of the captured ironclad now lying in Gorath Bay. I fear that even the most cursory analysis must suggest that—"

Someone knocked sharply on the cabin door's frame.

Thirsk's eyes popped open in an instant scowl of irritation, but the irritation changed almost as quickly into something much closer to concern as he saw Commander Ahlvyn Khapahr standing in the open doorway and Khapahr's expression registered.

"I beg pardon for interrupting, My Lord."

"Somehow I doubt you would have interrupted unless it was important, Ahlvyn." Thirsk smiled faintly. "This is your poker night aboard *Courageous*, I believe."

His sally drew no answering smile from Khapahr, and the earl straightened in his chair.

"Very well, Ahlvyn. What brings you here?"

"The guard boat reports that a vessel has just entered harbor, My Lord," Khapahr said, meeting his eyes very levelly across the desk. "It's *Prodigal Lass*."

▼ ▼ ▼

"What sort of repercussions is this likely to have for young Mychysyn and the others, My Lord?"

It was morning. The early sunlight sent bright lines dancing across the overhead as it bounced off the harbor water and reflected through the stern windows, and more sunlight poured down through the cabin skylight. Earl Thirsk stood, leaning one shoulder against the bulkhead with his arms crossed as he faced Bishop Staiphan Maik. He'd been up most of the night, and his eyes were bloodshot and his voice was harsh with more than simple fatigue.

"I can't answer that yet, Lywys." Maik sat in one of the earl's armchairs, hair gleaming like true silver in the sunlight, but his normally lively brown eyes were grim and his expression was somber. "It's too early to say.

The first semaphore messages will only have reached Zion an hour or so ago. I'm sure the Grand Inquisitor is . . . considering them even as we speak, but you know as much as I do about how the Inquisition is likely to react."

Thirsk started to snap out a reply to that, his own expression angry. But he stopped himself. Partly from prudence, but mostly because Staiphan Maik wasn't the person who'd awakened that anger. So instead of venting his temper on the auxiliary bishop he straightened and made himself take a quick turn around the cabin. He stopped when he reached the stern windows, then stood staring out across the harbor's wind-ruffled water at the anchored *Prodigal Lass*.

The merchant galleon lay to her anchor like a plague ship, guarded by no less than three armed launches, all flying the golden scepter of the Church of God Awaiting and not the banner of the Royal Dohlaran Navy. Each of those launches had a swivel-mounted nine-pounder in its bows, and they rowed constantly, steadily, circling the anchored vessel like hungry krakens.

*At least they let us send the wounded ashore*, he reminded himself. *Surely that has to be at least a hopeful sign!*

He closed his eyes, resting his forehead lightly against the window glass, remembering the look on Rubyn Mychysyn's face as he'd presented his verbal report. Mychysyn was a year younger than Urwyn Guhstahvsyn, but he'd held his rank six months longer, which made him the senior unwounded officer from the entire convoy. Zhorj Kurnau would live, although he lost both legs at the knee. The healers were less confident about Sir Lywys Audhaimyr's survival, and Thirsk wondered if it might not be more merciful of them to grant him Pasquale's Grace rather than put him through the long, drawn-out suffering of recovery only to deliver him to the Inquisition.

*Stop that! You don't* know *the Inquisition's going to hold them responsible for what happened. After all, they* aren't *the ones who're responsible. If anyone is, it's* you, *Lywys. You should have sent a bigger escort. No doubt that butcher Clyntahn's going to think so, anyway!*

He made himself take a deep breath and accept that possibility. No reasonable person could fault him for his decision, but "reasonable person" and "Zhaspahr Clyntahn" were words that didn't belong in the same sentence with one another. It wasn't likely to matter to Clyntahn that there'd been not one single reported sighting of a Charisian galleon after the Battle of the Kaudzhu Narrows. *Not one.* Five galleons ought to have been a case of gross overkill for any of the handful of Charisian schooners which might still have been prowling about the Gulf of Dohlar! For that matter, the Inquisition had seen and approved his orders for the prison transport because *they'd* thought they were more than sufficient, as well. They'd been as wrong about that as he'd been, but how in Langhorne's name could even the *Charisian* Navy have found no less than fifteen galleons—that was Mychysyn's minimum estimate—and sent them *fifteen hundred* miles from Talisman Island so soon after the battle? And even if they'd had the ships, how could they have intercepted the prisoner convoy so perfectly, under cover of night when the escorts never even saw them coming? Lywys Gardynyr had been a seaman for his entire life, and he knew—*knew*—how impossible that was. Yet somehow the Charisians had done it, and there was going to be Shan-wei to pay for it.

He knew that, too.

At least Fraidareck Chalkyr was unlikely to be called before the Inquisition for his part in this fiasco. Thirsk would have felt much better if he'd been more confident of that. Unfortunately, he wouldn't put it past Clyntahn to decide Chalkyr's failure to anticipate the squall which had damaged his ship was somehow an act of disloyalty to Mother Church. As for the officers who'd actually lost their ships—or, far worse, surrendered Mother Church's prisoners to the "heretics" . . . .

*And I'm certain Sarmouth figured on that. He didn't have to return our people. In fact, it's been Charisian—*

*and now Siddarmarkian—policy* not *to return them, and he didn't even try to extract a parole from them. Is he really coldblooded enough to send them home because he knows* exactly *how Clyntahn's going to regard them . . . and how the Navy's likely to react when the Inquisition punishes them for something* no one *could have prevented? His message says he sent them home for "humanitarian reasons," but sometimes mercy can be deadlier than any sword, can't it? Especially when Charis' "mercy" gives Clyntahn a chance to display his own . . . or not.*

Behind his closed eyes, he saw once more the letter from the Charisian baron. The one he'd given Captain Kurnau to deliver directly to Thirsk. The one which had driven a searing wave of humiliation through Thirsk . . . because it had contained nothing but the truth.

*Their Majesty's Ship* Destiny,
*Malansath Bight off Dial Island,*
*September 1, 897.*

*To Lywys Gardynyr, Earl of Thirsk, greetings.*

*My Lord, I return to you the men and officers honorably surrendered to the vessels under my command after a most gallant defense.*

*They were unfortunate enough to be taken unaware in a night attack with no warning by a greatly superior force. Despite that surprise, they sought only to bring their ships into action as rapidly and effectively as possible. I commend to you especially the officers and men of* Saint Kylmahn, *who continued a courageous resistance even though Captain Bryxtyn must have been fully aware the day was irretrievably lost. I commend also Captain Audhaimyr and the men and officers of* Riptide, *who most gallantly attempted to bring their ship into action while actually under fire at very close range and abandoned their effort and their vessel only when she had taken fire and was heavily aflame.*

*Such gallantry, it seems to me, deserves better than*

to spend the next several years in a Charisian prison camp. The mission upon which they had been dispatched was as foul a blot upon the honor of the Kingdom of Dohlar as anyone might ever conceive, but they obeyed their orders with a courage and a devotion which must inspire respect from any adversary.

Since you and I are both fully aware that the human-shaped corruption calling itself Zhaspahr Clyntahn would never permit any paroled prisoner to honor the terms of his parole—indeed, that he would condemn anyone who offered parole to the Punishment—I have made no such request of your personnel. Perhaps we will meet them in battle again, but simple decency requires me to return them to you aboard Prodigal Lass. You will understand, I am certain, why neither Father Tymythy nor Father Ahndyr or any members of their staff are available to be returned.

It seems likely you and I will also meet in battle in the fullness of time, for there can be no peace between those who have given their souls and their swords to the Dark and those who serve the Light. I look forward to a just resolution under God of the many crimes which have been committed against the officers and men of the Charisian Navy and against every other Godfearing citizen of Safehold in the Group of Four's service. I do not think those who have chosen to serve Zhaspahr Clyntahn's foulness will enjoy that resolution.

Until that day, I remain—
    Sir Dunkyn Yairley,
    Baron Sarmouth,
    Commanding Officer,
    Their Majesties' Squadron in Dohlaran waters.

No fair-minded man could fault a single line in that letter. And no more deadly letter could have been written. He wanted to rail at Sarmouth for putting the contrast between the Imperial Charisian Navy's behavior and that of the Royal *Dohlaran* Navy into such stark and pitiless contrast, but he couldn't. Even knowing how every word of it must strike Zhaspahr Clyntahn like salt in an open wound, he couldn't.

He deserved it . . . and so did his Kingdom.

"It wasn't their fault, Staiphan," he said softly, never turning from the windows, his eyes fixed on the single ship the Charisian commander had released to return his prisoners to Gorath. "It wasn't their fault, not outnumbered by four-to-one and taken by surprise in the middle of the night. Chihiro Himself couldn't have done any better—or fought any *harder*—than they did!"

"You don't have to tell *me* that, Lywys," Maik said, equally quietly. "I know it already, and I've said as much in my own dispatches to the Bishop Executor, the Archbishop, and the Grand Inquisitor. The problem's going to be convincing *them* of that."

Thirsk wheeled back around to face him and saw the other truth Maik had left unsaid in the bishop's eyes.

*Well, it's only fair that I should face Clyntahn's rage right along with them, I suppose. I am the one who sent them to deliver his prisoners to him. And I'm also the one who argued against surrendering our first Charisian prisoners to him. I'm sure all the rest of the Navy's heard about that, and I don't suppose it's very surprising the bastard thinks I was the one who convinced the Royal Council to suggest we turn this lot of them over. Hell, if I'd had the guts for it, I should have been the one who suggested it! But either way, I'm sure my initial resistance to handing over his proper prey affected the rest of the fleet. That's going to be his conclusion, anyway. No doubt it contributed to the moral rot that led my galleon captains to strike their colors when no more than three-quarters of their people had already been killed!*

A shiver of cold terror went through him, not for himself—although the thought of facing Zhaspahr Clyntahn's enmity was enough to terrify any rational man—but for his daughters and his grandchildren. It shamed him to realize he felt more fear for them than for the survivors of the prisoner convoy, but he wasn't prepared to lie to himself about that. And the worst of it—the pure, unmitigated *hell* of it—was that despite everything, he was immensely relieved the Charisians had escaped. The fresh, savage defeat they'd handed his Navy was something else entirely, yet even there he felt a sense of something almost like . . . gratitude. That defeat had been so total—the toll in dead, wounded, and lost ships so high—that even Zhaspahr Clyntahn might recognize the odds against which his men had fought.

▼ ▼ ▼

"And I want every one of those surviving 'officers' here in Zion to be sifted, Wyllym!" Zhaspahr Clyntahn snapped. "*Every* one of them, you understand?"

"According to Bishop Staiphan's report—and the senior Pasqualate in Gorath concurs—moving some of them would probably kill them, Your Grace," Wyllym Rayno replied.

The Archbishop of Chiang-wu stood in his familiar position, hands tucked into the sleeves of his cassock as he faced Clyntahn across the Grand Inquisitor's massive, gleaming desk. The mystic, ever-changing murals of Clyntahn's office showed a snowy winter mountainside today, and as the Grand Inquisitor's fiery glare enveloped him, Rayno found himself wishing he actually was on a mountainside somewhere far, far away from Zion.

"And what makes you think I give a flying fuck if the 'gallant' bastards drop dead on the trip?" his superior snapped. "That son-of-a-bitch Sarmouth would've done us all a favor if he'd just cut their throats and dropped them overboard like he probably did to our Inquisitors!" Clyntahn's fury when he perused Sir Dunkyn Yairley's letter to Earl Thirsk had been truly monumental. "I don't give a good goddamn how many of them survive their little journey!"

"Your Grace, that decision is up to you. I merely offered it as a point of information. At the same time, perhaps I should also point out that, should they die en route to Zion, there will be no opportunity to question them and compare their accounts to one another in order to detect any discrepancies."

Clyntahn's nostrils flared, but he made himself sit back in his chair and consider Rayno's argument—if that was what it was—for several fuming seconds. Then he nodded.

"Point taken." The words might have been bitten out of a slab of granite, yet they were at least a little calmer and he inhaled sharply. "Consult with the healers. I want them here, but you're right; I want them here *alive*."

"Of course, Your Grace. How would you wish to have them transported?"

"Not aboard a frigging *Dohlaran* galleon, that's for damned sure! The useless piece of crap would probably sink halfway here. And if *that* didn't happen to it, no doubt more of the Shan-wei-damned heretic galleons the Dohlarans are too fucking stupid to know are out there would swoop down and capture *it*, too!"

Rayno nodded and forbore to mention that the Inquisition had been as firmly convinced as anyone in Dohlar that the five galleons Thirsk had assigned to escort the prisoners would be fully adequate to the task. Clyntahn himself had approved the transport plans . . . and that, too, was something it would be . . . impolitic to bring up.

"If not aboard a Dohlaran vessel, then how, Your Grace? We could move them overland, but it would almost certainly be faster—and easier on the wounded—to move them by sea."

"Allayn must have at least one or two galleons of his own left," Clyntahn growled.

"I can certainly look into that possibility, Your Grace," Rayno said.

In fact, virtually all of the Navy of God's surviving galleons had been transferred to the Royal Dohlaran Navy or Imperial Harchongese Navy once the Sword of Schueler had forced Maigwair to concentrate his full attention on raising, training, and equipping the *Army of God*. That was probably another of those small matters with which it would be wiser not to burden the Grand Inquisitor at the moment, however.

"And then there's that bastard Thirsk," Clyntahn growled. One meaty fist smacked down on his desktop. "Don't think for a moment I don't know who to thank for the defeatism that led those *gallant heroes* to surrender Mother Church's prisoners back to the heretics! And turn over consecrated priests of God for murder, as well!" The Grand Inquisitor's face darkened again. "I'll bet every frigging officer in the entire Royal Dohlaran Navy knows Thirsk never wanted those heretical sons-of-bitches handed over to us in the first place! No wonder they gave up so easily!"

A casualty rate of over seventy percent didn't exactly strike Wyllym Rayno as giving up "so easily," but that was yet another point it would be wiser to leave unmade. And in fairness to Clyntahn's ire, those casualties had been suffered by the escorting galleons, not the transport crews who'd actually handed the captured heretics back to their friends. Of course, exactly what else they'd been supposed to do when they found themselves outnumbered seven- or eight-to-one by heavy galleons was a bit of a puzzle. He knew what *Clyntahn* thought they should have done, but Rayno was realist enough to know it was far easier to exhort someone else to die in Mother Church's name from the comfort of a Temple office than it was to face that cold, grim reality one's self.

*And whether or not they acted reasonably is really beside the point, isn't it, Wyllym? The point is that examples must be made, especially when so many of God's faithful are beginning to . . . question the inevitability of Mother Church's victory. Which brings up another rather delicate consideration.*

"Your Grace, while I agree with you entirely about the no doubt unfortunate consequences stemming from the example of Earl Thirsk's intransigence on this question, there is one other point which must, perhaps, be considered."

Clyntahn glared at him. He recognized that calm, reasonable tone and knew he wasn't going to like whatever Rayno was about to say. He considered simply refusing to let the archbishop say it. Tempting as that was, however, he also knew Rayno was the only man in the entire Office of the Inquisition who was even remotely willing to risk his temper by telling him something Rayno believed he needed to hear whether he *wanted* to hear it or not.

"And that point would be what, precisely, Wyllym?" he asked acidly after a moment.

"The Kaudzhu Narrows, Your Grace." Rayno bent his head in a slight bow, then straightened. "I'm afraid many of the Faithful still see that battle as Mother Church's one clear, unambiguous victory out of this entire year," he reminded his superior in a careful tone. "To move precipitously against the admiral they believe produced that victory might cause questions and . . . uncertainty on their part. I fear that hasn't changed since the last time we discussed this matter."

"I am *so* sick and tired of hearing about how 'irreplaceable' that miserable, motherless Dohlaran bastard is."

Clyntahn's almost conversational tone was far more frightening to Wyllym Rayno than his customary choleric ranting. But the Grand Inquisitor inhaled sharply and shook himself.

"On the other hand, that's a valid point," he acknowledged. "And not just about Thirsk, for that matter, damn it. If we drag those other bastards in and give them to the Punishment for their failure, it's likely to raise some of those same questions, isn't it? After all, they're in the same frigging navy's *he's* in, so that makes all of them Shan-wei-damned *heroes*, too, doesn't it?"

"Possibly, Your Grace. Perhaps not as much as it would in Thirsk's case, but the possibility should probably be considered."

Clyntahn's jaw clenched, yet once again he made himself sit silently for several seconds, thinking about it.

"All right," he said then. "First, I want you to draft a message to Archbishop Trumahn, Bishop Executor Wylsynn, Father Ahbsahlahn, and Bishop Staiphan. Inform them that I've determined that it's more important Mother Church's justice be truly just in this case than that it be as swift as possible. Tell them I've further determined that, given the serious wounds suffered by so many of the convoy escort's officers and men, it would be wisest to wait until all of them are fit to travel before sending any of them to Zion. I'm authorizing Father Ahbsahlahn and Bishop Staiphan to take statements from all of the survivors and begin compiling a comprehensive report on this debacle immediately, and I have no intention of acting until I've received that report."

Despite decades of experience, Rayno felt his eyebrows rising, and Clyntahn grunted a harsh, humorless laugh.

"I'm not giving them a pass, Wyllym, whatever they may think when they hear about my instructions. They *will* answer for this—fully, right here in the Plaza of Martyrs—but you're right. Given how important the Kaudzhu Narrows battle's proving in the struggle to sustain the hearts and minds of Mother Church's children, it would be wiser to . . . delay the day of accounting, shall we say? It's clear enough Allayn and Rainbow Waters are determined to dig in where they are for the winter, so we're unlikely to see any stirring victories before spring. The Kaudzhu Narrows may be the only thing we have to keep the Faithful's hearts warm over the winter. There'll be time enough to settle with these useless excuses for naval officers after we've taken the field next spring and kicked the heretics' arses on land for a change. In fact, I want you to spend some of that winter quietly putting the pieces in place for Thirsk to accompany his loyal subordinates to Zion next summer. I've got a ledger entry or two to settle with *him*, too."

"Of course, Your Grace." Rayno bowed again. "I'm sure the Office of Inquisition can develop the evidence to justify moving against him at a . . . more propitious time."

"Yes, but I don't trust that slippery little prick," Clyntahn growled. "He's too damned good at surviving, and he and *General* Ahlverez—" the Grand Inquisitor's tone made the rank title an obscenity "—seem to be getting a little too friendly for my taste. I'm not convinced the pair of them haven't been looking over their shoulders at Desnair and thinking about how the Desnairians are running for the exit. I think Thirsk would love to do the same thing with Dohlar, and given how badly Ahlverez fucked up by the numbers in the South March, Thirsk might well be able to convince him to go along with the idea!"

"Perhaps he might, Your Grace. But he *is* just an earl, and one with enemies of his own on the Royal Council."

"We've just decided he's also such a successful admiral and so frigging important we can't simply order him to Zion," the Grand Inquisitor pointed out icily. "If that's true for us here in Zion, don't you think it might also have a little bearing on how much . . . influence he might wield in Dohlar?"

Personally, Rayno strongly doubted Earl Thirsk was likely to succeed in convincing even his own strongest supporters, like the Duke of Fern, to form some sort of cabal opposed to Mother Church's commands. As for the Duke of Thorast or *his* political allies, Thirsk would have a hard time convincing *them* water was wet! Still, the archbishop wasn't prepared to completely rule out the possibility Clyntahn seemed to be suggesting.

"Is there some measure you'd like me to take to discourage any disaffection on Earl Thirsk's part, Your Grace?"

"Yes, there is." Clyntahn smiled thinly. "I believe it's time we invited the Earl's daughters to make their pilgrimage to the Temple."

. III .
# Claw Island,
# Sea of Harchong

Guns thudded in salute, wreathing Claw Island's barren, sun-scorched hillsides in gunsmoke as the four galleons ghosted out of North Channel and into the waters of Hardship Bay. The protective berms of the onetime Dohlaran batteries, captured when Claw Island was retaken from the Royal Dohlaran Navy, were lined with wildly cheering Marines and Imperial Charisian Navy seamen, and seabirds and wyverns eddied about the heavens, crying out in protest of the hullabaloo rising from the island's human occupants.

Sir Lewk Cohlmyn, the Earl of Sharpfield, stood on the platform of one of the waterfront observation towers, gazing through his double-glass. He'd stood there for the past two hours as the tall, weather-stained pyramids of canvas resolved themselves into individual sails and the ships beneath them. Now they were close enough he could pick out individual men on their decks, see the rows of topmen spaced out along their yards. A slow, thundering salute to his own admiral's streamer rippled from the lead galleon, HMS *Vindicator*, and a fresh wave of cheers roared up from the crowds of men gathered along the harbor seawall to welcome her home.

Sharpfield lowered the double-glass and blinked hard. For some reason, it was difficult to see.

After a moment, he inhaled deeply and turned to the dark-haired, dark-eyed lieutenant at his elbow.

"I never would have expected even Baron Sarmouth to pull off something like this, Mahrak," he said. "Never in a thousand years."

"The Baron does seem to make something of a habit out of pulling people out of tight places, doesn't he, My Lord?" Lieutenant Tympyltyn smiled wryly. "Of course, this was a rather larger number of people, I suppose."

"Not large enough," Sharpfield said, then sighed heavily. "No, that's not right. It's an incredible accomplishment to get this many of our people back again. It's just that we've lost so many no one will ever be able to get back."

His flag lieutenant nodded somberly. Sir Bruhstair Ahbaht had sailed from Talisman Island with fifteen galleons, four schooners, and over eighty-four hundred men. Only three of those galleons and one of those schooners had survived, and according to the dispatch Sarmouth had sent ahead aboard HMS *Sojourn*, there were only four hundred and eighty-seven survivors aboard those incoming galleons. The other eight thousand men were dead, killed in battle or dead of wounds afterward . . . or of neglect and brutality, like the seventeen men who'd died in *Prodigal Lass'* filthy, reeking hold.

And that number didn't include the five hundred men who'd died with Kahrltyn Haigyl aboard HMS *Dreadnought*.

Sharpfield felt a familiar stab of pain as the thought of Haigyl and his magnificent ship ran through him, and he looked at the returning galleons once more. Sarmouth had remained on station at Talisman Island, but he'd sent all three of Ahbaht's surviving galleons—including *Firestorm*, now that her immediate repair needs had been met—to carry his surviving men home. The fourth galleon flew the Charisian standard above the green wyvern on the red field of Dohlar. Sarmouth had retained HMS *Truculent* when he dispatched *Prodigal Lass* back to Gorath with the survivors of Captain Ohkamohto's crews. He'd needed the extra passenger space, although he hadn't said why he'd kept *Truculent* instead of *Prodigal Lass*. His reasoning seemed evident reading between the lines of his tersely factual dispatch, however. The prisoners aboard *Truculent* had been treated with something as close to humanity as any Charisian was likely to find in the hands of the Church of God Awaiting's defenders. Those aboard *Prodigal Lass* had not.

Sarmouth had made a point of praising Commander Urwyn Guhstahvsyn and Commander Rubyn Mychysyn in his dispatch. More than that, he'd specifically mentioned the way in which Mychysyn had prevented Tymythy Maikyn from committing one last atrocity against the prisoners in his custody. Yet none of that could undo what Maikyn had done to those prisoners first. It wasn't all that surprising, Sharpfield thought, that Sarmouth had released the ship which had been a floating chamber of horror for the Charisians aboard it and retained the one aboard which they'd been decently treated.

He watched the galleons' canvas vanishing as sails were furled. They continued slowly forward under jibs and spankers alone, losing speed steadily. Then white water spouted under their bows as the waiting anchors were dropped, and he nodded.

"I believe it's time we headed down to dockside ourselves, Mahrak," he said.

▼ ▼ ▼

"You did good, Dunkyn," Cayleb Ahrmahk said quietly over the com as he watched the returning prisoners' tumultuous welcome. "You and Hektor both did. Thank you."

"Even with the SNARCs, we were lucky, Your Majesty," Sarmouth said frankly. He stood on *Destiny*'s sternwalk with Hektor Aplyn-Ahrmahk, savoring a cigar as they gazed out over the galleon's bubbling wake. "And we couldn't have managed it if everyone hadn't done his job exactly right."

"Yes, they did. And when something like that happens, it's never the result of blind chance," Sir Domynyk Staynair commented from his predawn flagship in Tellesberg Harbor. "It happens because the men and officers involved were *trained* to do their jobs 'exactly right,' and you know it."

"There's something to that," Cayleb agreed. "In fact, there's a lot to that."

"That letter of yours is likely to turn up the Inquisition's wick under Thirsk, too," Phylyp Ahzgood put in. "That was a nice touch, Sir Dunkyn."

"I agree," Nahrmahn Baytz said. "Rayno's probably smart enough to realize that's exactly what it was intended to do. Clyntahn's *certainly* smart enough, but he's too invested in hating anything to do with Charis—and in distrusting anyone on his own side with anything resembling a moral spine—to think about it. Your little note's going to go a long way towards undermining any confidence he still has in Thirsk, and that can't be a bad thing from our perspective."

"All that's probably true, but to be honest, I was less concerned with 'turning up the wick' for Thirsk out of any Machiavellian motivation—" Sarmouth smiled briefly as he used what had become one of the inner circle's more popular adjectives "—than I was simply pissed off. I think you and Cayleb are probably right about what's going on inside Thirsk's head, Merlin, but he had that letter coming. Especially because he *is* a man of honor with—what did you call it, Narhmahn?—something 'resembling a moral spine.' He damned well *knows* better than to believe this kind of crap could be anything *God* wanted!"

"I agree, Sir Dunkyn," Irys Aplyn-Ahrmahk said. "On the other hand, I wouldn't be too surprised if what you sent to him didn't help to . . . clarify some of those things going on inside his head."

"And if it does 'clarify' them, what does he do about it, Irys?" Hektor asked.

"I have no idea," his wife replied. "He's not exactly an inept sort, though, now is he?"

"No, he certainly isn't," Sharleyan said. She sat gazing out of her tower window at the harbor where Rock Point's flagship lay at anchor, anchor lights burning like tiny stars above the mirror-smooth water. "But even more to the point—and the one thing about your letter that truly concerns me, Dunkyn—*Clyntahn* knows he isn't just as well as we do."

"Exactly what I was thinking, Your Majesty," Aivah Pahrsahn said. Her expression was troubled as she sat brushing her long, lustrous hair before her bedchamber's mirror. Now she laid the brush down and sat back in her chair in a rustle of steel thistle silk kimono. "If Clyntahn thinks there's a chance Baron Sarmouth's letter's going to goad Thirsk into some sort of action, he'll take steps to preempt that action."

"Yes, he will," Maikel Staynair agreed. "And the most likely step, given how that man's diseased excuse for a brain works, would be to insist that Thirsk's family be formally taken into 'protective custody' by the Inquisition."

"And probably not in Gorath," Nimue Chwaeriau said from her own Manchyr bedchamber.

"No, not in Gorath," Merlin concurred, his voice as hard as his sapphire eyes as he sat across the fireplace from Cayleb in the emperor's sitting room. "He'll order them sent to Zion, where he can 'protect' them properly."

"I wonder if Thirsk's smart enough to realize that once they go to Zion he's personally doomed," Aivah said quietly. "The temptation to believe otherwise—to *make* himself believe otherwise, when there's so little he can do about it—must be enormous. But there's no way someone like Clyntahn's going to let him survive indefinitely after taking a step *guaranteed* to turn him into a mortal enemy. Eventually, he'll have Thirsk—and his family—permanently eliminated. He may settle for a simple, anonymous murder rather than the full Punishment, given the way Thirsk's become one of the jihad's few genuine heroes, but he *will* have them all killed."

"I'd hate to see that happen." Cayleb's expression was grim, almost haunted. "Eliminating him from the opposition's talent pool would be a huge gain, however it happened, but I'd hate to see it happen that way."

"We all would, love," Sharleyan told him gently.

"I wonder how he'd have them transported to Zion?" Nimue mused.

"That's an excellent question." Merlin leaned back in

his armchair, eyes thoughtful. "Somehow, given the suspicions he's probably nursing, I tend to doubt he'd be happy trusting an RDN galleon to deliver them. Send them overland?"

"If I were him, that's how I'd do it," Rock Point said after a moment. "Especially with you lurking in the Gulf, Dunkyn."

"He might not want to go overland after what 'Dialydd Mab' did to the Camp Tairek guards and inquisitors, either, though." Nimue's tone was as thoughtful as Merlin's eyes. "That's the biggest strike the 'seijins' have carried out yet, and none of Clyntahn's trackers or investigators have a clue how so many of them could have gotten in and out without being spotted. He might be afraid we'd manage to intercept Thirsk's family the same way. We already did it with you and Daivyn, Irys. And Thirsk's children and grandchildren are almost as important to the Church as you two were. Worse, unlike the camp's prisoners, they'd be a small enough group those wicked seijins might smuggle them out the same way the Demon Merlin got you two and Phylyp out of Delferahk."

"Are you suggesting you'd like him to worry about that sort of thing?" Aivah asked.

"I don't see where it could hurt anything," Nimue replied.

"In that case, Seijin Zhozuah could have a word with Ahrloh Mahkbyth. We may've gotten Father Byrtrym out, but Helm Cleaver still has at least a few contacts in the Inquisition. Mostly through people the agents inquisitor in question have recruited as sources rather than actual agents themselves. And in addition to that, we're quite good at starting 'whispering campaigns,' you know. I think we could come up with a few artfully designed rumors to encourage Clyntahn's paranoia in that respect."

"I don't see where that would be likely to have any downside," Cayleb said after a moment. "Are you going somewhere with this, though, Nimue?"

"Well, if Dunkyn is kind enough to cooperate with what I have in mind, it might just be that we can steer Clyntahn into transporting them *our* way instead of his."

## . IV .
## Shyan Island,
## Gulf of Dohlar

"Were you born stupid, Naiklos, or did you have to study?" Sergeant Major Allayn Mahgrudyr inquired in less than dulcet tones. Corporal Naiklos Hairyngtyn stopped and looked at him, and the sergeant major pointed. "Up *there*," he said. "You know—where the chief petty officer with the pretty little flag is waving it back and forth over his head trying to get your attention?!"

Hairyngtyn looked in the direction of the pointing finger, then nodded.

"Gotcha, Sar'Major!" he said cheerfully, nodded to his fatigue party, and went slogging through the loose sand towards the aforesaid chief petty officer. Sergeant Major Mahgrudyr watched him go, hands propped on hips, then shook his head and returned his attention to Major Brahdlai Cahstnyr.

"I swear, Hairyngtyn's head would make a damned good round shot. It might even be *useful* that way!"

"Now, now, Allayn," Cahstnyr said soothingly. "You know you don't mean that. And even if you did, Captain Lathyk wouldn't let you do it. It'd make an awful mess on deck when you disconnected it."

"I'd promise to clean it up afterward, Sir!" Mahgrudyr looked at his CO entreatingly, his tone wheedling. "Wouldn't take more than twenty, thirty minutes with a pump and a hose."

"No," Cahstnyr said firmly around a bubble of laughter. "Besides, he may not be much of a thinker, but he's a hard worker . . . once you get him pointed in the right direction. And he *is* Second Platoon's best shot."

"What do the Bédardists call that, Sir? 'Idiot savant,' isn't it?"

"I'm impressed, Sar'Major! And now that we have that mostly out of your system, what's our status?"

"Once Hairyngtyn gets his party in position and they start swinging those shovels and filling those sandbags instead of just carting them around, we'll be almost on schedule, Sir," Mahgrudyr said in a much more serious tone. "We'll have the first three emplacements finished by evening."

"Good. Master Wynkastair and Lieutenant Skynyr want to bring the guns ashore first thing tomorrow morning."

Mahgrudyr nodded, but his expression showed rather more concern than he was accustomed to displaying, and Cahstnyr cocked his head at him.

"Something on your mind, Sar'Major?"

"Well, Sir, it's just—" Mahgrudyr paused and shook his head. "Nothing, Sir."

Cahstnyr gazed at him for another second or two, then nodded.

"In that case, I'll leave you to it. Lieutenant Sygzbee will be bringing the rest of Second Platoon ashore with another load of bags as soon as I get back to the ship."

"Aye, aye, Sir!"

Mahgrudyr touched his chest in salute and Cahstnyr nodded to him before he turned and started slogging back down the beach to the launch waiting just beyond the surf line. He waded through the thigh-deep water, climbed over the side of the boat, and took his seat on the third thwart as the oarsmen bent to their oars.

The launch gathered way quickly, heading back towards where HMS *Destiny* lay to her anchor a thousand yards from the shore of Shyan Island, and the Marine captain's lips twitched in a sour smile as he watched the galleon grow larger. He knew exactly what was on Mahgrudyr's mind, and he didn't blame the sergeant major one bit.

Like most of the officers and men serving in Baron Sarmouth's squadron—and like *all* of them actually serving aboard *Destiny*—Cahstnyr had immense faith in the baron's judgment. He'd served as the commander of *Destiny*'s Marine detachment for the last two years, and Sir Dunkyn Yairley had never gotten his ship or her people into something he couldn't get them back out of again. And that didn't even consider his most recent feat. Sailing an entire squadron into exactly the right position to intercept that convoy of prisoners was an accomplishment worthy of Emperor Cayleb himself. Anyone who could pull that off had an almost unlimited line of credit where Brahdlai Cahstnyr was concerned!

But still . . . .

*Oh, be still, Brahdlai!* he scolded himself. *If the Admiral wants to seize an island, then we'll by Langhorne seize an island. And we'll damned well* hold *it, too, if that's what he wants!*

Still, it did seem a little . . . audacious for someone with Sarmouth's reputation for carefully calculating and planning before he committed his command to action. And exactly what might have brought him here, of all places, eluded Cahstnyr.

*Well, hopefully if it "eludes" you, it'll do the same thing to the frigging Temple Boys!*

He hoped so, although if nothing else it was certain to draw a . . . spirited response from the other side.

Shyan Island lay smack in the middle of the entrance to Saram Bay in the Province of Stene, the primary western anchorage of the Royal Dohlaran Navy now that the Dohlarans had lost Claw Island. Unfortunately, "smack in the middle" was a somewhat misleading term. It was almost a hundred and sixty miles from Saram Head to Cape Rhaigair. For that matter, it was seventy-five miles from Shyan Island to Shipworm Island on the other side of the Basset Channel, and the channel was sixteen miles wide at its narrowest point. Even at low water, the navigable channel was over twelve miles wide, and that meant no one was going to be forced into range of batteries on Shyan, "smack in the middle" or not, under any conceivable normal circumstances. That was why the *Dohlarans* hadn't bothered to put guns on the island.

So far as Cahstnyr could see, there was absolutely no strategic or tactical value to occupying Shyan. The forty-odd-mile-long island didn't even offer a decent anchorage or a reliable source of fresh water. The only thing seizing it was likely to accomplish was to really, really piss off the Dohlarans—and the Harchongians to whom Saram Bay and all of its islands legally belonged. And since the island lay less than two hundred and fifty miles from the city of Rhaigair, which was home to both a major Harchongese dockyard and the primary support facilities for the RDN, it was likely that they'd try to do something about it.

*Maybe that's what the Baron has in mind*, the captain reflected as the launch neared the squadron flagship. *We know they got hurt pretty damned badly themselves at the Kaudzhu Narrows. Even if we hadn't already figured that out for ourselves, the people we took back from the Inquisition have confirmed it in spades. And you overheard the Baron telling Captain Lathyk they can't have* Dreadnought *back into action yet yourself, Brahdlai. So maybe what he wants is to draw them into attacking us here, without* Dreadnought *and before they get all of their own ships back into service.*

It made a sort of sense, and whether it did or not, it was up to Baron Sarmouth to decide what the squadron did, not Major Brahdlai Cahstnyr.

"Well, your good friend Thirsk doesn't seem to be doing very well these days, does he, Allayn?"

There was a typically cutting edge in Zhaspahr Clyntahn's tone, but there were others present, and Allayn Maigwair reminded himself not to roll his eyes. Instead, he simply paused in his walk across the Courtyard of Saint Mahrys and turned to face the Grand Inquisitor. It was unusual for Clyntahn to buttonhole someone—especially another member of the Group of Four—outside his office or a council chamber, and especially not when there were other witnesses, like the dozen or so priests and upper-priests taking advantage of the morning sunlight. He usually had an ulterior motive when he did, and that was a pity, the Captain General thought. Up until that very moment he'd been rather enjoying his own walk. The early-September air had just enough bite to be bracing and the leaves were just reaching the truly spectacular point in their seasonal change. There wouldn't be many more clear, enjoyable mornings like this one and he resented the interruption. Especially since Clyntahn was clearly in one of his moods.

He wasn't the only one who'd realized that. It was amazing how quickly their departing juniors created a bubble of privacy about them, and he wondered if the loss of his audience disappointed the Grand Inquisitor.

"I've never actually met the Earl, you know, Zhaspahr." He allowed just a hint of impatience into his own voice. "On the other hand, I'm unaware of any disastrous reports from Dohlar. Or are you still talking about the prisoner convoy?" He showed his teeth briefly. "I thought you'd instructed Kharmych and Lainyr to

'investigate thoroughly' before you leapt to any conclusions?"

There wasn't much doubt in Maigwair's mind about
the conclusions to which the Grand Inquisitor intended
to leap as soon as his "thorough investigation" was out
of the way, but there also wasn't a great deal he could
do about it.

He'd personally read all the initial reports, and he
couldn't see a great deal the convoy commander might
have done differently. Zhaspahr could moan and complain about how they should have been sailing with
darkened ships to conceal themselves from the Charisians, but that was a lot more than merely being wise
after the fact. It was also a case of being willfully stupid. There was a reason ships sailing in company—
which rather described transports sailing under
escort—showed lights at night; it helped them keep
track of one another and maintain station. That was
hard enough to do with sailing ships in broad daylight,
given the fact that every single one of them handled differently from every other one ever built, but it was
hard for an escort to protect a transport when they
couldn't even *find* one another! And he'd noticed that
Clyntahn's Inquisition still hadn't explained exactly
where all those fresh *Charisian* ships had come from,
either. It seemed most likely to him that they'd sailed
from Corisande, but that was only a guess at this
point. And since no one had warned either Thirsk or
his escort commander about the mysterious enemy reinforcements, and since Clyntahn's office had specifically approved Thirsk's plans, it seemed just a little
irrational—even for him—to condemn people who'd
been doing exactly what they were supposed to be doing for having done it.

Of course, the officers who'd surrendered the transports rather than sending them and all of the heretics
chained aboard them to the bottom . . . *those* officers
would have some serious explaining to do in the eyes
of Clyntahn's agents inquisitor. Maigwair didn't like to
think about what their decision to do the only sane

thing was likely to cost them, yet he also knew he'd be unable to protect them from the Inquisition.

"I'm not talking about *that* fiasco," Clyntahn said unpleasantly. "I'm talking about the fact that despite the 'magnificent victory' at the Kaudzhu Narrows, he seems incapable of preventing the Shan-wei-damned heretics from doing whatever the hell they want in the Gulf of Dohlar."

"Excuse me?" Maigwair cocked his head. "He's dispatched half of the Dohlaran Home Fleet to the Malansath Bight to drive out the heretic commerce-raiders, and I'm not aware of any reports of fresh depredations in that area. And according to the last estimates your people gave me, the heretics have at least twenty-five of their galleons—possibly as many as thirty—in the Gulf."

*Although*, he added to himself, *so far you haven't given me a single clue as to how you came up with that number. Frankly, I'm pretty damned sure it's only a guess, and probably not a very good one. But I sure would love to see whatever information that guess is based on. Of course, I'm only Mother Church's Captain General, aren't I? Why should I possibly need the best numbers available and some sort of an idea as to how reliable they might be?*

"Until he's completed repairs to the ships damaged in the Kaudzhu Narrows," he continued out loud, "his margin of superiority is dangerously thin, especially if the frigging heretics bring up another one of their ironclads before his gun founders have been able to produce new ammunition for the one Admiral Rohsail captured." He shrugged. "Under the circumstances, it seems to me that keeping at least the eastern end of the Gulf clear of raiders and open to our commerce rather than dissipating his strength by sending detachments all over the Gulf chasing heretic squadrons—which will probably outnumber any detachment that actually catches up with them—is a reasonable and prudent policy on his part."

"And while he's doing that, the heretics are getting

ready to take Saram Bay away from him," Clyntahn half snapped.

"Who told you that?" Maigwair demanded.

"The information came in from your own local commander! I saw the same semaphore report *you* did, damn it! The bastards are digging in on that island—what's its name? Shyan?"

"And it's doing them exactly no good," Maigwair retorted. "Not even their guns have the range to cover the entry channel effectively, and without an ironclad of their own, they aren't going to challenge the batteries protecting the anchorage. There are almost two dozen of Brother Lynkyn's eight-inch rifles covering the approaches to Rhaigair, Zhaspahr, and six of the new ten-inch guns will be arriving there within the next three five-days."

"Then why are they occupying it?" Clyntahn shot back.

"Probably because they hope Thirsk will do exactly what *you* seem to want him to do. The only way he could evict them would require him to send a big enough piece of his fleet off to defeat them, and they're clearly hoping for a chance to defeat a portion of his forces in isolation. On the other hand, once he's completed his repairs—and once he has the captured ironclad back in service—he'll have plenty of firepower to drive off their galleons. At which point, Shyan Island ceases to have any importance one way or the other. It's possible the heretics might think they could hold off Thirsk's fleet if they have sufficiently powerful batteries of their own on the island, but I wish to Langhorne they'd try it! There's no water on Shyan, Zhaspahr. That means they couldn't stand any lengthy sieges the way their garrison at Talisman Island can. So as soon as Thirsk is strong enough to operate freely in the western Gulf again, they'll almost certainly pull their troops off of Shyan rather than leave them there to be blockaded into surrender."

"So you're prepared to tolerate this . . . this *lethargy* on his part?"

"At the moment he's doing exactly what I want him to do," Maigwair said flatly. "If you object to the strategy, then offer me a better one and we'll debate it. I'm not a perfect strategist and I never claimed to be one, so it's entirely possible you or someone else may have thought of something I haven't. Until you bring it to my attention, though, there's not much I can do with it."

He held Clyntahn's eyes with his own for a heartbeat or two, until the Grand Inquisitor shrugged his beefy shoulders irritably.

"I'm telling you the heretics are up to something. No doubt they're getting ready to run rings around your precious Thirsk all over again. But, no, I haven't 'thought of something' you haven't. I'd just feel a lot happier if Thirsk and your other commanders seemed to be capable of thinking of *anything*—especially something remotely smacking of *offensive* thinking—on their own."

He jerked a curt nod at his fellow vicar, then turned on his heel and strode away across the now deserted courtyard.

Maigwair watched him go, feeling the implicit threat in his final sentence. The problem wasn't that Maigwair and his commanders didn't have plans; it was that Clyntahn didn't like the ones they had. Unfortunately for what the Grand Inquisitor might have preferred, however, Rainbow Waters was right. They had neither the time, nor the mobility, nor the resources to launch any sort of offensive action in the northern lobe of the Republic of Siddarmark before winter shut down operations. Given that unpalatable truth, and coupled with the degree of mobility the Charisians had displayed in the winter just past, it was time to disaster-proof their positions to the greatest possible extent for the winter while preparing to resume the offensive as early next summer as weather conditions permitted.

All indications from Clyntahn's spies were that the Charisians' newest weapons went through ammunition the way a hungry dragon went through a cornfield.

Those same weapons gave even relatively small Charisian formations spectacular hitting power, as Eastshare had demonstrated in Cliff Peak, but the need to keep those formations provided with adequate ammunition reserves seemed to be putting a cap on the total number of weapons they could provide. It might well be a transitory problem, but it was clearly a factor at the moment—assuming Clyntahn's spies could find their arses with both hands and a candle—and the recently confirmed report about the disastrous fire at Ehdwyrd Howsmyn's Delthak Works suggested it might persist longer than Maigwair had originally hoped it would.

In the meantime, the second wave of the Mighty Host of God and the Archangels had reached the same camps in which Rainbow Waters' men had overwintered. The Army of God training cadres who'd worked with the first wave had already begun improving the new troops' training, and they'd learned a great deal about how to go about that over the previous winter. By spring, an additional Harchongese army, three-quarters of a million strong, would be ready to take the field. They'd be short on rifles, but relatively well equipped with artillery, and another half-million or so men were being raised, trained, and equipped for the Army of God, as well. Their weapons wouldn't be as good as the heretics', but that was a situation with which Mother Church's defenders had become unfortunately accustomed to coping, and coupled with the forces already in the field, it would allow him to send the better part of three million men against Charis and Siddarmark.

The thought of armies that huge was enough to boggle anyone's mind, but Mother Church's manufactories were actually attaining a rate of production which should let him equip and supply all of them. For a time, at least, and assuming the Charisians and their allies couldn't get in behind them and cut the canals through which every pound of food, every boot, and every bullet must travel. Neither Maigwair and Rhobair Duchairn nor Earl Rainbow Waters and Earl Silken Hills had forgotten what the ICN's canal raid had done to the Army of the Sylmahn. That was why Rainbow Waters was so insistent on building up the largest possible supply magazines at his present positions. It was costing a pretty copper, and it gave someone like Zhaspahr Clyntahn entirely too much ammunition for complaints about "inactivity" and "timidity," but that firm logistics base also meant Maigwair's field armies wouldn't find themselves starving to death if something unfortunate happened to the canals supplying them.

*And we'd damned well* better *have a "firm logistics base" come summer*, he thought grimly, resuming his walk with rather less pleasure than before. *I think Rhobair might be a little overly pessimistic about the state of our finances, but if he is, it isn't by much. We've got to score a significant victory next year. I'd love to see one decisive enough to inspire Stohnar to sign a separate peace, but that's not bloody likely after Zhaspahr's frigging "Sword of Schueler" and that bastard Edwyrds' concentration camps! Either way, though, we* have *to hammer them at least hard enough to drive them back onto the defensive and buy ourselves some breathing space to get our economy reorganized into something more sustainable.*

He tried very hard not to think about the fact that he didn't have a clue how to do that.

▼ ▼ ▼

"The prick isn't going to do a damned thing about Thirsk," Clyntahn growled. "If anyone does, it's going to be up to us. Have you finalized plans for bringing his family to Zion for a winter vacation?"

"Not entirely, Your Grace." Wyllym Rayno replied from the other side of the Grand Inquisitor's desk. "We've been considering the possibilities. Our original intention was to bring them here overland, especially in light of what happened to the prisoner convoy."

He shrugged ever so slightly. The Church's official position was that the convoy interception had been a fluke, a matter of luck which had favored the heretics this time. Privately, Rayno was less confident of that explanation, and he knew Clyntahn was, as well, whether or not the Grand Inquisitor was prepared to admit it.

"Unfortunately, I'm not convinced that would be the safer avenue," he continued. "As you know from our intendants' reports, that 'Fist of God' terrorists are operating increasingly brazenly behind Earl Silken Hills' lines. There's evidence the murderer Mab is personally leading them, and they've carried out a half-dozen 'reprisal' attacks against our inquisitors and the guards on Inquisitor General Wylbyr's new Border State camps."

"And I assume no one's done anything about it?" Clyntahn said caustically.

"Your Grace, there isn't a great deal anyone *can* do." Rayno really, really didn't like telling his superior that, but he forced himself to meet Clyntahn's glare levelly. "We have no evidence any of the local inhabitants are assisting the terrorists in any way," he continued. "It seems clearly evident that the attackers are themselves '*seijins*,' since we have yet to kill or capture a single one of them. And I know this is something you won't wish to hear, but the terrorists have been relentless in hunting down any of our inquisitors who distinguish themselves in efforts to root out their local supporters."

"Relentless enough that no one's willing to 'distinguish themselves' any longer?" Clyntahn asked very softly, and Rayno sighed.

"Some of them are, Your Grace. But their superiors—with my agreement—have instructed them not to."

"And why have you agreed to any such policy, Wyllym?" Clyntahn's voice was even softer than before, and Rayno squared his shoulders.

"Because our previous policy had become counterproductive, Your Grace. It was clear we were failing to deter the terrorists' attacks. At the same time, we were creating anger towards—even hatred for—Mother Church. This is no longer happening only in Siddarmark; it's happening in Sardahn, Jhurlahnk, and Faralas, as well. It's clear the attackers are coming over the border from the Republic, however. The Faithful of the Border States are already nervous, Your Grace. In some cases 'terrified' would probably come closer to their mood, and our agents inquisitor report that their courage and readiness to stand forth squarely for the Faith in the face of all trials and tribulation is wavering in far too many cases. I judged it was wiser to moderate the severity of our efforts to root out the terrorists coming into their lands from Siddarmark in order to reassure them of Mother Church's concern for them and to strengthen their willingness to stand with her against the foreign terrorists murdering Mother Church's own priests on their soil. If you believe my judgment was in error, I will of course instruct the local intendants and inquisitors to resume a more active policy."

*Which some of them may or may not do, even if I tell them to*, he thought. *Dialydd Mab and his "seijins" have made their own position on "active policies" abundantly clear, after all. Slitting throats in the middle of the night has a way of doing that. That's not something I need to be pointing out to Zhaspahr at the moment, however.*

Clyntahn sat silently for several endless, smoking seconds. Then he shook himself like an irate boar rising from a mud wallow.

"Very well, Wyllym," he said harshly. "I understand your position . . . and I won't countermand it at this time. It may even be the correct policy, at least for the moment." He looked like a cat-lizard passing fish bones, but at least he got it said. "So I'm not going to overrule you. Not immediately, at any rate. If the terrorists expand the nature or the frequency of their attacks, that may well change, however."

Rayno bent his head in silent acknowledgment . . . and to hide the relief in his eyes until he was sure his expression was back under control.

"In the meantime," Clyntahn continued, "I assume you're concerned about the possibility of this Mab kidnapping Thirsk's family, the way Athrawes kidnapped Irys and Daivyn, if you use the overland route?"

"That concern has crossed my mind, Your Grace," Rayno acknowledged, although "kidnap" wasn't the verb he'd been using in his own mind.

"Well, in that case perhaps it's fortunate after all that Thirsk has allowed the heretics free rein in the Gulf of Dohlar." The Grand Inquisitor smiled unpleasantly. "Since the combination of his tireless efforts in the eastern Gulf and the fact that he doesn't have a single damned rowboat in the *western* Gulf has inspired the heretic Sarmouth to take his entire fleet off to blockade Saram Bay, it would seem that it would be not only faster but safer to transport his daughters and their children in comfort by water, so long as they stay well away from Saram Bay. And so long as they make the voyage aboard one of Mother Church's own vessels, of course."

## . VI .
## City of Gorath,
## Kingdom of Dohlar

"Good evening, My Lord. I came as quickly as I could," Commander Ahlvyn Khapahr said as he entered the lamplit study and bent to kiss Staiphan Maik's ring of office. "How may I serve you?"

"I'll need to speak to Earl Thirsk as early as possible tomorrow, Commander," Maik said, speaking a bit more formally than had become his habit where Khapahr was concerned. "I've received a message from Father Ahbsahlahn on Bishop Executor Wylsynn's behalf. Apparently, the Bishop Executor has received a semaphore message from Archbishop Wyllym and Father Ahbsahlahn wishes to acquaint the Earl with its content. He's . . . requested that the Earl and I attend upon him in the Archbishop's palace tomorrow afternoon.

I thought it would be best if he and I traveled to the palace together."

Although Maik, as an auxiliary bishop, was technically superior to a mere upper-priest like Absahlahn Kharmych, Kharmych's position as the Kingdom of Dohlar's intendant made him Maik's de facto superior in many areas, and Khapahr half bowed in acknowledgment and understanding.

"Of course, My Lord. May I tell His Lordship what the meeting is to discuss? In case he needs to bring any documents or reports, I mean."

"I doubt any reports will be necessary. The Intendant hasn't confided anything of a sensitive nature to me, you understand, but my impression—" the auxiliary bishop's eyes bored very levelly into Khapahr's "—is that he wishes to discuss something of a . . . personal nature with him."

"I see." Khapahr met Maik's eyes steadily for a heartbeat before he gave another of those slight bows. "I'll see to it that he's informed, My Lord."

"Thank you, Commander. I was confident I could rely upon you."

▼ ▼ ▼

"Yes, Mahgdylynah?" Lady Stefyny Mahkzwail looked up, fair hair gleaming in the warm lamplight, as Mahgdylynah Harpahr knocked quietly on the frame of the sewing room's open door.

"I'm sorry to disturb you, My Lady," her housekeeper said, "but you have a visitor."

"At this hour?" Lady Stefyny stuck her needle into the canvas stretched on the stand-mounted embroidery frame.

"Yes, My Lady. It's Commander Khapahr."

"No doubt he's here to speak to Sir Ahrnahld," Lady Stefyny said. "Did you tell him Sir Ahrnahld told us he'd be delayed at the office tonight?"

"I did, My Lady. He said to tell you that in that case he humbly begs a moment of *your* time."

Lady Stefyny removed the glasses she wore for close

work and frowned slightly. Ahlvyn Khapahr was a
cousin of her husband, Sir Ahrnahld Mahkzwail, although the connection was distant. He and Sir Ahrnahld had known one another all their lives, but they'd
never been especially close until Commander Khapahr
became the personal aide of Lady Stefyny's father. Since
then, she'd come to know the commander quite well,
yet he'd never called upon her this late at night with
no previous warning and without his cousin's being
present.

"Did he say why he needs to speak to me?" she asked
calmly.

"No, My Lady. He just emphasized that it was important."

"I see."

The two women's eyes met. Mahgdylynah was fifty-
three years old, twenty years Lady Stefyny's elder, and
while she'd been the Mahkzwails' housekeeper for only
five years, she'd been Stefyny *Gardynyr's* personal maid
long before that. In fact, she'd been Lady Stefyny's
nanny after her mother's death, and she'd filled that
same role for all three of Stefyny's children . . . and for
her older brother's orphaned children for the last eight
years, as well. If there was a single person on the face
of Safehold whose loyalty Stefyny Mahkzwail trusted,
it was Mahgdylynah. And at the moment, Mahgdylynah's eyes were dark with worry.

"I suppose if it's important, you should show him
in," Stefyny said after a moment.

"Of course, My Lady."

Mahgdylynah disappeared. Minutes later, she returned with the handsome, dark-complexioned commander. Stefyny stood, holding out her hand, and he
bent over it to kiss its back gallantly, then straightened
and stroked his moustache with one finger.

"I apologize for intruding at this hour, My Lady," he
said. "Something's come to my attention, however.
Something which I believe concerns your father . . . and
you."

"Indeed?" Stefyny looked at him for several seconds,

then waved a graceful hand at the large, deeply upholstered leather armchair set aside for her husband's oc-
cupancy three nights out of the five when he joined
her in the sewing room after dinner. "In that case, perhaps you'd better have a seat." She glanced at the
housekeeper. "Mahgdylynah, would you bring the Commander a glass of Sir Ahrnahld's whiskey? The Glynfych, I think."

"Of course, My Lady."

Mahgdylynah dropped an abbreviated curtsy and
withdrew, and Stefyny seated herself once more in her
own chair behind the embroidery frame. She put her
glasses back on, recovered her needle, and began setting neat, precise stitches as she looked across the top
of the frame—and her glasses—at her visitor.

"And now, Commander, how can I help you?"

▼ ▼ ▼

Ahlvyn Khapahr leapt easily from the boat to the waiting battens and swarmed up HMS *Chihiro*'s tall side.
It was a climb he usually made at least twice a day and
frequently rather more often than that, and no one
watching him this morning would have suspected he'd
been up throughout the night.

He reached the galleon's entry port, stepped through
it onto the main deck, and paused for a moment as he
found himself facing Mhartyn Rahlstyn, *Chihiro*'s first
lieutenant, rather than the midshipman of the watch.

It was only a brief pause. Then he touched his chest
in salute.

"Permission to come aboard, Sir?" he asked formally,
and Rahlstyn returned his salute.

"Permission granted," he said, equally formal. His
eyes met Khapahr's. "I believe His Lordship is expecting you."

"Indeed?" Khapahr asked calmly, one eyebrow
quirked.

"Yes. Father Chermyn and two officers of the Temple
Guard are with him."

"I see." There might have been the slightest of pauses. Then Khapahr nodded. "In that case, I'd best not keep them waiting."

▼ ▼ ▼

"Lieutenant Rahlstyn said you wished to see me, My Lord?"

Lywys Gardynyr turned quickly from the stern windows as Commander Khapahr entered the day cabin. Only someone who knew the Earl of Thirsk well would have recognized the anxiety in his dark eyes, but Ahlvyn Khapahr had come to know him very well. He saw not simply the anxiety but the stark appeal—and the despair—behind it, and he smiled ever so slightly before he glanced quickly around the cabin.

Captain Baiket sat in a chair to one side and Sir Ahbail Bahrdailahn, Thirsk's flag lieutenant, sat next to his flag captain. Baiket's expression was calm, but Bahrdailahn looked a bit nervous.

Two Temple Guardsmen, both with officers' insignia, stood to either side of the door through which Khapahr had just stepped, and he nodded casually to them as he moved several more paces into the day cabin, coming to a halt under the central skylight, facing the earl. The skylight's louvers were open, and a gentle breeze wafted in through them to stir his dark hair as he tucked his hat under his left arm. His expression was calm and respectful, the perfect model of an attentive staff officer. As always, he was immaculately groomed—it was easy to see why he'd attracted the eye of so many females over the years—although his tunic was unbuttoned this morning.

"Yes. Yes, I did ask Mhartyn to send you straight to me when you arrived, Ahlvyn," Thirsk said after the briefest of pauses, and there was a slight but unmistakable edge to his voice.

"How may I serve you, My Lord?"

"I'm afraid Father Chermyn has a few matters he needs straightened out."

"Of course, My Lord." Khapahr turned to face the fair-haired, broad-shouldered cleric in the purple cassock of the Order of Schueler badged with the sword and flame of the Inquisition in the green of an upper-priest. "How may I be of service, Father?"

"As the Earl says, I have a few minor questions that need . . . clarification, Commander."

Father Chermyn Suzhymahga was easily the tallest man in the cabin. He'd been born and raised in the Episcopate of St. Cahnyr at the western end of Lake Pei and handpicked to serve as Ahbsahlahn Kharmych's senior agent inquisitor in the Kingdom of Dohlar. He had the smooth accent and exquisite manners only to be expected from one of the Temple Lands' great ecclesiastic dynasties and they'd served him well over the years. But now, as he smiled pleasantly at Khapahr, that smile somehow never reached his still, watchful blue eyes.

"Of course, Father," the commander said courteously.

"Did you meet with Auxiliary Bishop Staiphan last night, Commander?"

"I did."

"May I ask why?"

"I'm not sure I have the right to tell you that, Father," Khapahr said, still courteously. "It was pursuant to my duties as Earl Thirsk's senior aide."

"I'm sure Earl Thirsk would permit you to answer my question, Commander."

"My Lord?" Khapahr looked at the earl.

"You may answer Father Chermyn's questions, Ahlvyn, unless you have reason to believe it would compromise sensitive military information." Suzhymahga seemed to bristle ever so slightly, but Thirsk continued in the same measured tones. "If there *is* something you feel might compromise that sort of information, you and I can step out onto the sternwalk to discuss it before you share it with Father Chermyn." He smiled briefly, fleetingly. "I doubt the Father is a serious security risk, and I'm sure a brief discussion would set both our minds at rest."

"I appreciate the offer, My Lord, but I don't think that will be necessary or advisable," Khapahr said, then turned back to Suzhymahga. "Given what His Lordship's just said, Father, I believe I can answer your question. Bishop Staiphan sent a note to my shore lodgings asking me to call upon him at my earliest convenience. When I did, he told me Father Ahbsahlahn wished to speak to him—that is, to the Bishop—and to Earl Thirsk this afternoon at the Archbishop's palace. He knows I have primary responsibility for keeping His Lordship's calendar, and he wanted to make sure time was cleared for the meeting."

"I see. And did he tell you what that meeting was to be about?"

"No, Father, he didn't. Nor did I ask him. I felt that if there was some reason for me to know, he'd tell me about it."

"I see," Suzhymahga repeated. Then he cocked his head. "May I ask where you went after leaving Bishop Staiphan, Commander?"

"I went to call upon my cousin, Sir Ahrnahld Mahkzwail," Khapahr replied calmly. Behind him, Thirsk stiffened ever so slightly, but Suzhymahga's eyes were on Khapahr's face.

"May I ask why?" the Schuelerite asked softly, almost gently.

"I'd made a mistake, Father." Khapahr shrugged with a whimsical smile. "I thought I was engaged to dine with him and his family last night, but I had the wrong five-day. He not only wasn't expecting me for supper, but he'd been detained in his office at the waterfront. So I spoke briefly with Lady Stefyny, made my apologies, and left."

"And returned directly to your lodgings, I presume?"

"No, Father. I had several other minor errands, and Bishop Staiphan had made it clear—or I certainly thought that was what he was suggesting, at any rate—that His Lordship would be occupied for some time today with Father Ahbsahlahn. Since it seemed likely my schedule would be the same as his, I thought it best to deal with them last night and get them out of the way."

"And one of those 'minor errands' took you to Bruk-fyrd Alley?"

The question came sharp and sudden, snapped out so abruptly Lieutenant Bahrdailahn twitched in surprise, but Ahlvyn Khapahr only smiled.

"Why do I think you already know the answer to that question, Father?"

"Because I *do*, Commander," Suzhymahga said coldly. "What I don't know is why one of your 'minor errands' took you to the lodgings of a known smuggler. Or why you booked passage aboard his ship for five adults and eight children. Or why you did that *after* speaking to Lady Stefyny Mahkzwail. Who sent you there, Commander, and why?"

"No one sent me, Father," Khapahr said calmly.

"So if we were to ask Lady Stefyny we'd find she had nothing to do with those arrangements?" Suzhymahga's voice was colder than ever, and his eyes drifted at last from Khapahr to the Earl of Thirsk, standing very, very still against the stern windows.

"If you were to ask Lady Stefyny, Father," Khapahr said, "I'm sure she'd tell you I informed her that the increased tempo of terrorist attacks in Jhurlahnk and Faralas have caused her father some concern. That he feared they might choose to target the families of senior Dohlaran officers, especially naval officers and particularly here in the capital itself, because of that business in the Kaudzhu Narrows and the Malansath Bight. And, for that matter, as a belated reprisal for the Charisian prisoners who were sent to Zion for Punishment year before last. That because of his concern for her personal safety he wished her and her family—and her sister and *her* family—to return to Thirsk, where they would be safer from such attacks."

"And you expect me to believe a woman as intelligent as Lady Stefyny is widely known to be believed she could be transported to Thirsk aboard Captain

Kartyr's *schooner*? I believe Thirsk is in the Duchy of Windborne, is it not? Just a bit far *inland* for someone to sail to it, wouldn't you say, Commander?"

"No," Khapahr said. "Obviously, Lady Stefyny is far too intelligent to believe anything of the sort. However, I never suggested to her that she and her family would be traveling to Thirsk aboard the *Mairee Zhain*. In fact, I never mentioned a ship to her at all. I'm afraid she thought we'd be traveling overland."

Earl Thirsk stiffened again, this time much more noticeably, and Khapahr glanced at him and smiled almost repentantly.

"I apologize for being less than honest with your daughter, My Lord. It seemed the . . . best way to proceed." He reached casually into his unbuttoned uniform tunic. "After all, the truth would have upset her so."

His right hand came out of his tunic, and every person in the cabin froze as the pistol hammer came back with a clearly audible click.

No one moved, and Khapahr beckoned gently with the muzzle of the pistol.

"Forgive me, My Lord, but I think you should join the others before you do something . . . intemperate."

Thirsk stared at him, then drew a deep breath.

"Please, Ahlvyn," he said very, very softly. "*Please*, don't do this."

"I'm afraid I don't have a great many options, My Lord," the commander said. "Now, please, do as I ask."

Thirsk looked at him for another moment. Then his shoulders slumped and he crossed to stand beside Captain Baiket's chair.

"Thank you, My Lord." Khapahr looked back at Suzhymahga, whose eyes were fixed in disbelief on the weapon in his hand. "And now, Father, perhaps you'd care to tell me what Captain Kartyr had to say when you asked *him* about my visit?"

Suzhymahga blinked and dragged his eyes away from the pistol, then glared at him wordlessly, and Khapahr shook his head.

"I wondered why you were conducting this little interrogation in front of the Earl. You didn't take Kartyr alive, did you? Or else you—or possibly these two gentlemen with you—were a bit overenthusiastic about how you asked him? They didn't know about his heart condition, did they?"

By rights, Suzhymahga's fiery eyes should have reduced the commander to a pile of flaky ash.

"That's what this is all about, isn't it? You think—you *honestly* think—His Lordship had something to do with this? You're standing there hoping he'll suddenly confess to sending me to Kartyr. That would be a little difficult for him to do, though, since he didn't."

"Where did you get *that?*" the upper-priest demanded suddenly, pointing at the weapon in Khapahr's hand. It was a Charisian-made revolver.

"Where do you *think* I got it?" Khapahr retorted contemptuously. "I—"

His eyes flicked suddenly to the side, and the muzzle of the revolver twitched to the right.

"Captain Baiket, I would truly regret shooting an officer I respect as much as I respect you. Take your hand off your dagger hilt, please."

Steward Baiket stared at him, then carefully lifted his empty right hand and showed it to the commander.

"Thank you," Khapahr said, and returned his full attention to Suzhymahga.

"Where were we?" he asked. "Ah, yes! You were about to trick the Earl into confessing his complicity in some plot to smuggle his family somewhere else. Actually, it would have made my job much simpler if he'd been willing to consider anything of the sort. After all, he would have relied upon me to make all the arrangements. Which, I'm afraid, would have been rather foolish of him."

"What?" Suzhymahga frowned. Then he shook himself. "What sort of lie are you trying to spin now?" he demanded.

"It's a bit late to be spinning lies, Father. Obviously, you and your agents inquisitor couldn't find your arses with both hands, but despite yourself, you've managed to thoroughly fuck up my own plans. I'd congratulate you if I thought you'd actually had a single clue about what those plans were."

"You don't think you're getting off of this ship—or even out of this cabin—alive, do you?" Suzhymahga asked almost pleasantly.

"And you don't think *you're* getting me off this ship alive, either, do you, Father?" Khapahr retorted. "I'm sure you'd like to, and I'm sure that's exactly what the Grand Fornicator would expect you to do. I rather regret that I won't have the opportunity to see you explain this colossal fuck-up to him."

"What are you talking about now?"

"The one thing you've actually managed to accomplish, despite what's obviously monumental stupidity," Khapahr told him, "is to unmask the most highly placed Charisian spy in Dohlar."

Absolute silence invaded the cabin. It hovered there for perhaps ten seconds before Suzhymahga shook himself like a golden retriever who'd just come ashore.

"Charisian spy," he repeated softly. "You actually *admit* that?"

"I might as well." Khapahr shrugged. "If Kartyr's dead—and he *is* dead, isn't he?—you'll probably eventually find his codebook." He glanced at a white-faced Thirsk. "When I suggested you release him and his ship because he'd make a suitably disreputable spy to keep an eye out for people selling information to the Charisians and planting our own spies on them, I truly did think he'd be perfect for the part. But I'm afraid I neglected to tell you that I was so confident of his abilities because he already *was* a spy . . . for Charis."

"*Kartyr* was a Charisian spy?" Suzhymahga said.

"Of course he was." Khapahr chuckled mirthlessly. "If your agents inquisitor were so stupid they hadn't figured *that* out, it may not've been his heart that killed him. Didn't you even think to check him for poison?"

Suzhymahga darted a venomous look at one of the Temple Guardsmen and Khapahr shook his head.

"Good help is hard to find, isn't it?" He sounded almost commiserating.

"What did you hope to accomplish?" Suzhymahga asked.

"Well, for the last couple of years, I've accomplished quite a bit in passing information to the Charisians," Khapahr told him. "I'm sure that had a little something to do with how handily they managed to retake Claw Island. They paid quite well for it, too. Of course, all that money's been held in an anonymous account in Siddar City. It's a pity I'll never see it after all. I was looking forward to a long and wealthy retirement."

"You're a *traitor*?" Bahrdailahn demanded from his place beside Captain Baikyr. "All these years, you've been a *traitor*?!"

"Not *all* these years, Ahbail," Khapahr disagreed. "Only the two and a half years or so since I convinced His Lordship to release Kartyr."

"Where was he going to take my family?" Thirsk's voice was strangely dead, flattened with something which sounded far more like disappointment—or grief—than the fiery outrage of betrayal.

"To Claw Island, My Lord." Khapahr met the earl's eyes levelly. "I was assured they'd be unharmed. Of course, the Charisians might not have told *you* that. It was their belief you might be inclined to be . . . cooperative if you felt the safety of your daughters and your grandchildren depended upon it. When Bishop Staiphan told me Father Ahbsahlahn wanted to speak with you today, it occurred to me that the Inquisition might have gotten some hint of mine and Kartyr's intentions. I suspected they might be planning to move them to Zion or somewhere else in the Temple Lands, so I found myself forced to set my own plans in motion sooner than I'd intended. And apparently I wasn't quite careful enough when I left Lady Stefyny's. You did have me followed, didn't you, Father?"

He turned back to Suzhymahga, and the Schuelerite's jaw muscles clenched.

"You're a dead man," he grated.

"No doubt. But I'm not the only one, Father. When you know that if you're captured you'll automatically be given to the Punishment, there's not much of an incentive to surrender. I won't pretend I wasn't in it mostly for the money, but I do take a certain pride in doing what I set out to do. So since I've failed to neutralize His Lordship one way, I'm afraid I'll have to do it another way."

He looked Thirsk in the eye.

"I'm very sorry about this, My Lord," he said quietly. "I've always deeply respected you."

Thirsk looked back at him . . . and Khapahr squeezed the trigger.

The heavy bullet hammered the earl out of his chair in a crack of thunder. He fell heavily, and suddenly everything was in motion. Captain Baiket lunged up, dagger hissing out of its sheath. Both of the Temple Guardsmen reached for their own swords. Lieutenant Bahrdailahn flung himself out of his own chair, going to his knees beside the earl, ripping open Thirsk's tunic to get at the wound. And Ahlvyn Khapahr brought the revolver back around, smiled at Father Chermyn . . . and shot him squarely between the eyes.

The back of Suzhymahga's skull exploded, spraying blood and brain matter over the Temple Guardsmen behind him. One of them stopped, pawing at his eyes, but the other kept coming. Voices could be heard shouting in alarm from the deck above their heads. Feet came thundering down the companionway, and Khapahr put a bullet into the guardsman who hadn't been blinded by Suzhymahga's brains.

The wounded guardsman went down, screaming, and the cabin door smashed open. Mhartyn Rahlstyn charged through it, sword in hand, followed by *Chihiro*'s senior Marine officer, and Khapahr darted back to the stern windows.

"Time to go," he said, and his right temple disintegrated as he fired one last shot.

"My God."

Cayleb Ahrmahk sat back in the armchair before the hearth in his embassy study, his face ashen, as the imagery from the SNARC's remote finished playing on his contact lenses. Outside the windows, a cold early-afternoon rain—not yet the bitter cold of winter, but enough to chill the bone and depress the heart—fell heavily, beating against the diamond-paned windows, and a coal fire hissed on the grate. It burned more for spiritual comfort than for physical, that fire.

It failed in its purpose.

"I never expected anything like that," the Emperor of Charis said softly. "Not in a million years."

"No one did, love," Sharleyan told him from distant Tellesberg. "How could we have?"

"It was brilliant," Aivah Pahrsahn said, almost as softly as Cayleb had spoken. "What a brilliant, brilliant young man."

"May God gather him to Him as His own," Maikel Staynair said quietly.

"I agree with you, Aivah—and with you, Maikel," Nahrmahn Baytz put in from Nimue's Cave. "But will it work?"

"It almost has to work, at least to some extent," Merlin said from the armchair facing Cayleb's. "Someone as smart as Rayno or as paranoid as Clyntahn may not buy it entirely, but they have to give it at least some credence."

"I'm not sure Clyntahn will question it as deeply as you might be afraid, Nahrmahn." Nimue Chwaeriau was the only member of the inner circle currently awake in Manchyr. Now she smiled crookedly as the others looked at her com image. "Clyntahn counts on the fanaticism of people like his Rakurai to work *for* him, but he doesn't really believe in the sincerity of anyone who *opposes* him. It's part of the same mind-set—if I can use the term 'mind' in reference to him—which lets him recognize how threats to someone's loved ones can be used to keep her in line without fully appreciating—or worrying about—the ultimate consequences of how much pure, distilled hatred that generates."

"You may have a point," Merlin said after a moment. "Everything we've learned about Clyntahn only underscores his fundamental narcissism. He can believe people are prepared to die for *him*, but he doesn't really believe anyone could be prepared to die for someone *else*. Someone that person loves."

"Rayno could believe that." Aivah sounded thoughtful. "But, as Merlin says, you may have a point about Clyntahn, Nimue. He can accept it as an intellectual proposition, but emotionally, it just doesn't resonate with him. He's . . . pre-programmed—" she smiled briefly, fleetingly, as she used the very un-Safeholdian term "—to accept bribery and corruption as a motive before he even considers something remotely like selflessness. And when I said Khapahr was brilliant, I wasn't using the term lightly. He not only gave Clyntahn a motive he's naturally inclined to accept but managed to provide alibis for all the rest of Thirsk's personal staff with the same move."

Merlin nodded, sapphire eyes dark as he thought about the decision Ahlvyn Khapahr had made.

Despite everything Owl and Nahrmahn could do, the sheer amount of data flowing in through the network of SNARCs—especially now that Owl was building additional remotes for them—continued to exceed their ability to process information. Since the cataclysmic events in HMS *Chihiro*'s admiral's quarters, however, they'd been back over every scrap of imagery of Commander Khapahr in those enormous data files. They'd actually found the imagery of him quietly appropriating the revolver from the weapons captured aboard HMS *Dreadnought*. It was one of the smaller Navy pistols, chambered in .40 caliber rather than .45, with a shorter barrel for use in close quarters on shipboard and a somewhat lighter load. That was the only reason he'd been able to hide it under his tunic, and Merlin suspected that the fact that it could never be mistaken for anything but a *Charisian*-made weapon had been part of his thinking from the beginning. It was unlikely he'd planned from the outset to sacrifice himself, but he'd clearly recognized what would happen to him if he was taken alive. Once he'd realized the Inquisition was about to arrest him, whatever else happened, he'd deliberately diverted suspicion from Thirsk, and that revolver had been part of the evidence to "prove" he'd been suborned by Charis, not working to liberate his commander's family from Church custody.

They still hadn't found any imagery of the moment when Thirsk had taken Khapahr fully into his confidence. He doubted they ever would, at this remove. From what they'd observed of Thirsk and Khapahr, it was entirely likely that Khapahr had been proceeding independently of any instructions from the earl. Cutting Thirsk out of the direct planning was one way to reduce the risk of detection by the inevitable spies keeping the earl under the Inquisition's eye. Yet it was virtually certain Stywyrt Baiket, Ahbail Bahrdailahn, and probably Mahrtyn Vahnwyk had been at least peripherally privy to what Khapahr was doing. One clue in that direction was the fact that Baiket's hand had been nowhere near his dagger hilt when Khapahr threatened him. Bahrdailahn's obvious nervousness from the very beginning might be another indication . . . but it might not, as well.

*They may not have known a thing about it, really, whatever we thought earlier. Khapahr must have known suspicion would fall on the rest of Thirsk's most trusted subordinates if he was caught, however "inno-*

cent" they might be. And Aivah's right about how smart he was. He might very well have been operating in just-in-case mode where they were concerned.

"It took a lot of nerve to shoot Thirsk," Cayleb said. "He could easily've killed him himself!"

"It took a lot of nerve to do *any* of that, and especially to do it so well," Nimue countered. "For that matter, it took a lot of nerve for Thirsk to stand still and *let* himself be shot, and it's obvious that's exactly what he did. He never even flinched when Khapahr squeezed the trigger."

"Agreed." Cayleb nodded. "I wonder if the surgeons will be able to save the use of his arm?"

"Speaking from personal experience, I think they've got a chance," Hektor Aplyn-Ahrmahk said. He sat on *Destiny*'s sternwalk, tipped back in his chair with both boot heels propped on the top of the railing while he watched the sun set beyond Cape Samuel. "Not a very good one, I'm afraid, but a chance."

On balance, Merlin suspected Hektor was probably correct. The bullet had struck Thirsk in the bony part of the left shoulder, mushroomed, and partially disintegrated. The main body of the bullet had punched a ragged hole through the scapula, shattered the clavicle, and fractured the first rib on that side, while lead fragments had broken the *second* rib and badly damaged the coracoid process, as well. The earl was fortunate Bahrdailahn had gotten pressure on the wound quickly enough to slow the bleeding until *Chihiro*'s healer could arrive. He was also fortunate that despite the rote nature of their training, the supernatural explanation of physical processes, and the total absence of the sort of medical technology the Federation—or even pre-space Old Earth—had taken for granted, Pasqualate surgeons were very good.

"But the severity of the wound should make it obvious Khapahr truly was trying to kill him," Aivah pointed out.

"As long as someone doesn't ask why he shot the

Earl through the body and that bastard Suzhymahga through the *head*," Nahrmahn agreed. "If he could manage a head shot when Suzhymahga was coming at him and everyone else was in motion, why couldn't he do the same thing with Thirsk, when everyone—including Thirsk—was still simply standing there?"

"He shot the Temple Guardsman in the *leg*, Nahrmahn," Merlin observed. "I think the hits are broadly enough distributed to deflect that sort of question."

"I hope so," Nimue said. "And I think you're probably right, but it wouldn't do for anyone to figure out he deliberately *didn't* kill the guardsman, either."

"I wonder if he killed Suzhymahga because he was more worried about him going over the entire conversation later and picking out flaws or because he was just really, really pissed at him?" Kynt Clareyk murmured from his office in the comfortable winter barracks being thrown up just outside the town of Lakeside on the northeast shore of Lake Isyk.

"I wouldn't put it past him to have done it for your first reason," Aivah said. "He left both of the guardsmen as witnesses—witnesses the Inquisition's going to have to take seriously—but much as I'd always loathed Suzhymahga, he was smarter than both of them put together. Khapahr led him to the conclusions he wanted him to draw and actually got him to put them into words for the guardsmen, then got rid of him before he had a chance to question his own conclusions." She shook her head. "*God*, that young man was brilliant."

"And the most loyal friend anyone could ever ask for," Sharleyan agreed softly.

Silence hovered for several seconds. Then Cayleb shook himself.

"So the question now is what Clyntahn does next. Any ideas?"

"I'd like to say I think it will cause him to decide Thirsk is actually trustworthy from his perspective," Merlin said after a moment. "Unfortunately, what I *actually* think is that that's about as likely as the sun rising in the west tomorrow morning."

"Probably." Nimue sat in the lotus position on her bed in her darkened Manchyr bedchamber and nodded. "I'd say it's likely to have diverted *immediate* suspicion from him—suspicion that he was actively trying to get his family out of Church custody, at least—but it's not going to change Clyntahn's fundamental distrust. And let's be honest here. All the indications are that Clyntahn's absolutely right to fear what will happen if and when he finally pushes Thirsk to the breaking point. Best possible outcome from *Clyntahn's* perspective is that when the earl reaches that point he kills himself as the only escape that might leave his family unharmed. But I think it's pretty clear Clyntahn's figured out Thirsk won't oblige him that way *unless* it's the only escape that leaves his family unharmed."

"Nimue's right," Aivah said. "He'll still want Thirsk's family under his thumb in Zion as the one lever he can be certain will keep Thirsk under control. And the one downside of Commander Khapahr's strategy—aside from the absolute tragedy of losing *him* that way, I mean—is that it gives Clyntahn a pretext to move quickly to *get* them to Zion."

"The 'terrorist threat,' you mean?"

"Exactly, Merlin." Aivah nodded. "Everyone will know it's bogus, that Khapahr the 'Charisian spy' manufactured it out of whole cloth as a pretext for maneuvering Thirsk's daughters and sons-in-law into a position which would let him and his accomplices 'kidnap them' for us. But it's still there on the table, and Clyntahn and Rayno are going to pounce on it the instant they read Kharmych's analysis of the witnesses' testimony."

"Then we're just going to have to do something about that, aren't we?" Merlin said, and smiled very, very thinly.

"Is Granddaddy really going to be all right?"

Lyzet Mahkzwail's eyes were anxious in the lamplight as she and her cousin Kahrmyncetah finished their bedtime prayers and climbed into their hammocks.

"The healers think so, sweetheart," her mother said, bending to kiss her forehead as she tucked the blanket around the nine-year-old. Four-year-old Zhosifyn had been put to bed two hours ago and slept blissfully through her cousin's and older sister's arrival. "And they're very good healers, you know, and Aunt Zhoahna agrees with them." Lady Stefyny straightened, touching the tip of Lyzet's nose with an index finger, and smiled. "And Granddaddy, even if I shouldn't be saying this, is very, very tough and very ornery," she added in a conspiratorial whisper. "He's way too stubborn *not* to be all right."

Lyzet crossed her eyes to stare at the fingertip on her nose and giggled, and Stefyny Mahkzwail patted her gently on the chest.

"I wish he could have come with us," Kahrmyncetah said wistfully from her own hammock.

Like Lyzet—and Stefyny, too, for that matter—Kahrmyncetah had inherited the blond hair and gray eyes of her maternal grandmother, for whom she'd been named. She was a year older than Lyzet, and the two of them were far more like sisters than cousins. Not surprisingly. She and her brother Ahlyxzandyr had been raised by Stefyny and Sir Ahrnahld since their parents' deaths in a house fire just over eight years ago.

"I'm sure he wishes the same thing, love." Stefyny managed to keep her voice tranquil while she tucked in Kahrmyncetah's blanket as she had Lyzet's. "But, you know, Granddaddy's a very busy man. I'm sure as soon as the healers let him out of bed he'll be right back at work running the Navy."

Kahrmyncetah considered that for a moment, then nodded, and Stefyny nodded back to her.

"Now go to sleep, both of you," she said, turning down the lamp wick. "I'll be along soon, and I want to hear those musical snores of yours when I climb into *my* hammock. Understood?"

"Yes, Momma," Lyzet promised demurely, and Stefyny stroked her older daughter's hair once, glanced at Zhosifyn, winked at Kahrmyncetah, and closed the cubbyhole of a cabin's door behind her.

"You got them corralled?" Sir Ahrnahld Mahkzwail asked, putting an arm around her and kissing her above the left ear as she entered what had been designed as the captain's day cabin.

"Yes." She leaned into his embrace for a long, grateful moment, then straightened and nodded to her middle sister and brother-in-law, seated at the captain's dining table. "What about your two?"

"Lywys is bedded down with Gyffry and Ahlyxzandyr," Hailyn Whytmyn told her. She, too, had Kahrmyncetah Gardynyr's gray eyes, although her hair was dark. "Mahgdylynah has Zhudyth right now, and bless Bédard she's here!"

Stefyny nodded in heartfelt agreement as she and Ahrnahld crossed to the table. Her husband pulled out her chair and seated her, then took his own place across the table from Hailyn's husband Greyghor.

"Is she any better?" Stefyny asked. Six-year-old Zhudyth was obviously ill-suited to follow in her seaman grandfather's footsteps. She'd been miserably seasick from the moment NGS *Saint Frydhelm* made sail.

"Mahgdylynah and I have dosed her with golden berry again," Zhoahna Gardynyr, Stefyny's youngest sister, said with an off-center smile. Zhoahna—dark-haired and dark-eyed—wore the green, caduceus-badged habit of a Sister of Pasquale with the white band of a novice. "At least it's made her drowsy enough she's stopped wailing, poor baby."

"It seems dreadfully unfair that Lywys has an iron stomach when his sister's the exact opposite," Hailyn said, and bared her teeth at her husband with mock ferocity. "That's probably your fault, now that I think about it," she told him. "She's always been a chip off the Whytmyn block, except for her coloring, so she probably got that tender tummy from you. Not that I'm complaining about Lywys, mind you! The last thing we need would be to have both of them down—or up, as the case may be—with it! Especially since you'd probably claim the weary weight and ancient decrepitude of all your years—your many, *many* years—made *you* too feeble to sit up with them both all night."

Stefyny smiled faintly. Greyghor Whytmyn was neither ancient nor decrepit, but he *was* twelve years older than his wife. And Hailyn had a point about Zhudyth's twin brother Lywys. *He* was clearly his grandfather's grandson, in more than name alone. He'd never been seasick for a single moment in his life and he thought sailing ships were the most wonderful thing God had ever created.

She sat back in her chair, looking around the cabin Father Syndail Rahdgyrz had made available to them. She hadn't had much opportunity to form an impression of the captain, and at the moment she wasn't especially fond of anyone with "Father" in front of his name, but Rahdgyrz seemed a competent seaman and he'd been the soul of courtesy as he showed them to the quarters he'd made available to them aboard his ship. He himself had evicted his first lieutenant from his cabin, in turn, in order to make the biggest and most comfortable space aboard ship available to his passengers.

They were still cramped—*Saint Frydhelm* had never been designed as a passenger vessel—but things might have been far worse. And at least with space at such a premium, there was no room for anyone else in the same quarters. That meant that except for the single sentry outside the cabins tucked under the quarterdeck, their "escort" had been forced to bunk elsewhere . . .

and that they had as much privacy as they could possibly have hoped to find.

"At least *Saint Frydhelm* seems like a well found ship," Stefyny observed, looking at her husband.

"She is." Her husband nodded. "We built five just like her from the same plans for King Rahnyld in the first run of orders. In fact, the *Riptides* are basically the same design; we just scaled them up and lengthened them enough for the extra sixteen guns."

"I thought she seemed familiar," Stefyny said. Sir Ahrnahld Mahkzwail's modest little shipyard had turned into a sprawling complex over the last few years. She'd been grateful for the way it had improved the family fortunes, but even more for the way it had supported Dohlar's contribution to the Jihad. Of course, that had been then and this was now.

The conversation slid to a halt for several seconds. Then, after a moment, Hailyn raised her head.

"Gyffry's worried," she said, her soft voice barely audible above the background noises of a sailing vessel underway. Stefyny looked up sharply, and her sister gave her a quick headshake. "He's not going to say anything he shouldn't, Stefyny! And he hasn't said anything to you because he doesn't want *you* to be worried. He asked me not to mention it to you, but I didn't promise I wouldn't. I hope that doesn't make me a tattletale aunt."

"No, of course it doesn't." Stefyny laid a hand lightly on her sister's forearm. "And I promise I won't betray your faithlessness to him. Did Ahlyxzandyr say anything?"

At thirteen—he'd turn fourteen in little more than a month—Ahlyxzandyr Gardynyr was the eldest of the Earl of Thirsk's grandchildren. He was also the earl's heir, and he, too, had his grandmother's eyes, although he'd clearly inherited his height from his mother's side of the family. He was almost six feet tall, despite his youth, and bidding fair to be at least a foot taller than his grandfather before he was done growing. Despite his youth, he was an insightful and thoughtful young man, who reminded Stefyny almost painfully of her dead brother Lanfyrd.

"I'm afraid Ahlyxzandyr has a very clear notion of what's happening, Stefyny," her husband said now, before Hailyn could reply. "You noticed how little he had to say about Ahlvyn, didn't you?"

"Yes," Stefyny sighed. "He *didn't* say much, did he?"

Neither the twins nor Zhosifyn had any clear idea of the last two five-days' tumultuous events, but the older children did. Lyzet and Kahrmyncetah had been stunned when Bishop Staiphan gently informed them that Commander Khapahr had shot and badly wounded their grandfather and then killed himself. They clearly didn't understand the implications, only that someone their entire family had trusted had turned upon their grandfather, and Bishop Staiphan hadn't passed along any of the details about the commander's treason. Despite that, Stefyny had been afraid Ahlyxzandyr would be able to add two plus two and come up with four. It seemed he had, and that could be dangerous to everyone.

"Ahlyxzandyr's a smart kid, Stefyny," Greyghor said, keeping his own voice low enough to be barely audible. "He's not going to say anything he shouldn't to anyone."

"Not in normal conversation, no," she agreed, equally softly. "And not on his own. But what about that bastard Rudahry?"

None of Lywys Gardynyr's daughters were anything remotely like prudes, but that particular noun was one Stefyny Mahkzwail used only very, very rarely. Especially about ordained clergy. No one seemed inclined to reprove her for her language, however. Zhoahna's expression flickered slightly, but with regret and anger, not disagreement.

Father Aimohs Rudahry was a Schuelerite priest who'd served as one of Ahbsahlahn Kharmych's troubleshooters in the Dohlaran Inquisition since the beginning of the Jihad. He was intelligent, he was ruthless, and he was a fervent supporter of Zhaspahr Clyntahn's policies. In fact, aside from coloration, he had a great deal in common with the late Chermyn Suzhymahga, with whom he'd worked closely. He was a man whose natural passion for ferreting out secrets had been honed and shaped to a razor's edge by the Inquisition, and like most inquisitors, he understood that the unguarded remarks of children were often keys to what those children's parents actually thought.

"You're right about Ahlyxzandyr's being smart, Greyghor," she continued, "but so is Rudahry. What happens when he starts pumping the kids for information?"

"That could be bad," Ahrnahld acknowledged with a wintry smile of his own. "Maybe we shouldn't have worked as hard as we did at teaching all of them to trust the clergy."

"It seemed like a good idea at the time, sweetheart," Stefyny said. "No one saw all this insanity coming then."

Ahrnahld cocked his head at her, remembering certain pre-Jihad conversations with his father-in-law, but chose not to mention them. Zhoahna was rather less reticent.

"It *did* seem like a good idea, Stefyny," she agreed, fingering the caduceus on the breast of her habit. "A lot of things seemed like a good idea then. But Rodahry's almost enough to make me think the Reformists have been right all along."

Her eyes were shadowed with mingled regret and anger, and Hailyn reached across to grip her forearm comfortingly. Zhoahna had completed her novitate as a Pasqualate before the Jihad was formally proclaimed. Since then, her plans to complete her vows had been put on hold, and both of her sisters knew her faith in the Church had been badly shaken. She was far too intelligent not to understand the way in which the three of them had been used as weapons against their father by Zhaspahr Clyntahn and the Inquisition. Her bitter disillusionment with the Group of Four hadn't been enough to make her doubt her own vocation, but it *had* been enough to make her delay that final step of commitment. Clyntahn had enough swords to hold over Earl Thirsk's head without a daughter whose ecclesiastic superiors could order her to Zion at any moment.

Not that it seemed to have prevented that from happening in the end, of course.

"I'll have a talk with Ahlyx in the morning, preferably out on the sternwalk where none of the big-eared little pitchers will overhear us," Ahrnahld said. Stefyny looked slightly alarmed, and he grimaced. "Honey, we can't hide this from him forever. He's three years older than Gyffry, and he's already figured out a lot more than any of us might really want him to have put together. We can't put the cork back into that bottle. But he *is* smart—scary smart, sometimes—and he's old enough to understand what could happen if . . . someone decided your father had had anything to do with Ahlvyn's actions. Which, of course," he looked around the table with no expression at all, "we all know he didn't."

The other four adults looked back at him without speaking.

▼ ▼ ▼

"Any problems with our guests this evening, Ahntwahn?" Father Syndail Rahdgyrz asked.

"No, Sir," Lieutenant Ahntwahn Kuhlhani, NGS *Saint Frydhelm*'s second lieutenant, replied. "Except the little girl's still seasick." The lieutenant shook his head, his expression sympathetic. "I hope it doesn't get any rougher than it is now. I'd hate to put her through a heavy blow if she's this unhappy right now!"

"You've got a point," Rahdgyrz acknowledged.

The two of them stood on the poop deck of the forty-gun galleon. The overcast night was moonless and starless, black as Shan-wei's riding boots, and cool, promising rain before dawn. A stiff topgallant breeze blew out of the north-northwest, and the ship moved north-northeast, close-hauled on the larboard tack, at a steady six knots. The waves were little more than four feet in height and *Saint Frydhelm*—a solid ship and a good seaboat, over a hundred and forty feet long and almost forty feet in the beam—pitched gently, almost sedately as she took them on her larboard bow. They were eight days and almost thirteen hundred miles out of Gorath Bay, just over halfway between Gorath and the port of Erthayn on the Princedom of Tanshar's Kahrvyr Bay.

Erthayn was Tanshar's largest—and only real—seaport, but it was perhaps a quarter of Gorath's size, at best. It was, however, barely a hundred miles overland from the even smaller town of Mahrglys, at the mouth of the Tanshar River. The Tanshar Estuary was shallow and liberally seeded with treacherous mudbanks, so it made much better sense to deliver Earl Thirsk's family to Erthayn. They could travel by road to Mahrglys, then upriver to the Schueler Canal and on to Lake Pei for the final leg of their journey to Zion. In many ways, Rahdgyrz would have preferred sailing to Malantor in the Duchy of Malansath rather than Erthayn. The voyage would have been about four hundred miles longer, which would have extended the sailing time by three days or so, but Malantor offered a much larger—and deeper, not to mention better sheltered—harbor than Erthayn, and his passengers' river and canal journey to Lake Pei would have been five hundred miles shorter.

His orders had been crystal clear on that point, unfortunately, and he couldn't argue with the logic behind their choice of destinations, however little he might care for it. From all reports, the heretics' galleon strength remained fully occupied blockading Saram Bay, and no one had reported seeing a single one of their light commerce-raiders east of Whale Island in five-days. That wasn't to say there *couldn't* be any of them farther east, however, and there was absolutely no point taking chances with his ship or its passengers, especially after what had happened to the prisoner convoy in the Trosan Channel. Far better to take the longer route through the Fern Narrows, staying within sight of Dohlar's friendly coastline—and, hopefully, within reach of a port of refuge—for the entire voyage. He'd moved a little farther west once night fell because the shoals along the Duchy of Malikai's coast stretched a bit farther out to sea, squeezing the Narrows down to little more than a hundred and thirty miles. With the wind from the north-northwest, he wanted a bit more sea room to leeward. They were forty-odd miles off the coast, and ports of refuge were thin on the ground in Malikai, but there were still a couple of them he could scrape into if he had to.

He wasn't too proud to run for it if anything untoward turned up, either, although he had to admit that skulking his way through what were supposed to be Mother Church's own waters . . . irritated him. That was one reason he would have preferred to sail straight to Malantor, and if the Church had possessed the wherewithal to provide *Saint Frydhelm* with a powerful escort, that was exactly what he would have done. Unhappily, Rahdgyrz' ship was one of only a scant handful of galleons still flying Mother Church's banner. By far the majority of the hulls remaining to the Navy of God after the Markovian Sea disaster had been transferred either to the Imperial Harchongese Navy or to the Royal Dohlaran Navy. Those which hadn't been transferred had simply been laid up so that their artillery could be used for coast defense and their manpower could be transferred to the *Army* of God. In fact, there were only five NOG galleons left in the entire Gulf of Dohlar, and it was pure luck *Saint Frydhelm* had been available in Gorath when Mother Church needed her.

*Of course it was "pure luck," Syndail*, the captain told himself now. *It couldn't possibly have been anything else, now could it? After all, how could anyone have known Admiral Thirsk's own aide would turn out to have been a Charisian spy?*

Unfortunately, Syndail Rahdgyrz was not a great believer in "pure luck," especially in this case. His ship had been ordered to Gorath to deliver a small group of inquisitors to Father Ahbsahlahn Kharmych. Any of the Church's rather smaller schooners or brigs could have made the same delivery, but she'd been chosen, and then there'd been some sort of confusion about her further orders. For some reason *Saint Frydhelm* had found herself anchored in Gorath Bay for almost two full five-days, waiting for someone to find something else for her to do, before Commander Khapahr's spectacular suicide. How *conveniently* that had worked out in the end, he reflected dryly.

And then, of course, there was the question of why the *Royal Dohlaran Navy* couldn't have provided the escort the Navy of God no longer could. Or, for that matter, have provided transport for its own commander's family aboard one of its vessels. Unless, of course, there was some reason someone in Mother Church might entertain reservations about the Dohlaran Navy's loyalty to the Jihad. And so, again, wasn't it fortunate that *Saint Frydhelm*'s wanderings just happened to have made *her* available for the duty, instead?

Fortune was another one of those things in which Father Syndail was not a great believer.

"And how's Father Aimohs?" he asked after a moment. "I missed him at supper . . . again."

Kuhlhani smiled slightly. Aimohs Rudahry was almost as bad a sailor as little Zhudyth Whytmyn. Worse, he was over six feet tall, which was an inconvenient height aboard a war galleon. He seemed to have trouble remembering that, unfortunately—possibly because of how thoroughly miserable the seasickness made him—and he'd nearly knocked himself unconscious against one deckbeam or another several times since coming aboard. Coupled with the queasiness he'd experienced, especially over the last few days, that had been enough to insure he spent most of his time in his hammock, tippling golden berry and trying to keep down a diet of soft bread and soup.

"I believe the Father's feeling somewhat better, Sir," the lieutenant said after a moment. "He was up on deck shortly after sunset, in fact."

"Good. I'm glad to hear he's feeling better. Maybe he'll even be up to joining us for dinner tomorrow night. Remind me to have the cook prepare something bland."

"Aye, aye, Sir," Kuhlhani said with a broader smile.

Rahdgyrz nodded to the lieutenant, folded his hands behind him, and began pacing slowly up and down the weather side of the poop deck for his nightly constitutional.

The air felt even damper and cooler than it had when he'd come on deck, and the glass had been falling steadily if slowly most of the day. The night promised to be full of rain, but it was unlikely the wind would pick up appreciably, which he was sure both Father Aimohs and young Mistress Zhudyth would appreciate. Although, if he'd been Mistress Zhudyth's parents, he would have voted for heavier weather to keep Rudahry right where he was and well away from them.

Syndail Rahdgyrz had served Mother Church and the Temple for his entire adult life. His own ordination as an under-priest of the Order of Chihiro had come about only because he was a skilled seaman who'd been tapped for command in the Navy of God, but before that, he'd captained Church couriers and transports for almost twenty years. That duty had brought him into contact with more priests, upper-priests, and bishops than he could count, and even a handful of *arch*bishops. As a consequence, he had rather fewer illusions about the Church's priesthood than many, and he'd recognized Aimohs Rudahry's type—and purpose—the instant he'd come aboard.

That was another of the several reasons he was confident *Saint Frydhelm* hadn't "just happened" to be available in Gorath Bay.

Rahdgyrz had nothing at all against the Earl of Thirsk. From everything he'd ever seen or heard, Thirsk was a superior officer who fully deserved the position he held. Although Rahdgyrz had never crossed swords with the Imperial Charisian Navy himself, he'd read

Father Greyghor Searose's heavily edited report on the Battle of the Markovian Sea. He'd also read the available reports on the Battle of Iythria, and he and *Saint Frydhelm* had visited Claw Island after the Dohlarans had retaken it from the heretics. He'd seen how effectively they'd fortified its approaches . . . which also told him a great deal about the fighting qualities of the Charisians who'd taken it back yet again. And all the world had heard about what had happened in the Kaudzhu Narrows. As far as he could tell, Thirsk's navy was the only one on Safehold which had ever given the heretics pause, and it was difficult not to conclude that that was because of the man who'd commanded and trained it.

In a reasonable world, that ought to have earned Thirsk the trust, support, and confidence of Mother Church. In the world that actually existed, things were seldom as clear cut as the *Holy Writ* said they should be, and Father Syndail Rahdgyrz had a very unhappy suspicion about why the obviously close and loving family currently occupying his quarters was bound for Zion.

In a reasonable world, it wouldn't have been his job to take them there. In the world that actually existed . . . .

▼ ▼ ▼

The rain fell steadily—and as heavily as Father Syndail had anticipated—as the night crept past midnight and into Langhorne's Watch. Here and there aboard NGS *Saint Frydhelm* the more zealous members of her crew paused in the prayer and meditation the *Holy Writ* enjoined all faithful sons and daughters of Mother Church to dedicate to the well-being of their souls during that special and sanctified time of the night. In the captain's quarters, Earl Thirsk's family slept soundly, except for young Zhudyth, who tossed fitfully in her seasickness while her mother napped beside her. On the galleon's decks, the duty watch went about their tasks, and high above those decks the masthead lookouts huddled in their oilskins. There was nothing to see in the rainy dark, however hard they might look, but at least the same wretched visibility meant no one else was likely to see them, either.

▼ ▼ ▼

"*Easy* there!" Lieutenant Hektor Aplyn-Ahrmahk called quietly from HMS *Fleet Wing*'s quarterdeck. "Let's not be breaking any legs or—or making any damned noise—we don't have to."

"Sorry, Sir."

The unfortunate seaman who'd slipped on the rain-slick planking and dropped the five-gallon demijohn of hot tea—and the dozen tin mugs—he'd been carrying on deck for the watch standers picked himself up. Miraculously, the heavy clay demijohn's wickerwork jacket had preserved it from breakage. It hadn't even spilled. The tin cups, on the other hand, had burst apart, breaking the string tied through their handles for ease of carry, and gone clattering and rolling into the scuppers.

Now the seaman stood cradling the demijohn in his arms while several of his grinning crewmates rescued the cups.

"Sorry, Sir," he repeated. "Won't happen again, Sir!"

"As long as you're all right, Fewmihyroh," Hektor said, trying not to grin himself, despite the tension ratcheting steadily higher along his nerves. "Just watch where you're going."

"Aye, aye, Sir!"

Fewmihyroh Kaspyr braced to attention, staying that way until Hektor nodded for him to continue on his tea run, and more than one of the other drenched seamen on *Fleet Wing*'s deck turned away or raised hasty hands to hide grins that threatened to get out of control. At nineteen and a half—less than eighteen, in Old Earth years—Fewmihyroh was very young, and he looked it as he faced his commanding officer. That commanding officer, on the other hand, had only turned *seven*teen—

sixteen and a half in Old Earth years—a month and a half earlier. He was also a good four inches shorter than Kaspyr, and might have weighed two-thirds as much.

Yet however amusing his ship's company might have found the tableau, not one of them questioned the Duke of Darcos' right to stand upon that deck as the eighteen-gun schooner's captain. Nor, for that matter, did he look nearly as young as Kaspyr, despite his lack of inches and his wiry build. By now, there might have been five sailors in the entire Imperial Charisian Navy who hadn't heard the story of the duke's rescue of Princess Irys and Prince Daivyn after all his superior officers had been killed or wounded. There couldn't have been *six* of them, however, and the tale of how he'd saved the princess' life a second time on their wedding day was just as widely known.

Everyone knew Baron Sarmouth had stretched naval regulations almost—*almost*—to the breaking point to name someone of Duke Darcos' age to the command of one of Their Majesties' warships. But the ICN's schooners were young men's commands, and "the Duke" (as he was known to the whole squadron, as if there were not another duke in the entire Empire), had amply proved his fitness to command. Courage, even *reckless* courage, youngsters of his age normally had in plenty. The Duke had demonstrated both moral courage, which was far rarer, and the ability to keep his head with cool calculation even in the midst of combat, which was rarer still. Those qualities were there in his eyes for any to see, just as the scars and the stiffened left hand showed the experience which had helped him gain them.

What none of HMS *Fleet Wing*'s crew realized was that he possessed one more quality, even more important than the others at the moment, which had made him the perfect choice for his current command.

Now he watched Kaspyr dispensing hot tea into the rescued mugs with half his attention while the other half stayed glued to the imagery projected onto his contact lenses.

*Soon*, he thought. *Soon.*

▼ ▼ ▼

"Are you sure about this, Merlin?" Nimue Chwaeriau asked softly as the recon skimmer's tractor lowered their fishing boat towards the rain-lashed surface of the Fern Narrows.

Merlin looked at her through the rain, and she reached out to touch his arm.

"I understand the logic," she said. "I just want to be sure you're ready to live with it."

"I am."

Merlin's tone was flat, very unlike his usual speaking voice. And, at the moment, he looked as unlike Merlin Athrawes as Nimue looked unlike Nimue Chwaeriau. Nimue was at least still female, although she'd become a brunette who was rather more full figured than her normal persona, but Merlin was obviously Harchongese.

"If we do it any other way, the consequences for Thirsk will be as bad as they'd have been if he'd tried to fight Clyntahn on this one. I don't say I like it, because I don't, but I understand why it has to be this way."

That wasn't precisely what Nimue had asked, and she studied his expression—daylight clear to her enhanced vision despite the rain and darkness. The basic idea had been hers, but it had been Merlin and Nahrmahn Baytz who'd recognized the most critical component of the entire operation, and she wondered if subconsciously she'd deliberately missed recognizing it herself from the beginning. For that matter, she wondered how much of her concern for Merlin was actually concern for herself. Despite the fact that both of them remembered being Nimue Alban, they were different people now, and she'd seen at least some of what the brutal demands of fighting the Group of Four had cost Merlin Athrawes. Had her subconscious tried to keep her from recognizing the costs of her own plan? To protect her from assuming her share of Merlin's crushing weight of responsibility and regret? And was that the real reason she was so worried about whether or not *he* could deal with it? Or—

*Stop that,* she told herself. *Stop worrying about whether you're projecting things onto him and remember that* he *faced up to the implications squarely as soon as you opened your mouth. If he says he's ready to live with it, then he's ready to live with it, and you damned well owe him the respect of taking his word for it.*

"All right," she said aloud. "In that case I suppose we should be about it."

Merlin nodded, then looked up at the recon skimmer.

"Time to go, Owl," he said.

"Acknowledged, Commander Athrawes," the AI replied, and the fishing boat shuddered as the skimmer's tractor beam eased it into the water.

The tractor didn't release the boat, however. Instead, the skimmer used it to tow the boat through the four-foot seas. With the skimmer's assistance, the forty-foot craft sliced through the waves in a cascade of blown spray, moving twice as rapidly as *Saint Frydhelm*. The fishing boat overtook the galleon rapidly from astern and the two PICAs checked their equipment one last time.

▼ ▼ ▼

"It looks thoroughly unpleasant out there," Lieutenant Zhurgyn Ahlzhernohn remarked, shrugging into his oilskins as he joined Ahntwahn Kuhlhani on the quarterdeck. The tall, narrow poop deck was a roof overhead, protecting them and the helmsmen from the rain—for now, at least—and Kuhlhani nodded in greeting as he turned to Ahlzhernohn and sketched Langhorne's scepter in salute.

"It's not all *that* bad," he said, "but it's miserable enough if you stand around in it for an hour or two.

Which is why I'm so delighted to see my relief arriving promptly, Sir."

"If Captain Hainz didn't snore so loudly, you probably wouldn't have," Ahlzhernohn said acidly, and Kuhlhani chuckled with remarkably little sympathy.

Gyairmoh Hainz commanded the fifteen-man detachment of the Gorath Temple Guard which had been assigned to escort Earl Thirsk's family to Zion. A native Dohlaran, he was in his mid-thirties, tough-minded, disciplined, a pleasant dinner companion, and always perfectly turned out and professional on duty. And at night, he sounded like a sawmill with a faulty waterwheel that stopped and started unpredictably. When Father Syndail handed his quarters over to their passengers, he'd appropriated Ahlzhernohn's cabin. Ahlzhernohn, in turn, had appropriated Ahntwahn Kuhlhani's, and Kuhlhani had moved in with the third lieutenant. Captain Hainz, however, shared the cabin which had once been Kuhlhani's with the first lieutenant.

"Far be it from me to say there's such a thing as poetic justice," Kuhlhani said now, "but if there *were* such a thing as poetic justice, then—"

He broke off, expression puzzled as he heard a sound. Sailing ships underway in a seaway were much noisier places than most landsmen would have believed, but sailors learned to recognize all of those noises. They knew what they were, why they were there, and what caused them. And when they heard one they couldn't identify, it got their attention quickly.

In this case, the sound Lieutenant Kuhlhani couldn't identify was the clatter of a pair of grappling hooks as they arced into the air from astern of the galleon and hooked their prongs over the taffrail on the poop deck above him.

As in most of the Navy of God's galleons, *Saint Frydhelm*'s poop deck was fairly short, forming a roof above the after part of the quarterdeck in a feature adopted from merchant galleon design. In a merchant ship, it provided a raised platform from which to con the ship but, even more importantly, it protected the quarterdeck-mounted wheel from the effects of rain, wind, and—especially—waves in heavy weather. If a ship was pooped, overtaken from astern by a heavy sea, the wave could sweep the full length of her decks, causing serious damage and washing men overboard. It could also wash away the men on the wheel, with potentially catastrophic consequences for control of the ship, especially in the midst of stormy weather. There'd been no galleon warships in the days of pre-Merlin Athrawes artillery, but the war *galley's* sterncastle had served much the same function as the merchant galleon's poop deck and, in addition, protected the men on the wheel from enemy fire.

As galleons were adapted for war, replacing galleys and growing rapidly larger on the seas of a post-Merlin Safehold, average freeboard had increased, raising the level of the quarterdeck (and so decreasing the likelihood of being pooped) while retaining the massive sterncastles could only have made the ships far less weatherly and maneuverable. Charisian naval architects had simply deleted them completely, but the Church's more conservative designers had substituted the merchant galleon's lighter poop deck as a compromise. Charisian experience with captured Church galleons suggested that the poop decks offered little practical defensive advantage and had a measurable negative impact on maneuverability, but the Church and her subject navies had stuck with them.

Most merchant galleons used their longer poop decks as the roofs of cabins built at the quarterdeck level. In *Saint Frydhelm* it simply formed a space—open at the front, closed at the back—almost like a cave, over the wheel, the stern chasers, and the last two guns in each broadside. There was no sternwalk at that level, but there were no lids on the quarterdeck gunports, any more than there were on the spardeck broadside ports. Now the grappling hooks sank their points firmly into the wood of the taffrail at poop deck level, and two figures in the blackened breastplates and hauberks of the Imperial Charisian Guard sailed in through those open stern gunports feet-first, hit the deck, rolled, and came smoothly upright.

If anyone had been watching at that moment, they might have noticed that the guardsmen had actually made no use at all of the grappling hooks. Tractor beams were so much more convenient, after all. Those hooks, like the lines attached to them and the fishing boat towing at the ends of those lines, were there for an entirely different reason.

But no one had been watching. Indeed, Kuhlhani was just beginning to turn towards the rather louder sound of their arrival when Merlin Athrawes squeezed his trigger.

The shotgun in Merlin's hands would have been called a 10-gauge on Old Earth, because a spherical lead bullet for it would have weighed one-tenth of a pound. Its bore was just over three-quarters of an inch in diameter, and each shell was loaded with sixteen of what had once been called "double-ought buckshot."

Each pellet was a separate .32 caliber lead ball, traveling at just over fourteen hundred feet per second. All of them hit the lieutenant squarely in the chest, and he flew backward without even a scream.

Ahlzhernohn whirled. He hadn't heard the grappling hooks, but the thunderous shotgun blast, trapped under the poop deck "roof," hit his ears like a sledgehammer.

He'd made it less than halfway around when Nimue Chwaeriau squeezed *her* trigger.

There were shouts in plenty now. The men on the wheel turned, staring in disbelief at the smoke-shrouded apparitions behind them, and metal clicked as the PICAs worked the shotguns' slides smoothly. Their weapons and ammunition had been manufactured not by the Delthak Works, but by an AI named Owl, and they boasted certain refinements Taigys Mahldyn's designs had not yet attained. One of those refinements was a box magazine which contained eight rounds, and as long as the firer held the trigger back, the Owl-built weapon fired each time the slide was worked.

The amount of carnage a pair of 10-gauge shotguns could wreak, each firing once per second, was indescribable. Every man on the quarterdeck was dead or dying before Ahlzhernohn's body hit the deck and stopped rolling, and Merlin and Nimue stepped across the corpses with faces of stone.

▼ ▼ ▼

*"Mommy!"*

Stefyny Mahkzwail thrashed upright in her hammock as thunder exploded overhead and Lyzet screamed. The other girls jerked awake right with her, and she heard their panicky cries, as well.

"It's all right, Lyzet!" she called, fighting the confinement of her hammock. "It's all right! Mommy's here!"

"What is it?! *What is it?!*"

"I don't know, honey, but Mommy's here!"

She half fell to the deck as she finally escaped the hammock. All three girls were already out of theirs, and they hit her like hunting wyverns striking a rabbit. She staggered at the impact, but she got her arms around them as she went to her knees, hugging them tightly.

"I'm here!" she told them again and again. "*I'm here!* Be brave!"

▼ ▼ ▼

Gyairmoh Hainz was a landsman. He'd never claimed or wanted to be anything else, and while he had to admit free-swinging hammocks were far more comfortable than beds would have been aboard a ship, he hadn't yet acquired the knack of climbing in or out of one of them gracefully. Now he tumbled out of his hammock with all the grace of a pig in swamp mud and landed flat on his backside, but he hardly noticed the impact. He was too busy springing back upright and snatching for his sword belt.

The sounds which had awakened him were the stuff of nightmares, and his blood ran cold as the cacophony of gunfire and the screams of the wounded and dying crashed over him. There'd been rumors that Earl Thirsk's family was being moved to Zion on the Grand Inquisitor's orders because Vicar Zhaspahr was less than confident of the earl's total loyalty to Mother Church and the Jihad. They'd been very quiet, those rumors, whispered only in dark corners, and Father Aimohs had addressed Hainz' entire detachment on that very subject before they ever boarded ship. The rumors, he'd said, were simply untrue. They were to convey the earl's family to Zion because of specific threats against their safety made by the infamous terrorist Dialydd Mab and his murderers, apparently because of the Royal Dohlaran Navy's successes against the heretics. That was the only reason Vicar Zhaspahr and Vicar Allayn had decided they must extend Mother Church's protective hand over them.

To his shame, Hainz had been less than positive Father Aimohs was telling them the truth. He'd hated admitting that to himself, but he couldn't help remembering the stories about how Earl Thirsk had resisted delivering captured heretics to the Inquisition to face the Punishment. And, whether Mother Church wanted to admit it or not, Hainz knew the Jihad was going badly—*very* badly—in Siddarmark. Under the circumstances, Mother Church had to be alert for any sign Dohlar might try to follow Desnair's example. In which case, he'd thought, it was only too possible, even likely, that the rumors about Vicar Zhaspahr's suspicion of the earl were entirely accurate.

Now, as he heard the impossible rapidity of that thunderstorm gunfire, he knew he'd been wrong to doubt.

He flung the sword belt across his shoulder like a bandolier, snatched up the pair of loaded, double-barreled pistols he'd laid ready with his uniform, and dashed for the cabin door barefoot, wearing only the boxer shorts in which he customarily slept.

▼ ▼ ▼

Merlin stepped down the short quarterdeck ladder to the main deck, shotgun held hip high and belching flame. The muzzle flashes were enormous, huge bubbles of blinding light in the darkness and the rain, but they had no effect on *his* vision. He swept the deck with a broom of fire, ejected an empty magazine, slapped in a loaded one, and opened fire once more as the first members of *Saint Frydhelm*'s off-watch crew erupted from the main hatch.

Behind him, Nimue followed down the ladder but turned aft, towards what should have been the captain's quarters. The single rifle-armed Temple Guardsman posted in the vestibule outside the passengers' cabins—solely to protect their privacy, of course—was waiting when she kicked open the doorway under the break of the quarterdeck. He fired as the door flew open and a sledgehammer struck her chest. But the flattened bullet whined viciously as it ricocheted from the battle-steel breastplate, and her PICA's strength shrugged off the impact.

The guardsman goggled in disbelief as his short, obviously female target ignored a direct hit and continued straight towards him. He had time to get his rifle up, to begin a bayonet thrust, but Nimue's left hand darted out. Her right retained its grip on the shotgun; the left twisted the guardsman's rifle, and he started to cry out in shock as she snatched it effortlessly from his grip. He never completed the exclamation; the butt plate of his own rifle, driven horizontally with piledriver force in a one-handed blow, shattered his forehead and killed him in mid-syllable.

▼ ▼ ▼

Syndail Rahdgyrz erupted from his cabin, one deck below Nimue, sword in hand, and almost collided with Gyairmoh Hainz. For an instant, Rahdgyrz glared at the Temple Guardsman. *He* was *Saint Frydhelm*'s captain; it was *his* job to get on deck first! But Hainz wasn't slowing down, and he had a pistol in each hand. Rahdgyrz had only his sword, and the cascade of gunfire told him a sword alone wasn't going to be enough.

He paused for a single heartbeat, letting Hainz bull past him, then followed at a run.

▼ ▼ ▼

*"Pistols!"* Sergeant Sedwei Garzha bawled as the men of Captain Hainz's detachment rolled—and fell—out of their berth deck hammocks, rubbing at sleep-crusted eyes while their brains tried to catch up. All around them, members of the galleon's crew were jerking awake, rolling out, hitting the deck, and his voice rose over the tumult like a trumpet.

"*Take* your fucking *pistols!*" he shouted. "Let's move! *Move, Shan-wei take you!*"

▼ ▼ ▼

Nimue opened the door to the captain's day cabin rather more sedately than the last one she'd encountered. She stepped through it, then stopped suddenly on the threshold. Sir Ahrnahld Mahkzwail and Greyghor Whytmyn might have been sound asleep when the attack began, but they were waiting inside the cabin. Somehow, they'd gotten daggers past the watchful eyes of their "escort," and steel gleamed in their hands as they stood shoulder to shoulder between her and their families. She saw the combined desperation and determination in their postures and expressions, and she raised her left hand quickly, elevating the shotgun muzzle to point at the deckhead instead of them.

"Wait!" she said sharply while Merlin's fire rolled and thundered behind her. "We're not here to hurt you. We're here to *rescue* you!"

Mahkzwail had already begun a hopeless lunge. Now he managed to abort it somehow and skidded to a halt, staring at her. She turned slightly, letting the lamplight fall fully on the blazon of the Charisian Imperial Guard on her breastplate, marred now with a long smear of lead from the sentry's bullet, and his eyes narrowed.

"I don't have time to explain," she said quickly, wondering if that sounded as idiotic to them as it did to her. Of *course* she didn't have time to explain! There was a damned *firefight* going on on deck! "Clyntahn wants you in Zion to control Earl Thirsk. Eventually, he's going to kill the Earl, and both of you know it as well as I do. What do you think Clyntahn's going to do with his children and his grandchildren when that happens?"

The two men darted glances at each other, and she saw the grim recognition in their eyes. They knew exactly what would happen to their wives and children on that day.

"We don't want that to happen," she went on hurriedly. "I don't know exactly what *will* happen; that's going to depend on things no one can predict right now. But Emperor Cayleb and Empress Sharleyan have instructed me to give you their personal word that you and your families will be safe in Charisian custody, no matter what else happens."

Mahkzwail and Whytmyn looked at each other again, and then, in unison, they lowered their daggers. Nimue heaved a huge sigh of relief, PICA or no PICA, and nodded to them.

"Get everyone together in the stern cabin," she said. "Keep them there." She smiled coldly. "No one's getting past me to hurt them."

▼ ▼ ▼

Gyairmoh Hainz charged up the steep ladder to the main hatch and hurled himself through it. He saw a tall, black shape turning towards him, and the double-barreled pistol in his right hand belched fire and recoiled sharply. He rode the recoil, brought it down, reacquired his target, and—

A charge of buckshot hit him in the head, effectively decapitating him, and his corpse fell back down the ladder.

▼ ▼ ▼

Merlin saw Hainz disappear in an explosion of blood, but there was someone else right behind the captain. Whether it was courage, or faith, or simply an instinctive reaction by men who hadn't yet realized what they faced, *Saint Frydhelm*'s crew and Gyairmoh Hainz' guardsmen swarmed up the ladders to defend their ship.

Another shotgun thundered behind him and he knew Nimue had reemerged from beneath the quarterdeck. That was her position, her task: to be the fortress between Thirsk's family and any threat, and nothing was going to move her. He'd seen her expression when he laid out the plan for this attack, known she realized why he'd assigned her to guard the civilians. She'd wanted to protest, but she hadn't, and he'd been grateful.

But that didn't mean she couldn't watch his back, and her shotgun bellowed again and again.

He advanced on the main hatch, working the slide, firing another round each time his right foot came down, ripping the mass of men trying to reach him with fire and gunsmoke and lead. He drove them back into the hatch, then down the ladder. He hit the release button inside the trigger guard and another empty magazine dropped free. He reloaded on the fly, worked the slide, squeezed the trigger, and reached the edge of the hatch. Pistol fire ripped up at him as he silhouetted himself against the dim glow of the deck lights. At least half a dozen bullets hit his breastplate or hauberk and ricocheted, and his eyes were pitiless, frozen sapphire come fresh from the heart of hell as he fired straight down the hatch into the crowded men at the foot of the ladder again and again.

▼ ▼ ▼

Syndail Rahdgyrz went down as a charge of buckshot amputated his right leg at the knee. The same buckshot killed another man and wounded two others, and Sergeant Garzha flew backward with the next racketing blast. The deck was hot and steamy-slick with blood, the bodies heaped at the foot of the ladder blocked it like some crazed butcher's barricade, and *still* that implacable black shape towered above the hatch, raining death down upon them.

Rahdgyrz saw it happening. He felt the blood—and life—pumping from his shattered leg, felt the darkness coming down, and in those fading moments, he saw his crew break. Saw them realize no one could dare that hatch and live. Saw them falling back.

"Open the armory, lads!" he said weakly. "Get to the muskets! Get to—"

His world dwindled into darkness.

No one heard him at all.

▼ ▼ ▼

"That's right, Gyffry," Stefyny Mahkzwail said encouragingly. "Just slide down the rope, like the *seijin* says."

As she'd hoped, the word "*seijin*" worked its charm. Gyffry had all of any eleven-year-old boy child's fascination with fantastic tales and bloody adventures. *Seijins* were a staple of his favorite stories, and the exotic dark-haired, armored woman smiling as she effortlessly boosted him over the sternwalk rail to reach the rope hanging down from the taffrail was the very embodiment of those selfsame stories.

Stefyny was grateful the *seijin* had been able to return to them, leaving the deck to her companion, and she was grateful for the strength of the arms lifting Gyffry, yet her heart was in her throat as her son shinnied down the knotted line. Ahrnahld had gone first, with four-year-old Zhosifyn strapped tightly to his back, sliding down to steady the rope and catch anyone who slipped on their own way to the *seijins'* fishing boat. Mahgdylynah Harpahr had gone second, displaying a surprising agility for someone in her fifties, and she stood in the boat as it rose and fell on the waves, with one arm around Ahlyxzandyr, who'd been the first of the children to dare the descent, and the other around Zhosifyn.

Stefyny had no idea where this night's madness was likely to end, and part of her screamed to turn around, to retreat from the *seijins*' false promises of safety. They served Cayleb and Sharleyan of Charis. Surely they hoped only to find a way to use her family against her father! And even if they didn't—her father had always said Cayleb was an honorable man, so perhaps they wouldn't—what about her children's *souls*? If Mother Church was right, these weren't *seijins*; they were demons, claiming to be the reincarnation of those ancient champions of God and the Archangels only so that they might entice ever more souls into damnation!

Yet at this time, in this world, Mother Church spoke with *Zhaspahr Clyntahn*'s voice, not God's. She believed that—she *knew* that—just as she knew why Clyntahn had wanted her, and her sisters, and their children in Zion. And so, even as terror pulled her in one direction, reason and courage drove her towards those ropes and that wave-surging fishing boat.

"Help me tie this."

She turned towards Zhoahna's voice. Hailyn had Zhudyth on her back, clinging like a terrified spider monkey, and Stefyny smiled at her niece as bravely as she could. She kissed the little girl on the top of her head, then helped Zhoahna loop the rope around Hailyn and Zhudyth and tied it with one of the knots their sailor father had taught them as children.

"Never thought it would come in handy *this* way," she said.

"Me neither," Hailyn agreed as Zhoahna ran another rope around her, under her armpits, and tied it off, as well.

Stefyny double-checked her own knot and met her youngest sister's eyes. Zhoahna's expression was grim and as frightened as her own, yet she seemed less worried about trusting Cayleb Ahrmahk's emissaries than any of the other adults. It was odd, Stefyny thought, but then she'd always admired and secretly envied the serenity of her sister's faith. Perhaps that was what lent her the calm acceptance to navigate through this night's screaming madness?

"Greyghor!" she called, and her brother-in-law appeared beside her. He reached out to cup the back of his daughter's head in one hand, then kissed Hailyn and took the rope from Stefyny.

"All right, love," he told Hailyn. "I've got both of you. Climb down the line, and I'll steady you. You can't fall as long as I hold on, and you know I'll hold on no matter what."

"Of course we do," Hailyn said very firmly, as much or more for Zhudyth's benefit as for herself. "Ready, baby?"

"Y-yes, Ma'am," Zhudyth said in a tiny voice, and Hailyn backed over the sternwalk rail holding the knotted climbing rope, and started down it.

Behind them, a shotgun boomed again, and then again, as the *seijin* still holding the deck covered their flight.

"Lots of time, honey," Stefyny said, hugging Kahrmyncetah against her side. "Lots of time."

▼ ▼ ▼

"Time to go," Nimue's voice said over Merlin's built-in communicator.

His eyes never flickered, never stopped their sweep of the body-choked ladder to the main hatch or the bulwark of bodies he'd piled around the fore hatch when they'd tried a pincer up both approaches. A dozen of them had tried climbing out gunports and scaling the ship's side, as well, but the hovering SNARC had spotted them, and his merciless shotgun had been waiting when they topped the bulwark.

They'd gotten to the ship's armory, and he'd been hit at least fifteen more times now. A remote corner of his brain, somewhere down below the icy control he'd fastened upon himself, said the defenders deserved far better than those bullets had accomplished. His armor and antiballistic clothing had stopped all of them, not that they could have significantly damaged a PICA even if they'd gotten through.

No one seemed willing to risk another rush, yet they hadn't given up entirely. They knew he was the most deadly enemy any of them had ever faced, that not a single man who'd gone up one of those hatches had survived, yet even now they had the courage to try yet again. They weren't whispering to each other down there in the bloody, reeking, slaughterhouse horror which had once been a galleon's gundeck because they'd given up. They were trying to come up with a plan that would work.

But they were out of time for planning.

He didn't have to look away from the hatches, away from the bodies. The images Owl projected into his vision showed him Nimue sliding down the rope one-handed, the other arm crooked around Kahrmyncetah Gardynyr while Stefyny Mahkzwail and Zhoahna Gardynyr stood on the fishing boat's deck reaching up to receive their niece. Nimue and Kahrmyncetah were the last. Now Merlin stood alone on *Saint Frydhelm*'s bloody deck, and he backed steadily towards the stern.

"Ready, Owl?" he asked over the com.

"Yes, Commander Athrawes," the AI replied, and Merlin grunted in satisfaction.

While everyone's attention had been concentrated on him and Nimue, four of Owl's smallest remotes had crept stealthily aboard the ship and spiked the vents of *Saint Frydhelm*'s upperdeck guns. None of them that could be used against the fishing boat, assuming anyone thought of that and was prepared to kill Thirsk's family in order to prevent them from being "kidnapped."

Of course, they wouldn't have very long to think about it.

He passed the wheel, which was lashed to hold the galleon on a steady course. That had been Nimue's work, and he nodded approval as he reached the after end of the quarterdeck and the open ports for the chasers.

*This would all have been a lot simpler if we didn't need an explanation for the Mahkzwails and the Whytmyns,* he thought. *But the butcher's bill would be the same in the end, either way. Maybe it's only fair we have to get the blood on our own hands directly.*

He slung the shotgun across his back, bent and stepped through the porthole, gripped the rope in one hand, and slid swiftly down it. By the time his boots hit the deck, Nimue had cut the lines tethering the fishing boat to the galleon and *Saint Frydhelm* began to draw rapidly away into the night. Merlin turned towards the tiller, then paused, and Nimue grinned at him.

"One advantage of rescuing an admiral's family!" she said almost gaily, flinging out an arm in a broad, sweeping gesture, and Merlin had to nod. He and Nimue could have managed the twin-masted fishing boat just fine by themselves; it was actually smaller than the yacht Nimue Alban had sailed a thousand years ago on another planet. But Thirsk's sons-in-law and the two older boys clearly knew what they were doing. Sir Ahrnahld was at the tiller, and he put it hard over, bearing away to the southwest and taking the wind on the starboard beam while Greyghor Whytmyn, Gyffry, and Ahlyxzandyr managed the sails. The fishing boat was only fifty-five feet long, but she was much younger—and faster—than her unprepossessing appearance might have led the casual observer to assume. She was actually only two five-days old, her artfully aged hull's lines taken from something called a "pilot boat schooner" from Old Earth. She was made for speed in moderate and light weather, and she heeled sharply as she went scudding through the waves.

"I see what you mean," he said.

He stood beside Nimue for several minutes, watching the galleon fade into the rain in the darkness. Then, once it had disappeared completely, beyond even the reach of his enhanced vision, he turned to Stefyny, Hailyn, and Zhoahna. The sisters stood side by side, facing him warily, and he bowed.

"I wish your children had never had to see or

experience any of this," he told them quietly, sincerely. "In the end, however, what they would have seen—what they would have experienced at Clyntahn's hands—would have been far worse. And as my companion's already told you, you have Emperor Cayleb and Empress Sharleyan's personal guarantee of your safety."

"She also promised we wouldn't be used against our father," Stefyny said, and Merlin's enhanced vision saw the fear, the despair, in her eyes despite the darkness. "And maybe you won't actually *use* us against him. But how do you think Clyntahn's going to react when he hears you've 'rescued' us? He's certain to assume you *will* use us . . . and that Father will do whatever you tell him to to keep us safe."

"But Clyntahn won't hear anything of the sort," Merlin assured her.

"Don't *lie* to me!" Stefyny snapped, her sudden fury fanned to a white heat that astounded even her as all of the night's terror and fear whiplashed through her. "Of course he'll hear! As soon as that ship makes port—"

The night turned into terrifying dawn.

▼ ▼ ▼

NGS *Saint Frydhelm* was three miles away from the fishing boat, her surviving crew creeping cautiously back up onto her decks. They went warily, expecting another deadly fusillade of shotgun blasts, but there was nothing, and their surviving officers and petty officers began shouting orders. Discipline reasserted itself, order grew out of chaos, and men ran to the braces while the galleon's fourth lieutenant gathered his helmsmen. They had no idea where their attackers had gone—none of them had actually seen the fishing boat—but unless they truly had been assailed by Shanwei's own demons, there had to be a boat out there *somewhere* in the darkness. If they could find it, all the shotguns in the world wouldn't protect it from a forty-gun galleon's broadside.

Unfortunately, none of them noticed the stealthed recon skimmer hovering far above them.

Merlin Athrawes had learned a bitter lesson in helplessness when Sir Gwyllym Manthyr's men were consigned to the Punishment. He'd been unable to sink the ships on which they were transported for the overwater portion of the trip, unable to give them the far more merciful death of drowning. There'd been several reasons for that, but one of them had been the very high probability that the emissions of his skimmer's normal energy weapons would have been detected by the sensors serving the orbital bombardment platform. There'd been no way to predict how the bombardment system might have reacted to that, and so he'd been powerless to intervene. But he'd also been determined that would never happen again, and so the remotes in Nimue's Cave had built the skimmer an anachronistic nose gun—a multi-barreled auto-cannon—to replace its original internal weapons. And to go with it, those same remotes had produced a small stock of ancient, laser-guided bombs. They were loaded only with old-fashioned chemical explosives, but Owl had built them in several sizes . . . including a two-thousand-pound version filled with half a ton of explosives far better than anything Sahndrah Lywys had ever produced.

In this instance, however, a rather smaller weapon would do.

▼ ▼ ▼

Stefyny and Hailyn, and every member of their families, whirled back to the north as the five-hundred-pound bomb punched through *Saint Frydhelm*'s decks as if they'd been made of paper. It detonated squarely in the galleon's magazine, surrounded by fifteen tons of gunpowder, and a pillar of fire raged into the heavens.

The long, echoing roll of thunder rolled over them fourteen seconds later.

▼ ▼ ▼

"That's what we been waiting for, boys!" Lieutenant Aplyn-Ahrmahk announced as the column of flame flashed against the darkness.

The rain reduced visibility, but not enough to keep *Fleet Wing*'s company from seeing the explosion when he'd been able to con the schooner to within five and a half miles before the bomb struck. And not when the explosion was that vast, that brilliant.

"Come to north-by-northeast, Master Slokym," he said, bending over the compass card and then straightening.

"North-by-northeast, aye, Sir!" the sailing master responded, and Hektor turned to Zosh Hahlbyrstaht, *Fleet Wing*'s first lieutenant.

"Go forward and . . . encourage the lookouts, Zosh," he said with a smile. "I'm sure they're already as alert as we could possibly ask for, but it never hurts to show them we care."

"On my way." Hahlbyrstaht agreed with a nod and an answering grin, and Hektor turned back to his helmsman. It wouldn't do to steer *straight* to Merlin and Nimue's fishing boat, but his lookouts were just as alert as he'd suggested. It was unlikely they'd miss the boat's masthead light, even in the rain, when he swept past within a few hundred yards or so . . . and if they did, Merlin had three of the Imperial Charisian Navy's signal rockets on board.

*You're not the only one on your way, Zosh,* the Duke of Darcos told himself silently. *You're not the only one.*

# OCTOBER
# YEAR OF GOD 897

✦

# . I .

## The Earl of Thirsk's Townhouse,
## City of Gorath,
## Kingdom of Dohlar

The rain pounded down as winter extended its grip over the city of Gorath. The drops hammered on slate roofs and clay shingles, and waterfalls cascaded from the eaves. Rivers ran down gutters and downspouts and gurgled down street drains. The torrents poured into the Gorath River, carrying refuse and debris with them, swelling the river dangerously toward the top of its confining embankments, and the night was a black, wet mystery that swallowed the feeble illumination of oil-fed street lamps like a monster.

The raw, drenching chill was worse, more enervating, than a fiercer, harder cold might have been. Not that there wasn't more than sufficient cold and the first heavy snows of winter farther north, where the Mighty Host of God and the Archangels hunkered in its entrenched positions and the Imperial Charisian Army and Republic of Siddarmark Army settled into winter quarters of their own. Behind the advanced Charisian and Siddarmarkian positions, engineers and fatigue parties continued to labor frantically, racing the inevitable frozen ground of October in their efforts to complete repairs to the canal system and high roads the Church's retreating armies had destroyed in their wake. Along the line of the Sheryl-Seridahn Canal, shoulders hunched in rain-lashed, muddy misery, the dug-in Royal Dohlaran Army faced the steady, pounding pressure of the Earl of Hanth's reinforced Army of Thesmar.

And in the study of a Gorath townhouse, a man who'd lost everything he'd loved sat staring into the fire on his hearth with a half-empty whiskey bottle at his elbow.

It was very quiet. He heard the crisp, steady ticking of the clock even through the drum of rain, and the fire crackled and seethed softly. Those were the only sounds, a background that perfected the vaster, echoing stillness behind them. The voices of his daughters, his sons-in-law, and—always and especially—his grandchildren haunted his memory, but those voices would never stir his house's silence again. The residual pain in his shoulder, the dull and unyielding ache of knitting bones that would never be quite the same again, was nothing beside that deeper, infinitely more bitter anguish.

The Earl of Thirsk closed his eyes, raised his glass, and threw back another swallow. The expensive whiskey, undiluted by water or ice, might have been the cheapest rum from some tumbledown dockside tavern. Its false promise of oblivion seared its way down his throat, but he'd always had a hard head. When he'd been younger and more foolish, he'd prided himself on his ability to drink other men, men twice his size, under the table. Now, when he longed for the forgetfulness—or at least the stupor—of drunkenness it was hard to come by.

"Will there be anything else, My Lord?" a quiet voice asked.

The earl hadn't heard the study door open. He didn't turn his head as the voice spoke. He only swallowed more whiskey.

"No, Paiair," he said flatly.

Paiair Sahbrahan stood in the open doorway for a long, still moment gazing at the man sitting before the fire. No one who'd ever had the misfortune to deal with the Earl of Thirsk's irascible valet would have accused Sahbrahan of sensitivity or anything remotely approaching sentimentality. But the look in the sharp-edged little valet's eyes at that moment might have given those people pause. There was helplessness in those eyes, and grief. Not simply for the man he'd served for so many years, either. His memory, too, heard those youthful voices neither of them would ever hear again in this world, and he longed—needed—to comfort the earl.

And he couldn't. No one could, not where this wound cut into the very soul of him.

"I'll be in the pantry, My Lord. If you need me, just ring."

"No," that stark, defeated voice said. "Go to bed. There's no point your sitting up, too."

"I—"

"I said go to bed!" Thirsk flared suddenly, never looking away from the fire. "I'm not in the habit of repeating myself. Do I need to find myself a valet who *understands* that?!"

"No, My Lord," Sahbrahan said after a moment. "No, you don't. Good night, My Lord."

He withdrew, closing the door soundlessly behind him, and Thirsk finished the whiskey in his glass. He set it on the table beside his chair, uncapped the whiskey bottle with his good hand, poured, and set the bottle back down. He took another swallow, and a corner of his mind jeered at him for taking out his own pain, a tiny fraction of his vast anger, upon Sahbrahan.

*Tomorrow*, he told that corner drearily. *You'll have to make it up to him somehow tomorrow. Assuming you're unfortunate enough to be sober in the morning.*

The self-pity in the thought cut deep, but he'd taken too much at last.

He'd given all he had to the resurrection and the re-creation of his navy. He'd fought the bureaucratic battles, made the enemies, known the men he'd infuriated would turn upon him and repay all his effort and labor with his own destruction the instant the Jihad no longer required his services. He'd sent the men and officers under his command off to fight an enemy whose weapons were always superior to their own, and they'd won the victories no other navy had. He'd risked the Inquisition's ire to protect men like Dynnys Zhwaigair because of how desperately his navy—and Mother Church herself—needed them. He'd sacrificed even his honor, standing by, acquiescing in the shameful surrender of honorably surrendered men to the vindictive savagery of Zhaspahr Clyntahn because his fealty to his king, his obedience to God's Church, had required even that of him.

And now, at the end of it all, he sat broken and alone, wishing with all his heart and soul that the bullet fired by the most gallant and loyal man he'd ever known had killed him where he stood. That it had spared him the knowledge of the price Ahlvyn Khapahr had paid to protect him, to *cover* for him. If it had, if he'd died that day with Ahlvyn, then perhaps the family Ahlvyn had given his own life trying to save might have survived. If he'd died, Clyntahn would have required no lever to use against him, and so his daughters could have buried him with honor in the family tomb, beside his beloved wife, and they would have been *safe*.

He swallowed more whiskey, cradling the memory of his dead, mourning the sacrifice of honor, integrity, and love Mother Church had inflicted upon him, and wondered why he hadn't ended his own life.

Stywyrt Baiket and *Chihiro* had personally led the squadron which had been sent to search the waters of the Fern Narrows. Thirsk had wanted to lead the search himself, but the horrendous damage to his shoulder had prevented that. The healers wouldn't hear of his leaving their care, and he'd been too weak, too diminished, to fight them over it. Besides, as Baiket and Staiphan Maik had pointed out when they joined their arguments to the healers', there was absolutely no proof—then—that anything was truly amiss. All they had was the unsupported report of a single fisherman that a ship had blown up in the Narrows. They didn't even have the man who'd supposedly seen it happen.

The fisherman had given his report to the commanding officer of the battery—if it wasn't abusing a perfectly good noun to call a half-dozen twenty-five-pounders and a garrison of old men and boys, all under the orders of a fifty-year-old lieutenant with one leg and one eye, a "battery"—placed to protect the small fishing town of Azhinkor. Thirsk couldn't think of a single reason Azhinkor might need protecting, any more than he could think of a Charisian threat which might be deterred by that pathetic defense, yet it was still a military outpost—of sorts, at least—and most fishermen had as little as possible to do with the military or any other branch of officialdom. Yet this one had sought out the lieutenant to inform him that he'd seen an "explosion like one o' the Rakurai its own self, if you take my meanin', Sir" through the previous night's rain.

Azhinkor was too small to be tied into the Church's semaphore chain, but the lieutenant had sent a runner to the nearest station of the coastal chain and the report had reached Gorath within hours. By the time instructions to query the fisherman for more details had gotten back to Azhinkor, of course, the man had disappeared out to sea once more, duty done and probably congratulating himself for having made a clean break of it.

Maik and Baiket might have argued that there'd been no reason to assume the explosion—if there'd actually been one in the first place—had to be *Saint Frydhelm*, but Thirsk had known. From the instant he'd heard the initial report, he'd known. If there truly had been an explosion as violent as the one the fisherman had described, it could only have been a warship's magazine. Nothing else carried enough gunpowder to explain something like that. And there'd been only one war galleon in the Fern Narrows that night.

And so the squadron had been sent out—ten galleons, a dozen schooners, and all eight of the new screwgalleys in Gorath. He'd been strong enough to stand at his window in the Pasqualates' Saint Sysaroh's Hospital and watch their sails depart. He'd known the men of his navy would do everything in their power; he'd also known there would be nothing they *could* do.

Baiket had crowded on all the sail his ships could carry, and they'd been favored with a fresh, favorable wind. And as Thirsk had known they would, they'd been too late. They'd found a few drifting bits of wreckage, and lucky to find even that, and half a dozen bodies had washed ashore near Azhinkor. That was all the sea had given up. But the bodies had worn the uniform of the Navy of God, and so whatever they hadn't had before the search fleet sailed, they'd had confirmation in plenty before it returned.

*Saint Frydhelm* had been three days overdue before Baiket ever reached its search area. By the time *Chihiro* and her captain returned to Gorath, the official messages of condolence from Zion had already begun coming in by semaphore.

They'd been wormwood and gall, choking him with fury and despair. His family—his *family*—had been taken from him, put aboard that ship, and *died* because Zhaspahr Clyntahn had wanted to control him, and now that bastard was sending him *condolences* for his loss. The official Church version of what had happened only made it still worse. The Inquisition reported that *Saint Frydhelm* had been attacked by half a dozen heretic galleons and fought gallantly until she blew up in action, sinking one of the heretics who'd come alongside just before the explosion. His agents inquisitor behind the heretics' lines, spying upon God's enemies at deadly peril to their own lives, had secured that information from the heretics themselves, Clyntahn asserted.

No doubt at least some of Mother Church's children would actually believe that. For the Earl of Thirsk, it was only one more example of Zhaspahr Clyntahn's cynical deceit, his casual murder of the truth whenever it suited his purposes. It didn't matter to Clyntahn how preposterous a lie might be. Indeed, Thirsk had come to the conclusion that Clyntahn had decided Mother Church's faithful were more likely to believe a falsehood because it was so preposterous it *had* to be true.

After all, everyone knew truth was stranger than fiction, and surely Mother Church, the keeper of men's souls, would never knowingly lie to her children!

The earl knew better. The fisherman had reported the explosion; if any other galleons had been involved, he could scarcely have missed the smoky thunder and blinding flashes of their broadsides, rain or no rain. Not if he'd been close enough to see the explosion itself. Even Clyntahn had to know that, although he supposed it was remotely possible the Grand Inquisitor might think for as much as twenty or thirty seconds that Thirsk could actually believe Charis had been responsible somehow for the galleon's spontaneous explosion.

He hadn't publicly denounced the story of Charisian warships. Not yet. Baiket and Ahbail Bahrdailahn—even Bishop Staiphan—knew what he truly thought, but he'd managed, somehow, not to say as much to another single soul. As long as he didn't challenge Clyntahn's fabrication, the Grand Inquisitor might take his silence as yet another acquiescence. Might interpret Thirsk's failure to contest the Inquisition's version of events as a flag of surrender . . . or perhaps simply the despair of a beaten and broken old man in whose heart grief and despair had crushed any dream of defiance.

It was unlikely the Grand Inquisitor would accept that for very long. If he hadn't already, he would quickly realize that the loss of his family had removed the only sword the Inquisition truly had to hold over Thirsk's head. And when he realized that, he would take action to remove the threat the earl might well have become.

*If I really wanted to survive*, he thought now, harshly, staring into the fire while the whiskey burned his tongue, *I'd tell the bastard I didn't believe for a moment there'd been any "heretics" involved in the actual explosion . . . but that it didn't matter. That if the Charisians hadn't begun the Jihad by their defiance of Mother Church, if they hadn't sent all the world to war, and if their agents hadn't corrupted Ahlvyn—may God receive him as His own—then Mother Church wouldn't have felt compelled to take them to Zion to protect them from Dialydd Mab and his "terrorists." Clyntahn would probably be smart enough to realize I was lying out my arse when I blamed Charis and not him, but as long as I said it, as long as I acted as if I believed it, he'd probably leave me in command of the Navy . . . and alive. Until I did the first thing he could conceivably interpret as "betrayal," at least.*

He had another two or three five-days before the healers would certify him as fit to return to duty. If he wanted to be allowed to return, though, he should probably start publicly blaming the Charisians soon. But he didn't have the heart. He just . . . didn't. Deep down inside, the man he'd once been, the man who'd faced Cayleb Ahrmahk after the Battle of Crag Reach, who'd thrown himself into the rebuilding of the Royal Dohlaran Navy—*that* man—cried out that he had to. That it was time—*past* time—that he stood up to redeem the honor Zhaspahr Clyntahn's butchery had befouled forever with blood and betrayal. That now, when no one could ever harm his family again, he was free to decide what the ghost of his murdered honor and God Himself demanded of him and to do it. And for that to happen, he had to survive.

But he paid no attention to the man he'd once been, because that man was dead. That man was broken beyond repair. That man no longer cared, and the man who was left in his place was willing for all the world to go down in wrack and ruin because God had allowed Mother Church to take every person in the world he loved away from him. And so he sat in front of the fire, drinking whiskey instead, and cherished his anguish because it was the only thing he had left.

A hinge creaked behind him, and sudden fury washed through him. He slammed the whiskey glass down on the table so hard it shattered, and alcohol stung in the cut on his palm as he flung himself up out of his chair and wheeled towards the door and the valet who'd dared to defy him.

"I damned well *told* you to—!"

Shock cut him off like a garrote.

He knew that man. Anyone would have recognized that scarred cheek, those unearthly eyes and that dagger beard, from Mother Church's own newspapers and broadsheets, from her fiery denunciations and anathemas. But the Earl of Thirsk needed no one else's description. He'd seen him with his own eyes, in the admiral's cabin of a galleon named HMS *Dreadnought* on the morning after the Battle of Crag Reach, standing at Crown Prince Cayleb Ahrmahk's shoulder. Yet he couldn't be *here*, couldn't have walked through the very heart of Gorath in the blackened armor blazoned with the colors of the Empire of Charis. He . . . simply couldn't.

But the intruder seemed unaware that he couldn't be there. He only bowed deeply, then straightened and stroked one fiercely waxed mustachio. His sapphire eyes met the earl's incredulous stare as levelly as they had aboard that Charisian galleon six years and a dozen lifetimes before, and his deep, resonant voice was preposterously calm.

"Forgive me for intruding, My Lord," Merlin Athrawes said, "but you and I need to talk."

# Characters

Book title abbreviations:

ABERNETHY, AUXILIARY BISHOP ERNYST—Schuelerite upper-priest; Bishop Militant Bahrnabai Wyrshym's assigned intendant, MT&T.

ABERNETHY, CAPTAIN BRYXTYN, Imperial Charisian Navy—CO, bombardment ship HMS *Earthquake*, 24, LAMA.

ABYKRAHMBI, GENERAL TYMAHN, Imperial Charisian Army—CO, 10th Infantry Division, 2nd Corps, Army of the Daivyn, HFQ.

ABYKRAHMBI, KLYMYNT—an assistant to Brygham Cartyr in the Charisian technical support mission to the Republic of Siddarmark, LAMA.

ABYKRAHMBI, PLATOON SERGEANT CHESTYR, Royal Dohlaran Army—senior noncom, 2nd Platoon, 5th Company, Sheldyn's Regiment, Army of the Seridahn, HFQ.

ABYKRAHMBI, TAHLMA—Klymynt Abykrahmbi's wife, LAMA.

ABYLYN, CHARLZ—a senior leader of the Temple Loyalists in Charis, BSRA.

AHBAHT, CAPTAIN RUHSAIL, Imperial Desnairian Navy—

CO, HMS *Archangel Chihiro*, 40; Commodore Wailahr's flag captain, HFAF.

**AHBAHT, CAPTAIN SIR BRUHSTAIR**, Imperial Charisian Navy—CO, broadside ironclad HMS *Thunderer*, 30, LAMA.

**AHBAHT, LYWYS**—Edmynd Walkyr's brother-in-law; XO, merchant galleon *Wind*, BSRA.

**AHBAHT, ZHEFRY**—Earl Gray Harbor's personal secretary. He fulfills many of the functions of an undersecretary of state for foreign affairs, BSRA. Same post for Trahvys Ohlsyn, HFAF.

**AHBRAIMS, MAJOR KREG**, Imperial Charisian Army—CO, 1st Battalion, 9th Mounted Regiment, 5th Mounted Brigade, Imperial Charisian Army, LAMA.

**AHDYMS, COLONEL TAHLYVYR**—Temple Loyalist ex-militia officer; "General" Erayk Tympyltyn's executive officer, Fort Darymahn, South March Lands, Republic of Siddarmark, MT&T.

**AHDYMS, ERAYK**—a junior partner and associate of Zhak Hahraimahn who serves on the Council of Manufactories, LAMA.

**AHDYMSYN, BISHOP EXECUTOR ZHERALD**—Erayk Dynnys' bishop executor, OAR. Now one of Archbishop Maikel's senior auxiliary bishops, HFAF.

**AHDYMSYN, CAPTAIN MOHRTYN**, Army of God—Major Zhefytha Chestyrtyn's second-in-command in the Camp Lairays guard force, HFQ.

**AHDYMSYN, FATHER BRYNTYN**—a Schuelerite under-priest; pre-Sword of Schueler schoolmaster in Maiyam, later appointed as Colonel Lyndahr Tahlyvyr's intendant, LAMA.

**AHLAIXSYN, RAIF**—well-to-do Siddarmarkian poet and dilettante; a Reformist, HFAF.

**AHLBAIR, EDWYRD**—Earl of Dragon Hill, MT&T.

**AHLBAIR, LIEUTENANT ZHEROHM**, Royal Charisian Navy—first lieutenant, HMS *Typhoon*, OAR.

**AHLBYRTSYN, COLONEL RAIF**, Imperial Charisian Army—CO, 2nd Scout Sniper Regiment, Imperial Charisian Army, LAMA.

AHLDARM, MAHRYS OHLARN—Mahrys IV, Emperor of Desnair, HFAF.

AHLGYRNAHN, COLONEL KYNT, Republic of Siddarmark Army—CO, 63rd Infantry Regiment, 3rd Brigade, 2nd Rifle Division, 2nd Corps, Army of New Northland, HFQ.

AHLKOFAHRDOH, LIEUTENANT CAHNYR, Royal Dohlaran Army—XO, HMS *Tide*, 52, HFQ.

AHLVAI, CAPTAIN MAHLYK, Imperial Desnairian Navy—CO, HMS *Emperor Zhorj*, 48; Baron Jahras' flag captain, HFAF.

AHLVEREZ, ADMIRAL-GENERAL FAIDEL, Royal Dohlaran Navy—Duke of Malikai; King Rahnyld IV of Dohlar's senior admiral, OAR.

AHLVEREZ, SIR RAINOS, Royal Desnairian Army—senior Dohlaran field commander in the Republic of Siddarmark, MT&T; CO of the Dohlaran component of the Army of Shiloh. First cousin of Faidel Ahlverez, Duke of Malikai.

AHLWAIL, BRAIHD—Father Paityr Wylsynn's valet, HFAF.

AHLYXZANDYR, MAJOR TRAI, Royal Dohlaran Army—CO, 1st Company, Ahzbyrn's Regiment (cavalry), part of Sir Rainos Ahlverez' component of the Army of Shiloh. Age 30 and 896, LAMA.

AHLZHERNOHN, LIEUTENANT ZHURGYN, Navy of God—XO, NGS *Saint Frydhelm*, 40, HFQ.

AHNDAIRS, TAILAHR—a Charisian-born Temple Loyalist living in the Temple Lands recruited for Operation Rakurai, HFAF.

AHRBUKYL, TROOPER SVYNSYN, Army of God—one of Corporal Howail Brahdlai's scouts, 191st Cavalry Regiment, MT&T.

AHRDYN—Archbishop Maikel's cat-lizard, BSRA.

AHRMAHK, CAYLEB ZHAN HAARAHLD BRYAHN—son of King Haarahld VII of Charis, Duke of Ahrmahk, Prince of Tellesberg, Crown Prince of Charis, OAR. Prince Protector of the Realm, King Cayleb II of Charis, Emperor Cayleb I of Charis and member of

Charisian inner circle. Husband of Sharleyan Ahrmahk, BSRA.

AHRMAHK, CROWN PRINCE ZHAN—see Zhan Ahrmahk.

AHRMAHK, CROWN PRINCESS ALAHNAH ZHANAYT NAIMU—infant daughter of Cayleb and Sharleyan Ahrmahk; heir to the imperial Charisian crown, MT&T.

AHRMAHK, EMPEROR CAYLEB—Emperor of Charis (see Cayleb Zhan Haarahld Bryahn Ahrmahk), BSRA.

AHRMAHK, KAHLVYN CAYLEB—Kahlvyn Ahrmahk's younger son, younger brother of Duke of Tirian, Cayleb Ahrmahk's first cousin once removed, OAR.

AHRMAHK, KAHLVYN—Duke of Tirian, Constable of Hairatha; King Haarahld VII's first cousin; traitor and attempted usurper (deceased), OAR.

AHRMAHK, KING CAYLEB II—King of Charis (see Cayleb Zhan Haarahld Bryahn Ahrmahk), BSRA.

AHRMAHK, KING HAARAHLD VII—Duke of Ahrmahk, Prince of Tellesberg, King of Charis, member of Charisian inner circle, KIA Battle of Darcos Sound, OAR.

AHRMAHK, PRINCESS ZHANAYT—see Zhanayt Ahrmahk.

AHRMAHK, QUEEN ZHANAYT—King Haarahld's deceased wife; mother of Cayleb, Zhanayt, and Zhan, BSRA.

AHRMAHK, RAYJHIS—Cayleb Ahrmahk's first cousin once removed, elder son of Kahlvyn Ahrmahk, becomes Duke of Tirian, Constable of Hairatha, OAR.

AHRMAHK, SHARLEYAN ALAHNAH ZHENYFYR AHLYSSA TAYT—Duchess of Cherayth, Lady Protector of Chisholm, Queen of Chisholm, Empress of Charis; wife of Cayleb Ahrmahk, BSRA. Member of Charisian inner circle, BHD. See also Sharleyan Tayt. See also Empress Sharleyan.

AHRMAHK, ZHAN—younger son of King Haarahld VII, OAR; younger brother of King Cayleb, younger brother and heir of Emperor Cayleb, betrothed husband of Princess Mahrya Baytz of Emerald, BSRA.

**AHRMAHK, ZHANAYT**—Cayleb Ahrmahk's younger sister, second eldest child of King Haarahld VII, OAR.

**AHRMAHK, ZHENYFYR**—Dowager Duchess of Tirian; mother of Kahlvyn Cayleb Ahrmahk; daughter of Rayjhis Yowance, Earl Gray Harbor, OAR.

**AHRNAHLD, SPYNSAIR**—Empress Sharleyan's personal clerk and secretary, HFAF.

**AHRTHYR, SIR ALYK**—Earl of Windshare, CO of Sir Koryn Gahrvai's cavalry, BSRA; cavalry CO, Corisandian Guard, HFAF.

**AHSTYN, LIEUTENANT FRANZ,** Charisian Royal Guard—the second-incommand of Cayleb Ahrmahk's personal bodyguard after he becomes king, BSRA.

**AHTKYN, LIEUTENANT ZHERALD,** Republic of Siddarmark Army—Colonel Phylyp Mahldyn's aide, MT&T.

**AHUBRAI, FATHER AHNSYLMO**—Schuelerite underpriest; senior Temple Loyalist clergyman, Fairkyn, New Northland Province, Republic of Siddarmark, MT&T.

**AHZBYRN, CAPTAIN REHGNYLD,** Imperial Charisian Army—CO, Company A, 4th Battalion, 1st Scout Sniper Regiment, Imperial Charisian Army, LAMA.

**AHZBYRN, COLONEL SIR AHGUSTAHS,** Royal Dohlaran Army—CO, Ahzbyrn's Regiment (cavalry), Dohlaran component, Army of Shiloh (cavalry), Dohlaran component of the Army of Shiloh, LAMA.

**AHZGOOD, PHYLYP**—Earl of Coris, Prince Hektor's spymaster, OAR; Irys and Daivyn Daykyn's legal guardian, chief advisor, and minister in exile, BHD; member Prince Daivyn's Regency Council, LAMA.

**AHZWAIL, MAJOR ZOSHYA,** Imperial Charisian Army—CO, 3rd Battalion, 5th Mounted Regiment, 3rd Mounted Brigade, Imperial Charisian Army, LAMA.

**AIMAIYR, FATHER IGNAZ**—Archbishop Arthyn Zagyrsk's upper-priest Schuelerite intendant in Tarikah Province, MT&T.

**AIMAYL, RAHN**—a member of the anti-Charis resistance

in Manchyr, Corisande. An ex-apprentice of Paitryk Hainree's, HFAF.

AIRNHART, FATHER SAIMYN—Father Zohannes Pahtkovair's immediate subordinate. A Schuelerite, HFAF.

AIRYTH, EARL OF—see Trumyn Sowthmyn.

AIWAIN, CAPTAIN HARYS, Imperial Charisian Navy—CO, HMS *Shield*, 54, HFAF.

ALBAN, LIEUTENANT COMMANDER NIMUE, Terran Federation Navy—Admiral Pei Kau-zhi's tactical officer, OAR.

ALLYKZHANDRO, COLONEL RAYMAHNDOH, Army of God—XO, Sulyvyn Division, Army of Glacierheart, LAMA.

ALLYRD, COLONEL KLYMYNT, Imperial Charisian Army—CO, 23rd Infantry Regiment, 13th Infantry Brigade, 7th Infantry Division, Imperial Charisian Army, LAMA.

ALYSYN, MARZHO—a milliner in Zion, a Sister of Saint Kohdy, and a senior cell leader for Helm Cleaver, HFQ.

ANVIL ROCK, EARL OF—see Sir Rysel Gahrvai.

APLYN-AHRMAHK, HEKTOR, Imperial Charisian Navy—midshipman, galley HMS *Royal Charis*, OAR; Cayleb Ahrmahk's adoptive son and Duke of Darcos; promoted to ensign, HMS *Destiny*, 54, BSRA; promoted to lieutenant HMS *Destiny* and becomes Sir Dunkyn Yairley's flag lieutenant, MT&T; married to Irys Daykyn and member Charisian inner circle, LAMA.

APLYN-AHRMAHK, PRINCESS IRYS ZHORZHET MHARA DAYKYN—daughter of Prince Hektor Daykyn of Corisande, sister of Daivyn and Hektor Daykyn, OAR; named legal guardian of Prince Daivyn Daykyn of Corisande, appointed to Prince Daivyn's Regency Council, married to Hektor Aplyn-Ahrmahk, Duchess Darcos, member Charisian inner circle, LAMA.

APLYN, CHESTYR—one of Hektor Aplyn-Ahrmahk's

younger brothers; newly admitted student at the Royal College of Charis, MT&T.

APLYN, SAILMAH—Hektor Aplyn-Ahrmahk's biological mother, MT&T.

APLYN-AHRMAHK, LIEUTENANT HEKTOR, Imperial Charisian Navy—CO, HMS *Fleet Wing*, 18. Hektor is placed in command of this schooner for the rescue of Earl Thirsk's family. Remember that he turned seventeen on August 6 of 897, HFQ.

ARBALEST—Aivah Pahrsahn's codename in Helm Cleaver, HFQ.

ARCHBISHOP AHDYM—see Ahdym Taibyr.

ARCHBISHOP DAHNYLD—see Dahnyld Fardhym.

ARCHBISHOP ERAYK—see Erayk Dynnys.

ARCHBISHOP FAILYX—see Failyx Gahrbor.

ARCHBISHOP HALMYN—see Halmyn Zahmsyn.

ARCHBISHOP KLAIRMANT—see Klairmant Gairlyng.

ARCHBISHOP LAWRYNC—See Lawrync Zhaikybs.

ARCHBISHOP MAIKEL—see Maikel Staynair.

ARCHBISHOP MILITANT GUSTYV—see Gustyv Walkyr, HFQ.

ARCHBISHOP PAWAL—see Pawal Braynair.

ARCHBISHOP PRAIDWYN—see Praidwyn Laicharn.

ARCHBISHOP URVYN—see Urvyn Myllyr.

ARCHBISHOP WYLLYM—see Wyllym Rayno.

ARCHBISHOP ZHASYN—see Zhasyn Cahnyr.

ARCHBISHOP ZHEROHM—see Zherohm Vyncyt.

ARTHMYN, FATHER OHMAHR—senior healer, Imperial Palace, Tellesberg, HFAF.

ASHWAIL, COMMANDER SAHLAVAHN, Imperial Charisian Navy—CO, 5th Provisional Battalion, 1st Independent Marine Brigade (one of Hauwerd Breygart's Navy "battalions" at Thesmar), MT&T.

ATHRAWES, MERLIN—Cayleb Ahrmahk's personal armsman; the cybernetic avatar of Commander Nimue Alban, OAR.

ATWATYR, COMPANY SERGEANT BRYNT, Royal Dohlaran Army—senior noncom, 5th Company, Sheldyn's Regiment, Army of the Seridahn, HFQ.

**AUDHAIMYR, CAPTAIN SIR LYWYS,** Royal Dohlaran Navy—CO, HMS *Riptide*, 56, HFQ.

**AUXILIARY BISHOP RHOBAIR**—see Rhobair Makswyl.

**AYMEZ, MIDSHIPMAN BARDULF,** Royal Charisian Navy—a midshipman, HMS *Typhoon*, 36, OAR.

**AZKHAT, BROTHER LAIMUYL**—a very skilled Pasqualate healer assigned to Archbishop Zhasyn Cahnyr's personal staff, HFQ.

**BAHCHER, COLONEL SIR ZHORY,** Royal Desnairian Army—CO, Bahcher's Regiment (medium cavalry), assigned to Sir Fahstyr Rychtyr's invasion column, MT&T.

**BAHKMYN, BARON OF**—see Hairwail Bahkmyn.

**BAHKMYN, COLONEL SIR HAIRWAIL,** Imperial Desnairian Army—Baron Bahkmyn; CO, Bahkmyn's Regiment (heavy cavalry), Army of Shiloh, LAMA.

**BAHLTYN, ZHEEVYS**—Baron White Ford's valet, OAR.

**BAHNYFACE, LIEUTENANT DAHNEL,** Imperial Charisian Navy—third lieutenant, ironclad HMS *Eraystor*, 22, HFQ.

**BAHNYR, HEKTOR,** Royal Corisandian Army—Earl of Mancora; one of Sir Koryn Gahrvai's senior officers; commander of the right wing at Battle of Haryl's Crossing, BHD.

**BAHNYSTYR, LIEUTENANT HAIRAHM,** Royal Corisandian Guard—CO, Princess Irys Aplyn-Ahrmahk's personal guard detail, LAMA.

**BAHR, DAHNNAH**—senior chef, Imperial Palace, Cherayth, HFAF.

**BAHRDO, SISTER KLAIRAH**—the Sister of Saint Kohdy who recruited Nynian Rychtair as a member of the order when she was only fifteen, HFQ.

**BAHRKLY, BISHOP HARYS,** Army of God—CO, Rakurai Division, Army of the Sylmahn, LAMA.

**BAHRMYN, ARCHBISHOP BORYS**—Archbishop of Corisande for the Church of God Awaiting, BHD.

**BAHRMYN, TOHMYS**—Baron White Castle, Prince Hektor's ambassador to Prince Nahrmahn, OAR.

**BAHRNS, ALAHNAH**—an employee of Marzho Alysyn, but not a member of Helm Cleaver.

**BAHRNS, CAPTAIN HALCOM,** Imperial Charisian Navy—CO, ironclad HMS *Delthak*, 22, MT&T.

**BAHRNS, CROWN PRINCE RAHNYLD**—second eldest child of King Rahnyld and Queen Mathylda of Dohlar. King Rahnyld IV's heir.

**BAHRNS, KING RAHNYLD IV**—King of Dohlar, OAR.

**BAHRNS, PRINCESS RAHNYLDAH**—youngest child of King Rahnyld and Queen Mathylda of Dohlar, HFQ.

**BAHRNS, PRINCESS STEFYNY**—eldest child of King Rahnyld and Queen Mathylda of Dohlar, HFQ.

**BAHRNS, QUEEN MATHYLDA**—Queen Consort of Dohlar, HFQ.

**BAHRDAHN, CAPTAIN PHYLYP,** Imperial Charisian Navy—CO, HMS *Undaunted*, 56, HFAF.

**BAHRDAILAHN, LIEUTENANT SIR AHBAIL,** Royal Dohlaran Navy—the Earl of Thirsk's flag lieutenant, HFAF.

**BAHRTALYMU, BRIGADIER DAIRAK,** Imperial Charisian Army—CO, 10th Mounted Brigade, 1st Corps, Army of New Northland, HFQ.

**BAHSKYM, COLONEL HYKAHRU,** Imperial Desnairian Army—CO, Bahskym's Regiment (infantry), Army of Shiloh. CO, Kharmych garrison, LAMA.

**BAHSKYM, GENERAL SIR BREYT,** Imperial Charisian Army—Earl High Mount, CO, Army of Cliff Peak, LAMA.

**BAHSKYM, SIR TRAIVYR,** Imperial Desnairian Army—Earl of Hennet, the Duke of Harless' third-in-command; CO, "Cavalry Wing," Army of Shiloh, LAMA.

**BAHZKAI, LAIYAN**—a Leveler and printer in Siddar City; a leader of the Sword of Schueler, HFAF.

**BAIKET, CAPTAIN STYWYRT,** Royal Dohlaran Navy—CO, HMS *Chihiro*, 50; the Earl of Thirsk's flag captain, HFAF.

**BAIKYR, CAPTAIN DUSTYN,** Imperial Charisian Army—CO, Company B, 2nd Battalion, 6th Regiment, Imperial Charisian Army, LAMA.

**BAIKYR, CAPTAIN SYLMAHN,** Imperial Charisian

Navy—CO, HMS *Ahrmahk*, 58. High Admiral Lock Island's flag captain, HFAF.

BAIKYR, COLONEL PAWAL—a regular officer of the Republic of Siddarmark Army who went over to the Temple Loyalists; commander of Temple Loyalist rebels in the Sylmahn Gap, MT&T.

BAILAHND, SISTER AHMAI—Mother Abbess Ahmai Bailahnd of the Abbey of Saint Evehlain, HFAF.

BAILUKHAV, COLONEL SAISAHR, Imperial Charisian Army—CO, 20th Mounted Regiment, 10th Mounted Brigade, 1st Corps, Army of New Northland, HFQ.

BAIRAHT, DAIVYN—Duke of Kholman; effectively Emperor Mahrys IV's Navy Minister, Imperial Desnairian Navy; flees to Charis following Battle of Iythria, HFAF; stripped of title by Emperor Mahrys, LAMA.

BAIRYSTYR, COLONEL MAYNSFYLD, Army of God—CO, 73rd Cavalry Regiment, Army of the Sylmahn, LAMA.

BAIRYSTYR, LIEUTENANT ZHAK, Imperial Charisian Navy—senior engineer, ironclad HMS *Delthak*, 22, MT&T.

BAIRZHAIR, BROTHER TAIRAINCE—treasurer of the Monastery of Saint Zherneau, MT&T.

BANAHR, FATHER AHZWALD—head of the priory of Saint Hamlyn, city of Sarayn, Kingdom of Charis, BSRA.

BANISTER—see Father Byrtrym Zhansyn.

BARCOR, BARON OF—see Sir Zher Sumyrs.

BARHNKASTYR, MAJOR PAITRYK, Imperial Charisian Army—XO, 3rd Regiment, 2nd Brigade, Imperial Charisian Army, MT&T.

BARON JAHRAS—CO, Imperial Desnairian Navy; Daivyn Bairaht's brother-in-law, HFAF; flees to Charis for asylum following Battle of Iythria, MT&T.

BARTYN, FATHER MAHKZWAIL—a Langhornite underpriest; one of Rhobair Duchairn's transport personnel, LAMA.

BARYNGYR, COLONEL BRYGHAM, Army of God—CO,

1st Regiment, Fyrgyrsyn Division, Army of Glacierheart, LAMA.

BAYLAIR, COLONEL NOHBYRO, Imperial Charisian Army—CO, 10th Mounted Regiment, 5th Mounted Brigade, Imperial Charisian Army, LAMA.

BAYTZ, COLONEL RAHDRYK, Imperial Charisian Army—CO, 27th Infantry Regiment, 14th Infantry Brigade, 7th Infantry Division, Imperial Charisian Army, LAMA.

BAYTZ, FELAYZ—Princess Felayz; youngest child and younger daughter of Nahrmahn and Ohlyvya Baytz, OAR.

BAYTZ, HANBYL—Duke Solomon, Prince Nahrmahn of Emerald's uncle and the commander of the Emeraldian Army, BSRA.

BAYTZ, MAHRYA—Princess Mahrya; oldest child and older daughter of Nahrmahn and Ohlyvya Baytz, OAR; betrothed to Prince Zhan of Old Charis, BSRA.

BAYTZ, NAHRMAHN GAREYT—son and second child of Prince Nahrmahn and Princess Ohlyvya Baytz, OAR; becomes Prince Nahrmahn Gareyt of Emerald, HFAF.

BAYTZ, NAHRMAHN HANBYL GRAIM—Prince Nahrmahn II of Emerald, OAR; swears fealty to Cayleb and Sharleyan Ahrmahk, imperial councilor for intelligence, BSRA; member Charisian inner circle, AMF; killed in terrorist attack, HFAF; virtual personality online, MT&T.

BAYTZ, OHLYVYA—Princess of Emerald, wife of Prince Nahrmahn of Emerald, OAR; member Charisian inner circle, AMF; Dowager Princess of Emerald, HFAF.

BAYTZ, TRAHVYS—Prince Nahrmahn of Emerald's third child and second son, OAR.

BÉDARD, DR. ADORÉE, PH.D.—chief psychiatrist, Operation Ark, OAR.

BEKATYRO, ELAIYS—previous Temple Loyalist mayor of Ohlarn, New Northland Province, Republic of

Siddarmark; unjustly denounced to the Inquisition by Bynno Leskyr, who wanted his position, MT&T.

**BEKHYM, MAJOR DAHNEL,** Imperial Charisian Army—CO, 1st Battalion, 6th Regiment, Imperial Charisian Army, LAMA.

**BEKYT, MAJOR OLYVYR**—CO, 1st Raisor Volunteers, Shilohian Temple Loyalist militia, LAMA.

**BISHOP AMILAIN**—see Amilain Gahrnaht.

**BISHOP CHESTYR**—see Chestyr Dahglys.

**BISHOP EXECUTOR BAIKYR**—see Baikyr Saikor.

**BISHOP EXECUTOR DYNZAIL**—see Dynzail Vahsphar.

**BISHOP EXECUTOR MHARTYN**—see Mhartyn Raislair.

**BISHOP EXECUTOR WYLLYS**—see Bishop Executor Wyllys Graisyn.

**BISHOP EXECUTOR ZHERALD**—see Bishop Executor Zherald Ahdymsyn.

**BISHOP FAILYX**—see Failyx Mahkgyvyrn.

**BISHOP KLYMYNT**—see Klymynt Rohzynkranz.

**BISHOP LYNAIL**—see Lynail Qwentyn.

**BISHOP MAIKEL (1)**—see Maikel Staynair.

**BISHOP MAIKEL (2)**—see Maikel Zhynkyns.

**BISHOP MARKYS**—see Markys Gohdard.

**BISHOP MILITANT TAYRENS**—see Tayrens Teagmahn.

**BISHOP MYTCHAIL**—see Mytchail Zhessop.

**BISHOP SEBAHSTEAN**—see Sebahstean Taylar.

**BISHOP STYWYRT**—see Bishop Stywyrt Sahndyrs.

**BISHOP ZHASYN**—see Zhasyn Howail.

**BLACK HORSE, DUKE OF**—see Payt Stywyrt.

**BLACK WATER, DUKE OF**—see Sir Ernyst Lynkyn and Sir Adulfo Lynkyn.

**BLAHDYSNBERG, LIEUTENANT PAWAL,** Imperial Charisian Navy—XO, ironclad HMS *Delthak*, 22, MT&T.

**BLAHNDAI, CHANTAHAL**—an alias of Lysbet Wylsynn in Zion, HFAF.

**BLAIDYN, LIEUTENANT ROZHYR,** Dohlaran Navy—second lieutenant, galley *Royal Bédard*, OAR.

**BOHLGYR, MAJOR TYMYTHY,** Imperial Charisian Army—CO, 3rd Battalion, 9th Mounted Regiment,

5th Mounted Brigade, Imperial Charisian Army, LAMA.

BOHLYR, WYLLYM, CANAL SERVICE—lockmaster, Fairkyn, New Northland Province, Republic of Siddarmark, MT&T.

BORYS, ARCHBISHOP—see Archbishop Borys Bahrmyn.

BOWAVE, DAIRAK—Dr. Rahzhyr Mahklyn's senior assistant, Royal College, Tellesberg, HFAF.

BOWSHAM, CAPTAIN KHANAIR, Royal Charisian Marines—CO, HMS *Gale*, OAR.

BRADLAI, LIEUTENANT ROBYRT, Royal Corisandian Navy—true name of Captain Styvyn Whaite, OAR.

BRAHDLAI, CORPORAL HOWAIL, Army of God—scout patrol commander, 191st Cavalry Regiment, MT&T.

BRAHDLAI, LIEUTENANT HAARAHLD, Royal Dohlaran Navy—third lieutenant, HMS *Chihiro*, 50, MT&T.

BRAHKMYN, COLONEL DAIVYN, Republic of Siddarmark Army—the Army of Hildermoss' chief Siddarmarkian engineer, HFQ.

BRAHNAHR, CAPTAIN STYVYN, Imperial Charisian Navy—CO, Bureau of Navigation, Imperial Charisian Navy, MT&T.

BRAHNDYN, FATHER ZHEROHMY—Rhobair Duchairn's senior representative with the Army of the Sylmahn, HFQ.

BRAHNSYN, DOCTOR FYL—member of the Royal College of Charis, specializing in botany, MT&T.

BRAHNSYN, MAJOR PAWAL, Imperial Charisian Army—CO, 1st Battalion, 10th Mounted Regiment, 5th Mounted Brigade, Imperial Charisian Army, LAMA.

BRAIDAIL, BROTHER ZHILBYRT—under-priest of the Order of Schueler; a junior inquisitor in Talkyra, HFAF.

BRAISHAIR, CAPTAIN HORYS, Imperial Charisian Navy—CO, HMS *Rock Point*, 38. POW of Earl Thirsk, surrendered to the Inquisition, HFAF.

BRAISYN, AHRNAHLD, Imperial Charisian Navy—a seaman aboard HMS *Destiny*, 54; a member of Stywyrt Mahlyk's boat crew, HFAF.

**BRAISYN, BRIGADIER MOHRTYN**, Imperial Charisian Army—CO, 3rd Mounted Brigade, Imperial Charisian Army, LAMA.

**BRAISYN, CAPTAIN DYNNYS**, Imperial Charisian Navy—CO, Bureau of Supply, Imperial Charisian Navy, MT&T.

**BRAIZHYR, BRIGADIER SIR EDGAIR**, Imperial Charisian Army—CO, 14th Infantry Brigade, 7th Infantry Division, Imperial Charisian Army, LAMA.

**BRAUHYLO, FATHER AHNDYR**—a Schuelerite underpriest and inquisitor assigned to the transport *Truculent* to oversee the transport of Charisian POWs from the Battle of the Kaudzhu Narrows to the Temple Lands, HFQ.

**BRAYNAIR, CAPTAIN LYWYS**, Imperial Charisian Army—Duke Eastshare's aide, LAMA.

**BRAYNAIR, PAWAL**—Archbishop of Chisholm for the Church of Charis, AMF.

**BRAYTAHN, MAJOR BAHNYFACE**, Imperial Charisian Army—CO, 3rd Battalion, 10th Mounted Regiment, 5th Mounted Brigade, Imperial Charisian Army, LAMA.

**BRAYTAHN, PLATOON SERGEANT RAIMYND**, Imperial Charisian Army—senior noncom, 1st Platoon, Company B, 1st Battalion, 1st Scout Sniper Regiment, Imperial Charisian Army, LAMA.

**BREYGART, FHRANCYS**—younger daughter of Hauwerd and Fhrancys Breygart; Lady Mairah Breygart's stepdaughter, MT&T.

**BREYGART, FRAIDARECK**—fourteenth Earl of Hanth; Hauwerd Breygart's great-grandfather, OAR.

**BREYGART, HAARAHLD**—second oldest son of Hauwerd and Fhrancys Breygart; Lady Mairah Breygart's stepson, MT&T.

**BREYGART, LADY MAIRAH LYWKYS**—Queen Sharleyan's chief lady-in-waiting, cousin of Baron Green Mount, OAR; Countess of Hanth and second wife of Sir Hauwerd Breygart, Earl of Hanth, MT&T.

**BREYGART, SIR HAUWERD**, Royal Charisian Marines—rightful heir to the Earldom of Hanth, OAR; resigns commission and becomes Earl of Hanth, BSRA; recalled to service, promoted general; CO, 1st Independent Marine Brigade, MT&T; CO, Thesmar garrison, LAMA.

BREYGART, STYVYN—elder son of Hauwerd and Fhrancys Breygart; Lady Mairah Breygart's stepson, MT&T.

BREYGART, TRUMYN—youngest son of Hauwerd and Fhrancys Breygart; Lady Mairah Breygart's stepson, MT&T.

BREYGART, ZHERLDYN—elder daughter of Hauwerd and Fhrancys Breygart; Lady Mairah Breygart's stepdaughter, MT&T.

BROTHER AHLPHANZO—see Ahlphanzo Metyrnyk.

BROTHER LAIMUYL—see Laimuyl Azkhat.

BROUN, FATHER MAHTAIO—Archbishop Erayk Dynnys' senior secretary and aide; Archbishop Erayk's confidant and protégé, OAR.

BROWNYNG, CAPTAIN ELLYS—CO, Temple galleon *Blessed Langhorne*, OAR.

BROWNYNG, CORPORAL AHLDAHS, Imperial Charisian Marines—senior member of Klymynt Abykrahmbi's assigned security detail, LAMA.

BROWNYNG, LIEUTENANT EHLYS, Imperial Charisian Navy—CO, Tymkyn Point battery, Thesmar Bay, LAMA.

BRUHSTAIR, STYVYN—a master clockmaker now serving as Ehdwyrd Howsmyn's chief instrument maker and inspector, LAMA.

BRYAHNSYN, LIEUTENANT AHRNAHLD, Royal Dohlaran Army—CO, 2nd Platoon, 5th Company, Sheldyn's Regiment, Army of the Seridahn, HFQ.

BRYAIRS, TAHLBAHT—Brother Lynkyn Fultyn's assistant in charge of production, St. Kylmahn's Foundry, LAMA.

BRYGSYN, COLONEL TRYNT, Royal Dohlaran Army—CO, Brygsyn's Regiment (infantry), Dohlaran component, Army of Shiloh, LAMA.

BRYGYR, LIEUTENANT SYMOHR, Royal Dohlaran Navy—second lieutenant, screw-galley HMS *Sword*, HFQ.

**BRYNDYN, MAJOR DAHRYN**—the senior artillery officer attached to Brigadier Clareyk's column at Battle of Haryl's Crossing, BHD.

**BRYNKMYN, LIEUTENANT CHESTYR**, Imperial Charisian Army—CO, 2nd Platoon, Company B, 1st Battalion, 9th Mounted Regiment, 5th Mounted Brigade, Imperial Charisian Army, LAMA.

**BRYNTYN, SIR YAHNCEE**—Baron Wheatfields' personal aide, HFQ.

**BRYNYGAIR, COLONEL SIR ZHADWAIL**, Royal Desnairian Army—CO, Brynygair's Regiment (medium cavalry), assigned to Sir Fahstyr Rychtyr's invasion column, MT&T.

**BRYSKOH, MAJOR HAIMLTAHN**—CO, 1st Greentown Militia, Midhold Province Temple Loyalist militia; CO, Greentown garrison, LAMA.

**BRYSTAHL, COLONEL FHRANKLYN**, Imperial Charisian Army—CO, 7th Regiment, 4th Infantry Brigade, Imperial Charisian Army, LAMA.

**BRYXTYN, CAPTAIN HONSHAU**, Royal Dohlaran Navy—CO, HMS *Saint Kylmahn*, 52, HFQ.

**BUKANYN, LIEUTENANT SYMYN**, Imperial Charisian Navy—CO, Navy Redoubt, Thesmar, LAMA.

**BYRGAIR, COLONEL SIR ZHADWAIL**, Royal Dohlaran Army—CO, Byrgair's Regiment (heavy cavalry), Royal Dohlaran Army, MT&T.

**BYRK, CAPTAIN ZHORJ**, Imperial Charisian Navy—CO, HMS *Volcano*, 24, one of the Imperial Charisian Navy's bombardment ships, MT&T.

**BYRK, FATHER MYRTAN**—upper-priest of the Order of Schueler; Vyktyr Tahrlsahn's second-in-command escorting Charisian POWs from Gorath to Zion, HFF.

**BYRK, MAJOR BREKYN**, Royal Charisian Marines—CO, Marine detachment, HMS *Royal Charis*, OAR.

**BYRKYT, FATHER ZHON**—an over-priest of the Church of God Awaiting; abbot of the Monastery of Saint Zherneau, BSRA; resigns as abbot and becomes librarian, HFAF.

**BYRMAHN, COLONEL ZHAKSYN**, Temple Loyalist Militia—

CO, 2nd Maidynberg Militia, Temple Loyalist Militia, assigned to Fort Tairys' garrison, LAMA.

BYRNS, BRAISYN—Earl of White Crag; former Lord Justice of Chisholm, currently first councilor, replacing Mahrak Sahndyrs, MT&T.

BYROKYO, LIEUTENANT AHTONYO, Army of God—CO, 2nd Platoon, 1st Company, 1st Regiment, Zion Division, Army of Glacierheart, LAMA.

CAHKRAYN, SAMYL—Duke of Fern, King Rahnyld IV of Dohlar's first councilor, OAR.

CAHMMYNG, AHLBAIR—a professional assassin working for Father Aidryn Waimyn, HFAF.

CAHNYR, ARCHBISHOP ZHASYN—Archbishop of Glacierheart, OAR; member of Samyl Wylsynn's circle of Reformists, BHD; a strong Reformist leader in Siddar City, AMF; returns to Glacierheart to lead his archbishopric against the Group of Four, MT&T.

CAHNYRS, CAPTAIN ALYK, Imperial Charisian Navy—CO, ironclad HMS *Eraystor*, 22, Admiral Hainz Zhaztrow's Old Charisian born flag captain, HFQ.

CAHNYRS, LIEUTENANT ZHERALD, Imperial Charisian Navy—second lieutenant, ironclad HMS *Delthak*, 22, MT&T.

CAHRTAIR, MAJOR HAHLYS—rebel Temple Loyalist; CO, 3rd Company, 3rd Saiknyr Militia Regiment, MT&T.

CAHSTNYR, COLONEL BRYSYN, Temple Loyalist Militia—CO, 3rd Mountaincross Rangers, Mountaincross Province Temple Loyalist partisans, LAMA.

CAHSTNYR, MAJOR BRAHDLAI, Imperial Charisian Marine Corps—senior Marine officer, Marine detachment, HMS *Destiny*, 54, HFQ.

CAHSTNYR, SIR BORYS, Imperial Desnairian Army—quartermaster, Army of Justice; quartermaster, Desnairian component, Army of Shiloh, LAMA.

CARLSYN, CAPTAIN EDWYRD, Imperial Charisian Army—CO, Company A, 1st Battalion, 5th Regiment, Imperial Charisian Army, LAMA.

CARTYR, BRYGHAM—Ehdwyrd Howsmyn's senior

representative to the Republic of Siddarmark's Council of Manufactories, the body set up by Greyghor Stohnar to rationalize Siddarmarkian contributions to the war effort, LAMA.

CARTYR, MAJOR BRYXTYN, Imperial Charisian Army—XO, 5th Mounted Regiment, 3rd Mounted Brigade, Imperial Charisian Army, LAMA.

CASTANET—see Zhorzhet Styvynsyn.

CELAHK, BRIGADIER HYNRYK, Imperial Charisian Army—Duke Eastshare's senior artillery officer, army of the Branaths. Promoted to brigadier, HFQ.

CELAHK, COLONEL HYNRYK, Imperial Charisian Army—Duke Eastshare's senior artillery officer, 1st Brigade (reinforced) and Army of the Branaths, LAMA.

CHAHLMAIR, SIR BAIRMON—Duke of Margo; a member of Prince Daivyn's Regency Council in Corisande who does not fully trust Earl Anvil Rock and Earl Tartarian, HFAF.

CHAIMBYRS, LIEUTENANT ZHUSTYN, Imperial Desnairian Navy—second lieutenant, HMS *Archangel Chihiro*, 40, HFAF.

CHALKYR, CAPTAIN FRAIDARECK, Royal Dohlaran Navy—CO, HMS *Challenger*, 54, HFQ.

CHALKYR, CORPORAL SLYM, Imperial Charisian Army—Duke Eastshare's batman.

CHALMYRZ, FATHER KARLOS—Archbishop Borys Bahrmyn's aide and secretary, OAR.

CHANDLYR, MAHRAK—Sir Bruhstair Ahbaht's steward aboard broadside ironclad HMS *Thunderer*, 30, HFQ.

CHANSAYL, COLONEL PAITYR, Republic of Siddarmark Army—CO, 43rd Infantry Regiment, Republic of Siddarmark Army, a part of General Trumyn Stohnar's Sylmahn Gap command, MT&T.

CHARLTYN, MAJOR KRYSTYPHYR, Imperial Charisian Army—CO, 3rd Battalion, 5th Mounted Regiment, 3rd Mounted Brigade, Imperial Charisian Army, LAMA.

Kyznetzov Province and Mayor of Yu-kwau, Kyznetzov's largest city, HFQ.

CHUSAI, SERGEANT MAJOR TWYANGCHU, Imperial Harchongese Army—senior noncom, 1st Squadron, Company B, 3rd Kyznetzov Lancers, HFQ.

CHWAERIAU, *SEIJIN* NIMUE—the second, "younger" PICA identity of Lieutenant Commander Nimue Alban on Safehold, LAMA.

CLAITYN, COLONEL SAMYL, Imperial Charisian Army—CO, 22nd Infantry Regiment, 13th Infantry Brigade, 7th Infantry Division, Imperial Charisian Army, LAMA.

CLAREYK, KYNT, Royal Charisian Marines—major, originator of the training syllabus for the Royal Charisian Marines, OAR; as brigadier, CO, 3rd Brigade, Royal Charisian Marines, made Baron Green Valley, BHD; transfers to Imperial Charisian Army as general and as advisor to Duke Eastshare, member Charisian inner circle, AMF; acting viceroy Zebediah, HFAF; CO, 2nd Brigade (reinforced), Imperial Charisian Army, MT&T; CO, Army of Midhold, LAMA.

CLOUD SHADOW, BARON OF—see Bauzhyn Kau.

CLYFFYRD, MAJOR CAHNYR, Imperial Charisian Army—XO, 6th Regiment, Imperial Charisian Army, LAMA.

CLYMYNS, FATHER ZHEROHM—a Schuelerite upperpriest serving as Bishop Wylbyr Edwyrds' chief of staff, LAMA.

CLYNTAHN, LIEUTENANT HAIRYM, Imperial Charisian Army—CO, Sup- port Platoon, 1st Battalion, 2nd Regiment, Imperial Charisian Army, MT&T.

CLYNTAHN, VICAR ZHASPAHR—Grand Inquisitor of the Church of God Awaiting; one of the so-called Group of Four, OAR.

COHLMYN, ADMIRAL SIR LEWK, Chisholmian Navy—Earl Sharpfield; Queen Sharleyan's senior fleet commander, OAR; second-ranking officer, Imperial Charisian Navy, HFAF; CO, Gulf of Dohlar Squadron, LAMA.

CORIS, EARL OF—see Phylyp Ahzgood.

CRAGGY HILL, EARL OF—see Wahlys Hillkeeper.

CRAHMYND, PETTY OFFICER FYRGYRSYN, Imperial Charisian Navy—senior helmsman, HMS ironclad *Delthak*, 22, MT&T.

CRAHNSTYN, CORPORAL LAIRMAHNT "SHADOW," Army of God—a section leader in 1st Platoon, Company A, 191st Cavalry Regiment, HFQ.

CRAWFYRD, SIR BRYNDYN, DUKE HOLY TREE—a conservative Chisholmian noble, concerned by changes involved in the industrial revolution, whose duchy lies between the Earldom of Swayle and the Duchy of Green Tree, HFQ.

CROSS CREEK, EARL OF—see Ahdem Zhefry.

CROWN PRINCE RAHNYLD—see Prince Rahnyld Bahrns.

CRYSTAL SKY, BARON OF—see Wynshyng Pahn.

CUDD, *SEIJIN* DAGYR—an alter ego of Nimue Chwaeriau, HFQ.

CUMYNGS, COMMANDER ZHERYKO, Imperial Charisian Navy—CO, HMS *Restless*, 18, HFQ.

CUMYNGS, FATHER ZHERYLD—a Chihirite under-priest (Order of the Quill); Bishop Maikel Zhynkyns' chief clerk/office manager at Camp Dynnys, HFQ.

CUPYR, LIEUTENANT COMMANDER AIZAK, Imperial Charisian Navy—CO, HMS *Sojourn*, 16, HFQ.

CUPYR, MAJOR BARTAHLAIMO, Imperial Charisian Army—CO, 1st Battalion, 5th Regiment, Imperial Charisian Army, LAMA.

CYSGODOL, *SEIJIN* GANIEDA—an alter ego of Nimue Chwaeriau, HFQ.

DABNYR, MAJOR WAHLTAYR, Imperial Charisian Army—CO, 4th Battalion, 9th Mounted Regiment, 5th Mounted Brigade, Imperial Charisian Army, LAMA.

DAHGLYS, BISHOP CHESTYR, Army of God—CO, St. Cehseelya Division, Army of Glacierheart, HFQ.

DAHGLYS, CAPTAIN LAINYR, Imperial Charisian Navy—CO, ironclad HMS *Tellesberg*, 22, MT&T.

DAHGLYS, MASTER SYGMAHN—an engineer attached to

Father Tailahr Synzhyn's staff to assist with canal repairs for the Church of God Awaiting, LAMA.

**DAHNEL, LIEUTENANT CHARLSYN**, Royal Dohlaran Army—CO, 1st Platoon, 5th Company Sheldyn's Regiment, Army of the Seridahn, HFQ.

**DAHNSYN, LIEUTENANT CHARLZ**, Republic of Siddarmark Army—Colonel Stahn Wyllys' senior aide, MT&T.

**DAHNTAHS, LIEUTENANT TAYDOHR**, Army of God—Colonel Bryntyn Olyvyr's personal aide, St. Yura Division, Army of the Sylmahn, HFQ.

**DAHNVAHR, AINSAIL**—Charisian-born Temple Loyalist living in the Temple Lands, recruited for Operation Rakurai, HFAF.

**DAHNVAHR, RAHZHYR**—Ainsail Dahnvahr's father, HFAF.

**DAHNVAIR, CAPTAIN LAIZAHNDO**, Imperial Charisian Navy—CO, HMS *Royal Kraken*, 58, HFAF.

**DAHNVYRS, COMMANDER BRYXTYN**, Imperial Charisian Navy—CO, HMS *East Wind*, 18, HFQ.

**DAHNZAI, LYZBYT**—Father Zhaif Laityr's housekeeper at the Church of the Holy Archangels Triumphant, HFAF.

**DAHRNAIL, SIR SLOHKYM, DUKE OF SHAIRN**—inheritor of Duke Kholman's position as Mahrys IV's Navy Minister, HFQ.

**DAHRYUS, MASTER EDVARHD**—an alias of Bishop Mylz Halcom, BSRA.

**DAICHYNG, LORD ADMIRAL OF NAVIES SHIANGZHU, DUKE OF MOUNTAIN SHADOW**, Imperial Harchongese Navy—effectively the navy minister of the Harchong Empire, HFQ.

**DAIKHAR, LIEUTENANT MOHTOHKAI**, Imperial Charisian Navy—XO, HMS *Dart*, 54, HFAF.

**DAIKYN, GAHLVYN**—Cayleb Ahrmahk's valet, OAR.

**DAIRWYN, BARON OF**—see Sir Farahk Hyllair.

**DAIVYN, PRINCE**—see Daivyn Daykyn.

**DAIVYS, MYTRAHN**—a Charisian Temple Loyalist, BSRA.

**DAIYANG, LORD OF HORSE TAYCHAU, EARL OF RAINBOW**

WATERS, Imperial Harchongese Navy—CO, Mighty Host of God and the Archangels, HFQ.

DANTAS, MAJOR SIR AINGHUS, Royal Dohlaran Army—CO, 1st Company, Sulyvyn's Regiment (infantry), Royal Dohlaran Army, LAMA.

DARCOS, DUCHESS OF—see Irys Aplyn-Ahrmahk.

DARCOS, DUKE OF—see Hektor Aplyn-Ahrmahk.

DARYS, CAPTAIN TYMYTHY ("TYM"), Royal Charisian Navy—CO, HMS *Destroyer*, 54. Flag captain to Domynyk Staynair, BSRA.

DAYKYN, CROWN PRINCE HEKTOR—Prince Hektor of Corisande's second oldest child and heir apparent, BSRA; assassinated with his father, BHD.

DAYKYN, DAIVYN DAHNYLD MHARAK ZOSHYA—Prince Hektor of Corisande's youngest child, sent to safety in Delferahk, and Prince of Corisande in Exile following his father's and older brother's assassination, BHD; rescued from Zhaspahr Clyntahn's assassination attempt, HFAF; in exile in Empire of Charis, MT&T; crowned minor Prince of Corisande and swears fealty to Cayleb and Sharleyan Ahrmahk, LAMA.

DAYKYN, IRYS—see Irys Zhorzhet Mhara Daykyn Aplyn-Ahrmahk.

DAYKYN, PRINCE HEKTOR—Prince of Corisande, leader of the League of Corisande, OAR; assassinated 893, BHD.

DAYKYN, PRINCESS RAICHYNDA—Prince Hektor of Corisande's deceased wife; born in the Earldom of Domair, Kingdom of Hoth, BSRA.

DEEP HOLLOW, EARL OF—see Bryahn Selkyr.

DEKYN, SERGEANT ALLAYN, Delferahkan Army—one of Captain Tohmys Kairmyn's noncoms at Ferayd, BSRA.

DEZMYND, FATHER TRYNT—a Schuelerite upper-priest entrusted with marching the inhabitants of Camp Tairek to the Princedom of Sardahn, HFQ.

DOBYNS, CHARLZ—son of Ezmelda Dobyns, sometime supporter of the anti-Charis resistance in Manchyr,

Corisande, AMF; convicted of treason but pardoned by Empress Sharleyan, HFAF.

DOBYNS, EZMELDA—Father Tymahn Hahskans' housekeeper at Saint Kathryn's Church, AMF.

DOWAIN, COLONEL TYMYTHY, Army of God—XO, Zion Division, MT&T.

DOYAL, MAJOR DUNKYN, Imperial Charisian Army—CO, 3rd Battalion, 8th Regiment, 4th Infantry Brigade, Imperial Charisian Army, LAMA.

DOYAL, SIR CHARLZ—Sir Koryn Gahrvai's senior artillery commander, Battle of Haryl's Crossing, BHD; Sir Koryn Gahrvai's chief of staff and intelligence chief, Corisandian Guard, AMF; Corisandian Regency Council's chief of intelligence, MT&T.

DRAGON HILL, EARL OF—see Edwyrd Ahlbair.

DRAGONER, CORPORAL ZHAK, Royal Charisian Marines—a member of Crown Prince Cayleb's bodyguard, OAR.

DRAGONER, SIR RAYJHIS—Charisian ambassador to the Siddarmark Republic, BSRA; retires as ambassador, MT&T.

DRAGONMASTER, BRIGADE SERGEANT MAJOR MAHKYNTY ("MAHK"), Royal Charisian Marines—Brigadier Clareyk's senior noncom, BSRA.

DUCHAIRN, VICAR RHOBAIR—Minister of Treasury, Council of Vicars; one of the so-called Group of Four, OAR.

DUNSTYN, LIEUTENANT TRUMYN, Imperial Charisian Army—CO, 1st Platoon, Company B, 2nd Battalion, 6th Regiment, Imperial Charisian Army, LAMA.

DYASAIYL, MAJOR AHRKYP, Imperial Charisian Army—CO, 4th Battalion, 1st Scout Sniper Regiment, Imperial Charisian Army, LAMA.

DYLLAHN, CHIEF BOATSWAIN'S MATE CHESTYR, Imperial Charisian Navy—boatswain, ironclad HMS *Delthak*, 22, LAMA.

DYMYTREE, FRONZ, Royal Charisian Marines—a member of Crown Prince Cayleb's bodyguard, OAR.

DYNNYS, ADORAI—Archbishop Erayk Dynnys' wife,

OAR; her alias after her husband's arrest is Ailysa, BSRA.

DYNNYS, ARCHBISHOP ERAYK—Archbishop of Charis. Executed for heresy 892, OAR.

DYNNYS, MAJOR AHBNAIR, Republic of Siddarmark Army—CO, 1st Company, 37th Infantry Regiment, Republic of Siddarmark Army, MT&T.

DYNNYS, STYVYN—Archbishop Erayk Dynnys' younger son, age eleven in 892, BSRA.

DYNNYS, TYMYTHY ERAYK—Archbishop Erayk Dynnys' older son, age fourteen in 892, BSRA.

DYNNYSYN, SIR MAHRAK, Imperial Desnairian Army— Earl of Hankey, Duke Harless' second-in-command; CO, Desnairian infantry force, Army of Justice and Army of Shiloh, LAMA.

DYNVYRS, SIR CLAIRYNC, BARON OF WHEATFIELDS— Prince Grygory of Jhurlahnk's senior army officer and the commander of his contribution to the Army of Glacierheart, HFQ.

DYTMAHR, MAJOR SIR ZHAN-CHARLZ, Imperial Charisian Army—CO, 2nd Battalion, 10th Mounted Regiment, 5th Mounted Brigade, Imperial Charisian Army, LAMA.

EASTSHARE, DUKE OF—see Ruhsyl Thairis.

EDMYNDSYN, MAJOR MAIKEL, Imperial Charisian Army—CO, 4th Battalion, 8th Regiment, 4th Infantry Brigade, Imperial Charisian Army, LAMA.

EDWAIR, FATHER SHAINSAIL—Schuelerite upper-priest; senior inquisitor attached to the Sylmahn Gap Temple Loyalists in Mountaincross, MT&T.

EDWYRDS, BAHRTALAM—Siddarmarkian master gunsmith and the Gunmakers Guild's representative on the Council of Manufactories, LAMA.

EDWYRDS, BISHOP WYLBYR—Schuelerite bishop; Zhaspahr Clyntahn's personal choice as "Inquisitor General" to head the Inquisition in territories occupied by the Army of God, MT&T.

EDWYRDS, KEVYN—XO, privateer galleon *Kraken*, BSRA.

EDWYRDS, SERGEANT MAHTHYW, Imperial Charisian

Army—an engineer attached to Earl Hanth's Thesmar command. He is a Chisholmian who worked as a salvage diver before his enlistment, HFQ.

EKYRD, CAPTAIN HAYRYS, Royal Dohlaran Navy—CO, galley *King Rahnyld*, OAR.

EMPEROR CAYLEB—see Cayleb Ahrmahk.

EMPEROR MAHRYS IV—see Mahrys Ohlarn Ahldarm.

EMPEROR WAISU VI—see Waisu Hantai.

EMPRESS SHARLEYAN—see Sharleyan Ahrmahk.

ERAYKSYN, LIEUTENANT STYVYN, Imperial Charisian Navy—Admiral Staynair's flag lieutenant, BSRA.

ERAYKSYN, WYLLYM—a Charisian textiles manufacturer, BSRA.

FAHBYAN, CORPORAL SHAIN, Army of God—assigned to Camp Chihiro guard force, HFQ.

FAHRKYS, MAJOR RHOBAIR, Imperial Charisian Army—CO, 1st Battalion, 8th Regiment, 4th Infantry Brigade, Imperial Charisian Army, LAMA.

FAHRMAHN, PRIVATE LUHYS, Royal Charisian Marines—a member of Crown Prince Cayleb's bodyguard, OAR.

FAHRMYN, FATHER TAIRYN—the priest assigned to Saint Chihiro's Church, a village church near the Convent of Saint Agtha; complicit in attempt to assasinate Empress Sharleyan, BHD.

FAHRNO, MAHRLYS—one of Madam Ahnzhelyk Phonda's courtesans, HFAF.

FAHRYA, CAPTAIN BYRNAHRDO, Imperial Desnairian Navy—CO, HMS *Holy Langhorne*, 42, HFAF.

FAHSTYR, COLONEL BAHZWAIL, Army of God—CO, 3rd Regiment, Sulyvyn Division, Army of Glacierheart, LAMA.

FAHSTYR, VYRGYL—Earl of Gold Wyvern, MT&T.

FAINSTYN, LIEUTENANT GHORDYN, Army of God—Bishop Militant Bahrnabai's junior aide, Army of Glacierheart, LAMA.

FAIRCASTER, SERGEANT PAYTER, Royal Charisian Marines—senior noncom, Crown Prince Cayleb's bodyguard, OAR; transfers to Royal Guard as King

Cayleb's bodyguard, BSRA; transfers to Imperial Guard as Emperor Cayleb's bodyguard, BHD.

FAIRSTOCK, MAJOR KLYMYNT, Republic of Siddarmark Army—CO, Provisional Company, Republic of Siddarmark Army, Fort Sheldyn, South March Lands, MT&T.

FAIRYS, COLONEL AHLVYN, Imperial Charisian Marines—CO, 1st Regiment, 3rd Brigade, Imperial Charisian Marines, HFAF.

FALKHAN, LIEUTENANT AHRNAHLD, Royal Charisian Marines—CO, Crown Prince Cayleb's personal bodyguard, OAR; CO, Crown Prince Zhan's personal bodyguard, BSRA.

FALLING ROCK, BARON OF—see Gwainmyn Yiangszhu.

FARDHYM, ARCHBISHOP DAHNYLD—Bishop of Siddar City, elevated to Archbishop of Siddarmark by Greyghor Stohnar after the rebellion of the "Sword of Schueler" ordered by Vicar Zhaspahr Clyntahn, MT&T.

FATHER AHNDAIR—see Ahndair Seegairs.

FATHER AHNDRU (1)—see Ahndru Fyrn.

FATHER AHNDRU (2)—see Ahndru Hainz.

FATHER AHNDYR—see Ahndyr Brauhylo.

FATHER AIZAK—see Aizak Mohmohtahny.

FATHER AIZYKYAL TRYNCHYR—see Aizykyal Trynchyr.

FATHER ALLAYN—see Allayn Wynchystair.

FATHER BYRTRYM—see Byrtrym Zhansyn.

FATHER CHARLZ—see Charlz Kaillyt.

FATHER CHERMYN—see Chermyn Suzhymahga.

FATHER CHESTYR—see Chestyr Thompkyn.

FATHER ELARYN—see Elaryn Ohraily.

FATHER KUHNYMYCHU—see Kuhnymychu Ruhstahd.

FATHER MAHKZWAIL—See Mahkzwail Bartyn.

FATHER MICHAEL—parish priest of Lakeview, OAR.

FATHER MYRTAN—See Myrtan Byrk.

FATHER SAIRAHS—see Sairahs Tyrnyr.

FATHER SYNDAIL—see Syndail Rahdgyrz.

FATHER TRYNT—Trynt Dezmynd.

FATHER TYMYTHY—see Tymythy Maikyn.

FATHER ZHAMES—see Zhames Symmyns.

FATHER ZHEROHMY—see Zherohmy Brahndyn.

FATHER ZHERYLD—see Zheryld Cumyngs.

FAUYAIR, BROTHER BAHRTALAM—almoner of the Monastery of Saint Zherneau, HFAF.

FERN, DUKE OF—see Samyl Cahkrayn.

FHAIRLY, MAJOR AHDYM, Royal Delferahkan Army—senior battery commander on East Island, Ferayd Sound, Kingdom of Delferahk, BSRA.

FHARMYN, SIR RYK—a foundry owner/ironmaster in the Kingdom of Tarot, HFAF.

FHRANCYS, CAPTAIN TEAGMAHN, Army of God—Bishop Gorthyk Nybar's personal aide, HFQ.

FHRANKLYN, PRIVATE TOHMYS, Army of God—a member of the Camp Lairays guard force, HFQ.

FOFÃO, CAPTAIN MATEUS, Terran Federation Navy—CO, TFNS *Swiftsure*, OAR.

FOHRDYM, MAJOR KARMAIKEL, Imperial Charisian Army—CO, 2nd Battalion, 3rd Regiment, Imperial Charisian Army, MT&T.

FOHRYSTYR, LIEUTENANT CHARLZ, Imperial Charisian Navy—second lieutenant, HMS *Fleet Wing*, 18, HFQ.

FORYST, VICAR ERAYK—a member of Samyl Wylsynn's circle of Reformists in Zion, BSRA.

FOWAIL, CAPTAIN MAIKEL, Royal Desnairian Army—CO, "Fowail's Battery," six-pounder horse artillery assigned to Sir Fahstyr Rychtyr's invasion column, MT&T.

FRAIDMYN, SERGEANT VYK, Charisian Royal Guard—one of Cayleb Ahrmahk's armsmen, later transfers to Charisian Imperial Guard, BSRA.

FRAIMAHN, COLONEL ZHUSTYN, Republic of Siddarmark Army—chief of staff, 2nd Corps, Army of New Northland, HFQ.

FRAYZHYR, SERGEANT WYNSTYN, Royal Corisandian Army—a noncommissioned officer serving as plainclothes security for Irys Daykyn and Hektor Aplyn-Ahrmahk's wedding, LAMA.

FRYMYN, DOCTOR ZHAIN—a member of the Royal

College particularly interested in optics; a member of the Charisian inner circle, LAMA.

FUHLLYR, FATHER RAIMAHND—chaplain, HMS *Dreadnought*, 54, OAR.

FULTYN, BROTHER LYNKYN—a Chihirite lay brother; supervisor/manager St. Kylmahn's Foundry; Allayn Maigwair's and Rhobair Duchairn's chosen industrial manager, LAMA.

FURKHAL, RAFAYL—second baseman and leadoff hitter, Tellesberg Krakens, OAR.

FYGUERA, GENERAL KYDRYC, Republic of Siddarmark Army—CO, Thesmar, South March Lands, MT&T; CO, Thesmar Division, LAMA.

FYNLAITYR, MASTER LYNYX, Imperial Charisian Navy—gunner, broadside ironclad HMS *Rottweiler*, 30, LAMA.

FYNTYN, BRIGADIER FRAYZHYR, Imperial Charisian Army—CO, 13th Infantry Brigade, 7th Infantry Division, Imperial Charisian Army, LAMA.

FYRGYRSYN, COLONEL TAYRENS, Army of God—the Army of the Sylmahn's senior quartermaster.

FYRGYRSYN, PETTY OFFICER CRAHMYND, Imperial Charisian Navy—senior helmsman, ironclad HMS *Delthak*, 22, MT&T.

FYRLOH, FATHER BAHN—a Langhornite Temple Loyalist under-priest in Tellesberg nominated by Father Davys Tyrnyr as Irys and Daivyn.

FYRMAHN, ZHAN—a mountain clansman and feudist from the Gray Wall Mountains; becomes the leader of the Temple Loyalist guerrillas attacking Glacierheart, MT&T.

FYRMYN, FATHER SULYVYN—a Schuelerite upper-priest assigned as Sir Rainos Ahlverez' special intendant, MT&T.

FYRN, FATHER AHNDRU—Bishop Militant Ruhsail's intendant, HFQ.

FYRNACH, BARON OF—see Sir Graim Kyr.

FYSHYR, HAIRYS—CO, privateer galleon *Kraken*, BSRA.

FYTSYMYNS, MAJOR TAHD, Imperial Charisian

Army—CO, 1st Battalion, 11th Mounted Regiment, 6th Mounted Brigade, Imperial Charisian Army, LAMA.

GAHDARHD, LORD SAMYL—keeper of the seal and chief intelligence minister, Republic of Siddarmark, HFAF.

GAHDWYN, STAHNLY—the Delthak Works' fire brigade commander, HFQ.

GAHLVAYO, CAPTAIN GAIYR, Imperial Charisian Army—CO, Company B, 1st Battalion, 1st Scout Sniper Regiment, Imperial Charisian Army, LAMA.

GAHLVYN, CAPTAIN CAHNYR, Imperial Charisian Navy—CO, ironclad HMS *Saygin*, 22, MT&T.

GAHNZAHLYZ, MASTER PAITYR, Imperial Charisian Navy—gunner, broadside ironclad HMS *Dreadnought*, 30, HFQ.

GAHRBOR, ARCHBISHOP FAILYX—Archbishop of Tarot for the Church of God Awaiting, HFAF.

GAHRDANER, SERGEANT CHARLZ, Charisian Royal Guard—one of King Haarahld VII's bodyguards, KIA Battle of Darcos Sound, OAR.

GAHRMAHN, TAYLAR—Duke of Traykhos; Emperor Mahrys IV of Desnair's first councilor, LAMA.

GAHRMYN, LIEUTENANT RAHNYLD, Royal Delferahkan Navy—XO, galley *Arrowhead*, BSRA.

GAHRNAHT, BISHOP AMILAIN—deposed Bishop of Larchros, HFAF.

GAHRNET, SIR AHLVYN, Imperial Desnairian Army—Duke of Harless, senior Desnairian commander in the Republic of Siddarmark; CO, Desnairian Army of Justice; CO, Army of Shiloh, LAMA.

GAHRNET, SIR RHOBAIR, DUKE OF HARLESS—the son of Sir Ahlvyn Gahrnet, inherited his father's title following Sir Ahlvyn's fatal heart attack during the Battle of the Kyplyngyr Forest, HFQ.

GAHRNET, SYMYN—younger brother of Sir Rhobair Gharnet, HFQ.

GAHRVAI, GENERAL SIR KORYN, Corisandian Guard—son of Earl Anvil Rock, Prince Hektor's army field commander, BHD; CO, Corisandian Guard, in the service of the Regency Council, AMF; CO, Royal Corisandian Army, LAMA.

GAHRVAI, SIR RYSEL, EARL OF ANVIL ROCK—Prince Hektor's senior army commander and distant cousin, BSRA; Prince Daivyn Daykyn's official regent and head of Daivyn's Regency Council, AMF.

GAHZTAHN, HIRAIM—Ainsail Dahnvahr's alias in Tellesberg, HFAF.

GAIMLYN, BROTHER BAHLDWYN—under-priest of the Order of Schueler; assigned to King Zhames of Delferahk's household as an agent of the Inquisition, HFAF.

GAIRAHT, CAPTAIN WYLLYS, Chisholmian Royal Guard—CO of Queen Sharleyan's Royal Guard detachment in Charis, KIA Saint Agtha assassination attempt, BSRA.

GAIRLYNG, ARCHBISHOP KLAIRMANT—Archbishop of Corisande for the Church of Charis, HFAF.

GAIRWYL, COLONEL DAHNYLD, Imperial Charisian Army—CO, 5th Mounted Regiment, 3rd Mounted Brigade, Imperial Charisian Army, LAMA.

GAIRWYL, COLONEL SIR NAHTCHYZ, Royal Dohlaran Army—CO, Gairwyl's Regiment (infantry), Royal Dohlaran Army, Dohlaran component, Army of Shiloh, LAMA.

GALVAHN, MAJOR SIR NAITHYN—the Earl of Windshare's senior staff officer, BSRA.

GARDYNYR, ADMIRAL LYWYS, Royal Dohlaran Navy—Earl of Thirsk; senior professional admiral of the Dohlaran Navy; second-in-command to Duke Malikai, OAR; in disgrace, BSRA; restored to command of RDN, AMF.

GARDYNYR, AHLYXZANDYR—the orphaned son of Lanfyrd and Zhudyth Gardynyr, grandson of Sir Lywys Gardynyr, and heir to the Earldom of Thirsk, HFQ.

GARDYNYR, COLONEL THOMYS, Royal Dohlaran Army—CO, Gardynyr's Regiment (cavalry), Dohlaran component, Army of Shiloh; distant cousin of Lywys Gardynyr, Earl of Thirsk, MT&T.

**GARDYNYR, KAHRMYNCETAH** (1)—deceased wife of Lywys Gardynyr, Earl of Thirsk, HFQ.

**GARDYNYR, KAHRMYNCETAH** (2)—the orphaned daughter of Lanfyrd and Zhudyth Gardynyr, granddaughter of Sir Lywys Gardynyr, HFQ.

**GARDYNYR, LANFYRD**—deceased son of Sir Lywys Gardynyr, Earl of Thirsk, HFQ.

**GARDYNYR, ZHOAHNA**—youngest daughter of Lywys Gardynyr, Earl of Thirsk, and a Pasqualate novice, HFQ.

**GARDYNYR, ZHUDYTH**—deceased daughter-in-law of Sir Lywys Gardynyr, Earl of Thirsk, HFQ.

**GARTHIN, EDWAIR**—Earl of North Coast; one of Prince Hektor of Corisande's councilors serving on Prince Daivyn's Regency Council in Corisande; an ally of Earl Anvil Rock and Earl Tartarian, HFAF.

**GARZHA, SERGEANT SEDWEI**, Temple Guard—senior NCO of Captain Gyairmoh Hainz temple guard detachment aboard NGS *Saint Frydhelm*, HFQ.

**GENGCHAI, LORD OF ARMIES YITANGZHI**—Grand Duke of Omar, the Harchongese Army Minister, LAMA.

**GHADWYN, SAMYL**—a Temple Loyalist mountain clansman from the Gray Wall Mountains; one of Zhan Fyrmahn's cousins, MT&T.

**GHATFRYD, SANDARIA**—Ahnzhelyk Phonda's/Nynian Rychtair's personal maid, HFAF.

**GHORDYN, VICAR NICODAIM**—an ally of Zhaspahr Clyntahn on the Council of Vicars.

**GODWYL, GENERAL SIR OHTYS**, Royal Desnairian Army—Baron Traylmyn; General Sir Fahstyr Rychtyr's second-in-command, MT&T.

**GOHDARD, BISHOP MARKYS**—a Schuelerite bishop and a member of the Inquisition, Wyllym Rayno's deputy, with specific responsibility for Rayno and Zhaspahr Clyntahn's personal security details, HFQ.

**GOLD WYVERN, EARL OF**—see Vyrgyl Fahstyr.

**GORJAH, FATHER GHARTH**—Archbishop Zhasyn Cahnyr's personal secretary; a Chihirite of the Order of the Quill, HFAF; Archbishop Zhasyn's executive assistant upon his return to Glacierheart, MT&T.

GORJAH, SAHMANTHA—daughter of Archbishop Zhasyn Cahnyr's previous housekeeper, Father Gharth Gorjah's wife, HFAF; a trained healer assigned to the archbishop upon his return to Glacierheart, MT&T.

GORJAH, ZHASYN—firstborn child of Gharth and Sahmantha Gorjah, HFAF.

GOWAIN, LIEUTENANT FAIRGHAS, Imperial Charisian Navy—XO, HMS *Victorious*, 56, HFAF.

GRAHSMAHN, SYLVAYN—employee in city engineer's office, Manchyr, Corisande; Paitryk Hainree's immediate superior, HFAF.

GRAHZAIAL, LIEUTENANT COMMANDER MAHSHAL, Imperial Charisian Navy—CO, schooner HMS *Messenger*, 6, HFAF.

GRAINGYR, CAPTAIN MAHTHYW, Imperial Charisian Army—Earl High Mount's personal aide, HFQ.

GRAINGYR, COLONEL BRYSYN, Imperial Charisian Army—senior quartermaster, 2nd Brigade (reinforced); later senior quartermaster, Army of Midhold, LAMA.

GRAINGYR, FATHER AHNDRU—a Pasqualate underpriest who serves as broadside ironclad HMS *Thunderer*'s surgeon and chaplain, HFQ.

GRAISYN, BISHOP EXECUTOR WYLLYS—Archbishop Lyam Tyrn's chief administrator for the Archbishopric of Emerald, OAR.

GRAISYN, LIEUTENANT STYVYN, Imperial Charisian Navy—second lieutenant, broadside ironclad HMS *Rottweiler*, 30, LAMA.

GRAIVYR, FATHER STYVYN—Bishop Ernyst Jynkyns' intendant, BSRA; hanged on Sir Domynyk Staynair's flagship, BHD.

GRAND VICAR EREK XVII—secular and temporal head of the Church of God Awaiting (the Group of Four's puppet), OAR.

GRAUSMYN, MAJOR STYVYN, Army of God—CO, Company A, 191st Cavalry Regiment, HFQ.

GRAY HARBOR, EARL OF—see Rayjhis Yowance.

GRAY HILL, BARON OF—see Byrtrym Mahldyn.

GREEN MOUNTAIN, BARON OF—see Mahrak Sahndyrs.

GREEN VALLEY, BARON OF—see Kynt Clareyk.

GREENHILL, TYMAHN—King Haarahld VII's senior huntsman, OAR.

GREGORI, LIEUTENANT ZHAIKYB, Imperial Charisian Navy—XO, ironclad HMS *Eraystor*, 22, HFQ.

GUHSTAHVSYN, COMMANDER URWYN, Royal Dohlaran Navy—CO, HMS *Truculent*, 18, HFQ.

GUYSHAIN, FATHER BAHRNAI—Vicar Zahmsyn Trynair's senior aide, OAR.

GWAY, CAPTAIN OF SWORDS JWEIPAHNG, Imperial Harchongese Army—CO, Company B, 3rd Kyznetzov Lancers (a militia regiment), HFQ.

GYLLMYN, COLONEL RAHSKHO, Republic of Siddarmark Army—General Kydryc Fyguera's second-in-command, Thesmar, South March Lands, MT&T; XO, Thesmar Division, LAMA.

GYLLMYN, MASTER AHLAHNZO, Imperial Charisian Navy—sailing master in broadside ironclad HMS *Dreadnought*, 30, HFQ.

GYRARD, LIEUTENANT ANDRAI, Royal Charisian Navy—first officer, HMS *Dreadnought*, OAR; Imperial Charisian Navy, CO, HMS *Empress of Charis*, 58, BSRA.

HAARPAR, SERGEANT GORJ, Charisian Royal Guard—one of King Haarahld VII's bodyguards, KIA Battle of Darcos Sound, OAR.

HADOR, MAJOR SAHLAVAHN, Imperial Charisian Army—CO, 1st Battalion, 5th Mounted Regiment, 3rd Mounted Brigade, Imperial Charisian Army, LAMA.

HAHL, LIEUTENANT PAWAL, Royal Dohlaran Navy—second lieutenant, HMS *Chihiro*, 50, MT&T.

HAHLBYRSTAHT, LIEUTENANT ZOSH, Imperial Charisian Navy—XO, HMS *Fleet Wing*, 18, HFQ.

HAHLCAHM, DOCTOR ZHER—member of the Royal College of Charis, specializing in biology and food preparation, MT&T.

HAHLCAHM, VICAR ZAKRYAH—a Chihirite of the Order of the Quill and seminary classmate of Rhobair Duchairn, HFQ.

HAHLEK, FATHER SYMYN—a Langhornite under-priest, Archbishop Klairmant Gairlyng's personal aide, HFAF.

HAHLMAHN, PAWAL—King Haarahld VII's senior chamberlain, OAR.

HAHLMYN, FATHER MAHRAK—an upper-priest of the Church of God

HAHLMYN, MIDSHIPMAN ZHORJ, Imperial Charisian Navy—a signals midshipman aboard HMS *Darcos Sound*, 54, HFAF.

HAHLMYN, SAIRAIH—Queen Sharleyan's personal maid, BHD.

HAHLTAR, ADMIRAL GENERAL SIR URWYN, Imperial Desnairian Navy—Baron Jahras; CO, Imperial Desnairian Navy; Daivyn Bairaht's brother-in-law, HFAF; flees to Charis for asylum following Battle of Iythria, MT&T.

HAHLYND, ADMIRAL PAWAL, Royal Dohlaran Navy—one of Earl Thirsk's most trusted subordinates; CO, antipiracy patrols, Hankey Sound; a friend of Admiral Thirsk, BHD; Admiral Thirsk's senior subordinate admiral, HFAF; CO of screw-galley fleet; uncle of Greyghor Whytmyn, Earl Thirsk's son-in-law, HFQ.

HAHLYND, COLONEL BRAISYN, Royal Dohlaran Army—CO, Hahlynd's Regiment (infantry), Dohlaran component, Army of Shiloh, LAMA.

HAHLYND, MAJOR RAHZHYR, Imperial Charisian Army—CO, 2nd Battalion, 5th Mounted Regiment, 3rd Mounted Brigade, Imperial Charisian Army, LAMA.

HAHLYS, BISHOP GAHRMYN, Army of God—CO, Chihiro Division, Army of Glacierheart (Bishop Militant Cahnyr Kaitswyrth's favored division), MT&T.

HAHNDAIL, CORPORAL WAHLYS, Imperial Charisian Marines—Marine section commander attached to Brigadier Taisyn's forces in Glacierheart, MT&T.

HAHPKYNS, PLATOON SERGEANT RUHFUS, Imperial Charisian Army—platoon sergeant, 1st Platoon,

Company A, 1st Battalion, 5th Regiment, Imperial Charisian Army, LAMA.

**HAHPKYNSYN, COLONEL NATHALAN**—CO, 1st Maidynberg Militia, Shilohian Temple Loyalist militia; assigned to Fort Tairys garrison, LAMA.

**HAHRAIMAHN, ZHAK**—a Siddarmarkian industrialist and foundry owner, HFAF.

**HAHRLYS, LIEUTENANT KLYMYNT**, Imperial Charisian Army—an engineering officer attached to Earl Hanth's Thesmar command, HFQ.

**HAHSKANS, DAILOHRS**—Father Tymahn Hahskans' wife, HFAF.

**HAHSKANS, FATHER TYMAHN**—a Reformist upper-priest of the Order of Bédard in Manchyr; senior priest, Saint Kathryn's Church, murdered by Temple Loyalist extremists, HFAF.

**HAHSKYN, LIEUTENANT AHNDRAI**, Charisian Imperial Guard—a Charisian officer assigned to Empress Sharleyan's guard detachment. Captain Gairaht's second-in-command, KIA Saint Agtha assassination attempt, BSRA.

**HAHVAIR, COMMANDER FRANZ**, Imperial Charisian Navy—CO, schooner HMS *Mace*, 12, HFAF.

**HAIGYL, CAPTAIN KAHRLTYN**, Imperial Charisian Navy—CO, broadside ironclad HMS *Dreadnought*, 30, LAMA.

**HAIMLTAHN, BISHOP EXECUTOR WYLLYS**—Archbishop Zhasyn Cahnyr's executive assistant in the Archbishopric of Glacierheart, HFAF.

**HAIMYN, BRIGADIER MAHRYS**, Royal Charisian Marines—CO, 5th Brigade, Royal Charisian Marines, BSRA.

**HAINAI, COMMANDER FRAHNKLYN**, Imperial Charisian Navy—one of Sir Ahlfryd Hyndryk's senior assistants; Bureau of Ordnance's chief liaison with Ehdwyrd Howsmyn and his artificers, MT&T.

**HAINE, FATHER FHRANKLYN**—upper-priest of the Order of Pasquale; the senior healer attached to Archbishop Zhasyn Cahnyr's relief expedition to Glacierheart Province, MT&T.

HAINREE, PAITRYK—a silversmith and Temple Loyalist agitator in Manchyr, Princedom of Corisande, HFAF; attempts to assassinate Empress Sharleyan, AMF.

HAINZ, CAPTAIN GYAIRMOH, Temple Guard—CO of the Temple Guard escort detailed to "escort" Earl Thirsk's family to Zion, HFQ.

HAINZ, FATHER AHNDRU—a Chihirite under-priest serving as Colonel Gylchryst Sheldyn's regimental chaplain, Sheldyn's Regiment, Army of the Seridahn, HFQ.

HAIRYNGTYN, CORPORAL NAIKLOS, Imperial Charisian Marine Corps—Marine NCO, Marine detachment, HMS *Destiny*, 54, HFQ.

HAITHMYN, COLONEL SIR AHLGYRNAHN, Imperial Desnairian Army—CO, Haithmyn's Regiment (medium cavalry), cavalry wing, Army of Shiloh, LAMA.

HALBROOK HOLLOW, DUCHESS OF—see Elahnah Waistyn.

HALBROOK HOLLOW, DUKE OF—see Byrtrym Waistyn and Sailys Waistyn.

HALCOM, BISHOP MYLZ—Bishop of Margaret Bay, becomes leader of armed Temple Loyalist resistance in Charis; KIA Saint Agtha's assassination attempt, BSRA.

HALMYN, ARCHBISHOP ZAHMSYN—Archbishop of Gorath; senior prelate of the Kingdom of Dohlar, OAR.

HAMPTYN, CAPTAIN MARKYS, Royal Dohlaran Navy—CO, HMS *Defiant* (ex-*Dancer*), 56, and Admiral Sir Dahrand Rohsail's flag captain, HFQ.

HAMPTYN, MAJOR KOLYN—Temple Loyalist ex-militia officer, Fort Darymahn, South March Lands, Republic of Siddarmark, MT&T.

HANSYLMAN, COLONEL BAHRTALYMU, Army of God—Bishop Gorthyk Nybar's chief of staff, HFQ.

HANTAI, WAISU—Waisu VI, Emperor of Harchong.

HANTH, COUNTESS OF—see Mairah Lywkys Breygart.

HANTH, EARL OF—see Sir Hauwerd Breygart; see also Tahdayo Mahntayl.

**HARLESS, DUKE OF**—see Sir Rhobair Gahrnet.

**HARMYN, MAJOR BAHRKLY**, Royal Emeraldian Army—an Emeraldian army officer assigned to North Bay, BSRA.

**HARPAHR, BISHOP KORNYLYS**, Navy of God—bishop of the Order of Chihiro; admiral general of the Navy of God, HFAF.

**HARPAHR, CAPTAIN BRYAHN**, Army of God—CO, 1st Company, 73rd Cavalry Regiment, Army of the Sylmahn, LAMA.

**HARPAHR, MAHGDYLYNAH**—Sir Ahrnahld Mahkzwail and Lady Stefyny Mahkzwail's housekeeper, HFQ.

**HARRISON, MATTHEW PAUL**—Timothy and Sarah Harrison's great-grandson, OAR.

**HARRISON, ROBERT**—Timothy and Sarah Harrison's grandson; Matthew Paul Harrison's father, OAR.

**HARRISON, SARAH**—wife of Timothy Harrison and an Eve, OAR.

**HARRISON, TIMOTHY**—mayor of Lakeview and an Adam, OAR.

**HARYS, CAPTAIN ZHOEL**, Royal Corisandian Navy—CO, Corisandian galley *Lance*, BSRA; CO, galleon *Wing*; responsible for transporting Princess Irys and Prince Daivyn to Delferahk, BHD.

**HARYS, COLONEL WYNTAHN**, Imperial Charisian Marine Corps—senior officer in command Marines detailed to support Captain Halcom Bahrns' operation ("Great Canal Raid"), MT&T.

**HARYS, FATHER AHLBYRT**—Vicar Zahmsyn Trynair's special representative to Dohlar, OAR.

**HASKYN, MIDSHIPMAN YAHNCEE**, Royal Dohlaran Navy—a midshipman aboard HMS *Gorath Bay*, OAR.

**HASKYNS, COLONEL MOHRTYN**, Imperial Charisian Army—CO, 11th Mounted Regiment, 6th Mounted Brigade, Imperial Charisian Army, LAMA.

**HAUKYNS, CAPTAIN ZHAK**, Imperial Charisian Navy—CO, HMS *Powerful*, 58; Admiral Payter Shain's flag captain, LAMA.

**HAUWYL, SHAIN**, Royal Dohlaran Army—Duke of

Salthar, senior officer, Royal Dohlaran Army, MT&T.

HAUWYRD, ZHORZH—Earl Gray Harbor's personal guardsman, OAR.

HAYSTYNGS, LIEUTENANT JYROHM, Royal Dohlaran Navy—first lieutenant, screw-galley HMS *Sword*, HFQ.

HENDERSON, LIEUTENANT GABRIELA ("GABBY"), Terran Federation Navy—tactical officer, TFNS *Swiftsure*, OAR.

HIGH MOUNT, EARL OF—see Breyt Bahskym.

HILLKEEPER, WAHLYS—Earl of Craggy Hill; a member of Prince Daivyn's Regency Council; also a senior member of the Northern Conspiracy, HFAF.

HOBSYN, COLONEL ALLAYN, Imperial Charisian Army—CO, 5th Regiment, 3rd Brigade, 2nd Division, Imperial Charisian Army, LAMA.

HOLDYN, VICAR LYWYS—a member of Samyl Wylsynn's circle of Reformists, BSRA.

HOLY TREE, DUKE OF—see Sir Bryndyn Crawfyrd.

HOTCHKYS, CAPTAIN SIR OHWYN, Royal Charisian Navy—CO, galley HMS *Tellesberg*, OAR.

HOWAIL, BISHOP ZHASYN, Army of God—CO, St. Thadyus Division, Army of the Sylmahn, HFQ.

HOWAIL, COLONEL BRYNTYN, Republic of Siddarmark Army—CO, 37th Infantry Regiment, LAMA.

HOWAIL, MAJOR DAHNEL, Army of God—XO, 1st Regiment, Zion Division, Army of Glacierheart.

HOWSMYN, EHDWYRD—a wealthy foundry owner and shipbuilder in Tellesberg, OAR; member of the Charisian inner circle, BHD; "the Ironmaster of Charis," Created Duke of Delthak, HFQ; the wealthiest and most innovative Old Charisian industrialist, MT&T.

HOWSMYN, ZHAIN—Ehdwyrd Howsmyn's wife, daughter of Earl Sharphill, OAR.

HUNTYR, LIEUTENANT KLEMYNT, Charisian Royal Guard—an officer of the Charisian Royal Guard in Tellesberg, OAR.

HUNTYR, ZOSH—Ehdwyrd Howsmyn's master artificer, MT&T.

HWOJAHN, CAPTAIN OF HORSE MEDYNG, Imperial Harchongese Army—Baron of Wind Song; Earl Rainbow Waters' chief of staff and nephew, HFQ.

HWYSTYN, SIR VYRNYN—a member of the Charisian Parliament elected from Tellesberg, BSRA.

HYLDYR, COLONEL FRAIHMAN, Republic of Siddarmark Army—CO, 123rd Infantry Regiment, Republic of Siddarmark Army, a part of General Trumyn Stohnar's Sylmahn Gap command, MT&T.

HYLDYRSHOT, PRIVATE SYMYN, Royal Dohlaran Army—1st Section, 2nd Platoon, 5th Company, Sheldyn's Regiment, Army of the Seridahn, HFQ.

HYLLAIR, SIR FARAHK—the Baron of Dairwyn, BSRA.

HYLMAHN, RAHZHYR—Earl of Thairnos, a relatively new addition to Prince Daivyn's Regency Council in Corisande, MT&T.

HYLMYN, CAPTAIN HENRAI, Royal Dohlaran Army—CO, Hylmyn's Battery, Sylvstyr's Artillery Regiment, HFQ.

HYLMYN, CAPTAIN SEBAHSTEAN, Imperial Charisian Navy—CO, HMS *Dynzayl Tryvythyn*, 68, HFQ.

HYLMYN, FRONZ—Earl Sharpfield's personal clerk and secretary, LAMA.

HYLMYN, LIEUTENANT MAINYRD, Imperial Charisian Navy—senior engineer, ironclad HMS *Saygin*, 22, MT&T.

HYLMYN, LIEUTENANT STYVYN, Imperial Charisian Army—CO, 1st Platoon, Company A, 1st Battalion, 5th Regiment, Imperial Charisian Army, LAMA.

HYLSDAIL, LIEUTENANT FRAYDYK, Imperial Charisian Navy—second lieutenant, HMS *Trumpeter*; detached to serve as CO, Redoubt 1, Thesmar garrison, LAMA.

HYNDRYK, SIR AHLFRYD—Baron Seamount; captain, Royal Charisian Navy, senior gunnery expert, OAR; commodore, Imperial Charisian Navy, BSRA; admiral, HFAF; CO, Bureau of Ordnance, MT&T.

HYNDYRS, DUNKYN—purser, privateer galleon *Raptor*, BSRA.

HYNRYKAI, COLONEL AHVRAHM, Imperial Charisian

Army—Army liaison with the Navy Bureau of Ordnance and the Delthak Works, LAMA.

HYNTYN, SIR DYNZAYL—Earl of Saint Howan; Chancellor of the Treasury, Kingdom of Chisholm, MT&T.

HYRST, ADMIRAL ZOHZEF, Royal Chisholmian Navy—Earl Sharpfield's second-in-command, OAR; Imperial Charisian Navy, CO, Port Royal fleet base, Chisholm, BHD.

HYRST, SIR ABSHAIR—Earl of Nearoak, Lord Justice of Old Charis and, effectively, of the Charisian Empire, LAMA.

HYSIN, VICAR CHIYAN—a member of Vicar Samyl Wylsynn's circle of Reformists (from Harchong), BSRA.

HYWANLOHNG, CAPTAIN OF HORSE KAISHAU, Imperial Harchongese Army—effectively, Earl Silken Hills' chief of staff, HFQ.

HYWSTYN, LORD AVRAHM—a cousin of Greyghor Stohnar, and a midranking official assigned to the Siddarmarkian foreign ministry, BSRA.

HYWYT, ADMIRAL SIR PAITRYK—Royal Charisian Navy, CO, HMS *Wave*, 14 (schooner), transferred Imperial Charisian Navy, BSRA; promoted captain, CO, HMS *Dancer*, 56, BHD; promoted admiral, CO, Inshore Squadron, Gulf of Mathyas, MT&T.

IBBET, AHSTELL—a blacksmith convicted of treason as part of the Northern Conspiracy in Corisande; pardoned by Empress Sharleyan, HFAF.

ILLIAN, CAPTAIN AHNTAHN, Royal Corisandian Army—one of Sir Phylyp Myllyr's company commanders, BSRA.

INGRAYAHN, CAPTAIN VALTYNOH, Army of God—CO, 1st Company, 1st Regiment, Zion Division, Army of Glacierheart, LAMA.

IRONHILI, BARON OF—see Ahlvyno Pawalsyn.

JAHRAS, BARON OF—see Urwyn Hahltar.

JYNKYN, COLONEL HAUWYRD, Royal Charisian Marines—Admiral Rock Point's senior Marine commander, BSRA.

JYNKYNS, BISHOP ERNYST—Bishop of Ferayd, BSRA.

**KAHBRYLLO, CAPTAIN AHNTAHN**, Imperial Charisian Navy—CO, HMS *Dawn Star*, 58, Empress Sharleyan's transport to Zebediah and Corisande, HFAF.

**KAHLDONAI, SERGEANT ZHYKOHMA**, Army of God—Sergeant, 1st Platoon, Company A, 191st Cavalry Regiment, Army of Glacierheart, LAMA.

**KAHLYNS, COLONEL ZHANDRU**, Army of God—CO, 1st Regiment, Sulyvyn Division, Army of Glacierheart, LAMA.

**KAHLYNS, GENERAL SIR FRAIZHER**, Imperial Charisian Army—senior Imperial Charisian Army commander in Chisholm, HFQ.

**KAHLYNS, LIEUTENANT ABERNETHY**, Republic of Siddarmark Army—1st Siddarmarkian Scout Regiment, Army of Hildermoss; Colonel Dahrdyn Tymythy's senior aide, HFQ.

**KAHMELKA, COLONEL GOTFRYD**, Royal Dohlaran Army—CO, Kahmelka's Regiment, Dohlaran component, Army of Shiloh, LAMA.

**KAHMERLYNG, COLONEL LUTAYLO**, Imperial Charisian Army—CO, 2nd Regiment, 1st Brigade, 1st Infantry Division, Imperial Charisian Army, LAMA.

**KAHMPTMYN, MAJOR HAHLYND**, Imperial Charisian Army—XO, 4th Regiment, Imperial Charisian Army, MT&T.

**KAHNKLYN, AIDRYAN**—Tairys Kahnklyn's older daughter, Rahzhyr Mahklyn's older granddaughter and oldest grandchild, BSRA.

**KAHNKLYN, AIZAK**—Rahzhyr Mahklyn's son-in-law; a senior librarian with the Royal College of Charis, BSRA.

**KAHNKLYN, ERAYK**—Tairys Kahnklyn's oldest son, Rahzhyr Mahklyn's older grandson, BSRA.

**KAHNKLYN, EYDYTH**—Rahzhyr Mahklyn's younger granddaughter; twin sister of Zhoel Kahnklyn, BSRA.

**KAHNKLYN, HAARAHLD**—Tairys Kahnklyn's middle son; Rahzhyr Mahklyn's second oldest grandson, BSRA.

**KAHNKLYN, TAIRYS**—Rahzhyr Mahklyn's married

daughter; senior librarian, Royal College of Charis, BSRA.

**KAHNKLYN, ZHOEL**—Tairys Kahnklyn's youngest son, Rahzhyr Mahklyn's youngest grandson; twin brother of Eydyth Kahklyn, BSRA.

**KAHRLTYN, CAPTAIN ZOSHUA**, Imperial Charisian Navy—CO, HMS *Firestorm*, 30, HFQ.

**KAHRNAIKYS, MAJOR ZHAPHAR**, Temple Guard—an officer of the Temple Guard and a Schuelerite, HFAF.

**KAHSIMAHR, LIEUTENANT SIR LAIMYN**, Imperial Desnairian Army—youngest son of the Duke of Sherach; Sir Borys Cahstnyr's senior aide and effective chief of staff, Quartermaster Corps, Army of Justice and Army of Shiloh, LAMA.

**KAILLEE, CAPTAIN ZHILBERT**—Royal Tarotisian Navy, CO, galley *King Gorjah II*, Baron White Ford's flag captain, OAR; Imperial Charisian Navy, CO, HMS *Fortune*, 58; Baron White Ford's flag captain, LAMA.

**KAILLEE, MAJOR BRUHSTAIR**, Royal Dohlaran Army—CO, 3rd Company, Ohygyns' Regiment (infantry), Dohlaran component, Army of Shiloh, LAMA.

**KAILLWYRTH, MAJOR ZHAIK**, Imperial Charisian Army—CO, 4th Battalion, 6th Regiment, Imperial Charisian Army, LAMA.

**KAILLYT, CORPORAL RAIMAHN**, Royal Dohlaran Army—SNOIC, 1st Section, 2nd Platoon, 5th Company, Sheldyn's' Regiment, Army of the Seridahn, HFQ.

**KAILLYT, FATHER CHARLZ**—a senior Schuelerite priest who was Gorthyk Nybar's senior chaplain in Langhorne Division, serves as the Army of Fairkyn's intendant, HFQ.

**KAILLYT, KAIL**—Major Borys Sahdlyr's second-in-command in Siddar City, HFAF.

**KAIREE, TRAIVYR**—a wealthy merchant and landowner in the Earldom of Styvyn, Temple Loyalist, BSRA; complicit in the attempt to assassinate Empress Sharleyan, BHD.

**KAIRMYN, CAPTAIN TOMHYS**, Royal Delferahkan

Army—one of Sir Vyk Lakyr's officers, Ferayd garrison, BSRA.

KAISI, FHRANCYS—one of the Republic of Siddarmark's greatest composers who wrote, among many other works, "The Stand at Kahrmaik," commemorating one of the greatest Siddarmarkian victories against the Desnairian Empire, LAMA.

KAITS, CAPTAIN BAHRNABAI, Imperial Charisian Marines—CO, Marine detachment, HMS *Squall*, 36, HFAF.

KAITSWYRTH, BISHOP MILITANT CAHNYR, Army of God—a Chihirite of the Order of the Sword and ex-Temple Guard officer; CO, western column of the Army of God, invading the Republic of Siddarmark through Westmarch Province, MT&T; his command redesignated the Army of the Sylmahn, LAMA.

KARMAIKEL, COMMANDER WAHLTAYR, Imperial Charisian Navy—CO, 3rd Provisional Battalion, 1st Independent Marine Brigade (one of Hauwerd Breygart's Navy "battalions" at Thesmar), MT&T.

KARMAIKEL, LIEUTENANT DYNTYN, Imperial Charisian Marines—Earl Hanth's personal aide, LAMA.

KARMAIKEL, MAJOR DYNTYN, Imperial Charisian Army—the Earl of Hanth's personal aide, promoted from lieutenant since LAMA, HFQ.

KARNYNKOH, CAPTAIN MAIKEL, Imperial Charisian Army—CO, Company A, 2nd Battalion, 12th Mounted Regiment, 6th Mounted Brigade, Imperial Charisian Army, LAMA.

KARSTAYRS, SERGEANT THOMYS, Army of God—regiment command sergeant, 191st Cavalry Regiment, MT&T.

KARTYR, CAPTAIN LAZYMYR—a Dohlaran smuggler who becomes a spy for the Royal Dohlaran Navy, HFQ.

KARTYR, MAJOR ZHON, Imperial Charisian Army—CO, 2nd Battalion, 8th Regiment, 4th Infantry Brigade, Imperial Charisian Army, LAMA.

KASPAHRT, SERGEANT LAIJAH, Army of God—Sergeant Ahzwald Mahthyws' replacement as Major Che-

Styvyn V of Sardahn's cousin and first councilor, LAMA.

KHLUNAI, COLONEL RHANDYL, Imperial Charisian Army—General Ahlyn Symkyn's chief of staff under the new staff organization, MT&T.

KHOLMAN, DUKE OF—see Faigyn Makychee; see also Daivyn Bairaht.

KHOWSAN, CAPTAIN OF WINDS SHOUKHAN, Imperial Harchongese Navy—Count of Wind Mountain; CO, IHNS *Flower of Waters*, 50. Flag captain to the Duke of Sun Rising, HFAF.

KING CAYLEB II—see Cayleb Ahrmahk.

KING GORJAH III—see Gorjah Nyou.

KING HAARAHLD VII—see Haarahld Ahrmahk.

KING RAHNYLD IV—see Rahnyld Bahrns.

KING ZHAMES II—see Zhames Olyvyr Rayno.

KLAHRKSAIN, CAPTAIN TYMAHN, Imperial Charisian Navy—CO, HMS *Talisman*, 54, HFAF.

KLAIBYRN, GENERAL ZHAMES—CO of the Temple Loyalist militia garrison of Sangyr in Cliff Peak, south of Aivahnstyn, HFQ.

KLAIRYNCE, CAPTAIN HAINREE, Republic of Siddarmark Army—acting CO, 3rd Company, 37th Infantry Regiment, Republic of Siddarmark Army, MT&T.

KLYMYNT, MAJOR ZAHNDRU, Imperial Charisian Army—CO, 1st Battalion, 7th Regiment, 4th Infantry Brigade, Imperial Charisian Army, LAMA.

KLYNKSKAYL, SIR ZHERYD, BARONET GLYNFYRD, Imperial Desnairian Army—CO, Glynfyrd's Regiment (light cavalry), Imperial Desnairian Army, Army of Shiloh, LAMA.

KLYNKSKAYL, SIR ZHERYD, Imperial Desnairian Army—Baronet Glynfyrd; CO, Glynfyrd's Regiment (light cavalry), cavalry wing, Army of Shiloh, LAMA.

KNOWLES, EVELYN—an Eve who escaped the destruction of the Alexandria Enclave and fled to Tellesberg, BSRA.

KNOWLES, JEREMIAH—an Adam who escaped the destruction of the Alexandria Enclave and fled to

Tellesberg, where he became the patron and founder of the Brethren of Saint Zherneau, BSRA.

**KOHLCHYST, BARON OF**—see Vyktyr Tryntyn.

**KOHMANDORSKY, COLONEL STYVYN**, Republic of Siddarmark Army—the Army of Hildermoss' chief artillerist, HFQ.

**KOHRAZAHN, SERGEANT AINGHUS**, Army of God—Lieutenant Ansyn Mahafee's platoon sergeant, HFQ.

**KOHRBY, MIDSHIPMAN LYNAIL**, Royal Charisian Navy—senior midshipman, HMS *Dreadnought*, 54, OAR.

**KRAHL, CAPTAIN AHNDAIR**, Royal Dohlaran Navy—CO, HMS *Bédard*, 42, HFAF; promoted admiral, CO, Claw Island, LAMA.

**KRESTMYN, COLONEL BYNZHAMYN**, Army of God—CO, Mighty Host of God and the Archangels' Camp Number Four, Duchy of Gwynt, LAMA.

**KRUGAIR, CAPTAIN MAIKEL**, Imperial Charisian Navy—CO, HMS *Avalanche*, 36. POW of Earl Thirsk, surrendered to the Inquisition, HFAF.

**KRUGHAIR, LIEUTENANT ZHASYN**, Imperial Charisian Navy—second lieutenant, HMS *Dancer*, 56, HFAF.

**KRYSTYPHYRSYN, ALYK**—a manufactory supervisor and night-shift supervisor, the pistol and rifle shop, Delthak Works, LAMA.

**KUHLBYRTSYN, CHIEF PETTY OFFICER MYRVYN**, Imperial Charisian Navy—a senior noncom aboard ironclad HMS *Delthak*, 22, LAMA.

**KUHLHANI, LIEUTENANT AHNTWAHN, NAVY OF GOD**—second lieutenant, NGS *Saint Frydhelm*, 40, HFQ.

**KULMYN, RHOBAIR**, Canal Service—pump master, Fairkyn, New Northland Province, Republic of Siddarmark, MT&T.

**KURNAU, CAPTAIN ZHORJ**, Royal Dohlaran Navy—CO, HMS *Saint Ahndru*, 54, HFQ.

**KWAYLE, TYMYTHY**, Imperial Charisian Navy—a senior petty officer and boatswain's mate, HMS *Destiny*, 54, HFAF.

**KWILL, FATHER ZYTAN**—upper-priest of the Order of

Bédard; abbot of the Hospice of the Holy Bédard, the main homeless shelter in the city of Zion, HFAF.

KYLMAHN, LIEUTENANT DAIVYN, Imperial Charisian Navy—XO, broadside ironclad HMS *Thunderer*, 30, LAMA.

KYNDYRS, PRIVATE ZHAKSYN "ZHAKKY," Army of God—a cavalry trooper in 1st Platoon, Company A, 191st Cavalry Regiment, HFQ.

KYNKAYD, BRIGADIER SAHLAVAHN, Imperial Charisian Army—Sir Bartyn Sahmyrsyt's chief artillerist in the Army of New Northland and youngest brother of the Earl of Shayne, HFQ.

KYR, SIR GRAIM—Baron of Fyrnach, Duke Harless' senior aide; age twenty-seven in 896, dark hair, brown eyes, handsome in a somewhat flashy sort of way; cousin of the Duke of Traykhos and Harless' grandnephew, LAMA.

KYRBYSH, COLONEL BRYAHN—CO, 3rd Maidynberg Militia, Shilohian Temple Loyalist, assigned to Fort Tairys' garrison, LAMA.

KYRST, OWAIN—Temple Loyalist, mayor of Fairkyn, New Northland Province, Republic of Siddarmark, MT&T.

LACHLYN, COLONEL TAYLAR, Army of God—senior regimental commander, Chihiro Division, Army of Glacierheart, MT&T.

LADY MAIRAH LYWKYS—see Lady Mairah Lywkys Breygart, Countess Hanth.

LAHANG, BRAIDEE—Prince Nahrmahn of Emerald's chief agent in Charis before Merlin Athrawes' arrival there, OAR.

LAHFAT, CAPTAIN MYRGYN—piratical ruler of Claw Keep on Claw Island, HFAF.

LAHFTYN, MAJOR BRYAHN—Brigadier Clareyk's chief of staff, BSRA.

LAHKYRT, COLONEL ZHONATHYN, Royal Dohlaran Army—CO, Lahkyrt's Regiment (infantry), Royal Dohlaran Army, Dohlaran component, Army of Shiloh, LAMA.

LAHMBAIR, LIEUTENANT LYNYRD, Royal Dohlaran

Navy—Lieutenant Henrai Sahltmyn's XO, Claw Island defensive batteries, LAMA.

LAHMBAIR, PARSAIVAHL—a prominent Corisandian greengrocer convicted of treason as part of the Northern Conspiracy, pardoned by Empress Sharleyan, HFAF.

LAHRAK, NAILYS—a senior leader of the Temple Loyalists in Charis, BSRA; complicit in attempt to assassinate Empress Sharleyan, BHD.

LAHSAHL, LIEUTENANT SHAIRMYN, Royal Charisian Navy—XO, HMS *Destroyer*, 54, BSRA.

LAICHARN, ARCHBISHOP PRAIDWYN—Archbishop of Siddar; the ranking prelate of the Republic of Siddarmark. A Langhornite, HFAF; archbishop in exile, MT&T.

LAIKHYRST, SIR ZHORJ, BARON OF YELLOWSTONE—a member of King Rahnyld IV's Royal Council and, effectively, the Kingdom of Dohlar's foreign minister, HFQ.

LAIMHYN, FATHER CLYFYRD—Cayleb Ahrmahk's confessor and personal secretary, assigned to him by Archbishop Maikel, BSRA.

LAINYR, BISHOP EXECUTOR WYLSYNN—Bishop Executor of Gorath. A Langhornite, HFAF.

LAIRAYS, FATHER AWBRAI—under-priest of the Order of Schueler; HMS *Archangel Chihiro*'s ship's chaplain, HFAF.

LAIRMAHN, FAHSTAIR—Baron of Lakeland; first councilor of the Kingdom of Delferahk, HFAF.

LAIROH, COLONEL SIR ZHONATHYN, Royal Dohlaran Army—CO, Lairoh's Regiment (medium cavalry), Dohlaran component, Army of Shiloh, LAMA.

LAITEE, FATHER ZHAMES—priest of the Order of Schueler; assistant to Father Gaisbyrt Vandaik in Talkyra, HFAF.

LAITYR, FATHER ZHAIF—a Reformist upper-priest of the Order of Pasquale; senior priest, Church of the Holy Archangels Triumphant; a close personal friend of Father Tymahn Hahskans, HFAF.

LAKE LAND, DUKE OF—see Paitryk Mahknee.

New Northland Province, Republic of Siddarmark, MT&T.

LOCK ISLAND, EARL OF—see Bryahn Lock Island.

LOCK ISLAND, HIGH ADMIRAL BRYAHN, Imperial Charisian Navy—Earl of Lock Island; CO, Imperial Charisian Navy, Cayleb Ahrmahk's cousin, OAR; KIA Battle of the Gulf of Tarot, AMF.

LOHGYN, MAHRAK—a Temple Loyalist mountain clansman from the Gray Wall Mountains; one of Zhan Fyrmahn's cousins, MT&T.

LOHGYN, MAJOR HAIMYN, Army of God—CO of the troops assigned to Father Trynt Dezmynd for the evacuation of the Camp Tairek prisoners, HFQ.

LOPAYZ, MAJOR BEHZNYK, Imperial Charisian Army—CO, 4th Battalion, 10th Mounted Regiment, 5th Mounted Brigade, Imperial Charisian Army, LAMA.

LORD PROTECTOR GREYGHOR—see Greyghor Stohnar.

LOWAYL, MAJOR FRAHNK, Imperial Charisian Army—senior engineer, 1st Brigade (reinforced) and Army of the Branaths, LAMA.

LYAM, ARCHBISHOP—see Archbishop Lyam Tyrn.

LYBYRN, FATHER GHATFRYD—Schuelerite under-priest; senior clergyman, Ohlarn, New Northland Province, Republic of Siddarmark, MT&T.

LYCAHN, PRIVATE ZHEDRYK, Imperial Charisian Marine Corps—a Marine private in Brigadier Taisyn's forces in Glacierheart; ex-poacher and thief, MT&T.

LYNDAHR, SIR RAIMYND—Prince Hektor of Corisande's keeper of the purse, BSRA; Prince Daivyn's Regency Council in the same capacity; an ally of Earl Anvil Rock and Earl Tartarian, AMF.

LYNKYN, ARCHBISHOP ULYS—Archbishop of Chisholm, replacing the murdered Archbishop Pawal Braynair, MT&T.

LYNKYN, SIR ADULFO—Duke of Black Water; son of Sir Ernyst Lynkyn, HFAF.

LYNKYN, SIR ERNYST, Corisandian Navy—Duke of Black Water, CO, Corisandian Navy; KIA Battle of Darcos Sound, OAR.

**LYNTYN, MAJOR CAHNYR,** Imperial Charisian Army—CO, 4th Battalion, 6th Mounted Regiment, 3rd Mounted Brigade, Imperial Charisian Army, LAMA.

**LYPTAKIA, MAJOR GHORDYN,** Imperial Charisian Army—CO, 3rd Battalion, 12th Mounted Regiment, 6th Mounted Brigade, Imperial Charisian Army, LAMA.

**LYWAHN, CAPTAIN OF FOOT RUHNGZHI,** Imperial Harchongese Army—Battery commander, Kyznetzov Narrows, HFQ.

**LYWKYS, FATHER AHMBROHS**—a Bédardist under-priest; chaplain, broadside ironclad HMS *Dreadnought* 30, HFQ.

**LYWKYS, LADY MAIRAH**—see Lady Mairah Lywkys Breygart.

**LYWKYS, SERGEANT REHGNYLD,** Royal Dohlaran Army—platoon sergeant, 3rd Platoon, 1st Company, Ahzbyrn's Regiment (cavalry), Dohlaran component, Army of Shiloh (cavalry), LAMA.

**LYWSHAI, SHAINTAI**—Trumyn Lywshai's Harchong-born father, MT&T.

**LYWSHAI, TRUMYN**—Sir Dunkyn Yairley, Baron Sarmouth's secretary, HFAF.

**LYWYS, COMMANDER FRAIZHER,** Imperial Charisian Navy—CO, HMS *Foam*, 18, HFQ.

**LYWYS, DOCTOR SAHNDRAH**—senior chemist of the Royal College of Charis, HFAF; member of Charisian inner circle, MT&T.

**LYWYS, SIR SHAILTYN**—Baron of Climbhaven, Duke Harless' senior artillerist, LAMA.

**LYWYSTYN, CAPTAIN KRYSTYPHYR,** Royal Dohlaran Navy—XO, Claw Island, LAMA.

**MAB, *SEIJIN* DIALYDD**—one of Merlin Athrawes' alternate identities, created especially for reprisals against the Inquisition, LAMA.

**MAGWAIR, VICAR ALLAYN**—Captain General, Council of Vicars; one of the so-called Group of Four, OAR.

**MAHAFEE, CAPTAIN DYOZHO,** Army of God—Major Lainyl Paxtyn's second-in-command in the guard force marching the Camp Tairek inmates from Westmarch to the Princedom of Sardahn, HFQ.

MAHAFEE, LIEUTENANT ANSYN, Army of God—the most junior commissioned officer of the troops assigned to Father Trynt Dezmynd for the evacuation of the Camp Tairek prisoners, HFQ.

MAHCLYNTAHK, MAJOR ZHAIKYB—CO, 3rd Company, 1st Glacierheart Volunteers, LAMA.

MAHFYT, BRAHDLAI, Imperial Charisian Navy—ironclad HMS *Delthak*, 22; Halcom Bahrns' personal coxswain, LAMA.

MAHGAIL, CAPTAIN BYRT, Delferahkan Royal Guard—a company commander, Telkyra Palace, HFAF.

MAHGAIL, CAPTAIN RAIF, Imperial Charisian Navy—CO, HMS *Dancer*, 56. Sir Gwylym Manthyr's flag captain, HFAF.

MAHGAIL, COLONEL PAYT, Royal Dohlaran Army—CO, Mahgail's Regiment (cavalry), Dohlaran component, Army of Shiloh, LAMA.

MAHGAIL, LIEUTENANT BRYNDYN, Imperial Charisian Marines—senior Marine officer assigned to Sarm River operation, HFAF.

MAHGAIL, MAJOR KYNAHN, Imperial Charisian Army—CO, 4th Battalion, 7th Regiment, 4th Infantry Brigade, Imperial Charisian Army, LAMA.

MAHGAIL, MASTER GARAM, Imperial Charisian Navy—carpenter, HMS *Destiny*, 54, HFAF.

MAHGENTEE, MIDSHIPMAN MAHRAK, Royal Charisian Navy—senior midshipman, HMS *Typhoon*, OAR.

MAHGRUDYR, LIEUTENANT TYMYTHY "TYM," Imperial Charisian Navy—purser, broadside ironclad HMS *Thunderer*, 30, HFQ.

MAHGRUDYR, PRIVATE TYMYTHY, Imperial Charisian Army—2nd Platoon, Company B, 1st Battalion, 9th Mounted Regiment, 5th Mounted Brigade, Imperial Charisian Army, LAMA.

MAHGRUDYR, SERGEANT MAJOR ALLAYN, Imperial Charisian Marine Corps—senior Marine NCO, Marine detachment, HMS *Destiny*, 54, HFQ.

MAHGYRS, CAPTAIN AHLFRYD, Royal Dohlaran Navy—

CO, screw-galley HMS *Sword*; Admiral Pawal Hahlynd's flag captain, HFQ.

**MAHGYRS, COLONEL ALLAYN**, Republic of Siddarmark Army—General Fronz Tylmahn's senior Siddarmarkian subordinate in support of Captain Halcom Bahrns' operation ("Great Canal Raid"), MT&T.

**MAHKAID, MAJOR PAITYR**, Royal Dohlaran Army—CO, 2nd Company, Ahzbyrn's Regiment (cavalry), Dohlaran component, Army of Shiloh, LAMA.

**MAHKBYTH, AHRLOH**—"Barcor," a Zion shop owner and a very senior cell leader in Helm Cleaver in Zion, HFQ.

**MAHKBYTH, DAHNYLD**—Ahrloh and Zhulyet Mahkbyth's deceased son, HFQ.

**MAHKBYTH, LIEUTENANT AHMBROHS**, Imperial Charisian Navy—first lieutenant, broadside ironclad HMS *Rottweiler*, 30, LAMA.

**MAHKBYTH, ZHULYET**—Ahrloh Mahkbyth's deceased wife, HFQ.

**MAHKDUGYL, MAJOR ZHERYLD**, Republic of Siddarmark Militia—CO, 1st Company, 1st Glacierheart Volunteers, LAMA.

**MAHKEEN, CAPTAIN DAHNYLD**, Imperial Charisian Navy—CO, HMS *Cherry Bay*, 68, HFQ.

**MAHKELYN, LIEUTENANT RHOBAIR**, Royal Charisian Navy—fourth lieutenant, HMS *Destiny*, 54, BSRA.

**MAHKGRUDYR, LIEUTENANT CAYLEB**, Imperial Charisian Army—Sir Bartyn Sahmyrsyt's personal aide, HFQ.

**MAHKGRUDYR, SAIRAHS**, Siddarmarkian Canal Service—Temple Loyalist canal pilot working to repair the damage done during the Great Canal Raid, LAMA.

**MAHKGYVYRN, BISHOP FAILYX**—a Schuelerite placed in command of Camp Chihiro, HFQ.

**MAHKHAL, BISHOP ZHAKSYN**, Army of God—CO, Port Harbor Division, Army of the Sylmahn, LAMA.

**MAHKHOM, WAHLYS**—Glacierheart trapper turned guerrilla; leader of the Reformist forces in the Gray Wall Mountains, MT&T.

**MAHKHYNROH, BISHOP KAISI**—Bishop of Manchyr for the Church of Charis, HFAF.

**MAHKLUSKEE, CAPTAIN LYWYS**, Royal Dohlaran Army—CO, 5th Company, Sheldyn's Regiment, Army of the Seridahn, HFQ.

**MAHKLUSKEE, MAJOR AHRYN**, Imperial Charisian Army—XO, 8th Regiment, 4th Infantry Brigade, Imperial Charisian Army, LAMA.

**MAHKLYMORH, GENERAL TOBYS**, Republic of Siddarmark Army—CO, 8th Division, Republic of Siddarmark Army, HFQ.

**MAHKLYMORH, MAJOR DYNNYS**, Imperial Charisian Army—CO, 1st Battalion, 2nd Scout Sniper Regiment, Imperial Charisian Army, LAMA.

**MAHKLYMORH, MAJOR KHEEFYR**, Imperial Charisian Army—CO, 2nd Battalion, 9th Mounted Regiment, 5th Mounted Brigade, Imperial Charisian Army, LAMA.

**MAHKLYN, AHNGAZ**—Sir Domynyk Staynair's valet, HFAF.

**MAHKLYN, DOCTOR RAHZHYR**—chancellor of the Royal College of Charis, OAR; member Charisian inner circle, BSRA.

**MAHKLYN, TOHMYS**—Rahzhyr Mahklyn's unmarried son, BSRA.

**MAHKLYN, YSBET**—Rahzhyr Mahklyn's deceased wife, BSRA.

**MAHKNAIL, COLONEL THYADOHR**, Imperial Charisian Army—Sir Bartyn Sahmyrsyt's chief engineer in the Army of New Northland, HFQ.

**MAHKNARHMA, MAJOR SIR SYMYN**, Imperial Desnairian Army—XO, Glynfyrd's Regiment (light cavalry), cavalry wing, Army of Shiloh, LAMA.

**MAHKNASH, SERGEANT BRAICE**, Royal Delferahkan Army—one of Colonel Aiphraim Tahlyvyr's squad leaders, HFAF.

**MAHKNEE, PAITRYK**—Duke of Lake Land, MT&T.

**MAHKNEE, SYMYN**—Paitryk Mahknee's uncle, MT&T.

**MAHKNEEL, CAPTAIN HAUWYRD**, Royal Delferahkan

Navy—CO, galley *Arrowhead*, Delferahkan Navy, BSRA.

**MAHKNEEL, LIEUTENANT DAHNEL**, Imperial Charisian Navy—first lieutenant, HMS *East Wind*, 18, HFQ.

**MAHKSWAIL, COLONEL CLAIRDON**, Army of God—Bishop Militant Bahrnabai's senior aide and effective chief of staff, LAMA.

**MAHKWYRTYR, COLONEL PAIDRHO**, Royal Dohlaran Army—CO, Mahkwyrtyr's Regiment (infantry), Dohlaran component, Army of Shiloh, LAMA.

**MAHKYNTY, MAJOR AHRNAHLD**, Republic of Siddarmark Army—CO, 4th Company, 37th Infantry Regiment, Republic of Siddarmark Army, MT&T.

**MAHKZWAIL, GYFFRY**—the eldest child of Sir Ahrnahld and Lady Stefyny Mahkzwail and grandson of the Earl of Thirsk, HFQ.

**MAHKZWAIL, LADY STEFYNY**—the elder daughter of Sir Lywys Gardynyr, Earl of Thirsk.

**MAHKZWAIL, LYZET**—the second child of Sir Ahrnahld and Lady Stefyny Mahkzwail, granddaughter of Lywys Gardynyr, HFQ.

**MAHKZWAIL, SIR AHRNAHLD**—husband of Lady Stefyny Mahkzwail and son-in-law of Earl of Thirsk, HFQ.

**MAHKZWAIL, ZHOSIFYN**—youngest child of Sir Ahrnahld and Lady Stefyny Mahkzwail, granddaughter of Sir Lywys Gardynyr, HFQ.

**MAHLDAN, BROTHER STAHN**—a Reformist sexton in Siddar City; Order of the Quill, HFAF.

**MAHLDYN, BYRTRYM**—Baron Gray Hill; replacement on Prince Daivyn's Regency Council in Corisande for the Earl of Craggy Hill after Craggy Hill's execution for treason for his part in the Northern Conspiracy, MT&T.

**MAHLDYN, COLONEL PHYLYP**, Republic of Siddarmark Army—CO, 110th Infantry Regiment, Republic of Siddarmark Army; acting CO, Fort Sheldyn, South March Lands, MT&T.

**MAHLDYN, FHRANKLYN**—Taigys and Mathylda's youngest son, admitted to Royal College, MT&T.

**MAHNYNG, MAJOR CLYNTAHN,** Imperial Charisian Army—CO, 2nd Battalion, 6th Mounted Regiment, 3rd Mounted Brigade, Imperial Charisian Army, LAMA.

**MAHRAK, LIEUTENANT RAHNALD,** Royal Charisian Navy—first lieutenant, HMS *Royal Charis*, OAR.

**MAHRAK, MAJOR ZHEFRY,** Imperial Charisian Army—CO, 4th Battalion, 12th Mounted Regiment, 6th Mounted Brigade, Imperial Charisian Army, LAMA.

**MAHRCELYAN, COLONEL AHNDRU,** Royal Dohlaran Army—CO, Mahrcelyan's Regiment (infantry), Dohlaran component, Army of Shiloh, LAMA.

**MAHRKOHNE, GENERAL SIR KYNYTH,** Imperial Charisian Army—CO, 3rd Corps, Army of Midhold, HFQ.

**MAHRLOW, BISHOP EXECUTOR AHRAIN**—Archbishop Zahmsyn Halmyn's executive assistant, Archbishopric of Gorath, Kingdom of Dohlar, HFAF.

**MAHRLOW, FATHER ARTHYR**—priest of the Order of Schueler; assistant to Father Gaisbyrt Vandaik in Talkyra, HFAF.

**MAHRTYN, ADMIRAL GAHVYN**—Baron of White Ford; senior officer, Royal Tarotisian Navy, OAR; admiral, Imperial Charisian Navy, HFAF; port admiral, Bedard Bay, Siddarmark, MT&T.

**MAHRTYN, COLONEL THE HONORABLE FAYDOHR,** Royal Dohlaran Army—CO, Mahrtyn's Division (infantry), Dohlaran component, Army of Shiloh; CO, Brahnselyk garrison, LAMA.

**MAHRTYN, MAJOR LAIRAYS,** Imperial Charisian Marines—CO, 2nd Provisional Battalion, 1st Independent Marine Brigade, LAMA.

**MAHRTYNSYN, LIEUTENANT LAIZAIR,** Imperial Desnairian Navy—XO, HMS *Archangel Chihiro*, 40, HFAF.

**MAHRYS, CORPORAL ZHAK "ZHAKKY"**—a member of Prince Daivyn Daykyn's Royal Guard in exile (Tobys Raimair's junior noncom), HFAF; Royal Corisandian Guard, the junior noncom on Irys' personal detail, LAMA.

**MAHRYS, ZHERYLD**—Sir Rayjhis Dragoner's senior secretary and aide, BSRA.

**MAHSTYRS, PRIVATE ZHUSTYN**, Royal Dohlaran Army—3rd Company, Wykmyn's Regiment (light cavalry), Dohlaran component, Army of Shiloh, LAMA.

**MAHTHYWS, SERGEANT AHZWALD**, Army of God—an NCO assigned to the "cleansing" of Sarkyn; killed in his own bunk in the middle of the night, HFQ.

**MAHZYNGAIL, COLONEL VYKTYR**, Republic of Siddarmark Militia—CO, 14th South March Militia Regiment, Fort Sheldyn, South March Lands, MT&T.

**MAHZYNGAIL, LIEUTENANT AHBRAIM**, Imperial Charisian Army—CO, 2nd Platoon, Company B, 2nd Battalion, 6th Regiment, Imperial Charisian Army, LAMA.

**MAHZYNGAIL, LIEUTENANT HAARLAHM**, Imperial Charisian Navy—High Admiral Rock Point's flag secretary, HFAF.

**MAIB, MAJOR EDMYND**, Army of God—CO, 20th Artillery Regiment, senior officer present, Ohlarn, New Northland Province, Republic of Siddarmark, MT&T.

**MAIDYN, LORD HENRAI**—chancellor of the exchequer, Republic of Siddarmark, HFAF.

**MAIGEE, CAPTAIN GRAYGAIR**, Royal Dohlaran Navy—CO, galleon HMS *Guardian*, BSRA.

**MAIGEE, PLATOON SERGEANT ZHAK**, Imperial Charisian Marines—senior noncom, Second Platoon, Alpha Company, 1/3rd Marines (1st Battalion, 3rd Brigade), Imperial Charisian Marines, HFAF.

**MAIGOWHYN, LIEUTENANT BRAHNDYN**, Royal Delferahkan Army—Colonel Aiphraim Tahlyvyr's aide, HFAF.

**MAIGWAIR, CORPORAL STAHNYZLAHAS**—Temple Loyalist rebel, garrison of Fort Darymahn, South March Lands, Republic of Siddarmark, MT&T.

**MAIGWAIR, VICAR ALLAYN**—Captain General of the

Church of God Awaiting; one of the so-called Group of Four, BSRA.

**MAIK, BISHOP STAIPHAN**—a Schuelerite auxiliary bishop of the Church of God Awaiting; effectively intendant for the Royal Dohlaran Navy in the Church's name, HFAF.

**MAIKEL, CAPTAIN QWENTYN**, Royal Dohlaran Navy—CO, galley HMS *Gorath Bay*, OAR.

**MAIKELSYN, LIEUTENANT LEEAHM**, Royal Tarotisian Navy—first lieutenant, galley HMS *King Gorjah II*, OAR.

**MAIKSYN, BRIGADIER ZHORJ**, Imperial Charisian Army—CO, 1st Brigade, Imperial Charisian Army, LAMA.

**MAIKSYN, COLONEL LYWYS**—CO, 3rd Saiknyr Militia Regiment; a Temple Loyalist who joined the Sword of Schueler in the Sylmahn Gap, MT&T.

**MAIKYN, FATHER TYMYTHY**—a Schuelerite underpriest and inquisitor assigned to the merchant galleon *Prodigal Lass* to oversee the transport of Charisian POWs from Battle of Kaudzhu Narrows to the Temple Lands. A personal favorite of Father Ahbsahlahn Kharmych, HFQ.

**MAINDAYL, COLONEL WYLSYNN**, Army of God—Bishop Militant Cahnyr Kaitswyrth's chief of staff, LAMA.

**MAIRNAIR, LIEUTENANT TOBYS**, Imperial Charisian Navy—XO, ironclad HMS *Hador*, 22, MT&T.

**MAIRWYN, RAHZHYR**—Baron of Larchros; a member of the Northern Conspiracy in Corisande, executed for treason, HFAF.

**MAIRWYN, RAICHENDA**—Baroness of Larchros; wife of Rahzhyr Mairwyn, HFAF.

**MAIRYAI, COLONEL SPYNCYR**, Army of God—CO, 2nd Regiment, Langhorne Division, Army of the Sylmahn, MT&T; Army of Fairkyn in HFQ.

**MAIRYDYTH, LIEUTENANT NEVYL**, Royal Dohlaran Navy—first lieutenant, galley HMS *Royal Bédard*, OAR.

**MAITLYND, CAPTAIN ZHORJ**, Imperial Charisian Navy—CO, HMS *Victorious*, 56, HFAF.

**MAITZLYR, CAPTAIN FAIDOHRAV,** Imperial Desnairian Navy—CO, HMS *Loyal Defender*, 48, HFAF.

**MAIYR, CAPTAIN ZHAKSYN**—one of Colonel Sir Wahlys Zhorj's troop commanders in Tahdayo Mahntayl's service, BSRA.

**MAIYRS, MAJOR TYMAHN,** Corisandian Royal Guard—senior officer, Corisandian Royal Guard, LAMA.

**MAIZUR, KHANSTANC**—Maikel Staynair's cook, MT&T.

**MAKAIVYR, BRIGADIER ZHOSH,** Royal Charisian Marines—CO, 1st Brigade, Royal Charisian Marines, BSRA.

**MAKFERZAHN, ZHAMES**—one of Prince Hektor's agents in Charis, OAR.

**MAKGREGAIR, FATHER ZHOSHUA**—Vicar Zahmsyn Trynair's special representative to Tarot, OAR.

**MAKGRYGAIR, COMMANDER SYMYN,** Imperial Charisian Navy—CO, shore establishment, Imperial Charisian Navy base on Talisman Island, HFQ.

**MAKKBYRN, GENERAL SIR TAMYS,** Imperial Charisian Army—CO, 7th Infantry Division, 2nd Corps, Army of Cliff Peak, LAMA.

**MAKSTYVYNS, MAJOR DUGAHLD,** Imperial Charisian Army—CO, 2nd Battalion, 1st Scout Sniper Regiment, Imperial Charisian Army, LAMA.

**MAKSWYL, AUXILIARY BISHOP RHOBAIR**—Bishop Militant Tayrens' intendant in Army of Tanshar, HFQ.

**MAKYCHEE, FAIGYN**—Duke Kholman; raised to Duke Kholman following Daivyn Bairaht's defeat in Battle of Iythria and flight to Charis, LAMA.

**MAKYN, COLONEL AHLYSTAIR,** Imperial Charisian Army—CO, 1st Scout Sniper Regiment, Imperial Charisian Army, LAMA.

**MAKYNTYR, COLONEL AHLFRYD,** Royal Dohlaran Army—Sir Rainos Ahlverez's senior artillery specialist, LAMA.

**MAKYSAK, LIEUTENANT ZHAIF,** Imperial Charisian Army—CO, 1st Platoon, Company B, 1st Battalion, 1st Scout Sniper Regiment, Imperial Charisian Army, LAMA.

MAKYSAK, PRIVATE BYNZHAMYN, Imperial Charisian Army—1st Platoon, Company A, 1st Battalion, 5th Regiment, Imperial Charisian Army, LAMA.

MALIKAI, DUKE OF—see Faidel Ahlverez.

MALIKAI, MAJOR STYWYRT, Imperial Charisian Army— Chief of Staff, 10th Mounted Brigade, 1st Corps, Army of New Northland, HFQ.

MALKAIHY, COMMANDER DAHRAIL, Imperial Charisian Navy—Captain Ahldahs Rahzwail's senior assistant; senior liaison between the Bureau of Ordnance and Sir Dustyn Olyvyr, MT&T; CO, Bureau of Engineering when it is formally organized, LAMA.

MANTHYR, SIR GWYLYM—Royal Charisian Navy, captain, CO, galleon HMS *Dreadnought*, 54; Cayleb Ahrmahk's flag captain, OAR; Imperial Charisian Navy, commodore, BHD; admiral, CO, Charisian expedition to Gulf of Dohlar, POW, AMF; surrendered to Inquisition and executed, HFAF.

MARDHAR, COLONEL ZHANDRU, Army of God—CO, 191st Cavalry Regiment, Army of Glacierheart, MT&T.

MARGO, DUKE OF—see Sir Bairmon Chahlmair.

MARSHYL, MIDSHIPMAN ADYM, Royal Charisian Navy— senior midshipman, galley HMS *Royal Charis*, OAR.

MASTER DOMNEK—King Haarahld VII's Harchongese court arms master, OAR.

MASTYRS, LIEUTENANT ZHON, Royal Dohlaran Army—one of Colonel Ohygyns' aides, LAMA.

MASTYRSYN, CAPTAIN SYMYN, Imperial Charisian Navy—CO, broadside ironclad HMS *Rottweiler*, 30, LAMA.

MASTYRSYN, LIEUTENANT BRYAHN, Imperial Charisian Navy—XO, HMS *Dynzayl Tryvythyn*, 68, HFQ.

MATHYSYN, BRIGADIER ZHAMES, Imperial Charisian Army—CO, 4th Infantry Brigade, Imperial Charisian Army, assigned Thesmar, LAMA.

MATHYSYN, LIEUTENANT ZHAIKEB, Royal Dohlaran

Navy—first lieutenant, galley HMS *Gorath Bay*, OAR.

MATTHYSAHN, AHBUKYRA, Imperial Charisian Navy—signalman, ironclad HMS *Delthak*, 22, MT&T.

MAYLYR, CAPTAIN DUNKYN, Royal Charisian Navy—CO, galley HMS *Halberd*, OAR.

MAYSAHN, ZHASPAHR—Prince Hektor's senior agent in Charis, OAR.

MAYTHIS, LIEUTENANT FRAIZHER, Royal Corisandian Navy—true name of Captain Wahltayr Seatown, OAR.

MEDGYRS, COLONEL LAINYL, Imperial Charisian Army—CO, 28th Infantry Regiment, 14th Infantry Brigade, 7th Infantry Division, Imperial Charisian Army, LAMA.

METYRNYK, BROTHER AHLPHANZO—a Chihirite lay brother of the Order of the Quill; one of Father Zheryld Cumyngs' senior clerks at Camp Dynnys, HFQ.

METZLYR, FATHER PAIRAIK—an upper-priest of Schueler; General Sir Fahstyr Rychtyr's special intendant, MT&T.

METZYGYR, MASTER HAHNDYL—a senior master of the Gunmaker's Guild in Gorath, LAMA.

MHARDYR, SYLVYST—Baron Stoneheart; current Lord Justice of Chisholm, replacing Braisyn Byrns, MT&T.

MHARTYN, COLONEL DAHGLYS—former Republic of Siddarmark captain, CO, 6th Regiment, a regular regiment which went over to the Sword of Schueler; second-ranking officer, Fort Tairys garrison, LAMA.

MHARTYN, MAJOR ABSHAIR, Imperial Charisian Army—CO, 3rd Battalion, 4th Regiment, Imperial Charisian Army, MT&T.

MHARTYN, MAJOR LAIRAYS, Imperial Charisian Marines—CO, 2nd Provisional Battalion, 1st Independent Marine Brigade, Thesmar, MT&T.

MHATTSYN, PETTY OFFICER LAISL, Imperial Charisian Navy—a gun captain in Lieutenant Yerek Sahbrahan's battery under Commander Hainz Watyrs in Glacierheart Province, MT&T.

**MHULVAYN, OSKAHR**—one of Prince Hektor's agents in Charis, OAR.

**MKWARTYR, COLONEL MHARTYN**, Imperial Charisian Army—senior engineer 2nd Brigade (reinforced) and Army of Midhold, LAMA.

**MOHMOHTAHNY, FATHER AIZAK**—a Pasqualate underpriest assigned to Camp Dynnys as the garrison's healer, HFQ.

**MOHZLYR, MAJOR ZHAIRYMIAH**, Imperial Charisian Army—CO, 2nd Battalion, 12th Mounted Regiment, 6th Mounted Brigade, Imperial Charisian Army, LAMA.

**MOUNTAIN SHADOW, DUKE OF**—see Shiangzhu Daichyng.

**MUHLKAYHE, MASTER EDWYRD**, Imperial Charisian Navy—gunner, broadside ironclad HMS *Thunderer*, 30, HFQ.

**MULDAYAIR, COLONEL HAARAHLD**, Imperial Charisian Army—CO, 1st Regiment, 1st Brigade, 1st Infantry Division, Imperial Charisian Army, LAMA.

**MULLYGYN, SERGEANT RAHSKHO**—a member of Prince Daivyn Daykyn's Royal Guard in exile (Tobys Raimair's second-ranking noncom), HFAF; sergeant, Royal Corisandian Guard, junior member of Prince Daivyn's personal detail, LAMA.

**MURPHAI, LIEUTENANT DUNKYN**, Imperial Charisian Army—CO, 3rd Platoon, 1st Company, 19th Mounted Regiment, 10th Mounted Brigade, 1st Corps, Army of New Northland, HFQ.

**MURPHAI, *SEIJIN* ZHOZUAH**—one of Merlin Athrawes' alternate identities; theoretically a spy stationed in the Temple Lands to keep an eye on events in Zion, HFQ.

**MYCHAIL, ALYX**—Rhaiyan Mychail's oldest grandson, BSRA.

**MYCHAIL, MYLDRYD**—one of Rhaiyan Mychail's married granddaughters-in-law, BSRA.

**MYCHAIL, RHAIYAN**—a business partner of Ehdwyrd Howsmyn and the Kingdom of Charis' primary textile producer, OAR.

**MYCHAIL, STYVYN**—Myldryd Mychail's youngest son, BSRA.

**MYCHYSYN, COMMANDER RUBYN**, Royal Dohlaran Navy—CO, *Prodigal Lass*, a transport taken into Royal Dohlaran Navy service to move Charisian POWs from the Kaudzhu Narrows to the Temple Lands, HFQ.

**MYKLAYN, ZHAIMYS**, Canal Service—a senior canal pilot of the Siddarmarkian Canal Service assigned to assist Captain Halcom Bahrns, MT&T.

**MYLLYR, ARCHBISHOP URVYN**—Archbishop of Sodar, OAR.

**MYLLYR, SIR PHYLYP**, Royal Corisandian Army—one of Sir Koryn Gahrvai's regimental commanders, BSRA.

**MYLLYR, ZHAK**—Ahrloh Mahkbyth's employee and a paid Inquisition informer, HFQ.

**MYLZ, BRIGADIER ZHEBYDYAH**, Imperial Charisian Army—CO, 2nd Brigade, Imperial Charisian Army, LAMA.

**MYNDAIZ, CORPORAL RAYMAHNDOH**, Army of God—2nd Platoon, 1st Company, 1st Regiment, Zion Division, Army of Glacierheart, LAMA.

**MYRDOHK, MAJOR AHLZHERNOHN**, Imperial Charisian Army—CO, 2nd Battalion, 11th Mounted Regiment, 6th Mounted Brigade, Imperial Charisian Army, LAMA.

**MYRGAH, MAJOR ADULFO**, Imperial Charisian Army—CO, 2nd Battalion, 7th Regiment, 4th Infantry Brigade, LAMA.

**MYRGYN, SIR KEHVYN**, Royal Corisandian Navy—CO, galley *Corisande*, Duke Black Water's flag captain, KIA Battle of Darcos Sound, OAR.

**NAHRMAHN, LIEUTENANT FRONZ**, Imperial Charisian Navy—second lieutenant, HMS *Destiny*, 54, MT&T.

**NAIGAIL, SAMYL**—son of a deceased Siddarmarkian sailmaker; Temple Loyalist and anti-Charisian bigot, HFAF; arrested and executed for murder, LAMA.

NAIKLOS, CAPTAIN FRAHNKLYN, Corisandian Guard—CO of Sir Koryn Gahrvai's headquarters company; later promoted to major, HFAF.

NAISMYTH, MAJOR CAHRTAIR, Imperial Charisian Army—CO, 2nd Battalion, 6th Regiment, Imperial Charisian Army, LAMA.

NARTH, BISHOP EXECUTOR TYRNYR—Archbishop Failyx Gahrbor's executive assistant, Archbishopric of Tarot, HFAF.

NAVYZ, WYLFRYD—Siddarmarkian Temple Loyalist guide attached to General Sir Fahstyr Rychtyr's Dohlaran invasion column, MT&T.

NEAROAK, BARON OF—see Sir Rahnyld Khettsyn.

NEAROAK, EARL OF—see Sir Abshair Hyrst.

NETHAUL, HAIRYM—XO, privateer schooner *Blade*, BSRA.

NEWYL, CAPTAIN ELWYN, Imperial Charisian Army—personal aide of Brigadier Sir Laimyn Seacatcher; CO, 5th Mounted Brigade, Imperial Charisian Army, LAMA.

NOHRCROSS, BISHOP MAILVYN—Bishop of Barcor for the Church of Charis; a member of the Northern Conspiracy in Corisande, executed for treason, HFAF.

NORTH COAST, EARL OF—see Edwair Garthin.

NYBAR, BISHOP GORTHYK, Army of God—CO, Langhorne Division; Bishop Militant Bahrnabai Wyrshym's senior division commander, MT&T; CO, Army of Fairkyn, HFQ.

NYLZ, KOHDY, Royal Charisian Navy—commodore; CO of one of High Admiral Lock Island's galley squadrons, OAR; admiral, Imperial Charisian Navy, BSRA; senior squadron commander, HFAF.

NYOU, GORJAH ALYKSAHNDAR—King Gorjah III, King of Tarot, OAR; swears fealty to Cayleb and Sharleyan Ahrmahk, HFAF.

NYOU, MAIYL—Queen Consort of Tarot; wife of Gorjah Nyou, HFAF.

NYOU, PRINCE RHOLYND—Crown Prince of Tarot; infant son of Gorjah and Maiyl Nyou; heir to the Tarotisian throne, HFAF.

NYTZAH, CORPORAL DAIVYN, Army of God—2nd Platoon, 1st Company, 1st Regiment, Zion Division, Army of Glacierheart, LAMA.

NYXYN, DAIVYN, Royal Delferahkan Army—a dragoon assigned to Sergeant Braice Mahknash's squad, HFAF.

OARMASTER, SYGMAHN, Royal Charisian Marines—a member of Crown Prince Cayleb's bodyguard, OAR.

OBAIRN, PRIVATE ZHYNKYNS, Royal Dohlaran Army—2nd Section, 3rd Platoon, 1st Company, Ahzbyrn's Regiment (cavalry), Dohlaran component, Army of Shiloh, LAMA.

OHADLYN, BROTHER LAHZRYS—a Schuelerite lay brother assigned to Camp Chihiro, HFQ.

OHAHLYRN, CAPTAIN MERYT, Imperial Charisian Army—CO, Company C, 3rd Battalion, 10th Mounted Regiment, 5th Mounted Brigade, LAMA.

OHBRYN, COMMANDER LYWYS, Imperial Charisian Navy—CO, HMS *Wanderer*, 18, HFQ.

OHCAHNYR, LIEUTENANT CHARLZ, Imperial Desnairian Army—CO, 2nd Platoon, 3rd Company, Bahskym's Regiment, Army of Shiloh, LAMA.

OHDWIAR, COLONEL MAHTHYW, Royal Dohlaran Army—CO, Ohdwiar's Regiment (infantry), Dohlaran component, Army of Shiloh, LAMA.

OHKAMOHTO, CAPTAIN FRAHNCHESKO, Royal Dohlaran Navy—CO HMS *Tide*, 52, and SO of the convoy delivering the Charisian POWs from the Kaudzhu Narrows to Zion, HFQ.

OHKARLYN, COLONEL BRYAHN, Royal Dohlaran Army—CO, Ohkarlyn's Regiment (cavalry), Dohlaran component, Army of Shiloh, LAMA.

OHLSYN, TRAHVYS—Earl Pine Hollow, Prince Nahrmahn Baytz' cousin, first councilor of Emerald, OAR; first councilor of the Charisian Empire and member Charisian inner circle, HFAF.

OHMAHLY, MAJOR QWENTYN, Imperial Charisian

Marine Corps—CO of the Talisman Island Marine garrison, HFQ.

OHRAILY, FATHER ELARYN—a Schuelerite priest and agent inquisitor who serves as a special trouble-shooter for Bishop Markys Gohdard, HFQ.

OHYGYNS, COLONEL SIR BRAHDFYRD, Royal Dohlaran Army—CO, Ohygyns' Regiment (infantry), Dohlaran component, Army of Shiloh; CO, Roymark garrison, LAMA.

OLYVYR, AHNYET—Sir Dustyn Olyvyr's wife, OAR.

OLYVYR, COLONEL BRYNTYN, Army of God—CO, 1st Regiment, St. Yura Division, Army of the Sylmahn, HFQ.

OLYVYR, SIR DUSTYN—senior naval constructor and designer, Royal Charisian Navy, OAR; senior naval constructor, Imperial Charisian Navy, BSRA; member Charisian inner circle, HFAF.

OMAHR, GRAND DUKE OF—see Yitangzhi Gengchai.

ORAISTYS, LIEUTENANT RYDOLF, Army of God—CO, 1st Platoon, Company A, 191st Cavalry Regiment, Army of Glacierheart, LAMA.

OVYRTYN, COLONEL LUDYVYK, Imperial Charisian Army—CO, 8th Regiment, 4th Infantry Brigade, Imperial Charisian Army, LAMA.

OWL—Nimue Alban's AI, based on the manufacturer's acronym: Ordones-Westinghouse-Lytton RAPIER Tactical Computer, Mark 17a, OAR.

PAHLMAHN, ZHULYIS—a Corisandian banker convicted of treason as part of the Northern Conspiracy, pardoned by Empress Sharleyan, HFAF.

PAHLMAIR, COLONEL BRYNTYN, Army of God—CO, 53rd Cavalry Regiment, Army of the Sylmahn, LAMA.

PAHLOAHZKY, PRIVATE SHYMAN, Army of God—2nd Platoon, 1st Company, 1st Regiment, Zion Division, Army of Glacierheart, LAMA.

PAHLZAR, COLONEL AHKYLLYS—Sir Charlz Doyal's replacement as Sir Koryn Gahrvai's senior artillery commander, BSRA.

PAHN, LORD OF FOOT WYNSHYNG, BARON CRYSTAL SKY,

Imperial Harchongese Army—Lord of Horse Falling Rock's senior brigade commander and second-in-command, HFQ.

**PAHRAIHA, COLONEL VAHSAG,** Imperial Charisian Marines—CO, 14th Marine Regiment, HFAF.

**PAHRKYNS, LIEUTENANT HYDYZHI,** Imperial Charisian Navy—second lieutenant, broadside ironclad HMS *Dreadnought*, 30, HFQ.

**PAHRSAHN, AIVAH**—Nynian Rychtair's public persona in the Republic of Siddarmark, HFAF.

**PAHSKAIL, COLONEL AHLBAIR,** Royal Dohlaran Army—CO, Pahskail's Regiment (infantry), Dohlaran component, Army of Shiloh, LAMA.

**PAHSKAL, MASTER MIDSHIPMAN FAYDOHR,** Imperial Charisian Navy—a midshipman assigned to HMS *Dawn Star*, 58, HFAF.

**PAHTKOVAIR, FATHER ZOHANNES**—Schuelerite intendant of Siddar, HFAF.

**PAIRMYN, MAJOR TOBYS,** Imperial Charisian Army—CO, 3rd Battalion, 6th Mounted Regiment, 3rd Mounted Brigade, Imperial Charisian Army, LAMA.

**PARKAIR, ADYM**—Weslai Parkair's eldest son and heir, MT&T.

**PARKAIR, COLONEL SIR PAWAL,** Imperial Desnairian Army—CO, Parkair's Regiment (heavy cavalry), cavalry wing, Army of Shiloh, LAMA.

**PARKAIR, LORD DARYUS**—seneschal, Republic of Siddarmark, HFAF.

**PARKAIR, SISTER EMYLEE**—the senior Keeper of the Tomb of Saint Kohdy, HFQ.

**PARKAIR, WESLAI**—Lord Shairncross; Lord of Clan Shairncross and head of the Council of Clan Lords, Raven's Land, MT&T.

**PARKAIR, ZHAIN**—Lady Shairncross, Weslai Parkair's wife, MT&T.

**PARKAIR, ZHANAIAH**—Daryus Parkair's wife, HFAF.

**PARKMYN, COMMANDER ZHORJ,** Imperial Charisian Navy—Charisian naval officer assigned to the Army of Hildermoss; CO of the flotilla of gunboats and troop barges assembled to cross Wyvern Lake, HFQ.

**PARKYR, COMMODORE AHRTHYR,** Imperial Charisian Navy—the Earl of Hanth's senior engineer, LAMA; promoted to commodore in HFQ.

**PARKYR, FATHER EDWYRD**—upper-priest of the Order of Bédard; named by Archbishop Klairmant to succeed Father Tymahn at Saint Kathryn's Church, MT&T.

**PARKYR, GLAHDYS**—Crown Princess Alahnah's Chisholmian wet nurse and nanny, HFAF.

**PARKYR, LIEUTENANT EHVRYT,** Royal Dohlaran Navy—third lieutenant, HMS *Defiant* (ex-*Dancer*), 56, HFQ.

**PAWAL, CAPTAIN ZHON,** Imperial Charisian Navy—CO, HMS *Dart*, 54, HFAF.

**PAWALSYN, AHLVYNO**—Baron Ironhill, Keeper of the Purse (treasurer) of the Kingdom of Charis and later of the Empire of Charis, a member of Cayleb Ahrmahk's council, BSRA.

**PAWALSYN, MAJOR SAMYL,** Imperial Charisian Army—XO, 6th Mounted Regiment, 3rd Mounted Brigade, Imperial Charisian Army, LAMA.

**PAXTYN, MAJOR LAINYL,** Army of God—CO of the guard force marching the inmates of Camp Tairek from Westmarch to the Princedom of Sardahn, HFQ.

**PEI, ADMIRAL KAU-ZHI,** Terran Federation Navy—CO, Operation Breakaway; older brother of Commodore Pei Kau-yung, OAR.

**PEI, COMMODORE KAU-YUNG,** Terran Federation Navy—CO, Operation Ark final escort, OAR.

**PEI, DOCTOR SHAN-WEI, PH.D.**—Commodore Pei Kau-yung's wife; senior terraforming expert for Operation Ark, OAR.

**PEZKYVY, MAJOR AHNDRAIR,** Army of God—XO, 191st Cavalry Regiment, Army of Glacierheart, LAMA.

**PEZKYVYR, MAJOR AHNDRAI,** Army of God—XO, 191st Cavalry Regiment, MT&T.

**PHALGRAIN, SIR HARVAI**—majordomo, Imperial Palace, Cherayth, HFAF.

PHANDYS, CAPTAIN KHANSTAHNZO—an officer of the Temple Guard, assigned to head Vicar Rhobair Duchairn's bodyguard, HFAF.

PHONDA, MADAM AHNZHELYK—proprietor of one of the City of Zion's most discreet brothels (an alias of Nynian Rychtair), OAR.

PINE HOLLOW, EARL OF—see Trahvys Ohlsyn.

PLYZYK, CAPTAIN EHRNYSTO, Imperial Desnairian Navy—CO, HMS *Saint Adulfo*, 40, HFAF.

POHSTAZHIAN, BISHOP AHDRAIS, Army of God—CO, Sulyvyn Division, Army of Glacierheart, LAMA.

PORTYR, COMMANDER DAIVYN, Imperial Charisian Navy—CO, 4th Provisional Battalion, 1st Independent Marine Brigade (one of Hauwerd Breygart's Navy "battalions" at Thesmar), MT&T.

PORTYR, MAJOR DANYEL, Imperial Charisian Marines—CO, 1st Battalion, 3rd Regiment, 3rd Brigade, HFAF.

POTTYR, MAHLYK—lockmaster, Sarkyn, Tairohn Hills, Princedom of Sardahn, LAMA.

POTTYR, MAJOR HAINREE, Imperial Charisian Army—CO, 4th Battalion, 4th Regiment, Imperial Charisian Army, MT&T.

POWAIRS, COLONEL ALLAYN, Imperial Charisian Army—chief of staff, 2nd Brigade (reinforced), Imperial Charisian Army, Army of Midhold, LAMA.

PRAIETO, LIEUTENANT ORLYNOH, Army of God—CO, Battery B, 20th Artillery Regiment, Ohlarn, New Northland Province, Republic of Siddarmark, MT&T.

PRAIGYR, STAHLMAN—one of Ehdwyrd Howsmyn's senior artificers, particularly involved with the development of steam engines, MT&T.

PRESKYT, BISHOP QWENTYN, Army of God—CO, St. Fraidyr Division, Army of the Sylmahn, LAMA.

PRESKYT, MAJOR SIR ALYKZHANDYR, Royal Dohlaran Army—CO, 3rd Company, Wykmyn's Regiment (light cavalry), Dohlaran component, Army of Shiloh, LAMA.

PRESMYN, SERGEANT ZHAIKYB, Imperial Charisian

Army—senior NCO, 1st Company, 19th Mounted Regiment, 10th Mounted Brigade, 1st Corps, Army of New Northland, HFQ.

PRINCE CAYLEB—see Cayleb Ahrmahk.

PRINCE DAIVYN—see Daivyn Dahnyld Mharak Zoshya Daykyn.

PRINCE GRYGORY—see Grygory Velahsko.

PRINCE HEKTOR—see Hektor Daykyn.

PRINCE NAHRMAHN GAREYT—see Nahrmahn Gareyt Baytz.

PRINCE NAHRMAHN II—see Nahrmahn Hanbyl Graim Baytz.

PRINCE RHOLYND—see Rholynd Nyou.

PRINCE STYVYN—see Styvyn Khettsyn.

PRINCE TRAHVYS—see Trahvys Baytz.

PRINCE ZHONAH—see Zhonah Rahdryghyz.

PRINCESS CONSORT BETHNY—see Bethny Velahsko.

PRINCESS FELAYZ—see Felayz Baytz.

PRINCESS IRYS—see Irys Zhorzhet Mhara Daykyn Aplyn-Ahrmahk.

PRINCESS OHLYVYA—see Ohlyvya Baytz.

PRINCESS RAHNYLDAH—see Rahnyldah Bahrns.

PRINCESS STEFYNY—see Stefyny Bahrns.

PROCTOR, ELIAS, PH.D.—a member of Pei Shan-wei's staff and a noted cyberneticist, OAR.

PRUAIT, CAPTAIN TYMYTHY, Imperial Charisian Navy—newly appointed captain of prize ship *Sword of God*, HFAF.

PRUAIT, GENERAL FHRANKLYN, Republic of Siddarmark Army—CO, 76th Infantry Regiment, Sylmahn Gap, MT&T; promoted general, CO, 2nd Rifle Division, LAMA.

PYANGTU, CAPTAIN OF HORSE BAYZHAU, Imperial Harchongese Army—CO, 231st Volunteer Regiment, 115th Volunteer Brigade, Mighty Host of God and the Archangels, LAMA.

PYGAIN, FATHER AVRY—Chihirite upper-priest of the Order of the Quill; Archbishop Arthyn Zagyrsk's secretary and aide, MT&T.

PYMBYRTYN, CAPTAIN LYWELYN, Imperial Charisian Navy—CO, HMS *Vindicator*, 68, HFQ.

PYNHALOH, COLONEL SIR SELVYN, Imperial Desnairian Army—CO, Pynhaloh's Regiment (light cavalry), cavalry wing, Army of Shiloh, LAMA.

QUEEN CONSORT HAILYN—see Hailyn Rayno.

QUEEN MAIYL—see Maiyl Nyou.

QUEEN MATHYLDA—see Mathylda Bahrns.

QUEEN SHARLEYAN—see Sharleyan Ahrmahk.

QUEEN YSBELL—an earlier reigning Queen of Chisholm who was deposed (and murdered) in favor of a male ruler, BSRA.

QWENTYN, BISHOP LYNAIL, Army of God—CO, St. Yura Division, Army of the Sylmahn, HFQ.

QWENTYN, COMMODORE DONYRT, Royal Corisandian Navy—Baron Tanlyr Keep, one of Duke of Black Water's squadron commanders, OAR.

QWENTYN, OWAIN—Tymahn Qwentyn's grandson, HFAF.

QWENTYN, TYMAHN—the current head of the House of Qwentyn, which is one of the largest, if not *the* largest banking and investment cartels in the Republic of Siddarmark. Lord Protector Greyghor holds a seat on the House of Qwentyn's board of directors, and the cartel operates the royal mint in the city of Siddar, BSRA.

RAHDGYRZ, FATHER SYNDAIL, Navy of God—CO, NGS *Saint Frydhelm*, 40, HFQ.

RAHDGYRZ, GENERAL SIR SHULMYN, Royal Dohlaran Army—Baron Tymplahr; Sir Rainos Ahlverez' quartermaster, LAMA.

RAHDGYRZ, SIR HAIMLTAHN—Duke Harless' seneschal and the CO of the defenses of the city of Geyra, HFQ.

RAHDRYGHYZ, PRINCE ZHONAH—Prince of Sardahn, ruler of the Princedom of Sardahn in the Border States, HFQ.

RAHLSTAHN, ADMIRAL GHARTH, Royal Emeraldian Navy—Earl of Mahndyr, CO, Royal Emeraldian

Navy, OAR; third-ranking officer Imperial Charisian Navy, BHD.

**RAHLSTYN, COMMODORE ERAYK,** Royal Dohlaran Navy—one of Duke Malikai's squadron commanders, OAR.

**RAHLSTYN, LIEUTENANT MHARTYN,** Royal Dohlaran Navy—XO, HMS *Chihiro*, 50, MT&T.

**RAHMAHDYN, CAPTAIN LYWYS,** Army of God—second-in-command, Camp Dynnys guard force, HFQ.

**RAHS, MAJOR KAYVAIRN,** Imperial Charisian Army—CO, 1st Battalion, 1st Scout Sniper Regiment, Imperial Charisian Army, LAMA.

**RAHSKAIL, AHNDRYA**—Barkah and Rebkah Rahskail's youngest child, MT&T.

**RAHSKAIL, COLONEL BARKAH,** Imperial Charisian Army—Earl of Swayle; a senior supply officer, Imperial Charisian Army, executed for treason, HFAF.

**RAHSKAIL, REBKAH**—Dowager Countess of Swayle; widow of Barkah, mother of Wahlys, MT&T.

**RAHSKAIL, SAMYL**—Wahlys Rahskail's younger brother, MT&T.

**RAHSKAIL, WAHLYS**—Earl of Swayle, son of Barkah Rahskail and Rebkah Rahskail, MT&T.

**RAHZMAHN, LIEUTENANT DAHNYLD,** Imperial Charisian Navy—Sir Gwylym Manthyr's flag lieutenant, HFAF.

**RAHZWAIL, CAPTAIN AHLDAHS,** Imperial Charisian Navy—XO, Bureau of Ordnance; Sir Ahlfryd Hyndryk's chief assistant following Commander Urvyn Mahndrayn's death, MT&T.

**RAICE, BYNZHAMYN**—Baron Wave Thunder; King Haarahld VII's spymaster/royal councilor for intelligence and a member of his Privy Council, OAR; same positions for Cayleb Ahrmahk following King Haarahld's death, BSRA; member Charisian inner circle, BHD.

**RAICE, LEAHYN**—Baroness Wave Thunder; wife of Bynzhamyn Raice, HFAF.

**RAIGLY, SYLVYST**—Sir Dunkyn Yairley's valet and steward, HFAF.

RAIMAHN, BYRK—Claitahn and Sahmantha Raimahn's grandson; musician and Reformist, HFAF; CO riflemen sent to Glacierheart by Aivah Parsahn, MT&T; CO, 1st Glacierheart Volunteers, Republic of Siddarmark Army, LAMA.

RAIMAHN, CLAITAHN—wealthy Charisian expatriate and Temple Loyalist living in Siddar City, HFAF.

RAIMAHN, SAHMANTHA—Claitahn Raimahn's wife and also a Temple Loyalist, HFAF.

RAIMAHND, BYNDFYRD—a Chisholmian banker deeply involved in spreading Charisian-style manufactories to Chisholm, LAMA.

RAIMAIR, LIEUTENANT TOBYS, Royal Corisandian Guard—late Sergeant Raimair of the Royal Corisandian Army, senior noncom of Daivyn Daykyn's Royal Guard in exile, HFAF; member Royal Corisandian Guard and CO, Prince Daivyn Daykyn's personal guard detachment, LAMA.

RAIMYND, SIR LYNDAHR—Prince Hektor of Corisande's treasurer, BSRA; royal treasurer and member of the Regency Council, HFAF.

RAINBOW WATERS, EARL OF—see Taychau Daiyang.

RAISAHNDO, ADMIRAL CAITAHNO, Royal Dohlaran Navy—captain, CO, HMS *Rakurai*, 46, HFAF; promoted admiral and second-in-command, Western Squadron, HFQ.

RAISLAIR, BISHOP EXECUTOR MHARTYN—Archbishop Ahdym Taibyr's executive assistant, Archbishopric of Desnair, HFAF.

RAISMYN, LIEUTENANT BYRNHAR, Imperial Charisian Marines—a lieutenant attached to Colonel Wyntahn Harys' Marines in support of Captain Halcom Bahrns' operation ("Great Canal Raid"), MT&T.

RAIYZ, FATHER CARLSYN—Queen Sharleyan's confessor, BSRA; killed in Sharleyan's attempted assassination at Saint Agtha's, BHD.

RAIZYNGYR, BRIGADIER SIR AHDRYN, Imperial Charisian Army—CO, 6th Mounted Brigade, Imperial Charisian Army, LAMA.

RAIZYNGYR, COLONEL ARTTU—CO, 2/3rd Marines

(2nd Battalion, 3rd Brigade), Charisian Marines, BSRA.

RAYNAIR, CAPTAIN EKOHLS—CO, privateer schooner *Blade*, BSRA.

RAYNO, ARCHBISHOP WYLLYM—Archbishop of Chiang-wu; adjutant of the Order of Schueler, OAR.

RAYNO, HAILYN—Queen Consort Hailyn, wife of King James II of Delferahk; a cousin of Prince Hektor of Corisande, BSRA.

RAYNO, KING ZHAMES OLYVYR—King Zhames II of Delferahk; a kinsman by marriage of Hektor Daykyn of Corisande and a distant cousin of Wyllym Rayno, Archbishop of Chiang-wu, BSRA.

RAZHAIL, FATHER DERAHK—senior healer, Imperial Palace, Cherayth. Upper-priest of the Order of Pasquale, HFAF.

REJ, MAJOR KRYSTYN, Imperial Charisian Army—CO, 1st Battalion, 12th Mounted Regiment, 6th Mounted Brigade, Imperial Charisian Army, LAMA.

RHOBAIR, VICAR—see Rhobair Duchairn.

ROCK COAST, DUKE OF—see Zhasyn Seafarer.

ROCK POINT, BARON OF—see Sir Domynyk Staynair.

ROHSAIL, SIR DAHRAND, Royal Dohlaran Navy—captain, CO, HMS *Grand Vicar Mahrys*, 50, HFAF; admiral, CO, Western Squadron, Royal Dohlaran Navy, based on Claw Island, LAMA.

ROHZHYR, COLONEL BAHRTOL, Royal Charisian Marines—a senior commissary officer, BSRA.

ROHZYNKRANZ, BISHOP KLYMYNT, Army of God—CO, 1st Temple Division, HFQ.

ROPEWALK, COLONEL AHDAM, Charisian Royal Guard—CO, Charisian Royal Guard, OAR.

ROWYN, CAPTAIN HORAHS—CO, Sir Dustyn Olyvyr's yacht *Ahnyet*, OAR.

ROWZVEL, ARCHBISHOP TRUMAHN—Archbishop of Gorath, a Langhornite, HFAF.

RUDAHRY, FATHER AIMOHS—a Schuelerite priest and inquisitor selected to oversee the "escort" of Temple Guardsmen detailed to transport Earl Thirsk's family to Zion, HFQ.

**RUHSAIL, PRIVATE AHNTAHN,** Army of God—assigned to Camp Chihiro guard force, HFQ.

**RUHSTAHD, FATHER KUHNYMYCHU**—a Schuelerite upper-priest assigned to Camp Chihiro, HFQ.

**RUSTMYN, EDYMYND**—Baron Stonekeep; King Gorjah III of Tarot's first councilor and spymaster, OAR.

**RYCHTAIR, NYNIAN**—illegitimate daughter of Grand Vicar Chihiro IX, adopted sister of Adorai Dynnys, BSRA; see Ahnzhelyk Phonda, Frahncyn Tahlbaht, Aivah Pahrsahn, and Arbalest. Mother Superior of the Order of Saint Khody and creator and leader of Helm Cleaver, a covert action organization directed against the Group of Four, HFQ.

**RYCHTYR, GENERAL SIR FAHSTYR,** Royal Desnairian Army—CO of the vanguard of the Dohlaran Army invading the Republic of Siddarmark, MT&T; CO, Trevyr garrison, LAMA.

**RYDACH, FATHER ZHORDYN**—Rebkah Rahskail's Temple Loyalist confessor; officially an under-priest (actually an upper-priest) of the Order of Chihiro, MT&T.

**RYDMAKYR, KAHLVYN, EARL OF CHESHYR**—physically incapacitated Earl of Cheshyr, HFQ.

**RYDMAKYR, KARYL, DOWAGER COUNTESS OF CHESHYR**—regent for her son, Kahlvyn Rydmakyr, Earl of Cheshyr, HFQ.

**RYDMAKYR, STYVYN**—son and heir of Kahlvyn Rudymakyr, HFQ.

**RYDNAUYR, MAJOR KAHLVYN**—CO, 5th Mountain-cross Rangers, Temple Loyalist partisans; CO, Chestyrtyn garrison, LAMA.

**RYNDYL, FATHER AHLUN**—General Trumyn Stohnar's chaplain, MT&T.

**SAHBRAHAN, LIEUTENANT YEREK,** Imperial Charisian Navy—a naval battery commander serving under Commander Hainz Watyrs in Glacierheart Province, MT&T.

**SAHBRAHAN, PAIAIR**—the Earl of Thirsk's personal valet, HFAF.

**SAHDLYR, LIEUTENANT BYNZHAMYN,** Royal Charisian

Navy—second lieutenant, galleon HMS *Dreadnought*, 54, OAR.

**SAHDLYR, MAJOR BORYS, Temple Guard**—a guardsman of the Inquisition assigned to Siddar City as part of the Sword of Schueler, HFAF.

**SAHLAHMN, PETTY OFFICER AHGUSTAHS,** Imperial Charisian Navy—Sir Bruhstair Ahbaht's personal coxswain, HFQ.

**SAHLAVAHN, CAPTAIN TRAI**—cousin of Commander Urvyn Mahndrayn; CO, Hairatha Powder Mill, HFAF.

**SAHLMYN, SERGEANT MAJOR HAIN,** Royal Charisian Marines—Colonel Zhanstyn's battalion sergeant major, BHD.

**SAHLTMYN, LIEUTENANT HENRAI,** Royal Dohlaran Navy—one of Captain Lywystyn's battery commanders on Claw Island, LAMA.

**SAHLYS, MAJOR GAHVYN,** Republic of Siddarmark Army—CO, 5th Company, 37th Infantry Regiment, Republic of Siddarmark Army, MT&T.

**SAHLYVAHN, LIEUTENANT DAHGLYS,** Republic of Siddarmark Army—General Trumyn Stohnar's aide, MT&T.

**SAHMYRSYT, GENERAL BARTYN,** Imperial Charisian Army—CO, Army of Old Province, LAMA; knighted and CO, Army of New Northland, HFQ.

**SAHNDAHL, COLONEL FRAIMAHN,** Delferahkan Royal Guard—XO, Delferahkan Royal Guard, HFAF.

**SAHNDFYRD, TAHVYS**—a junior partner and representative of Ehdwyrd Howsmyn sent to Chisholm to assist Sharleyan in creating Chisholmian manufactories, LAMA.

**SAHNDHAIM, BISHOP MERKYL**—a Schuelerite and Earl Rainbow Waters' intendant with the Mighty Host of God and the Archangels, HFQ.

**SAHNDHAIM, COLONEL STYWYRT,** Army of God—CO, 1st Regiment, Zion Division, Army of Glacierheart, MT&T.

**SAHNDYRS, BISHOP STYWYRT**—Reformist Bishop of Solomon, Princedom of Emerald, MT&T.

**SAHNDYRS, GENERAL SIR LAIMYN**, Royal Desnairian Army—Sir Rainos Ahlverez' senior field commander in the main body of the Dohlaran Army invading the Republic of Siddarmark; effectively, Ahlverez' second-in-command, MT&T.

**SAHNDYRS, LIEUTENANT WAHLTAYR**, Imperial Charisian Army—Colonel Hynryk Celahk's aide, LAMA.

**SAHNDYRS, MAHRAK**—Baron Green Mountain; Queen Sharleyan of Chisholm's first councilor, OAR; first councilor of Chisholm within Charisian Empire, BSRA; wounded and incapacitated by terrorist attack, HFAF. Effectively Sharleyan Aplyn-Ahrmahk's second father, having served her father, King Sailys, in the same role, HFAF.

**SAHNDYRSYN, LIEUTENANT DAIRYN**, Imperial Charisian Navy—CO, Trumpeter Redoubt, Thesmar, LAMA.

**SAHNDYRSYN, MAJOR BRYNTWYRTH**, Republic of Siddarmark Army—CO, 4th Company, 63rd Infantry Regiment, 2nd Rifle Division, 2nd Corps, Army of New Northland, HFQ.

**SAHNGYRMAIN, COLONEL EDWYN**, Army of God—Bishop Gorthyk Nybar's senior artillerist, Army of Fairkyn, HFQ.

**SAHRKHO, FATHER MOHRYS**—Empress Sharleyan's confessor, HFAF.

**SAIGAHN, CAPTAIN MAHRDAI**, Royal Charisian Navy—CO, HMS *Guardsman*, 44, HFAF.

**SAIGYL, CAPTAIN ZEBDYAH**, Imperial Charisian Navy—CO, HMS *Vortex*, 30, HFQ.

**SAIGYL, COMMANDER TOMPSYN**, Imperial Charisian Navy—one of Sir Ahlfryd Hyndryk's senior assistants; Bureau of Ordnance's chief liaison with Sir Dustyn Olyvyr, MT&T; CO, Bureau of Ships, LAMA.

**SAIKOR, BISHOP EXECUTOR BAIKYR**—Archbishop Praidwyn Laicharn's bishop executor; a Pasqualate, HFAF.

**SAINT HOWAN, EARL OF**—see Sir Dynzayl Hyntyn.

**SAIRAH HAHLMYN**—Queen Sharleyan's personal maid, BSRA.

**SAITHWYK, ARCHBISHOP FAIRMYN**—Reformist Archbishop of Emerald for the Church of Charis, HFAF.

**SALTAIR, HAIRYET**—Crown Princess Alahnah's second nanny, HFAF.

**SALTHAR, DUKE OF**—see Shain Hauwyl.

**SANDKARAN, LIEUTENANT ERAYK,** Royal Dohlaran Army—CO, 4th Platoon, 5th Company, Sheldyn's Regiment, Army of the Seridahn, HFQ.

**SARFORTH, COMMANDER QWENTYN,** Imperial Charisian Navy—senior officer in command, Brankyr Bay, Kingdom of Tarot, MT&T.

**SARMAC, JENNIFER**—an Eve who escaped the destruction of the Alexandria Enclave and fled to Tellesberg, BSRA.

**SARMAC, KAYLEB**—an Adam who escaped the destruction of the Alexandria Enclave and fled to Tellesberg, BSRA.

**SARMOUTH, BARON OF**—see Sir Dunkyn Yairley.

**SATYRFYLD, MAJOR LAREK,** Republic of Siddarmark Militia—CO, 2nd Company, 1st Glacierheart Volunteers, LAMA.

**SAWAL, FATHER RAHSS**—an under-priest of the Order of Chihiro, the skipper of one of the Temple's courier boats, BSRA.

**SAWYAIR, SISTER FRAHNCYS**—senior nun of the Order of Pasquale, Convent of the Blessed Hand, Cherayth, HFAF.

**SAYLKYRK, MIDSHIPMAN TRAHVYS,** Imperial Charisian Navy—senior midshipman, HMS *Destiny*, 54, HFAF; fourth lieutenant, HMS *Destiny*, 54, MT&T.

**SAYRANOH, CORPORAL BRUNOHN,** Imperial Charisian Army—squad leader, 1st Squad, Company B, 1st Battalion, 1st Scout Sniper Regiment, Imperial Charisian Army, LAMA.

**SCHAHL, FATHER DAHNYVYN**—upper-priest of the Order of Schueler working directly for Bishop Mytchail Zhessop; attached to Colonel Aiphraim Tahlyvyr's dragoon regiment, HFAF.

SCHMYD, PRIVATE MAHKZWAIL, Royal Dohlaran Army—2nd Section, 3rd Platoon, 1st Company, Ahzbyrn's Regiment (cavalry), Dohlaran component, Army of Shiloh, LAMA.

SCHYLLYR, FATHER AHMBROHS—a Schuelerite priest; intendant, Fyrgyrsyn Division, Army of Glacierheart, LAMA.

SCOVAYL, BISHOP TYMAHN, Army of God—CO, Fyrgyrsyn Division, Army of Glacierheart, LAMA.

SEABLANKET, RHOBAIR—the Earl of Coris' valet, HFAF.

SEACATCHER, BRIGADIER SIR LAIMYN, Imperial Charisian Army—elder son of the Baron of Mandolin; CO, 5th Mounted Brigade, Imperial Charisian Army, LAMA.

SEACATCHER, SIR RAHNYLD—Baron Mandolin; a member of Cayleb Ahrmahk's Royal Council, BSRA.

SEAFARER, ZHASYN—Duke of Rock Coast, MT&T.

SEAFARMER, SIR RHYZHARD—Baron Wave Thunder's senior investigator, OAR.

SEAHAMPER, SERGEANT EDWYRD, Charisian Imperial Guards—Sharleyan Ahrmahk's personal armsman since age ten, member Charisian inner circle, BSRA.

SEAMOUNT, BARON OF—see Sir Ahlfryd Hyndryk.

SEAROSE, FATHER GREYGHOR, Navy of God—CO, NGS *Saint Styvyn*, 52. Senior surviving officer of Kornylys Harpahr's fleet. A Chihirite of the Order of the Sword, HFAF.

SEASMOKE, LIEUTENANT YAIRMAN, Imperial Charisian Navy—XO, HMS *Dancer*, 56, HFAF.

SEATOWN, CAPTAIN WAHLTAYR—CO of merchant ship *Fraynceen*, acting as a courier for Prince Hektor's spies in Charis, OAR. See also Lieutenant Fraizher Maythis, OAR.

SEEGAIRS, FATHER AHNDAIR—a Schuelerite upperpriest; technically Ernyst Abernethy's senior assistant as the intendant of the Army of the Sylmahn but actually Zhaspahr Clyntahn's senior agent inquisitor in the Army of the Sylmahn's hierarchy, HFQ.

SEEGAIRS, FATHER HAHSKYLL—a Schuelerite upper-priest

and inquisitor; a senior member of Inquisitor General Wylbyr Edwyrds' staff, LAMA.

SEEVYRS, LIEUTENANT ALYK, Royal Dohlaran Navy—first lieutenant, screw-galley HMS *Lance*, HFQ.

SEIDYNG, LORD OF HORSE ZHOWKU, EARL OF SILKEN HILLS, Imperial Harchongese Army—CO, Southern Mighty Host of God and the Archangels (the forces being detached to shore up the Church's position following the destruction of the Army of Glacierheart), HFQ.

SELKYR, BRYAHN—Earl of Deep Hollow; a member of the Northern Conspiracy in Corisande, executed for treason, HFAF.

SELKYR, PETTY OFFICER AHNTAHN, Imperial Charisian Navy—a boatswain's mate, HMS *Destiny*, 54, HFAF.

SELLYRS, MAJOR ZHORJ, Royal Dohlaran Army—CO, 3rd Company, Ahzbyrn's Regiment (cavalry), Dohlaran component, LAMA.

SELLYRS, PAITYR—Baron White Church; Keeper of the Seal of the Kingdom of Charis; a member of Cayleb Ahrmahk's Royal Council, BSRA.

SEVYRS, TRYNT, Imperial Charisian Navy—ironclad HMS *Delthak*, 22; Halcom Bahrns' steward, LAMA.

SHAIKYR, LARYS—CO, privateer galleon *Raptor*, BSRA.

SHAILTYN, CAPTAIN DAIVYN, Imperial Charisian Navy—CO, HMS *Thunderbolt*, 58, HFAF; "frocked" to commodore to command the squad- ron escorting the Charisian Expeditionary Force to the Republic of Siddarmark, MT&T.

SHAIMUS, DAHNVYRS, LIEUTENANT, Imperial Charisian Army—CO, 1st Platoon, 1st Company, 19th Mounted Regiment, 10th Mounted Brigade, 1st Corps, Army of New Northland, HFQ.

SHAIN, PAYTER, Imperial Charisian Navy—captain, CO, HMS *Dreadful*, 48. Admiral Nylz' flag captain, BSRA; admiral, flag officer commanding ICN squadron based on Thol Bay, Kingdom of Tarot, HFAF; CO, Inshore Squadron, Gulf of Jahras, LAMA.

**SHAIOW, ADMIRAL OF THE BROAD OCEANS CHYNTAI,** Imperial Harchongese Navy—Duke of Sun Rising; senior officer afloat, Imperial Harchongese Navy, HFAF.

**SHAIRN, DUKE OF**—see Sir Slohkym Dahrnail.

**SHAIRNCROSS, LADY**—see Zhain Parkair.

**SHAIRNCROSS, LORD**—see Weslai Parkair.

**SHANDYR, HAHL**—Baron of Shandyr, Prince Nahrmahn of Emerald's spymaster, OAR.

**SHARGHATI, AHLYSSA**—greatest soprano opera singer of the Republic of Siddarmark; friend of Aivah Pahrsahn's, HFAF.

**SHARLEYAN, EMPRESS**—see Sharleyan Alahnah Zhenyfyr Ahlyssa Tayt Ahrmahk.

**SHARPFIELD, EARL OF**—see Sir Lewk Cohlmyn.

**SHARPHILL, EARL OF**—see Sir Maikel Traivyr.

**SHAUMAHN, BROTHER SYMYN**—hosteler of the Monastery of Saint Zherneau, HFAF.

**SHELDYN, COLONEL GYLCHRYST,** Royal Dohlaran Army—CO, Sheldyn's Regiment, Army of the Seridahn, HFQ.

**SHELTYN, LIEUTENANT CHARLZ,** Royal Corisandian Guard—an officer of the Royal Guard who deeply resents and distrusts Nimue Chwaeriau, LAMA.

**SHEWMAKYR, LIEUTENANT ZHASPAHR,** Imperial Charisian Navy—XO, HMS *Vortex*, 30, HFQ.

**SHOWAIL, LIEUTENANT COMMANDER STYV,** Imperial Charisian Navy—CO, schooner HMS *Flash*, 10, HFAF.

**SHOWAIL, STYWYRT**—a Charisian foundry owner deliberately infringing several of Ehdwyrd Howsmyn's patents, MT&T; charged with several illegal practices and financially ruined, LAMA.

**SHRAYDYR, COLONEL TOBYS**—CO, 2nd Raisor Volunteers, Shilohian Temple Loyalist militia, Fort Tairys garrison.

**SHULMYN, BISHOP TRAHVYS**—Bishop of Raven's Land, MT&T.

**SHUMAKYR, FATHER SYMYN**—Archbishop Erayk Dynnys'

secretary for his 891 pastoral visit; an agent of the Grand Inquisitor, OAR.

**SHUMAY, FATHER AHLVYN**—Bishop Mylz Halcom's personal aide, killed during Saint Agtha assassination attempt, BSRA.

**SHYLAIR, BISHOP EXECUTOR THOMYS**—Archbishop Borys Bahrmyn's bishop executor, BSRA.

**SHYLLYR, FATHER ZEFRYM**—a Langhornite under-priest who attached himself to Major Kahlvyn Rydnauyr's 5th Mountaincross Rangers as its chaplain, LAMA.

**SHYNGWA, CAPTAIN OF SEAS RYANGDU**, Imperial Harchongese Navy—CO, Alexov Defense Squadron, HFQ.

**SHYRBYRT, COMMANDER ALLAYN**, Imperial Charisian Navy—Earl Sharpfield's chief of staff, LAMA.

**SHYRBYRT, GENERAL FRAIDARECK**, Republic of Siddarmark Army—CO, Cavalry Corps, Army of Hildermoss, HFQ.

**SILKEN HILLS, EARL OF**—see Zhowku Seidyng.

**SILKIAH, BRIGADIER ESTMYN**, Imperial Charisian Army—Sir Bartyn Sahmyrsyt's chief of staff for the Army of New Northland, HFQ.

**SISTER CLAUDYA**—see Claudya Zhansyn.

**SISTER EMYLEE**—see Emlyee Parkair.

**SISTER KLAIRAH**—see Klairah Bahrdo.

**SISTER MARZHO**—see also Marzho Alysyn.

**SISTER TYLDAH**—see Tyldah Zhansyn.

**SKRYVNYR, ZHASYN**, Imperial Charisian Navy—Captain Kahrltyn Haigyl's secretary in broadside ironclad HMS *Dreadnought*, 30, HFQ.

**SKYNYR, LIEUTENANT MHARTYN**, Imperial Charisian Navy—third lieutenant, HMS *Destiny*, 54, MT&T.

**SLAYTYR, ZHAPYTH**—one of Merlin Athrawes' alternate identities, LAMA.

**SLOHVYK, COMMANDER PAIDRHO**, Imperial Charisian Navy—CO, schooner HMS *Termagant*, 18, Gulf of Jahras, LAMA.

**SLOKYM, CAPTAIN THOMYS**, Army of God—CO, 2nd Company, 73rd Cavalry Regiment, Army of the Sylmahn, LAMA.

**SLOKYM, LIEUTENANT BRYAHN,** Imperial Charisian Army—Baron Green Valley's aide, 2nd Brigade (reinforced), Charisian Expeditionary Force, MT&T.

**SLOKYM, MASTER TAYRENS,** Imperial Charisian Navy—sailing master, HMS *Fleet Wing*, 18, HFQ.

**SMOLTH, ZHAN**—star pitcher for the Tellesberg Krakens, OAR.

**SNELYNG, CAPTAIN TYMYTHY,** Royal Dohlaran Navy—CO, screw-galley HMS *Lance*, HFQ.

**SOLAYRAN, LIEUTENANT BRAHD,** Imperial Charisian Navy—XO, ironclad HMS *Tellesberg*, 22, LAMA.

**SOLOMON, DUKE OF**—see Hanbyl Baytz.

**SOMERSET, CAPTAIN MARTIN LUTHER,** Terran Federation Navy—CO, TFNS *Excalibur*, OAR.

**SOMYRS, COLONEL KHOLBY,** Army of God—CO, 112th Infantry Regiment, St. Ulstyr Division; senior officer in command, Five Forks garrison, HFQ.

**SOWTHMYN, TRUMYN**—Earl of Airyth; one of Prince Hektor of Corisande's councilors serving on Prince Daivyn's Regency Council. He is an ally of Earl Anvil Rock and Earl Tartarian, HFAF.

**SPRYNGYR, CAPTAIN ZHEROHM,** Royal Dohlaran Navy—CO, HMS *Scepter*, 52, HFQ.

**STAHDMAIYR, PRIVATE LEWSHYS,** Army of God—assigned to Camp Chihiro guard force, HFQ.

**STAHDYRD, LIEUTENANT SIR WAHLYS,** Royal Dohlaran Army—CO, 3rd Platoon, 1st Company, Ahzbyrn's Regiment (cavalry), Dohlaran component, Army of Shiloh, LAMA.

**STAHKAIL, GENERAL LOWRAI,** Imperial Desnairian Army—CO, Triangle Shoal Fort, Iythria, HFAF.

**STAHLYNG, COMMANDER ZHAMES,** Royal Dohlaran Navy—CO, screw-galley HMS *Saber*, HFQ.

**STAHNTYN, GENERAL CHARLZ,** Republic of Siddarmark Army—CO, Aivahnstyn garrison, Cliff Peak Province, Republic of Siddarmark, MT&T.

**STANTYN, ARCHBISHOP NYKLAS**—Archbishop of Hankey in the Desnairian Empire; a member of the Reformists, BSRA.

**STAR SONG, BARON OF**—see Wyukau Chinzho.

STAYNAIR, MADAME AHRDYN—Maikel Staynair's deceased wife, BSRA.

STAYNAIR, MAIKEL—a Bédardist, Bishop of Tellesberg, King Haarahld VII's confessor, member Royal Council, member Charisian inner circle, OAR; created Archbishop of Charis, defies the Temple and the Group of Four, BSRA; creates Church of Charis following the merger of Kingdom of Old Charis and Kingdom of Chisholm, BHD.

STAYNAIR, SIR DOMYNYK, Royal Charisian Navy—younger brother of Bishop Maikel Staynair; commodore, specialist in naval tactics, CO, Experimental Squadron, Cayleb Ahrmahk's second-in-command, Battle of Rock Point and Battle of Darcos Sound, OAR; promoted admiral, created Baron Rock Point, BSRA; CO, *Eraystor* blockade squadron, BHD; member Charisian inner circle, promoted high admiral, Imperial Charisian Navy commander-in-chief, AMF.

STOHNAR, GENERAL TRUMYN, Republic of Siddarmark Army—a first cousin of Lord Protector Greyghor Stohnar; commander of the reinforcements sent to hold the Sylmahn Gap, MT&T; CO, Army of Hildermoss, HFQ.

STOHNAR, LORD PROTECTOR GREYGHOR—elected ruler of the Siddarmark Republic, OAR.

STONEHEART, BARON OF—see Sylvyst Mhardyr.

STONEKEEP, BARON OF—see Edymynd Rustmyn.

STORM KEEP, EARL OF—see Sahlahmn Traigair.

STORMYNT, LIEUTENANT AHDYM, Imperial Charisian Navy—Sir Hainz's Zhastro's flag lieutenant, HFQ.

STOWAIL, COMMANDER AHBRAIM, Imperial Charisian Navy—Sir Domynyk Staynair's chief of staff, MT&T.

STYLMYN, BRAHD—Ehdwyrd Howsmyn's senior civil engineer, MT&T.

STYVYNSYN, MAJOR AHLYK, Imperial Charisian Army—CO, 2nd Battalion, 2nd Scout Sniper Regiment, Imperial Charisian Army, MT&T.

STYVYNSYN, MAJOR ZHORJ, Republic of Siddarmark

Army—CO, 2nd Company, 37th Infantry Regiment, Republic of Siddarmark Army, MT&T.

STYVYNSYN, ZHORZHET—"Castanet"; Marzho Alysyn's senior employee and a member of Marzho's Helm Cleaver cell, HFQ.

STYWYRT, CAPTAIN AHRNAHLD, Imperial Charisian Navy—CO, HMS *Squall*, 36, HFAF.

STYWYRT, CAPTAIN DAHRYL, Royal Charisian Navy—CO, HMS *Typhoon*, 36, OAR.

STYWYRT, MAJOR LAIMUYL, Republic of Siddarmark Militia—CO, 4th Company, 1st Glacierheart Volunteers, LAMA.

STYWYRT, PAYT—Duke Black Horse, MT&T.

STYWYRT, SERGEANT ZOHZEF, Royal Delferahkan Army—noncom in Ferayd garrison, party to Ferayd massacre, BSRA.

SULYVYN, COLONEL CHERMYN, Royal Dohlaran Army—CO, Sulyvyn's Regiment (medium cavalry), Dohlaran component, Army of Shiloh, LAMA.

SULYVYN, DAHMBRYK, Imperial Charisian Army—CO, 5th Brigade, 3rd Infantry Division, LAMA.

SUMYR, FATHER FRAHNKLYN—Archbishop Failyx Gahrbor's intendant, Archbishopric of Tarot, HFAF.

SUMYRS, GENERAL CLYFTYN, Republic of Siddarmark Army—CO, Alyksberg, Cliff Peak Province, Republic of Siddarmark, MT&T.

SUMYRS, SERGEANT DAHLTYN, Imperial Charisian Marines—a senior Marine noncom attached to Brigadier Taisyn's forces in Glacierheart, MT&T.

SUMYRS, SIR ZHER—Baron of Barcor; one of Sir Koryn Gahrvai's senior officers, Corisande Campaign, BHD; later member of Northern Conspiracy, HFAF.

SUN RISING, DUKE OF—see Chyntai Shaiow.

SUTYLS, MIDSHIPMAN TAIRAINCE, Imperial Charisian Navy—ironclad HMS *Delthak*, 22, LAMA.

SUVYRYV, MAJOR AHRNAHLD, Royal Desnairian Army—Colonel Sir Zhadwail Brynygair's executive officer, assigned to Sir Fahstyr Rychtyr's invasion column, MT&T.

SUWAIL, BARJWAIL—Lord Theralt; Lord of Clan Theralt, Raven's Land, MT&T.

SUWAIL, COLONEL ZHORDYN, Republic of Siddarmark Army—CO, 93rd Infantry Regiment, Republic of Siddarmark Army, MT&T.

SUWYL, TOBYS—an expatriate Charisian banker and merchant living in Siddar City; a Temple Loyalist, HFAF.

SUWYL, ZHANDRA—Tobys Suwyl's wife; a moderate Reformist, HFAF.

SUZHYMAHGA, FATHER CHERMYN—a Schuelerite upper-priest and inquisitor attached to the office of father Ahbsahlahn Kharmych, Archbishop Trumyn Rowzvel's Intendant, HFQ.

SVAIRSMAHN, MIDSHIPMAN LAINSAIR, Imperial Charisian Navy—a midshipman, HMS *Dancer*, 56, AMF; youngest of Charisian POWs surrendered to Inquisition by Kingdom of Dohlar, HFAF.

SWAYLE, DOWAGER COUNTESS OF—see Rebkah Rahskail.

SWAYLE, EARL OF—see Barkah Rahskail and Wahlys Rahskail.

SYGAYL, FRAYDRYKHA—Zhustyn Sygayl's twelve-year-old daughter, raped and killed by Temple Loyalists attacking the Siddar City Charisian Quarter, LAMA.

SYGAYL, LYZBYT—Zhustyn Sygayl's widow and Fraydrykha Sygayl's mother, LAMA.

SYGAYL, ZHUSTYN—Klymynt Abykrahmbi's uncle, killed defending his daughter against Temple Loyalists attacking the Siddar City Charisian Quarter, LAMA.

SYGHAL, COLONEL TREVYR, Imperial Charisian Army—senior artillery officer, 2nd Brigade (reinforced), Charisian Expeditionary Force, MT&T; same position, Army of Midhold, LAMA.

SYGZBEE, LIEUTENANT ZHORJ, Imperial Charisian Marine Corps—XO, Marine detachment, HMS *Destiny*, 54, HFQ.

SYGZBEE, MAJOR STYWYRT, Imperial Charisian Army—

XO, 2nd Scout Sniper Regiment, Imperial Charisian Army, LAMA.

**SYLVELLA, SERGEANT DAIVYN**, Imperial Charisian Army—2nd Platoon, Company A, 2nd Battalion, 12th Mounted Regiment, 6th Mounted Brigade, Imperial Charisian Army, LAMA.

**SYLVSTYR, MAJOR FAILYX**, Royal Dohlaran Army—CO, Sylvstyr's Artillery Regiment, HFQ.

**SYLZ, PARSAHN**—a Charisian foundry owner and associate of Ehdwyrd Howsmyn, MT&T.

**SYMKEE, LIEUTENANT GARAITH**, Imperial Charisian Navy—second lieutenant, HMS *Destiny*, 54, HFAF; XO, *Destiny*, 54, MT&T.

**SYMKYN, GENERAL AHLYN**, Imperial Charisian Army—CO, 3rd Infantry Division, Imperial Charisian Army, and CO of the second wave of the Charisian Expeditionary Force, MT&T.

**SYMMYNS, BISHOP MILITANT RUHSAIL**, Army of God—CO of the army Allayn Maigwair has been recruiting and training in the Temple Lands, HFQ.

**SYMMYNS, FATHER ZHAMES**—a Schuelerite priest, serving as Father Trynt Dezmynd's second-in-command, HFQ.

**SYMMYNS, LIEUTENANT ZHORJ**, Royal Dohlaran Navy—second lieutenant, HMS *Tide*, 52, HFQ.

**SYMMYNS, SENIOR CHIEF PETTY OFFICER MAIKEL**, Imperial Charisian Navy—boatswain, HMS *Destiny*, 54, HFAF.

**SYMMYNS, TOHMyS**—Grand Duke of Zebediah, senior member and head of Council of Zebediah, OAR; swears fealty to Cayleb and Sharleyan Ahrmahk, BSRA; joins Northern Conspiracy in Corisande, AMF; executed for treason, HFAF.

**SYMPSYN, CAPTAIN LYWYS**, Imperial Charisian Marines—Earl Hanth's senior artillerist at Thesmar, LAMA; promoted admiral, HFQ.

**SYMPSYN, LIEUTENANT COMMANDER BRYAHN**, Imperial Charisian Navy—CO, Kaihrys Point battery, Thesmar Bay, LAMA.

**SYMPSYN, MHARGRYT**—Alyk Krystyphyrsyn's assistant

supervisor at the Delthak Works, part of Ehdwyrd Howsmyn's program to promote female management personnel, LAMA.

**SYMYN, LIEUTENANT HAHL,** Royal Charisian Navy—XO, HMS *Torrent*, 42, BSRA.

**SYMYN, SERGEANT ZHORJ,** Charisian Imperial Guard—a Charisian noncom assigned to Empress Sharleyan's guard detachment, KIA in Saint Agtha assassination attempt, BSRA.

**SYNGPU, SERGEANT TANGWYN,** Imperial Harchongese Army—standardbearer (color sergeant) 1st Company, 231st Volunteer Regiment, 115th Volunteer Brigade, Mighty Host of God and the Archangels, Imperial Harchongese Army, LAMA.

**SYNGYLTYN, COLONEL CLAREYK**—CO, 9th Cavalry Regiment, Shilohian Temple Loyalist militia, LAMA.

**SYNKLAIR, AHDYM,** Imperial Charisian Navy—a member of Laisl Mhattsyn's gun crew in Glacierheart Province, MT&T.

**SYNKLYR, LIEUTENANT AIRAH,** Royal Dohlaran Navy—XO, galleon HMS *Guardian*, BSRA.

**SYNZHYN, FATHER TAILAHR**—a Hastingite upper-priest and native Chisholmian serving as Duchairn's engineering expert for the canal system, LAMA.

**SYRAHLLA, CAPTAIN MARSHYL,** Royal Desnairian Army—CO, "Syrahlla's Battery," six-pounder horse artillery assigned to Sir Fahstyr Rychtyr's invasion column, MT&T.

**SYRKUS, MAJOR PAWAL,** Imperial Charisian Army—CO, 2nd Battalion, 4th Regiment, Imperial Charisian Army, MT&T.

**SYVAKYS, SERGEANT CLAYMAHNT,** Army of God—platoon sergeant, 1st Platoon, Company A, 191st Cavalry Regiment, Army of Glacierheart, LAMA.

**TAHLAS, LIEUTENANT BRAHD,** Imperial Charisian Marines—CO, 2nd Platoon, Alpha Company, 1/3rd (1st Battalion, 3rd Regiment) Marines, Imperial Charisian Marines, HFAF.

**TAHLBAHT, FRAHNCYN**—a senior employee (and actual

owner) of Bruhstair Freight Haulers; an alias of Nynian Rychtair, HFAF.

**TAHLBAHT, MAJOR ERNYST,** Royal Dohlaran Army—CO, 5th Company, Sheldyn's Regiment, Army of the Seridahn, HFQ.

**TAHLBAHT, SERGEANT ALLAYN,** Army of God—company sergeant major, 1st Company, 231st Volunteer Regiment, 115th Volunteer Brigade, Mighty Host of God and the Archangels, Imperial Harchongese Army, LAMA.

**TAHLMYDG, COLONEL GAHDARHD,** Royal Desnairian Army—CO, Tahlmydg's Regiment (infantry), assigned to Sir Fahstyr Rychtyr's invasion column, MT&T.

**TAHLYVYR, COLONEL AIPHRAIM,** Royal Delferahkan Army—CO, dragoon regiment assigned to "rescue" Princess Irys and Prince Daivyn, HFAF.

**TAHLYVYR, COLONEL LYNDAHR**—ex-lieutenant Republic of Siddarmark Army; CO, Maiyam Militia, Temple Loyalist militia; CO, Maiyam garrison, LAMA.

**TAHLYVYR, COLONEL SYMYN,** Army of God—XO, Fyrgyrsyn Division, Army of Glacierheart, LAMA.

**TAHLYVYR, MAJOR FRAIDARECK,** Imperial Charisian Army—CO, 1st Battalion, 2nd Regiment, Imperial Charisian Army, MT&T.

**TAHNAIYR, COLONEL PRESKYT,** Imperial Charisian Army—CO, 6th Regiment, 3rd Brigade, 2nd Division Regiment, Imperial Charisian Army, LAMA.

**TAHNGUCHI, EYSAMU**—Sir Dustyn Olyvyr and Ehdwyrd Howsmyn's senior foreman, Delthak Yards, Larek, HFQ.

**TAHRLSAHN, FATHER VYKTYR**—Schuelerite upperpriest and one of Zhaspahr Clyntahn's handpicked inquisitors detailed to deliver Charisian POWs from Dohlar to the Temple, HFAF; assigned to Bishop Wylbyr Edwyrds' staff, LAMA.

**TAIBAHLD, FATHER AHRNAHLD,** Navy of God—upperpriest of the Order of Schueler; CO, NGS *Sword of God*; Bishop Kornylys Harpahr's flag captain, HFAF.

TAYLAR, MAJOR PAIDRHO, Imperial Charisian Army—CO, 1st Battalion, 4th Regiment, Imperial Charisian Army, MT&T.

TAYSO, PRIVATE DAISHYN, Charisian Imperial Guard—a Charisian assigned to Empress Sharleyan's guard detachment, KIA Saint Agtha assassination attempt, BSRA.

TAYT, ALAHNAH—Dowager Queen of Chisholm; Queen Sharleyan of Chisholm's mother, BSRA.

TAYT, KING SAILYS—deceased father of Queen Sharleyan of Chisholm, BSRA.

TAYT, MAJOR CHARLZ, Imperial Charisian Army—CO, 4th Battalion, 3rd Regiment, Imperial Charisian Army, a distant cousin of Empress Sharleyan, MT&T.

TAYT, QUEEN MOTHER ALAHNAH—Queen Sharleyan of Chisholm's mother, BSRA.

TAYT, SHARLEYAN—Empress of Charis and Queen of Chisholm. See Sharleyan Ahrmhak.

TEAGMAHN, BISHOP MILITANT TAYRENS, Army of God—CO, Army of Tanshar, HFQ.

TEAGMAHN, FATHER BRYAHN—upper-priest of the Order of Schueler, intendant for the Archbishopric of Glacierheart, HFAF.

THAIRIS, RUHSYL, Imperial Charisian Army—Duke of Eastshare; CO, Imperial Charisian Army, HFAF; CO, Charisian Expeditionary Force; CO, 1st Brigade (reinforced), MT&T; CO, Army of the Branaths, LAMA.

THAIRNOS, EARL OF—see Rahzhyr Hylmahn.

THERALT, LORD OF—see Barjwail Suwail.

THIESSEN, CAPTAIN JOSEPH, Terran Federation Navy—Admiral Pei Kauzhi's chief of staff, OAR.

THIRSK, EARL OF—see Lywys Gardynyr.

THOMPKYN, FATHER CHESTYR—a Schuelerite underpriest and Admiral Sir Dahrand Rohsail's chaplain, HFQ.

THORAST, DUKE OF—see Aibram Zaivyair.

THYRSTYN, LEEAHM GRYGORY—Sir Paitryk Thyrstyn's son and heir, HFQ.

THYRSTYN, LEEAHM, EARL OF USHER—Earl of Usher in the Border States; father-in-law of Prince Grygory of Jhurlahnk, HFQ.

THYRSTYN, SIR PAITRYK—Leeahm Thyrstyn's older son and heir, HFQ.

THYRSTYN, SYMYN—a Siddarmarkian merchant; husband of Wynai Thyrstyn, HFAF.

THYRSTYN, WYNAI—Trai Sahlavahn's married sister; secretary and stenographer in Charis' Siddar City embassy, HFAF.

TIANG, BISHOP EXECUTOR WU-SHAI—Archbishop Zherohm Vyncyt's bishop executor, BSRA.

TIDEWATER, NAHRMAHN—one of Ehdwyrd Howsmyn's senior artificers, MT&T.

TILLYER, CAPTAIN VYNCYT, Army of God—CO, 3rd Company, 73rd Cavalry Regiment, Army of the Sylmahn, LAMA.

TILLYER, LIEUTENANT COMMANDER HENRAI, Imperial Charisian Navy—High Admiral Lock Island's chief of staff; previously his flag lieutenant, HFAF.

TILLYER, LIEUTENANT HENRAI, Royal Charisian Navy—High Admiral Lock Island's personal aide, OAR; lieutenant, Imperial Charisian Navy, High Admiral Lock Island's flag lieutenant; commander, Imperial Charisian Navy, High Admiral Lock Island's chief of staff, AMF.

TIRIAN, DUKE OF—see Kahlvyn Ahrmahk and Rayjhis Ahrmahk.

TOBYS, WING FLAHN—Lord Tairwald's senior "wing" (blooded warrior), MT&T.

TOHBYAIS, CAPTAIN RAIMAHND, Imperial Charisian Navy—CO, HMS *Sickle*, 54, HFQ.

TOHMPSYN, COLONEL SIR SAHLMYN, Royal Desnairian Army—CO, Tohmpsyn's Regiment (infantry), assigned to Sir Fahstyr Rychtyr's invasion column, MT&T.

TOHMYS, FRAHNKLYN—Crown Prince Cayleb's tutor, OAR.

TOHMYS, FRAIDMYN—Archbishop Zhasyn Cahnyr's valet of many years, HFAF.

TRAIWYRTHYN, COLONEL SIR BRAHDRYK, Imperial Desnairian Army—CO, The Perlmann Grays (imperial guard light cavalry), cavalry wing, Army of Shiloh, LAMA.

TRAYKHOS, DUKE OF—see Taylar Gahrmahn.

TRAYLMYN, BARON OF—see General Sir Ohtys Godwyl.

TRAYLMYN, COMMANDER AHNTHYNY, Royal Dohlaran Navy—CO screw-galley HMS *Cutlass*, HFQ.

TREDGAIR, CAPTAIN SYMYN, Army of God—CO, 3rd Company, 16th Cavalry Regiment, Army of the Sylmahn, LAMA.

TRUMYN, ZHORJ—an assistant to Brygham Cartyr in the Charisian technical support mission to the Republic of Siddarmark, LAMA.

TRYFELD, BARON OF—see Sir Daivyn Wynstyn.

TRYMOHR, MIDSHIPMAN AHLYN, Imperial Charisian Navy—a midshipman in broadside ironclad HMS *Dreadnought*, 30, HFQ.

TRYNAIR, VICAR ZAHMSYN—Chancellor of the Council of Vicars of the Church of God Awaiting; one of the so-called Group of Four, OAR.

TRYNCHYR, FATHER AIZYKYAL—a Schuelerite upperpriest serving as Bishop Failyx Mahkgyvyrn's second-in-command at Camp Chihiro, HFQ.

TRYNTYN, CAPTAIN ZHAIRYMIAH, Royal Charisian Navy—CO, HMS *Torrent*, 42, BSRA.

TRYNTYN, COLONEL VYKTYR, Imperial Desnairian Army—Baron Kohlchyst; CO, Empress Consort Gwyndolyn's Own Regiment (imperial guard light cavalry), cavalry wing, Army of Shiloh, LAMA.

TRYVYTHYN, CAPTAIN SIR DYNZYL, Royal Charisian Navy—CO, galley HMS *Royal Charis*, flag captain to King Haarahld VII, KIA Battle of Darcos Sound, OAR.

TSAUZHYN, CAPTAIN OF WINDS MAIDAHNG, Imperial Harchongese Navy—CO, HMMIMS *Celestial Music*, 58, Captain of Seas Shyngwa's flag captain and senior subordinate, HFQ.

TSHANGJYN, LORD OF FOOT BANGPA, Imperial Harchongese Army—CO, 115th Volunteer Brigade, Mighty Host of God and the Archangels, LAMA.

TSYNZHWEI, CAPTAIN OF SWORDS YAUNYNG, Imperial Harchongese Army—CO, 1st Company, 231st Volunteer Regiment, 115th Volunteer Brigade, Mighty Host of God and the Archangels, LAMA.

TUKKYR, COLONEL SIR BAHRTALAM, Imperial Desnairian Army—Baron Cliff Hollow; CO, Emperor Mahrys' Own Regiment (imperial guard heavy cavalry), cavalry wing, Army of Shiloh, LAMA.

TUKKYR, LIEUTENANT MAIRYN, Royal Dohlaran Navy—XO, HMS *Saint Ahndru*, 54, HFQ.

TYBYT, GYFFRY—Paidryg Tybyt's thirteen-year-old son, MT&T.

TYBYT, MAJOR KLAIRYNCE, Royal Dohlaran Army—CO, 1st Company, Gardynyr's Regiment (cavalry), Dohlaran component, Army of Shiloh, LAMA.

TYBYT, PAIDRYG—Temple Loyalist barge crewman and farmer, Fairkyn, New Northland Province, Republic of Siddarmark, MT&T.

TYDWAIL, FATHER ZHORJ—Schuelerite upper-priest; Zion Division's special intendant, Army of Glacierheart, MT&T.

TYLBOR, COLONEL SAIRAHS—CO, 7th Regiment, Usherite Army; one of Baron Tryfeld's regimental commanders, HFQ.

TYLLYTSYN, PLATOON SERGEANT GYFFRY, Imperial Charisian Army—Lieutenant Hahrlys' platoon sergeant, HFQ.

TYLMAHN, FATHER VYKTYR—Pasqualate upper-priest; senior Reformist clergyman in Thesmar, South March Lands, MT&T.

TYLMAHN, GENERAL FRONZ, Republic of Siddarmark Army—senior officer in command, Siddarmarkian infantry detailed to support Captain Halcom Bahrns' operation, MT&T.

TYMAHK, COLONEL AHGUSTAHN, Army of God—CO, Camp Dynnys guard force, HFQ.

TYMKYN, FATHER ZHAMES—Langhornite under-priest,

chaplain, 191st Cavalry Regiment, Army of Glacier-heart, MT&T.

**TYMKYN, LIEUTENANT TOHMYS,** Imperial Charisian Navy—fourth lieutenant and later third lieutenant HMS *Destiny*, 54, HFAF.

**TYMKYN, ZHASTROW**—High Admiral Rock Point's secretary, HFAF.

**TYMPLAHR, BARON OF**—see Sir Shulmyn Rahdgyrz.

**TYMPYLTYN, GENERAL ERAYK**—Temple Loyalist ex-militia officer whose mutinous troops seized Fort Darymahn, South March Lands, Republic of Siddarmark; the promotion to general is self-awarded, MT&T.

**TYMPYLTYN, LIEUTENANT KLAIRYNCE,** Imperial Charisian Navy—CO, Western Battery, Thesmar, LAMA.

**TYMPYLTYN, LIEUTENANT SIR MAHRAK,** Imperial Charisian Navy—Earl Sharpfield's flag lieutenant, LAMA.

**TYMYNS, MAJOR RHOBAIR,** Republic of Siddarmark Army—CO, 2nd Provisional Cavalry Regiment, LAMA.

**TYMYOZHA, COLONEL SIR ZAHLOH,** Imperial Desnairian Army—CO, Tymyozha's Regiment (light cavalry), cavalry wing, Army of Shiloh, LAMA.

**TYMYTHY, COLONEL DAHRDYN,** Republic of Siddarmark Army—CO, 1st Siddarmarkian Scout Regiment, Army of Hildermoss, HFQ.

**TYOTAYN, BRIGADIER BAIRAHND,** Imperial Charisian Marines—CO, 5th Brigade, Imperial Charisian Marines. Sir Gwylym Manthyr's senior Marine officer, HFAF.

**TYRN, ARCHBISHOP LYAM**—Archbishop of Emerald, OAR.

**TYRNYR, ADMIRAL ZHORJ,** Royal Dohlaran Navy—shoreside officer in charge of developing and producing artillery for the Royal Dohlaran Navy's galleons, MT&T.

**TYRNYR, CAPTAIN TYMYTHY,** Imperial Charisian Navy—CO, HMS *Valiant*, 56, LAMA.

**TYRNYR, COLONEL SAIDRYK,** Imperial Charisian

Maikel's personal secretary and most trusted aide, BSRA; member Charisian inner circle, HFAF.

VAHLAIN, NAIKLOS—Sir Gwylym Manthyr's valet, AMF; one of the Charisian POWs surrendered to Inquisition by the Kingdom of Dohlar, HFAF.

VAHLVERDAY, COLONEL HELFRYD—CO, 3rd Raisor Volunteers, Shilohian Temple Loyalist militia, Fort Tairys garrison, LAMA.

VAHNHAIN, FATHER NAIKLOS—a Schuelerite underpriest and intendant, Fort Tairys garrison, LAMA.

VAHNWYK, MAHRTYN—the Earl of Thirsk's personal secretary and senior clerk, HFAF.

VAHNWYK, MAJOR ZHERYLD, Army of God—XO, 73rd Cavalry Regiment, Army of the Sylmahn, LAMA.

VAHRNAY, CAPTAIN HORAYSHYO, Imperial Charisian Navy—CO, HMS *Vengeance*, 68, HFQ.

VAHRTANYSH, COLONEL KATHYL, Imperial Charisian Army—CO, 9th Mounted Regiment, 5th Mounted Brigade, Imperial Charisian Army, LAMA.

VAHSPHAR, BISHOP EXECUTOR DYNZAIL—Bishop Executor of Delferahk; an Andropovite, HFAF.

VANDAIK, FATHER GAISBYRT—upper-priest of the Order of Schueler; an inquisitor working directly for Bishop Mytchail Zhessop in Talkyra, HFAF.

VELAHSKO, PRINCE GRYGORY II—Prince of Jhurlahnk and son-in-law of Leeahm Thyrstyn, the Earl of Usher, his neighbor to the north. Grygory and Thyrstyn get along well and generally closely coordinate their diplomatic and military policies, HFQ.

VELAHSKO, PRINCESS CONSORT BETHNY—Princess Consort of Jhurlahnk, the wife of Prince Grygory II, and the daughter of Leeahm Thyrstyn, Earl of Usher, HFQ.

VELDAMAHN, BYRTRYM ("BYRT"), Imperial Charisian Navy—High Admiral Rock Point's personal coxswain, HFAF.

VELDAMAHN, COLONEL MAHKSWAIL, Imperial Charisian Army—CO, 19th Mounted Regiment, 10th Mounted Brigade, 1st Corps, Army of New Northland, HFQ.

VERRYN, CAPTAIN DYGRY—senior Temple Loyalist officer, Fairkyn, New Northland Province, Republic of Siddarmark, MT&T.

VICAR ALLAYN—see Allayn Maigwair.

VICAR HAUWERD—see Hauwerd Wylsynn.

VICAR NICODAIM—see Nicodaim Ghordyn.

VICAR SAMYL—see Samyl Wylsynn.

VICAR STAUNTYN—see Stauntyn Waimyan.

VICAR ZAHMSYN—see Zahmsyn Trynair.

VICAR ZAKRYAH—see Zakryah Hahlcahm.

VICAR ZHASPAHR—see Zhaspahr Clyntahn.

VOHLYNDYR, SERGEANT ROLLYNS, Imperial Charisian Army—platoon sergeant, 2nd Platoon, Company B, 1st Battalion, 9th Mounted Regiment, 5th Mounted Brigade, Imperial Charisian Army, LAMA.

VRAIDAHN, MISTRESS ALYS—Archbishop Maikel Staynair's housekeeper, HFAF.

VYKAIN, LIEUTENANT MAHRYAHNO, Imperial Charisian Navy—XO, HMS *Ahrmahk*, 58, HFAF.

VYNAIR, BISHOP ADULFO, Army of God—CO, Holy Martyrs Division, Army of the Sylmahn, MT&T.

VYNAIR, SERGEANT AHDYM, Charisian Royal Guard—one of Cayleb Ahrmahk's armsmen, BSRA.

VYNCHOZY, LIEUTENANT CHARLTYN, Imperial Charisian Navy—CO, gun brig *Grenade*, HFQ.

VYNCYT, ARCHBISHOP ZHEROHM—primate of Chisholm, BSRA.

VYNTYNR, MAJOR FRAYDYK, Imperial Charisian Marines—Colonel Wyntahn Harys' senior Charisian subordinate in support of Captain Halcom Bahrns' operation ("Great Canal Raid"), MT&T.

VYRNYN, LIEUTENANT TRUMYN, Royal Dohlaran Navy—third lieutenant, HMS *Saint Ahndru*, 54, HFQ.

VYRNYR, DOCTOR DAHNEL—member of the Royal College of Charis specializing in the study of pressures, MT&T.

WAHLDAIR, LIEUTENANT LAHMBAIR, Imperial Charisian Navy—third lieutenant, HMS *Dancer*, 56, HFAF.

Queen Sharleyan's uncle and treasurer; ex-CO, Royal Chisholmian Army, does not favor an alliance with Charis but has long tradition of loyalty to Sharleyan, BSRA; betrays Sharleyan to Temple Loyalists, killed by Temple Loyalists during Saint Agtha assassination attempt, BHD.

WAISTYN, ELAHNAH—Dowager Duchess of Halbrook Hollow; widow of Byrtrym Waistyn; mother of Sailys Waistyn, MT&T.

WAISTYN, SAILYS—Duke of Halbrook Hollow; Empress Sharleyan's cousin; only son and heir of Byrtrym Waistyn, MT&T.

WAISTYN, SHARYL—Byrtrym and Elahnah Waistyn's older daughter, MT&T.

WALKYR, ARCHBISHOP MILITANT GUSTYV—a Chihirite archbishop who is Allayn Maigwair's second-in-command in the Army of God, HFQ.

WALKYR, EDMYND—CO, merchant galleon *Wave*, BSRA.

WALKYR, GENERAL LAIRYS, Temple Loyalist Militia—ex-Republic of Siddarmark Army captain; CO, Fort Tairys, LAMA.

WALKYR, GREYGHOR—Edmynd Walkyr's son, BSRA.

WALKYR, LYZBET—Edmynd Walkyr's wife, BSRA.

WALKYR, MIDSHIPMAN FRAID, Imperial Charisian Navy—midshipman in HMS *Shield*, 54, HFAF.

WALKYR, MIDSHIPMAN MAHRLYN, Royal Dohlaran Navy—a midshipman serving aboard the screwgalley HMS *Sword*, HFQ.

WALKYR, MYCHAIL—Edmynd Walkyr's youngest brother; XO, merchant galleon *Wind*, BSRA.

WALKYR, PRIVATE STYV, Army of God—a private assigned to 1st Regiment, Zion Division, MT&T.

WALKYR, SIR STYV—Tahdayo Mahntayl's chief advisor, BSRA.

WALKYR, ZHORJ—Edmynd's younger brother; XO, galleon *Wave*, BSRA.

WALLYCE, LORD FRAHNKLYN—chancellor of the Siddarmark Republic, BSRA.

WATYRS, COMMANDER HAINZ, Imperial Charisian

Army—one of Colonel Aiphraim Tahlyvyr's junior platoon commanders, HFAF.

**WYLLYMS, MAJOR AHRTHYR**, Army of God—XO, 16th Cavalry Regiment, Army of the Sylmahn, LAMA.

**WYLLYMS, MARHYS**—the Duke of Tirian's majordomo and an agent of Prince Nahrmahn of Emerald, OAR.

**WYLLYS, COLONEL STAHN**, Republic of Siddarmark Army—CO, 37th Infantry Regiment, Republic of Siddarmark Army, a part of General Trumyn Stohnar's Sylmahn Gap command, MT&T; CO, 1st Rifle Division, Republic of Siddarmark Army, LAMA.

**WYLLYS, DOCTOR ZHANSYN**—member of the Royal College of Charis with an interest in chemistry and distillation, MT&T.

**WYLLYS, GENERAL STAHN**, Republic of Siddarmark Army—CO, 37th Regiment, Sylmahn Gap, MT&T; promoted general, CO 1st Rifle Division, LAMA.

**WYLLYS, STYVYN**—Doctor Zhansyn Wyllys' estranged father, MT&T.

**WYLSYNN, ARCHBAHLD**—younger son of Vicar Samyl and Lysbet Wylsynn; Father Paityr Wylsynn's half-brother, HFAF.

**WYLSYNN, FATHER PAITYR**—a priest of the Order of Schuelcr, the Church of God Awaiting's intendant for Charis, OAR; becomes Maikel Staynair's intendant and head of Imperial Patent Office, BSRA; member Charisian inner circle, HFAF.

**WYLSYNN, LYSBET**—Samyl Wylsynn's second wife; mother of Tohmys, Zhanayt, and Archbahld Wylsynn, HFAF.

**WYLSYNN, SERGEANT THOMYS**—Temple Loyalist rebel, garrison of Fort Darymahn, South March Lands, Republic of Siddarmark, MT&T.

**WYLSYNN, TANNIERE**—Samyl Wylsynn's deceased wife; mother of Erais and Paityr Wylsynn, HFAF.

**WYLSYNN, TOHMYS**—older son of Samyl and Lysbet Wylsynn; Father Paityr Wylsynn's half-brother, HFAF.

**WYLSYNN, VICAR HAUWERD**—Paityr Wylsynn's uncle; a

member of Samyl Wylsynn's circle of Reformists; ex-Temple Guardsman; a priest of the Order of Langhorne, HFAF.

**WYLSYNN, VICAR SAMYL**—Father Paityr Wylsynn's father; the leader of the Reformists within the Council of Vicars and a priest of the Order of Schueler, HFAF.

**WYLSYNN, ZHANAYT**—daughter of Samyl and Lysbet Wylsynn; Father Paityr Wylsynn's half-sister, HFAF.

**WYNCHYSTAIR, FATHER ALLAYN**—a Schuelerite upperpriest; one of Wyllym Rayno's senior assistants and the equivalent of a divisional commander among his agents inquisitor, HFQ.

**WYNDAYL, MAJOR BRAINAHK**, Imperial Charisian Marines—CO, 1st Battalion, 14th Marine Regiment, HFAF.

**WYNKASTAIR, MASTER PAYTER**, Imperial Charisian Navy—gunner, HMS *Destiny*, 54, HFAF.

**WYNSTYN, LIEUTENANT KYNYTH**, Royal Corisandian Navy—first lieutenant, galley *Corisande*, OAR.

**WYNSTYN, MAJOR ZAVYR**, Imperial Charisian Army—XO, 7th Regiment, 4th Infantry Brigade, Imperial Charisian Army, LAMA.

**WYNSTYN, SIR DAIVYN, BARON OF TRYFELD**—the senior Usherite field commander of the combined Jhurlahnkian and Usherite army, HFQ.

**WYRKMYN, COLONEL MALIKAI**, Imperial Charisian Army—CO, 4th Regiment, 2nd Brigade, 1st Division, Imperial Charisian Army, MT&T.

**WYRSHYM, BISHOP MILITANT BAHRNABAI**, Army of God—a Chihirite of the Order of the Sword and ex-Temple Guard officer; CO, Army of the Sylmahn, MT&T.

**WYSTAHN, AHNAINAH**—Edvarhd Wystahn's wife, BSRA.

**WYSTAHN, SERGEANT EDVARHD**, Royal Charisian Marines—a scout sniper assigned to 1/3rd Marines, BSRA.

**WYTYKAIR, CAPTAIN BYNZHAMYN**, Imperial Charisian Army—General Ahlyn Symkyn's aide, MT&T.

Loyalist, Archbishop of Tarikah Province, Republic of Siddarmark, AMF.

ZAHMSYN, ARCHBISHOP HALMYN—Archbishop of Gorath; senior prelate of the Kingdom of Dohlar until replaced by Trumahn Rowzvel, OAR.

ZAHMSYN, COLONEL MAIKEL—ex-Republic of Siddarmark Army captain; CO, 15th Regiment, Temple Loyalists, Fort Tairys, LAMA.

ZAIVYAIR, AIBRAM—Duke of Thorast, effective Navy Minister and senior officer, Royal Dohlaran Navy, brother-in-law of Admiral-General Duke Malikai (Faidel Ahlverez), BSRA.

ZAVYR, FATHER SEDRYK—Schuelerite upper-priest; Bishop Militant Cahnyr Kaitswyrth's special intendant, MT&T.

ZEBEDIAH, GRAND DUKE OF—see Tohmas Symmyns and Hauwyl Chermyn.

ZHADAHNG, SERGEANT WYNN, Temple Guard—Captain Walysh Zhu's senior noncom transporting Charisian POWs to Zion, HFAF.

ZHADWAIL, CAPTAIN ADYM, Army of God—CO, 1st Company, 16th Cavalry Regiment, Army of the Sylmahn, LAMA.

ZHADWAIL, MAJOR BRYWSTYR, Imperial Charisian Army—CO, 3rd Battalion, 3rd Regiment, Imperial Charisian Army, MT&T.

ZHADWAIL, MAJOR WYLLYM, Imperial Charisian Marines—CO, 1st Provisional Battalion, 1st Independent Marine Brigade; Earl Hanth's senior Marine battalion commander at Thesmar, MT&T.

ZHADWAIL, PRIVATE BRYGHAM, Royal Dohlaran Army—3rd Company, Wykmyn's Regiment (light cavalry), Dohlaran component, Army of Shiloh, LAMA.

ZHADWAIL, TRAIVAHR—a member of Prince Daivyn Daykyn's Royal Guard in exile, AMF; sergeant, Royal Corisandian Guard, senior noncom on Irys Aplyn- Ahrmahk's personal detail, HFAF.

ZHAHNSYN, COLONEL HAUWERD, Republic of Siddarmark Army—the senior Siddarmarkian officer sent to Glacierheart with Brigadier Taisyn, KIA Battle of the Daivyn River, MT&T.

ZHAIKYBS, ARCHBISHOP LAWRYNC—Langhornite; Archbishop of Sardahn, LAMA.

ZHAIMSYN, COLONEL MAIKEL, Republic of Siddarmark Army—CO, 15th Regiment, a composite "regular regiment" that went over to the Temple Loyalists, Fort Tairys garrison, LAMA.

ZHAKSYN, AHLDAHS, Royal Dohlaran Navy—gunner, screw-galley HMS *Lance*, HFQ.

ZHAKSYN, CAPTAIN TYDWAIL, Imperial Charisian Navy—CO, HMS *Broadsword*, 60, HFQ.

ZHAKSYN, LIEUTENANT AHLBER, Imperial Charisian Navy—second lieutenant, broadside ironclad HMS *Thunderer*, 30, HFQ.

ZHAKSYN, LIEUTENANT AHRNAHLD, Imperial Charisian Navy—senior engineer, ironclad HMS *Tellesberg*, 22, MT&T.

ZHAKSYN, LIEUTENANT TOHMYS, Imperial Charisian Marines—General Chermyn's aide, BSRA.

ZHAKSYN, PHYLYP—Lord Tairwald; Lord of Clan Tairwald, Raven's Land, MT&T.

ZHAKSYN, SERGEANT GROVAIR, Republic of Siddarmark Army—senior noncom, 2nd Company, 37th Infantry Regiment, Republic of Siddarmark Army, LAMA.

ZHAKSYN, SERGEANT RAHZHYR, Royal Dohlaran Army—company sergeant, 3rd Company, Wykmyn's Regiment (light cavalry), Dohlaran component, Army of Shiloh, LAMA.

ZHAMES, COLONEL EVYRTYN, Army of God—a Langhornite lay brother and a member of Bishop Militant Cahnyr Kaitswyrth's headquarters staff, HFQ.

ZHANDOR, FATHER NEYTHAN—a Langhornite upperpriest and lawgiver accredited for both secular and ecclesiastic law; assigned to Empress Sharleyan's staff, HFAF.

ZHANSAN, FRAHNK—the Duke of Tirian's senior guardsman, OAR.

ZHANSTYN, BRIGADIER ZHOEL, Imperial Charisian

Marines—CO, 3rd Brigade, Imperial Charisian Marines; Brigadier Clareyk's senior battalion CO during Corisande Campaign, BHD.

ZHANSYN, FATHER BYRTRYM—"Banister"; a Schuelerite priest and agent inquisitor, one of Markys Gohdard's more trusted investigators and a member of Helm Cleaver, HFQ.

ZHANSYN, SISTER CLAUDYA—Byrtrym Zhansyn's deceased paternal aunt and a Sister of Saint Kohdy, HFQ.

ZHANSYN, SISTER TYLDAH—Byrtrym Zhansyn's older sister and a Sister of Saint Kohdy, HFQ.

ZHARDEAU, LADY ERAIS—Samyl and Tanniere Wylsynn's daughter; Father Paityr Wylsynn's younger full sister; wife of Sir Fraihman Zhardeau, HFAF.

ZHARDEAU, SAMYL—son of Sir Fraihman and Lady Erais Zhardeau; grandson of Vicar Samyl Wylsynn; nephew of Father Paityr Wylsynn, HFAF.

ZHARDEAU, SIR FRAIHMAN—minor Tansharan aristocrat; husband of Lady Erais Zhardeau; son-in-law of Vicar Samyl Wylsynn, HFAF.

ZHASTROW, FATHER AHBEL—Father Zhon Byrkyt's successor as abbot of the Monastery of Saint Zherneau, HFAF.

ZHAZTRO, ADMIRAL SIR HAINZ, Imperial Charisian Navy—as commodore, Prince Nahrmahn Baytz' naval commander following the Battle of Darcos Sound; as admiral, CO, 2nd Ironclad Squadron, Imperial Charisian Navy, HFQ.

ZHAZTRO, CAPTAIN AHNTAHN, Royal Emeraldian Navy—Sir Hainz Zhaztro's deceased younger brother, KIA at the Battle of Darcos Sound, HFQ.

ZHEFFYR, MAJOR WYLL, Royal Charisian Marines—CO, Marine detachment, HMS *Destiny*, 54, BSRA.

ZHEFRY, AHDEM—Earl of Cross Creek, MT&T.

ZHEPPSYN, CAPTAIN NYKLAS, Royal Emeraldian Navy—CO, galley *Triton*, OAR.

ZHERMAIN, CAPTAIN MAHRTYN, Royal Dohlaran Navy—CO, HMS *Prince of Dohlar*, 38, HFAF.

**ZHWAIGAIR, THOMYS**—Lieutenant Dynnys Zhwaigair's uncle; an innovative Dohlaran ironmaster in the Duchy of Bess, MT&T.

**ZHYNG, CAPTAIN OF SPEARS HAIGWAI,** Imperial Harchongese Army—XO, Captain of Foot Ruhngzhi Lywahn's battery, Kyznetzov Narrows, HFQ.

**ZHYNKYNS, BISHOP MAIKEL**—a Schuelerite bishop and inquisitor commanding Camp Dynnys, the Church concentration camp on Lake Isyk, HFQ.

**ZHYNKYNS, COLONEL SIR RHUAN,** Imperial Desnairian Army—CO, Crown Prince Mahrys' Own Regiment (imperial guard medium cavalry), cavalry wing, Army of Shiloh, LAMA.

**ZHYNKYNS, LIEUTENANT AIMOHS,** Royal Dohlaran Army—CO, 4th Platoon, 5th Company, Sheldyn's Regiment (replaces Lieutenant Erayk Sandkaran), HFQ.

**ZHYWNOH, COLONEL LEWSHIAN,** Imperial Charisian Army—CO, 12th Mounted Regiment, 6th Mounted Brigade, Imperial Charisian Army, LAMA.

**ZOAY, FATHER ISYDOHR**—a Schuelerite under-priest and intendant, Sulyvyn Division, Army of Glacierheart, LAMA.

**ZOHANNSYN, PRIVATE PAITRYK**—Temple Loyalist rebel, garrison of Fort Darymahn, South March Lands, Republic of Siddarmark, MT&T.

**ZYLWYKY, MAJOR SYMYN,** Imperial Charisian Army—CO, 1st Company, 19th Mounted Regiment, 10th Mounted Brigade, 1st Corps, Army of New Northland, HFQ.

**ZYMMYR, CORPORAL FRAIDARECK,** Royal Dohlaran Army—noncommissioned officer in command, 2nd Section, 3rd Platoon, 1st Company, Ahzbyrn's Regiment (cavalry), Dohlaran component, Army of Shiloh, LAMA.

**ZYWORYA, PLATOON SERGEANT NYCODEM,** Army of God—platoon sergeant, 2nd Platoon, 1st Company, 1st Regiment, Zion Division, Army of Glacierheart, LAMA.

# Glossary

*Abbey of Saint Evehlain*—the sister abbey of the Monastery of Saint Zherneau.

*Abbey of the Snows*—an abbey of the Sisters of Chihiro of the Quill located in the Mountains of Light above Langhorne's Tears. Although it is a working abbey of Chihiro, all of the nuns of the abbey are also Sisters of Saint Kohdy and the abbey serves as protection and cover for Saint Kohdy's tomb. The Abbey of the Snows is built on the foundation of a pre-Armageddon Reef structure, which is reputed to have been a resort house for Eric Langhorne before his death.

*Angle-glass*—Charisian term for a periscope.

*Angora lizard*—a Safeholdian "lizard" with a particularly luxuriant, cashmere-like coat. They are raised and sheared as sheep and form a significant part of the fine-textiles industry.

*Anshinritsumei*—"the little fire" from the *Holy Writ*; the lesser touch of God's spirit and the maximum enlightenment of which mortals are capable.

*Ape lizard*—ape lizards are much larger and more powerful versions of monkey lizards. Unlike monkey lizards, they are mostly ground dwellers, although they are capable of climbing trees suitable to bear their weight. The great mountain ape lizard weighs as much as nine hundred or a thousand pounds, whereas the plains ape lizard weighs no more than a hundred to a hundred and fifty pounds. Ape lizards live in families of up to twenty or thirty adults, and whereas monkey lizards will typically flee when confronted with a threat, ape lizards are much more likely to respond by attacking the threat. It is not unheard of for two or three ape lizard "families" to combine forces against particularly dangerous predators, and even a great dragon will generally avoid such a threat.

**Archangels, The**—central figures of the Church of God Awaiting. The Archangels were senior members of the command crew of Operation Ark who assumed the status of divine messengers, guides, and guardians in order to control and shape the future of human civilization on Safehold.

**ASP**—Artillery Support Party, the term used to describe teams of ICA officers and noncoms specially trained to call for and coordinate artillery support. ASPs may be attached at any level, from the division down to the company or even platoon, and are equipped with heliographs, signal flags, runners, and/or messenger wyverns.

**Bahnyta**—the name *Seijin* Kohdy assigned to his *hikousen*.

**Blink lizard**—a small, bioluminescent winged lizard. Although it's about three times the size of a firefly, it fills much the same niche on Safehold.

**Blue leaf**—a woody, densely growing native Safeholdian tree or shrub very similar to mountain laurel. It bears white or yellow flowers in season and takes its name from the waxy blue cast of its leaves.

**Borer**—a form of Safeholdian shellfish which attaches itself to the hulls of ships or the timbers of wharves by boring into them. There are several types of borer: the most destructive of which continually eat their way deeper into any wooden structure, whereas some less destructive varieties eat only enough of the structure to anchor themselves and actually form a protective outer layer which gradually builds up a coral-like surface. Borers and rot are the two most serious threats (aside, of course, from fire) to wooden hulls.

**Briar berries**—any of several varieties of native Safeholdian berries which grow on thorny bushes.

*Cat-lizard*—furry lizard about the size of a terrestrial cat. They are kept as pets and are very affectionate.

*Catamount*—a smaller version of the Safeholdian slash lizard. The catamount is very fast and smarter than its larger cousin, which means it tends to avoid humans. It is, however, a lethal and dangerous hunter in its own right.

*Chamberfruit*—a native Safeholdian plant similar to a terrestrial calabash gourd. The chamberfruit is grown both as a food source and as a naturally produced container. There are several varieties of chamberfruit, and one common use for it is in the construction of foamstone pipes for smoking.

*Cherrybean tea*—a "tea" made from the beans (seeds) of the cherrybean tree, especially favored in Emerald and Tarot and a highly esteemed luxury in North Harchong and the Temple Lands, although its expense limits it to a very wealthy group of consumers.

*Cherrybean tree*—the Safeholdian name for coffee trees. There is only one variety on Safehold, a version of robusta genetically engineered to survive in a wider range of climates. The cherrybean tree is still limited to a fairly narrow belt of equatorial and near equatorial Safehold because of the planet's lower average temperatures.

*Chewleaf*—a mildly narcotic leaf from a native Safeholdian plant. It is used much as terrestrial chewing tobacco over much of the planet's surface.

*Choke tree*—a low-growing species of tree native to Safehold. It comes in many varieties and is found in most of the planet's climate zones. It is dense-growing, tough, and difficult to eradicate, but it requires quite a lot of sunlight to flourish, which means it is seldom found in mature old-growth forests.

*Church of Charis*—the schismatic church which split from the Church of God Awaiting following the Group of Four's effort to destroy the Kingdom of Charis.

*Church of God Awaiting*—the church and religion created by the command staff of Operation Ark to control the colonists and their descendants and prevent the reemergence of advanced technology.

*Cliff bear*—a Safeholdian mammal which somewhat resembles a terrestrial grizzly bear crossed with a raccoon. It has the facial "mask" markings of a raccoon and round, marsupial ears. Unlike terrestrial bears, however, cliff bears are almost exclusively carnivorous.

*Cliff lizard*—a six-limbed, oviparous mammal native to Safehold. Male cliff lizards average between one hundred and fifty and two hundred and fifty pounds in weight and fill much the same niche as bighorn mountain sheep.

*Commentaries, The*—the authorized interpretations and doctrinal expansions upon the *Holy Writ*. They represent the officially approved and Church-sanctioned interpretation of the original Scripture.

*Cotton silk*—a plant native to Safehold which shares many of the properties of silk and cotton. It is very lightweight and strong, but the raw fiber comes from a plant pod which is even more filled with seeds than Old Earth cotton. Because of the amount of hand labor required to harvest and process the pods and to remove the seeds from it, cotton silk is very expensive.

*Council of Vicars*—the Church of God Awaiting's equivalent of the College of Cardinals.

*Course lizard*—one of several species of very fast, carnivorous lizards bred and trained to run down prey. Course lizard breeds range in size from the Tiegelkamp course lizard, somewhat smaller than a terrestrial greyhound, to the Gray Wall course lizard, with a body length of over five feet and a maximumn weight of close to two hundred and fifty pounds.

*Dagger thorn*—a native Charisian shrub, growing to a height of perhaps three feet at maturity, which possesses knife-edged thorns from three to seven inches long, depending upon the variety.

*Dandelion*—the Safeholdian dandelion grows to approximately twice the size of the Terrestrial plant for which it is named but is otherwise extremely similar in appearance and its seeds disperse in very much the same fashion.

*De Castro marble*—a densely swirled, rosy marble from the de Castro Mountains of North Harchong which is prized by sculptors, especially for religious and Church art.

*Deep-mouth wyvern*—the Safeholdian equivalent of a pelican.

*Doomwhale*—the most dangerous predator of Safehold, although, fortunately, it seldom bothers with anything as small as humans. Doomwhales have been known to run to as much as one hundred feet in length, and they are pure carnivores. Each doomwhale requires a huge range, and encounters with them are rare, for which human beings are just as glad, thank you. Doomwhales will eat *anything* ... including the largest krakens. They have been known, on *extremely* rare occasions, to attack merchant ships and war galleys.

*Double-glass* or *Double-spyglass*—Charisian term for binoculars.

*Dragon*—the largest native Safeholdian land life-form. Dragons come in two varieties: the common dragon (generally subdivided into jungle dragons and hill dragons) and the carnivorous great dragon. *See* Great dragon.

*Eye-cheese*—Safeholdian name for Swiss cheese.

*Fallen, The*—the Archangels, angels, and mortals who followed Shan-wei in her rebellion against God and the rightful authority of the Archangel Langhorne. The term applies to *all* of Shan-wei's adherents, but is most often used in reference to the angels and Archangels who followed her willingly rather than the mortals who were duped into obeying her.

*False silver*—Safeholdian name for antimony.

*Fire striker*—Charisian term for a cigarette lighter.

*Fire vine*—a large, hardy, fast-growing Safeholdian

vine. Its runners can exceed two inches in diameter, and the plant is extremely rich in natural oils. It is considered a major hazard to human habitations, especially in areas which experience arid, dry summers, because of its very high natural flammability and because its oil is poisonous to humans and terrestrial species of animals. The crushed vine and its seed pods, however, are an important source of lubricating oils, and it is commercially cultivated in some areas for that reason.

*Fire willow*—a Safeholdian evergeen tree native to East Haven's temperate and subarctic regions. Fire willow seldom grows much above five meters in height and has long, streamer-like leaves. It prefers relatively damp growing conditions and produces dense clusters of berries ranging in color from a bright orange to scarlet.

*Fire wing*—Safeholdian term for a cavalry maneuver very similar to the Terran caracole, in which mounted troops deliver pistol fire against infantry at close quarters. It is also designed to be used against enemy cavalry under favorable conditions.

*Fist of Kau-Yung*—the unofficial name assigned to Helm Cleaver and its operatives by agents inquisitor attempting to combat the organization.

*Five-day*—a Safeholdian "week," consisting of only five days, Monday through Friday.

*Fleming moss*—an absorbent moss native to Safehold which was genetically engineered by Shan-wei's terraforming crews to possess natural antibiotic properties. It is a staple of Safeholdian medical practice.

*Foamstone*—the Safeholdian equivalent of meerschaum. This light-colored, soft stone takes its name from the same source as meerschaum, since it is occasionally found floating in the Gulf of Tanshar. Its primary use is in the construction of incense burners for the Church of God Awaiting and in the manufacture of tobacco pipes and cigar holders.

*Forktail*—one of several species of native Safeholdian

fish which fill an ecological niche similar to that of the Old Earth herring.

*Fox-lizard*—a warm-blooded, six-limbed Safeholdian omnivore, covered with fur, which ranges from a dull russet color to a very dark gray. Most species of fox-lizard are capable of climbing trees. They range in length from forty to forty-eight inches, have bushy tails approximately twenty-five inches long, and weigh between twenty and thirty pounds.

*Gbaba*—a star-traveling, xenophobic species whose re-action to encounters with any possibly competing species is to exterminate it. The Gbaba completely destroyed the Terran Federation and, so far as is known, all human beings in the galaxy aside from the population of Safehold.

*Glynfych Distillery*—a Chisholmian distillery famous throughout Safehold for the quality of its whiskeys.

*Golden berry*—a tree growing to about ten feet in height which thrives in most Safeholdian climates. A tea brewed from its leaves is a sovereign specific for motion sickness and nausea.

*Grasshopper*—a Safeholdian insect analogue which grows to a length of as much as nine inches and is carnivorous. Fortunately, they do not occur in the same numbers as terrestrial grasshoppers.

*Gray-horned wyvern*—a nocturnal flying predator of Safehold. It is roughly analogous to a terrestrial owl.

*Gray mists*—the Safeholdian term for Alzheimer's disease.

*Great dragon*—the largest and most dangerous land carnivore of Safehold. The great dragon isn't actually related to hill dragons or jungle dragons at all, despite some superficial physical resemblances. In fact, it's more of a scaled-up slash lizard, with elongated jaws and sharp, serrated teeth. It has six limbs and, unlike the slash lizard, is covered in thick, well-insulated hide rather than fur.

*Group of Four*—the four vicars who dominate and effectively control the Council of Vicars of the Church of God Awaiting.

*Hairatha Dragons*—the Hairatha professional baseball team. The traditional rivals of the Tellesberg Krakens for the Kingdom Championship.

*Hake*—a Safeholdian fish. Like most "fish" native to Safehold, it has a very long, sinuous body but the head does resemble a terrestrial hake or cod, with a hooked jaw.

*Hand of Kau-Yung*—the name applied by agents of the Inquisition to the anti-Group of Four organization established in Zion by Aivah Pahrsahn/Ahnzhelyk Phonda.

*Helm Cleaver*—the name of *Seijin* Kohdy's "magic sword," and also the name assigned by Nynian Rychtair to the covert action organization created in parallel with the Sisters of Saint Kohdy.

*High-angle gun*—a relatively short, stubby artillery piece with a carriage specially designed to allow higher angles of fire in order to lob gunpowder-filled shells in high, arcing trajectories. The name is generally shortened to "angle-gun" by the gun crews themselves.

*High Hallows*—a very tough, winter-hardy breed of horses.

*Highland lilly*—a native Safeholdian perenial flowering plant. It grows to a height of 3 to 4 feet and bears a pure white, seven-lobed flower 8 to 9 inches across. Its flower is the symbol of martyrdom for the Church of God Awaiting.

*Highland lily*—a tulip-like native Safeholdian flower, found primarily in the foothills of the Langhorne Mountains and the Mountains of Light. Its snow-white petals are tipped in dark crimson, and it is considered sacred to martyrs and those who have fought valiantly for Mother Church.

*Hikousen*—the term used to describe the air cars provided to the *seijins* who fought for the Church in the War Against the Fallen.

*Hill dragon*—a roughly elephant-sized draft animal commonly used on Safehold. Despite their size, hill dragons are capable of rapid, sustained movement. They are herbivores.

*Holy Writ*—the seminal holy book of the Church of God Awaiting.

*Hornet*—a stinging, carniverous Safeholdian insect analogue. It is over two inches long and nests in ground burrows. Its venom is highly toxic to Safeholdian life-forms, but most terrestrial life-forms are not seriously affected by it (about ten percent of all humans have a potentially lethal allergic shock reaction to it, however). Hornets are highly aggressive and territorial and instinctively attack their victims' eyes first.

*Ice wyvern*—a flightless aquatic wyvern rather similar to a terrestrial penguin. Species of ice wyvern are native to both the northern and southern polar regions of Safehold.

*Inner circle*—Charisian allies of Merlin Athrawes who know the truth about the Church of God Awaiting and the Terran Federation.

*Insights, The*—the recorded pronouncements and observations of the Church of God Awaiting's Grand Vicars and canonized saints. They represent deeply significant spiritual and inspirational teachings, but as the work of fallible mortals do not have the same standing as the *Holy Writ* itself.

*Intendant*—the cleric assigned to a bishopric or archbishopric as the direct representative of the Office of Inquisition. The intendant is specifically charged with ensuring that the Proscriptions of Jwo-jeng are not violated.

*Journal of Saint Zherneau*—the journal left by Jeremy Knowles telling the truth about the destruction of the Alexandria Enclave and about Pei Shan-wei.

*Jungle dragon*—a somewhat generic term applied to lowland dragons larger than hill dragons. The gray jungle dragon is the largest herbivore on Safehold.

*Kau-yungs*—the name assigned by men of the Army of God to antipersonnel mines, and especially to claymore-style directional mines, in commemoration of the "pocket nuke" Commander Pei Kau-yung used against Eric Langhorne's adherents following the destruction of the Alexandria Enclave. Later applied to all land mines.

*Keitai*—the term used to describe the personal coms provided to the *seijins* who fought for the Church in the War Against the Fallen.

*Kercheef*—a traditional headdress worn in the Kingdom of Tarot which consists of a specially designed bandana tied across the hair.

*Knights of the Temple Lands*—the corporate title of the prelates who govern the Temple Lands. Technically, the Knights of the Temple Lands are *secular* rulers who simply happen to also hold high Church office. Under the letter of the Church's law, what they may do as the Knights of the Temple Lands is completely separate from any official action of the Church. This legal fiction has been of considerable value to the Church on more than one occasion.

*Kraken* (1)—generic term for an entire family of maritime predators. Krakens are rather like sharks crossed with octopi. They have powerful, fish-like bodies; strong jaws with inward-inclined, fang-like teeth; and a cluster of tentacles just behind the head which can be used to hold prey while they devour it. The smallest, coastal krakens can be as short as three or four feet; deepwater krakens up to fifty feet in length have been reliably reported, and there are legends of those still larger.

*Kraken* (2)—one of three pre-Merlin heavy-caliber naval artillery pieces. The great kraken weighed approximately 3.4 tons and fired a forty-two-pound round shot. The royal kraken weighed four tons. It also fired a forty-two-pound shot but was specially designed as a long-range weapon with less windage and higher bore pressures. The standard kraken was a 2.75-ton, medium-range weapon which fired a thirty-five-pound round shot approximately 6.2 inches in diameter.

*Kraken oil*—originally, oil extracted from kraken and used as fuel, primarily for lamps, in coastal and seafaring realms. Most lamp oil currently comes from sea dragons (*see* below), rather than actually being extracted from kraken, and, in fact, the sea dragon oil actually burns much more brightly and with much less odor. Nonetheless, oils are still ranked in terms of "kraken oil" quality steps.

*Kyousei hi*—"great fire" or "magnificent fire," from the *Holy Writ*. The term used to describe the brilliant nimbus of light the Operation Ark command crew generated around their air cars and skimmers to "prove" their divinity to the original Safeholdians.

*Langhorne's Tears*—a quartet of alpine lakes in the Mountains of Light. Langhorne's Tears were reportedly known as Langhorne's Joy before the destruction of Armageddon Reef.

*Langhorne's Watch*—the 31-minute period which falls immediately after midnight. It was inserted by the original "Archangels" to compensate for the extra length of Safehold's 26.5-hour day. It is supposed to be used for contemplation and giving thanks.

*Levelers*—a reformist/revolutionary Mainland movement dedicated to overturning all social and economic differences in society.

*Marsh wyvern*—one of several strains of Safeholdian wyverns found in saltwater and freshwater marsh habitats.

*Mask lizard*—Safeholdian equivalent of a chameleon. Mask lizards are carnivores, about two feet long, which use their camouflage ability to lure small prey into range before they pounce.

*Master Traynyr*—a character out of the Safeholdian entertainment tradition. Master Traynyr is a stock character in Safeholdian puppet theater, by turns a bumbling conspirator whose plans always miscarry and the puppeteer who controls all of the marionette "actors" in the play.

*Messenger wyvern*—any one of several strains of genetically modified Safeholdian wyverns adapted by Pei

Shan-wei's terraforming teams to serve the colonists as homing pigeon equivalents. Some messenger wyverns are adapted for short-range, high-speed delivery of messages, whereas others are adapted for extremely long range (but slower) message deliveries.

*Mirror twins*—Safeholdian term for Siamese twins.

*Moarte subită*—the favored martial art of the Terran Federation Marines, developed on the colony world of Walachia.

*Monastery of Saint Zherneau*—the mother monastery and headquarters of the Brethren of Saint Zherneau, a relatively small and poor order in the Archbishopric of Charis.

*Monkey lizard*—a generic term for several species of arboreal, saurian-looking marsupials. Monkey lizards come in many different shapes and sizes, although none are much larger than an Old Earth chimpanzee and most are considerably smaller. They have two very human-looking hands, although each hand has only three fingers and an opposable thumb, and the "hand feet" of their other forelimbs have a limited grasping ability but no opposable thumb. Monkey lizards tend to be excitable, *very* energetic, and talented mimics of human behaviors.

*Mountain ananas*—a native Safeholdian fruit tree. Its spherical fruit averages about four inches in diameter with the firmness of an apple and a taste rather like a sweet grapefruit. It is very popular on the Safeholdian mainland.

*Mountain spike-thorn*—a particular subspecies of spike-thorn, found primarily in tropical mountains. The most common blossom color is a deep, rich red, but the white mountain spike-thorn is especially prized for its trumpet-shaped blossom, which has a deep, almost cobalt-blue throat, fading to pure white as it approaches the outer edge of the blossom, which is, in turn, fringed in a deep golden yellow.

*Narwhale*—a species of Safeholdian sea life named for the Old Earth species of the same name. Safeholdian narwhales are about forty feet in length and equipped with twin horn-like tusks up to eight feet long. They live in large pods or schools and are not at all shy or retiring. The adults of narwhale pods have been known to fight off packs of kraken.

*Nearoak*—a rough-barked Safeholdian tree similar to an Old Earth oak tree. It is found in tropic and near tropic zones. Although it does resemble an Old Earth oak, it is an evergreen and seeds using "pine cones."

*Nearpalm*—a tropical Safeholdian tree which resembles a terrestrial royal palm except that a mature specimen stands well over sixty feet tall. It produces a tart, plum-like fruit about five inches in diameter.

*Nearpalm fruit*—the plum-like fruit produced by the nearpalm. It is used in cooking and eaten raw, but its greatest commercial value is as the basis for nearpalm wine.

*Nearpoplar*—a native Safeholdian tree, very fast-growing and straight-grained, which is native to the planet's temperate zones. It reaches a height of approximately ninety feet.

*Neartuna*—one of several native Safeholdian fish species, ranging in length from approximately three feet to just over five.

*NEAT*—Neural Education and Training machine. The standard means of education in the Terran Federation.

*Nest doll*—a Harchongian folk art doll, similar to the Russian Matryoshka dolls in which successively smaller dolls are nested inside hollow wooden dolls.

*New model*—a generic term increasingly applied to the innovations in technology (especially war-fighting technology) introduced by Charis and its allies. *See* new model kraken.

*New model kraken*—the standardized artillery piece of the Imperial Charisian Navy. It weighs approximately 2.5 tons and fires a thirty-pound round shot with a diameter of approximately 5.9 inches. Although it weighs slightly less than the old kraken (*see* above) and its round shot is twelve percent lighter, it is actually longer ranged and fires at a higher velocity because of reductions in windage, improvements in gunpowder, and slightly increased barrel length.

*Northern spine tree*—a Safeholdian evergreen tree, native to arctic and subarctic regions. Spine tree branches grow in a sharply pointed, snow-shedding shape but bear the sharp, stiff spines from which the tree takes its name.

*Nynian Rychtair*—the Safeholdian equivalent of Helen of Troy, a woman of legendary beauty, born in Siddarmark, who eventually married the Emperor of Harchong.

*Offal lizard*—a carrion-eating scavenger which fills the niche of an undersized hyena crossed with a jackal. Offal lizards will take small living prey, but they are generally cowardly and are regarded with scorn and contempt by most Safeholdians.

*Oil tree*—a Safeholdian plant species which grows to an average height of approximately thirty feet. The oil tree produces large, hairy pods which contain many small seeds very rich in natural plant oils. Dr. Pei Shan-wei's terraforming teams genetically modified the plant to increase its oil productivity and to make it safely consumable by human beings. It is cultivated primarily as a food product, but it is also an important source of lubricants. In inland realms, it is also a major source of lamp oil.

*Operation Ark*—a last-ditch, desperate effort mounted by the Terran Federation to establish a hidden colony beyond the knowledge and reach of the xenophobic Gbaba. It created the human settlement on Safehold.

*Pasquale's Basket*—a voluntary collection of contributions for the support of the sick, homeless, and indigent. The difference between the amount contributed voluntarily and that required for the Basket's purpose is supposed to be contributed from

Mother Church's coffers as a first charge upon tithes received.

*Pasquale's Grace*—euthanasia. Pasqualate healers are permitted by their vows to end the lives of the terminally ill, but only under tightly defined and stringently limited conditions.

*Persimmon fig*—a native Safeholdian fruit which is extremely tart and relatively thick-skinned.

*Prong lizard*—a roughly elk-sized lizard with a single horn which branches into four sharp points in the last third or so of its length. Prong lizards are herbivores and not particularly ferocious.

*Proscriptions of Jwo-jeng*—the definition of allowable technology under the doctrine of the Church of God Awaiting. Essentially, the Proscriptions limit allowable technology to that which is powered by wind, water, or muscle. The Proscriptions are subject to interpretation by the Order of Schueler, which generally errs on the side of conservatism, but it is not unheard of for corrupt intendants to rule for or against an innovation under the Proscriptions in return for financial compensation.

*Rakurai* (1)—literally, "lightning bolt." The *Holy Writ*'s term for the kinetic weapons used to destroy the Alexandria Enclave.

*Rakurai* (2)—the organization of solo suicide terrorists trained and deployed by Wyllym Rayno and Zhaspahr Clyntahn. Security for the Rakurai is so tight that not even Clyntahn knows the names and identities of individual Rakurai or the targets against which Rayno has dispatched them.

*Reformist*—one associated with the Reformist movement. The majority of Reformists outside the Charisian Empire still regard themselves as Temple Loyalists.

*Reformist movement*—the movement within the Church of God Awaiting to reform the abuses and corruption which have become increasingly evident (and serious) over the last hundred to one hundred and fifty years. Largely underground and unfocused until the emergence of the Church of Charis, the movement is attracting increasing support throughout Safehold.

**Rising**—the term used to describe the rebellion against Lord Protector Greyghor and the Constitution of the Republic of Siddarmark by the Temple Loyalists.

**Round Theatre**—the largest and most famous theater in the city of Tellesberg. Supported by the Crown but independent of it, and renowned not only for the quality of its productions but for its willingness to present works which satirize Charisian society, industry, the aristocracy, and even the Church.

**Saint Evehlain**—the patron saint of the Abbey of Saint Evehlain in Tellesberg; wife of Saint Zherneau.

**Saint Kohdy**—a *seijin* who fought for the Church of God Awaiting in the War Against the Fallen. He was killed shortly before the end of that war and later stripped of his sainthood and expunged from the record of the Church's *seijins*.

**Saint Zherneau**—the patron saint of the Monastery of Saint Zherneau in Tellesberg; husband of Saint Evehlain.

**Salmon**—a Safeholdian fish species named because its reproductive habits are virtually identical to those of a terrestrial salmon. It is, however, almost more like an eel than a fish, being very long in proportion to its body's width.

**Sand maggot**—a loathsome carnivore, looking much like a six-legged slug, which haunts Safeholdian beaches just above the surf line. Sand maggots do not normally take living prey, although they have no objection to devouring the occasional small creature which strays into their reach. Their natural coloration blends well with their sandy habitat, and they normally conceal themselves by digging their bodies into the sand until they are completely covered, or only a small portion of their backs show.

**Scabbark**—a very resinous deciduous tree native to Safehold. Scabbark takes its name from the blisters of sap which ooze from any puncture in its otherwise very smooth, gray-brown bark and solidify into hard, reddish "scabs." Scabbark wood is similar in coloration and grain to Terran Brazilwood, and the tree's sap is used to produce similar red fabric dyes.

**Sea cow**—a walrus-like Safeholdian sea mammal which grows to a body length of approximately ten feet when fully mature.

**Sea dragon**—the Safeholdian equivalent of a terrestrial whale. There are several species of sea dragon, the largest of which grow to a body length of approximately fifty feet. Like the whale, sea dragons are mammalian. They are insulated against deep oceanic temperatures by thick layers of blubber and are krill-eaters. They reproduce much more rapidly than whales, however, and are the principal food source for doomwhales and large, deep-water krakens. Most species of sea dragon produce the equivalent of sperm oil and spermaceti. A large sea dragon will yield as much as four hundred gallons of oil.

**Seijin**—sage, holy man, mystic. Legendary warriors and teachers, generally believed to have been touched by the *anshinritsumei*. Many educated Safeholdians consider *seijins* to be mythological, fictitious characters.

**Shan-wei's candle** (1)—the deliberately challenging name assigned to strike-anywhere matches by Charisians. Later shortened to "Shan-weis."

**Shan-wei's candle** (2)—a Temple Loyalist name given to the illuminating parachute flares developed by Charis.

**Shan-wei's footstools**—also simply "footstools." Charisian name for nondirectional antipersonnel mines which are normally buried or laid on the surface and (usually) detonated by a percussion cap pressure switch. See Kau-yungs.

**Shan-wei's fountains**—also simply "fountains." Charisian name for "bounding mines." When detonated, a launching charge propels the mine to approximately waist height before it detonates, spraying shrapnel balls in a three-hundred-and-sixty-degree pattern. *See* Kau-yungs.

**Shan-wei's sweepers**—also simply "sweepers," Charisian name for a Safeholdian version of a claymore mine. The mine's backplate is approximately eighteen inches by thirty inches and covered with five hundred and seventy-six .50-caliber shrapnel balls which it fires in a cone-shaped blast zone when detonated. *See* Kau-yungs.

**Shan-wei's War**—the *Holy Writ*'s term for the struggle between the supporters of Eric Langhorne and those of Pei Shan-wei over the future of humanity on Safehold. It is presented in terms very similar to those of the war between Lucifer and the angels loyal to God, with Shan-wei in the role of Lucifer. *See also* War Against the Fallen.

**Shellhorn**—venomous Safeholdian insect analogue with a hard, folding carapace. When folded inside its shell, it is virtually indistinguishable from a ripe slabnut.

**Sisters of Saint Kohdy**—an order of nuns created to honor and commemorate Saint Kohdy. The last of the "angels" used kinetic weapons to obliterate their abbey and the tomb of Saint Kohdy shortly after the last of the original Adams and Eves died.

**Sky comb**—a tall, slender native Safeholdian tree. It is deciduous, grows to a height of approximately eighty-five to ninety feet, and has very small, dense branches covered with holly tree-like leaves. Its branches seldom exceed eight feet in length.

**Slabnut**—a flat-sided, thick-hulled nut. Slabnut trees are deciduous, with large, four-lobed leaves, and grow to about thirty feet. Black slabnuts are genetically engineered to be edible by humans; red slabnuts are mildly poisonous. The black slabnut is very high in protein.

**Slash lizard**—a six-limbed, saurian-looking, furry oviparous mammal. One of the three top land predators of Safehold. Its mouth contains twin rows of fangs capable of punching through chain mail and its feet have four long toes, each tipped with claws up to five or six inches long.

*Sleep root*—a Safeholdian tree from whose roots an entire family of opiates and painkillers are produced. The term "sleep root" is often used generically for any of those pharmaceutical products.

*Slime toad*—an amphibious Safeholdian carrion eater with a body length of approximately seven inches. It takes its name from the thick mucus which covers its skin. Its bite is poisonous but seldom results in death.

*Snapdragon*—the Safeholdian snapdragon isn't actually related to any of the other dragon species of the planet. It is actually a Safeholdian analogue to the terrestrial giant sea turtle. Although it is warm-blooded, its body form is very similar to that of a terrestrial leatherback sea turtle, but it is half again the leatherback's size, with fully mature male snapdragons running to body lengths of over nine feet. No living Safeholdian knows why the snapdragon was given its name.

*SNARC*—Self-Navigating Autonomous Reconnaissance and Communications platform.

*Spider-crab*—a native species of sea life, considerably larger than any terrestrial crab. The spider-crab is not a crustacean, but more of a segmented, tough-hided, many-legged seagoing slug. Despite that, its legs are considered a great delicacy and are actually very tasty.

*Spider-rat*—a native species of vermin which fills roughly the ecological niche of a terrestrial rat. Like all Safeholdian mammals, it is six-limbed, but it looks like a cross between a hairy gila monster and an insect, with long, multi-jointed legs which actually arch higher than its spine. It is nasty-tempered but basically cowardly. Fully adult male specimens of the larger varieties run to about two feet in body length, with another two feet of tail, for a total length of four feet, but the more common varieties average only between two or three feet of combined body and tail length.

*Spike-thorn*—a flowering shrub, various subspecies of which are found in most Safeholdian climate zones. Its blossoms come in many colors and hues, and the tropical versions tend to be taller-growing and to bear more delicate blossoms.

*Spine fever*—a generic term for paralytic diseases, like polio, which affect the nervous system and cause paralysis.

*"Stand at Kharmych"*—a Siddarmarkian military march composed to commemorate the 37th Infantry Regiment's epic stand against an invading Desnairian army in the Battle of Kharmych.

*Steel thistle*—a native Safeholdian plant which looks very much like branching bamboo. The plant bears seed pods filled with small, spiny seeds embedded in fine, straight fibers. The seeds are extremely difficult to remove by hand, but the fiber can be woven into a fabric which is even stronger than cotton silk. It can also be twisted into extremely strong, stretch-resistant rope. Moreover, the plant grows almost as rapidly as actual bamboo, and the yield of raw fiber per acre is seventy percent higher than for terrestrial cotton.

*Stone wool*—Safeholdian term for chrysotile (white asbestos).

*Sugar apple*—a tropical Safeholdian fruit tree. The sugar apple has a bright purple skin much like a terrestrial tangerine's, but its fruit has much the same consistency of a terrestrial apple. It has a higher natural sugar content than an apple, however; hence the name.

*Surgoi kasai*—"dreadful" or "great fire." The true spirit of God. The touch of His divine fire, which only an angel or Archangel can endure.

*Swamp hopper*—moderate-sized (around fifty to sixty-five pounds) Safeholdian amphibian. It is carnivorous, subsisting primarily on fish and other small game and looks rather like a six-legged Komodo dragon but has a fan-like crest which it extends and expands in response to a threat or in defense of territory. It is also equipped with air sacs on either side of its throat which swell and expand under those circumstances. It is ill-tempered, territorial, and aggressive.

*Swivel wolf*—a light, primarily antipersonnel artillery piece mounted on a swivel for easy traverse. *See* Wolf.

*Sword Rakurai*—specially trained agents of the Inquisition sent into the enemy's rear areas. They operate completely solo, as do the Inquisition's regular Rakurai; they are not suicide attackers or simple terrorists. Instead, they are trained as spies and infiltrators, expected to do any damage they can but with the primary mission of information collection.

*Sword of Schueler*—the savage uprising, mutiny, and rebellion fomented by the Inquisition to topple Lord Protector Greyghor Stohnar and destroy the Republic of Siddarmark.

*Talon branch*—an evergreen tree native to Safehold. It has fine, spiny needles and its branches are covered with half-inch thorns. It reaches a height of almost seventy feet, and at full maturity has no branches for the first twenty to twenty-five feet above the ground.

*Teak tree*—a native Safeholdian tree whose wood contains concentrations of silica and other minerals. Although it grows to a greater height than the Old Earth teak wood tree and bears a needle-like foliage, its timber is very similar in grain and coloration to the terrestrial tree and, like Old Earth teak, it is extremely resistant to weather, rot, and insects.

*Tellesberg Krakens*—the Tellesberg professional baseball club.

*Temple, The*—the complex built by "the Archangels" using Terran Federation technology to serve as the headquarters of the Church of God Awaiting. It contains many "mystic" capabilities which demonstrate the miraculous power of the Archangels to anyone who sees them.

*Temple Boy*—Charisian/Siddarmarkian slang for someone serving in the Army of God. It is not a term of
endearment.

*Temple Loyalist*—one who renounces the schism created by the Church of Charis' defiance of the Grand
Vicar and Council of Vicars of the Church of God
Awaiting. Some Temple Loyalists are also Reformists (*see* above), but all are united in condemning
the schism between Charis and the Temple.

*Testimonies, The*—by far the most numerous of the
Church of God Awaiting's sacred writings, these
consist of the firsthand observations of the first few
generations of humans on Safehold. They do not
have the same status as the Christian gospels, because they do not reveal the central teachings and
inspiration of God. Instead, collectively, they form
an important substantiation of the *Writ*'s "historical accuracy" and conclusively attest to the fact that
the events they describe did, in fact, transpire.

*Titan oak*—a very slow-growing, long-lived deciduous Safeholdian hardwood which grows to heights
of as much as one hundred meters.

*"The Pikes of Kolstyr"*—a Siddarmarkian military
march composed to commemorate a Desnairian
atrocity in one of the early wars between the Republic of Siddarmark and the Desnairian Empire. When
played on the battlefield, it announces that the Republic of Siddarmark Army intends to offer no
quarter.

*Tomb of Saint Kohdy*—the original Tomb of Saint
Kohdy was destroyed by the same kinetic weapons
which destroyed the Abbey of Saint Kohdy. Before
that destruction, however, the Sisters of Saint Kohdy
had secretly moved the saint's body to a new, hidden tomb in the Mountains of Light, where it
remains to this day.

*Waffle bark*—a deciduous, nut-bearing native Safeholdian tree with an extremely rough, shaggy bark.

*War Against the Fallen*—the portion of Shan-wei's War

falling between the destruction of the Alexandria Enclave and the final reconsolidation of the Church's authority.

**Wing warrior**—the traditional title of a blooded warrior of one of the Raven Lords clans. It is normally shortened to "wing" when used as a title or an honorific.

**Wire vine**—a kudzu-like vine native to Safehold. Wire vine isn't as fast-growing as kudzu, but it's equally tenacious, and unlike kudzu, several of its varieties have long, sharp thorns. Unlike many native Safeholdian plant species, it does quite well intermingled with terrestrial imports. It is often used as a sort of combination hedgerow and barbed-wire fence by Safehold farmers.

**Wolf** (1)—a Safeholdian predator which lives and hunts in packs and has many of the same social characteristics as the terrestrial species of the same name. It is warm-blooded but oviparous and larger than an Old Earth wolf, with adult males averaging between two hundred and two hundred and twenty-five pounds.

**Wolf** (2)—a generic term for shipboard artillery pieces with a bore of less than two inches and a shot weighing one pound or less. They are primarily antipersonnel weapons but can also be effective against boats and small craft.

**Wyvern**—the Safeholdian ecological analogue of terrestrial birds. There are as many varieties of wyverns as there are birds, including (but not limited to) the homing or messenger wyvern, hunting wyverns suitable for the equivalent of hawking for small prey, the crag wyvern (a flying predator with a wingspan of ten feet), various species of sea wyverns, and the king wyvern (a very large flying predator with a wingspan of up to twenty-five feet). All wyverns have two pairs of wings, and one pair of powerful, clawed legs. The king wyvern has been known to take children as prey when desperate or when the opportunity presents, but they are quite intelligent. They know that humans are a prey best left alone and generally avoid inhabited areas.

*Wyvernry*—a nesting place or breeding hatchery for domesticated wyverns.

*Zhyahngdu Academy*—perhaps the most renowned school for sculptors in all of Safehold, located at the port city of Zhyahngdu in the Tiegelkamp Province of North Harchong. It dates back to the days of the War Against the Fallen and has trained and produced the Church of God Awaiting's finest sculptors for almost nine hundred Safeholdian years.

## *The Archangels:*

| Archangel | Sphere of Authority | Symbol |
|-----------|---------------------|--------|
| Langhorne | law and life | scepter |
| Bédard | wisdom and knowledge | lamp |
| Pasquale | healing and medicine | caduceus |
| Sóndheim | agronomy and farming | grain sheaf |
| Truscott | animal husbandry | horse |
| Schueler | justice | sword |
| Jwo-jeng | acceptable technology | flame |
| Chihiro (1) | history | quill pen |
| Chihiro (2) | guardian | sword |
| Andropov | good fortune | dice |
| Hastings | geography | draftman's compass |

| Fallen Archangel | Sphere of Authority |
|------------------|---------------------|
| Shan-wei | mother of evil/evil ambition |
| Kau-yung | destruction |
| Proctor | temptation/forbidden knowledge |
| Sullivan | gluttony |
| Ascher | lies |
| Grimaldi | pestilence |
| Stavraki | avarice |

## The Church of God Awaiting's Hierarchy:

| Ecclesiastic rank | Distinguishing color | Clerical ring/set |
| --- | --- | --- |
| Grand Vicar | dark blue | sapphire with rubies |
| Vicar | orange | sapphire |
| Archbishop | white and orange | ruby |
| Bishop executor | white | ruby |
| Bishop | white | ruby |
| Auxiliary bishop | green and white | ruby |
| Upper-priest | green | plain gold (no stone) |
| Priest | brown | none |
| Under-priest | brown | none |
| Sexton | brown | none |

Clergy who do not belong to a specific order wear cassocks entirely in the color of their rank. Auxiliary bishops' cassocks are green with narrow trim bands of white. Archbishops' cassocks are white, but trimmed in orange. Clergy who belong to one of the ecclesiastical orders (see below) wear habits (usually of patterns specific to each order) in the order's colors but with the symbol of their order on the right breast, badged in the color of their priestly rank. In formal vestments, the pattern is reversed; that is, their vestments are in the colors of their priestly ranks and the order's symbol is the color of their order. All members of the clergy habitually wear either cassocks or the habits of their orders. The headgear is a three-cornered "priest's cap" almost identical to the eighteenth century's tricornes. The cap is black for anyone under the rank of vicar. Under-priests' and priests' bear brown cockades. Auxiliary bishops bear green cockades. Bishops' and bishop executors' bear white cockades. Archbishops' bear white cockades with a broad, dove-tailed orange ribbon at the back. Vicars' priests' caps are of orange with no cockade or ribbon, and the Grand Vicar's cap is white with an orange cockade.

All clergy of the Church of God Awaiting are affiliated with one or more of the great ecclesiastic orders, but not all are *members* of those orders. Or it might, perhaps, be more accurate to say that not all are *full* members of their orders. Every ordained priest is automatically affiliated with the order of the bishop who ordained him and (in theory, at least) owes primary obedience to that order. Only members of the clergy who have taken an order's vows are considered full members or brethren/sisters of that order, however. (Note: there are no female priests in the Church of God Awaiting, but women may attain high ecclesiastic rank in one of the orders.) Only full brethren or sisters of an order may attain to rank within that order, and only members of one of the great orders are eligible for elevation to the vicarate.

The great orders of the Church of God Awaiting, in order of precedence and power, are:

**The Order of Schueler**, which is primarily concerned with the enforcement of Church doctrine and theology. The Grand Inquisitor, who is automatically a member of the Council of Vicars, is always the head of the Order of Schueler. Schuelerite ascendency within the Church has been steadily increasing for over two hundred years, and the order is clearly the dominant power in the Church hierarchy today. The order's color is purple, and its symbol is a sword.

**The Order of Langhorne** is technically senior to the Order of Schueler, but has lost its primacy in every practical sense. The Order of Langhorne provides the Church's jurists, and since Church law supersedes secular law throughout Safehold that means all jurists and lawgivers (lawyers) are either members of the order or must be vetted and approved by the order. At one time, that gave the Langhornites unquestioned primacy, but the Schuelerites have relegated the order of Langhorne to a primarily administrative role, and the head of the order lost his mandatory seat on the Council of Vicars several generations back (in the Year of God 810). Needless to say, there's a certain tension between the Schuelerites and the Langhornites. The Order of Langhorne's color is black, and its symbol is a scepter.

**The Order of Bédard** has undergone the most change of any of the original great orders of the Church. Originally, the Inquisition came out of the Bédardists, but that function was effectively resigned to the Schuelerites by the Bédardists themselves when Saint Greyghor's reforms converted the order into the primary teaching order of the church. Today, the Bédardists are philosophers and educators, both at the university level and among the peasantry, although they also retain their function as Safehold's mental health experts and councilors. The order is also involved in caring for the poor and indigent. Ironically, perhaps, given the role of the "Archangel Bédard" in the creation of the Church of God Awaiting, a large percentage of Reformist clergy springs from this order. Like the Schuelerites, the head of the Order of Bédard always holds a seat on the Council of Vicars. The order's color is white, and its symbol is an oil lamp.

**The Order of Chihiro** is unique in that it has two separate functions and is divided into two separate orders. The Order of the Quill is responsible for training and overseeing the Church's scribes, historians, and bureaucrats. It is responsible for the archives of the Church and all of its official documents. The Order of the Sword is a militant order which often cooperates closely with the Schuelerites and the Inquisition. It is the source of the officer corps for the Temple Guard and also for most officers of the Temple Lands' nominally secular army and navy. Its head is always a member of the Council of Vicars, as Captain General of the Church of God Awaiting, and generally fulfills the role of Secretary of War. The order's color is blue, and its symbol is a quill pen. The Order of the Sword shows the quill pen, but crossed with a sheathed sword.

**The Order of Pasquale** is another powerful and influential order of the Church. Like the Order of Bédard, the Pasqualates are a teaching order, but their area of specialization is healing and medicine. They turn out very well-trained surgeons, but they are blinkered against pursuing any germ theory of medicine because of their religious teachings. All licensed healers on Safehold must be examined and approved by the Order of Pasquale, and the order is deeply involved in public hygiene policies and (less deeply) in caring for the poor and indigent. The majority of Safeholdian hospitals are associated, to at least some degree, with the Order of Pasquale. The head of the Order of Pasquale is normally, but not always, a member of the Council of Vicars. The order's color is green, and its symbol is a caduceus.

**The Order of Sóndheim and the Order of Truscott** are generally considered "brother orders" and are similar to the Order of Pasquale, but deal with agronomy and animal husbandry respectively. Both are teaching orders and they are jointly and deeply involved in Safehold's agriculture and food production. The teachings of the Archangel Sóndheim and Archangel Truscott incorporated into the *Holy Writ* were key elements in the ongoing terraforming of Safehold following the general abandonment of advanced technology. Both of these orders lost their mandatory seats on the Council of Vicars over two hundred years ago, however. The Order of Sóndheim's color is brown and its symbol is a sheaf of grain; the Order of Truscott's color is brown trimmed in *green*, and its symbol is a horse.

**The Order of Hastings** is the most junior (and least powerful) of the current great orders. The order is a teaching order, like the Orders of Sondheim and Truscott, and produces the vast majority of Safehold's cartographers, and surveyors. Hastingites also provide most of Safehold's officially sanctioned astronomers, although they are firmly within what might be considered the Ptolemaic theory of the universe. The order's "color" is actually a checkered pattern of green, brown, and blue, representing vegetation, earth, and water. Its symbol is a compass.

**The Order of Jwo-jeng,** once one of the four greatest orders of the Church, was absorbed into the Order of Schueler in Year of God 650, at the same time the Grand Inquisitorship was vested in the Schuelerites. Since that time, the Order of Jwo-jeng has had no independent existence.

**The Order of Andropov** occupies a sort of middle ground or gray area between the great orders of the Church and the minor orders. According to the *Holy Writ*, Andropov was one of the leading Archangels during the war against Shan-wei and the Fallen, but he was always more lighthearted (one hesitates to say frivolous) than his companions. His order has definite epicurean tendencies, which have traditionally been accepted by the Church because its raffles, casinos, horse and/or lizard races, etc., raise a great deal of money for charitable causes. Virtually every bookie on Safehold is either a member of Andropov's order or at least regards the Archangel as his patron. Needless to say, the Order of Andropov is not guaranteed a seat on the Council of Vicars. The order's color is red, and its symbol is a pair of dice.

▼ ▼ ▼

In addition to the above ecclesiastical orders, there are a great many minor orders: mendicant orders, nursing orders (usually but not always associated with the Order of Pasquale), charitable orders (usually but not always associated with the Order of Bédard or the Order of Pasquale), ascetic orders, etc. All of the great orders maintain numerous monasteries and convents, as do many of the lesser orders. Members of minor orders may not become vicars unless they are also members of one of the great orders.

The lines are drawn, the navies and armies raised—and only one side can survive.

# DAVID WEBER

## AT THE SIGN OF TRIUMPH

After eight years of war the Church stands upon the brink of defeat. But it still commands immense resources, and—faced with the unthinkable—the Church has decided that it, too, must embrace the forbidden technology that has carried Charis so far.

★ "Gripping…Shifting effortlessly between battles among warp-speed starships and among oar-powered galleys, Weber brings the political maneuvering, past and future technologies, and vigorous protagonists together for a cohesive, engrossing whole."
—*Publishers Weekly* (starred review) on *Off Armageddon Reef*

★ "A superb cast of characters and plenty of action… This fine book gives new luster to Weber's reputation and new pleasure to his fans."
—*Booklist* (starred review) on *By Schism Rent Asunder*

**TOR**
tor-forge.com